## About the author

After many years in Dundee, Nora Kay now lives in
Aberdeen with her husband. She has written forty short
stories and a newspaper serial. Her first novel, *A Woman
of Spirit*, was published by Hodder & Stoughton in 1994.
Other wonderful sagas by Nora Kay – *Gift of Love*, *Tina*
and *Lost Dreams* – are available in Coronet paperback.

*Also by Nora Kay*

Gift of Love
Tina
Lost Dreams

# Beth
# Best Friends
# A Woman of Spirit

Nora Kay

CORONET BOOKS
Hodder & Stoughton

First published as three separate volumes

*Beth* © 1995 Nora Kay
First published in Great Britain in 1995 by Hodder and Stoughton
First published in paperback in 1996 by Hodder and Stoughton
A division of Hodder Headline PLC

*Best Friends* © 1995 by Nora Kay
First published in Great Britain in 1995 by Hodder and Stoughton
First published in paperback in 1995 by Hodder and Stoughton
A division of Hodder Headline PLC

*A Woman of Spirit* © 1994 by Nora Kay
First published in 1994 by Hodder and Stoughton
A division of Hodder Headline PLC

This edition published in 1999

A Coronet Paperback

ISBN 0 340 76720 0

Printed and bound in Great Britain by Mackays of Chatham plc, Chatham, Kent

Hodder and Stoughton
A division of Hodder Headline PLC
338 Euston Road
London NW1 3BH

# Beth

For Bill and Raymond and my brother Syd

# Chapter One

The last of the children to come out of Sandyneuk Primary School were two small girls. One of them pointed to a woman standing alone and well apart from the young mothers gossiping at the school gate.

'Is that lady your mummy?'

'Yes,' Beth answered shortly, and her small mouth buttoned. Mary Watson had no need to ask, she knew it was her mother.

'My mummy thinks she's your gran and not your mummy.'

'Well, she isn't, she's my mummy,' Beth said indignantly.

'She looks old, that's why. She looks like my gran only she doesn't because my gran looks nicer.' Having said her say the child skipped ahead and out of the gate.

Beth watched her go, wanting to put out her tongue, but afraid to in case her mummy saw her and Beth knew she'd be very cross. Her mummy did look old, that was the worst of it, but Mary Watson didn't have to go and say so. Crossing to where her mother stood Beth wished with all her heart that she had a mummy who was young and wore pretty clothes.

Harriet Brown smiled to her daughter, then frowned.

'Must you always be last, Beth?' She wore a drab brown coat on this bright, breezy April day, with a cloche hat of the same colour.

'I couldn't help it, my shoe lace came undone and I had to stop and tie it.'

'At your age you should be able to tie them so that they don't come undone.' They moved off together, the tall, thin woman and the child. For all her drab clothes Harriet Brown was a good-looking woman with a smooth, oval face and a nice figure. The child with her long, skinny legs would likely be tall, too. Beth resembled her mother in all but her hair which was dark like her father's. Harriet's was light brown with traces of grey.

Beth was deep in thought. Should she or should she not tell her mother? She decided she should.

'Mummy, do you know what Mary Watson said?'

'That's just silly, Beth, how could I possibly know since you haven't told me.'

With the tip of a pink tongue Beth moistened her lips and said the words into herself first. It was important to get them right. 'She said that – her mummy – said that my mummy – looked like a grandma.'

Beth watched the angry colour flood her mother's face. 'That was an extremely rude thing to say.'

'Are you very old, mummy?' Beth persisted.

'No, I am not very old, I am not old at all, just older than – than—'

'The other mothers,' Beth added helpfully.

'Yes.'

'Is daddy very old?' Beth thought about her daddy and decided he must be a hundred.

'No, he is not. We are what you could call older parents, dear. Do you understand now?' But of course the child didn't, it was obvious she didn't, her little face was puckered in concentration.

'No, I don't, mummy, I don't really understand why you had to wait until you were old to have me borned.'

Harriet had to smile. The child could be quite amusing, some of the things she came away with.

'I wasn't old,' she said sharply, 'just old to be having a first baby.'

'You're hurting my hand,' Beth complained, 'you're holding it too tight.'

'Sorry, I didn't mean to,' Harriet said letting the small hand go free, 'but do keep up.'

Beth was almost running. 'You don't need to meet me from school. I can come home all by myself.'

'If I were to allow you to do that, would you promise to come straight home and not have me worried?'

'Yes, mummy, I promise.'

'Very well, Beth, starting Monday I won't come to meet you.' Harriet smiled to herself as she said it. She had been thinking about allowing the child to find her own way home but she was pleased that Beth had suggested it herself. Though it wasn't far from number three Sycamore Lane to the school, the double journey and the waiting about dug into her day. Then there was the embarrassment of being so much older than the other mothers and feeling their eyes on her.

As for six-year-old Beth, she was just hugely delighted with her victory. No one would call her a baby now or worse, say that her mummy looked like a grandma. They wouldn't if they didn't see her.

Running ahead, Beth went round to the back door of the neat little cottage that was home to George, Harriet and Beth Brown. The front door, with its shining brass door knob and letterbox, was seldom used. Only the occasional visitor or the minister, who visited his flock twice a year (more often if they were ill), came in that way. All the houses in the lane were similar but the garden at number three was the best kept.

The garden was Harriet's hobby and she spent as much time as possible in it. To the front of the house there was a small patch of grass kept short, and in spring and summer the borders were a blaze of colour. Just now the long trumpeted golden daffodils were at their best with the tulips alongside just beginning to show their pinks and reds. The ground to the back was long and narrow and on a slight slope and much of it was given over to the growing of vegetables. In one corner there was a chicken coop, and eggs surplus to their requirements were sold.

'Keep your coat on, dear, we'll take a walk to Inverbrae with the eggs.'

'It's too hot, I don't need my coat,' Beth complained.

'Yes, you do, that wind has a real chill in it and I don't want you getting a cold.'

Beth sighed. She knew better than to argue and stood with her coat on watching her mother pick up the box from the pantry shelf with each egg carefully wrapped in newspaper. Then they set off along the lane and up the steep hill to Inverbrae House.

Sandyneuk was a seaside village on the east coast of Scotland and a pleasant place to live. In the summer months day-trippers flocked to the beach laden with baskets of food, thermos flasks of tea, extra cardigans in case the weather got chilly, buckets and spades and all the other paraphernalia so necessary for a family day out. The more affluent holiday-makers rented a house for one or two weeks and did for themselves. At the end of the season, when the visitors had gone, there was a curious silence which took a little time to get used to. Most of the villagers, though not the shopkeepers, were glad to have Sandyneuk to themselves.

Harriet and George were among those who appreciated

the quietness. They were a placid couple, always ready to give a helping hand but who generally kept themselves to themselves.

George earned his living as a clerk with a local building firm. He was very efficient at his job but his heart wasn't in it. He longed for a different life, a worthwhile life spent doing missionary work in Africa, India or wherever the Lord had need of his services. As a lay preacher, George felt himself well qualified and it was at a Prayer Meeting that he had met the woman who was to become his wife. Discovering that they both had an interest in missionary work drew them together. Love didn't enter into it and neither Harriet nor George looked for more than liking and respect. Marriage, however, was desirable. A couple, legally tied, could do so much more and accommodation was less of a problem for a couple than two single people.

Harriet was thirty-eight and George five years older when they married. A year later they were making arrangements to go to Africa when Harriet discovered she was pregnant. It was difficult to know which of them was the more appalled. Nearing forty, Harriet had been so sure that motherhood was no longer a threat, but it had happened. She couldn't go but she insisted that George should go without her. George was torn between his desire to go and his duty to his wife. Harriet did have a sister who might be called on to help, though they weren't particularly close. In the event it was the doctor who made the decision for them. His patient, he said bluntly, was not having a trouble-free pregnancy and there was her age, old to be having a first baby. At a time like this a husband should put his wife first. His own opinion, not voiced, was that visiting heathen countries was a waste of money and that there were plenty of folk in this country in need of spiritual help.

'Mummy, do you think we might see the little girl today?'

'No, Beth, I think that highly improbable. The child won't be allowed to wander about in the servants' quarters, nor the kitchen.'

'Is that because she is better than us?'

'She and her family have advantages that we don't have but if you listened properly in church you would know that in the sight of our Lord we are all His children, we are all equal.'

'Then why does she have a big house and we have a little one?'

Harriet sighed. She shouldn't complain, asking questions was a sign of intelligence, but it was very wearing when the questions went on and on.

'Her family is one where wealth and property are handed down to the next generation.'

'Why doesn't she go to my school?'

'I expect the daughter of the house will have a governess.'

'What's that?'

'Someone who teaches,' Harriet said wearily. Her arms were beginning to ache, not so much from the weight of the eggs, but from the careful way in which they had to be carried.

There was silence while Beth thought this over. 'You mean, mummy, that she has a teacher all to herself?'

'Yes, that is it exactly.'

'Will she be cleverer than me?'

'Not necessarily,' Harriet smiled, 'you have a good teacher.'

The answer pleased Beth, she'd got a star for spelling and all her sums right but she was keeping it a secret until daddy came home. She wanted to tell them together.

They were almost there. Beth wondered what it would be like to live in a big house with servants to do everything. The thought of a little girl like herself living at Inverbrae House fascinated Beth and she longed to see her.

# Chapter Two

Set on a rise and sheltered by mature trees, Inverbrae House was surrounded by acres and acres of land, much of it rented out. When it was built it was considered a monument to wealth, though there was nothing vulgar or showy about it. Rather it had a classic simplicity that was pleasing to the eye and the ivy, twisted round the pillars at the entrance, gave it a welcoming look.

The wrought-iron gates were just ahead of them and a wide, tree-lined driveway led up to the imposing stone frontage. As always Beth took a long look at all this grandeur before turning left to walk along a gravel path that led to the rear of the house. After passing a number of outbuildings and the stables, they reached the servants' quarters. The lesser orders had tiny rooms at the top of the house with windows little bigger than portholes. Each room was furnished with a cheap wooden wardrobe with a drawer at the bottom. There was a narrow bed beneath the fall down roof and many a young maid forgetting the danger and rising quickly, was reminded of it by a painful crack on the head.

As befitted their positions, the housekeeper, Mrs Murdoch and Mrs Noble, the cook, were provided with a comfortably furnished bed-sitting room. The placing of Miss Mathewson, the governess, was more difficult since she was neither family nor servant, but at Inverbrae

House they had solved the problem by giving her a room on the same floor as the nursery. Nanny Rintoul had a room next to her charge.

The outer door was open and Harriet pushed Beth ahead of her. 'On you go, dear, and knock.'

Beth did as she was told and rapped her knuckle on the door as hard as she could.

'Come in,' a voice called.

'Go on, Beth, open it.'

Beth turned the knob and pushed and a wonderful, mouthwatering smell of baking wafted out.

'Thought it might be you, Mrs Brown. Yes, that's right, just put them there on the table. I keep yours for the breakfasts and Cunningham's do fine enough for the baking.' She was a dumpling of a woman with reddish fair hair cut short and her round face was usually smiling. A huge white apron tied at the back with strings enveloped her ample frame.

Harriet had little social chat but it went unnoticed since Mrs Noble had plenty to say. Some would call the cook a gossip and perhaps they were right, but she was never deliberately hurtful.

'I was going to wait until tomorrow to bring them.'

'Glad you didn't, I'm down to my last dozen.' Clouds of white flour rose as she pounded and kneaded the dough and Beth watched in fascination. The punishment went on until Mrs Noble declared it was ready then, picking up a cloth, she opened the oven door and shot the tray in. 'Now I can relax for a wee while and enjoy a cuppie. You'll join me, Mrs Brown?'

'That's very kind of you,' Harriet smiled as she sat down. The cup of tea would be very welcome.

'Undo your coat, it gets that hot in here.'

Beth stood as her mother loosened her coat. Her eyes

were on the biscuits cooling on the tray.

'That you just come from school, Beth?'

'Yes.'

Waddling to the pantry she returned with a jug of milk and, after removing the cloth weighted with beads, filled a cup.

'There you are, lass, drink that and help yourself to a biscuit. No, make that two, you're a growing girl.'

Beth had one biscuit in her hand and the other was hovering as she stole a glance at her mother. Harriet gave a slight shake of the head.

'One is quite enough, Mrs Noble.'

'Away with you.' Picking one up she put it in Beth's hand. 'Drink your milk and eat your biscuits outside if that is where you'd rather be.'

Beth smiled and nodded. She liked Mrs Noble and not just because she got something to eat from her, but because she knew that listening to grownup talk wasn't any fun for little girls.

'My, that's a warm winter coat you're wearing,' Mrs Noble said looking at Beth's navy nap coat, 'you must be sweating in that?'

Beth nodded again. Nodding was rude, she knew that, but if she said anything she would have to swallow the piece of biscuit and she would lose all the lovely taste.

'There's a chill air outside,' Harriet said but half-heartedly.

'Bairns don't feel the cold the way we do and I see she has a warm jumper on.' With what could have been a wink she helped Beth off with her coat and opened the door for her.

Once outside Beth began walking without paying any attention to where she was going. Her first biscuit had slipped over too quickly and she was determined to make the other one last as long as possible.

Coming to the high hedge surprised her, she didn't remember coming this way before but she wasn't lost. She could quite easily find her way back to the kitchen. What, she wondered, was on the other side of the hedge? A break in it couldn't be ignored and allowed her to peer through. As she did voices drifted across. Beth kept as quiet as a mouse, she didn't want anyone to know she was there. Moving nearer to get a better view, she was thrilled to see what to her looked like a very big doll's house. The windows of it had pretty flowered curtains, the chairs were cushioned and she could see right in to where a little girl was sitting at the table and chewing the end of a pencil. Beth nearly giggled out loud. She did that and got into trouble.

This, then, must be the little rich girl, the girl she longed to meet, and the woman bending over the table as though explaining something would be the governess. Beth could hardly contain her excitement.

'It's too difficult, Mattie.'

'Of course it isn't, Miss Caroline, you are just not paying attention.'

Fancy being called Miss Caroline! Beth began putting 'Miss' before her own name but it didn't sound nearly as nice as Miss Caroline. She tried it with her real name and decided that Miss Elizabeth sounded even better than Miss Caroline.

'I'm tired, I've been paying attention for ages and ages and when I'm tired I don't have to do lessons. Daddy said so, so there!'

'That was when you were unwell, Miss Caroline, but you are very much better now.' The woman paused then added, 'And what would your grandmother have to say if

I were to tell her that you are falling behind with your schoolwork?'

The mention of her grandmother had the desired effect as the governess knew it would.

'You don't have to tell her, Mattie, and truly, truly I'll work very hard tomorrow. No, I won't, tomorrow is Saturday, but Monday, I'll work very hard on Monday.'

'Is that a promise you mean to keep?'

'Yes, honestly it is, and now will you please go away and let me sit here by myself for a little while?'

'Very well,' came in a resigned tone, 'I'll take these things to the schoolroom and come back for you.'

'You don't need to.'

'Nevertheless I intend to. I'll give you ten to fifteen minutes, no more, and keep that rug over your legs.'

Beth watched a pair of thick legs in lisle stockings and brown flat-heeled shoes walk away. She was about to walk away too in case her mother was looking for her, but she was stopped in her tracks.

'I know you are there, I saw you moving so you might as well come out.'

Beth was in two minds. She knew it would be safer to run away but curiosity nagged at her and won. Parting the foliage she stepped out and her eyes widened at what she saw. She was in another world where the explosion of space was overwhelming. Vast areas of grass like green velvet spread out before her and dotted all around were carefully tended flower beds. Further away heads bobbed as the gardeners heaped the cuttings into the barrows to wheel away for compost.

The six-year-olds looked at each other, the one so dark with blue black hair, dark eyes and cheeks that were a healthy pink. The other had pale yellow hair, pale blue eyes and pale skin. The yellow ringlets swung as she spoke.

'What were you doing hiding?' she demanded.

Beth didn't have an answer.

'Cat got your tongue?' It was what her grandmother said to her when she didn't have an answer.

The expression was new to Beth and she thought it funny. How could a cat get hold of her tongue, and anyway she couldn't see one. 'I'm waiting for my mummy.'

'Where is she?'

Beth pointed vaguely. 'With Mrs Noble.'

'Our cook, oh, she'll be ages then,' she said matter-of-factly. 'Grownups do a lot of talking.'

'If that lady finds me here, will she be angry?'

'I expect so but it doesn't matter. Mattie's just my governess,' she said dismissively.

'Mattie's a funny name.'

'That's not her real name, silly, I just call her that.'

'What is her name?'

'Miss Mathewson. What is yours?'

'Beth.'

'Beth what?'

'Beth Brown, but my real name is Elizabeth.'

'Mine is Caroline Parker-Munro.'

'That's a long name.'

'You would have to call me Miss Caroline.'

'Why?'

'Because you would, that's why.'

'Then you have to call me Miss Elizabeth, that's only fair,' Beth said with a toss of her head.

'Is it? Oh, well, you can call me Caroline when nobody is about and I'll call you Beth.'

'Why have you got a blanket over your legs?'

'It's not a blanket, it's a rug and the doctor said I have to keep warm. I'm not very strong, you see.'

14

'You're lucky,' Beth said enviously, 'having a little house to play in.'

'It's a summer house. Mattie doesn't like being outside, she'd stay in the schoolroom for ever, but when the weather is good I make her come out.'

'My mummy says it isn't good to get all your own way.'

'I don't have a mummy, she went to heaven when I was born.'

Beth thought that was dreadful, not to have a mummy. 'Who looks after you?'

'Well, daddy does of course, then there's my nanny, she was daddy's nanny when he was a little boy.'

'She must be very old,' said Beth who was greatly taken up with age.

'I expect so.'

'My mummy and daddy are old.'

'Nanny must be a hundred.'

'My daddy's more than that, he's a hundred and something.' A movement caught her eye. 'She's coming, your governess,' Beth said, alarm in her voice, 'and my mummy will be cross if she's waiting for me.'

'You'll come back? Please say you will?' There was a pleading note in the voice.

'I'll try.'

'Try very hard.'

Beth nodded, then ran back through the hedge and didn't stop running until she was in sight of the kitchen. At that moment the door opened with Harriet saying her goodbyes. She was carrying Beth's coat and the empty egg box.

'There you are, Beth, slip on your coat quickly or daddy will be home and no meal ready for him.'

George Brown was a mild-mannered man who looked his

age. He was of medium build with the beginning of a paunch and had a pleasant face, though it was marred by worry lines. Most of his worries were matters over which he had no control. Disasters that made newspaper headlines gave George sleepless nights. Other people would shake their head and be suitably shocked, but not unduly concerned since it wasn't happening on their doorstep.

When her father joined Beth at the table he had changed out of his dark blue business suit into clerical grey which was more suitable for his duties as a lay preacher.

'Did you work hard at school today, Beth?' he asked as he always did.

'Yes, daddy.'

Harriet was flushed with hurrying. 'Sorry, dear, I spent rather too long at Inverbrae,' she said as she came out of the tiny scullery that was off the kitchen.

'That's all right,' he smiled, 'I'm not in a desperate hurry.'

She served her husband his helping of meat, home-grown vegetables and fluffy boiled potatoes, then went back for her own and Beth's. Harriet didn't eat a lot and her portion was small. Beth, who disliked meat, but had to eat it – how often had she heard about those poor starving people who would be glad of it and how often had she longed to say it, but didn't dare, that they were welcome to hers – had hers cut up small.

Swallowing the meat first was what she liked to do, then she could enjoy forking down the potatoes into the rich brown gravy. But not yet – not a knife or fork could be lifted until the grace was said. Following her mother's example Beth bowed her head, shut her eyes tight, and wished her daddy would say the words a bit quicker.

'Amen.' It came at last and she could open her eyes.

16

Talking at the table wasn't forbidden but it wasn't encouraged either. Eating was a serious business. One piece of meat on Beth's plate had a horrible bit of fat hanging on to it. She tried to get it off with her knife but it stubbornly refused to move and the thought of it going down her throat right into her stomach made her feel sick.

Harriet had been watching the performance and tut-tutted. 'For goodness sake, child, it won't poison you,' she said as she forked it off Beth's plate and on to her own.

Beth gave a satisfied smile, ate the rest of her meal and decided now was a good time to tell them.

'Mummy, daddy, I got a star for spelling and all my sums right *and* we got our places changed, *and* I'm top of the class,' she said triumphantly.

'Well done, Beth, you're a clever girl,' her father said, his fork arrested half way to his mouth.

'Yes, well done, dear,' her mother added.

'Keep it up, lass, stick into your lessons, there's nothing to beat a good education.' He nodded several times as if to emphasise the point.

Harriet agreed wholeheartedly with her husband. If any good came out of that dreadful war, it was the difference it had made to women. They were just beginning to enjoy a freedom never experienced before. The war years had seen women doing men's work, like driving trucks, working on munitions, and they had shown themselves to be every bit as capable as men. Now there was a marked reluctance to return to the drudgery and boredom of housework and men returning from the war in 1918 were shocked, angered and bewildered to face wives no longer willing to go back to what had been, for them, the bad old days.

Young girls like Beth were the most likely to benefit. No longer would the choice of job be limited to a factory, going into service, or standing behind a counter. The dull jobs would still require to be filled but the less intelligent or those lacking in ambition would be available to do them. The brighter girls would be demanding the right to be as well educated as their brothers.

Before her marriage, Harriet had worked long hours in a draper's shop for a pittance and like everyone else had just accepted her lot, although in her case she had much to be grateful for. She had her Prayer Meetings where she could have intelligent discussions with like-minded people.

It was half past eight and Beth's bedtime. She'd had her glass of milk and taken as long over it as she could, then said her goodnights. The room that was her bedroom was small with the walls painted cream and pretty pink and white curtains at the window. Her narrow bed had brass knobs and beside the bed was a small table with a weak leg. A bookcase had been fashioned out of a wooden box and there was a rag rug to protect small feet from the cold linoleum.

Her mother came up to hear her say her prayers, then Beth climbed into bed. She wished now that she had told her mother straight away about Caroline at the Big House, and she couldn't remember why she hadn't. She would have to now, she couldn't go to sleep without telling her.

Harriet was busy folding up Beth's clothes and putting them on the chair. The school clothes went in the wardrobe since tomorrow was Saturday, and the soiled blouse she took with her for the wash. Beth was sitting up.

'Mummy?'

'Yes, dear?'

'I've got something to tell you.'

'Hurry, then, I have a pile of ironing to do.'

'I saw the little girl and she spoke to me.'

'Who spoke to you?'

'Mummy, I've just told you,' Beth said impatiently. Why was it that grownups didn't have to pay attention and children had to? 'The little girl from the Big House.'

She had her mother's attention now. 'Where was this?'

'You know that place where the high hedge is?'

'Yes, I do know and you've been warned not to stray over that way,' Harriet said severely.

'I didn't know I was walking that way, I just came to it, mummy, and I found a hole in the hedge that I can squeeze into.'

'Why would you want to do that?' The eyebrows shot up.

"Cos I heard someone and I just wanted to peep through.' She paused and her eyes widened. 'And that was when I saw the little girl.'

'And obviously she saw you. Really, Beth, that was too bad of you.'

'I wasn't hiding and I wouldn't have spoken to her only she spoke to me first.'

'Wondering what you were doing there, no doubt?'

Beth ignored that. How did her mummy know, anyway? 'It was nice and warm and do you know this, the girl had a blanket over her legs only she said it wasn't a blanket, that it was a rug and it was because she had been ill. That's funny isn't it, mummy, calling it a rug when rugs go on the floor?'

Harriet didn't trouble to answer. 'If I had been looking for you I would have been frantic wondering where you'd got to.'

'I didn't stay long and I told her you were with Mrs

Noble and she said she was their cook and you would likely be there for ages.'

Harriet's lips twitched.

'And I ran all the way back,' Beth said as if that made everything all right.

'Very well, we'll say no more about it.'

Beth was on the verge of tears. 'She's called Caroline and I like her and she likes me and she made me promise to come back and I said I would try and she said I had to try very hard – and – and – and—' The eyes brightened and the tears overflowed. 'Why can't I play with her? I haven't got anyone to play with.'

Harriet handed her own handkerchief to Beth. 'Wipe your eyes. I didn't expect a big girl like you to act like a baby.'

Beth used the handkerchief. 'I'm not a baby,' she sniffed.

Harriet did feel some guilt. Only a very few of the school children lived up their way and no one in Beth's class. Some lived in the centre of the village beside the Main Street, but most were in the fishermen's cottages clustered down beside the harbour. Harriet knew she wouldn't have a moment's peace if she allowed Beth to play there. It was much too dangerous.

'When you are a little older you can play with your school friends.'

'I'd rather play with Caroline.'

Harriet sighed. 'Although I have nothing against you playing with the girl, I doubt if she would be allowed to play with you.'

'Why not?' The tears had gone and there was outrage in her voice.

'You would not be considered suitable.'

'I would so, but she can't ask her mummy because she

hasn't got one. Did you know that, mummy?'

'Yes, Beth, I knew that.' She well remembered the village's grief when the young woman had died in child-birth.

'Next time you go with eggs, it'll be Friday, won't it?'

'More than likely.'

'I can just go and see if she's there, can't I?' she pleaded. 'Please, mummy, and you did say promises had to be kept.'

'Very well, but you are not to be forward or make a nuisance of yourself.'

Beth didn't know what forward meant but the impor-tant thing was that she hadn't been forbidden to go.

'No, mummy.'

'Get to sleep now, goodnight, dear.'

'Goodnight, mummy.'

The door closed quietly. Beth never got a goodnight kiss or cuddle. Harriet wasn't the demonstrative type and George was of the same mould. A pat on the head and a smile was all their child could expect.

George Brown took all of his duties seriously and that included making time for his small daughter. Saturday afternoons were devoted to this, when, if the weather was favourable, they would go for a walk. If it wasn't Beth would have to listen to Bible stories. Sometimes she got quite interested and listened eagerly but she much pre-ferred going for walks.

Today it was bright and breezy with a blue sky and no sign of rain clouds. Beth was ready with her coat buttoned and waiting for her daddy to take his off the coatstand.

'Think I'll need it?'

'Your coat? Yes, it's quite chilly out and it'll be worse where you are going.'

'How do you know where we are going, mummy?'

'Isn't it always the harbour?'

'Nearly always.'

'The fresh air would do you good, Harriet.'

'That may well be but I have too much to do and with you both out of the way I'll get on all the quicker.'

George smiled. 'In that case we'll get on our way. Come along, Beth.'

Beth liked it best when it was just daddy. He didn't walk fast the way mummy did and he always answered her questions without sighing. Hand-in-hand they walked down the lane, then down the steep brae to the fishermen's cottages and then along by the harbour wall. There they could hear the screeching of gulls and see the small boats bobbing about the harbour. Far into the distance could be seen the outline of a steamer.

'Breathe in deeply, Beth, let your lungs fill with the fresh sea air, nothing like it to get rid of germs and keep healthy.'

Beth took a deep breath, she loved the smell of the sea and wished that their house was down at the harbour instead of up the hill. They walked on and along the coast road and Beth studied the white house. It fascinated her the way it jutted out and she was filled with a fear that one day it would topple into the sea and disappear.

'How can you be so sure it won't, daddy? What if there was a big wind and it blew the house into the sea?'

This time she heard him sigh the way mummy did.

'Beth, we've been through all this before. The house is perfectly safe and even a gale force wind won't unsettle it. You only think it is in danger because of the angle and the way you are looking at it. Tell you what, one Sunday the three of us will take a walk up to the white house and you will see for yourself that it is nowhere near the cliff edge and absolutely safe.'

'Would you like to live in it, daddy?'

'I would indeed, the house has a superb outlook but we cannot afford to live there.'

'Is it very big?'

'Compared to ours, yes it is, but it wouldn't be considered a large house, just a good family size.'

'When I'm big I'll buy it for you and mummy.'

He smiled down at her. 'And where would you get all that money?'

Her blue eyes looked at him gravely. 'You said I was clever and if I'm clever I'll make a lot of money, won't I?'

'It doesn't always work out that way and remember this, Beth, because it is very important. Money is not, it is not important, we need just enough to cover our basic needs,' he said firmly.

Beth didn't say but she knew he was wrong. Everything in the shops cost money and if you didn't have any then you couldn't buy things.

'Daddy,' she said coming to a stop, 'this is far enough. I want to go back.'

'We could go back home by the top road instead of retracing our steps.'

She looked stubborn. 'No, daddy, the harbour, please.'

'All right, you win this time,' he said, turning round to face the other way.

Back by the harbour wall Beth tugged at his sleeve. 'Daddy, someone is painting, I want to see what he is doing. Please, daddy.'

'He may not object but don't go too near.'

The artist looked up as they approached. He was a tall, gangling youth and he didn't seem to mind at all. Beth went over to the easel to have a good look and turned away disappointed.

'You haven't done hardly nothing,' Beth said accusingly and heard them both laugh.

'Beth, will you never learn to think before you speak. What you should have said is, you've hardly done anything.'

'I finished one earlier on if you would like to see it,' he said eagerly, and before they could answer he had gone to get it.

'That's the harbour,' Beth said excitedly.

'It's very good,' her father said quietly.

'Thank you.'

George pondered. He would like to buy it for Beth but he couldn't afford very much. Still, unless he was very much mistaken the artist was desperate for a sale but trying not to show it.

'Daddy, I like it.'

'How much would you want for it?'

'You are interested?'

'If I can afford it.'

'Make me an offer.'

George did and felt ashamed to be offering so little.

'It's yours.'

'Are you sure you want to let it go for that?' George hated to think he was cheating anyone.

'Absolutely sure.'

'You haven't signed it.'

'Neither I have. I'll do it now.' His hand was shaking as he scrawled his signature.

'Daddy, is it for me?'

'Yes, we'll hang it in your bedroom.'

Beth was flushed with excitement. 'Let me carry it.' Then she looked at the tall youth and remembered her manners. 'Thank you very much. Are you going to paint another one the same?'

'No, no two paintings are ever exactly alike.'

'This one will be best?'

He smiled and Beth thought he had a very nice smile. 'Special anyway,' he said.

'Good luck,' her father said, moving away.

'I have a feeling you have brought me that,' the youth said quietly as he picked up his brush.

# Chapter Three

Colonel Nigel Parker-Munro was a tall, handsome man in his late thirties who worried about his delicate small daughter and tried, whenever possible, to spend an hour or so with her each day. Well-meaning friends, his elderly mother among them, hinted that, after six years, it was time he took another wife. For Caroline's sake perhaps he should, he told himself, a girl needed a mother, but he hadn't met anyone with whom he wanted to share his life. Margaret had been very special and losing her in childbirth had been a tragedy that had embittered him for a long time. Some worried that he would blame the baby and have little time or love for her, but they were quite wrong. He saw their child as a living part of Margaret and each day Caroline seemed to grow more like her mother.

Before going down for dinner, Nigel gave a light knock on the nursery door and went in. A small figure usually hurtled herself at him and he would swing her in the air until she was screaming with delight, but not tonight. He glanced questioningly at his old nanny. Miss Rintoul got up stiffly to leave father and daughter together, then caught his eye and shook her head. He knew that look, it said it all, Miss Caroline was being difficult and a good talking to was what she needed. He sighed and forced himself to face the truth. Nanny Rintoul had seemed old when he was a little boy but he remembered, too, that strict though she had been, she could be fun, too. Now she was old and done and sometime soon he would have to make some provision for her and engage someone else. Poor Caroline was surrounded by old people.

'What's the matter, poppet, doesn't daddy get a smile?'

'I haven't got any smiles, I'm too unhappy and it's all grandmama's fault and nanny's, and Mattie's most of all because she told tales.'

'Dear me, I'd better hear about this,' her father said, adopting a serious air. Sitting down in the chair that Nanny Rintoul had vacated he gestured for Caroline to come over. With a whimper she got up on his knee and put her arms round his neck.

'I love you the best in the whole world.'

'Cuddle in then and tell me what is troubling you.'

'I've got a new friend, she's nice and Mattie asked grandmama and I'm not being allowed to play with her.'

'Who is this new friend of yours?'

'Her name is Beth, daddy, she's six same as me, and her mummy brings eggs for Mrs Noble.'

'How did you two meet?'

Caroline giggled. 'She was hiding, she said she wasn't but she was and when Mattie went away I made her come out.'

'That was naughty, making her do something she didn't want to do.'

'I didn't make her, she wanted to.'

Nigel tried to hide his amusement. 'So you two did manage to meet again?'

She nodded vigorously. 'Her mummy said she could play with me but she wasn't to be a – a—' Her brow puckered.

'A nuisance?' Nigel raised an eyebrow.

'Yes,' said a delighted Caroline, 'that's what she said, a nuisance.'

For himself Nigel didn't mind who Caroline played with just as long as she was happy, but his mother, Nanny and even Mattie were of the old school. Shades of Upstairs, Downstairs and, in their eyes, this child was plainly Downstairs.

'I'm lonely, daddy, I don't have anyone to play with.'

'That just isn't true, Caroline, your cousins come over and the Watson children.'

She looked scornful. 'They are all older and bigger than me and they are rough. Nanny Rintoul said so, too.'

She had a point, no denying that, and he just wished that she were strong enough to join in a rough and tumble but doubted if that day would ever come.

'Please, daddy, let me play with Beth.'

'Darling, the little girl will go to school and she'll have lots of her own friends.'

'No, she hasn't. She goes to school but her friends all live far away and she hasn't got anybody.' She paused and looked at him with all the wisdom of her six years. 'Everybody has to do what you say.'

'Can't say I've noticed,' he said drily.

'They have to, daddy.'

'No promises but I'll see what I can do.' He glanced at the time. 'If I'm to read you a story we'd better get started.'

'I don't want a story. I want you to tell me what it was like when you were a little boy and you were naughty and climbed up a tree and Nanny Rintoul couldn't find you anywhere.'

'Mother, I honestly don't see any harm in it.'

'No, perhaps you don't, Nigel, and more's the pity.'

'Things have changed,' he said gently, 'the great divisions are no longer there.'

'The war was responsible for that, it was an unsettling time, but the old values will come back, just you wait and see. No, Nigel, it isn't snobbishness, that was what you were about to say, it is a case of knowing one's place. Whatever is said to the contrary, there will always be the gentry and there will always be the servant class. Master and servant, how else could it be?'

Nigel looked at his mother with affection and exasperation. She would never change and perhaps he didn't want her to. She was a proud, imposing woman who held herself very straight and was a firm believer that posture was important to well-being. No member of the family was allowed to slouch in her presence. No member of the family would dare.

'You could be right.'

She smiled and as she did the harshness in her face softened. Nigel was her first born and held a special place in her heart. Her second son had died in infancy and James, three years younger than Nigel, had caused a lot of heartbreak to his parents. He had been the rebel, and even as a schoolboy had just escaped expulsion for some of his pranks that had got out of hand. Many of his misdemeanours would have been overlooked had it not been for his ability to charm others astray.

James had neither the wish nor the brains to follow Nigel to university and his father decided for him that the army would be the making of him. Unfortunately, James had other ideas, he wanted to see a bit of the world but not as a soldier. In the first year of his absence postcards arrived from various places in Europe informing them that he was fine and taking whatever job came his way. Then, quite suddenly, the postcards stopped and they had no means of getting the information to him that his father had died of a heart attack.

Nigel got up and kissed his mother. 'Rest assured, mother, I'll see this friend of Caroline's and satisfy myself that she isn't going to lead your grand-daughter astray.'

Wearing an ancient Harris tweed jacket with leather patches on the elbows and trousers that had long since lost their crease, Colonel Nigel Parker-Munro strode across the lawn and over to the two small figures. It was a Saturday morning and the May sunshine had a lot of warmth in it. Beth and Caroline were sprawled out on the grass and re-arranging the furniture in the doll's house. Both wore summer dresses, white ankle socks and sandals. Beth's dress was pale blue cotton with pink dots and had a white Peter Pan collar. Caroline's dress was pink with sprigs of blue flowers and the cotton of her dress had a lovely sheen to it. Unlike Beth she wore a white cardigan over it to protect her fair skin and give her the extra warmth she always required.

'Silly you, that table goes in the dining-room, not the drawing-room.'

Beth removed it. 'We haven't got a drawing-room.'

'Where do you entertain your guests?'

'We don't hardly have any.' Beth paused. 'We've got a living-room, though.'

Caroline had ceased to listen. 'Look! It's my daddy,' she said excitedly and, dropping the furniture at her feet, ran to meet him.

Beth watched the tall man swing Caroline up high then kiss her cheek before lowering her to the ground. She wished that he would do the same to her, her own daddy never did.

Taking her daddy's hand Caroline dragged him over. 'Daddy, I want you to meet my new friend. She's called Beth.'

Beth had got to her feet and was looking at him shyly. He wouldn't send her away, she was sure of that, because Caroline had said he didn't mind them playing together, it was just her grandmama who objected.

'Hello, Beth, I've heard so much about you from Caroline that I came especially to make your acquaintance.'

'Did you?' she said, then blushed, not at all sure what was expected of her.

'I did indeed.' It was Nigel's turn to search for something to say. 'Spring-cleaning the doll's house are you?'

'Of course not, daddy, the servants do that,' his daughter said scornfully. 'I've been showing Beth where the furniture goes. She isn't very good at it.'

Beth wasn't standing for that. She did so know what went in each room. 'The only one I didn't know was that silly drawing-room.'

'It's not silly,' Caroline said and turned to her daddy. 'Beth doesn't know about a drawing-room because her mummy and daddy don't have one.'

'We've got a living-room,' Beth said defensively.

'Same thing, different name,' Nigel said soothingly though he wanted to laugh. His daughter looked outraged and Beth's mouth was set in a stubborn line. This child, he thought, was going to be good for his daughter, she wouldn't give in to her the way others did, including himself. Because she was delicate they all spoiled her dreadfully, even his own mother who had been so strict with her own.

What an enchanting child had been his first thought on seeing Beth. With those huge, expressive, dark eyes and those incredibly long lashes she was going to grow up to be a real beauty. Beside her dark-eyed friend his pretty little daughter was just a pale shadow. Later he was to learn that Caroline was the older by a month but Beth was taller with her long, thin legs giving her a coltish look.

Lowering himself to the grass, Nigel sat down beside them and began to select pieces of the tiny, exquisitely made furniture, but his clumsy attempts to put them in place had both girls laughing delightedly as they insisted on showing him how it should be done. Perhaps that was when he became Beth's hero. She thought him the most perfect daddy in the whole world. It wasn't that she didn't love her own daddy, she truly did, but he never played with her. Of course, she told herself that it wasn't his fault, he couldn't help being a hundred and something, and Caroline's daddy was young.

Nigel got to his feet and dusted the grass off himself. 'Much as I would like to spend more time with you both duty calls and I have work to do.'

That surprised Beth, she didn't think rich gentlemen worked, only men like her daddy who needed the money. Her Mother had warned her not to be forward and she thought she knew what that meant now. She'd asked and been told that being forward was being cheeky. But asking questions wasn't cheeky and daddy had told her before that asking questions was the only way to learn.

'Do you do real work, Colonel Parker-Munro?' She was glad she had managed to get his name right. Her mummy called it a right mouthful.

'Real work, Beth? Yes, I think you could call it that,' he smiled.

'My daddy does very important work, he looks after the estate. I know that because grandmama told me.' She looked meaningfully at Beth as she said it.

'My daddy has two jobs,' Beth added her bit and it was

true, she didn't have to make it up. 'He's a clerk in an office doing lots of sums and he's a preacher – a lay preacher,' she corrected herself, 'and if I hadn't been borned my mummy and daddy would have been missionaries.'

That was quite a speech for a six-year-old, Nigel thought to himself. A very interesting child, this Beth Brown. Given Beth's background or rather her religious background, his Mother could hardly object, he thought as he prepared to go. Religion didn't play a big part in his own life but his family had always given generously to the church and he'd followed the tradition.

Before he left, Caroline threw herself at him and as he hugged her he caught a wistful expression on Beth's face.

# Chapter Four

Beth had been going to Inverbrae House for close on two years. On Mondays and Wednesdays she went straight from school for an hour, and most Saturday mornings were spent there. On good days she walked the three quarters of a mile – there and back – but in rain or darkness a car was provided. Word very quickly spread round the village that Beth Brown was going regularly to Inverbrae House to play with the colonel's daughter. It caused much shaking of heads and not a little jealousy. No good came out of mixing the classes it was agreed, and this would only result in the lass getting ideas above herself.

Having no dealings with the village women, Harriet was unaware of the talk and the undercurrents of resentment, but even had she known it wouldn't have troubled her. She knew that Beth was safe at Inverbrae House and she didn't have the worry of her playing down at the harbour. Mrs Noble, the cook at Inverbrae House, would no doubt have had something to say but the two no longer met. One of the maids collected the eggs.

Beth loved the walk to the Big House. She liked to play make believe and imagine herself the daughter of Colonel Parker-Munro, and with her head held high she would go through the gates and up to the House. Once there a maid would come to escort her along the hallway and then left to a stairway that led to the nursery, now used as a

35

play-room. There she would usually find Caroline and Nanny Rintoul and on the occasions when Caroline was still with her governess, Nanny Rintoul would greet Beth with a smile and tell her to occupy herself until Miss Caroline was free.

It hadn't always been like that. The first few weeks had been a difficult time for everyone but, of course, the colonel's orders had to be obeyed. Eventually the staff began to see that life with Beth there was easier than life without Beth. There were fewer tantrums, Caroline was more biddable and even her health seemed much improved.

Disapproval still came from one quarter. Caroline's grandmother strongly objected to this totally unsuitable friendship but there was nothing she could do about it apart from ignoring the girl.

A heavy mist was coming off the sea, shrouding the buildings and making the October day more like bleak November. The car came to a halt outside 3 Sycamore Lane and the young man came round to hold the door open for his young passenger. Beth was glad that it was Tommy who brought her home and not the real chauffeur because he made her feel shy and awkward. Tommy was fun. He was employed as the head gardener's assistant but acted as a chauffeur when required. Beth knew all about him, he had a special young lady he was walking out with and he was going to marry her one day when he had saved up a lot of money. And after that he was going to save up more money and buy a car and charge people for taking them where they wanted to go.

'Thank you, Tommy,' Beth said politely.

'My pleasure, nothing I like better than having a bonny wee lass sitting beside me,' he grinned, showing even white teeth in a face brown from being so much out of doors.

Beth laughed delightedly at the compliment then left him to run round to the back door.

'I'm home, mummy,' she called unnecessarily as she shut the back door and went through the kitchen and into the living-room. 'Daddy, you shouldn't be home yet,' she said showing surprise at seeing him seated at the fireside.

'Took myself off early,' he smiled.

'No, Beth, you do not leave your coat on the chair, you hang it up in the lobby.'

'I was going to later.'

'Do it now. It must be wet.'

'No, it isn't, it can't be because Tommy brought me home.'

'Even a few moments out in this weather would have made it damp.'

'Do as you're told,' her father said irritably, 'hang it up then come and sit down, we have something to tell you.'

Beth picked up the coat and went out, wondering what the something was. When she returned she noticed that her mother had seated herself opposite her husband with her hands clasped in her lap. Her father looked ill-at-ease as he knocked his pipe against the side of the grate.

'George?'

'No, you do it, you'll make a better job of explaining.'

'Explaining what?'

'I'm about to tell you.' Harriet cleared her throat and suddenly Beth was afraid of what she was about to hear. 'We, that is daddy and I, have been asked by the church authorities to go out to Bengal to work there,' she said slowly and clearly.

'Where is Bengal?' Beth asked in a small voice.

'I thought you would have known that. It is in India and

we shall be going as missionaries, spreading the Word of God,' her mother said, quite unable to keep the awe and excitement out of her voice.

'Will there be a school for me?'

'No, Beth, you won't be coming with us.'

'Why not?' she demanded, her voice rising as she became more frightened.

'The life out there is totally unsuitable for children. We shall be in the back of beyond, going from village to village and living in very primitive conditions. No, Beth,' she said, putting up her hand as Beth made to interrupt, 'it is completely out of the question and there is your education to be considered.'

Beth's eyes were round as she stared at her mother, unable to make sense out of what was being said. 'What about me? What is going to happen to me?'

'Your Aunt Anne and Uncle Fred have agreed to look after you. The likelihood is that we'll be home for a short spell after two or three years.'

'Two or three years?' Beth couldn't believe what she was hearing.

'Yes, we'll just have to wait and see what happens then.'

Beth's face showed her horror. Her aunt and uncle and their sons, Adam and Luke, lived in the Lochee district of Dundee. Her cousins were much older than Beth, Adam had started work in the shipyard and Luke hoped to be taken on in eighteen months. She barely knew them for they disappeared with their friends on the rare occasions when Beth and her parents visited Dundee and they didn't accompany their mother and father on the return visit to Sandyneuk. Beth wasn't too concerned about her cousins or her Uncle Fred. Uncle Fred was quite kindly but didn't have much to say for himself. She remembered her daddy saying that it was Anne who wore the trousers and she couldn't understand what he meant. She couldn't imagine her prim, thin-lipped aunt in trousers. Furthermore, she didn't like her aunt and she had the sneaking feeling that the dislike was mutual.

'I am not going to live with Aunt Anne, I don't like her and she doesn't like me, I know she doesn't.' She was pale with shock and fright.

'That is nonsense,' her mother said sharply.

'No, it isn't, and daddy doesn't like her either and that's why he never wants to go to Dundee. And – and – and,' she sobbed, 'I'm not going to live with her and if you try and make me I'll run away.' One look at her father's face told her that she had gone too far. He'd half risen from his chair.

'You will do as you are told, my girl,' he said sternly. 'In this life we all have to make sacrifices. Your mother and I are giving up a comfortable home to work in very difficult conditions.'

'And doing it gladly,' his wife murmured.

'You want to go,' Beth said through noisy tears, 'you've always wanted to go. It isn't a sacri– a sacrifice when you want to do something. It's just horrid for me and you don't care, you don't care what happens to me.' She didn't have a handkerchief, searched her pockets for one to blow her nose, and silently took the one her mother held out.

Her father was pointing to the door. 'Go to your bedroom this minute and don't return until you are ready to apologise for that disgraceful conduct.' After she'd gone, George had the grace to feel ashamed. The child had spoken the truth. They were about to fulfil their own hopes and dreams and the one to suffer was Beth. It was going to be hard on her.

Beth flung herself out of the door, banging it behind her

and in her bedroom gave vent to her rage and frustration by lying on the bed and thumping the pillow. She wasn't ever going to come out of her bedroom. She would die rather than apologise and her parents were hateful. Forty-five minutes later her stomach was rumbling with hunger and with a murmured apology, she sat down to the meal that had been kept hot for her.

'I knew it wasn't going to be easy,' Harriet said to George later in the evening when they were alone, 'but she is being more difficult than I expected.'

'Pity there wasn't someone else we could leave her with.'

'Well, there isn't and I can trust Anne to look after her properly.' Harriet sounded annoyed, which she was.

'I could go alone, Harriet, in fact it might be better with all the unrest there is just now. It could be dangerous.'

'All the more reason for me going. I'm very aware of the dangers, George, and I intend to be at your side.'

George nodded. Harriet was determined and there was nothing more to be said.

'Don't worry so much about her, Beth will get over the shock. She is a sensible child and she'll make the best of it once she realises that there is no alternative.'

They retired to bed to spend a sleepless night.

Next door their eight-year-old daughter was tossing and turning before sleep claimed her and her dreams were of a figure chasing after her and wearing a witch's hat on her head. When hands caught at her, the face under the hat was her Aunt Anne's.

In the morning Beth looked round her bedroom with a vague sense of terror but the sun glinting through the curtains dispelled some of her fears. In that time between sleeping and waking the dream had faded but she was remembering something else. Her parents were going to India in six weeks and they were leaving her behind with Aunt Anne.

It was a silent and unhappy Beth who got through the schoolday and set off for Inverbrae House. Not today did she imagine herself Beth Parker-Munro, she was plain Beth Brown about to leave Sandyneuk to live in Dundee. In six weeks time she wouldn't be coming to Inverbrae House to play with Caroline, maybe she would never see Caroline or the Big House again. A sob escaped her and she swallowed to hold back the rest. She didn't want to cry any more.

When she entered the playroom, Caroline was on her stomach with a colouring book and crayons. She knew it was Beth but she finished filling in the petals of a daffodil with bright yellow before looking up. The greeting died on Nanny Rintoul's lips and her voice held concern.

'Beth, is something the matter, dear?'

The sympathetic voice was Beth's undoing and her eyes filled. Suddenly she was in Nanny Rintoul's arms being comforted, and with her face pressed to the soft bosom. Sobbing with gasps like retches she blurted it all out.

Nanny Rintoul didn't catch everything but she got the main facts.

'Your parents are going to Bengal?'

'Yes.'

'But you're not going?' Caroline said as she came to stand beside them.

'No.'

'That's all right then, you wouldn't want to go to that horrible place anyhow.' Caroline had no idea where Bengal was but she wasn't going to admit to it.

'It isn't all right, Caroline,' Beth said raising her head

and looking a bit self-conscious, 'I'm being made to go and live with my Aunt Anne and Uncle Fred in Dundee and I'll have to go to a new school and I won't ever see you again,' she ended tragically.

'You can't do that! What about me?'

'Miss Caroline, you have nothing to do with it, dear, if Beth's parents wish her to live with her relatives in Dundee—'

'I'll tell my daddy,' Caroline interrupted rudely, 'he'll think of something and Beth,' her eyes gleamed, 'I've just thought of something clever, you can come here and I'll hide you.'

'How do you think you are going to manage that, young lady?'

'I don't know, Nanny, but there's lots of rooms and you wouldn't tell, would you?'

Colonel Parker-Munro was dismayed at the news but like Nanny Rintoul felt it was none of his business. They would all, with the exception of his mother, miss Beth, but life would go on. That, however, was where he was wrong. His daughter had inherited some of his stubbornness, a little of her dead mother's persuasiveness, and her own brand of behaviour to get her own way.

'Daddy, you must do something, Beth doesn't want to go to Dundee and her aunt is a cruel witch.'

'Now, now, Caroline, that is quite enough!'

She burst into tears, sobbed uncontrollably and had everyone in a state when the sobbing turned to hysterics and the doctor was sent for.

He was annoyed at being called away in the middle of dinner, but hid his displeasure. He couldn't afford to offend the Parker-Munros.

'What caused this?' he demanded. 'The child has been so much better lately.'

'Her friend's parents are going to India and leaving their child in Dundee,' Nigel said worriedly. 'As a matter of fact Beth is in a state herself, she doesn't want to go.'

'Ah, the Browns. Going out as missionaries, I believe. I did hear something of the sort.' He paused. 'I'll leave something to calm her but it's only temporary and she is going to continue to be upset until she gets over losing her friend. In the meantime her health is going to suffer.'

# Chapter Five

Harriet tapped the letter which had arrived with the morning post.

'It's from Anne, she wants us over on Saturday.'

'Count me out, Harriet, I've too much to do,' George said looking up briefly from reading his own mail.

'No, George, you can't get out of it. She particularly asks that the three of us come and I think it is the least we can do,' his wife said reproachfully.

'Perhaps you're right, what time does she want us?' he said resignedly.

'We're invited for high tea so if we get there late afternoon, we'll have time for a talk before the meal.'

Beth knew that it would be about her but she said nothing, just studiously avoided looking at her mother.

Squally showers in the early part of Saturday meant the wearing of raincoats and Harriet carrying an umbrella to keep her good hat dry. She couldn't go emptyhanded and the previous day had busied herself baking a two-pound sultana cake which, with an unusual touch of humour, George declared had risen to the occasion.

It was now carefully wrapped in greaseproof paper and inside a shopping bag. George had on his best blue suit and carried his raincoat. Harriet wore her Sunday charcoal grey costume under her beige raincoat and Beth had on her navy school trench coat over her dress.

Beth's parents had little in the way of small talk and it was usually Beth who kept up a running commentary when they were on a journey. But not today and it was a silent trio who waited for the bus to Dundee and then a further wait for a tram to take them from the city centre out to Lochee.

After leaving the tram it was a short walk to the home of the Farquharsons at number six Walton Street, a street of tenement dwellings of the better class since they had a bathroom.

'Here we are,' Harriet said with forced cheerfulness as they turned into the close. The close and stairs had been painted a bottle green with a thin yellow line to break the monotony. Harriet went ahead and when it came to the curve she kept to the broader side of the stone stairs. She stopped at a door on the second floor, or two stairs up as Aunt Anne would have it. There she waited until the other two had arrived before knocking.

In a few moments quick footsteps were heard, then the door opened.

'Not too early, are we?' Harriet smiled. It wasn't like her sister to come to the door with an apron on over her dress.

'No, of course you're not,' she said untying her apron. 'Just putting the final touches to the table and I knew it was you, heard the clatter on the stairs. Come in.' They followed her – George closed the door – along a narrow lobby to the front room where a fire burned.

Uncle Fred got to his feet. 'Hello, there, nice to see you all again, it's been a long while.'

'You're looking well, Fred,' Harriet smiled.

'Can't complain. The rain kept off for you, did it?'

'Yes, we were lucky.'

'In that case I won't need to hang up your coats, they

46

can go on the bed,' Anne said as she collected the garments over her arm.

'Sit yourself down, Harriet, over here beside the fire. My Beth, but you're getting to be a big bonny lass. In a year or two, George, she'll be having the lads after her.'

'And me after them,' George laughed, 'seems to me that they are courting these days as soon as they finish school.'

'You're not so daft, are you?' Fred turned to Beth.

'No, Uncle Fred.' Beth sat next to her mother. She had on a pale green dress with tiny brass buttons down each side to the waist. It had been let down twice and no amount of pressing with a damp cloth had taken out the marks.

'And this is you for pastures new, George?'

'That's right, Fred, a big change for us all.'

'It's that all right and I don't envy you. Not that I wouldn't mind a change of scenery but that kind of life isn't for me.'

'I should think not,' his wife agreed and with a sound that could have been a sniff as she brought a straight-backed chair forward for herself, 'but some folk just have itchy feet I'm thinking.'

Beth laughed, she couldn't help it, it was seeing the expression on her father's face, one of tolerant amusement with just a trace of anger.

'Neither of us has itchy feet, Anne, we are going on God's work.'

'If that is the way you like to put it. To me it's just an excuse to see a bit of the world.'

There was an uncomfortable silence eventually broken by Fred.

'I know better than to offer you a refreshment, George, but Anne, lass, how about making a pot of tea, it's a long while yet until we get something to eat.'

Anne got up. 'I'll put the kettle on.'

Harriet got up, too. 'Let me help with the cups and oh, that parcel I put down is a sultana cake I made.'

'Thanks, but you didn't need to. I did a baking myself.'

'I'm sure you did,' Harriet said gently, 'but none of it will go to waste with two big strapping lads—'

They were through in the kitchen by now.

'Like filling a bottomless pit, heaven alone knows where they put it all. Away and get the cake then and I'll put it in the tin.'

Harriet went to collect it from the half moon table in the lobby then left Anne to unwrap it. The look of surprise as she did was unflattering, but even Harriet had to admit that she seldom produced anything so professional looking. The cake was perfectly browned and the fruit well distributed.

'Good for you, Harriet, it might have taken a prize at one of your village fêtes.'

'Never do have a success when it really matters,' Harriet laughed as she took cups and saucers from the press. 'How are the lads?'

'Fine. Adam's got himself a lass.'

'Not serious, though?'

'Better not be, as I told him it'll be a long while before he's able to support a wife.'

'And Luke?'

'A worry, that one, clever like your Beth, but can't get himself away from school quickly enough. I'm tired telling him that paying attention to his lessons will get him a better job.'

'He'll maybe change and you've done your best.'

'I have that. Playing truant, too, would you believe? I was up at the school about that, but enough about Luke.

When I was there I mentioned that my niece would be coming to live with me and transferring from Sandyneuk Primary.'

'Any problems?' Harriet asked anxiously.

'None.' She filled the teapot. 'You take that tray with the cups and I'll follow. A few fairy cakes is all I'm putting out, I don't want to put them off their meal.'

A stool, a wooden one that Fred had made, was put beside Beth to hold her cup in case she spilled. The others got theirs in their hand. Harriet and Anne had long since mastered the art of holding cup and saucer in one hand and eating a cake with the other. Their spouses hadn't and looked for a suitable resting place for their cups. Fred chose the mantelpiece and George put his on the floor beside his feet.

'Got your sailing date?' Fred asked as he waited for the sugar bowl to reach him.

'Yes, Fred, everything is arranged as far as possible and we've managed to get a chest to take our belongings.'

'Will it take the lot?'

'No, Anne, we'll have a case as well but that will go with us.'

'What about your house?'

'A bit of luck there, Fred,' George said as he swallowed the last of the fairy cake, 'the landlord belongs to our church and he is to let the house furnished until such time as we know our future plans.'

'Hope it's someone who will look after your things.'

'We'll just have to take that chance. It would cost us a lot to store the stuff.'

'Anything you want, Anne, you must just take,' Harriet said.

'There's a bed that will do the bairn but I've no spare wardrobe for her clothes.'

'We'll get that over with bedding and various other things.'

Beth was looking from one to the other, taking it all in.

'You haven't much to say for yourself, Beth,' her aunt said sharply, 'I've no time for sullen bairns.'

'Beth's just a bit bewildered.'

Beth bit her lip. She'd finished her tea and cake and was sitting hunched up, looking every bit as miserable as she felt. She had to get out of the room and she was going to make the excuse that she wanted the bathroom, though she did not. She looked hard at her mother who thought she knew the signs and indicated by the faintest of nods that it would be in order to excuse herself.

'Excuse me,' Beth mumbled as she got to her feet and was careful not to come against the stool and send the cup and saucer flying. It wasn't very steady.

Once she was safely in the smallest room of the house with the door locked, she looked about her. Of course she had been in it before, but she was looking at it with different eyes. The bathroom was smaller, though not much, than the one at home and the white bath was the same with its clawed feet. The walls were cream painted and a shelf held Uncle Fred's shaving things. How much water would she be allowed? How far up the bath would it come and how often would she be allowed to have a bath? At home it was Tuesday nights and Friday nights and the rest of the time she had, what her mother called, a good wash.

Then she thought about her cousins, those big boys she barely knew and wondered what it would be like living with them. Mummy didn't allow her to lock the bathroom door when she was having a bath in case she fell getting in the high bath or lost her balance getting out – as if she would. One thing she was absolutely sure about was that the door would be locked when she was having a bath in Aunt Anne's house. She wasn't going to let anyone see her without clothes.

How long had she been? She flushed the toilet then wished she hadn't. All of a sudden she wanted to go and she knew it would take ages for the cistern to fill up again. She knew about these things, her daddy had told her.

'Poor bairn, it's no wonder she's quiet,' Uncle Fred was saying once Beth had left the room. 'What an upheaval for her.' He puffed at his pipe, then took it out of his mouth and jabbed it at them. 'While you're busy preparing yourselves to go and do your Good Works, I wonder if you've given much thought to how that lass feels about it?'

George looked distinctly uncomfortable. He was changing his mind about Fred. The man was far from being hen-pecked. Probably he just thought it was easier to go along with his wife than face up to the tirades, unless it was something he felt keenly about.

Harriet was slightly flushed but she spoke in her usual calm way.

'You are being rather unfair, Fred. I can assure you that Beth's welfare has been uppermost in our minds and it is only because we know she is to be well taken care of that we can leave with an easy mind.'

'Oh, she'll be that, I promise you,' Anne said and like the other two was surprised at the outspokenness of her usually easy going husband. 'I'll see that she doesn't get up to any mischief. In fact it'll be real fine having someone to help with the housework.'

'Have a heart, Anne,' Harriet laughed, 'remember she's only eight.' But for the first time she was feeling uneasy.

'Going on nine.' Her small eyes darted to Harriet.

'Don't tell me you still do everything for her?'

'Well, yes, I suppose I do.'

'More fool you. My laddies have their tasks to do. Well, not Adam now that he's working, but Luke has to do his before he leaves for school. High time you had that lass doing something, but don't you worry, I'll take her in hand. I'll see she gets a proper training, I'll take a leaf out of mother's book.'

Being the elder daughter with an ailing widowed mother, or one who pretended poor health, the bulk of the housework had fallen to Harriet when she was about Beth's age. Remembering her own lost childhood and the resentment that had built up in her, she had determined that her daughter's life would be different.

'Anne, I have no objections to her helping a little but I don't want Beth neglecting her homework. And I certainly don't want her over-burdened with household tasks. To my mind mother made little effort to do much herself and was far too hard on us. Perhaps not so hard on you since you were the younger.'

'Did us no harm.'

'I don't agree.'

'The trouble with you, Harriet, is that you never liked housework, to you it was drudgery. Believe me the day will come when Beth will thank me.'

They broke off when Beth came in quietly and took her same seat.

No one could have faulted the meal or the way it was set in the large kitchen which was also the family's living-room. Over the white starched tablecloth was a lace-trimmed teacloth embroidered in a lazy-daisy stitch and the best china was set out.

Fred had been well warned by his wife about grace

being said but she gave him a look in case he had forgotten.

'You'll say grace, George,' Anne said from her place at the top of the table.

Before bowing her head and closing her eyes, Beth caught the tiniest flicker of an eye that could have been a wink from Uncle Fred.

Beth enjoyed the home-made meat roll, it was tasty with no bits of fat to put her off. When asked she took another slice and more potatoes. Once the meat plates had been removed the teacups were filled and passed down the table. Beth's eyes were on the three-tiered cakestand. On it were scones, some plain, some with currants, fruit loaf, gingerbread, a cut-up jam sponge and plain Abernethy biscuits.

George wiped his mouth with the linen napkin then sat back.

'That was a lovely meal, Anne, I thoroughly enjoyed it.'

Anne's putty-coloured skin reddened at the compliment. She didn't understand her brother-in-law, never had, but he was always polite and well mannered. Her own men folk ate heartily but without comment. A clean plate, she supposed, was a compliment of sorts.

'It was lovely, Anne, and you went to a lot of trouble,' Harriet added.

'What about you, Beth, did you enjoy your Aunt Anne's cooking?'

'Yes, thank you, it was very nice,' Beth said politely. She wished that she'd managed to get her thank you in before her aunt asked, particularly when she noticed the slight fleeting frown on her mother's face. But it wasn't her fault, she wasn't allowed to interrupt, and she couldn't get a word in anyway.

★ ★ ★

It was time to go, the coats had been carried through.

'We'll see you at Sandyneuk, there are things we need to discuss.'

Anne nodded. 'I'll let you know which day.' She knew it would be about money for Beth's keep and her clothes. She could say that in their favour, neither of them was mean with money, and spent as little as possible on themselves. Anne felt sure that the authorities would make provision for family left behind. She was wrong there. Money was in very short supply for missionary workers but George and Harriet, living in hope of being selected, had put a certain amount away each month. George was to arrange with his bank to pay a regular allowance to Anne, and perhaps it was guilt at abandoning their small daughter that the amount was so generous.

# Chapter Six

The knock at the front door in mid-afternoon surprised Harriet who was in the kitchen ironing the last but one shirt. She put the iron on its heel and went to answer it. Who could be calling? Then she decided it must be someone from the church.

Harriet wasn't vain, far from it, but just that morning she had washed her hair and being so fine it was flyaway. A quick glance in the kitchen mirror had her patting it in place and hoping it would remain that way. She opened the door and straight away knew who the tall gentleman was. Everyone in Sandyneuk knew Colonel Parker-Munro by sight, but the unexpectedness of seeing him on her own doorstep had Harriet flustered. She hoped it didn't show.

'Good afternoon, Mrs Brown. Do forgive me if this is an inconvenient time to call.' He had a pleasant voice and a nice smile.

'Not at.all, Colonel Parker-Munro, do come in,' Harriet said, opening the door wider.

'Thank you.' He stepped into the narrow lobby and waited until Harriet had closed the door, then she went ahead of him and along to the living-room. The room was reasonably tidy and had a homely, lived-in look. Harriet wasn't too houseproud, she didn't feel bound to put everything back in its rightful place. Books her husband had left lying about remained there until he decided to return them to the book-shelf, and the same went for Beth.

The colonel accepted a chair but remained standing until Harriet was seated. His well-cut tweed suit had seen better days but he wore it with the careless style that only a member of the aristocracy could get away with.

'I'm sorry my husband isn't at home.'

'I am, too. I should have liked to have made his acquaintance but I made a point of choosing a time when Beth would be at school.'

'Then this is about Beth?'

'Yes, Mrs Brown, my visit concerns your daughter and mine. The two girls get on very well together and Caroline is making herself quite ill at the thought of losing her friend.'

'I'm very sorry to hear that,' Harriet said quietly, 'we are not having an easy time with Beth, either.'

'So I gathered.' He was silent for a few moments and Harriet wondered if she should offer to make tea, then decided against it. No doubt the colonel would prefer to say whatever he had to, then depart. 'Beth is to be living with her aunt and uncle in Dundee?'

'Yes, my sister and her husband. They have two boys, older than Beth, but company nevertheless.'

'It must be a worry for you both in case she doesn't settle happily in Dundee?'

'She will in time, I – we – are sure of that.'

'May I make a suggestion?'

She didn't immediately answer but when he raised an eyebrow she nodded.

'Please don't think that you have to give me a reply now. This is something that you and your husband need to consider carefully.'

'I can't answer for my husband but I can answer for myself.'

'Would you consider allowing Beth to live at Inverbrae House under my care, Mrs Brown?'

Harriet was speechless. She didn't know what she had expected but it wasn't this.

'Think about it, Mrs Brown. It would make two little girls very happy.'

'I'm afraid it's out of the question. You see arrangements have already been made and it would be extremely awkward if I were to—'

'Change those arrangements?'

'Yes, it would and my sister would be dreadfully hurt.'

'Is a temporary awkwardness more important than your child's happiness?'

He saw anger in her eyes and hastened in with, 'I'll be completely honest with you, Mrs Brown. Caroline is delicate and highly strung and as a result gets more of her own way than is good for her.' He smiled. 'Beth handles her better than any of us. She doesn't give in to her demands, indeed she doesn't, and I think my daughter quite likes that.' He smiled as though amused. 'Whatever it is I'd say those two are good for one another.'

'Beth can be a determined little monkey and if I am to be honest, too, I know how very much she enjoys the company of your daughter.'

'There is another plus, an important one, I think you'll agree. Beth wouldn't have the upheaval of changing schools, she could continue to attend Sandyneuk Primary and Caroline will, of course, remain with her governess until such time as she goes off to boarding school.'

Harriet nodded. She couldn't deny that it was a big plus. Moving to Dundee and living with virtual strangers would be an ordeal without changing schools as well. Even so she couldn't possibly accept this offer. 'Children adapt very quickly, Colonel Parker-Munro, and Beth would make new friends.'

'No doubt.' He got up. 'May I take it that you and your husband will give the matter some thought?'

'Most certainly, it is very generous of you to make such an offer.' She got up to see her unexpected visitor to the door.

Before departing he held out his hand and she felt the firmness of his grip. 'I do admire you and your husband, it isn't easy to uproot oneself for the unknown.' He paused. 'I know something of that part of India and the difficulties that lie ahead for you. It won't be a picnic.'

'We wouldn't want it to be.' She smiled into his face and the light in her eyes shone out. It was a look the colonel was to remember. 'The dangers have been spelt out to us, and no, colonel, I am not brave, but I do have my faith. He gives his love and protection to those who do His Works.'

He smiled. It was the sort of answer he expected and for a moment he allowed himself to wonder what it would be like to have such faith.

'Perhaps we'll meet again before your departure, Mrs Brown, but in case we don't, let me wish you both a safe journey, good luck – and take the greatest care, won't you?'

'Thank you,' she whispered. The words and the sincerity in his voice touched Harriet and brought an unexpected lump to her throat.

Harriet was in a fever of impatience to tell George about her visitor but managed to wait until Beth was in bed and they were free to talk.

'Sounds wonderful and we would be foolish to turn it down. Indeed, Harriet, I can tell you it is the answer to my prayers.'

She was taken aback. 'You mean—'

'I've been very worried.'

'You didn't trust Anne to look after Beth?'

'On the contrary, she would have looked after her very well but in her own way. You've told me how much you resented the way you were treated as a child and I'm afraid Anne takes after your mother.'

'Perhaps she does, a little, though she doesn't pretend ill health.'

'That's not very Christian, perhaps your mother was genuinely ill.'

'She was eventually,' Harriet said drily.

'Let them have Beth at Inverbrae. She'll be happy and we'll go away with an easier mind, I know I shall.'

'It's more or less settled, then. You're in favour?'

'Absolutely. Aren't you?'

'I suppose so but with some reservations.'

'And what are those?'

'What happens when that child goes to boarding school?'

'That's a long while yet and in the meantime Beth will be well looked after.'

'She'll be neither fish nor fowl as the saying goes. I don't see her accepted as family and I can see Beth becoming very confused.'

'You're looking for difficulties.'

'I'm seeing them. After Inverbrae House how is she going to settle in Sycamore Lane when we come home?'

'She has to adjust now, she'll have to adjust then. Stop worrying.'

'All right for you but I'm the one who has to break it to

Anne and I'm not looking forward to that.'

'Take the coward's way out and write first, then go and see her. And when you do take her a gift, something she'll appreciate.'

'How like a man, but I may just do that.'

On a cold, cheerless late November night, a group of church people stood on the platform at Dundee station to see two of their flock, George and Harriet Brown, leave on the first stage of their journey. Anne and Fred were not at the station, they had said their goodbyes earlier with the coolness that was still there since the change of plans concerning Beth.

In the final weeks Beth had put a brave face on it and kept her tears for her pillow. She was in the bewildering limbo of seeing her parents packing their belongings and of people they hardly knew coming to the house to say goodbye. The initial excitement of hearing that she was going to stay with Caroline at Inverbrae House was fading as Beth thought of the long, long months, even years, without her parents.

Most of all she was dreading the final goodbye and here it was.

As the moment of departure drew near, well-wishers moved back. The last few minutes were for parents and child. One part of Beth's mind noted that her mother wore her old brown coat. She had bought nothing new, declaring that cotton garments were all that she would require in the heat and they could be purchased cheaper out there.

When George lifted her off her feet and held her tight in his arms, she was struggling with her tears.

'You'll be fine, Beth, you'll have a grand time at Inverbrae House.'

Beth gave a muffled 'Yes'.

'Be good, pet.' His voice was rough with emotion. 'Remember us in your prayers as we will remember you in ours.'

'Don't leave me! Please, please, daddy, don't leave me. I want to go with you,' she burst out as she tried to hang on to him.

He shook his head, patted her shoulder, looked helplessly at his wife, then thrust their child into her arms. Harriet was pale but much more composed.

'Be brave, my dearest Beth. We'll write as often as we can and you must write regularly, each week without fail. We'll be longing for your letters and you must tell us all your news, all you are doing.'

'Oh, mummy!'

'Where's my brave little girl?' She dabbed at Beth's eyes with her handkerchief and wiped a tear from the corner of her own. 'Don't forget to send a little letter, a few lines will do, to your Aunt Anne. She is your nearest relative and it is important to keep in touch. Letters from the villages are sometimes held up for weeks and you'll get a whole batch at one time. When you do tell Aunt Anne and I've asked her to do the same.'

Doors further up the train were slammed as the guard showed his green flag. Her parents got on, a porter clicked the door shut after them. They stood at the window. The others moved forward to wave farewell and a man came from behind to lift Beth up. She glanced down and saw that it was Tommy. Then she was waving until her parents disappeared from sight as the train took the curve. As it did Beth felt a strange premonition and a ripple of fear went through her.

Tommy set her down gently. He saw the state she was in and his own feelings were that people weren't fit to be parents when they could go off and leave their only child with strangers.

Beth clung to his hand as though to a lifeline and he could feel her fear as they left the station and went out into the poorly lit street.

'I'm glad you came, Tommy.'

'The master sent me but I would have come anyway.'

'Would you really, Tommy?'

'Wild horses wouldn't have kept me back. You and me is friends and don't you ever forget it, Beth. If you're ever in trouble you come to me, you come to Tommy. Promise?'

'I promise,' she said solemnly.

They were almost at the parked car. 'Is something wrong, Beth?'

'N–no, just – you won't laugh or anything, or tell anybody?'

'I won't laugh or anything or tell anybody.'

'When the train went away I got a funny feeling that something bad was going to happen.'

'Nothing bad is going to happen, Beth.'

'How can you be sure?'

'I'm just sure that's all.' He opened the car door and she got in the front seat then he went round to the driver's side and started up.

'I wish—'

'What do you wish?'

'That I was going back to Sycamore Lane,' she said brokenly.

He patted her knee. 'Put your hand in my jacket pocket and see what is there.'

She brought out a bar of Fry's Cream.

'Break it in two. No cheating, mind, equal pieces.'

She was smiling and sniffing away her tears. 'Will I

break off a bit and put it in your mouth?'

'Have to since I'm not supposed to take my hand off the steering wheel.'

'Like feeding the ducks,' she said, popping a piece of chocolate into his mouth.

'Cheeky.'

The lamps were on at the gate and Tommy drove up to the front door. The house lights were bright and as Beth stepped out of the car the front door opened.

'It's the master himself, Beth, you're getting a royal welcome. Off you go then, can't keep his Lordship waiting.'

'Thank you, Tommy,' she whispered, then she walked up the stone steps and into the house.

'Come away, Beth, I wanted to be here to meet you. Nanny Rintoul has milk and biscuits waiting for you.'

Her new life had begun.

# Chapter Seven

Her eyes were flooding with tears that wouldn't be held back and Beth couldn't find her handkerchief. Giving up the search she wiped at them with the back of her hand.

Nigel Parker-Munro saw the trembling lips, the traces of tears and the misery on the young face and wondered what kind of people could go off to distant lands and leave a child of that age. But, of course, he did know what kind of people they were. He had met them both, and to the colonel, they were a genuinely nice couple, older than he had expected, which made it all the more surprising that the man would give up a steady job and the pair of them forego the joy of seeing that delightful little girl growing up. But then these religious people looked at things in a different way, he supposed.

'Beth, my dear child, come along,' he said, putting an arm round her shoulder. 'Caroline so wanted to stay awake but I'm afraid she fell asleep in the chair and had to be carried to bed.'

'Is it very late?' she asked in a small voice.

'Late for little girls, it's after ten.'

She nodded, suddenly too tired to talk.

'You're dead beat and no wonder, but after a good night's sleep you'll feel very different,' he said kindly.

'Yes.'

He took her hand and together they walked down the

spacious hall, passed a table with brass ornaments that shone like gold in the light and above it was a stag's head. Beth had seen it before but now it took on a menacing appearance. Her cold hand was being warmed in the comforting heat of the colonel's large hand as they went up the thickly carpeted stairs to the first floor and then onwards to the room where Nanny Rintoul, stifling a yawn, was waiting.

'Here she is, Nanny, here is Beth, and a very tired little girl almost sleeping on her feet.'

'I can see that, the poor little lamb, but don't you worry, I'll have her tucked up in bed in no time.'

'Goodnight, Beth, sleep well,' the colonel said patting her shoulder and, before turning away, nodding to Nanny Rintoul.

Nanny helped her off with her coat and Beth saw that a corner of the table had been set with a lace cloth and on it was a glass of milk and a plate of biscuits.

Beth had eaten a half bar of Fry's Cream with Tommy and she had no appetite for milk and biscuits. She took a small sip of the milk that was slightly warm and put down the glass.

'Don't you want it, Beth?'

'No, thank you, I don't want anything.'

'Just your bed, that's what you want. Come along then.'

Beth got up and it seemed as though they were walking along an endless corridor before Nanny Rintoul stopped and opened a door.

'This is your room, Beth.'

The child was too exhausted to notice her surroundings. She hadn't known where she was to sleep but at this moment she didn't care where it was. All she wanted was to get her head down on the pillow.

The choice of bedroom had come as a shock to Nanny

Rintoul but she was informed that it was the one the servants had been instructed to prepare. She couldn't even recall the last time it had been used as a bedroom. At one time she remembered that there had been plans to turn it into a storeroom for surplus furniture but nothing had come of it. The reason for the bedroom remaining largely unused was the tall, very old oak tree which blocked out much of the daylight.

Beth undressed and put on her nightdress which had been folded neatly and placed on the pillow. Then with a small sigh she slipped between the sheets and almost at once the dark lashes fluttered then settled. Nanny Rintoul waited until she heard the steady breathing before tiptoeing out and going along to her own room.

Perhaps it was the strange bed, but whatever it was Beth had a disturbed night with confusing dreams. In them she was running alongside the slow-moving train and pleading with her mummy to open the door and let her in. But she wouldn't and just kept on telling Beth to get back. For one brief moment their fingers touched and they were united, then the train gathered speed, tore them apart and in a blackened cloud of smoke it disappeared into the distance leaving Beth alone and frightened in the dark, deserted station.

When Beth opened her eyes it was quite dark with just a faint light coming through the curtains and outlining the heavy Victorian furniture. Why, she wondered, was everything so strange? It wasn't her own bed she was in, this wasn't her bedroom. Where was she? Her fuddled brain could make no sense of it. Perhaps if she closed her eyes then opened them again she would be in her own room in Sycamore Lane. She tried it but when she opened her eyes it was still the same. Then she was brought fully awake by the noise, a swishing, mournful sound followed by a sharp tap! tap! tap! that made her jump and her eyes widen in terror. What was it? There it was again and her flesh crept. Wildly her eyes sought for the door, then she was out of bed and wrenching at the knob until she got herself out and into the passage. Running along the dimly lit passage the sounds seemed to follow her and she opened her mouth to scream but no sound came. When it did it was a thin screech but enough to alert Nanny Rintoul who was a poor sleeper, and she moved with all the speed of which her old limbs were capable.

She wasn't to know it but the sight of that white nightgowned figure coming out of the door so terrified the child that she was close to collapsing.

'Beth! Beth! It's only me, Nanny Rintoul,' the woman said, keeping her voice as calm as she could, but at her approach Beth was flattening herself against the wall, shaking her head from side to side. 'There's nothing to be afraid of.'

The soothing voice eventually got through the terror and Beth let herself be held until the shaking lessened.

'You must have had a bad dream, dear.'

'No, it wasn't! You've got to believe me, it wasn't,' Beth cried as she held tightly to a hand that felt as dry as old parchment. 'I heard it, I know I did.'

'No, Beth,' Nanny Rintoul said in her no-nonsense voice, 'you've had a bad dream.'

'I'm not going back there, I'm not.' Beth was becoming hysterical.

'Hush, dear, or you'll waken the household.'

Another time and the sight of Nanny Rintoul in her night attire, her hair in a long plait down her back, and her mouth all sucked in, would have had Beth giggling. And as if this had just occurred to the woman, she took Beth's arm and guided her along to her own sitting-room and sat her down on a chair. Then with her back to Beth she went over to the bedside table and took something out of a china dish. When she turned round again her mouth was filled with large, very white teeth. The woman hadn't felt the cold until now and she gave a shiver. Her warm, pale pink robe was on the back of the door and she took it down and put it over her nightgown. Her feet were already in pink, fluffy slippers. Beth's feet were bare.

The child was slowly recovering but desperately anxious to have Nanny Rintoul believe her.

'Honestly, it wasn't a dream, nanny,' she said, her eyes imploring to be believed.

'You've certainly had a bad fright and your poor little feet must be cold.'

'They don't feel cold.'

'We'll go along together, and don't worry, you'll be quite safe with me.'

Reluctantly and fearfully Beth allowed herself to be led back to her own room. The door was wide open just as she had left it in her headlong flight but more of the daylight was getting in.

'No! No! Please don't shut the door, leave it open,' Beth cried as her frightened eyes raked the room.

'You can see for yourself, Beth, can't you, that there is nothing, absolutely nothing, to be afraid of,' Nanny Rintoul was saying when Beth clutched at her arm.

'That's it again! Listen!'

They both stood and listened to the gentle taps, then a flurry of more urgent taps. After a moment or two Nanny Rintoul left Beth and, going over to the window, drew back both curtains.

'Look, child, that's all it was, the branches of that tree knocking against the window. The wind must have got up during the night.'

'I'm – is that all it was – I'm very sorry,' Beth said looking shamefaced and feeling very foolish.

'No need to apologise, bairn, anyone hearing that in the middle of the night would have been alarmed.'

'You're not just saying that, are you?'

'No, I am not.' She paused. 'You've no need to feel ashamed.' And to herself she added, it's the one who put you in that bedroom who should be ashamed.

'Did I waken anyone else, do you think?'

'Couldn't have, else they would have been here. I'm a light sleeper, that's why I heard you.'

'I'm glad it was you.'

'So am I,' Nanny Rintoul smiled. 'Now into bed with you and sleep for what is left of the night.'

'What is the time?'

'I couldn't say for sure, probably between half past five and six.'

'Will you manage to sleep? My mummy—' her voice faltered, 'my mummy said she could never get over again if she wakened in the middle of the night.' The tears overflowed. 'I don't like this bedroom and I wish I was back home.'

'Now, now, we'll have no more tears, and didn't you say you liked coming to Inverbrae House?'

'That was when I could go home at night.'

'Well, Beth, my dear, you're here now and you'll just have to make the best of it.' Then, thinking that was rather harsh, she softened it with, 'Once you start getting letters with foreign stamps on them your school friends are going to be very envious.'

Beth smiled at that. It would be nice to show off a little but she decided there and then that she wouldn't give any of the stamps away. She would keep the stamps and envelopes with the letters and when mummy and daddy came back they would be pleased that she had kept their letters. Maybe Colonel Parker-Munro would let her have a big box to keep them in because if she got one every week she'd have a big pile.

Nanny Rintoul checked that Beth was asleep, then got up stiffly from her chair and made her way back to her own room, knowing there was little hope of any further sleep for her. Anger had taken away any chance of that. She couldn't recall a time when she had been so angry. Years in this household had given her the freedom to speak out and she would use it – oh, yes, she would use it.

'Are you trying to tell me that Beth was given that bedroom at the end of the corridor?' the colonel said disbelievingly.

'That is exactly what I am telling you, Colonel Parker-Munro.'

'But why? What was wrong with the spare bedroom beside my daughter's?'

'Nothing that I know of, but apparently the servants were given orders to prepare that room for Beth.'

'Who gave those orders may I ask?'

'The Mistress,' she said, looking him fully in the face.

'Thank you.' The Master of Inverbrae House turned on his heel, his lips set, his eyes furious.

'How could you, Mother? How could you be so cruel to a small child?'

She was sitting in the back sitting-room with the morning sunshine streaming in. There was no heat in it but a log fire gave off plenty of warmth. She wore a long mauve skirt and matching twin-set and on the small table beside her was a cup of tea and the untouched morning papers.

'Do sit down, Nigel, you look quite menacing standing

there with that look on your face. And stop making such a fuss about something so trivial.'

He sat down. 'I wouldn't describe scaring the child half out of her wits as trivial. Had that been Caroline it could have sent her over the edge.'

'Caroline is a nervous, highly-strung child and that girl is most certainly not.'

'That girl as you call her was already distressed after the ordeal of seeing her parents off to India.'

'What right have those people to expect others to shoulder the responsibility for their offspring?' she said in clipped tones.

'That is not the point, though you should remember, Mother, that Beth was to be living with her aunt and uncle and I persuaded, yes I had to use persuasion on them to allow Beth to come here and be a companion for Caroline.'

'If we had all ignored a few tantrums Caroline would have got over the separation.'

'A view not shared by the doctor.'

'What does Dr Grieve know about it? The man panics far too easily.'

'You were concerned yourself.'

'Of course I was. With Caroline it is difficult to know how much is genuine. That young lady knows how to get her own way.'

'You may well be right but personally I wasn't prepared to take the risk.'

She nodded. 'I can understand that. But to get back to what this is all about, the accommodation in question is a guest bedroom, not a servant's room, and I imagine a great deal better than the girl has been accustomed to.'

'When was it last used as a guest room? Everyone knows that it gets precious little daylight with that huge oak blocking the window. Perhaps we should consider having it ruthlessly lopped or taken away altogether.'

She drew herself up. 'Indeed and you will do no such thing, not as long as I am Mistress of this house you won't. The girl must have been over-wrought to imagine something outside the window. Had it been on the ground floor there might have been some excuse.'

'She was in quite a state according to nanny and it is the unknown that frightens us all. Aren't you ever afraid, Mother?'

She didn't answer, just looked at him coldly. In truth she was afraid, afraid of what the advancing years might bring. Her own mother had spent her final years in a wheelchair and now she seemed to have the same symptoms, the pain and the stiffness.

'We all have our secret fears, Mother,' he said gently.

'Even you?'

He laughed. 'Even me.'

It eased the tension and lightened the atmosphere.

'I find that hard to believe.'

He paused. 'Incidentally, you should know that Beth's parents insisted on money coming from their bank account for Beth's clothes and other necessities.'

'A gesture.'

'No, I don't think it was, more like a need to feel that they were making a contribution.'

'Surely you didn't accept—' she laughed, 'this small sum?' She made it sound ridiculous.

'To Mr and Mrs Brown, Mother, that money must have meant a great deal of saving and sacrifice. I happen to know that most missionaries live a hand to mouth existence, money is a very scarce commodity,' he said reprovingly.

She had the grace to look ashamed. 'Yes, I'm sorry,

that was unforgivable of me.'

He stood up. 'I must go. And, mother, I have personally instructed the servants to transfer Beth's belongings
to the bedroom next to Caroline's.'

She inclined her head. 'Hardly your place, but since you
have taken it on yourself there is nothing more to be said.
Before you go, ring that bell if you please. This tea must
be stone cold.'

# Chapter Eight

Among the range of emotions Beth went through were a deep sense of shame, and humiliation that her parents could so easily abandon her. Other parents didn't leave their children so hers, she decided, hadn't loved her enough. Then there was the memory of her night of terror when she had made such a fool of herself. She had expected to be embarrassed, instead of which she had received a lot of sympathy and understanding and, most important of all, no one had laughed.

Settling in at Inverbrae House was difficult, it was all so different from what she had been used to, but after a few bewildering weeks she learned to adapt to this new life and began to feel happier. A routine had been established and twice a day Tommy did what came to be known as the school run. Beth took to school with her a packed lunch of sandwiches and fruit prepared by Mrs Noble, the cook. She ate them in the classroom with the other children who lived too far away to get home.

As for school, it was not without its difficulties, and Beth quickly found a change in the attitude of those she had once considered her chums. They weren't exactly unfriendly, just no longer natural with her. She had become different, they imagined a change in her. For one thing no one else had parents who were missionaries in India, a country that conjured up for them all kinds of mysteries. Letting them see her foreign stamps might have helped but she wasn't going to do that now.

What really set her apart was that she should be living at Inverbrae House, that mansion, and living as rumour had it as one of the family. Only occasionally was she asked to join in their play and she was frequently to be seen standing apart and alone, very much as her mother had once stood outside the school waiting for her small daughter.

The arrival of the posh vehicle at the school gate had caused some excitement and there was a rush of children to examine it. Beth would not forget in a hurry that first time she stepped out of the car. When play stopped and curious eyes followed her she went pink with embarrassment. A few shouted, 'Look, it's Beth Brown!' Another voice called out 'swank' and others took up the chant.

'Don't mind them, pay no attention, Beth,' Tommy said when she told him later.

'I don't like being called a swank,' she said unhappily.

'Of course you don't.'

'I'm not one, am I, Tommy?'

'You are not and if any of them bothers you just you tell them that Tommy here will sort them out.'

'You'll give them a good talking to?'

'More than that,' he said darkly. 'Tell you what, Beth—'

When he stopped she said, 'Tell me what?'

'How about if I just come to the gate when it's raining?'

'Where would you wait?'

'In Sea Braes. I'll let you off there in the morning and pick you up at four o'clock.'

'I used to go home to Sycamore Lane by myself.'

'Inverbrae House is a good bit further on, Beth, and I

have my orders to get you to school and back, and that's what I'm going to do.'

With most of her pupils having reached the age of nine, Beth's teacher began giving out homework. Beth did hers in the schoolroom at Inverbrae House and Miss Mathewson offered her help should it be required.

'Do you mind if I see your schoolwork, Beth?' she asked one day.

'No,' said Beth handing the books over.

Turning the pages the governess nodded her head a few times, then looked up.

'Very good, Beth, and extremely neat. Come and see Miss Caroline.'

Caroline made a face but went over and, after looking at the pages of neat figures and the red tick beside each, she turned angrily to her governess.

'Matty, why can she do these sums and I can't when Beth is only at a silly little village school?' she demanded.

'It is not a silly little village school,' Beth said indignantly. 'And anyway, it can't be silly if I can do harder sums than you.'

'Now, now, you two, that is quite enough of your bickering!' the governess said sternly. 'As for you, Miss Caroline, you are perfectly capable of the same standard, but unlike Beth you are not prepared to work.'

'Well I am now, I'm not having her beat me,' she said and burst into tears.

'Caroline, don't cry. You're better at some things than me,' Beth said generously, 'and I'm better at some things than you,' she felt obliged to add.

The crying stopped. 'You are not allowed to be better than me in anything.'

It was all getting too much for the governess and since it was her time off she left them to argue. Actually she was delighted, feeling the victory was hers. Miss Caroline was a spoilt child, a difficult and at times rude pupil, but she was far from stupid. This was what was needed, a bit of rivalry, a bit of competition from Beth. From now on she saw life as being easier, particularly with the old mistress who blamed her for her grand-daughter's lack of progress.

'Why am I not allowed to be better than you in anything?'

'Because you're not.'

'That's not an answer, you've got to give a reason.'

'I don't have to but I will. It's because – because one day I'll be a lady.'

'So will I.'

'No, you won't, you can't ever be one.'

'Why not?'

'Because you're poor.' She paused. 'My grandmama doesn't like you.'

'I don't care, I don't have to like her, she isn't my grandmother.'

'I told her you were my friend and she said you weren't a suitable companion and if you don't know what a companion is I'll tell you. It's something like being a lady's maid.'

'I am not your maid,' Beth said furiously.

'Not that kind of maid, you are a silly thing, Beth. The queen has a lady's maid but she doesn't have to do any housework.'

'What does she do?' Beth was curious to know. Being lady's maid to the queen would be a very important job and you would get to live in a castle. She smiled to herself. A castle would be even bigger and better than Inverbrae House.

Caroline was tiring of the subject, she didn't know much about it anyway.

'I can't remember exactly, but I think she follows the queen about and tells her what to wear. I'll ask my grandmama again and then I'll tell you.'

Beth was finding out things about her friend that she didn't much like. Things that she hadn't known when she was just going back and forward to the Big House. Like how spiteful Caroline could be if she thought that Beth was getting too much attention. But worst of all in Beth's eyes was that Caroline wasn't above cheating at board games.

'Why does Caroline always have to win?' Beth asked Nanny Rintoul one day after her friend had flounced out of the room banging the door behind her.

The old woman sighed. She was getting too old for all this noise and bother and maybe she should think again about making her home with her widowed sister, risk though it was. It wouldn't be easy for either of them, there would be skin and hair flying as her old father used to say after one of their many quarrels. Still, neither of them would have the energy for that now and in the loneliness of old age they would be company for one another. She turned her attention back to the child.

'Did your parents allow you to win at games?'

'Only if I really and truly won, otherwise it wouldn't be winning, would it? I never cheat, nanny. My daddy said that cheating is wrong and that if you do it your – your sins will find you out.'

Quaint little thing, Nanny thought with amusement. Obviously she'd been brought up very strictly with a good understanding of what was right and what was wrong.

'No, I know you wouldn't cheat, Beth, and Miss Caroline doesn't mean to, either.' She felt a need to protect her charge for, difficult though she could be, she had a lot of affection for the motherless girl.

Beth was like a dog with a bone, she wouldn't give up and worried at it until she was satisfied.

'Then why does she? I told her if she didn't stop cheating she would go to a bad place when she died.'

'Oh, dear me, that was a dreadful thing to say and you shouldn't have.' She paused and shook her head. The words spoken so freely had shocked her. 'Miss Caroline's daddy is partly to blame, he always used to let her win.'

'My daddy wouldn't ever do that.'

'No, I'm sure he wouldn't,' Nanny said drily. She didn't like the sound of Beth's father one little bit. 'It's wrong, no denying that, but you have to make allowances for Miss Caroline. You have a mother, Beth, though she isn't with you just now, but Miss Caroline's mother died when she was a tiny baby and she never knew her.'

Beth looked crestfallen. 'I shouldn't have said those nasty things to her but I'll go and tell Caroline that I'm sorry.'

'No, don't do that, better leave well alone. She forgets very quickly.'

'I'll forget too and be especially nice.'

'That's what to do, Beth, forgive and forget. We all make mistakes and Miss Caroline needs a good friend like you. Don't give in to her all the time, that wouldn't be good for her, but be kind.'

'Because she's delicate?'

'She's not so delicate now but she isn't a big strong girl like you.'

'I don't want to be big and strong, I'd rather be small and – and dainty.'

Nanny smiled. Strange how so few of us were satisfied with the looks and figure we were given, but this child beside her had a God-given gift. She was lovely and in a few short years would become a tall, strikingly beautiful young lady with young and not-so-young men beating a path to her door. Caroline would have her admirers, too. She was a pretty little thing, but could she ever be sure of whether her admirer's interest lay in herself or her position and money?

Beth loved her new bedroom. It was next to Caroline's and was a bright room with cream, embossed wallpaper and pretty, flowery curtains. The same material had been used for a bedspread and in place of the heavy Victorian furniture which had added to the gloom in the other bedroom, the furniture here was in a lighter wood. Her clothes hung in the wardrobe and her underwear in the drawers. Gradually new clothes were appearing and some of her older garments were missing.

She asked Caroline about it but she had merely shrugged, saying that she didn't know anything about it. When the colonel came unexpectedly to find out if the bedroom was to her satisfaction she had been overcome with shyness.

'Beth, you don't have to be shy with me. I want you to feel comfortable and be able to tell me if anything is troubling you or making you unhappy.'

She smiled and bit her lip.

'You like your bedroom?'

'Oh, yes,' she breathed, 'it's lovely.'

'As nice as the one in Sycamore Lane?' he teased.

'Better, 'cept for one thing.'

'Oh, dear, then I had better hear where we have fallen down.'

'My daddy made me a bookcase, he made it all by himself out of a box and I kept my books in it.'

'That was very clever of your daddy but I'm afraid my talents don't stretch to that. Do you like reading, Beth?'

'Yes and I like all kinds of stories.'

'Then I'll know to give you books for your birthday and Christmas.'

She blushed with pleasure and decided this was the moment to ask him before she lost her nerve.

'Colonel Parker-Munro, I've got some new clothes and a brush and comb set and I don't know who I have to say thank you to.'

'You don't have to thank anyone, Beth. Your parents left some money with me to buy whatever you needed.' In truth that money was an embarrassment and the colonel had been relieved when the bank manager had suggested transferring the money directly into an account in Beth's name.

Beth looked at him, only half believing. She supposed they must have if the colonel said so, but she was old enough to know that the dresses, petticoats and knickers were much nicer than mummy could afford to buy.

'Missionaries don't get paid a lot of money, they get hardly any,' she said bluntly.

'That is very true,' he said seriously. He would have to go carefully here. 'Beth, your parents did leave money for your requirements but I would be very sad if you denied me the pleasure of buying you the occasional little gift.' He smiled. 'I'm told all little girls like pretty clothes.'

She was standing beside him, looking up and smiling and at the same time going over the side of her shoe.

He pointed. 'If you do that too often you'll have a good shoe and a badly shaped one.'

'I don't even know when I'm doing it.'

'Then I must remind you since you are in my charge.'

Beth liked the sound of that, it made her feel that she belonged.

'I won't let myself forget, and I won't do it, and thank you for buying me things, Colonel Parker-Munro.'

He wished he could do something about the name. She got round it pretty well but it was a mouthful. In the army he had been 'Parky' and had no desire to hear himself called that again. He would have to come up with something, even if it was Uncle Nigel. He thought of his mother's face when she heard it and her reaction, and grinned.

'Before I go, tell me, are your parents well?'

'Yes,' she said eagerly. 'I didn't get a letter for a long time then I got three all at once. Mummy says they are always busy, there is so much to do and they are starting up a Sunday School for the little boys and girls.' She took a deep breath and went on. 'Daddy only adds a little bit at the end. He doesn't mind the heat but he says mummy doesn't like it, it makes her tired.'

He smiled down at her. 'They must long for your letters. Do you write often?'

'Every week. Mummy made me promise to do that even if sometimes it is only a little letter.'

That very next day when she returned from school there was a mahogany bookcase against the wall. It had three shelves and some children's books were already on one of them.

Beth was dancing with excitement and rushed to find Caroline and tell her.

'A bookcase, is that all?'

'Well, I think it is lovely.'

'Those books are old,' she said dismissively, 'daddy had them when he was little. Don't you have any of your own?'

'Yes, I do, that's them on the floor. I haven't had time to put them away.'

'Is that a Bible?'

'Yes.'

'Do you still say your prayers every night?'

They were both remembering when Caroline had barged in and found Beth on her knees beside the bed.

'Yes, I do,' she said defensively. It was true that she did still say them, but only when she was in bed. She felt guilty about it but it was better to feel guilty than have Caroline poke fun at her.

'You only say them because your daddy is a minister.'

'He isn't a minister, he's a lay preacher, and now he and mummy are missionaries.'

'Same thing.'

'No, it isn't.'

'What is the difference, then, and I bet you can't tell me.'

That was a poser for Beth and something she hadn't questioned herself. 'I think, and I only think, it is because ministers are paid and they get a free house called a manse and a lay preacher doesn't get any money and that is why they have to take another job.'

'When you pray what do you say?'

'I ask God to bless mummy and daddy and keep them safe, and I pray for other things, but secret things and I can't tell you them.'

'Do you pray for me?'

'No.'

'Why don't you? I'm your friend.'

'Only sometimes you are. You can pray yourself.'

'I don't want to.'

'You won't go to heaven.'

Caroline seemed scared. 'My mummy's in heaven and I

84

want to go there when I die. I've got lots of photographs of her so I know what she looks like. Will you tell me what to say?'

'Yes, only you have to think of things yourself.'

'I don't want to now, I'll tell you when.'

But she never did.

Before Beth fell asleep she would sometimes think about her parents and wonder what they were doing. The letters she got were full of the good works they were doing and the great need there was in that vast country for missionaries and helpers. Unfortunately, neither of them had the knack of bringing that faraway land to life. Beth wanted to know about India, not the good works her parents were doing, but what the natives were like and what they did. In her own letters she tried to ask but got no satisfactory answers. If they made the country sound exciting she might want to go out there when she was big, but by that time her mummy and daddy would be very, very old.

In nearly every letter she was asked if she was sticking in at school and being good and she was getting tired of it. They added at the end that they were missing her and she wondered if that were true. She couldn't honestly say that she was missing them – not now. The life she had shared with them in Sycamore Lane was fast fading, and when she tried to remember their faces she couldn't. Sometimes that worried her, but not very much.

# Chapter Nine

Beth raised her eyes from the letter she was reading. 'Honestly, my mother's writing is getting absolutely awful, I can hardly read this,' she announced to anyone who was listening.

Caroline's grandmother had dropped the book she was reading, her mouth was half open and she was snoring gently. Caroline was on the couch with her legs tucked under her and flicking over the pages of a magazine which had been left at one time by one of her father's lady friends.

The colonel lowered his paper. 'Maybe your mother is busy, Beth, and just scribbles a few lines when she gets the chance.'

'But she always takes such a pride in her writing and look at it.'

He put out his hand for the flimsy sheet, meaning to do no more than glance at it, but he looked again and was careful to hide his concern. He was remembering Mrs Brown's writing from early correspondence and recalled it as being very neat. This, unless he was very much mistaken, was the writing of someone who could barely hold a pen. The thin scrawl told its own tale.

'Not very clear, Beth, I have to agree. When did you notice a change in the writing?' he asked, keeping his voice casual. He didn't want to alarm her.

'The last few letters weren't very good,' she said after pondering a few moments, 'but not nearly as bad as this.' Then she added spiritedly and with a mischievous grin. 'I'm going to say something about the writing in my next letter because if I had sent writing like that to India there would have been plenty said. I wouldn't have got away with it.'

'Do you hear from your father?'

'Not actually from him, but I hear about him. My mother' – he noticed that she now referred to her parents as mother and father – 'wrote to tell me that he's travelling between the villages, but my mother has decided to stay in one place.'

The girls were now eleven years of age. Caroline had grown but was still small for her age, her health had improved and she was less delicate looking. Beth was a good head taller than her friend, and the long thin legs were becoming shapely. She held herself well and moved with an unconscious grace.

For some months Mrs Parker-Munro had been saying that it was high time that Caroline joined them for dinner in the dining-room. The child, she said, could be excused after the dessert. Her son was in total agreement, and left to him it would have happened sooner. The problem had been, and still was, Beth. The old lady didn't want Beth to dine with them and Nigel refused to exclude her.

'How ridiculous can you get, Nigel! Anyone but you would see how out of place it would be,' his mother said, trying to contain her anger. 'And I am sure the girl would be a lot more comfortable if she were to continue to have her meals with Nanny Rintoul.'

'I've said it before, Mother,' he said patiently, 'and I'll say it again. Beth is a guest in this house and she will be treated as one.'

'And may I ask,' she said sarcastically, 'how long this state of affairs is to continue? Do her parents have any intention of coming home? They must be more than due leave or whatever the term is.'

'I imagine they will be coming home in the near future.'

'What then? Do they go off again and leave their daughter?'

'That I don't know, Mother, we'll just have to wait and see what happens.'

'All highly unsatisfactory.' She played her trump card. 'Miss Mathewson tells me that Caroline has been working extremely hard and, in her opinion, has now reached the entrance standard for Rowanbank. When Caroline goes off to boarding school, what then? Have you asked yourself that?'

'Yes, Mother,' he said wearily, 'it is giving me cause for concern but I'm sure something can be worked out.' He left her and went along to his study. Much as he loved his mother he found her a trial at times.

Behind his desk and comfortably settled in his leather chair he pondered the situation he had got himself into and wondered what could be worked out. His own fault and no one to blame but himself. He had been too anxious to keep his small daughter happy and had given no thought to the problems that might arise in the future. They had arrived and he had to find a solution.

His mother was right. Beth was becoming a problem and would be a bigger problem if and when Caroline left Inverbrae House for boarding school. If the parents were to remain abroad then Beth would have to join them, he was quite sure that arrangements could be made for her education. In the event of it not being possible then Beth would have to take up residence with this aunt and uncle in Dundee. He did feel a fleeting sense of guilt about that, knowing as he did that Beth had little affection for her aunt, but dash it all he was horribly and awkwardly placed.

Beth was looking unhappy and feeling extremely nervous.

'For goodness sake, Beth, what a state to get into about nothing,' Caroline said scornfully. 'My grandmama won't eat you.'

'She would if she could.'

'More likely to spit you out once she'd chewed you to bits.'

At the same moment this struck both girls as enormously funny and they dissolved into fits of laughter.

Nigel, passing on his way out, smiled. It was good to hear Caroline so happy and, though Beth was now causing him problems, he couldn't but bless the day that he had persuaded her parents to allow her to come to Inverbrae House. How much easier it would have been for all concerned if his mother had taken to the girl. Nigel was wrong there. His mother did not dislike the girl, in fact she admired Beth's spirit and her quiet thoughtfulness. When she dropped a book, Beth immediately picked it up whilst Caroline would have stepped over it. If her shawl slipped from her shoulders it was quietly adjusted. It shamed her to think that she seldom said thank you, but it was important to get Beth away from Inverbrae House before it was too late. Thinking herself disliked and unwanted, she would be more inclined to go to those relatives she should have been with in the first place.

Although she would only admit it to herself, the girl had done her grand-daughter a power of good. Miss Mathewson had taken the credit and she supposed some of it was her due. However, the old lady was well aware of the real reason for Caroline's sudden thirst for knowledge as she

put it. It was that she couldn't bear to have Beth, her
social inferior, shine while she trailed behind. She smiled.
Caroline was a Parker-Munro and already showing the
family pride.

The reason Mrs Parker-Munro wanted to see the back
of Beth was for a reason that would never have occurred
to her son, indeed it would not have occurred to the
majority of males. She was seeing the situation a few
years ahead. Already Beth was blossoming and very
soon she would have the figure and striking good looks
that would turn heads. Caroline, pretty little thing
though she was, would never do that. Far better to
separate them now than run the risk of Beth being
accepted into the same social circle and spoiling Caroline's chances. In her day the door would have remained
firmly shut to anyone of low birth, but in this modern
age one could never be sure.

The table was beautifully set, the crystal sparkled and the
silver shone. Beth took her place opposite Caroline and
wished herself anywhere but where she was. Her hands in
her lap were shaking so much that she had to lock her
fingers together. Perhaps she would have had more confidence if she had been aware of the attractive picture she
made in her pale green dress with its cream lace collar and
matching cuffs. Caroline's dress was blue with white tiny
flowers on a cream background. It had a wide skirt and a
tiny v-neck and had been her own choice. The neckline
was wrong and she would have looked so much nicer with
a Peter Pan collar.

The colonel in a dark suit sat at one end of the table and
his mother, looking very stiff and regal in burgundy and
black, at the other. Wine glasses were set in front of the
adults and a glass to hold water was in front of the girls.

Beth felt annoyed with herself and, as Caroline had so forcefully said, there was no reason at all for her to be nervous. Certainly her table manners were every bit as good as Caroline's. It was those old, unfriendly eyes that upset her and they would keep resting on her as though willing her to make a mistake.

At a signal from the mistress, the maids began to serve the soup and when they withdrew the colonel and his mother exchanged the day's news. Caroline was occasionally brought into the conversation by her grandmother but Beth hadn't uttered a word and no one had spoken to her. To give the colonel his due he didn't address his daughter either. As a young boy, he had always been silent at the table, as had his brother. Only the parents spoke with occasional remarks about forthcoming events, but largely meals were eaten in silence. The old master had appreciated good food but not idle chatter.

Beth finished her soup and placed her spoon on the empty plate ready for it to be removed. At this point the wine was poured and the girls had their glasses half filled with water from a jug.

Beth was just congratulating herself that she'd got through the soup course without mishap when her cuff caught her fork and sent it to the floor. She had been well taught by Nanny Rintoul and she knew very well that dropped cutlery, or for that matter dropped anything, remained where it fell until the meal was over when it would be picked up by a maid. In her nervousness Beth forgot and bent down to retrieve her fork. The moment her finger touched the silver Beth was aware of her mistake but it was too late, the damage was done. The disapproving silence terrified her and it was only broken by a small giggle from Caroline.

'I'm – I'm so sorry, Mrs Parker-Munro,' Beth stammered, crimson-faced, 'I forgot, I didn't mean to pick it up.'

'But you did,' the old lady said coldly and her meaning was clear. Beth wasn't fit to be at the dining-room table. The old lady signalled to a maid who quickly brought a fork from the sideboard and placed it in its correct position.

'No harm done, Beth,' the colonel muttered, but she felt that she had let him down.

'What a very stupid thing to do,' Caroline said later when they were alone.

'I know, I don't know why I did it,' Beth said wretchedly.

'Neither do I. It's something I would never have done, it simply wouldn't have occurred to me.' She paused. 'That is the difference between us, Beth, I just know what is correct and how to behave and you have had to learn it all.'

Maybe the others had forgotten the incident but it took Beth longer to get over what she thought of as her disgrace and it was several days before she was relaxed enough to enjoy the food placed before her.

# Chapter Ten

Beth fingered the letter feeling a curious reluctance to open it. The writing was her father's and she wondered what she was afraid of. Putting a finger under a small unsealed part of the flap she opened it carefully, then took out four sheets of paper in her father's large and well spaced writing. She began to read.

*My dear Beth,*

*Your mother is ill and unable to write to you herself. As you know the heat out here has been a great trial to her, as have the primitive living conditions, although she wouldn't admit to finding it so and has battled on bravely.*

*Now, I am afraid, she is much too weak to be of assistance here. Everyone has been kind and helpful but nursing an invalid takes up so much time and their talents are desperately needed elsewhere. Your mother recognises this. The doctor says that her condition is worsening and that she must return home. It is out of the question for me to accompany her, my place is here, and the Lord has directed that I remain.*

*Fortunately, and there is always an answer to our prayers, a Mr and Mrs Deuchars are returning home in a few weeks – I haven't an exact date as yet – and they are to look after your mother on the journey. I personally feel that she will recover her health once she leaves India.*

*And now to the arrangements, Beth. With your mother returning home always a possibility, I set the wheels in motion in good time. The family occupying our home in Sycamore Lane have been given notice to vacate it. Your Aunt Anne should receive a letter about the same time as you get this. I have asked her to get the house in order for your mother's return and I know that she will be happy to oblige. You, Beth, must give your aunt every assistance.*

*You will inform Colonel Parker-Munro yourself of the contents of this letter and I know that you will be so happy to return to your own home and welcome your dear mother. She has missed you very much and is longing to see you again.*

*I trust you, my daughter, to put aside all else and give your love and support to your mother. Of course I am not forgetting your schoolwork and during school hours someone from the church will take over the responsibility.*

*from*

*Your loving father.*

Beth was glad that she was in her bedroom and alone. She couldn't face questions just yet. She was just too numb with shock and quite unable to take it in at the first reading. This time she read it very slowly. Her mother was ill and she felt dreadful about that, but she wasn't dangerously ill. Didn't her father say that it was mainly the heat and once she was away from India she would quickly recover?

The awful, shameful truth was that she didn't want to go back to Sycamore Lane. She no longer thought of it as her home, yet she would have to return, she had no choice in the matter. How could she fit in there again after life at Inverbrae House? She wanted to weep. She should be so happy yet she had never felt so miserable, so mixed up.

The letter had come with the second post and on her return from school she had picked it up from the hall table. It was now a quarter to five and more than likely the colonel would be in his study. She would go there now. Once she would have been shy to do so but now she was more relaxed with Colonel Parker-Munro. In any case, the sooner he knew the contents of the letter the better. Wistfully she hoped that he would be as unhappy to see her go as she was going to be to leave.

She rapped on the door with her knuckles.

'Come in.'

Beth, still in her school outfit, went in and over to the desk, the letter in her hand.

'It's you, Beth,' he smiled. 'And what is troubling you if trouble it is?'

Suddenly the lump in her throat was too big to swallow and silently she handed him the letter.

'You want me to read it?'

She nodded.

The colonel read the letter and felt an overwhelming relief that his problem should be this easily solved. Of course he was sorry about Mrs Brown's illness, but he'd known others who had had to come home after a few months in that awful heat and Mrs Brown had put up with it for three years.

Her eyes searched his face but she couldn't tell what he was thinking from his expression.

'Don't worry too much about your mother, Beth, because as your father says, once she is on her way home her health should improve.'

'Yes,' she said listlessly, disappointed that he hadn't

immediately said how much she would be missed.

'Your aunt lives in Dundee, doesn't she?'

'Yes.'

'Perhaps not too easy for her getting back and forward to the house to get it in order for your mother. Do remind me nearer the time and I'll get Mrs Murdoch to arrange for two of the maids to do what is necessary. That will relieve your aunt and, of course, yourself, of some of the preparations.'

'Thank you.'

Didn't he know or couldn't he guess that after having everything done for her, she wouldn't know where to begin?

Smiling, he handed her the letter, then dropped his eyes to the papers on his desk and picked up a pen. She was dismissed but in the kindest way, or so he would believe it to be. She put the pages back in the envelope, got up and left the study.

On hearing the door click shut the colonel put down his pen and thought about that letter. To him it was clear that Beth's father would be relieved to see his wife depart for these shores. No doubt her illness worried him but not sufficiently to let it interfere with his work. He would put it stronger and say that George Brown was in his element, feeling himself to be indispensable.

Then he thought about Beth. Judging by the look on her face she was none too happy to be going back to her own home. Still, he thought, that was only to be expected. Three years was a long time in a child's life and he could remember the state she was in when her parents had gone off and left her. She had got over that and she would get over this. All it needed was time. Give it that and she would settle back to the life she had once known.

He got up, his concentration gone. Perhaps he should

go and see his mother and give her the news.

'Yes, of course I'm relieved, dear, very relieved and I imagine that you are too?'

'Yes, I am, especially now that we expect Caroline to go to Rowanbank.'

She smiled.

'It also saves a lot of soul searching on my part.'

'Soul searching?' Her brows shot up.

'We have rather made use of Beth and, quite frankly, the thought of sending her to live with an aunt for whom she has so little affection was making me feel decidedly uncomfortable. This, I have to admit, has come at a very opportune time.'

'You dear boy,' she smiled fondly. 'You can live with yourself again?'

'Just about. Actually, I'll quite genuinely miss the child when she goes, which is something you won't.'

She frowned. 'Strange though it may sound to you I shall miss the girl. Having admitted to that, it is better for all concerned that it is the parting of the ways. We have Beth to thank that Caroline is a different girl and I'm sure she'll settle happily and enjoy boarding school. Her cousin Ruth is there after all and—'

'Ruth is two years older, Mother, and I remember enough about boarding school to know that senior pupils are most definitely not interested in taking juniors under their wing.'

'That is as maybe but I am sure that she'll settle.'

'That's absolutely awful, Beth,' Caroline said, close to tears. 'Of course I am sorry about your mother but it'll mean I'll hardly ever see you.'

'Mattie said that you'd be going off to that school—'

'Rowanbank. Some time in the future I may have to, but I don't think Mattie will be in too much of a hurry to see me go. After all she'll be out of a job, won't she?'

'Unless she has something else lined up?'

'Dreadful, these changes,' Caroline said glumly. 'Nanny has been threatening for ages and ages to leave us and go and live with her sister. I never believed her and now it's actually going to happen.'

'Be honest, Caroline, you don't really need a nanny.'

'I know that but it will be strange without her. I mean she has always been here and I suppose she has been a sort of mother to me. Which reminds me of something I was going to talk to you about,' Caroline said in the quick way she had of moving from one subject to another.

'What was it?'

'It was told to me in confidence by my grandmama but I'll tell you.' Her voice dropped. 'She thinks that daddy is serious about a certain lady and she is absolutely delighted.' Caroline kept looking at Beth, waiting for her reaction.

'I hope it is Mrs Cuthbert.'

'It is and I do like her.'

'That makes a change,' Beth said laughing.

'I like Jenny better than the others because she doesn't treat me like a little girl and fawn over me in that sickening way. Keeping in with daddy, that's all it is.'

Beth looked surprised. She had been mistaken about Caroline, she wasn't so easily taken in after all.

'You wouldn't mind if you got Mrs Cuthbert for a step-mother?'

'That really is funny, Beth. I never expected ever to say yes but I think it would be rather fun to have Jenny as my step-mother.'

They were both silent for a few moments, each thinking

of what the future might hold.

'Sometimes I wish that things would stay the same,' Beth said wistfully.

'Can't, though.'

'No, I know that.'

'Still, I know what you mean,' Caroline said in a small voice. 'We've got used to each other and what I am going to miss most is telling you things that I know won't reach another soul.'

'When I go I'll miss Inverbrae House an awful lot but you most of all, even though sometimes you make me very angry.'

'Do I?'

'You know you do but I suppose you can't help it, you've always got all your own way.'

'Not now, I don't always get it now. You like my daddy?'

'Yes.'

'You'll miss him?'

Beth nodded.

'Not grandmama, though?'

'Sometimes I nearly like her.'

'Sometimes I think she nearly likes you, too.'

'Because I'm going away.'

'Maybe it is. Grownups are strange.'

Beth couldn't have agreed more. She pondered then said, 'When I'm grown-up and have children I won't be strict with them. I'll let them know that I love them and I'll give them lots of hugs.'

'Didn't you get cuddles from your parents?'

'Hardly ever.'

'Why not?'

'Don't know.'

'My daddy cuddles me because he loves me. Not so

much now because he says I'm getting a big girl which I am not.' She giggled. 'I expect he cuddles and kisses Jenny now.'

Old Mrs Parker-Munro had all but given up hope of seeing her son remarry, and thus it was with a good deal of surprise and pleasure that she saw him look at Jenny Cuthbert in that unmistakable way. The young widow who had recently come to this part of the country had bought and settled into a house a few miles away from Inverbrae House. Discreet enquiries had satisfied the old lady that Jenny was of good family, not quite the equal of the Parker-Munros, but perfectly acceptable.

Attracting women had never given the colonel any trouble but most of them bored him after a while. That he was considered a catch he could not fail to know. A spare man, particularly when he is a handsome widower, is much sought after to make up the numbers at a dinner party. Many a fading beauty who had lost or missed out in the marriage stakes had looked at the colonel with hope in her heart.

In the colonel's case one could add that he was under forty, wealthy and owned an estate. None of this made any impression on Jenny Cuthbert. She was charming and polite when in his company but neither encouraged nor discouraged him, and it was this very indifference that set her apart. She intrigued him as no one else had and aroused feelings that he had not experienced since he lost his beloved Margaret. He had made love to women more beautiful than Jenny, women who had satisfied a physical need. But that was all it was – his feelings weren't involved.

Jenny was quite tall with a slim figure and small, firm breasts. Her eyes were light hazel, her hair, with a hint of a wave, was auburn and cut short in the style of the day. She had a smooth complexion and her face, though it wasn't beautiful, had something compelling about it. Other men saw it, he could tell, and jealousy was a new and not very pleasant experience for Nigel. Often he would find himself wondering about her late husband and what he had been like.

Proposing marriage to Jenny was constantly on his mind but he was desperately afraid of being refused.

'Pay attention, Beth, you'll have to direct me from here,' Tommy said as they approached the Lochee district of Dundee.

Beth had been lost in her own thoughts and looked up quickly.

'Follow the tramcar, that would be best,' she said.

Tommy was amused. 'Fair enough until it stops, what then?'

'I've only ever come by tramcar,' Beth said worriedly, 'go slowly and I'll try to remember where to turn off.'

It wasn't the correct turn-off, she knew it the moment they were in the street and she apologised to Tommy.

'Not to worry, we'll get back on the main road and if we get lost you can always get out of the car and ask.'

She didn't have to, the next turn-off was Walton Street and Tommy stopped the car outside number 6.

'She'll be at home?'

'My aunt? Oh, yes, she doesn't go out a lot.'

'How long will I give you? Half an hour or nearer the hour?'

'Make it about an hour then come up if you want, Tommy. Aunt Anne will give you a cup of tea, she's all right that way.'

'I won't, thanks all the same. Just you come down when

you're ready and you'll find me waiting.'

'How will you pass the time?'

'Take myself for a wee dander. First, though, I'll wait until I'm sure you've got in.'

Beth got out of the car, went in the close and climbed the stairs. Perhaps she should have let her aunt know that she was coming but it had happened so quickly. The colonel's suggestion had just come the previous night that Tommy should drive her to see her aunt and discuss the arrangements for her mother's homecoming. Beth wondered at the haste, it was almost as though he were hurrying her departure. Her mother wouldn't even be on her way home yet and the sea trip took a long time. She was beginning to feel very let down. Apart from Caroline, and sometimes her friend didn't seem too bothered about her going away, she didn't feel that anyone would miss her. Had it something to do with her, was there something wrong, that made people not love her enough? Her parents had left her behind and her mother was only returning home because of poor health. Life at Inverbrae House would go on as before and in a very short time she would be forgotten. Caroline would make friends at her school and those friends would be acceptable to Mrs Parker-Munro. Beth felt very depressed.

Her knock brought hurrying feet and the door was opened.

'Bless my soul, it's you Beth. Come away in.'

'Hello, Aunt Anne.'

'Why didn't you let me know you were coming? Not that I'm often out, I'm not the gadding about type, but this could have been one of the times and then you would have had a wasted journey.' She shut the door and Beth followed her aunt into the kitchen. The ironing cloth was covering the table and the flat iron was on its heel. There was the smell of damp clothes ready to be ironed.

Beth waited to be invited to, before sitting down.

'You've caught me in the middle of ironing, not my usual day, but I didn't want too much for Monday. Take off your coat, no need to act like a stranger, though that is what you are.'

Beth took off her coat with its little fur collar and her aunt took it and put it on the back of a chair.

'Right bonny coat, fine piece of cloth, too.'

Beth nodded. She knew what her aunt was thinking and she was right, her parents could not have afforded to give her a coat like that.

'Managed the journey by yourself?' she said as she prepared to clear the table.

'Please don't stop the ironing, Aunt Anne, we can talk while you do it.'

'No doubt we could but it isn't my way. There's time enough for this when you've gone. I was asking if you managed the journey on your own?'

'No, I got a lift in the car.' She knew that she sounded apologetic.

'Of course, keep forgetting that you're a toff now.'

Beth looked at her quickly but her aunt was smiling.

'Is Uncle Fred well?'

'Nothing coming over him. My, but you're growing into a fine big lass,' she said looking Beth up and down. 'Good to you, are they?'

'Yes.' Beth nodded vigorously, feeling she hadn't sounded sure enough.

The table was cleared, the iron put beside the fire, and the cloth folded. Her aunt did everything very quickly.

'Your Uncle Fred is at the timber merchants looking for bits of wood to make something he has in mind. You won't know but Adam is getting wed and they've managed to get a house. It's not much I'll grant you and I would have liked something better for them. Wanted them to wait awhile but not them, they were in a hurry to get married.' She looked sharply at her niece as though she had said something she shouldn't. 'Not that kind of hurry, she's a nice lass is Morag, a real sensible kind.'

'Have they set a date?'

'Not yet. Morag's folk want to make a splash of it and take St David's rooms for the reception, but it isn't that easy getting a suitable date with it being so well booked in advance.' She smiled. 'I'm happy enough about the delay. It lets them put a wee bit more by them, and more important to me your ma might be home by that time. I'd like it fine if she was well enough to attend, and you too of course.'

'She wouldn't want to miss it.'

'No, she wouldn't and I think that's the kettle boiling. I'll make a pot of tea, you won't be in a hurry to get away?'

'Tommy said an hour.'

'Plenty of time then.'

Beth took the cup of tea and a currant bun. 'Thank you.'

'Still haven't a lot to say for yourself, have you? Thought you would have had with all the posh training.'

'I'm sorry, Aunt Anne, I don't mean to be rude and you've been very kind, it's just – I don't know – I feel so—'

'Unsettled?'

'Yes.'

'Not to be wondered at, feel a bit that way myself. It's the not knowing what to expect. Knowing Harriet I'd say she was in a bad way.'

'You mean very ill?' Beth said, looking anxious.

'No, no, not very ill, that was stupid of me to alarm you. The heat would take it out of her but in her last letters I thought she sounded depressed, as if things hadn't worked out the way she had expected them to. But then that is perhaps just my imagination. What did you think?'

'I just thought that her writing was terrible and I wrote to tell her that.'

Aunt Anne laughed heartily. 'Did you now, Harriet wouldn't take kindly to that. Nice writing she always did, got a few prizes at school for it. I did notice but thought it was your mother in a hurry to get it off, maybe someone waiting to take it to the post. Never mind, once we get her home to her own house we'll nurse her back to health.'

'Yes.'

'You've got mixed feelings because you're going to miss that life you've got used to.' She paused. 'Even so, you've never felt yourself one of them, have you?'

'Is there anything wrong with people trying to better themselves if they want to? And I have been made welcome,' Beth said, stung.

'Bettering yourself is one thing, lass, and good luck to those who try and succeed, but trying to be accepted into another class that's a different matter altogether. Mostly it ends in heartache and resentment. Not that I am suggesting for a moment that those Parker whatever-you-call-them folk haven't been good to you. It has suited them to be. After all, they wanted a companion for their daughter and the lass had taken a liking to you.' She paused to take Beth's cup and put it on the table. 'What is to become of the girl?'

'Caroline will be going to boarding school.'

'There you are then, worked out very nicely for them hasn't it? Very convenient indeed to have your mother coming home at this time. They must be relieved. After all, it stands to reason they wouldn't want you in the house and their daughter away at school.'

What her aunt said made sense and Beth had the horrible feeling that it was all true. She hadn't wanted to accept what must have been clear to everyone else. She had served her purpose and the colonel would be relieved to see her go.

Beth wanted away before her aunt said any more. She got up, anxious to be gone and hoping that Tommy was waiting. 'I'll need to watch my time, Aunt Anne,' she said as she reached for her coat.

'Run downstairs and bring the lad up, he'll be glad of a cup of tea and I'll make fresh.'

'I knew you'd say that, Aunt Anne, and I asked Tommy before I came up but he said no, he had to get back.'

'Doesn't matter. You've got the road now so come again.'

'I'll try.'

'Make it a Sunday and you'll see your Uncle Fred, he'll be fair disappointed at having missed you.'

# *Chapter Eleven*

He had to read it again and yet again. He couldn't
believe it, the news was just too awful to take in. How
could he tell that child? How could he break such
dreadful news to her? Yet somehow he had to find the
words to do it. There was the aunt in Dundee, of
course, but because Beth was in his care the church
authorities had notified him.

The need to tell someone was great and he went along
to the sitting-room where he knew his mother would be.

She looked sharply at him. 'Nigel, is something the
matter, you look a bit white?'

'Yes, Mother, something is very much the matter, read
that.'

'My spectacles – over there on the cabinet.'

He got them for her and she put them on.

Her face was shocked. 'Oh, my dear, this is absolutely dreadful!' She shivered. 'What a wicked world we
live in.' From over her spectacles she looked at her son.
'That poor, poor child.' Then she clutched at his hand.
'You must not be the one to tell her, Nigel. This will
have to be broken to her gently and it needs a woman to
do that.'

'Considering your treatment of Beth, Mother, don't
tell me you are suggesting yourself?' he said with mild
sarcasm.

She had the grace to look ashamed but even so her eyes were stormy. 'Men can be very stupid and shortsighted on occasion.'

'Explain my stupidity to me.'

'No, Nigel, I won't for the simple reason that you wouldn't understand.'

'Whatever I wouldn't understand, Mother, you are not the person to tell Beth.' He frowned. 'What a pity Nanny Rintoul isn't still with us, they got on so well together, and she could have done it and saved me,' he said as he turned away.

She stopped him at the door. 'If you are determined to take on this responsibility, Nigel, do be careful. Eleven is a very impressionable age.' Her voice grew weary and she closed her eyes.

'I'll be as gentle as I can, Mother, but she must be told at once.'

'Yes, I can see the need for that. The news will soon get out.'

'My relationship with Beth is good. I'll manage.'

'Very well.'

Beth was surprised and a little apprehensive to get a summons to the colonel's study and she went along quickly. She knocked at the door and a voice immediately said, 'Come in.'

Beth went in and closed the door behind her. She smiled, then grew uncertain when he didn't return it. He looked very grave.

'Sit down, Beth,' he said gently. When she did and her dark eyes rested on him he wondered if the study was perhaps the wrong place to break such news. The sitting-room would have been better, less formal, and he could have made sure that they wouldn't be interrupted. Too late for that and he could see that he had already alarmed her.

He was clearing his throat and Beth couldn't wait any longer. She had to ask.

'Is it about my mother, Colonel Parker-Munro, is she worse?' Beth said anxiously. There must be something very wrong when the colonel was taking such a long time to tell her.

He hesitated then said, 'Beth, my dear, it is my painful duty to tell you that I have just now received very bad news—' It was so formal but how else could he say it?

'It is my mother – please tell me, is she very ill?' Then, fearfully, as a terrible thought struck her, 'She's not—' She couldn't bring herself to say more, just looked over at him with frightened eyes.

'There has been a terrible tragedy—' She saw him swallowing before going on and Beth wanted to scream. Why was he taking so long about it? 'A terrible massacre—' He stopped, appalled at himself, he hadn't meant to use that word though that was what it had been.

'A massacre,' Beth repeated the word wonderingly. A massacre was what happened in a war. What was the colonel talking about?

'An uprising is the expression I should have used, Beth, and a number of the missionaries and their helpers have been killed.'

Her mouth went dry. 'My father—'

She saw a look of great sadness cross his face. 'Beth, my dear child, both your parents are dead.'

Her eyes, like saucers, never left his face and Nigel shook his head, took the handkerchief from his pocket and wiped the perspiration from his hands. His mother had been right, it wasn't a job for a man and he was making a mess of it. The minister, now why hadn't he thought of him before? The man was trained for such tasks, he should have been sent for.

Beth felt very strange as though she were floating and everything unreal. What was it the colonel had said? That her parents were dead, but that couldn't be. Her mother was coming home, maybe on her way by now.

'Beth, I can't tell you how sorry I am.'

'They aren't dead, it isn't true. You have made a mistake.'

'Beth, I'm afraid it is true, I have had official word from the church authorities.'

'Why would anyone want to kill them? Who did it?' She had spoken very softly as if to herself.

'Pardon?' He hadn't heard what she said.

'Who killed my mother and father?'

'The very people they were trying to help.'

'But why?'

He raised his hands, then let them fall on the desk. It was a question that would remain unanswered.

'My mother was wrong, she said that God would look after them.'

'Your mother said that to me too.' He remembered the way Mrs Brown's eyes had shone when she said it and hoped that her end had been swift and painless. 'We none of us understand how these things happen, Beth, but we have to believe that it is all for a purpose.'

'Would you like to know what my father would have said?'

'Yes, Beth, I would.'

'He would have said that it was His will.'

'They had their faith, Beth, they wouldn't have been afraid. And they wouldn't have suffered, it would have been very quick.' If only she would cry, scream even, but this calm acceptance, the flat voice, were unnatural and he was growing increasingly concerned.

The strange, floating sensation was going but now the walls seemed to be closing in on her and Beth had a desperate urge to get out of this room. She saw the colonel get up from his chair and come round, and when his arm went round her shoulder she got up and pushed him away.

'Leave me, I don't want anyone,' then before he could stop her she had run from the study. She heard him calling her name but paid no heed. In her haste to reach her own room she almost knocked into old Mrs Parker-Munro. She, too, called out but Beth ignored her and ran on until she was in her own bedroom and the door shut. Then she threw herself on the bed.

Mrs Parker-Munro had been unable to settle and, seeing Beth's fleeing figure, she hurried to the study as fast as her protesting limbs would allow. Her son was at the door.

'Don't scold, Nigel, I was too upset to stay away.'

'I'm not scolding,' he said wearily. 'Come in and sit down, you look all in.' She let him help her into a chair.

'Just tell me.'

'She was very calm, mother, much too calm for my liking. Then suddenly, I wasn't prepared for it, she bolted out of the door. I saw she was heading for her room.' He shook his head and pulled his fingers through his hair, a habit he had when he was bewildered and worried. 'All I was doing was trying to comfort her but she didn't want that.'

'Phone for Dr Grieve, Nigel,' she said urgently, 'I don't like the sound of this at all.'

'I'll phone right away and Caroline will have to be kept away.'

'I've spoken to Caroline and told her that Beth's

parents have been killed in an accident and that the kindest thing would be to leave her alone with her grief.'

'Thank you.'

The middle-aged family doctor came very quickly.

'Just terrible! Unbelievable! I had heard the news before you telephoned. By this time it will be all round Sandyneuk and I think everyone's thoughts will be with that bairn.'

'Will she be all right?' Nigel asked worriedly.

'In time. That is the great healer, and remember she hadn't seen her parents for three years. If I know the lass she'll put a brave face on it.' He paused, closed up his bag, then looked with concern at his elderly patient. 'A tragedy like this affects everybody and I'd suggest, Mrs Parker-Munro, that you try to get a good night's sleep. Take two of your pills.'

'Never mind me, what about Beth?'

'She wants to be left alone and it is better at this stage to give in to her wishes.' He nodded thoughtfully. 'I'd leave her for an hour or so then try her with some food. Come to think about it, it would be better for a maid to take it in, then she won't have to talk unless she wants.'

'Are you leaving something to help her sleep?'

'Yes, but she may not require it. Children are not like us, sleep overtakes them no matter what.'

'One feels so helpless,' the old lady said.

'It's times like these when relatives can give support,' the doctor said. 'There is a need in us all to be able to talk about the dead with someone who knew them.' He smiled sadly. 'That is why grieving relatives, who never see each other from one year's end to the next, gather round at funerals and talk in hushed tones of the dear departed.'

That brought a smile. 'How very sad and how very true,' the old lady said.

'Beth has an aunt in Dundee, she will have been notified,' the colonel said, 'her only close relative as far as I know, but there is no strong bond there.'

'Well, as I say it is just a suggestion.'

The door opened and Beth saw a tray being placed on the table but, before the maid could look over at the bed, Beth had closed her eyes and was feigning sleep.

She couldn't eat, the thought of food made her feel ill. In any case she didn't deserve kindness. This was her punishment. As her father had often said there was no hiding anything from God. He would know that deep down she hadn't wanted her mother to come home. She had wanted them both to stay in India and let her go on living at Inverbrae House. As to boarding school, she didn't believe that Caroline wanted to go and if she made a big enough fuss she wouldn't have to. Caroline always got her own way.

Her thoughts were feverish as she began to toss about on the bed. Because she had these wicked thoughts God had let her parents die and she didn't believe what the colonel said, that they wouldn't have suffered. He couldn't know and he was only saying that to make it easier for her to accept.

Had they been killed together or had one seen the other die? Who would have been the braver? Her mother, she thought, and didn't know why she thought that.

In her mind's eye she began to see black figures with evil eyes and spears in their hands. She saw them stealing towards the camp then – then – the horror was too much for her and she had to get away, had to get out and far away from Inverbrae House. She looked at the clock and

115

her eyes registered that it was well after six. A good time to make her escape and if she was quiet and careful no one would see her go.

From its hanger in the wardrobe Beth got out her school coat and fastened the buttons. Her scarf and gloves were on the shelf but she ignored them. Then she stood for a moment listening before opening the door and checking that no one was about. No one was, all was quiet, and she ran lightly along the passage. In a few minutes she was down the stairs with the only sound the click of the outside door as she let herself out. The cold damp of the November night touched her face but she felt nothing. The grey dark that she so disliked held no fear for her, instead she found it comforting since it would hide her from searching eyes. Keeping well into the side of the drive and brushing against the shrubs, she hurried until she was clear of the gates, then she adopted a steady walking pace. She knew where she was going.

The smell of the sea came to her and she breathed deeply as she made her way along the cobbled path that twisted its way down to the harbour. When she was little it had been her father's favourite walk. Together they would stand and watch the waves crashing against the harbour wall and if the sea was angry, huge mountains of frothy foam would boil over and spray them, forcing them to step back. The shrieking of the gulls as they swooped and dived both terrified and excited her but with her hand held firmly in her father's, she had felt safe.

For three years she hadn't seen them, hadn't greatly missed her parents, but she had known where they were and she had their letters. Now they were gone and she would never see them again. As her aunt had said, those at Inverbrae House had been kind because it had suited them to be. But that couldn't go on much longer, she didn't belong there and Caroline didn't really need her now. Well, perhaps for a little longer, but what after that? What was to become of her? With no money coming from her parents for her keep, Aunt Anne wouldn't be keen to have her, especially since she was so useless. She walked on – down – down – down – towards the sea.

'Daddy, I've looked and looked and Beth isn't anywhere.'

'She has to be somewhere, Caroline.'

'She wouldn't have run away, would she?'

'Don't be silly.' Worry was making him irritable and it showed in his voice. 'Why would she do a thing like that?'

'Well, she isn't anywhere in the house,' Caroline pouted. There was no need for daddy to use that tone of voice to her. 'I've looked, the maids have looked, everybody has looked.' She almost added, 'so there'.

There was no doubt that Caroline was deeply and genuinely concerned for her friend but she was enjoying the excitement, too. It was even worse about Beth's parents than she had thought. Her grandmama had wanted her to believe it was an accident but she knew better. She'd heard two of the maids discussing the tragedy and one had told the other that Beth's mother and father had been murdered by natives with long spears.

A full hour had gone before the search for Beth had got under way. An alarmed maid, coming from Beth's bedroom, had rushed to report Beth's disappearance to the housekeeper. Mrs Murdoch had gone along to check for herself that Beth was, indeed, not in her bedroom and finding it so had straight away reported the matter to the colonel. He in turn ordered a thorough search of house and grounds.

The grey-black November darkness was hampering the

search of the grounds and outhouses but a dogged, determined small band of searchers continued with the task until they were satisfied that the child was not in the grounds of Inverbrae House.

A very worried Tommy saw his employer on the steps of the house and went up to him. The colonel looked at him questioningly and Tommy shook his head.

'Nothing, sir, but could I make a suggestion?'

'Of course, if you have the least idea of where she might be then out with it.'

'Beth and me talked a lot, sir, and she used to tell me about the walks she took with her da. It was always down to the harbour they went.'

'The harbour! Dear God! Not there!' the colonel said as a real, crawling, dreadful fear gripped him. The child had acted strangely and in the state of mind she was in, there was no knowing what she might do. 'Come on,' he said urgently, 'into the car, I'll drive and you keep your eyes skinned.'

The car shot away before Tommy had the door shut. Driving down that road in this weather would be hell and good driver though he was, Tommy was glad it was the colonel who was at the wheel. With the fine mist clinging to the windows the windscreen wipers were of little use, and the car lights didn't give much assistance either. Neither man spoke as the car hurtled round the narrow, steep, twisting road. One concentrated on the driving, the other was looking for a lost, frightened child who could be anywhere.

The colonel was particular about his cars and the tiniest scrape or mark on the bodywork would result in a very severe reprimand. Judging by the scraping noises a great deal of the paintwork must be damaged by now, Tommy thought, but no mention was made of it.

'Sir!' Tommy just stopped himself from grabbing his employer's arm. 'There's something there, I'm sure of it.'

'Where, for God's sake?'

'Down at the bottom. If you could let me out, sir, I'll go and investigate.'

'Stay where you are, I've got us down this far, I'll manage the rest. In any case, I'll need to get to the flat before I can turn.'

'It is her, it's Beth,' Tommy said, trying to keep the excitement out of his voice. He longed to jump out of the moving car and run to Beth but years of obeying orders held him back.

'I'll go to her. You take the car back, Tommy, and watch how you turn it, enough damage has already been done,' he muttered as he put on the brake and got out. Tommy slid over to take the wheel. 'Be as quick as you can and get the news to everyone that Beth has been found, then come back for us.'

'Down here?'

'Good God, no! We'll walk up the Braes and get you there.'

Tommy felt a surge of anger as he watched the tall figure of the colonel walk away. He had wanted to be the one to find Beth and bring her back but typical of that lot to take all the credit, yet he had been the one to think of the harbour.

The shifting of the stones under the colonel's feet made plenty of noise but the figure sitting on the low wall gave no sign that she had heard. So still was she that she could have been fashioned in stone, and the lapping of the water against the harbour wall added an eeriness to the scene.

A damp cold was worse than an icy chill, he thought, and got through to the very bones. The child must be frozen. He would have to be careful how he went about this, the last thing he wished to do was to scare her. If he sat by her for a little – she must be aware that someone was there, he thought, as he sat down on the cold, wet wall and felt the icy cold seep through his heavy coat. He waited for Beth to turn her head but she made no move to see who it was, just kept on staring ahead. Down here it was less dark, he noted, or perhaps it was just his eyes becoming accustomed to the darkness.

'Beth,' he said softly. He wanted to touch her but was afraid to. It was as though the Beth he knew wasn't there and this was a small stranger. He tried again. 'Beth, dear, you must be very cold, come back with me and get a hot drink and then off to a warm bed. You'll feel much better then.'

Had she heard? He didn't know.

'It was my fault,' she said tonelessly.

'What was your fault?'

She turned to him then, a white face with anguished eyes but without a trace of tears. She gave no answer to his question.

'Give me your hand, Beth.'

Obediently, she let him take it. It was icy.

'Come along, dear, we must get back. Everybody is very worried. You shouldn't have run off like that.'

'Is everybody angry with me?' She asked the question but didn't seem concerned.

'No, Beth, no one is angry with you. Everybody was just very worried, but Tommy has gone ahead to let them know that you are all right. By the time we walk to the top of the Braes, he'll be there with the car.'

'Tommy?' she said surprised.

'Yes, it was his suggestion that you might be down here.'

She gave a ghost of a smile. 'Tommy is my friend and I

120

told him about the walks I used to take with my father.' She was chatting now and he was glad, though the sing-song voice wasn't Beth's. 'My mother would never let me play with my friends at the harbour.'

'Very wise, too, it is dangerous.'

Hand-in-hand the man and the girl walked up the steep brae. She was calling him 'daddy' now and he was afraid to correct her.

How strange it was, she thought, that she should be with her daddy, yet it was Colonel Parker-Munro who was doing all the talking. Weariness was making her drag one foot in front of the other and, picking her up, the colonel carried her the last few yards to where Tommy was waiting.

# Chapter Twelve

Before the car had stopped, the door to Inverbrae House was opened and a blaze of light shone out and down the stone steps. To avoid the sudden influx of cold air into the hallway, Mrs Parker-Munro stood well back and held a restraining hand on Caroline. Behind them was the governess ready to take charge of her pupil once the old lady had satisfied herself that no real harm had come to Beth.

The housekeeper went forward and the colonel, thankful that his part was over, gave Beth into her care. Mrs Murdoch was visibly shocked to see the state Beth was in.

'Poor wee lass, you look frozen to the bone, and is it any wonder and you out on a night like this.' She took Beth's arm. 'Come along with me, dear, I've had two hot water bottles heating your bed and we'll soon have you nice and cosy,' she said soothingly.

'Daddy, why can't I go to Beth, she'll want me, I know she will.' Caroline was just a little bit peeved at all the attention Beth was getting.

'Not just yet, Caroline, Beth isn't well enough.'

'When will she be?'

'Very soon I hope.'

His mother spoke. 'Nigel, you had better change out of your wet clothes, we don't want you down with a chill.'

Nigel laughed. 'Honestly, Mother, you make me feel like a ten-year-old.'

'At that age you had enough sense to do what you were told,' she said tartly. Caroline giggled.

'Don't worry, Mother, I'm just going up and, speaking of chills, you shouldn't be out here.'

'Jenny arrived a short time ago. She heard the news and said she just had to come over.'

'Where is she?'

'In the drawing-room. She said she would prefer to wait there and I'll go along now and keep her company.'

'You do that and I'll be with you shortly,' he said, feeling a warm rush of pleasure at the thought of seeing Jenny.

The brightening of his face didn't go unnoticed, and the old lady was well pleased. She could hear wedding bells.

Wearing a light grey suit and feeling more like himself, Nigel joined the ladies in the drawing-room. There was a roaring fire that gave out a good heat and they each had a glass of sherry in front of them. Jenny was wearing a royal blue, long-waisted dress with large white lapels. She never dressed fussily, he thought, and always managed to achieve a look of elegant simplicity.

As he went forward he had a huge smile on his face. 'Jenny, how very kind of you to come over and enquire about Beth.' But for his mother sitting there, he would have taken her in his arms and kissed her properly, instead of which he had to content himself by touching his lips to her cheek.

'Such tragic news, that poor, poor child,' she said quietly, 'I couldn't stop thinking about her and I wanted to know if there was anything I could do to help.'

Before answering, Nigel poured himself a whisky,

added water then took himself and it to sit next to Jenny. 'I doubt if there is anything anyone can do,' he said stretching out his long legs to the heat. 'I was for getting the doctor but mother wasn't in favour.'

They looked over at the elderly lady sitting very straight in her chair and with her feet on a small padded stool. Jenny's pale-coloured, well-shaped eyebrows were raised in enquiry.

'Jenny, dear, I am afraid I am of the old school and in my opinion Dr Grieve would be of little help at the moment. A good night's sleep can do wonders, and since he comes to see me tomorrow morning he can take a look at Beth then.' She made to get up, feeling that she should leave them together, and Nigel was on his feet quickly to help her.

'Assist me to the door, Nigel, if you please, and I'll manage perfectly well after that. What you can do is tell the maid to have a tray brought to my bedroom. I shan't eat much but I must attempt a little.'

'Won't you wait and have dinner with us?'

'No, Nigel, it's been postponed twice already and it'll be a while yet. I expect it was ruined and they had to start again.' She sounded annoyed. 'Goodnight, Jenny.'

'Goodnight, Mrs Parker-Munro.'

Nigel, closing the door after his mother, showed his relief, and Jenny laughed outright. Drinking the rest of his whisky, he looked to Jenny but she shook her head. 'Mind if I do?'

'You carry on, darling, I'd say you need it.' She paused. 'Before you came in your mother was saying that you haven't been able to replace Rutherford.'

'I haven't. Butlers, my dear Jenny, I am discovering, are a dying breed but Maxwell is standing in and doing rather well. Perhaps I should just let him carry on and have young Tommy take over the driving.'

'Sounds like a good idea,' she said absently. 'Tell me truthfully what condition that child is in?'

'Very confused, worryingly so.' He poured himself a good measure of whisky and sat down. 'Do you know, Jenny, I didn't mention it to mother, but when I had Beth by the hand and we were walking up the Braes to the car, she began to address me as daddy.'

'Did you correct her?'

'No, I didn't.'

'That was sensible, darling,' she said with obvious relief. 'In her confused state she would very naturally connect the harbour and holding your hand with the walks she probably took with her father when she was a small child. I shouldn't worry too much about that.' She paused. 'I didn't bother to say it in front of your mother but I have already eaten.'

'Couldn't you take something and keep me company?'

'I'll have coffee with you, that's all. What I would like to do, Nigel, is go and see Beth. If she's asleep I won't disturb her.'

'She'll be asleep,' he said firmly, 'Mrs Murdoch would have given her something to make her sleep.'

'Let me go to her, Nigel, I may be able to help.'

He was trying to hide his annoyance. In his opinion Beth had caused enough trouble and worry for one day. She wasn't family after all and he had done all that could reasonably be expected of him. 'If you must.'

'Hers is the bedroom next to Caroline's isn't it?'

'Yes. I'll come with you.'

She put her hand on his arm. 'You stay where you are, have your drink, then go and have dinner.' As she finished talking there was a tap at the door and a maid announced that the meal was ready to be served.

★ ★ ★

Beth allowed herself to be undressed and the warmed nightdress to be slipped over her head.

'Into bed with you now,' Mrs Murdoch said.

Beth climbed into bed. Her feet touched the hot water bottle but she felt nothing.

'Don't be putting your feet on the bottle or it's chilblains you'll be getting, and painful things they are. Here, I'll push the bottles to the side,' she said slipping her hand below the bedclothes, 'you keep your feet on the warm patch. No, lass, don't go down, not just yet, you drink this. It'll give you a nice warm feeling inside and make you sleep.'

'I don't want it.'

'Drink it, Beth, it'll do you good.'

'I don't want it, please don't make me take it.'

'Force you? Never. What I'll do, lass, is leave it here on the table beside you and take it when you're ready. The light can stay on for a while.'

'Thank you.'

'Snuggle down like a good girl.'

Beth went under the bedclothes and turned her face to the wall. She was back in Inverbrae House, in her own bed, and she had never felt so frightened in her whole life or so alone. That was strange, she thought, since she wasn't alone.

Jenny gave the lightest of taps on the door before opening it and going in. She saw that the light had been left on and was glad that Mrs Murdoch had had the good sense not to leave the child in darkness.

'Beth, are you sleeping?' she said softly.

It was a strange voice, yet not totally strange, Beth felt sure that she had heard it before. She turned round and looked into Jenny Cuthbert's concerned face.

Jenny saw the dumb misery on the young face and without a word gathered Beth into her arms. Beth felt the comfort of being held in a warm embrace and then at last they came. Hard, painful, retching sobs that seemed to be torn from the small body and all the time Jenny went on holding her and making soothing noises. Only when the racking sobs changed to a soft crying did Jenny lower Beth's head, with its still damp curls, on to the pillow.

'I – I'm sorry,' Beth whispered, using the back of her hand to wipe the tears from her eyes.

An overwhelming feeling of compassion came over Jenny as she looked at the blotched face, the swollen eyelids, and the frightened, haunted expression. The child needed far more than she would get at Inverbrae House. She needed love and understanding and, perhaps most important of all, someone who would listen. She could be that person, she could help Beth, and in her usual impulsive fashion Jenny made up her mind there and then to have Beth stay with her.

'There is absolutely no need to apologise, Beth, dear. There is no shame in crying and we are all the better for a good weep. I've cried myself to sleep and felt a lot better for it.'

'Have you?'

'Yes, and I was a lot older than you.' She paused and took Beth's hand in hers. 'Listen, dear, how would you like to come and stay with me for a few days? Apart from my housekeeper, my treasure I call her,' she smiled as she said it, 'we should be alone. If you want to go for walks, we go for walks, if you don't we do something else or nothing, just as you please.'

Jenny saw the look of interest, then it faded.

'What is it, dear? Don't you like the idea?'

'Oh, I do, I wish I could, Mrs Cuthbert.'

'I'm Jenny to you.'

'I'd like to but I don't think I would be allowed—'

'A few days – a week with me? Can't see how anyone could object to that but, tell you what, I'll have a word with Colonel Parker-Munro, but I don't foresee any difficulty.'

'What about Caroline? I'm her companion.'

'You are her friend and a very good friend, and as for Caroline she can manage very well without you for a few days. Just stop worrying about other people.'

Beth gave a watery smile and Jenny kissed her on the brow. 'Now you can do something for me. You can drink that up, it's to make you sleep.' She handed Beth the glass and Beth took it and drank it all.

'Well done! Close your eyes and you'll be asleep in no time.'

'I love you, Jenny,' she murmured. Already everything was blurring and in less than five minutes Beth was sound asleep. For twelve hours she slept solidly and when she wakened it wasn't the tragedy that came first to her mind, it was the thought of spending some days with Mrs Cuthbert – Jenny as she was being allowed to call her.


'It's kind of you, my darling, but absolutely unnecessary to put yourself to all that trouble.'

'For me it would be a pleasure not a trouble.'

'Beth is my responsibility meantime.'

'Meantime?' she said, picking him up at once on that word.

He frowned, Jenny was becoming a nuisance taking all this interest in Beth. 'It was a temporary arrangement, no more than that. Her mother, poor soul, if only she had left

India sooner, would be living in Sandyneuk in her own house and Beth with her.'

'But the woman and her husband are dead,' she said abruptly.

'Yes,' he said heavily. 'I had met them both, but that first time I went to see Beth's mother she made quite an impression on me.'

'Beth had to get her good looks from somewhere,' Jenny said, amused at the turn the conversation was taking.

'Don't pick me up wrong. She was a pleasant looking woman, Jenny, but it wasn't that, and she was older than I would have expected. Rather it was a kind of innocence—'

'Innocence?' Her brow puckered.

'I'm not explaining this very well, but innocence is the only word that fits. That is what it was, a childlike faith, an absolute and total belief that she and her husband had been called to do God's Work and that no matter what, they would be protected from all harm.'

'Yet this could happen?'

'Makes one question one's beliefs, doesn't it?'

'I prefer not to think about it, but we've rather strayed from the point.'

'What were we talking about?'

'Beth coming to stay with me.'

'You are a very determined woman, Jenny Cuthbert.'

'I can be if something means a great deal to me.'

'Very well, I'll get Mrs Murdoch to arrange what is necessary and I'll drive Beth over to Greystanes.'

'Thank you, darling.'

'What about us? I feel terribly neglected.'

'Poor darling, but as you said yourself, you have a lot of paperwork to get through and not having me around will let you get on with it.'

'I'd rather have you around and blow the work,' he said taking her in his arms and, when their lips met, she returned his kisses but with less passion.

'Dearest,' she said pushing him away, 'I never feel relaxed when there is the possibility of someone coming in.'

'Why don't we get married then? Why keep putting me off? I love you but I'm beginning to wonder about your feelings for me.'

'Then don't wonder. I like you very, very much Nigel, I may even love you, but I do not want marriage.'

'Is it because of your first husband? I would understand, you know, you have nothing to fear. I loved Margaret and, like you, I have my memories but I am ready to love again. I didn't think there would be anyone until you came into my life.' He sighed. 'Oh, Jenny, what is it that is truly holding you back? A woman needs a man and I need you.'

'A lot of women need a man, I agree, but not all by any means. I have had marriage. Derek was good to me and I have pleasant memories, but now that I am on my own, I am finding a great deal of enjoyment in my independence.'

'You don't need me,' he said flatly, 'is that it?'

'No, it is not. I do need you.' The look she gave him made her meaning abundantly clear.

'You can't mean—' he said scandalised.

'Why not?' she said, opening her eyes wide, 'I don't imagine you've lived like a monk?'

He flushed. 'That's rather different.'

'Is it? It shouldn't be. Women have needs too, or do you imagine that not to be the case?'

'I don't think I have ever given the matter any consideration,' he said stiffly.

131

'How like a man.'

'Are you by any chance trying to make fun of me, darling?'

'Far from it. This is a serious conversation.'

'Let me get this right. You are suggesting a relationship rather than marriage?'

'Yes.'

'I can't believe you are saying this.'

'You're shocked at this moment but you'll get over it. Think about it seriously, Nigel. You have been a bachelor for – how long – eleven years?'

'I've told you before that there has been no one in that time whom I wanted to marry until you came along.'

'I'm flattered but not convinced. Had I been like those other women—'

'Not such a large number as you're trying to make out.'

'If you say so,' she smiled. 'The fact is that had I thrown myself at you, you would have quickly tired of me.'

'You would never have done that, you are just not the type.'

'That is perfectly true.' She paused. 'I have really shocked you, haven't I?'

'A little. You are a very remarkable woman, Jenny.'

'I'm honest and I want you to be that too. What we both want and need is companionship and, on occasion, perhaps more, but neither of us wants to lose our independence.'

'I'd still like to marry you.'

'But the alternative has its attractions?'

'I wouldn't deny that.'

'Bang goes your mother's hopes of wedding bells.'

'She's been disappointed before and survived,' he said drily. 'Her real fear is departing this life and leaving Inverbrae House without a mistress.'

'She takes good care of herself, I'd say she's likely to live to a ripe old age. As for Caroline she will manage beautifully, she's been brought up to it.'

'Then hopefully my daughter will marry a suitable young man,' he smiled. 'Talking of Caroline, mother and I are extremely pleased with her progress in every way.'

'Much of it I'd say thanks to Beth, even your mother admits to that. Strange that she hasn't taken to the girl, I find her a particularly charming child,' Jenny said musingly.

'Mother doesn't dislike Beth, she just doesn't want her at Inverbrae House. Don't ask me why. When I asked the reason I was told that I wouldn't understand, and that she was only thinking of Caroline. It's the future she is concerned about and I as a mere male wouldn't understand.'

'Ah!'

'What's that supposed to mean?'

'The most likely explanation – first, though, tell me what you see when you look at Beth?'

'What do I see when I look at Beth?' he said mystified. 'I suppose I see a bright, attractive child.'

'And that bright, attractive child in a few years time will turn into a tall, dark-eyed beauty.'

'So?'

'Poor boy, you haven't a clue. Your mother is looking ahead to the time when young men will come a-courting – and she would prefer Beth not to be on the scene.'

'Meaning my daughter won't attract young men?' he said angrily.

'Caroline, my dearest, is a pretty little thing and she will have her share of admirers. Some will love her for herself, others for her money and position. Those who already have money have no need to marry it and they will find

Beth irresistible. That is how I see it, though of course I could be wrong.'

He was thoughtful. 'I see. My mother is afraid that Beth may make a better marriage than her grand-daughter?'

'It shouldn't matter but I rather think it would.'

His smile didn't hide his concern. 'The girls are not yet twelve and long before young men come on the scene they will have gone their separate ways.'

'It's not fair,' Caroline said, two spots of angry colour on her cheeks, 'why can't I go and stay with Jenny as well? I've never been in her house.'

'It'll only be for a week,' her father said, frowning over his newspaper.

She went out, banging the door behind her, and the old lady winced. 'No need for her to get into that state and bang the door, but I can understand the child being annoyed. In my view Beth is getting far too much attention. That said, this separation has my approval.'

'Why?' he said sourly and put down the paper.

'Caroline depends far too much on Beth and this break will help. We must see that she is happily occupied and if I were you, Nigel, I would put Caroline's name down for next term. She badly needs the discipline of boarding school.'

'That's what I'd like, but what do I do about Beth?'

'Obviously we can't have her here without Caroline. You should go along with what Dr Grieve suggested. Didn't he say that after such a tragedy it would be better for the girl to be with her own people?'

'Yes, I recall that.'

'It's where she belongs.' She pursed her thin lips. 'Had she been with this aunt from the beginning the woman would have been receiving an allowance for Beth. That, of course, has ceased with the death of Beth's parents but perhaps if you offered a little money, it needn't be much—'

'Enough to cover her needs until she leaves school and takes up employment? Yes,' he nodded several times, 'that could be the answer.'

# Chapter Thirteen

'Almost there, Beth,' the colonel said as the car took the corner. They were in a quiet, tree-lined avenue of detached houses with long, well-kept gardens that sloped down to the road. A few stubborn leaves clung to the branches of the tall trees, and on the lawns were signs of the overnight frost that hadn't lifted.

Strathvale was about eight miles from Sandyneuk and consisted of one long street of shops. The church was at the far end. It was small, had a spire, and was built of weathered stone. To each side of it were a number of headstones partly covered with moss and with much of the writing gone. An old villager made weekly visits throughout the growing season and used a scythe to keep down the grass, and shears for the verges. A rather dreary looking manse was nearby. At the other end of the village was the hall where everything of importance, and a lot besides, took place. The nearby field owned by a kindly farmer was much in use during the summer months for church fêtes, school sports, and various other activities.

Beth wore a cherry-red coat with a black velvet collar and matching buttons. A red beret covered her head and on her feet she had shoes with a strap. Mrs Murdoch was of the opinion that Beth should have been wearing a black armband as a mark of respect to her dead parents but, since it did not appear to have occurred to anyone else, and it was hardly her place to raise the matter, nothing was done.

Beth looked pale and wan. Her appetite was poor, she merely picked at food, and the doctor, informed of the forthcoming short holiday, was sure that the complete change was just the thing and likely to do Beth the world of good.

In a few moments the car slowed down and stopped. Beth saw the front door of the house opening and Jenny waving. Dressed in a calf-length tweed skirt with box pleats and a heavy-knit cream and brown jumper, she ran down the path, avoiding as she did the overhanging branches of trees. The late November day was bright but there was no heat in the sun and it was bitterly cold.

Beth got out first. Then, with a broad smile on his face, the colonel swung his long legs out, shut the door and went to meet Jenny. Beth saw them embrace, then exchange a kiss. She should have looked away but by the time she thought of it, it was too late. The kiss wasn't a casual one on the cheek but one with his mouth on hers that lasted a little while. Beth wondered if that meant that they were going to get engaged but keeping it a secret meantime. If so, Caroline would be getting Jenny for a step-mother and she thought wistfully of how lovely that would be, then immediately she felt a rush of shame and the awful feelings of guilt were back with her. To have thoughts like that was wicked when her own parents had so recently met their death in such a dreadful way.

Beth waited by the car. Her case was in the boot and she would have to stay until the colonel opened it, then she could carry it in. While Jenny and the colonel were talking, Beth took the chance to study her surroundings. Compared with Inverbrae House, Jenny's home was tiny, but compared to the cottage in Sycamore

Lane, Greystanes was huge. It was a substantial, two-storey-high structure of stuccoed stone and over the doorway was a graceful fanlight. On the ground floor were two bow-fronted windows and the long narrow ones above had ivy growing round them.

Beth was enchanted.

'Jenny,' the colonel said sternly, 'will you please get back indoors before you catch your death of cold.' Then he called over his shoulder, 'I'll bring Beth's case. On you go, Beth, with Mrs Cuthbert and I'll follow.'

'I've told Beth to call me Jenny, Mrs Cuthbert is far too formal. Come along, dear, we'll do what we are told for once and get out of this cold,' she said taking Beth's hand and hurrying them both indoors.

'Do you want the case taken upstairs, Jenny?'

'No, thank you, dear, leave it in the hall and come and have a drink.'

'I won't, thanks all the same. I have an appointment and I'm running it rather neat,' he said, depositing the case at the foot of the stairs.

'It was kind of you to bring me, Colonel Parker-Munro, thank you very much,' Beth said politely.

He smiled. 'You get the roses back in your cheeks, Beth.'

'She will if I have anything to do with it. I'll take your coat, dear, and I don't suppose you thought about bringing wellingtons?'

'No, I didn't.'

'Hardly time for those, the real snow doesn't come until after the new year.'

'Miss Harris smells it in the air, Nigel, and she is very often right.'

'Then I hope to goodness that she's wrong this time, I hate an early start to winter,' he growled before sketching a salute and letting himself out.

'I've got heavy shoes with me, Jenny.'

'Not to worry, if we do get a fall I've got a selection of rubbers somewhere and with a thick pair of socks, or a couple of pairs for that matter, we should manage to get you fitted. Oh, here she is, my Miss Harris.'

A pleasant-faced woman in her mid-fifties smiled to Beth and took her coat and beret from Jenny. 'What a lovely shade of red,' she said admiringly. She had a sallow complexion and blue-grey eyes that lit up when she smiled.

Jenny nodded. 'Just what I thought. A Christmas colour, I do love these bright happy shades. Beth, dear, let me introduce you. This is Miss Harris, my treasure, I'd be lost without her. And this is Beth Brown, my very special young friend.' Beth didn't know whether to shake hands or not and waited to see what Miss Harris would do. When she just smiled, Beth did the same.

'I've coffee prepared, Mrs Cuthbert, but I'll bring tea as well if the young lass would prefer that?'

'Yes, please.' Beth had tasted coffee but hadn't as yet acquired a taste for it.

They went through to the sitting-room overlooking the front garden where a log fire burned brightly. Deep blue velvet curtains were at the window and a selection of pot plants were on a table in front of it. Between the two armchairs at either side of the marble hearth was another table covered with an embroidered cloth, and on it were cups and saucers, sugar and cream and a plate of sponge cakes and biscuits. Miss Harris came in with a coffee jug in one hand and a pot of tea in the other.

'Thank you, Miss Harris. Just leave those beside me and I'll pour.'

'If that's all meantime, Mrs Cuthbert, I'll take myself to

the shops. When it comes to butcher meat I do like to see what I'm getting instead of taking what they send.' The door closed softly, then opened again. 'I've taken Beth's case up to her bedroom and I'll unpack it before I go out. That'll save the lass the trouble.'

Beth smiled her thanks and Jenny nodded.

'Are you comfortable there, Beth, or would you like another cushion?'

'No, this is fine, thank you.'

'Once we've finished I'll take you on an inspection of the house,' she laughed. 'That won't take us long, but I want you to know your way around so that you can feel completely at home.'

'We only had a tiny cottage in Sycamore Lane,' Beth's voice wobbled, 'and I think this is the nicest house I have ever been in.'

'Beth, sweetheart, you haven't seen it.'

'But I know, I just know.'

Was this the best time, Jenny was wondering, and decided, since they were on their own, it was.

'There are times, Beth, when it helps to talk to someone. I know in the past it has helped me. I'm a good listener and you can be assured that nothing you tell me will be repeated to another soul. Perhaps I too may tell you things that I wouldn't want others to know.'

Beth looked very solemn. 'Jenny, I would never, ever say anything or tell anybody, honestly I wouldn't.'

'I know that. We are friends and we can trust each other.'

Beth moistened her dry lips. 'I think I must be wicked, Jenny.' She dropped her eyes to the floor.

'That you most certainly are not.'

'I am. You see my father told me, and he must have got it from the Bible, that you don't have to do wrong things to be wicked, thinking them is nearly as bad.'

'In that case there's not much hope for most of us,' Jenny said drily. 'Tell me what bad things you were thinking.'

'I didn't really want my mother to come home from India because it meant I would have to leave Inverbrae House.'

'That wasn't wicked, Beth, it was perfectly natural in the circumstances. Your parents wanted to go to India, it was their wish and they put their wishes first, although it meant leaving you behind. In my book that squares it up. You have nothing to feel guilty about,' she said firmly.

'They wouldn't have gone if they had loved me enough,' Beth burst out. 'You see, Jenny, they never – except for once at the station—' she stopped and struggled with her tears.

'Take your time, dear, we have plenty of it.'

Beth swallowed, dabbed at her eyes with her handkerchief and continued, but in a whisper that Jenny could only just make out. 'Caroline and girls at my school get lots of hugs and kisses, but I only got a hug before they left. My mother never even kissed me at night before I went to sleep.'

'That doesn't mean they didn't love you, I'm sure they loved you very much, they just weren't demonstrative, it wasn't their way. I can understand the hurt, though, probably better than most.' She paused to fill up her cup. 'Come on, dear, have a little sponge, there is only a bite in them. I'm making a beast of myself, this is my third,' she said, picking one up and putting it on her plate.

Beth wasn't the least bit hungry but to please Jenny she took one and bit into it.

'Where was I? Oh, yes, I was pretty much in the same boat, Beth, my parents weren't demonstrative either. I don't even recall them showing affection to each other, but they were happy enough. It wasn't in their nature to show, in a physical way, what they felt, but they both loved me and I have absolutely no doubts that your parents loved you. Am I making myself clear?'

'Yes, you are, but I wish my parents hadn't been like that. You aren't.'

'No, I'm the other way, I'm rather too demonstrative.'

'You aren't and anyway it is much better.'

Jenny smiled and had a faraway look on her face. 'I was lucky to have a grandmother with whom I spent most of my holidays. She was a lovely person, Beth, and I absolutely adored her.' She waved a hand round the room. 'This was all hers and in the Will she left me this house, the contents, and enough to keep me, if not lavishly, then without need for worry. My late husband left me a little, too, and I feel very fortunate to be in the position I am. Independence is a fine thing, Beth.'

'Does that mean you won't want to get married again?' Then she looked worried. 'I shouldn't have said that, should I?'

'I don't mind, and since you are unburdening yourself to me I'll be honest with you. Never is a long time and I can't say for sure that I'll never marry, just that I have no plans to enter into matrimony in the foreseeable future.' She gave a chuckle that made Beth laugh. 'In a few years time I'll be so old and wrinkled that no one will want me and that, I suppose, will serve me right.' She jumped up. 'Good, I've got you laughing, but that is enough of serious talk just now. Come on and I'll show you the house. Will you be warm enough? Upstairs is cold during the day but the bedroom fires go on in the early evening and the rooms are easily heated.'

'This is warm,' Beth said, plucking at the Fair Isle

jumper she was wearing over her navy blue pleated skirt.

'My grandmother used to knit the loveliest Fair Isle jumpers and gloves and she kept me supplied, but sadly my stock is now well past its best.' They crossed the hall to a lounge that looked out on to a landscaped back garden and, beyond that, to trees and shrubs that gave complete privacy to the house. Beth walked over to the window.

'Do you do any gardening, Jenny?'

'In the spring and summer I potter about a bit, but I have a regular gardener who comes and he takes on casual labour when it is needed.'

'My mother was very good, we had the best garden in Sycamore Lane.'

'Perhaps you have green fingers, too?'

'I don't think so.'

'You don't know. Wait until you have your own garden and you may take a great pride in it.'

'This is nice,' Beth said, looking at the Regency striped curtains, the chintz-covered furniture and the water colours on the plain cream walls.

'Yes, I like it myself. Nigel – the colonel is of the opinion that I should get rid of the lot and start again.'

'You wouldn't, though?'

'Probably not. Not for a long time, anyway.'

'Was the furniture your grandmother's?'

'A lot of it. The beds I got rid of, they sagged a bit, and I've added a few pieces of my own but, yes, it is largely as it was in her day. Now we come to the dining-room,' she said going to the next door and opening it. This was a slightly smaller room with an Adam fireplace, a long dining table and high-backed chairs pushed under the table. One picture hung on each wall. The pictures were of country scenes. Miss Harris hadn't as yet returned and they took a peep into the kitchen. There was the appetising smell of recent baking and a fruit cake was cooling on a tray. A cooker and oven occupied one wall and cupboards covered the others. There was a walk-in pantry.

'On the coldest days I envy Miss Harris the warmth of the kitchen, but on hot, sunny days she has my sympathy.' Jenny closed the door and pointed. 'Nothing of interest, just cupboards, and the door at the very end is a toilet. The bathroom is on the half landing,' she said as she went ahead and up the carpeted stairs and stopped. 'That's a bedroom, or could be if required. Miss Harris calls it the lumber room, I refer to it as the glory hole. We won't bother with it but feel free to look around, you never know what you may find there. This is the bathroom,' she added, pushing the door wider. 'Functional but hardly luxurious. One day I've promised myself a whole new bathroom, but the thought of all the upheaval puts me off.'

A further flight of stairs brought them to the three bedrooms. 'This is mine.' Beth saw a double bed with a gold-coloured bedspread, then she was being shown her own where there was a single bed.

'It's lovely, Jenny, and blue is my favourite colour.'

'Good! I'm glad you like it. This was my room when my grandmother was alive. I did have the painters in for this one to freshen it up. And when I was in Perth I saw that blue-sprigged curtain material and couldn't resist it.'

Beth's eyes were shining and Jenny said a silent prayer that she had had the foresight to invite the child to Greystanes, she needed away from Inverbrae House. It wasn't so much grief for her parents that had brought her down to this low, but rather that she didn't feel enough grief. She was very mixed up and Jenny surmised that there was a great deal more worrying her, but all in good time. Beth was beginning to trust her and when she was ready it would all come out.

They went downstairs and could hear Miss Harris singing as she went about her duties.

'She has a good voice, Beth, and with proper training Miss Harris would have been very good. I once said that to her but I couldn't convince her that I wasn't joking. She is totally unaware of her gift.'

'Maybe there are lots of people like that, Jenny?'

'I have no doubt there are and it is such a waste. Come and see this,' she said walking away and opening a door that Beth believed to be a cupboard. It was far from that, it was a studio.

'You paint? You are an artist?' Beth exclaimed as her astonished eyes took in the easel and board, a table cluttered with brushes and paints and a mixture of colours on a palette. A paint-stained smock hung on a hook at the back of the door and a worn rug covered the linoleum beside the easel.

'No, I am not, and more's the pity. My grandmother was the artist and though I know I should, I haven't as yet been able to bring myself to clear the lot out. The paint and stuff won't be much good but some struggling artist could make use of the rest. One day I'll get down to it. The paintings downstairs in the dining-room are my grandmother's work.'

'I didn't get a proper look at them.'

'I showed them to someone knowledgeable and he said there was talent, but what she produced was amateurish because she hadn't had the benefit of tuition.'

'Why didn't she?'

'Money wasn't the problem. My great-grandparents were not wealthy but comfortably off, but in those days it was just not done. Young ladies were not encouraged to have a career and art, in all its forms, was very much a man's world.'

'Then it shouldn't have been,' Beth said indignantly, 'and I bet some women were even better than men.'

'And so say all of us!' She laughed. 'I couldn't agree more, but here we are approaching the 'thirties and things haven't improved all that much, but give it time, Beth, and we may get something approaching equality.'

'Do you really think that?'

'Alas, no, just wishful thinking on my part. Too many women are happy enough with their lot for the others to be taken seriously.'

'One day I hope to have a career.'

'Don't you want to fall madly in love with some handsome young man?'

'And live happily ever after like a princess,' Beth laughed.

'Not all of them are happy. You, my dear, are going to grow up to be a beautiful woman and it may well be that you can have a happy marriage and a career.'

Beth blushed and looked uncomfortable. 'I wanted to be small and slim and graceful when I grew up but I just keep growing.'

'You are to be tall and slim and graceful and believe me, that is very much more desirable. My dear child, you don't know how lucky you are.'

'Caroline is small and pretty,' she said wistfully.

'Yes, she is, and with a little less spoiling she could be a delightful girl.'

'She can't help that though, can she?'

'I think she could, and a dose of boarding school may be just what she needs.'

Beth didn't answer but it brought back all her fears.

'Miss Harris will have tidied up by now, we'll go and see.'

Miss Harris had, the table was back in its own place and logs had been added to the fire. Jenny went over to the fire and stretched out her hands before the warmth. 'Aren't your hands cold?'

'No, they aren't and I'm not in the least cold.'

'Lucky you, my hands go dead. Bring in your chair, dear. No, nearer than that.' Beth brought it forward and sat down and Jenny moved hers even closer to the heat. 'Not desperate to go out of doors, are you?'

'No, I like it here.'

'Fine. For your first day we'll make it a quiet one.'

Beth felt very contented. It was such a novelty for her to be able to talk to an adult the way she could with Jenny.

'We'll have what my old gran used to call a good old chin-wag, and for the rest of your stay we'll have walks in the country and afternoon tea in a darling little tea-room. It's quite a distance from here, but we'll have rested before the return journey.'

'Sounds lovely to me,' Beth smiled.

They were both silent for a few minutes, a comfortable silence, then Jenny touched Beth's hand. 'Forgive me for saying so but you, my dear, are too sensitive for your own good. In this world we have to fight for our own little corner and all of us suffer from guilt feelings at some time in our life.' She paused. 'What I am about to tell you is for your ears only.' She paused again. 'I married Derek for all the wrong reasons. No, don't misunderstand, I had a tremendous affection for him, but I wasn't in love. To my shame I used him to escape from being stifled at home. Mind you, looking back I must have been a trial to my parents, but I longed for freedom and they were old-fashioned and terribly strict. Derek, poor lamb, came along. I saw my chance and took it.'

'Did you regret marrying Derek?'

'No, I didn't, Beth. I never regretted my marriage, only that I had cheated Derek. There you are, you see, my guilt feelings.'

'He must have loved you?'

'Yes, he did,' she said softly, 'and he was very good to me.' She sighed. 'He made no secret of his love, while for me there was a great deal of pretence.'

'Perhaps he never knew that it was pretence?'

'That, my dear Beth, is the nicest thing you could have said and what I have always secretly hoped.'

'Did Derek become ill and die?'

'No, it was an accident. He was a little bit of a show-off, was Derek, ignored the warnings and went too far out. It would have been to impress our friends and he was a strong swimmer. Poor Derek, by the time people realised that he was in difficulties and got help it was too late to save him.'

'That was awful, Jenny.'

'Yes, it was. Had I been there at the time perhaps I might have got help sooner, but I wasn't.' She looked at Beth. 'I'm over it just as you will get over your loss.'

'I think I am getting over it, Jenny, but sometimes I have bad dreams and in them I'm – I'm—'

'Imagining terrible things?'

She nodded and her mouth trembled. 'Colonel Parker-Munro said they wouldn't have suffered, but how could he know that, Jenny?'

'He couldn't, of course.' She paused and looked thoughtful. 'I'm not a particularly religious person, Beth, but occasionally I do go to church and one minister, a visiting minister, said something that stuck with me. He said that no one gets more than they can stand. He was talking about suffering, suffering pain. No one can know for sure but I am of the firm opinion that it would all have happened so quickly that there would have been no time to feel pain. Does that help?' she asked gently.

'Yes, it does.' She gave a deep, shaky sigh. 'Do you know what I wish?'

'No. What do you wish, Beth?'

'That this go on for ever, just us talking like this.'

'You really are a sweet child and you are holding something back, my dear. Remember what I said – a worry shared is a worry halved.'

'It's only that – well, I can't expect to be at Inverbrae House much longer.'

'Why not?'

'Caroline has changed her mind and she doesn't mind going to boarding school now, especially since she would be going as a weekly boarder.'

'You'll see each other at the weekend.'

Beth shook her head. 'No, it won't be like that. Caroline tells me things.'

'What has Caroline been saying that she shouldn't?'

'Only that she overheard her father and grandmother discussing me and they said they could hardly be expected to be responsible for me for much longer, or something like that. They don't want me, Jenny.'

'Caroline may have got it wrong.'

'No, Jenny, it's true,' Beth said miserably. 'Colonel Parker-Munro has been encouraging me to visit my aunt.'

'So that you can go and live with her?'

'Yes.'

Jenny was thoughtful as she lifted the poker, poked at a log, then replaced the poker. What Beth was afraid of could very easily happen.

'Don't worry too much about it, Beth, things have a way of working out.'

They were silent, looking at the fire, then Beth spoke. 'I wonder what will happen to our house in Sycamore Lane?'

'Was it rented?'

'Yes, someone, a family, had the use of it, but they had to get out when—' she swallowed, remembering the letter, 'my father told them to vacate it for—'

'Your mother coming home?' Jenny finished for her.

'Yes.'

'Very likely you and your aunt will have to see to disposing of the furniture and clearing out the house completely.'

'Aunt Anne can have everything.'

'Perhaps some if it could be sold and you would be entitled to whatever it raised.'

'No, I wouldn't want that. Aunt Anne can have it all.'

Beth would look back and remember those wonderful days at Greystanes as being one of the happiest times of her life. Jenny's sympathy and understanding had removed the burden of guilt that had hung so heavily on her. Of course, she still had worries. She couldn't help worrying about what was to become of her when Caroline went off to boarding school. Jenny hadn't been able to help there, Beth thought. In all likelihood she would end up with Aunt Anne and, if she did, perhaps it would have been for the better, as her aunt said, if she had gone there in the first place. Then she wouldn't have had the awful change from Inverbrae House to a tenement in Dundee.

When she awakened on her last day snow was falling steadily beyond the window and a snowy white blanket stretched for as far as the eye could see. Beth dressed quickly.

The small sitting-room was the easiest to heat and, since it had a table, it doubled as a breakfast room and occasionally as a dining-room.

'I like eating in here,' Beth had said on one occasion.

'So do I, but I remember my grandmother saying how easy it was to fall into bad habits, and that rooms in a house should be used for what they were intended. In this case, my dear Beth, it means using the dining-room at least for the evening meal. If I don't I feel guilty.'

'Even when you are eating on your own?'

'Even then, but I hasten to add that I don't dine all that often on my own. I'm either out or have friends in.' They both turned as the door, off the catch, was pushed open and the housekeeper came in carrying a tray and on it plates of fluffy scrambled eggs and a rack of nicely browned toast. 'Is this weather to last, Miss Harris? Beth is hoping it will.'

Miss Harris smiled indulgently. 'Well, Beth, I have it on good authority that this won't last the day. There is a definite change on the way, it'll become milder and all that snow will have disappeared before your head touches the pillow tonight.' She poured tea into the cups and put down the teapot. 'If you want to make the most of it, lass, I'd suggest you get out when you finish your breakfast.'

Beth looked hopefully in Jenny's direction.

'You win, my young friend,' Jenny said in mock surrender. 'I'll look out my wellingtons and then I'll—'

'All done, Mrs Cuthbert,' Miss Harris said smugly, 'I've three old pairs looked out for Beth and some thick socks.'

'Wonderful, isn't she, Beth?'

'I think you both are.'

In her red coat, her beret, a scarf of Jenny's tied round

her neck and her hands in warm gloves, Beth looked cosy and happy. The roses were back in her cheeks, her eyes were clear and bright, and she laughed delightedly at the deep hollows made by her much too large wellington boots. Inside them, over her slim feet, she wore two pairs of thick, hand-knitted socks.

Jenny arrived outside in a bottle green coat with huge pockets and a storm collar. On her head was a woollen cap that covered her hair completely and her boots were shiny black. Looking at the happy eleven-year-old, Jenny felt a deep sense of satisfaction. It just showed what a little loving kindness could do, she thought. Miss Harris had produced meals that looked appetising and would appeal to a child. Small helpings were served with the dish left should either of them want more. No one was more delighted than the housekeeper when Beth's appetite returned and she waited hungrily for the next meal to be served.

'Come on, Beth, we'll take a walk down to the shops and save Miss Harris the trouble.'

'Have you got a list?' Beth said cheekily.

'Meaning I won't remember what to get?'

'Miss Harris says you forget what you are supposed to buy and come back with something totally different.'

'Very true, I'm afraid, but I do have a list this time and a shopping bag which you can carry,' she said handing Beth a crocheted bag that stretched to accommodate a remarkable number of purchases.

The shopkeeper had taken the list, then carefully selected the items before packing them into the bag. Beth giggled as Jenny kept adding whatever took her fancy, and only with difficulty did they all go into the bag.

'It's a mite heavy when you have a fair walk,' the shopkeeper said. 'I could have them delivered to Greystanes once my laddie gets back, but in this weather I wouldn't like to say when that will be.'

'That's kind of you, Mr McGregor, but I'd better say no. Miss Harris is sure to be requiring something straight away, and it is as much as my life is worth to go back emptyhanded.'

'Well, if you put it that way, and you've a helper I see.' He was a red-faced, jovial man with a huge stomach, bristling moustache and keen eyes that missed very little. He needed to have eyes in the back of his head to watch those young scallywags. Take off with an apple or what takes their fancy, they would, if they thought they would get away with it, he told them.

'Let me carry the bag, Jenny,' Beth said eagerly.

'There you are, then. You take it the length of the church, that'll be far enough, and I'll take it from there.'

They set out and after a while Jenny took a bar of chocolate from her coat pocket and broke off two squares. She gave one to Beth and the other to herself.

'Normally I like two squares in my mouth to get the taste, but we'll be dainty today and make it last out.'

When they came in sight of the house Beth stopped talking.

'You're quiet, Beth, and you look sad.'

'I'm sad because this has to end.'

'It has gone quickly, hasn't it?'

'Much too quickly and I wish I had the right words to tell you – to tell you—' she broke off, too choked to go on.

'Beth, dear, I have enjoyed it too and I know that Miss Harris has loved having you. You'll come back when the better days arrive.'

'You mean that?'

'Beth, you should know me well enough to know I don't say things out of politeness. Of course I mean it.'

★  ★  ★

'Jenny, what time is Colonel Parker-Munro expected?'

'He didn't say, but I imagine late morning or early afternoon, and as patience isn't his strong point you had better be packed and ready.'

'I'll go and get my case packed this very minute,' Beth said, making to get up from the breakfast table. She had finished hers but Jenny took a long time over her second cup of tea. Beth could please herself, she could either wait or excuse herself from the table. Jenny didn't stand on ceremony.

'No, Beth, dear, leave the packing to Miss Harris,' Jenny said stifling a yawn. She was in her dressing-gown but Beth was dressed.

'I can easily do it myself,' Beth protested.

'I daresay you could but it would be a waste of time since it would end up being unpacked. Miss Harris has a special way of arranging everything neatly into the smallest possible space. Left to me I usually have to sit on the case to get the wretched thing to close.'

'I'd better leave it then.'

'Sit still and tell me something I keep forgetting to ask.' She drained the last of her tea. 'Has the colonel ever suggested some other way of addressing him?'

'No.'

'Colonel Parker-Munro is such a mouthful.'

'That's what my mother once said.'

'Did she?' Jenny pursed her lips. 'Not an easy one, it's difficult to know what would be acceptable.' She flicked a crumb across the table and grinned. 'Don't tell him or anyone else for that matter, or he'll kill me, but in the army, among his fellow officers, he was known as Parky.'

Beth looked shocked. She couldn't imagine anyone being sufficiently disrespectful to shorten the colonel's name like that. 'He doesn't look like someone you could call Parky,' she said.

'I have to agree there, but apparently they did and he hated it.' Jenny wiped her mouth with her napkin. 'To call him colonel is a bit too casual and I doubt he would approve. Personally, I see nothing wrong with Uncle Nigel, not after three years in his household, but the old lady would have something to say about that I'm afraid.'

'I could never call him Uncle Nigel,' Beth said firmly. She knew that Mrs Parker-Munro would be horrified and she rather thought that Caroline wouldn't be too happy about it either.

'Sorry, love, but you appear to be stuck with that mouthful.'

'I don't mind, I'm used to it.'

As forecast by Miss Harris and the villagers the snow quickly disappeared and by afternoon it had turned to slush and a dreary dampness was in the air. Lunch over, Beth was at a loose end and with the colonel due to arrive at any time she couldn't venture far. After a last look in at all the rooms, Beth went along to see Miss Harris. She wanted to say thank you for all the kindness shown to her.

'Was that the car, Beth?'

'No, not yet, but when it does I won't have the chance to thank you properly.'

'Nothing to thank me for, lass,' the housekeeper smiled as she emptied the water from the basin where she had been scraping and peeling the vegetables. After carefully holding back the scrapings from going down the sink and choking it, she dried her red roughened hands on a towel and gave her whole attention to Beth.

'You've been very kind and I wish I didn't have to go,' she said wistfully, then, afraid to have given the wrong impression, she hastened in with, 'I don't mean I'm unhappy at Inverbrae House, I'm not, but this has been special.'

'You're looking a lot better. Mrs Cuthbert has been a comfort to you and from time to time we all need a bit of that and a shoulder to cry on.'

'Jenny is the only grown-up I've been able to talk to – to – about—'

'What's been worrying you.'

'She told you!' Beth felt an overwhelming disappointment. She had been so sure that Jenny would keep her promise and not repeat a word of what she had said.

Miss Harris was watching the young face. Beth wasn't old or experienced enough to hide her feelings.

'All Mrs Cuthbert told me, Beth, was that you had your own private worries but you were getting to grips with them. She is not a lady to break her promise but I didn't need to be told, I could see that you were sorely troubled. Mind this, lass, worrying doesn't do any good.'

'Jenny said that.'

'Easier said than done, but you're a bit easier now?'

'Yes, and I feel a lot better.'

She smiled. 'I'm glad. At your age you shouldn't have worries.'

'Have I been much trouble?'

'Anything but. What you have been is a very nice, well-behaved young lady.'

'I never did anything to help.'

'And do me out of a job? Now I wouldn't want that, would I?'

'My aunt thinks all girls should do some housework, but my mother never made me. She said I would get plenty of it when I was older.'

'A lot of folk are like your aunt but I would say with your mother, and if I had been blessed with a daughter I hope I would have allowed her to enjoy her childhood with just the occasional wee help. Something tells me that you are going to grow up to be a very lovely lady.'

'Caroline, she's Colonel Parker-Munro's daughter, says I can't ever be a lady because I was born poor. But that is not true, Miss Harris, we were never poor, we just didn't have a lot of money.'

Miss Harris burst out laughing. 'Beth, you are a caution, and as to being a lady, to my mind it has nothing to do with wealth or position. A lady is someone who is kind and gentle and good inside.'

'Like Jenny?'

'Yes, like Mrs Cuthbert.'

'Is that my name I hear—'

'Miss Harris was telling me what a real lady is like and you are one, we both said that.'

'And I am going to say something else. Will you both kindly leave my kitchen and let me get on?'

'Come on, Beth, we know when we are not wanted.'

Lunch was over and cleared away before the colonel arrived. Jenny went out to meet him. Beth stayed indoors, she wanted to keep out of the way until they had greeted each other.

The colonel was bare-headed and wore a heavy tweed suit, one that Jenny, in her outspoken way, had said was only fit for a beggar and one who wasn't too particular. They were arm-in-arm when they came into the house.

'I hope Beth is ready.'

'She is and has been since morning,' Jenny said tartly.

'Don't blame me, it wasn't my fault, I got held up and couldn't get over any earlier.'

'Didn't matter, I was in no hurry to part with my guest.'

'No problems with her?'

'None.'

'Mother said to be sure to tell you how grateful she is for you taking Beth for a few days.'

'It was a pleasure, I assure you, and be sure to tell Mrs Parker-Munro that.' There was a small frown on Jenny's face. Were they trying to make out that Beth was a burden when nothing could be further from the truth? Then again she could be wrong and it was kindly meant. It didn't do to jump to conclusions.

'Yes, I'll give mother the message.' They were now in the sitting-room with the colonel standing until Jenny had seated herself. She saw that he looked well satisfied. 'Just shows how quickly children adapt to change. I expected Caroline to have missed Beth, be lost without her, but it wasn't the case.'

'Perhaps the break from each other did them both good.'

'Could be. Certainly Caroline didn't weary.' With the arrival of Beth they broke off their conversation. 'Ready, Beth?'

'Yes, I'm ready, Colonel Parker-Munro.'

'Good! Go and wait in the car and I'll be out directly.'

Her case was by the door and as she made to pick it up, Jenny gave a small shake of her head.

'A week is a long time, Jenny, and I've missed you.'

'Have you, darling?'

'You know I have.' He paused and just wished that Jenny would say that she had missed him too. 'Since you didn't enjoy the last play I didn't get tickets for this one,' he said.

'It was poor, you have to admit that. The players are so wooden Nigel, or am I being over critical?'

'No, Jenny, you aren't. Attendances are falling. It wasn't a full house when we were there but I blame the choice of plays rather than the players.'

'You may be right. I do wish we had an Opera House close by.'

He raised his eyebrows. 'Nothing to hinder us having a weekend in Edinburgh and enjoying what is on offer, is there?'

She smiled. 'Nothing that I can think of.'

'As regards this evening – dinner at the Majestic, I thought?'

Her eyes lit up like a child promised a treat. 'Wonderful, for want of a better word,' she said. Jenny made no secret of what pleased her and what didn't. Her total lack of pretence was one of the things Nigel loved about her.

The newly built luxury Majestic Hotel, with its commanding view of the snow-peaked hills and a glimpse of the sea, had opened its doors only the previous week and those who had wined and dined there were loud in their praise.

'Come early, Nigel, and I promise to be ready. It'll give us time for a talk before setting out.'

'Should manage that, and the talk, is it about anything in particular?'

'Something I would prefer to discuss here rather than over a meal. In any case I want to give my complete attention to the food.' She got up. 'Nigel, that poor child is waiting in the car.'

'Sorry, I forgot. Being with you puts everything else out of my mind,' he said, getting to his feet and picking up the case.

'Off you go, darling, I won't come out. I'll watch you leave from the window.' She blew him a kiss.

When the car had disappeared from sight, Jenny was still deep in thought. All that talk about Caroline not missing Beth, had it more significance than just a casual remark? She was uneasy and Beth could be right about her days at Inverbrae House drawing to an end. Surely, though, Nigel wouldn't be so cruel? He wasn't by nature uncaring yet where his mother was concerned he was inclined to give in to her. And the old lady was determined to be rid of Beth.

In his well-cut dinner suit the colonel looked very handsome and Jenny's heart gave a lurch. He really was a charming and attractive man.

'Darling, you look very handsome.'

'And you look enchanting.'

'Rubbish! Quite the wrong word, I couldn't look enchanting no matter how much I tried. Elegant and attractive, I'll settle for those.'

'Elegant and attractive and so much more,' he laughed.

'Tell me what you think of my gown, then pour yourself a drink and I'll have a sherry.' She stood quite still waiting for his approval.

Looking at her his eyes softened. The deep blue gown hugged her figure then fell in soft folds. The low neckline showed off the long stem of her neck and was bare.

'Quite perfect, my dearest, and you are the only woman I know who can resist jewellery, and how right you are to do so.'

'Thank you and now we can relax with a drink.' She sank back on the cushions with her sherry and Nigel, whisky in hand, joined her. A table was at hand.

'This talk, I'm curious.'

'It's about Beth.'

She saw that he was annoyed. 'Beth is getting rather too much attention.'

'Losing her parents in such horrifying circumstances I think she should be getting a great deal of attention,

Nigel. More than attention, loving care.'

'You seem to forget she isn't family.'

'And that holds you back?'

'Obviously it makes a difference.' He lifted his glass and Jenny put hers down on the table.

'Why should it, Beth is in your care?'

'She is and has been very well looked after.' He moved the amber liquid in the glass and studied it. 'Forgive me, Jenny, but Beth is hardly your business. As a matter of fact our family doctor was of the opinion that Beth would be better with her own relatives. Tragedy draws families together.'

'Which in Beth's case means an aunt for whom she has little affection.'

He shrugged. 'The woman is still family and Beth likes her uncle.'

'All this is because you want rid of her,' she said quietly.

'I don't care for the expression but I do think the time is right for Beth to make her home with her relatives.'

'In other words, she has served her purpose and it is time to go.' Jenny turned sideways to look him straight in the eyes and, under her scrutiny, he shifted in his chair and looked both annoyed and uncomfortable.

'I can't for the life of me understand why we are having this conversation at all,' he said stiffly, 'and isn't it about time we were setting off?'

'Not really, it is early enough. Nigel,' she said softly, 'I'm not quarrelling with you or at least I don't want to, but I've grown very fond of Beth and in a funny sort of way I feel responsible for her.'

'That, my darling, is simply ridiculous.'

'Ridiculous or not it is how I feel.' She paused. 'You know, Nigel, I can't help remembering you saying that you had a hard time persuading Mrs Brown to let you have Beth. That is true, isn't it?'

'Yes,' he said reluctantly.

'If she had refused to let you have her child, Beth would have been living with this aunt and uncle and by now have accepted that way of life.'

'Exactly my point and that is what will happen. Give it time, that is all it needs.'

'You honestly believe that, or do you just want to make yourself believe it?'

'I do believe it.'

'You can say that,' she said incredulously. 'For heaven's sake, Nigel, the change from a cottage to a tenement is very, very different to a change from Inverbrae House to a tenement, and remember she's had three years of it, a very large slice of a child's life.'

'She will adapt I tell you,' he snapped. 'Now can we kindly end this conversation?'

'In a few minutes.'

'I have nothing further to say.'

'But I have. You are being very cruel and I won't have Beth treated like this.'

'What, pray, do you intend doing about it?' he said sarcastically.

'Beth can come and live with me,' she said quietly.

She saw by his expression that she had shocked him. 'With you?' he said, then gave a half laugh. 'For a moment I thought you meant it.'

'I do mean it. Miss Harris will be more than delighted to help look after her, and Beth can attend a good day school.'

'Out of the question, I won't allow it.'

'Are you her legal guardian?'

'No.'

'Then you have no say in the matter. The choice will be

Beth's. Her aunt or Greystanes and I know which one she will choose.'

For a long time he was silent, not looking at her, then with a sigh he got up to refill his empty glass. Jenny had hardly touched her sherry.

'I can't have you doing this, Jenny,' he said at last, 'but you must see that having Beth at Inverbrae House with Caroline away at school—'

'Why can't Beth go to Rowanbank with Caroline? I can't believe the expense would upset you?'

'The expense – no, of course not,' he said dismissively, 'but even if I were to entertain your suggestion it would never come to pass.'

'Your mother would object?'

'Too true she would, but it was of the school I was thinking.'

'Meaning Beth wouldn't be accepted?'

'She wouldn't.'

'Nonsense. Your position, not forgetting your charm.'

'Flattery will get you nowhere,' he said lightly, the anger leaving him.

'She's a bright girl and you have her to thank that Caroline has reached the entrance standard.'

'Pity I tell you everything, I must watch in future,' he said glumly. 'Remember, though, that Caroline has been introduced to subjects that are not taught at Beth's village school.'

'No great problem. Beth will soon pick up what she needs.'

He leaned back. 'You have precisely two minutes to state your case, Jenny, and then we either go to the Majestic or it will be too late and we'll have to forget about it.'

'Two minutes will do.' She took a deep breath. 'Take

Beth away from her school now and let her share lessons with Caroline's governess.'

'You have it all worked out, haven't you?'

'Nigel, you owe it to Beth and I think if you did abandon her you'd feel horribly guilty and you would deserve to be.' She jumped up. 'I'll get my cloak,' and when he got to his feet she put her arms round his neck. 'Thank you, darling.'

'For what?'

'For doing the right thing.'

He held her close but didn't answer. He hadn't promised anything. Jenny, he thought fondly, got so easily carried away, the dear girl was so impetuous. By tomorrow she would be regretting her offer to give Beth a home, and with Beth away from Greystanes, it would all be forgotten.

As to the future, he would get in touch with this aunt and make the necessary arrangements.

# Chapter Fourteen

'I didn't miss you, at least not very much,' Caroline said when Beth joined her. They had moved on from the playroom to their own sitting-room, leaving behind all childish things except books and a few favourite games. The square-shaped room had a fire burning brightly and a guard in front of it in case of sparks flying. At first Caroline had strongly disapproved and had removed the offending fireguard. When this had been discovered by the colonel and Mrs Parker-Munro, there had been a stormy scene with Caroline stamping her foot in a rage, but all to no avail. The fireguard would remain in place or it was a return to the playroom. Caroline was discovering that throwing a tantrum did not get her her own way as it once had.

Beth was turning the pages of a book showing pictures of the beautiful Swiss Alps. Usually the scenes gave her a lot of pleasure and she would imagine herself ski-ing down those slopes. Not that it was ever likely to happen, it was a sport for the privileged few, but there was a lot of pleasure to be derived from dreaming.

'I'm glad, I didn't want you to be lonely,' Beth said quietly.

'I was anything but that.'

'What did you do?' Beth closed the book and sat back in her chair. Caroline was stretched out on the sofa with a selection of glossy magazines.

'Mrs Watson invited me over,' she touched the magazines, 'that's where these came from. Most of them are about fashion and Mrs Watson says it is never too early for young girls to be interested in clothes.'

'Was Emma there?'

'Of course.' Emma was coming up for ten, a podgy, sweet-tempered child who had been teased mercilessly by her brothers, Leonard and Ralph, until boarding school claimed them and peace reigned between the holidays. 'Mrs Watson took us shopping and we had tea and lovely cream cakes and there was an orchestra playing.' She looked to see if Beth was impressed and was disappointed that she didn't seem to be. 'Then I spent another day with Aunt Gwen,' she continued, 'and she said I must come when Ruth is there so that she can tell me about Rowanbank.'

'Do you know when you will be going?'

'To Rowanbank? No, I don't, daddy hasn't mentioned it for a while. I expect he's wondering what to do about you when I do go.'

Beth felt the breathlessness that was the beginning of panic. With Jenny beside her she hadn't felt like this. Jenny had been able to smooth away her fears but with those words Caroline had brought them back.

'You're not saying anything,' Caroline said accusingly.

'What do you want me to say?'

'Don't you care what happens to you?'

'Of course I do but Jenny said worrying about things won't change them.'

'Jenny this, Jenny that,' Caroline said nastily, 'she just took you away to please daddy, and grandmama was pleased about it too. You'll have to go and live with that aunt of yours and you'll be poor again like you used to be.'

Then, seeing Beth's stricken face, she hesitated. She hadn't really meant to be nasty and in truth she didn't think she wanted Beth to go away. Being with Emma Watson and the other day with her Aunt Gwen had been all right, it put in the time, but Beth was much more fun. Sometimes she couldn't understand herself. She wanted Beth, then she didn't. 'I'm sorry, I didn't mean to say that and truly I did miss you.'

Beth smiled. 'I'm glad, it's nice to be missed.'

'What did you do when you were with Jenny?'

'Went for walks mostly.'

'Is that all, how dull.'

'It wasn't, it was fun.'

'I suppose Jenny is your most favourite person.'

'Yes, she is.'

'I wonder when daddy will marry her,' she said, letting the magazines slide off her knees to the floor and bending down to get them.

Beth remembered what Jenny had told her, that she enjoyed her independence and had said in confidence that she had no plans to remarry and perhaps she never would. Beth hugged this knowledge to herself and, though she liked the colonel very much, she preferred to think of Jenny and Miss Harris together at Greystanes. She was saved an answer by a maid giving a knock and popping her head in the door.

'What do you want?' Caroline asked, putting on her mistress of the house voice.

The maid ignored her. 'The master wants you, Beth. He said you are to go to his study at once.'

Beth looked shattered. This was it and much sooner than she had expected. The maid withdrew.

'Better go, Beth, then come back here and tell me what it is all about. It'll save me asking daddy if you tell me.'

Beth nodded.

She closed the door on Caroline but Beth didn't hurry to the study. Bad news was something you put off hearing for as long as possible. She took her time and tried to let her mind go blank. The maid who had brought the summons passed her as she reached the stairs, and stared curiously at Beth. She certainly wasn't hurrying herself and the master could be a crabbit devil if folk didn't jump to do his bidding.

'Come in.'

Beth opened the door and went in. The colonel's smile was to put her at ease, she thought, or maybe it was just to soften the blow before it came. He indicated the chair with a movement of his hand and she sat down on the very edge of it.

'Usually I manage to open my mail early on but with a busier than usual morning and having to collect you from Greystanes, I've only just worked my way through it.'

Beth nodded. She wondered what that had to do with her. Was he blaming her because he had to collect her from Greystanes? She thought he would have been pleased, after all it gave him a chance to see Jenny.

He fingered a letter. 'It appears that there is some urgency about clearing out the furniture in your old home. This is to allow new tenants to take possession. I, of course, have nothing to do with it, Beth, other than to inform you that the authorities have also contacted your aunt on this matter.'

Beth wished the colonel wouldn't talk in that business-like manner, but relief was flooding through her that it wasn't the news she had feared.

'You do understand what I am saying, Beth?'

'Yes. The house in Sycamore Lane has to be emptied.' Why couldn't she bring herself to say her parents' house or even her old home? The colonel had been speaking and she hadn't heard. 'I'm sorry, I didn't hear—'

'Pay attention, Beth.' He sounded irritable as if already he had spent too much time with her. 'What I was saying was that you and your aunt must get together to arrange for the house to be emptied.'

'Yes.'

'And, Beth?'

She looked at him enquiringly.

'I feel that you should spend more time with your aunt and her family, get to know them better. They are, after all, the only family you have. Perhaps a weekly visit, Tommy can take you if he is not otherwise engaged but you are of an age now to be able to travel by public transport.'

'Tommy doesn't need to take me at all,' she said spiritedly. Anger was driving out the fear and she was beginning to see this family, the much respected Parker-Munros, in a less flattering light. Their generosity, she was discovering, only extended to those who were of use to them. She had been a companion for Caroline, his delicate daughter, and mistakenly she had thought of herself, not as family, she wouldn't presume that, but as a sort of extended family.

'Very well, you can take public transport and I must remember to give you a little money.' He smiled. 'In your situation it is important to learn to be independent.'

'Yes.'

'Oh, I'd better mention this now in case I forget. Your parents insisted on leaving a little money—'

'Yes, you've already told me that,' she interrupted.

The colonel frowned heavily. He was not in the habit of being interrupted.

'As I was saying,' he continued in clipped tones that

showed his annoyance, 'the money, needless to say, was not touched by me and it is in an account at the bank in your name.'

'Thank you, Colonel Parker-Munro.'

Beth wanted to weep. To weep for her parents who had been so anxious to support their own daughter. They hadn't wanted her to be totally dependent on the Parker-Munros. That her mother and father had gone to India and left her behind, Beth had forgiven them that. She was older now and perhaps her parents had been singled out as very special people to do the kind of work that was required. They had known the dangers before they went and had been prepared to risk their own lives but not the life of their young daughter. She would never know if that were true, but she wanted to believe it.

Her mind kept wandering but she really must keep her attention on the colonel and his voice was droning on.

'—a very small sum, but a start. Once you leave school, Beth, and take up employment you should be able to add to it.' He wasn't an unkind man, she knew that, but he couldn't completely hide his amusement. To him the sum was so paltry, yet for her parents it had been a lot of saving. Just to provide for their daughter they would have considered it no hardship to do without all but the basic necessities. At this moment she felt very proud of them.

'That's it, you may go now, Beth.'

'Thank you.'


'Well, what was it all about?' Caroline was very curious and didn't bother to hide it.

'I've to arrange with my aunt to have my old home cleared out.'

'What for?'

'So that another family can live there.'

'That was all?' She sounded disappointed.

'Yes, what did you expect?'

'Something more interesting than clearing out a lot of rubbish.'

'It is not rubbish.'

'Well, maybe not exactly rubbish but since you were poor the furniture can't be up to much.'

'I do wish, Caroline, that you had the good manners to stop calling me poor. My father was in a good job and we always had proper clothes and my mother cooked nice meals.'

'Not as good as you get here.'

'Sometimes they were better.'

'I'm going to tell my grandmama what you said.'

'Go and tell her then and see if I care. Sometimes, Caroline, you can be hateful.'

'I am not hateful.'

'Yes, you are.' Beth made for the door.

'Where are you going?'

'Out.'

'That is no way to speak to me,' Caroline began haughtily. She had been precariously near to the edge of the sofa and, with her legs in the air and a splendid show of underwear, she toppled over and landed on the floor in an undignified heap.

Beth had her hand on the door knob but turned and came back. Caroline's face was a picture of wounded pride and in spite of her anger and hurt, Beth burst out laughing.

'I have seldom witnessed such unladylike behaviour,' Beth said sounding, though she didn't know it, remarkably like Caroline's grandmother.

As so often happened the quarrel ended in laughter.

'If I am hateful you are worse, Beth Brown, a real lady

would have turned her eyes away.'

'And missed that spectacle?'

Caroline got herself back on the sofa. 'Friends again?' she asked.

'Until the next time,' Beth grinned. Caroline could be infuriating, the absolute limit, but she was still her friend.

The December day was cold and raw as Beth, well wrapped up against the chilly air, waited for her aunt. In her coat pocket was the key to 3 Sycamore Lane but she had no intention of opening that door. She wanted to be with someone when she did. Although it was just two o'clock in the afternoon, already the day was darkening. Beth shivered, not from cold, just from a dread that she couldn't explain. Her aunt would probably say that she should have gone inside to get out of the cold wind but the chilly dampness of an unheated house could be worse than standing outside.

Her own suggestion had been that she should meet her aunt off the bus but for some reason this hadn't been acceptable. Meeting at the house would be better, she had said, and that way there would be no danger of missing one another. Since the Dundee bus made only one stop in the village, Beth, for the life of her, couldn't imagine how they could possibly miss each other but it was always better to fall in with Aunt Anne's wishes.

She didn't stand directly outside the house; Beth did not want neighbours coming out to talk to her. Her mother had never had much coming and going with them, just passing the time of day unless there was illness and then she would enquire. And in her own case, with Tommy transporting her to and from school, there had been no need for her to go anywhere near her old home.

The end of the lane was the best place to stand and from

there she would be able to see her aunt climbing the hill. Her wrist watch told Beth that the bus was due and after five more minutes a straggle of passengers began the climb. Ahead of them was Aunt Anne. Beth set off to meet her.

'Hello, Aunt Anne. Coming to meet you was better than standing waiting.'

'I daresay,' said her aunt. There was no physical contact, no kiss on the cheek, no hug. 'You're colder here than Dundee, that's what I always told Harriet.' They had fallen into step. 'I'm still not taking it in, Beth, and the little faith I had I'm in danger of losing.' She was out of breath. 'Slow down, lass, once I could have run up this brae but those days are gone.'

Beth didn't think she had been hurrying but she reduced her pace.

'How could a God in heaven let that happen to folk doing His work, I keep asking myself?'

Beth shook her head. 'My father would have answered that it was His will.'

'So he would and meaningless words they are to my way of thinking. Why does God take good living folk like Harriet and her man, not forgetting those others who died with them, and spare murderers and robbers?'

'I know, I wonder those things too, Aunt Anne.'

'Do you? Aye, I suppose you do.' There was a weariness in her voice.

'Yes, I do and I feel angry, then I'm afraid to be angry.'

'Stands to reason, you are their bairn.' She gave a half smile. 'Some of it must have rubbed off.'

Beth smiled at that as they walked to the top of the hill. Now that she was looking at her aunt properly, Beth thought that she looked poorly and there were dark shadows under her eyes. Like her mother had, Aunt Anne wore a lot of drab colours. Something brighter and she might have looked better, Beth thought, then she remembered that her aunt was in mourning and she didn't know for how long that went on.

'Are you keeping well, Aunt Anne?'

'Well enough, I have my worries but they'll keep for the now anyway.'

Did that mean that she was going to hear about them? Beth wondered.

'Is the house clean?' she asked abruptly.

'Should be, two of the maids spent a whole day in it.'

'That's not to say they were working. Without supervision I doubt they would do all that much.'

'I think they are quite dependable, Aunt Anne.'

'Doesn't matter all that much. It would have if your mother had been coming home. Still it's easier and nicer to handle stuff not thick in dust.'

In silence they reached 3 Sycamore Lane and walked up to the front door.

'Gives you a peculiar feeling.'

'Yes,' Beth said fighting a lump in her throat. It was far worse than she had expected. If only her aunt would take the key from her and open the door but she made no move.

'Just given the front door key, were you?'

'Yes.'

'Not many got to come in this way, just those and such as those. For the rest of us it was the back door. Of course, you'll be minding all that?'

'Yes.' She was remembering it clearly, the shining brass door knob and letter box. So dull now, no shine at all on them.

'Come on, lass, open up and get it over.'

Beth inserted the key, surprised to find that it turned so

easily when before she recalled it being stiff to turn. Those who had followed her mother must have come in and out this way.

The door opened on to a small, narrow passage with enough light getting in to let them see to go about. Beth went ahead. The door to the living-room was slightly ajar and she pushed it wide. There was a box of matches on the mantelpiece and Beth picked them up, meaning to light the mantle, but she was stopped.

'No, lass, never take chances with gas, we'll manage well enough.'

It was a strange feeling returning to a house that had once been home and Beth shivered.

'Upsetting you, is it?'

'Yes, a little. It looks familiar and strange at the same time. That sounds silly, I know. I remembered it as being so much bigger and surely it wasn't as shabby?'

'Told you, didn't I, that no one looks after a house the way you would yourself?'

'Yes, you did.' The chair that her father had once sat in looked sad and lost as did the smaller one that had been her mother's. Daft to think like that but she couldn't help it. Aunt Anne was watching her face. 'It's more than shabby, Aunt Anne, it looks so neglected.' She wanted to weep.

'Worse for you after that posh place you've been living in. It's clean enough, there isn't a lot of dust in here.' She rubbed her finger over the surface of the sideboard. She paused and then sat down, not in either armchair but on a hard wooden chair beside the table. 'Have you thought of what you are to do with everything? It's all yours now.'

'There is nothing I want. Oh, yes, there is, just one thing and I hope it is still there.' They had both been talking in low voices, just above a whisper, but Beth raised hers.

'What is it?'

'A picture.' Beth went quickly into the room that she had slept in for nine years. How pokey it was, she thought, looking about her and comparing it with her bedroom in Inverbrae House. Her eyes went to the bookcase, the one her father had lovingly made from an old orange box, perhaps two orange boxes. It was stacked in a corner, the shelves broken and now only fit for firewood. The lump in her throat returned but she would fight her tears, Aunt Anne wouldn't like her to break down.

The picture was there, on the wall above the bed and was just as she remembered it. The bedcover was stained and tatty looking and there was no one to scold her for standing on the bed in heavy outdoor shoes. Carefully she removed the painting from the hook on the wall and got down from the bed. Then she went through to her aunt who had got up and was examining the sideboard.

'Look, Aunt Anne, my father bought it for me.'

'That's the harbour! Good likeness, I'd say, but I'm no expert on paintings.'

'Take whatever you want, Aunt Anne, I'd like you to and the rest will just have to be disposed of somehow.' She looked about for something to wrap the picture in but there was nothing, nothing in the kitchen either. It didn't matter, she would carry it under her arm.

'Pity to throw out what could be of use to someone. Not me, lass, I've enough to do me all my days but Adam and Morag are just starting out and what is here would be a grand start to them, tide them over nicely until they can afford to replace them with new. Not the sideboard, though, I was with your mother when she bought that.

Cost a bit it did but as I always say you get what you pay for. A good polish and it'll take pride of place in Adam's house.'

'I'm so glad,' Beth smiled and she was glad. It was nice to think of her parents' furniture still being in the family. 'How will they manage to get all this to Dundee?'

'Adam knows a lad with a van. Mebbe need two journeys but you don't need to worry yourself about it. The pair of them will clear the lot and Morag will give it a good brush out.' She paused. 'Gone through the cupboards and drawers, have you?'

'No.'

'Neither have I, better do it though.'

They went round the house checking on everything.

'Nothing much just some china and cutlery and other odds and ends. Morag might find some of it useful.'

'Sure to and, of course, your mother had away with her what she valued. The pity of it is you'll never see any of it.'

They were both silent. They knew that everything that Harriet and George had possessed would have long gone and that there would be no money. What little they had would have been spent on those they considered less fortunate than themselves. That was their way.

'Sit yourself down, lass, I've something to tell you,' she said abruptly.

Beth sat down on a wooden chair and looked expectantly at her mother's sister and wondered what was coming.

'I'll not beat about the bush, Beth, your Uncle Fred has been put on short time.'

'Oh, I am sorry to hear that.'

The woman sighed and straightened her back. 'Aye, it's come as a shock. Bad though it is, there are some who have been harder hit and lost their jobs. Luke's working but for all he brings in it doesn't keep him or anything like it. Adam was a help, or becoming one, but he'll be away from the house before long. Which brings me to the wedding. I don't suppose you would want to go?'

Beth would very much have liked to attend and meet the cousins she hardly knew and be introduced to Morag but it didn't sound as though Aunt Anne wanted her there. She wondered about that, it wasn't like her aunt, then she thought that she understood. Aunt Anne had hoped her sister would be home from India and able to join in the festivities whereas Beth, on her own, would be a constant reminder of the tragedy. A tragedy that needed to be forgotten on that special day.

'I would have liked to be at Adam's wedding but it would be awkward – I mean, getting back to Inverbrae House could cause problems and I wouldn't like to be a nuisance,' she ended lamely.

'Who said anything about being a nuisance? You wouldn't be that but, as you say, transport could be difficult. You could hardly expect your folk to send a car for you.'

The 'your folk' had a false sound. 'No, I wouldn't expect it of them.'

Her aunt smiled. Beth thought it was of relief. 'These affairs can go on long enough when folk get cheery.'

Beth nodded. 'I suppose so. You'll give Adam and Morag my very best wishes, won't you?'

'I'll do that, lass.'

'Poor Uncle Fred, he'll be miserable about being on short time.'

'Miserable and worried like myself. Yon's a good house we have but it's a steep rent and that has to be paid before anything else.' She paused. 'I'm just that glad to know that you are happy with those Parker folk. You are, aren't you?'

'Yes.' Beth wondered if that were strictly true. It wasn't easy to be happy when you felt yourself to be unwanted but that was her own worry and by the sound of it her aunt had enough of her own.

'Well, now, that's a big load off my mind because, lass, I couldn't take you now, I couldn't afford to. You've still two years to go before you can leave school and whatever job you managed to get it would only pay a pittance.' She smiled sadly. 'You do understand, Beth?'

'Yes, of course I do, Aunt Anne.' Not wanting her face to betray her, Beth spoke quickly. 'But before we go I would like a look out the back.'

'On you go, then, but don't be long.'

'I won't.'

Now that it was sinking in the shock was devastating and with it came a feeling of unreality. This couldn't be happening to her, it couldn't. Blindly she went through to the kitchen. The key was in the back door, she turned it and went outside. A greyness added to the gloom and after seeing the condition of the house, Beth had no great hopes for the garden. Fortunately the semi-darkness hid most of the neglect but in any case did she really care? She had cared but not any more. The new occupants could deal with the neglected house and garden and lucky they were if that was all they had to worry about. Her own position, her uncertain future, could hardly be worse.

Standing just outside the door, her eyes went down to the foot of the garden where once had been the chicken coop. Her mother had had it removed and that corner tidied before they had set out for India. That chicken coop, she thought, had been the means of altering her life. Had it not been for taking the eggs to Inverbrae House she would not have met Caroline and she would not be facing this crisis that loomed ever more threatening. Instead she would have been living with her aunt and uncle in Dundee and by this time considered part of the family. Changed circumstances would not have meant her being shown the door. They wouldn't have put her out or rather put her into an orphanage when times got hard. She would have shared those hard times with them.

She must go inside now. Beth forced a smile to her face and rejoined her aunt.

'Well?'

'Much as I expected, Aunt Anne. Whoever gets the house will have a lot to do.'

'Hard work never killed anyone and I'm getting anxious about that bus,' she said, getting to her feet and picking up her handbag. 'Is it due soon, do you know? I wouldn't want just to miss one and have a long, cold wait for the next.'

Beth consulted her watch. 'If we leave now you should be all right.'

'No need for you to come.'

'Of course I'll see you off and about the key—' Beth began as she locked up.

'Give it here, good job you reminded me.'

'It has to be handed in—' Beth began anxiously.

'I know, Beth, I have the address, it was on the letter I got. Rest assured the key will be handed in once the house has been cleared out and the place swept clean.'

'That's fine then.' She handed over the key and her aunt opened her bag and dropped it to the bottom.

They had almost reached the square when the bus arrived and three people got out. A few were waiting and they quickly got on.

'Better hurry, Aunt Anne, it just turns and leaves.'

'Not without me, it doesn't,' but she hurried all the same and got herself on to the step of the bus. 'Look after yourself, Beth,' she said, turning briefly to her niece before going forward to a seat.

'Goodbye, Aunt Anne.'

'Goodbye, lass.'

The bus moved away and Beth felt a lump in her throat. Her hand went up to wave but her aunt was already looking for her fare. She let her hand fall and turned to walk back the way she had come. At least she had been able to hide her shock from her aunt and she was thankful for that. It was certainly true that she had never wanted to go to Dundee and live with her aunt and uncle, indeed she had dreaded the thought, but now that the offer was no longer there Beth realised that, at the back of her mind, she had always thought of it as a home if the worst came to the worst. And it had, and she had no place to go.

No one cared about her. No one cared what happened to her. She was about to be alone, an orphan in a frightening world. Fear made her stomach knot. She had never felt so utterly and completely alone.

With her painting under her arm, her head down, she trudged the road back to Inverbrae House. Almost without realising it she was at the gates of the house and ahead of her a gardener raked smooth the gravel on the drive. Beth didn't feel ready to talk, she needed time to calm herself and still the panicky fluttering in her stomach. Leaving the main drive she took one of the winding paths that circled the landscaped gardens. The bleakness of winter was all around, the trees were bare and the gardens without colour. Only very infrequently did Caroline and Beth venture far from the summer house and the smooth velvety lawn where once two six-year-olds had met. In the cold weather Caroline was unwilling to leave the warmth of the house unless it was to be driven to a house party or some other entertainment.

Calmer now, remembering that Caroline would be having her music lesson, she went in through the servants' entrance and unseen slipped up to her bedroom. Looking about her for a suitable hiding place for the picture, her first thought was of the floor of the wardrobe with something covering it. She decided that the drawer where she kept her underwear would be better. She couldn't bear it if someone ridiculed the picture and she knew that she would not be permitted to hang it on the wall in her bedroom.

Beth would have loved to master the piano and had secretly hoped that she would receive lessons but in this the colonel and his mother were in total agreement. Young ladies in Caroline's position were expected to have mastered the piano and be able to give a reasonable performance to invited guests. Beth would have no need of such an accomplishment.

Her head ached and for a little while she sat on the bed refusing to let herself think. She tried to let her mind wander to happier times and for a short while she succeeded. Feeling better, she went to their own sitting-room and found Caroline already there.

'Hello, I thought you would still be having your music lesson.'

'My dear Beth,' she said haughtily. 'I have had my lesson and if I have to do another scale for that stupid teacher I'll go mad.'

'You should be grateful for the opportunity to learn.' Beth knew what was going to follow but it was helping her to act normally.

'I – do – not – have to be grateful for anything.'

'Lucky you.'

'And poor you, always having to be grateful for every little thing. If I were you, I'd be sick of the word "grateful".'

'I am sick of the word. And if I have children, that word will never be used to them.'

'How did it go?'

'All right.'

'Not very forthcoming, are you?'

'Didn't expect you to be interested.'

'Well, I am. Did you get all your stuff disposed of?'

'Disposed of, yes I did. My cousin, Adam, is getting married very soon and my aunt suggested it would start them off.'

'Will you be going to the wedding?'

'No.'

'Why not?'

'I don't want to,' she lied.

'Because it is too soon after – you know—?'

Beth was surprised and a little touched. Caroline could be thoughtful at times.

'Yes, that is the reason.'

'You'll have to give your cousin a gift and how do you do that when you have no money?'

'That's where you're wrong,' Beth said lifting her head high. 'I do have an account in my own name at the bank. Your father told me about it, it was money my parents sent towards my – my upkeep.'

'Wouldn't be very much.'

'A little to you is a lot to me.'

'You sound very sorry for yourself all of a sudden.'

'I don't mean to.'

'Ask daddy, he'll give you money to buy a gift and we can go together and choose something.'

'Adam and Morag are getting plenty from me. I'm just

about furnishing their home.'

Caroline giggled.

'What's so funny?'

'You and me. We are poles apart but we still manage to laugh together.'

Beth nodded. It was true.

# Chapter Fifteen

On Christmas eve and again on Christmas day there were flurries of snow and the forecast was for snow after the new year. In preparation for a heavy fall, and in case the village was cut off, folk took the precaution of getting in emergency supplies. At Inverbrae House the fires burned brightly. Stocks of fuel and food were plentiful and there was an abundance of everything, enough to last for a number of weeks in the unlikely event that the roads remained impassable for that length of time.

There had been the usual festivities at Inverbrae House with the exchange of Christmas gifts. Below the tree in the drawing-room the gifts were piled up. Caroline's pile was by far the largest and her presents the most expensive. From the colonel, Beth had been given a sum of money to choose her own books. Her other gifts were small, mostly boxes of handkerchiefs or gloves with only Jenny treating them alike. She had given both girls beautiful silk squares, Caroline's in shades of pink and Beth's in shades of blue.

By the middle of January most of the snow had disappeared and the hazard had changed to icy roads. The road to Sandyneuk School was particularly dangerous for the car and Beth insisted that Tommy took her only part of the way. She didn't mind slithering and sliding to school, others did it.

In preparation for Rowanbank, Caroline was being

taught French and a little Latin and she was particularly proud of her progress in French.

'You don't get taught languages in your village school,' she said, preening herself. 'When I go on holiday to Paris I'll be able to use my French.'

'You mean you hope they'll understand you?'

'Of course they will understand me. Mattie is a fluent French speaker and she is teaching me how to raise my voice at the end, as though everything were a question.'

'I wish we got to learn French but when I go up to the secondary, I'll get it there.'

'If I taught you, you'd know some before you went.'

'Would you really teach me?'

'I could try and, Beth Brown, if I decide to give you homework, I would expect you to do it.'

'Yes, Miss Parker-Munro,' Beth said meekly. She wanted very much to learn another language and wondered if Caroline meant it. 'This isn't a joke? You would really teach me?'

'Haven't I just said so and it could be fun. When you reach the stage that I am, it will be easier, you'll just be one lesson behind me.' She paused. 'Not Latin though, it's horrible, all those ghastly verbs. Mattie says it is a dead language and all I can say to that is that I wish to goodness it could be well and truly buried.'

Beth laughed. Caroline was such a mixture. Here she was being kind and helpful but in a few short minutes that could change and she would become rude, difficult and impossible to please.

As the dullness of winter changed to the delicate colours of spring, boarding school was seldom mentioned. But it was always at the back of Beth's mind, a nagging worry that wouldn't go away. Only to Jenny could she have poured out her worries but it was as though they were deliberately keeping them apart. On those occasions when Jenny was at Inverbrae House, Beth would be sure to be sent on some errand that kept her away and only at the dinner table did they set eyes on one another. Then Jenny would smile across to her in that special way she had and make some remark that Beth would answer. Quickly the colonel or Mrs Parker-Munro would claim Jenny's attention and occasionally bring Caroline into the conversation. Beth never spoke unless she was spoken to. It didn't upset her being left out, she had become used to it.

On one occasion Jenny and Beth did meet. Caroline had left that morning to spend the day with her aunt and her cousin who was home for half term. The invitation had not included Beth. Jenny was coming out of the study on her way to the drawing-room, intending to sit with the old lady until the colonel had attended to work that required his immediate attention.

'Beth, wait!' she called as she caught sight of her.

Beth swung round. 'Jenny! I didn't see you,' she said smiling broadly.

'I know you didn't. We never do seem to get the opportunity to have a talk.' She laughed. 'You are not by any chance trying to avoid me?'

Beth looked wounded. 'I would never do that. You didn't really think that did you, Jenny?'

'Of course not, you silly goose. Where are you making for?'

'Our sitting-room, Caroline's and mine.'

'We could be interrupted there, what about your bedroom?' She raised her eyebrows. 'Caroline, I believe, is taken care of and I don't imagine anyone else would barge in?'

'No, they wouldn't.'

'Lead on. I can't stay long or there will be a search party sent out.'

Beth giggled. A few minutes in Jenny's company and she forgot her worries. Once inside the bedroom with the door shut, Beth said, 'There is something I want to show you, Jenny. It's a painting my father bought for me and I went over and got it from the house.'

'A jolly good job you did, someone might have taken a fancy to it.'

Beth shook her head. 'No, Jenny, the people who lived in my house were careless but honest. I don't think they took anything that didn't belong to them.'

Jenny was sitting on the bed looking bandbox fresh in a long black skirt and primrose yellow blouse with a frilled neckline and matching cuffs. From where she was she watched Beth open a drawer and bring out a framed picture.

'Why keep it hidden? It should be hanging up on the wall where you can see it.' Taking the small painting from Beth, she began to study it.

'Beth, dear, this is very good. Mind you, I wouldn't call myself an expert but I would say that the artist has a lot of talent. This is Sandyneuk harbour and he has captured it exactly.' She smiled at Beth with her eyes sparkling. 'Who knows, one day it might be worth quite a lot of money.'

'I would never sell it, no matter how much it was worth.' Beth's voice faltered. 'It's all I have to remind me of my parents.'

'You must have photographs?'

'A few. I wish I had more.'

'You have your memories, no one can take those away from you,' Jenny said gently.

Beth looked down at her hands. 'I find it harder and harder to remember them.'

'That is the way of the world, my dear,' Jenny said, giving the picture back to Beth. 'We are meant to forget the pain and heartbreak of losing those nearest and dearest to us but from time to time you will be given glimpses of your old life, special moments that will never leave you.'

'I'd like to think that.'

'Then you must.' She watched Beth take another look at the harbour scene then prepare to put it back in the drawer.

'Would you like it hung on the wall?'

Beth shook her head. 'No,' she said firmly.

'What would you like?'

Beth's dark blue eyes looked into hazel eyes that were full of understanding. 'Would you take it and keep it for me?'

'If that is what you want?'

'It is. You don't have to hang it up unless you want.'

'I do want. I shall hang it up in the hallway for all to see. Would you mind very much, Beth, if I got another frame for it? That one is—'

'A bit awful,' Beth finished for her. 'My father said that one day he would get a new frame for it only – only—'

'Only he never managed it. Talk about your parents, Beth. Believe me, it is better to do so and each time it will get a little easier. Regarding the frame, I'll get a friend of mine to see to it and since this is to be our secret we have to find a way of getting it from here to my home. Any suggestions?' She began whispering as though they were conspirators.

'I can't think of one.'

'I can,' she said. 'Listen to this. On my way here Colonel Parker-Munro very kindly stopped the car so that I could collect a dress from the dress-maker. It is in a box on the back seat and you, my child, must find something to wrap the painting in then take it out to the car, it won't be locked, and tuck it under the box.'

'Won't Colonel Parker-Munro wonder how it got there?'

'Not him. Men don't notice these things, Beth, and even if he did I'd think of something.'

Beth didn't doubt it for a moment. 'I can get paper and string from the kitchen,' she said eagerly.

'Good, we've got that settled and now before I fly, tell me is all well or is something worrying you?'

Beth hesitated. It didn't seem fair to burden Jenny with her worries.

'Come on, there is something so out with it.'

'It's only that I am almost sure that Caroline is going to Rowanbank and I think it might be soon. When she goes I won't be able to stay here and I don't know what is going to happen to me.'

'You are right that she is going, that is definite enough, but as to when I wouldn't know.'

Beth nodded miserably.

'It is the thought of living with your aunt and uncle in Dundee that is making you unhappy?'

Beth looked at Jenny but said nothing. How could she tell Jenny that she was no longer welcome in her aunt's home, that the door was closed?

Jenny misunderstood the silence. The poor child was dreading the thought of life in a tenement and who could blame her? There could hardly be a bigger contrast to this life and the life she would be going to.

Jenny gave her a quick hug before leaving. 'Try not to worry. Things will work out, you'll see.'

Beth forced a smile. It was easy to say not to worry but Jenny didn't know just how bad it was. Right now she

would have given a lot to have her Uncle Fred in full
employment and the door once again open to her.

On her way to the drawing-room, Jenny was thoughtful.
That poor child was making herself ill with worry and
Jenny was getting angrier by the minute. It was monstrous
to treat a child the way they were doing and unless she
herself did something about it, Beth's fate was sealed. She
was still thinking what she could do when she joined the
old lady who had wakened with a start when Jenny
entered.

'Never in all my born days have I heard anything so
ridiculous. Have you gone completely mad, Nigel?'

'No, Mother, but I am in danger of losing my patience.'

'Then kindly listen to me—'

'No, Mother, I am doing the talking for a change.' He
saw her colour was high and her breathing harsh but this
time he was ignoring the signs. Heartless and unlike him
though it was, he had just about had all he could take.
'Like it or not, Beth is going to Rowanbank with Caroline
because I have no choice in the matter,' he said slowly and
distinctly.

'Who may I ask is holding a gun to your head?' she said
sarcastically.

'Jenny, if you must know.'

'What has Jenny to do with it?'

'The answer to that should be nothing but unfortunately
Jenny is making Beth her business.'

'And you are allowing her to dictate to you?' The
eyebrows shot up and she glared.

'As I have already told you, Mother, I have no choice in
the matter.'

'Kindly explain yourself.'

'Should I not agree, Jenny is to take Beth to live with

her and her housekeeper and enrol Beth at a good day school.'

'I wouldn't have believed this of Jenny.'

'Neither would I, but apparently she and Beth had grown very close in the week they were together at Greystanes.' He looked closely at his mother, at her angry face. 'And if you recall, Mother dear, you were very much in favour of Beth going there.'

'Yes, I was. I saw it as a way of separating Caroline and that girl. I see my mistake when it is too late but there is no use dwelling on that.'

'I agree with you there,' he said wearily.

'Jenny doesn't mean it and you should realise that, Nigel.' She took out her handkerchief and dabbed at the corner of her mouth. 'She has no intention of saddling herself with Beth. It is no more than a threat to get her own way. Scheming woman that she is,' she said viciously. 'How wrong we can be about people.'

'Jenny does mean it, every word of it. If we are to keep our good name, we cannot afford to go against her.'

'Keep our good name? What on earth are you talking about?'

'The tragedy in India made the headlines throughout the country not just here. Our friends and acquaintances got to know that Beth was living here as a companion for Caroline and she came in for a lot of sympathy.'

'Of course such a gruesome tragedy was on everyone's lips. We have all been very sympathetic and understanding. No one could have been kinder than you during that difficult time when she disappeared and had us so worried. We were all very supportive, we couldn't have done more for her even if she had been family.' She paused and said forcefully, 'We have nothing at all with which to reproach ourselves.'

'True, but our friends are going to have something to say if Beth goes to live with Jenny and she will tell them the reason that we no longer want her.'

'You are convinced that Jenny is serious?'

'I have no doubts whatsoever.'

Mrs Parker-Munro was thoughtful for a long time and Nigel drummed his fingers on the spindly-legged table beside him.

'Do stop that, it is getting on my nerves.'

'Sorry.'

Suddenly she smiled. 'How silly we are to be worried about something that won't happen. Rowanbank would never accept Beth.'

'At one time that would have been true.'

'Still is.'

'No, Mother, times are changing I'm afraid. More people are going abroad and firms anxious to entice the best are offering perks. One is to have their children's fees paid at a good boarding school and to meet that demand new schools are opening up and offering a first-class education together with all the extras that would appeal to parents forced to make a painful separation.'

'Even so, Rowanbank is very exclusive. It always has been and they wouldn't want to lower their standards.'

'I'm sure you are right, Mother. They won't want to lower their standards, no one does, but if they have vacancies they can't afford not to fill them.'

She threw up her hands. 'This is a world gone mad and I can't say I'll be reluctant to leave it.' It wasn't true, of course, the will to live was stronger than ever. She was needed at Inverbrae House since marriage between Nigel and that woman, a union she had once encouraged, would never happen. Her son had had a narrow escape.

Inverbrae House needed a woman and that woman in a

few years time would be Caroline. She would see to it, if God spared her, that her grand-daughter made a suitable marriage and not to take too long about it either. She was in favour of girls marrying young. Beth must be kept out of sight. It could be done, it would have to be done.

Caroline, she knew, would not be returning home until after the evening meal and the old lady had no intention of eating with Beth present. Her reluctant admiration for this quiet-spoken girl had changed to a bitter resentment. It wasn't the girl's fault, she accepted that, but nevertheless she had caused nothing but trouble.

Attending the village school, Beth was a nobody but once she was accepted at Rowanbank, and Nigel thought it more than probable, she would have the kind of school behind her that would open all doors. With her appearance and all the signs of respectability that Inverbrae House had given her, eligible males seeking a wife would be queuing up and poor, pretty little Caroline would have to take a back seat.

Pressing the bell brought the maid.

'Yes, m'am?'

'The master and I will be dining at the usual time but Beth will have her meal in the girls' sitting-room. See to that.'

'Very good m'am.'

'Just the two of us, Mother?'

'Yes.'

He nodded. It was a relief. At the moment, the less he saw of Beth the better he would be pleased. It was all getting completely out of hand and he cursed the day, instead of blessing it, when Beth Brown had captivated his daughter and he, too, had been charmed.

Left to dine on her own, Beth had a book propped up in front of her and couldn't have been more pleased. The very thought of sitting at the dining-room table without Caroline had terrified her. Once it had been the old lady who had made her feel uncomfortable but now it was both of them. The colonel was always perfectly polite but there was a coldness that hadn't been there before.

'Who is your letter from?'

Beth had picked it up from the hall table, an envelope addressed to herself in a large school hand.

'Don't know.'

Caroline glanced at it. 'Cheap envelope and from someone not very well educated. I could write better than that even before I was nine years of age.'

'But you are a real clever clogs and think of the opportunities you've had.'

'Oh, come on, open it or aren't you going to?' she said impatiently.

'I'll open it when I feel like it and you know what curiosity did?'

'Killed the cat. Go on open it, I'm dying to know who is writing to you.'

'I don't ask about your letters.'

'You could hardly since I never get any unless on my birthday. I don't have secrets from you.'

'Yes you do, lots of them. How often do you go and leave me on my own?'

'That's not my fault or are you blaming me?'

'No.'

'I can hardly force Aunt Gwen to invite you to her house since she doesn't like you, now can I?'

'No.' She had been looking at the envelope but raised her eyes. 'I wouldn't want to go.' Beth didn't much care for Caroline's mother's sister. Her Uncle Robert was all right and his appearance had come as a bit of a surprise.

She had expected someone more like the colonel for Mrs Esslemont. Robert Esslemont was a stout, bald-headed man with a pleasant manner and much given to wearing plus-fours. Ruth, the cousin at Rowanbank, took after her father in appearance and nature. She was an ungainly, plain girl with a lovely nature that was sorely tried by her mother's constant reference to her bulging figure and she was the despair of her small, neat mother who secretly wished that Caroline were her daughter. Her niece, though two years younger, was already interested in fashion and, being so pretty and dainty, was a joy to dress.

'Ruth was asking for you.'

'That was nice.'

'She wondered why you weren't with me.'

'Did you tell her?'

'I didn't have to. Aunt Gwen overheard her and said that now that I was growing up, I would be mixing with other young people. She said it wouldn't be possible to include you, Beth, that it was different when we were small children. Oh, well, if you aren't going to open that wretched letter, don't,' she said tossing her head and turning away.

Beth left her and went to her bedroom. Opening the letter she drew out the pages of lined paper that had been taken from a jotter. Both sides of them were filled with the large writing. Beth could tell that the sender was not in the habit of writing letters but that a great deal of care had been taken in the writing of it. She began to read.

> 19 Broomfield Road,
> Dundee

Dear Beth,

 Adam's mother said that she had thanked you for all the furniture you let us have but I wanted to write to you

*myself. Adam and me could hardly believe it. We
expected to wait for a long time to get furniture except for
what we couldn't do without, of course. Adam's mother
is a very good worker, well you would know that and we
have polished everything until you can nearly see your
face in it.*

*Adam says he only remembers you as a little bairn.
The wedding went off well. I was in a white dress with a
veil, it was my cousin's but we are about the same size so
it didn't need much alteration. Only when it was nearly
the end did my Uncle Joe make a fool of himself. He isn't
used to the drink and I don't know who got him into that
state. Adam thought he was funny but his mother did not
and she wasn't very pleased. Still it was a wedding after
all and my mother said it was to be expected and she
thought our side behaved themselves quite well.*

*Thank you very much again and if you want to come
and see me and Adam we'll be very pleased.*
*Your cousin-in-law*
*Morag*

Beth read it over again and again and found herself
smiling. It was such a nice letter, a genuinely friendly
letter and she wanted very much to meet Morag and
Adam too. She was smiling when she went to join
Caroline.

'The letter was from my cousin's wife, thanking me for
the furniture and inviting me to their house.'

'Will you go?'

'Yes, I'm looking forward to it.'

# Chapter Sixteen

She closed the door and the colonel looked up briefly.

'Sit down, Beth,' he said curtly.

A shaft of sunlight came through the window and showed up the hairs on the back of his hand. Beth pulled out the chair and sat down with her hands folded in her lap. She had on a grey flannel skirt, white blouse and a grey cardigan that was unbuttoned. For so long she had dreaded this summons and now that it had come she was curiously relieved. There was no doubt in her mind about what she was to hear. Bad news was something she had come to associate with a summons to the colonel's study.

Her eye followed his pen as it raced over the headed paper then stopped while he read over what he had written. It must have satisfied him because he scrawled his signature at the foot of the page and returned the pen to the marble stand. That done he looked across at Beth, subjecting her to a lengthy and unsmiling scrutiny. Once she would have hung her head in confusion wondering what she had done to displease but no longer. Her dark eyes held his gaze.

'What I am about to say, Beth, will come as a surprise to you,' he said making an arc of his fingers. She had begun to notice that it was something he did when he was either thoughtful or annoyed.

With his eyes still on her, Beth wondered if he was waiting for her to speak. Or could it be that he was just postponing the moment, searching perhaps for words to soften the blow?

'I am arranging for you to go to Rowanbank with Caroline.'

Beth stared at him stupidly. What was he saying?

'Well?'

'I am to go to Rowanbank?' she squeaked.

'I believe that is what I have just said.'

'I don't know what to say, Colonel. I never thought – I never expected—'

He screwed up his face in annoyance and cut her off. 'The reason for you going to Rowanbank need not concern you. However, no pressure will be put upon you to accept. Indeed it would be better for you and understandable—'

'Oh, please, I would like to go, I—'

'Kindly do not interrupt. The one thing you must understand is that in no circumstances can you continue to live at Inverbrae House once Caroline is away at school.'

'I do understand that,' she said quietly.

'An ordinary secondary school would be more suitable for a girl in your position who must earn her own living. Your education in such an establishment would prepare you for suitable employment.' He smiled. 'Rowanbank is for young ladies—'

'Who don't have to earn their living,' she added without thinking.

'Precisely – and I do wish you would get out of that deplorable habit of interrupting. It is the mark of bad manners.'

'I'm very sorry. I didn't mean to be rude and I

202

appreciate all you've said but I would still very much like to go to Rowanbank with Caroline.' She stopped breathless but she just had to get that in.

'One day you may regret the choice.'

'I'll work very hard, Colonel, I promise you that,' she said earnestly, 'and I am very grateful.'

'Your academic progress is of no interest to me,' he said cruelly, 'and as to being grateful so you should.' He paused and spoke in a resigned voice. 'Since you have set your mind on going to Rowanbank I would expect, indeed I insist that you help Caroline at all times and put her interests before your own.'

'I can promise that.' Beth was bewildered. There was a lot she didn't understand but her relief was so great that she wasn't to be homeless after all, that she had no wish to question her good fortune.

The colonel saw the relief and bewilderment on Beth's expressive face and felt a rush of shame. Why was he taking it out on the child? She was in no way to blame for this mess. He it was who had brought her to this house expecting it to be for a short period but fate had dealt them all a bitter blow. The death of Beth's parents was having unforeseen repercussions. He gave a wry smile. The real culprit was Jenny. Not many dictated to him and he deplored his weakness but Jenny had become necessary to his happiness. He had never known anyone like her. No matter the bitterness of the disagreement, she never let it spoil their relationship, declaring that the two were quite separate. If anything, their relationship had improved. She had become more loving and as a result even more desirable.

Jenny could forgive and forget, she wasn't petty and never vindictive. Pity, he thought, that his Mother wouldn't take a leaf out of her book but alas she was not the forgiving kind and Mrs Cuthbert, as she had now become, was no longer welcome at Inverbrae House. It made it dashed awkward for him.

Beth waited while the colonel appeared to be lost in thought. She pondered often at the change in him. Not that he was ever unkind, just distant, as though he didn't have a great deal of time for her. Yet how could that be? Having her educated at Rowanbank would cost a great lot of money and he hadn't wanted her to accept. Why offer her the chance then?

Was he under some kind of pressure, but if so by whom? Count out Mrs Parker-Munro, most certainly count her out, Beth thought grimly. That only left Caroline. Had she demanded it as being the only way to get her to go to Rowanbank? Mentally she shook her head. That wouldn't do, Caroline wasn't too concerned about going on her own to boarding school. Then she smiled to herself as something just occurred to her. Of course it was Caroline, she could be quite the actress when she chose. She'd had it planned all along. Those lessons in French were to keep her from being too far behind. Her friend had done this for her. Beth felt a surge of pure happiness. If Caroline wanted to keep it a secret then she would be happy to go along with it.

'You have a very unfortunate habit of letting your attention wander,' the colonel said testily.

'I am sorry, I do apologise.'

'A display of bad manners such as that will not be tolerated at Rowanbank.'

Beth hung her head.

'Persuading the headmistress to accept you was difficult in the extreme but, since she has now consented to have you as a pupil, it is essential that you work hard to reach the necessary standard.'

'Yes. When do I—?'

'The school year starts at the end of September. It will be necessary for you to leave the village school immediately and from now on to share lessons with Caroline.'

Beth wouldn't shed any tears over leaving her school. She had been happy enough there but had no close friends.

He smiled, the cold unfriendliness gone. 'This has come as a shock to you but remember that school for Caroline will be a much greater ordeal than it will be for you.'

'I'll look after her.'

'Yes, you must do that.' He stood up. 'That is all, Beth, off you go.'

'Thank you, Colonel.' She got up and closed the door quietly behind her. Then she let out a long, shaky breath, hardly able to take it in. It was just too wonderful to be true. She just managed to stop herself from jumping for joy and hurried along to her bedroom. Once inside she shut the door and dashed to the mirror. Her face was flushed, her eyes sparkling and turning away she danced round the room before collapsing on to the bed. With her hands behind her head, she thought back to those scenes in the study and the wonderful opportunity that had come her way.

When she did go along to the sitting-room her heart was singing with happiness.

'Where have you been?' Caroline demanded. 'It is very nearly lunch time.'

'I was in the study, your father wanted to see me.'

'What about?'

'As if you didn't know.'

'I don't and I won't until you tell me.'

Beth smiled happily. 'Caroline, you could make a name for yourself on the stage.'

'I am that good?'

'You are and I'm over the moon about going with you to Rowanbank.'

Caroline looked puzzled. 'What on earth has that got to do with the stage?'

'Nothing at all but thank you for teaching me French.'

'I'm a good teacher?'

'Oh, yes, you are and it will make it so much easier. Mattie won't have to start at the beginning.'

'That's what you think. She'll say I haven't taught you properly and the reason for that is she won't want to admit how good I am.' She looked very pleased with herself.

'You can take it from me that you are good. Now, we are going for lunch, aren't we?'

'Yes, come on,' Caroline said jumping to her feet.

'A walk after it, it is such a lovely day.'

'We'll see.'

'Caroline, you need fresh air. It isn't good to be cooped up indoors.'

'A short walk then, no further than the village.'

'That'll do me,' Beth said as both girls went along to the breakfast room where a light meal awaited them.

'Remember this, I am not allowed to go to the harbour. For one thing it is too far and for another it is dangerous. I told my grandmama about being there with you and she was very angry. She said it was perfectly all right for you but not for me. I suppose she thought that I might go too near the edge or something and fall in and drown.'

'Wouldn't matter if I did, though?'

'She would be sorry but not half as sorry as she would be if it was me.'

'Incidentally, that day you are talking about, Caroline, you suggested the harbour yourself. You said you had only ever seen it from the car.'

'Did I? I don't remember.' They had reached the breakfast room. 'I hope Mrs Noble has produced something decent for a change.'

Beth's appetite was good and she ate hungrily. Caroline picked at hers but in the end had eaten a reasonable amount.

The signs of spring were everywhere and the gardeners were busy tending the flower beds and hoeing the ground. Clumps of long trumpeted daffodils surrounded the tree trunks and, with the blues and pinks of the crocuses, made a glorious splash of colour. Together the girls walked down the drive, past the thick bushes with their buds just opening and on to the road. Behind the sun there was a coldish wind and both of them wore warm coats. Caroline wore a scarf and her hands were inside lined gloves. She always said that her hands were the coldest part of her. Beth, delighting to be outside, breathed in the clear fresh air and raised her face to the sun. She needed neither scarf nor gloves.

'Did I tell you that grandmama is absolutely livid, I've never seen her so angry?'

'What about?'

'You, of course. And I have to say it came as a complete shock to me – don't look so dim, of course I mean you going to Rowanbank.'

'Oh, that,' Beth said offhand. If Caroline wanted to carry on with the joke she wouldn't spoil it.

'She says it will be very difficult for you at Rowanbank.'

'Why should that be? I'm not stupid.'

'That has nothing to do with it. It's being born into the

right family, that sort of thing, and you weren't.'

'Unless you tell them they won't know.'

'I won't but I'm afraid you'll have to be prepared. Miss Critchley, she's the Head, has to know everything about her pupils so daddy, whether he wanted to or not, would have had to tell her.'

'Everything? What do you mean by everything?'

'Your humble beginnings, your parents being poor—'

'Not that again,' Beth said furiously.

'Poor to her and poor to you don't mean the same thing.'

'If I am so unsuitable why has Miss—'

'Critchley.'

'Miss Critchley condescended to accept me?'

'You want to know what I really think?'

'Yes, I would.'

'Daddy wants me to be happy at Rowanbank and he thinks that it might be a bit much – you know, separating us and me going off to school.'

'You were coming round to it.'

'Yes, I was. I was prepared to put on a brave face because I thought I had no choice. Daddy can be quite grumpy at times and I don't always get my own way now.'

They had reached the village shops. 'Do you want anything?' Beth asked. 'No use deciding you do when we are half way home.'

'I am not giving in to temptation and buying chocolate. Aunt Gwen says it makes one fat and she blames Ruth's weight problem on eating too much of it when she was younger. And you, Beth Brown, are not going to buy any either.'

'Can't, I haven't any money with me.'

'What were we talking about?'

'School. Caroline, are you really glad that I'm going with you to Rowanbank?'

'Of course, you ninny. You'll be there to look after me,' she said smugly, 'but enough about boring school. Have you noticed how grumpy daddy is these days?'

'Could be he's worried about something.'

'Can't think what.' Then she giggled. 'Yes, I can. I think he has had a tiff, a lover's quarrel, with Jenny.'

'What makes you think that?'

'Well you must have noticed that she hasn't been at Inverbrae House for two whole weeks?'

Beth had noticed and wondered if Jenny had tired of the colonel. She wasn't in love with him after all, or so she said. Maybe she had met someone she liked better. 'Perhaps she has gone off on holiday or something.'

'No, it won't be that. I think daddy must still be seeing Jenny but it will have to be in her house and that's making him mad.'

'Why?'

'Because of grandmama,' she said opening her eyes wide. 'I just happened to mention Jenny's name to her and that I hadn't seen her and she got all starchy.'

'What do you mean by starchy?'

'Stiff, that's what it means. What she said to me was, kindly do not mention Mrs Cuthbert's name in my presence. Her lips were pursed in that disapproving way.'

'Sounds as though your grandmother and Jenny have had words.'

She nodded. 'Pity, I liked it when Jenny came here.'

'Me too, she's the very nicest person I know.' It was in that moment that Beth made up her mind to write to Jenny and tell her about Rowanbank. She was certainly going to be surprised about that. Beth felt wonderfully happy and a little sorry for Caroline. Being the much-loved daughter of the house, she was denied freedom and couldn't go where she wished. No such restrictions were put on her.

They were indoors, their coats off and back in the sitting-room.

'Put that book down, you are not going to read. I want to talk,' Caroline said flinging herself on the sofa.

'What about?' Reluctantly, Beth put down her book and gave her attention to Caroline.

'For a start when are you going to visit your cousin and his wife?'

'Soon, I hope. Sunday is best if I am to see both of them.'

'Do you know how to get to their house?'

'Aunt Anne gave me directions. I know the tramcar to get and the stop to get off at. I'll manage perfectly well.'

'I've never been on a tramcar,' Caroline said wistfully.

'I don't expect you ever will.'

'Why not?'

'There is always a car at your disposal.'

'You could get Tommy to take you.'

'No, thanks, I quite enjoy the bus run then catching the tram.'

'Would you take me to meet your cousin and Morag, that's her name isn't it?'

'Yes, that is her name and no, I wouldn't.'

'Why not?'

'My Aunt Anne lives in what is considered a good neighbourhood but you wouldn't think so. Adam and Morag are in a run-down area, I haven't seen it yet but I know you would be horrified and turn up your nose.'

'You think I am a snob,' Caroline said indignantly.

'I know you are,' Beth grinned.

'Maybe I was but I'm not like that now.'

'You'll never change.'

'That isn't the word of a friend. I thought you liked me.'

'I do, but it is the way you've been brought up, Caroline. You can't help it.'

'Which is just a way of saying that you don't want me to meet your cousin and his wife?'

'That's right, I don't.'

'If I demand to be taken?'

'Demand all you like but I won't take you.'

'You've been with me to see my relatives.'

'Exactly,' Beth said grimly, 'and they made sure I felt out of it.'

'Not really. They aren't like that, the fault was yours.'

'Because I didn't fit in? I didn't, I knew it and that's the way it would be if you met my relatives. They would try to make you welcome but all they would do would be to make you feel uncomfortable. We would all be glad when the visit was over.'

Beth could have stayed in bed longer but she couldn't, she wanted up, she was too wide awake. Padding across the room in her bare feet, she drew back the curtains. The window was open top and bottom and the welcome cool air coming in was pleasant. The sun shone out of a cloudless sky to welcome this very special day. Beth dressed in her usual school clothes, navy skirt and white blouse, and went down for breakfast. A maid was always on duty to replenish the dishes and those who wanted breakfast helped themselves.

Beth was alone in the breakfast room. Caroline didn't get up until the last minute. The colonel was an early riser and ate a hearty breakfast of bacon, eggs and sausage, before setting out. He had long gone. Mrs Parker-Munro had a tray taken to her room.

She helped herself to porridge and followed it with a rasher of bacon and scrambled eggs. After that she had toast and marmalade. Excitement hadn't taken away her appetite. She felt very proud that she, Beth Brown, was to be taught by a governess. Even yet she had difficulty in believing it.

What was lifting was the nagging fear that she would be made to feel inferior. No one need know that she had been educated at the local school, there was no need for it to be mentioned. She could with perfect honesty, say that she had shared lessons with Caroline.

When told of the changes, Tommy had been glad for her but disappointed that the school run was to cease. Theirs had been an easy friendship with plenty to talk about. Not a lot happened to her but Tommy had a fund of stories that he swore blind were true. Beth knew that they were exaggerated, sometimes, she guessed, made up but she didn't mind, they were amusing and made her laugh. Six months previously Tommy had married his sweetheart and now Mabel's name was constantly on his lips.

She remembered that his dream had once been to have his own taxi service but since becoming chauffeur to the colonel, it had lost its appeal. No one, that is no one with any sense, would throw up a steady job with a reasonable wage, uniform provided and a tied house with a nominal rent, in exchange for a dream.

The schoolroom at Inverbrae House was a large airy room with a fireplace, a scuttle of coal at one side and a filled log basket at the other. Miss Mathewson saw to the fire herself but other hands cleaned it out and checked that there was always plenty of fuel. Two desks and seats, similar to the ones in the village school were set well apart. There was a blackboard and a box of chalk at the far end of the room and this was seldom used. Miss Mathewson had her own table and chair, a large cupboard for school books and a very old-looking cabinet that held jotters, pencils and rulers.

Beth had gone back to the breakfast room to collect Caroline so that they could go along to the schoolroom together. Caroline was drinking the last of her tea.

'Why didn't you wait for me, you know I dislike eating alone?'

'You've always done it before. By now I would have been half way to Sandyneuk School.'

'Well, you don't go there now so in future wait for me.'

'If you are late I won't. Come on, Caroline, I don't want to be late and get a bad mark on my first morning.'

'It doesn't bother me one little bit if I am late.'

'It bothers me so hurry up.'

'Good morning, Miss Caroline,' the governess said giving her tight little smile.

'Good morning, Mattie.' Caroline yawned and sat down at her desk.

'Good morning, Beth.'

'Good morning, Miss Mathewson,' Beth said shyly.

'You take that desk.'

Beth sat down and looked at the jotter on the desk. In the groove were a pencil and ruler. She made to lift the lid of the desk and stopped herself.

'It's empty. Your teacher kindly let me have some of your work, Beth. She said she was sorry to lose you, that you were one of her best pupils.'

Beth blushed. 'Thank you.'

'Why are our desks so far apart?' Caroline demanded to know.

'I prefer it that way.'

'In case Beth copies from me?'

'No, in case you copy from Beth,' Miss Mathewson said swiftly but with a smile.

'As if I would. I don't need to.'

'Neither of you needs to.'

'I've been teaching French to Beth.'

'She has, Miss Mathewson.'

'Indeed!'

'Beth won't have to start at the beginning now.'

'She most certainly will.'

'Why?'

'Miss Caroline, you make mistakes which I have to correct.'

'Not many.'

'One is too many. Nevertheless it was nice of you and I am sure Beth appreciated that.'

'I did, Miss Mathewson.'

'Enough of this, we cannot waste any more time. Miss Caroline, while I am with Beth you will do some calculations. You are weak in mathematics and that won't do.'

'I won't ever need maths so why bother about it? It's a waste of time teaching me.'

'That may well be true but it is my duty to get you to the required standard and that, Miss Caroline, is what I intend doing. Kindly get on with your work,' she said firmly. 'Neat figures if you please and all workings at the side.'

Caroline looked at Beth, raised her eyes to heaven then got her head down.

Miss Mathewson brought her chair over beside Beth.

'Je suis—' Caroline said softly.

'Miss Caroline, are you going to behave?'

'Yes, sorry, couldn't resist it.'

There was no more trouble. Beth could see that Caroline was wary of going too far.

# Chapter Seventeen

On a hot windless afternoon in May, Beth set out for Broomfield Road. It wasn't the best day to be going to the town with its smoke-filled air, and those who could would be heading for the beach.

For her visit she had decided on a cap-sleeved green and white patterned cotton dress with a narrow black patent belt. On her feet she wore white ankle socks and brown sandals and over her arm she carried a white cardigan. In her purse was enough money for her fares and a bit over. Since it had been the colonel's wish that Beth visit her relatives, he had arranged for her to receive a weekly sum to cover her expenses.

Beth was feeling very grown-up and she was enjoying the experience of making these trips on her own. This was her first visit to her cousin and his wife but she had already paid two visits to Aunt Anne and Uncle Fred.

After getting off the bus in Dundee she walked smartly to the tram stop only to see one disappearing into the distance. During the week the wait would have been of only five minutes but this was Sunday and there were ten minutes between trams. No one else was at the stop and when the tram arrived Beth got on and sat down on the wooden seat that stretched down one side. A few people sat opposite. The conductor came for her fare and gave her a ticket. Two passengers got up and were standing ready to get off when the tram trundled noisily to the next stop. After they alighted three women and a child got on. Near to the stop was a cluster of shops and since it was a Sunday all but the newsagents had their shutters up. From her seat Beth could see that the window was festooned with advertisements and a few youths and one girl were studying them. The next stop but one was hers and she got up in plenty of time. The conductor said a smiling cheerio and she smiled. For a moment Beth stood looking about her, then having got her bearings she continued for a few yards to a side street, went down it and running across the foot of it was the sign saying Broomfield Road.

Here the tenements stretched uniformly on either side and Beth, used to space, felt hemmed in. It was a shabby, depressing area and much as her aunt had described it. Dirty-faced, snotty children played happily in the road. The boys were shouting and kicking a tin can about and the girls had bits of rope and were skipping. One girl in a clean dress had a proper skipping rope with handles and was holding tightly to it. An older child, or perhaps a parent, had used white chalk to make neat squares on the pavement. Beth knew the game and slowed down to watch a small stone being thrown to land in one of the squares. Then a girl in a torn dress made complicated movements as she jumped about. Beth moved away and quickened her pace.

She checked the numbers where they still existed and fortunately the number nineteen was quite clear. The close was clean from a recent washing and the smell of disinfectant mingled with the cooking smell of cabbage coming from upstairs. The door to the left was the one she wanted and a piece of white cardboard held on by two drawing pins told her that she had come to the right house. Printed on it was the name A. FARQUHARSON.

Beth knocked and after a few moments it opened. A girl in a thin beige skirt and a blue hand-knitted, short-sleeved, string jumper gave a welcoming smile. She was smallish with an elfin face, even white teeth and straight fair hair with a fringe. Beth thought her very pretty.

'You are Beth, aren't you?'

'Yes, and you're Morag?'

'Come in, you managed to find us then?'

'Without any trouble,' Beth smiled as she stepped into the lobby with its floor covered in faded linoleum. 'Aunt Anne gave me very detailed directions.'

'So she would. Still, better that than directions you couldn't follow.' Morag went ahead and into the front room and immediately she was in it her eyes went to her mother's sideboard which graced one wall, and graced was the correct word, Beth thought. In Sycamore Lane she couldn't recall it ever shining this bright. An embroidered cover hung over both ends and on it was a marble clock with a spotted china dog on either side. The clock was broken or it hadn't been wound up. The hands pointed to half past ten.

'That doesn't go, that's why we got it. My mother said we could have it if we got it mended.'

'You will, won't you?'

'Sometime. Adam is going to hunt around to see who will do it cheapest. He'll be here in a minute, Adam I mean, he was just getting ready when you knocked.' She laughed. 'Speak of the devil.'

Adam was slightly above average height with broad shoulders, good features, dark brown springy hair and blue eyes.

'Hello, Beth.' His grip was firm. 'Glad you managed to make it and give us the chance to thank you properly. You could have got a tidy bit for the furniture and we know that.'

'I wanted you to have it and I'm sure it would have been my mother's wish,' Beth said quietly.

'Are you over that awful tragedy?' His blue eyes were concerned.

'I think so, Adam. It was difficult but I'm over the worst now.'

'Why are we all standing?' Morag wanted to know.

'Because you haven't invited our guest to be seated,' Adam teased.

'Beth, sit down. I'm not very good at this – we haven't had much practice. Isn't that right, Adam?'

'Not counting our folks and a couple of my pals and one of Morag's friends, you are our first real visitor, Beth.'

'Adam, are you going to or—?'

'That's my wife's broad hint to put the kettle on,' he said as he made to go.

'Remember, the water must be boiling,' she called after him.

She waited until the door closed before saying, 'Adam is really very helpful, Beth. He sees to the fire before he leaves for work and he's not like some I know who won't lift a hand because they think all housework is woman's work.'

Beth was sitting in what had been her mother's chair and Morag on the sofa. There was none of the strangeness that is common at a first meeting and they were talking about the furniture.

'We hardly have anything that is new, Beth, only the bed and a basket chair,' she grinned.

Beth smiled and saw Morag looking anxiously at the door. 'You won't mind if I leave you a minute? You see, I've only one set of china and the odd bits we use ourselves and I'd rather carry the good ones through myself.'

Just then Adam put his head round the door. 'Everything is ready, tea infused and pancakes buttered. See what a hen-pecked husband I am?'

'You don't look it and incidentally, Adam, I have a bone to pick with you. Why did you and Luke always disappear when we visited Dundee?'

'Did they?' Morag stopped to hear the answer.

'Beth, you were just a wee bairn and we were two strapping laddies – or rather I was a strapping laddie and Luke a bean pole.'

'All right, I forgive you.'

The small table, Uncle Fred's handiwork, was pulled forward so that they could set their cups and saucers on it.

'Morag, how did you manage to get that shine on the sideboard? My mother never did, I'm sure.'

Morag drank some tea then put down her cup. 'I can't take the credit. Honestly, Beth, I do not know where that woman gets her energy. My mother thinks herself a good worker but she says Adam's mother puts her to shame. Not just polishing either. This house was pretty mucky, wasn't it, Adam?'

'Filthy.'

'That's true. I don't think it had ever had a proper clean in years. Adam and me didn't know where to begin.'

'Until ma took us in hand.'

She giggled. 'Talk about being organised. Adam's ma got her sleeves up.'

Adam took over the story. 'Out came the buckets and scrubbing brushes and the three of us set to like nobody's business,' he recalled.

Morag nodded. 'Even when we were more than half

dead she kept us at it. We're laughing, Beth, but I was very grateful. Maybe she works everybody until they are on the point of dropping but she doesn't spare herself.'

'At one time I was scared of Aunt Anne, not Uncle Fred—'

'He's a lamb,' Morag said.

'I remember I was just coming up for nine and Aunt Anne was horrified that my mother didn't make me do housework but my mother said that I would get enough of that when I was older. She didn't want me to work the way she had to when she was little.' Beth swallowed remembering. 'She was all for me enjoying my childhood.'

'I like the sound of your mother, Beth. Mind you, I haven't much to grumble about. We did have to help but my mother did all the hard jobs herself.' She turned to her husband. 'You had to do your stint, didn't you?'

'Certainly did but you shouldn't complain, Morag, it's thanks to ma that I can just about turn my hand to anything.'

'Your mother, Adam, told mine that I would grow up to be useless and she's right. I don't know a thing about housework.'

Adam groaned. 'No help with the dishes, I can see that, and it'll be yours truly as usual.'

'Thinks himself hard done by that one. Don't mind him, Beth.'

'Seriously, ma's bark is worse than her bite, Beth,' Adam defended his mother. 'She means well but like my da says, she's just naturally bossy. She can't help it.'

'I do understand her better now, Adam.' Beth had eaten a pancake and was accepting another. 'These are very good, Morag, did you make them?'

Adam choked over his tea and his wife glared.

'I had hoped to get away with you thinking they were

mine but I might have known better. No, Beth, my mother made them this morning and came over in the tram with them still warm and wrapped in a tea towel. She never has a baking failure and I hardy ever have a success.'

'That I do not believe.'

'It is true but supposing I say it myself, I'm a good cook.'

'She is, Beth, makes a grand steak and kidney pie does our Morag.'

'That's what you are getting for your tea.'

'Lovely. Steak pie is my favourite.'

Morag looked pleased.

Beth had been shown round the house by a proud new housewife with Adam hovering nearby. In the kitchen where they were to eat, the table was set with a white tablecloth with a yellow border. The pepper and salt pots – vaguely familiar to Beth – sat in the middle. Four places were set with cutlery. The wallpaper had a flowery pattern and the cream painted ceiling showed a number of cracks. The linoleum was new and in brown and gold and the curtains picked up the colours. Beth thought it all very pleasing and said so.

'Out the back is awful,' Morag said apologetically.

And it was. Beth looked out of the window to a row of cellars, one for each house. They were in a dilapidated state, one had no door at all.

'Never mind, we'll get something better in a year or two, won't we, Adam?'

'Long before then,' Adam said firmly. 'It's just a case of keeping eyes and ears open and being first there when someone moves.'

'Before that, Adam, you've to be there when someone

is just thinking about moving,' Morag laughed. She opened a door. 'Our bedroom.'

Beth stood at the door, she could see it all from there. The flooring was of linoleum so threadbare that the original pattern and colours were long gone. There was a double bed with a pretty blue cover and two pairs of slippers sat side by side between the wardrobe and the basket chair.

Adam moved away and Morag whispered, 'The "you know" is in the close, that's the real drawback to living here. My mother was more concerned that we might have bad neighbours but we haven't, they are all quite nice in this close. The woman upstairs from us,' she pointed to the ceiling, 'said she had a bonny house like ours when she got married but between losing her man—'

'You mean he's dead?' Beth asked.

'That or he walked out. You don't ask questions like that, Beth, not hereabout. They'll tell you what they want you to know. Anyway between losing her man, three bairns in three years, and poor health because of it, she lost heart. I feel sorry for her but Adam's mother says she could do more for herself if she tried. She looks so old yet she's a lot younger than my mother.'

The "you know" was worrying Beth since she would have to make use of it sometime. Then she thought how foolish she was. It was a toilet in the close instead of one in the house, that was all. Adam had been used to a bathroom, very likely Morag had too, but they must have been so anxious to get married that they had been prepared to put up with any inconvenience. The real problem, she imagined, would be having to get up in the middle of the night. She never had to and perhaps it was only very old people who were troubled that way.

'Does it give you a strange feeling to see your parents' things here?'

'No, it doesn't,' Beth said truthfully. 'It's a nice feeling and the furniture suits the house.'

'That is what everybody says.'

Beth gave a start when there was a sharp knock at the door and she saw husband and wife exchange smiles.

'No prizes for guessing who that is. You answer it, Adam.'

They heard him say, 'It's you. You don't live here, you know.'

A very tall, painfully thin youth came in. He had reddish fair hair, a healthy complexion and a crop of freckles on his forehead and across the bridge of his nose.

'This lad just can't stay away.'

'Morag likes me coming.'

'Of course I do, Luke, you know you are always welcome.'

'Came specially to see my wee cousin, ma said she'd be here.'

'She's not so wee,' Morag said.

'No, I'm not, I just keep growing and growing. Hello, Luke.'

She expected them to shake hands but Luke bent down from his great height and kissed her cheek. 'I'm allowed that since you're family.'

Beth blushed but she was pleased.

'That's a liberty I didn't take,' Adam said and promptly touched his lips to Beth's brow.

'The pair of them are awful teases, Beth. You'll get used to them, I've had to.'

'I hope they are looking after you,' Luke said as he began to unbutton his jacket.

'Oh, they are.'

'Let me take your jacket, Luke, and I'll put it in the bedroom.' Luke gave it to her. He had on a pale blue open-necked shirt.

'Don't tell me you were allowed to come out without a tie and this a Sunday?'

'I'm a big lad now, Morag, and I do what I like.' For a split second he scowled and Adam, raising an eyebrow, glanced at his wife. Beth wondered what had brought on the scowl or perhaps she had imagined it. Luke was all smiles again.

'You staying for tea?' Adam asked his brother.

'Is there enough, Morag?'

'Plenty, I had a feeling you would come.'

'Any tea in that pot?' he asked hopefully.

'No, but I'll make a fresh pot.'

'Don't do that. I'll have a couple of pancakes and that'll do me until I get my tea. What's for it?'

'Steak and kidney pie.'

'Great! She can make a good steak pie, Beth.'

'I know.' Beth was loving it. This was family life and already she felt herself being drawn into their circle.

It was five o'clock and they were seated round the table in the kitchen. With no scullery, the gas cooker, their most expensive buy, was next to the window. The bunker used to keep the coal was covered with a cloth and the ashet was balanced on a square of thin wood to take the heat. Morag was cutting up the pie with its nicely browned flaky pastry and sharing it between the four plates. Adam had the task of carrying them to the table. Morag, flushed from the heat and her efforts, emptied the mashed potatoes from the pot and into a large tureen. It went to the centre of the table with a big spoon so that they could help themselves.

'That's the only serving dish—'

'Tureen, sweetheart.'

'Tureen then, I couldn't think of the word.'

'Didn't know it, be truthful.'

'Hit him over the head with something, Morag.'

'I'm coming very close to it, Luke.' She went back to the cooker. 'Excuse the pots,' she said as she dished the vegetables straight from the pot on to the plates.

Beth was hungry, the steak pie was very good and she ate heartily. There was no ceremony here, just plenty of laughter and good-natured teasing. How different from the dining-room at Inverbrae House, where there was little laughter and only a low hum of conversation, to which she contributed nothing.

Luke dropped his fork and immediately bent down to get it, and for a moment Beth was back in time. How dreadful she had felt, and had been made to feel, when she had broken the rules and did what Luke had done.

'Beth, come on and tell us what it is like to live with the toffs and have servants to do all the work.'

'Maybe she doesn't want to, Adam, and Luke, you greedy scamp, that's enough potatoes, leave some for the rest of us.'

'Sorry, can't resist them. Ma says I'll turn into a tattie if I don't cut down.' He looked at his cousin. 'Come on, Beth, you're the nearest we've come to gentry.'

'I was just wondering where to begin. For one thing there is never any hilarity at the table.'

'Not done in the best of circles?'

'Not done at Inverbrae House anyway but there is another house I go to. After – after they died I went to stay with Jenny and she was wonderful to me. She's a real lady and we were always laughing in her house.'

'Are you happy with those people, Beth?'

'They have been good to me, Morag,' Beth said quietly, 'so I shouldn't complain.'

Morag nodded. 'Like Adam's mother said, they are good to you because you keep that lass of theirs happy.'

'I suppose that's true. When I was younger I felt myself the same as Caroline because her Nanny treated us alike. Then when I was a bit older I could tell that they were relieved because my mother was coming home.'

'Then the tragedy?'

'Yes. I caused them a lot of worry at that time and they were kind. Even so, I don't know how to describe it. It all seemed to be on the surface and that I had become an embarrassment. Honestly, I'd never felt so miserable and alone.'

'Some people make me sick,' Morag looked on the verge of tears. 'You wanted a lot of loving and understanding and anybody with any decency would have known that.'

'I got some from Jenny but no one else. I've always felt starved of love—' She stopped, embarrassed.

'Your parents, surely—?'

Beth looked sad. 'They loved me in their own way but they were quite incapable of showing it.'

'No hugs or kisses?' Luke had been silent until then. 'A family thing, Beth. I mind when I was a bairn and coming in with a bloody nose or scraped knees and just getting cleaned and bandaged and a raging. The others, my pals, got a good telling off and a hug. I just got the telling off.'

'Was that the way it was with you, Adam?'

'Yes, but it didn't worry me, I wasn't bothered.'

'I tell you here and now, Adam Farquharson, that our bairns will get plenty of love. And don't look at me like that, we all need it.'

'Help! What have I done to deserve this?'

'You mean what have I started?' Beth laughed.

'Shut up you two I want to hear Beth's story.'

'Jenny was a friend of Colonel Parker-Munro—'

'You didn't have to call the old fellow that, did you?'

'Yes, I did, at first anyway.'

Morag giggled. 'Heavens! I would never have got my tongue round it.'

'I got used to it. Jenny was marvellous to me and after a week with her I felt much better.'

'I bet you have to be meek and grateful,' Luke said.

'Not meek, I could never be that. Having to be grateful is bad enough.'

Morag got up to collect the dishes and Adam helped her. They exchanged smiles. Luke and Beth were hitting it off well.

'I bet.'

'Something inside me won't let me feel grateful for what others, like Caroline, take for granted. That's wrong, I suppose. Caroline was born into this family and she has the right to feel superior.'

'You don't really believe that?'

'No, but I should.'

'No, you shouldn't, you are every bit as good as them.'

'Oh, I almost forgot to tell you, I am being sent away to school.'

Morag stopped what she was doing. 'Sent away where?'

'Caroline is going to Rowanbank after the holidays and I've just been told that I'll be going with her.'

'Boarding school you mean?' Morag said with awe in her voice.

'We'll be weekly boarders.'

'Will you still manage to come and see us?' Morag

asked and then, more slowly, 'Maybe you won't want to come here.'

Beth looked hurt. 'If I'm invited I'll come and it'll be because I want to.'

'She'll always be welcome, won't she, Adam?'

'Beth knows that. She might be living with the toffs but we are her family. Better keep it to a Sunday.'

'That won't be easy, Adam. We've got to be back in school by seven at the latest.'

'Are you looking forward to going?'

'Yes, I am, Luke. I'll get a good education and I'm going to work hard to get qualifications. When I have those I'll hopefully get a good job and be independent.'

'Until you get married?'

'I won't be in a hurry, I want to taste independence.' She glanced at her wrist watch. 'Goodness, it is time I was on my way.'

Adam got up but Luke said hastily, 'No need for you to leave Morag on her own. I'll see Beth to the bus.'

'No, please, I can manage on my own,' Beth protested.

'Maybe, but you're not going on your own. Is someone meeting you at Sandyneuk?' He paused and added, 'Or is it not very far?'

'It's quite a bit but I don't mind and nobody knows where I am.'

'Then they should,' Adam said angrily. 'You're just a bairn and someone should be concerned about you.'

But Beth was already at the door. 'Thank you both for a lovely day,' she said.

'When will you manage to come again?'

'It might have to be in the holidays, Morag, but I'll write and let you know how I'm getting on at school.'

Morag nodded. 'Yon letter I sent you was the first I'd ever written. Didn't ever need to before.'

'It was a lovely letter.'

She got a hug and a kiss from Morag and Adam before she left. The streets were quiet as they set out, the children all indoors.

'I must be taking you a lot out of your way, Luke?'

'Not much.'

The tram was just moving away and they both sprinted. Beth jumped on and Luke followed. The conductor shook his head. 'You'll do that once too often, that's the way accidents happen.'

'Surefooted,' Luke laughed as he handed over the money for the fares. Beth wanted to pay her own but he wouldn't hear of it.

'Surefooted until you fall,' came the sour reply.

'Where do you work, Luke?'

'The foundry.'

'Adam still in the shipyard?'

'Yes, he's doing all right. Ma keeps on at him to try and get me in.'

'Would he manage that?'

'Possible and it's better than the foundry, better money.'

'But not what you want?'

'No, Beth, not what I want but my wishes don't seem to be important,' he said bitterly.

'What do you want to do?'

'Go off to sea. It's all I've ever wanted and I'd take any job going.'

'What's holding you back?'

'Ma, she goes on at great length about me being too young – I'm nearly nineteen – to know what I want and that I would live to regret it. Just a lot of tripe, she doesn't want me to go that's the sum total of it.'

'She's afraid for you.'

'That's stupid. Danger is everywhere, you just have to look out for yourself.' He glanced out. 'Come on, it's our stop.'

'So it is,' Beth said, springing to her feet. 'It's a good job someone was paying attention.' They were walking when she said, 'What has Uncle Fred to say?'

'Da doesn't say much but he isn't keen. The reason for that is he had a brother lost at sea.'

'Understandable then?'

'Suppose so.'

In a companionable silence they walked to the bus station. The Sandyneuk bus, though not due to leave for eight minutes, was already in the station. The driver was leaning against the bonnet and smoking a cigarette.

'Thank you, Luke, and good luck.'

'Same to you, I'll be thinking of you in that posh school and don't let them push you around.'

'I won't.'

He gave her shoulder a squeeze just like a brother, she thought, and she got on the bus and took a seat at the front. He turned once and waved then he was lost to sight.

Beth sat and thought about her day. It had been hugely enjoyable. She liked her cousins and Morag very much but she didn't think she could ever live in such conditions. Perhaps being in love made the discomforts bearable. It must. Adam and Morag had made a choice, either wait until a better house was available or take what was on offer and get married right away.

Beth didn't hurry when she got off the bus. It was a balmy night and it was pleasant to breathe deeply of the fresh air that smelt of flowers. In the distance was Inverbrae House, aloof and proud like its owner. They had a privileged status in life, the colonel and Mrs Parker-Munro, but were they happy? She supposed they were – it was the only life they knew. As to herself, she was about to be given the benefit of an education at a top school and that was something for which she would be grateful.

Caroline was in their sitting-room, drooping like a wilting lily.

'You've got back? Mrs Watson came over for me and I'm absolutely exhausted. Leonard and Ralph are home and you won't believe the difference in those two. Remember how rough they used to be?'

'I haven't seen them more than twice.'

'Neither you have, then take my word for it. They have become so nice and polite and we played the gramophone. Imagine what grandmama would have said about playing it on a Sunday! Beth, I've come to the conclusion that I quite like boys. I always said I didn't but I've changed my mind. Was your day awful?'

'Why should it have been?'

'I don't know that is why I am asking.'

'I had a perfectly lovely day.'

# Chapter Eighteen

The postal van was never late. Folk could very nearly set their watches by it, because business and other institutions depended on the mail being delivered on time and now the post office had let them down. It just wasn't good enough. Muttering his annoyance, the colonel left Inverbrae House without having seen the mail. Damn it! he thought. More than likely there would be a letter requiring his immediate attention.

One mile from Inverbrae House, the post office van was parked at the side of the narrow country road with its bonnet up. A mechanic was half inside it and a worried looking postman, a cup of tea in his hand, stood nearby and watched. The tea had come from the young woman who lived in one of the farm cottages. A toddler and an older boy arrived to see what was going on.

'Will it no' go?' the older boy, who would be about five, wanted to know.

'No.'

'Is it broken?'

'Yes.'

'Are you a different postie?'

The postman sighed. He couldn't be bothered with bairns, not right now, but it was their ma's tea he was drinking so he'd better not ignore them. 'Your own postie's on holiday.'

'Where's he gone?'

'Don't know.'

'We never go a holiday.' The woman was back. 'We never go a holiday do we ma?'

'Hold your sheesht, Bobby, and take Herbert inside.'

'Don't want to, I want to watch.'

'Inside I said.' Her hand shot out and pointed to the open door.

Taking his wee brother's hand they walked away, with Bobby turning round once to see if his mother had had a change of heart. She hadn't.

The mechanic's head appeared. 'Try it now.'

'I'll keep my fingers crossed,' the woman said as she took his cup.

'Ta, that was fine,' the postman said. He got behind the wheel, turned on the ignition and the engine spluttered into life. 'Thank the Lord for that.'

'Let it run for a wee while to make sure.'

They listened. There was a slight hiccup when they looked at each other anxiously then came the sound for which they had been waiting.

Before moving off the postman called out, 'Thanks, lad, what was the trouble?'

The mechanic scratched his head with his oily hands. 'Can't rightly say, just one of those things I suppose.'

The postman nodded. It was the answer he had expected.

'Thanks again for the tea.'

'You're welcome.' She smiled and waved. It made a nice break in her day.

The van shot off with the first stop Longacre Farm then it was on to Inverbrae House. There would be complaints, he thought bitterly, and the blame would be his. Not the van's fault, not sloppy maintenance, no one else's fault just his. That was life and silence, he had discovered, was the best policy if he wanted to keep his job. It didn't do to lose your rag.

Mrs Parker-Munro was annoyed. She usually read her letters in bed. They arrived with the breakfast tray but not this morning. It was too bad and it upset the routine of her day.

When the van did eventually arrive the maid collected the mail, carried it through to the hall table and placed the letters on the silver tray left there for the purpose. A few minutes later Mrs Parker-Munro's stick could be heard on the parquet floor, and seeing the pile she went over. Sitting down on the tapestry covered chair she took her spectacles from her cardigan pocket, put them on and prepared to go through the letters. Most were for her son. Two were marked 'Urgent' and underlined in red ink. Her frown deepened. Not good enough. Nigel would have something to say and with good reason. There could be no excuse, this wasn't the winter after all, and even then the greatest effort had to be made. Wasn't it their boast that no matter what the post got through?

She fingered one, a pink envelope and spidery writing, that would be from Leonora. Her letters were always a delight, so full of news and gossip, pity it wasn't easier to read. That one she would keep to the end. She put it aside along with another two from friends and several accounts that required settling. What was this? She looked at it closely, examining the stamp and the postmark. Australia? Who did she know in Australia? No one. She checked that it was addressed to her. It was. Written very clearly on the envelope was Mrs Euphemia Parker-Munro. Who could be writing to her? At her age she didn't like shocks, they quickened her heartbeat and that could be dangerous. Perhaps she should wait until evening when Nigel would be here. He would read it first then break it to her whatever it was.

Gathering up her letters and leaving the rest in an untidy pile, the old lady picked up her stick and went slowly along to the sitting-room. She would ring for tea, even though it was just an hour since she'd had breakfast. Tea was one of her greatest comforts.

By midday Mrs Parker-Munro had done fingering the letter. She was being ridiculous, she told herself, acting as though she were in her dotage. The letter could be from a friend of a friend, for goodness sake. But she knew it wasn't. Something told her that it was important, important to her.

Using her letter opener she slit the envelope and drew out several flimsy sheets. She looked at the address in the right hand corner and then began to read. As she read, her eyes widened in shock and her face lost the little colour it had. After coming to the end of the first page she went back to the beginning to go over it again before turning to the next.

*Dear Mrs Parker-Munro,*

*This is a very difficult letter to write and I don't quite know where to begin. Perhaps it would be best to tell you who I am, that I am your daughter-in-law. I was married to your son, James, for sixteen years, and sadly he died six months ago from a brain haemorrhage. He was a good husband and father and our three children are finding it hard to accept his death. For me it was a devastating blow but life must go on and ours is a close and loving family. My children and I are being well looked after.*

*James spoke little of his early life but I knew there were times when he regretted losing touch. On these occasions I would plead with him to write to his family but he said that he had left it too late. Though I didn't agree with that I had to respect his wishes but I did feel he was wrong in depriving his children of grandparents and you and your late husband of knowing about your Australian grandchildren.*

*Shall I now tell you about our family? Robert is fifteen and there is a resemblance to James. I think so but others think he takes after our side of the family. People see what they want, don't they? William is thirteen and resembles neither of us but he has the look of his grandfather Reid. Emily, the baby, is nine. She is a lovely sweet child and James adored her. He loved his sons dearly but when Emily was born it was as though I had given him the greatest gift of all.*

*My thoughts are wandering and the letter is getting a bit disjointed. How did I get your address? Going through James's papers I found letters dating from far back, long before I knew him. Not knowing the position at Inverbrae House I got our solicitor to make enquiries and I learned from him that James's father had died.*

*I met James when he came to work for my father. We have a very large sheep farm and all the family are involved in it in one way or another. Robert and William are both away at school and are happy enough although they would much rather be at home. Emily is taught by a governess who is very good but in a year or two Emily too will have to go away. I try not to think of it.*

*Robert, our eldest, is fascinated to learn about his Scottish family. Unlike William who has no wish ever to leave Australia, Robert would like to see a bit of the world, and once his education is completed, he intends to do just that. Most of all he would like to see where his father grew up and to meet you all. Perhaps one day this will happen.*

*I feel sure that you would like to have photographs of James and the family and once I hear from you I'll sort out the best and post them on. Would you be kind enough to send on one or two photographs of James as a boy? I would so love to have them for myself to see the little boy that was James, and for the children to treasure and add to the family album.*

*I'm so sorry that I failed to persuade James to write to you and I can only imagine as a mother myself, what you have been going through.*

*We have a large ranch-style house and three smaller homes nearby. This gives us the privacy needed in all families and yet the nearness to work together which is so essential out here. My grandfather, who is ninety on his next birthday, lives with my parents. He is still active and takes an interest in everything as well as keeping us all in order! He loves nothing better than a good argument and he always said that James was the only one who could hold his own. Such happy times.*

*The news of your son's death will sadden and distress you, and my heart goes out to you and your son, Nigel. I hope that I have managed to convey in this letter the happiness we all enjoyed. Your son got on well with everyone, Mrs Parker-Munro, and was a much-loved member of our family. We all miss him so much.*

*Before I end this very difficult letter I had better tell you that James called himself Munro not Parker-Munro. Out here they would have shortened it anyway!*
*Very sincerely,*
*Your daughter-in-law,*
*Dorothy Munro.*

Euphemia Parker-Munro kept the pages between her fingers. How often had she read it? The tears, unheeded, rolled down her cheeks and lodged for a moment in the deep crevices round the mouth. Her son was dead. She would never see James again, not in this life. For years his name had been barely mentioned but always there had been hope in her heart that one day he would return to Inverbrae House. Now all hope was gone. Just lately it had been easier to remember the past than what had taken place a few short weeks ago. A sure sign of age.

James so different from Nigel. He had been such a naughty little boy, unable to keep out of mischief but so lovable. Certainly he had been a trial to everyone, especially to his father who was bewildered and angered by such behaviour. If only they hadn't taken such drastic action and believed mistakenly that the army would be the making of him. A little more time, a little more understanding, and he might well have outgrown his rebelliousness. The letter was proof of that, James had settled down to be a responsible family man.

She moved in the chair and winced at the pain, sharp for a few moments then dulling to the usual ache that she had learned to live with. Her husband was gone and so was her son James but James's children were very much alive and he had called his first born Robert, after his own father. She smiled.

Robert Munro. Robert Munro he might be in Australia but when he came to Scotland that would change. Time was ticking away for her and she tried to calculate how long it would be before her grandson, Robert, would be old enough to travel to Scotland and come to Inverbrae House. Eighteen would likely be the school leaving age unless, of course, he wanted to go on to university or college. His father had not wanted that but his son might be different. She was tired in body but her mind was working feverishly.

Robert could come to Scotland when he left school and attend a Scottish university if that was what he wanted. Perhaps St Andrews, where Nigel had gone? That could be easily arranged. What was important was Robert coming to Inverbrae House. She would have liked to see her other two grandchildren but that seemed unlikely.

If only Nigel would come. She kept looking at the clock and willing the hands to go round. In a fever of impatience, unable to eat, but drinking endless cups of tea and between them giving the maids frequent and strict instructions that the master was to come and see her the moment he arrived.

The master, thus informed as he stepped inside his home, was irritated and showed it. He marched along, knocked out of habit and went in.

'Mother, what is it that can't wait? I don't have much time with the mail not turning up and having to be dealt with now.'

'You can deal with that later.' There were times, she thought, when her son annoyed her and this was one. She wasn't in the habit of demanding his attention on frivolous matters, she thought indignantly. He should know that it was important.

Something in her face, perhaps its greyness alarmed him and he regretted his brusqueness. 'What is it, Mother?' he said gently. 'What is troubling you?'

'I've had a letter about James,' she said shakily.

'James! You've had a letter from James,' he said disbelievingly.

She shook her head. 'If only that were so. James is dead, Nigel.' The letter was on the table and she put her hand over it. He saw that it shook.

Nigel was shocked and upset and he sat down abruptly

as though his legs had given way.

'James dead – I can't believe it!'

'His wife – his widow has written a long letter, such a nice brave letter. Read it, Nigel, read it for yourself. I think I know it almost off by heart.'

He read it through quickly then read it again.

'My poor, poor James,' his mother said brokenly.

'He had a happy life, Mother, that leaps off the pages.'

'But so young to die?'

'Yes. I like the sound of my sister-in-law very much, I think she must be a very remarkable woman.'

'Her letter moved me deeply. She has taken such care to break the news as gently as possible and at the same time to bring the family to us.'

'A very carefully worded letter. Mother, you'll have to get used to the idea of having four grandchildren,' he smiled.

'I find that quite wonderful and I only wish there weren't so many miles between us.' She paused and looked at Nigel. 'Fancy James settling so far away, right at the other end of the world.'

'Father made a mistake thinking the army would be the making of James.'

'I seem to recall you agreeing with him,' his mother said drily.

'If I did then I was wrong. I remember James telling me once that he felt trapped here. I suppose he thought of the army as another trap. He yearned for the open spaces and Australia offered him that.'

'How anyone could feel trapped in Inverbrae House is beyond me.'

'From all accounts he landed on his feet. There is plenty of money there and if the son wants to travel, I don't imagine anything would be put in his way.'

'The boy must come here,' she said firmly, 'and you, Nigel, must go and see to that urgent business of yours.'

He got up. 'Indeed I must.'

'You aren't going out this evening?' She looked wistful.

'No, and had I been it would have been cancelled.'

'You are a dear boy.'

'Shall I send Caroline in?'

'No, I don't want the child's chatter just at present. What I do need is to talk about James.'

He kissed her cheek. 'Directly I finish, we shall talk of James and tomorrow Caroline will be told of her Australian cousins.'

'She will be thrilled and perhaps the teeniest bit jealous,' the old lady smiled.

'No, just thrilled, I think.'


'You'll never guess, the most exciting thing ever has happened.'

Beth, used to Caroline's exaggeration, looked up briefly. She was on the floor sitting on a cushion and trying to concentrate on her French reader. 'Mmm,' was all she said.

'Kindly stop reading that and listen to me. Beth, I am talking to you.'

'All right! All right! Hurry up and say what you are going to, I'm not even half way through this.'

'You don't have to work as hard as all that. You heard what Mattie said that we are well up in what we are supposed to know. You, Beth Brown, are in danger of turning into a horrible little swot.'

'Not a chance since you never stop chattering.'

'I'll let that pass and now listen. Grandmama has had a letter from Australia.'

'So your grandmother has had a letter from Australia?'

'Telling her that she has grandchildren. I've got three cousins I didn't know existed.'

She had Beth's attention now.

'Daddy's brother, James. I think he was a rebel. Isn't that exciting? Apparently he ran away from home, from Inverbrae House, and for a while he sent postcards from different parts of the world then that stopped and nothing was heard of my Uncle James.' Her pale blue eyes grew round.

'Until now?'

She nodded. 'Uncle James is dead and his wife, she's called Dorothy, that means I have an Aunt Dorothy—'

'I managed to gather that.'

'She wrote to my grandmama to let her know that she has three grand-children, that makes four counting me.' She grew very serious. 'Robert is fifteen, William is thirteen and Emily, she's just nine.'

'You'll have to start writing to them.'

'Sometime. I'll wait until I see the photographs when they come. Grandmama says Robert is supposed to be a little like his father and she says that Uncle James was quite nice looking so I expect this Robert will be too. He is to be invited to come here when he leaves school, that'll be when he is eighteen. He's three years older than me, than us.' She said all this barely stopping for breath.

'That's a long time and maybe he won't want to come to Scotland.'

Caroline looked scornful. 'He does want to come, he wants to see where his father lived and that's only natural.'

'I saw my cousins and Morag in Dundee. You never asked about them?'

'Forgot all about your visit to Dundee. Anyway it's much, much more exciting having cousins in Australia than boring old ones in Dundee.'

Beth let that pass. 'I had a lovely, lovely day and I'll be going back to see them.' Beth was determined to get her cousins a mention.

'That may not be possible since you are going off to school. Oh, I nearly forgot, Aunt Gwen is taking us both to Perth on Tuesday to get our uniform and all the other dreary things on the list.'

Beth felt excited at the thought of the uniform but wished it hadn't been Caroline's Aunt Gwen who was to take them. She wasn't exactly rude, that would never do, but the woman had a habit of ignoring Beth almost as though she weren't there. Beth thought if it wasn't rude it was certainly bad manners.

'What is the uniform like?'

'Haven't you seen Ruth in hers?'

'No.'

'Well, it's grey and red.'

'That should be nice.'

'Glad you think so, I find all talk about uniform and everything else utterly boring.'

'Boring seems to be your favourite word just now.'

Caroline grinned. 'One ordeal we are going to miss.'

'Oh!'

'Ruth says it is normal to visit the school, be shown around then introduced to the Head but for some unknown reason the Critchley female won't be available and instead she is to meet the new girls when they arrive.' She made a face. 'Thank goodness you are coming with me, Beth. Now that it's getting near the time I'm getting butterflies in my stomach when I think about it.'

'You shouldn't. Ruth likes it so it can't be too bad.'

'Oh, her! Aunt Gwen says she is so easy going that nothing ever bothers her.'

'That's the best way to be.'

'Not according to Aunt Gwen, she gets very annoyed at Ruth. It is easy enough for you, Beth Brown, not to be worried. You know what school is like, I've only ever been taught by Mattie.'

'You'll be all right, I'll look after you.'

'You'll have to, that's why you are getting to go to Rowanbank.'

'Something you are going to remind me of constantly.'

'For your own good. In case you haven't noticed, I look after you too. One learns by example,' she said haughtily, 'and I've been your model. You used to watch me before you did anything.'

'Maybe I did but I don't have to now.'

'My cousins in Australia are very wealthy, even better off than we are or so daddy says. They have a huge sheep farm.'

'One day you might go to Australia to visit them.'

'No, Beth, I wish I could but grandmama has been reading about Australia, the climate and everything. She says the dry heat wouldn't do with me.'

# Chapter Nineteen

On the day the school broke up for the Christmas holidays, there was a lot of noise and excitement from the full boarders but less from the weekly boarders. The classroom windows were open and there was the smell of chalk and polish as cleaning got under way. Outside it was crisp and cold. Cars began to arrive with parents or chauffeurs to take the girls back home for the two-week break. Tommy, smart in his uniform, stood outside the colonel's car waiting to drive his boss's daughter and Beth to Inverbrae House.

On several occasions Caroline had made it clear that she did not approve of any familiarity with the chauffeur. She frowned on Beth for engaging Tommy in conversation. Tommy was aware of this and, fearful of losing his job, contented himself with a wink to Beth when the young madam wasn't looking.

Tommy dealt with the trunks when they arrived back in Inverbrae House. Both girls ran up the steps and into the house.

'The decorations look a bit dull,' Caroline said with critical eyes as she looked about the hall. 'These same ones appear each year.'

'Look all right to me and there is plenty of holly.'

Caroline shrugged and went over to the silver tray. 'No letters for me.'

'Were you expecting some?'

'One anyway. I wrote to Aunt Dorothy in Australia.'

'Takes ages for letters to get there and the reply to come.'

'Suppose so.' She began to unbutton her coat and Beth did the same. 'Come on, leave our coats here and show ourselves to grandmama.'

Mrs Parker-Munro was sitting by the fire when they went in. It was stiflingly hot but even so she had a shawl round her shoulders.

'You've arrived then?'

'Yes, grandmama,' Caroline said going over and giving her a kiss.

'Nice to have you home, dear.'

'We are both glad to be home, aren't we, Beth?' There were times like now when Caroline tried to include her friend.

As though just aware of another presence she inclined her head but gave no word of greeting.

'You are happy at school, Caroline?'

'It isn't too bad, could be worse.'

Her grandmother smiled. 'That means you have settled down as I knew you would.'

Beth remained standing. She would have liked to go and leave them together but required permission to do so and she wasn't going to ask. Caroline had gone to sit beside her grandmother.

'Those decorations in the hall have seen better days. Who is supposed to see to having them renewed?'

'That would be my responsibility, dear. Mrs Murdoch arranges for them to be put up and after the new year they go back into the attic. You, my dear child, can see to that come another year. It will be a beginning for the time when you will have the responsibility for this house. A very great responsibility, Caroline.'

'Surely the servants see to that,' she said carelessly.

'They do but the orders must come from you.'

'Not daddy?'

'His duty is to the estate and yours will be to the house.'

'Unless daddy gets married and that would make a difference.'

'I think we can rule that out.' She frowned as though just remembering that she and her grand-daughter weren't alone. 'Beth?'

Beth was startled out of her day-dreaming. 'Yes, Mrs Parker-Munro?'

'I had forgotten you were there. Go along to the kitchen if you please, and have tea for two sent to the sitting-room.' She smiled to Caroline. 'You and I, my dear, have things to talk about.'

It was a dismissal and Beth went along to the kitchen. The journey she knew to be unnecessary since ringing the bell would have brought the maid. Beth gave the order and went back to the hall. The coats were still where they had left them and Beth put hers on. She would go outside and have a chat with Tommy if he was cleaning the car.

He looked up. 'Safe to talk now? How are you getting on at that posh school?'

'All right.'

'Better than the secondary where you would have gone?'

'Different.'

He laughed. 'Understatement of the year.'

'How are things with you, Tommy?'

'Can't complain. Life's pretty good. I reckon it's what you make it.'

'I reckon you're right.'

'What do you plan to do when you finish school?' He

stopped the polishing and looked at her.

'Get a job.'

'And live here?'

'I wouldn't want to do that. I want to be independent.'

'That'll be all right for a wee while. Know what I see for you?'

'I'm listening.'

'You're going to have a lot of admirers, me among them if I hadn't been caught.'

'Pull the other one. You wouldn't change Mabel for the world and don't try and tell me otherwise.'

'That's true enough but, kidding apart, Beth, there are going to be a few after you. Know it or not, you're going to be a smasher.'

'What about those few after me,' she laughed.

'Take care and choose carefully. The nobs,' he jerked his head, 'set more store on suitable marriages than a love match. Don't you make that mistake, Beth. What me and Mabel have is special and money can't buy that.' He stopped and grinned. 'Sound soppy, don't I?'

'No, you don't, Tommy, and one day if and when I marry I hope we'll be as happy as you and Mabel.'

'No ifs about it.'

She went away laughing.

Caroline's coat was still in the hall and Beth picked it up and took it to the cloakroom along with her own. With being so near Christmas the mail had been late and there were letters on the silver tray. Beth went through them to see if there was one for Caroline from Australia. There wasn't, but there was one addressed to Miss Beth Brown. The address was printed and Beth put the letter in her pocket and went along to her room to read it. Opening it she smiled, it was from Jenny. A short scrawled note.

*My dearest Beth,*

  *In the unlikely event of you being alone on Christmas day do please take an early bus and come to Greystanes for luncheon. I am to be with friends in the evening and we shall drop you off at Inverbrae House.*

  *Don't bother to reply. If you don't come I'll know that you are being entertained. If you do decide to come Miss Harris and I will be so delighted.*

*In haste,*
*love*
*Jenny.*

There was nothing she would enjoy more than being with Jenny on Christmas day but she couldn't accept. She would be expected to have the meal at Inverbrae House. There wouldn't be much celebrating in Dundee, Christmas day wasn't a holiday in Scotland. New Year's day was. For some lucky children there would be a trip to the pantomime and in the morning they would rush to see what Santa Claus had left in their stocking. Others would get an apple and an orange and perhaps a new penny. For the very large number where the breadwinner was unemployed there would be nothing. Did these children question why Santa Claus always forgot them or were they so used to poverty and want that they had lost the ability to wonder?

  Beth sat in her usual place in the dining-room. Earlier in the day the colonel had spoken briefly to her and then, with Caroline hanging on to his arm, they had gone to join Mrs Parker-Munro. How very stiff and formal the meals were and how different from that meal with Adam and Morag where there had been laughter and good-natured banter. Jenny had brought laughter to Inverbrae House but now her name was never mentioned.

Caroline chatted about school and from time to time brought Beth into the conversation. Beth responded then ate what was before her and drifted into her own thoughts.

After the maid had removed the plates Mrs Parker-Munro touched her lips with her napkin and began to speak.

'Caroline, dear, there is a change of plan for Christmas day.'

'Why, what is happening?'

'Your Aunt Gwen has very kindly invited us to spend Christmas day with them. It is to be a family gathering.' She turned her head to look at Beth. 'Since it is family only, you will understand, Beth, that the invitation does not include you but I'm sure the kitchen will put on something special. You can take your meals with Mrs Murdoch, who is quite agreeable to this, or you can have them on your own, just as you please.'

Beth felt the colour rush to her face. She felt humiliated and wished, oh, how she wished, that she could get up from the table and never have to eat there again. Then she remembered the invitation from Jenny and a little of the devil was in her.

'How very, very kind of you, Mrs Parker-Munro, to put yourself to all that trouble on my behalf,' Beth said sweetly.

The old lady looked at her sharply. Had there been a hint of impertinence in that answer? But the girl's expression gave nothing away.

Caroline looked displeased and was frowning. She knew it was going to be dull and boring at Aunt Gwen's. Everybody old except Ruth and they never had a lot to say to one another. Beth and she could have had a giggle and really it was too bad the way they were treating her friend.

It hadn't always been like that and she wondered what had brought it on.

'I think it is too bad of Aunt Gwen not to invite Beth. Don't you agree, daddy?'

The colonel raised his eyes and avoided looking at Beth. 'Your Aunt Gwen is kindly arranging a family party and since she has emphasised that it is to be family only and Beth isn't family, there is no reason why she should have been included in the invitation.'

The old lady nodded her approval.

'I still think it is too bad and I know someone who is going to agree with me.'

'Caroline!' Her father said warningly.

'Thank you, Caroline, but it is all right.' Beth smiled across at her friend. Her eyes were bright and she was going to enjoy the next few minutes. 'Even had I been invited I would not have accepted.'

There was a gasp of outrage from the old lady. Beth smiled and carried on. 'You see, I have already had an invitation for Christmas day so no one need worry about me.'

Caroline opened her mouth to say something then thought better of it.

'How very suitable, Beth, I am very pleased.' Indeed the colonel seemed to be inordinately pleased. 'It is a time for family and your place is with yours.'

Beth saw no reason to correct him.

On Christmas eve there had been a few flurries of snow but to the disappointment of many, mostly children, it wasn't to be a white Christmas. Instead the morning dawned bright and cold and was pleasant for getting about. With breakfast over there was a movement to the drawing-room where the gifts were set beside the

Christmas tree. It all looked very festive and the four people were smiling as they awaited the exchange of gifts. Caroline had appointed herself to be the one to read the names on the gift cards.

As always both girls had been given a modest sum of money to buy small inexpensive gifts for the tree. After a good deal of thought, Beth had purchased a bottle of eau de cologne for Mrs Parker-Munro and a leather bookmark for the colonel. Her gift to Caroline was the same as Caroline's gift to her. Unwrapping them they thanked each other effusively for their very first box of make-up. The old lady frowned heavily.

'Good skin needs nothing but soap and water,' she said severely. 'That cheap rubbish can only do harm.'

The girls paid no attention and the colonel chuckled and shook his head.

Beth's gift from Caroline's grandmother was a box of lace-edged handkerchiefs and from the colonel she had been given money to buy books. Since there were a great many books at Inverbrae House to suit all ages, Beth had begun to save the money she got for birthdays and Christmas. She had her account at the bank and knew the procedure for making deposits. Seeing her savings grow was giving Beth a great deal of satisfaction.

Her father and grandmother gave Caroline jewellery, a beautiful necklace and bracelet that had cost a great deal of money. After a quick glance at them she kissed her father and grandmother, said a dutiful thank you, and returned to the box of make-up which was giving her the greatest amount of pleasure.

On Christmas eve Beth had gone into the village for two last-minute gifts. There wasn't much choice but a small glass ornament of a horse took her fancy and she bought it for Jenny.

'Would you like me to wrap it for you?' the woman assistant asked.

'Yes, please,' Beth answered with such a dazzling smile that the woman, after wrapping it, added a bow of red and gold ribbon.

'That should give someone a lot of pleasure,' she smiled.

'I'm sure of it and thank you for being so kind.'

Beth left the shop and went to look at the other windows. She would like to take something to Jenny's housekeeper but what could she get for Miss Harris? It was a problem. In the end she settled for a box of chocolate gingers and had to ask for it to be wrapped in Christmas paper. There was no ribbon for this one. The girl behind the counter looked tired and dispirited, and Beth thought that perhaps she didn't have much to look forward to. She sympathised, knowing that she could well have been in the same boat.

Since the buying of the school uniforms, Caroline's Aunt Gwen had taken on the responsibility for her niece's wardrobe. A fashionable figure herself, she was delighting in Caroline's interest in clothes, more especially since her own daughter had to be dragged protesting to the shops. Only when a spurt of growing demanded new clothes did Beth accompany them.

Mrs Esslemont picked out a chocolate brown pinafore dress with a lighter brown blouse. 'Is that her size?' she asked the saleslady.

She looked at the label. 'Yes, it is.'

'Then that should do you nicely, Beth.'

That Beth was not taken with the outfit was obvious but it was ignored.

The head saleslady who always attended to Mrs

Esslemont felt sorry for this tall, quiet girl and wondered about the relationship. The fair-haired girl was the daughter of Colonel Parker-Munro and a niece of Mrs Esslemont. The dark-haired girl must be a poor relation, judging by the way she was being treated.

'Excuse me, Mrs Esslemont, I'll take the young lady to one of the cubicles.'

'Since it is the correct size, is that necessary?'

'A fitting would make sure.'

'Very well but, before you do so, have you anything else to show my niece?'

'I'm afraid not.'

'We'll consider these again, Caroline.'

'I do like the pink one with the shawl collar.'

'Do you, dear? I thought the style a little old for you.'

Caroline made a face.

'All right, dear,' she said fondly, 'we'll take it and the peach one which is quite perfect with your colouring.'

The assistant left them to it and hurried to where Beth was waiting. She was in her petticoat and looking glumly at the pinafore dress.

'Doesn't look much on a coat hanger but really it is very nice on.' The saleslady touched the cloth. 'A good material like this always hangs well.'

Beth wasn't convinced. 'It is dull though, isn't it?'

'With that blouse, yes, I agree but slip this one on and see the difference.' She handed Beth a cream satin blouse with a delicately embroidered collar.

Beth's eyes brightened as she put on the outfit. 'Don't the two have to go together?'

'Supposed to but, to my mind cream and brown, coffee and cream, are made for each other.'

Looking in the mirror and turning to see herself at different angles, Beth couldn't hide her delight. The slightly flared skirt suited her girlish figure and the cream shade was perfect with her lovely colouring.

'I didn't expect to like it and now I love it,' Beth said happily.

The saleslady smiled, she was well pleased. The fair-haired little madam, no matter what she eventually chose, would not look as well as this dark-eyed, graceful girl.

'Do you want to ask Mrs Esslemont if you can see something else?'

'Oh, no, I want this, please, but is the blouse more expensive than the other?' she said anxiously.

It was double the price but the account was going to Colonel Parker-Munro and, in any case, Mrs Esslemont would consider it vulgar to discuss the cost.

'Not by very much.' She waited until Beth was dressed and then they joined Caroline and her aunt.

'Was it all right for you, Beth?' Caroline looked up briefly from examining the dresses draped over the chairs.

'Yes, a perfect fit, thank you.'

'The blouse was rather too wide at the neckline, Mrs Esslemont, but I managed to get one that is a better fit.'

'Very well. Have them all sent to Inverbrae House.' She got up in a cloud of perfume. 'Come along, Caroline and you too Beth, we'll have afternoon tea before thinking about shoes. A small dainty heel for you, Caroline.'

Caroline smiled. 'With straps?'

'If that is what you want.' She turned to Beth and frowned. 'You're such a big girl, you can only wear flat shoes.'

Beth was furious but said nothing. She was being made to feel that she was a big heavily-built girl when in fact she was tall and slim. She used to want to be smaller but now she wasn't so sure.

For her visit to Greystanes, Beth wore a herring-bone,

belted coat. Her head was bare and at her neck was a small colourful scarf. Her gloves were in her pocket in case she needed them. Under her coat she had on her pinafore dress and the cream satin, long-sleeved blouse. Her gifts she carried in her hand.

The ten o'clock bus, surprisingly busy, left punctually and an hour later Beth was being ushered in and hugged by a delighted Jenny. Jenny had on a very fine knitted suit in a pale peach and a matching blouse and looked her usual bandbox-fresh self.

'You look wonderful, Beth. Happy Christmas, dear.' She kissed her on both cheeks.

'A happy Christmas to you too, Jenny,' Beth said shyly. 'It was very kind of you to ask me.'

'And nice of you to come. No standing on ceremony, you know your way about the house so just make yourself at home. Hang your coat up in the cloakroom.'

Beth did so then handed Jenny the gift.

'For me? Oh, Beth, my dear, how lovely of you and so beautifully wrapped too.'

'The shop lady did that. It isn't very much, Jenny, but I hope you like it.'

'Darling, I know I'm going to love it but you must never, never apologise for a gift.' She smiled as she said it. 'I have something for you and we'll open them together and in the proper spirit.' She laughed and took Beth's hand. 'Miss Harris made her famous ginger cordial since you are too young for sherry.'

'That's funny, ginger cordial I mean, I bought chocolate gingers for Miss Harris.'

'You darling girl, she'll be so pleased and what a very nice thought. But before we go to the sitting-room come and see this.'

'My picture! It looks much better now.'

'The frame sets it off and, my dear, it is a good painting and has been much admired. Now let me look at you. You've grown, Beth, and in that pinafore dress and the lovely blouse you look a very attractive young lady.'

'When I saw it first I didn't like it. This isn't the blouse that should go with it.' She began to tell Jenny about the shopping expedition. Hearing about it, Jenny was seething with anger. Beth wasn't telling all but she could imagine the rest. Silently she blessed the kindly saleslady.

The sitting-room was warm but not stuffy and there was a Christmas tree at the window. Jenny poured cordial for Beth and sherry for herself and set them on a table between them.

'Now we shall open our gifts,' she said as she handed Beth a small, neatly packaged box. Jenny had hers open first. 'Charming, simply charming, Beth, thank you so much and see how it sparkles in the light from the fire. I wonder – I wonder – where shall I put it? On the cabinet, I think, but not before I show it to Miss Harris.'

Beth had unwrapped her gift. Lying on a velvet pad was a brooch in the shape of a butterfly studded with tiny stones in every shade of blue.

Beth caught her breath. 'Jenny, I've never had anything so pretty and I'll be afraid to wear it in case anything happened to the catch and I lost it.'

'No fear of that, it has a safety catch and you are to wear it, Beth, not stick it in a drawer. It really wasn't so very expensive and it won't bankrupt me.' Taking it from the pad she pinned it on to Beth's dress. 'There now.'

'Thank you,' she whispered, 'thank you very much.'

When they went along to the kitchen Miss Harris was putting the finishing touches to the trifle.

'There's Christmas pudding too, Beth, but I thought you might prefer this.'

261

'Take some of each, Beth, or I'll be eating them until the new year.'

Jenny produced her gift from Beth. 'Look what I got from my young friend.'

'That's pretty and something else for me to dust,' she smiled as she moved the trifle and wiped her hands on a towel.

'That's for you, Miss Harris, it isn't very—' then stopped as Jenny coughed delicately. 'I mean, I do hope you like them.'

Miss Harris went a rosy pink. 'How very kind of you, lass,' she said as she undid the wrapping. 'Chocolate gingers that's a treat for me.'

'You like them?'

'Too much. I'll have to ration myself. That was a very nice surprise.' Her eyes were suspiciously moist and Jenny took Beth's arm. 'We'll let Miss Harris get on.'

They were back in the sitting-room and Beth took rather too much cordial. It caught at her throat and sent her into a paroxysm of coughing.

'Easy does it, Beth. I should have warned you that Miss Harris's brew is quite strong.'

'I like it but I took too much at one time,' Beth said as she recovered and wiped her eyes.

'Satisfy my curiosity if you will. How did you get away from Inverbrae House?'

'The Christmas luncheon was to be at Caroline's aunt's house and it was for the family only.'

'Don't tell me you weren't invited? You are practically family.'

'I wasn't but I was so glad when I got your letter, Jenny.' She dimpled prettily. 'I was a bit naughty,' she added.

'This I want to hear.'

'Mrs Parker-Munro said that the invitation didn't include me but that the kitchen would put on something special and I could have mine with Mrs Murdoch.'

'What had you to say to that? I know what I would have been tempted to say but go on tell me.'

'Well, Jenny, I thanked her for all the trouble she had put herself to—'

'Naughty! Naughty!'

'I know,' Beth grinned. 'I said I couldn't have accepted even if I had been invited because I was going somewhere else for Christmas luncheon.'

'Taken aback, was she?'

'Oh, yes, she didn't say anything.'

'That would make a change.'

'The colonel said that he was delighted to hear that I was to spend Christmas with my family in Dundee and I just let him go on thinking that.'

'Very wise in the circumstances.' She took a sip of her sherry. 'What is life like at Rowanbank? Are you happy?'

'I did write.'

'You did and nothing could be as perfect as you made out.'

'Oh, dear.'

'Is that all you are going to say?'

'Honestly, Jenny, everything is fine. I'm very grateful to be getting such a good education.'

She smiled. 'I won't question you further. I have enough confidence in you to know that you will deal with any difficulties in your own way. Remember, too, that you will come out of it all the stronger.'

# Chapter Twenty

Beth knew by Caroline's face that she was bursting to tell her something but the opportunity for confidences didn't come until the morning of Boxing day. A friend of Jenny's had driven Beth back to Inverbrae House. He was a married man with charming manners and the brother of the hostess who had been grateful to have him chauffeur any unescorted ladies. Asked by Jenny if he would drop Beth off at Inverbrae House, he had declared himself only too willing to do so and dismissed as nothing the extra few miles involved.

Nine o'clock had already chimed when Beth let herself in by the side door. Before going up to her room, she decided it would be wise to tell Mrs Murdoch that she had returned.

'Did you have a nice Christmas, Beth?' the housekeeper smiled. She was quite flushed and Beth thought with amusement that she must have been quite free with the sherry or perhaps it had been wine. She was glad. Her own day had been so very enjoyable that she wanted everyone else to be happy.

'I had a lovely time, Mrs Murdoch.'

'Glad to hear it. With everybody away we took advantage and had a bit of a party.' She gave a small hiccup followed by a giggle. 'Mrs Noble did us proud, and the men folk produced two bottles of wine. Normally I wouldn't approve of such carryings on but well, what's the harm when it's only once a year?'

'No harm at all, Mrs Murdoch.' She paused. 'If Miss Caroline asks for me, please tell her that I've gone to bed.'

'I don't blame you, all that excitement fair tires you out.' She yawned. 'I'll be making tracks myself in a wee while.'

Before going to bed Beth put her brooch back in the box and into her drawer. She would have to be going to some very special occasion before she wore it. Caroline already had a social life and her day would come.

'What time did you get home, Beth?' They had eaten breakfast and were in their own sitting-room.

'About nine o'clock. You were well after me.'

'I know. I don't remember the actual time but I know I almost fell asleep in the car coming home. Grandmama snored in the chair all afternoon then when she did waken up she said she was as fresh as a daisy. Then, of course, everybody just talked and talked and the gentlemen disappeared with Uncle Robert. I am quite sure a lot of drink must have been consumed because they were all very happy and as you know Uncle Robert and daddy don't usually have much to say to one another.' She paused. 'Better ask did you have a good day with your cousins?'

'I had a marvellous day but I wasn't with—' Beth had been about to tell Caroline that she hadn't been with her cousins but with Jenny, and that she should keep the information to herself. But she didn't get the chance. Caroline cut her off, so anxious was she to have her say. Beth thought it would be safer to say nothing about Greystanes unless it couldn't be avoided.

'Wait until I tell you, you just have to hear this.' Her

eyes were dancing. 'When Ruth said what she said I think Aunt Gwen could have willingly strangled her.'

'Poor Ruth, she does tend to put her foot in it,' Beth laughed.

'Both feet more like. But listen, this is serious and you were the cause of it.'

Beth looked annoyed. 'Since I wasn't there I find that difficult to believe.'

'That was why, silly. Oh, do stop interrupting and let me tell it in my own way.'

'Knowing the time you take to tell anything I'll get myself into a more comfortable chair,' Beth said as she dropped herself into one of the armchairs.

'There we all were sitting round the table and I had better tell you it was beautiful but then you know with Aunt Gwen that everything has to be just perfect.'

'How many were round the table?'

'Just ourselves and Uncle Robert's two unmarried sisters. What a pair!' Caroline rolled her eyes. 'One is as deaf as a door post and the other yelled in her ear to keep her up with the conversation but that is just by the way. Ruth came in wearing a navy and white dress and I think it made her look slimmer. Aunt Gwen was already annoyed with her because Ruth was the last to come to the table and then when she sat down and looked around she asked me where you were and before I got a chance to say that you were in Dundee, Aunt Gwen looked daggers at Ruth and said that since it was a family party, you had not been invited. Ruth said that was ridiculous and since you lived at Inverbrae House as family, then you were practically family and you should have been invited.'

Beth looked uncomfortable. 'I do wish Ruth hadn't said that.'

'I'm not finished,' Caroline glared, 'so do be quiet.

Grandmama, I could see, was about to put in her bit to support Aunt Gwen when Uncle Robert, who as you know likes a quiet life and seldom crosses Aunt Gwen, announced that he thought it was just terrible, and he absolutely agreed with Ruth, and what was his wife thinking of? Wasn't this Christmas and a time of goodwill to all? Well by this time Aunt Gwen was glaring at husband and daughter and everyone was feeling very uncomfortable and glad when the maids arrived to serve the meal.' Caroline giggled. 'The funniest bit for me was those two old dears. Uncle Robert, I'm positive, must have been a late baby, because they looked ancient. The deaf one felt she was missing out on the fun and demanded to be told what was going on.'

'It didn't spoil the day, did it?'

'Of course not, Beth Brown, you are not that important.'

'Never suggested I was. I just didn't like the thought of being the cause of any unpleasantness.'

'You weren't, at least not after the food arrived and daddy was at his most entertaining. The same funny stories come out year after year but no one seems to notice but me.'

'The others are probably too polite to say so.'

'Could be, I suppose. Grandmama was talking about the Australian side of the family and Ruth said she wished she was there, in Australia she meant. She winked at me but I knew what she meant. After we'd gone she would be in for a good talking to from Aunt Gwen.'

'Poor Ruth.' Beth got up and wandered over to the window. 'I think it is going to stay fair so how about a walk?'

Caroline swithered. 'Perhaps I should, all that food yesterday and today will be just about as bad. Being small I can't afford to put on weight.'

'You won't.'

'How do you know?'

'Someone said if both your parents are thin then you will be too or it is true most of the time.'

'Oh, good, that means I can eat as many chocolates as I like and not get fat.'

'Make yourself sick, that's all. Are you coming or not? I'm going anyway.'

Caroline sighed. 'Anything for a quiet life but not too far remember!'

'Just a short brisk walk.'

The wind whipped the colour into their cheeks and both girls were enjoying being outside. Caroline was a lot less delicate now, particularly since starting school. She was excused games but just occasionally Beth thought there was a wistful longing in her face as if she would like to join in but was afraid to in case her health suffered.

'Beth, I hope you know that it was no fault of mine that – that—'

'I got left out? No, and I honestly don't mind.'

'You know, Beth, I had a thought in bed last night. Poor you, you're not going to meet anyone special, you never get the chance, but wouldn't it be funny and nice too, if my cousin came over from Australia and he liked you and you liked him.'

Beth laughed.

'It could happen. If you got married one day, then you would be really part of the family.'

'You can forget that, Caroline. I don't want to get married for ages and ages and only if I fell in love.'

Caroline didn't look convinced. 'Tell me honestly, Beth, if you had the choice of marrying a boy you loved who had no money and a boy who was wealthy, whom would you choose?'

'Love and poverty,' she said immediately, 'but we wouldn't need to be all that poor because I would take a job and earn money.'

'Not after you were married, surely?'

'Yes, I see no wrong in that.'

'What about when the children arrive?'

'Then, of course, I wouldn't be able to work.'

'What would you do for money?'

'Wait until we could afford to have children.'

'Can you do that? Choose your own time I mean?'

'I don't know.'

'You see, Beth,' Caroline said seriously, 'sometimes I get very frightened.'

'What about?'

'Having babies. My mother died having me,' she whispered.

'Caroline, you mustn't worry about that. No two persons are alike, not even mother and daughter. In any case, doctors are much cleverer now and know far more than they did when you were born.'

'I'll try to remember that.'

With Caroline spending so many of her Saturdays with her Aunt Gwen, Beth felt very alone. She decided to visit Dundee more often. She would go and see Aunt Anne and Uncle Fred this very day and another Saturday she would visit Adam and Morag.

The day was pleasant with no sign of rain when Beth set off to catch the bus. Once she would have asked permission, or at least stated where she was going, since the colonel approved of her having closer links with her family. She didn't bother this time, for the very good reason that no one cared, no one was the least concerned where she went or what she did. She had all the freedom she could want yet deep down she was unhappy about that. Having to account for where she went would have shown that someone had her welfare at heart. Knowing no one did made her feel very isolated.

Her aunt's face beamed with pleasure and Beth felt a glow at her welcome.

'Now this is a nice surprise, come away in, Beth.'

'Hello, Aunt Anne,' Beth smiled as she went in. 'Is this you on your own or is Uncle Fred at home?'

'He's got a wee job on a Saturday and that helps to fill in his time. You'll mind he's handy with a saw and he's cutting up lengths of wood over at McGregors. Doesn't get much for his labours but it's something for his pocket. Hang your coat in the lobby. I take it you're staying awhile?'

'If you aren't going out?'

'Not me, I don't venture far and I've got the messages in. Sit yourself down, lass.'

Beth sat down. 'Aunt Anne, could I ask a favour?'

'Well you could ask. But as to whether I grant it, that's another matter.' She was smiling as she said it. 'Let's hear it then.'

'Would you teach me to cook?'

'Mercy me! Am I hearing right? And what's given you this notion?'

'I don't know what I'll be doing when I leave school and I think it might be useful to be able to cook. Just simple cooking, nothing complicated.'

'No complicated dishes in this house, just good wholesome food,' she said, shaking her head. 'All that expensive schooling, filling your head with a lot of stuff you'll never need.' She tut-tutted. 'I doubt if you're capable of making yourself a pot of tea.'

'Don't make me out to be worse than I am,' Beth

laughed. 'I can just about manage that. Pouring boiling water over the tea leaves is all there is to it.'

'That's where you're wrong. There's a lot more to it, as you'll find out before I'm finished with you.'

'You're going to take me on?'

'That I am. Away and get yourself a pinny from that top drawer in the sideboard. I'll do the stew now instead of later. First though we'll prepare the vegetables.'

Beth got an apron from the drawer and put it on over her skirt. She hadn't expected to start this early but, as her aunt would say, there is no time like the present. She went over to the sink to await instructions.

'That's the best knife, you take it and scrape those carrots. I've topped and tailed them and mind a thin scraping.'

Beth put her hands in the water and gasped. 'Aunt Anne, this water is absolutely freezing.'

'You didn't expect hot water did you?'

'I'm not saying another word,' Beth laughed.

'No, just you concentrate on the job you're doing. Get that done and the meat browned then we'll have ourselves a cup of tea.'

By the time Beth had finished the carrots Aunt Anne had peeled a pot of potatoes. 'Will that do?' Beth asked.

'Not too bad, we'd all to crawl before we could walk.'

'How is Luke? I suppose I'll be away before he gets home?'

'More than likely.' Her lips pursed. 'Never a moment's worry with Adam but Luke,' she shook her head, 'right from the time he started school he's been in some kind of trouble.'

'Not serious trouble though?'

'Serious enough, skipping school when the wee devil felt like it.'

Beth smiled. 'That was a long time ago.'

'Time to have mended his ways but he hasn't. Oh, he turns up for work, if he didn't he would be out on his ear. No, lass, it's more than that. He's that moody, your uncle says it's just a phase and he'll grow out of it but that is all he ever says.' She paused and went to see to the meat. 'Men don't worry the same as we women and of course mothers are worst of all, as you'll no doubt find out one day. If I just knew what was bothering him—'

'Have you asked Luke?'

'Have I asked him? Time without number and I could have saved my breath. Nothing is wrong is all I ever get.'

'Probably because nothing is and you are worrying yourself needlessly.'

'I don't look for trouble, lass, I don't have to.' She brought down the biscuit tin. 'Here, put some of those on a plate. Where was I? Oh, yes, moods I expect from young lads and lasses too, all part of growing up, but his have gone on too long.' The kettle boiled and she went over to it. Come along and make your first decent pot of tea.'

Beth waited.

'Heat the teapot by putting in some boiling water, leave it a second or two then pour it out.'

Beth did that. 'There's the caddy, two good spoons of tea then fill up with boiling water and make sure it hasn't gone off the boil. Now leave that until it draws, a good three or four minutes.' She smiled. 'That should give us a good cup of tea.'

Beth returned to Inverbrae House feeling well satisfied with her day. How wrong she had been about Aunt Anne. It was only that abrupt manner that made her seem unapproachable. Underneath it was a genuinely kind and caring woman.

★ ★ ★

Back in school, Caroline was telling Beth about the photographs that had arrived from Queensland.

'I've seen them but grandmama won't let them out of her sight.'

'What are they like?'

'Very good. Uncle James isn't, or I should say wasn't, as nice looking as daddy but quite nice all the same. Robert looks a bit like him but not so tall but then maybe he hadn't stopped growing when they were taken. William is two years younger but you can see by his loose build that he is going to be tall. Grandmama was a bit annoyed with me for saying so and I can't think why—'

'Saying what?'

'Only that William is nicer looking than Robert. She said they were both good looking boys and that photographs weren't always a true likeness.'

'True, I suppose.'

'Aunt Dorothy looks nice and friendly just the way she writes if that makes sense. Emily looks all right too. The house, Beth, is huge or looks to be but not a bit like Inverbrae House. Daddy says it is ranch style and there are a few others but smaller homes nearby for the rest of the family.'

'Is your cousin, Robert, coming over?'

'Yes, but no date is fixed. Aunt Dorothy says both boys will be given a year to travel where they want. William doesn't want, at least that is what he is saying at the moment, but Robert intends doing the capitals of Europe or some of them. Doesn't that sound wonderful?'

'Certainly does. Will he be on his own?'

'Yes. Aunt Dorothy says it is good for them, character building and had Uncle James lived, he would have been all for it.'

★ ★ ★

Another weekend and they were back in Inverbrae House.

'I told daddy and he is all for you doing business studies.'

'I rather thought he would approve.'

'Approves of it because it'll help you to get a job. But he agrees with Miss Critchley that it is bad for the school's image and if the Board of Governors aren't careful, he says Rowanbank will cease to be an exclusive school. Another thing he said, before I forget. He said he could do with some clerical assistance and it will be good experience until you get fixed up.'

'That suits me.'

'See this,' Caroline said holding up a large brown envelope. 'Guess what is in it.'

'Photographs.'

Caroline's face fell. 'How did you know?'

'Educated guess,' Beth grinned. 'Thought it probable since you have spoken of little else since they arrived.'

'I couldn't get them earlier because grandmama would hardly let them out of her sight.'

'You managed?'

'Nipped them when she was snoring her head off. Funny how she snores worse than ever now. When I told her she snored, she almost took my head off. "Ladies do not snore and you would do well to remember that, Caroline," her grand-daughter mimicked. Then she returned to her normal voice. 'Bring your chair nearer mine,' she said, 'and I can hand them over and explain who everyone is.'

One by one Caroline brought out the photographs of her Australian relations, making some remark about each. What struck Beth first was how happy they looked, their very ordinariness. They couldn't have been more different from the Parker-Munros of Inverbrae House, with their stiffness and formality, especially in the dining-room. Beth thought those on the photograph would have quite happily sat down at the kitchen table.

'That is Uncle James, one of the last taken before he died. Take note of the large brimmed hat, that is the badge of the true Aussie,' she grinned.

'Maybe your uncle was more at home in his adopted country than he was when he was here.'

'That's probably true. Robert looks a little like him. I'm a teeny bit disappointed, he's quite ordinary looking isn't he?'

'I think he looks nice.'

'But not handsome. William might be when he is a bit older, pity he wasn't the elder brother, he looks rather fun – see that mischievous grin on his face?'

'The little girl Emily is pretty.'

'Not bad.' She handed over another photograph. 'That's a good one of Aunt Dorothy.'

'She didn't know it was being taken and those always turn out best.'

Caroline jumped up. 'That'll have to do and I'll pop along before she wakens but don't you go – I have something else to tell you.'

'What about?'

'Ruth, but I'll tell you when I get back.'

Beth waited for Caroline's return. She wanted to hear about Ruth. Caroline's cousin had always been kind to her. Once she had confided in Beth her wish to take up nursing but knew there would be stiff opposition from her mother who was desperately looking for a young man, or failing that a not-so-young man of good family, who would marry Ruth and take her off her hands. An unmarried, clumsy daughter at home was something she could do without.

As had been predicted, Mrs Esslemont was both shocked and horrified. Nursing was perfectly acceptable for a working- or even middle-class girl but most certainly not for her daughter. It was a hard life, she pointed out, with unspeakable tasks to perform, and never, never would she give her consent.

Ruth sulked, refused to have her wardrobe renewed, would not accompany her mother on social rounds and in general made life miserable for everyone herself included. Ruth's father had reservations himself. His daughter was stubborn and of strong character but he rather doubted that she would last the course. After much discussion Mr Esslemont won over his wife by saying that their daughter would be unlikely to complete the course and after a few months would be only too willing to return home. A further inducement was that Ruth could train at Edinburgh Infirmary and during that time live with an acquaintance of his, a senior doctor and his wife who had their home in Morningside.

Caroline flung herself in the door. 'Just made it, she was just stirring.'

'Come on, what is the news about Ruth? Done exceptionally well in her exams, is that it?'

'No, it is not, though actually she has done well but I would hardly call that exciting. My cousin, believe it or not, has got herself engaged. Engaged to be married,' she added unnecessarily.

'But that is wonderful,' Beth exclaimed, 'and I only hope he is worthy of her.'

Caroline shrugged. 'He's a doctor, five years older than Ruth and his name is Ian Melville. Aunt Gwen and Uncle Robert have met him.'

'Did he pass the test?' Beth said drily.

'With Uncle Robert, yes and his doctor friend is high in his praise. A clever lad who could go far in his profession was his opinion.'

'Couldn't fault that, surely?'

'Not his profession but he comes from a working-class background and like you his parents are dead.'

'His working-class background is against him as far as your aunt is concerned,' Beth said sarcastically.

'Beth, you have been very slow to understand this but one's background, the family one is born into, is very important. Much more important than money, I may say, and I think it is extremely generous of Aunt Gwen to accept this engagement without having to rejoice in it.'

Beth laughed. 'You really are a pompous little madam and I think you and your aunt are well matched. You, not Ruth, should have been her daughter.'

'The pompous bit I shall ignore but the rest I accept. Aunt Gwen has never made a secret of the fact that she would have liked to have me as a daughter.'

'What does he look like?'

'Ian? Tall and skinny.' She giggled. 'Actually—'

'Do you have to say actually quite so often?'

'I don't know when I'm saying it. But, actually, Ruth has lost quite a lot of weight and needless to say is happy about it. She says it is the result of being so happy. When she was miserable, which was a lot of the time when she was at home, she used to stuff herself with sweet things.'

'All that running about the wards will help too.'

'Do they have to run?' Caroline asked.

'They run because they are in a hurry. Nurses never walk. Next question. Have they fixed a date for the wedding?'

'No. Battle two commences before that.'

'Won one, good chance of them winning the next.'

'My daddy says it will end in a compromise.'

'Why?'

'Ruth and Ian want a quiet wedding and you must remember that Ian has no close family. He is all for tying the knot in the Registry Office and Ruth wouldn't mind. But to please her mother she would be married in church, but quietly and with only close relatives.'

'Ruth should stick out for that.'

'Probably will. Uncle Robert offered to buy them a house in Edinburgh and Aunt Gwen favoured that. Her daughter and son-in-law in a good practice and living in a desirable residence, she could just about live with that.'

'All satisfactory then?'

'No, it isn't. The wretched Ian wants to work with the poor and needy and, as he says, not sit in some posh surgery listening to imaginary ailments. The cheek of him, as though we couldn't be ill the same as everybody else.'

'I know what he means and I admire him.'

'Well you would, wouldn't you? Actually – yes I know I am saying it again – Ian would have been a good match for you.'

'He happens to be in love with Ruth.'

'Enough about my cousin. I am not going to Aunt Gwen's next Saturday so we can go somewhere together.'

'Sorry I can't.'

'Can't or won't?' Caroline said huffily.

'Take your pick. For goodness sake don't go off in one of your huffs. This is serious. Morag wrote to tell me that my aunt is in a terrible state. Luke has run away to sea.'

'How exciting! Did he leave a message for them to find?'

'Yes, saying he couldn't stick it any longer and since

they wouldn't let him go to sea he is doing it this way but not to worry.'

'As a sailor?'

'An extra hand he called it but same thing I suppose.'

'Shades of Uncle James.'

'I hope not. Your uncle never came back but I think Luke will. He did say he would write as soon as he could. My uncle told them that he would most likely be on a boat going to India since they leave from Dundee. He said they are always short of hands and glad of anyone and Luke is a strong, healthy lad.'

Aunt Anne had shed her tears but her eyes were anguished.

'Good of you to come, lass.'

'I wanted to as soon as I heard.' Hardly aware of what she was doing, Beth put her arms round her aunt. 'Try not to worry, Aunt Anne. Luke will be all right and in a few weeks you'll be getting letters and postcards from different countries.'

Her aunt didn't immediately push her away and seemed to get comfort from the embrace. She gave a little smile then patted Beth's shoulder. 'You're a good lass, Beth. You've turned out better than I ever expected.'

'That's a relief,' Beth said trying to hide her amusement. 'You sit down and I'll make you a good strong cup of tea the way you like it. Uncle Fred, you're not going out, are you?'

'Not the day, lass, so you can make that two cups, no three counting yourself.'

Beth had put down a shopping bag on the floor and her aunt picked it up.

'Fair weight in that.'

'Open it.'

She did. 'Grand looking potatoes and fine vegetables you have there.'

'For you.'

She bristled. 'I don't accept charity from those posh folk of yours.'

'You are not being asked to,' Beth said quietly, knowing she would have to go carefully. 'How often do you complain about waste? The gardeners have too much and the surplus is just left to rot.'

'Sinful that would be. In that case, thanks. I can make good use of it.'

Beth sighed with relief. She hadn't been honest. Nothing went to waste at Inverbrae House. What wasn't required in the kitchens went to any of the staff who would take the trouble to carry it home.

Beth made the tea and they had it with buttered scones.

'Why would he do that to us, Beth? He would know I'd be worried out of my mind.'

'He left a note, Aunt Anne, and it would have been far worse if he hadn't.'

'Just what I've been trying to get into her head, lass,' Uncle Fred said as he clattered his cup down. 'We can blame ourselves, Anne. The lad told us often enough that he hankered after a life at sea. We should have given him his head. If we'd let him do what he wanted, we would have been spared this.'

His wife shivered. 'I have a horror when I think about a wee boat being—' her voice broke.

'Lass,' her husband said patiently, 'he'll no' be on a wee boat that I can promise you. It'll be a sturdy, sea-worthy vessel.'

'So you say,' she sniffed, 'and you with a brother that was drowned at sea.'

'Aye, that's true enough, Danny got a watery grave but

281

others lose their lives in accidents at work or get run over in the streets. Too many cars on the road with idiots inside them. They'll mow down a few, you mark my words.'

'Is that supposed to comfort me?'

'Just my way of telling you that the sea doesn't claim any more than any other occupation.'

She turned to her niece. 'Still doing well at that school?'

'Yes, thank you. Another year and I'll be job hunting.'

'And what had you in mind?'

'Probably an office job.'

'Wouldn't hold out much hope for you there. At seventeen you'll be a bit old, the lasses hereabout have office jobs, taken on at fifteen when they left school. No boss is going to pay a seventeen-year-old when he can get a fifteen-year-old to do the same work.'

'A proper ray of sunshine your aunt is.' Uncle Fred shook his head. 'Don't you worry, Beth, your good education won't be lost but you'll maybe need to wait a while until the right job comes along.'

For the first time Beth felt less confident. Her aunt, after all, was only stating what Miss McAndrew, the English teacher, had said. Far from being an asset, her expensive education could well be a drawback.

# Chapter Twenty-One

Her schooldays were over. As the colonel was driving the car down the drive and through the gates for the last time, Beth could not bring herself to turn round for that final look at Rowanbank School for Young Ladies. She wondered how, in the years to come, she would look back on her schooldays at Rowanbank. Would she manage to forget the bad times and only remember the good days, or would it be the other way round? A bit of both, she decided.

Father and daughter were not concerned with her, they were talking and she was in the back seat with her own thoughts and they were taking her back to what had happened a short time ago. Where on earth had she found the courage?

The other girls had behaved properly, saying what was expected. Goodbye, Miss Critchley, I shall miss Rowanbank and all the happy times or some such words but they would have stuck in Beth's throat.

Somehow she had managed to say and in a voice loud enough to carry, 'I have no wish to shake your hand, Miss Critchley, and I certainly have nothing for which to thank you.'

There were gasps, shocked looks. Someone had giggled. She had walked out of the hall with her head held high.

★ ★ ★

The car stopped in the drive and the three of them went up the steps and into the house.

An hour later the colonel approached Beth. 'I want you to come to my study in half an hour, Beth.'

'Yes.' She wasn't surprised – this was only to be expected. She was to be asked to go but she was older now, she was seventeen and she rather thought she wouldn't be left homeless. She had her savings and they had grown to a sizeable sum. Not that it would last long if she had to pay for lodgings while she looked for a job but Aunt Anne had softened and she thought she would be welcome to stay in her house for a short time. Then there was Jenny who had made it clear that she would always be welcome at Greystanes. It was a comforting thought but most of all Beth wanted to be independent. That was the way to self respect.

She knocked and wondered if this might be the last time she would enter this study. His voice: 'Come in.'

Closing the door behind her, she did not wait to be invited to do so but sat in the chair facing him. His elbows were on the desk and his fingers pressed together.

'This commercial course you have completed, what qualifications has it given you?'

'My shorthand is about a hundred words a minute and my typing is good. I have a certificate to prove—'

He stopped her. 'That is of no interest to me.' He paused. 'What I have in mind, Beth, is for you to assist Mr Blair. He manages the estate, as you know, and fulfils that position to my satisfaction. Sadly, he is very slipshod regarding the paperwork and though he says he has a filing system, I am at a loss to understand it.'

Beth smiled with relief. 'You would like me to take over the filing and put it in order?'

'That and other things. Blair can spend more time seeing to his other duties if he doesn't have to worry about the paperwork. Come along,' he said getting up, 'and I'll show you where you will be working.' Beth followed him. Outside the sun was shining and there was the merest whisper of a breeze as they walked together to the office building. She knew it, of course, but she had never been inside. The colonel unlocked the door and went in, leaving her to follow. Once it had been home to a family, a cottage with three rooms, a tiny scullery and a toilet. The wall between two of the rooms had been knocked down and this was the office. There were two windows that gave plenty of light and both were curtained in brown and gold material. The walls were painted cream but in need of a freshen up. A desk with a chair behind it was over at one of the windows. There was an Underwood typewriter on a table. The cover was on and there was a lot of dust. Filing cabinets against one wall were only partly filled and bundles of papers were piled on the floor. The fireplace was empty, Beth supposed for the summer months, and there was a brass scuttle for coal or logs.

The colonel was over at the desk examining papers and Beth wandered through the rest of the office. The small room where she stood was obviously where the manager made himself a meal. There was an old dresser containing crockery and cutlery, a table and two chairs. In the scullery just off it was a rather ancient cooker. There was also a kettle and two pans. The toilet was tiny and she was glad to see that it had a lock.

'Have you seen all you wish?' He was behind her.

She turned. 'Yes, thank you.'

'Better sit down while we discuss one or two things.' She did and he went to the chair behind the desk. 'You must have realised, Beth, that you cannot continue to live at Inverbrae House.'

'I'm prepared to leave now or as soon as I have accommodation arranged,' she said coldly.

'Kindly listen to what I have to say and don't be so prickly,' he frowned. 'You would agree, I hope, that you owe me some repayment for all that has been done for you?'

'Yes.'

'Until such time as you find suitable employment, I want you to take over the office here.'

'What about Mr—?'

'Blair won't trouble you. He will have his meals at home and, apart from calling in occasionally, you won't see much of him.'

'What are my duties to be?'

'Normal office work. You will type my letters.'

'I can take them down in shorthand.'

'I prefer to write them out in longhand.' He cleared his throat. 'First and foremost, you must get a good filing system going and then see that accounts are paid before the final date. Remember to file the receipts. You are following me?'

'Very easily.'

'This is to be a business arrangement, Beth. You will work office hours 9 am to 5 pm with the whole of Saturday off. As to your meal times,' he paused and avoided looking at her, 'you will continue to have your meals up at the house but you will not dine with the family. Instead you will take yours in the breakfast room.'

'That will suit me very well.'

'That is all, I think.'

'Not quite, Colonel Parker-Munro,' Beth said quietly. 'Since this is to be a business arrangement and I am to be working office hours, there is the matter of remuneration.'

He looked startled. 'I – I—'

'I would expect the going rate for the job,' she said boldly, 'with a deduction for board and lodging.'

She had angered him but he was trying not to show it. 'I'll see to it,' he said stiffly.

'Thank you.' Her eyes were suspiciously bright and there was a tremor in her voice. 'When do I begin?'

'Immediately.' He smiled. 'Caroline's life and yours will be very different from now on. Now that you are a working girl, you will see a lot less of each other. Start tomorrow. This will be good experience for you.' He dangled the keys. 'You had better have these. You can stay as long as you wish but remember to lock up.'

'Yes.'

He went. Beth waited until the door closed and the sound of his footsteps had died away. Then she sat down to do some thinking. She wouldn't stay in Inverbrae House a day longer than necessary and from now on she was going to look after herself. Newspapers came to the house including the *Courier & Advertiser* which was the newspaper for the area. Apart from *The Times*, many of the papers remained unread and by evening were seized on by the staff. She would get the 'situations vacant' pages and begin to apply for jobs straight away. If she was lucky enough to get an interview, she would go with or without permission and whenever they wanted her to start she would be happy to oblige. On the other hand, if no job came along as had been hinted by Aunt Anne, she would continue to work for the colonel and get valuable experience which should help her to get a position in the future.

Caroline was avoiding her, that was obvious. But Beth didn't blame her. It couldn't be easy for Caroline and it was likely that she had been told to keep her distance.

With her now an employee she was not a suitable companion. It was hurtful but she had a lot of experience of being hurt.

She knew Mr Blair by sight only but he proved to be a pleasant man of middle age who was clearly delighted to be rid of the paperwork. Beth had a free hand but it was a daunting task to start a new filing system. Nevertheless it had to be done and the quicker she got the papers off the floor the better. The colonel had his own keys and he made use of them because quite often in the morning she would find letters on her desk waiting to be typed.

She was neither happy nor unhappy. The work filled her day and most weekends she spent in Dundee, even staying overnight and sleeping in Luke's bed. As yet no letter had arrived but there had been a postcard from Calcutta. Not much on it. He was well. He was happy. But it was enough to take away the anguished look from Aunt Anne's face.

'You can stop worrying, that is great news,' Beth said when told.

'Surely he could have taken the trouble to write a proper letter,' Aunt Anne grumbled.

'He may have and the letter hasn't arrived.'

'No address, I can't even write to him and give him a piece of my mind.'

'He won't have an address,' Uncle Fred said from behind his paper. 'Just be content with what you've got and change the subject. Tell Beth the good news.'

'I was going to if you'd give me time. What I would give to have you back working full time and out from under my feet,' she said irritably.

'And me I wish I was away from that tongue of yours.'

Beth knew that it was the worry about Luke that had them at each other's throats. Worry and sleepless nights could strain even the best marriage.

'What's the news, Aunt Anne?'

'Adam and Morag have got another house after spending all that time and money on the one they are in.'

'Where is it?'

'Ten minutes' walk from where they are. A better district or a bit better anyway and there is an inside toilet which is the main attraction.' She smiled. 'Morag has put her foot down and says there will be no more flittings until they get the key to a corporation house and that will be a long while, the waiting list is as long as your arm.'

'Tell them I am delighted.'

'I'll do that, and happy though I am to see you, I'm thinking you're not spending much time with those Parker folk. You and the lass fallen out, have you?'

'No, we haven't, but Caroline has a busy social life.'

'Which does not include you?'

'No reason why it should.'

'That's as maybe. They'll be looking for a good match for the lass.' She shook her head. 'Times I'm sorry for the family of gentry.'

'Why? They have it made as far as I can see,' Beth said a little sourly.

'All that talk about arranged marriages in those foreign countries but to my mind it is the same with the nobs. Nobody is going to choose your husband for you, Beth.'

'You're right there, but wrong about Caroline. Provided she doesn't choose someone totally unsuitable, she will marry whom she wants.'

With each passing month Beth was becoming increasingly disheartened. She had written numerous applications for clerical vacancies in Perth and Dundee and had, as requested, enclosed a stamped, addressed envelope. In due course the envelope came back and inside it a small typed note thanking her for her interest and informing her that the post was now filled. Her experience hadn't improved her chances since there were fewer jobs for seventeen-year-olds and those that did appear from time to time demanded more in qualifications than she could offer. The trouble was that she was over-educated in subjects that were of little use in her present circumstances and when asked to state the school she had attended, Beth was reluctant to do so. Far from being an advantage, it merely hastened her application into the wastepaper basket.

One person was extremely pleased with her and the arrangements were very much to his satisfaction. Beth had proved to be a good and conscientious worker with a real grasp of what was required. What was more she was on the spot and willing to do work outside the stipulated hours. The filing system she had introduced was simple and efficient and the office had changed out of all recognition. Beth had made her own small demands and had the maids come in regularly to clean out the premises and wash the windows. New curtains had replaced those that were badly faded with the sun and a rug of good quality had been brought down from the attic and was on the floor beside the desk. During the cold winter months a fire blazed and Beth thought of the office almost as her home. Here she was king of her castle. There was tea and a bottle of Camp coffee and in the mornings she made herself a cup of coffee and in the afternoon she had tea. The biscuits and the occasional bar of chocolate she bought in the village shop.

Most days Tommy called for the mail and took it to the post office but on others she posted the letters herself and enjoyed the walk. Speaking nicely to the gardeners meant she was given choice blooms or flowering plants for the window sills.

'This is all very attractive,' the colonel said approvingly as he prepared to sign his letters.

'I work better in pleasant surroundings.'

He nodded. 'You are doing a good job for me, Beth, and I am well pleased.'

'Thank you.'

He smiled. 'In a month or two we must reconsider your salary or should I call it wages?'

'Wages since I am paid weekly,' she said quietly.

'Would you prefer to be paid monthly?'

'No, the present arrangements suit me quite well.'

'As long as you are happy—' He signed the letters, the final one with a flourish. 'By the way has Blair been in about those repairs to the dyke, the one dividing the north fields?'

'Yes, it is being dealt with and he wants your attention drawn to the roofs of two of the cottages. They are in a bad condition and urgently require new roofing before the next heavy rainfall.'

The colonel gave an exaggerated sigh. 'A nominal rent is all they are charged and for that they expect a palace. Some people don't know when they are well off.'

Beth didn't answer. She was getting her eyes opened. Doing this job meant she was getting to know a great deal about the estate and the way it was run. The colonel was quick enough to have workmen see to any fault, major or minor, at Inverbrae House but there was absolutely no urgency about work being carried out on leaking roofs. Pails were constantly in place to collect the drips and a long wet spell was a nightmare and an ever-increasing worry.

The colonel was thoughtful as he left the office. Beth was very quiet and distant and that should please him but it didn't. It was a tricky situation trying to keep her at Inverbrae House and at the same time distancing her from Caroline.

Once she was an employee, Beth's sleeping arrangements had been changed. Her bedroom would be required for guests, she was told, and her belongings had been transferred to a much smaller bedroom in the little-used wing nearest to the servants' quarters. Caroline had been apologetic and embarrassed about the move but as she said there was nothing she could do about it. That could well be true Beth thought but she didn't much care. This family had lost the power to hurt her – or so she thought.

No one is irreplaceable but when she did leave, the girl who succeeded her would need training and that would have to come from the colonel or his manager, neither of whom would relish the task.

To be independent was Beth's goal and she longed to be free of Inverbrae House. But she had to be sensible. Staying where she was had a lot of advantages for, apart from buying clothes and other personal items, the money was found and she was able to save. Entertainment took little of her money and only occasionally did she meet up with girls she had known in the village school to accompany them to a cinema or a local dance. Boys asked her out but she didn't accept and this amazed the other girls. After all, they were nice boys and it didn't do to be too choosy and get a name for yourself. A date was a date and a way of keeping in circulation until someone more exciting came along.

Over at Inverbrae House mother and son were together in the drawing-room. It was the end of January and outside a blizzard was blowing. Inside the house the fire gave out a good heat. Nigel finding it too much for him moved his chair back. His mother leaned forward and held her hands out to the blaze.

'Hard to believe that our little Caroline will be eighteen next month,' she smiled.

'Shouldn't be, Mother,' he smiled back at her, 'since you've talked of little else but her eighteenth birthday.'

'Such an important day, dear, and I'm very grateful to Gwen for offering to see to all the arrangements.'

'Very good of her and a relief to me. A ball, even with modest numbers, takes a bit of arranging.'

'Oh, but I were younger,' she sighed. Then she brightened. 'Gwen has it from me that no expense is to be spared and I am to pay for Caroline's gown. She must get something extra special.'

'She will, I'm sure.'

'What is making it perfect for me is having Robert with us. It couldn't have been better timed.' She paused. 'How long does Robert intend staying in London before travelling up, or don't you know?'

'I do as it happens. I have written to Robert and his mother to say that I'll meet Robert in London and he can spend a few days there if he wishes or travel up here and visit London on another occasion. In either event I'll accompany him on the journey and that will give us an opportunity to get to know one another before he meets the family.'

'Gwen is in her element and I rather think she is looking on Caroline as her daughter. Do you mind?'

'No, why should I?' He laughed. 'Caroline is the daughter she would have liked, Ruth is what she got.'

'Ruth's wedding won't take any arranging. The affair is to be as quiet as possible. Her intended has no one of his own. Rather sad really.'

'Yes.'

The old lady sniffed or as near as elegance would allow. 'Poor family background, I believe, and that is so important. One has to think of the children of the marriage and how they would turn out.'

'Which brings us to Beth.'

'I had hoped we had finally got rid of that girl.'

'Beth does a very good job for me, Mother, in fact I would go as far as say I would be lost without her. We have come to depend on her.'

'Nonsense, any girl from a business college could meet your requirements.'

'I am afraid you are wrong there but we'll let the matter rest. Incidentally, Caroline feels that she cannot leave Beth out of the guest list and in any case she wants her there. No, don't say what you were going to: that Beth is a working girl and no longer a threat to Caroline. To be honest, I feel very offended that you should think so little of your grand-daughter's charms that you would consider Beth a threat.'

'I do consider that, I always have. You, my dear, are blinded by love of your daughter and her resemblance to Margaret. I am not, I see what is there. Caroline is pretty, Beth is beautiful. Take it from me there will be no invitation going to Beth Brown and you can leave Caroline to me.'

# Chapter Twenty-Two

On a bitterly cold February day when the wind was at its strongest, Robert Munro, with a fellow traveller, stepped on to British soil and shivered. The two young men got on so well that they had decided to enjoy what London had to offer before going their separate ways. They booked in at a cheap boarding house which supplied a comfortable bed at night and a hearty breakfast in the morning. Robert was not short of funds and neither, as it turned out, was his companion but, being unaware of the other's circumstances, they settled for inexpensive accommodation.

Uncle and nephew had arranged to meet in the small private lounge reserved for residents of the Grand Hotel in Tottenham Court Road. Nigel had booked two nights for himself and one night for Robert.

Both were a little anxious, a little apprehensive. The exchange of letters was one thing, but meeting face to face was quite another. In the event it went off very well.

Nigel sat in a large, leather armchair, a drink to hand. Each time the door opened, though it was not yet the appointed time, he lowered his newspaper to see if the incomer was his nephew. Robert was punctual, however, and immediately he entered and looked about him, Nigel sprang to his feet, dropped the paper, and with a welcoming smile extended his hand.

'Robert, my boy, you have the look of James without

resembling him,' he said. 'Make of that what you will,' he said, laughing.

The handshake between uncle and nephew was firm and each was weighing up the other.

'Great to meet you, sir, and I do know what you mean,' he said and grinned. 'My Mother says much the same thing only she is a little more direct and says my dad was better looking.'

Nigel laughed. 'Now that I did not say. Come on, Robert, sit down, we'll talk better over a drink.' He pushed the bell on the wall and in a few moments it was answered.

'What will yours be, Robert?'

'A beer if that is all right,' he said in a voice that held only the faintest suggestion of a drawl.

Nigel glanced up at the waiter. 'A beer and bring me another whisky.'

'Very good, sir.'

'For an Australian born and bred you don't have a pronounced drawl.'

'Mine got ironed out. Dad loved his adopted country and its people but not the way they speak.' He paused. 'I miss him,' he said simply and for a moment his eyes were bleak.

'I'm sure you do,' Nigel said quietly, 'and we will be forever grateful to your mother for getting in touch. She wrote such a wonderful letter, Robert, and your grandmother has read it so often that she has it off by heart.'

'It wasn't for want of trying. Mum tried hard to get dad to write and maybe if he had been spared longer she might have succeeded.' He shrugged. 'Who knows?'

The drinks arrived. Robert's luggage had been taken to his bedroom and his short leather coat was over a nearby chair.

'Judging by the photos sent out to us, you have a very pretty daughter.'

'Yes, Caroline is a pretty girl,' his uncle said proudly. 'As a young child she was very delicate but her health has improved though she can't do anything strenuous.' He paused to drink the remainder of his first drink and move the glass aside. 'I have to confess that, being an only child and motherless, Caroline has had a lot of her own way.'

'Like my sister, she gets away with murder.'

'Girls do. I gather you and your brother were made to toe the line.'

'You could say that but, if dad was firm with us, he was always fair.'

They talked for an hour and then decided to go for a walk to stretch their legs.

Nigel was all but a head taller than his nephew. He wore a dark, double-breasted suit and over it a Crombie coat. The military style looked well on him. Robert, at his mother's insistence, had packed a dark suit and this he wore with a blue shirt and a rather gaudy tie in blues and reds. Over the suit and to keep out the cold, he had on a leather coat with a fleecy-lined collar. As they left the hotel, older women turned to look at the colonel but Robert got barely a glance from their daughters. For all that he was a pleasant looking young man of average height with thick light brown hair, a tanned skin, grey eyes and an open, friendly face.

Tommy was at the station to meet the train which was ten minutes late. Nigel would have hailed a porter to deal with the luggage until Tommy took charge of it but Robert waved away assistance and carried his own baggage to the car, leaving Tommy to pack it all into the very large boot. The London streets had been wet with slushy snow swept to the side. Here the countryside was blanketed in white. 'Take a good look, Robert,' said the colonel. 'You are seeing snow at its best before it turns into filthy slush. Add to that severe overnight frost and driving becomes a nightmare. Black ice can take one unawares and spin the car out of control.'

'How do you manage?' Robert brought Tommy into the conversation, much to his uncle's annoyance.

'By keeping down my speed and putting up a prayer,' Tommy answered. Nice bloke this Australian, no side with him, must tell Beth, he promised himself.

It was late afternoon by the time they reached Inverbrae House and already darkness was falling. The gloaming they called it. The lamps to either side of the house were lit and as the car travelled up the long drive, Robert got his first look at the house which had been home to his father. What he had expected he couldn't rightly have said but the photographs hadn't prepared him for this magnificence. Perhaps it was due to the semi-darkness and the flood of lights coming from the house that gave it a fairyland appearance.

'Here we are,' Nigel got out to go ahead and Robert followed him up the stone steps that had been swept clean of snow earlier on but already had a fresh covering. The heavy door opened and the wind sent a shower of dry snow inside and on to the floor of the hall. Then they were inside and the door hastily shut against a further onslaught.

Here I am in Inverbrae House, Robert thought. He had the strangest feeling that he had come home.

Mrs Murdoch was waiting with a maid beside her to take their coats. Then Caroline came in, her face pink with excitement. She had taken care over her appearance and wore a warm dress in a shade of burnt orange. The colour suited her and the style emphasised her tiny waist. On her feet she wore black patent shoes with straps and a medium heel. High heels would have been her choice but she lacked the confidence to wear them. Not to worry, her aunt said, that would come.

'Caroline, dear,' her father said kissing her brow and giving her a hug, 'this is your cousin, Robert.'

They smiled to each other. Caroline wondered if he would kiss her cheek or just shake hands. Robert wondered that too. Back home it was all so easy and natural, and his mother's parting advice hadn't been especially helpful.

'Be yourself,' she had said.

Caroline put out a small, slim hand and he took it in his. Solemnly they shook hands until his cousin, with a hint of mischief in her eyes, said mockingly, 'Being a relative you are permitted to kiss me on the cheek. Or don't they do that in Australia?'

'Stop teasing, Caroline.'

Robert was about to kiss his cousin when a noise made them all turn. Mrs Parker-Munro stood at the open door, leaning on her stick.

'You were taking your time and I couldn't wait a moment longer to meet my grandson.'

Robert went forward with a big smile on his face. 'Hello, grandma.'

She winced at being addressed as grandma and this would be conveyed to him at a later time but nothing must be allowed to spoil this moment. Putting her stick against the door post she held out both hands.

'Robert,' she said and her eyes were moist.

Her grandson took her hands in his and kissed her on both cheeks. He was used to old people and good with them. Her appearance had surprised him, knowing as he did that she was just in her mid seventies. She looked so old and wrinkled but haughty too and very much the lady of the manor. This was only to be expected, he supposed, since she was mistress of Inverbrae House. Could be her health wasn't too good. His great-grandad never gave in to age, indeed he said the minute you did you were finished. His recipe for a long life was to look after the body, take an interest in life, be concerned with what was going on in the world and keep the brain active. And, at the end of the day, never to forget to count your blessings.

She was subjecting him to a long, steady look from those faded blue eyes.

'A little of James there but you must take after the other side of the family.'

'They don't see it, but I must take after someone,' he grinned.

'You are a Parker-Munro, no doubt about that.'

'Begging your pardon, grandma, but I'm Robert Munro or Bob Munro to my friends.'

'Whatever you call yourself, young man, you are a Parker-Munro,' she said firmly, 'and very, very welcome in Inverbrae House.'

Nigel moved forward. 'Mother, you are standing too long, we should go along to the drawing-room and you had better take my arm.'

'No, Nigel, my grandson will help me.'

'Delighted to,' Robert said quickly and with a gentleness that surprised them, he took his grandmother's arm and together they went through the spacious hall and along to the drawing-room.

'Thank you, my dear, I shall manage now,' Mrs Parker-Munro said as she crossed to her usual chair. Robert stood in the centre of the room and looked up at the high frescoed ceiling and then to the solid, old-fashioned furniture and the cabinets that held priceless ornaments.

'This is going to take some describing when I write home. Our house is considered pretty good and it is but nothing remotely like this.'

His grandmother nodded. Caroline said, 'Have you seen a fire before or is it always too hot to need one?'

'We have coolish nights when we do light a fire but, far from dominating the room, it is tucked away in a corner and not much noticed.'

'Are you going to like Scotland?'

'Caroline, give your cousin a chance,' her father laughed, 'Robert has only just got here.'

'Sure to and you'll have to forgive me if I ask a lot of questions.'

'Ask as many as you like.'

'Thanks. I've had strict instructions to write home at least twice a month and tell them about you all and this house. A tall order, how can I do justice to it? To me it is magnificent and I wonder how dad could have turned his back on it.' He stopped, 'Or is that something that isn't spoken about?'

'Not at all, Robert, but this isn't quite the time,' his grandmother said. 'Once you have settled we'll have a talk, you and I, and I'll tell you about your father. He was a rascal, James was, a lovable rascal who couldn't keep out of mischief. But that is all I am going to say just now.' She paused, took a breath and smiled to him. 'What I will say, however, is that we are all just so happy that you are to be with us for Caroline's eighteenth birthday.'

'Having a big splash?' he asked, turning to Caroline and thinking that she really was a very pretty girl but too delicate for his liking. Not like Gemma back home. That had been the worst part about leaving Australia, having to leave Gemma behind. Since small children they had played together, quarrelled and made it up. Pals they were until the night before he had to set sail and neither of them knew how it had happened. Just that they were in one another's arms, clinging to each other. He had tasted the salt of her tears when their lips met in a long kiss that left them both shaken.

Would she wait for him? Nothing had been said, no promises made. Gemma was a fun-loving, attractive girl with no shortage of admirers. He would write but would she reply? He thought not. He couldn't imagine her sitting down to write a letter. Riding, swimming, any outdoor activity and dark-haired Gemma would be taking part.

They were talking to him and his mind had wandered. 'Robert?'

'Sorry,' he apologised, 'what were you saying, Caroline?'

'Only that my birthday is being celebrated here and for the first time in years the ballroom is to be opened up—'

'A ballroom!' He stretched his eyes.

'It isn't huge, just big enough for family and friends,' she said primly.

'Sounds to me like a dress affair and I had better warn you what I stand in is the only formal suit I possess.'

'Of course it is a dress affair,' Caroline said, outraged. She was becoming just the teeniest bit annoyed with this Australian cousin. For heaven's sake, they were wealthy and must surely attend some functions that demanded the correct clothes.

'Robert, we didn't expect you to bring your entire wardrobe,' Nigel said laughing. 'It will be my pleasure to take you along to my tailor to have you measured for a dress suit and anything else you require.'

'Good of you, Uncle Nigel, but I couldn't possibly accept, I mean I can—' he floundered to a stop. He was about to say that he had money and more would follow when it was needed.

'That could be James talking,' the old lady came in swiftly to avoid any awkwardness. 'He had absolutely no interest in clothes and your Uncle Nigel wasn't all that keen either. Often my son wears clothes that are shabbier than the ones his workers wear.'

'Not the cut though, Mother, and that is what counts.'

'I wouldn't deny that.' She frowned. 'When is that wretched maid coming with the tea? Caroline, give that bell a pull and see what is going on. Where was I? Oh, clothes, I remember now. Robert, my dear, do accept your Uncle Nigel's offer and get what is required. I imagine that you have lightweight suits that are totally unsuited to this climate of ours.'

There was a tap at the door then a maid, looking flustered, came in with a tray and went over to put it on a table. Another maid followed with plates of daintily cut sandwiches.

The mistress examined the food and nodded. It would do until the evening meal.

'The weather is colder than I expected. Thanks, Uncle Nigel, your offer is accepted and I'll accompany you to your tailor's and not disgrace the family,' he grinned.

'Good! Good!' Nigel nodded his head a few times. 'Seeing round the estate will be of more interest I imagine?'

'Much more.'

'Weather permitting, I'll show you around tomorrow.'

The maids poured the tea and handed round the cups and, at a nod from the mistress, departed. Caroline got up to hand round the plate of sandwiches.

'Robert, I simply must hear about Queensland,' she said as he took a sandwich.

'Great country but why don't you come back with me and see it for yourself?'

His grandmother and her son exchanged looks. 'Caroline couldn't stand the heat, I'm afraid. Extremes of temperature are bad for her and she is better to remain indoors in the coldest weather.'

'I understand.' He looked sympathetically at his cousin who was pulling a face.

'Have another sandwich, Robert,' Nigel said taking the plate from Caroline.

'Thanks.'

'Take two, hardly a bite in them.'

Robert agreed and reached for another. The kitchen at home never produced anything this small.

'Did your family make their money out of sheep?'

'Caroline, that was rude,' her grandmother said sharply.

'I don't mind answering that, grandma. Yes, the money comes from sheep, Caroline – don't you ever get called Carrie?'

'Never.'

'The real hard work was done by my great-great-grandfather. He sweated it out and against all the odds it began to show a profit. The sons followed him, did their bit, and now,' he said proudly, 'ours is the biggest and best sheep farm in the whole of Queensland.'

'A family concern?' Nigel asked.

'Very much so and not just close family either, there is enough work for everybody.'

Next morning the weather was bright and cold. The overnight frost had not been as severe as expected and, in heavy footwear, Nigel and Robert set out. They would go on foot, the colonel said, and take it in easy stages. The farm cottages interested Robert, and he was amazed at the smallness of them. How, he wondered, did they manage to bring up a family in such cramped conditions? He asked the question of the colonel.

'They manage because it is what they are used to. Like everything else, Robert, one accepts what one has and makes the best of it.'

'How about ambition?'

'That doesn't enter into their lives.'

'Surely they would want to better themselves for the sake of their children?'

'They have a roof over their head, food for their stomach and enough sense to know when they are well off,' Nigel said shortly.

Robert said no more. This, then, was the class system of which his father had spoken on those rare occasions when he had mentioned his homeland. Had that been the reason for his turning his back on his own country? Remembering the man his father had been, the way he judged people for themselves and not their possessions, he rather thought it possible. Being the younger brother, the ties would be less since Inverbrae House and all it stood for would never be his.

They left the row of cottages and came to one well apart from the others. Smoke was coming out of the chimney and a girl was sitting at what could be a table or a desk. His uncle surprised him by saying, 'This is the manager's office, but I have a girl in doing the paperwork. She may have letters for me to sign so we'll pop in for a minute or two.'

With a turn of the knob the door opened into a small passageway that took them to where the girl was working. Robert saw a good-sized room fitted out as an office, with everything neat and tidy. A fire burned in the grate and there was the crackle of logs. The girl had stopped typing when her visitors entered.

'Anything for me to sign, Beth?'

'Two, Colonel Parker-Munro. You can have this other if you wait a few minutes.'

'No, these two will do, I'll sign them.' He took out his fountain pen, uncapped it and after reading them, signed his name. Then he smiled. 'Come along, Robert, there is much to see.'

Robert was appalled and embarrassed at what he took to be a display of bad manners. There had been no attempt made to introduce them. Was this the way they behaved to all employees? If it was, give him Australia any day. They had their snobs but very few. Before following his uncle, Robert smiled and she did too and he rather thought the eyes held amusement.

She was a looker, as they would say back home, and there was a quiet dignity about the girl that made him wonder why she worked in such a lowly position. He would have expected someone like her to be in a streamlined office, as secretary to some prominent businessman. On the other hand, maybe that didn't appeal to her and this was just to fill in time until she got married. He laughed at himself for taking so much interest in the girl but even so he was already promising himself that one day, on his own, he would come this way again.

'Carrie?'

'I do not answer to that, Robert.'

'Carrie is nice and you can call me Bob.'

'No, thank you, we'll keep to our proper names if you don't mind.' She pursed her lips. 'Bad enough that you call yourself Munro when your surname is Parker-Munro.

Grandmama is going to keep on at you until you agree to use your full name.'

'Not a chance.' He saw her give a small shiver. 'You're cold, do you want that fire attended to?'

'I was about to ring for the maid.'

'No need, I'll see to it.' He lifted the shovel, put on coal and added a log. 'That please your ladyship?'

'No, it does not. Our maids are employed to do that and you are a guest as well as being family.'

'Know something?' he said as he sprawled in the easy chair.

'Quite a lot, I should hope.'

'Smart girl! Touch of Gemma there.'

'Who is Gemma?'

'A girl back home.'

'Your sweetheart?'

'Hope so.'

'Don't you know?'

'No, it just hit us when I was leaving.'

'Robert, can't you be serious for a minute?'

'I am serious, Caroline, and it is just as I said.'

'Then for goodness sake write and tell the poor girl how you feel.'

'That would sound better coming from your grandma.'

'What do you mean by that?' she said indignantly.

'Just that you are a sweet, little, old-fashioned girl,' he teased.

'I am not old-fashioned.'

'It was intended as a compliment.'

'Telling a young lady that she is old-fashioned is anything but. It seems to me, Robert Parker-Munro, you have a great deal to learn.'

'Meaning I lack polish?'

'Would you be very angry if I said yes?'

'No, since you mean it.'

She laughed. 'Robert, I do like having you here. It is almost like having a brother and being able to insult each other without either of us taking offence. Let's get back to Gemma. Are you really serious about her?'

'I am dead serious, but I am not at all sure that Gemma is. Until our final goodbye, we were just good pals.'

'Poor you. You're afraid to tell her in case you embarrass the girl and you lose the easy friendship you had.'

'Quite a bit of sense in that little head of yours and yes, you've just about got it right.'

'Want my advice?'

'Yes, but no guarantee I'll take it.'

'Write and tell her all you are doing and say how much you are missing her. Then add, as a sort of afterthought, that you are going to my ball, tell her it is my eighteenth and it is to be a very grand occasion.'

'So?'

'So, silly boy, she'll know that there are bound to be a lot of young ladies invited and that you might fall for one. It could make her jealous.'

'Some hope.'

'Nonsense,' Caroline said sharply. 'You want to know where you stand, don't you?'

'I suppose so and, speaking of young ladies, I met one in your manager's office.'

'Oh!'

'Uncle Nigel went in to sign letters.'

'Does she interest you?'

'Not in the way that look suggests.' He smiled. 'I steer clear of tall girls but she certainly is easy on the eyes and wasted, I thought, in a small office like that.'

'Obviously she doesn't think so.'

'Do you know Beth?'

'You were introduced?'

'No, her name came up that's all. Does she live around here?'

'Yes.'

'In one of the cottages?'

'No.'

'Not very forthcoming, are you?'

'What is your interest in Beth or is it curiosity?'

'Bit of both. Where does she live?'

'At present she is living here in Inverbrae House but you are unlikely to see her.'

'Don't tell me servants' quarters!'

'Of course not. Beth is not a servant, she is in charge of the clerical duties for the estate or something like that,' she said vaguely. 'It was grandmama's suggestion that she ate her meals with Mrs Murdoch and she has a pleasant bedroom which, Robert, isn't bad and much better than she would get elsewhere.'

'Board and lodgings thrown in?' he said sarcastically and wondered why he felt so annoyed.

'Exactly.' Caroline felt a twinge of conscience. It would have been far better for all concerned if Beth had taken employment in the town and made a complete break instead of this unsatisfactory state of affairs. It was her father's fault, she knew that, she was useful to him and he was holding on to her. She wondered what Beth thought and how she had taken to being told she could no longer have her meals in the breakfast room.

Beth was not too concerned. In fact, it suited her quite well. She had no desire to meet any of them, not even Caroline, and had taken to using, not the servants' entrance, but the little-used side door. She would put up with anything until she could afford to walk out.

The vacancies columns had yielded nothing suitable and she wondered if Jenny would be able to help. There was an open invitation to Greystanes but, even so, she had to check that it was convenient before taking the bus over.

Jenny was her usual charming self and embraced Beth warmly.

'Miss Harris and I were just talking about you the other day and hoping you would put in an appearance and here you are. Take your coat off and we'll go through.' Miss Harris had heard the voices and came to take Beth's coat.

'Picture of health and bonnier every time I see her, don't you agree, Mrs Cuthbert?'

'I do indeed.'

Beth blushed.

On their way to the sitting-room Beth took a long look at her picture hanging on the wall.

'I'm going to miss that when it goes,' Jenny smiled.

'That won't be for a long time.'

'We'll exchange our news first then tea, does that suit you?'

'Yes, but I'm afraid I'm about to ask another favour.'

'Ask away and don't sound so apologetic.'

'You know I've been applying for jobs but I can't get one that pays enough to cover a rented room somewhere. That is the only reason I stay where I am.'

'Tell me about the position at Inverbrae House. Not too comfortable?'

'I don't see any of them except the colonel when he comes in to sign his letters or he wants me to do something.'

'Don't you see Caroline? You must, you sleep next door to each other.'

'Not now. I'm over at the other end of the house and I have my meals with Mrs Murdoch.' She saw Jenny's face and rushed in with, 'Honestly, Jenny, I don't mind, in fact I actually prefer it.'

'That may well be but I think it is dreadful. Sadly I can't help since Nigel and I decided to part as good friends.'

'Oh, I didn't know.'

'Far better since the poor dear was horribly embarrassed not to be able to invite me to his home. I made him angry by saying that he gave in to the old lady far too much.'

'You've done such a lot for me, Jenny, and I only discovered by chance that I owe my education at Rowanbank to you.'

'A mixed blessing, as it turned out.' She began to laugh.

'Don't I get to share the joke?'

'My dear Beth, you have become quite famous. That waspish Miss Critchley has few friends but what is said is usually behind her back. You, my brave girl, told her to her face just what you thought of her and I am so proud.' She took Beth's face in her hands and kissed her brow. 'Now tell me about this favour you want.'

'Do you know of anyone who needs secretarial help? Or if you hear of something, please let me know. I also need a room to rent.'

'My dear girl, you are welcome to stay here.'

'I know and I am grateful but I remember what you once told me.'

'What was that? I seem to have told you a lot of things.'

'That independence is something to be treasured. I want to make my own way, Jenny, but,' and here she smiled, 'I need a bit of help to get started.'

'Be sure I'll keep my ears open. As it happens, I do know of one vacancy but I hardly think it would appeal to you.'

'Try me. You never know.'

'Does the name Anna Martin ring a bell?'

Beth shook her head.

'Hardly thought it would. She is an elderly, rather eccentric woman who writes historical books. Her home is between here and Sandyneuk.'

'She wants someone to do her typing?'

'Yes, she wants her manuscripts typed and from what I gather they are none too easy to make out.'

'Very bad?'

'Apparently her writing is atrocious.'

'Could be a challenge, if nothing else.'

'The only plus as far as you are concerned is that accommodation goes with the job if wanted.'

'She wants someone to live in?'

'She would prefer it.'

'Like a companion?' Beth said dismissively.

'Far from it. Our Anna Martin keeps herself to herself but she likes the thought of someone else in the house.'

'She sounds a bit weird.'

'I like her, as it happens, but it is not what you are looking for. As I said, I'll keep my ears open—'

The tea arrived and the conversation was general until Miss Harris left.

'Tell me about the Parker-Munros. I confess to still being interested.'

'There is to be a ball for Caroline's eighteenth birthday, a very grand affair. Mrs Murdoch says the ballroom has been taken out of mothballs and freshened up for the occasion.'

'I see the fair hand of Mrs Esslemont in this!'

'She is seeing to all the arrangements and the nephew from Australia, Caroline's cousin, has arrived in time to attend.'

Jenny's eyes opened wide. 'This I want to hear. What is he like?'

'Very pleasant.'

'Your heart didn't miss a beat?'

'No, absolutely not.'

'How did you two come to meet?'

'The colonel was taking him over the estate and they dropped in.'

'To introduce you?'

'No, to sign letters.'

'And what did this Australian say?'

'Nothing. He smiled and I smiled and they departed.'

'From that I gather you were not introduced?'

'That's correct but it didn't upset me. After all I am just an employee. Robert seemed surprised, though.'

'Being an Australian, he would. They are a friendly bunch and don't stand on ceremony. I like them.' She paused. 'Cinderella isn't going to the ball?'

'Cinderella wasn't invited but even had I been I would have refused.'

'Why?'

'Because a gown for such an occasion would not only make a dip in my savings, it would clean me out.'

# Chapter Twenty-Three

Robert had not forgotten Beth but there were few occasions when he was left alone. Today, surprisingly, he was. Caroline was having the final fitting for the much spoken-of gown. Her excitement, with only eight days to go, was bordering on the feverish and Robert wished that they would stop going on and on about the forthcoming event. He was sick of hearing about it but had gone to be measured for an evening suit and a dinner jacket. Being honest with himself, he had been pleasantly surprised. The young man in the mirror looked passably handsome.

The suggestion had come from Mrs Parker-Munro that Robert should accompany his uncle to Edinburgh but he had managed to get out of that. It was a business meeting and Nigel freely admitted that there was no saying how long it would last. In truth, the colonel hadn't been too disappointed at Robert's reluctance to join him. He was rather looking forward to meeting his friends and, with Robert to be considered, he would have had to leave before the customary drinks in the private bar.

When Robert set out a pale wintry sun was bravely peeping out from between the clouds. In a short time he was knocking at the door of the office. Expecting it to be Tommy, Beth shouted, 'It's open,' and didn't immediately turn round but finished what she was doing. When she did turn she was flustered.

'I'm so very sorry,' she said, 'I thought it was someone else or I would have gone to the door.'

He smiled. 'No apology necessary. Is this an awkward time to barge in and are you very busy?'

'No to both questions. Is there something I can do for you?' she asked politely.

'For a start you could sit down, then I would be able to do likewise.'

Beth went over to sit behind the typewriter and Robert sat down in the nearest chair.

'We weren't introduced. I'm afraid it was an oversight on my uncle's part but let me put that right. I'm Robert Munro.'

She liked the sound of his voice and she liked this Robert Munro. Not Parker-Munro, she noted. The colonel not introducing them had been no oversight but it was nice of his nephew to suggest it had been.

'I'm Beth Brown,' she said.

'I know it is short notice but may I ask if you are doing anything special this evening?'

Beth was taken aback. 'Why?' she asked at last.

'If you aren't, I wondered if you would take pity on a lonely Australian and have dinner with me?'

'The bit about being lonely doesn't impress me in the least since I don't believe you.'

'Then would you believe it if I said I would like a change of company?'

Beth thought she could believe that. 'It's kind of you, but I won't accept, thank you all the same.'

His face fell and he looked genuinely disappointed. 'I do wish you would. Let me say that this is friendship pure and simple. I have a girl back home.'

She shook her head and he sighed.

'I suppose I should have known that a nice-looking girl

like you wouldn't be likely to have a free evening.'

Why shouldn't she accept? Beth thought. It would be very pleasant to have a night out and she appreciated his honesty. She would be honest too.

'I'm not doing anything this evening.'

'Then you'll change your mind?'

Beth laughed. 'I have changed it and I'll be happy to accept, thank you.'

'You choose where we should go and make it somewhere nice.'

'But not too far away,' she said thoughtfully.

'That doesn't matter I can borrow a car.'

'No,' she said firmly. She wouldn't feel comfortable in a vehicle belonging to the colonel.

'A taxi then?'

'What is wrong with the bus?'

'Nothing as far as I am concerned but, for the return journey, I must insist on a taxi.'

'May I ask why?'

'Hanging around in this freezing weather waiting for a bus would be a poor end to what I hope will be a very pleasant evening.'

Beth smiled and looked apologetic. 'I'm sorry. That was thoughtless of me. You must be taking bad with this cold.'

'Takes a bit of getting used to I have to admit.' Then he grinned. 'No problem seeing you home.'

'How do you know that?'

'Caroline told me.'

'Ah!' Beth wondered just how much Caroline had told her cousin, and was reasonably confident it had been very little.

'Have you made up your mind where we should go?'

'The choice is limited unless we go much further afield and I'd rather not.'

'As I said, you choose.'

'There is a rather old-fashioned hotel' – Jenny had called it quaint – 'just beyond Strathvale and I can recommend the food. It has another advantage, someone runs a taxi service close by.'

'Sounds perfect. Better book,' he pointed to the phone.

'I don't make use of it for private calls.'

'Then get the number for me and I'll make the booking.'

'Probably wouldn't be necessary.'

'Better to be sure.'

Beth found the number for him and Robert got up.

'A table for two for this evening, please,' he said into the phone. 'Time? Oh, about eightish.' He looked at Beth for confirmation and she nodded. 'The name is Robert Munro of Inverbrae House. You've got that? Thank you, goodbye.' He replaced the receiver. 'Charming lady, she said she would look forward to seeing us.'

Beth wound a sheet of paper into the typewriter and Robert, taking the hint, began to walk towards the door.

'When do we leave?'

'Seven-thirty should do.'

'And where do we meet?'

'At the side entrance,' Beth said firmly.

He seemed about to object. 'That's where I'll be,' she said.

'Your wish is my command.' He sketched a salute and went out closing the door quietly behind him.

After he had gone Beth sat thinking and made no attempt to type. Perhaps she had been wrong to accept but she was in a rebellious mood, born out of anger and frustration against the humiliating position in which she found herself. Why should she deny herself a social life? She wasn't answerable to anyone. Stupid though, when she considered it. Here she was just waiting her time to be free of the Parker-Munros and accepting an invitation from the Australian nephew. Would she never learn?

If they found out, the Parker-Munros would be none too pleased. They might even go as far as suggest to Robert that he had made an unfortunate choice. The Australian would have his answer to that, she felt sure, but it made her more anxious than ever to get away. And that brought her thoughts to the eccentric woman writer of whom Jenny had spoken. Maybe it was worth serious consideration and, if it came to anything, and the woman wanted her to start right away, then she would oblige. Since she was paid weekly, the legal entitlement was for one week's notice. If it upset the smooth running of the estate, which she uncharitably hoped it would, then so be it. She would feel no guilt.

As he walked away from the cottage, Robert whistled happily. Instead of the dull evening he had been contemplating, he was to be in the company of a very lovely young lady. Very soon now he would be packing his bags and setting out on his travels. Paris and Rome were a must and after that he would just go where the mood took him. The final week or two he would spend at Inverbrae House. He had an affection for his relatives but he wouldn't be heartbroken to leave them. Poor Caroline didn't have much of a life, he thought, and as far as he could see had absolutely no freedom. Everything was arranged and she just had to fall in with the plans made for her. Beth, now, where did she come in? There was a mystery here and perhaps tonight he would learn something.

His lounge suit had not been in need of sponging and

pressing but it had been taken away and duly brought
back ready for him to put on. Making work for themselves, that's all it was. Back home no one looked for
work – there was always plenty of it.

The bus rattled its way along the country roads and let
them off at the far end of Strathvale near to a garage that
advertised a taxi service. A short distance from that was
the Halfway Hotel. It was a lovely old building that had
started life as a coaching inn, and the atmosphere inside
was warm and inviting. The dining-room had an open fire
set into an alcove and it gave out a good heat. A lighted
candle in a holder was on each table. Two of the tables
were taken and at one there was an animated conversation
going on between two couples, punctuated by peals of
laughter.

The table Beth and Robert were shown to was some
distance away and, as if the other diners were suddenly
aware of them, the noise grew less and the laughter more
subdued. Beth wore a dress in duck-egg blue with a
matching embroidered bolero. Having stopped growing
when she was in her final year at school meant that she
still had a reasonable wardrobe of clothes. Those she
bought from now on would be from the inexpensive
stores.

'You suit that colour, in fact you look delightful,'
Robert said admiringly.

'And you look very nice too,' she laughed.

'I'm glad about that. Compliments on my appearance
don't come flying this way all that often.'

'Mostly casual wear back home, is it?'

'Don't forget the big hat,' he grinned.

'Tell me about Australia, Robert, I'm interested.'

'I wouldn't know where to begin and, presumably, you

320

would have got some of it from your geography lessons at school.'

'Not all that much, I think we were short-changed on Australia and New Zealand.'

'That was disgraceful.' They looked up and accepted menus but didn't immediately study them. Robert was leaning across the table. 'Did you know that Australia is the largest island in the world?'

'I'm not sure but if you are telling me then, of course, I believe you.'

He opened the menu. 'Better study this and get the order in.'

For her main course Beth decided on roast beef and Yorkshire pudding. Robert swithered between that and steak, eventually settling for the same as Beth. The waitress arrived in her stiffly starched apron and Robert gave the order.

'Where were we?'

'Improving my education.'

'Ah, yes, so we were. Australia, my dear girl, has everything. Wide open spaces, spectacular scenery, and miles and miles of soft white sands. And as to culture we are not starved of that either nor city life.'

'Sounds perfect,' Beth sighed.

'Although I say it myself it is pretty good.' He paused when the meal arrived and watched the wine bottle being opened then left on the table. 'For your information this is summer time back home and it will be very, very hot and my folk will be sweltering.' As they ate he spoke of his family with such warmth that he brought them alive for Beth.

'Does Scotland come up to your expectations?' she asked.

'It does. I love what I have seen of it. My dad didn't talk

a great deal about his homeland but when he did there was a lot of pride in his voice. Much as he loved Australia, Beth, he never thought of himself as an Australian.'

'You do?'

'Of course I do, that's where I was born and brought up and I'm proud to call myself an Australian.'

'Could you settle here or would you always be homesick for Queensland?' She took a sip of her wine while waiting for his reply.

'Difficult one that,' he said thoughtfully, 'because Inverbrae House pulls me in a way I find difficult to describe. When I arrived I had the strangest feeling that I had come home.'

'Inverbrae House is very beautiful,' she said softly. 'I have always thought so.'

He leaned back. 'That is my turn over and now I await the story of your life.'

'Not a great deal to tell.' And that was far from the truth, she thought.

'I rather think there is,' he said gently.

Just then the waitress came to collect the dessert plates.

'Would you like coffee served at the table or would you prefer a more comfortable seat at the fire?'

'That sounds like a good idea.'

Beth laughed. 'He means he would like a comfortable seat at the fire.'

They moved to sit in the chintz-covered armchairs and partly facing each other. A small table was pulled over. The coffee arrived together with a plate of tiny triangles of shortbread.

Beth drank some coffee and hoped Robert had forgotten and they would talk of something else but no such luck, she thought. He was looking at her with his eyebrows raised.

'I'm waiting, Beth.'

'That was a lovely meal, Robert,' she said playing for time. 'I think the wine has gone to my head. I feel deliciously drowsy.'

'Don't fall asleep on me and if that is an excuse—'

'No, it isn't but, before I begin, I need your promise that you won't repeat any of what I tell you.'

'You have my promise,' he said solemnly, 'that not a word of it will be repeated.'

She gave a deep sigh. 'It all began when I was six years of age—'

Beth had not intended to tell Robert very much but it was as though she couldn't stop herself. To this man, the nephew of the colonel, she poured out her miseries, especially those after the tragic death of her parents. The lighter moments came when she told of her speech on the final day of school.

'Good for you,' he said admiringly, 'and the girls rushing over to the car to congratulate you must have made you proud?'

'I didn't feel proud, Robert, and Caroline was very shocked.'

'What about uncle?'

'He was disgusted with me and with good cause, since he had paid my fees.'

'Not willingly, I gather, but I'm glad this Jenny has your interests at heart. You need someone to look after you.'

She frowned. 'I don't, Robert. I can look after myself.'

'You won't need to. Someone else will want to do that. A lovely girl like you should have plenty of admirers and you would if you didn't keep yourself hidden away.'

'I'm doing something about another job.'

'That's the spirit. Beth,' he took her hand. 'I wish you all the luck in the world, you deserve it.'

'You do believe what I've told you?'

'Every word. As you know, Beth, my father walked out on this family and according to my grandma he was a bit of a handful, a difficult boy to control and a worry to everybody. Probably all true, dad never gave his reasons for running away to pastures new.'

Beth was showing distress. 'Robert, don't think badly of your uncle and grandmother on my account. They truly believed they had done their duty by me and many would agree they had.'

'I'm not one of them.'

'I'm not family so it was understandable.'

'Back home you would have been one of the family from day one.'

'To begin with they were very kind—'

'Exactly,' Robert said grimly. 'They used you and when you ceased to be necessary to them they wanted rid of you. That in my book is despicable.'

'We'll stop there. That is quite enough about my problems. I don't usually talk this freely and I blame the wine.'

'What you told me was in confidence but I'm glad you did.'

To get off the subject, she said, 'Tell me about the preparations for Caroline's big day.'

He groaned. 'Absolutely not, that's all they ever talk about.'

'Mrs Parker-Munro will be so delighted to have you here for Caroline's ball. You'll be expected to partner her.'

'So I gather but I make myself scarce when someone more interesting comes along. This elaborate do is just an exercise to find a suitable husband for Caroline.'

'You think so?'

'I know so. Wealth isn't all that important, family is and a younger son would be more acceptable.'

Beth looked puzzled.

'Should have worked that one out, Beth. Caroline's husband-to-be must be willing to live at Inverbrae House and assist in the running of the estate.'

'You could be right.'

'My little cousin is a spoilt brat but I like her and I just hope she has some say in whom she is to marry.'

'Don't worry, Caroline always gets her own way.'

'In things that don't matter all that much, yes she does. But this concerns the future of Inverbrae House. I just hope that the chosen one will bring Caroline happiness.'

'I hope so too.' Beth gave a start when she saw how late it was. 'Robert, look at the time, I had no idea!'

'Neither had I, but there is no danger of us being locked out.' He smiled as Beth reached for her coat and he helped her into it. 'Don't panic, I'll get the bill and the taxi is taken care of, I thought to mention it when we arrived.'

The waitress brought the bill. 'Did you enjoy the meal?' she asked with a tired smile.

'Very much and apologies for the lateness of the hour.' He settled the bill and added a tip that had her protesting.

'You've more than earned it.'

'Thank you very much, sir and I took the liberty of calling your taxi. It should be here by now but I'll check.' She came back. 'Yes, it is.'

They left the warmth and got into the taxi. The engine was running and there was a little heat in the car.

'Are you and Caroline the same age?'

'I'm a little younger, my birthday, my eighteenth isn't until the fifteenth of next month.'

'Too bad I'll be on my travels by then or we could have celebrated it.'

The taxi drew up and when it had gone Robert opened the side door to Inverbrae House. 'Thank you, Beth, for an evening I shall long remember.'

'And thank you for an unforgettable evening.'

Robert kissed her lightly on the cheek as he turned the key in the lock. Together they walked quietly along the passageway. At the end they separated, one going to the right, the other to the left. There was no sound, nobody was astir.

Beth took the bus into Perth. There was no invitation for her to the birthday ball but even so she couldn't let the day pass without a small gift. Going from shop to shop she despaired of finding something that would appeal to Caroline. What did one give a girl who had everything? In the end she bought a glass ornament similar to the one she had given Jenny. Caroline could put it on her dressing-table and when the light touched it the glass would sparkle. She found a suitable card and returned satisfied. She would wrap up the gift and give it to one of the maids to put on the hall table. There were moments when Beth was wistful, imagining the glitter of the occasion and thinking how wonderful it would be. Perhaps the music would reach her bedroom and with an imaginary partner she would dance round the room. Dreams! Dreams! But what would life be without them?

Replenishing the postage stamps was Beth's responsibility and she chose a time when her work was well advanced. She had letters to post and set off for the village. The weather was cold and frosty but she was warmly clad. After popping the letters in the pillarbox she went inside the post office for stamps. Daydreaming was still a failing of Beth's and, coming out of the door, it was entirely her fault that she collided with someone.

'Sorry! Sorry! Sorry!' said a male voice as he steadied her.

'My fault – I wasn't watching where I was going.'

Laughing blue eyes were looking into hers and Beth felt the colour rush to her face. He was the most handsome man she had ever met and her heart was doing a somersault. Becoming aware that she was still in the stranger's arms and feeling desperately embarrassed, Beth broke away and as she did a sheet of stamps fluttered from her hand and on to the pavement. He was there before her to pick it up.

'Someone is going to be very busy,' he smiled as he handed the stamps over.

She smiled back. 'Thank you.'

'Which way are you going?'

She pointed.

'May I walk with you?'

'Yes, if you wish.' Beth felt breathless as though she had been running. The young man, whom she took to be about twenty-five, was having a most disturbing effect on her. Could it – was it possible that what she was experiencing was love at first sight? Not so long ago she had ridiculed the idea but now she wasn't so sure. Then she tried to talk sense to herself. He was an exceptionally handsome young man and there weren't too many of those around Sandyneuk. Tall and well built with thick, dark brown hair, blue eyes and a face that, were he a film star, would have women swooning. Was it possible for a man to be too handsome? When she was unobserved, she searched his face for some fault and found one. The chin could have been firmer.

As they walked they spoke mainly of the invigorating

weather and other generalities until they reached the gates to Inverbrae House.

'This is where I leave you.' She saw his start of surprise.

'You live here?'

'Yes.'

'Don't go, please, not just yet.' He held out his hand. 'I'm Adrian Scott-Hamilton.'

'Beth Brown,' she said. It was time to move away but she couldn't bring herself to and he was in no hurry either.

'Would it be possible for us to meet? I'm staying at Rockville Manor.' His hand went vaguely in its direction. 'Leonard Watson and I were at school together.'

She nodded then shook her head. 'I don't know—' she began hesitantly.

'Tomorrow evening? Could you manage that?'

Very easily, she thought but would it be wise to accept? The Watsons were close friends of the Parker-Munros—

'Well—?'

'Perhaps for a short time,' she said weakening.

'Tell you what, I'll slip away after dinner and meet you here at eight-thirty. You'll find me parked round the corner. A drink somewhere, a place where we can talk.'

He was so sure of himself, so sophisticated but she wasn't certain what going out for a drink meant.

'I don't drink.'

She saw the amusement in his eyes, they were dancing with merriment, and she felt foolish but she would stick to her guns.

'You don't have to drink. There is a charming little inn that Leonard introduced me to and if you would prefer a soft drink or a coffee for that matter—'

'Yes, all right, thank you.'

'Had this been the summer we could have walked and talked but in this weather we could either sit and shiver in the car and talk, or be comfortable beside a fire.'

Her face felt hot and she wanted away to hide her confusion. There had been none of this when she had accepted an invitation from Robert Munro. The difference was that she saw Robert as a friend and no more, whereas she didn't know what to think about Adrian Scott-Hamilton.

He saw her confusion and had a quiet smile to himself. His charm never failed.

'Until this evening,' he said softly.

'Yes,' she smiled and, in a daze, walked up the drive to Inverbrae House.

'Leonard?'

'What?' The Watsons kept open house and the boys had been encouraged to invite their friends for the school holidays. Adrian Scott-Hamilton had taken full advantage and was a frequent visitor to Rockville Manor.

'I met a smashing-looking girl in the village.'

'Did you now?' Leonard didn't take his eyes from his paper.

'The name Beth Brown mean anything to you?'

The paper was dropped and there was a look of surprise on his friend's face. 'Where did you see Beth?'

'Coming out of the post office,' he laughed. 'We bumped into each other. It was her fault, I hasten to add, but being the gentleman I am, I took the blame.'

'Made a date?'

'This evening.'

Once Leonard had thought Adrian could do no wrong but now he was actually beginning to dislike him.

'We parted company at the gate to Inverbrae House. Is she a relative of the Parker-Munros?'

'No.' He showed his annoyance as Adrian got up to

help himself to a drink. 'Better go easy on that stuff. The old man is beginning to notice. He complained the other day that he had never known whisky to evaporate before.'

'You wouldn't deny me a small one, would you?'

'It's going out of sight and that is hardly a small one.'

'What's got into you?'

'Nothing.'

'No love life, that is your problem.'

'Shut up, Adrian.'

Leonard Watson was of medium height and plump. He was a good-natured, shy young man who longed to have a steady girl friend but few spared him more than a glance when Adrian was around. Of late he was wishing that Adrian wouldn't visit so often but his mother, who thought him charming, told him to come when he wished. There was always a welcome for him.

There was never an invitation to Adrian's home in Stirling and the reason given was that his mother did not enjoy good health and was troubled with her nerves.

'Tell me about Beth.' Adrian eyed the amber liquid and drank it down.

'Wasting your time there. Beth is as poor as the proverbial church mouse.'

'With her speech and manner I would say—'

'Beth's parents moved to India and, as Beth and Caroline got on so well, Beth was invited to live in Inverbrae House until the parents returned.'

'Only they didn't.'

'Exactly. Since they could hardly throw the child out she continued to live at Inverbrae House.'

'One of the family?'

'No, never like that. She works in the colonel's office and I believe she has her meals with the housekeeper. So you see, she is not for you, old boy.'

'Pity she wasn't the daughter of the house. I fancy her, I fancy her like mad.'

'Don't play around with Beth,' Leonard said sharply.

'Any chance of her being at this birthday "do"?'

'I think it unlikely.'


Beth left the office punctually and had her meal alone. This was Mrs Murdoch's day off and she always spent it with her sister and her family.

A bath, a long, leisurely bath, then she would take her time over dressing. She wanted to look her best but not in something too dressy. Her hair, never a problem, was cut short and needed only a brush to shape it the way she wanted. A pleated skirt in a soft shade of green was her eventual choice. It was mid-calf length and the fine woollen jumper in the same colour made it look like one garment. She swithered about shoes, her newest ones were quite high but she didn't want them ruined and there might be a bit to walk from the car to the inn. Better to be safe than sorry and wear her medium heels.

A dab of perfume behind her ears and on her wrists and she was ready.

Beth smiled at her reflection in the mirror and felt a surge of pure excitement at what lay ahead. She took a deep breath, knowing that she must keep calm. Someone like Adrian Scott-Hamilton would expect a small show of sophistication and she didn't want to let herself down. Happily, her appearance pleased her. Her long black coat with its astrakhan collar suited her figure and had been the last garment to be charged to the colonel's account. There had been mild opposition from Caroline's Aunt Gwen who thought it much too old for her but she hadn't been all that interested and the coat became Beth's.

In the semi-darkness the car was not easy to see and

Beth approached carefully. She started slightly when the door opened.

'Beth?'

'Yes,' she whispered and heard the laughter in his voice.

'In you get.'

Beth went round and got herself in. She felt flustered and a little ridiculous. 'I couldn't be sure it was you.'

'I know and a girl can't be too careful. Think how awful it would have been to find yourself in someone else's car.'

'It doesn't bear thinking about,' she laughed.

'Comfortable?' he asked turning to her briefly before starting up the engine.

'Yes, thank you.'

Not until he had negotiated the double bend did he speak again. 'Dangerous bit of the road this, particularly at night and it doesn't do to take chances.' He smiled to himself as he said it. The only reason he was taking extra care was because his own car was off the road meantime and this was borrowed from the Watsons.

'I'm sure it doesn't.' She wished she could think of something to say instead of just answering but her brain seemed to have stopped working.

In a short time they turned into a narrow road full of pot-holes that had Beth hanging on to her seat.

'Sorry about that,' he apologised.

'Why doesn't someone fill them up?'

'You may well ask. One reason given me was that it acted as a warning and slowed down a getaway. The inn is very isolated, Beth.'

'Tell them of a car approaching and anyone up to no good would be hampered making their escape.' She paused to peer out of the window. 'Makes sense I suppose.'

'Yes, it does but it is damned hard on the car.'

Beth was out before Adrian got round and together they went up to the entrance. Lights shone from a few of the windows and a lamp was at each side of the door. It looked welcoming. Adrian's arm went round her shoulders and Beth felt the thrill of his nearness.

The door pinged when it was opened and a roar of men's laughter came from nearby. Adrian took hold of her arm.

'Don't be alarmed, that's coming from the bar. It'll be quiet where—' he broke off as a man in a white apron and carrying a tray stopped.

'It's all right, I know the way,' Adrian said pleasantly.

'You do? There's a good fire burning and I'll be coming for your order just as soon as I get rid of this.'

The room they found themselves in was warm and welcoming after the cold of outside. There were a number of small tables, one with empty glasses. Four people got on their feet and were preparing to go.

'The table beside the fire, Beth, or would it get uncomfortably hot?'

'It might.' The flames were leaping high and there was a pile of logs ready to go on when necessary.

'The corner one then.' He pulled out a chair for her and, after loosening her coat, she sat down. The man arrived to take their order.

Adrian looked enquiringly at Beth.

'A glass of orange, please.'

'Whisky and bring water.'

'Very good, sir.' He used a cloth to wipe the surface of the table and brought over a glass ashtray which he placed in the middle. Then, with a smile to Beth, he left.

The room fascinated Beth. It was so unusual and could have been a small library in a private house. From floor to ceiling books lined every wall. Most of them were huge volumes and very old. Some had broken spines, others had tattered covers and the lettering was faded and difficult to read. Only a very few looked in good condition.

'Pure show,' Adrian smiled.

'Nice, like being in a library.'

'A reference library. On one occasion Leonard and I had a good look round and we were of the opinion that the lot had been picked up very cheaply at an auction sale hoping it would bring a touch of class to the place.'

'Which it does and full marks to whoever it was.'

Their drinks arrived and the orange set before Beth.

'The young lady was admiring the books.' Adrian smiled lazily, moving his long legs to a more comfortable position.

The man put down the whisky. 'For myself I like a good thriller but there's no accounting for taste, is there? Still it's a talking point and if it keeps the customers happy, who is complaining? My old lady wouldn't give them house room, I can tell you.' He went away chuckling.

The small exchange had relaxed Beth and she drank some of her orange. The logs crackled and burned and she thought this was so much nicer than sitting in a hotel.

'Cosy, isn't it?' he said. 'And all to ourselves.'

'You chose well.'

'Oh, I have excellent taste and not only in this.'

She couldn't mistake his meaning. She blushed, and lowered her eyes to hide her confusion.

'Tell me about yourself, Beth,' he said softly.

'There isn't much to tell.' Not so long ago she had been asked the same question. For a moment she remembered Robert and how easy it had been to tell him about herself. That was different, though. Robert was a Parker-Munro, he had been sympathetic and understanding and the outpouring had done her a lot of good. Adrian was only being polite. He didn't want her life story just a little about herself.

'For a start, what is your connection with Inverbrae House?'

What a strange question she thought. She must have looked surprised.

'I have to confess I did ask Leonard Watson about you.'

'He hardly knows me.'

'Not the impression I got, most certainly it is not. Poor old Leonard doesn't have much success with girls and I suppose he admires you from afar.' He paused and lifted his glass. 'All he told me, Beth, was that you and the daughter—'

'Caroline.'

'Yes, Caroline, were childhood friends and that you now work for the colonel.'

'You know it all then.'

'Far be it for me to pry.' He was looking across and holding her gaze. 'Beth, you are very lovely but no doubt many have told you that.'

She shook her head. No one who mattered had told her that.

'Leonard called you a lovely girl but that isn't how I would describe you.'

'It isn't?'

'No.' His voice was like a caress. 'To me you are a beautiful young woman who has completely bewitched me. I hope I am not alone in thinking that this is the start of something very special.' Leaning forward he gently touched his lips to hers. 'Tell me it is the same for you, that is what I want to hear.'

Her heart sang. She wanted to shout it from the roof

tops. Yes, Yes, Yes, I feel it and it is wonderful, wonderful. She wanted to tell him that he was the handsomest, most exciting man she had ever met. One day she would but not yet.

'Your shining eyes are answer enough – or at least I am taking that as an encouraging sign.' He had been holding her hands but let them go. 'Drink up your orange and later you must let me introduce you to the delights of something a bit stronger – nothing to go to your head—'

'But more acceptable than orange?' Suddenly she didn't want to drink any more of it.

'Yes, my darling. You are no longer a schoolgirl and I have a great urge no, wrong word, a great wish to introduce you to a whole new world.'

Beth felt thrilled but disappointed too. 'Do I seem so very naïve?'

'A little but I find that utterly charming. My joy and pleasure will come as each day that passes makes you more beautiful and more desirable.'

Beth reached for her glass for another drink and shivered. It wasn't from the cold drink, the shiver had come from a strange new feeling that both alarmed and excited her.

'Your turn now, Adrian,' she said shakily. 'I know nothing about you.'

He shrugged. 'My second home is with the Watsons and I am grateful to them for making me so welcome. My home, or rather my parents' home, is in Stirling.'

'Do you have a large house in Stirling?' she found herself asking.

'Yes. Once it was a house to be proud of,' he began, but she heard the bitterness creep into his voice. 'Sadly it is now in poor condition but since the family fortunes have gone not a lot can be done about it.'

'Perhaps your fortunes will change,' she said gently.

'That is in our nightly prayers,' he said flippantly. 'So you see, my dear Beth, I am poor.'

Beth wondered about the degrees of poverty. She had seen real poverty in the poorer quarters of Dundee and Adrian saying he was poor was just laughable. He couldn't want for much when he drove a car, ordered drinks and spoke of taking her out to dinner.

'You must do something, have some kind of job?'

'If you could call it that,' he said looking at her with amusement. 'I have business interests which require my attention from time to time.'

'Yes, yes,' she nodded but she thought it could hardly be called hard work. Still, that was the way the upper classes lived. Come to think about it, the Watson boys didn't appear to do anything but then again they would be involved in the family business.

'I'm sorry I don't understand these things,' she murmured, anxious to get off the subject.

'Women, particularly beautiful young women, are not expected to. But back to you – tell me, what really is your position at Inverbrae House?'

'I told you. I do clerical work for the estate and meantime I have accommodation in the house.'

'Part of the family?' he asked though he already knew the answer.

'No, not family and not servant. Just something between.'

'Don't you have anyone of your own, Beth?'

'Not here but I do have relatives in Dundee and I visit them occasionally.'

'An independent young woman who can do much as she pleases. No checking up on when you get in at night.' Or even if you get in at all, he added to himself.

337

'No one checks on me, that is true, but there is no reason why they should. I keep respectable hours and that's the way it stays,' she said firmly.

'I should think so too, I am all for keeping respectable hours but it does mean that there is no need to panic if by chance you were delayed.'

'That's true.'

Adrian ordered another whisky but Beth wanted nothing more. He drank his quickly then glanced at his watch.

'Ah! Time we were getting on our way. I don't want to keep you late on this our first date.' He smiled as he said it then drained his glass.

Beth was relieved that she hadn't had to remind him of the time. He was a real gentleman and she could trust him absolutely.

When they reached the gates of Inverbrae House he switched off the engine and turned to face her.

'Beth, I come and go a lot, I have to.'

'Yes.'

'How do I get in touch with you? What are your hours in that office?'

'Usual office hours, though sometimes I work later.'

'Then I can pop in to see you! Honestly,' he said with his disarming smile, 'I wouldn't keep you off your work, it would just be to make arrangements to meet.'

'No problem, Adrian,' she said eagerly. 'I'm on my own for most of the time so you can come into the office.'

'Or tap at the window and have you come out?'

'If you prefer.'

'Whereabouts in the grounds is this office?'

She told him.

He leaned over and kissed her on the cheek and she thanked him for the evening.

'My pleasure and I hope the first of many.' This time he

gently turned her face towards him and pressed his lips against hers.

Beth felt herself slip into a world of warmth and excitement as he took her into his arms and, unable to stop herself, she put her arms round his neck and returned his kisses.

'I must let you go, my darling,' he said huskily.

She could only nod. Her voice seemed to have deserted her and her eyes were gazing at him adoringly. She got out, still in a daze, and watched him drive away.

Adrian Scott-Hamilton was well satisfied. Beth was very different from his usual women, which made her all the more desirable. He knew how to handle women and Beth was so young and trusting that she was going to be a walkover.

As for Beth, in those following days, she was experiencing first love with all its pain and wonder. And Adrian discovered to his relief that the estate office was well away from the workers' cottages and out of sight of the Big House. He took to calling on her and though she invited him in, he didn't do so, preferring that she came out. The back of the office had the benefit of trees and shrubs and no one was likely to see them.

# Chapter Twenty-Four

Smiling warmly, Jenny welcomed her guests and gave a special smile to the new faces. It was a warmish night and none of the men, who were in the majority, wore coats. They were ushered through the hall and into the drawing-room. Food and liquid refreshments, including some of the hard stuff as Jenny called it, were set out in the dining-room which was being used as a buffet. There was the low murmur of voices from those who had just arrived, and were at the polite, not-quite-at-ease stage with strangers. That would change before long as groups with similar interests gathered round to hear and discuss what was happening in their own small world.

A ring at the door and Jenny excused herself and went to answer it.

'David! Lovely to see you,' Jenny said as his lips brushed her cheek.

'Looking lovely as ever, my darling, and I know you won't mind that I have brought a friend with me.'

Jenny turned her attention from the heavily-built, middle-aged man to the younger one who was standing a little apart and clearly not happy at the situation in which he found himself.

'Jenny, this is Peter Nicholson and Peter, your hostess, Mrs Cuthbert.'

They shook hands. 'Peter is a talented artist and already

making a name for himself. Let me add that I almost had to drag him here.'

'Now why was that, Peter?' Jenny looked amused. 'Not many have to be forced to attend.'

'I'm sure they don't, Mrs Cuthbert, but I feel this is an imposition landing on you like this.'

'Nonsense, a new face is always welcome. Next time, I hope you will want to come and not have to be dragged!' She smiled into his face as she ushered them both indoors.

David closed the door behind him, beamed at them both then went ahead to where the laughter and talk was coming. Jenny looked at Peter and they both laughed. 'Like a homing pigeon,' she whispered.

Together they went along the well-lit hall until Peter stopped abruptly.

'How on earth do you come to have that? Where did you get it?'

Jenny was taken aback at the brusqueness of his manner but she saw that he was unaware of it, that genuine amazement had caused it. The look on his face was almost comical.

'If you are referring to the picture it does not belong to me. Why, may I ask, does it interest you so much?'

He went nearer. 'Not easy to make out the signature but I remember I was so shocked to get a sale that when it was pointed out to me that I hadn't signed it, I just scrawled my name.'

Jenny was all smiles. 'Now aren't you just glad you came?'

'Most certainly I am.'

'I've always thought it very good.'

'Thank you. It's not bad,' he said modestly, 'but hopefully I've improved since then.' He paused then turned away from the picture to face Jenny. 'If it isn't yours, would you mind telling me to whom it does belong?'

'A young friend of mine,' Jenny said carefully.

'Would your friend sell it back to me, do you think?'

'I doubt it. Are you very anxious to have it?'

'Only because selling it was the turning point in my life. I was very young and impatient, Mrs Cuthbert, and hope was dying. In fact I had reached the stage when I was agreeing with my parents that this should be kept as a hobby and that it was time I found myself a proper job.'

'Peter, I do understand your wish to have the painting but then again I can understand my friend's wish to keep it.' Her eyes went to the clock. 'Should be any time now if she is coming and if she does, I'll introduce you. Meantime do circulate Peter.'

He smiled and Jenny left him looking at the painting.

Beth had been in two minds as to whether it was worthwhile going to Greystanes since it was so late, but then she decided it was. She didn't want to miss it. She changed quickly into a long-waisted dress in a strawberry shade, pulled a comb through her hair, a touch of colour to her lips, and she was ready.

Miss Harris answered her ring.

'Just about giving you up, Beth,' she smiled as Beth walked in.

'Nearly didn't come, thought it was too late.'

'Just warming up by the sound of it. I'll take your coat and you go right through.'

The door was half open and groups of people, a glass in hand, were engaged in animated conversation. Beth saw Jenny trying to get her attention and went over.

'Hello, dear, and don't you look charming? In fact,' she said, 'I would go as far as saying you look blooming. Is there a special reason for the happiness shining out of your eyes?'

'Oh, Jenny, is it so obvious? I've met the most wonderful man—'

'Tall, dark and handsome, a perfect specimen of manhood and you've fallen very, very badly,' she said softly.

'Yes, I have,' she said just a little put out and Jenny saw it.

'I'm a tease but truly I'm happy for you. But I won't say more until I hear about him and that will have to wait until later. Meantime there is someone here who is very anxious to meet you. A young man, tall, fair and utterly charming.'

Beth looked mystified and Jenny took her by the hand and over to where a young man had moved away from a group to join them.

'Beth, dear, this is Peter – sorry, Peter, I've forgotten your other name.'

'Nicholson, Peter Nicholson.'

'Beth Brown, the young friend of whom I spoke.'

They shook hands.

'Now come along and see what this is all about.' She had them each by the hand like children and led them into the hall. Stopping beside the picture of the harbour at Sandyneuk she let go of them. 'I'm going to leave you, and Beth, when you get over the shock do see that Peter gets some food. I do love the lean, hungry look but it worries me too.'

Peter laughed and his eyes crinkled. 'It used to worry my mother as well but I do eat like a horse, Mrs Cuthbert.'

'Peter isn't going to tell you but I will. I have it from David that he is a very talented artist with a bright future.'

'Spare my blushes, please, and David exaggerates. I've

344

had a few lucky breaks that's all.'

'Which wouldn't have come your way unless you had that extra special something.' She pointed to the picture. 'Beth, meet the artist in the flesh.' She gave them a mischievous smile and walked away.

'You – you painted it?' Beth said incredulously.

'Guilty, and if you look very closely you will just about make out my signature.'

She nodded and he saw the hint of tears. 'I was with my father when he bought it for me.'

'I know. You were the little dark-eyed girl and long ago though it was, I remember you both very well.'

- 'He died,' she said quietly. 'Both of my parents are dead.'

'I'm sorry,' he said gently. 'Is this distressing for you?'

'No, it isn't, far from it. It's just that I can't get over it. Please tell me why, after all these years, you should remember us?'

'Because that sale shaped my life. Without it my life would have been very different.'

'In what way?'

'Because I had reached the end and was about to return to my parents' home to admit that they had been right and art should be kept as a hobby.'

'You were going to look for a job that brought in a regular wage?'

'Yes.'

'That would have been such a waste.'

'Thank you.' They smiled, both a little shy and Beth, remembering her instructions said, 'Peter, food, we'd better go and see what is left.'

Miss Harris piled sandwiches on a plate. 'That should start you off.'

'Lovely.' Beth said looking and finding a place apart

from the others. 'This do, Peter?'

'Perfect.' They used a corner of the table for their cups and ate the sandwiches in a companionable silence. Peter broke it. 'Would it upset you to talk about your parents?'

'No, it was a long time ago, I can talk about it now. They went out to India as missionaries and were killed – murdered by the very people they were trying to help. I didn't go with them, they left me behind.'

'And a good thing.'

'Yes.'

He looked shocked, stricken almost. 'That was dreadful, just awful.' He shook his head. 'I feel an almost personal loss. I can't explain it but because your father had a small but important part in my life it somehow makes it so much worse. Are you an only child?'

'Yes. I was looked after and in many ways I was fortunate. Jenny, Mrs Cuthbert, has been marvellous to me.'

'I've just met her but she strikes me as being a good friend to have.'

'She's kind, helpful and completely honest.' She looked up at him. 'Not too many people are, honest I mean, have you noticed that?'

'Well—'

'No, I'm explaining it badly. What I mean is that she would never lie, no matter what it cost her to tell the truth.'

'The truth, the whole truth and nothing but the truth.' He shook his head. 'Not in complete agreement with you there. A white lie can often save a great deal of distress and I'm sure Mrs Cuthbert has told one or two but who is to know?'

She laughed. 'I suppose you are right. Where do you live, Peter?'

'If you mean where do I belong it is in Edinburgh. My parents' home is there as I think I mentioned. I have a younger brother, Alex, and a married sister. Ruby and Norman have a two-year-old boy, a bundle of mischief. Foolishly I agreed to do a portrait of their offspring.' He clapped a hand to his brow. 'The wee monkey couldn't or wouldn't keep still for more than a minute but happily I caught enough of his expression to please his doting parents and grandparents.'

'Are you specialising?'

'Yes and no to that. Portraits are what I want to concentrate on and I've had a few good commissions. Even so, I like to keep my hand in with landscapes and coastal scenes, mostly from around here.'

'You must live nearby.'

'Number five Summer Street.'

'I know it.'

'This is an evening I am going to remember and to think I was reluctant to come.' She blushed under his scrutiny. 'Don't mind me, Beth, when I see a face that interests me, good manners fly out of the window.'

'Why does my face interest you?'

'The bone structure. I see a perfect oval with high cheekbones, delicate features and a warm mouth with its hint of a smile as though from some inner happiness.'

I'm in love, she wanted to tell him. Had he experienced love, did he know what it was like? She could tell him. She only had to think of Adrian and the sun shone on the darkest day.

'One day perhaps you will sit for me?'

'I would like that.'

'Don't be passing Summer Street without coming in to see me or I would feel very hurt.'

'Don't worry. I had no intention of passing. I wanted an

excuse to see you at work and now I don't need one. I'll accept your invitation.'

'Knock and come in, the door is always open.'

'Terribly sorry to break this up, you two. Hello, Beth,' David said as he put on his coat. 'Problem is it is always difficult to tear ourselves away from Greystanes – oh, dear me, have I spoilt something, Peter, were you going to see Beth home?'

'No, he wasn't, I'm staying overnight with Jenny. There is a lot of clearing up to do—'

'Which we shall leave until tomorrow,' Jenny said appearing at their side.

Goodnights were said and Peter's parting words were, 'Don't leave it too long before you come.'

'I won't.'

'What a very nice, charming young man, not all that young, he must be in his late twenties.'

'Yes, he must,' Beth said doing a quick calculation and ignoring Jenny's amused expression. 'He has invited me to see his studio.'

'I hope you accepted.'

'Of course I did, I've never seen an artist at work, not in a studio.'

'Don't you find him attractive? I know I do. Not disgustingly handsome, I do hate very handsome men, they are all so sure of themselves—' Then, seeing Beth's face, she began to apologise. 'Why don't I think before I speak? Of course, there are always exceptions to every rule and this young man of yours is one.'

'Yes, he is, Jenny, and he can't help being handsome.'

'Of course he can't. Come along into the kitchen. I've made a fresh pot of tea and we'll have it and a postmortem of the evening. Someone once said that and I thought it apt and amusing.'

Beth giggled and took the cup handed to her.

'Is this wonderful young man local?'

'No, his home is in Stirling but he spends a lot of time with friends who live nearby.'

'May I ask his name?'

'Adrian Scott-Hamilton.'

'A very impressive name and what does this Adrian do? Or is he one of the idle rich?'

'He isn't rich, far from it, and he doesn't actually work but he has business interests.' It sounded a bit lame but it was all she could say.

Jenny nodded her head but said nothing. Scott-Hamiltons of Stirling, it shouldn't be difficult to find out about them if she ever thought it necessary.

'I love him, Jenny.'

'And needless to say he loves you?'

'I hope he does. He says he does and he wouldn't say it if it wasn't true. What would be the point? Jenny, he could have any woman and yet he wants me,' she said shakily.

'This is serious then?'

'For me it is. I'll never love anyone the way I love Adrian but I worry sometimes—'

'What about? Do eat up. Have another sandwich and I'll have one as well since I didn't eat much earlier on.'

'I shouldn't, but to please you—' She took one and put it on her plate. 'Jenny, he's so marvellous and sophisticated, what can he see in me?'

'Someone very lovely and completely unaware of her own charms. That must make a change for this sophisticated young man.' She didn't know why, she hadn't met this Adrian but already she disliked him and that wasn't like her.

Beth didn't answer. She hardly heard.

'Darling, you'll be falling asleep in the chair. Off you go

to bed for what is left of the night.'

She got up and yawned. 'Goodnight, Jenny.'

Jenny sat nursing her cup for a while. This Adrian wasn't for Beth but there wasn't much she could do about it and of course she could be wrong and he could be a thoroughly nice young man. Peter, now, had it been Peter – she was very taken with the young artist and if she wasn't very much mistaken, Peter was attracted to Beth.

That first dinner she had with Adrian had been perfect, quite, quite delightful. How handsome he had looked in his dinner jacket and how proud she had been to be with him. Heads had turned to look at him but other heads had turned to look at the handsome young couple being shown to their table. Beth had worn a long black skirt with a lovely pale green chiffon blouse. Jenny had come to her rescue when she complained of having nothing suitable to wear and that she would have to go and buy herself a new gown.

'Nonsense, dear,' she had said. 'That would be an unnecessary extravagance and after two or three times you wouldn't be able to wear it again. Take my tip and buy yourself a couple of long skirts, one of them black. Teamed up with different blouses you will get away with it again and again. Have different necklines too so that you can dress it up with jewellery for a special occasion, and on another go for simplicity and wear no jewellery of any kind.'

It had been good advice and Beth was glad now that she had followed it.

'My darling, you do have very good dress sense,' Adrian remarked. He had said as much on more than one occasion and she had been so pleased.

True to his promise, he had introduced her to various

wines and other drinks, sherry among them. To please him she had tried to like them. Occasionally she failed and made a face and she had expected him to laugh but he hadn't and she had felt miserable. Much as she loved him, she didn't always understand him.

Another niggling worry was the amount Adrian drank. Admittedly it didn't seem to affect his driving but she was beginning to have to fight him off when he would pass beyond kissing and go too far for her liking. No, that wasn't true and that was the worry. Still Adrian always took no for an answer and was most apologetic afterwards.

'Sorry, my darling, but it gets harder and harder to resist you.'

'I'm sorry, Adrian, it's difficult for me too. I do love you but I would never give myself before marriage and deep down you wouldn't want me to.'

He had almost choked keeping in the laughter. Did the silly girl really think that marriage was on the cards? But she must. He would break down her resistance when the time was right. Strangely enough, he was enjoying the situation, finding it a novelty. Not many resisted his charms; most of them were only too happy to oblige. Good God! he wasn't in love with the girl, was he? He couldn't afford to be but on the other hand he had no intention of letting her go. He had to marry money and that couldn't be put off much longer.

Why Peter Nicholson should come into her thoughts this particular morning Beth had no idea but suddenly she wanted to visit Summer Street and this very evening, she decided, she would go and surprise him.

It was only a fifteen-minute walk from Inverbrae House or a short bus run. She arrived at the stop with minutes to spare but since no one was waiting there was a good chance that the bus had gone before its scheduled time. She didn't mind too much since it was pleasantly cool and dry and her feet were in flat-heeled shoes.

Perhaps he wasn't at home or too busy to welcome a visitor – these were her thoughts as she knocked at the door. She didn't like to open it and walk in. Beth knocked again and was on the point of leaving, feeling more disappointed than was reasonable, when the door was thrown open. A startled but clearly delighted Peter stood there and Beth couldn't but think of the contrast between the artist and her Adrian. Even in casual clothes, Adrian always managed to look immaculate. But now Beth had a sudden urge to giggle. Peter wore a pair of paint-stained baggy flannels and a loose cotton jacket with huge pockets. A rag protruded from one pocket and Beth thought he had used it to wipe his hands before answering the door. The jacket had started life as charcoal grey but now sported cheerful streaks and blobs of various colours. The thick blond hair had fallen over his forehead and Beth had a silly wish to push it back.

'Beth! by all that's wonderful, I'd all but given you up. Come in! Come in!'

What a lovely welcome! Beth was smiling as he closed the door then led her along a narrow corridor and into a room that had a coal fire burning in the grate.

'This is where I eat and sleep and through there' – the rooms were connected by a door which was open – 'is where I work.'

'Have I interrupted something, Peter? I don't know but I imagine artists don't like to be disturbed when they are working.'

'Depends,' he grinned. 'Go on, take off your jacket and

put it over a chair or on the bed. You are staying for a while?'

'I'd like to.' She took off her jacket and he was about to take it then drew back.

'Better not, can't guarantee that my hands are paint free.'

Beth put it on the back of a chair and began to look about her.

'This is nice, Peter, cosy too.'

'Suits me.' He smiled. 'I don't have far to walk for anything.'

There was a table and two chairs tucked under it. A single bed was against the wall and a woven bedcover kept it looking tidy. Two shabby but comfortable-looking armchairs were at either side of the fireplace which had a fender and a brass stand. Hanging on the stand were a poker and a pair of tongs. Small rugs covered most of the linoleum but what surprised her was the total absence of pictures. There were plenty of picture hooks but no pictures.

Peter must have anticipated the question. 'The craft shop took the lot. Most of them were small and of local scenes.'

'To display and sell?'

He smiled. 'Apparently they do bring people into the shop. Not necessarily to buy a painting, more to browse. Then they end up buying some ornament.'

'That doesn't tie up with what Jenny said. She says your paintings are much in demand.'

'Can't grumble,' he said, walking away and into the other room. Beth felt honoured to be invited into Peter's world and it *was* like stepping into another universe. The room, a twin of the other, was a happy, friendly clutter of artist's tools, canvases, paints and brushes. Paintings were stacked against the walls, some awaiting frames and a few unfinished and sad, looking as though the painter had lost interest and withdrawn from them disheartened. Perhaps he hadn't quite captured what he had seen with the eye.

She went over to the easel to see what Peter had been working on when he'd had to leave it to answer the door. There was enough done for Beth to call out delightedly, 'Peter, the white house—'

'Good! You recognised it?'

'Of course. It brings my childhood back. I used to worry myself sick that it would topple and end up in the sea and it took my father to show me the house before I was convinced it was safe.'

'What an imaginative child you must have been. It's the angle, of course.'

'Is it commissioned or are you just doing it because it appeals to you?'

'Only because it appeals. To live in such a house is an artist's dream. Can you imagine, Beth, the sheer delight of getting up each morning and looking out at a different scene. The sea is forever changing— Oh, listen to me going on and not remembering to offer hospitality. Sadly there isn't much to offer, just tea and biscuits. Tomorrow is my day for stocking up and I'm afraid even the coffee jar is empty.'

'I don't need anything.'

'Tea and biscuits, you must.'

'All right. Let me help.'

'Never refuse help.' The scullery was smaller than her Aunt Anne's, she thought, and remarkably tidy. It had an uncurtained window with a white sink under it. There was a geyser that gave hot water and a cooker crowded one corner. Shelves covered the remaining spaces.

'Very compact.'

'Tight fit for two but not of our build.' He filled the kettle, got down a biscuit tin and a plate and put them down on the board beside the sink. 'You see to that and if you're lucky you'll find two cups and saucers that match.'

'A nearly match, Peter,' she said as she leaned over to get them from the shelf. 'One odd saucer.'

The gas was turned fully up and before long Peter had the tea made. Beth was amazed at how comfortable they were. It was as though they had known each other all their lives and even when they bumped into each other there was no awkwardness. Beside the fire, dunking ginger snaps, they talked of everything that came to mind.

'Beth?'

She looked up and studied his face. Not a handsome face, the features were irregular and the face rather long but it was an interesting face, full of character and something else was there – kindness. It was in the eyes, a caring person. He would be attractive to women, some would want to mother him. 'Beth, I can squeeze another cup or make fresh?'

'No, no thank you, Peter. That was lovely but I must go.'

'Must you?'

'I'm afraid so, I have a bus to catch and I don't want to be late.'

He didn't argue. 'I'll see you on the bus but before you go would you do me the honour of having dinner with me? Any evening that suits you.'

'Peter,' she said getting up for her jacket, 'it is very kind of you but I'm afraid I can't—'

'There is someone and he would object?'

'Yes. You do understand?'

He nodded. 'Someone very special?'

Her face softened. 'Very, very special.'

355

'Lucky fellow, I hope he appreciates his good fortune but I'm sure he does. Sorry I haven't time to change but a mac and the darkness will cover my shabbiness.' He took her hand and, with a show of olde worlde charm, kissed it. 'Thank you for coming.'

'I've really enjoyed it.'

'Then you'll come again?'

'If you want me to?'

'I do. Beth, we are friends and I want you to promise me that if you should need help in any form you will come to me. I do mean it, Beth.'

'I know you do and thank you.' She wondered what had made him say that but it was nice to have Peter for a friend.

In the end there was a rush to catch the bus and no time for further talk.

Going back, Peter was thoughtful and strangely depressed. Mrs Cuthbert, or Jenny as she had become, didn't believe that this Adrian Scott-Hamilton had serious intentions and was afraid that Beth was going to be badly hurt. He hadn't asked how she knew and in all likelihood she wouldn't have divulged that information but she would have her own method of finding out what she wanted.

Peter wasn't a violent person, quite the opposite, but he knew he would cheerfully strangle the person who brought unhappiness to Beth. In her short life she had had more than her share.

# Chapter Twenty-Five

When she was with Peter everything was so easy, Beth thought, but then that was because they were friends. With him she could be herself and not give a thought to her appearance. He certainly didn't give a thought to his, though he could dress smartly when the occasion demanded.

Refusing Peter's invitation to dinner hadn't been easy. She had wanted to accept because he was such fun and they seemed to have so much to say to each other. But she was right to refuse, she had done the right thing.

Adrian was waiting in the car at the usual placc. He always arrived punctually and so did she and that meant that the car was never parked for any length of time beside Inverbrae House. Beth saw no need for this, no need for secrecy, and wondered at Adrian thinking there was. He said it was for her sake, and he said it so firmly that she hadn't pursued the matter.

When it was to be a dress affair Adrian always told her, even suggesting what she should wear. She didn't mind, welcomed it really, and it saved any unfortunate mistakes.

She missed him dreadfully when he was home in Stirling and lived for that tap on the office window, the signal for her to rush out to the back of the premises and for a few precious moments be in his arms.

Dinner this evening was to be at a small hotel, somewhere new where they hadn't been before. Beth was spending more than she wanted to on clothes but she had to be smart for Adrian. The latest buy was a navy blue fine-knitted suit with brass buttons and to complete the outfit she wore navy court shoes and a navy handbag.

'Very nice,' he said approvingly then seeing she was settled and the door shut he moved off. 'How did you spend your time when I wasn't here?'

He often asked that and expected the usual answer that she had done nothing much.

'Nothing much apart from going to see a friend of mine.'

'Male or female?' he smiled.

'Peter is an artist. We met in a friend's house and strangely enough he met my father—'

'Old, getting on a bit, nothing for me to be worried about,' he smiled.

'Late twenties,' she said and then added mischievously, 'He's talented and charming and one day I think he may well become famous.'

'What were you doing with – this artist?'

'What's that supposed to mean? What would I be doing with him?' she said angrily.

'That is what I am asking you. I understood that you were my—'

'Of course I am yours. I belong to you, Adrian, but there is such a thing as trust.'

'I'm sorry, Beth,' he said softly, 'I can't bear to think of you with someone else, that is all. Forgiven?'

'Adrian, of course you are forgiven, if there is anything to forgive and you have nothing to fear. I love you and only you.'

'Thank you, darling, I shouldn't want anything to spoil this evening.'

They arrived at the Grange Hotel. It was a small, rather shabby hotel but according to Adrian it had a good reputation for food and offered a fine selection of wines. Adrian always took a long time over the choosing of a wine and had been known, to Beth's embarrassment, to have tasted one and sent it back.

Beth had her usual sherry before the meal and allowed her wine glass to be topped up more than once. It pleased Adrian and it was a small price to pay. A sweeter wine and she might have liked it but Adrian preferred a dry wine and he was the expert.

The dining-room was warm and getting warmer. A number of people were dining though no one known to them. Beth began to feel pleasantly drowsy, not enough to want to sleep, just to lean back in the chair and let the murmur of voices drift by.

'More coffee?' The waitress was over with the coffee pot.

'Beth?'

Beth roused herself. 'No, thank you.' The waitress went away and Adrian excused himself. She didn't think anything of it, for in a short time she too would be asking to be excused. The minutes ticked away. Surely this was a very long time? Perhaps he was unwell but, if she asked someone to find out and he suddenly appeared, she would feel all kinds of a fool. Just as she was seriously thinking of asking a waiter Adrian appeared and was looking very apologetic.

'Sorry, darling. Did you think I'd got lost or something?'

'I did. Another few minutes and I was to ask the waiter to check and see if you were all right.'

'Good God! You wouldn't have done that, surely?'

'What else was there for me to do?'

'True. The truth is, Beth, that something very unfortunate has happened.'

She looked startled. 'What?'

'You remember the car was playing up on the way here?'

She didn't, everything had seemed normal to her but obviously something had been wrong. 'Yes, I think so.'

'No use explaining to you the mechanical fault that has developed but—'

'You mean you can't drive, something's broken?'

'Yes.'

'Can't you get a mechanic to see to it?'

'At this time of night?'

No, she supposed not. 'Then someone will have to drive us back.' She did feel light-headed but her brain was still functioning and better than Adrian's by the sound of it.

'That's what I was taking so long about. No one is available but not to worry, we can stay here overnight and a mechanic will look at the car first thing in the morning and you'll be in the office at your usual time. Should you be a little later no one will bother?'

'No.' It was true she wouldn't be missed, not for a while.

'You're tired?' He sounded concerned.

'I am a bit.' She saw that he had keys in his hand, not his car keys, she would have recognised them by the lucky charm on the ring. They went upstairs and he opened a door.

'Is this yours or mine?'

He didn't answer and she followed him in. It was a large room and nicely furnished but all Beth saw was the double bed.

'Plenty of room for you,' she said with an attempt at humour but really she was dreadfully tired. She yawned. 'I didn't get much sleep last night and I am hopeless without sleep. Do you mind if I go to my bedroom now?'

'This is the only room available.'

'The only room available,' she said stupidly.

'Afraid so.'

'What happens now?'

'What do you think?' He was smiling.

The lightheadness was beginning to go. She didn't know why, but she was suddenly very frightened. Was this a trick? No, it wasn't, Adrian wouldn't do this to her or would he? She swung round to face him. 'You did try, didn't you?'

He looked hurt. 'Darling, don't you trust me?'

'I – I don't know, I think so but I am not going to sleep with you. I'm not sharing this room.'

'Not even if I sleep in the chair?'

Beth thought about that. Where was the harm? Then she pictured it. Adrian in the chair and she in the double bed. What if – no she couldn't risk it, there had to be another way. She would go to the desk and ask, the hotel didn't seem busy.

'I'm sure there must be a spare room, I'm not fussy just provided it has a bed and I'll make do with anything.'

He turned away to hide the scowl. Worth one more try.

'Beth, look at me.'

She did.

'You love me don't you?'

'Yes, you know that but—'

'And I love you very, very much. I want you and I think if you are honest with yourself you want me. Beth,' she could feel his breath on her face, 'when two people love each other the way we do it can't be wrong.'

'I'm sorry, Adrian, I think it wrong and I won't change my mind.'

'If you won't then come on and I'll drive you home.'

She stared. 'This was all – the car isn't—'

'If I tell you I'm deeply ashamed would you believe me?'

'Yes, I suppose so, Adrian, but why – why go to all this—' She looked at him helplessly.

'I need you Beth, and now I've spoilt everything.'

He did look genuinely upset and in a way he was paying her a compliment.

'No, we'll just forget all about it.' She went to him and put her arms round his neck. After a moment he put her aside.

'If you want home we'd better be on our way.'

'Yes.' She thought about the room, would he have to pay for it? 'Adrian, what about—'

'The room? Since I've booked it it'll have to be paid. I'll come back and sleep in my lonely bed and think of you in yours.'

She giggled. 'Adrian, you're hopeless.'

Yes, I am, he thought. It would have taken time but he could have seduced her. Why hadn't he? He couldn't understand himself.

It didn't come as a surprise, she had expected it since Adrian was such a regular visitor of the Watsons but it upset Beth more than she was prepared to admit. She wondered what would have happened if the invitation to Caroline's birthday ball had included a partner but it hadn't.

'A shortage of young males that's why I was included in the invitation,' Adrian said. 'Unfortunately I was not in a position to suggest I bring you.'

'I know that and you can tell me all about it.'

'Won't be much to tell. You don't expect me to describe the gowns, do you?'

'Not in detail.'

Alone in her room on the evening of the ball, Beth tried not to imagine the scene but it kept coming before her eyes. The dimmed lights, the haunting music of the waltz, the lovely gowns and beautiful women all eager for Adrian's arms to hold them as they danced the evening away.

Trying desperately to sound off-hand, Beth had asked Adrian if he had enjoyed himself.

'How could I not, since nothing was spared to make the evening a success? With you there, darling, it would have been quite, quite perfect.'

She smiled into his eyes. 'Did Caroline look very lovely?'

'Yes, very nice, pretty little thing but far too excitable for my liking. You aren't, you cannot be jealous?' One eyebrow lifted in that special way he had.

'I don't want to be but I am,' she said with complete honesty.

'Foolish girl, you have no need. Not one woman there could hold a candle to you. Satisfied now?'

She nodded feeling the tears sting the back of her eyes. He was a dear and those were the words she had wanted to hear. Where they were, behind the office and in the shelter of the trees, she fell into his arms. Adrian loved her and if he was slow to mention marriage then he must have his reasons and she would be content to wait. He would propose in his own time.

'Darling, I have to go away,' he murmured, nibbling at her ear.

'Oh, no, not again,' she said moving back to look into

his face. 'I've hardly seen you,' she whispered.

'The Watsons will be getting sick and tired of me and I must go home. I have things to see to, you know.' She thought she detected the faintest touch of irritability in his voice.

She couldn't hide her misery. 'Sorry, I know I'm being unreasonable but I'm lost without you.'

'Nonsense. You've managed before. Just be a good girl and I promise to come back as soon as possible.' He took out his cigarettes, put one in his mouth and lit it with a gold cigarette lighter.

Beth was completely under his spell, he thought smugly. Adrian enjoyed his power over women but only a very few earned his respect. Beth was one. A wife with money was essential and he needed Beth. Having both would take a little arranging but it could be done.

It was only very rarely that Beth and Caroline set eyes on one another and when they did there was a slight awkwardness. To Beth's knowledge, Caroline had never set foot in the office so it came as a surprise when, two days after her birthday, she tapped at the door and entered.

'Hello!' Beth said startled.

'Not bad in here,' Caroline said glancing around.

'I've added the homely touches. Have a seat.'

'Haven't time, Beth, just popped in to thank you for the gift.'

'That's all right, did you like it?'

Caroline looked vague. 'Ye – es, I got so many—'

'It was a small ornament for your dressing table.'

'So it was, I remember now, sweet little thing.'

'Did everything go well?'

'Everything was absolutely perfect, it couldn't have been better.' She did sit down. 'My gown was heavenly, everyone said so and told me that I was looking lovely. One person,' she blushed, 'said I looked enchanting.'

'What colour was your gown?'

'Peach, my favourite colour.'

'Yes, I remember.'

'Wish you had been there to see me.' Her eyes grew dreamy. 'It was the most wonderful night of my life, Beth, and I'll just whisper it.' She dropped her voice and gave a small giggle. 'Someone very, very special was there.'

'Caroline, you've fallen in love?'

'I have and don't you dare laugh, it happened the moment I saw him and this is absolutely true, Beth, he said it had been the same for him. I don't expect you to understand—'

'I think I can, Caroline,' Beth said softly. 'It's—'

'Magic?'

'Yes, that is it exactly.'

They were laughing together like they once had. Caroline got quickly to her feet. 'There is so much going on, so much excitement, that I don't know whether I'm coming or going. Robert leaves for London tonight, then it is Paris and dear knows where after that. Grandmama is quite pleased to have him travel and see places of interest just so long as he spends some time with us before he goes back to Australia.' She walked to the door. 'Must go and let you get on with whatever you are supposed to be doing. 'Bye.'

'Goodbye, Caroline, thanks for calling.'

The days went in, empty days that seemed endless and the nights when she couldn't sleep were worse. Each morning she looked for a letter and each morning she was disappointed. Adrian knew when her birthday was, it had come up in conversation, but would he remember?

The morning of her eighteenth birthday came and she

wondered if anyone would remember. Not many knew the date. Aunt Anne wasn't one for remembering birthdays. There was only one gift she longed for or even a card, just something to show that Adrian hadn't forgotten her.

Mrs Murdoch fetched the letters and any for Beth were put on a table. Today there were three. Three small packets addressed to Beth. Two had come by post. The one without a stamp was in Caroline's writing, the other from Jenny. The third one had her heart racing, the postmark was smudged but she didn't need to examine it, it could only be from Adrian.

Shaking with excitement she took the packages to her room. Adrian's she would keep until last. She fingered it lovingly then put it aside. Caroline's gift was a pretty string of beads and Jenny's a bottle of perfume, a heavenly choice. Adrian liked a whiff of expensive perfume. Now to open his gift – carefully she undid the wrapping and then tissue paper and she was looking at a slim box. Opening it she found a lovely silver bracelet. She slipped it on and her eyes were shining. There was a card and she turned it over and read the words. To Beth on her eighteenth birthday with my very best wishes. Perhaps we'll meet again when I return from my travels – Robert.

How long did she stand there? From the heights to the depths. She wondered how she was going to cope with the disappointment. Fancy Robert remembering? How very, very kind of him but if only – if only – it had been from Adrian.

He came when she had all but given up. The small tap on the window had her on her feet and running out to fling herself into his arms. In her joy at seeing him she gave no thought to them being seen. Someone had, however, someone who was too shocked to move as she stared at the couple locked in each other's arms. For several disbelieving moments she stared at them and then, her feet making no noise on the grass, she ran towards Inverbrae House. Once there she was panting for breath and had to lie down until she could breathe normally.

When he left Beth, Adrian was whistling happily. He went out and returned by a different entrance. One had to be careful. He had been back living with the Watsons for a week, much of it spent in Caroline's company. Everything was going well and according to plan. The girl was besotted with him, he thought smugly. The old woman, bless her heart, was completely won over and the colonel had accepted him. And why not? The Scott-Hamiltons were county, their name much respected by all but those who had suffered financially, their bills unpaid and likely to remain that way. Adrian smiled grimly. Gambling was a mug's game and not a weakness of his but it had been the ruin of his family.

It was no crime for the gentry to be in debt but it made living conditions difficult. A skeleton staff was all they could afford and only a wing of Bankhead House was used. The thought disgusted him as he compared it to the lavish living at Inverbrae House.

He had missed Beth, missed her more than he would have believed possible but Caroline was the catch. If he played his cards right he could have marriage to Caroline and Beth as the love of his life.

# Chapter Twenty-Six

Her face a frozen mask of fury and her hands clenching and unclenching, Caroline barged into the office.

'How dare you, Beth Brown! How dare you embarrass Adrian with your unwanted attention. He was disgusted and so am I.' She almost spat the words.

Sheer disbelief held Beth silent and she could only stare at Caroline.

'You stupid, stupid creature. To think you had a chance with Adrian! Did you really believe he would have anything to do with the likes of you, a nobody? Adrian happens to come from a good family and is a perfect gentleman.'

Beth was pale and shocked but she had found her voice.

'It is simply not true to suggest that I—'

Caroline cut her off. 'Useless to deny it. I saw you with my own eyes.'

'Saw what?'

'You tearing out of the office and throwing yourself at Adrian.' Her lips curled.

Beth was about to hotly deny it when she remembered that it was partly true. She had rushed out to see Adrian, she had been so happy to see him. But surely it couldn't be true what Caroline was saying? Surely the arms that held her were willing arms? Desperately she searched for some explanation. Adrian wouldn't do this to her? He wouldn't, he couldn't, not after – not after— After what? she asked herself dully. The endearments, his kisses, how much had they meant to him? Nothing if what Caroline said was true.

'Caroline, it wasn't quite what it appeared to be,' Beth said unsteadily.

'Adrian had just come back and—'

She gave a self satisfied smirk. 'For your information, Adrian has been back in Sandyneuk for the last seven days—'

'But that is impossible, he couldn't have, he told me—'

'Of course he did. To be rid of you was worth a white lie,' Caroline said smugly. She had relaxed a little but her eyes were hard. 'Adrian came with the Watsons to my birthday ball and hardly left my side all night.'

Caroline was telling the truth, Beth was sure of that now. Adrian had been amusing himself with her and she had been fool enough to read more into it. Her face burned at the thought but she wasn't alone in being taken in. Adrian wasn't in love with Caroline, had she been a nobody he would not have spared her a second glance.

Beth was sickened and shattered at her own naïvety but she was the lucky one. Her eyes were opened and she was seeing Adrian for what he was. She was probably setting herself an impossible task but she must try to warn Caroline.

'Caroline?'

'Yes?' she said haughtily. 'If this is a belated apology you can save your breath.'

'It is far from an apology. The fact is, Caroline, Adrian has made a fool of me and yes I am humiliated and hurt but I'll recover. We have both been taken in by a handsome face and a great deal of charm.'

'So that is it! You just can't accept that Adrian is in love with me because you want him for yourself. This time, you have gone too far.' Her pale blue eyes showed outrage and her face hardened. 'Daddy isn't here but in his absence I am ordering you out of Inverbrae House and what is more I wish never to see you or speak to you again.'

Beth gave her a long, steady look. Then she got up from her chair where she had been sitting all this time while Caroline stood. Without hurrying herself, she took her coat from the coat-stand, put it on, fastened the buttons, drew the belt round her slim waist and buckled it. That done she collected her handbag and made to walk to the door.

'Where do you think you are going?'

'Obeying instructions – yours.'

'I said to remove yourself from Inverbrae House. No doubt daddy will terminate your employment as soon as he gets a replacement.'

'As far as I am concerned the job and the accommodation go together,' Beth said quietly. She touched the keys. 'I'll leave them with you.' She turned the knob. 'Goodbye, Caroline. Perhaps the day will come when you wished you had taken my warning seriously.'

She left Caroline looking uncertain and a little afraid.

Somehow Beth got herself to her bedroom at Inverbrae House, though she had no recollection of what she did after leaving the office. Throwing her coat on to a chair, seeing it falling off and doing nothing about it, Beth sat down, put her hands over her face and tried to think. Her whole world had collapsed, lay in ruins at her feet and how was she ever to pick up the pieces? Did one get extra strength at a time like this? She tried to picture life without Adrian and couldn't. For so long she had just lived for the times they were together but that was over. She let out a shuddering breath. This couldn't be happening to her! She must be dreaming? But it was no dream.

How could he be so cruel? And it was the spark of anger, faint though it was, that gave her the courage to go on. She had been in deep despair before and had come through it. Now she was older and it should be easier to hide her hurt and humiliation. Only it wasn't.

Other more pressing worries were surfacing in her mind. What am I to do? she thought in panic. She had no home, she had no job. The luxury of grieving over Adrian would have to take a back seat while she thought of her position.

Jenny was always there and she was tempted to phone, only she wouldn't. The time had come for her to stand on her own two feet. It was then that she remembered Anna Martin though, after all this time, it was very unlikely that the writer would still be seeking a typist.

Once, out of curiosity, she had gone to see Lilac Lodge and found it to be an attractive house and bigger than she had expected.

No time like the present – she would go now. Beth walked to the bus stop and after a few minutes a bus came along. She got off at the foot of the brae, went along to the house and up to the door. Taking a deep breath she tugged at the bell-pull. She heard footsteps and the door opened. The woman was tall and thin with a pleasant face free of make-up and she wore her short grey hair with a fringe. Round her neck was a double string of wooden beads and Beth thought she looked charmingly Bohemian. Her long shapeless garment was in silver grey and over it was a loose black cardigan.

'Are you Miss Anna Martin?' Beth asked.

'I am.'

'I'm Beth Brown, Miss Martin. Perhaps Mrs Cuthbert, Mrs Jenny Cuthbert, mentioned my name?'

'Not that I recall.'

'Oh!' Beth swallowed and wondered what to say next. 'I – I do typing and I'm looking for a position but perhaps you don't require anyone,' she said in a defeated voice.

'That all depends but we'll talk better indoors. Do come in.'

Beth entered a modest hall, square-shaped, with a polished wood floor on which were two fringed rugs. Against one wall stood a grandfather clock and in a corner was a coat-stand with an umbrella, a collection of walking sticks, and an ancient raincoat hanging on one of the pegs. A stairway curved upwards, and to the right was a room, quite large, with a bow-window. There was an Adam fireplace and the fire was set ready to light with curled up paper, sticks, and a few pieces of coal. A gas fire stood in front of it and Miss Martin lit it.

'Instant heat and so handy to take the chill off the room.' Beth was standing. 'Please sit down.' She gestured to an armchair.

'Thank you.'

A cat was curled up in another chair and Miss Martin lifted it and sat there herself. With a look of outrage at having been disturbed the cat padded round the chair, then jumped up on its mistress's knees and curled up into a ball.

Beth laughed.

'Likes his home comforts but then don't we all?' Her hand gently smoothed the fur. 'My apologies, my dear. Thinking about it, I do seem to remember Jenny mentioning a young friend who might be interested in typing my manuscripts. I don't think she mentioned your name and, of course, it was a long time ago.'

'Yes, and you must have engaged someone by now.'

'Yes and no to that. My typing is done by an agency that charges the earth and refuses to have the mistakes corrected unless they receive further payment. I am not mean but I hate to feel I have been cheated.'

'Miss Martin, I'll be honest, until this afternoon I did clerical work including a lot of typing for Colonel Parker-Munro—'

'Ah!' A look of understanding crossed her face. 'I see the connection with Jenny but do go on.'

'I had a disagreement with his daughter, an unpleasant scene and because of that I am without a job and with nowhere to live.'

'Jobless and homeless, you poor thing.'

Beth had believed herself to be in control but without warning she gave a gulp and the tears began to flow. 'I'm so – so very, very sorry—' she sobbed, 'I can't help it but I'll be all right in a minute.'

Anna Martin touched her arm gently. 'The kindest thing I can do is leave you alone. Cry your heart out, my dear, you'll feel the better of it. I'll go and put the kettle on – come on, puss.'

'No, please—'

'My usual time for having a cup of tea and making two cups is as easy as making one.'

Beth was feeling all kinds of a fool. Why did she let herself get so upset? Heaven knows, she had plenty of practice of getting hurt and humiliated. She should be used to it. It wasn't Adrian's shameful behaviour but the look on Caroline's face that stuck with her. The look had been one of hatred.

She was composed and shamefaced when Anna Martin came in with a tray. On it was a teapot, two white china cups and saucers, sugar and milk and, on a plate, slices of Madeira cake.

'Very plain fare with me, I'm afraid.'

'Miss Martin—' Beth bit her lip.

'No apologies, my dear, it's totally unnecessary. A good weep is like a refreshing shower of rain. Just tell me, are you feeling better?'

'Yes, I am, much better, thank you.'

'Good! You owe me no explanation, we shall talk of other things such as your reason for coming here. You have secretarial skills and let me point out that those will be wasted here—' she put up her hand as Beth made to interrupt. 'Let me acquaint you with my requirements. First I need someone to type my manuscripts and my writing has been described as atrocious. It isn't, of course, and I'm sure you would master it in no time. Like most writers I make a great many changes but again you will get used to that.'

'May I ask what you write, Miss Martin?'

'Obviously you are not a fan of mine,' she sighed, then laughed as Beth looked uncomfortable. 'I am a historian with a great love of the past and do a lot of research into the lives of people who have shaped this country of ours. My following is small but genuinely interested and I ask no more. Fortunately my parents left me this house and enough for its upkeep. If not I would have been unable to indulge in what I find to be a fascinating hobby.' She paused to take a drink of the tea and to insist that Beth take another piece of Madeira cake.

'Thank you, it is very good.'

'Now where was I? Oh, yes, from time to time you

would be required to do some research for me and that would mean a trip to town and a lengthy spell in the library. The staff are helpful.'

'I would enjoy that.'

She smiled. 'Should you wish to remain in town to do shopping or whatever feel free to do so. No set hours here Miss—'

'Brown, Beth Brown.'

'You are much too young and pretty to be Miss anything – how old are you?'

'I've just turned eighteen.'

'Neither child nor woman, a difficult age but in your case I'd say a mature eighteen. Life hasn't always been kind to you, my dear, that much I have gathered. It is obvious, really, when you are looking for a home. You never know but this could be the turning point in your life. I hope so.'

'I hope so too, Miss Martin,' Beth said quietly.

'More tea?'

'No, thank you.'

Miss Martin took the cup from Beth and put it on the tray. 'I shall call you Beth, a pretty name. Is it short for Elizabeth?'

'Yes.'

'Provided the work is done, Beth, you can do it when it suits you. By the way, can you cook?'

'Just about,' Beth smiled. She was blessing Aunt Anne for having taught her.

'Just about should do it. I eat when I feel like it, I have no set meal times and I cook to suit myself. You must do the same. A Mrs McLeod comes in to do the housework and the laundry, sheets and towels – your personal laundry you would see to yourself. Am I making sense?'

'Yes.'

'My thoughts take off and I'm inclined to wander but you'll get used to my peculiar little ways.' She glanced round her. 'This is my sitting-room or the parlour as it was called in my parents' day. Mrs McLeod is very thorough and cannot bear to see anything out of place which is why she is on pain of death to enter my sanctuary. Come along and I'll show it to you.' They crossed the hall and Beth tried to hide her surprise when the door was opened. It was quite large, the ceilings were high, and a very large desk dominated the room. Two of its drawers were pulled out and papers were strewn over the floor. On the desk were books, many of them open and pages and pages of handwritten notes. A child's mug held a quantity of sharpened pencils and beside it was a pencil sharpener. There was a glass ashtray half filled with cigarette stubs. 'I only smoke when I am waiting for inspiration so you'll be able to tell from the state of the ashtray whether or not I am having a good day.'

Beth looked at the stubs and laughed. 'Not too good?'

Miss Martin laughed ruefully. 'As you say, not too good. Incidentally, let me make this point, believe it or not I can straightaway put my hand on what I want.' She waited a moment or two. 'We'll now go to the back of the house where you would be working. The reason for you being so far away is because the constant tapping of the typewriter keys would drive me mad.'

This room had flowery curtains at the window and the view was of a well-kept garden. There was a desk, a filing cabinet and a covered typewriter sitting on the table.

'That's a Royal. Is that the make you are used to?'

'No, but it is very similar.'

'Now to where you would sleep. Oh, by the way there are gas fires in all the rooms to save work but I've kept the fireplaces and occasionally I have a coal fire in my sitting-room. To work well one must be comfortably warm, Beth, and I don't grudge heat. What I do object to is waste and by that I mean a fire on and no one in the room.'

'I would be very careful.'

The bedroom was small with a single bed, a wardrobe, and a dressing-table. There were two chairs, one with arms and both had cushions. The curtains and bedcover were matching in a pleasing pattern of yellows and blues.

'Suit you?'

'Perfectly,' Beth said beginning to feel excited at the prospect of working and living here.

They went into the room next to the bedroom. It was larger and was furnished as a sitting-room. 'When I was a young girl these two rooms were mine. No doubt you will have a few possessions of your own, Beth, so please change things around to suit yourself. If this is to be your home you must feel comfortable in your surroundings.'

'You are very kind.'

'Method in my madness. If I can leave everything to you, the payment of accounts and all the day-to-day trivia, I shall be free to concentrate on my own work.'

Beth followed the flowing skirt down the carpeted stairs. 'There is a bathroom upstairs and a cloakroom with a toilet and wash-hand basin downstairs. The kitchen,' she waved vaguely in its direction, 'is your average kitchen with a fairly new cooker which works very well.' They were downstairs and back in Miss Martin's sitting-room.

'What do you think?'

'Am I being offered the job?'

'Would I have shown you over my home otherwise? Of course I am offering you the job.'

'Thank you very, very much and I accept.' Beth's eyes were shining.

'Sit down and tell me when you can start.'

'Now if you want.'

Miss Martin raised her eyebrows. 'You do need to give notice to your employer.'

'His daughter told me to leave the house at once and since job and accommodation go together—'

'Now, my dear, don't be hasty, a very common fault of the young. The daughter would have no authority over your employment. You must give notice to your employer—'

Beth looked stubborn. 'I was told to go so I wouldn't think that necessary.'

'Nevertheless it is. Don't put yourself in the wrong, Beth. Only your employer can dispense with your services and not his daughter.'

'In that case, Miss Martin, it would be one week since I am paid weekly.'

'A week will pass very quickly. You must first arrange for your belongings to be brought here.'

'When should I do that?'

'Would you like to move in now?'

'Yes, please, and I am really very grateful. Tommy, he's the chauffeur, he would help me. I'm friendly with him.'

She shook her head. 'Not a good idea, it could get this Tommy into trouble. I have someone who sees to transport when I require it. How long would it take you to pack?'

'Not long.'

'What about cases?'

'I have two.'

'Harry can take an extra case or boxes. Excuse me and I'll see when he could be available.'

'Miss Martin, it would have to be the side entrance.' Beth was becoming more bewildered by the minute at the speed of events.

'All this speed is alarming you but I am someone who likes to get things done immediately then I can forget about them.'

'I am only too happy to have you take over because frankly I'm in a daze.'

Miss Martin went away and came back five minutes later. 'All arranged. I've just remembered one important omission – we haven't discussed salary.'

'I wouldn't expect much, not with living here.'

'May I ask what your present salary is?'

Beth told her.

'Including board and lodgings?'

'Yes.'

'Well, Beth, I'll match the salary but you will have to buy in your own food and cook it so you will be worse off.'

'I shouldn't mind that. In fact I'm going to enjoy doing something for myself.'

Anna Martin smiled. 'As I said all arranged. Harry is to be at the side entrance to Inverbrae House at seven o'clock.'

'In a minute I am going to waken up.'

'Poor child, you shouldn't be going through this ordeal at your age. If you want my advice, I would suggest you go now and do your packing then I would—' she stopped and chewed at her lip.

Beth waited for her to go on.

'Your letter of resignation, I'd write that out, and make

it clear that you are giving the legal requirement of seven days' notice. That should take the wind out of his sails for I doubt that he would expect you to know that.'

Beth nodded eagerly. 'I'll do that and I'll get the work as far forward as possible to make it easier for whoever takes over.'

'Good girl. Just this once I'll have a meal ready for you when Harry brings you and your belongings. After that I'll show you where to get sheets and pillowcases for the bed.'

When Beth returned to Inverbrae House she went straight to the office. There was the possibility that it would be locked but it wasn't. Mr Blair, the manager, was there and looking glum.

'Beth, tell me it isn't true, you aren't going?'

'Yes, Mr Blair, I am. As a matter of fact I was told to go.'

'Not by the boss, you weren't. That Miss Caroline, was it?'

'Same thing.'

'No, it isn't. You two had a row and Miss Caroline lost her temper—'

Beth stopped him. 'A lot more to it than that but as it happens she did me a good turn. I've got another job and accommodation.'

'Just like that?'

'Just like that,' she smiled.

'You'll stay until he gets someone else,' he said anxiously.

Beth knew he was thinking of himself and felt sorry for him. 'I'm giving one week's notice, Mr Blair, but I'll get everything as far forward as I can.'

'You'll be difficult to replace.' He cheered up. 'Maybe you'll be offered a rise to stay on?'

'I won't change my mind.'

The manager grunted and went out, leaving the keys behind. Once he'd gone Beth put paper in the typewriter and typed out her resignation. She signed it and put it in an enveloped addressed to the colonel. That small but important job done, she placed it in a prominent place on the table. Satisfied, she left the office and went to the house to do her packing.

Coats and jackets could be carried over her arm and the rest of her clothes would go in the cases. Boxes would be required, since her worldly possessions proved to be more than she thought. Over the years she had received gifts and all these would go with her. Jenny could keep her picture, meantime.

She was as ready as she could be and at five to seven she was downstairs carrying one case and two coats over her arm. A car slowed down and a voice called, 'Would you be Miss Brown?'

'Yes.'

He smiled. 'Harry at your service. Give me that case and I'll put it in the boot. Put your coats on the back seat.'

She did that. 'I'll be as quick as I can and I'll take two of these boxes.'

'I'll come up with you, then the one journey will do.'

Beth looked uncertain. 'I'm only an employee—'

'And me the removal man,' he grinned. 'I don't see me meeting much opposition, do you?'

She had to laugh. He was a very large, well-built, middle-aged man. 'No, I don't.'

For all his bulk, Harry was quick on his feet and in a short time everything was in the car. Beth didn't look back and she just wished that the next seven days were over.

The remainder of that eventful day passed with Beth not quite sure if she was coming or going. Anna Martin had busied herself preparing a tasty meal but Beth was too choked to do justice to it. When she tried to apologise, her expressions of regret were waved away.

'It has been a traumatic experience and it takes a day or two to recover. Get the next seven days behind you and you'll feel very different.'

Next morning on the dot of nine, Beth was at her desk. The colonel had been in, the letter was gone and there was a pile of letters waiting to be typed. Beth was glad, it would keep her occupied and her mind off what was ahead. Perhaps there would be no unpleasantness and the colonel would be glad to see the back of her. He came in just before four o'clock. She looked up from her typing.

'Good afternoon, Colonel Parker-Munro,' Beth said quietly. She was nervous and her heart was racing.

'Good afternoon,' he said coldly.

He hadn't used her name and abruptly he turned away to pick up the letters that were ready for his signature. He sat down to read them and scrawled his signature.

'Stop typing, if you please.'

Beth took her fingers off the keys and sat back.

'Your disgraceful behaviour has greatly upset my daughter.'

'May I ask what I am supposed to have done?'

His eyes were icy, like blue pebbles and she heard the anger in his voice, 'You are a selfish, ungrateful girl. You tried to ruin my daughter's happiness.'

'Far from it.' Beth was calm now, she had nothing to lose. 'All I did was try to warn Caroline about Adrian. He is not to be trusted.'

'Enough! That is quite enough. The gentleman in question was reluctant to condemn you—'

'Condemn me, that's rich,' Beth said furiously. 'You are as blind as your daughter and I pity Caroline if she marries him.'

'Just as she said, you are eaten up with jealousy.'

'It is easier to accept than the truth, isn't it?'

'That you, of all people, should behave like this after all that has been done for you.'

'Done for me? As a child I accept that you were kind to me but then it suited you to be. In fact, Colonel Parker-Munro, you were a sort of hero until I got older and realised that your kindness was extended to me just as long as I was of use.'

She saw her outburst had surprised him.

'We took care of you after your parents died.'

'For a short time. Since it was you who persuaded my mother to let me live at Inverbrae House it was difficult to remove me. What would people say?' To her own ears she sounded breathless but she knew that she could hold her own.

'I have more than fulfilled my obligations.' He permitted himself a wintry smile.

'Let me finish, please.' Now that she had started, Beth couldn't stop herself.

'Regarding my schooldays at Rowanbank, you deliberately set out to make my life as difficult and unpleasant as possible.'

'I beg your pardon?' he said, fixing her with cold eyes.

'Miss Critchley, that odious woman, did not require to know my family history. I am not ashamed of it, nothing could be further from the truth, but you must have known that the information would not remain confidential.' She paused. 'Only a small number tried to make my life a misery but I wouldn't let them succeed.' Beth smiled. 'I'm just so glad I had the guts to tell her publicly what I thought of her.'

'You made an exhibition of yourself.'

'Yes, I did and it was much appreciated by a great many.'

'The fees for that school are quite considerable and you should be grateful—'

'Grateful – grateful – always grateful, how I hate that word. Strange, I thought, that you were paying my fees when you clearly didn't want me in the school and stranger still how we come to hear things.'

'Go on,' he said sarcastically, 'this is interesting.'

'I know now that I have Mrs Cuthbert to thank for my education at Rowanbank. She persuaded you to let me go with Caroline. That is true, isn't it?'

'It is.'

For the first time Beth saw the colonel lost for words.

'You do realise that I am working my notice?'

'With no consideration for me. How am I supposed to get a replacement in seven days?'

'Mr Blair and you will just have to manage,' she said sweetly.

She saw the struggle. 'Would you consider staying another month?'

'I'm sorry, I have already accepted another position.'

'I see,' he said tersely and without looking at her went out.

Beth knew it was a victory but even so she could have wept. In spite of all the hurtful things that had been said she hated leaving this way.

There was no problem getting from Lilac Lodge to the office. She now had a bicycle. Miss Martin had told her that there was one in the shed and she was welcome to it.

On her final day but one, Beth locked up and went round to the back of the office to collect her bike. It was then that she saw him and, for a moment, the breath went from her body.

'Hello, Beth!' he smiled.

She didn't answer, just looked at him coldly and reached for her bicycle. He had put himself between it and her.

'Would you kindly get out of my way?'

'We need to talk, Beth.'

'I have nothing to say to you.'

'I've hurt you and that was the last thing I wanted to do.'

'How very touching.'

'Please don't be like that, I only want to explain.'

'I have no wish to hear.'

The patience had given way to anger. 'You might as well listen, since you can't get at your bicycle.'

'I can always get a bus.'

'You aren't going anywhere until you hear what I have to say.'

'Make it quick,' she snapped.

He spread out his hands in a gesture of despair. 'Beth, I had no choice in the matter.'

'You are hoping to marry Caroline for her money?'

'Yes. Don't look like that. It happens in families like ours. And it works. Caroline wants me, her family wants me.'

'She believes you love her.'

'I'll let her go on thinking it. We can all be happy, Beth. Much better, of course, if you had been the daughter but we love each other. That is what is important and, since you are no longer at Inverbrae House, it should be easier to arrange to meet.'

'Your conceit is unbelievable. It takes my breath away. If you imagine even for one moment – if you think I would dream of – of—' She found she couldn't go on and just looked at him with cold contempt.

He shrugged. 'Nothing unusual about what I am suggesting, Beth, but if it doesn't appeal to you—'

'Appeal? It sickens me. I hope and pray that Caroline comes to her senses and sees you for what you are.'

He grinned maliciously. 'Not a hope and don't try anything, my dear Beth, because Caroline wouldn't believe a word against me.' He moved away from the bicycle. 'Don't let me detain you any longer.'

He walked away with that easy grace and arrogance that she had once admired. How confident he was, so sure that she could do nothing and, of course, he was right. She had tried and failed.

# Chapter Twenty-Seven

It was wonderful, this new-found freedom, and Beth was thoroughly enjoying life. At Inverbrae House she had known freedom but that had been different. No one there had cared sufficiently about her to bother where she went. By contrast, Lilac Lodge had become home, a place where she felt happy and contented. She had her own bedroom and sitting-room and could cook a meal or make a cup of tea for herself whenever she felt like it. She could also entertain friends if she so wished. When her book was going well, Anna Martin would be shut in her study for much of the day but there was always a point when they were together and theirs was an easy relationship that suited them both.

Over coffee one morning, when the writer had finished explaining changes in her manuscript, Anna Martin asked Beth if she was happy or if she felt it was too quiet for her.

'I love it here, Miss Martin. I think of it as the luckiest day of my life when I came to your door.'

'Bless you for that but you are young, my dear, and I worry that you are missing out. I was always a bit of a loner but thankfully there aren't too many like me.' She smiled and sipped at her coffee. 'You make a good cup, just the way I like it.'

'I'm learning and I'm becoming quite good at cooking.

One evening you must let me prepare you a meal.'

'Be your guest?'

'Yes.'

'I'll keep you to that.' She paused and looked apologetic. 'You must know by now that I hate stopping for meals and much prefer to work on until I finish whatever it is.'

'I do understand and I've wanted to say for some time that I don't earn my salary.'

'That you do. My manuscripts are neater than they ever were. Added to that, I like to think of someone else in the house.'

'I'm reasonably good at figures, Miss Martin, and if I can be of any assistance in that way—' she broke off and looked at her employer who was nodding and obviously pleased at the offer.

'You could, and I would be most grateful. There are financial matters that I find confusing but they probably wouldn't be to you.'

'You trust me—'

'I pride myself that I am a good judge of character and I imagine Jenny Cuthbert is too. She speaks highly of you.'

'Do you know Jenny well?'

'I got to know her well when I was ill.'

'She came to help you – that would be like Jenny.'

'Yes, as you say, that was like Jenny. Knowing that, for most of the day, I would be on my own, she called round to see how I was. I must have looked a poor soul because she had her housekeeper prepare small nourishing meals and stood over me until I ate them.'

Beth laughed, picturing the scene.

'Proper bossy boots I told her she was and she heartily agreed.'

'Jenny was so good to me when I lost my parents.'

'I did hear about your tragic loss, Beth, and the difficult life you have led since.'

'One day I'll tell you about my parents. I would like to.'

She gave a small nod of her head. 'Thank you, and now I am going to tell you something that you may think peculiar coming from me. It concerns our mutual friend, Jenny, and I tell it only because you will hear it anyway and now you will be prepared.'

Beth looked mystified. 'Jenny would never do anything wrong,' she said stoutly.

That brought a delighted laugh from Anna. 'My dear child, none of us is perfect, Jenny included, we have all sinned. It is just that some folk make a habit of it, and for others it is just an occasional slip.'

'Yes, I know,' Beth said self-consciously. 'You see, Jenny is my very best friend.'

'Such loyalty and I do like that. Jealousy, Beth, is at the root of all evil or a large part of it, and Jenny happens to be an attractive widow of independent means with a number of male admirers. In a small village like this, platonic friendship is met with scepticism. No one believes in it and, with having men friends, it is only too easy to become the victim of gossip.'

Beth could believe that.

'Should you hear gossip, don't be tempted to vent your anger. Jenny wouldn't thank you. Ignore it and treat it with the contempt it deserves.'

'Why are some people so horrid?'

'Because, my dear, their own lives are so drab that they resent others enjoying theirs.'

'I find that sad.'

'So do I. Jenny has many friends, particularly among struggling artists. More than one, on the brink of despair, has left Jenny's house with food in his stomach and words of encouragement ringing in his ears.' She smiled. 'Some have gone on to do great things.'

'Jenny's grandmother was an artist.'

'Was she? That could account for her interest.' Miss Martin got up and walked to the window where the bright sunshine was streaming in. 'Such a pity to waste the summer, Beth, and since you live on the premises the work can be done at any time. You should make use of that bike of mine and get out and enjoy the best of the day.'

Beth enjoyed cycling and the freedom it gave her. The rain had fallen overnight, leaving the countryside fresh and green. Today she would get one or two bits of shopping in the village and then take the coast road, since there was nothing to hurry her.

Cycling along, she saw the artist in the distance. There was something familiar about the figure. She propped her bicycle against a post and began walking over the stony beach. Beth stopped well short of where he was working. She had no wish to disturb but she would enjoy watching him. Eventually it was he who turned.

'Don't move, just stay exactly as you are,' he said urgently. As she obeyed, he left his easel and took up his sketching pad. Just as she was beginning to get a crick in her neck, Peter smiled. 'Relax now, Beth, and thank you very much. That was a moment I wanted to capture.' He closed his sketching pad.

'Don't I get to see it?'

'Not yet.'

'I didn't think you knew I was there.'

'I knew someone was but that someone was obeying the rules.'

'What rules?'

'Never disturb an artist when he is working. Look by all means but do not give advice. We get heartily sick of that.'

'Surely no one would?'

'You'd be surprised and they think they are doing us a good turn.'

She was about to get up and go. 'No, don't go yet. I want to know what I have done that you haven't paid a return visit to 5 Summer Street.'

'It's not an excuse, Peter, I have been very busy. A lot has happened just lately, like getting myself a new job and accommodation.'

'I know about that.' He broke off a piece of chocolate and gave it to her.

'Thanks. What do you know?'

'Some writer has given you a job.'

'Anna Martin.'

'A bit eccentric, I hear.'

'She isn't, she's lovely.'

'Could be both. I like eccentric people, usually find them a lot more interesting.'

'Who told you?'

'Jenny. Who else could it have been?' He paused. 'It was just in case I put my foot in it and said the wrong thing – but I didn't get the chance to say anything. You didn't come and I was disappointed.'

She smiled. 'Maybe I would have wept all over you.'

'He's not worth a single tear.'

'I know.'

He saw the bleak expression and knew that she wasn't over it, the hurt had gone too deep. For a while they sat in a companionable silence and gazing out to sea.

'How lucky you are, Peter.'

'Am I?'

'You can lose yourself in your work and forget disappointments.'

'That is only partly true. We all have our hopes and dreams and when they don't look much like being realised we are just as likely to be hurt and depressed as the rest.'

She looked at him in surprise. It sounded as though he had been disappointed in love.

She got up. 'I'd better get my bike and be on my way.'

Peter got up too, fished in his pocket and drew out a bundle of keys. Selecting one he took it off the ring.

'Take that.'

'Why?'

'Because I want you to have it. Take that shocked expression off your face. We are friends and friends like to help one another. Could be a change of scenery would do you good. If you want to make yourself useful, I don't eat when I am working but I do like cups of tea.' His lips curved into a cheerful smile.

She put the key in her pocket. 'Thank you,' she said. 'I make a good cup of tea.'

The newspapers made a big splash of it. Beth saw it in the local paper. It was expected but it still came as an unpleasant shock when she read the announcement of the forthcoming marriage of Caroline Parker-Munro and Adrian Scott-Hamilton.

Robert Munro returned to Inverbrae House while it buzzed with excitement over the forthcoming marriage of the daughter of the house. He was to spend ten days with his relatives before returning to Australia. Caroline pleaded with her cousin to postpone his departure until after the wedding as did the colonel and Mrs Parker-Munro. If Robert had approved of the union, he may well have done so. But he had disliked Adrian on sight and the dislike was mutual.

Robert saw behind the charm, and wouldn't have trusted Adrian an inch, but he recognised that there was nothing he could do. He hadn't expected his grandmother to be taken in but she was captivated by all that charm and his uncle appeared to be well pleased with his future son-in-law.

Adrian was glad to see the back of Robert Munro. Once he was away, he began to spend most of his time at Inverbrae House. Already he was very much one of the family but Caroline did wish that he were more ardent. Why wasn't he? she thought crossly. She could hardly throw herself at him and there were some she knew who would say that it only showed the great respect he had for her.

She wished, too, that Adrian was a bit more forthcoming. Caroline was discovering that he didn't like to be questioned but surely, as his future wife, she had a right to know what he did. And since his family was in such straightened circumstances, and he the younger son, surely he must have some occupation. It was worrying Caroline enough to mention it to her father.

The colonel looked at her fondly. 'Darling, you must have embarrassed Adrian. He wouldn't expect that kind of question from you.'

'I can't see why not. I'm not a child and, for heaven's sake, this isn't the Victorian age.'

'Most men find women more attractive when they don't try to enter a man's world. Poor boy, he feels badly enough about having so little money. I am not in the least concerned, my dear, because Adrian will be involved in the running of the estate and I'll be glad to ease off.'

'Ease off? Are you ill, daddy?' Caroline said anxiously.

'Of course not, don't be silly, I'm as fit as a fiddle but I want my future son-in-law to be able to take over when the day comes that I am not so able.'

Caroline nodded. She could forget her niggling doubts since her father had none.

'I miss Robert,' Caroline said when she and Adrian were alone in the drawing-room.

'Do you? I don't.'

'You didn't like him. Why was that?'

He shrugged. 'Fellow doesn't know how to behave.'

'Rubbish, just because he has a friendly word with the servants.'

'Didn't you find it out of place?'

'Perhaps at first I did but life in Australia is very different to what it is here.'

'Don't give me that, Caroline. There is class difference down under just as there is here. Know what I think?'

'What do you think?'

'I'd say he comes from poor stock on his mother's side.' He paused and looked at her. 'Could be that his forebears were criminals shipped out there to do their sentence and stayed on.'

Caroline was shocked and angry. 'That is a terrible thing to say. Robert's family is very nice and his mother writes such lovely letters.'

'My sweet innocent, of course she does. There is plenty of money to be made on a sheep farm and the family would have received a good education but be totally lacking in—'

She didn't let him finish. 'Since Robert's father was daddy's brother, I find your remarks insulting and to suggest he has no—'

'Breeding?' He laughed a little unpleasantly. 'Your cousin Robert is short on that.'

He saw by her face that he had gone too far and quickly tried to make amends. 'Darling, apart from Robert, you haven't met the family.'

'We correspond regularly.'

'Hardly the same thing.' They were sitting together and he drew her near, kissed her lightly on the mouth and sighed. 'Darling, I do love you and I can't wait to make you mine. Only I'll have to—' He gave a wry smile.

Caroline snuggled closer and her annoyance disappeared. 'I love you, Adrian,' she said pressing her lips to his.

'Steady on, darling, I am only human.'

'Sorry,' she said blushing and giggling.

'We have all our tomorrows and the years ahead, just remember that.'

'It's a lovely, lovely thought,' she said blissfully.

'Know what suddenly came into my mind?'

She shook her head.

'Wouldn't it be awful if one day Robert were to inherit Inverbrae House? Don't look like that, my love, it could happen.' He paused and looked very serious. 'We must make sure it doesn't and that means having our family right away.'

Caroline felt the cold hand of fear grip her heart. One day, but well into the future, she supposed they would have a child but a family and right away—

Adrian saw her look of alarm.

'You do want children, my children, surely you do?'

'Yes, but I don't want the responsibility of motherhood for some years. I am young.'

'Young and pretty and adorable and all the more reason to get it over in the first years of marriage.'

'This is something that should be discussed after marriage and not before,' she said frostily.

'It embarrasses you?' he said gently.

'Yes, it does.'

'Then not another word on the subject and just as well because I hear voices and your grandmother's stick.'

There was a discreet knock at the door then Nigel and his mother entered. Adrian dashed over to help the old lady into a chair.

Caroline was quieter than usual and she was shivering with a nameless fear. Only it wasn't a nameless fear, she knew of what she was afraid. Her mother had died in childbirth.

The colonel and Adrian had gone round the estate and were now back and in the drawing-room. Adrian, in country tweeds, lounged with his legs out-stretched towards the fireside. There was no fire because the day was warm. Both were smoking cigars and the nearby table held drinks.

Mrs Esslemont had arrived to whisk her niece away for the first fitting of the wedding dress. After that it would be necessary to choose lightweight costumes, gowns and dresses for all occasions. Then would come the choosing of hats that were the very latest fashion. Aunt Gwen was in her element, loving every moment, while her niece tried to hide her tiredness.

The colonel was pleased with Adrian's show of interest in the estate and the questions he put. But like his daughter, though he had hidden it from her, other areas were giving him concern. Better to have it out now.

'Adrian?'

Adrian looked across at his future father-in-law with the satisfied smile that was so often on his face these days.

'We are sorry about your mother not being well enough to come with your father and spend a few days here. But time is getting on and I think you should take Caroline to meet your family.'

'Exactly what I had in mind,' Adrian said smoothly, though it was far from the truth. Making his mother the excuse, he had hoped that their first meeting would be at the wedding. He might have known that that wouldn't have gone down well with colonel and his mother. 'Actually, sir, I was to seek your permission to take Caroline to Bankhead next weekend when my brother and his wife would be there.'

'Splendid, my boy, and I know that Caroline is looking forward to meeting your family.'

Since money was so scarce, her expectations had not been too high but would she ever forget that weekend in Adrian's home?

When they set out it was a soft summer's day with the gentlest of breezes and the countryside was at its best. Adrian drove the colonel's car, having said that it would be more comfortable for Caroline than his own. She was happy knowing that she looked fresh and pretty in a fine linen dress in a lovely shade of lime green. It had a matching jacket which was on the back seat of the car.

'Know your history, do you?' Adrian smiled as they approached Stirling.

'A little but I haven't been this way before. Oh, look! The castle,' she said pointing to it eagerly.

'Difficult to miss. That castle, my dear Caroline, has a dark history, a tumultuous past, and it was the Stewarts who built the castle as you see it now.'

She was pleased that Adrian had an interest in history. 'I believe I read somewhere that Mary Queen of Scots, married her second husband, Lord Darnley, in Stirling Castle.'

'Clever girl.'

'Have we much further to go?'

'No, not far now.'

Adrian fell silent for the last few miles then he pointed to a building. 'That, before you, is Bankhead.'

Set on a rise with the sun glinting on it, the house looked impressive and Caroline began to look about her with interest. The approach through the wrought-iron gates was pleasant since the trees lining the drive hid the untidiness behind. Only when they drew near to the house did it become apparent that Bankhead, home of the Scott-Hamiltons, was run down and in a poor state of repair. An attempt had been made to keep the garden in front of the house tidy but the rest was overgrown and had been long neglected. Broken slates lay about the ground, blown down after the recent gales and never replaced.

Caroline looked for movement from the house but there was none. Getting out of the car, she couldn't hide her dismay.

'Should have warned you, I suppose. The place is a bit of a shambles and will be for as long as money is tight.'

'Pity to let it go like this. The worse it gets, the more will need to be spent on it.'

'That is father's problem and my brother's, not mine, thank God.'

She watched him take her case from the boot and still no one appeared. 'My jacket,' she said, seeing it on the back seat. 'I had better have it with me.'

Adrian got it for her and she took it from him to carry over her arm. They walked to the heavy door which was half open. In the large, dreary hall, an elderly maid came forward and took the case from Adrian.

'Take it to the room prepared for the young lady.'

'Very good, sir.'

After the heat of the car and the few minutes in the sunshine, indoors seemed chilly. Caroline was in two minds as to whether she should put on her jacket or not. Her arm was all goose pimples but she decided to suffer the cold for the moment. No doubt it would be warmer where they were going.

Taking her arm Adrian guided her through long corridors where some of the paintwork was peeling.

'It gets better,' Adrian said with an attempt at humour.

Caroline smiled weakly. She thought it could hardly get worse.

'Only one wing of the house is used and that I can promise you is quite comfortable.'

He proved to be right. This was more like it, Caroline thought with relief. There was a brightness here denied the rest of the house, or what she had seen of it and Caroline cheered up. Adrian stopped to open a door.

'Come and meet the family.'

Caroline had heard the low murmur of voices which stopped as they entered. Adrian stood aside to let her go ahead and her immediate impression was of a comfortable but over-furnished drawing-room. Four people were there and all eyes turned to the stranger. The two women were sitting together on the sofa.

'This is Caroline,' Adrian said bringing his fiancée forward, 'and Caroline,' he smiled down to her, 'this is my mother, my father, my brother and his wife Virginia.'

Caroline smiled and, feeling her lips quivering, wondered at her nervousness. She was used to being in company, to meeting people but, of course, this was different. These people were Adrian's family and she wanted them to like her.

Both men had got to their feet, and the florid-faced man

who was Adrian's father, came forward. He was smiling hugely.

'Such a pleasure to have you here. Welcome to Bankhead, my dear.'

'Thank you.'

Roderick Scott-Hamilton was as tall as Adrian and there was a strong resemblance between father and son. Caroline thought the older man must once have been as handsome as his younger son. They had the same regular features and charm of manner but the years or perhaps the lifestyle had not been kind. The face was fleshy, the eyes slightly bloodshot, and the figure was thickening.

Caroline felt his lips on her cheek and then he was taking her arm and leading her across the room. This wasn't as it should be. Adrian should be with her and not his father but Adrian had moved away to look out of the window. For someone who complained of bad manners in others, she thought crossly, his were quite appalling at times.

Adrian's mother was not as she expected her to be and yet, if someone had asked her what she had expected, she could not rightly have said. Marjorie Scott-Hamilton was nondescript, a plain woman who made no attempt to improve herself. She wore no make-up and with her sallow skin a light foundation and powder would have made a difference. Her hair was pepper and salt and she had a slide in it to keep it off her face. She did, however, have a nice smile and an attractive husky voice.

'Caroline, I am delighted to meet you and do let me apologise for being unable to accept your father's kind invitation. You see—'

'Mother!' Adrian had turned from the window and said swiftly, 'I explained to Caroline that you have been in poor health.'

'Yes, Adrian did, Mrs Scott-Hamilton. We were disappointed you couldn't come. Are you feeling better now?'

'My wife has been in delicate health for some time but she is determined to be well enough to attend the wedding.'

Caroline was irritated that Adrian's mother wasn't allowed to speak for herself. She seemed perfectly capable.

'I'll make sure she is.'

'Yes, Virginia, you do that.'

Virginia smiled. 'You sit here beside mother-in-law,' she said, getting up from the sofa. She was of medium height and on the plump side but her soft brown eyes held a warm smile.

'Let me introduce myself. I'm Michael.' Adrian's brother came over with an outstretched hand. Caroline took to him immediately. Like his mother he was very ordinary-looking but there was a gentleness that appealed to her and a message in the eyes, a hint that he recognised this was an ordeal.

Adrian's father spoke. 'While you are on your feet, Virginia, ring that bell, if you please.' The voice was clipped and angry.

'No need, I hear someone coming,' Virginia said shortly.

It was the same elderly servant who came in with the laden tray. With her was a very young girl who had the rest of the things.

'Shall I pour, m'am?' the elderly woman asked her mistress.

'No, I'll see to it.' She smiled. 'Thank you.'

'Very good, m'am.'

Virginia touched her mother-in-law on the shoulder. 'No, you sit still and keep Caroline company. I'll pour and Michael, dear, you'll hand them round, won't you?'

'A pleasure.' He looked at Caroline. 'How was the journey?'

'Before you answer that, Caroline, tell me how you like your tea.'

'A little sugar and rather a lot of milk, please.'

'That's the way I take it too. Michael calls it baby tea.'

'I suppose it is,' Caroline laughed, 'and as to the journey, Michael, it was very pleasant. Coming into Stirling, Adrian gave me a history lesson.'

'Did you now, my boy?' His father looked pleased, then frowned. 'Virginia, what is in those sandwiches?'

'I don't know. Shall I be naughty and take a peep inside to see?'

'Safer not to. I'll let myself be surprised.'

'Roderick, that was completely unnecessary as well as being unkind,' his wife said sharply. 'With so little help in the house, I think the servants do extremely well.'

'I couldn't agree more, Mother,' Michael said.

Adrian scowled. Roderick looked daggers at his wife and Virginia's lips quirked as though she were amused.

Caroline looked from one to the other in bewilderment. She was beginning to see this as a divided house – but why? Adrian and his father appeared to be close and the mother was supported by Virginia and Michael.

Whatever was in the sandwiches was tasty and Caroline, faddy with food, enjoyed hers.

'More tea, Caroline?'

'No, thank you, Mrs Scott-Hamilton, but that was very refreshing and I enjoyed it.'

'Perhaps you would like to see your room?'

'Yes, I would, please.'

'I'll come with you, Caroline,' said Virginia, putting down her cup. They excused themselves and left the room.

'Poor you, you are wondering what to make of them, aren't you?'

'I suppose I am.'

'Families can be the limit. The maid position is pretty desperate and that upsets mother-in-law.'

The bedroom was very nice and Caroline was well satisfied.

'The flowers were mother-in-law's idea. She is rather sweet.'

'Do you always call her mother-in-law?'

'Yes, can you think of something better?'

'Tricky?'

'Exactly.'

'Do you address your father-in-law that way too?'

She grinned. 'That and a few other names.'

They emptied the case and Virginia hung up the two dresses that Caroline had brought with her. 'Very pretty,' she remarked.

'Thank you.'

'Nice to be slim and dainty. No chance for me. I am too fond of my food.'

'May I ask you something, Virginia?'

'Ask away.'

'Why won't they let Mrs Scott-Hamilton speak for herself?'

'Afraid what she'll come away with. No, no, not quite as bad as that. I don't like my father-in-law, as you may have gathered. Like Adrian he was blessed with good looks and that brand of charm which frankly makes me sick – sorry, I'm just talking of the old man. He married for money, had his fling with other women and now, I believe, he has a mistress tucked away somewhere.'

'That's awful. But surely Adrian's mother put her foot down? I mean she was bringing money into the family—'

'Until he got the money into his own hands – and women in love are fools – he would act the loving husband.'

'If he wanted he could leave her since he has all her money.'

'Which is what would have happened according to Michael if she hadn't been left money by an aunt who had the sense to leave it in such a way that Roderick couldn't get his hands on it.'

'Why doesn't she leave him?'

'She wants to keep Bankhead going until Michael takes over and that might be sooner than you think. The old boy drinks heavily and when he has the money gambles the night away. The doctor has warned him to cut down on the drink but frankly I don't think he can. Look, we'd better go down now but don't worry, there will be time for a chat later on if you want to hear more.'

'Since I am to be part of this family I had better know about them and Adrian doesn't tell me much. It won't make any difference to my feelings for Adrian,' she hastily added.

'If you are truly in love nothing else matters. Michael and I are very lucky,' she said softly.

Later on, Adrian was at his most charming and drove her into the countryside where he pointed out places of interest. Some of the amusing tales he told her had her laughing delightedly. This was the Adrian she loved and she could have forgiven him anything.

'You do love this part of the country don't you, Adrian?'

'Yes, I do,' he said quietly.

'There must be times when you wished you were the elder brother?'

'What good would that do, wishing something that can

never be? You are right though, there are times—'

'Tell me what happened to the family fortunes.' She kept her voice light.

'You are one for questions, aren't you?'

'I want to know about your family, Adrian. After all, you know about mine.'

'The sad tale of Bankhead? All right, my dearest, here it is. Once upon a time, if I may borrow the fairytale beginning, ours was one of the finest houses for miles around. But sadly my grandfather was what is now termed a compulsive gambler. We can stop here for tea if you wish,' he said, slowing down opposite a tea-room.

'No, go on, please.' Stop now and she would never hear the story of the Scott-Hamiltons. It was just an excuse to change the subject.

'Grandfather's gambling set the rot in and when he died my father inherited a load of debt and with every chance of being declared bankrupt.'

'That must have been dreadful!'

'It was and, very stupidly, my father tried his hand at gambling himself, hoping to be lucky. And he was. Luck was with him and everything would have been fine if he had had the sense to leave it at that but no, he thought his luck would hold.'

'It didn't?'

'Very nearly back to square one.'

'He doesn't gamble now?'

Adrian laughed. 'He doesn't have the money, Michael sees to that, but I am afraid it is once a gambler always a gambler.' He glanced sideways. 'Don't look so worried, Caroline. Neither Michael nor I have the least interest in gambling. We saw at first hand what it could do.'

'I'm glad you've told me, Adrian. I understand now why you didn't want to talk about your home.' She smiled and studied his profile and thought again how lucky she was to be marrying someone so handsome. Then, hoping to cheer him up, she said, 'In time Michael may bring Bankhead back to its former glory.'

'Might well have, had he married wealth instead of Virginia.'

'That wasn't a very nice thing to say and I like Virginia,' Caroline said reprovingly.

'Do you? I don't and happily our paths seldom cross. This was just a special occasion in your honour.'

Caroline was silent for a little then decided she would say it.

'Adrian, in Michael's place would you have married for money?'

'Perhaps.' Then, seeing her face, he added, 'It was a joke, Caroline.'

'I sincerely hope so.'

He took one hand off the steering wheel and squeezed hers. 'Darling, I am honest enough to admit that I am glad you are not penniless. But had you been, it would have made no difference. You are, for me, the girl of my dreams.'

She smiled tremulously. Nothing else mattered, they loved each other and once they were married and living in Inverbrae House, only an occasional visit to Bankhead would be necessary.

When they returned Caroline was flushed and happy. She would have a leisurely bath and take special care over her appearance.

In the long dress with its full skirt and sweetheart neckline, Caroline looked sweet and pretty and the gentlemen eyed her with appreciation.

Virginia gave a nod of approval and Mrs Scott-Hamilton spoke softly.

'Caroline, my dear, you look enchanting.'

'Picked a peach, my boy.'

Was it the voice or something in the older man's face that made Caroline uncomfortable? She was deciding that, like Virginia, she didn't much like her future father-in-law.

'Thank you for the flowers in my bedroom, Mrs Scott-Hamilton. They are lovely and it was a nice thought.'

She smiled. 'Flowers are my greatest joy but sadly we cannot afford the gardeners—'

'Shall we sit down?' a voice said loudly.

'Yes, Roderick, we shall all take our places.'

The dining-room was well decorated and well furnished. The silver and crystal sparkled and Caroline could not have faulted the table. She rather thought that it wouldn't be this grand most of the time but she was pleased someone, most likely Mrs Scott-Hamilton, had gone to this trouble on her behalf.

Virginia wore a long, black skirt and an emerald green blouse. She looked nice. Adrian's mother had on a cerise silk suit that when new must have cost a lot but it looked old-fashioned and where her figure had expanded it showed unbecoming bulges.

There were no awkward silences during the meal and everybody appeared to be making an effort to keep the conversation going. Dinner was as formal as at Inverbrae House, only the service was slower. Roderick Scott-Hamilton, from his place at the head of the table, had them laughing at some amusing stories and she was reminded of Adrian who had had her smiling at his. In many ways Adrian resembled his father but in what really mattered they were totally unalike. She knew quite a bit about this family but she knew there was more to learn, particularly about her future mother-in-law. She watched her when this was possible. She smiled a lot, as nervous people did, and her hands when not engaged with cutlery were never still. She said very little but when Michael spoke, the smile she bestowed on him was full of mother love. Not once did she look in her husband's direction and when he spoke she looked down at the table. How could they live like that, Caroline wondered.

After coffee Mrs Scott-Hamilton excused herself and went upstairs to her bedroom. Michael and his father disappeared to discuss some business and Adrian got up and stretched himself.

'The very last thing I want to do this evening is go out.'

'Then don't, stay in. I'm quite happy.'

'You are?' he said, looking immensely relieved. 'That makes me feel less guilty, Caroline, because I simply must get some business done while I am here and in a way you are to blame—'

'Me?'

'Haven't I been spending most of my time at Inverbrae House?'

'True,' she dimpled prettily.

'And because of it I have neglected my business here.'

Virginia shot him a look of amusement mixed with contempt but Caroline didn't notice.

'If you say so.'

It was all so easy and he wanted to hoot with laughter. His business tonight was with an actress whose voluptuous figure partly compensated for her poor acting ability. She knew to expect him and would be ready and waiting.

'May I go?'

'Of course, darling.' She held up her face for his kiss. 'Virginia and I will have lots to talk about.'

'Lots and lots,' Virginia said and saw his scowl. Caroline missed it.

★ ★ ★

They were on their own. 'Adrian did tell me about his grandfather being a compulsive gambler and his father inheriting a lot of debt and how he tried to pay it off by more gambling.'

'You know it, then.'

'Not all, and it doesn't explain Mrs Scott-Hamilton.'

'I like her but let us be brutally frank. I am no oil painting but mother-in-law is plain and she was as a young woman. No sparkling conversationalist either, so what was the attraction for the handsome Roderick?'

'Money,' said Caroline quietly.

'Exactly.'

'But you told me that before.'

'I wanted to repeat it. Her family were very wealthy and after her parents died she was brought up by her grandmother. She tried everything to stop her marrying Roderick Scott-Hamilton but she was determined and she defied her grandmother and eloped with Roderick.'

'With a happy ending, that would have been very romantic.'

'Sadly her happiness didn't last long. But she had her pride and she pretended all was well and that suited his lordship. They had two sons.'

'And Michael is her favourite?'

'No use denying what is obvious but she did try always to treat the boys alike. Their father didn't. He had no time for Michael but he adored his handsome son.'

'Adrian can't help being good looking.'

'Of course not, but I'm just trying to give you a picture of what this family was like. There comes a time in a person's life when she can take no more and mother-in-law had reached it. She did have a sort of breakdown and it resulted in depression.'

'But not mentally disturbed?' Caroline had heard her grandmother use the term for one of her friends.

'Not seriously, and she is perfectly all right now. But just to spite her husband and get her own back, and I'm sure that is what it is, she pretends not to be. Roderick is always afraid of what she will come out with.'

'Oh, dear, it is all so different from my own family.'

Virginia smiled. 'Adrian, naturally enough, wanted to keep the family difficulties from you.'

'Not much happiness in this house?'

'No, as you say, not much happiness. Michael and I have suggested that she make her home with us and she says nothing would please her more but she is determined that Michael will one day have Bankhead. For that to happen, she has to keep an eye on her husband.'

'Adrian loves this house, you know.'

'Yes, we know that.'

# Chapter Twenty-Eight

The great day had arrived and, after the long dry spell, there were fears that it couldn't last. In fact, there had been short sharp showers the previous day, which had served to freshen the countryside and make this July morning quite perfect for Caroline's wedding. The sky was clear, the sun shone and there wasn't a breath of wind. Inside Inverbrae House, the servants had been up since the crack of dawn, and a great deal of the activity was coming from the kitchens.

After a lot of careful consideration, the marquee had been erected on the lawn to the side of the house. This area near to the rose gardens and flower beds was favoured because guests standing nearby would be able to smell the heady perfume drifting across. Quietly and efficiently a small band of workmen were going about the business of erecting tables and placing chairs for the less able who might require them. About nine o'clock a van drew up in front of the house and armfuls of flowers were taken indoors, while other blooms and a number of floral baskets were left beside the marquee.

Caroline had spent a restless night and woke early sick with excitement and an uneasy fear. Of what was she afraid? She kept telling herself there was nothing. After all, Adrian could hardly be held responsible for his family, indeed his reluctance to have her meet them was understandable and stemmed from embarrassment. Everything was going to be lovely and this was just silly pre-wedding nerves. Adrian loved her, had told her so repeatedly and he had completely bewitched her grandmother and charmed Aunt Gwen. Even daddy was won over and he wasn't easy to hoodwink.

Why, on this morning of all mornings, did Beth have to come into her thoughts? Was it because Beth had never lied to her? But there was a first time for everything, and the truth could only be that Beth was consumed with jealousy. There could be no other explanation for her conduct.

Had it just been Beth, she could have dismissed it. But Caroline thought now of that other person who didn't approve of Adrian, although he hadn't actually said so. That, she reminded herself, had been no more than a clash of personalities, and the dislike had been mutual.

There was a light tap at the door and a maid came in with a breakfast tray, interrupting her thoughts and perhaps just as well.

'Take it back,' she said sharply.

The girl looked uncertain as to what to do.

'I said take it back.'

'Yes, Miss Caroline.' She went out and returned later with fingers of dry toast and a pot of tea.

'I may manage that. You can leave it.'

Looking relieved, the maid put the tray on a table beside the bed and hurried out. Caroline lifted a piece of toast and nibbled at it, then took another. She drank a cup of tea and felt a little better.

The thought that this would be the last time she would sleep alone and in this room gave her a peculiar lost feeling but at least she wasn't leaving Inverbrae House. This would continue to be her home and in many ways her life would not change all that much. Perhaps she should start exercising her authority, insist that she was consulted on all matters that concerned herself. She had been more than annoyed, she had been extremely angry that they – her husband-to-be, her father and her grandmama – had gone over her head in a matter that concerned her personally.

Starting their married life in another wing of the house would have given them privacy and be much more romantic. She had been very much in favour of it. But, no, all that had been taken care of, and daddy and grandmama couldn't hide their delight when Adrian had expressed a wish that they live as a family and dine together. Much better, he explained and showing great concern, that Caroline should not be alone when he had to be away on business which would be necessary from time to time. What business? For all her questions, Caroline hadn't had a satisfactory answer to that one.

The ceremony was over. They were married. Handsome, darling Adrian was her husband and Caroline was blissfully happy with all the attention she was getting. She looked lovely, a radiant bride, everybody said so. Her wedding dress, with the many hours of work spent on it, was beautiful and brought gasps of delight from those gathered around the church. Eagerly they watched the arrival of guests and then the great excitement came when the bride and her father arrived. Emma Watson, no longer plump, made an attractive bridesmaid and was receiving a lot of attention from the best man, a cousin of Adrian's.

A few miles away in Lilac Lodge, Beth's thoughts were with Caroline. She hoped and prayed that this would turn out to be a happy marriage. And perhaps it had a good chance. With Adrian living in Inverbrae House and under the watchful eyes of the colonel and the old lady, he would surely have the sense to be on his best behaviour. Adrian knew on which side his bread was buttered.

Beth was at Greystanes having afternoon tea with Jenny.

'More tea, Beth?'

'No, thank you, Jenny, that was lovely and now I really must—'

'Another few minutes, do stay a little longer, dear, there is something I want to ask.' She got up and put the tray on a table ready for Miss Harris to collect, and then went back to her chair.

'Something you want to ask me?'

'Yes. Tell me, do you have any contact with Inverbrae House?'

'None at all. Have you?' she asked in surprise. She wondered if the old romance with the colonel was on again.

'Not directly, but I do hear and the news is not good. Colonel Parker-Munro has suffered a slight stroke.'

Beth looked shocked and concerned. 'That's terrible and hard to believe, I mean he always looked so – so—'

'Healthy? Yes, poor Nigel, I feel so very, very sorry about it. But thankfully it was not severe and though it is unlikely that he will ever be one hundred percent, there is no reason why he shouldn't enjoy a full and happy life. Unfortunately he is making little effort to help himself and appears to have lost interest in everything, including the estate.' She stopped to drink some tea, then put down her cup. 'Knowing Nigel as I do, Beth, I can understand it. He's never had a day's illness in his life, apart from the minor complaints we all have from time to time, and this must have been a devastating blow.'

'It's all so sad, so terribly sad.'

'You are wondering how Caroline is managing?'

'Yes.'

'Then be assured Caroline is coping extremely well. All the more credit to her since the poor girl has had such a bad time.'

'Why? What? Has she been ill?'

'Very ill, indeed for a while it was touch and go. Caroline had a miscarriage, Beth, and things went badly wrong. That could well have been what brought on Nigel's stroke.'

'That could be, Jenny. The colonel would have been nearly out of his mind with worry and Caroline would be so afraid—' Beth's voice wobbled. 'She once told me that she was afraid to have a baby—'

'Because her mother had died in childbirth? Poor little Caroline, and she would have had no one to turn to.'

'I wish, I wish, I wish I could have been there to help her.'

'It wasn't your fault that you weren't and perhaps some good has come out of it. Caroline knows now that she is perfectly able to stand on her own two feet and that will help in the years to come.'

'Is she happy with Adrian?'

'No is the short answer to that but she is pretending that all is well.' She frowned. 'In a few weeks, when I think Nigel has come to terms with his slight disability, I shall go to Inverbrae House.' She smiled across to Beth. 'The old lady, bless her, is so confused that she may even welcome me with open arms.'

Beth tried to smile but made a poor job of it.

Beth was usually the one to answer the door to callers but Anna did since she was nearest. The woman standing on the doorstep was a stranger.

'Would it be possible for me to see Miss Brown?' she asked.

'Yes, I'll get Beth for you but do come in.'

Anna Martin showed the woman into the sitting-room, got her seated then went along to where Beth was pouring over a manuscript before beginning to type.

'Don't tell me that after all this time you are finding difficulty with my writing,' Anna laughed.

'No, I can make it out but find it safer to read it over first.'

'Wise, and you, Beth, have a visitor, a woman, I've shown her into the sitting-room.'

'Who is it, do you know?' Beth asked. Aunt Anne wouldn't come here but who else could it be?

'I didn't enquire but on you go quickly and find out.'

The woman got to her feet when Beth entered.

'Mrs Murdoch!' Beth couldn't hide her surprise at seeing the housekeeper from Inverbrae House.

'Hello, Beth. I hope you don't mind me coming like this but I'm so worried.'

'Sit down, Mrs Murdoch,' Beth said gently, and when she did Beth sat down herself. 'Of course I don't mind you coming but does it mean that something is wrong?'

'Very far wrong, Beth. Inverbrae House is nothing like it used to be.'

'Is Caroline – Mrs Scott-Hamilton, ill again?'

'You heard then?'

'I heard she had lost her baby.'

'Poor lass, the doctors despaired of saving her and the master was nearly out of his mind. In a state I was myself, I can tell you. But you must be wondering what I am doing here and I have to say I have no business.'

'Mrs Murdoch, if I can be of any help you have only to ask. Did Mrs Scott-Hamilton suggest you get in touch with me?'

'No, Beth, she didn't but that is just pride. Whatever the quarrel you two had was about, it is time to make it up. I'm speaking out of turn but I know the young mistress needs you. She has no one else to turn to.'

'What about her husband?'

Mrs Murdoch all but sniffed. 'That gentleman does exactly as he pleases. It's God's truth that he wasn't there when his wife was at death's door. He is away a lot and I'm glad to see the back of him.'

'Surely with Colonel Parker-Munro the way he is, Mr Scott-Hamilton should be seeing to the estate.' Beth spoke indignantly, then remembered that it was none of her business.

'That's what you would expect. There is a lass doing the job you did in that office but Mr Blair says she doesn't get through half the work you did.'

Beth smiled. 'Would you like me to come with you now?'

'Nothing I would like better.'

'I'll tell Miss Martin and get my coat.'

'Bless you, lass.'

It was as it had always been with no outward sign of the unhappiness within. Mrs Murdoch expected the old lady to be in the sitting-room and most likely dozing. She had cat-naps all day. She smiled as she said it.

They went in by the side door and Beth was left to wait in the breakfast-room. Looking around her, Beth thought of the times she had eaten in this room and then of her dismissal from the house and for some unaccountable reason began to feel nervous. She couldn't blame her sudden appearance on Mrs Murdoch since that woman had exacted a promise from Beth that her part would not be mentioned.

Beth need not have worried about her welcome. Caroline opened the door of the breakfast room and stared for a few unbelieving moments. Then, with a choking sob, she dissolved into floods of tears.

'You came! Oh, Beth, the times I've wanted you.' Caroline tried to smile through her tears as Beth's comforting arms went round her.

'If I had known you wanted me I would have come.' Now that she had her first good look at Caroline, Beth was shocked at the change. The little-girl look had gone. This was the face of a young woman who had suffered and was still suffering.

'This is my prayer answered.'

'Caroline, why didn't you get in touch?' Beth said gently.

'How could I after all the dreadful things I said? How do you like living and working with that eccentric writer, I can't remember her name?'

'Anna Martin is a lovely person, Caroline, and she is both my friend and employer.'

'Come on, we can't talk here, we'll go to our own room. Would you believe, it is exactly as it was, I didn't want to change anything. When I'm feeling low,' she gave a mirthless laugh, 'which is most of the time, I go there and remember happier days.'

They were in the room they had shared as girls and Beth looked about her. 'All just as I remembered,' she said softly.

'We'll have tea brought here later but for now I just want to talk and talk and talk. You see, Beth, there hasn't been a single soul that I could confide in. Only you. Did you ever miss me?' she said wistfully.

'Often and I never stopped thinking of you as my friend.'

'More like sisters until things started to go wrong. Mostly my fault but there is no use crying over spilt milk, is there?'

'None at all,' Beth answered as Caroline led her to the sofa. They sat together, half-facing each other.

'So much to tell but where to begin.'

'Remember I was always a good listener.' Beth put one hand over Caroline's. Her hand was warm and Caroline's cold.

She nodded. 'Am I forgiven?'

'Forgiven and all forgotten.'

'Forgiven, I hope so, but forgetting is too much to expect.' She was very pale, her face had thinned down and her eyes were enormous in her small face. Pretty would no longer be a fitting description. Beth thought she looked delicately beautiful but as if a puff of wind would blow her away.

'All forgotten, Caroline. I have a convenient memory and I can blot out what I don't want to remember.'

'Lucky you. I have such a confusion of thoughts going through my mind that I don't know where to begin.'

'At the very beginning and take it slowly. My employer is very understanding and I can do the work at anytime.'

'The beginning,' Caroline said with a grimace. 'Had I paid attention to your warning there would be no sad tale to relate. You do know about daddy?'

'Yes, I heard and I'm very, very sorry.'

'Who told you?'

'Jenny.'

'You still keep up?'

'Yes.'

'That was all grandmama's fault. I liked Jenny and I missed her when she stopped coming. As a matter of fact, next to you, she was the only person I could have confided in. Daddy missed her too, I'm sure he did.'

'Would your father like Jenny to come and see him? She would like to, I know, but she doesn't want to upset him.'

'She wouldn't. I think he is beginning to accept the situation and the doctor has been at pains, and so has the specialist, to make him understand that this was a very slight stroke, a warning to take things easier and stop worrying.'

'Easier said than done.'

'I know. Poor daddy never expected anything like this. You tell Jenny from me that she is just the tonic daddy needs. She is both bossy and kind and he gets enough sympathy. A good talking to from Jenny will stop him feeling so sorry for himself.'

Beth was amazed. This was a new Caroline.

'I lost my baby,' Caroline said abruptly, 'and don't say you are sorry because I am not. I was glad. It was never a real baby, I mean I never held it in my arms. Beth, I love babies but I didn't want Adrian's because by the time I was pregnant I knew he was cheating on me. He had a mistress in Stirling, still has, and makes frequent visits there – it's supposed to be on business but it wasn't long before I knew exactly the kind of man I was married to.' She spoke bitterly, talking fast.

'Calm down, Caroline, take it easy. We can talk into the evening if necessary.'

'I have so much to tell you but, all right, I'll calm down.' She took a deep breath and began again but this time she spoke naturally. 'You cannot even begin to imagine what it is like for me to talk to you and know what I'm saying will never reach another soul. The baby, I was telling you about the baby—' She clutched at Beth's hand. 'Adrian nearly went mad when I lost it.'

'Then that showed—'

'That he cared about me?' Caroline's laughter was verging on the hysterical. 'Beth, Adrian cares nothing for me, even when it was touch and go as to whether or not I would live, he wasn't here. Had I died he would have wept no tears but losing the baby was different. If I can put it crudely, that was to be his meal ticket, his hold on Inverbrae House and all it stands for. With his child, the heir, his future was assured but with no child he could not be sure. He knew that I was wise to his wicked ways. Am I making sense?'

'Yes, Caroline, you are.'

'His hope was to get me pregnant again and this time produce a baby. I told him there would be no more babies. I told him I couldn't have one now but he wouldn't believe me. He told me I was a coward and called me a few choice names that he felt I deserved.'

'Caroline, I am so shocked I don't know what to say.'

'Not surprised though, are you?'

'I thought him ruthless but this is so much worse, you are painting a picture of a monster.'

'I am married to a handsome monster but one day, and very soon I hope, I'll be free of him.'

'Divorce him?'

'Yes. When I die, and since I can't have children, Robert is the next heir.'

'I begin to see now.'

'Good.'

'I don't know much about these things, Caroline, but I imagine you need proof. Are you quite sure that Adrian has a mistress?'

'His sister-in-law, who has no time for him, told me. I like her and I like my mother-in-law.' She made a face. 'Not my father-in-law though and that should have warned me. Once he must have been very like Adrian, same looks, same charm, but those have gone and he just looks dissolute.'

'What about your mother-in-law?'

'She is what I could become if I don't watch myself. She has been unwell for a long time and no wonder, all her money has gone or the bulk of it. She does have some, a bequest from an aunt I think, and that is left in such a way that her husband can't get his hands on it. Michael watches that his mother doesn't weaken and let him have it.'

'Does your father know all this? He can't or surely he would act.'

'You are thinking of daddy as he was, not as he is. Honestly, Beth, there are times when I get so angry with him that I could scream.'

'When he is himself again he will come down on Adrian.'

'Better be soon then.'

'What do you mean by that?' Beth felt a cold shiver down her spine.

'Since he had the stroke daddy just signs anything Adrian puts before him.'

'You need advice, Caroline, professional advice,' Beth said urgently. 'You must not let this run on. Adrian could be ruining you.'

'Exactly. He doesn't even bother to lock up his papers because he thinks I am too stupid to understand.'

'Then he certainly under-estimates you.'

'Yes, Beth, he does.' She looked suddenly drawn and tired and put a hand to her head. 'There is so much more to tell.'

'Not until we have tea. You look as though you could do with a cup.'

'I wouldn't say no and you could do with one as well. Excuse me.' She crossed the room, opened the door and called out to someone. 'Wait! Mrs Murdoch! I'm glad I caught you. You'll never guess whom I have beside me. Beth.'

'Beth!' the housekeeper exclaimed and Beth heard the exaggerated surprise. 'Well, I never!'

'Bring tea, will you?'

'That I will, m'am, and right away.'

Caroline came back. 'Not another word about my troubles until we have had tea. Tell me about yourself. You look happy but then you are, aren't you?'

'Yes, I am very lucky. Miss Martin couldn't be nicer. I can come and go as I please but she would worry if I were very late and I like it that way. It means that she cares about me.'

The tea came and they drank it, each having a second cup and a fairy cake. Beth gathered up the dishes and carried the tray to a table near the door for the maid to collect.

'Caroline, why don't you write to Robert and get his advice?'

'I already have. That is the next bit you were to hear. Robert is married.'

'To Gemma?'

'You knew about Gemma?'

'Robert asked me to have dinner with him one evening and just in case I got any wrong ideas he told me that there was a girl back home.'

'I do love Robert, he's closer than a cousin and more like the brother I never had.' She laughed, 'This must sound so silly, cloak and dagger stuff, but I don't want Adrian to get hold of Robert's letters. He would read them you know. Imagine me asking this kind of favour of a housekeeper but Mrs Murdoch has a good idea that things are not as they should be and she has difficulty hiding her dislike of Adrian. Robert puts my letters in an envelope addressed to Mrs Murdoch and that way there is no danger of them falling into Adrian's hands. Is your head buzzing or can you take more?'

'I'll try. I want to understand as much as possible and that way I may be able to help.'

'You are, just by being here and listening.' She paused and seemed to be trying to organise her thoughts. 'Adrian's home, as you may know, is in Stirling. When he took me to meet his parents, Beth, the place was a shambles. No use going into the details but gambling debts were responsible. As I said previously, Adrian thinks he is married to a simpleton and it suits me to let him go on thinking that. It makes him careless and I have proof that he is taking money from Inverbrae and spending it on Bankhead.'

'Bankhead being the family home?'

'Yes. Gradually and at our expense, Bankhead is being restored to its former glory.'

'But that is stealing, a criminal offence!' Beth was horrified.

'He has daddy's signature and I told you daddy signs anything.'

'Then you must put a stop to it.'

'I have,' Caroline said triumphantly. 'I had a long session with our solicitor and put him fully in the picture.'

'Very sensible.'

'Nothing goes through now without my signature and a particularly big withdrawal has been cancelled.'

'How was that managed?'

'The solicitor had our doctor issue a certificate to the effect that his patient is not sufficiently recovered to be in control of his affairs.'

'I'm so glad,' Beth breathed. 'I couldn't bear to think of Adrian getting away with it though I suppose he has got away with some.'

'Not as much as he believes. I rather think the work has gone ahead on the strength of that large withdrawal and he is going to be one very worried man when he finds out.' She gripped Beth's hand with such ferocity that Beth winced. 'I sound brave and I am anything but. Beth, I'm so scared, scared of what he'll do to me if, when, he finds out.'

'There has to be a way out of this.'

'There is but it is the waiting. Robert and Gemma are due here in three weeks but that is still three weeks to get through.'

Beth gave a sigh of relief. 'Don't worry, Caroline. Your solicitor is in possession of the facts and he has the legal jargon. He is sure to come up with a plausible reason why the money must remain where it is for a further twenty-one days or whatever.'

'And by that time Robert will be here! If it works out like that, it will be wonderful.'

'It will and Robert will be well able for Adrian.'

'I've kept him informed so he's coming prepared. Beth, I'm divorcing Adrian but I'm not facing him with it until I have Robert's support.'

'How long will Robert and Gemma stay?'

Caroline stared. 'Haven't I made it clear?'

'No, not to me.'

'This is to be their home. Robert will help daddy with the estate and one day it will belong to him.'

'Caroline,' Beth said gently. 'All this has been terrible for you but soon you will be able to put it behind you and find happiness with someone else.'

'No,' she said firmly. 'I will never marry again but I

shall spend the rest of my life here in Inverbrae House. Gemma and I have been corresponding and I told her they could be quite separate in a wing of the house, that we don't have to fall over each other, and do you know what she wrote back?'

'No.'

'She said both Robert and she are used to families and there would be no separate wing. We would all dine together and she would help me with grandmama since she is used to old people.'

'She sounds lovely.'

They sat and looked at one another, the two friends who had met as six-year-olds.

'Thank you for listening, Beth.' Her eyes were moist.

'Caroline, I am just so proud of you. Once your father is his old self, he is going to be very proud of his daughter and so he should.'

Caroline giggled and for a moment it was a glimpse of the old Caroline. 'When Aunt Gwen hears about the divorce, she is going to be reaching for the smelling salts. In her family and ours too, divorce is a dirty word.'

'I shouldn't worry about that. Cheap at the price just to be rid of him.' She smiled. 'Speaking of your Aunt Gwen, how is Ruth?'

'Blooming. Happy and contented. They have two children, a girl and a boy. Ruth helps out in the practice when she can. They live in a poor quarter of the city and do a lot of good work. Ian is very much thought of and not only by those he helps but others in high places. Aunt Gwen is quite chuffed about that. I think she has hopes of some honour for her son-in-law.'

'I'm glad Ruth is happy. She deserves to be. And now, Caroline, I must go and get my bus.'

'You'll do no such thing. Tommy will drive you back

and promise me you'll come again and soon?'

'I promise but phone if you need me in a hurry. Remember now!'

They hugged each other and a maid was sent to find Tommy. When he came he could hardly believe his eyes.

'Quite like old times,' he said as she got in beside him. There was a baby now and most of the talk was about Tommy junior and just how bright the child was. Beth was happy to listen.

So anxious was Beth to share her worries with Jenny that, when the door to Greystanes opened, she was breathless from hurrying. As always, Jenny greeted Beth with a light kiss and a warm welcome.

The early spring day was bright and cold and Beth wore a tweed skirt in a mixture of golds and browns and over it a boxy jacket in a light shade of camel. Her dark hair was cut short and shaped to her head, and the cold wind had whipped the colour into her cheeks.

'A picture of health,' Jenny said admiringly. She gave a mock shiver and closed the door. 'You obviously don't feel the cold.'

'Only because I was hurrying. Jenny, I have so much to tell you.' She almost babbled the words.

'All in good time, my dear. Slip off your jacket and hang it up, then come along to the sitting-room. News good or bad, is better received when one is sitting comfortably. At least it is for those of us who have gone beyond the first flush of youth!' She spoke drily but with a twinkle in her eye.

'Jenny, it isn't good, in fact it is all very sad,' Beth called after her as she put her jacket on a coat hanger and hung it up on a peg.

The sitting-room was comfortably warm with the heat

of the sun playing on the window and a small fire burning. They sat in a chair at either side of the fireplace. Jenny wore a dress in an unusual shade of mustard with long amber beads round her neck.

'This can only concern Inverbrae House?'

'Yes, it does.' Beth leaned forward. 'Mrs Murdoch came to see me. Anna let her in and honestly, Jenny, I nearly fainted when I saw her there, I was so surprised.'

Jenny raised her eyebrows. 'If Mrs Murdoch went the length of calling on you then she must be very worried.' She paused. 'Unless, of course, she was just bringing a message from Caroline?'

Beth shook her head vigorously. 'Caroline knew nothing of her visit and Mrs Murdoch made me promise not to tell her.'

'And you gave that promise?'

'Yes. Jenny, I was so worried that I asked Anna if I could go back with Mrs Murdoch. When we got to Inverbrae House I was shown into the breakfast-room and a maid went to tell Caroline.'

'What kind of reception did you get?'

'I was nervous but I needn't have been.'

'She was delighted to see you?'

'Yes, she was. Jenny, the change in Caroline is frightening.' She didn't realise what she was doing but she had gripped Jenny's hands.

'What do you mean?' Jenny said sharply. 'Or is it just that you haven't seen Caroline since she lost the baby?'

Beth shook her head slowly. 'It is more than that. She told me everything, Jenny, about Adrian and the dreadful life she has with him.'

'That shouldn't surprise you, since you had first-hand experience of the type of person he is. To your credit, you did your best to warn Caroline.'

'I know but I can't blame Caroline for thinking it was jealousy on my part. I may have thought the same in her place, particularly when Adrian is so well thought of by those whose opinion she values.'

They were both silent for a little while. Miss Harris came in with tea and the conversation became general.

'Let me hear the rest,' Jenny said when they were alone again. 'Then we can discuss it and see what, if anything, can be done. Help is one thing and interference quite another.'

'I know that, Jenny, but you'll want to help Caroline when you hear what I have to tell you.'

Jenny poured tea into the cups.

'This is really quite dreadful,' Jenny said looking shocked and angry. 'That odious creature must not get away with it and as to Nigel—'

'Forgot to tell you that bit. Caroline said she did wish you would come, she's missed you. Not like Caroline but she did say this, that her father gets too much sympathy and that you are the one to talk some sense into him.'

'She said that? Poor, brave little soul, I always thought there was more to Caroline than the spoilt little girl she always appeared.'

'You will go to Inverbrae House, won't you, Jenny?'

'Yes, Beth, I'll go and see Nigel. From all accounts his was a very mild stroke but it was a terrible shock to his system. Nigel was never the most patient with illness in others and he obviously hasn't faced up to his. But he will if I have anything to do with it,' she said firmly.

'You won't turn him against Adrian. He won't hear anything against him.'

'Probably no one has said anything against him and that is the trouble. An intelligent man like Nigel is bound to know that things are not as they should be. In the helpless state he considers himself to be in, though, he's just opted for the easy way out and done the unforgivable. He signed his name without knowing what he was signing away.'

The tea was cold by now but they both drank and made a face. 'Shall I get fresh, have you time?'

'No, Jenny, I haven't,' Beth said preparing to rise, 'but thank you for listening. I don't know what I would do without you.'

Jenny patted her arm. 'You would manage but, never fear, we'll get this sorted out.'

# Chapter Twenty-Nine

Over in Inverbrae House, there were obvious signs of preparation for the arrival of Robert and Gemma Munro from Australia. Caroline had made no mention of it to her husband and, strangely enough, no one else had either. Had Adrian been his normal self he would have noticed and questioned what was going on but worry clouded the handsome face. The restoration of Bankhead was well advanced but accounts demanding payment were beginning to arrive. Their non-payment was causing consternation and Adrian pictured ahead the nasty scenes when no money was forthcoming.

Plausible excuses for withholding the money had been made by the smooth-tongued solicitor for Inverbrae House but Adrian was uneasy and he was no fool. Something had gone very far wrong but how? He had been so careful, and he was almost convinced that his father-in-law was not responsible. After all, wasn't he just too relieved to have his son-in-law see to everything? The old lady could be ruled out, since she hardly knew the time of day. That left his silly, bird-brained wife but had he been wrong about Caroline? Had he under-estimated her? There had been times when he had been careless about locking up documents. His face hardened. If it turned out to be the truth he would make her suffer. Already she had cheated him out of an heir and a comfortable future and if she were to die – the doctor had warned him about Caroline's weak heart, worsened by that miscarriage – the thought of her death sent a shiver of fear through him. Losing Caroline wouldn't upset him, he had never had much time for her, but were she to die he would have no hold on Inverbrae. That cousin Robert would come and claim everything.

He cursed her. Caroline, and only Caroline, was responsible for the mess in which he found himself. Had there been a child he would not have set out on this course of bringing Bankhead to its former glory. Now he and his own family were to be faced with ruin and disgrace. Declared bankrupt and when that happened, Bankhead would fall into other hands. It didn't bear thinking about. And it wasn't going to happen, there must be a way of getting his hands on money. His wife had money, a substantial amount, and that rat of a solicitor would have to pay out if it was at Caroline's request. He smiled cruelly. She was afraid of him, he thought contemptuously, and almost cringed when he was near. He drew himself to his full height and there was a smile on his face. He was the master and his wife would do exactly as he ordered or else – or else what? The truth was he had no hold over her. The love she had once had for him had turned to hate. Now she feared him and fear of him would be his weapon.

It was an emotional meeting. Caroline was in floods of tears as she hugged Robert and met his wife. They were tears of relief that she could hand over responsibility and feel safe. So afraid was she, that she locked her bedroom door at night and made sure that she was never alone with her husband. This had frustrated Adrian but he could afford to wait a little. The little money his mother had left had bought time and her failing health was made the excuse for the length of time he spent in Stirling.

Her husband's absence had Caroline jubilant. Things couldn't have worked out better, because it gave Robert and Gemma a chance to settle in. Gemma had been utterly fascinated with the house and its history. She endeared herself to all, maids included, because she was so natural and friendly. She and her husband were very much in love. It was there in the glances they exchanged but they didn't seek to be alone, declaring themselves only too happy to be part of the family.

Robert couldn't hide his shock at the change in his cousin, and felt a murderous rage towards the man who had brought her to this. Gemma, however, thought her delicately lovely and she was. Her face, thinned by grief and illness, had achieved a mature beauty.

The decision to come and live in Scotland had not been taken lightly. It was a big step into the unknown for Gemma but she hadn't hesitated. Her place was with her husband, she said, and now that she was here her practical capabilities were being put to good use. The frail young woman needed protection from that brute of a husband and as for the old lady, there was a great deal more she could do for herself. Elderly people could rest too much, light exercise was good for them, a short walk in the grounds when the weather was good. The fresh air would help her sleep at night.

Far from rebelling, old Mrs Parker-Munro was enjoying this new experience. She was a nice girl, this Gemma. Funny way of speaking, she had, but once one got used to it, it was quite pleasant. The name, though – that was just not acceptable. Parker-Munro was the family name and Robert must take it. Gemma liked to hear about the old days, had an interest in Inverbrae's history, and she would see the importance of Robert taking the family name. One day they would have children and then it would be more important than ever. She smiled tiredly, she could die happy knowing that the family name lived on.

Jenny had made progress with the colonel and he was beginning to feel thoroughly ashamed of himself. How selfish he had been to put such a strain on Caroline and as for Adrian, he didn't know what to believe—

Adrian had been drinking. He wasn't drunk, just happy and that made a welcome change. The demands had ceased, at least for the present, and he could relax. There was time for his wife to come up with the cash or, better still, for that solicitor to release the money which had to be legal and binding since it had the colonel's signature. Time to call that solicitor's bluff.

The May sunshine was streaming through the window and, being Sunday, they had all eaten lunch in the dining-room and were now settled in the drawing-room. For the benefit of the old lady and those used to a warmer climate, a small fire had been lit and the large room was comfortably warm. Robert and Gemma had brought laughter and they were a family happy to be together.

Caroline's sharp ears had caught the sound first. Adrian must have parked the car round the back and walked round to the front door. Those were his footsteps, and as they drew nearer she caught her breath. She had promised herself to be brave but her heart had begun to hammer alarmingly. Robert heard the approach of feet and Caroline's look of alarm and whispered something to Gemma. She nodded and he got up and went to sit beside his cousin just as the door opened.

'Well! Well! Quite a party we have here.' The worry lines had smoothed out and the face was as handsome as before. He wore a well-cut suit and looked smart and relaxed. 'Caroline, my dear, you must have forgotten to tell me.'

She remained silent. Robert spoke.

'Sit down, Adrian.'

'Do I need an invitation to be seated in my own home?'

'Adrian,' the old lady said plaintively, 'close that door, if you please, you know how I dislike a draught.'

'Sorry.' He closed the door, hesitated, then sat down. He looked over at the young woman, presumably Robert's wife, and found she interested him. He liked that healthy, sporty type and she looked as though she could be fun – not like his wishy-washy wife. He would use his charm and he needed someone new in his life. His mistress was causing him some annoyance, withholding her favours and accusing him of meanness. He was tired of her anyway.

'Robert, aren't you going to introduce me to your wife?' he said. 'At least, I presume the very attractive young lady is your wife?'

'My wife, Gemma, Adrian Scott-Hamilton,' he said stiffly.

He wanted to go over and kiss her hand, the gentlemanly thing to do, but her cool nod was hardly encouraging.

Caroline had recovered. 'How is your mother, Adrian?'

'My mother,' he said blankly then remembered she was the excuse for his prolonged stay. 'There is a little improvement but she is far from well.'

'I'm sorry to hear that.'

He smiled. 'Darling, I haven't eaten. Do ring the bell and have the kitchen prepare a meal.'

'Do it yourself.'

'I beg your pardon.'

'I said do it yourself or better still wait and hear what I

have to say. It may put you off eating.'

'My poor dear, you are not yourself. Perhaps we should go elsewhere and have our talk.' He smiled. 'The others will excuse us, I'm sure.'

With Robert beside her, Caroline was gaining strength. 'I am not moving from here and now seems like a good time to tell you—'

'Tell me what?'

'I am divorcing you, Adrian. I want you out of my life.'

His face had whitened and he looked incredulous. 'What are you saying?'

'My cousin spoke clearly. It is your hearing that is at fault.'

'I'll thank you to mind your own damn business,' Adrian said furiously.

The old lady was looking outraged. 'Robert and Adrian, I'll remind you that this is the Sabbath day. You should be ashamed of yourselves, using such language. Had you been younger I would have sent you to your room.'

She got up and asked Caroline to take her to her room.

'No, grandma, I'll take you,' said Gemma.

'You'll stay for a while?'

'Of course and see more of your photographs. I would like that.'

They went out. The door closed and for a few moments no one spoke.

'On what grounds, Caroline?' Adrian said at last.

'On what grounds, you ask? Such a question only shows your arrogance. My solicitor is in possession of all that is necessary.'

'How about proof? A jealous wife would make up anything and any good solicitor would know that.'

'I have the name and address of your mistress.' Her

lips curled. 'And I am far from being a jealous wife. For a time I was taken in by your charm but I soon found out the type of man I was married to. You are a bully, a cheat, and a liar and you will not spend another night under this roof.'

This wasn't Caroline, this woman with her blazing eyes. He couldn't believe it but he had to. It was all happening.

'I would advise you to be careful what you say or you could find yourself in serious trouble.'

Robert gripped her arm to stop her answering. 'Well done, Caroline, but I'll take over now.'

'And what, pray, has the Australian to say?' Adrian said contemptuously.

'Plenty, as it happens. For what you have done you could go to prison, do you know that?'

'What am I supposed to have done?' he sneered. 'My father-in-law,' he smiled over to the colonel but he was staring into the fire, 'handed over responsibility for Inverbrae to me. Any transaction I made had his signature, nothing can alter that.'

'That is where you are wrong. Some time ago my uncle's doctor signed a certificate stating that his patient was unable to conduct his affairs at present. No document would be legal without his daughter's signature.'

Robert smiled. He was enjoying this and it gave him tremendous satisfaction to see Adrian's look of horror.

He was blustering now, desperately trying to salvage something. 'This place needs me. I have the experience to run an estate and what happens when you return to that Godforsaken land?'

'Robert isn't returning to Australia, Adrian,' Caroline said quietly. 'He and Gemma are making their home here.'

The colonel had said nothing all this time but now he sat

up straight in his chair. 'It is time I spoke up.'

Adrian gave a huge sigh of relief. 'Thank you, sir, I knew I could depend on you.'

'Depend on me to do what?'

'Speak up for me.'

'You disgust me but I have greater disgust for myself for letting things develop to this stage. I have been all kinds of a fool and I am to blame.' The speech was slightly slurred and there was a small hesitancy between some of the words but he had their attention. He shook his head. 'I prided myself on being a good judge of character, but how wrong I was to trust you. You have stolen and cheated for your own ends and believe me, Adrian, I was hard to convince. Only when I saw the evidence for myself did I believe it.' He wiped his brow and Caroline looked at him anxiously.

Robert gave a small shake of his head. His uncle was doing all right and this could be a turning point for him. From now on he would take some interest in what was going on.

'Bearing in mind your home situation, I might have been able to forgive you in time but for the unhappiness you have caused my daughter. That is something I will never forgive nor forget. Indeed, I would like to see you horse-whipped.'

Adrian got unsteadily to his feet. Ruin and possibly worse faced him but his father had come through much the same and he had survived. Come to think about it, a divorce would suit him nicely. He still had his looks and could turn on the charm when he wanted. Better to do something and quickly about finding himself a rich wife. To get his hands on money he was prepared to marry a plain woman just as his father had. Already he was beginning to feel better. Like father, like son.

Robert had the door open. 'Collect what belongs to you and get out.'

Adrian looked across to Caroline and wondered if his charm would work with her, even at this late stage. But one look at her face gave him his answer. He left without another word.

A career as a portrait artist is not easily established and is probably the most difficult to achieve. But when one does reach the heights, the rewards are great. For Peter it was a dream beginning to come true but he did not make the mistake of neglecting his other work, what had been his bread and butter. He still did small paintings of seascapes, harbour scenes and the rest which were snapped up and the monies saved.

Painfully thin though he was, Peter enjoyed good health and there were no ill effects from his early struggles. Those times spent in freezing rooms when he would have worked at his easel wearing two jumpers, a coat and gloves with the fingers cut out, would not easily be forgotten. All creative people, or the large majority, have agonising moments of self doubt and often go through deep despair. Peter had done his share but a dogged perseverance, together with a slice of luck, had put him on the path to success.

Peter knew his worth now and accepted that he was good. But these days he was achieving so much more. He felt inspired and for that he knew he had Beth to thank. Just to know she was near and he worked better. For her part, she seemed to understand his moods and never intruded other than to take in cups of coffee or tea. Food did not interest him until evening and then he would eat ravenously.

The two rooms, bathroom and tiny kitchen at Summer

Street became a second home to Beth. She spent happy, happy hours there but her work for Anna was not neglected and she continued to do the many extras she had taken on.

The house in Summer Street was showing evidence of a woman's touch as fresh curtains went up at the windows and flowering plants took up a place on the sills. At what he termed a decent hour, Peter escorted Beth to her door, kissed her lightly on the lips and left her feeling strangely dissatisfied. She wanted more, hoped that Peter did too, but could not be sure.

Peter and Anna hit it off immediately. Peter thought her delightfully eccentric, and she found him intelligent, interesting and charming. As a way of showing her approval Anna took them to the Excelsior Hotel where they dined extravagantly. It was a wonderfully enjoyable evening and the start of a long and happy friendship.

In the cool of the evening and after a long hard day, Peter needed to relax and stretch his limbs and he and Beth would take a walk along the coast road. Her eye never missed it and since she was a small child the white-painted house had fascinated Beth. From a distance and with its peculiar angle, the house looked as though it would topple into the sea. As a little girl, she had feared for the safety of those who lived in it. To reassure her and probably to stop the flow of questions, her father had taken her to the house and she had been both relieved and disappointed to find it set firmly on the ground and at a safe distance from the cliffs.

'Beth, I have to go to Edinburgh for a few days, maybe a week,' he said one day.

'To see your parents?'

'Partly. I'll be living at home – no correction, this is home – I'll be staying with my parents.' He paused and looked slightly embarrassed. 'Actually it is a small exhibition of my work.'

'But, Peter, that is marvellous,' Beth said delightedly. 'I couldn't be more pleased.' She went over to hug him. 'When is this to be?'

'In three weeks.'

'I'll be thinking of you and keeping my fingers crossed but I just know it will be a big success.'

'Hope so.' Should he ask her? No, she would just go out of politeness.

Beth was so sure he would invite her but he hadn't. Certainly it was in Edinburgh but she could have got the morning train and one back in the early evening. Why should he? Edinburgh was where he had been brought up and there would be plenty of relatives and friends to flock to see Peter's paintings. She told Anna.

'My dear child, did you show a willingness to go to Edinburgh?' her friend asked.

'Not exactly.'

'That means no and you must know that he isn't aware of our working arrangement.'

Beth looked at her enquiringly. 'That didn't apply to a whole day.'

'Of course it does. You must go, my dear, if for no other reason than to swell the numbers. I'm sure it will be well attended but he isn't to know that. One hopes but one can never be sure.'

'Anna, I'm only a friend.'

'A very special friend. Now, as you know, I am not one for interfering but this time I am going to chance it. You get yourself to Edinburgh and go and see Peter's paintings. If you don't, the day will come when you will regret it.'

'You think I should surprise him?'

'I most certainly do.'

★ ★ ★

The train thundered along the track and Beth was getting cold feet and wishing she hadn't listened to Anna. Out of good manners and kindness, Peter would make her welcome but if he had really wanted her there he would have said so.

Coming out of Waverley Station the strong breeze whipped her hair about her face. It was to be expected, it was always windy coming out of the station. Beth spent some time wandering about Princes Street admiring the fashions in the shop windows. A walk in the gardens would have been nice, but she had better get herself something to eat and a cup of tea before going out to the exhibition. Anna, it turned out, knew Edinburgh well and had drawn a remarkably clear map for which Beth was grateful. She had no difficulty finding the street and the old Victorian mansion house. Shabby but still stately, it had been divided into apartments. Outside the large ground-floor room there was a notice and Beth felt a burst of pride when she read, 'Exhibition of Paintings by Peter Nicholson'. A few people were in the spacious hallway and she saw with relief that some of the women wore tweeds. She was glad then that she had worn hers and not something more dressy. She went in.

There was low-murmured talk as people stood before the paintings and gave their opinion before moving on to the next. Beth had moved from the doorway into the room and saw him immediately. He looked very smart in a dark suit, a crisp white shirt and a blue tie and was moving about answering questions. Beth was just on the point of going over when a young blonde woman put her hand on his arm and Peter, turning round gave a delighted smile. She saw the two heads together and laughing at what could only be a private joke.

People were pushing by, she was in the way but did nothing about it. She was jealous, there was no other way to describe the feeling that gripped her. The shock of the discovery kept her standing there dumbly. She loved Peter but when had it happened? When had her feelings changed from friendship to love? She didn't know. Perhaps she had always loved him but had been blinded by her infatuation for Adrian.

He must never know. Her pain had to be private and in the next few minutes she must put on an act. Just as she was moving towards him, a set smile on her face, he saw her. She saw his start of surprise, his quick word to the blonde girl, then he was beside her.

'Beth! It really is you? I thought I must be dreaming. Why didn't you tell me you were coming?'

'Just a sudden decision. Thought I would combine it with a look round the Edinburgh shops.'

'Excuse me, I wanted to ask you—' They were all around him, all anxious to speak to the artist. A word here, a word there, he tried to get away but someone else buttonholed him and with a wry smile he caught Beth's eye and she smiled.

'You must go, Peter, I'll have a look round on my own.'

'As soon as I can I'll be with you, so don't you dare disappear.'

Beth didn't answer. She would slip away but not before she saw the paintings. Many she had seen but it was different to see them in these surroundings. People were smiling and there was a lovely atmosphere. They weren't just looking, as was shown by the large number of paintings with the small stick-on sign that said they were sold.

A small group stood before one painting that was a little apart from the others and she went over to look. The group obligingly parted to let her through and she found herself open-mouthed with astonishment. She was looking at herself, the one taken from the sketch he had made of her on the stony beach at Sandyneuk. He must have worked on it when he knew he was to be alone. There was no sold sign on this one but there was a card to the side. She read it. Not for sale.

Beth felt a lump in her throat and was about to rush away but Peter was beside her and looking at her strangely.

'And I thought it was good. One of my best. Others must have thought so too because I've had a few tempting offers. But nothing,' he said softly, 'would let me part with that one.'

'Oh, Peter,' was all she could say, her lips were trembling so much.

They were motionless, staring at one another. A smile played around Peter's mouth and Beth's eyes were shining.

'At last,' he whispered, 'at last you are putting the past behind you. I was beginning to despair that you ever would.'

'You mean – all this time—' she said wonderingly.

'All this time, from the moment I saw you as it happens, I've loved you. No, the first time you were a child but the next time, in Jenny's home.'

'You never gave a hint—'

'Of course not. I always hoped that the right moment would come and it has.'

'I've been over Adrian for a very long time.'

'There was another reason—'

'What possible reason could there be?'

'The age gap. You see, my darling, I didn't want to risk telling you of my feelings and losing your friendship. Ten years or near enough is quite a lot.'

'Ten years is nothing,' she said dismissively. Then she remembered the blonde girl. 'You were with a fair-haired girl—'

'Snakes alive, I forgot all about her,' he said dragging her along with him.

The girl was there. 'Fine one you are—'

'Sorry, Susie, I got tied up.'

'So I see,' the blonde girl said smiling to Beth.

'Susie, this is Beth from Sandyneuk and Beth, this is my cousin.'

They shook hands. 'Nice to meet you, Beth.' She looked at her cousin. 'Am I right in thinking that Beth is the reason we see so little of you?'

Peter laughed and Beth blushed.

'Not saying. All right, Peter, I'll keep your secret.' She waved her hand and left them.

'That's a joke, Susie couldn't keep a secret. I give it two hours then the entire family will know.'

'Will you mind?'

'Far from it.'

'Peter, I must go for my train.'

'Miss it and come home with me. Mother would be delighted to put you up.'

'I can't, I'm a working girl, remember. And I have Anna to thank for me being here.'

'You mean you needed to be persuaded?'

'I can't recall being invited.'

'I didn't want you searching for an excuse to spare my feelings.'

The minutes were ticking away. 'Peter, I must go.'

'I can't even see you on the train, I have to lock up here.'

'I know.' Their lips met for that first brief kiss. Then she was outside and all but running to catch her train.

# Chapter Thirty

Peter was back in Sandyneuk. The exhibition had been an outstanding success and people were congratulating him. The people of Sandyneuk claimed him as their own and the small craft shop was desperate for more paintings. Everything was wonderful for Peter and Beth but their love was too new to share with others. They needed this time to themselves before shouting out their happiness to the world. As if they needed to – it was plain for all to see. Jenny and Anna had a quiet smile. They saw the way things were between the young couple and they couldn't have been more delighted.

Beth could feel Peter's excitement as they set out for a walk along the coast road. She wondered where they were going. It had nothing to do with his paintings, she knew that. What could it be? She wouldn't ask.

She had heard rumours that the white house was to go on the market but there had been rumours before and nothing had come of them. Only when they turned off the coast road to the rough path did her heart begin to flutter with excitement.

'Is it really for sale, Peter?'

'Yes, it really is for sale and we are expected.'

'You mean we—' But she didn't get to finish.

Peter knocked on the door and in a short while the bolt

was pulled back and a little old lady peered at them shortsightedly.

'Mrs Cameron?'

'Yes.'

'I'm Peter Nicholson and this is—'

'Your lady wife?'

'Not yet.'

Beth blushed becomingly and dropped her eyes to the steps.

'Come in.'

First they were in the vestibule then into the hallway. The old lady was dressed in black and looked old-fashioned and rather sweet.

'My legs are not what they used to be but then if they were I wouldn't be selling the house.'

'You must be very sad.'

'Where would be the sense in that? I am, of course I am, but relieved too. Help in the house is becoming difficult to get and expensive. I shouldn't complain, I've had a good life and if I see my home going to folk who will look after it I'll be satisfied. You look like a couple who would. Go ahead and have a good look round. Take your time.'

'Thank you,' they both said.

'May I ask what you do, young man?'

'I'm an artist.'

'An artist.' She nodded two or three times. 'You'll be the lad that has caused a wee bit of a stir? I still manage to read the papers. No artists in my family but my late husband and I had a great love of the sea. The room above this is where we sat of an evening and at the weekends. You won't find a view like it. But here I am talking and you anxious to see the house.' She smiled a little sadly. 'Comes from being so much on my own, I did have a dog and he was fine company but I had to have him put down.'

'That must have been sad and distressing for you,' Beth said sympathetically.

'Yes, but not for him. A happy release it was. He was in a lot of pain but he'll be all right wherever he is.' She turned away and they began to look around the house.

The sitting-room was large, the dining-room smaller. There was another room between them that was quite small. It had a single bed and a wardrobe and Beth thought it likely that Mrs Cameron slept there rather than climb the stairs.

Together they went up the carpeted stairs and she heard Peter gasp as he went ahead. The doors were wide open but one room drew him. It stretched the whole length of the house and could have been purposely built as a studio. Peter needed to see no more but he accompanied Beth to see the rest then they went to join the old lady.

She was smiling as she got up from the chair. 'Well?'

'It's lovely, absolutely lovely,' Beth breathed.

'Perfect, need I say more?' Peter said.

'You've fallen in love with it just as I did all those years ago. I can see by your faces that you both have.'

'Yes, we both have.'

'I'll see the solicitor and put in my offer tomorrow morning,' Peter said.

She looked pleased. 'Put in a reasonable offer, Mr Nicholson, and it will be accepted.'

'Perhaps your solicitor will want to hold out for more? It would be to his advantage.'

'That is probably true but we know each other well. We go back a long way, and he'll carry out my wishes.'

'Thank you very, very much,' Beth said as they prepared to go.

★ ★ ★

By the end of the month the house was theirs and Beth didn't know how to contain her happiness. The two rooms in Summer Street were given up and Peter's worldly possessions moved to the white house, now to be known as Cliffend Cottage. Until they were married he would live and work there. He shut himself in the studio while willing hands stripped the wallpaper from the rooms and did a thousand and one jobs.

There was so much to do, so much going on, that Beth didn't know whether she was coming or going. Peter had taken her to Edinburgh to meet his family. His mother had arranged it so that Alex, unmarried and three years younger, and sister Ruby, husband Norman and their little boy, would be there to meet Beth.

John Nicholson, Peter's father, was tall and both sons resembled him. Mrs Nicholson was a happy-faced woman with a weight problem which she totally ignored. Ruby was small and slim and reminded Beth of the younger Caroline. Husband Norman doted on his wife and son and they could not have been more welcoming. She was immediately drawn into the family and she loved them all.

Aunt Anne and Uncle Fred liked Peter but how could they not, Beth thought. No one could dislike Peter.

'Fixed the big day?' Aunt Anne asked. 'Need time to save up, you know.'

'Early September,' Beth smiled, 'and Aunt Anne, would you and Uncle Fred take the place of my parents?'

'Oh, lass, I would and willingly but not if it is to be one of those posh affairs, your uncle wouldn't like it either.'

'Speak for yourself, woman. With no lass of my own I'm only too happy to give Beth away. Not to anyone mind, but Peter, here, will look after her, I've no fears there.'

'Nothing posh about our wedding. Only close relatives

including cousins and friends. Jenny, you know who I'm talking about?'

'I should I've heard about her often enough.'

'She wants us to be married in the village church and the reception in her home.'

Aunt Anne pursed her lips and nodded. 'Since it is to be a quiet affair I'll manage to take Harriet's place.'

On her wedding day, Beth was up early to look out of the window at the lashing rain but nothing could dampen her spirits. She was too excited to eat breakfast but Anna and she had a cup of tea together.

'I was so sure it would be a lovely day,' Beth said as rivulets of rain ran down the window.

'It's early yet and it could well clear up before midday.'

'Anna, is it possible to be too happy?'

'No, my dear. You have a right to every moment of happiness. Wherever you are, we are all touched by it.'

'You have such a lovely way of putting things, such a lovely way with words.'

'Oh, I was getting quite crusty until you came into my life. I am just so glad that I am not to lose you – at least not for a while yet.'

'I want to go on working for you, Anna, and thank you a thousand times for all you have done for me. This has been home to me, you know.'

Anna patted her hand. 'Perhaps it is true to say we needed one another. But now, would you just go and take a look out of that window.'

They had been talking and she hadn't even noticed. 'It's clearing, it is going to be a good day after all,' Beth said joyfully. And it was – the clouds had dispersed, the sky was blue and the sun had appeared.

The small church was filling up and well-wishers were

gathered round the gate eager to catch a glimpse of the bride. The heat of the sun had miraculously dried up the paths and pavements and no puddles remained to wet the shoes of unsuspecting guests. Beth had decided against having a bridesmaid. She had friends, but no one she wanted in that role. Instead she would have a matron-of-honour unless Caroline refused. But she hadn't, she was touched and honoured to be asked.

Beth was radiantly beautiful, her gown simplicity itself with a froth of white net over it. Any nervousness had gone and Uncle Fred, looking proud, squeezed her arm and whispered, 'All right?'

'Just fine,' she answered as they entered the porch.

The bridegroom and best man looked smart and solemn. But Peter's face broke into a smile of pure delight as the bride, on the arm of her uncle, and followed by Caroline, came slowly down the aisle. Caroline wore a lovely gown of pale apricot. She looked frail but her eyes were clear and she looked quietly happy.

Soon they were man and wife and, leaving the confetti-strewn path, they climbed into the car that was to take them to Greystanes for the reception. Beth, with Peter by her side, had cut the cake and it was being handed round with a tray of assorted drinks following.

She looked at them, all the smiling faces and felt a lump in her throat. Once she had thought herself unloved and unwanted but all that had changed. She had a loving family and good friends, like Jenny and Anna who between them had done so much for her. Caroline had come back into her life and it was lovely to be friends or near sisters as Caroline was telling everybody.

Peter's arm drew her close. 'Darling, you are miles away.'

'Just thinking.'

'Thinking what?'

'That I am so lucky to have you beside me. I love you so very much, Peter.'

'I love you, Beth, and we will be together—'

'For always.'

'Until the end of time.'

# Best Friends

**For Bill and Raymond**

# Chapter One

All day long fog had hung over Dundee but as darkness fell it had thickened and was like an icy-cold wet blanket. In the eerie light of the gas lamps the cobblestones glistened black as George Donaldson carefully picked his way to avoid the deep ruts caused by the cart wheels. A tram loomed out of the fog then with a clanking noise disappeared into the haze like a phantom monster. Fifteen minutes took George Donaldson to his tenement home at 23 Blackford Street in the west end. Here most of the houses consisted of a room and kitchen but as befitted a foreman of the Tayside Jute Mills, number 23 boasted a kitchen with a bed recess, a good-sized, square-shaped room that his wife, Amelia, referred to as the parlour, a small bedroom, a tiny scullery and an inside lavatory.

In his late thirties George Donaldson was a tall, well-built man with unruly black curly hair and regular features. Anxious to reach home he took the stairs two at a time to the second landing and opening the door let himself in. After hanging up his coat and cap on a peg he opened the kitchen door and immediately felt the familiar pity and despair.

She was huddled in a chair beside the blackleaded range where a fire burned and crackled. To him just in from the damp chill of the November night the heat was overpowering but Amelia had drawn the plaid tighter around her thin shoulders as though the opening of the door had lowered the temperature. She was always cold, had forgotten what it was like to be warm, yet Amelia was only thirty years of age.

'George!' Her blue eyes opened wide in welcome and the smile she gave him was the same smile that had captivated him from that moment when her pert little hat had blown away on a frisky wind and he'd caught it before it reached a puddle of dirty water.

'That's a filthy night out there, typical November,' he said stooping to plant a kiss on her forehead.

'Look, Papa, I'm making toast,' the child said unnecessarily. Nine-year-old Rachel, her black curls tied up in a ribbon and wearing a clean

1

white pinafore, was sitting in front of the fire flushed with the heat and with a thickly cut slice of bread on the end of the toasting fork.

'So I see and if you're not careful it's a burnt offering I'll be getting.'

'Oh!' Hastily pulling back the fork she looked at it in dismay. 'It's gone all black.'

He laughed and rumpled her hair. 'No, just nearly black; it's all right, lass. I'll scrape it but see and make a better job of the other side.'

The child had her mother's small, neat features but in all else she resembled her handsome father. One day she would be beautiful.

'How was your day, dear?'

'Much as usual but I sense a bit of unease in the jute trade and I'm not the only one.'

'But not serious?' she said alarmed.

'Not yet, love, but India could become a real threat and I'm thinking the bosses had better take heed.'

'Why?' Amelia had always shown an intelligent interest in the jute trade and George, knowing how it pleased her, kept her up-to-date.

'Unlimited cheap labour, that's why. But never mind that just now, what did Mary say?'

'As I expected. She'll be happy to come in to see to the house and cook the meals but said there was no charge for being a good neighbour.'

'Even so it's too much to expect.'

'That's what I told her and I made it clear that I wouldn't be able to call on her if she didn't accept payment.'

'So it's all settled?'

'Yes, George, it's settled. She'll stay with me until Rachel gets home from school.' She paused and leaned back. The effort of speech tired her but she added. 'I think she enjoys being needed and the wee extra will be a help.'

After arranging the toast on a plate the child carried it over to the table. 'Papa, everything's ready,' Rachel said importantly before moving quickly to the range where the meal prepared by Mary Rodgers was simmering gently in the big black pots. She had just taken the pot holder from its hook when George was over, a constraining hand grasping her arm and making her wince with pain.

'Don't you ever do that again, do you hear?' he said sharply, more sharply than he intended but she had given him a fright. The pots were heavy, far too heavy for her skinny arms and wrists.

Amelia saw Rachel struggling to hold back the tears and with a reproachful look at her husband said soothingly, 'Papa didn't mean to shout at you, dear, but he is right; you're too little to do that.'

'Sorry, pet, but you gave me a fright,' George said hugging her to him and for a few moments she leant into him feeling his strength.

She was so precious to them both and they worried about her but in different ways. George worried because Rachel seemed to have no friends of her own age and the blame for that he placed firmly at her mother's door. Amelia had been determined that her daughter was to be brought up properly and that meant talking nicely and being well-mannered, not like the children round about. They had broad Dundee accents, wore ill-fitting hand-me-downs and spoke of their parents as Ma and Da whereas Rachel had been taught to address hers as Mama and Papa. George, remembering his own school days, could well imagine what Rachel had to put up with. Children could be so cruel and to be labelled as stuck-up was torture to a sensitive child.

Rachel had been bewildered and hurt to be singled out for ridicule and she had even tried to have a playground language but that had been greeted with hoots of laughter and she'd quickly abandoned it. Instead she'd concentrated on her lessons, getting praise from Miss Melville and earning herself yet another name – teacher's pet.

Earlier in the day Amelia had managed to take a little beef tea and now sat watching her husband and child tucking into their plates of potato soup followed by Irish stew. Mary was a good plain cook and she would have been hugely pleased to see each plate wiped clean with the last of the toast.

'Amelia, lass, tell Mary that was champion,' George said as he scraped back his chair. Rolling up his sleeves he went over for the black kettle and half emptied the hot water into an enamel basin. Rachel carried the dishes into the scullery and George washed them. The nightly ritual had gone on for a long time and both were accomplished at their tasks. George finished the job, emptied the basin, dried his hands and sat down with the newspaper. Rachel carefully dried the dishes and put them away in the dresser before returning to the table to cover it with the dark red chenille cloth with its edging of bobbles.

Amelia knew that death was near but she wasn't afraid, only saddened to be leaving George and Rachel, particularly Rachel. Her blue eyes clouded with distress as she wondered what would happen to her darling child when she was no longer here. George, after a decent interval would remarry. He was still young with a man's needs and though the woman might be good for George, would she be good to Rachel? A cold-water chill went through her at the thought of Rachel with a stepmother.

She was trembling, getting herself into a state and she knew that it was bad for her. What if she slipped away tonight before she had a chance – George wouldn't like what she was going to ask of him but he was a man of his word and if she got his promise then she could die with an easy mind.

She kept looking at the clock; would nine o'clock, Rachel's bedtime, never come? It wasn't quite that but Amelia was so dreadfully tired that even another five minutes seemed like an eternity.

'Rachel, dear, bedtime.'

'It isn't, Mama, it's not nine o'clock yet,' Rachel sounded aggrieved.

'By the time you drink your milk it will be,' Amelia said with unaccustomed firmness.

George sensed that there was something. 'Do as you're told, Rachel,' he said in a voice that brooked no argument and Rachel, with the smallest of sighs, closed her book and got up. The cup of milk was warming on the range and Rachel took as long over drinking it as she dared then said her goodnights.

Closing the kitchen door she went along to her bedroom. The gas mantle was lit and Rachel knew how to turn it up to give her enough light to read but it was forbidden. Other children got walloped if they misbehaved, she knew that, but no one had ever lifted a hand to her. Instead, if she was found out it would be a raging or the withholding of some treat.

When had she last had a treat? Feeling hard done by, Rachel sat on the bed and wished her mother would hurry up and get well. It had been so long since she had had any fun, not one picnic all summer, not even one. She sighed, remembering those lovely sunny afternoons and the dainty sandwiches her mama used to make and her papa saying there wasn't a decent bite in them. Later on they would play hide-and-seek and once she had come across her mama and papa kissing behind the bushes, and feeling strangely embarrassed, she'd pretended she hadn't seen them. Slowly Rachel undressed and put on her warm white nightie. Last night

4

she had been too tired to say her prayers so God might be angry with her – but if she explained. Kneeling beside the bed Rachel put her hands together and closed her eyes.

'I'm very sorry about last night, not saying my prayers, I mean, but I was too tired. Bless Mama and Papa and please God make Mama well again as quickly as you can and make me a good girl. Amen.'

In the kitchen Amelia had moved from the chair to the couch which George had dragged nearer to the heat. He adjusted the cushions and tucked the blanket round her. 'Comfortable?'

'Yes, George, thank you, I'm fine.' It wouldn't do to let him see just how exhausted she was or else he'd be putting her to bed like a baby.

'You don't look fine to me and you'd be a lot more comfortable lying down in bed.'

'No.' She patted the place beside her. 'Dearest, we have to talk.'

He sat down suddenly apprehensive. 'Something is troubling you, isn't it?'

'Yes, George, something is.' She paused to push a strand of fair hair from her eyes and he took the fine-boned hand and folded it in his. 'I'm not going to get better, dear, and we have to stop pretending.'

'Oh, God, Amelia, don't, just don't! I can't bear it, can't bear to think—' George's voice was low and rough with pain.

'Sh, darling, don't upset yourself, I'm not afraid of death – just – just—' her voice wavered, 'leaving you both is so difficult.' Her blue eyes, too large in the small face, were filled with love and sadness as she saw his distress. Her mind went back as it so often did these days to the hardship that marriage to George had meant, but then she would remember their lovemaking and a tender smile touched her lips. Their love had been an unleashing of passion that had brought undreamed of ecstasy but there were other times when she had had to fight the loneliness, times when her body ached with weariness and it was then that she regretted her marriage. But those times were rare and George never knew of them.

She struggled a bit before beginning, wondering where to start, the words she had prepared already forgotten.

'George, I want you to promise me something.'

'Anything.'

She moistened her lips. 'Sitting here day after day I've done a lot of thinking and I know now that I want Rachel to be told about her grandparents.'

There was a silence, a tightening of the lips, then with difficulty the words came out. 'You always said you'd never – do you want me to get in touch, tell them—?'

'About me?' She shook her head. 'No, it's too late for that but Rachel has a right to know and neither of us should deny her that.'

'Then tell her.'

'No, George, she's too young to understand.' Amelia looked at him imploringly. 'Wait until she's twelve and old enough to understand.'

'Very well, I'll tell the bairn when she's twelve.'

'Your promise on it, George.'

She saw the hesitation then the rueful smile. 'I'm not so sure you're doing the right thing but you have my word.'

'Thank you, darling.' Amelia knew only too well what it cost him to give that promise. 'It was a very long time ago, dear, people change, we all do.'

George wasn't so sure. 'She's my child too,' he found himself saying. 'Don't you trust me to look after her?'

'George, that was unworthy of you and this is difficult enough for me. Of course I trust you but you could remarry.' She put up her hand as he started to speak. 'You're young and you have a right to happiness with someone else but Rachel's position could be awkward.' Her voice had grown weaker. 'One last thing, that box—'

'Your secret hoard,' he said trying to infuse some lightness.

She smiled. 'No secret hoard as you very well know. The key has always been in the vase on the mantelpiece. George, do you remember how angry you were when I took in sewing?'

'And rightly so, a man likes to see himself as the provider.'

'You were always that and not a penny of that money did I spend. All of it went into that box for Rachel. Not that my efforts brought in much but it is something for her and the brooch I got for my eighteenth birthday. It's valuable, dear,' she said anxiously, 'so do make sure that the child takes great care of it.'

'Look at you, you're absolutely exhausted!' Her face was completely grey and she made no demur when he began unbuttoning her blouse then undressing her. The nightgown had been warming beside the fire and he slipped it over her head, then taking the almost weightless body in his arms laid her on the bed in the recess. She moved herself nearer the wall hoping George wouldn't be long in retiring. Her only comfort now was the warmth of his body next to hers.

# Chapter Two

The year was 1926 and the January night was bitterly cold. The wind was rattling the window frames when George fell into an uneasy sleep. Amelia, lying beside him, gave the smallest of sighs and quietly left this world.

Through the wall Rachel wakened at her usual time. Why hadn't her Papa knocked to make sure she was awake? Not that she was in any hurry to leave the warm bed but she was sure it must be morning. Throwing back the bedclothes she was about to get up when the door opened and Mrs Rodgers came in. That in itself showed that something was wrong. Mrs Rodgers never came before nine o'clock.

'Don't get up, lass, stay there the now.'

'I can't, I'll be late for school,' Rachel protested.

'There'll be no school for you the day.' Mary Rodgers looked at the bewildered face framed by a mop of springy curls, and wondered how she was going to break it to the poor wee lamb. But there was no one else. George, that big strapping lad, had gone to pieces and Mary's feelings were a mixture of pity, anger and something bordering on contempt. A man had no right to display his grief so openly, he should be able to control it by her way of thinking.

Sitting herself on the narrow bed, her weight a test on the springs, Mary took Rachel's hands in her own work-roughened ones and looked into the young face. 'Now, lass, you've got to be brave.'

Rachel's eyes widened and a terrible fear gripped her. 'It's Mama, she's worse?'

'She's gone, Rachel,' Mary forced the words out, 'but peacefully and God be thanked for that.'

'Gone!' Rachel whispered not understanding then suddenly she did and would have wrenched herself free had Mary not held on to her firmly. 'Mama! Mama! Mama!' she screamed shrilly. Then the tears came, painful gulping sobs that racked the small body. Mary rocked her in her arms until the shuddering stopped and she too wept but silently for that brave lass who had tried so hard to fit into a life so different from the one she had known.

At the table, her porridge untouched, Rachel stared at her father in acute embarrassment. Seeing him like that with his eyes all red and swollen and tears pouring down his face was awful. Mary saw the expression on the child's face and quickly moved over to the dresser. She knew where the drink was kept, never a great deal of it but enough for an emergency or for an unexpected guest. Taking it on herself she poured a good measure of whisky into a glass, added water from the tap and without a word put it beside George.

Rachel saw it all and that was when the nine-year-old first began to suspect that it had been her gentle mama who had been the strong one.

Wearing her darkest dress for the occasion, Rachel was taken through to the front room to say goodbye to her mother. The parlour, as her mother had always referred to it, looked different. The big sideboard with its large mirror was the same. The marble clock still sat in the centre of a crocheted cover with a charging horse on either side. The straight-backed chairs, the spindly-legged table and a footstool were just as always and now she saw that it was the couch that made the difference. It had been moved to the middle of the floor. Fearfully and reluctantly Rachel approached the couch and looked down on the still, white face. Her papa took her hand and squeezed it in reassurance. What had she expected? Something dreadful, something terrifying and it wasn't like that at all. Her mama looked pretty and she was wearing her best nightie.

'She looks pretty,' Rachel whispered to her father.

'She's beautiful,' George said hoarsely. His hand touched the cold brow. 'Goodbye, my darling Amelia,' then gently he pushed Rachel forward. 'Say goodbye to your mama, Rachel.'

'Goodbye, Mama.'

Mary Rodgers was at the door, a deep frown on her plump face. She'd advised George against it. Surely it was better for the child to remember her mother as she had been, but he'd been adamant and of course it was none of her business.

Neighbours came to pay their respects, to commiserate with George and to cast sympathetic glances at the motherless lass. They were completely natural with George as they had never been with his wife. She had been a strange one and no mistake but the woman was gone and it didn't do to speak ill of the dead.

Amelia's funeral took place in the early afternoon and when the men returned from the cemetery the womenfolk were already sitting in the parlour talking in hushed voices. Mary Rodgers had taken charge of arrangements and tea was handed round to the women. There was a murmur of 'Ta, lass' as Rachel dutifully followed with the sandwiches. George was kept busy pouring whisky for the men and very soon voices grew louder as the talk became general.

Rachel sat apart eating a sandwich and feeling appalled as someone laughed at a remark. How could anyone laugh when her mama was dead! Even her papa had smiled and she wondered what her mama was thinking. It was different for those in heaven, they could see and hear everything or so she had been told. She remembered her mama saying that God even knew what we were thinking. Rachel wasn't too happy about that, sometimes she thought naughty things but you couldn't help what you were thinking. Funny that she couldn't cry now; she'd tried to make the tears come but they wouldn't. Now why should that be when she was still sad? When would they go away? Would Papa be angry if she slipped away to the kitchen and read her book? Better not, she didn't want Papa to be cross with her.

'I think we'd better get on our way,' Mrs McDonald from the close wheezed as she got to her feet. Others followed, but reluctantly, they had just been beginning to enjoy themselves. Knowing this Mary Rodgers hastened their departure then shooed Rachel to her bed. Rachel needed no encouragement and she was asleep as soon as her head touched the pillow.

The day after the funeral at Balgay Cemetery a man, with his head bowed and a child by his side, stood before the loosened ground gazing down at the already wilting flowers. Rachel wore a navy pleated skirt and white school blouse and over it a navy nap coat. On her head was a velour hat held on by elastic under the chin. The two were hand-in-hand and after a few minutes they turned away to squelch through the sodden ground. George would have preferred to walk home, he was in no hurry to return to an empty house, but it was a fair step, too far for Rachel so they joined the others waiting at the tram stop.

'Papa, we can ride on the top?'

'Aye, if you want.'

★ ★ ★

The piercing scream shattered the silence bringing George instantly awake. The dying embers of the fire gave a little light but even so he swore as he stubbed his big toe on the leg of the chair. Thankfully he'd left the gas on at a peek and as soon as he went in he turned it up. Rachel was sitting bolt upright, her blue eyes huge and terrified in a white face.

'You've been dreaming, that's all,' George said soothingly as he went to her.

'It wasn't – it wasn't a dream. Papa, it wasn't,' she said wildly. Her arms went round his neck so tight that he had to force her to loosen her grip.

'Look about you, Rachel. Go on, have a good look. There's absolutely nothing to be afraid of.'

'Not here,' she whispered. 'It's Mama, I saw her waken up and she can't get out.'

George felt an icy chill go through his body and lifting the child on to his knee he cuddled her to him then spoke slowly and distinctly.

'Rachel, your mama is dead. You know that and you know she isn't going to waken up. Like I said you've just been having a bad dream.'

But Rachel wasn't satisfied, the horror had been very real and it had been in Balgay Cemetery where her mama was under the ground. What if she wasn't dead at all, just sleeping? Papa could be wrong, grown-ups did make mistakes.

'Mrs Rodgers said Mama was sleeping and when she wakened up she'd be in heaven but what if she wakened up before she got to heaven?' Rachel said fearfully.

George cursed Mary Rodgers. Rachel had always been one for questions, not giving up until she was satisfied. And now what in God's name was he going to say? Amelia had been religious, a believer, she would have known what to say but religion had never played a big part in his life. Just so long as a man led a decent life that was all that could be expected and if there was such a place as heaven he felt that he had a reasonable chance of getting there. Now he sought for the unfamiliar words.

'Death isn't like sleeping, people just use that expression. What happens is the body dies and the soul rises to heaven.' There, he'd done quite well, George congratulated himself.

'Will Mama be with the angels?'

'Sure to be and she'll be happy, but mind she wouldn't like you carrying on like this.'

'I'm sorry,' her lips quivered. 'I wish, I wish, I wish she'd come back.'

'So do I, pet, but we've got to be brave,' George said bleakly. In truth he wondered how they would manage. 'Snuggle down and you'll soon be asleep.'

'I'm still frightened,' she clung to his sleeve. 'Please, please, Papa,' she implored, 'let me sleep with you, just this once.'

George shook his head then relented. It was probably the only way to get any sleep and there was precious little of the night left. 'And it will be just this once,' he warned.

Slipping off his knee, Rachel hurried through to the kitchen before he changed his mind. Clambering into the bed she quickly got below the bedclothes and moved over to the place where until a short time ago Amelia had slept.

There were no more nightmares and though Rachel begged to be allowed to sleep in the big bed George was deaf to her pleas and she returned to her own bedroom.

During those early difficult days Mary Rodgers was a tower of strength and came in daily to prepare meals and tidy up the house. Once long ago she had felt sorry for George's young bride. The lassie had never cooked a meal in her life, that was clear enough, and she knew next to nothing about keeping a house. But she'd been very willing to learn and a lasting friendship had developed. Now it was Amelia's daughter she took in hand. Gradually, not pushing her too much, she showed the motherless lass how to prepare and cook a plain appetising meal. Later would come the harder work, the black-leading of the range, the scrubbing and the washing and ironing that were all a part of a woman's lot.

The pain of loss was an excruciating agony for George and he felt no shame at showing his grief. Why shouldn't he weep for the wife he had adored? He wasn't a coward, he could stand physical suffering as well as the next man but this was different, this was so much worse.

He had been surprised by Rachel's behaviour. After the early bouts of weeping there had been no more tears and she had become quiet and composed. He had remarked on it to Mary Rodgers.

'The poor lass hasn't faced up to it yet.'

'You mean she hasn't fully taken it in?' George said worriedly.

'She understands well enough that her mother is dead but it's the finality of it that hasn't registered.'

'What can we do?'

'Nothing, she'll cope in her own way.' She paused. 'Pity she wasn't back at school. I know she has a nasty cough—'

'I only did what Dr Maxwell advised and he thought she needed another week at home.'

'You couldn't do anything else.' She sniffed. 'Supposed to know best but being with other bairns would have helped.'

'She'll be back on Monday and that should keep her mind off things,' George answered, but he was none too happy. Rachel was in no hurry to return. She had no friends.

In those early days Rachel had clung to the hope that God, who could make anything happen if He wanted to, would let her mama come back. It could be the way it was in a dream when you wakened up. But with God showing no sign of changing His mind hope faded and she became listless just picking at her food. The very thought of returning to school was making her physically sick.

In the playground a group of girls surrounded Rachel who wore a black band round her sleeve to show that she was in mourning, but there was none of the taunting and jeering that had once made her life a misery. Instead, in their clumsy way they were trying to offer sympathy but unable to find the words. Agnes Boyd, auburn-haired and freckled, and who had once jeered the most, offered Rachel a sticky toffee.

Rachel had been about to refuse, to say no, thank you, but something in the girl's face stopped her. There was almost a pleading for forgiveness and Rachel, wise beyond her years, recognised it.

'Ta,' she said only just holding back the 'thank you' which so readily came to her lips.

That night Rachel waited in a fever of impatience for her papa to get home from work. She couldn't wait to tell him.

'Half a minute, lass, let me get my coat off.'

Rachel returned to the kitchen, keeping her eye on the bubbling pots.

'I'm ready to listen, so what is it all about?' he said as he stuck a fork in the potatoes to test them. 'A wee bit hard yet, we'll give them another minute or two.' She was dancing from one foot to the other.

'I know it's because of Mama but everybody is nice to me and Agnes

Boyd gave me a toffee and she's always been the nastiest.'

Poor lass, George thought, so touchingly grateful for that show of friendship and it was the best thing that could have happened. It would help her get over Amelia's death.

'And Agnes Boyd said I could be her chum. I've never had a chum.'

'Well, that's just grand. Over to the table with you and get this while it's hot.'

Rachel sat down obediently and picked up her knife and fork but couldn't help her lips curving into a smile.

'God!' George thought, 'it had to be that Boyd family, and shuddered to think what Amelia would have said. A hovel, that was the only way to describe the Boyd home. Big, fat, lazy and uncouth, Eddie Boyd was unable to hold down a job for more than a few weeks and most of what he got went on drink. Poor Jenny, he thought with a pang of genuine sympathy, she'd been a right bonny lass with her thick auburn hair and her laughing eyes and there had been a time when he'd fancied her himself but then he'd found Amelia and after that no other lass existed for him. Worn out with too many pregnancies Jenny had seemed to give up the struggle. Folk said the house was never cleaned and the bairns were allowed to run wild, but the more charitable admitted that the older ones were fiercely protective of the wee ones and heaven help anyone who laid a finger on them.

'Miss Melville said Agnes had—' Rachel searched for the word and came out with it triumphantly – 'ability but said she's too lazy to do any work.'

'Her mother was a clever lass.'

Rachel looked astounded. 'You know Agnes's mother?'

'She was in my class at school but it's years since I spoke to her.'

'Papa—'

This was something he could change, George thought, and it would make life easier for the lass. 'Rachel, how about calling me Da? It's no disrespect to your mother but I've never felt comfortable with this papa and mama business.'

Rachel nodded happily. 'Yes, all right – Da,' she said experimentally and liking the sound of it, then she added thoughtfully, 'Why did Mama like it?'

'It was the way she was brought up.' He smiled ruefully remembering his own difficult days. 'I had to watch my ps and qs I can tell you.'

'What are ps and qs?'

'Watching your ways, watching your manners. I had to watch mine but when you love someone the way I loved your mother,' he swallowed the lump in his throat and went on quickly, 'you'd do anything to please them. There were times I can tell you when I felt a bit of an ass but och I managed no' bad.'

Rachel smiled, her eyes dancing, she loved it when her papa – no, her da – spoke to her like this, it made her feel grown-up.

'In the mill was a different story; there I was as broad Dundee as the rest.'

'Why did Mama never speak about the time when she was a little girl?'

George was silent for a while and Rachel wondered if she had said something wrong, but she wanted to know so badly.

'Why, Papa? Why, Da?' she corrected herself.

'It made her unhappy.'

'Because they are dead?'

He frowned. 'Away and warm some milk for yourself.'

Rachel got up reluctantly. She knew that there was to be no answer to her question.

It all came crowding back to George, the unanswered questions. Had Amelia been unhappy? She had never complained but then she wouldn't, it hadn't been her way, but in the secrecy of her own heart had she sometimes admitted to regrets? There had been times when she had thought herself unobserved and he'd glimpsed a sadness in her eyes and been afraid to question it, too afraid of the answer. Had her love for him been enough to compensate for all she had given up? He would never know or perhaps she had given it away at the end. There was that promise, a promise she knew had been dragged from him and one he had to honour when the time came. The bitterness of being rejected without even a chance to speak for himself had never left him, the sour taste was still in his mouth. He had never met them, never set eyes on them but the hatred remained.

# Chapter Three

The school bell had just gone and Miss Melville's class of boys and girls were impatiently waiting to escape from the confines of the classroom. Their behaviour had been worse than usual and she kept them waiting a few minutes, any longer and she would be punishing herself, she decided.

'You may go. Quietly!' she shouted as a desk banged and there was a scuffle to get to the door. 'Not you, Rachel Donaldson,' her eyes swivelled round. 'I want you to stay behind.'

'Yes, miss.'

Agnes Boyd slipped across the room to Rachel, her eyes anxious.

'What does she want you for? What've you done?' she whispered.

'Nothing that I know of.'

'I'll wait.'

'No, don't. Honest I don't think it's trouble,' she whispered back. Rachel knew that Agnes had to hurry home to look after the youngest Boyd who had only weeks ago put in her appearance. A puny infant, she was surviving against all the odds and taking up room in that already overcrowded house.

'Agnes Boyd, don't you have a home to go to?'

'Yes, miss.' At the door Agnes turned her freckled face and stuck out her tongue at Miss Melville's back giving Rachel a hard time trying to keep her face straight.

At twelve, Rachel was tall for her age. Miss Melville had watched this child grow, could see in her the promise of beauty and a natural grace that set her apart from the others. She, who prided herself on having no favourites, was drawn to Rachel Donaldson. Her good manners and pleasant speaking voice had served to alienate her from her peers, yet she had suffered it all with a quiet dignity and it had taken her mother's death to break down the barriers. Miss Melville had seen it all and the extraordinary friendship that had developed between Rachel and Agnes

Boyd. Yet was it so extraordinary? she asked herself. They were both intelligent, indeed Agnes Boyd was by far the brightest girl in the class but mostly she was inattentive and not prepared to work.

'Bring over a chair for yourself and sit down.'

Rachel obeyed and sat with her hands in her lap. All of a sudden she found that she was nervous and began to worry her lower lip, a habit she had developed.

'Don't do that!' Miss Melville said sharply, then more kindly, 'I'm not going to bite your head off.'

Rachel smiled weakly.

Miss Melville, Miss Charlotte Melville, was a tall, sallow-faced woman in her late forties with fine light brown hair drawn severely back from her face and fixed in a neat bun at the back. Her best feature, her eyes, were slate-grey and showed a sharp intelligence.

'It's early days yet, Rachel, but have you given any thought to what you'll do when you leave school?'

'No, miss.'

'You are quite intelligent and you work hard.' She paused. 'I think you would make a good teacher.'

Rachel blushed scarlet. 'I – I'd love to teach,' she stammered, 'and I would work ever so hard, Miss Melville.'

'You'd have to,' her teacher said dryly. 'Teaching calls for dedication and more than average patience – much more,' she added. Then she smiled. 'Nevertheless, I can assure you that it is a very worthwhile and rewarding profession.'

Rachel didn't know if a comment was expected so she merely nodded.

'Your friends will have left school to take up whatever jobs are available whilst you will be staying on and studying hard.'

'I shouldn't mind that at all.'

'And if you do well, Rachel, it means going on to college to get the necessary qualifications and this, of course, would depend upon your father's willingness or indeed his ability, to keep you on at school.'

'I'll ask my father tonight, Miss Melville.' It would be all right, Rachel thought, her da would be proud of her if she became a teacher.

'You do that, talk it over, and now run along.' She pointed to the chair. 'Put that back before you go.'

Rachel's stomach was churning with excitement but she forced herself not to run and make a noise in the corridor. Once in the playground, though, she ran nimble as a mountain goat, her curls flying, her cheeks rosy, until she reached home with a painful stitch in her side.

The key was under the mat and she let herself in. For about a year she had hated coming into an empty house and Mrs Rodgers had tried to be there when she got in from school. Now it didn't trouble Rachel at all. She was becoming independent. Cooking was something she enjoyed and if she didn't like black-leading the grate – who in their right mind would – she tackled it and those other jobs that Mrs Rodgers could no longer manage.

Mary had tried to deny it but was forced to accept that her rheumaticky joints were making it difficult to do as much as she would have liked. Still Rachel was getting on, she was twelve and a fine wee housewife and for that she could take the credit.

Rachel was bursting to tell her da the unbelievable news but she would have to be patient. Her da was never home before half past six.

There was an apple tart ready for the oven and Mrs Rodgers had put out the potatoes for peeling. Once she had taken half the potato away with the skin but Mrs Rodgers had shown her how to take a thin paring. The potatoes seen to she began on the vegetables. Cutting up the meat she browned it in the pot the way she had been taught, turning it around with a spoon. Satisfied that it was all nicely browned she added the vegetables, a little boiling water and put on the lid. It would be ready in plenty of time.

Half past six came and went. The apple pie was ready, the meat tender and the potatoes soft. If only he would come. Constantly her eyes went to the clock and it was on seven before she heard his heavy step on the stairs, the door opening and shutting and then the minute or two it took to hang up his jacket in the lobby.

'That smells good, lass,' he said, coming into the kitchen and sitting down at the table.

'It's stew and Mrs Rodgers made an apple tart.' Rachel wished that her da would remember to wash his hands before he sat down at the table. In her mama's time he wouldn't have forgotten – he'd even change out of his heavy serge trousers but his standards were slipping.

'You're late, Da,' she said as she spooned the meat and vegetables on to the plate added a good helping of potatoes and carried it over.

'You're going to turn into a right wee nark if you're not careful,' he said and she could see that he was annoyed.

She bit her lip wishing she hadn't said that, particularly tonight, and bent her head to concentrate on filling her own plate. He was already eating his before she sat down and taking huge mouthfuls as if he were starving. Rachel deplored his table manners then was immediately ashamed. Her da worked hard and he still got up in the morning to see to the fire before he left for work.

Rachel was on the point of blurting it out but stopped herself. Timing could be important and her da had never approved of talking at the table preferring to concentrate on the food and enjoy what he was eating. Far better to wait until the table was cleared, the dishes away and he was relaxed.

Everything was done and Rachel sat down in the chair that had once been her mother's. Her throat felt dry and she felt a kind of despair. What if he laughed at the idea of her becoming a teacher, getting above herself he might say and could he afford it? Would he want to afford it?

'Da, Miss Melville made me stay behind.'

The newspaper dropped to the floor. 'And why would she do that? What have you been up to?'

'Nothing – it wasn't like that. She wanted to know if I'd like to be a teacher, to train to be one.'

His eyes opened wide. 'A teacher! She thinks my Rachel could become a teacher!' He was shaking his head and looking absolutely delighted.

'You're pleased then?' All the tension had gone and she felt gloriously happy.

'Pleased? 'Course I'm pleased, what a daft thing to ask. I'm pleased as Punch.' Then his face clouded. 'Your mother should have been here, she would have been that proud. Not a job, a profession, aye she would have liked that fine.'

'Da, I'd be a trainee teacher then only if they are satisfied—'

'Of course they'll be satisfied.'

'It means going to college to get qualifications. I wouldn't be earning money for a long time.'

'Never you mind about that, I've a bit put by and we'll manage.'

Rachel got up to fling her arms round his neck. 'Thank you, Da, and one day when I'm earning money I'll pay you back.'

'That you won't,' he said frowning. 'It's my privilege to see to my daughter's education.' He was almost preening himself.

20

★  ★  ★

Agnes caught up with Rachel before she reached the school gate.

'What did old Melly want?'

'I'll tell you if you keep it to yourself.'

'Cross my heart.'

'You're not a Catholic.'

'I can still cross my heart. Honest, Rachel, I won't tell.'

'Miss Melville said I could be a teacher when I leave school.'

'She never!'

'She did.'

'You're lucky,' Agnes said wistfully. 'It's the mill for me or a shop assistant or mebbe I'll be a skivvy in a big house, only way I'll see the inside of one.' She laughed but it had a hollow sound.

'I wish, oh I really do wish that we could both be teachers,' Rachel said generously then honesty forced her to add, 'You're clever and you're quicker than me in learning things.'

'Mebbe.' Agnes saw no point in denying what she knew to be the truth. 'You could be top of the class if you wanted.'

Rachel saw a hint of tears in the brown eyes, then saw her give an impatient shake of her head. 'Reading and writing is all I need, what use is the rest to me? I'd like fine to learn and I ken I'm clever, my ma was too but like she says too much learnin' just makes you discontented. Your ma made you talk posh and that's why old Melly likes you.'

'You could talk like me and it's not posh just proper. If you want I'd teach you.'

'No, ta, I dinnae need your help.' She drew herself up the way Miss Melville did. 'If it was my wish to speak properly then I should do so.'

It was so like their teacher, Agnes was a good mimic, that Rachel took a fit of the giggles. Agnes joined in and the pair of them went into the playground falling about laughing.

Groups of girls were whispering and giggling among themselves and Rachel had a vague idea of what they were discussing but she had no wish to join them. Agnes did but not very often. It was Agnes who had prepared Rachel for her monthlies and a good thing too, Rachel thought, or she might well have panicked.

'You don't like talking about it, do you?' Agnes asked, jerking her head towards the group.

Rachel shrugged.

'Better to know what it's all about,' Agnes said matter-of-factly, 'you'll have to know one day.'

'Know what?'

'What happens.'

'What does?'

'You mean you don't know?' Agnes said incredulously.

Rachel looked shamefaced. 'I haven't got a ma to tell me.'

'It wasn't my ma, it was my sister telt me. If you want to know I'll tell you.'

Rachel wanted to say no but curiosity got the better of her. 'All right, tell me then.'

Agnes whispered into her ear.

Rachel looked shocked. 'I don't believe a word of that. My parents would never have—'

'You daft thing, they must have or you wouldn't have got born.'

Rachel felt sick. 'If it's true I'm never going to get married.'

'You won't be getting married anyway,' Agnes said scornfully. 'You'll be a teacher and become an old maid like your precious Miss Melville.'

'And you, Agnes Boyd, are just jealous.'

Agnes's eyes were bleak. 'I know I'm jealous, I can't help it.' She paused, gulped and looked down, scraping the loose stones with her boot. 'When you're a teacher you won't want anything to do with me.'

'That is just not true, Agnes Boyd,' Rachel said indignantly, 'you're my best chum and you always will be.'

Agnes cheered up but all she said was, 'Mebbe aye, mebbe no.'

'Lass, stop that and come and sit down,' her father said irritably.

'I'm almost finished cleaning the brasses.'

'Leave them I said.'

'What's wrong, Da?'

'Nothing is wrong. Your mother wanted me to have a little talk with you when you came twelve.'

He looked uncomfortable and Rachel felt herself go hot and cold with embarrassment. 'A little talk.' Surely that could only mean one thing, that he was going to talk to her about 'those things' and she didn't want to hear about them, not from her da. Dropping her eyes to the floor she tried to close her ears to the sound of his voice.

'Your grandparents, your mother's parents, are alive.'

Rachel's head shot up. 'What? What did you say?'

'You have grandparents living.'

She stared at him as though he had taken leave of his senses. 'But they are dead, Mama said . . .'

'They were dead to your mother from the time they disowned her.'

Rachel moistened her lips. 'Why did they disown Mama?'

'She married me, that's why,' George said bitterly. 'An ignorant millhand was no match for the daughter of a mill owner. Aye, Rachel, a mill owner. Your grandfather is Albert Craig of the Craig Mills in Lochee.'

Rachel knew of the Craig Mills. Who didn't? It was one of the biggest in Dundee. She was too stunned to say anything, her mouth hung open and she stared fixedly at her father.

'Mebbe I should begin at the beginning.'

She nodded.

'It started with a wee hat.' He gave a short laugh. 'I saw the thing and caught it before it landed in a puddle. And there was I feeling right stupid I can tell you when these two lasses came hurrying over.'

'One of them was Mama? That's right, isn't it?'

She saw his face soften and a faraway look come into his eyes. 'That was the first time I saw your ma. She was a bonny wee thing and I knew right then that she was the lass for me.'

'What happened?' Rachel asked eagerly.

'Well, I handed over the hat and your ma thanked me real prettily then they walked away.'

'Don't stop.'

'I was still standing when Amelia turned round and smiled and I took that as a wee sign of encouragement and began to haunt the Esplanade in the hope of seeing her and unknown to me she was doing the same thing. To this day I don't know how she managed it.'

'But you met and fell in love?' Rachel said, her face pink with excitement.

'Your mother was just looking for a bit of excitement before she became officially betrothed to one of her own kind.'

'Da,' she said impatiently.

'I was for doing the right thing, the honourable thing, and asking for her hand in marriage but Amelia had other ideas. She wanted to prepare them, make it easier for me when we did meet, but I never met them, Rachel, never got beyond the gate.'

'Oh, Da,' Rachel said feeling anguish for what he must have suffered. He was a proud man and she could imagine how dreadful it must have been for him.

'That's the way it was, lass,' he said heavily. 'Your mother was kept a virtual prisoner and told that if she had anything more to do with me she'd be disowned. They thought threatening her with an impoverished future would bring her to her senses but they didn't know their daughter.'

'Why didn't you just go up to the house?'

'And get my marching orders from some maid or their snooty housekeeper?'

'But it wasn't fair, Da, you couldn't help falling in love.'

'Love, real love is a very a powerful emotion, lass, one day you'll mebbe find that out for yourself. It makes slaves of us all.'

'How did Mama and you get married?'

'Amelia got one of the maids to act as a go-between and get notes to me. When she knew her parents were to be away on a social visit she packed a couple of suitcases and I was waiting.'

Rachel looked at her da with a new respect. It had taken a lot of courage but for her mother it had been a great deal more to give up all she had known.

'Where did you go?'

'Your Aunt Gwen and Uncle John had a house in Dundee at that time and Amelia stayed with them until I arranged things. The pity was that Gwen, John and the bairns were booked to go to America. Gwen would have been a great help and God knows your mother needed all the help she could get. Still, there is always a way and Mary Rodgers—'

'Mama always said that Mrs Rodgers was a godsend.'

'That she was and still is.'

'Why did Mama not tell me this herself?'

'I don't know, lass. She didn't mean you to know at all but she must have changed her mind. She asked me, saying you were too young at nine.'

'You didn't want me to know, did you?'

'No, lass, it was the last thing I wanted, but a promise to a dying woman is something that has to be honoured. Anyway, you know now and that is an end to it.'

'They sound horrible,' Rachel said close to tears, 'and I never want anything to do with them.'

George looked relieved. 'That's what I hoped you'd say.'

'Where do they live, Da?' George's relief vanished.

'At that time they had a big house on the Esplanade but the family home is somewhere in Perthshire. Your mother got snippets of information now and again. Your great-grandfather died and as the only son, your grandfather inherited the estate.'

Rachel was having difficulty taking it in. 'Does Mama's father still work in Lochee?' She couldn't bring herself to say Grandpa.

'His kind don't work, lass. A manager is put in charge to see to things.'

'Da, have I any cousins on mama's side?'

'Quite possibly. She had an older sister, Maud, but that's all I can tell you. One more thing – that box on the shelf.' They both looked at the wooden box out of reach on the shelf.

'That's where Mama kept her papers.'

'Is that what she told you? You've a fine memory. Mebbe there's papers too but there is a brooch, one your mother got for her eighteenth birthday. It's valuable, Rachel, so you'll need to take great care of it. Then there is a little money, what your mother earned from her sewing, that's yours too.'

'Da, that'll help with college when I go,' Rachel said eagerly.

'No, it won't. It doesn't amount to much but it'll buy you something nice to wear when you're older. Or when you go off to college.'

'May I see the brooch?'

'Not the now.'

# Chapter Four

Amelia had been dead for four years and though Rachel often thought of her mother, still shed a few tears into her pillow, the pain of loss had gone leaving just an aching longing for what might have been.

At thirteen Rachel was a head taller than Agnes and both girls were still best friends though Rachel had gone on to the academy. They were together for their Sabbath day stroll. Leaving Blackness Road they approached Victoria Park then on to Balgay Hill and climbed the flight of steps known locally as Jacob's Ladder and on to the top of the hill. They looked at the clear, sparkling water which gurgled through an opening to trickle over stones, smooth and whitened over the years, then cupping their hands drank noisily until their thirst was quenched. Summer was nearly over and the first of the leaves had fluttered from the trees to make a soft carpet. Agnes flopped down.

'I'm tired, let's have a rest.'

Rachel dropped down beside her and watched as Agnes took off her boots and wiggled her toes. 'These are pinching,' she said as she adjusted the piece of newspaper inside.

Rachel looked away feeling uncomfortable. She was always well-dressed and her boots never worn through.

'Agnes?'

'What?' She turned to Rachel screwing up her face against the sun.

'There is only me and I've outgrown some things. I mean I have school boots that are too small and if you or one of your sisters—' she stopped. 'Agnes, I'm not trying to—' she stopped again.

'If you mean am I too proud to accept them the answer is no. Like you said, you haven't anyone coming behind you and there's plenty of us.'

Rachel was relieved that Agnes was anything but offended.

'What about coming to my house tomorrow after school and I'll have things looked out?'

'What about your da? Will he mind you giving me—'

27

'No, why should he?'

They sat in a companionable silence broken by the drone of a bee as it circled them, then as Agnes waved a boot at it, circled once more as if in defiance, then disappeared. Putting her boots back on Agnes stood up and Rachel, who had been lying with her hands behind her head, slowly got up. Instead of using Jacob's Ladder for the return journey they slithered down the grass to the path below.

'Folk are talking about your da and Peggy McKenzie.'

'That blonde woman with the awful laugh? Don't be daft, Agnes, he just blethers to her when he's in for his tobacco.'

'That's enough to set tongues wagging around here,' Agnes said knowingly. 'My ma says Peggy's no spring chicken and your da is a good catch.'

A vague disquiet touched Rachel then she shrugged it off. Her da would never replace her mama with the likes of Peggy McKenzie. The woman was common and vulgar.

Agnes touched her arm. 'Don't worry about it, you can bet it's only wishful thinking on Peggy's part.'

'I'm not worried, not in the least.'

But she was and Rachel worried about it long after she and Agnes parted company, Agnes to her home in Spinner's Lane off the Hawkhill and Rachel to her home. Little things, unimportant at the time, were coming back. Like how she had always gone for her da's tobacco until a month or so ago. And her da going out after his meal and not coming back until late. With a little shudder she recalled the time, the one and only time, that she'd waited up for him and unable to stay awake he'd found her curled up in his chair. She recalled too how he'd shaken her roughly.

'What's this? Why are you no' in your bed?' he'd demanded to know and leaning over her she'd got a whiff of his breath and knew that he had been drinking.

'I – I thought you might want something when you got in.'

'You thought wrong then.' Then his voice softened. 'There's no need for you to stay up for me. You just get to your bed at the usual time, at your age you need your sleep.'

After that she'd gone to bed and had no idea of the time he got in.

Agnes was greatly impressed with Rachel's home and that visit remained in her memory for a long time. The contrast to her own home could not have been greater. In her house the table was never without a clutter but in Rachel's it was cleared and a cover spread over. Her eyes settled on the range.

'Would you look at that grate, you can nearly see yoursel' in it.'

Rachel preened herself. 'My own work I'll have you know. Mrs Rodgers used to do it but she's not so able.'

'You mean you do everything?'

'Just about. Da sees to the fire and fills the coal bucket.'

'Proper little housewife.'

'I've Mrs Rodgers to thank; she said I would need to learn to look after my da. Want to see the rest?' she said carelessly not wanting to appear to be showing off.

'Wouldn't mind.'

Rachel opened the door into the front room, no longer called the parlour, and Agnes walked in.

'Gawd, it's like a blinkin' palace. Is it ever used?'

'Not very often. My mother used to sit and sew at the window. She liked the view.'

Agnes joined her at the window. 'Marvellous view of the Law hill. My ma would like this. When I was wee she used to take us up the Law hill and point out the pencil shape of the mill chimneys and make us count them. Maybe I should take the wee ones up, let them play there instead of the gutter. Listen to me. I'm full of good ideas but that is as far as it ever gets.' She grinned and followed Rachel out.

'This is my bedroom.'

'A room all to yourself?'

'Who else is there?' Rachel asked amused.

'Daft thing to say wasn't it? With us it's three in a bed and as for the house itself, it's a midden. Not my ma's fault,' she said loyally, 'it's a' they bairns, she never gets a chance.'

Rachel bent down and hauled the kist over. Under protective paper were the clothes that had belonged to her mother, all carefully folded. Mrs Rodgers had advised George to keep them, the material was good, she said, and they could be altered for Rachel.

'There,' she said, handing Agnes a navy blue serge skirt. 'It's too short for me and that's a blouse you can wear with it. One of the buttons is hanging off but you can sew it on, can't you?'

29

'No bother. But are you absolutely sure, Rachel?' Agnes said holding the skirt against herself then doing the same with the blouse.

'Of course I'm sure. They are no good to me and there is no one I'd rather give them to.' She looked over at Agnes. 'My mother kept some of the clothes I had when I was little and I thought they would do for your wee sisters.'

'Oh, ta, my ma will be over the moon.'

Rachel put out two pairs of boots, one pair well worn but the other pair had been a bad buy. She should have made sure that she had plenty of room to allow for growth but instead she had chosen a pair that just fitted. She added some underwear and left Agnes to wrap up the bundle in an old blanket.

'Rachel, did you notice Maggie Thomson was wearing shoes with a cross-over strap?'

Rachel nodded. 'I liked them and my da's going to let me buy a pair.'

'You're dead lucky, do you know that?'

'In some ways I am, Agnes, Rachel said quietly, 'but remember you have a mother and I don't.'

Agnes didn't answer. She loved her mother but even so, given the chance she knew she would willingly change places with Rachel.

'Look at the time,' Agnes shrieked, 'I'll better go.' At the door she stopped and said almost shyly. 'Ta, Rachel, ta very much, you're a good chum to have.'

# Chapter Five

Jenny Boyd was leaning against the door post, the sleeping infant in her arms when Agnes arrived out of breath and clutching her precious bundle.

'About time too! Where do you think you've been?'

'Rachel's.' She followed her mother into the house and dumped the bundle. 'She's given me things she's outgrown.'

'Oh, aye, let's have a look.' There was a commotion at the door. 'Here, put the bairn in the cot and careful she doesnae waken.' The four-year-old twins, Daisy and Rose, came in, their faces filthy and Rose's nose was running.

'A piece,' Daisy demanded for them both. She was the dominant twin and Rose happily followed where she led.

Poor Rose squirmed as her mother, with a quick and none too gentle twist of the rag, cleaned the runny nose then cut two slices of bread and spread them with jam. 'Here,' she said handing one to each, 'and bide outside till you're telt to come in.'

Agnes had undone the bundle and her mother picked up the navy blue skirt. 'This'll be just grand for Meg; with her workin' she needs something decent to wear.' Meg, at fourteen and the eldest, had started work in the baker's shop just round the corner. To compensate for the meagre wage she was given a bag of stale buns and once a week a bag of broken biscuits.

'No, Ma,' Agnes said firmly, 'that's not for our Meg, it's mine.'

'What you have is good enough for school.'

'If Rachel doesn't see me wearing it she won't give me anything else,' Agnes said cunningly.

'Och, well, in that case—'

'I'm having the skirt, the blouse and the best pair of boots and one of the petticoats. Meg can have the others and Rachel put in some things for the wee ones.'

Jenny Boyd picked up the garments and shook her head. 'Poor lass, she must have wanted another bairn to keep a' this.' A tender smile crossed her face. 'Right bonny things, I heard tell she was good with the needle. Ta, Agnes, lass, this'll be a grand help.' She got up off her knees and took the blanket. 'It's a double; it'll do on oor bed.'

'I'm hungry.'

'It's herrin the day, I'll away and fry ours and we can have it in peace.'

For so long Agnes had lived with squalor that she took the untidiness and dirt for granted but coming from Rachel's spotless house she looked about her with disgust. The smell of herring was strong but not unpleasant and Agnes's stomach was rumbling with hunger. The house was a midden just as she'd told Rachel. The room was both kitchen and her parents' bedroom, the baby's cot was next to the bed which hadn't been made. The table was cluttered with dirty dishes, a loaf of bread, a jar of jam which without the lid was attracting flies as was the pot of congealed gravy and there were various other items that should have had no place beside food. With a grimace of distaste Agnes removed the pot to the floor and cleared a space.

'You never bring that lass, Rachel, here.'

'And I'm not going to either, you should see her house.'

'Huh! Easy for them – her da's a gaffer.'

'He was at school with you, wasn't he?'

'Aye. Geordie Donaldson was a fine lad, I fancied him for a bit.' For a moment her face lit up and showed something of the attractive girl she had once been, but her hair, her once beautiful hair, hung in straggles.

'But you married Da,' Agnes said accusingly as her mother dished up the herrings.

'Mebbe he's no' much now but your da was good-lookin' in them days and anyway Geordie wed that stuck-up piece.'

'Rachel's going to be a teacher, she'll be going on to college and it's not fair, I'm the cleverest.' Agnes hated herself for sounding resentful. She was glad for Rachel, she had to keep telling herself that but she felt a hatred of the system that deprived her of the opportunity to better herself. Surely it should be ability that counted and not the ability to pay.

'Nothin' is fair in this world, Agnes, I'm surprised it's taken you so long to find that oot. The likes of us are trapped in poverty from the day we were born.'

'If Da drank less and worked harder we wouldn't be.' Agnes said greatly daring.

A flush of anger settled on her mother's face. 'You watch that tongue of yours, my lass. A man needs a drink.'

'A drink mebbe but not a bucketful. Why should he need it anyway?'

Jenny Boyd gave an unpleasant laugh. 'Helps him forget he's a failure. And as for you, Agnes, take my advice and get yoursel' a job in one o' they big hooses.' She paused to cut herself a slice of bread to clean her plate. 'Keep on the right side o' them that can dae ye a favour and mebbe you'll end up a cook or a hoosekeeper.'

Agnes, her good humour restored, grinned across at her mother. 'Mebbe I'll wed someone with money.'

'Be an auld man's darlin'?'

'Or better still a young ane's.'

'Dinnae expect him to put a ring on your finger or you'll be dafter than I thought.'

Just then the twins trailed in dirtier than ever. Eddie and Bobby, a year between them, were fighting as usual and eight-year-old Peter, in trousers several sizes too big for him, was yelling encouragement.

'In the lot of you,' Jenny Boyd bawled, separating the fighters and cuffing Peter's ear. 'Gawd, who would hae bairns?'

Agnes picked up the infant now known as Ruby, and cuddled her in her arms.

'You can't complain about this one, Ma, she's always good.'

'More's the pity, times I'd welcome a bit of temper.'

'Why?'

'I'm not sure, just a feeling.'

Jenny had noticed right away that this one was different and she was proved right. The youngest Boyd was a mongol and would need to be looked after all of her life.

# Chapter Six

Swirls of sea mist chilled the very bones and there was the moist feel of snow in the air. On Hogmanay morning an overnight sprinkling, like a dusting of icing sugar, appeared on the distant Sidlaw Hills.

Dundee housewives were up early that morning cleaning the house from top to bottom and polishing the brasses until they shone. Carrying unfinished handwork into the New Year was said to be unlucky and the more superstitious had been known to unravel knitting that could not be completed in time rather than risk misfortune.

Rachel had been up since six and she was flushed and happy as she looked over to the table. Cooling on it were cakes of shortbread, scones and a light fruit cake. Mary Rodgers had baked a black bun and this, too, was on the table. Rachel didn't care for it, it was much too heavy for her taste, but to Mary the New Year was just not the New Year without a piece of black bun to go with a dram.

George had disappeared to the Tally-Ho to collect some bottles to add to those already in the cupboard. And that was his step she heard in the lobby.

'By, there's a right nip in the air,' he said putting down his purchases and blowing on his hands.

'Da, look at that!' Rachel said indicating the table.

'Looks grand, lass, a fair treat and I'm thinking you're going to make some man a fine wife one day. And now you can give me a hand by opening that dresser and I'll pack away this lot.'

'Who is coming anyway?' Rachel asked as she began handing him the bottles.

'Never know who might cross the door and I'd think shame if I was caught out.'

Now was the moment when he was in a good mood.

'Da, Agnes is getting to go into the town to see the New Year in and she's asked me if I'll be allowed.'

George stopped what he was doing. 'What, just the pair of you?'

'No. Davie Burnside and Tommy Allardyce are going.' She played her trump card. 'Davie said to tell you he'd see me right to the close. Please, Da, I'd like to go,' she pleaded.

George Donaldson looked into the young face pleading with him and sighed inwardly. His lass was growing up and he didn't know how much freedom she should be allowed. He knew that he would prefer to err by being overcautious, no doubt about that, but the lass had the right to some enjoyment. She worked hard at school and in the house and she was sensible.

'By all accounts Alex Burnside's son is a nice lad and I think I could trust him to look after you but that doesn't mean to say I'm entirely happy. To my way of thinking you are all too young to be gallivanting in the town.'

Rachel let out her breath in relief. 'Then I can go?'

'On one condition,' George said sternly. 'The four of you keep close together all the time. I know what I'm talking about, Rachel, I've been often enough in the High Street to bring in the year. It'll be crowded and a lot of them far gone on drink and it could get rough.'

'We'll keep together, Da.' She would have promised anything.

'Mind you do then and what time is this lad coming?'

'Half past ten, we've to meet Agnes and Tommy at the Pillars about eleven.'

George nodded. 'That's all right then but you're not to stay out too long.' He knew he was beginning to sound like an anxious mother hen but the responsibility for her safety was all his.

Rachel chose to ignore that. If they were to stay together she could hardly dictate and she didn't want to anyway. She felt the thrill of approaching independence, of what it was going to be like when she was grown-up and this, her first experience, she was going to enjoy.

'What about you, Da? What are you doing?'

'Oh, a few neighbours will drop in I wouldn't wonder. Don't worry about me, lass.' There was a small, satisfied smile on his face but Rachel was too busy thinking of the evening ahead to notice.

Davie Burnside looked a little self-conscious as he was shown into the kitchen. Just short of fourteen and a few months older than Rachel, Davie was tall and painfully thin. He had a pleasant, open face and a surprisingly firm chin for one so young. His hair was the colour of sand and thick and his eyes were blue-grey. He would likely broaden out and end up like his father, a tall, broad-shouldered man with thinning fair hair and a good, friendly manner for the grocer's shop which he owned. With three daughters and one son the shop would one day belong to Davie.

After school Davie served in the shop to relieve his mother and she saw to it that her son had smart clothes and coppers in his pocket. In a year or two the lasses would be looking hopefully in his direction for Davie Burnside would be a fine catch.

They were on their feet and George put his hand on Davie's shoulder.

'She's in your keeping, lad.'

'Don't worry, Mr Donaldson, I'll look after Rachel and bring her safely home.'

Rachel was beginning to feel distinctly annoyed. Agnes wouldn't have to put up with this, she thought resentfully.

At last they were outside and she could begin to enjoy herself.

She was wearing a warm skirt and a high-buttoned thick blouse and over it a lovely rose pink cloak that had belonged to her mother. Amelia had been small and some of her clothes already fitted Rachel.

'That's bonny and you look nice in it,' Davie said shyly as he touched the cloak.

'It was my mother's,' Rachel answered then wished she hadn't said it. All that was called for was 'thank you', she would have to learn how to accept a compliment.

With matching steps they walked smartly down Blackness Road, not saying a great deal but comfortable with each other. Once they reached the West Port Davie tucked her arm in his.

'Better hang on to me.'

Rachel thought that she'd better as they were swept along and into the Overgate where stalls were doing a roaring trade in gifts for first footing. All afternoon the city centre had been throbbing with excitement which intensified with the hour. For the revellers Dundee had much to offer, so many places of attraction.

Leaving the stalls Rachel and Davie wound their way to the Town House affectionately known as the Pillars. The impressive stone building was designed by William Adam in 1731 and consisted of a vaulted ground-floor arcade with shops and a bank. Above those were the council chambers, courts and jail. Enjoying a good position in the town centre made it a popular meeting place for Dundonians. It was somewhere to shelter from the rain and pass the time by looking at the various window displays. Rumours were about that the Pillars was to be demolished but few believed that it would actually happen.

Straining their eyes they soon picked out Agnes and Tommy from the noisy crowd congregated there.

'Look that's them yonder,' Davie said pulling Rachel with him just as Agnes waved and screamed their names across the length of the Pillars. There were shouts and laughter as the four friends got together. Tommy Allardyce cast an admiring glance at Rachel.

'You look like a princess in that pink thing.'

Rachel blushed. 'Don't be so daft.'

'When does it come to me?' Agnes whispered with a hopeful grin.

'Never. This is something I keep for ever, it was my mama's favourite.'

Agnes was always decently dressed and if she took it for granted that Rachel's outgrown clothes would continue to come her way, Rachel didn't mind. She knew that they eventually reached the younger Boyds and made things a little easier in that household. The three of them were warmly clad and Rachel just wished that the same could be said for Tommy Allardyce. The threadbare coat he wore would do little to keep out the cold but he was always clean and tidy. Like Agnes, Tommy knew poverty but unlike Jenny Boyd his widowed mother kept a clean house and took in other people's washing to help earn enough to feed and clothe her family.

The old year was slowly but steadily drawing to a close and a magical air of expectation was all around. Time seemed to stand still as silence fell for the last few moments. In the hush that was almost eerie, Rachel felt a lump in her throat and she could see that others were affected too, some were openly weeping. Amidst the joy of welcoming in the New Year there was sadness at seeing the old year slipping away and the feeling of anxiety of what the New Year might bring. Then cares were forgotten as the awaited signal, the firing of the time-gun, shattered the silence and was followed by the pealing of the bells from the Steeple and St Paul's.

As the sky filled with the coloured lights of rockets lighting up the heavens the crowd screamed its delight. Friends and strangers alike shook hands wishing one another a guid new year and four young people were unusually subdued as they gripped each other's hands in friendship. A year from now would they be together or would fate have sent them in other directions?

By one o'clock a tired but happy foursome was heading for home and in the early morning frost the boys' heavy boots rang hollowly as they left the crowds. At the West Port they parted company, Agnes and Tommy to go along the Hawkhill and Rachel and Davie into Brook Street and Blackness Road.

Rachel gave a deep sigh and yawned.

'Tired are you?'

'Just a bit but I wouldn't have missed it for the world.'

'My da said it's always a marvellous occasion when people are just happy to be together.'

'It was, it was very special but sad too. Did you think that, Davie?'

'Everybody gets emotional at the New Year and those with a good drink in them are the worst.'

They laughed as they saw two men trying to hold each other up as they struggled to keep their balance.

'Happy New Year,' Davie shouted across the road.

'An' you as weel and your bonny lass,' came the reply.

For one awful moment Rachel thought they were going to stagger across the road and she gripped Davie's arm.

'That was daft.'

'A harmless pair, Rachel.'

'How can you possibly know that?'

'Through the shop and watching my da. He knows the type itching for a fight and gets them out before it develops. That pair are just at the happy stage when everybody is a friend.'

'And the world a lovely place,' Rachel added softly.

'It is an' all, wouldn't you say?'

'Pretty good,' she agreed.

'Doesn't all that swotting—'

She stopped him. 'Davie, I'm happy to work hard and I'm grateful to my da for giving me the chance to stay on at school.' She paused. 'You could easily stay on for your certificate. Why don't you?'

'Waste of time, I'm going into the shop with my da.' He grinned. 'And he says as long as I can coont he's no' bothered by the rest.'

They had now reached her close and she was taken completely by surprise when he bent his head to touch his lips to hers in a feather-light kiss. Pushing him away she voiced her indignation.

'What did you have to go and do that for?'

'Just wanted to and anyway you're supposed to like it.'

'Well, I did not, Davie Burnside,' but Rachel wasn't telling the truth. That touch had sent a strange, tingling sensation through her body that both alarmed and delighted her.

'Never mind,' Davie said not in the least put out. 'I'll get better at it.'

She tried to hold back the giggle and put her hand over her mouth but it came out and Davie laughed with her. 'He's really nice,' Rachel thought as she moved inside the close.

'I'll wait until I hear the door shutting.'

Each landing had its own gaslight between the two doors but more often than not the gas wasn't lit or the mantle was broken but this was the New Year and negotiating the stairs in darkness after a few drams could be a risky business. No one wanted to be held responsible for a broken limb or worse, so tonight the close and stairs were well lit.

Even before she reached and opened the door Rachel could hear voices and laughter and was glad that her da had company. No one heard her until she opened the door of the front room and she immediately saw that they were neighbours from round about. Her da had seen her and was getting up from the horsehair sofa, his faced flushed with too much celebrating and then she saw with a sinking heart who was still on the horsehair sofa.

'Happy New Year, my own wee lass,' George Donaldson said, his whisky-warm breath on her face as he kissed her.

'Happy New Year, Da.'

'You enjoyed yoursel' and the lad brought you home?'

'It was great, really great, Da.'

With a hand not quite steady George was pouring out some ginger cordial.

'My Gawd, Geordie, you're no' on that stuff!'

'No, Bella, this is for the young lass.'

'Rachel, that's surely no' you wi' a lad already and you not turned fourteen?' Lizzie Skinner said as she helped herself to a piece of black bun. Her own two plain, ungainly daughters were eighteen and nineteen with no lad showing an interest in either.

'Of course not, Mrs Skinner,' Rachel said furious with herself for blushing, 'it was only Davie Burnside and – some of my friends.'

'Take my tip and hang in there,' Bob Skinner nodded knowingly, 'that shop is a wee gold mine and it'll go to the lad one day.'

'No wonder it's a gold mine,' Bella McDonald added her twopence worth, 'with the prices Alex Burnside charges. Fair disgrace that he gets away with it.'

'My lass has more to do than bother her head wi' lads. She's going to be a teacher,' George said proudly.

There was a moment's silence then a few mutterings. 'Would you credit that?' followed by words of congratulations.

'Only if I pass the examinations,' Rachel said desperately and wishing her father hadn't told them. It was so unlike him but then drink was loosening his tongue.

'Wouldn't you say that calls for drinks all round?' Bill Webster shouted after draining his glass. 'A toast to the lass.'

'If your hand is steadier than mine you can pour.'

'Steady as a rock,' Bill Webster declared as he lurched forward and earning himself a warning from his grim-faced wife. One small sherry hadn't sweetened the night for her.

Rachel did the round of the room shaking hands and suffering a kiss if there was no escape.

'You've missed Peggy,' her da said pushing her towards the horsehair sofa, 'I want my two lasses to be friends.'

Rachel didn't miss the look that passed between her da and Peggy McKenzie and as the implications of that look took shape she knew with a dreadful certainty that the relationship had gone far beyond friendship. If only she didn't dislike the woman so much, Rachel thought wretchedly, it wasn't just the loud, coarse laugh, it was more than that. She didn't trust her. To be fair, Rachel accepted that there would be some who found Peggy attractive – her da for one obviously – though how he could admire someone so different from her mama was hard to understand. Her mother had been small and dainty whereas Peggy was the big blousy type. She looked well in her black skirt and red blouse, though to the women present, the plunging neckline showed too much of the heavy bosom. George was called away and Peggy settled her hard eyes on Rachel.

'A happy New Year.'

'And to you,' Rachel answered as their hands touched briefly.

'Fancy you wantin' to be a teacher! Wonder Geordie didn't mention it afore now.'

'Why should he? If my father hadn't been drinking it wouldn't have come out at all. Incidentally, Peggy, my father's name is George, my mother wouldn't have dreamt of calling him Geordie.' They were speaking quietly but the others were too busy among themselves to pay attention.

'I'm sure your ma wouldn't.' The bold eyes flashed with anger mixed with amusement. 'Your ma thought herself a cut above the rest of us and tried to mould her man to her ways and Geordie being the big, soft lump he is did his best to please her.'

'That's a lie. How dare you say such a thing.'

Her father was back, his face wreathed in smiles. 'Now isn't that just grand, my two lasses getting acquainted,' he said drawing Rachel down with him on the sofa and putting an arm round each of them.

How much longer were they going to stay? Rachel wondered. It had gone three o'clock and still no sign of a move. Sheer determination to see Peggy off the premises kept her awake. And then just as she thought she would have to give in Bella McDonald heaved herself out of the chair.

'Would you folk take a look at the time?'

'My, it's fair flown but we'll hae to be like the beggars,' someone said.

'That was a rare night, Geordie.' Bella gave him a resounding kiss before he helped her on with her coat.

They were all on their feet, all except Peggy.

'Where is your coat, Peggy?'

'It's all right, Rachel, it's in the lobby with mine,' George answered for her.

Anxious to be given her rightful place, Rachel stood with her father at the door while the departing guests made their slow way down the stairs.

'Is Peggy waiting for you to take her home?'

'She won't be going for a while yet,' he said shutting the door and walking back to the front room. Peggy lived about ten minutes away in Ure Street where she shared two rooms with her invalid mother and Aunt Kate, her mother's unmarried sister.

'Geordie, I could murder a cup of tea.'

'I'll make it,' Rachel said.

They both turned almost as though they had forgotten her existence.

'It's bed for you, my lass.'

'Don't I get a cup of tea?'

'No, you do not. I said bed and I meant it.' If only he hadn't winked to Peggy, Rachel thought miserably. Perhaps it had been the look on her face but George added, 'I'll escort Peggy home just as soon as—'

'We have that cuppie,' Peggy finished for him. 'And I'll see your da hurries back home, Rachel, if it's staying in the house on your own that is worrying you.'

'It doesn't, not in the least,' Rachel said as she marched from the room still smarting from being treated like a little girl. She undressed, put on her nightgown, pulled the bedclothes over her head and slept the sleep of the dead.

At a quarter past eleven Rachel got up, opened the curtains and went through to the kitchen. Only when she was in there did the events of the previous night come crowding in. A little apprehensively she looked over to the recess. Surely she hadn't expected to see them in bed together? Of course not, she blushed at the very idea. Her da would never do anything like that, shame on her even to have considered it. But then drink did strange things to people, she mused, and her da had had a skinful. For a moment she looked at him lying in the middle of the big bed, his mouth slightly open and giving out an occasional snort. She had always thought of her da as handsome but he didn't look it now. His skin had coarsened and the black curly hair was peppered with grey. Would he still have aged if her mama had been alive or would love have kept him young-looking?

Suddenly she shivered, the fire hadn't been backed up and only the cold ashes remained. Quickly she returned to her room to dress in an old skirt and warm jumper. She would get the fire going, her da would be pleased to get up to a warm room and his breakfast all ready for him. He would see that she could look after him and that Peggy McKenzie wasn't necessary in his life.

# Chapter Seven

The shrill sound of the hooter brought sighs of relief from the mill workers as they hastened to leave their looms. Soon they were a laughing, noisy crowd bursting through the gates to join shop assistants and others all homeward bound. Propping herself against the newsagent's window, Agnes Boyd watched them and bitterness rose like nausea in her throat.

With her brains she should be at the academy with Rachel and studying for a worthwhile career instead of being forced to leave school when she was still short of her fourteenth birthday. Agnes hated herself for being jealous and resentful of a friend, particularly a good friend like Rachel, but she couldn't help it. And each time she saw Rachel in the distinctive uniform of the academy it was like adding salt to the wound.

Standing there waiting for the crush of workers to pass, Agnes began to think about the unfairness of life. Why, she wondered, didn't God see to it that everyone got an equal chance? And that brought to mind the earnest, bespectacled minister who came twice in term-time to address the pupils in the school hall. Droning on in that ministerial voice that always made her want to laugh, he had stressed the importance of being good and obedient and showing fitting gratitude for all His loving kindness.

Yet how could He expect her to be grateful for being born into a family like the Boyds? She had even begun to have secret doubts about His existence but thoughts like that scared her too. Even if He hadn't been fair to her, and some others she could name, it was comforting to think of a God in heaven.

Something else was troubling her, the gulf between them was growing wider though Rachel strongly denied it. She needed Rachel, needed her chum's quiet good humour and her kindness to help forget the poverty and squalor of her own home.

Over and over again a slightly impatient Rachel had assured her that attending different schools would make no difference to that friendship but they were both aware of the lengthening silences when they were together. If she detected a change in their relationship Rachel put the blame on Agnes. More often than not she was short-tempered and forever moaning as though only she had problems.

Officially it was spring but hard to believe. The east wind was bitingly cold and the drawn faces of the passers-by were pinched and blue. Rachel reached the corner of Tay Street, the arranged meeting place, hoping to find Agnes already there but of course she wasn't, Agnes wasn't strong on punctuality. Stamping her feet to keep the circulation going Rachel waited almost ten minutes before Agnes put in an appearance.

'Come on, Agnes, this isn't good enough,' Rachel fumed, 'you're late as usual and it's perishing standing on this corner.'

'Sorry.'

'What's wrong? You've got a face on you like a wet Sunday.'

'So would you in my shoes. I start work on Monday.'

'How can you when you're not fourteen?'

'Easy enough. My ma went up to the school and told them I had a job if I could start straight away. Laying it on thick about needing the money and jobs being hard to come by.'

'That's true enough, Agnes, my da says the mill isn't taking on any weavers meantime.' Then seeing the misery on her friend's face she said gently, 'What kind of job?'

'Our Meg's got a living-in job as a maid in one of the big houses in the Broughty Ferry Road and I've to take over hers in that bloody baker's.'

Rachel was shocked. 'Agnes, you shouldn't swear, not that terrible word.'

'Why not? It's the way I feel and bloody is tame to what you'd hear in our house.' She gave a cheeky grin. 'Finish your education it would if you heard what my da and ma yell at each other.'

Rachel had no desire to further her education that way.

'You don't have to stick it for long, you can look for something better.'

'That's exactly what I mean to do. I'll do the same as Meg.'

'You don't like housework, Agnes.'

'Neither does Meg. Mind you, come to think about it how do we know— neither of us has had any experience. Only the minimum gets done in our house.'

Rachel had no answer to that.

'She's to share a room with another maid but she'll have her own bed and that must be bliss.'

Rachel nodded. She knew that Agnes had the twins, Daisy and Rose, sleeping beside her and that a damp bed was nothing unusual. Poor Agnes, she did have a lot to put up with and if she moaned who could blame her?

'Mind telling me where we're heading?'

'The Wellgate. We could have a look round Hunter's unless you have a better suggestion,' Agnes said.

'No, that's fine by me provided you behave yourself.'

'What do you mean by that?'

'As if you didn't know! And, Agnes,' Rachel said severely, 'it isn't fair to pretend you're going to buy something, have the assistant go to the trouble of bringing things out, then tell her it isn't quite what you were looking for.'

'No harm in it and it gives her something to do. I don't do it when they are busy.'

'Wait until someone does that to you when you're behind the counter.'

'In a baker's?' Agnes said scornfully.

'Yes, even in a baker's. I could come in, ask for half a dozen pancakes, four scones, four morning rolls, a loaf of bread and when you'd got them in bags ready to hand over, I'd tell you I've changed my mind.'

'Gawd! I'd murder you.'

'Then behave yourself in Hunter's and just by way of a change, Agnes Boyd, you can listen to my troubles.'

'Heavens! What have you got to moan about?'

'Plenty, as it happens. Honestly, Agnes, I'm sick of the sight of Peggy McKenzie, she's never away from our house.'

'Your da must invite her?'

'Her kind don't need an invitation.'

'Could be you are about to get a stepmama.'

'Don't joke about it, Agnes.'

Agnes wasn't but she kept silent and Rachel took a deep breath, relieved to be able to unburden herself even though Agnes was unlikely to be very sympathetic.

'That awful laugh of hers makes studying impossible.'

'Tell her to shut up.'

'Wish I could.'

'Well if you can't bring yourself to do that take your books elsewhere. No great problem I would have thought.'

'And freeze? The bedroom is like an ice box I'll have you know, and the front room fire is only on when we have visitors.'

'Not counting Peggy?'

'That one considers herself family.'

'My heart bleeds for you.'

'Thanks,' Rachel said huffily, 'I should have known better than expect sympathy from you.'

'What good is sympathy, but I'll give you some advice.'

Rachel shrugged but looked at her friend questioningly.

'Better learn to stick up for yourself because once Peggy gets the ring on her finger—'

'*If* she gets the ring on her finger.'

'Have it your own way, but Peggy knows you dislike her and she'll do her best to blacken you in your da's eyes.'

'What rubbish! What utter trash you do talk, Agnes Boyd. My da wouldn't believe any bad of me.' She stormed ahead with Agnes hurrying to keep up.

'I hope it does turn out to be rubbish, Rachel,' Agnes said in an unusually quiet voice.

Rachel slowed down and smiled. 'Sorry, Agnes, I know you mean well and I didn't mean to bite your head off. It's looking after the house and keeping up with a mountain of homework.'

'Not finding it too difficult are you?' Wasn't that her secret hope?

'No, not really but it's frustrating when you can't get a bit of peace and quiet. Stop here,' she said taking Agnes's arm. 'I want some barley sugar or something that lasts.'

Agnes made to stay outside. 'For goodness sake, Agnes, come on, Da gave me money for both of us.'

'Ta, tell him ta from me.'

The table was cluttered with books and Rachel was scribbling furiously.

'Rachel, take a break from that.'

'I can't, Da, I have to get this done before Peggy comes.'

'Why?'

'Why? You ask me why? Because, Da, I need peace and quiet and there is precious little of that when Peggy is around.'

'No need to be sarcastic.'

'It happens to be the truth and if it wasn't so cold I'd study in my bedroom.'

She saw his face harden. 'You'd better get used to Peggy being about the house.'

Rachel put down her pencil and stared at him. 'Da, are you trying to tell me something?' She could feel a sudden tension emanating from him as though he were steeling himself to get something off his chest.

'Yes, Rachel,' he said sitting forward in his chair, 'I do have something to tell you.'

'And I know what it is. You are going to marry her, aren't you? That is what you're trying to tell me.' She was almost shouting and sobbing at the same time.

'Yes, Rachel, I have asked Peggy to be my wife and she—'

'Accepted like a shot.' She saw his colour rise, saw the anger but she was uncaring. 'Oh, I heard the rumours but I wouldn't believe them and I almost quarrelled with Agnes.'

'I'm not bothered about rumours but I would have thought that my happiness would have meant something to you.'

'Da,' she was over and sitting in the chair the other side of the fire, 'of course it does. Of course I want your happiness.'

'Then give Peggy a chance, she's willing enough to be friends.'

What was the using of saying any more, Rachel thought dully.

'Your mother has been dead over four years, Rachel, and it is a lonely life.'

'You have me.'

He smiled and bent forward to pat her knee. 'You're a good lass and you've done wonders but in a few years you'll want to get married yourself.'

'Maybe, but, Da, it's just that – just that Mama was so different. I remember her you know,' she added.

'I know you do, lass, and I agree that Amelia and Peggy are very different.' He turned away so that she couldn't study his face. 'Let me tell you something, Rachel, and it is no disrespect to your mother. I'm comfortable with Peggy, we talk the same language, laugh at the same things, I can be myself.' Then turning back to her she saw the pleading in his face. 'Amelia will always have a place in my heart, nothing is going to change that, but remember this, only the deep love I had for your mother made me change into the person she wanted me to be. And trying to be something you're not can be a big strain.'

'More difficult for Mama though, wasn't it?' she said accusingly.

'Yes,' he said slowly, 'I was only too well aware of what Amelia had given up and trying to please her and keep her happy was what I was determined to do.'

They were both silent, both staring into the fire and thinking their own thoughts. George sighed and was the first to speak.

'Give Peggy a chance, Rachel, do that and I'll guarantee that the three of us will get along just fine.'

'I'll do my best,' Rachel promised but she had to steel herself when Peggy, a triumphant look on her face, went over to kiss her da on the mouth.

'Told Rachel our news, have you?'

'Yes, Peggy, Da told me,' Rachel said forcing a smile, 'Congratulations and just you be sure to make my da happy.'

'Och, I'll make him happy, never fear. Made for each other, aren't we, Geordie?' She winked and he laughed and something about that exchange sickened Rachel.

Peggy proved to be a reasonably good cook but admitted that she was hopeless at baking and Rachel was happy enough to see that the cake tins were filled. All-in-all the marriage that Rachel had dreaded made little difference to her. True there was that first embarrassment of going through to the kitchen and seeing them in bed together but mostly she managed to avoid the kitchen until they were both up.

Afterwards, Rachel was to remember it as the calm before the storm as Peggy, tiring of housework, pushed more and more of it on to a resentful and hostile stepdaughter.

Rachel had grown a lot in the last year and was already an inch taller than Peggy. Standing straight she faced up to her stepmother. Her dark curls reached to her shoulder and she had her hair tied back with a black, velvet ribbon that was almost invisible. Her skin was clear and healthy with a faint blush of colour and though her body was unformed and flat she carried herself well.

'Peggy, I am not going to black-lead that grate, I do enough already and you are supposed to be the housewife.' She almost added that she had tried hard enough for the position but stopped herself in time.

'Listen, you,' Peggy said in her roughest voice, 'don't you dare take that attitude with me. You'll do as I say, my lass, or your da's goin' to hear of it.'

'Your version of it anyway,' Rachel flung back. 'I know you're trying to turn my father against me but you won't succeed.'

'No? Want to bet on it?'

Rachel turned her back and went through to her bedroom. The cold, damp weather had seeped into the room but Rachel's anger kept her warm. For weeks now she had been irritated at the treatment she was receiving from Peggy when her da was absent and then the smiling show of friendship when the three of them were together. Collecting her books she put them beside the bed and pulled down the bedclothes. Then fully dressed apart from her shoes, she went into bed to do her studying.

Rachel stuck to her guns about the housework and continued to tidy her own bedroom, clear the breakfast table and wash the dishes before she left for school. The wash house was out at the back and shared by all the tenants. The Donaldsons were allocated Tuesdays and George had the boiler fire going before he left for work ready for Peggy to do the washing. If the weather was good the clothes were hung out to dry and Rachel got all the ironing done in the evening but if it rained the wet clothes were draped over the 'horse' and put in front of the fire and the ironing completed sometime the following day. The grate had long since lost its shine.

As part of her homework Rachel had three chapters of David Copperfield to read and putting up her feet she settled on the couch looking forward to an hour or two of uninterrupted reading. Peggy was visiting friends. Her da had just gone into the scullery to add water to the drink he had poured himself. When he came out he drank some of the whisky but instead of returning to his chair towered over her. Startled, Rachel looked up then got to her feet.

'Rachel, I want to talk to you.' He had never used that tone of voice to her before and she knew that it spelt trouble.

Though shaking inwardly Rachel faced him bravely. 'What has Peggy been saying? No, let me guess. I'm lazy and rude and never lift a finger to help. And, of course, you believe every word she says.'

'I do as it happens and get that defiant look off your face.' He stabbed his finger towards her. 'Peggy has bent over backwards to gain your friendship, I've heard her myself, and you've gone out of your way to be nasty.'

'That is simply not true, I have never been nasty but what you don't understand because you don't want to, is that Peggy is only pleasant to me when you are about.'

'She called you a spoilt brat.'

'She what?'

'A spoilt brat and that is exactly what you are. Since you've gone to that academy you've become impossible and I'm warning you, Rachel, I won't stand for Peggy being upset.'

Rachel could say nothing, only stare at her father. She felt choked but tears were the last thing she would allow herself.

As if regretting his harshness George's voice softened. 'I'm not asking much, lass, just for you to give Peggy her place and give her a hand with the housework.'

'I already do,' she managed to get out.

'A wee bit more wouldn't hurt.' His eyes went to the clock. 'I'll away and meet her and that'll give you time to think on what I've said.'

After he'd gone Rachel sat for a long time and wondered how she was going to stand it. But, of course, she had to while she was at school. And then it would be college and eventually independence. But those years between still had to be lived through.

# Chapter Eight

The kitchen door was shut. Rachel had just come into the lobby but she could hear Peggy.

'Geordie, I tell you it's a monstrosity and I want rid of it and a fireplace put in.'

'But, Peggy—'

'Don't Peggy me, it's got to go. It's a devil to clean and that little madam doesn't like to get her hands dirty.'

'She used to—'

'Well, she doesn't now. And a lot of folk are getting rid of them. Jeannie Forbes for a start, Her man wasn't in favour at the beginning but now he's highly delighted.'

'It's kind of homely, Peggy, I'd miss it,' George said wistfully. 'And come to think about it how to you propose to do the cooking?' He brightened thinking he'd found a flaw in her argument.

'A gas stove or a cooker as Jeannie calls it.' Peggy was now in full flow. 'Their house is similar to this and they have a cooker in the scullery. Yon shelf would have to go but that's no problem.'

Rachel had come into the kitchen but they seemed unaware of her presence.

'Cost a tidy bit,' George said worriedly.

'Don't start that, Geordie, we can afford it and Jeannie says not having that fiend to clean has given her a new lease of life.'

Rachel bit her lip. She felt guilty, for in a way it was her fault. Before Peggy came she'd black-leaded the range and, filthy job though it was, she could have gone on doing it. And her da wanted to keep it that was clear enough. She wanted to please him.

'I like it too, Da, and I'd hate to see it go. Tell you what, if Peggy does the ironing I'll black-lead the grate.'

'You keep out of this,' Peggy said furiously, 'this is between Geordie and me and none of your business.'

53

George looked from his wife to his daughter and for a moment she saw approval, was sure of it, and believed that she had won a small victory until he turned away.

'Mebbe Peggy's right, lass, and we should move with the times.'

A glance at her stepmother and Rachel saw the satisfied smile on her face. Defeated, she bowed her head and closed her eyelids tightly and, as the tears welled up, she turned abruptly and went into the scullery. The dirty dishes were piled high, and keeping her face averted she went to pick up the black kettle, carried it through, filled the basin with the hot water then topped the kettle up with cold. They were still talking when she returned with the kettle but her ears were closed to them.

Washing the dishes wasn't a favourite occupation of Rachel's but she found the simple task therapeutic and her hands in the hot, soapy water was calming her. It was obvious that her opinion counted for nothing, she wasn't allowed any say and come to that her da's wishes didn't count for much either. It was easy to see that he was completely under Peggy's thumb and the worst part of all, Rachel thought, was the certain knowledge that he didn't mind. Her one time hero, her big, strong father was a weak man, a man who allowed a woman to rule his life. If she ever married she wouldn't want her husband giving in to her every whim. Maybe there was a lot to be said for being a teacher, staying single and keeping her independence.

At Peggy's insistence, George accompanied her to the Forbes's house to see how it looked with its modern fireplace and how the gas cooker fitted into the scullery. Jeannie and Danny Forbes spoke through each other in their eagerness to explain the working of this wonderful invention and George nodded dutifully but was far from convinced that it was a worthy successor to the old-fashioned range.

'Cannae go wrong with it, Geordie,' Danny said as he slapped George on the back. 'Mebbe takes a wee bit getting used to but once you get the hang of it you'd never go back to the auld way.'

'That's right, Geordie,' his wife nodded vigorously.

'What about baking?' Peggy asked in a subdued tone. She wouldn't admit it for the world but seeing the gas flames and hearing that peculiar hiss was terrifying her and she wondered how she was going to cope on her own.

'You'll get an instruction book and it tells you everything including the oven.' Then Jeannie admitted shamefacedly that she'd never used theirs. 'I just use the top for cooking and, well, that's what bakers' shops are for after all. Didn't know you baked, Peggy.' She made it sound like a fault.

'She doesn't,' George said, 'Rachel's a good wee hand with the baking though.'

'Och, she'll manage then,' Danny said as he turned away to get them seated round the fire with its tiled front instead of a fender. 'Rachel's a bright lass, she'll understand the instructions though I'll admit I couldnae mak' head nor tail of them but then that's them with their fancy words. Call a spade a spade I always say.'

Peggy was unusually silent as they walked home.

The men arrived with the gas cooker, carefully protected by cardboard and settled it in it position in the scullery. One of them seeing the worried look on Peggy's face tore a bit of the cardboard away and fished inside until he found the instruction book.

'They'll be up the morn to fit it in so I'd suggest you studied the book the night. My missus managed the cooking a treat but took a long time to get her baking to rise the way it did with the range oven, but then the daft besom never bothered reading the instructions.' He went away chortling to himself. Rachel, who had witnessed it all went to her bedroom to hide her amusement but Peggy followed.

'You'd better read that book, Rachel.'

'Why?'

'You're still goin' to do the bakin', aren't you?'

'I didn't think I would be allowed to touch the cooker.'

'Don't be so daft. Come on, I'll make us a cup of tea and you study the instructions so we can tell Geordie we've mastered it.'

Only too happy to encourage this show of friendship though well aware of the reason, Rachel read the instruction book from cover to cover and found it easy to follow.

'Seems simple enough, Peggy.'

'Still we'd better make the meals together for the first while.'

'When are they coming to take out the range?'

'Tuesday.'

'Then we've the range to fall back on – until Tuesday that is.'

'You're goin' to rub it in, aren't you?' Peggy said fiercely, 'Just because I want to improve things.'

For the first time Rachel felt a prick of sympathy for her stepmother.

'No, I'm not going to rub it in, in fact, I'm quite looking forward to using the oven.'

'You are?'

'Yes, I am. I'll have to adjust some of the timings so maybe we'll have a few flops to begin with.'

'Never mind,' Peggy said hastily as she filled up Rachel's cup, 'we can have something in reserve from the baker's.'

George, coming in at six thirty, saw the change, the absence of hostility and smiled. His two girls were getting on at last.

The fitter arrived in the early morning and by the time Rachel arrived home from school the cooker was in place, the scullery tidied and an excited Peggy going back and forward for yet another look at the brand new cooker.

'You know something, Peggy?'

'Oh, God, what now?'

'The pots, we'll have to buy lightweight ones.'

'Won't what we have do?' she said anxiously.

'For the time being, but getting through that thickness is a waste of heat. It's all in the instructions, didn't you read them.'

'No, I did not, I'm not much good at understanding—' she flushed, 'we weren't all at the academy, you know.'

Rachel felt like saying that it didn't need more than an elementary education to understand it but she was suddenly sorry for this flustered and worried woman.

'Don't worry, we'll manage.'

'That'll mean new pots and a new kettle. Gawd, Geordie's goin' tae go his dinger about that.'

'You don't have to splash out all at once.'

'No, that's right, we don't, do we?'

By the time the workmen arrived with their hammers and chisels, Peggy had mastered the top of the cooker and bought a lightweight kettle and two pots. Rachel had done her first batch of baking and declared herself well satisfied.

Then it began. The neighbours were up in arms about the noise as the dreadful hammering went on and on and the once pride and joy was dragged out and broken up. The dust was everywhere, on table and furniture and even finding its way into the other rooms. Peggy's blonde hair looked grey, her nostrils were filled with the fine dust making breathing difficult and her eyes felt gritty.

Rachel came home to find the close and stairs under a thick film of dust and wondered just what to expect. What met her eyes was so awful that her mouth hung open. Where the range had been wrenched out, bits of the wall had gone too and loose plaster covered the linoleum. Then she looked at Peggy, grey from head to foot and she began to giggle, the giggle gave way to laughter and soon she was helpless with mirth. After an indignant outburst, Peggy's laughter, that loud laughter that had once grated on Rachel, joined her own.

'Gawd, Rachel, what am I goin' to do? There's goin' to be murder done this night.'

Rachel was beginning to recover. 'Peggy, make a cup of tea, please, and I'd like a scone or something that isn't covered in dust.'

'Och, the food's all right, everything in the scullery is covered and I kept that door shut.'

'Good, I'll get out of my school uniform and get dug in here.'

'Thanks, lass.'

'We'd better set the table in the front room and have the meal there.'

'Just what I was thinkin'.'

Refreshed after the tea and the dust now reasonably settled, Rachel and Peggy set to with a will and sooner than they could have expected, they had the worst of the rubbish away. Old dusters made out of worn-out clothes took care of the dirt and dust and gradually the kitchen became ship-shape, all except the wall and that looked even uglier now that the furniture was back in place.

'Time we were gettin' somethin' ready for your da.'

'Yes, you're right.' Rachel lifted an exhausted face streaked with dirt. 'I feel absolutely filthy.'

'You look it and I'm an even bigger mess.'

'Any hot water?' Rachel asked.

'Oh, Gawd no, I'll have to fill the kettle and it takes a while to heat up.'

'Not if you turn it up full, the gas I mean.' She gave a sly look at her stepmother. 'One thing about the old range, there was always hot water.'

'Well, what is done is done and I'm not one to cry over spilt milk.'

'Neither am I,' Rachel smiled, 'We'll get used to it.'

'We'll have to,' Peggy said grimly.

George, forbidden the kitchen, had eaten his meal in the front room and was now in the kitchen and looking with horror and disbelief at the broken wall.

'God's truth, what have you done, Peggy?'

'Da, it isn't all that bad. The plasterers are coming tomorrow to even up the wall and then you'll get your nice new fire.'

'Nice new fire,' he said bitterly, 'I'm goin' out for a drink and don't expect me back this side of bedtime.'

'Peggy?' Rachel said uncertainly once the door banged after George.

'What?'

'May I make a suggestion?'

'If you think it'll help.'

'The coal bunker's about empty, isn't it?'

'Aye.'

'Get it filled and all the dirty jobs over at one time.'

'That's sensible. Wait till I mind,' she puckered her brow, 'I mind now, Jock comes this way tomorrow late afternoon. I'll get him to bring up four bags.'

The plasterers had filled the holes and evened the wall where it was bumpy. They arrived as George departed with his 'piece' to see him through the day. Rachel had her dinner 'piece' too and promised to come home smartly.

'Peggy, that's the coal cart turning the corner.'

'Go on then, catch him and tell him to bring up four bags and I'll get the bunker ready.' Raising the lid she reached down and brought to the surface a number of flue brushes and a shovel and placed them on the floor in front of the bunker. In a little while heavy footsteps sounded on the stairs. Rachel opened the door and it was pushed wider as Jock, a bag of coal on his back came into the kitchen, crossed to the bunker then let the bag slither from the leather protector which eased the pressure on his back. Then picking up the corners of the bag emptied it out to send coal dust flying in all directions.

'Think it'll take four, Jock?'

'Nae bother.'

A young lad, his face streaked with coal dust arrived with the second bag passing Jock as he went down for another. With the last bag in the lid would only half close. Peggy, not noticing, got out her purse.

After taking the money Jock began shaking his head. 'You've made a big mistake there, lass.'

'What are you talkin' about?'

'Getting' rid of your range. Best friend a man could have.'

She shot him a look that would have warned another to drop the subject. 'I'll have you know that Jeannie Forbes told me it was the best thing she ever did.'

He raised his eyebrows. 'What would you expect her to say? She's not goin' to admit her mistake and I'll tell you this, lass, and mind I see it first hand, many a wife thought it would make life easier and mebbe it has in one way but they wee fireplaces don't send out the same heat and a man feels at home with his old-fashioned range and a place to put up his feet.'

'Quite finished have you, Jock Thomson?'

'Aye, Peggy, I've had my say and now I'll be gettin' on my way, but mark my words this'll no' endear ye tae Geordie.'

She banged the door behind him and with a great show of energy and a few muttered oaths, arranged the coal so that eventually the lid went down properly. Wisely Rachel kept silent but was ready with a duster to clean the top and replace the wilting plant.

Peggy was smiling. A fire burned brightly and if the heat was less than that given out by the range it was enough to heat the small room. Geordie had done the redecorating and everything looked fresh and clean. The coal bucket had been replaced by a brass scuttle that shone with newness and the upheaval was now a distant memory as was the old range.

In the last few weeks the atmosphere in the house had improved but Peggy's swift changes of mood kept Rachel wary. What did concern her, though she said nothing, was the worry she saw in her da's face. Once she would have demanded to know what was wrong but now she held back. No longer did she feel close enough to her father to expect him to confide in her.

She was to find out very shortly and he arranged it for a time when they were alone.

'Come over here, Rachel, lass, and take Peggy's chair.'

Rachel welcomed the prospect of a comfortable chair and went over to sit on the chair that had once been hers. The kitchen had two easy chairs, sagging a bit, but comfortable nonetheless and four wooden, straight-backed chairs. These were pushed under the table and in the evenings one was brought out for Rachel to sit on. She would have welcomed a cushion but none was provided.

'You like it then?' her father said indicating the room.

'Yes, I do, you made a good job of the papering.'

'Aye, I think I could take some credit there.'

She could see he was pleased with what she had said. 'You don't miss the range after all?'

'For the first week or two mebbe I did, but I think Peggy was right and it gives her a bit less to do.'

He was working up to something and Rachel wondered what it could be.

'Cost a good bit more than I expected.'

'Is that why you've been looking worried?'

'Oh, I've been worried all right.' He was looking more uncomfortable than she had ever seen him. 'Worried, lass, because of what it will mean for you.'

'For me?' Rachel felt the blood drain from her face. 'I don't understand what has it got to do with me?'

'Obvious I would have thought.'

'You can't,' she whispered, 'you can't mean what I think you mean.'

He nodded. 'I'm sorry it's come to this.' He lifted the poker and poked away at the coal though it didn't need it, 'but the truth is it's goin' to cost too much to put you through college. I'm right sorry, lass, but that is the way it is.'

She was on her feet her eyes blazing with anger. 'You've a short, convenient memory, Da, haven't you? Who was to be so proud to have his daughter a teacher? And the money,' she said bitterly, 'not to worry my little head about it, was I, the bit you had put by would take care of that.'

'And so it would but—'

'But Peggy wanted a whole new kitchen, to be able to show off to her friends and that was more important than the promise you made to your daughter.' She shook her head in disbelief. 'At one time I thought you were the most marvellous da on earth and now,' he heard the cold contempt in her voice, 'I think you are just pathetic.' For a moment she thought that he was going to hit her with the poker, his hand was clenched round it, but he put it down.

'You watch that tongue of yours or you'll be shown the door. And I'm thinkin' the sooner you leave that academy and get yourself a job the better it will be for everybody.'

'That is just what I intend to do and don't worry I won't be a burden to you a moment longer than necessary.'

'You're not a burden, lass, and I'll forget those harsh words of yours.' The anger had left him and he looked at her with the beginning of a smile but Rachel stared back with eyes which were hard and unforgiving. Without another word she left him, got her coat and slammed the door after her.

Slipping her arms into it, Rachel walked the whole length of the road without noticing, registering nothing but the fact that she had teaching no longer as her goal. All her hard work had been for nothing, her dreams trampled upon, finished. The sour taste of bile rose in her throat and she thought she was to be physically sick. With some surprise she found herself in the Hawkhill and not far from the baker's shop where Agnes worked. It was Thursday, Agnes worked until eight, she would still be there. The shop was on the corner of the lane where the Boyd family lived. Rachel had never been in Winter's the baker's, there was no reason why she should shop in the Hawkhill. The Blackness Road shops were almost on the doorstep and most of them had well-maintained premises and windows that in the early part of the day showed an attractive selection of home-baking together with bought-in bread and fancy teabread. In contrast, this part of the Hawkhill was run down with peeling paint work and shabby doors too often kicked open. Rachel turned the knob and went in. There were no customers and if not bright and welcoming the inside of the shop was clean enough.

The woman had been staring out of the window but she turned to smile. Not much was left to sell but it was nice to get rid of what wouldn't keep until the next day.

'Yes?'

'Is Agnes in, please?'

The smile turned to a frown as she went into the back shop and reappeared with Agnes showing her surprise.

'Rachel, you look awful, is something wrong?'

She couldn't speak, just nodded.

'This is my friend, Rachel Donaldson,' Agnes said to her employer. The woman was small and stout and could be difficult at times but she'd come to rely on the Boyd family. In time the younger ones would take over from Agnes and rough though they were they had been brought up to be honest.

'Looks like your friend is upset so you can go but mind be here tomorrow mornin' on time,' she warned.

'Ta, Mrs Winter and I'll mebbe even manage to be early.'

'Cheeky devil,' she said, but she was smiling as Agnes took off her overall and collected her coat. Then she stopped them at the door with two dough-rings hastily picked up from a plate in the window. 'Nobody's goin' to come in now and the sugar will be gone afore long.'

'She's a besom but no' bad at times, like now,' Agnes said as she bit into a dough-ring. 'Come on, eat that up then tell me what's the matter.'

Rachel could have done without the dough-ring. It was heavy, not to her liking, but she managed to eat it.

The day had been warm but a coolish breeze had got up and both girls were glad of their coats. They walked to the Sinderins then sat down on the wooden bench that, during the day, was occupied by old men with nothing better to do than pass the time.

'Peggy's doing, of course?' Agnes said when Rachel had poured out her misery, hating herself for the leap of joy she felt. Rachel wasn't going to be a teacher after all, she would have to get an ordinary job and be no better than herself.

'No, my da's more at fault than Peggy.' A great sob burst from Rachel's throat. 'How could he, Agnes? How could he break his promise?'

'Maybe he'll change his mind.'

'No, absolutely not,' she choked. 'I gather it's going to take every penny he has to meet the bills and our Peggy has extravagant tastes.'

'In that case you've got to accept it, Rachel, and working yourself into a state won't help. Things'll go from bad to worse if you carry on like that.'

Rachel dried her eyes, swallowed and looked over at Agnes. 'I suppose you're right,' she said at last. 'And thanks for listening.'

'That's what chums are for. And if I sit here much longer I'll be frozen to the seat.' They both got up and parted in the Hawkhill, Rachel to walk up Peddie Street. She wasn't ready to go home yet.

Mary Rodgers was baking when the knock came and after wiping the flour from her hands went to see who her caller was.

'Rachel!' she exclaimed in surprise, 'Come away in, lass.'

Rachel was breathing hard and trying to get a grip on herself.

'Sit yoursel' down and not a word till you get a cup of tea into you.'

Rachel sat down and watched Mary Rodgers make the tea then rush to the oven to take out a sponge. It had risen beautifully and Mrs Rodgers sighed with relief.

'Just in time,' she said as she put it on the wire tray to cool then buttering two scones she put them on a plate beside Rachel and poured tea into both cups.

Rachel lifted the cup and took a sip. 'Thank you, Mrs Rodgers, but nothing to eat. The woman in Agnes's shop gave us a dough-ring.'

'Then you'll need that to put the taste away. I'm never that sure what goes on in the back o' they shops. Mebbe better not to know,' she added with a smile as Rachel bit into a scone.

'I've a nerve, haven't I? I haven't been near you in weeks and when I come it's to load you with my troubles.'

'Och, lass, I was young mysel' once and I'm only too happy that you come to see me. It's nice to be needed, you know,' she said wistfully.

Rachel took a deep breath. She'd done her crying and she wasn't going to do any more. 'I'm not getting to go to college. My da says he can't afford it.'

Mary nodded, her face showed nothing but there was a seething anger in her. Those two had a lot to answer for, she thought grimly, making the bairn suffer for their own extravagances. It wasn't just the money spent on the house, it was what went on drink. George Donaldson, to give him his due, had never been a heavy drinker but Peggy liked a drink and as George couldn't take her into the rougher public houses, it meant paying out more for a better class bar. She knew all this, it was common knowledge.

'And now you've to leave school and get a job?'

Rachel nodded miserably. 'I'm not going into the mill.'

'I thought they were payin' off?'

'So they are but Da would find a place for me but he can't force me to work there and I won't.'

'What do you have in mind, lass?' she said gently.

'Nothing, Mrs Rodgers, but I suppose it will have to be a shop, that's to say if I can even manage that,' she said bitterly.

Mary was silent for along time, her head bowed and Rachel wondered if she'd nodded off. Then the head went up.

'Mebbe this'll help and mebbe it won't.' She reached for a scone and nibbled at it. 'Lizzie Reid, you know, the dressmaker?'

'Yes, I know of her.'

'She's very busy and I hear tell that she is thinkin' of takin' on a lass to help. Needs to be good with a needle.' Her eyes held Rachel's. 'Your ma was neat with the stitches, did some fine work and I'm wonderin' if her daughter could mebbe learn to be a dressmaker.'

A genuine look of interest crossed Rachel's face. 'I'm quite good at sewing. We get one period a week and my teacher complimented me on my small even stitches.' Her face dropped as she remembered that there would be no more classes of any kind.

'Can't promise anythin', lass, but Lizzie's been a friend of mine for years and if she has no one in mind I'm thinkin' I could persuade her to take you.'

'You've been very good to me, Mrs Rodgers,' Rachel said with a catch in her voice, 'and I hope some day that I can repay you in some way.'

Mrs Rodgers looked embarrassed. 'Och, lass, your happiness is all I want, but mind if you do land the job it won't be all roses. Lizzie has a sharp tongue and she'll expect plenty for the pittance you'll get. But look at it this way, you'll be learnin' a trade and able to make your own clothes one day.' She smiled. 'If she shouts at you dinnae heed, Lizzie's bark is worse than her bite.'

'When will you ask her?'

'I'll take mysel' along there first thing the morn.'

Rachel was dry-eyed as she said goodbye to her teachers and the friends she had made. They were all sorry to see her go. The school had a shop where outgrown uniforms were sold to the more needy. Rachel handed hers in and pocketed the money. Saving had suddenly become important and the first seeds of a plan were taking root. Fifteen was too young but when she was sixteen she would make her move. Had her mother foreseen this when she left her daughter an address in Perthshire?

# Chapter Nine

Before taking up her position as helper to Miss Lizzie Reid, Rachel had expected to be interviewed, but apparently Mrs Rodgers' recommendation had been enough. The house was in Ainslie Park, off the Perth Road, a respectable cul-de-sac of cottages with their doors giving directly on to the pavement. That it was a dressmaker's establishment no one would have guessed from the outside and only the number told Rachel that she had come to the right place.

Swallowing nervously, she knocked and it was immediately opened by a small, sharp-featured woman.

'Good morning, Miss Reid, I'm—'

'I know fine who you are, come in.'

Shutting the door she led Rachel through a narrow lobby and into a cluttered room. There was a fireplace against one wall and being September and still warm the black iron grate was filled with pink crêpe paper. Against another wall were a few bales of material and a box of odds and ends. The centre was taken up with a table on which was a large pair of scissors and tweed cloth in the process of being cut to a pattern. Nearby was a Singer sewing machine. Fine net curtains adorned the window and gave privacy without noticeably darkening the room.

Rachel stood awaiting instructions. For her first day she wore a dark blue skirt with box pleats and a pink-striped cotton blouse and over it a short beige jacket. The packet clutched in her hand held a cheese sandwich and an apple.

'Take your jacket off, you'll be bidin' I take it,' Miss Reid said with an attempt at humour.

Rachel smiled and some of her earlier nervousness disappeared. 'Where shall I put it?'

'Ben there,' she said pointing to a door that led directly into another. 'You'll find a nag on the back of the door.' Rachel went through to what was obviously the living quarters. She hung up her jacket and took a

65

quick look round. The room was of similar size to its neighbour but there was a door off it which Rachel took to be a scullery. A tall dresser had a row of plates in the Willow pattern and on the table was a teapot hidden under a knitted cosy. After a brief hesitation Rachel put her 'piece' beside it.

'Now, lass,' her employer said as Rachel reappeared, 'you bring that chair over and we'll have a wee chat.' She was sitting at the sewing machine but turned to face Rachel. 'I'm particular, very particular, and with a reputation for good work I have to be.'

'I'm very neat, Miss Reid,' Rachel said quietly.

'I'm glad to hear it but I'll be the judge of that when I see your work.'

'Yes, of course,' Rachel murmured. She had been sitting on the edge of the chair but moved to a more comfortable position. The seat was cushioned and Rachel was relieved that she wouldn't have to sit on a hard chair all day. Its comfort was more than she was accustomed to at home.

'Most nights you'll be away at six but occasionally I have a rush order and I'd expect you to stay on and help.' She looked over at Rachel with her eyebrows raised.

'Yes, I'd be prepared to do that.'

'Good and for that there'd be a wee extra at the end of the week.' She paused. 'Did Mary Rodgers tell you to bring something to eat?'

'Yes, I left it through on the table, was that all right?'

She nodded. 'I supply the tea and I'm partial to a cuppie in the morning, mebbe in the afternoon too. Take it as I'm workin' so don't feel guilty. You'll see to that, Rachel, and if I need a bit of shoppin', you'll not mind goin' for a few messages, will you?'

'I'll be happy to.' Rachel was warming to this woman, who though she had a sharp voice didn't order but rather asked. She couldn't imagine Peggy saying 'you'll not mind'.

'Ever worked a sewing machine?'

'No.'

'Nothin' to it, I'll teach you when I've the time. Only use it for straight seams, the rest is done by hand, time-consuming but the result makes it well worthwhile. 'Here,' she said handing Rachel a piece of material. 'Let's see what you can do. Take up a half inch hem on that.'

This was work Rachel could do easily. After pinning then tacking, she threaded a needle with matching thread and began to sew. Meantime

Miss Reid had risen to pick up the scissors and finish the cutting out she had begun. They worked in silence until Rachel finished her task.

'Give it here.'

With growing confidence Rachel handed it over.

'Mmmm. Quite good but why rush the last bit? See,' she said putting the material in front of Rachel, 'compare your stitching at the beginning then at the end. Would you call that regular?'

Rachel bit her lip. 'No, it isn't. I'm sorry, shall I unpick it?'

'No, but I saw by your face that you thought you'd done a good job and I'm just showin' you that it doesn't meet my high standards. But don't look so worried, lass, I'm sure I'll make a dressmaker of you given time.' She smiled. 'Am I right in thinking that Mary Rodgers told you I'd be a tartar to work for?'

'No, Mrs Rodgers didn't, really she didn't.'

'What did she say?'

Rachel blushed and stayed silent.

'Come on tell me, I'm not easily offended.'

'All she said was that your bark is worse than your bite.'

'Oh, she did, did she? Well, mebbe she's right and mebbe she's wrong but you'll find out in time and now this won't do. I can't be talkin' here and me with all the work I've to get through.'

'What shall I do?'

'Put the kettle on. Through in the scullery, you'll find everythin' there if you use your eyes. Then I'll show you how to take up a skirt hem without the stitches showin' through.'

At ten past six, her first day's work over, Rachel felt contented as she walked home. The awful disappointment at having to leave school was easing and thanks to Mrs Rodgers she'd be learning something useful. That didn't mean she had forgiven her da, no, it would be a long time before she forgave him for breaking his promise.

Whenever possible Rachel and Agnes would spend part of Sunday together and if the weather turned out to be good they would often take a walk to Luigi's in Lochee High Street and treat themselves to an ice cream. Today it was warm with a pleasantly cool breeze and Agnes immediately suggested Luigi's.

'Fine by me,' Rachel said looking curiously at her friend and wondering what had brought the colour to her cheeks. Her eyes were dancing the way they did when she was bursting to tell something. But she wouldn't ask, she'd let Agnes come out with it in her own time.

They had reached Glenagnes Road and gone beyond the dairy before Agnes spoke of what was uppermost in her mind.

'I'm going into service, I'm getting Meg's job.'

'Meg's job? But where is she going?'

'Nowhere, just back home.'

'Back home?'

'Do you have to repeat everything I say? Yes, back home. For goodness sake, Rachel, think girl, why would she be sent home?'

'Oh, no! You don't mean—'

'Yes, I mean that my stupid sister has got herself into trouble or if you prefer someone has had his wicked way with her.'

'But that is awful and you shouldn't be joking about a thing like that.'

'I'm not joking but being miserable about it isn't going to help anyone.'

'What about whoever he is, isn't he going to marry her?'

'No chance of that and anyway she won't say who it is. Just stood there like a dummy with my ma and da yelling at her and my da threatening to throw her out if she wouldn't tell.'

'Would he do that?'

'No, he wouldn't.' She shook her head vigorously. 'Not that he has been much of a da to us but to give him his due he wouldn't throw any of us out no matter what we'd done.'

For all their rough ways, Rachel thought, the Boyds were a united family and for the first time in her life she felt the faintest touch of envy. Not having brothers or sisters hadn't troubled her before but now she wished that she had someone of her own, someone who cared what happened to her. Peggy didn't, she'd be only too happy to see the back of her stepdaughter and as for her da – Rachel pondered on that. Then she sighed, her da's life was bound up with Peggy, she was his wife after all and would always come first. His love for his daughter hadn't changed but she would have to learn to take a back seat.

'Sorry, Agnes, what were you saying/'

'Shows how much attention you've been paying; however, I shall repeat it. My ma thought she would get it out of Meg when they were alone but she's stopped asking now.'

'Maybe your sister just wants to protect whoever it is.'

'That would be like her.'

They walked in silence for a little while. 'What will happen to Meg's baby? Will she stay at home to look after it?'

'Good heavens, of course not. What's another bairn in our house,' Agnes said airily. 'My ma will look after it and like as not Meg will go back to the baker's shop. Mrs Winter wouldn't survive very well without the Boyds.'

They were in Lochee High Street and in sight of Luigi's café which being open on a Sunday did a brisk trade with hikers glad of a short break and a refreshment, and young children who pestered their parents for an ice-cream cone.

'Agnes, would you marry for money and security?'

'Like a shot and don't look so blooming superior and disapproving. If you'd known want you'd do the same.'

'I hope I wouldn't, Agnes. A marriage needs love if it is to be happy.'

'Granted a perfect marriage has both but how many perfect marriages are there?'

'I'm sure lots of people do marry for love and I know I'd rather stay single then enter into a loveless marriage.'

'Oh, I'd have to like the person but that's a far cry from being in love and a little pretence would keep everybody happy.'

'You are absolutely hopeless, Agnes Boyd.'

They were both laughing as they went into Luigi's and over to sit in one of the cubicles. The elderly Italian after finishing tying his blue striped apron came over for their order.

Agnes leaned her elbows on the mock-marble top. 'Two ice creams with raspberry sauce,' then added with a beaming smile, 'don't be sparing with the sauce.'

He turned away mumbling something they didn't hear.

'Any more news?' Rachel asked.

'Yes, nearly forgot to tell you, Tommy Allardyce is starting work in the Caledon Shipyard.'

'What to be doing?'

'Office work.'

'I am glad, he deserves to get on.'

'Apparently he is over the moon. The wage isn't much but he doesn't mind since the prospects are good.'

'Next time you see him tell him how delighted I am.'

'Can't say when that will be.'

'I forgot, I wasn't thinking, but we'll still be able to see each other, won't we?'

'I won't be a prisoner. Meg says I get one Sunday off in three and so many hours other days.'

'Broughty Ferry Road isn't that far. I can take a tram out to see you once in a while.'

'Certainly you may visit me in my mansion.'

'Servants' entrance, of course.'

Agnes gave her a strange smile. 'One day it's going to be different.'

In those moments Rachel believed it too.

The son of the proprietor placed the dishes in front of them. A liberal amount of raspberry sauce ran down the ice cream.

'That enough for you?' he asked with a cheeky grin.

'Lovely, thank you,' Rachel smiled.

'Just about,' Agnes grinned back as she lifted her spoon.

Conversation all but dried up as they let the ice cream linger in their mouths.

'That was delicious, you've got to hand it to Luigi, he knows how to make good ice cream,' Agnes said as she put down her spoon on the empty dish.

'Looks as though he agrees with you,' Rachel laughed as she pointed to a notice pinned on the wall behind Agnes. Agnes turned round. In bold print Luigi's customers were informed that the ice cream they were about to enjoy was the best in Dundee.

'Nothing like blowing your own trumpet,' Agnes laughed. With no one waiting for their seats they sat on and talked. 'You haven't said much about your job?'

'You haven't asked but now that you have I can tell you that I'm really enjoying it.'

'Told my ma about you landing the job. She'd heard it said that your Miss Reid is a pernickety wee besom.'

'If by that you mean particular, yes she is and it's because of that that people keep coming back to her. I can't complain; she's nice to me and I've learnt a lot in the short time I've been there.'

'Making your own clothes before long?'

Rachel laughed. 'Not for a very long time I'm afraid. I have to perfect each stage before I'm allowed to move on to the next.'

Agnes nodded her head but Rachel knew that she had been barely listening. It was a habit she'd developed of late that irritated Rachel.

'You'll let me know if I'm boring you,' she said sarcastically.

'What? Oh, you weren't, I heard all you said but I was thinking—' She looked apologetic and was immediately forgiven.

'Thinking about what?'

'About what I'm going to do with my life. Being a maid in Kerne House is just a beginning, the first rung of the ladder. And you can laugh if you like but I know, I just know that one day I'm going to be someone—'

'Who gives orders rather than takes them?'

'You don't believe me, do you?'

'On the contrary, Agnes, I can very easily picture you giving the orders.'

'Want to know how I'm going to go about it?'

'I'm all ears, I might get some tips.'

'You're in the wrong job for that. You see, Rachel, every chance I get I'm going to watch this family, study how the toffs behave, how they talk, their table manners, everything. I'll pick it up in no time. Mind you the Taylors are not gentry, the real gentry I mean, but it's a start.'

One moment Rachel wanted to laugh and then the next to cry. How improbable it all was but what would life be without our dreams, she thought.

'You're laughing inside, Rachel Donaldson, I can always tell with you.'

'No, I'm not. Maybe I think you're being a bit over ambitious but I know that if anyone can do it you can.'

'I've a long way to go before I'm a lady but you're halfway there already.'

'Flattery will get you nowhere.'

Agnes wasn't listening. 'It will mean going well away from Dundee and making a completely new start.'

'You'd drop me?'

'No, not you. I'd keep in touch but you would be the only one.'

'What about your family?'

'I'd have to drop them, be ruthless and cut myself free. Sounds awful I know but I'm intelligent enough to realise that they would always bring me down.'

'You wouldn't, Agnes. You couldn't.'

'I could, but I'm not all bad. Once I make a bit of money I'd send some home and I bet that would be more welcome than a visit from me.'

They got up, paid for their ices and left.

'Got over your disappointment?'

'About going to college? Had to.'

For a little while they walked in silence, the air was pleasantly warm for early spring and a lot of families were enjoying a Sunday stroll and stopping to talk to friends.

'Surely you've got some ambition, Rachel? I can't see you spending the rest of your life making clothes for other people.'

'Neither can I.'

'What do you want to do with your life?'

'I don't know, Agnes, but I've a feeling I'll be leaving Dundee too.'

# Chapter Ten

The spring day was soft, with puffballs of cloud against a blue sky. It was the fourteenth day of April 1933 and the sixteenth birthday of Rachel Donaldson. She should have been happy, she had expected to be happy but instead she was choked with disappointment and a deep, deep hurt. How could he have forgotten? How could her father have forgotten her sixteenth birthday?

Getting up in the morning she had gone through to the kitchen, so sure that there would be something at her place on the table but there had been nothing and her da had already left for work. Peggy, never at her best in the morning, had grunted that there was porridge keeping hot but to go easy on the milk.

By evening Rachel was still not without hope. Maybe her da had wanted to wait and hand over whatever it was himself. She gave Peggy a hand with the meal and when her da came in looked at him expectantly. He smiled. It was an evening no different from any other, just the usual routine before the three of them sat down to eat.

'You'll mind we're goin' to the Club Rooms, Geordie, so don't you be sittin' yoursel' down with the paper.'

'Five minutes, surely?'

'Not even five minutes. There's to be some good turns tonight and I want a seat near the front. If I'm stuck at the back I won't hear or see what is goin' on.'

'All right! All right! I'll get mysel' ready in good time.'

Rachel watched with distaste as Peggy gobbled her food then pushed back the plate. 'I'll get mysel' washed and changed first then you can get in.' She went into the scullery and shut the door.

'Had a good day, lass?' George looked across the table.

'Yes.'

'You're likin' the job?'

'It's all right.' She wasn't going to give him the satisfaction of saying that she liked it. Anyway it came a poor second to what she had expected to be doing.

'Geordie!' She was towelling herself as she popped her head out. 'That's me finished.'

'I'll be there in a minute. If I bolted food the way you do I'd suffer for it all night.' He smiled to Rachel and shook his head. But in a few minutes he was obeying instructions and taking his turn in the scullery.

They were gone. The house was silent. Tight-lipped Rachel went about the tasks left to her. She cleared the table, washed and dried the dishes and put them away in the dresser. To think she could have been out tonight enjoying herself. David Burnside had been a bit put out when she'd declined his invitation.

'There's a good picture on at La Scala.'

'I know and I'd love to see it, Davie, but I can't, not tonight.'

'Why not?' he'd asked suspiciously.

'I'm sorry, Davie, I just can't that's all.'

'Or don't want to?'

'That's not true but if you want to think it then you do just that.'

They had almost quarrelled and now she wondered why she hadn't told him the truth. That it was her birthday and she thought her da might have a surprise evening ahead. Instead of which he had gone off to the Club Rooms with Peggy. Not so long ago her da wouldn't have gone near the Club, not his kind of entertainment, he used to say. Changed days.

Plans that had been little more than dreams began to take shape. She was sixteen, a time to put childhood behind her and take her place in an adult world. Her secret hoard as she termed it, was on the floor of her wardrobe in her bedroom. Going there she took out the rosewood box that had once belonged to her mother. Until Peggy had started coming about the house the box had been on a shelf and out of reach, but Rachel had removed it to her bedroom. She couldn't bear the thought of Peggy touching anything that had belonged to her mother. If her da had noticed he'd kept quiet about it.

The key was in the drawer below her underwear and she went to get it. Once it had been stiff to turn but not now that it was opened regularly for the little she managed to save each week. Peggy frequently complained of the pittance she got from Rachel for her keep but in this her da had been firm. It was enough, he said, with the work the lass did about the house.

Inside the rosewood box was a small velvet jewel case and nestling in the white satin the brooch that had once belonged to her mother, a gift for her eighteenth birthday. Gently she lifted it out and held it up to the light as she always did. She loved the way the stones sparkled and she'd asked her da what they were but he couldn't tell her. All he said was that the brooch was valuable. Next she touched the heavy brown envelope addressed to 'Rachel'. The familiar lump was in her throat as she thought of her darling mama taking in sewing not to make life easier for herself but to have something to leave to her daughter. That money had never been touched, only added to. The knowledge that she had something of her very own was comforting.

Finally the folded sheet of notepaper, no need to look at it. Rachel knew it by heart. In her mother's neat script was a name and address. Two names. Albert and Katherine Craig, Duncairn House, Hillend, Perthshire. Her grandparents. Were they still alive? And if so did they know that their daughter, Amelia, was dead? Would they care? After all, she had been dead to them since that day so long ago when she had left her comfortable home to marry the man she loved. The man she loved. Rachel thought of her da as he was today. Would Amelia still love the man George was today? But that was unkind, unfair. Her da had made himself into the man her mama had wanted him to be – and was there greater love than that?

Her da wouldn't like it but it wouldn't stop her. One day, she promised herself, she would go to Duncairn House, announce herself as Amelia's daughter and see how she was received.

It was a full week later and possibly something in the paper had brought it to mind. Whatever it was, George dropped the paper and all but yelled at Rachel.

'You let me forget your birthday, you deliberately didn't remind me. Your sixteenth birthday.' He looked shattered and angry.

'It doesn't matter, Da,' Rachel said quietly.

'Of course it matters. You could have reminded me, you knew that I'd forgotten. If you wanted me to feel rotten then you've succeeded.'

'For Gawd's sake, what's all the fuss about? I'm only too happy to forget mine.'

But for once George was ignoring his wife.

'Of course I was disappointed, but as Peggy says it's only a birthday.'

'A very special one it should have been and now it's belated birthday greetings.' His anger never lasted long and he was taking the money out of his trouser pocket and counting it. 'Peggy, you got half a crown you could lend me?'

'No, I haven't.'

'Come on, woman, you'll get it back.'

'I'd better,' she muttered as she went for her handbag and threw half a crown on to the table.'

'There you are, lass, ten shillings should buy you something?'

'Thanks, Da.'

'Don't I get a kiss?'

She dropped a kiss on his brow and his hands went out to grip hers.

'Forgiven, am I?'

'Of course.'

'Don't you dare let me forget the next.'

'There'll be a few changes by then,' Peggy said looking pointedly at Rachel. 'Could be that lad of yours will have popped the question.'

'There's nothing like that between David Burnside and me,' Rachel said hotly.

'Then have the decency to tell the lad instead of stringing him along.'

Rachel's mouth tightened. 'Peggy, will you kindly mind your own business.'

'As long as you're under this roof you are my business.'

'Then the sooner I'm away the better.'

'That is enough, you two,' George thundered. 'It's my house and what I say goes, so you can both think on that.'

Rachel added the ten shillings to her savings, glad now that her da had given her money rather than bought her a gift. Every little was needed and ten shillings was a big help.

Was Peggy right? Was she being unfair to David Burnside? The trouble with childhood sweethearts, she thought, was that you grew away from them or one of you did. A few short weeks ago Davie had seemed all she had ever wanted. Compared to the other boys, she saw him as better looking and always polite and she'd been proud to be seen with him. Holding hands and the goodnight kiss had been pleasant, more than pleasant, enjoyable, but the boy was no longer a boy. Suddenly he was a grown man and when he had pressed himself against her she hadn't liked it and wriggled free. His face had darkened and he'd muttered something she hadn't caught before leaving her abruptly at her close.

So much for David Burnside. Her thoughts flitted to Miss Reid. Was the woman unwell? That something was wrong was obvious to Rachel. A few weeks ago she had kept the finer work for her own nimble fingers telling Rachel that it would be a long while yet before that kind of work came her way. Yet here she was getting it to do and having to stop that delicate work to thread a needle for Miss Reid.

'Sorry, lass, you'll need to thread that for me, these specs of mine are leavin' me and I'll have to see about getting another pair.'

She had come back from the optician's strangely quiet and withdrawn and had snapped at Rachel when she enquired as to how she had got on.

'Well enough,' then regretting her abruptness. 'I'm just in a bad humour, all those tests just a waste of time when all I need is a stronger pair of glasses.'

A month later Miss Reid seemed ill-at-ease as Rachel prepared to start work.

'Rachel, sit down, lass, I've something to tell you and it's not easy.'

'I thought you didn't look very well, Miss Reid.'

'Oh, my general health is fine. It's my eyes, Rachel, I've tried to deny the truth making out that stronger specs was the answer and knowing fine that it was more than that. No, no, lass,' she hastened on when she saw Rachel's expression, 'there is little danger of me goin' blind but my eyesight is deteriorating and I won't see well enough for this kind of work.'

'Miss Reid, let me do the fine work, I promise I'll be very careful.'

She shook her head sadly. 'You're a good lass and it was a lucky day for me when Mary Rodgers recommended you but I'm afraid my days as a dressmaker are all but over. In fact I've stopped taking orders and we'll just finish what is on hand.'

Rachel couldn't hide her dismay. 'That means—'

'The end of the business. My sister in Edinburgh, she's widowed and on her own, wants me to share her home and that's what I've decided to do. Mind you, we haven't always got on but we're older now and I'll say this for mysel', I've a sharp tongue but I never carry grievances.'

'I'll miss you, you've been good to me.'

'I'll miss it all, it's been a way of life to me and I'll have many a quiet greet I've no doubt, but you are young, Rachel, your whole life stretches before you. I won't be finishing off here for six or seven weeks but I wanted you to be the first to know. Needless to say I'll be glad, very, very glad to have you stay on but you must feel free to go whenever you want. You'll get a good reference, the best, and now, lass, that's been quite an ordeal and I think we both need a cuppie.'

For the remainder of the day Rachel worked steadily, taking care to keep her stitches even though she doubted that Miss Reid would notice the occasional stitch larger than its neighbour. All the time her mind was working. What good would a reference be if there were no jobs? And jobs like hers would be difficult to come by. Perhaps she should have done a commercial course and gone into an office. Too late now to be taken on as an office junior. Employers wanted cheap labour and a fourteen-year-old could be trained to do the job.

'You are worryin', Rachel,' Miss Reid said as she looked up from the sleeve she was pinning into a blouse.

'Just thinking.'

'When you come to my age you begin to see that all things in life have a meaning. What looks bleak just now, Rachel, may just be the turning point in your life. Added to which you are a bonny lass and I have no doubt more than one lad has his eye on you.' She got up as a customer arrived but something she had said stayed with Rachel. A turning point in her life – perhaps it was.

Miss Reid didn't ask but she showed her relief when Rachel offered to stay on to help finish an evening gown and an afternoon dress for Mrs Mildred Lyall-Black who was fussing about the garments not being ready on the promised day.

'Never liked that one, Rachel, but she's been a good customer and one who paid her bills promptly. It's that haughty manner of hers I can't be doin' with. Not the top drawer you know. The real gentry don't carry on like that.'

'They are just like the rest of us?'

'Oh, dear me, no. The proper gentry can dress in rags but still look right. Something to do with breeding and our Mrs Mildred Lyall-Black hasn't had that advantage.'

Well behind her usual time for getting home Rachel heard the voices as she let herself in. Peggy and her da must be sitting down to their meal. She wasn't deliberately quiet, it was just her way of coming in – no doubt when she was little her mother had discouraged a noisy entrance. Peggy banged doors and accused Rachel of creeping in and taking them unawares. She was on the point of opening the kitchen door and announcing her arrival when she heard her own name. Eavesdropping was something she deplored but there is something about hearing one's own name, a need to know what is being said. She stayed where she was, the voices carried clearly.

'Stop sticking up for Rachel, Geordie, you're just as sick as I am.'

'I'm not denyin' it would be fine just the two of us, but this is her home for as long as she needs it.'

'And that could be long enough. From what I hear she's coolin' off with that Burnside lad. Pity she didn't fancy goin' into service like that chum of hers.'

'Rachel is cut out for something better than that. Mebbe I should have tried to get her into the mill office.'

'It was the looms she thought you had in mind and turned up her nose.'

'The looms – I never suggested that.'

'Doesn't matter whether it's the mill or that Miss Reid, she'd still be livin' here.'

'Wheesht, that's the door, that's her comin' in.'

Rachel deliberately opened and shut the door with enough noise for them to hear. Anger was boiling up inside her but she forced herself to act normally, even to managing a smile.

'Sorry I'm late, we had a rush order to finish.'

'That's all right, lass,' her da said, 'nice to hear that some folk are doing well in these hard times.'

'She's not dependent on the workin' classes,' Peggy sniffed. 'Help yoursel' to what's left and don't complain if it's dried up.'

'Do I ever complain, Peggy?'

'Not in so many words, but it's there in your face.'

Going into the scullery Rachel looked into the pot. Most of the gravy had dried up but she spooned the meat on to her plate, added potatoes, mashed carrot and turnip and carried it to the table. The meat was tender, Rachel was hungry and she ate it all. For a pudding Peggy had tried her hand at an apple sponge but without much success. Rachel avoided the soggy sponge but scraped out as much of the apple as she could. Her da looked up.

'Peggy can't make an apple sponge like you, Rachel, you'll need to give her a lesson.'

In spite of her misery Rachel wanted to laugh. If looks could have killed her da was stone dead but with his head once again in the paper he didn't notice. Peggy had already started on the dishes when Rachel collected hers and took them through. Picking up the tea towel she began to dry them and marvelled that more weren't chipped with the rough treatment they received.

After drying her hands Peggy flounced out and sat down opposite her husband. Her knitting, a jumper for herself in royal blue wool, had been on the go for some time and was grubby. The back and front were complete and the stitches cast on for the sleeve. She picked it up and soon the clicking of the needles was the only sound in the room.

Should she go out? No, why should she? It had rained off and on all day and the evening didn't look much better. In any case where would she go? Agnes was no longer at home. She wondered how she was getting on. Davie would be preparing orders in the back shop. She'd helped him on occasions and enjoyed it. Mr Burnside had been pleased enough for her to be there and Davie's mother had brought through tea and biscuits. A wave of longing for those days to return gripped Rachel but she knew that it was impossible to recapture what had been. Davie and she were no longer comfortable with one another.

Taking out the hard wooden chair from below the table Rachel brought it nearer to the fire. Then she saw that it needed attention and making use of the paper bag added coal and a log without dirtying her hands. That done she settled on the chair and opened the magazine she'd got from Miss Reid that day. She made no sense of the written word but it gave her a chance to think. The plans that had once been but an idle dream were about to become reality. This could be the turning point in her life but only if she were brave enough to turn her back on all she knew for an unknown future. Turning her back on unhappiness was all it was she told herself. She was nearly sixteen and a half, old enough to make a fresh start but she would have to do it secretly. No one, least of all her father, must know what she was contemplating. It needed careful planning to get away from Dundee and if it should happen that she was not made welcome at Duncairn House then she would get a job. Perth was the nearest town to Hillend and if she was willing to turn her hand to anything, there would be something for her before her savings ran out. In an effort to boost her morale she began to number those jobs she could perform. Sewing, she could do that and she had a reference. Shop assistant shouldn't be beyond her capabilities and if all else failed she could copy Agnes and go into service. Feeling happier, Rachel went back to the beginning of the magazine and this time the words made sense.

# Chapter Eleven

The outside of the house was a big disappointment. She had never got around to seeing it when Meg worked there but from her description she had expected something better. Kerne House was a large dwelling made of stone blocks and not a patch on the beautiful houses out on the Perth Road. Agnes stood with her battered suitcase and looked up at the house at the end of the long drive then moved herself hastily as a motor car came speeding down before swinging out on to the road. Shaken at her narrow escape she had just time to see a red-faced man shake his fist at her and without taking time to think she stuck her tongue out at him.

Kerne House was set far back on a rise and had a panoramic view across to the Fife border. The present owners, Edwin and Margaret Taylor, had returned from Bengal four years previously with rather less money than they had expected and been forced to lower their sights and settle for the rather drab-looking Kerne House. Years in India with servants to see to their every need had made Edwin Taylor expect far too much from the small domestic staff who ran Kerne House. Used to shouting at the natives he had continued the practice and scared away more than one maid. Girls, as his wife kept reminding him, were less willing to go into domestic service these days and the point had been reached when new staff of reasonable intelligence was difficult to find.

Margaret Taylor was very different to her husband. She was a head taller and a quietly spoken woman with a gentle manner who accepted that servants, black or white, were human beings and should be treated properly. By that she meant that they should know their place, treat their employers with respect, and work diligently and uncomplainingly. Believing that a wife's duty was to be by her husband's side she had suffered the heat and boredom of India without complaint but had counted the days when she would be back in Scotland. Her one passion was the garden and her interference, as the gardeners saw it, infuriated them until they realised that she was knowledgeable. Now she was an

83

accepted and familiar figure kneeling on her rubber mat, tending the plants and flowers. Deploring the perfect borders and manicured lawns of their neighbours she delighted in a glorious, tangled growth. It wasn't until one got nearer that it was realised that the natural almost wild look was the result of a great deal of work and planning. Agnes went round to the back of the house and here the gardens were surrounded by high hedges. The stables, now empty, were a reminder of the elegant age of the horse and carriage. Motor cars did come into the poorer streets of Dundee but it was still a rarity and an object of interest. Gradually and to the regret of the older generation the horse-drawn vehicles were themselves becoming a rarity as vans and lorries took to the road.

Agnes felt hot and sticky as she knocked at the back door.

'Come in, my hands are all flour,' came the shouted command.

The door scraped the flagstone floor as Agnes got herself and her case inside. 'I'm Agnes Boyd,' she announced.

'So you are and Meg's sister, I see the resemblance. I'm Mrs Robertson as you'll know.'

'Yes,' said Agnes putting down her case.

'Bring a chair and sit yoursel' down, it's a fair walk from the tram.'

'It is lugging this thing,' Agnes smiled as she sat down.

The cook, Mrs Robertson, was a big woman with a face that could fold into laughter lines one minute then scowl the next. She was exacting and demanding but warm in her praise when she felt it was merited. In her fifties, she had never married but wore her mother's gold wedding ring on the third finger of her left hand and when addressed as a married woman by her first employers had seen no point in a correction. To her way of thinking that gave her the advantages of the married status without the demands of a husband. No one at Kerne House ever asked about Mr Robertson, no doubt believing him to be deceased and of course she never referred to her 'husband'.

She wore a voluminous white apron tied round her ample waist and her sleeves were rolled up as her hands worked the scone dough in the wide brown bowl. Flour was scattered on the table and a scone cutter ready for the dough once it was rolled out.

Agnes settled back in her chair. Only one had arms and was for the cook. As she viewed the kitchen, Agnes thought it was a bit of all right. She had never seen anything like this big room with its long table down the middle, its ovens that looked huge to Agnes, it array of pots and pans and shelves of jars all labelled and containing the essential ingredients for the preparing and cooking of food. Until she sat down Agnes hadn't noticed the girl, the kitchen maid, at the far end of the room. She was straining vegetables through a sieve into the deep sink. Briefly she turned her head to study the newcomer then got on with her work.

Agnes hadn't eaten since breakfast and even then had only half finished her plate of porridge. It was unusual and her mother had remarked upon it.

'Nerves, didn't think you suffered from them?'

'I'm not nervous,' lied Agnes, 'just wondering how I'm going to get on. Housekeeping skills are in short measure around here and they'll expect me to know something at sixteen years of age.'

There was an angry flush on her mother's face or was it that she was ashamed?

'Housekeeping skills indeed! You can keep that high falutin' talk for someone else. Meg managed without the benefit of household skills,' she said with heavy emphasis on the words, 'and you'll just have to swallow your pride and ask what you don't know.'

'Meg was younger, it was easier for her.'

'Not much, but she's a sight more humble and while I'm about it don't you dare come back here in the state she's in.'

'No fear, I'm not so bloody stupid.'

'Stupidity has little to do with it as you'll find out, my lass.'

'You don't like me, do you?' Agnes surprised herself by saying as she pushed her plate away and got up. 'Meg and the twins and the boys, of course, you like them better.'

'You've a brain so I won't insult you. I love all my bairns and that includes you but you're a bit of a cuckoo in the nest and there are times, I confess, when I don't much like you.'

'That's plain enough,' Agnes replied and finding that she wasn't deeply hurt.

'Rachel Donaldson's fault I would say; that lass has class and you're always trying to emulate her, big mistake that.'

'Oh, Ma, emulate, such words from Spinner's Lane.'

'Like you, Agnes, I have brains and like you no class. I've the sense to accept it and for your benefit it isn't something you pick up, it can't be learned. You have it or you don't.'

'Rachel's da is working class and so is Peggy.'

'True but her ma had whatever it is. That one was a lady married out of her class and I'll warrant she often went to bed with a sore heart.'

Agnes was starving, her stomach was rumbling with emptiness and Mrs Robertson could hardly fail to hear. Rachel would have come out with a quiet 'pardon me' but she didn't see why she should. It wasn't her fault, it was the mouth-watering smell of beef roasting in the oven and of freshly baked scones and cakes.

'You'd like a cup of tea?'

'I wouldn't mind, thanks.'

'Then I'll get Gloria here,' she jerked her head towards the sink, 'to show you to the room you'll be sharing with Polly. Nice lass, you'll get on fine with her. Gloria, dry your hands and make a fresh pot of tea then butter a couple of scones for – for—'

'Agnes.'

'I've a poor memory for names and I was about to call you Meg, and speaking of the lass, how is she?'

'All right.'

'Your folk standin' by her?'

'Yes.'

'Least said about it the better, but I was real vexed just the same,' then she turned with an irritated expression. 'Gloria, you'll have to stop that sniffin', it's gettin' on my nerves. I take it you do have a handkerchief?'

The thin mousey-brown-haired girl with a face the colour of a suet pudding finished infusing the tea then took out a greyish-white handkerchief, blew noisily into it them promptly gave another sniff. Speaking through her nose she said, 'Blowing makes no difference, Mrs Robertson, my ma says it's just a stuffed head and it'll go away in its own good time.'

'Then let's hope that it won't take too long,' the cook said with a wink to Agnes. 'Gloria comes in daily to do the vegetables and other odd jobs. We're a small staff here with only two live-in maids, that's Molly and yourself. Our last tablemaid left in a hurry about the same time as your sister and we were lucky to get Molly so quickly.' She looked at Agnes picking up the last of the crumbs from the scone. 'Take another but don't be spoiling your appetite.'

'Thanks,' Agnes smiled as she reached for another.

'The master and mistress dine at seven, no visitors tonight for a change, then the staff eat here in the kitchen and if Kerne House has its faults it isn't with the quality or quantity of the food. Mrs Taylor entrusts all that to me,' she said proudly. 'I'm never wasteful, hate to see good food left on the plate, but then there very seldom is.'

The official day for the closing of Miss Reid's dressmaking business was 30 June 1933 and it was just ten days short of that. Miss Reid was looking relaxed and almost happy.

'Rachel, that's us well on with everything and now I think we should spend a little time on you.'

'On me?' Rachel looked up from her sewing.

'Yes, my dear,' she got up to bring over two lengths of material. 'Plenty here of the paler blue to make you a blouse.'

'No, no, really, you've been good to me and I couldn't.'

'This is goin' to give me pleasure, Rachel, so don't spoil it.' She smiled. 'You're getting shapely—'

Rachel blushed scarlet under the close scrutiny. She knew that her body was changing. In the privacy of her bedroom she had looked at herself in the full-length mirror on the wardrobe door and felt the wonder of the changes from girl to woman. Her hips were swelling gently below her small waist, her bosom was rounded and even her face had altered. It was now a perfect oval.

'Blue is your colour, Rachel.' Miss Reid sighed. 'What I would have given to look as you do. That wonderful thick black curly hair is a gift from heaven and those dark-lashed eyes—' She stopped suddenly. 'Yes, I'm goin' to say it, you've no mother and a steppy doesn't count. My father inflicted one of those on us and I don't imagine you think any more kindly of yours than we did of ours. Mind you, it is a difficult relationship for all concerned but I'm digressin'.' She paused. 'Don't throw yoursel' away, lass. You've good appearance and more than that, a natural grace. There'll be a fine young man for you, so don't promise yoursel' before he comes on the scene.'

Rachel threw back her head and laughed but deep down wasn't that what she hoped? That she would meet someone very special who would sweep her off her feet – a fairytale romance.

'Now as I was sayin',' Miss Reid continued as she picked up the material and felt its texture. 'You'll choose a pattern for a blouse and this darker blue tweed made into a skirt will be perfect with it. I'll cut them out but you've enough expertise now to make up a skirt and blouse yoursel'.'

Rachel felt close to tears. 'Thank you very, very much, Miss Reid, and I'll tell you this, I'll never forget you.' She hesitated just for a moment, then made up her mind. Miss Reid was going to Edinburgh and it would be nice to tell someone, someone she could trust to keep it to herself.

'My mother's family live just outside Perth and I'm going to see them but I don't want anyone to know. You see my mother's people were fairly well-off and didn't approve of my father and he would hate to think of me going there.'

'I see, my dear, and you've thought it all out very carefully?' she said with her eyebrows arched.

'Yes, I have. Peggy and my father would be much happier on their own but Da feels responsible for me and I want that to end. I'm over sixteen and I should be able to look after myself.'

'Have you been in touch with these relatives of yours?'

'No.'

'Then I should make some enquiries before you decide to leave home. But, of course, you're sensible, you'll do that?' She looked worried and Rachel wanted to put her mind at rest.

'Yes, I'll do that.' But she had no intention of getting in touch and the reason for that, she could be honest with herself, was the fear that the letter would be ignored. Much better to go there and find out the position for herself.

The skirt and blouse were beautiful. Miss Reid complimented her on the neatness of the finished garments but Rachel knew that the cutting out was what really counted. As Miss Reid had so rightly pointed out, clothes had to hang right to have any appearance and that's where a good pair of scissors in the right hands made all the difference.

'Is this true, Rachel, that Miss Reid is giving up and you'll soon be out of a job?' Peggy said accusingly from the chair at the fire, and her da looked up from filling his pipe.

Peggy hated darning. George's big toe had come through his hand-knitted sock and Rachel was searching for matching grey wool to mend it. Finding a suitable match, she cut off a length, threaded it into the needle and began to darn. Then she answered.

'Yes, it's quite true,' she said quietly.

'And it didn't occur to you to tell us?' Peggy had got to her feet and stood with her hands on her hips looking from her husband to her stepdaughter.

'Miss Reid didn't want it common knowledge before—'

'Meaning I'd spread it?' Peggy said dangerously quiet.

'Yes, Peggy, if you want the truth. You wouldn't have been able to keep it to yourself, now would you?'

'The lass is right, Peggy love, you wouldn't have been able to resist that piece of gossip.' He turned from his wife's furious face to Rachel. 'Now that we do know have you anything in mind – a job I mean?'

'Nothing definite, Da.'

'So we've to keep you until you find somethin' that's suitable to your ladyship?'

Rachel stopped weaving the needle in and out and let the sock rest in her lap while she looked at her stepmother. 'Sit down, Peggy, you look menacing standing like that and now to put your mind at rest let me promise you this. My father will not have to keep me.'

'Then you do have the promise of a job?' Peggy said, sitting down.

'I didn't say that. What I did say was that I would not be a burden.'

'You are not a burden, Rachel.'

'Yes, she is, and be man enough to tell her that to her face instead of trying to keep in with both of us.'

George flushed with anger or embarrassment or perhaps both and Rachel had to admit that Peggy had scored there.

'Why is it, can anyone tell me, that two grown women can't be civil to each other?'

'That's the way it is, Geordie, in circumstances like this.'

In silence Rachel darned the sock and another two pairs needing attention. The job done she put the workbox away and handed the socks to Peggy.

'Ta.'

'You'll miss me for that,' Rachel smiled as she got up.

'Oh, I'll no' deny you've got your uses.'

'Da's hard on his socks and if I were you I'd reinforce the thin bits before they become a hole.'

'Proper wee housewife, aren't you?'

'Not so wee. And now if you'll excuse me I'm going out for a breath of fresh air.'

Tomorrow would be her last day. Miss Reid had insisted that she take an extra week's pay saying that she had more than earned it. They were both dreading the last day. A working relationship to the surprise of them both had developed into friendship and both knew that their paths were unlikely to cross. In the event the day passed off like any other, only the firm handshake that turned into a hug at the end making it different. Returning home, Rachel went over her plans and wondered anew why she hadn't told Agnes. She could have made a point of seeing her. Agnes was her best friend yet she didn't want her to know, not at present anyhow. Perhaps it was because she'd never talked about her mother with Agnes and Agnes knew nothing about her mother's background. Once out of curiosity she'd asked about Rachel's other relations. Her da's folk, her aunt and uncle and cousins in America, she knew of them but what of her other grandparents? At the time Rachel had believed them to be dead and after her da had spoken to her about his in-laws she had wanted to keep it to herself. There were some things one didn't discuss, not even with one's best friend.

And now the time had come to think seriously about her departure from Dundee and how she should go about it. For her plan to work she did need someone and Mrs Rodgers was really the only one she could approach. So far so good, she would go there this evening.

'Rachel, lass, come away in. I was fair wearied wonderin' what to do with mysel'. My knitting's finished and I've nothin' on the pins.' Rachel followed her in and closed the door. 'And what brings you?' Mary Rodgers said as she shuffled ahead in her carpet slippers.

'Oh, dear, does there have to be a reason?' Rachel smiled.

'Young folk comin' to visit the old, more than likely there's a reason, but that's as it should be.'

'Any tea in the pot?'

'There is and it'll be fresh enough. My, but it must be bad if you're askin' a cup of tea. No,' she said when Rachel made to speak, 'let's get ourselves comfortable first. Bring two cups and matching saucers out of that press and save my legs.'

Rachel opened the cupboard door. Some home-made jam was on the top shelf and a few empty jars ready for the next jam-making session. On the second shelf Mary Rodgers had what she called her stock. There were bags of sugar, packets of tea and packets of cornflour, semolina and sago all neatly arranged. The shelf under that had china and Rachel picked up two cups in a faded rose pattern and saucers to match.

'That's fine, lass,' as Rachel set them on the corner of the table where Mrs Rodgers had just covered it with an embroidered cloth. She brought over the cosy-covered teapot and poured the tea. 'Help yoursel' to milk and sugar, I forget what you take.'

Rachel put one teaspoonful into her cup and added milk.

'Bit late to be askin' if you're one of those that needs the milk in first.'

'No, it makes no difference to me.'

'Rich Tea biscuits, it's all I have,' she said offering the plate.

'Thanks.' Rachel stirred her tea, bit off a bit of biscuit, ate it, drank some tea then took a deep breath.

'You must know about Miss Reid?'

'I do, and this'll be about a new job you have in mind?'

Rachel shook her head. 'I haven't been looking for one. I'm going to see my mother's people, they live just outside Perth but I don't want my father to know.'

'You think he'd try to stop you?'

Rachel's voice hardened. 'Like Peggy, he'd be happy enough to see me go but he'd hate to think of me going there.'

'Your da doesn't want rid of you, it's just your imagination.'

'No, Mrs Rodgers, it isn't my imagination. They didn't hear me coming in and I heard with my own ears what my da said.'

'And what was that?' Mary Rodgers said gently, 'and drink that tea before it gets cold.'

Rachel drank some and put the cup down. 'He said,' she swallowed the lump in her throat, the hurtful words were still fresh with her, 'said that, like Peggy, he wished it was just the two of them and words to the effect that he couldn't do anything about it, that he was responsible for me and for a roof over my head.'

Mary sighed. She could imagine the scene. Peggy goin' on about life bein' better if it was just the two of them and George, no doubt to get peace, agreeing with her. But a sensitive lass hearing those words and believing herself unwanted, would take them to heart. Some folk should have been drowned at birth, she thought savagely. She leaned forward and patted Rachel's knee.

'The way I see it your da loves you both but he'll agree with Peggy because it's from her he gets his comforts and you can take what you like out of that.' She looked at the lovely young girl, no not a girl, a young woman. 'The days of bein' a bairn are over, Rachel, and though you're no threat to Peggy she's jealous of your youth and beauty now that she's lost whatever she had.'

'It's not that and I don't think I'm—'

'That's your great attraction, lass, but you'll need to be careful you don't know the effect youth and beauty can have on some men and I'd be a sight happier if I knew you were to be welcomed into your mother's family. Have you been in touch?'

This wasn't going the way Rachel wanted at all. 'No, I haven't been in touch,' she said sharply, 'and I don't intend to.'

'A letter would prepare the way. How do you know that your grandparents are still alive?'

'I don't, but I must have cousins, some relatives and my mother must have wanted to me to get in touch or she wouldn't have left me their address.'

'And if things don't work out, what then?'

'I have a little money my mother left me and I've saved some. Honestly, Mrs Rodgers, I'm not stupid. I've thought of all those things and the job position may well be better in Perth than Dundee.' She smiled. 'I can keep myself until a job turns up and I do have a good reference from Miss Reid.'

'That I would have expected, she was well pleased with you.' They were both silent. Mary drained her cup, set it on the saucer and sat back. 'You could be right with your ma leaving the address. Amelia was a happy enough soul before the illness took her but I always thought there was a sadness too. She was bound to have missed her own folk but being Amelia she would hide it from your da. Likely she wanted you to be accepted, wanted them to see their granddaughter.'

'Don't blame my da, Mrs Rodgers, it must have been very hurtful when they refused even to see him.'

'It would be their way of protecting their daughter. She was such a fine lass and I'm sure she would have been a much loved daughter and their bitterness all the worse for that.'

Rachel felt a burst of happiness. 'I love to hear you talk about my mama. Da never does, not now, and sometimes I think he's forgotten her.'

'No fear of that. He has his memories and you have yours, but life goes on and a second wife doesn't want to be reminded of a first, particularly a well-loved one.'

'You always make me feel better.'

'That's nice to know and perhaps it's time I knew where I come in to these plans of yours.'

'Only if you are agreeable.'

'And I'll know that when I hear them.'

'Like I said I don't want my father to know and if I could leave my suitcase with you I could collect it on my way to the station.'

'He'd be worried out of his mind. Mebbe he hasn't played fair with you, not letting you go on to college was a terrible disappointment and I doubt if you're really over that, but even so, disappearing without a word is cruel and I'm surprised and disappointed in you, Rachel Donaldson.'

Rachel hardened herself. 'He would do everything in his power to stop me. He hates them.'

'Hatred like that is unhealthy but after all this time it's more likely to be resentment caused by hurt pride.'

'It's more than that, I know it is, but once I'm away I don't mind them knowing.'

'You'll leave a note?'

'No, I won't. I'll leave at a time when I know they are both to be out. If you wish, you can tell them I've gone to Perth – my father will know what that means.'

'You're a stubborn soul I'll say that for you.'

'May I leave my case?' she wheedled.

'I suppose so.'

'Thank you,' Rachel said getting up and thankful that she'd got her way.

'And now you promise me one thing, Rachel. I'm not one for interfering but I'm dealing with Amelia's daughter and I think I'd have her blessin' in this.'

Rachel waited.

'Writin' is not for me so there'll be no reply but you send me a wee note to put my mind at rest and you won't insult me with anythin' less than the truth.'

'No, I won't insult you with anything less than the truth.'

# Chapter Twelve

Peggy wasn't one for the house and got out of it most afternoons. The highlight was going into town to do a little shopping with her married sister then having afternoon tea in one of the big stores and listening to the orchestra. Customers were encouraged to request a favourite tune and Peggy, along with some other matrons, was not slow to take up the offer.

The only suitcase was on top of the wardrobe. Rachel stood on a chair to bring it down then proceeded to give it a good dust. A cheap cardboard case would not have survived the passage of time but this was a leather case, darkened almost to black, and it still looked good. Rachel wondered if it was the same case that had transported her mother's possessions on the night she fled her parents' home.

She was alone when Mary Rodgers came round and for a heart-stopping moment Rachel thought the woman had had second thoughts about becoming involved. But it was only to say that she had been called away to a sick bed and that the key would be under the mat and to leave her case in the lobby.

The open suitcase was on the floor and her clothes on the bed. She had taken some tissue paper with Miss Reid's permission. First she wrapped her shoes in old newspaper and put them at the bottom of the case with toiletries and other items to fill in the spaces. Then carefully she folded the new skirt and blouse as she had been taught and slipped the tissue paper between the folds. The rest of the clothes went on top. Her mother's rosewood box would take up too much room and very reluctantly she decided to leave it behind. The velvet case with its precious brooch she put between the layers of clothes then she shut the suitcase. Into her handbag that she had bought herself when she started to work she put her purse with her money. Then a comb, a pale pink lipstick that both she and Agnes had bought for themselves in Woolworth's, and a lace-edged handkerchief that had been her mother's. Some of her oldest clothes still hung in the wardrobe and Rachel had no doubt that Peggy would soon get rid of them. She took a last long look at her mother's rosewood box, empty now and with its key in the lock. Should she give it to Mrs Rodgers, the woman who had been her mother's friend, or should she leave it in the bottom of the wardrobe? In the end she left it. Peggy would very likely use it for her cheap jewellery but her da might like to think that something belonging to his first wife still remained in the house.

Lifting the suitcase, heavier than she had expected it to be, Rachel hurried as fast as she could to Mrs Rodgers' house. She was both surprised and relieved to have met no one she knew. Flushed with nervous excitement and the effort of carrying the case, she picked up the key from under the mat, opened the door and put the case in the narrow lobby. Then making sure that the door was securely locked she replaced the key under the mat and had a quiet smile. Most of the folk round about were particular about locking up yet left an open invitation under the mat. Outside the close she lifted her face to the sunshine and gave a little shiver of excitement. So far so good.

Everything had gone to plan and it had been so easy. Her father had left for work and she'd helped Peggy with the housework.

'You doin' anythin' about a job?'

'No.'

'It won't come to you, you'll have to look.'

'I know.'

'You've somethin' in mind then?' she said suspiciously.

Rachel hung up the tea towel on its hook. 'Yes, Peggy, I've something in mind and I have paid you for this week.'

'Doesn't keep you.'

'I don't agree.'

'You wouldn't.'

'One day you may realise just how much work I do in the house, not forgetting the darning and mending which you profess to hate so much.'

'What am I supposed to do, go down on my knees and thank you?'

'A word of appreciation wouldn't have gone amiss.'

'Gawd! Is that the time? I'll have to get my skates on.'

Ten minutes later her face thick in pancake make-up and her mouth a red slash, she appeared in the kitchen.

'You're off then?' Rachel said.

'Aye. If you've a mind you can peel some tatties, save me when I come in.'

'I'll do them. Cheerio, Peggy.'

'Cheerio.'

It was time to go. Her stomach was behaving strangely, making her feel slightly sick as she gazed about her for the last time. The day was warm and she wore a print dress with a three-quarter-length oatmeal coat over it. She checked her appearance in the mirror then stood stock still. The enormity of the step she was about to take made her catch her breath. She was barely sixteen and a half, just becoming an adult and with nothing secure ahead of her. Had she taken leave of her senses? No, no, she was being cowardly and that was ridiculous after all her careful planning. Put it down to nerves and once she was on the train, turned her back on Dundee, she would be all right.

Silently she said goodbye to her bedroom that had been hers for all of her life. Tonight she would lay her head on a strange pillow. Not that she would be at Duncairn House, she liked the sound of Duncairn House, her grandparents' home and wondered how it had got its name. Arriving at the door clutching a suitcase would make her appear like a little lost orphan. Far better to put up the first night at a lodging house or perhaps she would make that two nights. Free of her suitcase and freshened up and in a more suitable outfit she would set out to make herself known to her relatives.

Mary Rodgers embraced her in a motherly hug then all but pushed Rachel and her case out of the door.

'Just go, lass, I cannae be doin' with partin's, no' at my time of life.'

'Thank you, dear, dear Mrs Rodgers,' Rachel called to her from the door, biting back her own tears. She had only a few minutes to wait for a tram. Someone helped her on with her case and in a short time she was walking down Union Street towards the station. Her new life had begun.

George Donaldson and his wife had finished their meal.

'Where on earth can she be?'

'I'm clearin' the table. She's not even workin' so there's no excuse.'

George grunted as Peggy began carrying the dishes to the scullery then removing the tablecloth.

It was half past seven before Peggy went through to Rachel's bedroom and her startled shout had George leaping from his chair as a ripple of fear went through him.

'What is it? What in God's name is the matter?'

'She's gone.'

'Gone!'

'Look,' she said and with a dramatic movement held the wardrobe door open. 'She's scarpered with all her stuff, the sly besom, and not a word of her intention.'

'Shut up, Peggy.' George was a sickly white as he stared about the room. Peggy was still holding the wardrobe door and his eyes moved to the rosewood box. 'No, she wouldn't,' he whispered.

'Wouldn't what?'

He ignored her and picked up the rosewood box then he lifted the lid. Peggy stood on tiptoe to peer in. 'It's empty.'

'I know where she's gone.'

'And where would that be?'

'It doesn't matter,' he said wearily.

'She'll come back in her own good time, just you wait and see.'

'No, Rachel won't be back. She knew you wanted rid of her and this is her way of going.'

'Don't start blaming me, George Donaldson.' Peggy shouted. 'You were just as anxious to be rid of her.'

'That's a lie, Peggy.'

'You said so yoursel'.'

'To shut you up, that's all.' He stopped suddenly. 'That time, Peggy, we were talking, I thought I heard the door earlier. Maybe she heard us, you have a loud enough voice.'

'Listeners never hear any good of themselves.'

'I remember what I said and I hope to God she didn't hear. Even if she did, she would know I didn't mean it.'

'No use upsettin' yoursel', that won't bring her back.'

'You've never got on with her but she's my daughter, Peggy, and I love her – perhaps I didn't realise how much until—' his voice broke and Peggy watched in appalled silence as the tears rolled down his cheeks. Almost motherly in her actions, Peggy led him through to the kitchen and into his chair, then she went to the sideboard poured a stiff whisky and handed it to him. Then she went back and poured an equally stiff drink for herself. She wasn't heartbroken, how could she be when she'd wanted rid of her stepdaughter, but she wasn't happy either. The lass was too stuck-up for her liking but she'd been good about the house and as for the mending and darning, those dreary jobs, she'd never complained. She had always done a baking at the weekend too and it was a lot better than bought stuff.

She didn't know what was wrong with her and George in the midst of his own grief didn't know either. Not someone to do anything by halves, Peggy broke into noisy sobs and all but collapsed into the chair.

Rachel Donaldson's disappearance was the main topic of conversation as groups of housewives gathered at the mouth of the closes to discuss it.

'That Peggy gave her a hard life, I hear. No wonder the lass up and went, only hope no harm's come to the lamb. She was a right nice lass, never let you pass without a smile.'

'From what I hear Peggy is real upset.'

'Puttin' it on more like.'

A stout woman dropped her voice. 'Got it from Bella McDonald, she bides beside them, and she says that her da knows where she's gone and so does Mary Rodgers but they're no' lettin' on to Peggy.'

'What about the laddie Burnside, they were goin' steady?'

'No, that had cooled a while ago and I've seen him mysel' with the lassie from the chemist but for all that he's in a bit of a state and cannae throw any light on it.'

'I'm real sorry for Geordie but I'm away for my half-loaf before the shop closes.'

Agnes had come home intending to see Rachel.

'Your chum's gone and done a bunk,' Meg said as she greeted her sister.

Agnes wasn't paying much attention, she was studying the strained skirtband. 'You're showing and what you're wearing makes it worse. That skirt was always too tight for you.'

'What am I supposed to do, buy maternity clothes?' she said sarcastically, but there was a trace of tears in her voice.

'My pink dress, it's loose enough and it looks awful on me, you can have it if you want.'

'Ta,' she said cheering up a bit. 'Kerne House, you gettin' on all right there?' she asked with studied indifference.

'So far, but you're a hard act to follow,' Agnes said generously. 'Seems you were a good worker and Mrs Robertson for one misses you.'

The tears began to flow and Agnes put her arms round the heaving shoulders.

'Want to tell me about it?'

'It was good, Agnes, everythin' was great. Good food, a bed to mysel' then I have to be a bloody fool and – and – it's too late now but I wish to God I'd got rid of it.'

'Why didn't you?'

'I don't know. In a funny sort of way I suppose I wanted it, even now – oh, I just don't know,' she ended wretchedly.

'Were you in love with him?'

She didn't answer, just wiped her eyes with the back of her hand and looked at Agnes with a tear-streaked face. 'Back here after Kerne House I'll go mad I think. It didn't seem so awful before but—'

'But you'll just get used to it.'

'Have to, won't I? And you didn't hear what I said about your chum.'

'What about Rachel?'

'She's cleared off.'

'Cleared off where?'

'That's what nobody knows.'

'Rachel wouldn't do that. I just don't believe it.'

'It's true,' Meg said, enjoying giving the sensational news, 'and you should just hear some of the rumours goin' about.'

'But where would she go?' Agnes said, her hands raking through her hair and a bewildered look on her face. 'She must have told somebody?'

'Mebbe she would have told you but when were you here last?'

'You didn't come home very often either did you, not to stay overnight, so don't start on me. And when I did try to see Rachel she was working – that's it,' she said excitedly, 'I'll go and see—'

'You can save yoursel' a journey, her da and Peggy are not sayin' anythin'.'

'Not them, but Miss Whats-her-name – Reid. They were pretty close and she'll know Rachel would want me to know her whereabouts. I bet she knows.'

'Mebbe she does but it's too late to find out. The business closed and she's gone to Glasgow or Edinburgh or some place.'

'Maybe Rachel's gone with her. Yes, that could be it.'

'Why would she leave a good home?'

'Peggy, that's your answer. Rachel felt she was only there on sufferance and yes, wait I'm remembering something – something she said but I didn't think anything of it at the time.' She puckered her brow. 'We were in Luigi's, it was when I was blethering about—' Agnes stopped, she had almost given herself away, she'd been about to say 'leaving Dundee to better myself.' Quickly she corrected herself, 'blethering about Kerne House and me starting in your job.'

'Go on then, what did she say?'

'She said,' Agnes spoke slowly, 'I have a feeling that I'll be leaving Dundee.'

'There you are then, mystery solved and you'll just have to wait until she writes to you.'

'Seems like it,' Agnes said quietly. She was hurt, deeply hurt, but she wasn't going to show that hurt to anybody.

Those first days at Kerne House had been bewildering but Agnes was coping. So far she had been kept to the kitchen and the back quarters and had seen nothing of the master and mistress. With unfamiliar work taking up all her attention she had all but forgotten the incident with the car and her unthinking and unfortunate response to the fist shaken at her. Visitors, as she was discovering, came frequently to Kerne House and more than likely it had been one of them.

The Taylors were childless, in their case from choice. India was not the best place to bring up children and Margaret Taylor had no intention of remaining in Scotland while her husband was free to take up with someone else in her absence. Since she didn't much care for children she didn't consider it a sacrifice. The owners of Kerne House enjoyed giving hospitality to former friends home for a holiday after a spell of four years in India. In many cases the novelty of staying with relatives quickly lost its appeal for all concerned and they were only too happy to descend on the Taylors for a few days or longer if they could manage it. Margaret Taylor was a gracious hostess though less enthusiastic than her husband about overnight guests. It meant being away from her beloved garden and engaging in conversation about the 'old days' and in her husband's hearing having to pretend a longing for them which she didn't feel. Edwin Taylor's heart and his interests were still in India and he enjoyed nothing better than to hear what was going on in the East. Wistfully he wished himself back there.

The steady breathing from the other narrow, iron bed showed Molly to be asleep. Usually she liked to chat but tonight she'd gone to sleep almost the minute her head touched the pillow. Agnes grinned into the darkness. The heady excitement of going on the back of a motor-bike must have been too much for her. In Agnes's opinion Molly was a bit of a dumb cluck but she was nice and she'd been helpful and shown Agnes how things were done that both the cook and housekeeper took for granted that she knew.

The letter was the cause of it all. It was from Tommy, her new boyfriend, to say that he was getting a loan of his brother's motor-bike, that he had mastered it without any trouble, and was coming to Kerne House to take Molly for a spin on her day off and that he could change his time off to suit hers provided it wasn't a Saturday when he worked all God's hours.

'What does he do?' Agnes had asked.

'Learnin' to be a butcher in his uncle's shop and he's keepin' in with him because he'll mebbe get the business one day.'

'This uncle has no children then?'

'None that counts. They do have a son but he's soft in the head.' She smiled happily. 'Tommy says he doesn't get it any easier because it is his uncle and that he can be a real, I won't say the word, but I told him he can't afford to cheek back else he'll lose out.' She suddenly switched to talk about the motor-bike. 'What if I fall off?' she asked anxiously.

'You won't if you keep your arms tight round his waist and hang on for dear life.'

'He wouldn't like it if I fell off.'

'I don't imagine you would be too happy about it yourself.'

'Not if I hurt mysel', 'course I wouldn't.' She paused. 'There's something else, Agnes.'

'What?'

'When he turns corners do I bend the same way as Tommy or the other way to help balance the bike?'

Agnes was stumped, she'd never been on the back of a motor-bike, didn't know anyone lucky enough to have one. 'You've got me there. Bend the same way he does I think but you'd better ask him.'

'I will.' She smiled dreamily. 'He's ever so nice, Agnes, and he's awfully good-lookin' just like a film star.'

'Sounds a bit of all right to me.'

'You'd like him I know you would.'

'Better watch out then, hadn't you?'

Molly was blessed with a good figure though perhaps a little on the heavy side and she was pretty. Her expression was almost smug as she looked at Agnes and shook her head.

'I'm not in the least worried.' She touched her dark blonde hair and twisted a strand of it round her finger. 'Tommy told me he didn't like girls with ginger hair.'

'Auburn if you please.'

'Same thing.'

'What has this Tommy of yours got against auburn-haired girls?' Agnes was just the teeniest bit annoyed. 'Come on he must have given a reason.'

'Well, if you must know he says they are – they are – I don't remember what he said.'

'Yes, you do and I'm waiting.'

'He didn't mean you, Agnes, how could he? He hasn't even met you.'

'What did he say?' Agnes almost shouted.

'That you are a fast lot and lead a fellow on.'

'What rubbish, what absolute tripe and you can tell him that from me.'

'I will not and I wouldn't have told you if you hadn't made me.'

Agnes lay with her hands behind her head and smiled at the memory of that exchange. She'd heard it said that red-haired girls were generally more passionate than their black, brown or fair-haired sisters but that didn't apply to her. She didn't believe it was in her nature to be passionate about any man but that didn't mean that she wouldn't like someone being that way about her. In any marriage, she'd heard it said, there was always one partner more in love than the other. And as for giving herself before marriage, there was no danger of that. Meg, silly girl that she was, had fallen for promises but she wouldn't. She would get that ring on her finger. She accepted that she might have to feign love but provided he was a person of means and intelligence that shouldn't be too difficult. Of course, he wouldn't have to be hideous or anything like that.

And what kind of bargain was he getting? Agnes asked herself and found the question easily answered. Admiring glances had only confirmed what the mirror told her. She was an attractive young woman of medium height with a good figure, a face that wasn't beautiful but passably pretty. Her thick, auburn hair she had always considered to be her crowning glory and if Molly's boyfriend didn't admire the colour then he was in the minority. It was silly of her to let a remark like that bother her but it had. One important quality she had omitted. She was intelligent and able to hold a conversation, not like some she could mention.

She stretched herself in the bed enjoying the still novel experience of having a bed to herself instead of sharing it with her sisters. In fact, the only fly in the ointment at Kerne House was the housekeeper, a proper tartar that one, and a frustrated old maid, Agnes decided, who delighted in taking out her frustration on the staff. She was a tall, thin, sharp-featured, middle-aged woman with iron-grey hair scraped back from her temples and secured in a tight little bun held in place by a large number of hair pins. Irene Templeton was the kind of woman who looked for faults and invariably found them.

In her presence poor Molly was a nervous wreck, the girl was highly strung at the best of times and was in fact extremely efficient in all tasks bar the one for which she had been primarily engaged. She knew how to set a table, how to place the cutlery, how to stand at the side of each guest, not too near, to serve the various courses. Left alone she was fine but a wrong word or a raised eyebrow from the mistress at some tiny omission was enough to throw her completely. It made her clumsy and had resulted in more than one unfortunate accident.

Agnes was well aware that Miss Templeton regretted giving in to cook and engaging Meg's sister without an interview. Nevertheless, Miss Templeton had to accept that the domestic position regarding new staff was difficult, very difficult indeed and the bold piece was intelligent. Too clever by half was her personal opinion. Molly was her biggest worry, the girl was a disaster at table and the Taylors (she thought of them as the Taylors but spoke of them as the master and mistress) were holding her responsible since it was she who had engaged the girl.

It left a sour taste in her mouth but the Boyd girl would have to be trained as a tablemaid and Molly demoted to housemaid.

# Chapter Thirteen

The train puffed into the tiny Hillend station and two passengers got off. One was Rachel. The other, a middle-aged woman carrying her shopping, walked briskly along the platform to be met by a man of similar age who relieved her of her packages and together they went out. Rachel followed more slowly and wondered which way to go. She stopped and put down her suitcase. The couple had turned right into a quiet country road. Rachel decided that their home was a secluded cottage or perhaps a farmhouse. She would walk the other way. Picking up her case she set off to where a few people were about and after a few minutes she was in a street of small houses with a corner shop – the sort of shop that appeared to sell anything and everything and the thought struck Rachel that here she might get information about a lodging house.

She went in and waited her turn.

'Yes, miss, what can I get you?' The woman was a cheery soul, her face wreathed in smiles at something her last customer had said.

'I'm looking for accommodation and I wondered if you could recommend someone.'

'How long for?'

'Two nights.'

She pursed her lips and seemed to be considering. 'Mrs McGregor, two doors down takes boarders but if it is just for a couple of nights you'd be better with Mrs Shepherd, her laddie's just gone to work out of town, and she'll have his room. She's a nice soul and you'll be all right with her.' She was pointing along the road.

'Which house?'

'Can't say the number but halfway along, the green door with the bonny shiny brasses, can't miss it. Tell her Mrs Mackay from the shop sent you.'

'Thank you, I'm very grateful.'

'You're not much more than a bairn to be lookin' for a room,' she said suspiciously as Rachel turned to go.

'I'm nearly seventeen,' Rachel said with as much dignity as she could muster. Sixteen years and seven months was near enough to seventeen she told herself.

The green door with the well-polished brasses stood out from the others. Rachel put down her suitcase and knocked. In a few moments it was answered by a woman who looked questioningly at the girl then at the case as if she were sure the caller was at the wrong house.

Rachel smiled to hide her nervousness – making plans and the reality were very different she was just finding out. The woman in the shop didn't seem to be sure of her. Perhaps a young girl with a suitcase and looking for accommodation did appear suspicious, like someone running away from home. She really must try to sound more confident, act like a mature person who knew what she was about.

She held her head high. 'I'm looking for accommodation for two nights and Mrs Mackay in the shop suggested I try you first.'

'I've a spare room right enough. Come away in and you can see if it'll be suitable.' She was a sturdy, pleasant-faced woman with short light brown fly-away hair and a complexion that many a young girl would have envied. Rachel's protests were swept aside as she leaned over the step and picked up the case. 'Straight ahead, the door to the left,' she instructed as she shut the outside door. It was a nice, homely, shabby room with photographs, probably of family, covering the surface of the sideboard. 'My but there is some weight in that, did you carry it from the station?'

'Yes, I did.' She smiled. 'I'm Rachel Donaldson, Mrs Shepherd.'

'You'd like to see the room now?'

'Yes, please.'

'Come along then. It was my son Eric's room but he's workin' out of town and he's been lucky enough to find a room with a nice old lady who seems glad of his company.' She laughed, a pleasant little tinkle of a laugh. 'Always falls on his feet, our Eric.' They went up a stairway covered in maroon and brown carpeting with brass rods to keep it in place. The door to the bedroom was wide open. 'Like to keep it well-aired. Well, what do you think? Will it do you?'

'It's perfect, Mrs Shepherd.' The room was similar in size to the one she had been used to. It had a single bed covered by a deep blue bedspread. There was no mirror on the wall but Mrs Shepherd opened the wardrobe and on the inside of the door was a full-length mirror. A basket chair was beside it and alongside that a table with a glass ornament in the centre.

'Looks empty without all the rubbish Eric used to accumulate. I used to go on at him complaining about the untidiness but I'll tell you this, lass, I'd willingly have the mess back if I could have my laddie.'

'You must miss him very much?'

'I do but I'm glad too that he's away. It was high time the lad learned to stand on his own two feet instead of expecting everything to be done for him. You like it then?'

'Yes, and of course I'll pay you in advance.'

'You've an honest face but if you'd prefer it that way?'

'Yes, I would.'

'We'll go downstairs and have a cup of tea and don't worry I won't be taking much from you, and that,' she pointed to a closed door and lowered her voice, 'that is the convenience if you want to make yoursel' comfortable. I'll away down and put the kettle on. Oh, by the way, I'd better know now about breakfast if you'll want something cooked. I take a plate of porridge and toast myself but the young people are mebbe not so keen on that.'

'Porridge and toast is what I'm used to, Mrs Shepherd.'

The woman looked relieved. 'That'll save me goin' to the shop for I don't keep a lot of food in the house, well you don't when you're on your own.'

Before Rachel could do more than open her case the call came that the tea was infused and just to leave everything and come down.

Feeling happier now Rachel ran down the stairs and into the living-room. A small table was set at the fire with two cups and saucers of fine china and there was a plate with slices of fruit loaf.

'Come late afternoon I usually put a match to the fire, it can get a bit chilly and it's cheerier than looking at an empty grate. Eat up, lass, don't be shy and I won't be charging you for this.'

Rachel took a piece of the fruit loaf and bit into it. 'It's lovely, did you make it?'

'Yes, I make two when I'm about it and send one in a tin box to Eric. There's mice in those sorting offices, you know, but they won't nibble through tin. Eric was always partial to fruit loaf and his landlady gets her share.'

She was such a friendly person, Rachel thought, and showing no curiosity in her unexpected lodger. All the same, she must tell her something.

'I'm from Dundee and before I visit my relatives I wanted to see Hillend. You see, someone I loved very dearly knew this village and spoke so well of it that I simply had to come and see it for myself.'

The woman smiled and nodded. That wasn't the whole truth, there was something the lass was keeping back and she had a perfect right to do that. Some folk around here, Mabel Mackay among them, wouldn't let it rest there, awful to be bothered with your nose. She was glad she wasn't like that and she'd put the lass at her ease. Nice lass, bonny too, she hoped Eric would choose well and not one of those silly, giggly types.

'Hillend is a bonny wee place and there's some fine walks. You've a sturdy pair of shoes with you, I hope?'

'Yes, I have, in the case,' Rachel said with a glance at her thin-soled shoes.

'There's the walk along the side of the burn and up to the auld kirk and then the village itsel' is worth a look at. Then you'll need to take the Glen Road, it's a fair climb and I've to stop halfway to get my puff back but it's an excuse to look over at Duncairn House.'

Rachel was tired and the strain of the last few hours was beginning to tell but at the mention of Duncairn House she was fully alert and wanting every scrap of information she could get without appearing to be curious.

'Is it a very grand house?'

'It's an estate, lass. The Craigs of Duncairn House are Hillend, if you see what I mean. The family has been here for generations but like others of their kind they hit hard times and jute has been their saviour.'

Rachel feigned surprise. 'Not the Craig Mills in Dundee, by any chance?'

'One and the same. The old master, gossip would have it, was quite a character and put the fear of death into his staff, yet he could be kindly too. He lived to a ripe old age and not many changes were made in his day. But when the son and family took over they spent a power of money bringing Duncairn House back to its former glory. That I may say was the time I got married to a Perth lad and went to live there.' She was silent for a little then gave a deep sigh. 'Bidin' with in-laws isn't the ideal way to start married life, so be warned. We had three years of it before we got our own wee place and Eric already a toddler. What on earth made me tell you that?'

'You had left Hillend to live in Perth?'

'That's it. Eric was twelve when I lost my man and I came back to Hillend with my laddie and hopefully I'll spend the rest of my days here.'

'Thank you for making it all sound so interesting, Mrs Shepherd,' Rachel said as she declined another cup of tea. 'Tell me, though, is the family still in residence?'

'The old lady is and she must be quite an age. It's a long while since she lost her man, I lose track of time, but it's some years. There's a married daughter living with her and a granddaughter I'd put to be ages with yourself.' She stopped, smiled and shook her head. 'Dear me, here I am goin' on about the folks at Duncairn House as if it was of any interest to you.'

Rachel smiled and got to her feet. She had learnt all she needed. 'May I wash these up for you?'

'And you a payin' boarder? No, thank you, lass, but it shows you've been well brought up.'

'I'll go up now and empty my case.'

'Do that and there should be a few spare coat-hangers. I'll be up shortly to put sheets on the bed.'

Tired though she was, sleep would not come. Maybe it was the silence, a country stillness different from the nights in Dundee to which she was accustomed. Even after the last tram had trundled by on its way to the depot, the silence was never complete.

Suddenly her face was wet with tears and Rachel was wishing with all her heart that she was back in her own bed at 23 Blackford Street with the dear familiarity of everything. She tried reasoning with herself that her tiredness was to blame, bringing to the front of her mind all the hurtful things that had driven her from home, but even Peggy at this distance didn't seem so bad. And her da, what would he think of her leaving in that manner?

She dried her eyes, put the sodden handkerchief under her pillow and closed her eyes. It was too late for regrets was her last unhappy thought before sleep overtook her.

Light filtered through the curtains and Rachel could hear movement downstairs. On first awakening in the strange bedroom she had wondered where she was or indeed if she was still sleeping and this was a dream.

As the previous day's events caught up with her she got out of bed and padded over to the window. The bedroom was to the front of the house and drawing back the curtains Rachel looked down onto the street. Not much activity, just a few people leaving their homes probably for their place of employment. Looking up she saw that the sky was overcast with the threat of rain. It decided her against wearing her best outfit. If it did rain, her new skirt would get wet under her short coat and she couldn't risk that. Instead, she would wear her workaday clothes and walking shoes. In any case she didn't want to approach her relatives today but there was nothing to stop her looking at Duncairn House. Tomorrow, dressed in her new blouse and skirt, she would know that her appearance would not let her down.

After breakfast and porridge that would have put Peggy's to shame she made her own bed and tidied up before setting out. How fortunate she had been with her accommodation – Mrs Shepherd was certainly not overcharging her. Most of those she met greeted her with a 'good morning' and a smile. Dundonians were friendly folk but they had to know a person by sight before passing the time of day.

Mrs Shepherd had been right. The dullness was no more than early morning mist and already the slight breeze was dispelling it. Rachel walked by the side of the burn enjoying hearing the sound of the water lapping against the stones but she didn't linger to admire her surroundings. She was too anxious to get on to the Glen Road and have her first look at Duncairn House.

She stopped halfway up the hill and drank in the soft beauty of the Perthshire hills and the lovely countryside.

Her first glimpse of Duncairn House was through a gap in the hedge and she caught her breath. It was so much more than she had expected. So beautiful was this majestic stone-built house with its well-proportioned windows and its wide, impressive entrance. Tearing herself away, Rachel left the Glen Road for a narrow path, not noticing the PRIVATE sign partly hidden by the overhanging branches of an oak tree. She walked on until she had Duncairn House in full view. The gates with their intricate pattern were open and two cars sat in front of the entrance. From that distance she could make out the figures of a man and a woman leaving the car and walking up the steps closely followed by a girl in a summery dress that ballooned out as she ran ahead of the other two and disappeared inside.

Rachel's throat was a tight knot. Was the girl her cousin and the woman her Aunt Maud? She stopped where she was and looked about her. Such a commanding position must have an unspoiled view of the gentle rolling hills of this lovely part of Perthshire. And this was where her mother must have spent many holidays with her grandparents before returning to the more modest residence in Dundee.

The gardeners were busy, gardens such as these must need a great deal of attention, Rachel thought. She was walking on when she heard the voice and stopped. It was one of the gardeners and he was shaking his head at her.

'Not this way, lass,' he shouted. 'Take the other fork and you'll find your way round to the back.'

'Thank you,' she called back and struck out in the other direction. She fell to wondering what he would say if she had told him that she was family and not trespassing as he had indicated she was doing. Probably would not have believed her.

For an instant, a single instant, she had felt as though her mother were there urging her on and she felt guilt at her lack of courage. Tomorrow and it couldn't be delayed, she had to bring herself to walk up that drive, ring the bell and announce to whoever answered it that she was Rachel Donaldson, Amelia's daughter, and that she wished to see her grandmother.

Deep in thought she was at the back of the house and a girl was hurrying towards the open door. The figure at the entrance hurried the girl inside then catching sight of Rachel signalled for her to get a move on. Not quite sure what to do she found herself hurrying forward.

'Follow that girl and take a seat.'

'But—'

The woman had gone and Rachel walked into a small room, like an anteroom was her first thought. The girl was already seated with her legs crossed and very much at her ease. She looked Rachel up and down with unfriendly eyes and the smile died on Rachel's face. The door leading into another room opened and a head popped out. 'I'll see you now.'

Less than ten minutes later the girl came out, glanced briefly across at Rachel and said. 'You've to go in.'

She really must apologise for the mistake. Rachel got up, gave a small tap at the door and went in. It was a sparsely furnished room she entered with a table not unlike the one at 23 Blackford Street, and behind it sat a woman her head bowed as she wrote on a pad. She didn't look up only indicating with a wave of a hand that Rachel should be seated at the other side of the table. In another minute the head went up and grey-blue eyes regarded her coolly. Difficult to determine her age but Rachel put the woman to be in her late forties or early fifties. Her brown hair, peppered with grey, was bobbed in the fashion that was becoming popular and her long face was sallow. She kept the pen in her hand.

'Name?'

'I—' began Rachel.

'You do have a name?'

'Rachel Donaldson.'

'And how old are you?'

'Sixteen.'

'Are you in employment?'

'No.'

'You will address me as Mrs Anderson,' she said coldly.

'I do beg your pardon, Mrs Anderson, I'm not – I mean—' she floundered and stopped.

The woman spoke irritably. 'That other girl ahead of you was sullen and disrespectful. You appear to be unable to answer a simple question when it is put to you. What is the matter with the younger generation? I take it that you are interested in the vacancy for housemaid or why else would you be here?'

Suddenly it dawned on Rachel that she was being interviewed for a job, a maid's job, in her grandmother's house. About to explain the true position she stopped herself. This was perfect. The ideal way to find out about her relatives and the woman who had disowned her own daughter. The housekeeper, or whoever she was, must think her an idiot the way she was acting and if she wanted this job, and suddenly she wanted it very much, then she had better start making a better impression.

Deliberately she moved to sit on the edge of the chair, a sign she knew that was associated with nervousness and being ill-at-ease.

'Mrs Anderson, please excuse me, I'm just nervous because I have so little experience but I am very willing.'

'Let me hear about the little you do have,' she said unbending a little.

'After my mother died I kept house for my father and did the cooking and baking.'

'That is rather different to working in a large house like this,' she said

112

looking amused. 'May I ask when this stopped and for what reason?'

'My father married again.'

She nodded. 'I see and now you are seeking a position, preferably a live-in position?'

'Yes, Mrs Anderson.'

'Do you live locally?'

Rachel hesitated then decided to keep as close to the truth as possible.

'Until very recently my home was in Dundee,' she said quietly and as she said it a picture of her father and Peggy came into her mind. Had her disappearance upset them? She thought not.

'Where are you staying at present?'

'I have accommodation in the village.' Rachel had a thought. 'Perhaps I should mention that I can sew.' She opened her handbag thankful that she had Miss Reid's reference with her, and handed it over. Mrs Anderson read it then handed it back.

'Very satisfactory,' she said as Rachel put the envelope back into her bag. 'It doesn't say but obviously you can use a sewing machine.'

'Yes.'

This seemed to please her and she kept nodding her head. 'We do have a woman who comes in to attend to the mending of the bed linen but she is far from satisfactory. Now if you could take on this task as part of your job I could see my way to offering you the position.'

Rachel almost laughed with relief but she kept her face straight. 'I would be happy to work in whatever capacity you feel I am best suited,' then wished she hadn't phrased it just like that.

'You don't talk like a maid.'

Rachel could think of no answer to that and remained silent.

'But then you weren't, you were keeping house for your father.'

Rachel smiled.

'How soon can you start? We are short-staffed at present.'

'Thursday,' Rachel answered promptly. She would stay at Mrs Shepherd's tonight, after all she had paid for it and she could have the whole day to explore.

'That would be very suitable. Usually the servant girls share a bedroom but there is a room available, much smaller of course, which you could have and it is next to the sewing-room.'

'I'd like that, thank you.'

'Very well,' she said getting up to show the interview was at an end, 'report to me on Thursday at nine a.m. Oh, we haven't discussed wages or your hours of work.' She proceeded to do so but remained standing no doubt expecting it to be satisfactory to the new maid, which it was.

After Rachel had gone Mrs Anderson smiled to herself, well pleased. Whatever the circumstances it was easy to see by the girl's appearance, manners and speech that she came from a good home. She could congratulate herself that the girl could sew. The old lady wasn't mean but she was of that dying breed that threw nothing away as long as there was wear in it. The sheets were badly in need of rehemming and there was plenty of work to be done in the linen cupboard. The old lady would be pleased, she was not above checking on the condition of the linen and voicing her disapproval of the frayed hems.

Rachel was outside and barely able to contain her excitement. How different it all was to what she had expected.

The ordeal of walking up that long drive, knocking at the door or ringing the bell, whichever it was, was no longer ahead of her. It was cowardly that she should feel such relief but she didn't care and in the fullness of time she could either announce to a startled household that she was Amelia's daughter or if she found that she disliked or wanted nothing to do with her mother's people then she could leave without anyone being the wiser.

The air was pleasantly cool as she walked away from the back door of Duncairn House. Like the front the gardens at the back of the house were well-kept and the borders were a blend of carefully chosen perennials their soft colours making Rachel think of peace and tranquillity. As that thought came into her head she wondered how her grandparents could ever have known real peace of mind. Had they ever tried to find out about their daughter? She thought not. After all, it shouldn't have been too difficult for people with money and authority to discover the couple's whereabouts. Her mother by all accounts had told them that her beloved worked in the Tayside Jute Mills. In the end was it just pride that kept them apart? Would she ever know?

# Chapter Fourteen

It was the deafening sound of a motor-bike arriving in the yard that sent Agnes flying out of the kitchen. What she had expected to see was an excited pillion-seat passenger, instead of which she saw a distressed Molly all but stumble in her effort to be free of the bike. Her face was almost green and Agnes hurried forward to help.

'Leave me, I'm goin' to be sick,' she said in an agonised voice and Agnes had her arm roughly shaken off.

'I'll come—'

'No,' she said wildly and with her hand pressed over her mouth ran behind a nearby clump of bushes.

'She'll be all right in a few minutes,' a voice said when the retching had stopped.

Agnes barely glanced at the young man.' No thanks to you,' she said curtly.

'And what exactly do you mean by that?' The voice was dangerously quiet and he'd moved away from the bike to tower above her.

'Showing off, that's what you'd be doing and driving like a maniac I bet.'

His eyes narrowed. 'Nothin' of the kind. For one thing I've more respect for other people's property.' He patted the bike with affection. 'Belongs to my brother.'

'You could still have been speeding,' but she was less aggressive now.

'Well, I wasn't. I've enough sense to know my own limitations.'

They were glaring at each other when a sheepish-looking Molly reappeared. The greenish tinge had gone from her face but she was still very white.

'Feelin' better?' Tommy asked as he put an arm round her shoulder.

'A bit, but I think I'll go to my room and lie down for a while,' she said beginning to move away, then stopped. 'Oh, sorry, I was goin' to introduce you. Tommy, this is Agnes Boyd and Agnes,' her voice softened, 'this is Tommy Kingsley.'

There was no way they could get out of shaking hands. Agnes saw the hesitation, or was it reluctance, as Tommy extended a lean brown hand and she met it with the tips of her fingers. For a moment she looked up into a pair of startlingly blue eyes and was shocked at her own feelings as he abruptly turned away to give Molly a hug.

'No bike next time, I promise,' he said as he mounted the machine and in a few minutes he was just a speck in the distance.

Molly had gone ahead to lie down and Agnes tried to make sense of her own feelings. Molly hadn't exaggerated, Tommy Kingsley was quite the most handsome young man she had ever met. He was quite tall with dark good looks and long lashes over those incredibly blue eyes. Duty called and for once she was thankful for something to do. She wanted to forget that arrogant, disturbing young man.

The kitchen at Kerne House was old-fashioned and a lot of work but Mr and Mrs Edwin Taylor saw no reason to spend money on something that had worked well in the past and continued to do so. There were faint mutterings of complaint from the cook but they never reached the master and mistress. In truth Mrs Robertson had no wish for change, indeed she would have fought it tooth and nail. It would be time enough for that when her days at Kerne House were over.

With just the three maids, Molly, Agnes and Gloria, the work had to be shared though Molly as tablemaid did fewer menial tasks. Gloria came in daily but she was never in a hurry to go home where more work awaited her and willingly tackled far more than her share of the work. A simple lad came when he felt like it and chopped wood and filled the buckets with coal.

Gloria and Agnes cleaned and black-leaded the grates once a week and each morning Agnes had to lay the fires and sweep and dust. She thought they were trying to make a fool of her when she was told to sprinkle tea leaves on the carpets before sweeping them.

'What for?'

'Doesn't your mother do that?' Molly asked her.

'Tea leaves on the mat,' Agnes said scornfully, 'no, she damn well doesn't, they go into the teapot.'

Molly giggled. 'Old tea leaves, silly. Mrs Robertson said you were a caution and so you are. It's to give a sweet smell to the rooms.' Agnes half smiled, she was unsure whether to believe it or not.

The one job Agnes really enjoyed and the other two didn't, especially on a cold and frosty morning, was taking the rugs out to the back-yard then throwing them over the clothes line to be punished with a carpet beater. If she was in a good mood she enjoyed it and if she was in a bad temper the exercise got it out of her system. The dust had long since gone but Agnes raised the beater for one last good wallop.

'God! I wouldn't like to be at the other end of that.'

Agnes lowered the carpet beater then turned to the voice. He wasn't very tall, quite broad-shouldered and with sandy-coloured hair. He smiled and it was a nice friendly smile.

'I'm looking for Meg Boyd, do you think you could get her for me?'

'She isn't here,' Agnes said carefully.

He looked disappointed. 'Know when she'll be back?'

'Why do you want her?'

A shadow of annoyance crossed his face and she came in quickly with, 'I'm her sister.'

'You're Meg's sister?' He came right up to her. 'Mebbe she's spoken of me? I'm Sam Robson.'

Agnes shook her head. 'Hang on here a minute, I'll shove these in.'

'I'll help you.' He gathered up the carpets and she opened the back door to let him put them inside. At the disturbance Gloria turned round.

'If anyone asks for me, Gloria, I'll be back in a few minutes.'

Gloria nodded and winked.

Sam Robson was looking puzzled as they walked away from the house. 'Is there something wrong?'

'You could say that.'

'Where is Meg?'

'She's left here and gone home.'

'But she liked it here, why would she go and do that?'

'Why, indeed?'

He stopped and gripped her shoulders and Agnes almost expected to be shaken. 'Just tell me what all this is about and stop monkeying around.'

'Were you her boyfriend?'

'You could say.'

'She left here because she's pregnant and if you don't know that word it means having a baby.'

'Cut that out,' he said angrily but she could see that he was shaken. 'I did odd jobs about here workin' on the cars, anythin' really and that's how I met Meg.'

Agnes waited, she wanted him to go on talking so she repeated – 'that's how you met Meg.'

He nodded. 'When I got this other temporary job it was only to be for a month to six weeks, I was coming back. I mean she knew I would.' He looked at her helplessly.

'A letter, it's not all that difficult to write one.'

'Shouldn't be but it is. I mean mebbe it's all right for you but I couldn't write on paper what I wanted to say, anyway I thought she would understand.'

From where she was Agnes could see Gloria waving frantically.

'I'll have to get back or I'll be like my sister and out of a job.'

'But about Meg, I've got to—'

'Tomorrow about half past six – can you make that?'

'No bother. I'll have the van.' But Agnes was already out of earshot.

Punctually the next evening at half past six Agnes was out of her uniform and into her own clothes and hurrying along the path. The day's work was over and she was free until nine thirty or ten at the very latest. She barely glanced at the van parked half on the path and half on the grass verge. He wasn't at the appointed place that was what registered. Typical, Agnes thought bitterly, Sam Robson was more than likely the father of Meg's unborn baby but no doubt after a night's sleep he'd wakened up to the cold reality that he could be trapped if he didn't put a few miles between them. Agnes was just about to turn round and go back to Kerne House when the van door opened and Sam Robson came to meet her.

'You're here,' she said stupidly.

'Did you think I wouldn't come?'

'There's some who would have taken to their heels.'

He smiled. 'You're Agnes, aren't you?'

'Yes.'

'Meg often spoke of you.'

'Did she?'

'Brains of the family, she said.'

Agnes laughed. She felt at ease with this young man and could almost envy Meg. No, that wasn't true, the shameful truth was that she had only to think of that arrogant Tommy Kingsley to feel – she couldn't put a name to what she felt but it was disturbing.

'I would have expected you to do more with your brains than—'

'Be a skivvy here. You're right, I do have plans but I have a lot to learn and this is a start. And now to the reason for us being here. Do you want to see Meg?'

'Of course I want to see Meg.'

'Well seeing as you have a van and I don't have to be back until half past nine we could go and see her.'

'Fine by me.' He paused. 'I'm no coward,' then he grinned. 'Yes, I am and I'd like to see Meg on her own.'

'Scared of my ma and da are you?'

'Should I be?'

She just smiled. 'Ever spoken to you, has she, about her family?'

'Only you.'

He had the passenger door open. 'Hop in.'

She got in and before she sat down he hastily removed a spanner. It was a very old van and it rattled along the road but Agnes wasn't troubled, her stomach wasn't easily upset.

'Learnin' to be a mechanic and I get the use of this to take me to jobs. Not much to look at but the engine's good. Which way, left or right?'

'Left here. You know Dundee?'

'Bits of it. Where are we headin'?'

'Spinner's Lane.'

'Never heard of it.'

'You haven't missed much but it's off the Hawkhill.'

'Should have said. I know the Hawkie, know most of the main roads.'

'Where is your home?'

'Barnhill. My mother has a wee shop there, took it over when my da died.'

Sam was a good careful driver who took no chances and they arrived safely at Spinner's Lane. The twins' eyes nearly popped out of their head when they saw Agnes getting out of the van. Sam remained inside.

'Listen, you two, is Meg in?'

'Yes.'

'Then go and tell her someone wants to see her but don't tell anyone else. Got that?'

'What's it worth?'

'Nothing but a thick ear if you don't do it.'

Agnes was all right but it was safer to do what she asked.

Meg appeared with a grey cardigan over the awful pink dress and

Agnes was glad to see that the miserable look had gone from her face. Now it was just resigned. She was smaller than Agnes with light brown wavy hair. Until now she had worn it to her shoulders but got a bit cut off since that way it would be easier to keep clean and she was particular about her hair. The sink was always cluttered with dishes and they had to be cleared away before there was any hair washing.

'Hello, Agnes, it's just you,' she said surprised. 'I'll kill those two, they said it was someone to see me.'

'So it is, look!'

Sam leaned forward so that she could see him but he kept within the van.

Agnes watched her sister's face go deathly white then flush a lovely pink.

'Sam?' she breathed.

'In you go, Meg,' Agnes said helping her sister into the van, 'and, Sam, you go slowly, she can't afford to be joggled about in her condition.' Then she winked to Meg who seemed to be undecided as to whether she should laugh or cry.

The van moved away, the twins were at the door as Agnes tried to push past. 'Move,' she said forcing her way in.

'Who was that?' Daisy demanded.

'Yes, who was that?' Rose asked.

'A friend of Meg's, that's all.'

Her mother had been at a neighbour's house and just come in. She gave an exaggerated start of surprise at seeing Agnes.

'My! My! We're honoured, two visits this month. What brings you?'

'I got the chance of a lift and just took it that's all. Where's Da?'

'The pub. No, here he is and before closing time, wonders will never cease.'

Her da nodded to her as if she were a stranger and without a word to anyone slumped into his chair which had long since lost its springs. After a few minutes the occasional snore showed that he was asleep.

'Is he still working?' Agnes jerked her head at the sleeping form.

'Still workin', Agnes, that's six weeks, must be a record.' She looked at him with some affection. 'Mind you it's back-breakin' work and it's takin' it out of him.'

Agnes looked about her and knew that she could never come back to Spinner's Lane to live. It was all so dreary. She felt a spurt of anger,

anger directed at her mother. Her da was working, so was Eddie, the laddies did messages after school and Meg was back in the baker's shop. She, herself, gave a little every month. Money couldn't be in such short supply and surely her mother could make some effort to tidy herself and the house. What on earth did she do with herself all day? Then she looked down at her youngest sister, the mongol child and largely ignored. She was sitting on the floor picking up a spoon and letting it fall with monotonous regularity. Her chin was wet and sore-looking, she slavered non-stop, her tongue was too big for her mouth, yet when given just the smallest bit of attention the reward was the sweetest of smiles. On an impulse Agnes picked her up and cuddled her. Chubby arms went round her neck and a wet face touched her own.

Agnes knew that her mother worried about her poor damaged babe and that she hoped the good Lord would see His way to take back the wee lamb before she, herself, departed this earth. For who else but a mother would look after the child? Agnes felt shame but she knew that none of them would be willing to shoulder the burden.

'Cup of tea?'

'Wouldn't mind.'

'Where's Meg?'

The twins didn't answer, just looked at Agnes.

'She's with a friend.'

'And who might that be?'

'She'll tell you herself.'

She shrugged and got on with infusing the tea. Agnes could be the limit but she wasn't going to quarrel with her.

It was nearly half past eight when Meg appeared. She was alone. Her eyes were bright and there was a flush of happiness on her face.

'Thanks, Agnes, thanks very, very much.'

'That's all right,' she said awkwardly.

'You've to go when you're ready, the van's at the corner.'

'Did you not ask him in or did he not want to come?'

'He wanted to but I said I would rather tell—'

'Tell what?' Mrs Boyd demanded. 'Will someone kindly tell me what this is all about?'

'I'm goin' to be married.'

'You're what?' The yell of surprise brought the sleeping figure to life.

'Can't a man sleep? What the hell's the racket?' he said as he tried to raise himself in the sagging chair then gave up and settled further into it.

'Your daughter is gettin' hersel' married.'

He looked at Agnes.

'No, not Agnes. It's Meg.'

'So she should and be quick about it by the looks of her.'

'Come on, lass, tell us about it,' her mother said kindly.

'Wait until I go,' Agnes said draining her cup and getting to her feet. 'I can't keep Sam waiting any longer.'

'So it's Sam is it – and, oh, afore you go, Agnes, cast your eyes over that.' She handed Agnes an official-looking letter.

Agnes opened it, read the letter and looked at her mother. 'That's great and not before time. It's taken them long enough to realise we're living in condemned property.'

'A corporation house,' her mother beamed, 'there's even a bathroom.'

'That's for keepin' the coal in,' Daisy said with a cheeky grin.

'So it is,' Rose agreed.

'That's enough, Daisy, you and your shadow are gettin' far too cheeky.'

'You'll be real toffs,' Agnes said as she took her departure.

Promotion was to come to Agnes quicker than she had dared hope. She was only too happy to be trained as tablemaid but she was upset that it meant Molly being downgraded to housemaid and general dogsbody.

'You're absolutely sure you don't mind, Molly?'

'I've just said so, haven't I?' She smiled. 'In fact it is a big relief.'

'In that case I'll stop worrying.'

'Mind you, Agnes, I was a bit bothered about the drop in wages but Miss Templeton isn't goin' to reduce them. She isn't so bad after all.'

So that's it, Agnes thought grimly. The rotten bitch isn't going to increase mine if she can help it. Fair enough until I'm competent at the job then just you wait, Madam Templeton. I'll get my rightful increase, you just see if I don't.

Agnes threw a bucket of water over the back steps then used a hard brush. She ought to have been on her knees to scrub it properly but there was no one about and she'd got away with it before. A little breather, she could do with it before going back in, and it was such an invitingly lovely, fresh morning.

'Hello, Carrot Nob.'

Agnes turned quickly, she was furious. She hated being called Carrot, Rusty or Ginger but most of all Carrot Nob. Heaven help him. It was Tommy Kingsley but a smiling Tommy Kingsley.

'We got off on the wrong foot and I want to apologise for my part in that.'

Agnes was taken aback, an apology was the last thing she expected from this arrogant friend of Molly's.

'You're still off on the wrong foot. I cannot stand being called Carrot Nob,' but a smile played around her mouth.

'Sorry. You've gorgeous hair, Agnes, I love the colour.'

'Liar.'

'What did you say?'

'You heard me or clean your ears if you didn't. Molly told me exactly what you said about auburn-haired girls.'

'And it nettled you?'

She shrugged and wondered why she didn't just walk away. She didn't even need an excuse, it was more than time she was back and inside Kerne House polishing the brasses. But still she stood.

'Now I remember the occasion. I'd taken Molly to the dancin' and there was this carrot – sorry, auburn-haired girl—'

'Giving you the glad eye?'

'How did you guess?'

'The conceit of some folk.'

'No, honestly, the girl comes into the shop, her folk are good customers, and I felt forced to give her a dance.'

'Keeping in with the customers?'

'Of course. Knew you'd understand, but Molly went in the huff and that's why I told her that load of rubbish.'

'I'll take that with a pinch of salt but what is a workin' man doing out at this time of day?'

'The benefit of bein' family means I don't have to work regular hours just as long as I'm at my uncle's beck and call.'

'You're here to see Molly?'

'I suppose so.'

'What do you mean you suppose so?'

'Could be I'm more attracted to someone else.'

The way he looked at her made the colour rush to her face and she turned as if to go.

'Don't, Agnes,' he pleaded. 'Don't go, not just yet.'

'I'm in trouble if I don't get back.'

He laughed. 'I'll bet you're seldom out of hot water and if it's Molly you're thinkin' of then don't. Her feelin's aren't involved any more than mine.'

'But you came to see her?'

'To tell her Friday is off, she knows it was a possibility. Will you tell her that from me? And I bet you anythin' she won't be upset.'

'I don't believe you but I'll tell her just the same.' With a determined effort she made herself walk away towards the back door of Kerne House but he was beside her.

'My brother's goin' to Canada.'

'What has that got to do with me?'

'He won't need his motor-bike.'

'You're buying it?'

'Yes.'

'Lucky you to have that kind of money.'

'I don't, but my uncle's goin' to lend me the money, take it off my wages every week I mean.'

'Very obliging uncle you have.'

The smile left his face. 'I'm no scrounger, Agnes, I work hard in that shop and at night I'm in the back making up orders. In a way I'm doin' two jobs for one wage and my uncle is shrewd enough to recognise that. He doesn't want to lose me.' He paused and touched her arm. 'Come out on the bike, you'd love it, I just know you would.'

Agnes was tempted, very tempted. She didn't know which was the bigger attraction, the bike or Tommy Kingsley. Together she was finding them irresistible.

'The last thing I want is to hurt Molly and I don't want any unpleasantness. I get enough of that from that sour-faced housekeeper.'

'Listen, Agnes, I wouldn't want to hurt Molly either but if I'm not very much mistaken I'm about to get the shove.'

'I'm going in.'

'Got a spare evening this week?'

'Wednesday,' she said, then could have bitten out her tongue.

'Great, I'll be at the end of the road sevenish.'

She was shaking and at the door she couldn't resist turning round and for a few moments she watched him walk away with his long swinging stride. What was she letting herself in for? This wasn't part of her plans. I'm letting myself in for nothing, she told herself, and that Tommy Kingsley can go and take a running jump. Too full of himself by far. Still just the once wouldn't do any harm and it was probably the only time she'd get the chance of being on the back of a motor-bike.

# Chapter Fifteen

It was just on eight forty-five on a close and clammy morning when Rachel arrived at Duncairn House and knocked at the door of the servants' entrance. The door was slightly ajar and the voices carried to Rachel standing on the step with her suitcase by her side. Her fingers ached, it had been a long way to carry a case that got heavier by the minute and she had had to keep switching it from hand to hand. The only transport she was informed was a bus service to the neighbouring villages and that didn't go near the Glen Road.

'See who that is.'

There was a clatter of feet and then the door was flung wide and a girl in a light green overall beamed at her.

'Don't tell me! You're the new maid, Rachel something-or-other?'

'Rachel Donaldson.' Some of the nervous tension left Rachel and in that first exchange she felt that she had found a friend.

'Come on in. Shove that case in the corner there, it won't be in the way and we'll get it up to your room later.' Another girl had dried her hands and was walking over. 'This is Janet. Janet Harris and I'm Hetty Porter, awful name I hate it.'

'Shut up, Hetty and stop moaning.' Janet shook hands with Rachel. The pale grey eyes were cool and assessing but not unfriendly. Hetty followed Janet's lead and shook hands too. The girls were very different in appearance but of a similar age, Rachel thought. She put that to be seventeen or eighteen. Hetty was small and plump with a round cheerful, face and mischievous brown eyes. Janet was almost as tall as Rachel. She was big-busted and with her slim figure it made her look slightly top-heavy but for all that she was an attractive young woman with short, thick, fairish hair and a pretty face.

'I've to see Mrs Anderson at nine o'clock.'

'That's a whole quarter of an hour yet,' Hetty said touching the teapot.

'Sit yourself down and have a cup of tea and I'll join you. What about you, Janet?'

'No, thanks. These things have to be put away and I can't do that until I clean the press out. Your fault, Hetty, you should be doing it. Honestly if you would just do what you were told.'

'How was I to know there was a tear in the bag?'

'That's not the point. The bag of lentils should have been emptied into the jar.'

'I know, I know, I know and I've said I'm sorry.' She grinned over to Rachel not in the least put out. 'I don't know why but I always seem to be in hot water with somebody.'

Rachel smiled and looked around her.

'If you are wondering where cook is she always has forty winks after breakfast.'

'A mighty long forty winks if you ask me,' Janet muttered as she wiped out the shelves and collected the stray lentils.

'She is getting on a bit,' Hetty said with just a touch of censure in her voice. 'Sugar?' She held up the sugar bowl to Rachel.

'Yes, please, and a spot of milk.'

'While she's snoozing we get it all our own way so who is grumbling? And don't look so worried, Rachel, she's nice you'll get on with her.'

'I hope to get on with everybody,' Rachel said as she took her cup.

'That's a tall order.' Janet stopped her cleaning for a moment.

'Pay no attention to her, we're a friendly bunch and you'll soon get used to Janet and her funny ways.'

'That's enough from you, fatty.' Rachel looked from one to the other but it was just friendly banter.

Janet came over to the table and sat down. 'I think I will have that cup after all. Pour me one will you, Hetty?'

'She always does this, Rachel,' Hetty grumbled, 'just when I was about to tell you something about Duncairn House but madam, here, thinks she can do it better.'

'At least I don't take so long about it.'

'Get a move on then before I take her to see Bluebell.'

Rachel looked from one to the other, she didn't know what to make of them.

'Bluebell is our housekeeper, Mrs Anderson.'

'Oh.'

'Bella Anderson by name but as you'll find out she's almost always dressed in blue. Someone, can't remember who, called her Bluebell, not to her face of course, and it stuck.' Janet stirred her tea slowly. 'The old lady, the mistress, doesn't keep very well.'

'Nothing wrong with her mind, she's right on the ball,' Hetty added, determined to be in on the telling. 'Janet has the job of looking after her.'

'I take her breakfast to her and if she doesn't feel like getting up for her other meals I serve them to her in her room.' She paused. 'Let me tell you this, Rachel, it is a properly set table if you please with all the niceties.'

'She is old-fashioned, so what, it is her home after all.' Hetty smiled to Rachel. 'Sometimes I see her crossing the hall and muttering to herself about things going from bad to worse.'

'Once she's gone there'll be changes.'

'And not for the better,' Hetty said darkly. Her face took on a gloomy expression. 'With your looks, both of you, you'll get married and it's only fatty here who'll be left.'

'Nonsense, Hetty, that new red-haired lad can't take his eyes off you.'

'The one come to help in the gardens? That one?'

'That one.'

'I haven't noticed. You're having me on, Janet Harris.'

'I'm not. Next time you see him give him a big smile and see what happens.'

Rachel was loving it all but worried about the time.

'It's almost nine,' she ventured.

'Lord, save us so it is,' Hetty said getting up. 'Come along, Rachel, Bluebell doesn't like to be kept waiting.' Rachel followed the broad figure hurrying out of the kitchen and along a passage that led into the hall, a beautiful hall with dark panelling, but there was no time to admire it. Hetty had turned into a narrow corridor and stopping halfway along she opened the door.

'That's Rachel for you, Mrs Anderson.'

'Come in, Rachel. Thank you, Hetty.'

'Sorry if we are a few minutes late, Rachel was early enough, it was us that kept her talking.'

'That I can well believe,' the housekeeper said dryly, but Rachel saw her mouth quirk. 'Sit down, Rachel, yes, there,' she said and Rachel sat down. Mrs Anderson was sitting in a comfortable armchair and a newspaper was neatly folded on a footstool. There was a spirit stove and a kettle beside it. She waited until Hetty had shut the door then shook her head. 'Hetty can be a problem at times and not at all dependable, I'm afraid, but she is such a sweet-natured girl that we tend to overlook her faults.'

'She is nice.' Looking about her Rachel could see that the name Bluebell was very apt. It wasn't just what she wore and that was a plain dark blue dress with a white lace collar and cuffs, the colour had been carried into her sitting-room. The fire was set but not lit and in front of it was a fireside rug in shades of blue and with fringes at each end. The blue scheme stretched to the wallpaper and curtains and the cushions were of a deep blue velvet. A collection of glass animals sat on a polished side table. There was a plant at the window.

'Have you been to see your room?'

'Not yet, Mrs Anderson.'

'It's rather bare at present and I apologise for that.' She frowned with remembered annoyance. 'The previous occupant was rather careless and the chest of drawers was damaged. It has been mended but is still in the attic. I had meant to get Benny, our handyman, to bring it down but it escaped my memory. Still it will allow you to choose one or two other pieces for which the family has no further use. Nothing big, there isn't the space.' She smiled as she said this.

'Thank you.'

'Hetty will show you and once you've selected what you want get Benny to bring it down.' She paused. 'That deals with that, now as regards your duties I have been giving some thought to them and I've decided that you should spend two hours each afternoon in the sewing-room. Once you get through the bulk of the work we can reduce your time there and you'll take on other duties.'

'Yes, Mrs Anderson.'

'I do like my staff to be flexible where possible but when it comes to looking after the mistress, Janet sees to most of her needs. When she is not available I see to Mrs Craig's requirements myself. Janet knows what is required and is very understanding. Like all elderly people who do not enjoy good health, Mrs Craig can be difficult. Nevertheless,' she said severely, 'she is mistress of this house and our employer and it is our duty to carry out her wishes.'

'I do understand.'

'Not for a moment am I suggesting that you would be guilty of it but I warn my staff that I will not tolerate gossip about any member of the household.'

'I do not gossip,' Rachel said feeling annoyed at the turn in the conversation.

Mrs Anderson smiled. 'Nevertheless, you do require to know something about the family you are about to serve. There is, as I have said, the mistress who is a widow. Her daughter, Mrs Maud Meldrum and her granddaughter, Miss Betsy, reside here. Mrs Meldrum's husband is frequently in London on business, and his son,' she laid emphasis on 'his', 'is away at business college. Until now Mr Brian has spent only holidays here but I believe he has now completed his studies and will be spending more time at Duncairn House.'

Rachel decided to risk a question. 'You did say Mr Meldrum's son, does that mean—'

'You are quick. Yes, it is a second marriage. Mrs Meldrum's first husband, Colonel Wood, was killed abroad before their daughter was school age. That is all you require to know about the family,' she said briskly.

'Thank you, and about my other duties, Mrs Anderson?'

'All in good time.' She looked over at the clock on the mantelshelf and registered surprise. 'Dear me, is that the time? Let me just say hurriedly, I'll go into details later, what your other duties are. You will assist Hetty with the washing-up and the making of the beds. There is a special way in which it should be done but Hetty has at least mastered that and it is Hetty's job to clean out the fires and set them. Benny brings in the coal and logs and Janet does the dusting and polishing of the downstairs rooms. You can take a share of that.' She was still talking as she got up and Rachel got up too. 'We have help from women in the village who come in for an hour or two as and when it is required. Have you taken in most of that?'

'Yes, thank you, Mrs Anderson.'

Hetty was flicking a feather duster over the ornaments on the hall table but stopped when she saw Rachel.

'How did it go?'

'All right.'

'We got Benny to take up your case.'

'I need to find him. Apparently I'm getting to choose some pieces of furniture from the attic.'

'Harriet, the girl before you, was a wrecker, she didn't last long, thank goodness. I get on with most people but I couldn't stand her.'

'Why was she engaged?'

'Good references and of course she was on her best behaviour at the interview.'

'If she was as bad as all that how did she manage to get a reference?'

'Good question.' She grinned. 'It's one way of getting rid of unsatisfactory staff without having to sack them.' She gave a final flick of the feather duster. 'Better let you see your room.' She went ahead to the end of the hall and along a corridor to a flight of uncarpeted stairs leading to the servants' quarters. Taste and elegance were left behind, what Rachel saw was gloomy brown paint work and badly scuffed linoleum underfoot. The door Hetty was opening would have been much improved with a lick of paint. It angered Rachel. Servants were entitled to something better than this. At little cost that dreary brown could have been replaced with something lighter and prettier. She followed Hetty inside and the room was as bare as Mrs Anderson had warned her it would be. There was a small washstand and on it a chipped china bowl with a jug inside, a narrow wardrobe and a single bed. On it was a lemon-coloured, freshly laundered top cover. A mirror, mercifully uncracked, hung on a nail beside the window. Linoleum covered the floor with a half-moon rug beside the bed. There was one hard wooden chair. The story of my life, Rachel thought and decided there and then that her first purchase would be a cushion. Faded curtains hung at the window and the light was a single ceiling bulb with a torn shade.

'You don't think much of it, do you?'

'Frankly I'm appalled but it has possibilities.'

'If it had been nice you wouldn't have got it. Janet would have taken it for herself. She'd rather be on her own; me now, I like someone to chat to.'

'I'm used to my own bedroom,' Rachel said as she tried but failed to improve the hanging of the curtains. 'I'm an only child.'

'You must have been lonely.'

'Not when you've known nothing else.'

'Suppose so. Where do you come from?'

'Dundee.'

'What brought you to Hillend if I'm not being too nosey?'

'My father married again.'

'And you wanted to put a few miles between you and your step-mother?'

'Something like that.'

'You'll get an overall for the mornings like this awful thing I'm wearing and for the rest of the day you'll wear a black dress. Mrs Anderson sees to all that. You'll get two dresses from a shop in Perth that specialises in that sort of thing.' She looked wistful. 'Janet looks lovely in black and when she puts on the white pinny, honest I'm not kiddin', it's the size of a postage stamp, she looks great. So will you. Me, now,' she patted her ample frame, tried to grin and failed, 'can you see a wee white pinny on this fatty?'

'Hetty, don't think of yourself as fat; my da would call you nicely rounded.' Thinking of her father she felt tears at the back of her eyes and blinked rapidly.

'You all right?'

'Yes, just got thinking.'

'Regretting leaving home?'

'No.' She smiled brightly. 'You're very kind going to all this trouble for me.'

'A pleasure and Mrs Anderson did tell me to take you under my wing until you find your way about.'

'Mrs Anderson is very nice.'

'Most of the time she is but Mrs Morton, that's the cook, is a real pet. Maybe she does take more time off than she should,' she began to giggle. 'Janet is convinced she doesn't go to her room for a rest but for a tipple. Don't be shocked, my ma told me most cooks do, it's one of the perks of the job.'

Rachel smiled. 'I'm not so easily shocked as I used to be.'

'Mrs Morton looks after us like a mother and if we have problems hers is a sympathetic ear and she doesn't gossip.'

Rachel pointed to the jug and basin. 'Where do I get the water?'

'Benny, this place would collapse without that man, gets it for you. Put your jug out at night and he'll fill it with hot water in the morning. Speaking of which, better show you the bathroom.'

They went out and further along the corridor, Hetty threw open the bathroom door letting it hit the wall. 'We are allowed one bath a week but no one would be any the wiser if you had an extra.'

The use of the bathroom even once a week pleased Rachel. All her life she had had to use the scullery, shutting the door to strip off and have a good wash all over. She went right inside for a better look. The walls were green and the bath had cast-iron feet. All around was a tide mark. There was also a brown stain caused by the small but steady drip of the cold-water tap which was in need of a new washer. A cake of Lifebuoy soap was on the window ledge and there was a cork mat in front of the bath.

'Don't forget to take your own towel along and believe me it's no joke if you forget it and no one around to get it for you.'

Rachel grinned. 'I get the picture. What's this wonderful Benny like?'

'Benny? He's old,' she said dismissively. 'After his wife died he didn't like to be alone in the cottage and spends most of his time here. Tomorrow do for your furniture?'

'Yes, fine.'

'I'll take you up in the morning and you can have a good nosey round.'

'Thanks for everything, Hetty, I'll go and hang up my clothes.'


Hetty took Rachel along to the kitchen which was warm and inviting. it wasn't quite time for the midday meal and no one was seated at the table.

'Brought our new maid to meet you, Mrs Morton. This is Rachel Donaldson.'

'Sit down, lass, it's all the same price,' she said continuing to beat the cake mixture. 'This is me all behind but a few more minutes and I'll have it in the oven. Test the potatoes, one of you,' she turned briefly to a woman and a girl. The woman went over to the pot and stabbed the potatoes with a fork.

'Ready for straining I would say.'

'Then do it.'

Mrs Morton was small and stout with a motherly face. She had a large white overall tied round her middle and judging by the effort going into the beating she had unlimited energy. Satisfied with the mixture she emptied it into a cake tin, evened off the top and placed it on the middle shelf of the oven. A rush of hot air came out and she shut the door hastily then put up a plump hand to tuck away a stray wisp of hair which hung damply to her forehead. A leg of pork sizzled on a spit and was being turned by a young boy, a relative of the cook's Rachel was to discover, who had not yet found suitable employment. It kept him out of mischief and gave him a few coppers for his pocket.

'No, Hetty,' lass, keep your eyes averted. The pork is for THEM but like as not there'll be enough to make a good meal for us tomorrow.'

Rachel was to remember that first meal in the warm kitchen. They were like a big family. The long scrubbed table had a bench down each side. Mrs Morton at the head of the table occupied a chair with arms and it was she who dished out the food which was then handed down the table. The hourly workers had departed but the two gardeners came in. The younger one had light ginger hair and Rachel saw Hetty colouring prettily as the youth gave a shy smile in their direction. Mrs Anderson was served her meals in her own room. Janet, who had been attending to the mistress, was the last to arrive.

For the servants and workmen this was the main meal of the day. It was good and substantial. Oxtail soup was followed by a rich stew thick with vegetables. The kind that sticks to your ribs was how her da used to describe it. She wished that she didn't keep remembering things. A huge tureen of potatoes was put in the centre of the table for everyone to help themselves. Apple tart with pouring custard followed and judging by the comments was a firm favourite. Hetty got up to bring the big brown teapot to the table but the two gardeners got up, mumbled something that could have been appreciation of the meal and went out. They preferred to make their own brew and take it in the shed that held their tools.

Forty-five minutes was the time allowed and as soon as it was up Mrs Morton pushed back her chair, got to her feet, and that was the signal for the kitchen to be cleared. Hetty rolled up her sleeves and began to pile up the dirty dishes and Rachel went to give her a hand. The cake was not yet ready to come out of the oven and Mrs Morton sat herself down beside the fire with her swollen feet on the wooden stool.

Her first day at Duncairn House was all but over. She lay in the creaking iron bed with sleep far away. Her brain was too active and in her mind she was going over all that had happened. On the whole she supposed it had been a satisfying day and she had learned something about life in her grandmother's house.

An alarm clock supplied to the servants gave them no excuse for sleeping in. It went off and Rachel groped over to silence it. A weak sunlight streaked in through the inadequate curtains and fleetingly changed the brown of the linoleum to a warm treacle. She got out of bed and opened the curtains then opened the door and brought in the jug of hot water. She poured it into the basin and washed as best she could. In a dark skirt and fresh blouse she went quietly through the sleeping household to the kitchen. The cook and Janet were already there. Good mornings were said but little else. It was too early for talking and time was precious with breakfast trays to be prepared for those who did not go down to the breakfast room. Rachel was getting it easy for the first day or two and after the breakfast dishes were washed and put away Hetty took her up to the attic. It was cold and cobwebby but with sufficient light from the small windows to see around.

'I'll leave you to it and get on with my chores. See and choose something decent.'

'I intend to. Thanks, Hetty.'

Dust was everywhere and Rachel was glad of her overall to protect her clothes. It was thick on some of the forlorn-looking articles of furniture that, along with boxes and wicker hampers, littered the floor area. Before long she found a small chest of drawers that would suit her and taking Mrs Anderson at her word put a tapestry stool in poor condition beside the drawers. Next she hunted for a chair and found one, small and comfortable-looking and in need of repair which she thought she could manage. No harm in having a look around to see what else was kept up here. As she moved along the head space grew less and there were more cobwebs, some getting into her hair. Her face broke into a smile when she saw the doll's house complete with furniture. There were games and grubby soft toys. It was over at the window and she had almost missed it – a large rocking-horse and she went over to touch it letting her hand glide over the smooth wood. Had her mother and her Aunt Maud played with these toys, she wondered? She pictured two small girls arranging and rearranging the tiny furniture. So engrossed was she that she didn't hear the light footsteps, only the sound of a voice that brought her quickly upright to bang her head against a rafter.

'Ouch! You didn't half startle me,' Rachel said as her fingers gingerly touched the top of her head.

'Obviously,' the voice said haughtily, 'and may I ask what you are doing sneaking about up here?'

'I was not sneaking,' Rachel said matching her tone for haughtiness and she noticed a flicker of surprise in the eyes looking at her. 'I happen to have Mrs Anderson's permission to choose furniture for my room.'

'And have you?'

'Yes.'

'Does that include the rocking-horse you seem to have taken a fancy to?'

Rachel coloured. 'I apologise for that, I'm afraid I couldn't resist touching it.'

'Very well, I shan't mention this to my grandmother but if she were to hear about it your days at Duncairn House would be numbered.'

She is my grandmother too, she wanted to say, but the time was not right. Perhaps it never would be.

'You had better get down and I'll follow.'

This could only be her cousin Betsy, Rachel thought. The girl wasn't very tall with straight fair hair cut in a fringe which suited her small face. Rachel thought her very attractive but could have wished to meet her cousin under happier circumstances. She sighed. It wasn't a very good start.

# Chapter Sixteen

Agnes was emptying the teapot when Molly joined her.

'You making fresh?'

'I am but it's not for us. Where have you been, I've been looking for you?' she said as she spooned in the tea.

'Well, I'm here.'

'Your boyfriend can't make it for Friday.'

'Where did you see him?'

'Out the back. Said he was in a hurry and to tell you.'

Molly sucked her lip and puckered her brow. 'I wanted to see him.'

'Why?'

'To tell him to his face that I wouldn't be goin' out with him again.'

'Thought he was the light of your life?'

'So he was for a while but I've gone off him. Anyway I hate that bike and he's mad about it.'

'He's buying it from his brother, he told me.'

'Not in much of a hurry when he took time to tell you that,' she said suspiciously.

'Just mentioned it as he was walking away,' Agnes said carelessly. 'You got your eye on someone else?'

'What's it to you?'

'Nothing.'

'I know better. You're keen on Tommy.' She smiled knowingly.

'No, I'm not.'

'Bet if you got the chance you would go on the back of his bike.'

'Quite like to go on the back of his bike and I've got a stronger stomach than you.'

Molly smirked. 'You're welcome to Tommy Kingsley and his bike. Geoffrey's lovely and he's a marvellous dancer,' she said dreamily.

'Sounds a bit of all right.'

Molly laughed. 'That tea is goin' to be stewed.'

'God! I forget all about it.' She hurried away.

Such hilarity had seldom been heard in the kitchen of Kerne House and it was obvious that Miss Templeton was out of earshot. The staff were seated at the long table and Mrs Robertson supervising the proceedings.

Agnes was doing her training and a dress rehearsal was the reason for the hilarity. Over her dark dress she had on a white frilly apron, the lace cap was all but lost in the thick auburn hair and only a wisp of it showed. She was unsmiling, she was concentrating hard for very soon now she would be serving the master and mistress in the dining-room.

Miss Templeton had thrust at her the book entitled DUTIES OF A TABLEMAID with instructions to read it and read it again until every word of it was understood. Agnes glanced at it then went back to read it properly. Most of it, she decided, was just plain common sense apart from the setting of the table and that she admitted had taken longer to master. The rest was straightforward enough and she wondered what all the fuss was about.

Now that she was actually handling plates filled with soup she was finding it rather more difficult. In theory she knew it all, in practice it was a different story.

'Keep your hand steady, Agnes, the soup shouldn't move in the plate.'

It was moving all right, it was splashing on her hand.

'Don't slouch, straighten your back and you'll find it easier,' Molly said. She was secretly pleased that Agnes, the know-all, was not finding the duties of tablemaid as easy as she had expected.

By the time she put down the last soup plate she was beginning to get the hang of it. Her trouble, she realised, was that she was too slow and careful. Quicker movements and she was getting better results.

'Not too bad, Agnes,' Mrs Robertson said kindly, 'and don't look so smug, Molly, everybody has to learn and you've had a few accidents in your day.'

Molly sulked through the main course. The others were full of praise though one or two had expected the soup to go down their necks.

'Hope there is plenty left for me,' Agnes said seating herself at the table.

'There's plenty since you refused second helpings,' someone muttered.

There was nothing wrong with Agnes's hearing. 'Demanding extra helpings is not done in the best of circles and you lot were supposed to be acting ladies and gentlemen for once in your life.'

'Mrs Robertson, I got ever such a little helping of rice pudding,' Gloria said.

'As much as we got,' the gardeners spoke together, 'and we are two growin' laddies.'

'Wheesht the lot of you,' the cook scolded but she was happy. The rice pudding would just have to be thrown out and with all those starving people in the world, she read all about it in the papers, it was a sin to waste good food. Plates were quickly handed up the table and after checking that the helpings were much the same for quantity, they were handed down again and the pudding disappeared in record time.

They left leaving just the cook and Agnes.

'I made a right mess of it, didn't I?'

'Och, not as bad as all that, you're needin' a bit more practice that's all. Better just practise on me. Serving one is no different from serving half a dozen so you just remember that and don't get flustered. You've one pair of hands and folk just have to be patient and wait.'

'Thanks, Mrs Robertson, you're a gem and you really think I'll make it?'

'Agnes, lass, I've no fear of you failin'.'

'You quite happy there?'

'Yes, fine,' Agnes said as she settled herself on the seat and put her arms around Tommy's waist.'

'I won't go fast.'

'I don't mind. I'm not Molly.'

'All the same, I'll go slow until you get used to it. It's a cold night and it's colder on the bike. Did you put something warm on?'

Agnes giggled. 'My da's drawers. No, honestly I'll be all right. I've a warm jumper under this jacket.'

'Right then, we're off.'

They weren't going fast but there was a wind and Agnes's hair was whipped round her face. Tommy had given her a pair of goggles that had belonged to his brother and Agnes longed to see herself in a mirror to see how they suited her. The wind sang, the countryside sped by and she wanted to burst out in song herself. She was so happy, she'd never been happier in her life.

'Mind if I go a bit faster?'

'Fast as you like,' she said throwing caution to the wind. Faster and faster they went and she clung to the figure in front and wished that she had worn gloves. Agnes seldom felt cold except for her hands. She could be warm all over and her hands go numb and they were going numb now. Her hands were slipping, she had no grip.

'Stop, Tommy.' But the wind blew away her voice and if anything he increased the speed.

'Stop! For God's sake stop, you idiot,' she screamed as her arms began to slip away from the leather jacket.

This time he did hear and brought the bike to a slithering stop at the side of the road. Agnes was almost in tears and Tommy's face was thunderous.

'Yelling like that could have caused a bloody accident. God, I thought Molly was bad but you're a damned sight worse, at least she suffered in silence.'

'I tried to get you to stop before,' Agnes whimpered. 'I couldn't hang on much longer.'

'I'm sorry.' Suddenly he was all concern as she raised a face pale with fright. 'What was it, Agnes? What frightened you?'

She started to speak but she was still reliving the moments when her hands, her useless hands, were slipping and she was going to be thrown off. She shivered and strong arms went round her, holding her close. She clung to him on that quiet country road and felt his comforting warmth. When her face came up from his jacket his mouth came down on hers. Agnes had been kissed before, light kisses that meant nothing but this was different. The first gentle butterfly kisses had given way to fierceness, an urgency, that both alarmed and thrilled her. This was different, this was exciting and all kinds of peculiar sensations were flowing through her body.

Then just as suddenly the old Agnes was back and she was pulling herself away ashamed and appalled at her show of weakness.

'Agnes! Oh, God, Agnes! That was wonderful.' His voice was rough with emotion. 'You felt it too, I know you did. You must have.'

'No, I did not,' she said furiously, 'and don't you ever do that to me again.' He was too angry and surprised to hear the tears in her voice.

'You asked for it,' he said brutally.

'That's a lie.'

'Is it, Agnes? Is it?' he demanded gripping her arms and bringing her close to him but she fought him off pounding at his chest.

'I'd got a fright, I was scared and you took advantage of me.'

'Wrong, I've never forced myself on any girl, I don't need to. For me it has to be a two-way thing. Your trouble, Agnes, is you're afraid of your own feelings.'

She shook her head and looked at him. She'd taken off the goggles as soon as the bike stopped and made as though to put them on.

'No, keep them off. Let me see the expression on your face.'

'I've got plans for my life, Tommy Kingsley, and they don't include you.'

'I've got plans too,' Tommy said quietly, 'and they could include you. Come on, sit down and let us talk it over.'

'There's nothing to talk about,' but she allowed herself to be led away and they sat down together on the grass verge.

'For a start I want to know what happened to scare you. I thought you were all right on the bike.'

'So I was, I was loving it but it was my hands,' she said shamefacedly, 'they go dead with the cold and I have no feeling at all in them. Stupid of me not to bring gloves but I didn't think.'

'You can have mine going back.' He took off the leather gauntlet gloves and she slipped her hands into them. They were deliciously warm and she began working her fingers inside the roomy gloves until a painful tingling returned them to life.

'Won't your hands get cold?'

'I'll manage.' She smiled. 'Those cosy enough for you?'

'Lovely.'

'Want to hear what my plans are for the future?'

'If you want to tell me.'

'I do. I'm a lad with ambition, Agnes, and I go after what I want. It doesn't depend on getting my uncle's shop though I expect it will come to me.'

'That could be ages, he can't be that old.'

'Getting on a bit, he is the eldest of the family and I see him wanting to take life a bit easier. Probably got quite a bit by him to see him through. He needs me, Agnes, more than I need him and that is nice to know.';

'You want your own business?'

'More than that. I want a shop and a fleet of vans on the road.' He laughed a little self-consciously. 'Can you see it, Agnes, KINGSLEY,

SUPPLIER OF PRIME BEEF in huge letters on the van?'

'Delivering orders you mean?'

'No, I do not. Folk out in the country, anybody away from the shops, would appreciate the shop coming to them. In the back of the van I'd have a slab to cut the meat to requirements, a scale to weigh, in short, the same as the shop. Must charge a wee bit more for the service but I don't see that a problem.'

'Neither do I, they would be saving the fare to the shops.'

'Exactly. What do you think of the idea?'

'Has merit. I'm impressed.' She was.

'More to being a butcher than people think,' he said importantly, 'have to know the cuts of beef for a start and just where to put the knife.' He watched the changing expressions on her face. 'I don't go after the impossible, Agnes, I'm a realist and I don't waste time dreaming. I don't expect to be wealthy but a comfortable living will do me fine.'

It sounded like a good life, Agnes told herself, much, much better than she'd known in Spinner's Lane but she knew it wasn't enough. It fell far short of her own ambitions. It wasn't only the money though that came into it. She wanted to be with educated people who would talk intelligently and effortlessly about things that mattered, not the awful trivia that was about all she ever heard. All the same, she conceded, for a working lad, Tommy spoke reasonably well but not good enough and his manners, hers were nothing to boast about, but there lay the difference, she would learn because she wanted to. Tommy would change as he became successful but his working roots would always show because he would have no wish to change that part of himself.

'Not saying much are you? But then it's money and position you're after isn't it?' he said heavily.

'Maybe it is. I'm certainly not going to throw myself away.'

'Is that what you would be doing if you ended up with me?'

'I didn't say that, you did. In any case there is no possibility of us ending up together.'

'You are afraid to admit it but you are just as attracted to me as I am to you. We belong together but you'd marry any ugly sod just so long as he had the means—'

'You go too far, Tommy Kingsley, how dare you say such a thing.' Her eyes were flashing fire as she got to her feet. 'When I marry it will be to someone who knows how to behave, not to an ignoramus like you.'

He got up but taking his time and she saw the contempt on his face. 'I'm sorry for you, Agnes,' he said quietly, 'there's no happiness in the road you're taking. A lady is born a lady. You'll aim high but like me you'll always be working class and those with breeding will make use of you for as long as it suits them.' He gave a cruel smile. 'Gold-diggers end up in the gutter where they belong.'

'Have you quite finished?' she said icily.

'I have.'

Going over to his bike, he swung himself into position and waited until her arms stole round his waist, then they were off. For the short journey he kept up a reasonable speed then stopped in front of Kerne House. Wordlessly she handed him his gloves and the goggles. He took them without looking at her then he was lost in a storm of dust and small stones.

Agnes was more shaken then she cared to admit. He had the measure of her as her mother would say, only she didn't believe it not for a single moment. She would be somebody and no one would look down on her.

Two weeks later Agnes had forgotten Tommy Kingsley or so she told herself. Her mind was concentrating hard on the ordeal ahead. Mostly she had been kept to the back of the house and rarely saw the mistress except as a hunched-up figure tending to her plants. As to the master, she had never laid eyes on him.

That was about to change. Miss Templeton had decided the time had come for Molly to step aside and Agnes take over the duties of tablemaid. To get to that stage had been nerve-wracking for all concerned. Twice or three times Agnes had only just stopped herself from emptying the plates into Miss Templeton's lap.

The housekeeper was to remain in the background to see that all went well. Agnes was dressed in the regulation dark dress with a small white apron and a frilly cap which Agnes had managed to secure at a jaunty angle. Her hands and nails had been inspected for cleanliness and now she stood against the far wall of the dining-room to await the arrival of Mr and Mrs Edwin Taylor.

The dining-room had two large windows that looked out onto the garden. The dining-table could be extended at either end to suit the number of guests but since it was to be only Edwin Taylor and his wife who were to be eating it was reduced to its smallest. Even so there was a good length of table between the master and his good lady. The straight-backed cushioned chairs were in the Regency pattern and had come from a sale in one of the big houses which had been bought over for a hotel. On the handsome sideboard were two heaters to keep the food warm.

The door opened and Margaret Taylor, in a burgundy dress that did nothing for her complexion, preceded her husband to take her place at the foot of the table. Agnes had glanced away from the door but now she turned back to it. A smallish, stout, red-faced man came in, shut the door, and Agnes nearly fainted. There was no question in her mind that this was the man who would have run her over had she not stepped smartly aside and at whom she had stuck out her tongue. Dear God! she thought in agony, would he remember her? But of course he wouldn't, not after all this time. Her eyes followed him until he sat down, took the white, stiffly starched napkin from its silver ring—'

'What are you waiting for, girl?' Miss Templeton hissed.

Agnes gathered her wits together. 'Do I start now?'

'Of course.'

Soup needed a steady hand but after a number of mishaps she had finally mastered the technique. A little less in the plate would have made it a bit easier, Agnes thought as she carefully placed the soup before the mistress. Mrs Taylor smiled and Agnes's confidence grew. When she lowered the plate before the master she would have sworn with her last breath that he moved and jerked her arm. For one nightmarish moment she expected the plate to empty over the table. The liquid swung from side to side and some of it went over the top and on to her hand. She bore with the pain, thankful that only a small amount had gone on the cloth.

'Sorry, sir, but you jerked my hand.'

'I did nothing of the kind,' he thundered, his face almost purple.

'You are new,' the quiet voice came from the foot of the table.

'Yes, ma'am.'

'First day nerves and don't worry, no great damage has been done.'

Agnes returned to her position at the sideboard. Miss Templeton's eyes were closed as if it was all getting too much for her. When she did open them Agnes was over collecting the empty plates. She dealt with the remainder of the meal with reasonable efficiency and Miss Templeton left after the sweet course. It was as she was going over with the cheese board that Agnes felt eyes watching her, and when she forced herself to look up and into his, she saw his puzzled frown.

★ ★ ★

The master and mistress were back in their sitting-room. Edwin with his cigar and brandy and Margaret with idle hands in her lap.

'Clumsy girl, bad as the other, maybe worse.'

'No, dear, I thought she did rather well particularly in the circumstances. You did knock her arm, accidentally, but you were to blame and you must have known it.'

His hand came down with a large smack on his knee. 'By God! I've got it. Never forget a face and that hair clinched it.'

'What are you talking about, dear?'

'That girl, how long has she worked here?'

'Let me think, it was just after – oh, I should think two months.'

'That fits.'

'What does?'

'That's her all right. Impudent madam put her tongue out at me.'

'Put her tongue out at you?'

'That is what I said.'

'Must have been a reason, and where did this take place?'

'Outside the gate, the fool girl was standing right plonk in the middle waiting to be knocked down.'

'You were in that car coming down the drive and into the roadway as if no one but you had the right to be there.'

'Nonsense, woman, the fool was standing there with no intention of moving.'

'What did you do?'

'Shook my fist at her and mouthed a few oaths which she couldn't hear, so don't upset yourself.'

'The truth is you nearly knocked her down – no wonder she stuck her tongue out at you. It's precisely what I would have done if I hadn't been so well brought up.'

'She's got to go, Margaret, I won't have that girl under my roof.'

'I refuse to dismiss her.'

'I insist that you do.'

'Insist all you like but the girl remains. You, Edwin, have no idea just how difficult it is to get honest and reliable staff these days. I can see it coming when we shall have to do a great deal more for ourselves.'

Edwin Taylor looked alarmed as well he might. He was a man who liked his creature comforts and someone at hand to see to his every need.

'Not as bad as that surely, you exaggerate, Margaret?'

'I assure you I am not exaggerating. All you need do is take a look in the paper for domestic help and you'll get some idea of what the position is.'

'I see,' he said tersely.

'The girl stays?'

'I suppose so.'

'Your chances of remaining at Kerne House are very slim after that exhibition.' Miss Templeton had sent for Agnes.

Agnes shuffled from one foot to the other. She was of the same opinion, it was just a question of how long it would take for Mr Taylor to remember the incident at the gate.

'He knocked my elbow,' Agnes said stubbornly, 'and I'd like to see you doing any better if someone knocked yours just as you were putting down a plate of soup.'

'That is not the point. I would have had the good manners to blame myself for the mishap. Really, to more or less tell your employer that it was his fault – words fail me they do, Agnes, they fail me.' She gave a deep, deep sigh. 'Just go away.'

'Thank you, Miss Templeton.'

For a whole week Agnes awaited her fate, certain that she was to lose her job but when it didn't happen she just assumed that Edwin Taylor had as yet not connected her with the incident. Life at Kerne House went on as usual and Agnes was quite happy. She had been too busy with unfamiliar tasks to give more than a passing thought to Rachel, but now she began thinking about her and wondering why she'd heard nothing. Surely she was sufficiently settled by now to let her best friend know where she was working and if she was staying with Miss Reid. There was a niggling worry, something wasn't right and she longed for a letter to clear up the mystery.

# Chapter Seventeen

Two extra bedrooms would be required for that night and Rachel was on her way down after preparing them. As she saw the solitary figure move away from the foot of the stairway Rachel felt her mouth go dry. This could only be her grandmother. A chill had confined the old lady to her room and this was the first day she had ventured downstairs.

Unaware of the watching eyes the woman moved on supported by her rubber-tipped stick and gazed out of the long, narrow windows that gave light to the hall. From where she stood she could see the sloping fresh green lawns and beyond that the soft rolling hills that seemed to merge with the blue-grey sky. Katherine Craig loved Duncairn House and the view from it. Was heaven to be compared to this? she wondered and how many years or months before the good Lord claimed her for that so-called Paradise in the skies? A small sigh escaped her. How lucky were those people with their faith and their absolute certainty that a better life lay beyond the grave. She could never be sure how much she believed and on the great Day of Judgment how would she fare? She closed her eyes. As God was her witness she had always done what she thought best. But best for whom? She gave another sigh. Useless to keep going over the past but it was becoming clearer than the present. Her thoughts these days were all for Amelia, that pretty child, that wicked young woman. No, wicked was too strong a word though Albert had used it. Thoughtless and silly more like, but, oh, the heartbreak she had caused.

Why? Why? Why? Life was full of questions that couldn't be answered. Why did she keep thinking of Amelia, feel her nearness? Amelia was dead, had been these long years. Perhaps it was of the child she was thinking. The girl child she knew existed, fathered by a rough, working-class nobody but still Amelia's child, the Craig blood in her. Her granddaughter.

How long was she going to stand there? Rachel asked herself. She made polishing the woodwork her excuse for remaining where she was. The woman moved at last but only to one of the chairs placed on either side of the hall table. Gingerly, and with a grimace of pain, she lowered herself into one and hung her stick on the edge of the hall table.

There was no way Rachel could avoid passing her grandmother and she couldn't linger any longer. A pile of sewing awaited her. Swiftly and holding the dusters in her hand, she went down the remaining stairs, made to pass the woman staring into space but the voice stopped her, a surprisingly strong voice.

'I don't recall seeing you before,' she rasped.

'I've only been here a few weeks, ma'am.'

Old and slightly stooped though she was, Katherine Craig had retained her haughty look. She had faded, watery blue eyes that must once have been beautiful. A myriad tiny lines criss-crossed the colourless face and the white hair was thinning to show patches of pink scalp. All this Rachel took in in those first moments.

'Don't rush away, girl,' she said irritably as Rachel made to go. 'What is your name?'

'Rachel Donaldson, ma'am.'

She pursed her lips and nodded. 'The seamstress.'

The description displeased Rachel. It made her sound like a hundred, she thought resentfully.

'I was a dressmaker's assistant, ma'am.'

'Is there a difference?'

'I would think so.'

'Sharp tongue you have, miss, doesn't become a maid.'

Rachel bit her lip and kept quiet. She wasn't going to apologise.

'Get on with your work then,' she said, fixing Rachel with a fierce look from those faded blue eyes.

Rachel needed no second bidding. Her grandmother had not endeared herself. She hadn't much liked her cousin either. Perhaps she would just stay long enough to get another job, perhaps as a dressmaker's assistant in Perth.

Nothing much was missed by Katherine Craig and this girl interested her. She was well-spoken and with a certain something she couldn't quite put her finger on. Perhaps it was pride though what a maid had to be proud about was hard to imagine unless it was in her work. Janet served her well and knew her likes and dislikes but this girl might be interesting to study, relieve the boredom too. She'd get Mrs Anderson to arrange it. A small groan escaped her as she saw the hurrying figure and from that distance could almost hear her tut-tutting.

'Mother, really, what are you doing sitting in the hall, you know how draughty it is and you just getting over that chill.'

Maud Meldrum had retained her slim figure but she had the face of a woman ten years older with pronounced bags under her eyes. She dressed well and suited what she wore. Her skirt was rough Harris tweed in a heather mixture and the cashmere twin-set picked out the palest shade of pink.

'Don't fuss, Maud, just help me up,' Mrs Craig said irritably, 'and if I want to sit here I'll sit here and if I get another chill then I get another chill and that'll maybe be the one that sees me off.'

'I do wish you wouldn't speak like that, Mother, it distresses me and it's childish.'

'Second childhood,' the woman said with a wicked grin, she liked to torment her daughter. She got her stick and with Maud's help started the slow painful process of walking.

'Is your arthritis playing up?' her daughter asked sympathetically.

'Arthritis doesn't play up, Maud, it is like bad toothache, the hell of all diseases, and it's in the family so you are not likely to escape.' She smiled grimly. 'That husband of yours, when is he expected?'

'Between six and six thirty, he's meeting Brian's train. Mother, I told you this before and I also told you that Mr and Mrs McGregor have been invited to dinner tomorrow evening and Peter too if he can manage.'

'Yes, I daresay you did.' They had reached the sitting-room where a fire was burning and a guard up to stop the sparks from flying. 'Take that thing away, keeps the heat from getting out and old bones need the heat.'

The guard was removed. The easy chair was refused and one with wooden arms replaced it.

'Are you quite comfortable now, Mother?'

'Yes, I'm fine, just fine,' but the tiredness was etched on her face. 'Leave me a while then come back and help me up to my room. I'll need a rest if I have to share a meal with that good-for-nothing husband of yours. You were a fool to marry him, Maud, you weren't the attraction,' she said brutally. 'All he's interested in is getting his hands on Duncairn House but that'll be over my dead body.' She gave a peal of laughter like someone demented and Maud looked at her with concern. 'I'm not mad just amused at my own remark "over my dead body" and that's exactly what he wants. He wants me dead and out of the way. You, he can twist round his fingers and Betsy is too young to be a problem but I'm a match for him and he knows it.'

'Henry is my husband and I refuse to listen to any more of this.'

'Your husband in name only, that is right isn't it, Maud?' her mother said with a new gentleness.

Maud's mouth quivered. 'That is our own affair, nothing to do with you.'

'It's none of my business I know that but I doubt if these trips are all business. You are too trusting, my dear.'

'Don't underestimate me, Mother, I may surprise everyone yet.' She paused. 'You are fond of Brian so don't make it difficult for him. Just try to be pleasant to Henry and particularly tomorrow when we have guests.'

'Hoping for a match between Betsy and Peter?'

'What if I am, it would be a good match.'

'I'd welcome it too but I'm afraid the spark isn't there, not with Peter, if I'm any judge of that sort of thing.'

The sewing-room next to Rachel's bedroom was a cold room and the uncurtained window made it feel even colder. The empty grate didn't help either and Rachel hoped that come winter, and some of the October days were cold enough for winter, she would be allowed a fire. The Singer sewing machine was similar to the one to which she had been accustomed and with her foot on the treadle the sheet was racing through her fingers. Two more and that would do for today. Hetty gave a light tap at the door and came in.

'Got the two bedrooms done, did you?'

Rachel raised her head. 'Yes. Who else is coming apart from Mr Meldrum and his son?'

'No one.' She nodded as if understanding. 'The extra bedroom is for Mr Henry. Separate rooms,' she giggled. 'Isn't it awful but maids know what is going on better than anyone.'

Rachel whipped out the sheet and tied the loose threads. 'What is he like, this Henry Meldrum?'

'Depends on your type I suppose,' Hetty said closing the door and ready for a gossip. 'Tall and broad with a moustache and thinks no end of himself.' She lowered her voice. 'Janet's smitten, I happen to know that.'

'Surely not, I mean, a married man,' Rachel said shocked and not really believing it. Janet didn't seem the type somehow.

'For some that makes it all the more interesting and I'm not saying this about Janet but he has plenty of money and a car and can give a girl a good time.'

'What about Brian Meldrum?' Rachel asked more to get off the subject of Henry Meldrum than genuine interest.

'As different to his old man as could be. Must take after his mother. He's not very tall, skinny, hardly any flesh on him. You know the half-starved-looking arty type, but he's nice.'

'Thought he was doing a business course?'

'Janet says he didn't make university and his father insisted he got some qualifications so that he can use his business connections and get him a job in the City. That's London.'

'I know that.'

'Brian would hate it, he's a real country lad at heart.'

'You know him?'

'I'd be so lucky. No, but he isn't in the least standoffish and talks to anyone. Tell you something else for good measure.'

'Go on then,' Rachel smiled as she began on the next sheet then decided it was so thin in places that it wasn't worth the trouble and tossed it aside.

'Mrs Craig has a soft spot for him and encourages him to make use of his artistic talents.,'

Rachel doubted if the woman she knew to be her grandmother would have a soft spot for anyone.'

'I'd better move my body.'

It was just as well she did for a minute later Mrs Anderson came into the sewing-room and Rachel took her foot off the treadle.

'You are doing very well, Rachel, but I think you can give the sewing a rest for a few days. Janet could do with some help in the dining-room. You could assist with the setting of the table and also help to serve the food.'

'The setting of the table, of course, Mrs Anderson, but I'd be a bit nervous about serving the meal, I've never done it before.'

'Neither you have but it is time you started. In any case, Janet will keep you right and she'll show you where to get a fresh white apron and cap.' She smiled. 'Just keep calm.'

She left and Rachel sat with idle hands thinking of the evening ahead. What worried her was having those faded blue eyes watching her and she had a sinking feeling they would be.

Rachel failed to hide her amusement. Janet was treating her as though she were a halfwit.

'What's so funny?'

'You! I have set a table before, you know.'

'Not in a proper dining-room.'

Rachel's thoughts went back over the years. She had been no more than eight or nine but her mother had been firm. To use the correct cutlery, to know how it should be placed, were so important to her and she had made sure that her small daughter would be no stranger to a properly set table. Sunday was the day everything was done just so and she could recall her father looking at the table and asking if royalty was expected. Looking back she wondered where all the cutlery had come from then supposed her mother must have bought six of everything when she could afford to.

Janet was waiting for an answer as she folded the white damask napkins.

'Perhaps not a proper dining-room but my mother set high standards.'

Janet's sharp look made Rachel think she had made her first mistake, she would have to be more careful. 'She was trained in a big house like this,' she added as a quick afterthought.

Janet nodded seemingly satisfied. 'I'm only following instructions from Mrs Anderson. She said I was in charge and you are to do as I say.'

'Yes, Janet, or should I say yes, m'am.'

'Cut it out.'

'Sorry.'

They worked in silence until Janet declared herself satisfied with everything.

Dinner was to be served at seven thirty and it was nearly that now. Dressed identically both maids were standing well back and near to the huge mahogany sideboard. It had a mirror along the back and Rachel took a hurried look at herself, the lace-trimmed cap was making her feel self-conscious, such a silly little thing. Watching her Janet felt irritation and jealousy and jealousy was a new experience. Aware of her attractive appearance, her power to attract men, she had always been full of confidence. Now here was Rachel and eyes that had followed her were showing an interest in the new maid.

'Done admiring yourself?'

'I wasn't.'

'I saw you.'

'You saw me looking at this stupid thing on my head that's all. I wish I could take it off.'

'Well, you can't.' Janet wished that she could take it off. The touch of white lace was barely noticed in her own fair hair but nestling in Rachel's black curls it was very eye-catching.

With time to spare Rachel took the opportunity to look around her and liked what she saw. Both windows were pelmeted and had floor-length curtains in rich green velvet. Matching material upholstered the dining chairs which were high-backed and cream embossed wall-paper made a fitting background for several large oil paintings and a few small watercolours which she thought could be of the gardens at Duncairn House.

There were no guests, the five for dinner were family. The seating arrangements surprised Rachel. As was expected, her grandmother was at the head of the table but it was her daughter, Maud, who sat at the other end. Rachel had expected it to be Aunt Maud's husband though maybe she was wrong there. Henry Meldrum had a side to himself and Betsy and Brian were opposite him.

A murmur of conversation prepared the two maids. Mrs Craig came in on the arm of her daughter. She was wearing a silver-grey dress with a black beaded top. Maud had on a cream silk dress with a red chiffon scarf at the neck. The old lady fussed until she was comfortably seated and the napkin spread over her knees. Henry Meldrum had advanced quickly to assist but a frosty look from his mother-in-law made him step aside. Before sitting down himself he waited until his wife was seated. The two young ones came in slowly, they were still talking but stopped when they reached the table. Like his father, Brian wore a dark suit, white shirt and tie. Henry Meldrum was a fine figure of a man and the touch of grey at the temples only enhanced his good looks. Brian's suit hung on him and he looked as though he could do with a few good meals inside him but in fact he had a hearty appetite and enjoyed good health. He was the type who would remain thin all through life.

Mrs Craig looked across at Janet and Rachel. 'You may serve now, Janet.'

'Thank you, m'am.'

Mrs Craig was served first with the tomato soup. Rachel carefully lowered it in front of her then hurried to serve the others. A warmed roll was on each side plate and little curls of butter decorated two dishes. Janet busied herself with the next course and having her offer of assistance refused, Rachel studied those around the table. Brian Meldrum was much as Hetty had described him though the description didn't do him justice. He had a thin, clever face and eyes that could be serious or fun-filled. Rachel liked him on sight.

Remembering Hetty's bit of gossip about Brian's father and Janet, she looked for signs but all she noticed was Janet's heightened colour and that could have been due to the heat of the room.

Janet's arm nudged her. 'Pay attention.'

'Sorry, what do you want me to do?'

'Be quite sure that everyone has finished before collecting the plates.'

Rachel stood back from the table until the old lady had put down her spoon.

'If you have finished, m'am, may I take your plate?'

'Yes, girl, take it away.'

Girl indeed, Rachel thought fuming inwardly. If she's forgotten my name surely she could ask. She carried the plates over to the sideboard. Until now conversation at the table had been subdued but with the main course served it all but dried up.

Under the eagle eye of her grandmother Rachel had expected to be nervous but the old lady had shown little interest and seemed tired. Instead it was Henry Meldrum who disturbed her, there was nothing obvious just moving to brush her when she served him. More disturbing was having those bold eyes follow her across the room.

'Not too bad,' Janet said condescendingly. 'You can get Hetty to help you clear the table and carry the dishes through to the kitchen.'

'What about coffee?'

'I prefer to see to that myself.'

Rachel smiled and nodded.

'You will remember that tomorrow evening will be more demanding. Three guests are expected.'

★  ★  ★

The table was fully out and three glasses were at each setting. There was to be a choice of starter followed by leg of lamb with fresh mint sauce, garden vegetables and even-sized small potatoes also from the gardens. The dessert was fresh fruit salad and cream or a light apricot sponge. By seven thirty the table looked very attractive with candles at either end. The only other light came from the corner lamps which together with the candles gave a soft glow to the room and added a sparkle to the silver and crystal.

Janet was fidgetting with the serving spoons. 'Dr McGregor hasn't turned up yet,' she said with a frown of annoyance. 'We've to hold back the meal for another fifteen minutes then serve it whether or not he has arrived. You could go and have a look out the hall window and see if his car is in sight.'

Rachel had just reached the hall when a loud ring proclaimed someone at the door. It was Hetty's duty to answer it but she wasn't in sight and Rachel opened the door herself. Standing there was a tall man with rugged good looks and an apologetic smile.

'Have they started?' he whispered as he stepped in.

This must be Dr McGregor. 'No, sir, they were giving you another fifteen minutes.' She found that she was whispering too. He wore a dinner jacket with the bow tie slightly crooked as though he had been in a rush to dress. Her fingers itched to straighten it but of course she couldn't.

From the drawing-room came the sound of animated conversation as they got up from their comfortable chairs.

'I'm so sorry to be late, my apologies, Mrs Craig,' he said lifting her hand and kissing it.

'No need to apologise, Peter, a busy doctor can never call his time his own. We are just delighted to see you here and now, young man, you can take my arm and escort me through to the dining-room.'

'My pleasure.'

There was more than a hint of the flirt in the old lady's manner and Rachel wondered if long ago her grandmother had flirted with handsome young men before settling down to marriage and raising a family.

With Janet, Rachel watched the company take their seats at the table. All the gentlemen wore dinner jackets and between John McGregor and his son, Peter, there was a strong resemblance. They were both about six feet tall, with the same straight, strong nose and the small cleft in the firm chin. What remained of John McGregor's hair was dark brown sprinkled with grey but Peter had inherited his mother's thick, dark blond hair. On his arrival mother and son had exchanged a warm smile. Waiting to begin her duties Rachel saw the pride in the motherly face as she watched her son and his gentleness with their hostess.

'No nine-to-five with the medical profession,' John McGregor said with a look along the table to Henry Meldrum.

'Nor in the City,' Henry answered a little too sharply and as if regretting his words, John McGregor nodded his head in agreement.

'I'm sure you're right. Like lawyers one can be working hard with precious little to show for it.'

'Not like Peter. He'll have bandaged limbs to show for his trouble,' Betsy said and flushed scarlet. She did so want to say something witty. There was a faint titter, then Mrs Craig gave the signal for the meal to be served.

The hostess looked regal in a deep purple velvet gown with a brooch at the neckline. Maud wore a café-au-lait lace dress which suited her slim figure but not her sallow skin. Peter's mother had favoured a black skirt with a white silk blouse. Her only make-up was a touch of pale pink lipstick, she needed nothing more. Betsy, occasionally bothered by spots, envied the woman her pink-and-white complexion. She had been so looking forward to this evening. Seated between Peter and Brian she had seen herself being gracious to both but letting Peter see where her heart lay. She knew too that she was looking fresh and pretty in her navy blue princess-style dress with its wide white collar and piping round sleeves and imitation pockets. It just wasn't fair that the new maid could look marvellous in that cheap uniform but worst of all was that special smile Peter had given her and the tell-tale flush on the servant's face.

There was an attraction there and some way would have to be found to get rid of that girl. The beginning of a plan was forming in her mind. Her stepfather, fool that he was, thought his affair with Janet had gone unnoticed and it suited her mother to let him think that. What if he switched his affections from Janet to Rachel. Janet would be out for revenge and a word to her grandmother about finding the girl snooping about the attic should seal her fate.

Rachel went round to Henry Meldrum with the basket of rolls. Before lifting one the thick fingers touched hers, pressing into them and Rachel felt her flesh crawl.

'He's a bit of all right, isn't he?' Janet whispered as they worked together at the sideboard.

'Who?'

'The doctor of course, you like him, don't you?'

'Don't be silly I've only just set eyes on him.'

'Waste of time if you are interested, he's Miss Betsy's property.'

'Not Brian?'

'He's keen enough but it's the doctor she wants and means to have and she usually manages to get her own way.'

Sleep was a confusion of dreams that night. Peter McGregor's face would slip away and then it would be her da and Peggy and her father's accusing eyes. Her thoughts went back to what she had done. Running away as she had was unforgivable, she could see that now when it was too late. She was trapped in her own stupidity, cut off from everyone she knew. At least Mrs Rodgers would have put her da's mind at rest. He would expect her to be comfortably settled at Duncairn House, accepted as Amelia's daughter. She moved restlessly. What would he have to say if he knew the true state of affairs, that she was a maid in her grandmother's house?

What remained of her money was in her purse in the drawer with the brooch. It wasn't a question of not trusting anyone but the money would be better in the bank. Hillend had its own post office and one day Rachel walked in, deposited her money and became the proud owner of a post office savings book with her signature inside the cover.

Her bedroom – what a difference there and at little cost she thought with justifiable pride. Approaching Mrs Anderson about old curtains a pair had been unearthed. They were maroon-and-cream-striped curtains that had once graced the dining-room. They were still good but faded with the sun. Being very long the faded material had been cut away and enough left to give a fullness at the window. With the remainder she made a cushion cover and recovered the stool. Earlier on, she had removed the ugly nail and replaced it with a hook for the mirror.

At long last Rachel sat down with pen and paper and wrote to Agnes. It took her an age, she had to be careful what she said. Agnes was quick to pick up something if it didn't sound right. She read it over again before putting it in the envelope and decided it would do. Much of it was about Agnes's job, how she was getting on and about family and friends. Only when she started on the envelope did Rachel discover that she couldn't remember the name of the house or the number in Broughty Ferry Road and it was a very long road. She would address it to Spinner's Lane.

Sadly it was all wasted effort. The houses in Spinner's Lane had been demolished and the Boyd family were in their new corporation house.

'Come in.'

'Oh, it's you, Janet,' Rachel said putting down the magazine she had been reading. 'You look very smart in that tweed costume. Where are you off to?'

'The village. I want a lipstick if the chemist has the shade. Fancy a walk?'

Rachel was surprised. Janet was a bit overdressed for a walk to the village and she had more make-up on than usual. She didn't remark on it, of course, Janet didn't have much of a sense of humour.

'Yes, I'll come. Sit down with that magazine and I'll get ready.'

'This is nice,' Janet said taking a look around her. 'Wish I'd taken it when I had the chance.'

'It was a mess then, that's why you didn't,' Rachel reminded her as she slipped off her uniform dress and stepped into a brown pleated skirt. Opening the drawer she took out a cream and brown jumper and pulled it over her head. Her lovely skirt and blouse, Miss Reid's gift, were still in the wardrobe awaiting a special occasion. She wondered when that would be.

'That's true,' Janet agreed looking up from the fashion page. 'When you are so good at sewing, what on earth made you take a job as a maid? I know for a fact that there is a shirt factory in Perth crying out for machinists.'

'A live-in job was what I required, Janet, and I don't imagine a machinist's wage, a beginner's anyway, would cover digs,' Rachel said shortly.

'I don't know, others must do it, everybody doesn't stay at home.'

'Most do.'

Rachel powdered her nose, drew a lipstick over her mouth and combed her hair. Her oatmeal jacket was hanging on the back of the door, she took it down and put it on. It was shabby and she was tired of it. Apart from money for the cinema and the fare to Perth she had few expenses and her wage, small though it was, was found money. She would save up for a coat withdrawing a pound or maybe two from her post office account so that she wouldn't have to wait so long. The helpful assistant had explained the procedure for withdrawing money but warned her always to leave in a little to save having to start all over again with a new book.

'I'm ready.'

They walked smartly down the drive and along the country road. It was the end of October and the countryside had already felt the sharpness of frost. Summer was reluctantly giving way to a short autumn then would follow a long bleak spell when roaring fires were the greatest comfort. Neither had much to say, and after a few desultory attempts at conversation, they gave up and walked in silence. Their feet crunched through the crisp, dry leaves lying thick on the ground. A few still clung determinedly to the trees flaunting their lovely scarlet and gold.

The village was one street of shops and housewives seemingly reluctant to return home, gossiped at shop doors. Hemmed between the butcher's and the grocer's was the chemist's shop. Two women, one with an irritating cough, were awaiting prescriptions; both looked miserable. Janet made for the selection of lipsticks and other make-up on display. The shade she wanted wasn't there but after uncapping some and testing the colour on the back of her hand, she decided on one. She paid for her purchase and they left.

'We'll go back by the station road,' Janet announced.

Rachel didn't mind but noticed that Janet was suddenly ill-at-ease. The road was vaguely familiar and Rachel realised then that this was the road she had taken when she had arrived in Hillend. She remembered the shop too.

'Hang on, I'm going in here for a tube of pastilles.'

'I'll wait outside.'

Three months was a long time but even so Rachel moved away from the window, only turning when she heard the door and Janet come out. Mrs Mackay was behind her to take in a bundle of newspapers dropped off by a passing van. A look of puzzlement crossed her face then she was smiling broadly.

'Took a wee while to place you but I have you now. You're the lass who asked about accommodation and I sent you to Mrs Shepherd?'

Rachel smiled and nodded but was aware of Janet's interest as she looked from one to the other.

'You were quite comfortable?'

'Yes, thank you.'

'You're from Duncairn House aren't you?' she asked, turning to Janet.

'We both are.'

'Well isn't that nice.' Her eye caught a customer going in. 'No patience some of them so I'll get back.' She hastened away.

'A bit of a dark horse, aren't you?' Janet said as they began walking.

'Why do you say that?'

'Just a feeling there is a mystery about you.'

'Nonsense, I could say the same about you.'

'No, you couldn't, but right away I wondered about you. I mean Mrs Anderson had three girls to interview for the vacancy and one wrote later to apologise for not turning up.'

'What conclusion did you draw from that?' Rachel was playing for time.

'None really. Mrs Anderson decided you must have heard about the vacancy and come along on chance.'

'Which is exactly what happened,' Rachel said, relieved that it sounded so plausible.

'Being able to sew clinched it for you.'

'It helped.'

'I'm going to ask a favour of you,' she said abruptly. 'Would you go back to Duncairn House on your own?' She paused. 'I'm meeting someone, you see.'

'Someone you don't want me to know about?'

'Someone I don't want anyone to know about. Look, Rachel, it isn't much to ask and I'd willingly do the same for you.'

'I don't mind, away you go and I'll go back the way we came.'

'Thanks, you're a pal.'

'Before you go tell me why you bothered to ask for my company, you didn't need to.'

'Oh, but I did. The two of us going out together wouldn't raise an eyebrow but on my own and dressed like this,' she touched her costume jacket, 'they would wonder—'

'You should just let them wonder.'

'Could you go now, please,' she was getting agitated. 'I'll be late and he'll think I'm not coming and not a word to Hetty or anyone.'

'You have my word.' Rachel walked quickly away only turning back once to look, but Janet was out of sight.

Janet was an adult, what she did was her own business but even so she was uneasy. Was Hetty right? Was she seeing Henry Meldrum? If it were true, poor Aunt Maud. She thought of the woman as her aunt, had come to like her which was more than could be said for her grandmother and her cousin. Even if it were a marriage in name only her aunt would feel humiliated if she were to find out about her husband and a servant girl.

So engrossed was she in her own thoughts that she was unaware of the car drawing up alongside.

'May I offer you a lift to Duncairn House if that is where you are heading?'

'It is and thank you.' Rachel found herself looking into the smiling face of Dr Peter McGregor. He leaned over to open the passenger door.

She got in and pulled the door; it didn't shut properly but it wouldn't open either. She felt a fool.

'Needs a good tug,' he said, leaning over her to secure it.

'Sorry.'

'Don't be, my mother never manages it. Were you in the village?'

'Yes.' She wasn't usually tongue-tied but she couldn't think of a thing to say and she felt breathless and excited.

'Where do you come from?' he asked as he changed gear.

'I was brought up in Dundee.'

'Know this part well?'

'No, but I hope to see a little of it before the winter sets in.'

'By bus?'

'Or train, whichever is more convenient.'

Peter McGregor knew that he was very, very attracted to this dark-eyed lovely girl. That she was a servant in a friend's house was of no importance. No maid he had ever seen had that quiet, ladylike grace nor spoke in such a beautifully modulated voice. He sensed there was a mystery here and he meant to solve it.

'When have you to be back on duty, if that is the correct term?'

'Not until half past six.'

'And I'm free until evening surgery. I could show you a little of our lovely countryside if the idea appeals to you.'

'Are you sure? I mean it is very kind of you.'

'My pleasure.'

She couldn't stop smiling and her eyes were shining, it was all so unexpected, so wonderful. It wouldn't do to show just how thrilled she was and Rachel was glad he was concentrating on his driving.

'My afternoon was to be a dreary session with medical journals which I'll gladly put off to another day.'

They were both smiling and happiness surged through her. She had never felt like this before. Only one thing was spoiling it for her, if only she had been wearing something smarter. Taking a sidelong look she was relieved that he had on an ancient tweed jacket with worn leather patches on the elbows and trousers that had lost their crease. Dr McGregor, she could see, was a man who put comfort before appearance and she liked that.

Very soon they were in Perth and in the busy centre. Peter concentrated on his driving until they were clear of the congested streets and out onto the quiet country roads. He kept his speed down while he pointed out places of interest.

'Where are we now?'

'Coming into Dunkeld. Pretty little place to stop in and the cathedral is worth a look. Pitlochry was where I was heading but I think we'll leave that for another time.'

Another time! Peter had said another time. She hugged the words to her then suddenly she was remembering about Betsy and her heart plummeted. Peter and Betsy, names linked, a union to delight both families. She had better stop her impossible dreams and come down to earth. Peter was being kind, a spur-of-the-moment invitation, but Pitlochry, that sounded as though he wanted to see her again. Safer, though, if she said nothing about Pitlochry.

'Have you always lived in Perthshire?'

'Born and bred. I share my time between my parents' home in Hillend and Perth.'

'Is that where your surgery is?'

'Yes, on the Crieff Road. Dr Smart, the senior doctor, is a widower with an absolutely marvellous housekeeper. I have a room in his house and can come and go as I please.' He paused at a junction. 'How do you like working at Duncairn House?'

'Quite pleasant. Much of my time is spent sewing and I'm glad of that. I find Mrs Craig rather terrifying.'

'Do you? To someone who doesn't know her well she could be, I imagine. I like her, she's quite a character with a lot of spirit and if she's difficult at times who could blame her. She suffers a lot of pain but tries to hide it.'

'Now that I know I'll make allowances,' she smiled. It was nice to hear her grandmother being praised.

'Peter was slowing down and looking about him. The frown changed into a broad grin as he pointed to a sign. 'Martha's Tearoom'. 'For one awful moment I thought the place had closed down.' He parked the car down a side road and they walked side by side.

'This is very kind of you, Dr McGregor.'

'Peter is the name and I don't knows yours. We should have introduced ourselves in the car.'

'I'm Rachel Donaldson.'

'Then Rachel Donaldson come and taste scones like you've never tasted before.' He took her arm and they went into the tearoom. A few elderly ladies having afternoon tea broke off their conversation for a moment to watch the good-looking young couple being shown a window table.

'Is it the set afternoon tea, sir?'

'If that includes scones?'

'It does,' she smiled. 'Afternoon tea for two.' She went away.

The teapot and hot-water jug were placed before Rachel. Then followed a tray with home-baking to replenish the cake stand. Last to arrive were the scones, hot from the oven.

'Do you like the milk in first, Peter?'

'Yes, please, and two of sugar, heaped ones.'

'Tut tut that's not what the doctor ordered! All that sweetness isn't good for you,' she said as their met across the table.

'I'm of the school that thinks a little of what you fancy does you good.'

She didn't know why but she blushed and he laughed as he cut open a scone buttered both sides and topped them with jam. 'Delicious,' he said.

She did likewise with her scone.

'Go easy if you're troubled with indigestion.'

'I'm not and I take it you aren't either?'

'No, but I'll probably pay the price in years to come.'

'Live for today and let tomorrow take care of itself.' It was what she was doing she told herself.

She's lovely, she's delightful, Peter was thinking to himself, and I want to go on seeing her. They were on their second cup of tea.

'Tell me about yourself, Rachel. I'm not curious but I am interested.'

An expression of sadness crossed her face then she shrugged. 'Nothing much to tell, Peter. As I said I was brought up in Dundee and I'm now working at Duncairn House.'

'Risking speaking out of turn I would say there is a great deal to tell, but it can wait.' His hand closed over hers and it was like a current of electricity. She tried to withdraw it but his hand remained firmly on hers. 'I'm very attracted to you, Rachel, and I hope we can go on seeing each other.' He let her hand go and she drank some of the tea then put down her cup.

'My story isn't all that unusual, Peter.' She liked the sound of his name on her lips. 'My mother died when I was nine years of age and there was just my father and I and a neighbour who came in to help.'

'Then your father decided to take a new wife?'

'How did you guess?'

'To me it seemed very obvious. The child and her father had been everything to one another then suddenly there was this stranger, this woman, and you felt yourself pushed out, unwanted.'

She smiled sadly. 'For as far as it goes that is more or less right and I'm certainly not blameless.'

'Do you feel like telling me the rest?' he said gently when she fell silent.

'Might as well finish what I've begun. I didn't get on particularly well with my stepmother, probably because she is so different from my real mother. It was an accumulation of things that drove me away from home but mostly it was because my father broke his promise to me.' She swallowed, painfully. 'I wanted to train to be a teacher, Peter, and my father was to be more than delighted to see me through college. Peggy, that's my stepmother, is very extravagant, the money put aside for me got spent and I had to leave school and get a job.'

'Even so, Rachel, with your intelligence and appearance you could have done a lot better for yourself than become a maid.'

'A roof over my head was a consideration,' she said shortly, 'and a live-in maid seemed like a good idea. And another thing, I rather resent your remarks suggesting a maid is a nobody.'

'Oh, dear, now I've put my foot in it and you couldn't be more wrong. All I meant and I think you deliberately took that the wrong way,' he said frowning at her, 'was that you are very obviously a superior girl who could have done a lot better for herself.'

'I did work for a dressmaker and it was when she was forced to give up the business that I decided to leave home.'

'Why Hillend?'

Twice she had been asked that. 'Why not? I just thought it would be a pleasant place to live.'

'Which it is.' He looked at his watch. 'Rachel, I could go on sitting here with you but unfortunately duties lie ahead for both of us.' He called for the waitress, settled the bill adding a good tip for the length of time they had occupied a table. Then they walked out to where the car was parked.

'We'll have to give the cathedral a miss, we spent rather longer in Martha's then I intended.' Peter knew that he had cut it fine and was forced to put his foot down though not to endanger life. The silence was comfortable with Peter turning occasionally to give her a smile.

Too soon for Rachel they were drawing up before the gates of Duncairn House. Peter got out to open the door for her just as a figure came flying down the drive.

'Peter, darling, how lovely to see you.'

'Hello, Betsy.'

She took his arm. 'Come along in.'

'Can't, I have a waiting-room full of patients.'

'A few minutes won't make much difference.'

Peter turned only to see Rachel's figure hurrying round to the back of the house. Drat Betsy, he thought uncharitably, he'd wanted to make arrangements with Rachel, now he would have to make it a letter.

'Two minutes to say hello to your grandmother,' he said, 'and not a moment longer.'

She linked him up the drive. 'Peter, dear, you are much too kind-hearted, you shouldn't be giving a lift to the maids, they can perfectly well walk from the village.'

Peter thought it best to say nothing.

Rachel turned the corner and almost bumped into Benny, the handyman.

'Steady there, knock an old man down, would you?'

'Sorry, Benny, my fault, I was rushing.'

'Mrs Anderson's been askin' for you.'

'For me?'

'Aye, for you. Better change into your workin' togs.'

Rachel smiled. 'I'll take your advice.'

There was no answer when she knocked at the housekeeper's door but just as she made to turn away Mrs Anderson arrived and unlocked the door.

'Come in, Rachel.'

Rachel stood in the centre of the room, she wasn't asked to sit.

'It has been decided, Rachel, that Janet and you are to take turns at seeing to Mrs Craig. This will relieve me and Janet's day off will cease to be a problem. Monday, Tuesday and Wednesday for you and Janet will do the rest of the week.'

This was what she wanted, a chance to get to know her grandmother but now that it was about to happen, Rachel could only feel panic. It must have shown.

'Good gracious! I wouldn't have expected you to be nervous,' Mrs Anderson said, showing annoyance. 'Your duties will be perfectly straightforward. At eight o'clock you will take a tray prepared by Mrs Morton to Mrs Craig's bedroom. She may want her breakfast in bed or she may prefer it at the small table. This will be properly set as if in the breakfast-room but Janet will keep you right there.'

Rachel nodded. It sounded easy enough.

'Some days she is in a lot of pain and won't leave her room all day. On those days you will attend to her every need. By that I mean her meals and seeing her comfortably seated with cushions for her back.'

# Chapter Eighteen

As each day went by Agnes was becoming increasingly uneasy. The darkening of Edwin Taylor's face whenever he saw her made Agnes believe that he was struggling with a memory, and she thought it just a question of time before he connected her with the incident at the gate and she got her marching orders.

At Kerne House, newspapers read by and cast aside by the master and mistress, were collected and used to light the fires. Before this happened, Agnes made a point of getting hold of them to tear out the pages headed SITUATIONS VACANT then studied them when she was alone. She could not have said rightly what she was looking for, only that she would know it when she saw it. The weeks went by and with them her seventeenth birthday without her having applied for a single vacancy. Then just as she was beginning to lose heart she saw it. Set apart from the others it had caught her eye immediately. Her eyes flew over it.

Domestic help urgently required for large country house on outskirts of Kirriemuir. Must be prepared to live in. Own room. Preferred age 17-19 years. Only girls of good character need apply. Applications in own handwriting to:

Mrs Harrison, housekeeper, Drumoaks,
near Kirriemuir, Angus.

This was it, Agnes thought with a flutter of excitement. She was meant to get this job, she was sure of it.

Pen, ink and cheap lined notepaper were provided, it being expected that even servant girls would occasionally wish to write home or to friends. Agnes disliked writing on lined paper, it reminded her of school. She was perfectly capable of writing in a straight line.

Fortunately for Agnes, Mrs Margaret Taylor was an enthusiastic correspondent and wrote regularly to her friends. For this purpose she kept a good supply of writing paper, some headed, some plain, and envelopes in the bureau which was usually kept open. The headed paper Agnes decided to ignore but the continuation sheets were of good quality. At the first opportunity, and that would have to be sometime today, she would help herself to a couple of sheets and an envelope. The stamp she would buy herself. Agnes saw nothing wrong in taking stationery but drew the line at stamps though her employer had a good supply to hand.

Mistakes were something she couldn't afford so on a page of cheap notepaper and in pencil Agnes scribbled down what she was going to say. Satisfied at last with the wording she copied it out in ink. Agnes could write well when she took the trouble and she was pleased with her effort. With the same care she addressed the envelope, sealed it then threw on her coat and took herself down to the corner shop. Though not permitted to sell stamps to the public, the elderly shopkeeper saw no harm in having a small supply for her own use and being able to oblige folk reluctant to walk the extra distance to the post office. It was good for business too.

'A letter for you, Agnes.'

Too soon to expect a reply to her advertisement; it could only be from Rachel.

'Thanks, Gloria.' She took the letter and her heart skipped a beat. It wasn't from Rachel, she knew her friend's handwriting. That could only mean it was from Drumoaks and to reply so promptly must be good news.

Gloria had disappeared but Mrs Robertson was there. 'Now that you've examined it aren't you goin' to open it?' She was trying unsuccessfully to hide her curiosity.

'No hurry, Mrs Robertson,' Agnes said carelessly, 'friend of mine getting round to writing at last.'

'Nice envelope,' Cook said suspiciously.

'Probably pinched it from her employer,' Agnes grinned.

Mrs Robertson nodded. 'Goes on I daresay.' She paused to take a handful of flour and scatter it liberally before rolling out the pastry. 'Gloria's got the sniffles again and I'm going to send her home in a wee while. No use spreading germs but it means you'll need to scrape those carrots, I've only one pair of hands.'

'All right.' Agnes scraped furiously at the carrots hoping the rest was already prepared. She was desperate to get away. 'That do?'

'For the now.'

Agnes made her escape and flew up the stairs and into her room. Shutting the door she went over and sat on the bed. Her hand was shaking as she took the envelope out of her overall pocket and opened it. She brought out a neatly folded single sheet of paper with an embossed heading and Agnes nearly died of excitement.

*Dear Miss Boyd*, (She'd never been called that and it gave her quite a thrill.)

> *Thank you for your application. Please attend for interview on the afternoon of Tuesday 24th. Drumoaks is about a mile and a half from Kirriemuir but there is a local bus to bring you the rest of the way.*
>
> *Information regarding transport can be obtained from the newsagent in the square. Travelling expenses will be refunded. On arrival go round to the side door and ask for Mrs Harrison. It is essential that you bring this letter with you.*
>
> *Lavinia Harrison.*

Agnes was hugging her knees and rocking herself. She was jubilant and refused to entertain the possibility that she could be unsuccessful. This was her future, her destiny. She looked again at the date. Tuesday, the twenty-fourth, that was a week tomorrow. Bad luck that it was Molly's day off and not hers but she didn't see it as too much of a problem. The big romance with Geoffrey was off, she was sure of it. Why did that immediately make her think of Tommy Kingsley? It maddened Agnes that she couldn't forget him.

'Why do you want my Tuesday? Where are you going'?'

'To Kirriemuir to see a friend I haven't seen for ages and this is the only chance we'll have.' Agnes thought it safer to keep as close to the truth as possible. There was always the outside chance that someone who knew her might see her stepping on the Kirriemuir bus.

'Male or female? Daft question,' Molly grinned, 'I don't see you goin' to all that trouble for a female.'

'Actually it is a girl.'

Molly looked her disbelief.

'Honestly, Molly, she's someone I was at school with, my best friend, as a matter of fact.' As she said the words Agnes asked herself if it was true. Would she have gone to all this trouble for Rachel and she believed the answer to be yes.

Molly took her time, not wanting to give in too easily.

'I'll think about it.'

'That won't do, I have to know now.'

She gave a big sigh. 'I suppose so, all right I'll change.'

'Thanks, Molly, you're a pal.'

'Seen anything of Tommy Kingsley?'

'No, I haven't, but there is no reason why I should, he's nothing to me,' Agnes said shortly.

'No need to snap, I was just askin'.'

'Sorry, didn't mean to.'

'In a way I'm sorry I gave Tommy up for Geoffrey.'

'All over with lover boy, is it?'

'Agnes, he had the nerve to stand me up,' she said indignantly, 'and no one does that to me,' she continued, forgetting that someone just had.

'Better without him if he's that type.'

She nodded. 'Mebbe I should try to get Tommy back – after all it was just that bike of his that caused the trouble.'

Agnes was shocked at just how much she disliked the thought of Tommy and Molly getting together again. Stupid, since she didn't want him herself.

'You are on a loser there, he worships that bike.'

Molly shrugged. 'You could be right.' She picked up the dusters and the Brasso and made to go, then stopped. 'How about comin' with me to the dancin' on Saturday, see what the talent is like?'

'Sorry, can't, I have to go home. I'm in trouble. They've been in their corporation house for over three weeks and I haven't seen it.'

'Some other Saturday?'

'Sure.'

Molly departed to polish up the brass candlesticks and Agnes returned to the kitchen to do more of Gloria's duties. As she opened the door Mrs Robertson stopped talking to Mrs Fairlie, the woman who came in to scrub the floors. They both looked at Agnes.

'You throw any light on it, Agnes?'

'On what?'

'Someone's been tearing pages out of the old newspapers, the "jobs vacant" ones and after me promising Mrs Fairlie here that she could take them home to her laddie.'

Mrs Fairlie got off her knees to give an explanation. She dried her hands on her coarse apron, tucked her hair behind her ears and began, 'When Mrs Robertson is kind enough, there's no need for me wasting money buying a paper that'll no' get read. You see, lass, it's just the job page I want.'

'Can't help you, I'm afraid,' Agnes said looking genuinely sorry, 'but I tell you what, I'll collect the papers myself before anyone else gets at them and bring them to the kitchen. How's that?'

'That's real good of you, lass, many thanks.' Mrs Fairlie smiled showing ill-fitting false teeth then dropped to her knees and set to with a will to scrub the floor.

It was warm and clammy the afternoon Agnes left Kerne House to catch two trams to take her to the West Port. Before making her way to the Boyds' new corporation house, Agnes decided to have a look at Spinner's Lane then wished she hadn't. Rubble was everywhere and it had become a playground for youngsters from the Hawkhill. The bigger boys were a menace as they threw bricks to break them up and generally make a nuisance of themselves.

Agnes hadn't meant to linger but watched with amusement as three little girls no more than five years of age played happily amongst the rubbish, their clothes and their faces filthy. Choosing the larger bricks and bowed down under their weight they began to build their own little house. The walls to their satisfaction they then went in search of linoleum and dragged back a torn piece which they managed to lay on the floor.

'I'll be the ma and I'll cook the dinner,' one said as she stirred an imaginary pot.

'And I'll be the da and do nothin',' another piped in.

The third child, hands on hips, looked belligerent. 'I am not bein' the bairn again and gettin' hitted, it isn't fair.'

Seeing it about to develop into a noisy quarrel, Agnes had a final look round then took herself away. She couldn't imagine anyone sorry to see the vermin-infested houses reduced to rubble. Ten minutes' smart walking took her to Brady Street, a short street with corporation houses down each side. Some had bright clean curtains at the windows and a few of the front gardens were being turned over. The houses were in blocks of four with a garden to the front and drying green to the back. Four poles had been hammered into the ground with jutting arms for the rope to be wound round. The washing was then pegged out and on a dry, windy day it dried in no time at all.

Opening the gates Agnes walked up the path to find her mother and Ruby sitting on the door-step. It was late afternoon and there was still some warmth in the sun.

'Hello, Ma,' Agnes said brightly and tickled her little sister under the chin.

'Took your time about comin'?'

'Better late than never.'

Only her hair was different, Agnes thought, as she looked at her mother. Was there to be an improvement now that she was better housed? It was shorter, looked clean and appeared thicker. She wore shabby carpet slippers showing a little of her big toe, her legs were bare and marbled through sitting too close to the fire. Her thin overall-style dress would have been acceptable had it been washed and ironed but it was stained and the material badly crushed.

'Do we go in or do I have to sit on the step?'

'We'll go in.' She got up and Agnes made to help Ruby.

'Leave her, she'll manage, she's just bone idle.'

'What do you mean she's just bone idle?'

'Had a visit from the nurse no' long after we came. Seems we've been doin' too much for her and if everything is done for her there's no need for her to do anything for herself if you get my drift.'

'Makes sense I suppose.' Agnes paused to watch Ruby lumber into the living-room then plonk herself down on her bottom. 'There should be a place for bairns like Ruby with trained people who understand them. Some could be taught to do something.'

'That depends on the severity of their handicap,' Jenny Boyd said wearily and repeating the nurse. 'Our Ruby is at the lower end of the scale.'

Agnes nodded. She'd seen other mongol children coping reasonably well but recognised that her sister was incapable of learning very much. To change the conversation she said, 'I like your hair short, makes you look younger.'

'Ta. Your da didn't even notice and what do you think of our new abode?'

'Nice what I've seen of it.'

'That brown linoleum goes all round the house, keep to one colour and you get it cheaper.'

Apart from the linoleum Agnes thought that Spinner's Lane might have been transferred to Brady Street. In fact there was a minus point in Brady Street. There was no recess for the bed, it wasn't intended to hold one, and the double bed took up a large part of the room. Her da's old, sagging chair was at one side of the fireplace and its neighbour in slightly better condition, at the other end. The dresser was cluttered, the table was cluttered, and the curtains removed from Spinner's Lane were six inches too short. The kitchenette referred to by her mother as the scullery was well fitted with cupboards and had a gas cooker. Agnes examined the wall cupboards and found most of them to be empty.

'Ma, that stuff on the table should be in here, there's plenty of room for everything and the dirty dishes go on the draining board until you get round to washing them.'

'The fire heats the water and it is only on at night.'

'Boil a kettle then.'

'And who is to pay the gas bill I'd like to know,' she shot back. 'Anyway I like things the way they are and it's my house. I've told that to Meg and I'm tellin' it to you,' she said with dangerous calm.

'Fair enough,' Agnes said carelessly, 'you must find a difference having a bathroom, though.'

'Your da still washes at the sink, he cannae be doin' with that wee wash-hand basin.'

'I meant the bath.'

'Friday night, the same water does the lot of them.'

'You don't look very happy, don't you like it here?'

She shrugged and walked into the kitchenette, Agnes followed. Her mother began filling the kettle and spoke through the rush of water. 'To tell you the truth I miss Spinner's Lane and so does your da. We miss the folk.'

'But you didn't even like them, you were always at loggerheads.'

'Mebbe we were but we understood each other and a good yelling match cleared the air.' She lit the gas and put the kettle on the ring then jerked her thumb upwards. 'That one up there had the nerve to say that this was a respectable district and sitting on the front step was common.'

'She didn't!'

'She did that and a bit more. Seems my bairns are out of control and more or less suggested that Ruby should be kept indoors.'

'What a cheek, what an absolute bloody cheek,' Agnes stormed. 'I hope you—'

'Don't worry she got a lot more than she bargained for and if anyone leaves here it'll be her I'm thinkin',' she said with a satisfied nod of her head. 'Meg'll be in any minute, I'll infuse the tea and you take a look round.'

Agnes went out to the narrow lobby and opened the first door. Again it was Spinner's Lane brought to Brady Street but the beds were made, the room quite tidy. The curtains like the others were well above the sill. The girls' room had an extra single mattress on the floor and this Agnes surmised would be where Ruby slept.

The outside door opened. 'It's me, Ma.'

'Tea's infused and see what the cat's brought in.'

'By that I suppose she means me,' Agnes said, following her sister to where she was emptying the bag of groceries.

Meg smiled her welcome. 'Thought we would have seen you last week.'

'Couldn't manage. You look great, positively blooming,' Agnes said and it was true. The loose coat covered her expanding waistline and there was a healthy look about her skin and a shine to her hair. Best of all she looked happy.

'Feel good now,' she smiled. 'Ma, better check that I've remembered everythin'.'

'Miracle if you have but let's get them away before that lot gets in from school.'

'Bit further for them to go,' Agnes said as she opened the cupboards and Meg put the groceries away.

'The bread is still hot, Ma, I'll leave it out.'

'Put it on the table.'

'No, I'll leave it here, make less crumbs when you come to cut it.'

Jenny Boyd, with a thunderous expression on her face, marched forward, grabbed the bread and banged it down on the table.

Agnes raised her eyes and Meg whispered. 'She's been like this since we came here, just wants to carry on the way she used to.'

'Better leave her, she'll come round in her own time,' Agnes said. She thought she could understand something of her mother's frustration. Those know-alls on the council should have had the good sense to keep the Spinner's Lane folk together instead of scattering them about Dundee.

'What are you two whisperin' about?'

'Nothin', Ma, and are we gettin' that tea before it's stewed?'

'It's poured and I'm puttin' jam on three pancakes.'

They sat down together at the table and ate in silence for a few moments.

'Well, tell her the news,' Mrs Boyd said impatiently.

'I'm just about to.' Meg swallowed the last of the pancake. 'Me and Sam are gettin' wed. Just the Registry Office of course,' she said, patting her stomach. 'We need two witnesses. Sam is askin' his cousin, John, and I want you.'

'Should think so too, I'd be furious if you hadn't asked me. When is it?'

'Tuesday, the twenty-fourth.'

Agnes's face fell. Oh, God, it had to be that day. 'I can't, Meg, any day but that day.'

'Tell them I'm gettin' married and you'll get off.'

'It isn't as easy as that,' Agnes said wretchedly.

'Me gettin' married isn't important enough, is that it?'

'Of course it isn't and I'd give anything to be there.'

'Then what's stoppin' you?'

'I'm askin' it too, what's stoppin' you?' Jenny Boyd added.

'I have an interview for a job that day.'

'Explain and say you'll attend another time.'

'There won't be another time.'

'Plenty of other jobs you can apply for later.'

'Not like this one, Meg,' Agnes said quietly.

'What's so special about this one and where is it?' Meg was looking hurt and angry and her mother grim.

'It's special, Meg, Ma,' Agnes said desperately, 'because it is the kind of job I've been looking for. It's in Kirriemuir, a mile or two out actually, but I get my expenses and it's all arranged.' She ignored her mother and looked pleadingly at Meg.

'Is it your day off?'

'No, I've got Molly to change. Honestly, Meg, if it were possible—' she broke off at the look on Meg's face and felt a spurt of anger. 'And just for the record, Meg, I doubt if there would be a wedding at all if it hadn't been for me. Give that some thought, will you?'

Meg crossed to the window and spoke with her back turned. 'It's something I hadn't forgotten, never will and it's all right, you go for your interview and I'll get another witness.'

'I'll come and haul your da with me.'

'No, Ma, that would mean askin' Sam's mother and her gettin' someone to look after the shop.' She turned back from the window and smiled. 'I'll get someone no trouble and as Agnes says there might not have been a weddin' and another bairn about your feet.'

'I wouldn't have minded that, you would have been company for me.'

Meg put her arms round her mother. 'Give this place a chance, Ma, everybody isn't like that besom upstairs and it could be that the other folk hereabout are waitin' for you to make the first move.'

'Wait a long time then, won't they?' She broke off and rushed to the window. 'Oh, God, here they come, and Bobby's been fighin' again by the look of him. Give me strength, I'll murder him.'

Bobby was first in, his brother just behind. Bobby had a black eye and an ugly bruise on one cheek and his mother gave him a sharp slap on the other.

'What was that for?' he yelled but backed away in case it was to be followed by another.

'Fine you know what for. I told you what you would get if there was any more fightin'.'

'That's not fair, Ma,' Eddie came to the defence of his brother. 'He was only sticking up for our Ruby.'

'What's this about Ruby?'

'Jimmy Cochrane said I had a daft sister.'

Jenny Boyd bridled. 'Don't tell me you let him get away with that?'

''Course I didn't. Told him she wasn't half as daft as his sister and that his da is a wee shrimp and my da would make mincemeat of him.'

Agnes and Meg were laughing helplessly and Bobby preened himself.

'He would have got a lot more than he did if old Matthews hadn't seen us.'

'The headmaster.' Mrs Boyd closed her eyes. 'What did he have to say?'

'We've to report to him in the mornin' for a beltin'.'

'You tell him what Jimmy Cochrane said about your sister.'

'No, Ma, that's like tellin' tales.'

'You big softie, he'll blame you.'

'No, he won't, we're pals most of the time.'

There was a further commotion as Peter, closely followed by the twins, Daisy and Rose, came in. Peter demanded a piece an' jam, and totally ignored Agnes. The twins were growing, she thought, both had long thin legs and though not identical there was a strong resemblance.

'What are you doin' here?' Daisy demanded.

'You don't live here any more,' Rose added.

'Thanks for the welcome, I came to see how you liked your new house.'

'We like it,' Rose said timidly.

'You do, I don't,' Daisy said firmly, 'Spinner's Lane was better.' She turned to her mother. 'Nobody likes us here, do they, Ma?'

'If you behaved yourselves they might.'

'When does Da get in?' Agnes asked.

'Your guess is as good as mine. Said he'd likely be workin' late and took a piece with him.'

'Can't wait very long.' Agnes was ashamed at how much she wanted to get away. She no longer felt part of the family and suspected that she wasn't greatly missed by any of them except perhaps by Meg.

'I'll come a bit of the way with you,' Meg said picking up her coat.

'No further than the tram stop,' her mother warned, 'you've done enough walkin' for one day.'

'I'll go then, Ma, tell Da I was asking for him.'

'When are we likely to see you again?'

'Not sure.'

'You'll not hurry yoursel' that's for sure.'

Outside there was a coolish breeze and it was very welcome. Meg linked her arm in Agnes's.

'How can you stand it, Meg?'

'After Kerne House you mean? Thought I'd go mad but you just get used to it again.'

Agnes smiled. 'Easier when you know it won't be for long.'

She nodded. 'Silly I know, but I worry in case somethin' goes wrong.'

'What could possibly go wrong?'

'That's what I don't know.'

'You'll get married to your Sam and make a good life for yourself.'

'I'll work at it. I'm determined we won't end up like Ma and Da.'

'You won't.'

'I don't think so either. I'm very lucky, Agnes, Sam is good and considerate and his ma couldn't be nicer. She's happy too about us stayin' with her until we get our own house.'

'Knowing you you'll be helping in the shop.'

'Because I want to, Agnes. She'll be a lot easier to get on with than Ma and there's been no sly remarks about me expectin' before the ring is on my finger.'

'His blame as much as yours I would say.'

'You're clever in some ways, Agnes, but you don't know everything. It's always the girl's fault. Lads can't control themselves but girls are supposed to.' She paused. 'What is so special about this job?'

'Probably nothing but I have a feeling I'm meant to get it. It's difficult to explain but believe me it had to be something very important when I put it before your wedding.'

'Don't worry about that. I would have liked you there but I do understand and I hope you get it and it proves to be all you wish.'

Agnes looked at her sister in surprise. 'Thanks, Meg, that means a lot to me.'

'Is it a bigger place than Kerne House?'

'Much bigger, it's an estate, a country estate.'

'Sounds posh. Fancy your chances there?'

'Stranger things have happened. Why shouldn't I fancy my chances?'

'No reason at all. You've got brains and you're not bad-lookin'.' She sounded worried. 'I always feel closer to you than the rest and I wouldn't like to think of you gettin' hurt.'

'In what way would I get hurt?'

'Aimin' too high.'

'Further to fall you mean?'

'I'm not sure what I mean,' Meg said slowly, 'only that happiness is bein' with someone you love even if it is a struggle to make ends meet.'

'You're wrong there, Meg. When poverty strikes love flies out the window.'

'You're sayin' that because our two are always at each other's throat.'

'Perhaps I am.'

'Stayed together though.'

'Out of habit or laziness.'

'No, Agnes, deep down they care about each other but have forgotten how to show it.'

'You'll better get back now.' They stopped and looked at one another. The Boyds were not given to an outward show of affection but the sisters were hugging each other.

'You know that I wish you and Sam all the happiness and luck in the world and when I save up some money I'll get you a decent gift.'

'Thanks, Agnes, and no hurry for the gift. Time enough when we get our own place.' She paused and brushed a tear away. 'I hope one day that you'll be as happy as I am.'

'Ma will blame me if you don't get back now.'

'In a minute. I didn't want to ask in front of her but do you ever hear anything about Rachel Donaldson?'

'No, and I can't understand it.'

'Mebbe wanted to make a clean break.'

'Looks that way but somehow I think she'll get in touch with me.'

# Chapter Nineteen

Rachel was watching the breakfast tray being prepared in the kitchen. The tray itself was of polished wood with a brass handle either end and on it Mrs Morton placed a snowy white embroidered tray cloth taking care that all the wood was hidden. Then she brought over cup, saucer and plate in delicate china followed by matching sugar bowl and cream jug.

'Rachel, lass,' Mrs Morton pointed to a large dish of prunes, 'choose four and put them in the wee plate.'

Very carefully, Rachel selected four fat, juicy prunes and using a big spoon added a little of the dark brown liquid.

'Will that do, Mrs Morton?'

'Lovely.' She put it on the tray. The toast browned to perfection was already cut into fingers, the butter into curls and there was a tiny amount of marmalade in a dish. A rolled-up napkin was secured in a silver holder and placed beside the cutlery.

'That the lot?'

'Dear me, no,' she said pouring boiling water into the silver teapot and picking up the tea strainer, set both in the centre of the tray. 'That way it'll help to keep it balanced. Don't want to spill, do you?'

Rachel tried lifting it. 'Goodness, it's heavy!'

'Surprising what the tray itself weighs but don't you worry you'll soon get used to it,' she said as she sat down to give her swollen legs a much needed rest.

Rachel was suddenly unsure as to how she would cope then ridiculed herself. Heavens! she was only carrying a tray to her grandmother's bedroom.

'Be as quick as you can, she doesn't like her toast cold. Janet would tell you the quick way to get there?'

'No, she didn't.'

'Must have forgotten. Difficult to explain, just muddle you. Just go the way you know but hurry.'

Inwardly fuming at Janet and not so sure that it had been a slip of memory, Rachel set off. More likely to be deliberate. Janet was proud to be the one to look after the mistress and sharing duties wouldn't be at all to her liking.

The tray was heavier by the minute, her arms were beginning to ache not so much from the weight but from trying to keep the tray steady. At last she reached the thickly carpeted stairs leading to the room she knew to be her grandmother's. Breathless she put down the tray and knocked at the door.

'Come in.'

Rachel turned the knob of the door then bending down picked up the tray, heard china knocking against china and pushed her way in.

'Close that door, there's a draught.' The voice was sharp and irritable.

'Sorry, m'am.'

She pressed it with her back until it clicked shut. Janet had told her to put the tray on the table at the window until Mrs Craig decided if she wanted her breakfast in bed or at the table. She put it down. Daylight was filtering into the room and Rachel went to draw back the curtains. It was a lovely morning and sunshine flooded the room.

'Half close them.'

Rachel did so. 'Good morning, m'am,' she said quietly, 'do you wish your breakfast in bed?'

'You're late.'

'I'm sorry, I came as quickly as I could.'

'Not good enough, need to smarten up. Janet has no difficulty getting here at the proper time.'

'No, m'am.'

Rachel felt a rush of compassion, she looked so old and frail and lost in the big bed. Going over she adjusted one of the pillows that had slipped. 'If you would raise yourself a little, m'am, I could make you more comfortable.' Putting her arm round the thin shoulders she kept it there until she had all three pillows in position.

'Thank you, but it was wasted effort since I intend getting up for my breakfast. Fetch my bed-jacket, no leave it, I'll have my dressing-gown.'

Rachel expected it to be on the chair nearest the bed in case the old lady required to get up during the night.

'On the back of the door, are you blind?'

Rachel swallowed her resentment and went over for the warm pink, fluffy dressing-gown. By now Mrs Craig had manoeuvred herself to the edge of the bed and Rachel bent down to put slippers on her feet. She helped her on with the dressing-gown.

'Tie the belt, my hands are useless at this time of the morning.'

She did as requested and the old lady sat down at the table.

'You should have had this set.'

'I haven't had time.' Quickly she spread the cloth over and from the tray collected the prunes and a spoon.

'A napkin if you please.'

'Sorry.' Rachel took it out of its holder, shook out the folds and placed it across her knees. While removing the dessert plate Rachel had noticed milk spilt on the tray cloth but that was a minor disaster. What horrified her was the sight of the soggy toast. If only she'd had the sense to turn the spout of the teapot the other way it wouldn't have happened.

'Do you think I could perhaps have a cup of tea?'

Swallowing nervously, Rachel went to remove the dessert plate. Four stones remained and she breathed a sigh of relief, at least she had something in her stomach. With a shaking hand she poured the tea then groaned when she remembered the milk.

'Do you take milk, m'am?'

'A little which I prefer in first but since it is too late for that you may add some.'

Rachel put the cup down in front of her and gave a silent prayer of thanks that none had gone in the saucer. She took a deep breath. It had always been her way to confess to failures rather than wait to have them pointed out.

'Mrs Craig, m'am, I'm very, very sorry but I'm afraid the toast is soggy, the tea must have – must have spilt when I was carrying the tray. I'll go back to the kitchen and make fresh.' She lowered her eyes waiting for the storm and when it didn't come she risked looking up.

Her grandmother was smiling, then chortling. 'You know, girl – what is your name?'

'Rachel.'

'You know, Rachel, I thought I'd like a change from Janet's super efficiency and I think you'll agree I'm getting it.'

Rachel dimpled. 'From one extreme to the other but I do assure you, m'am, that I am not usually so clumsy.'

'I should hope not or you wouldn't last long.'

'May I see to the fire?'

'Yes.' The old eyes were twinkling, 'better remove that toast to the fire and you can tell Mrs Morton that everything was satisfactory.'

'That is very good of you, m'am.'

There was a knock. 'Answer that, it'll be the morning papers.'

They had been left at the door and Rachel brought them in.

Mrs Craig had removed her own dressing-gown to reveal a flannelette nightdress with a trimming of lace at the neckline. Without bothering to ask, strong young arms clumsy with a tray were gentle as she assisted the frail old lady into bed. She helped her on with her bed-jacket and adjusted the pillows.

'Is that comfortable, m'am?'

'Yes, thank you, you would have made a good nurse.'

'It was a teacher I wanted to be.'

'Indeed! That's a far cry from a maid.'

Rachel smiled. 'Circumstances, m'am. May I remove the tray?'

'You may but I'll have the newspapers first and my spectacles.'

Rachel did as requested. She then threw the toast into the fire and collected the dishes together. Once all was tidied she made for the door.

'Either this print is getting smaller or my eyes weaker,' Mrs Craig said peevishly, then looked at Rachel. 'Get rid of that tray then come back.'

'Yes, m'am.'

Why had she to go back? Rachel pondered on that on her way to the kitchen.

'You've been a while.'

'I know, Mrs Morton, Mrs Craig required assistance to get back into bed and I had the fire to see to.'

'I'm not complainin',' Cook said as she uncovered the tray. 'My! My! the old dear must have been hungry, she's finished the toast.' Then she frowned. 'Dry toast, no butter or marmalade, mebbe the poor soul's stomach isn't right.'

Rachel started a giggle which she quickly managed to change into a cough. 'I've to go back.'

'What for?'

'Don't know. Will you tell Mrs Anderson if she comes looking for me?'

'I'll do that and hadn't you better get a move on, patience isn't your employer's strong point.'

Rachel almost ran across the hall but had to stop.

'Where do you think you're going?' It was Janet at her haughtiest.

'Mrs Craig wants me.'

'What for?'

'I don't know.

'Or aren't saying. How did you manage?'

'Not very well you'll be pleased to learn.'

Janet's eyes narrowed. 'What's that supposed to mean?'

'You didn't bother to tell me—'

'The shorter way – you could have worked that out for yourself, you've been here long enough.' She smirked as she walked away.

Part of the newspaper had been marked with a pencil.

'Bring over a chair for yourself and push the table back. That's it.'

Rachel sat down.

'Reading aloud should hold no problems for you since it was a teacher you wanted to be.'

'No problems at all,' Rachel smiled.

'Straining my eyes with the small print gives me a headache.'

Rachel missed reading the newspaper. There was usually one in the kitchen but Mrs Morton, though she didn't pay for it, considered it her property and woe betide anyone who dared remove it before she was finished reading it and she was a slow reader.

The room Rachel was in was large with a high ceiling. It had to be large to take the four-poster bed, a double wardrobe, a dressing-table, two small tables and a number of chairs. The dressing-table had a glass top and on it were a hand mirror, a brush and comb set and crystal ornaments that sparkled.

She was enjoying this, it wasn't work it was a pleasure. Occasionally her grandmother would make a remark berating some political figure for shortsightedness or more often plain stupidity.

'That'll do, girl.' She saw Rachel frown as she folded the paper and put it down. 'I'm sorry, Rachel, isn't it? I can see by your face that you object to being called girl.' She gave one of her chortles. 'If the years would roll away I wouldn't mind being addressed as girl.'

Rachel smiled as she took back her chair and thought that her grandmother was really rather nice once you got to understand her.

'You have a lovely clear voice and now if you don't mind an old lady's curiosity, what happened that you didn't take up teaching?'

'Lack of money. There would have been enough to see me through if my father hadn't remarried.'

'An extravagant stepmother?'

'Yes,' Rachel said shortly.

'Would you read to me when required?'

'I would be happy to, m'am.'

Her eyes were closing, she was beginning to nod and Rachel moved away.

'Thank you, my dear,' the words were little more than a murmur and Rachel wondered if she'd imagined them.

Had the time come to reveal her true identity? And if she did what kind of shock would it be for her grandmother?

'Leave those letters, Mrs Anderson, and I'll sort them.'

'Thank you, Miss Betsy,' the housekeeper said handing them over. Letters for the family went on a silver tray and those for the staff were distributed by Mrs Anderson.

'I'll leave those for the staff on the table and you can see to them later.'

Betsy was bored, glad even of this small task. The only pastime that gave her pleasure was playing the piano and that didn't give her the satisfaction it used to. Once her dreams had been of becoming a concert pianist but her teacher, though loud in his praise for his talented pupil, quickly brought her down to earth. Only a very, very few attained those heights and she was not in that class. Teaching music she might have settled for, but her mother hadn't wished such a lowly occupation for her daughter. Marriage to Dr Peter McGregor was what she had in mind.

She flicked through the bundle hoping there might be a letter from Joanna. Perhaps she should have gone to that school in Switzerland but she had expected it to be a disciplined life and she'd had enough of that. Joanna had written to tell her of the marvellous time she was having and hardly any discipline. Lucky Joanna.

Turning her attention back to the letters Betsy began to study them. Three for her grandmother, one of them highly scented. One for her mother. So far none for her. One, two, three, four for her stepfather. Her lips curled. More debts which her mother would feel obliged to meet. Why didn't she divorce him? Come to that why had she married him in the first place? All that charm, of course, that would have done it and he wasn't bad-looking. Pity her mother wasn't a strong character like her grandmother. Betsy smiled. She made it all too plain what she thought of her son-in-law but even so she was careful. If she threw him out of Duncairn House she couldn't be sure that his wife wouldn't go with him. Betsy shuddered. If that happened she might be dragged away too.

If only Peter were a bit more ardent. He was always charming and had partnered her on many an occasion but it only ended with a peck on the cheek. Her mother had pointed out that this was quite proper since she was a lot younger and he wouldn't want to rush things.

She gave a deep sigh. Oh, well, she'd have to do something about it herself – but what? She could hardly throw herself at him. She gave her attention back to the letters. That seemed to be all the letters for the family. The one for Mrs Morton made her smile, what atrocious writing, pity the poor postman or whoever sorted them. The letter under it, and she'd almost missed it, made her go pale. A local postmark and addressed to Miss Rachel Donaldson. Staring at it and willing it not to be what she suspected, Betsy kept looking at the writing. No two people could have that distinctive scrawl. It was Peter's writing but what would he be doing writing to a maid. Surely sensible Peter wouldn't be foolish enough to get involved with a girl of that class. Jealousy such as she had never experienced gripped her and the humiliation was almost more than she could bear. She wanted to scratch that girl's eyes out.

Bad enough that he had given her a lift from the village – or was that all it had been? Betsy had a desperate need to know, she had to know what was in that letter. What she was contemplating was dreadful, it was wicked, but she couldn't help herself. She wouldn't know a moment's peace until she knew for certain what Peter had written. Checking to make sure that no one saw her Betsy put the letter in the deep pocket of her skirt. Not a moment too soon either, here was her mother with the usual worried expression on her face.

'Any letters for me, dear?'

'Just one.'

She took it and examined the small, neat writing. 'I don't recognise the writing, I wonder whom it is from?'

'Open it and you'll find out,' Betsy said rudely.

'No, I'll wait and I'll take those for your grandmother.'

'What about his? Four, probably bills, do you want them?'

'I do not. Leave them and where are you off to?' she asked as Betsy tried to make her escape.

'Change out of this old skirt and spend a while at the piano.'

'That would be nice, dear, we miss hearing you play and it would be a pity to lose your touch. You know, Betsy, I'm far from convinced that being a concert pianist is beyond you.'

'Mother,' Betsy said wearily, 'we have been through all this before. I am not good enough. Like Brian with his painting we both lack that extra something and if we can accept that, isn't it time you did too?'

Maud smiled a little sadly. 'Perhaps you're right, dear, I won't mention the matter again.'

Some hope, thought Betsy as she hurried away. Once inside her bedroom she stood with her back against the door. Was it worth making a thief of herself for that's what it was? It was a struggle but one she wasn't going to win.

It was a young girl's room and after the austere school dormitories it had been her pride and joy. Allowed to make her own choice she had selected a pink bedcover with fringes, pink-and-white-striped wallpaper and white had been her choice of carpeting. She'd lost out there though and the carpet was pale grey. At fifteen she had loved it, at eighteen she hated it.

She fingered the envelope, bending the corners, putting off the moment, then tore it open. Two pages she drew out, one headed with Peter's home address. Her eyes blurred as she began to read: 'My dear Rachel,—'

Not a love letter just a sincere wish that they should meet again. Her hand clenched, her fingers screwed up the paper and she hurled it across the room. They had been together, had visited Dunkeld together, had had tea together, there was mention of a tearoom. How dare he? If he'd wanted company she was available but instead he had invited that maid. Throwing herself on the bed Betsy sobbed as though her heart would break. After a while she sat up and dried her tears. She had just had a thought that she could accept. Servant girls were easy, look at Janet and her stepfather. Not that Peter was a bit like him but all men had needs she had heard it whispered and the girl was nice-looking no use denying that. Yes, she could forgive Peter but it must not be allowed to continue, it would have to be nipped in the bud.

Getting no reply to his letter, Peter would begin to wonder. The post office wasn't guilty of losing letters but it couldn't be ruled out and Peter would no doubt give Rachel the benefit of the doubt. He would maybe write again so she would have to be on the look-out for the postman. Another thought struck her, she could use her stepfather. The fool thought himself the answer to a maiden's prayer and if she could just drop a hint to him that he had an admirer in the dark-haired maid then perhaps—

Feeling more like herself again. Betsy picked up the letter, smoothed out the pages and returned them in the envelope to her pocket. Burning it was the answer but there was only a fire in the drawing-room and sitting-room and there was a risk attached, admittedly small, but she wasn't willing to take it. Before flames devoured it someone might have come in and asked questions she didn't want to answer.

Putting a cardigan on, Betsy left the house, glad that the weather was warmish and dry. The leaves were well trodden into the path giving it a patterned appearance. Onwards through the gardens she went to where the burn, higher than usual after more than average rainfall, gurgled merrily. The wind, playfully boisterous, whipped at her skirt as she tore up the letter and envelope. She held her hand in the water fearful of some pieces escaping to land near the house. Opening her fingers she let the paper free and watched the tiny paper boats being swept away and out of sight. Only then did she dry her hands on her skirt and return to the house.

Working in the sewing-room Rachel could afford to let her mind wander to the family at Duncairn House. Her grandmother was a proud and difficult woman, a demanding one too but there was a kindliness that showed itself in different ways. The toast, the soggy toast was one example. Vague Aunt Maud she already liked but Betsy was the problem. Her cousin disliked her, made no secret of it, and Rachel was at a loss to understand. Certainly there had been the incident in the attic when Betsy had accused her of snooping around but nothing further had been said and Rachel had dismissed it from her mind. More than likely it was to do with Peter. Seeing a servant girl getting out of his car she must have wondered. Perhaps Betsy was in love with Peter, perhaps there was an understanding between them and Peter had merely been amusing himself. A spare afternoon, and she had been on hand. Rachel's face burned at the thought.

Work, what was needed was plenty of that to keep her from thinking of Dr Peter McGregor. Fortunately there was enough to keep her fingers busy. The linen was in good order and Rachel had expected her sessions in the sewing-room to be cut instead of which other work of another nature began to come her way. Shorter skirts had become the fashion and Mrs Anderson, moving with the times, made use of Rachel's expertise. Seeing an opportunity to improve her own lot, Rachel had requested curtains for the window and a fire in the room. The former she got without difficulty but a fire was not permitted until the last day of October though the temperature could have dropped before that.

How her Aunt Maud came to hear about her dressmaking skills Rachel never did find out but skirts and dresses requiring to be shortened or in need of minor repair such as the tightening of buttons, began to arrive. She was doing fewer and fewer household tasks.

Earlier on, Mrs Anderson had tried to be tactful. 'Do you mind, Rachel, if Janet goes back to being in charge of Mrs Craig's breakfast tray?'

'Not in the least, Mrs Anderson, in fact I'd be delighted.'

'Needs quick feet and a steady hand and we can't all be good at the same things.'

'Very true.'

Nights were the worst. Rachel tossed and turned unable to get to sleep and sometimes it was well into the small hours before she got over. Stupidly she had allowed herself to dream impossible dreams while Peter was no doubt regretting his impulsiveness, if not, surely he would have made some attempt to get in touch with her. All the time she had been at Duncairn House she had never had a letter. Only one person could have written and that was Agnes and she hadn't.

At times she was so unhappy that she thought seriously of applying for other jobs and leaving Duncairn House, yet she couldn't bear the thought of leaving it either. She had come to love the old house and this quiet part of Perthshire. Then there was the bond with her grandmother, it was getting stronger. With each passing week she wished for the courage to tell her grandmother that she was Amelia's daughter but something always held her back.

The waiting-room was empty, Dr Peter McGregor had seen the last patient off the premises himself then gone back to sit behind his desk. Some paperwork needed to be done and he saw to it then he put down his pen and sat looking at the blank wall. His thoughts were of Rachel. As a doctor he knew all about hope. One had it and one kept going, his had died slowly as October gave way to November and still no reply to his letters. One could have gone astray but not two. Peter was hurt, surprised, angry and unexpectedly depressed. At twenty-eight years of age he had had a few girlfriends, been quite keen on one or two, but when the romance ended he'd felt no real regret, no sense of loss.

Rachel had seemed to him to be so different. He had enjoyed talking to her and happy that there had been no need for non-stop chatter. The silences were comfortable, two people completely at ease with one another or so he had thought. He was wrong, he must be. The attraction had been all on his side or she would have replied to his letters. Twice at Dr Smart's request, he had visited Duncairn House to see Mrs Craig but though he'd lingered, there had been no sign of Rachel. No sign of Betsy either and he'd been glad of that. Just lately he'd got the impression that she was becoming possessive expecting him to escort her to this, that and the other. Being friendly with the family made it difficult to refuse but that was what he was going to do. Brian Meldrum would be more than happy to oblige, it was easy to see where his heart lay.

That other maid, Janet, had come to the door with him and he could have asked about Rachel, but he hesitated and the moment was lost.

Reading helped but it didn't throw off her depression and reading aloud to her grandmother was very much part of her daily routine. They had moved on from newspapers.

'Perhaps you could read a chapter or two of a book, Rachel, there isn't a great deal of interest in the papers these days.'

Rachel was touched. 'Of course, m'am, I'd be delighted.'

'You will have been into the library?'

'No, I haven't.'

'My husband used to collect books and I read them. He didn't have a great deal of time to do so himself but expected to do a lot of reading in later life. Sadly it was not to be.' She frowned as if she had said more than she intended. 'What I wanted to say was that you have my permission to choose a book for your own pleasure. I've watched you handle them and feel sure I can trust you to be careful.'

'That is very kind of you, m'am, and you have my word that I would take the greatest care.'

'Less of your time will be spent in the sewing room since the linen is now in good repair.'

'Not really, I'm there quite a lot.'

'Doing what?'

Rachel hoped she wasn't getting anybody into trouble. 'With the change in fashion I am getting a lot of skirts and dresses to shorten.'

'Is there a change? I hadn't noticed.' She smiled. 'Once upon a time I took a great interest in clothes but at my age one puts comfort first.'

She closed her eyes, an indication that she was tired talking and wished to be alone. Rachel left quietly.

Another day and she was with her grandmother. Outside a thin, grey November mist shrouded the countryside but there was a roaring fire in the bedroom. The old lady sat up very straight in her high-winged chair, her slippered feet on a pouffe.

'I've had enough of the papers today and all that talk of poverty. One gets heartily sick of it. Folk would be able to manage if they used a little common sense.'

'They would if they got enough to cover their basic needs.'

'Nonsense, that kind take things on credit without thought as to how they are going to keep up the payments. If they would just realise that they are paying a lot more for goods which I believe in many cases are repossessed if the payments fall behind. Save up then buy is what they should be taught.'

Rachel hadn't expected her grandmother to know about hire-purchase but she was going to put her right on a few things.

'M'am, those people you speak of are well aware that they are paying about half again for the goods but that is better than not having the basic essentials for living such as a bed, table and chairs.'

'Don't enter into marriage until you have something behind you.'

Rachel wanted to laugh. 'Precious few would get married if that were the case and don't lump them together. Many do manage to keep up payments, they budget for it and once the debt is nearly cleared they buy another article of furniture or clothes for the family.'

'And never get out of the bit,' came the sharp reply.

'They don't see it that way and incidentally that is why it is called the never-never.'

'Well named, I would say. Surely you don't approve of it?'

'My father saved before he bought but then he was in the fortunate position of being in a reasonably well-paid job.'

'Exactly, he was working not like those others just looking for handouts.'

Rachel was getting angrier by the minute but her grandmother hadn't finished. 'In this day and age all children receive an education to the age of fourteen and all but the most stupid should be able to read, write and count.'

'And all that is available for the majority of them are poorly paid jobs with no prospects. Indeed, m'am, many at sixteen find themselves unemployed through no fault of their own, merely that the job can be done more cheaply by a fourteen-year-old.'

'Go on.'

Rachel wasn't sure if it was sarcasm or not. She hesitated then decided as she'd gone this far she might as well continue. 'Walking the streets looking for a job with boots lined with newspaper or cardboard because they are beyond being repaired then returning to a cold house with no money to buy coal, not enough to eat and knowing that the next day and the next again will likely be the same,' she paused to take a breath, 'twenty or more after the same job, what chance, m'am, what chance have they?'

'You seem to be very knowledgeable on the subject,' her grandmother said tartly, 'yet I don't imagine you've known want.'

'No, it's true I haven't, but I've seen at first hand what poverty and hopelessness can do to people. My father has been reduced to tears by men coming to him pleading for work, prepared to do anything, and having to turn them away. Seeing in their faces the bitterness, the hopelessness, the guilt that goes with being unable to provide for a wife and family.'

'Where does your father work?'

'In the jute mill.'

'Yes,' she nodded her white head, 'times are difficult in the jute trade, I do know about that, my family has suffered too.'

Rachel felt like screaming that she knew nothing about it. How could she, brought up in luxury, wanting for nothing? The plight of those people was beyond her understanding. Rachel bit back the words waiting to be said, she had probably said too much already. Leaning over she picked up a leather-bound copy of *Jane Eyre* and opened it at the place.

'M'am, would you like me to begin reading?'

'If you've come down from that soap box.'

'I'm sorry, I shouldn't have said all that.'

She inclined her head as if to agree. 'Don't let that fire go down,' she said irritably, 'and get me my shawl, there is quite a drop in temperature.'

Rachel rose to see to the fire. It was stifling in the room but she added a few more lumps of coal then went for the shawl and draped it over the narrow shoulders. Already she was regretting her earlier impatience, a woman of her grandmother's age would have set ideas and newspaper accounts could be very misleading. The one way to understand real poverty and wretchedness was to experience it.

As Rachel began to read, the beautiful words soothed her. The story, familiar though it was, never failed to move her and she saw the glint of tears in the faded eyes. After two chapters Rachel closed the book.

'Thank you, I'll rest now.' Her head went back, her eyes closed and Rachel went quietly closing the door behind her. Hoping for a cup of tea she ran down the stairs, across the hall and through to the kitchen. She was thinking of nothing in particular when the name Kerne House was released from her memory. For long she had racked her brains trying to remember the name of the house where Agnes was employed. This very evening she would write to Agnes at Kerne House and if that brought no reply then she would just have to accept it that Agnes had no desire to keep up the friendship.

Mrs Morton produced a welcome cup of tea.

'Thanks, Mrs Morton, you've saved a life, I needed that.'

'Are you all right, lass, you've been lookin' a bit peeky this while back?'

'I'm fine, touch of the cold that's all.'

Mrs Morton nodded but she wasn't satisfied. The lass didn't have a cold but something was making her unhappy.

Hetty, too, was concerned about Rachel and voiced it to the cook.

'What is the matter with her, Mrs Morton. I've asked but she just says nothin' is the matter?'

'Noticed it mysel'. Lost all her sparkle, mebbe it's a lad and she's had a disappointment.'

'Can't be that. She's never been out with a lad or I would have known.'

'Mebbe it is something she doesn't want to talk about.'

Hetty nodded. 'Never mentions her home and that's strange, isn't it?

All she's ever said is that she belongs to Dundee.'

Mrs Morton pursed her lips. 'I'd say there is something far wrong when a lass doesn't mention her home.'

'No letters, she never gets any.'

'A mystery, Hetty, but it's none of our business.'

Hetty wasn't ready to go yet and Mrs Morton was in a chatty mood.

'Janet and Rachel hardly speak.'

'Nothin' more than jealousy on Janet's part.'

'Jealous of Rachel's appearance you mean? But Janet is good-lookin' hersel'.'

'Not in the same class, Hetty, and that to my mind is where the mystery comes in.'

Hetty was slightly offended. 'You think she's above us?'

'I think you'd better get those hands workin' and get those brasses shining.'

'Bloomin' awful brasses,' Hetty grumbled. 'I'm tellin' you this, Mrs Morton, when *I* get married there won't be a blinkin' piece of brass in my house or for that matter anything that needs polishin'.'

'Away with you and let me get on.'

'I'm just goin',' Hetty said heaving her body up and collecting the Brasso tin, a dirty rag and some clean dusters. 'What a life!'

Two hours off in the afternoon was a waste. A little longer and she could have taken the bus into Perth and done some window-shopping. The weather was mild for the beginning of December and Rachel decided on a stroll in the gardens to get some fresh air into her lungs. With it being so mild Brian Meldrum might be there. He called the scenery an artist's paradise and could well be busy painting. If he was around she would have a chat with him.

She liked Brian, liked his open friendliness and disarming smile. Absolutely no side with him, he spoke to everyone and being of the same generation he and Rachel found much to talk about. It was nothing more than friendship they shared and because of it there was no awkwardness. He told her a lot about Duncairn House knowing his disclosures would go no further.

'The old lady's been marvellous to me,' he'd said on one occasion, 'encourages me with my painting even to giving me a room—'

'Your own studio,' Rachel smiled.

'As good as. It has plenty of light and room for all my paraphernalia.' His face hardened. 'Or rubbish as my father would call it. Not likely to make my fortune and I accept that, but I know I'm reasonably good. Get better too if I get the chance to work at it.'

'What I've seen of your work I'd say you were very good.'

'Sweet of you, Rachel, but I know my limitations. Betsy is a very good pianist, did you know that? and we console each other that we just fail to be in the genius class.' He laughed but without mirth. 'A job in the City is what my father wants for me and for the present I am going along with it.'

'Then you'll please yourself?'

'When I'm twenty-one I'll make my own decisions and that won't be long. It's when I come into a little money from my mother. Enough to keep the wolf from the door until I make up my mind what to do with my life. The rest comes to me when I'm twenty-five.' He paused. 'I lost my mother when I was twelve and I didn't think I would ever get over it.'

'I can understand, Brian. I lost my mother when I was nine.'

'Did your father remarry?'

'Yes, my stepmother was the reason I left home.'

'Tough. My stepmother is very good to me and Betsy. I don't have a chance there, Betsy only has eyes for that doctor chap. Nice bloke but I could see him far enough at times.'

There was no sign of Brian today and Rachel decided to turn back. Suddenly and without warning it got colder, the daylight seemed to vanish and the grey bleakness of December take its place. What had seemed friendly countryside had taken on a menacing look and a rustle in the bushes made her start. An animal, nothing to be afraid of, then out of the greyness loomed a figure and she saw that it was a smiling Henry Meldrum. Her stomach muscles tensed.

'What a pleasant surprise, my dear, but I didn't mean to startle you.'

'It's all right but if you'll excuse me I'm in a hurry. Please let me through.'

'Oh, Rachel, my dear girl, I don't think you are in all that much of a hurry.' He gave her a knowing little smile. 'You see, a little bird whispered to me that my advances would not be unwelcome.'

# Chapter Twenty

It was Tuesday the twenty-fourth and Agnes who prided herself on never getting into a state was a bundle of nerves from the moment she put her bare feet to the cold linoleum floor and padded over to the window. Holding back the curtains she checked on the weather. There were puddles on the uneven ground after the heavy overnight rain but the clouds were breaking up with the promise of a good day. A good day for Meg's wedding. She couldn't help feeling guilty about it but Meg was a decent sort, she wouldn't hold it against her. Anything but this she would gladly have given up to be with her sister on this day of all days. Put it out of your mind, Agnes, and concentrate on what lies ahead.

Though the interview wasn't until the afternoon she was up early unable to stay in bed any longer. The other bed was empty, Molly would have started her chores by now. After enquiring at the bus station Agnes found the most suitable bus to be the one o'clock which would mean leaving Kerne House shortly after twelve to catch a tram into town.

First impressions were lasting impressions or so she had been told and with that in mind Agnes had the previous day made one of her rare visits to the hairdresser.

'Could you give me a Marcel wave or something? It's important I look nice so what style do you suggest?'

The hairdresser, young and stylish herself, played around with the auburn hair pulling it through her fingers. 'It's in good condition and you have a hint of a natural wave so I'd say all you need for a neat, fashionable look is a bit off the length then the ends turned in.'

'Just turned in, is that all?'

'Up to you, of course, but that is my professional opinion,' she said haughtily.

Careful, Agnes, she warned herself. 'Right! You're the expert and I'm in your hands.'

The girl knew her job. The new pageboy look was perfect with her small features.

'Happy with it?' the stylist asked as she held the mirror to let Agnes get a good view of the back.

'You're a genius so you are,' Agnes beamed, hugely delighted with the result and only wished as she handed over the money that she was in a position to add a tip. One day she would be but not quite yet.

'Good luck,' the girl said as Agnes went out.

'Thanks.'

An end-of-season sale had produced a bargain of a navy trench coat, perfect for fit. Tightly belted and with the collar turned up at the back Agnes felt attractive and well-dressed. She was less happy about what she wore under it, the grey skirt had seen better days and the pink blouse with its frilly neckline was too fussy and had been a poor buy. Still the likelihood of being asked to remove her coat was slim and even if she were it would be in the kitchen where she hoped to be offered something to eat before travelling back to Kerne House.

She looked down at her feet, the shoes, flat-heeled, brown and scuffed at the toes, were a let-down but there was no way her funds would stretch even to the cheapest pair. Agnes felt the familiar irritation at still being expected to contribute to her mother's household expenses. Without that she would be able to save a little.

Molly came in. 'You look quite smart,' she said, then frowned, 'except about the feet. I know you don't have big feet but those shoes make you look as though you did.'

'Thanks a lot, any more encouraging remarks like that and keep them to yourself.'

'You suit your hair like that, I may think about having that style myself.' She fingered her blonde tresses. 'My hairdresser says I have marvellous hair and she can do anything with it.'

'Lucky old you.'

'Molly, if you promise to keep it to yourself I'll tell you something.'

'Tell me what?'

Agnes remained silent.

'All right I promise and anyway I'm not a gossip.'

'I've got an interview for a job.'

Molly's mouth fell open. 'You haven't! But why, Agnes, why do you want to leave here? I thought you liked Kerne House.'

'I do, it's not that but I want to better myself and this could be just what I'm looking for.'

Molly looked put out. 'Where is this job?'

'Kirriemuir.'

Molly was silent, her fingers playing with her hair, then she said slowly, 'In one way, Agnes, I hope you get the job but in another I hope you don't.'

'Care to explain that.'

'I'll miss you and then you know yourself the bother it is trainin' someone new.'

'Don't worry about it yet, there's no guarantee I'll get the job.'

'I've a feelin' you will,' Molly said glumly then added. 'Not a very good service to Kirrie so you'd better check on the buses back unless you want to be stranded.'

'If I had a watch I'd know the time. What about giving me a loan of yours?' she asked hopefully.

'That's askin' a lot and I don't like folk borrowin' my things.'

'I hope I'm not just folk and honestly I would take great care of it.'

'I don't know, Agnes,' Molly said doubtfully.

'Please.'

Molly swithered and then decided to be generous. Going over to the set of drawers she took the watch out of its box. 'I wound it up last night and it keeps good time so don't you dare touch it.'

'Wouldn't dream of it.' Agnes took the silver watch with its black moiré ribbon band and slipped it on her wrist then secured the catch.

Molly looked as though she were already regretting her generosity. The timepiece had come to her through her uncle who had a pawnbroker's shop. Goods unclaimed after a specified time were frequently sold at a fraction of their worth and being family Molly's mother got the watch for next to nothing to give to her daughter for her eighteenth birthday.

Agnes was the first to board the Kirriemuir bus and sat near the front. By the time they left, two minutes late by Molly's watch, the bus was slightly more than half filled. There were a number of stops where passengers got off and others got on. Bush with her own thoughts Agnes hardly noticed the passing countryside as they sped through the small villages. only when they approached Kirriemuir did she begin to pay attention to her surroundings.

Kirriemuir was a quaint, attractive little town on the Braes of Angus with sandstone cottages lining the narrow streets. Agnes knew a little about it but this was her first visit. She did know that its most famous son was born at 9 Brechin Road and that Kirriemuir had been immortalised as Thrums in the tales of J.M. Barrie who also wrote *Peter Pan*.

The bus stopped in the square and after collecting their belongings the passengers stood waiting until it was their time to get off. Agnes had no belongings other than her handbag which she opened yet again to check that she had the all-important letter. Touching it she shut her handbag and looked about her. Sunshine flooded the square and a group of men she took to be farmers shouted greetings to those who passed.

The newsagent's shop was two-windowed and was on the corner. The floor was cluttered with cardboard boxes and bundles of newspapers and Agnes had to pick her way to get to the counter. A head turned from arranging packets of cigarettes on the shelf.

'Yes, lass?'

'I'm waiting for the local bus. When is it due?'

'Anytime now. Where would you be going?'

'Drumoaks.'

'Some parcels for them so he'll be stopping right at the gate. Don't be wandering far, Willie is his own timetable and that means he leaves when he's ready.'

Agnes smiled. 'Thanks very much.'

In less than five minutes a small, shabby vehicle with wooden benches for the passengers trundled into the square. Agnes had been alone but suddenly others arrived, cracked a joke to Willie who grunted a reply before his face creased into a smile. Fares were taken as they got on and the money dropped into a large brown pouch. Agnes climbed in. Since her expenses were to be refunded the cost didn't worry her.

'Drumoaks, please.'

'Tuppence.'

Agnes handed over two pennies. 'Will you tell me when I get there?'

'I'll give you a shout.'

Shopping baskets took up about as much space as the passengers and as Agnes sat down a stout woman in a woolly hat drew her shopping closer to her.

'Move up, lass, there's plenty of room.'

'I'm fine here,' Agnes said from her seat at the far end. The woman looked ready to talk but Agnes wasn't and she was relieved when she turned to someone else and drew her into conversation.

Some time later a voice from the back shouted. 'Let me off at the corner, Willie.'

'Take you all the way – save your legs.'

'No, it means you turnin' and I don't mind the wee walk.'

'Just as you say, Annie, and mebbe it's the exercise that keeps you looking so trim.'

Her ample frame shuddered with laughter as she heaved herself up. 'That's enough from you, you saucy old devil.' She got off and stood still to give a cheery wave.

Drumoaks was the next stop. 'This is you, lass.'

'Thank you,' she said getting up quickly.

'Biding there are you?' He jerked his thumb.

'No.'

'If you need a lift back I pass here between five and five thirty.'

'I'll keep it in mind, thanks for telling me.'

A lad in heavy working togs and big boots climbed on to get the parcels for Drumoaks. He nodded to Willie then got off and walked away smartly not giving Agnes a chance to speak to him. She began walking in the same direction. The drive had wide grass borders leading up to the house and the sun glinted on the stone walls washing them to a pale gold. Drumoaks was a lovely old house with no harsh lines about it, just a grace and gentleness in tune with the surrounding countryside. Agnes experienced a sense of awe that people could live in such a magnificent dwelling. There was an archway and stone steps led up to a door that could have belonged to a castle. Ivy clung to the wall above the archway and continued along the line of windows.

Remembering her instructions, Agnes looked for and found the narrow path which led to the side of the house. There was a short flight of steps much worn by the weather. She went down them and on to a short path to a door. On it was a heavy black knocker and Agnes gave it two sharp raps. Hurrying footsteps could be heard, a bolt was drawn back then the door opened. A small, thin girl and rosy cheeks and light-brown straight hair looked at Agnes and smiled showing white even teeth.

'I have an appointment with Mrs Harrison. I'm Agnes Boyd.'

'Come in, Mrs Harrison is expecting you.' The girl had a clear, pleasant voice with a lilt. 'Wait here till I get this door bolted.'

There was an inner door. Agnes shivered though she'd been quite warm until then. The stone floor and the stone steps leading from it gave it the chill of a cell.

'Don't worry, it isn't all like this,' the girl said noticing the shiver. 'Did you come with Willie's bus?'

'Yes.'

'He's very obliging and even in the worst weather he tries to keep the bus running.' Agnes followed her up a half-flight of stairs and through a door similar to the other but minus the knocker. Here a waft of welcome warmth greeted them and a bewildering number of passages. Out of one came a tall, bespectacled girl. She looked Agnes up and down and Agnes did the same to her.

'Where do you think you are going, Madge?'

Madge flushed. 'This is the girl from Dundee, Beatrice. Miss—' she floundered and Agnes came to her assistance having taken an instant dislike to Beatrice.

'Agnes Boyd.'

'I'm taking Agnes to Mrs Harrison,' she said nervously. 'Is she in the office or her own room?'

'In the office. You should know that she is always in the office at this time of day.' Then to Agnes. 'You'll be after the job of housemaid?'

'Yes,' Agnes said shortly.

'Get back to your duties, Madge,' she ordered.

'Are you going to take—'

She gave Madge a withering look. 'Follow me, Miss Boyd,' then not waiting to see whether Agnes was following or not went quickly through a passageway then down a particularly narrow stairway. 'Watch your head,' she called back carelessly and too late for Agnes to avoid the unexpectedly low ceiling at the foot of the stairs. Fortunately it wasn't a hard bang but it hurt. The oath died in her throat when Agnes remembered where she was.

'Sorry, did you bang your head?' Beatrice said sweetly.

'No,' Agnes lied.

The door they came to was slightly ajar and Beatrice knocked before putting her head in.

'The last applicant has arrived, Mrs Harrison.'

'Show Miss Boyd in, Beatrice.'

Agnes was annoyed that Beatrice hadn't bothered with her name. She walked in totally ignoring the other girl and Beatrice shut the door with unnecessary force.

Mrs Harrison frowned. 'Beatrice in one of her moods. Do sit down, Miss Boyd.' She indicated a chair and Agnes sat down knees and feet neatly together. She opened her bag and put the letter on the desk.

'Thank you. You had no difficulty getting here?'

'None at all.'

The housekeeper looked fortyish. She was of average height, thin and with a narrow face, brown hair parted down the middle and plaited into a neat bun. She had a sweet smile and Agnes began to relax.

'Your letter told me a little but I'd like you to go into more detail.'

Agnes proceeded to do so. She had it off by heart.

'You do realise that the vacancy is for a housemaid and not a tablemaid?'

'Yes, I understood that.'

'You would accept that drop in status?' Her eyebrows rose.

'Yes.'

'Did you bring a reference with you?'

Agnes's face dropped. 'I'm afraid not, Mrs Harrison, and may I tell you the reason for that?'

'I think you had better.' She looked amused, unaware that Agnes was playing for time, deciding what best to say.

'My employers returned to this country after many years in India and have had difficulty in getting and keeping domestic staff.'

'Why should that be?'

Agnes wanted to laugh out loud, it was all going to be so easy. She didn't have to make it up, she could tell the truth. 'My employer forgets that he is no longer in India and being used to shouting at the natives—'

'You don't need to go on, Miss Boyd, I get the picture for myself.'

'I don't much like being shouted at either but his wife is such a gentle charming lady that I just put up with it.'

'You feel that you have had enough?'

'Yes.'

'We do expect a high standard from our staff at Drumoaks but I can assure you that there will be no shouting.' She smiled then frowned. 'This is rather difficult, I had all but decided on one of the other applicants, a local girl whom I may say has excellent references but I am going to offer you the position, Miss Boyd, for the simple reason that your training as a tablemaid may come in useful. Beatrice carries out this duty with her usual efficiency but there are times when she could do with some assistance when there are guests. You wouldn't object to that?'

'I'd be more than happy to oblige.'

'You are paid weekly?'

'Yes.'

'Then one week's notice is all that is legally required, but perhaps you would prefer that to be two weeks?'

'I would, please.'

'We will match your present wage and in six months if you prove to be satisfactory, this will be reviewed.'

'Thank you, Mrs Harrison.' Better and better, Agnes thought.

'It would be more suitable and give you a chance to settle in if you were to come in on the Sunday ready to begin your duties on the Monday.'

'That would be no problem, Mrs Harrison.'

She smiled. 'Now do you have any questions?'

'No, I don't think so.'

'Oh, mustn't forget your expenses,' she said handing Agnes a sealed envelope.

Agnes breathed a sigh of relief. She hadn't wanted to ask for them and was glad it hadn't proved necessary.

Mrs Harrison got up. 'Come along and I'll introduce you to Mrs Tomlinson, our cook. You'll be glad of a cup of tea and something to eat then Madge can – have you met Madge?'

'Yes, she showed me in.'

'Nice girl, you'll get on with her I'm sure. After you've eaten and if you have time before your bus, Madge will show you the bedroom you will be occupying. Regarding your duties we'll decide those when you arrive.'

Another bewildering journey took Agnes to the kitchen premises.

'I'm beginning to think I'll need a map to find my way around.'

Mrs Harrison laughed. 'Difficult to begin with but you'll master it in no time.'

Mrs Tomlinson was elderly, a stout and pleasant-faced woman. After wiping her floury hands on her overall she extended a large hand with thick short fingers. For a moment Agnes's eyes went beyond her to the extremely well-fitted, modern kitchen.

'Mrs Tomlinson, this is Agnes Boyd, our new housemaid.'

'Welcome, lass, you'll be the one from Dundee?'

'Yes.'

'Give Agnes something to eat, will you? And get Madge to show her where she will be sleeping.'

'I'll do that. Sit down, Agnes.'

The lovely warm smell coming from the ovens made Agnes realise just how hungry she was.

'What a beautiful kitchen, Mrs Tomlinson.'

'You expected an old-fashioned kitchen?'

'I suppose I did, I mean parts of the house look ancient.'

'Most of the big houses are modernising the kitchens and I have to say this is a pleasure to work in. Mind you, at the start I was against change, made me nervous, you see, but now I wonder how I managed before. Hungry are you?'

'Starving.'

'Bacon, egg and fried bread?'

'Sounds wonderful.'

'The pan's still hot, it won't take me long.'

True to her word Agnes was soon tucking in.

'Enjoyin' that?' Mrs Tomlinson asked unnecessarily.

'I'll say I am.'

'Like a lass who enjoys her food, can't be doin' with those that just pick at it. I'll have a cup with you. Can't stand too long with these varicose veins of mine. I'll talk while you eat and tell you somethin' about the family. I take it you'd like to hear about them?'

Agnes nodded, her mouth too full to speak.

'A scullery maid I was when I first came to Drumoaks. The old master and mistress were a fine couple, did a lot for the people hereabout and they were sorely missed when they went, God rest their souls.' She paused to drink her tea and perhaps to think back to those days. After putting down the cup she wiped her mouth. 'The two sons, Mr Adrian and Mr Gerald, were a pair of rascals. The tricks those two got up to – and many a dressing-down they got. The gentry can be real hard on their own. Spare the rod and spoil the child is how they see it.' She smiled. 'They used to sneak down to the kitchen here and stand and eat whatever they were given and in a wee while tears gave way to smiles.'

'Did they go to the local school?'

'You've a lot to learn about the gentry, lass. The boys had a tutor then boarding school and university. Both clever lads but Mr Gerald, he's the younger, was by far the brightest. Such a tragedy—' She shook her head.

Agnes placed her knife and fork together on the empty plate and waited for Mrs Tomlinson to go on and when she didn't Agnes prodded her. 'What kind of tragedy, Mrs Tomlinson?'

'Terrible, terrible thing. There'd been a storm, you see, not unusual but this was a very bad one and Mr Adrian and Mr Gerald went out to see the extent of the damage for themselves. The grounds and gardens are lovely around Drumoaks, Agnes, a sight to gladden the eyes—'

Agnes wished she would keep to the point but tried to hide her impatience the best she could.

'The accident I was tellin' you about that—'

'Yes.'

'Mr Adrian saw it happen, yelled a warnin' to his brother but it was too late. You see, lass, a tree slackened by the storm came crashing down pinning Mr Gerald by the legs.'

Agnes shuddered. 'How awful!'

'A nightmare for poor Mr Adrian as well. What a state he was in, he couldn't move the weight from his brother and had to run to the house for help. By the time they got the lad free they thought he was gone, but there was a flicker of life and being a strong, healthy laddie he pulled through. A big, handsome lad who'll never walk again. Bitter too he is and difficult.'

'Who could blame him?'

'Aye, as you say, who could blame him?' Mrs Tomlinson, after filling up Agnes's cup, took up the story again. 'Now for the rest of the family. There's the master's wife, a proper lady and very involved in charities and good works. They have two bairns. Master Mark is seven and his sister, Mary, is five. With this new nanny I don't see much of them. Pity, I like the wee ones coming in and getting a biscuit but Miss Reynolds doesn't approve.'

'Perhaps she's got orders from above,' Agnes suggested.

'I doubt that, I doubt it very much. The master would mind when he liked to come in and get a tasty bite. Are you all right for time?'

'Yes, if I'm at the gate by five I'll get the bus.'

'You've a while then. Miss Gertrude comes between her brothers.

Should have been a laddie that one, daft about horses. She's no oil painting but I will say this, she looks well sitting on a horse.'

'All easy to get on with, are they?'

'I've no complaints. Keep out of Mr Gerald's way would be my advice. He gets into terrible rages about little or nothing.'

Agnes got up and began to collect her dishes meaning to take them over to the sink.

'No, lass, leave them and here's Madge.'

'Thank you for a lovely meal, Mrs Tomlinson.' She grinned. 'If for nothing else I'm looking forward to the food here.'

Mrs Tomlinson looked pleased. 'Fine to see food you've cooked being appreciated. Bye, lass, we'll look forward to you coming.'

'She's a gem, isn't she?' Madge said as they climbed to where the servants slept.

'She certainly is. The only fly in the ointment seems to be Beatrice.'

'She's terribly efficient, I'm a bit scared of her.'

'Don't be and you certainly won't be when I start.'

Madge looked impressed. 'Why, do you think you'll be able to stand up to her?'

'No bother, I've met that type before – face up to them and they soon stop their nonsense.'

'I'm glad you're comin'. Beatrice is worse than usual today and I can tell you why that is.'

'Go on then.'

'She was desperate for her friend to get the job and she very nearly did.'

'So I believe.' Agnes kept her face straight. 'She saw me and there was never any question but that I would get the job.'

'Are you terribly efficient too? I'm not.'

'I'm no great shakes but I muddle through. To be honest I have some experience as tablemaid and that clinched it for me. Heavens! Is this mine?' Agnes asked as Madge flung open the door letting her see right into the room.

Madge nodded happily. 'We're terribly lucky. You see the mistress did an inspection of the servants' quarters and she was horrified at what she saw and had the painters in to freshen up the rooms. We got new furniture too.'

'The room I have in Kerne House is pretty good but nothing like this.'

'I wasn't used to much at home, Agnes,' Madge said delighting Agnes with her honesty.

'That makes two of us.' Agnes went right in and had a good look round. The walls were cream-painted and the curtains were heavy flowered cotton with plenty of fullness. Patterned linoleum was on the floor and there was a rug beside the single bed and that was covered with a peach-coloured bedspread. A small dressing-table, a single wardrobe and two chairs completed the furnishings.

'When do you have to leave?'

With a well-practised flick of the wrist Agnes looked at Molly's watch. 'Just as well you asked, it's time I got my skates on.'

'I'm saving up for one of them.'

'One of what?'

'A watch.'

'This isn't mine, I borrowed it. Like you, I'd better start saving for one as well.'

Back in Kerne House, Molly was given the news first. 'I got the job, Molly, I start a week on Monday.'

Molly's face fell. 'Funny, you know, I didn't realise how much I like you, it's only now when you're leavin'.'

'Start looking around for something better yourself.'

'I could, you know, but I don't think I will. This place isn't bad and I might make a bad move.' She paused and looked searchingly at Agnes. 'Are you sure you're makin' a good one?'

'Time will tell.' Reluctantly she removed the watch from her wrist. 'Thanks, Molly, it was good of you letting me have it.'

Molly took it and placed it back in its box.

'Gift, was it?'

'Yes, from my mother for my eighteenth. My uncle got it for her.'

'He a jeweller?'

'Not exactly, well I suppose I could tell you. He isn't a jeweller, Agnes, but he does deal in jewellery and other things too.'

'Got a stall in the market you mean?'

'I do not,' she said indignantly. 'My uncle is a pawnbroker and he makes a very good livin'.'

'I bet he does.'

'What do you mean by that?'

'A lot of sharks.'

'They are not,' she said heatedly.

'Molly, I should know, folk where I used to live were regulars at the pawnbrokers.'

'My uncle gives a – a—'

'A service.'

'Yes, a service, and he says folk wouldn't manage without him.'

Agnes shook her head. 'Have you ever heard of a poor pawnbroker?'

'I only know one.'

'I've known folk, Molly, hand over something good, worth a lot of money but they are so desperate for the money that they accept the little they are offered hoping to reclaim whatever it is later, only they never do. Your uncle and his kind make a mint.' Agnes grinned. 'Maybe your watch came from some poor soul.'

'Mebbe it did but it didn't stop you borrowin' it.'

'I didn't know where it came from then but you're right. I would have borrowed it just the same.'

'And if I got you one cheap you'd take it.'

'Too true.'

'Well, I wouldn't.' Molly's colour was up. 'Are we fightin'?'

'No, just a friendly argument.'

'Well mind this, I don't like folk miscallin' my family.'

'I wasn't. I was just wishin' one of my stupid uncles had the brains to be a pawnbroker.'

Molly looked uncertain and Agnes gave her a hug. 'You've been a good friend to me, Molly, and I'm going to miss you.'

'Will you?' she said wistfully.

'Old Templeton will be glad to see the back of me.' But there Agnes was wrong.

'May I ask where you are going?' she asked, her brows drawn together in an angry frown.

'Drumoaks, it's an estate just outside Kirriemuir.'

'As a tablemaid?'

'No, a housemaid.'

'Isn't that a backward step?'

'Could be but I think I'm doing the right thing.'

'Before going the length of finding yourself another job surely you could have given some indication that you were dissatisfied. You could have come to me to talk the matter over.'

'You know, Miss Templeton, that never occurred to me.' Something in Agnes's voice made her look up sharply but Agnes's face showed nothing. She was enjoying herself. 'After all you never seemed pleased with my work.'

'Admittedly you were very careless at the start but you improved thanks to the training you got here.' She glared at Agnes. 'Just be sure that for the remainder of your time at Kerne House you fulfil your duties.'

On the whole Kerne House held happy memories for Agnes. Saying goodbye to Mrs Robertson, Molly and Gloria proved to be more difficult than she expected. Particularly when on her last day Mrs Robertson handed her a small packet.

'That's with our best wishes, Agnes, lass, and the gardeners chipped in too.'

'For me?' Agnes was taken aback.

'Open it, Molly said as they all drew nearer.

Agnes opened the package then gasped. Her face paled then flushed as she took out the wristwatch, not new, the metal was slightly tarnished, but a watch.

'I – I just don't know what to say—'

'That makes a change,' Mrs Robertson chuckled. 'Fancy our Agnes bein' tongue-tied.'

'It's the best, the very best gift I've had in my whole life,' she said, fighting back the tears.

'It was to be a nice warm scarf,' Mrs Robertson said, 'but Molly knew that you would like a watch and she knew where she could get a good one cheap. I'm tellin' you that just in case you think we've come into a bit of money.'

Agnes looked gratefully at Molly then put the watch on her wrist and could hardly take her eyes off it.

'Put some fancy biscuits on a plate, Gloria, and you, Molly, make a good cup of tea, none of your dishwater.'

'Strong tea is bad for you,' but she ladled in three heaped caddy spoons of tea before adding the boiling water.

'Agnes, I can't stand it a moment longer. Give me that watch, it's goin' back in the box till night or there won't be a stroke of work done.'

★ ★ ★

They were in the bedroom, Agnes was doing her packing.

'You won't forget us will you?'

'How could I with a watch to remind me?' She grinned cheekily. 'Three cheers for the pawnbrokers, especially your uncle. I take back all I said.'

'You are the limit, Agnes Boyd, and I nearly forgot to tell you I saw Tommy Kingsley and I told him you were leaving Kerne House.'

Agnes waited. Her face showed no change but her heart was hammering.

'What had he to say to that?'

'Nothin' much, just that he hoped it would all work out for you. Funny thing to say, why couldn't he have just wished you all the best or somethin'? In a way,' she said thoughtfully, 'you and Tommy are two of a kind.'

'In what way?'

'Neither of you comes out with what you're thinkin', you never say it straight.'

'Maybe that's because we don't know what we mean ourselves.'

'There you go again,' Molly said exasperatedly.

'When you see him again tell him it is all going to work out for me, that I'll make sure it does.'

'If I can remember all that,' she said doubtfully.

After giving in her notice Agnes never set eyes on either the master or mistress before she left Kerne House. Mrs Taylor was confined to her room with a feverish cold and the master had business in London requiring his attention.

One week after Agnes's departure from Kerne House Rachel's letter arrived. Miss Templeton had a forwarding address and to be fair to her she had every intention of redirecting it. But something claimed her attention and she put the letter in the drawer with receipted accounts meaning to deal with it later on in the day, but it completely slipped her memory.

Guilt at not attending her sister's wedding still bothered Agnes and she wrote two short notes, one before she got the position at Drumoaks and the other after being successful. With some impatience she awaited a reply and eventually one came. It was a happy letter, a bride clearly bursting with happiness and painting a picture, a very nearly perfect picture, of married bliss. As she said herself it wasn't many who praised their mother-in-law but Sam's mother was a gem. The wedding itself barely got a mention. It had been little more than the signing of names but it put the gold band on her finger and that was all she cared about. As a postscript and very much an afterthought, she hoped that Agnes had made a good move and wouldn't regret leaving such a nice place as Kerne House.

Was it envy Agnes was feeling? Perhaps just for a little it was. For the majority married bliss didn't last long. Hardship, unemployment, unwanted pregnancies saw to that. Meg could be the exception, she was getting a decent start and Sam was nice, dull but nice. Dull in her eyes but not in Meg's. Into her mind and unbidden came Tommy Kingsley, not the laughing lad she had gone off with on the back of his bike, but Tommy with his face showing only contempt for someone like her. Yet all she was doing was making sure she didn't end up like her mother. Admittedly what Tommy was offering was far above what she had been used to, it should be enough for her, but it wasn't. Something inside her would not let her be satisfied. She had to aim higher.

# Chapter Twenty-One

Wildly her eyes were seeking a way of escape but he was blocking the narrow path with his big, powerful body. What could she do? For a start, she told herself, she could stop panicking and letting him see that she was afraid. It was that strange knowing smile that was making her uneasy, unnerving her. She forced herself to be calm and repeated firmly, 'Mr Meldrum, you are blocking the path and I wish to get past.'

'Such a tease you are, my dear.' He wagged a finger as though to a naughty child.

Fear was quickly giving way to anger. 'Mr Meldrum,' she said icily, 'let me through at once.'

They were about a foot apart and she stepped to the side. It meant going nearer to the shrubs, thick in this area and menacing in the grey light, but she thought it her only chance of getting away. Turning back would plunge her into more of the thick growth and take her further away from the house. This was probably his idea of fun, scaring the maids and feeling safe to do so since they would be too afraid of losing their job to complain.

She made her move but he was quicker. An arm stopped her flight then both arms went round her and he drew her close.

'Relax, my dear Rachel, and let us enjoy this little while together.'

She felt the roughness of his coat as his sleeve brushed her face, then the prickly moustache as his mouth sought hers. She struggled, was fighting desperately to free herself but her strength was nothing against his. All she was doing was exhausting herself. With brutal hardness his mouth was on hers almost suffocating her and she tasted blood as he forced her lips apart. In those moments Rachel knew and understood what was meant by complete and hopeless despair. She made one last desperate bid for freedom then allowed her body to go limp. She felt his hold on her ease as he fingers fumbled with buttons and she took her chance. Her right foot was free and with all the pent-up fury of a caged animal she kicked out at his legs with her sturdy shoes. The sharp, unexpected, agonising pain made him throw her from him as he clutched at his leg.

'You bitch, you'll suffer for that, by God, you will,' he snarled but Rachel barely heard. Already she was running, the branches tearing at her clothes as she slithered, lost her balance, regained it and ran on only stopping when she reached the servants' entrance. As she tore up the back stairs her breath was coming in painful gasps. She reached her room without anyone seeing her, shut the door, put her back to it and slithered to the floor. Shaken and bruised she sat there for a long time then slowly got to her feet and went to look in the mirror. The eyes looking back were wild in a chalk-white face with traces of blood around her mouth and streaked down one side of her face. Her clothes were muddied where she'd fallen, her stockings ruined and a button was missing from her coat with another hanging by a thread.

A bath, she must have a bath, though she wasn't entitled to one. Janet would complain bitterly if there wasn't enough water. She liked a lot and she liked to soak in it but Rachel was uncaring, her need was greater.

It certainly helped and after it she gave her teeth a vigorous brushing to wash away the traces of that horrible mouth on hers. The memory of it made her almost throw up.

Of one thing she was certain and that was that she was in no fit state to assist Janet with the serving of the evening meal to the family. It wasn't far from the truth to say she was unwell and her white face would bear witness to that. Mrs Anderson was the one to approach but she couldn't bring herself to do that. She glanced at the clock. Hetty might be on her own. Dressed in a clean blouse and skirt she went along to the room shared by Janet and Hetty and knocked.

'Come in.'

Relieved to see that Hetty was on her own, Rachel opened her mouth to explain but the words wouldn't come and instead she burst into tears.

Hetty was full of concern and put her arm round Rachel's shoulder. 'What is it, Rachel, what is the matter?'

'I don't want Janet—' she managed to get out between sobs.

'She could be here any time. You get back to your room and I'm goin' along to the kitchen to make tea. You badly need a cup.'

Rachel smiled weakly as Hetty arrived with a tin tray on which was a chipped brown teapot and three cups. Two had some milk in the bottom and the extra cup held sugar and a spoon.

'No one about,' she said, spooning a liberal amount of sugar into Rachel's cup. 'Best thing for shock and that is obviously what you've had.'

'Thank you, I—'

'Not a word until you get that down you.'

The sweet tea did help but most of all it was Hetty's presence.

'Feelin' a bit better?' she asked kindly.

'Yes, I am.'

'Right,' she said, sitting herself firmly in the chair. 'I'm gettin' to the bottom of this and it's your Auntie Hetty talking so no fobbin' me off with half-truths.'

'Hetty, I want to tell you, you are the only one I can tell.' Haltingly she related all that had happened.

'The swine, I hope you crippled him.' She paused and said quietly, 'He didn't—'

'No, Hetty, he didn't harm me.' She knew what Hetty meant. 'Having you beside me is letting me remember things that didn't make sense. Things he was saying, Hetty. He more or less suggested that I was just teasing, that I – that I wanted him,' she said incredulously.

'Proper conceit of himself that one.'

'I know, Hetty, but he seemed genuinely to believe – wait, I can remember his words or near enough.' She took a deep, shaky breath. 'He said a little bird told him that his advances wouldn't be unwelcome.'

'Rachel, no one would say a thing like that.'

'I know, but why should he say it?'

'Dear knows and it wouldn't be Janet that's for sure. Better just put it all out of your mind and be thankful it wasn't any worse.'

'I know but I can't face him tonight.'

'Of course not, I'll say you're not feelin' well.'

'It means you helping Janet.'

She made a face. 'She'll just have to put up with me, in any case all I'll get to do is collect the dirty dishes and even I can do that.' She got up and turned at the door. 'Keep to your room and I'll get Mrs Morton to prepare a tray.'

'I won't be hungry, Hetty.'

''Course you will. Any leftovers I'll see to them, nothing wasted when I'm around.'

★ ★ ★

'Seemed well enough earlier on. What's the matter with her?' Janet said sharply.

'She's not feelin' well, that's all, and she's as white as a ghost.'

'That's me landed with you then?'

'You do most of it anyway.'

'How true.'

The table was set, everything in place when Mrs Maud Meldrum, looking flushed and not a bit like herself, came into the dining-room and over to where Janet and Hetty were standing.

'Janet, don't take the cups through to the dining-room, we'll have coffee served at the table this evening.'

'Yes, Mrs Meldrum.'

'I wonder why,' Janet said thoughtfully once the door had closed.

'Looked a bit on edge,' Hetty answered.

'Nothing unusual about that,' Janet said with unconcealed contempt. 'She's as nervous as a kitten.'

'Kittens can scratch.'

'Whatever that is supposed to mean.'

'Still waters run deep.'

'Good heavens! What's got into you?'

Hetty grinned. 'Not sure I know but anyway it means less work.'

'But I enjoy serving coffee in the drawing-room.'

'It'll be only for one night.'

'But why?'

'None of our business.'

Janet glowered. 'Once the dessert plates are cleared you can go. I'll see to the rest myself.'

'Good, that'll let me get a tray up to Rachel.'

'If she's as ill as you suggest she won't be interested in food.'

'Then I'll eat it.'

'No wonder you're fat.'

At the usual time the family came into the dining-room and sat down in their usual places. Betsy and Brian were having a good-natured argument. The old lady smiled to them as she sat bolt upright in her chair. Henry Meldrum had a bad-tempered scowl on his face and glared across at the young couple who studiously ignored him. With her back as straight as her mother's, Maud Meldrum spoke clearly.

'You may begin serving, Janet.'

Startled looks went to the old lady who always gave the orders but her face was expressionless. The meal was served in near silence. After dessert Hetty removed the plates. It was the signal to get up but Mrs Craig had to make the first move and she showed no sign of getting up.

'Coffee for this evening is to be served at the table,' Maud announced quietly. 'Janet, pour the coffee, then you and Hetty just go. I'll ring when you are required.'

'Very good, m'am.' Janet finished pouring and put down the coffee pot. She gave a quick glance to Henry Meldrum but he wasn't looking her way. The door gave a click leaving the family alone.

'Mother, why are we having coffee here?' Betsy demanded, 'and are you all right, Grandmother?'

'I'm perfectly well, thank you, Betsy.'

'Why the change of routine?' Henry Meldrum asked irritably as he added more sugar to his coffee.

'All in good time, Henry.' There was colour in the usually sallow cheeks and about her an air of suppressed excitement. Mrs Craig kept her eyes on her daughter and a little smile hovered round her lips.

'Brian, sugar if you please.'

'Sorry, Betsy, thought you'd had it.'

Maud lifted the cup to her lips then put it carefully down on the saucer having only wet her lips.

'The change in routine, Henry, is because I have something to say and I prefer to say it in front of you all, here in the dining-room where we are unlikely to be interrupted.' Her eyes went to her husband. 'Henry, I am divorcing you and I want you out of Duncairn House, my mother's home, by tomorrow morning at the latest.'

There was a shocked gasp. All were looking at this timid woman as though they couldn't believe the words had come from her.

'What – I—' Henry Meldrum blustered. 'Is this some sort of joke, Maud?'

'Since you always complain that I have no sense of humour you can be assured I mean every word.'

'This is ridiculous nonsense. You can't without—'

'Proof?'

'That is something you do not have,' he said, but some of the bluster had gone and a new wariness was in his expression.

'Does the name Miriam Brownlow mean anything to you?'

He smiled showing more confidence. 'A friend, no more than that, my dear. You are just letting your imagination run away with you, old girl.'

'A friend with a husband conveniently abroad and no children to complicate matters.'

'An acquaintance whom I see from time to time and always in other people's company.'

'Not good enough, Henry.' She gave a half laugh and moistened her lips. The hands in her lap were clenched but no one saw them. 'I've had you watched and the solicitor has in keeping all the evidence required.'

'I don't believe you.'

'That is your privilege.' She paused. 'Even without it, there is always Janet.'

That brought a look of shocked surprise to his handsome face, then he recovered. 'A maid, an ignorant servant, Maud, my dear. Give me credit for some sense and knowing you if you'd had the least suspicion of anything of that nature she would have been dismissed.'

'Wrong, Henry,' his mother-in-law said acidly. 'Why on earth should we get rid of Janet? She is a first-rate servant and those aren't so easily come by these days.'

Henry Meldrum made a last appeal to his wife. 'All this drama, my dear, is so unlike you. This could have been settled between us and any little problems ironed out. It still isn't too late to do that.'

'Oh, but it is, Henry. All those years you've humiliated me and I was fool enough to give you yet another chance. Don't waste your breath trying to get me to change my mind, there is no chance of that. I am divorcing you and our only contact from now onwards will be through my solicitor.'

'If that is the way you want it, very well.' He got up, pushed back his cup and spilled coffee on the white tablecloth leaving an ugly brown stain. 'Come along, Brian, we are not spending another night here.'

'You were told to go, it did not apply to Brian.' Maud smiled to her stepson who was looking bewildered. 'This is your home, Brian, and you are welcome to remain at Duncairn House for as long as you wish.'

'My son goes with me.'

Betsy had a restraining hand on him. 'Don't go, Brian.'

'Brian has no intention of going, have you Brian?' The faded eyes of Mrs Craig met his.

'He does as I say. There is a good job waiting for him in London.' He looked at his son. 'Time you saw a bit of life, began to enjoy yourself instead of being stuck in this dreary place.'

That was too much for the mistress of Duncairn House. 'You wanted Duncairn House, it was the perfect background to impress your business colleagues. Nice to be able to boast of an estate in the country especially when those same guests were entertained at my expense,' Mrs Craig said witheringly.

'Dad, I am not going with you,' Brian said quietly and firmly. 'London holds no attraction for me. I have never had any intention of going.'

'Rather live on the old woman's charity, would you?'

Brian flushed. The normally placid young man had a temper and Betsy was pleased to see it. 'You forget, sir, that I am almost twenty-one and Mother's money comes to me then. I don't need charity and it wouldn't be charity I'd be offered. My stepmother and my adopted grandmother have shown me nothing but kindness.'

'And me? What about me?' Betsy said huffed.

'Need someone to fight with, don't I?' They grinned at each other.

'That money you talk of should be mine not yours.'

'No, Mother meant it for me and in case I blew the lot when I became twenty-one she left it so that I wouldn't get my hands on the rest until I'm twenty-five.'

'Sensible woman your mother, Brian.' Mrs Craig nodded approvingly. 'Tell you what you could do.'

He smiled.

'Help your father pack and hasten his departure from Duncairn House. This'll be a happier place without him.'

Defeated, Henry Meldrum, in his haste to be gone from the room, knocked his damaged leg against the chair and winced with pain as he limped to the door. As if remembering the cause of his damaged leg he turned, and Betsy cringed under that look of loathing.

'You've a lot to answer for, you little—'

'No bad language in this house if you please, Mr Meldrum.' The old lady turned to her daughter. 'Quite an interesting evening, my dear. You

221

can ring for the maids to clear up then assist me to my room.'

Maud gave a pull at the bell that would bring Janet and Hetty then went to assist her mother. A smile passed between them and the quiet words were for Maud's ears alone.

'Well done, Maud, I couldn't have done better myself.'

All next day rumours and counterrumours went round the servants' quarters. Everyone knew that something momentous had happened, that it concerned Henry Meldrum, but no one knew what. Curious faces, smilingly satisfied faces but only one glum face and that belonged to Janet. She went about her work in her usual competent fashion but made no contribution to the conversation.

'He's gone and three cheers for that,' Hetty said gleefully with a special glance to Rachel.

'How can you be so sure?' Rachel asked.

'Because I do out his room, don't I? He didn't sleep in his bed last night and everythin' has gone, wardrobe cleared out and the drawers emptied.' They were in the kitchen drinking tea with work temporarily forgotten.

Mrs Morton sat in a chair with her feet up on a box ready for a gossip.

'Your young man was tellin' me, Hetty, he saw Mr Meldrum loading up his car and gettin' in it and drivin' off like the wind.'

'What do you mean my young man?' Hetty said going pink in the face.

'Stupid we may be but blind we are not. That's a fine laddie with his eye on you and you could do a lot worse.'

'Mr Meldrum is away for good then?' Rachel asked hopefully.

'Seems like it. You feelin' better now?'

'Much better.'

'Mrs Anderson told me to strip the bed and to put everything in the wash.'

'Hope you opened the window, Hetty,' Mrs Morton said.

'Wide as it would go.'

The door opened, Janet came in and there was an uncomfortable silence. The silence continued as Janet went to get a tin of polish from the cupboard. All the time she kept her face averted and went out again without a word.

'Poor Janet, she's been cryin', should I go after her?'

'No, let her be, Hetty,' Mrs Morton said sharply, 'The lass has feelings and mebbe she was genuinely fond of him. There's no accounting for taste if I've got the right expression.'

Rachel slipped away and along to Janet's room, knocked and put her head round the door. 'Wondered if you'd be here.'

'Well, I am.'

'Would you like me to bring you a cup of tea, Janet?'

She gave an odd little laugh. 'If you think it would help.'

'I'm sure it will. I won't be long.'

# Chapter Twenty-Two

Finding her way about Drumoaks wasn't as difficult as it first appeared and Agnes soon had it mastered. Heating such a large house was a problem and many of the passageways and corridors were icy cold during the winter months. Comfort was important to the family at Drumoaks and it had taken a great deal of thought and care to marry the old with the new but it had been done. The drawing-room and smaller sitting-room showed how to achieve comfort without losing its old-fashioned charm. Having dealt with their own creature comforts the master and mistress undertook a tour of the servants' quarters and were appalled by what they saw. Perhaps because of it and the guilt they felt, the upgrading went further than could reasonably have been expected.

Agnes kept congratulating herself on attaining such a desirable job, few in her position had such comfort. If there was a jarring note it came from Beatrice. She wasn't openly hostile but had an unpleasant way of examining the work done by Agnes and finding fault. Polishing was an example, she never got the desired shine.

'A bit more elbow grease, Agnes.'

'You got promotion to housekeeper or something?' Agnes snapped.

'Mrs Harrison is fully occupied and as the senior—'

'Don't give me that, you are only a tablemaid, Beatrice, and I was one myself at Kerne House.'

'So I believe and that strikes me as being very peculiar.'

'For your information I am not losing out financially and I am to be helping out in the dining-room on occasions.'

'That I find hard to believe and it is the first I've heard of it.' She began to move away.

'Suit yourself and before you go let me tell you this. It wasn't my fault that Mrs Harrison chose me rather than your friend.'

'It was a pity but I agree it wasn't your fault.'

'Then stop picking on me. If you do have the authority to boss me and Madge then just make sure it's fair.'

Beatrice took off her spectacles and there were dark violet shadows beneath her eyes. She had good features and a clear complexion and without the ugly steel frames she was a good-looking girl and Agnes said so.

'Why on earth do you wear those things, you look far better without them?'

'Why do people wear spectacles? Don't be so stupid, Agnes, do you think I would wear them if I didn't need to?'

'What I meant was, get yourself a decent pair. I've seen some really nice ones.'

Beatrice looked uncertain then came back to stand beside Agnes. She had the superior height and Agnes, sure that she had gone too far, waited for the storm.

'Maybe I have been hard on you.'

'No question about it you have and that applies to Madge too. She's scared stiff of you.'

'She's just plain silly.'

'No, Beatrice, she isn't. She's shy and nervous, we can't all be the same and what's more she's nice.'

Beatrice wasn't paying attention to what Agnes was saying. 'You think I should get other spectacles?'

'If you can afford it, of course.'

'I don't spend much, I have a bit saved.'

'Meaning you don't go out?'

'Hardly ever.' She bit her lip and Agnes could see the struggle she was having.

'If you want a second opinion—'

'You would come with me?'

'Of course. Any outing would be welcome, I'm a stranger remember.'

'You know Mr Bannerman?'

'Been introduced, yes.'

'Most Thursdays he takes the car into Perth and if I asked him he would give us a lift.'

'Great! I've never been in Perth.'

'You'll like it, it's a good shopping centre.'

'Could this mean we are friends?' she grinned.

'Just as long as you remember I'm the boss.'

'You'll keep reminding me, I'm sure.'

Beatrice walked away but she was smiling.

'She's all right, Madge, honest she is.'

Madge didn't look convinced.

'Know her real problem?'

Madge shook her head.

'Loneliness and she's doesn't want anyone to know it.'

'That's sad I suppose. Fancy you getting that out of her.' She paused. 'Know what Mrs T said?'

'No, but you're going to tell me.'

'She said, there's a lass who knows what she wants and like as not she'll get it.'

'Did she now? Well all I say is I hope she's right.'

'What do you want, Agnes?'

'I'm not sure I know but of one thing I am certain and that is I won't always be a maid.'

'Neither will I, I want to get married and I expect I will.'

'I'm sure of it too,' Agnes said with a smile. She spoke her thoughts out loud. 'One day I'll have a lovely house with maids to do the work and I'll be free to read books or do anything I want.'

'I was bein' serious and you are bein' funny.'

'Madge, I was never more serious in my life.'

'I never know whether you are kiddin' or not.'

November was mild, indeed much of it was warmer than October. Agnes had become an aunt, Meg had given birth to a son and straightaway Agnes had bought a rattle and teething rings which had made a hole in her savings. The wedding gift had never materialised but it wasn't forgotten. One day when funds permitted she would buy Meg and Sam something really good and they would know then that it had been worth waiting for.

By December winter had set in and Agnes and Beatrice made that visit to Perth. Mr Bannerman was to allow them three hours to do what they wanted then he would pick them up at the North Inch.

The optician was horrified. 'When did you get these?'

'I can't remember,' Beatrice mumbled, 'but it was a long time ago.'

'Were they meant for you in the first place?'

Beatrice blushed crimson. 'No, they were my sister's but she wouldn't wear them and since I could see better with them—' she swallowed. 'My mother said there was no use them going to waste.'

'Have you been suffering from headaches?'

Beatrice looked surprised. 'Yes, she admitted, 'they've got worse these last few months.'

'I'm not surprised,' he said drily. 'You could have permanently damaged your eyes, young woman.'

'I haven't though, have I?' she said anxiously.

'No, but you must stop wearing these,' he fingered the offending spectacles with distaste then smiled. He was fiftyish, stout and with greying hair. 'Why do you want to hide a bonny face behind those ugly steel frames?'

Beatrice dropped her eyes in embarrassment.

'Told her the same myself,' Agnes said.

'Good for you. Now, miss, I'm going to give you a pair of spectacles to wear until your own are ready.'

'Thank you very much but how much extra—'

'There will be no charge for these provided you bring them back in good condition.'

'I'll take very great care of them.'

'And these, my dear girl,' he said handing over the old ones, 'if you'll take my advice you'll put them where they belong in the nearest bin.'

'Better let her put them in yours.'

He smiled. 'I'll drop you a postcard when your spectacles are ready for collection,' he said, putting the old ones in his bin and wishing them both good day.

They were outside and walking towards the shops. 'Have you been troubled with headaches?'

'Off and on. An aspirin used to help but it isn't much good now.'

'Fancy you being stupid enough to wear specs meant for someone else.'

'Maybe it seems that way to you, Agnes,' Beatrice said quietly, 'but my parents were poor, and I do mean poor. My eyesight was always weak and those did help.'

'Is your home hereabout?'

'I used to live quite near but both my parents are dead, my father before I was at school and my mother,' her voice wobbled, 'nearly two years ago.'

'And what about your sister?'

'Elsie is very good with children and the family she was with were going to America and took her with them.'

'All right for some.' She paused to look at a shop window. 'Don't run away with the idea that you are the only one. Believe me, I know all there is to know about poverty.'

'Are you bitter about it?'

'Sometimes, but what's the point?' Agnes shrugged and decided to change the subject. 'What is Christmas like at Drumoaks?'

'Very good. There's a big tree, holly and the usual Christmas trimmings and Mrs T does us proud. The family eat first but we get the same meal except, of course, for the wine but Mr Bannerman and Mrs Harrison get together and buy a couple of bottles.' She laughed. 'Two sips and our Madge is at the giggly stage. Things don't get hilarious until the master and mistress have been to the kitchen to wish us all a Happy Christmas.'

'Just that – no more?'

'No presents if that is what you mean, but don't look so glum,' she said as Agnes's face fell, 'we get an extra week's wages and that to me is better than a box of hankies.'

'Couldn't agree more,' Agnes said cheering up instantly. She smiled to herself as she caught Beatrice looking into shop windows not so much to see the goods on display but to admire herself. The tortoiseshell frames suited her face.

'How long have we, Agnes?'

Agnes consulted her watch. 'Just over half an hour.'

'Time for tea and a bun, my treat.'

'No, I'll pay my own.'

'You will not and that is an order.'

Christmas went by and the last day sof December gave way to a cold, damp, depressing January. Stripped of their leaves the trees appeared black and all around was the dirty yellow tangle of old bracken. Until then there had been only flurries of snow but those born in the country could smell snow in the air and forecast a heavy and prolonged fall. Used to harsh conditions they were always well prepared. Emergency food was stocked up as well as a good supply of fuel. It was all hands on deck with the stable-boy, gardeners and odd-jobmen chopping up wood for the fires and piling up the logs in the cellars.

'You wanted to see me, Mrs Harrison?'

'Yes, Agnes, come in and sit down.'

Agnes sat with her hands folded in her lap.

'From time to time I change duties round and with winter upon us there is a need for more fires – even to those rooms that are seldom used dampness can spread very quickly. The library, as you know, is heated for most of the day, it has to be. There is a valuable collection of books and a degree of heat is necessary to keep them in good condition. That duty I am giving to you; you will see to the fire in the library.'

'Before or after the bed-making?'

'Before I think,' she said thoughtfully. 'Once you have cleared up the dishes in the breakfast-room and tidied up there go along and clean out the fire. Do remember, but I'm sure you will, to put a newspaper over the ashes to keep the dust from flying. Then you will lay the fire and light it.'

'When do I begin, Mrs Harrison?'

'Tomorrow morning.'

Wearing a dark blue overall over her dress, Agnes got down on her hands and knees and raked and cleaned out the grey ash using a small shovel to transfer it to the pail. That done she covered the pail with a double page of newspaper and used the rest rolled up to set the fire. Thin sticks of firewood went on next in criss-cross fashion then small pieces of coal. In Kerne House it hadn't been allowed but here a half firelighter was used to hasten the blaze. Satisfied with her handiwork Agnes put a match to the paper, watched as the small flame caught the firelighter and the sticks began to burn. She would have to wait until it got a good hold before adding more coal. Since her overall was soiled anyway, Agnes wiped her hands on it taking away the worst of the dirt. Coming in she had only taken a quick look round but now she took the time to study it. Books, hundreds of them, lined every wall and over at the window was a handsome desk with a leather-seated chair under it. On the desk was a crystal inkstand and a marble oblong-shaped dish holding an assortment of pens with some spare nibs.

Fascinated, Agnes wandered over to look at the books, some were protected by glass but others were on open shelves. So engrossed was she in examining the titles that she failed to hear the tap, tap of crutches. The angry bark made her nearly jump out of her skin and she swung round guiltily.

'What the devil do you think you are doing?' he bawled.

'N-nothing.'

'Nothing? Poking about where you have no right to be and you have the impudence to say – nothing.'

This could only be Mr Gerald Patterson. She knew of him but hadn't seen him and that was because he had been in hospital undergoing treatment. That he was blazingly angry was obvious and what was also obvious was that she had no right to be where she was. She began to move away.

'Don't you dare move. You'll stay where you are.'

Agnes watched his painful journey from the doorway to the desk and wondered how he was going to get himself into the chair. She longed to bring it out for him but dare not. Was it just bad temper or were those lines of pain? Putting one crutch against the desk he manoeuvred the chair to the desired position then managed to swing himself into it. For a moment his eyes closed and when he opened them she was looking into dark blue eyes that were almost black. His hair was crinkly and was a rich nut brown and without the scowl Gerald Patterson would be a handsome man.

'I am waiting for an explanation.'

'Before I give you one do you mind if I see to the fire or it will go out.'

'Be quick about it.'

Her hands were shaking but she managed to coax it back to life with a few more dry sticks. Soon it was burning well and she got off her knees.

'Over here.'

She swallowed nervously. 'I'm very sorry, sir.'

'I want to know what you touched with your filthy hands.'

'Nothing.'

'That I do not believe, not for a moment.'

Crippled or not Agnes wasn't standing for that. 'When I said I touched nothing that is exactly what I meant.'

'You mean you didn't touch anything.'

'That is what I said.'

'No you didn't.'

'All I did was look. I've never been in here before and I've never seen so many books.'

There are public libraries with many more, but what would someone like yourself do with books?'

'Read them same as you,' she shot back, 'or maybe you think I can't read.'

'Hardly, since everyone is entitled to an education of sorts these days.'

'Since I'm getting the sack let me tell you something.'

'If you've more to say, for God's sake sit down.'

Agnes sat. 'You and your kind don't know you're living.'

'That's true for me anyway. With two bloody useless legs life has very little meaning.'

The anger drained out of Agnes.

'I'm sorry, you've plenty to be bitter about.'

He smiled and it was a nice smile. 'One of my passions was trees, I had a great love of them and it was one of them that did this to me.'

'I heard about it, sir, and if I can borrow your language it was a bloody awful thing to happen.'

'I apologise for my bad language.'

'No need, I was brought up on that word.'

She saw he was trying to hide his amusement. 'What is your name?'

'Agnes Boyd.'

'New here are you?'

'Been here since November.'

'You've lasted that long.'

Those last few minutes and she was beginning to think her job might be safe after all, but not now. 'You've lasted that long,' was what he'd said and all there was to add was – but it won't be for much longer.

Without waiting for permission Agnes got up, added more coal to the fire, picked up the pail of ashes and let herself out of the library.

# Chapter Twenty-Three

Janet gulped down some of the tea then put the cup back on the tray. Her apologetic laugh rang out before she buried her face in her hands.

Rachel longed to give comfort but stopped herself. It would be unwelcome. Better to do nothing and stay silent and if Janet should indicate that she wanted to be left alone then she would get up and go. Janet didn't.

In a little while he dried her eyes and balled the handkerchief in her hands. 'Sorry, I feel all kinds of a fool.'

'Would you rather I went?'

'Not unless you want to go.'

'I don't.'

'Thanks. I need to talk, get things sorted out in my own mind.'

'Take your time, I'm a good listener and if you need the assurance nothing goes further than this room.'

'I know that.' She shook her head sadly. 'You should be gloating after the way I've treated you.'

'It's all right,' Rachel said awkwardly.

'Getting involved with a married man, you would never have done that and I suppose I'm getting what I deserve.'

Rachel didn't know how to answer that. 'We all make mistakes, Janet,' she said quietly.

'You never liked him?'

'No, I didn't.' She thought of what she had gone through with Henry Meldrum and only just managed not to shiver.

'If you'd really known him you would have liked him. Henry could be absolutely charming, Rachel. If I'm to be honest my head was turned with all the posh places he used to take me. I was terribly nervous at times particularly at the beginning, but Henry was so good, letting me know in a quiet way what was acceptable and what was not.'

'Didn't you feel guilty about Mrs Meldrum?' Rachel was forced to ask.

'He said I had no reason to be, that we were hurting no one and, Rachel, it's awfully easy to believe something you want to believe.'

'I know it is.'

'He said he wasn't cheating on his wife.'

'What did he call it then?'

She shrugged. 'His wife was so dull, he said. He'd thought of leaving her but couldn't bring himself to do it. Laughable in the light of what has happened.'

'From what I gather, Janet, Duncairn House was the attraction and poor Mrs Meldrum didn't realise that until it was too late.'

Janet didn't look convinced. 'I think you've got that bit wrong. A little of country life was enough for Henry, he was all for the bright lights, although he did admit to me that it was rather nice to boast of an estate in the country.'

'But he didn't own it,' Rachel said indignantly. 'Duncairn House wasn't his, it belongs to Mrs Craig.'

'Of course, everyone knew that,' Janet said impatiently, 'but in time it would have gone to her daughter. Maud Meldrum and Betsy are her only relatives.'

Wrong, Janet, Rachel said silently, her other granddaughter is sitting here talking to you. It set her off to wondering how long she could keep up this pretence yet with each passing day it was becoming more and more difficult. Her grandmother liked her but liked her as a servant girl with a pleasant voice. Even if her grandmother accepted her as Amelia's daughter there was Aunt Maud and there was Betsy and she could hardly expect a welcome from either, most certainly not from Betsy. Coming to Duncairn House had been a mistake, a foolish, impulsive action on her part. What a mess she had made of her life. Thinking back with the benefit of hindsight she saw Peggy with a reluctant stepdaughter and herself with a reluctant stepmother. They had both been at fault and her poor da caught up in the middle. It was too late for regrets, her father would never forgive her for what she had done. He knew where she was, that she had chosen her grandmother and Duncairn House and he had washed his hands of her.

'I'm sorry, Janet, you were saying—'

'He promised to take me to London, show me the sights and he would have done too, Henry kept his promises. You know this, I was to arrange my holidays to suit.' Her voice broke. 'I could have forgiven him a lot,

Rachel, if only he hadn't gone off like that without a word to me.'

'Maybe he didn't get the chance.'

'He had the chance all right, we had our own way of communicating,' Janet said bitterly.

They were both silent, everything seemed to have been said. Janet drank the rest of the lukewarm tea then cradled the cup in her hand.

'Better to hand in my notice rather than await my marching orders.'

'Don't do anything hasty, Janet.'

'Mrs Meldrum will want me out of Duncairn House.'

'That's possible and natural in the circumstances but Mrs Craig may or rather will have the final say and I rather think she'll want to hang on to you.'

'You really think so?' There was a glimmer of hope on Janet's face.

'You are very efficient and would be difficult to replace.'

'You could take over and do the job just as well.'

'No, I couldn't, and I'm going to tell you something no one else knows. That first breakfast tray—'

'Now you're making me feel rotten. I deliberately made it difficult for you.'

'Wouldn't have made any difference. I don't have steady hands and to make matters worse the spout of the teapot was turned towards the toast.'

Janet gave a scream of tearful laughter. 'Soggy toast, oh heavens, you didn't offer her that?'

'I apologised for it and offered to get fresh but she was very nice about it, said to put it in the fire and say nothing to Mrs Morton.'

Janet looked amazed and perhaps envious. 'No one else would have got away with that, she must really like you.'

'She likes me to read to her, Janet, but not to take up her breakfast, she made that clear.'

'You've just been the tonic I need.'

'Good, I'll get on my way then and, Janet, let me say one thing more before I go. Forget Henry Meldrum, he isn't worth a single tear so put him right out of your mind.'

'Better fish in the sea?'

'Much better.'

'Rachel, you don't go out much do you?'

'Not a great deal, why?'

'Fancy us going out together?'

'Yes, I do.'

'There's a dance advertised, a local hop.'

'I think I've forgotten how to dance.'

'No one forgets how to dance.'

'What do I wear?'

'Any old thing, no one dresses up and speaking of clothes that blue skirt and blouse you've been wearing I really do admire. Where did you buy them?'

'I didn't. The lady who taught me to sew gave them to me as a parting gift.'

'Lucky you.' Her face fell at the mention of the parting gift making her remember her own difficult position. 'You do think I have a chance of being kept on?'

'Personally I do, but I don't want to raise your hopes. I could be wrong.'

'I know,' she said glumly.

'It could be that nothing will be said and things will just go back to normal.'

'I need a friend,' she said abruptly.

'So do I.' It was true, Rachel thought, she had no one really close. Every day she had expected, hoped to get a letter from Kerne House but there had been nothing. Writing again would be pointless, she had done all she could. The next move would have to come from Agnes. Even though she had all but given up hope there was an aching longing inside her that one day they would meet again.

The village hall was well filled, the band was too loud but there was plenty of laughter. Three chairs were put together to hold the coats. Rachel and Janet added theirs.

'That's nice,' Janet said admiring the brightly coloured cotton skirt.

'Made it myself from a remnant I got at the sales.'

'Wish I could sew, takes me all my time to sew on a button.'

'When I've time I'll run up something for you but nothing complicated I'm not that good. I like what you're wearing.' The slightly flared primrose yellow dress with its square shaped neckline and stiffened belt set off her figure and looked fresh and attrractive.

'Henry bought it for me,' she said a little defiantly. 'It should be nice, it cost enough. I bet in my place you would have thrown it out.'

'Janet, there is no answer to that since I wouldn't have accepted it in the first place.'

'You and I are very different. It belongs to me, I like it, I wear it.'

'Fair enough.'

'I'm not broken-hearted, just terribly hurt at the way he treated me.'

'Then you weren't in love with him.'

'I was in love with what he could give me and I enjoyed being with him. There now I've shocked you.'

'That's what you are trying to do and I think we should drop the subject.'

'You could be right at that. Don't turn now but a couple of very presentable fellows have just come in and I think we are getting the once-over.'

The band struck up a quickstep.

'May I have this dance?' the taller of them asked Rachel while the other smiled to Janet.

Rachel smiled, bit her lip, went into his arms and just hoped that her feet obeyed the music.

'Been here before?'

'No, my first time.'

'What do you think of it?'

'Noisy but nice,' she smiled and he laughed.

'Live around here, do you?'

'I work at Duncairn House, I'm a maid.'

'Your friend too?'

'Yes. Are you local?'

'Born and bred these parts.'

'You asked my occupation, may I ask yours?'

'I work at Braelands, that's a farm.'

'You're a farmhand then?'

'You could say that.'

It didn't at the time, only later the peculiarity of the words struck her. He was either a farmhand or he wasn't; it would seem he wasn't.

'I'm Ian Thompson.'

'I'm Rachel Donaldson.'

She supposed him a good dancer, putting in all the twirly bits and after a few apologies when she'd stood on his toes, she was getting the hang of it.

★ ★ ★

'Fun wasn't it? Glad I persuaded you to go, aren't you?' Janet said as they began setting the table in the dining-room.

'Yes, I enjoyed myself.'

'Your fellow seems nice, quite good-looking too.'

Rachel nodded agreement. He was pleasant-looking in a boyish way, not like – she closed her eyes. Why had she to compare him with Peter McGregor. It angered her that he kept intruding in her thoughts.

'Bobby said they only intended popping in for half an hour or so but changed their minds when they saw us. Incidentally, in case he didn't tell you, Ian Thompson's father farms Braelands, one of the biggest here about.'

'Oh, dear, he said he was on the farm and I put him down to be a farmhand.'

'A bit well-spoken for a farmhand.'

'I don't know, Janet, you could say that about us.'

'Two superior maids,' she grinned. 'Asked you out again, has he?'

'Yes. He has to deliver some produce in Perth, then it's the first house of the pictures. What about you?'

'Bobby's a mechanic, his dad owns the garage opposite the school and he's taking me for a spin on my day off.'


'Sorry it's just the van, my brother has the car,' Ian apologised. He was dressed in dark trousers with a tweed jacket with leather patches on the elbow. Peter had leather patches on the elbows too and she wondered if it was to reduce wear or just for appearance.

'I don't mind.'

'I'll say this for it, it is dependable, it has to be to get us to the market in all weathers. The back is filthy but my sister cleaned out the two front seats so there is no danger of getting your clothes soiled.'

Rachel climbed in, it was clean and comfortable too.

'There's a tartan rug on the back seat and if it gets cold coming back you can wrap it round your legs.'

'Ian, I'm not a hothouse plant.'

'No, I didn't think you were, but the temperature is going to plummet. I've had it from a reliable source,' he paused, 'my father.'

'Farmers are good at predicting the weather or so it's said.'

'My dad's pretty good.'

He kept up a good speed but he was careful. 'Mind if I ask how old you are?'

'Eighteen in April. I might not be so keen to answer that question in a few years' time.'

'Women are funny like that. I'm twenty.'

Ian delivered the produce and got back in the van. 'Thought we would have high tea at the Grosvenor then go to the pictures if you'd like that.'

'Sounds lovely. What's on?'

'Never thought of looking to see but if we don't like it we can come out.'

'What a shocking waste of money.'

'It won't ruin me.' He took his hand off the steering wheel and went into his pocket to bring out two tickets which he put in Rachel's lap before returning his hand to the wheel.

'Keep the eighteenth of February free, that's three weeks tomorrow.'

'What for?'

'You've got the tickets in your hand, the Farmers' Ball.' He smiled and glanced sideways at her.

Rachel read it and gasped as her eye caught the corner and the price of the ticket.

'You'll come, won't you?'

'I'd be thrilled to but I don't think I can. I mean it will be very grand and nothing in my wardrobe would be remotely suitable.'

'Nonsense, you'd look lovely in rags.'

She laughed. 'Oh, I could do better than that.'

'Then it's a date?'

'Thank you very much.' It was true she didn't have an evening gown but she did have money in her Post Office savings account. Yes, she would treat herself even if it meant blowing the lot. Suddenly Rachel felt carefree. This was an occasion and she wanted to look her best.

As the date of the Farmers' Ball drew near, Rachel was filled with nervous excitement. Janet could have been of assistance, helped her choose something suitable, but they were seldom free at the same time. Nothing else for it, she would just have to choose carefully and hope she got a helpful shop assistant.

The small amount of money payable on demand was insufficient and Rachel sent off the necessary form leaving just enough in her account to keep it open. The gown might not take it all and she would be able to put some back.

The February day was bitter when Rachel, the money making a bulge in her purse, took the bus into Perth. She knew the Fair City by this time and where to find the best shops. Browsing was what she intended doing at the start and she stopped at one window. It was its stark simplicity that attracted her. No fussy window-dressing detracted from the beautiful black velvet gown displayed. It was for someone older and sophisticated but it was the sheer magnetism of that window that kept her glued. Almost without thinking, she went in, her feet making no sound on the carpet. There were two curtained cubicles and the air was faintly but pleasantly perfumed. Voices drifted from one of the cubicles and a girl came from the back and walked towards her. Her lips curled as she took in Rachel's shabby coat and Rachel wished herself a thousand miles away.

'Did you want something?' she drawled.

'A – an evening dress. I'd like to see what you have, please.'

'We don't go in for the cheaper models.'

That angered Rachel as it was no doubt intended to do. Her nervousness vanished, she wouldn't buy anything but she would put this insolent madam in her place.

'Perhaps you would be good enough to show me what you do have.'

The shoulders shrugged and the girl went away returning a few minutes later with two gowns over her arm.

'Just go into the cubicle.' She went ahead and laid the gowns over the back of a chair. Then she closed the curtain and left Rachel to it. One of the gowns was in a sweetie pink, a colour she disliked. A pale pink, yes, but not that shade. The other would have suited a mature woman, it was in a coffee colour with a matching bolero. The girl drew back the curtain.

'Neither of these appeals to me, I'm afraid.'

'You can't tell until you've tried them on.'

'I don't need to try them on, I don't like either.'

'If it is the colour that is bothering you try them on for style.'

Rachel swithered, maybe she was being awkward. She removed her skirt and blouse and allowed the gown to be slipped over her head.

'That shade of pink suits you very well. Your sort of gown I would say and it is one of our less expensive models.' The drawl was more pronounced as was the look of boredom.

'I don't agree, I don't think it suits me at all.'

'Try the other then.'

'No, thank you, if that is all you can show me I won't trouble you further.'

The curtain was gently pulled aside.

'Miss Brown, go and see to the stock at the back, I'll look after this young lady.'

Rachel bit her lip. 'I'm sorry I don't care for either of these.'

'Of course you don't, they are completely unsuitable.' Mrs McMaster who owned the shop was a small woman, plainly but fashionably dressed and Rachel knew instinctively that here was someone who would rather lose a sale than have a customer leave with something that did not suit her. 'Just excuse me, I shan't be long.'

The voices drifted through the half-open door and Rachel could not but hear.

'What on earth were you thinking about? These, as you very well know, are not part of my stock just what I inherited with the shop and they'll be got rid of at the next sale.'

'By the look of her she can't afford our prices.'

'That is not for you to decide. My regret is that I was persuaded to take you on but unless your manner improves, young woman, it will be the parting of the ways for you and me.'

She was back. 'Try these, my dear. You are so lucky to have such a nice slim figure and with that lovely colouring you could wear almost any shade.' She held up the peacock blue. 'Very simple and that is the secret of good style.'

'A friend of mine, a dressmaker, once told me that,' Rachel said shyly.

'She spoke good sense. I can't tell you the number of times I've wished for a pair of scissors to snip off those unnecessary bits and bows. There now, what do you think of that?'

Looking at herself, Rachel felt a tingle of excitement. The gown was lovely and could have been made for her. 'It's beautiful but before you go to any more trouble I'd better tell you how much I can afford to spend.'

The gowns cost more, a lot more, but there was something about this girl that she liked and she was still seething at her assistant.

'We'll manage to keep within your budget,' she smiled.

'Meaning I can afford this one?' Rachel asked.

'Yes, but one does not decide as quickly as all that on something as important as an evening gown. May I ask if this is a special occasion?'

Rachel felt a flush of colour rise in her face. 'I've been invited to the Farmers' Ball.'

'My dear, how perfectly splendid, it is the occasion of the year. Slip out of that and we'll try the turquoise.'

'I can't decide, they are both – both perfect. Which do you think? I'd value your opinion.'

'Not yet, my dear. I want you to try on one more then I'll give it.'

'What a lovely and unusual shade,' Rachel exclaimed when the gown was brought to her.

'Isn't it? It's called tangerine and what I, myself, would call a deep orange with just a hint of red. Not many can get away with that colour but it's an eye-catcher.'

As Rachel slipped it on, Mrs McMaster added, 'One or two of my regular customers were very taken with the shade but it wasn't right on them. It needs black hair like yours to set it off.'

Rachel looked at herself, turning this way and that. Mrs McMaster nodded.

'Your gown, my dear, don't you agree?'

'Oh, I do, I really do,' Rachel said with a sigh of happiness.

Mrs McMaster opened the curtain and called to her assistant, 'Miss Brown, come here, please.'

She came hurrying. 'You wanted me, Mrs McMaster?'

'Yes. The tangerine gown has always been your favourite?'

The girl swallowed and nodded.

'Unfortunately you have neither the figure nor the colouring to carry it off whereas it is quite perfect on this young lady. And this very lucky lady is going to the Farmers' Ball.' She smiled at Rachel. 'A few of my regulars will be wearing my creations but I can assure you that none will outshine you. On you go, Miss Brown, you can get on with your work now.'

Rachel felt sorry for the girl and it showed on her face. 'She deserved it, my dear, she was appallingly rude to you and I will not have my customers treated like that.'

Back into her own clothes Rachel approached the glass counter.

'Don't be tempted to wear a necklace of any kind no matter what anyone says. You have a lovely, long, graceful neck, let it be shown. A sandal with a small heel would suit best.' She was chatting as she carefully inserted tissue paper between the folds then gently lowered the gown into the dress box. While Rachel was getting out her money the woman disappeared and came back with a fine shawl. 'That has been lying about and is soiled and I can't sell soiled goods. A careful wash and it will come up like new.'

'I don't know what to say, you've been so kind.' Rachel was taken aback at this show of generosity.

'Caught me in a good mood.'

'Thank you very much indeed.'

'I hope you have an unforgettable evening.'

Flushed with her successful shopping expedition Rachel headed for the bus. A cup of tea would have been welcome but she wasn't going to spend a penny more. Only when she was on the bus did it hit her. She had cleaned out her savings on a gown that would perhaps only be worn on the one occasion. She was all sorts of a fool, she thought ruefully, yet even if she could take it back she wouldn't.

'Rachel, it's fantastic, gorgeous, beautiful and must have cost you the earth. On the never-never, is it?' The two were in Rachel's room.

'No, it's paid for, a lot more than I intended spending, but there it is, I need my head examined.'

'Need it examined if you let a creation like that slip by you,' Janet said openly envious.

Hetty came in and Rachel did a twirl for her benefit. 'You look like a princess,' there was awe in her voice.

As the lady had said, after a careful wash the shawl came up like new. She threw it around her shoulders. 'There, that's me ready for the Ball.'

'Need something over it.'

'I'd rather freeze than put on my old coat.'

'You are welcome to my cloak.'

'You mean it, Janet?'

'Yes, I rather like to think of it being at the Ball. Mind, I would have preferred if I had been inside it.' They all laughed.

'Rachel, I've got pearls – they belonged to my grandmother. I don't think they are real but they look nice.'

'Sweet of you, Hetty, but the lady in the shop made me promise I wouldn't wear jewellery of any kind.

'Probably got a point,' Janet nodded.

★ ★ ★

It was here, the longed for night of the Farmers' Ball, with the weather dry and blustery. Janet and Hetty were engaged in the dining-room but Rachel was glad to be alone. Excitement had given her petal-smooth skin a rosy glow and her hair shampooed the previous evening was the length she preferred – neither short nor long. Black springy curls framed her face and her blue eyes were shining like twin stars as she stared at herself in the mirror.

She wasn't vain but she knew she looked beautiful. The colour was right and the cut of the gown emphasised the long slenderness of her body. It was a young dress full of youthful promise yet with a subtle elegance. She thought how kind everyone had been, all so anxious to give something of theirs. Janet, her cloak and evening bag both very much appreciated, Hetty, with her pearls and Mrs Morton her amber beads. The jewellery she had gently but firmly declined but in a way that gave no offence.

Always sparing with make-up, sometimes she wore none at all, tonight she gave her face a dusting of powder and added colour to her lips.

Mrs Morton had requested that she pop into the kitchen before she left and half an hour before Ian was due she went along.

'A fair picture you are, lass. The lads won't be able to take their eyes off you.'

'I'm going with a partner.'

'I know that, lass, but some of them toffs is right persistent.'

'I'll do then?'

'You'll do. See and have a lovely time and if you were my daughter I would be tellin' you to mind yoursel'. I'll get them to leave a light on for you comin' in.'

'Thank you and I promise to be as quiet as a mouse.'

Time she went downstairs, then Rachel had an uncomfortable thought. She'd forgotten to tell Ian to come to the side door, but surely he would. He would remember she was a servant in the house. The knock came, she heard Hetty opening the door to him.

'Rachel ready?'

'Yes, I am,' Rachel smiled. 'Hetty, this is Ian, or should I have said Ian this is Hetty.' Ian shook hands and Hetty went beetroot red.

'Have a good time,' she said, waiting until they were well away from the door before closing it.

Taking Rachel's arm, Ian hurried her through the blustery, dry night to where the car was parked. Once she was comfortably settled he closed the door and went round to the driver's side.

The roads were narrow, it was grey-dark and Ian concentrated on his driving saying little until they reached the Grosvenor Hotel. All but a small part of it had been given over to those attending the Farmers' Ball. An attempt had been made to organise the parking with white lines indicating the space allotted to each car. This had been largely ignored by the first arrivals who had more or less abandoned their vehicles.

'Typical,' Ian fumed.

'What's typical?'

'Farmers, they don't obey any rules except their own.'

'Does that apply to your father?' she teased.

'It would if he was here. If I park where I am I'm blocking two cars from getting out – oh, what the blazes, if *I* don't someone else will.' He switched off and went round to open the door for Rachel and she carefully lifted the skirt of her gown lest her heel caught in it. The wind whipped around them but it was a short step to the entrance where the uniformed attendant had the glass door open. There was warmth and people congregating and greeting each other noisily. Most of the women had fur coats or fur jackets over their gowns and the men were in evening or Highland dress. A few smiled her way and gave a word of greeting to Ian.

'Ian, where do I leave my cape?'

'Over there, you'll have to join the queue.' A girl behind the counter was taking coats and handing over tickets.

'Don't lose your tickets, ladies, you'll need them to reclaim your belongings.'

Rachel put it carefully in the evening bag she had borrowed from Janet and turned to find Ian at her back.

'Nothing to wear! Heavens, you look ravishing.'

'You like it then?' she said shyly. His open admiration was embarrassing her.

'I'll say I do. Come to that I like what's inside it even better.' His arm went round her waist as he led her into a very large room with huge crystal chandeliers that glittered and sparkled as the dancers circled the floor. There was a mixture of old and young as Ian had said there would be. Some of the older women were heavily jewelled and wore gowns that were fashionable and no doubt very expensive, Rachel thought. There were others for whom fashion was unimportant and it looked as though the same gown came out of its mothballs year after year.

The band had just finished playing an old-fashioned waltz, a favourite of the older generation.

'Have to cater for all tastes,' Ian apologised.

'Nothing wrong with an old-fashioned waltz.'

He made a face. 'How are you with an eightsome reel?'

'I won't disgrace you,' she laughed.

'You couldn't,' he smiled. 'I much prefer modern dancing but I don't mind getting up for a reel.' The band at that moment struck up a quickstep and Ian immediately led her on to the floor. She was still nervous about the extra twirly bits he put in but she was managing to follow him though it meant concentrating.

After three dances in succession they sat down. 'Why do you keep putting in those complicated steps?' she complained. 'It must be obvious to you that I'm not in your class when it comes to dancing.'

'Rubbish. You have natural rhythm, you just have to learn to let yourself go.' They were chatting happily when someone drew near and they both looked up.

'Ian, do you mind if I borrow your partner for this dance, that is, of course, if the lady is willing?'

Rachel felt herself flush then go pale as she looked into the face of Peter McGregor.

# Chapter Twenty-Four

'You'll have to leave that, Agnes,' Mrs Harrison said as she came into the kitchen, 'you're wanted in the library.'

'Wanted in the library?' Agnes repeated in dismay.

'Yes, on you go,' she said, and gave a smile as though to reassure Agnes, but then she wasn't to know that this was the summons she had been dreading.

She dried her hands, smoothed down her skirt and went along, not hurrying, she needed the time to pull herself together. If only she hadn't let her tongue run away with her but it was too late for regrets. Her outspokenness was to cost her her job. She swallowed the lump in her throat and wondered even at this late hour if an apology would do any good. She doubted it but it was worth a try. She took a deep breath and knocked at the door.

'Come in.'

She did and closed the door behind her. Gerald Patterson looked up briefly then went on with his writing. After a few moments he put down his pen. 'What are you doing standing there? Come over here.'

She went to stand in front of the desk. 'Mr Gerald, sir.'

'Yes.'

'I – I just wanted you to know how very sorry I am for the way I spoke to you, I don't know what got into me.' She paused and swallowed. 'Please don't sack me, sir, please give me another chance.' She was grovelling and if it meant saving her job she would do any amount of it.

'Don't sack me!' he said with heavy emphasis on the words. 'For someone anxious to better herself that was a shockingly bad expression. Much better if you had said, "Please don't terminate my employment" or even "Please don't dispense with my services".'

Agnes flushed angrily. The rotten so-and-so was making fun of her. With difficulty she bit back the words she longed to say and instead lowered her eyes to the carpet and picked at the thick pile with her toe.

247

'When I am addressing someone I expect that person to look at me.'
Reluctantly she raised her head.

'I did not call you here to terminate your employment, someone else
would have done that.'

'You didn't?' Agnes felt dizzy with relief and let out a huge sigh.

He laughed, a real laugh that was full of amusement and chased away
the lines of pain and suffering. 'Nothing was further from my mind. What
I wanted was to find out if your declared interest in books was genuine or
not.'

'It's genuine all right.'

'Did you work hard at school?'

'No,' she answered truthfully.

'And why was that? Before you answer, bring over a chair for yourself.'

She did and was glad to be off her legs. Her hands, she never quite
knew what to do with them and she had been standing with them behind
her back. Now she put them in her lap and locked her fingers. 'The
answer to your question, sir, is it seemed like a waste of time and,' she
looked over at the fireplace she cleaned every morning, 'not much
learning is required to clean out the ashes.'

'Perhaps not but learning is never wasted.'

'I appreciate that now but I didn't then.'

'Given the opportunity what would you have done with your life?'

'I'm clever.'

'And modest.'

'Well, I'm only saying what my teacher said,' she defended herself.
'She said I had a good brain but I was too lazy to use it.'

'And was she right?'

'No, she wasn't. My ma, I mean my mother, said too much learning
just makes you discontented.' She stopped.

He nodded. 'Go on.'

'My best friend was staying on at school then going on to college, only
she didn't because her da married again and the money went on his new
wife.' Why on earth was she telling him all this and why didn't he stop
her.

'You must have been distressed for your friend?'

'Should have been, I know, but I wasn't. I wanted to be a teacher too
and her not getting to be one made us the same again.'

Gerald Patterson was having great difficulty in hiding his amusement.

It wasn't just amusement, the girl fascinated him. How refreshing to hear someone being so honest. Many would have felt the same but quite unable to admit to it.

'May I ask what you should be doing at this moment?'

'You took me away from my job helping in the kitchen, after that I was supposed to clean the silver.'

'Boring, repetitive jobs?'

'Yes and no to that. I do my thinking then.'

'Let me give you something to think about.' He paused to look at her. 'I have selected some reading matter for you.'

She beamed. 'That is very good of you, sir.'

'You won't hoodwink me, my girl. I'll know if you have read them, for I mean to question you on them.'

Agnes gave a broad grin, she couldn't help it.

'What is so funny?'

'You, you sound like a schoolmaster.'

A look of great sadness crossed his face. 'A schoolmaster is precisely what I would have been had it not been for these—'

'Bloody, useless legs,' Agnes finished for him, then appalled, clapped her hand over her mouth.

The roar of laughter could have been heard through the whole of Drumoaks and indeed it had been heard by Gerald's unmarried sister, Gertrude, who knocked first then poked her head in.

'What is going on, Gerald? I haven't heard you laugh like that in a very long time.'

'Never had very much to laugh about. Come in if you want.'

Agnes got up hastily. 'Excuse me, sir, I'd better get back to work.'

'Yes, perhaps you had. Here, take these and read them.'

Gertrude was frowning. 'Is that wise, Gerald?'

'She'll take good care of them.'

Gertrude sat down with her feet slightly apart in her sensible brogue shoes and studied her younger brother. 'Do you mind telling me what is going on?'

'Nothing is going on, my dear Gertrude, and if you will forgive the crudeness, my accident saw to that.'

She winced. 'Of course you are bored, I know you are, but if you weren't so rude to people they would come and see you. You can be horribly rude when you choose.'

'Their sympathy I can do without and the way they avoid looking at my legs makes me sick.' He looked down at them. 'Covered with trousers they look perfectly ordinary, wouldn't you say?' The peevishness disappeared and he gave a sudden grin. 'That red-haired piece referred to them as my bloody useless legs.'

'Only repeating what she heard you say I have no doubt. That red-haired piece as you call her should not be encouraged. She is after all only a maid in this house and you would do well to remember that.'

'Not your ordinary maid, Gertrude, not by a long way.' He gave her a sidelong look and a smile. It wasn't difficult to win over his sister and he wasn't above using his disability to get what he wanted. 'Do something for me, will you?' he asked.

The face that her brother Adrian sometimes described as 'horsey' softened. 'You've only to ask.'

'Her name is Agnes Boyd and she's intelligent. Her speech isn't too bad when she remembers and she wants to make something of herself.'

'Is that what she told you?'

'More or less. Given the chance she'll get on I'm sure of it.'

'She may feel that way just now.'

'What do you mean by that?'

'She'll get married, have a family and that will be that.'

'Not Agnes, not that redhead, she won't throw herself away on some ignorant lout. She interests me, Gertrude, and God knows I need something in my life.'

Better than anyone Gertrude knew her brother, knew too how close he had been to taking his own life. 'What have you in mind?' she said carefully.

'Perhaps a couple of hours' tuition here in the library. You know how that could be arranged?'

She was thoughtful. She didn't approve but where was the harm in it. The girl would be bored in no time and Gerald didn't tolerate fools gladly. It would burn itself out but meantime it would keep him happily occupied.

'Well?'

'I was thinking. If you're serious I'll have a word with Mrs Harrison, make out that you have plans for rearranging the books, or something of the sort.'

'Brilliant, that should do it.'

'If it goes on for long, Mrs Harrison can ask one of the others to do an extra hour or so.'

'Thanks, Gertrude.' He suddenly looked depressed and she glanced at him worriedly. He had such swings of mood.

'Yes, I think I am very much in favour of it after all. It would be a start. Tutoring here at Drumoaks could be a worthwhile career, Gerald, you have excellent qualifications and students wouldn't be in short supply. What you need is your confidence back and this little maid may be the answer.'

Mrs Harrison was none too happy, in fact she was very displeased. Agnes Boyd was a maid and maids were engaged to do household tasks not play around with books. This sort of preferential treatment could go to the girl's head, give her ideas above her station and cause discontent among the others. She pursed her lips and drew in her brows, but an order was an order and had to be obeyed. She had no say in the matter.

'Agnes, finish what you are doing and then come along to my room,' she said severely.

'Yes, Mrs Harrison.' The tone didn't sound too promising but she couldn't recall doing anything dreadful and she wasn't unduly worried.

The housekeeper was looking out of the window when Agnes entered. Taking her time she turned round to face Agnes.

'I have had a most peculiar request concerning you. It appears that Mr Gerald is once again taking an interest in things and wishes to catalogue the books in the library and apparently you are to do the fetching and carrying.'

Agnes could feel Mrs Harrison's displeasure and hid her excitement as best she could. She waited for the housekeeper to go on.

'You are required in the library at ten o'clock tomorrow morning. See that you do your usual duties before that time, and should your work fall behind I shall expect you to work extra in the evening.'

'Yes, Mrs Harrison.'

'That is all, you may go.'

Risking a reprimand Agnes went quickly to her own room and once there gave in to her excitement and hugged herself. Mr Gerald was going to help her, she just knew he was. It was happening, slowly but surely her dreams were coming true. She was to be given the right books to read and questioned on them. She was privileged indeed and Agnes couldn't help smiling at the thought of scruffy Agnes Boyd, formerly of Spinner's Lane, being taught by Mr Gerald who, but for his accident, would have been teaching the toffs in one of those posh schools. For a moment she felt a rush of compassion mixed with guilt that she should benefit from another's misfortunes. But that, she told herself, was life.

A moderate show of interest was all that Gerald expected from Agnes and he was deeply touched to see her genuine eagerness to learn. Daniel Defoe's *Robinson Crusoe* had delighted her as had John Buchan's *The Thirty-nine Steps*. Now as a complete change he had given her *Far From the Madding Crowd*.

'What did you think of Thomas Hardy, Agnes?' Gerald asked as they sat together in the library.

'Well, he must be a good writer,' she grinned. 'I mean I didn't know the first thing about country life but after reading that I think I do now.'

She saw him nod approvingly and relaxed. It was so very important for Agnes to please this gentleman who was giving her so much of his time.

'Did you study it as you were reading?'

'No, I read it quickly to see how it was going to end then I went back and read it properly.'

'Good girl.' He put his elbows on the desk. 'What is your opinion of Bathsheba?'

'In the beginning I thought her too concerned with her appearance.'

'Too vain?'

'Yes. Always wanting to make a good impression but I think by the end she was a stronger character.'

'Go on,' he said smiling encouragingly.

'Pretty rotten joke to send that valentine to that farmer whats-his-name?'

'Boldwood?'

'Yes, him.'

'Why was it cruel, Agnes? Lots of people send valentines, after all it is only a light-hearted piece of nonsense. Haven't you given or received one?'

She looked scornful. 'Folk where I come from have more to do with their money. Anyway it was a mistake. Boldwood took it seriously and once he discovered who it was from he set about courting her believing she felt the same way about him.'

'Was Bathsheba in love with anyone?'

'Mostly herself, I would say, but she was very taken with Troy or maybe it was the uniform.'

'Would Troy have appealed to you?' he asked with a mischievious grin.

'Absolutely not, I can see through that kind. Mind you, a bit of flirting might be fun but when it comes to marriage—' she stopped and flushed.

'Don't be embarrassed, go on.'

She hesitated then decided it would be better just to carry on and say what she was going to. 'Liking and respect are more important than love, more lasting too, but of course if you're lucky enough to get all three,' she broke off and looked at the ceiling.

'Improbable but certainly not impossible, Agnes, if we are to believe all we read.' A spasm of pain crossed his face and Agnes wondered if he were in actual pain or it was something he was remembering. 'The fire is going down, see to it.'

'Sorry, I should have noticed,' she said getting hastily to her feet. She used the poker to clear the ashes then added a log and placed coal around it. All this she managed without dirtying her hands. Once she had used a paper bag for her hand but now there was a large mitt for the purpose. She came back to sit opposite him and waited with her hands folded in her lap.

'You enjoy reading?'

'I love it.'

'Books are one of the greatest joys in life as you are just beginning to find out.' He paused and frowned as if in thought. 'You've read *Emma* and you've read *Pride and Prejudice* so I think we'll give Jane Austen a rest. How about Charles Dickens?'

'I've read *David Copperfield*.'

'So you have. Go and get down *Great Expectations*. It is a wonderful novel, Agnes, but after that we turn our attention to history. No use being well-read if you have no knowledge of what went on in this great country of ours to make it what it is today.'

She couldn't let that pass. 'That sort of depends on your position in this country,' she said tartly and he raised an eyebrow.

'My dear girl, I was not thinking of material things but rather of the wars and the bravery of our fathers who gave their lives that we should know freedom.'

'I suppose if you put it that way.'

\* \* \*

As the weeks went by and spring brightened the lawns with masses of large, golden-trumpeted daffodils, Agnes was to be seen poring over books. Sometimes she thought her head would burst with all this learning and occasionally she would suffer the lashing of his tongue if she was slow to grasp his meaning. That had bewildered her, made her angry too at the unfairness of it, but she kept quiet. In bed at night she fought tiredness to read and study the work he gave her, sometimes dozing off with the light still burning and having to get up later to turn it off. Did he forget, or perhaps he didn't know, that she still had to get through her chores?

Not that she would ever complain, she was too grateful for what he was doing for her. The highlight of her day was when he would tell her to stop what she was doing and they would have a discussion on a particular book, politics or whatever he had in mind. Politics had them at loggerheads. There would be heated arguments and sometimes Agnes would forget herself sufficiently to bring in a few choice adjectives. Far from angering him it had the opposite effect and Gerald Patterson was reduced to helpless laughter.

Beatrice and Madge at first accepted the explanation that Agnes was helping to reorganise the books in the library but as the weeks turned into months curiosity got the better of them and they all but demanded to know what was going on.

'Nothing is going on, you two, but it's confidential and just you remember that.' She stopped and wondered what to say but knew too that nothing short of the truth would satisfy.

'We wouldn't say a word, would we, Beatrice?'

'Of course not and Agnes knows that.'

'All right I'll tell you but no laughing. It's just that I showed an interest in the books in the library and it went on from there. Mr Gerald was going to be a schoolmaster so he knows how to teach. He, well, he sets me passages to read then questions me on them.'

'Better you than me,' Beatrice said feelingly. 'I had enough of school when I was there.'

'Me too.' Madge looked puzzled. 'What are you goin' to do with all that learnin', that's what I'd like to know?'

'I'm not sure myself, Madge, but at least I have the satisfaction of knowing things I never knew before.'

'I suppose there's that to it.'

As for Gerald Patterson, he was a changed man. Everyone noticed it but only his sister understood it. She was both pleased and disturbed. Gerald seemed to be obsessed with the girl and it worried her. Adrian and Olive knew nothing of it and she wondered what they would say if they did know. Blame her for encouraging it and try to talk sense into Gerald.

Gertrude wasn't the only one who worried. Gerald did a good deal of it himself. What had been intended as a way of helping to put in the day had become a necessary part of his life. Saturdays and Sundays when he didn't see her were just days to be got through. Strange that he should find her presence disturbing when he had thought never to be interested in a woman again. No longer did he see or think of her as a servant at Drumoaks; he saw her now as a young, attractive woman whom he could engage in conversation and get a lively response.

Looking at her bowed head he wondered what it would feel like to bring his fingers through that thick auburn hair. Her mouth fascinated him, so set and determined one moment then in the next turned up in the sweetest smile that churned at his insides and was the cause of those cruel, sarcastic remarks he hurled at her. She took it in silence but he would see the hurt in those brown eyes and hate himself.

His nightmare was that she would leave him, leave Drumoaks. Gertrude had warned him that it was to be expected, that girls of her class married young and started families almost immediately. What could he do about it? Nothing. There was nothing he could do. Or was there?

What was going on in his mind was impossible, laughable, yet it stayed with him.

He waited another month before plucking up courage. His hands under the desk were sweating and he wiped them on his trouser legs.

'Agnes, do you find the life at Drumoaks quiet for you?'

'I love it,' she said simply.

'You would miss all this if it were to stop?'

She looked away from him, the pain was a hard lump in her throat as she thought of these precious hours coming to an end and her return to full-time domestic duties. Yet she had known they couldn't go on.

'Yes, I would,' she said quietly and managing to steady her voice, 'you have been very good to me, sir, and very patient and I'll always be grateful to you.'

'You have been a joy to teach.'

There is something you will never know, Gerald Patterson, Agnes thought, and it would be embarrassing for both of us if you did, but I'm going to miss you as much as the lessons.

'I'm glad about that.' She had to get out before she made a fool of herself. 'Excuse me, sir, I'd like to go now if you don't mind.' Her voice was wobbling and she got up almost knocking the chair over in her haste to be gone.

'Sit down at once,' he bawled at her and when she didn't, he said quietly, 'Sit down, Agnes, and tell me what has upset you.'

'Nothing.'

'Agnes Boyd doesn't get into a state like this about nothing. Out with it, girl.'

She bit her lip. 'I'm just being foolish and yes, you're right, it isn't like me but these hours in the library have come to mean a great deal to me. Of course I knew they would have to come to an end but it was springing it on me like that.'

'Springing what on you?'

'That this is the end of the lessons.'

'I didn't say that, you went off on that tack on your own.' He was silent for a long time, then he spoke softly, so softly that she barely heard him. 'As far as I'm concerned, Agnes, these lessons can go on for a lifetime.'

'I don't understand.'

'Don't you? Have you no inkling?'

She shook her head.

'Agnes Boyd, I am asking you to marry me.'

She stared at him, then the swift colour came to her face flooding it.

'I am not in the mood for jokes.'

'This is no joke, I am being completely serious.'

'Would you mind repeating the question?'

'I was proposing marriage to you, Agnes.'

'You want me to be your wife?'

'That is what it usually means. Do you want time to consider?'

Her eyes widening in shock but thankful that her brain was functioning properly, Agnes wasn't prepared to risk delaying her answer but in the moments before accepting, Tommy Kingsley's words came back to her. 'You'll always be working class, Agnes, and those with breeding will make use of you for as long as it suits them.' He could very easily be right, she wasn't denying that, but wasn't she doing the same thing? She was using Gerald Patterson to get what she wanted.

Her mouth widened into a huge smile. 'I don't need time to consider, the answer is yes, please, sir.'

'Gerald. You'll have to get used to calling me that.'

'Take a bit of doing.'

'You'll manage.' He paused. 'How old are you, Agnes?'

'Eighteen going on nineteen.'

'I'm thirty-two. Does that seem very old to you?'

'Not for a man, but I'd be old if I were thirty-two.'

'You'll never be old, Agnes, in years perhaps but not in any other way.'

'I'm not sure if that is a compliment or not, sir, I mean, Gerald. Sounds as though I'll never grow up.'

He laughed then grew sober. 'You have to understand, Agnes, that this can never be a proper marriage,' he said slowly and keeping his eyes on her. 'You do know what I mean?'

'Yes,' she said gently and feeling an overwhelming compassion for him.

'No children – ever—'

'Truthfully, that wouldn't worry me. There were seven of us at home and at times it was sheer hell. That's not to say I don't like kids, as a matter of fact I do, but I don't need any of my own.'

He nodded, well pleased. He knew that Agnes could be relied on to tell the truth. 'I don't see a great deal of my nephew and niece but then they are usually with their nanny.'

She didn't say anything. She could see that there was something else he wanted to say and at last the difficult words came out.

'You would be getting a cripple for a husband and as you know as well as anyone I can be the very devil to get on with. As Gertrude could tell you it was my appalling behaviour that chased away more than one person from Drumoaks.'

'You shouldn't let that bother you. True friends wouldn't have let a few tantrums drive them away.'

'Tantrums? Is that how you would refer to them?'

She grinned. 'Never do get the right word, do I? But it's near enough.'

'You could put up with that?'

'Yes, but I would try very hard to make sure that you had no cause to fly off the handle.' She frowned. 'No, I take that back, a good burst of temper doesn't do any harm, does a lot of good actually. My parents go at it hammer and tongs, it clears the air and they are reasonably pleasant to each other until the next time.'

'What are your parents going to say about this?'

'It has nothing to do with them, it is my life and I knew a long time ago that I had to break away.'

'Why?' he asked gently.

'Because they would always hold me back. They won't change and the person I have become, largely through you, they wouldn't want to know.'

'You would make a complete break?'

'In the sense that we wouldn't see each other but I would like to go on sending them a little money.'

'How on earth have you managed that on the pittance you get?'

She grinned mischievously, 'You do admit it is a pittance?'

'The going rate I am informed.'

'Every little helps is what my mother would say.'

'We'll have to improve on that, give them a monthly allowance to cover their rent, heating and the like.'

She shook her head. 'Very nice of you, but that isn't the way to do it. What seems a very little to you is a great deal to them and it would be squandered. Saving is something they don't understand. The best way to help them is to pay the rent directly to the rent office.'

'In case they spend the money unwisely?'

'They would, no doubt about it. My mother would decide that something was more important than paying the rent and they would quickly get into arrears. I know them, Gerald.'

'Very well, my dear, we'll work that one out later.'

'Seems to me that I'm getting a lot out of this marriage and you very little.'

'I am getting a refreshingly honest, spirited girl of eighteen going on nineteen and you a man of thirty-two and a cripple at that.'

'I'm not afraid of the word cripple and you shouldn't be either. Apart from—'

'My bloody, useless legs.'

'Yes, apart from those legs you have everything. Brains, good looks, a privileged background and a beautiful home and that can't be bad.'

'Can't it, Agnes? What if I told you I would give up everything if I could throw away my crutches and walk?'

'I'd believe you and I wish with all my heart that it could be.' And if it could we wouldn't be talking like this, she added silently.

'To seal our engagement and forthcoming marriage and since I can't come round to you—'

She got up feeling suddenly shy and went round to stand beside him.

'Don't be afraid of me, Agnes.' Taking her face between his hands, he pressed his lips to hers. The sensation surprised her, she hadn't expected to feel anything, certainly not the little thrill that went through her as their lips met for that first kiss. Yet she shouldn't have been surprised, for hadn't she been drawn to him these last few weeks and on occasions disturbingly so.

Had it been the same for him? she wondered and decided it couldn't have been. Not once had the word love been mentioned and she would do well to remember that. Liking and respect were all she could expect and her own feelings she would keep well hidden. But did she know her own feelings? Tommy Kingsley was always there, unbidden his image would rise up, but now he must be banished for ever.

'The wedding as soon as possible, Agnes, no reason for delay.'

'What about the master and mistress and Miss Gertrude? They are going to be shocked.'

'Let them be shocked.' He frowned deeply and drummed his fingers on the desk. 'There is so much to talk about and this isn't the best place for it.'

'May I say something?'

'Of course.'

'Let me carry on with my duties as normal—'

'No, at least no longer than the next few hours. Tell you what – bring afternoon tea for two to my room about three thirty and that is to be your very last duty as housemaid. I'll see that Gertrude tells Mrs Harrison to engage another maid in your place.'

Gerald Patterson made his slow way to his own sitting-room and once there rang the bell for Bannerman, his manservant, who filled so many roles in his master's life. He came very quickly.

'Bannerman, do you know if Miss Gertrude is in the house or in those damned stables?'

'In the house. I saw her a few minutes ago.'

'Good! Tell her to come in, that I want to see her at once.'

★ ★ ★

'What's so urgent?'

'You are the first to congratulate me on my forthcoming marriage.'

She knew, of course, but she had to ask. 'To whom, dear brother?'

'How many women of marriageable age do I see?'

'Your fault. A few of them would be very happy to come and visit.'

'I've asked Agnes to marry me.'

She whitened.

'You must have guessed?'

'I suppose I just hoped against hope that I was wrong. You've actually proposed?'

'Yes, and been accepted.'

'I see.'

'Like the others will do, you are going to put forward every objection you can think of.'

'I can think of plenty.'

'Forget the objections and think of my happiness.'

'That is what I am thinking of. Gerald, you are rushing into something without giving it careful consideration. You have nothing, absolutely nothing in common and I doubt if she would ever be accepted by your own circle of friends.'

'My steadily declining circle of friends.'

'And we know whose fault that is.'

'Come on, Gertrude, you can't deny that I'm a changed man since Agnes entered my life.'

'I don't deny it and I'm grateful to the girl, but marriage – apart from your own position have you given a thought to how difficult it would be for her?'

'She'll cope, she's a quick learner.' He paused. 'Gertrude, Agnes is nobody's fool, she knows what is ahead but in a way I'm giving her what she wants. She's desperate to make a break with her old life and her family won't be a problem, she has made that clear.'

'That's something, I suppose.' She gave a deep sigh. 'All right, Gerald, if you are determined to go through with it I'll do what I can to help.'

'Thanks.'

'For a start her belongings will have to be transferred to one of the guest rooms and no more contact with the servants. See that she understands that, Gerald, and to ease matters, Mrs Harrison will need to know the circumstances.'

'I can leave that to you – and the marriage – I want that to take place as soon as it can be arranged.'

'Is she getting an engagement ring, or is that unnecessary?'

'She'll want one, I imagine. Get the jeweller to send up a tray. And clothes, Gertrude, organise that too will you, and have everything charged to my account.'

'Fashion as you know isn't my scene but I must just enjoy this. She is a pretty little thing and get that horrified look off your face. I'm not going to choose for her.' She grinned displaying large perfect teeth. The same features on a man would have been handsome but on a woman they were too heavy.

Gertrude was with her brother when Agnes arrived with a tray and it was she who opened the door.

'Want to join us, Gertrude?'

'No, I won't, thanks.'

He looked at her pointedly and Gertrude got the message.

'Gerald has just told me the news, Agnes. May I be the first to wish you every happiness.'

'You can't be pleased,' Agnes burst out, 'you don't have to pretend.'

Gerald frowned, but Gertrude smiled. 'Directness is something I admire and I propose to be equally direct. You are perfectly correct in thinking that I am against this marriage. It is no disrespect to you as a person but to the difference in your background. The way ahead, my dear, will not be easy.'

'You forget, Gertrude,' Gerald said irritably, 'that there will be very little socialising, if any at all. We'll be marooned on our own little island, won't we, Agnes?'

It was said in a jocular way but a little shiver went through her at Gerald's words. He was making it sound like a prison, a comfortable prison, but a prison nonetheless, then she ridiculed herself for such fanciful thoughts.

'Miss Gertrude – Miss Patterson – I'll do my best to make your brother happy.'

'I'm sure you'll do that, Agnes, and since you are about to become family you had better address me as Gertrude.'

'Thank you.'

'This tea is going to be stewed.'

'I'm just going, Gerald, but a word to Agnes before I do. Your clothes are being moved to one of the guest rooms and from now on there will be no contact with the servants. I'm sure you will appreciate the wisdom of that.'

Agnes was dismayed. She hadn't given any thought to it. So much had happened in such a short space of time that she was bewildered. The thought of losing the friendship of Beatrice and Madge upset her but Gertrude had spelt it out and she had to agree.

'Yes, I understand,' she said quietly.

'You'll need clothes. I'll bring the car round to the front tomorrow morning. Be ready at nine thirty.' She nodded to them both and left.

'Your first ordeal over and it wasn't too bad was it?'

She smiled. 'I've a feeling the others won't be so understanding.'

It was a masculine room they were in with no frills. The deep leather chairs looked comfortable in their shabbiness. Gerald occupied a wide, high-backed chair recommended by the surgeon as being the easiest to get in and out of. There was a wheelchair in the corner. He saw her eyeing it.

'My transport,' he said with a trace of bitterness, 'crutches can be damned tiring.'

'So I imagine. Gerald, do I have to be tactful all the time?'

'No.'

She took a deep breath. 'If you had been badly wounded in a war or some conflict would you have been ashamed to get yourself about in a wheelchair?'

He drank some tea and she thought he wasn't going to answer, but he had been considering his answer. 'No,' he said, 'no, I wouldn't.'

'Then what is so different about your situation? You had an accident, no one's fault, just an act of God.'

'I doubt if the Almighty would take the blame,' but he was laughing.

'Then use the blasted thing to get about.'

'Such language from my wife-to-be.'

'A lifetime of lessons was what you promised,' she said gently.

The silence was comfortable as they ate the sandwiches and Agnes poured second cups. When they had finished she lifted the tray and put it nearer the door meaning to remove it later.

'Agnes, someone will collect that later.'

'But—'

'Leave it, you are no longer a servant.'

She got up and wandered round the room knowing that his eyes were following her.

'You have a nice figure, Agnes, and in the right clothes you are going to be a very attractive young woman.'

She had no answer to that but her heightened colour showed that she was pleased. Most of the pictures were of country scenes but one was of a group of cricketers. She looked at it closely.

'That's you in the front?'

'Yes.' He reached for his crutches then changed his mind. 'Bring that damned thing over.'

She looked at him uncomprehending then her mouth stretched in a smile. Carefully she manoeuvred the wheelchair into the position he wanted, then with her heart in her mouth watched as he swung himself into the wheelchair. The perspiration was beaded on his brow and seeing it Agnes's quick temper got the better of her. 'Is it beneath you to ask for help?'

'I prefer to manage on my own,' he said stiffly.

'Then you are bloody stupid and I'm not apologising for the language, you use it often enough yourself.'

'From a gentleman it is acceptable.'

'Since I'm no lady—' she stopped and for a split second she was hearing Tommy Kingsley's words again. "A lady is born a lady and you'll always be working class like me".'

'You didn't hear what I said; you were miles away.'

'Sorry.'

'I said it is possible to be a lady without being ladylike.'

'There's hope for me then.'

He brought the wheelchair close to her and studied the picture.

'I was a good cricketer.'

'A good-looking lot especially that one in the front row,' she teased.

'I made captain for a couple of seasons.'

'Which means you weren't just good you were very good.'

'I loved the game,' he said wistfully.

'Do you ever go to watch?'

He shook his head.

'Then you should. You can look back on what you did and enjoy watching others play.'

'Maybe I will at that.'

'You can explain the game to me if women are allowed anywhere near, that is.'

'A few go to see to the tea.'

'Oh, that's typical, and speaking of tea I hate to bring up the subject of food but I'm starving. I've had nothing since breakfast apart from those tiny sandwiches with you.'

'You poor girl and I do apologise. For myself I seldom bother with lunch but you must learn to order for yourself.' He saw her face. 'I usually dine with the family but we'll have our meal together in the breakfast room – you'd rather that, wouldn't you?'

'Yes, Gerald, I would. Incidentally, which room am I getting?'

'I think Gertrude said the second guest room but pop into each until you see your own belongings.'

'Gerald, would you mind if I – if I went away for a bit.'

'Went away for a bit?' he said puzzled.

'No, what I meant was I'd like to go to my room for a while.'

'Of course, heavens, girl, you don't have to ask permission for everything. Do what you want to do. In any case you'll want out of that outfit and into something of your own.'

'Yes,' she answered but she knew that the maid's outfit was better than what she had in her wardrobe.

'Seven o'clock in the breakfast room.'

No one was about as she hurried to her new bedroom. Her duties had never included cleaning out the guest rooms so it was something of a shock when she opened the door. It was hers all right, she recognised a few of her things on the dressing-table. Slowly she went in and closed the door. She judged it to be three times the size of her old room with a double bed. The furniture was heavy and old-fashioned but looked what it was – top quality. Lined curtains in a leafy design were draped at the double window and there was a watercolour on one wall. She should have been delighted and impressed but she was neither. Her old room she had come to love; this was too big, she felt lost in it. If only she had been allowed to make the transfer herself, this was like being catapulted into a new life without being permitted a single backward glance.

Who, Agnes wondered, had taken her clothes from the wardrobe and emptied the drawers of her possessions? Beatrice? Madge? She thought not. More than likely it had been Mrs Harrison and she must have been given some explanation. The kitchen must be buzzing with gossip and soon they would all know and of one thing she was sure, it would not go down well. The servant classes did not like it when one of their own moved up in the world. It made them uncomfortable and resentful. Agnes Boyd, a nobody, to wed the master's brother. In her mind's eye she could see it all. The wise nod of the head, then the shaking of it as they reminded each other that the poor soul was a cripple and that Agnes wouldn't have her sorrows to seek. Not much of a catch really when you thought about it and as everyone knew he had a filthy temper.

Opening the wardrobe door she saw her few garments hanging up, lost in the vast space. One of the drawers, long and deep, was enough to hold her underwear and the rest. Deciding what to wear at night wasn't a problem. It would have to be her green accordian-pleated skirt and a pink-and-blue-striped blouse, her only white one was badly soiled at the neck. That was the worst of being an impulsive buyer, nothing ever matched up. Rachel used to laugh and say that her taste was all in her mouth.

The skirt could have done with a press, the pleats didn't stay the way they should for very long. Remembering four squares of chocolate in her coat pocket she went to see if they had survived the change over. They had and she sat down and ate them.

A good soak in plenty of water, she would enjoy that and the bathroom was right next door. Going through she saw a pink towelling robe hanging on the back of the door and took it with her into the bedroom. Better than wearing her petticoat to get from bedroom to bathroom. Taking off her clothes she slipped into it, a size smaller would have fitted better but tightening the belt would keep it up over her ankles. Back in the bathroom she turned on the water and looked about her. There was scented soap, a large tablet for the bath and a smaller one for the wash-hand basin. On the glass shelf were various bottles and a tin of talcum powder.

Lying back in the scented bath water, Agnes had her first experience of luxury and she was loving it. This was sheer bliss and best of all was the thought that she wouldn't have to clean up after herself.

Gerald's lips quirked into a smile as Agnes came into the breakfast-room. She smelt like a dream and looked like God-knows-what he thought. The girl had no dress sense, those colours screamed at one another and with that hair—

'That smells good,' she said appreciatively.

'Just arrived. I thought you would prefer to serve us yourself.'

'Thank you, I would.' That was thoughtful of him, she thought. For Gerald it wouldn't be awkward, people of his class could carry off anything, even dining with a maid. But for her it would have been acutely embarrassing. Beatrice would be in the dining-room serving the family and it would have fallen to Madge to serve them. Poor Madge would have got herself into such a state of nerves that she would probably have dropped the serving dish on the floor, or worse, over one of them.

'A sherry first, I think.'

'I don't care for sherry, thank you.'

'Have you ever tasted it?'

'No.'

'Then how do you know you won't like it?' He smiled. 'Just take tiny sips.'

'Is that to make it last out?'

'No, that is the correct way to drink it.'

Agnes took tiny sips.

'All right?'

'Nothing to write home about.'

'In time you'll acquire a taste for it and I had better tell you now that my brother and his wife wish to meet you.'

'Not for a while, I hope.'

'Thursday evening actually. We'll all dine together.'

He saw her shocked dismay and was irritated by it. 'For God's sake, Agnes, we have established that you have above average intelligence—'

'I'm blessed with brains not social graces.'

'Then we need to concentrate on your weaknesses. Adrian and Olive are not going to eat you, and speaking of eating, when are you to serve us?'

'Sorry.' She concentrated on the food. The main dish was tender chicken breasts with small roast potatoes and a selection of vegetables. A place had been set at either end of the table but Agnes had altered this, removing the place mat and cutlery to be next to Gerald. He nodded his approval.

'Is your head buzzing or can you take more?'

'Not much more. I'm in a kind of daze but I'll do my best.'

'You know the Laurels, of course, though I don't imagine you have been inside it.'

'It looks lovely and no I haven't been in it.'

'There is, of course, plenty of rooms at Drumoaks but it might be nice to start our married life a bit apart from the family.'

She brightened visibly. 'Gerald, what a lovely idea. I would love that, but only if it suits you.'

'Makes little difference to me. Bannerman will come too, he sees to my needs.'

Should she say it or should she keep quiet meantime? She decided to risk it. 'As your wife, shouldn't I be looking after you?'

He put down his knife and fork and subjected her to a cold stare. 'As I said, Bannerman comes with us and that is an end to it.'

They were silent during the dessert course. Madge knocked and brought in the coffee but studiously avoided looking at Agnes. Instead she looked at Gerald. 'Shall I pour, sir?'

'No, just leave it.'

'Very good, sir.' The door closed quietly.

Agnes hardly touched her coffee.

'Is the coffee not to your liking?'

'I prefer tea but no doubt in time I'll acquire a taste for this stuff.'

She hadn't meant to say that but she was tired, her head ached, and she longed for this day to end. 'Sorry, what was that about the Laurels?'

'Until about four or five years ago the house was occupied by an uncle of mine, an unsociable fellow who preferred his own company.'

'What happened to him?'

'He died. Since his death the house hasn't been lived in but it has been kept aired. Some redecorating will be required but that should be all.'

'May I see round it?' she asked eagerly, her tiredness temporarily forgotten.

'Yes, I'll get the keys for you and you can have a good look round. The wedding now, we'll discuss that then we'll call it a day. Naturally it will be very quiet, just immediate family and the ceremony here at Drumoaks.' He paused. 'Robert McLean, our local minister, will officiate.'

Agnes had seen his name on the board outside the church but she had never entered it. According to Mrs Tomlinson there had been a time when all the domestic staff were forced to attend the service but that rule had been relaxed. Only Mr Bannerman and Mrs Harrison put in an occasional appearance.

'Will you have a best man?'

'Michael, a friend from my schooldays, will undertake that duty.'

'May I have a friend from my schooldays to be my bridesmaid?'

'You told me you didn't want family,' he reminded her.

'Neither I do, but I said a schoolfriend. Trouble is, I don't know how to find her, we've lost touch.'

'Write to her family and get your letter forwarded.'

'I'll write to her father.'

The long, long day came to an end and Agnes lay in the strange bed in the darkness, staring up at the ceiling where the moonlight threw a pattern of branches. Through sheer exhaustion sleep claimed her and when she awoke at her usual time of six thirty her fuddled brain took some time to adjust. When it did she snuggled down again. Seven thirty, even eight o'clock would be time enough to get up.

She remembered her appointment with Gertrude and as she came down the front steps of Drumoaks a twist of excitement squeezed at her stomach and brought a flush to her cheeks. For this outing she wore a badly fitting checked costume, a bargain that had turned out to be not a bargain at all but a bad buy. Nevertheless, good money had gone on it and it had to be worn. She hurried the remaining steps, Gertrude was at the wheel with the passenger door wide open.

Good mornings were said and Agnes got in.

'Give that door a sharp pull.'

Agnes did and it clicked shut. After a noisy gear change the car shot off. Agnes sat well back in her seat and looking out at the passing scenery wondered what she could find to say.

''fraid I'm not sociable while I'm driving. With so many fools on the road these days one has to concentrate on one's driving.'

Agnes had a great urge to answer with, yes, one does, doesn't one.

'Yes.'

'Need to get Bannerman to teach you to drive, could come in useful.'

Almost swooning at the thought of herself at the wheel she managed to croak, 'Is it difficult?'

'Nothing to it.' After that exchange she lapsed into a silence that lasted until they were in Perth town centre. 'There is a lane next to McNeil's where I can park unless someone has beaten me to it.'

Agnes knew of McNeil's – who hadn't heard of the store that catered for the country folk of Angus and Perthshire? Leaving the car Agnes had almost to run to keep up with Gertrude's long strides. Her eyes darted to the windows where country tweeds and tartans filled two of them and the latest fashions were displayed in the others. The vulgarity of a price ticket was nowhere to be seen.

The heavy glass door was open and Gerald's sister strode purposefully in with Agnes following. In her shabby but well-cut tweed costume and flat sensible shoes heads turned to watch her. Agnes was seeing at first hand that it wasn't clothes that made a lady, it was that indefinable something called breeding.

Following Gertrude's tall figure Agnes was vaguely aware of the walls mirrored to reflect the pale gold carpet. Black leather chairs with gold studs were placed here and there for the convenience of the customers. Huge chandeliers added their brilliance to the scene. On they went through the departments showing exquisite lingerie, some of it plain wicked to Agnes's eyes. She only knew sensible knickers and plain petticoats. In passing, she glimpsed handmade leather shoes, belts, handbags and a heavenly perfume wafting over from the cosmetics counter. Gertrude stopped to look at a cashmere twin-set.

'May I help madam?'

'Tell Miss Inglis it's Miss Patterson.'

Miss Inglis must have been within earshot and wearing a welcoming smile she came forward.

'Good morning, Miss Patterson.'

'Good morning.' Gertrude turned to Agnes. 'This is Miss Boyd, she requires a number of outfits all to be charged to Mr Gerald's account.'

'Certainly.'

'A complete wardrobe from the skin out, you understand?'

'I do. Shall we start with a lightweight suit now that summer is approaching, two or three afternoon dresses, skirts and blouses—' Gertrude tiring of the flow had moved away then came back.

'That cream suit,' she pointed to the stand, 'You would suit that, Agnes, and get the accessories to go with it.'

Miss Inglis checked on the size. 'Yes, this should be your size, if not it can be altered to fit.' She beckoned to a young assistant.

'Take the young lady into a cubicle.'

Agnes had hoped to be left alone but no such luck, the girl in her attractive shop outfit was here to stay. Agnes took off her jacket and handed it over. Next she unbuttoned her blouse, stepped out of her skirt and handed both to the girl. Standing in her petticoat before the full-length mirror, Agnes felt self-conscious. It was her best and fresh on that morning but it was cheap and awful and clung unbecomingly. Spending money on what wouldn't be seen seemed to her like a criminal waste of money. She had gone for the very cheapest. Sometimes she didn't wear a petticoat at all.

Miss Inglis came in, took one look and despatched the assistant to the lingerie department. A kindly woman, she saw Agnes's embarrassment and said quietly.

'The undergarments must be of the correct length, yours is on the short side.'

Two slips arrived, both white, one in very fine cotton, the other in silk. She was left alone to make the change and chose the cotton slip.

All agreed that the cream two-piece suited Agnes and she agreed wholeheartedly. All it needed was a slight adjustment to the sleeve and could be done in the workroom right away.

Time flew as Agnes tried on garment after garment and she was amazed at Gertrude's ability to select outfits that suited her and as though she knew what Agnes was thinking, she looked amused.

'Agnes, I am large and clumsy and as a result I wear what I am comfortable in. You have the advantage of being small-made and neat and a joy to dress.'

'That is the nicest compliment anyone has ever paid me, do you know that?'

Gertrude smiled, then as Agnes was about to take off the pale green linen suit stopped her. 'Keep it on, Agnes. What should she wear over it, Miss Inglis?'

'The boxy jacket is very fashionable and the camel shade would look well with that shade of green.'

Agnes put it on. 'It's beautiful, Gertrude,' she said, digging her hands into the deep pockets.'

'Good, now it's my turn. I'm rather fond of that colour myself.'

'I have it in two shades of camel. Shall I send both jumpers on?'

'You might as well.' She turned swiftly. 'Agnes, you don't need to bother with those old clothes.'

'I want them,' she said stubbornly.

'I'll have them parcelled up.'

'Thank you.' She avoided Gertrude's eye. Her ma would be glad of them.

On the way out, Gertrude stopped at the handbags. She looked at several.

'Which one do you like, Agnes?'

'The crocodile one,' she said without hesitation and thinking it was for Gertrude herself.

'A good choice.' She spoke to the assistant. 'Charge that to Miss Patterson, Drumoaks. There you are, Agnes, my gift to you.'

'Oh, I didn't, I thought it was for yourself.'

'I've more than I'll ever need.'

'Thank you very much. It is very, very good of you to spend all this time on me. I really do appreciate it.'

Gerald was in the library where she had expected him to be. She had taken off her coat and given herself a quick freshen up.

'How did it go?'

'Gerald, I'm speechless and you are going to be the same when you get the bill in.'

'Bad as that is it?' His eyes softened as he looked at her. 'You look lovely in green, suits your colouring. Turn round slowly.' She obliged, 'Never noticed before,' he said with a mischievous gleam in his eyes, 'but you go in and out at all the right places.'

'I should hope so too and for your information the lady in McNeil's said with a few more inches I could have been a model.'

'I prefer my women slim and petite.'

The smile left Agnes's face, she was remembering what Gertrude had said in the car coming back.

'Agnes, money is not important.'

'It is if you haven't got any.' Agnes couldn't let that pass.

'Yes, well, I suppose that is true but I was about to tell you that I am not just doing this for you but for Gerald too. Most men like to see an attractive, well-dressed woman and Gerald falls into that category.' A look of great sadness crossed her face. 'Before his accident Gerald had everything. He had looks, charm, he was gifted academically and a good sportsman.'

'I know that, Gertrude, and I have no doubt he had a string of female admirers.' She tried to say it flippantly but a catch in her voice gave her away.

'He was engaged to a very lovely girl.'

Agnes moistened her lips. 'What happened?'

'Myra broke it off. She couldn't bear the thought of being married and tied to a cripple.'

'Precious little love there.'

'As you say, precious little'

'How did Gerald take it? Badly I suppose?'

'Once it was broken off he never spoke of it and neither did we.'

'That was a mistake I would have thought. Better surely to have spoken of it rather than let it fester.'

Gertrude looked at her in some surprise. 'Go on, you were going to say something else.'

'Only that if you'd all had a go at the Myra female, said what you thought of her, Gerald might have realised he wasn't missing much.'

'Lot of sense in that little head of yours.'

Agnes grinned. She was beginning to enjoy talking to Gertrude.

'Result of a deprived childhood. Brings out the fighter in you, or as you lot would say, brings out the fighter in one.'

'Oh, dear,' Gertrude said then bellowed with laughter.

'Come over here, Agnes, I have something to show you.'

She went over and watched him take from the drawer a velvet pad on which was a selection of engagement rings that winked and sparkled in the light.

'Take your time then choose the one you want.'

'I'm going to wake up any minute. I like that one,' she pointed.

'Give me your hand.' Agnes had never given much thought to her hands apart from keeping her fingernails clean and short. She put out her left hand and Gerald, after slipping it on, shook his head. 'The stones are too big, you need to have long slim fingers to show that to advantage.'

'Meaning mine are stumpy? You do know how to boost a girl's confidence,' she said pulling back her hand and taking off the ring.

'Short and fat then?' He was laughing at her.

'You wouldn't have lily white hands either if you'd cleaned out as many mucky grates as I have,' she answered, glaring at him.

'For someone as outspoken as yourself you are quick to take offence.'

'All right, you choose then.'

'This one.' The ring had three small diamonds and she had to admit it looked much better on her hand.

'You don't have to take that one but it suits your hand. How is the fit?'

'Needs a little pressure to get it over the knuckle but I prefer it that way.'

'Yes, better be firm and now to the wedding ring and the choice of it I leave entirely to you.'

Mindful of her short, fat fingers – it still rankled even though she knew he was teasing – she ignored the broad gold band and chose one that was narrower.

'Fine, that's that done.'

'Don't I get to wear the engagement ring?'

'Yes, of course, here it is, I wasn't thinking.'

She admired it on her finger. 'Thank you, Gerald,' she said softly and giving in to impulse kissed his cheek. If only he had taken the initiative then and kissed her properly but he hadn't. Maybe he didn't want to, perhaps she didn't appeal to him that way. She went back to her chair hiding her hurt.

Gerald wondered too why he had let the moment go. Heaven knew he desired her but that kiss on his cheek had been no more than a thank you, what else could it have been? he asked himself. Agnes was young and fresh, kind-hearted too, but it was only to escape the kind of life she knew and hated that she had agreed to tie herself to a cripple. What kind of marriage would it be? How long would it last?

He broke the silence. 'Remember we are dining on Thursday with Adrian and Olive. Gertrude will be there, of course.'

Agnes felt her mouth go dry.

'Wear something nice. Gertrude will advise you, she tells me you have some lovely clothes.'

'Yes, I do.'

'You'll be the prettiest there.'

'Gerald, don't treat me like a child. I don't want to disgrace you but acting the lady doesn't exactly come easy to me.'

'Just be yourself.'

'That's the daftest thing you've ever said.'

'Agnes, no matter how we come into this life we all have difficulties to overcome.'

'I know and I'm just being stupid.'

'You'll manage very well and now run along and do whatever you want.'

'Can't, I haven't any money. I didn't get my wages.'

'I don't believe what I'm hearing.'

'You don't understand. I want to get my hair done for Thursday and I need money for that and my fare into Perth.'

'Lord! I don't keep money on me. Ask Gertrude to get some for you. That is something I'll have to see to, opening an account for you once we're married.'

Gertrude was coming away from the stables and Agnes hurried to meet her. She looked well in her jodhpurs and smiled at Agnes. 'Hello, where are you off to?'

'Get my hair done.'

Gertrude had hers cropped short. It was light brown, thick, healthy-looking hair and Agnes wondered how she would look with it longer. 'Of course, you'll want to look your best for Thursday.'

'I hate to mention this after all that has been spent on me but I've no money. I didn't get my wages or I wouldn't have asked,' Agnes said desperately.

'Don't keep much myself, just charge it up. Did you ask Gerald? Come to think of it, he isn't likely to have any. Come back with me.'

In her room she emptied her purse. Agnes counted four pounds twelve shillings and sixpence.

'That won't be enough?' Gertrude said.

'It's more than enough, I'll just take -'

'Take it all for goodness sake and remember you can charge it up in McNeil's.'

'For my hair you mean?'

'They have a first-class hairdressing department.'

'I'm not known. I can't charge it up.'

Gertrude frowned then brightened. 'Get hold of Miss Inglis, better still I'll give you a note for her, that'll clear the way. In time you'll get your own account there. Sorry I can't take you in myself, but see if Bannerman is free.'

'If it's all the same to you I'd rather go by bus.'

Gertrude shrugged her shoulders. 'Up to you.'

Agnes enjoyed her day, enjoyed having money in her purse. After some thought she wore her fine tweed suit with a cream silk blouse, on her feet leather small-heeled shoes and carried Gertrude's gift, her crocodile-skin handbag. It might be the last time she would be able to do this, so she was going to make it a day to remember. First she treated herself to coffee – almost she'd weakened and had tea – but coffee was what they drank at Drumoaks other than in the afternoon. With cake thick with cream the coffee went down rather well. A second cake was a temptation but she resisted it and for the first time in her life she left a tip, a threepenny piece under the plate. She sailed out with her head high and made for McNeil's. To Agnes's surprised delight Miss Inglis recognised her and after reading the note she gave Agnes a printed card signed by herself with the instructions to allow the bearer, Miss Agnes Boyd, to purchase goods or services as required and the same to be charged to Mr Gerald Patterson of Drumoaks.

Thursday, the dreaded day, had arrived and all too soon for Agnes it was time to get herself ready. Applying the make-up she had bought in Perth, she was careful to keep it light. She had a good skin but it got shiny when she was excited and using the tips of her fingers she smeared on a little foundation then a dusting of powder. Lipstick next then in her own language a good squirt of perfume behind her ears and at her wrists.

Stepping into the turquoise silk dress, feeling the folds of the soft material about her legs, Agnes forgot her apprehension for the moment and revelled in the unaccustomed luxury. What would Rachel think of her now?

The high heels gave her the height she longed for and glancing at her watch – her parting gift from Kerne House – she went along to Gerald's room for his approval. She knocked and entered.

Sitting in his chair, he looked very handsome in his dinner jacket and his eyes lit up when he saw her.

'Enchanting, my dear Agnes,' he said and she blushed to the roots of her hair. 'You'll have to get used to compliments, my dear.'

'Not many have come my way up to now,' she said with some of the old sparkle. 'Do you like my hair?'

'Lovely. Get rid of that though.'

'What?'

'That watch.'

'No, I like it, it was my parting gift from Kerne House.'

'Get rid of it, it spoils your outfit.'

Reluctantly Agnes took it off and put it on the side table, she would collect it tomorrow.

'Agnes, I'll buy you a watch.'

She nodded. Gerald couldn't be expected to know how much the watch meant to her and she knew in her heart of hearts that no matter how much he paid for one it could never give her the thrill of owning that first timepiece.

'Are you ready then?'

'Yes.' As ready as I'll ever be, she thought. She watched him as he reached for his crutches.

Together they went along to the drawing-room and Agnes kept turning the ring on her finger and forcing herself to be calm. Her hands felt clammy and she worried about the handshake. Taking a handkerchief out of the small pouch she carried, she wiped them.

'Give a small knock then open the door. It isn't usual,' he said seeing her expression, 'but this is a special occasion.'

They were both in and she closed the door just as Adrian Patterson got to his feet. He was broad-shouldered, of slightly above average height with brown hair just beginning to recede. Like Gerald he wore a dinner jacket. Olive Patterson watched her brother-in-law until he was safely seated. From the chair he said.

'Adrian, Olive, this is my fianceé, Agnes.'

Just then Gertrude breezed in. 'Sorry I'm late, folks, I got tied up.'

'With a horse I expect,' her brother Adrian said.

She gave him a withering look then smiled as he crossed to Agnes and extended a hand. He said nothing but his piercingly blue eyes seemed to go right through her.

'How do you do, sir?'

Olive gave a small titter. 'Now that you are to be family, dear, you'll have to learn to call my husband Adrian. That right, Adrian?'

'Yes, yes, of course.'

Agnes was looking uncertain, she hadn't been offered a seat then she was and she was grateful.

'Come and sit beside me on the sofa, Agnes,' Olive said kindly. She was a plump woman in a flame-coloured dress.

'Thank you.'

'May I say how charming you look.'

'I take quite a lot of the credit for that,' Gertrude said as she drew her chair closer to Gerald's. 'And no wisecracks, Adrian, if you please.'

'Nothing was further from my mind and isn't it time we drank a toast to Gerald and Agnes?'

'You do the honours then,' his wife said.

Suitable words had been said and they were all holding a glass of champagne. Agnes felt her face stiff with having to keep a smile there and she was just congratulating herself that things were going better than she had expected when a little of the champagne went down the wrong way and Agnes spluttered into her handkerchief which she had fortunately taken out of her pouch.

'I'm sorry,' she said with an agonised look in Gerald's direction but he wasn't looking.

'Don't worry,' Olive said putting her own glass down, 'I've done that myself. Much overrated, I don't like it.'

Gertrude laughed. 'Olive used to check that no one was looking then pour hers into the nearest plant.'

'No wonder we have such a healthy lot of plants at Drumoaks,' Gerald said.

'That was when I was young and silly, but enough of this, isn't that the dinner gong I hear?'

Afterwards Agnes could never have said what she ate but from all accounts it was an excellent meal. It was served by Beatrice who looked at Agnes as though she had never seen her before. Back in the drawing-room where the coffee was served Beatrice handed a cup to Agnes. 'Thank you, Beatrice,' she said and smiled and was rewarded with what was very like a wink. The conversation had drifted to people she didn't know and Agnes was glad to sink into her own thoughts. Soon the staff would be settling down to their meal in the kitchen, tucking in and chatting and Agnes had a few moments of envy. It was all such a strain thinking before she spoke and watching her manners. Come to think about it, it was more exhausting than a day's work in the kitchen.

It was after breakfast the next morning and she'd left Gerald reading the newspapers. The May sunshine was streaming through the windows and she decided to have a walk in the grounds. Crossing the hall she came face to face with Beatrice.

'Hello!'

'Can't speak, not allowed,' she muttered.

'That's ridiculous, of course you can speak to me. Anyway I'm speaking to you.'

'Never got the chance to wish you all the best but I do.'

'Thanks.'

'There's a letter for you in that pile on the hall table,' she said as she began flicking a duster around.

Agnes found her letter, saw that it had a Dundee postmark and her heart began to thud. She put it in her pocket and on an impulse she took off the watch, her parting gift, and handed it to Beatrice.

'Tell Madge she can stop saving up for one, she can have mine.'

'She'll be thrilled. Somebody's coming,' she said agitatedly. 'I'm going or I'll be out of a job.'

'Not if I have any say in the matter.' But she didn't object to Beatrice scurrying away, she was anxious to be on her own to read the letter. There was an old summer house in a state of disrepair and Gerald had said that it wasn't worth the money to restore, and very shortly it would be removed and that part of the garden tidied up. No one would be there and she made for it. Rain had seeped through and damaged much of the interior but the cane chair looked reasonably clean and she sat down. With a shaking hand she opened the envelope and drew out – her own letter. The feeling of disappointment was so great that she could have wept. Then as she opened it out she saw that there was an address at the foot of the page. Nothing else, just the address but it was all Agnes wanted. Duncairn House, Hillend, Perthshire, she read it out aloud. Heavens! They weren't all that many miles apart.

Going back to the house she went in search of Gerald and found him in the library.

'Come for a lesson?' he joked.

'No, I have not. You can further my education some other time. Right now I have something important to tell you. I've got Rachel's address.'

'Good, you'll be able to write to her then.'

'She's at Duncairn House, the address is Hillend, Perthshire.'

He raised an eyebrow. 'Not so far away. If I recall correctly it belongs to the Craig family.'

'Do you know them?'

'Not personally.'

'I'm not going to write, Gerald, I'm going to see Rachel and surprise her. You won't know anything about buses but I'll find out.'

'Your days of travelling by bus are over, Agnes,' Gerald said firmly.

'Who says so?'

'I do.'

'I'll travel by bus if I want, we aren't married yet,' she said stubbornly and added silently, and after that too.

'Just listen to me will you? Since you are not writing to your friend you cannot know for sure that she will be there. What I suggest is that Bannerman drives you there, you will ascertain if your friend is available and if she is then tell him when to return for you. Should she not be there Bannerman will drive you back here. Now doesn't that make sense?'

She smiled sheepishly. 'Yes, it does and thanks.'

# Chapter Twenty-Five

'Hello, Dr McGregor,' Ian turned and smiled at Rachel and she got to her feet. The unexpectedness of seeing Peter had brought a tell-tale flush to her cheeks and her breathing had become fluttery. In casual clothes Peter was handsome, in formal dress even more so. She wished that she could be as relaxed as he appeared.

'May I say how very lovely you look, Rachel,' Peter said softly as he led her on to the dance floor.

'Thank you,' she murmured.

As she went into his arms the strains of the waltz filled the room. She liked the way he held her, firm but without the pressure Ian seemed to find necessary. Soon her breathing became normal and her nervousness vanished. Her feet were obeying the music, Peter was easy to follow, no silly little extra steps, and she gave herself up to the sheer enjoyment of being in his arms. As more couples took to the floor, the lights were dimmed to a romantic glow and Rachel willed the music to go on for ever. The touch of his lips on her brow sent her heart fluttering wildly and she closed her eyes. All too soon the music died away and stopped, the lights went on and was it her imagination or did she hear an echo of her own sigh?

Other eyes had followed them. Other eyes had seen that tender moment and Betsy was almost trembling with rage. How dare that girl be here. Had she known she would have declined to dance with Clive and hung on to Peter, but she had wanted Peter to see that she was desirable to other men. She wanted to make him jealous, instead of which she had sent him straight into the arms of that hateful creature. In fact he must have made a beeline for her. Just as infuriating was Clive asking about the stunning girl in the tangerine gown. Betsy had pretended not to hear.

She wanted to weep. Her own peach-coloured gown had been bought especially for the occasion and everyone had said how lovely she looked. In the mirror she had smiled happily at her reflection, enchanted at what she saw. Peter, she thought, couldn't fail to see that she was a beautiful, desirable woman and tonight she wanted a lot more than the usual peck on the cheek. If necessary, and she hoped it wouldn't be, she'd take the initiative. Now all that was ruined. Peter seemed obsessed with that servant girl and something would have to be done about it. It was just too humiliating. Destroying the letters hadn't been enough.

Her eyes narrowed. That tangerine gown, she knew it, had wanted it for herself but had had to agree with her mother and the woman in the shop that it just wasn't her. Where did a servant girl get the money to buy a model gown? There was something here that needed investigating.

Betsy left Clive abruptly and made her way to where Peter and Rachel were smiling into each other's eyes as though they were in a world of their own. The voice startled them and they drew apart.

'Come along, Peter, have you forgotten that we are going into supper with Marie and Angus?' Betsy said sharply.

'No, I hadn't.' She saw by his quick frown that she had annoyed him. 'Just let me take—' He turned but Rachel had already slipped away leaving him with only a glimpse of the tangerine gown before it was lost to sight.

'What's the matter, Betsy?' Marie asked as they joined the queue and Peter and Angus were in conversation.

'Nothing,' Betsy said shortly.

'Sorry, you seemed a bit upset that's all.'

'If I am it is because of this queue, I hate waiting like this.'

'We're moving quite quickly, I thought.' Betsy was a spoilt little madam and something had most certainly displeased her but she wasn't going to be the one to humour her, Peter could do that. The foursome hadn't been her idea.

Rachel had left her bag on the chair. She lifted it and sat down. Her feelings were mixed. She couldn't deny to herself that she was in love with Peter but she couldn't understand him and Betsy had been furious.

Her thoughts were interrupted as Ian returned after having danced with the petite and pretty daughter of a neighbouring farmer. He was still smiling.

'Stella's wee but boy can she dance,' then as an afterthought. 'Didn't know that you and the good doctor were acquainted,' he said as he sat down.

'Dr McGregor visits Mrs Craig.'

'Seems interested in the granddaughter, he's here with her.'

'Come on, Ian,' someone shouted, 'grub is up and you're not usually so slow.'

'Just coming,' he shouted back. He held Rachel's hand as they joined the group. There was a lot of laughter and hilarity among people very much at ease with one another. Most were farming people or with farming interests. 'I apologise for that rowdy lot.'

'No need, they are just enjoying themselves.'

'And you, are you enjoying it?'

'Very much indeed,' she said smiling into his face.

On the long white-clothed tables were every imaginable delicacy and on another were liquid refreshments of every kind.

'Some spread, wouldn't you agree?' Ian said as though he'd had a hand in its preparation.

'Never seen anything like it,' she said truthfully as Ian began to introduce her to his friends. Stella had joined the group and Rachel couldn't fail to see the way she looked at Ian, a wistful look that told its own story. The girl was in love with Ian but there was no resentment or jealousy in the smile she gave Rachel.

'I love your gown, everybody is remarking on it,' she said shyly.

'Thank you, it was kind of you to say so and may I say how very sweet and charming you look.'

Ian came and put an arm round each of them. 'Come on, girls, get a plate and help yourself.'

After the supper Ian did his duty dances and Rachel found herself much in demand. On the crowded dance floor she saw Peter and Betsy and flashed him a smile to let him see how much she was enjoying herself. Strangely enough he didn't appear all that happy himself.

She had the last dance with Ian. She knew that he didn't drink much but she had the uncomfortable feeling that he'd had more than usual. His cheek touching hers she could hardly object to that, but his murmured endearments made her increasingly uneasy. On the occasions she had been out with him he had behaved as she would have wished, a kiss after a pleasant evening. She hoped that what was ahead was no more than that. Unfair to Ian she knew it was, after all she owed the evening to him, but the truth was she couldn't help thinking of Peter and his arms were the only arms she wanted around her.

Car doors banged, good nights were shouted across the car park. Ian carefully tucked her gown in to be free of the door then went round to the driver's side.

'Thank you, Ian, for a very enjoyable evening, it has been lovely.'

One hand came off the steering wheel to pat her knee. 'Save it for later, then you can tell me just how much you enjoyed it.' He gave a secret, satisfied smile.

'Why later?' But she had the sinking feeling that she knew what he was leading up to.

'Perfect little spot and it's not far off the road.'

'No, Ian,' she said sharply. 'I don't want that.'

'Stop kidding yourself, of course you do.'

'I meant what I said. It's been a lovely evening, Ian, don't spoil it, please. I want back to Duncairn House, straight back to Duncairn House.'

'Know how to lead a fellow on, don't you?'

'That is just not true and if you got that impression I am very sorry.' She could sense his anger but was not prepared for his words.

'Bit high and mighty for a servant girl, aren't you? They don't usually put up much resistance, but could be you're just playing hard to get.'

'Stop the car this instant,' she said icily, 'I'll walk the rest of the way.'

'Shut up and don't be so ridiculous.' They had been going slowly but now his foot went down hard and she clung desperately to the seat as the car screeched round corners on the narrow, twisting road.

Believing it would only make him worse Rachel didn't shout to him to slow down but she was terrified that some other vehicle could be coming towards them. Thankfully they met no one and with a squeal of brakes he brought the car to a standstill then dropped his head on the steering wheel.

'Ian,' she said uncertainly.

His head came up and he gave her a sheepish, apologetic look. 'I'm sorry, I don't know what got into me.'

'It's all right,' she said shakily as she opened the door and got out, 'but please do be careful on your way home.'

'Is this the end for us, Rachel?'

'I think it has to be, Ian, and I'm genuinely sorry if I – if I—'

He shook his head. 'You didn't lead me on, that was just wishful thinking on my part. I'm sorry I spoilt the evening for you.'

'It was a wonderful, an unforgettable evening and thank you again.'

She could hardly tell him that it had been unforgettable for those precious minutes she had been in another's arms.

'Still friends?'

'Of course.'

'Goodnight then.'

'Goodnight, Ian.'

He drove off after she was inside. Not wishing to disturb anybody, Rachel went quickly and quietly to her own room glad of the light that had been left on for her benefit. Stepping out of the gown she wondered if there would ever be another occasion to wear it. Sighing, she put it on a coat-hanger and hung it on the outside of the wardrobe where it would remain until the morning.

Routine set in dulling the pain but the ache remained. One day followed the next, the fourteenth of April, her eighteenth birthday passed without notice. No one cared, no one sent her a card. Her own fault, a hint to Janet and Hetty and there would have been some kind of celebration but Rachel hadn't wished it. She was in no mood to celebrate.

The sky had darkened as she was returning from the village and hearing the growl of thunder she quickened her pace. As the first spots of rain fell on her face she wished that she'd had the sense to bring a raincoat or an umbrella but then when she left the weather had seemed settled. It was getting heavier with a flash of lightning followed by a roll of thunder. She looked about her for some place to shelter but there was nothing. Only the trees but she knew that to shelter there was dangerous in case lightning struck. With only a cotton dress, cardigan and flimsy sandals she was going to get well and truly soaked. At first she didn't hear the call, only the swishing of tyres warned her of an approaching car. She drew further into the side until it would pass.

'Rachel!'

This time she heard her name, saw the passenger door being opened and only then did she see that the driver was Peter.

'In you get, quickly.'

She needed no second bidding. 'Thank you very much for stopping. I didn't expect this kind of weather when I left.'

'So it would appear.' He was just beginning to get up speed when the heavens opened and sheets of rain came down. 'My windscreen wipers won't take this, Rachel, we'll have to pull in until it passes.' Inching along he got the car to where it would not be a hazard to oncoming traffic.

'Can't remember seeing rain like this before.'

'It doesn't happen often, thank goodness.' They were both silent for a few moments then he said, 'Did you enjoy the dance?'

'Yes, I did, very much.'

'Ian Thompson the steady boyfriend?'

'No, he isn't,' she said curtly, 'he's a friend that's all.'

'I'm really disappointed in you, Rachel.'

'And why should that be so?'

'Not replying to my letters. I sent a second in case the first had gone astray. You see I gave you the benefit of the doubt.'

'Peter, I did not receive either of your letters.'

'But you must have.'

'I assure you I did not. If I had I would have replied.'

'That is what I thought. Can't understand it,' he said sounding puzzled. 'My writing is shockingly bad but letters usually arrive at their destination.'

Her heart was singing. 'What – what were you writing about?'

'Can't you guess?'

'I'd rather you told me.'

'Very well. I wanted to see you again and you can't begin to know how disappointed I was. Surely you expected me to get in touch?'

She was smiling now. 'I must admit I hoped to hear from you and when I didn't—' she shrugged.

'You gave up on me. Oh, Rachel! Rachel!'

The smile left her face as she remembered Betsy. 'What about Betsy?'

'What about her?'

'I think she is in love with you and I know it's generally believed—'

'She's just a kid,' he exploded, 'and there is absolutely—' he seemed lost for words. 'Look Rachel, I get roped in to escort her to various functions – family pressure, but that stops now and would have stopped before this if I'd had an inkling of what was being said.'

'Peter, I think Betsy's in love with you. I'm sure she is.'

'Stuff and nonsense, if anything she is just using me to give Brian Meldrum a hard time. The poor lad is besotted with her.' He turned to smile into her eyes. 'Satisfied now?'

'Yes.'

'From now on I'm calling at Duncairn House and demanding to see you and if I'm not admitted then I'll stay put in the car until you come out.'

'You are Mrs Craig's blue-eyed boy', Rachel said mischievously, 'she wouldn't do that to you.'

Neither knew how it happened but in that cramped space she was in his arms, his lips on hers in a kiss that left them both breathless. He kept hold of her hand. 'By a stroke of bad luck I'm to be in Birmingham next week, a medical conference and impossible to get out of since I made such a fuss about wanting to attend.'

'You must go, of course you must.'

'The minute I get back we'll be together.'

'Provided I can arrange the time off. Incidentally it's stopped raining or hadn't you noticed?'

'What a pity. Not often I bless a storm but this one I do,' he said as he started up the engine. He drove to the gates of Duncairn House, kissed her lightly on the lips and waited until she was well up the drive before moving away.

Was it possible to be exhausted with happiness? She thought it must be. All she wanted was to throw herself on the bed and go over each detail of the time she had been with Peter but such a luxury would have to wait. After changing out of her damp clothes into her serviceable dress Rachel went along to her grandmother. She would have had her rest and be ready for a chapter of her book. Just recently the old lady had seemed confused, dwelling in the past she called it. Amelia's name was never mentioned yet Rachel felt sure that it was of her younger daughter she was thinking.

'Your voice, certain movements of your head and I'm reminded of someone—' she shook her head and seemed perplexed and there and then Rachel decided the time had come to reveal her identity but first she wanted to tell Peter.

Leaving her grandmother's room she saw Mrs Anderson hurrying over to her.

'Rachel, you have a visitor.'

'A visitor for me?' she said sounding her surprise.

'Yes, a very charming young lady. I've shown her into the morning-room.'

What was Mrs Anderson thinking of, the morning-room was for family guests.

'Come along, you don't want to keep her waiting.' Mystified, Rachel followed her along the passageway and pushed open the door. A girl got up from the chair and gave a squeal of delight.

'Agnes! Agnes! Oh, Agnes! I don't believe this,' she cried as the two friends hugged one another. Becoming aware of Mrs Anderson still hovering, Rachel broke away. 'Agnes is my school friend, my best friend, and we haven't seen each other for ages and ages.'

'Mrs Anderson, would you do me a great favour?' Agnes said in her recently acquired cultured voice.'

'You want some time together, of course I understand, and Rachel is excused her duties.' She smiled as though bestowing a great favour.

'How very kind of you. I have a car waiting, just let me run down and tell the driver—'

'Not at all. Hetty or one of the others can go down and give him your message.'

'An hour, is that asking too much?'

'No, that will be all right.'

'Agnes, you besom,' Rachel said as they both dissolved into helpless laughter, 'come on up to my room, no one will interrupt us there.'

Once inside Rachel's room and the door shut she took a long look at Agnes and shook her head. 'You look absolutely marvellous, hair, clothes, everything and what is this?' she said pouncing on Agnes's left hand and admiring the ring. 'An engagement ring, it's beautiful. This is you getting married,' she said softly.

'Yes. Oh, God, I've so much to tell you,' she said sounding like the old Agnes. 'Where to begin, yes I know where to begin, how could you leave without a word to me? I was hurt and angry.'

'Agnes, I wrote to you, wrote two letters as a matter of fact and I was hurt at not getting a reply.'

'Honestly, Rachel, I didn't get either.'

'The first I sent to Spinner's Lane.'

'Must have been after they moved house. The whole shooting match was knocked down. Ma's in a corporation house.'

'Does she like it?'

'Not much.'

'The other I sent to Kerne House.'

'Moved from there to Drumoaks in Kirriemuir. With the hope of hearing from you I left my new address. Tell you, I could murder that lot.'

'How did you get this address?'

'Your da, I wrote to him.'

'And he told you?' Agnes saw the look of pain.

'Just returned my own letter with this address on it.'

'I wish I could turn the clock back, Agnes.'

'Sorry you took off like that?'

'Yes, I am. I don't regret leaving Dundee, only the way I did it.'

'You could put that right.'

'Not so easy, there are complications – but enough about me.'

'I'm someone to talk about getting in touch. I never go near my family but then if you remember I made up my mind about that a long time ago.'

'Do you miss them?'

'In all honesty, no, just Meg, I miss her. Oh, better tell you, Sam, the man in her life, made an honest woman of her and they dote on the wee lad. Really happy they are.'

'I'm glad and now before I burst with curiosity, tell me about the man in your life and this wonderful new Agnes. Chauffeur-driven cars and the like.'

'We'll skip Kerne House, it served its purpose and from there I got a job at Drumoaks.' A born storyteller, Agnes embroidered on her first meeting in the library and had Rachel in stitches. Then her eyes widened as Agnes told her friend everything.

'Sounds like a fairy tale, younger son falls in love with the maid who blossoms into the lovely creature with me here. What is he like?'

'Gerald is thirty-two, very intelligent, nice-looking and by this time you must be wondering what on earth he sees in me?'

'He saw someone very special,' Rachel said softly then added, 'You are in love with him, aren't you?'

'You are remembering what I said, that respect and liking were enough?' She paused. 'I do love him, Rachel, I don't know when it happened, but I do. But I'm confused too, about love, I mean. There was an ordinary working bloke I thought I was in love with but he wasn't good enough for me or so I thought.'

'You got over him?'

'That's just it, I'm not sure.'

'Meet him again and you probably wouldn't give him a second look.'

'You could be right at that.'

'What does your fiancé do?'

'Gerald helps his brother to run the estate. He was to be a schoolmaster at one of those posh schools but he had this accident. Bloody tree fell on his legs and he'll never walk again.'

'Poor, poor man.'

'He gets frustrated and has a filthy temper and I'm the only one who can help him. That's because I don't give him sympathy, to my way of thinking he's had too much of it already.'

Poor Agnes, Rachel thought, life wasn't going to be a bed of roses.

'The girl he was to marry threw him over, couldn't bear the thought of being married to a cripple.'

'Well rid of her then and I hope he appreciates the treasure he's got in you.'

'Oh, Rachel, you can't know the relief it is to be able to talk freely and you are the only one with whom I can do that.' She giggled. 'Please note the "with whom". I'm hot on that. All this is a far cry from Spinner's Lane, isn't it?' There were tears in the brown eyes. 'I owe Gerald such a lot, he's made me the person I am and I want to be worthy of him.'

'You will be, Agnes,' Rachel said gently, then added, 'What about Gerald's family?'

'Not exactly thrilled, you wouldn't expect them to be, would you? But they are quite pleasant and I like his unmarried sister, Gertrude.'

'In time they will all love you.'

'No, that won't happen, I'll never quite fit but enough of that. Now I'm coming to the important bit. I want you to be my bridesmaid, Rachel.'

'Agnes, I'd love to be your bridesmaid and I'm very honoured.'

'Needless to say it will be very quiet, immediate family only, and no one from mine of course, but that is the way I want it.' She paused. 'That was why I was so desperate to find you. You were the only one I wanted with me.'

'I'm so glad we've found each other and we're never going to lose touch again,' Rachel said firmly. 'Is Gerald's brother to be best man?'

'No, an old school chum and immediately he said that I said I wanted my school chum too.'

'You like his sister and that's important. What is she like?'

'Gertrude? Very county if you know what I mean, tweeds, pearls and flat-heeled shoes. Mad about horses and Adrian, her brother, says she looks like one.'

'Beastly man.'

'Water off a duck's back, that lot can insult each other but it doesn't seem to bother them. Us now, we'd fly off the handle.'

'I most certainly would if someone told me I looked like a horse.'

'No danger of that, even in that maid's outfit you look terrific. Like my ma said you could wear a dishcloth and look marvellous.'

'Same old Agnes under all that finery.'

'Before I forget, when is your day off?'

'Tuesday.'

'Could you manage to get yourself to Perth?'

'No problem.'

'Meet you about eleven o'clock outside McNeil's.'

'Window shopping, I hope, I can't stretch to their prices.'

'All goes on Gerald's account and don't start objecting, it is the bride's privilege. Honestly, Rachel, he's terribly generous and he'll want us to get something very special. That said I must be careful to see that you don't outshine me.'

'Not a chance.'

'Unfortunately there is every chance. And now tell me about you, there must be someone in your life.'

It was too soon to talk about Peter. 'There is someone, Agnes, but there is a lot to tell you and there just isn't the time. I hate to say it, but the hour is up and I don't want Mrs Anderson to think I am taking advantage.'

'No, right enough, she's been very decent.'

'Only because you impressed her,' Rachel said getting up from the bed and smoothing the cover.

At the door they hugged each other. 'Until Tuesday,' Agnes said.

'Until Tuesday,' Rachel smiled and watched her friend hurry down the drive.

At Drumoaks the June sunlight streamed through the open windows and the air was scented with the flowers which had been picked that morning to grace the window-sills and tops of furniture. The joining together of Agnes and Gerald was to take place at two thirty and Bannerman had been despatched to Duncairn House in the morning to pick up Rachel.

She sat in the back of the car with her carefully wrapped parcel. The problem of a gift had at last been solved. She had chosen book ends, plain but good looking. Not exciting but she rather thought that Agnes would like them.

How was Agnes feeling, she wondered? Was she apprehensive now that the big day was here? Rachel just wished that there had been an opportunity to meet Gerald but there had been no time. The journey was completed in silence and then Rachel got her first look at Drumoaks. She couldn't but be impressed; it was very big and very grand. Much grander than Duncairn House, but to her mind not so attractive. There was a brooding look about it and her first impression was of a very old family house with its own dark secrets.

As Bannerman opened the door for her Agnes came flying down the steps to greet her. 'I told Gerald that I want you all to myself for the first hour at least.' She was trying to appear cool and calm but Rachel knew that she was far from that, that her nerves were taut as violin strings.

'For you,' Rachel said handing her the parcel.

'You shouldn't, you know. I seem to have everything, but thank you very much. Do you mind if I take you up to the bedroom? I always feel more relaxed there.'

'So do I.'

Inside the bedroom Agnes tore off the wrapping.

'Not very exciting,' Rachel apologised.

'It's perfect, quite perfect and very special because it is from you.'

Rachel looked at her worriedly, she didn't seem able to keep still.

A maid arrived with coffee. 'Thanks, Madge.' They smiled at each other then the girl went out.

'Awful, isn't it? She's my friend and she's not allowed to talk to me.'

'It's a difficult situation, but you'll get used to it, Agnes.'

'I'll have to, won't I? You pour the coffee, Rachel, I'm sure to spill it.'

'Yes, of course,' she said going over to the tray, 'but listen, Agnes, you were never the nervous type so calm down and just be yourself. Take a deep breath and say to yourself: this is my day and I'm going to enjoy every moment of it.'

'Some hope, I'll be glad when it's all over and if you drink up that coffee we'll go down to the sitting-room, they should all be there now.'

Rachel put down her unfinished coffee and got up. Agnes's

nervousness was affecting her too and she was glad to be going downstairs and getting the introductions over.

When they entered Adrian Patterson stood up but Agnes drew Rachel over to where Gerald sat.

'Gerald, this is Rachel.'

He held out his hand and Rachel felt its firm grip. 'You must excuse me for not getting up but may I say how delighted I am, how delighted we all are, to meet a friend of Agnes's.'

'Thank you, Mr Patterson, I'm very pleased to be here,' she said quietly.

'Gerald will do.'

I like him, she thought, and felt a wave of compassion for this man confined to a wheelchair or crutches.

'My brother, Adrian, the head of the household and his wife, Olive.'

Rachel smiled and shook hands. 'My sister, Gertrude.' A tall woman had got off her seat and gone over to Rachel. Keen eyes looked into hers then nodded as though satisfied.

'Welcome to Drumoaks.'

'Thank you.' A door banged, there were voices then a head popped round the door.

'Ah, this is where you all are.'

'Mike, come in,' Gerald called. 'I think this is what you call a full house now. Bride, groom, best man and bridesmaid all present and correct.'

It was said in a jocular fashion but Rachel had the impression that Gerald was almost as keyed up as Agnes.

'Like me, Agnes wanted her school friend to be present. Let me introduce you. Mike, this is Agnes's friend, Rachel Donaldson. Rachel, this is Michael Fairweather.' Another firm handshake.

He wasn't very tall with broad shoulders, his hair was dark and his complexion sallow, an ordinary-looking man except for the intensity of his grey eyes.

'Touch and go whether Mike would manage. A happy event is expected any time now but we are hoping Daphne will oblige by waiting another few hours.'

There followed a murmur of voices. 'Daphne looked positively blooming last time I saw her,' Olive smiled, 'but we do understand and you must just dash off after the ceremony.'

A light refreshment was served at midday then they separated. Agnes and Rachel went upstairs. 'So far so good,' she breathed.

'Gerald is charming, Agnes, and so are the others.'

'They took to you, that was easy to see. You can have a room to yourself to change or share mine.'

'Share yours, of course, silly question I would have thought.'

'Thought you would say that so had both our outfits spread out on the bed.'

Rachel thought back to when they were in McNeil's. Agnes suited green, it was her favourite colour but Miss Inglis had looked worried. She had the responsibility that both girls chose wisely.

In the end Agnes decided on a dress in eggshell blue, plain but stylish, with a bolero embroidered in a darker blue. Rachel let Agnes choose for her. And her choice was a dress in salmon pink with long sleeves that ended in a broad cuff secured by pearl buttons. It had a scooped-out neckline that showed Rachel's long, graceful neck.

'Put that away,' Agnes ordered as Rachel took out the thin chain she intended wearing round her neck. 'Your gift from Gerald,' she said, handing Rachel a long, narrow, velvet-covered case. Taken aback Rachel opened it and gasped. She didn't have to be told that she was looking at real pearls.

'I couldn't, Agnes, it is far too much.'

'It is not and you can. Turn round and I'll fasten them for you.'

Rachel stood admiring herself in the mirror then turned to the bride. A small smile played round her mouth as she looked at the lovely auburn-haired girl and just for a moment her thoughts went back to the child in the heavy clumsy boots and the ill-fitting hand-me-down clothes.

'What are you thinking about?'

'You, Agnes,' she said softly. 'Gerald won't be able to take his eyes off his beautiful bride.'

'I still expect to waken up and find it all a dream.'

'It's real, Agnes.'

'I'm scared, Rachel,' she whispered. 'I've just discovered the truth that I'm acting a part and I'm wondering how long I can keep up the performance.'

'It's not an act, this is the real you.'

She grimaced. 'The real Agnes is just under the surface, the Agnes

Boyd of Spinner's Lane. No,' she said as Rachel made to speak. 'That boy I told you about, he said – he said – that a lady was born that I'd always be working class. He was right, Rachel, he said they would accept me only for as long as I was of use to them.'

'He's wrong, so very, very wrong and I think he sounds horrible. Thank goodness you had nothing more to do with him. I bet he just said it because you wouldn't have him.'

'The family are accepting this marriage without too much show of opposition because I am relieving them of a burden.'

'What on earth do you mean?'

'Gerald has terrible bouts of depression and an explosive temper and there have been times, Gertrude told me, when the family has been at its wits' end. He has a manservant, Bannerman.'

'He drove me here?'

'Yes, and as you would see he is getting on a bit. Up to now he's looked after Gerald and drives him here and there. Later on Gertrude wants me to take lessons and learn to drive. To put it bluntly I am really a future replacement for Bannerman.'

'What absolute nonsense. If that was all he wanted he would have employed another manservant.'

Agnes managed a smile. 'He likes me, he likes being with me but that is a far cry from being in love with me.'

'I have a feeling that everything will work out for you.'

'Of course it will, just pre-wedding nerves. Ready?'

'Yes.'

'Then we'll get ourselves downstairs.'

'One minute, you didn't let me see your watch.'

'My gift from Gerald,' she said, holding her arm up to show the tiny wristwatch encrusted with diamonds.

'It's beautiful, you must be thrilled.'

Agnes smiled. 'I am but I'll let you into a secret. My first watch was a cheap little thing, from a pawnbroker's actually and was my gift from Kerne House when I left. Nothing but nothing could ever give me the same thrill again.'

Agnes opened the door to the knock. 'We're just coming, Gertrude, come in and give us the once-over before we go down.'

Gertrude nodded approvingly, 'Very nice, both of you.'

'That goes for you too, Gertrude,' Agnes said unsuccessfully hiding her surprise. The change was quite startling. In her lovat green soft wool suit and her small-heeled court hoes she didn't look the same person.

'Thank you,' she said gruffly, 'I do occasionally make the effort and this is one.' She smiled at them both. 'Since you two were such close friends you must keep in touch, but I expect we will see you occasionally at Drumoaks.'

'The Laurels, Gertrude,' Agnes reminded her.

'Dear me, yes, I almost forgot, but the invitation still stands.'

Gertrude led the way down the broad stair with its thick carpet and shiny brass rods keeping it in place. Not so long ago it had been Agnes's job to polish those same rods.

They were all there in the drawing-room. Gerald in his wheelchair, the minister having a few words with him then he spoke to Agnes and smiled at Rachel.

It was over, they were man and wife. No photographer was there to take photographs of the bride and bridegroom. It had been Gerald's wish and though saddened, Agnes had tried to understand. The cake had come from a leading Perth baker and bride and groom, their hands together on the knife, cut through it. Beatrice, solemn-faced, cut up the cake into dainty pieces and handed them round. Drinks were poured, the bride-groom made a short but fitting speech and everyone shook hands with Gerald and gave a peck to the bride's cheek.

Rachel managed a few words with Gerald. 'Thank you very much indeed, Gerald, for the lovely pearls. I shall always treasure them.'

'My pleasure to see them on such a lovely young woman.'

She would have had to be blind not to see the admiration in his eyes and she knew that this was a man who had appealed to women and who had probably flirted outrageously.

'Thank you.' Agnes had returned and he took her hand in his. 'Agnes, I was about to tell your charming friend that she will be a welcome visitor in our home.'

'Rachel knows that, I told her,' Agnes said shortly.

No one could have faulted the meal but Agnes found that she had no appetite. The demon jealousy had raised its ugly head and that sick, humiliating feeling attacked her again making her want to cry out her frustration. For heaven's sake, Rachel was just a maid, a nobody and she had thought to impress her. She should have known better, there was no envy in Rachel's heart only a genuine wish for her friend's happiness.

By rights, in such company, Rachel should have been paralysed with fright as she herself had been, but instead here she was, completely at ease and chatting away as if she were their equal. Yet she wasn't trying to impress, she was just being herself.

Everyone had gone home. After driving Rachel back to Duncairn House, Bannerman returned to drive the newly weds to the Laurels which had undergone a thorough cleaning. The decorators had been in and everything looked bright and fresh. Curtains had been cleaned and some replaced.

'Don't you want to change anything, Agnes?' Gerald had asked her.

'Not at the moment, everything looks fine to me.'

'In time you'll want to make your own mark but if you're happy as things are there is no rush.'

She looked about her, the house was as big as Kerne House and she was the mistress. Her dream had been realised, she had arrived but instead of being deliriously happy she felt flat and deep down she knew the reason for it. Rachel. Gerald was looking at her and it was though he were reading her mind.

'We all thought your friend quite charming, a delightful girl.'

'So I gathered.'

'If I may say so a strange relationship.'

'Why?'

'Because, my dear, although you like and admire Rachel, you also resent her. I'm recalling what you told me and at the time I admired you for your honesty. There is a lot about you that I admire, Agnes.'

'Do you, Gerald?' She swallowed painfully. 'Do you feel married? I know I don't.'

He didn't answer the question, just gave her a funny look. 'Did I hear Bannerman come in?'

'Yes. What do you want him for?'

'To help me into something more comfortable.'

'Why can't I do that?'

'Certainly not, that is what Bannerman is here for.'

'You use him as an extra crutch, you don't need him.'

She saw that she had angered him and was holding in his temper with difficulty.

'I am not going to answer that in case I say more than I want.'

Agnes had less control over her temper. 'Fine thing, Bannerman has the bedroom next to yours and mine is upstairs. How do you think I feel about that?'

'I told you that this could never be a proper marriage and you accepted it.'

'In the physical sense, I knew that, but what is wrong in sharing a room? God knows they are all big enough to take two beds.'

'This conversation is distasteful to me.'

'You didn't need to marry me. You could have engaged me as your companion,' she said, and burst into tears.

'A companion, how quaint,' he said trying to hide his amusement. 'Incidentally, Agnes, would you have accepted?'

'You never know, I might have,' she said rubbing at her eyes with a tiny, sodden handkerchief.

'Take mine,' Gerald said, taking a clean, unfolded handkerchief out of his pocket, 'and mop up for heaven's sake or folk will think I'm ill-treating you.'

'I'm not the weeping type and you're the only one who makes me this way I'll have you know.'

'Then I'm more than distressed that it should be I who reduces you to tears.'

'So you should be,' but she was half laughing now.

'As to your reply to my question—'

'What question was that that, I've forgotten?'

'Whether or not you would have agreed to be my – er – companion and your unsatisfactory answer. A refusal was a possibility and I couldn't risk that, hence my offer of a more permanent position.'

'You always manage to put me in the wrong but I'm sorry for the waterworks. I don't know what is the matter with me.'

'I do. Today has been a strain for both of us but it's over and after a night's sleep you'll waken up your old self again.'

Her old self – would she ever be that again? She very much doubted it. The suddenness of having all this responsibility thrust on her was terrifying and she was so afraid of making a fool of herself. Where was the old Agnes Boyd? she asked herself angrily, she was being pathetic.

Gertrude had bent backwards to be helpful insisting that she be present during the interviews for the position of cook/housekeeper and she had been in wholehearted agreement that Mrs Yuill was the most suitable. The woman was forty-five, had excellent references and before her husband's death they had both been employed in a large house, he as head gardener and she as cook. Since then Mrs Yuill had held only temporary jobs and the Laurels would suit her very well. As at Drumoaks extra domestic staff would come from the village, those employed full-time arriving at eight o'clock and the others for the number of hours required. The Laurels was to have one live-in maid and sixteen-year-old Brenda Black had been chosen. She was fair-haired and nondescript and assured them breathlessly that she wasn't afraid of hard work.

Mrs Harrison undertook the job of organising everything at the Laurels to make it ready for Mr Gerald and his bride.

Agnes had got up to wander over to the window then came back and sat on the arm of the chair beside Gerald. Better to say what she had to say now. 'Mind if we get one or two things settled?'

'Not at all.'

'Gerald, I do need some guidance.' She took a deep breath. 'Regarding the bedroom arrangements you've made that clear enough.'

He nodded.

'Now I want your promise that you'll back me up if there are any domestic difficulties.'

'Do you anticipate any?'

'I want to be prepared.'

'Anything you can't handle yourself see Gertrude, or Olive for that matter.'

'No, I don't want to do that.'

'Then you must deal with it yourself.' He paused. 'You will be quite a lot on your own since I'm now involved more in running the estate.'

'Why does Adrian have to be in London so often?'

'Didn't I tell you? Olive lost her father and since she is his only child Adrian has to protect her interests.'

She was biting her lip.

'Something else troubling you? Better deal with it now, Agnes, so out with it.'

'If you must know I'm scared of being laughed at.'

'Who would want to laugh at you?'

'Gerald, until a very short time ago I was a maid at Drumoaks and here I am at nineteen years of age and mistress of the Laurels. The new staff if they don't already know, very soon will.'

'Is that all that is bothering you? Where is Agnes, my brave, spirited girl?'

'She's well and truly lost.'

'No, she's just hiding.' He looked at her kindly and his voice was so gentle that the tears threatened to overflow but she blinked them back. 'Make it a challenge, Agnes, and remember that you are my wife and that is all the authority you need. Start as you mean to finish. Let them know straight away, my dear, that you are mistress and what you say goes and if you have reason to believe that you are not getting their respect then to use your own expression – sack them.'

'Rachel would carry it off better than me.'

'Stop always comparing yourself unfavourably with your friend. You are very different, so cease thinking of yourself as inferior to Rachel.'

'Crazy, isn't it? She's just a maid and I'm Mrs Gerald Patterson.'

He laughed. 'That's the spirit but don't let it go to your head.'

'Ta – thanks, I mean, for the words of wisdom, they've done me good.'

'It's made me thirsty, so pour me a drink if you will, then ring for Bannerman.'

She did so. 'I'll go up and change.'

'Do that then come down and talk to me.'

He watched her leave the room, her shoulders drooping a little, and he felt a rush of guilt. She was young and attractive and for how long would she be content with the life he offered her? There was so much loving in Agnes and she was offering herself to him. It was only his pride that was getting in the way and she was sensible enough to know that a satisfying relationship was possible for them. A crippled body, a crippled mind, was that how he appeared? Was he capable of love, he wondered, or had being jilted made him feel a lesser person and soured him for ever? If only Myra had waited, had let him be the one to break off their engagement. Surely she must have known he would.

Upstairs in the large, lonely room that was to be hers, Agnes looked about her. Dreary would have been her own description – it was essentially a masculine room apart from her own clutter on the dressing-table. There was her make-up, two bottles of perfume, a jewellery box and silver-backed hairbrushes, a gift from Adrian and Olive's children and one from which she got a great deal of pleasure.

There had been that one time when their nanny had been called away and she had been unexpectedly asked to keep an eye on the children. A lucky day though she hadn't thought so at the time. In the garden two pairs of eyes were regarding her unsmilingly.

'Couple of smilers, aren't you?' she mumbled to herself but their sharp ears had caught the words and it set them giggling. Agnes was very much at home with children and apart from speech and manners she didn't imagine these two any different from her own sisters and brothers.

'Want me to tell you a story?'

'Only if we haven't heard it before,' Mark said.

'All my stories are home-made so you can't possibly have heard them.' She sat down between them on the rug spread out on the grass. Stories that had delighted the Boyd children were now amusing Mark and Mary and the return of Nanny was greeted with dismay as she bade her charges to hurry themselves up and return with her to the house.

Olive, tired of hearing from her offspring about the stories, made a point of thanking Agnes personally.

'You obviously know what children like. Where do you get your material?'

'Material?' Agnes repeated, puzzled.

'Your children's stories, where do you get them?'

'Out of my head.'

'You mean you make them up?'

'As I go along.' She grinned. 'If their eyes get like saucers I'm doing all right.'

'My two were certainly impressed. Maybe you should start writing them down, Agnes.'

'What for?'

'Perhaps they are good enough to be published. Show them to Gerald and get his opinion.'

'He would laugh his head off.'

Changing into her green polka-dot dress she began to think seriously about Olive's suggestion. With Gerald occupied for some of the day she could use the time to write down a few of her stories. She wouldn't ask his opinion, she didn't want to be patronised. Perhaps he wouldn't be patronising but she wouldn't risk it. This was something she could do on her own and if, as she supposed likely, her efforts were returned with 'Thanks but no thanks', no one else would know. It would mean writing them out clearly then finding someone to type them. As for publishers she would get them from children's books.

The thought had cheered her, it was something to look forward to. Pleased with her appearance in the mirror she patted her hair into place and went down to join her husband, but this time she held her shoulders back.

# Chapter Twenty-Six

Time off was a problem for a busy doctor but it made their time together all the more precious and their love was blossoming.

In the small tearoom where they had become regulars Rachel and Peter were in their usual table tucked away in a corner and far enough away to carry on a conversation without being overhead.

He was looking at her thoughtfully as she poured the tea. 'Rachel, now that you have met my parents and visited my home, don't you think you should tell me about yours?'

She replaced the teapot and nodded her head. 'My mind was made up to tell you everything before I told – before I told someone else.'

He looked puzzled but remained silent.

To prepare herself Rachel took a few sips of the tea then put down her cup and began. 'Peter, did you know that Mrs Craig had a younger daughter by the name of Amelia?'

'Now you mention it I vaguely remember something about a younger daughter running off with some chap.'

'That chap was my father, is my father.'

'That means,' he said slowly and incredulously, 'that you are—'

'Mrs Craig's granddaughter. It's a long and not very happy story but let me begin at the beginning.'

Peter didn't interrupt, time seemed to stand still for them and only when the tearoom was about to close did he lead her out to the car where she finished telling her story.

'I'm not proud of my own part in this, Peter. I blamed my stepmother but looking back I was just as much at fault.'

'It is high time those hurts were healed, my darling.'

'But difficult after all this time.'

'True.' He drew her into his arms cursing the awkwardness of the front seats. 'Of one thing I am very glad.'

'What would that be?'

303

He grinned wickedly, 'That I proposed to you believing you to be a humble maid.'

She stroked his face and there was a tightness in her throat as she said unsteadily, 'Peter, I am so lucky to have you, you make me feel safe where before I used to feel so alone.'

His arms tightened round her and his voice was husky. 'We'll be together for always, my darling, I love you very, very much.'

'And I love you too, more than I can say.'

With great reluctance he consulted his watch and cursed under his breath. 'If time would just occasionally stand still but alas it won't. These split hours are the very devil,' he said, moving back to start up the car. 'I'll just have time to drop you at Duncairn House before getting myself to the surgery.'

'Will there be many waiting, do you think?' she asked.

'Too many. Half of them don't really need me, just think they do.'

'Reassurance?'

'That and a wee chat,' he laughed. 'Mind you, a friendly neighbour could do as much good, probably more. Of one thing I can assure you, my precious, nothing but nothing is going to spoil Thursday afternoon for us. We go for that ring and I refuse to accept that anything is an emergency.'

'That'll be right, Peter McGregor, and I don't think. With you, your patients will always come first and I wouldn't want you any different.'

'Bless you.'

Happiness was brimming over and her eyes were shining as she let herself in at the servants' door then hurried along the passage. She was late but perhaps no one would notice.

'Rachel!' Hetty was hurrying after her and looking agitated. 'I've been lookin' all over for you.'

'I know I'm late but not by very much. Is something the matter?'

'You're wanted in the sittin'-room, urgent like.'

A terrible fear gripped her. 'Mrs Craig—'

'No, she's fine. Go on, Rachel, don't keep them waitin' any longer.'

Curious rather than worried Rachel went along to the sitting-room, knocked on the door and when told to come in did so. Once inside the room the smile died on her lips and her happiness took a plunge. Rachel had the strongest feeling that something dreadful had happened and that in some way she was to be held responsible. Her grandmother's face was a stern mask as she sat in her chair with her back rod-straight. Sitting close by, Maud Meldrum dropped her eyes rather than meet Rachel's. Betsy, her colour high, was on her feet and going round the back of Rachel. Opening the door she called for Mrs Anderson and the housekeeper came quickly.

'Do be seated, Mrs Anderson,' Betsy said.

Rachel began to tremble without knowing why. 'What is it? What is the matter?' she asked and wishing that she too could sit down.

'You are about to find out though I imagine by the state you look to be in that you've guessed.' She took a deep breath. 'Perhaps you could explain how a brooch of mine came to be in your room. This brooch,' she said, displaying it in her mind.

Rachel was pale with shock but there was growing anger. 'I have never seen it before.'

'That won't do, I'm afraid. Unfortunately for you my memory is good and I recall wearing it when I went into the drawing-room but I didn't have it when I came out. The clasp is faulty and so positive was I that it had fallen off that I went back to check. You were coming out and it was your startled, guilty look that stayed with me.'

Rachel shook her head in bewilderment, made to speak, but Betsy silenced her.

'So sure was I of your guilt that I asked Mrs Anderson to accompany me to your room. Mrs Anderson,' she looked over to the woman, 'you saw this brooch in the girl's room?'

'Yes, Miss Betsy.'

Rachel's eyes were smouldering with anger. 'How dare you search my room when I wasn't present. You had no right to do such a thing.'

'The girl is right there, Betsy, you had no business to do that,' Mrs Craig said.

That hurt, that really hurt, to hear her grandmother call her girl rather than use her name. It meant she had been found guilty without a chance to defend herself.

'Are you denying that it was in your room?' Betsy said haughtily.

'If Mrs Anderson said she saw the brooch in my room then I'm sure she did, but since I didn't put it there someone else did.'

'A likely story,' Betsy sneered, 'and I wonder where you got your other treasures.' She opened a drawer and placed the articles for all to see. 'Such expensive jewellery for a maid to possess. Real pearls no less and what I recognise to be a very valuable brooch.'

Rachel had stopped shaking and a cold anger was urging her on.

'You are perfectly correct, the pearls are real and the brooch is valuable.'

'Where did they come from?'

'That has nothing to do with you.'

'Meaning you can't answer the question.'

'Betsy, I don't think—' her mother started then looked at Rachel. 'Perhaps it would be better and put an end to this unpleasant scene if you were to – if you were to—' she foundered to a stop.

'Very well, Mrs Meldrum,' Rachel said with icy coldness. 'You can decide whether I am a thief or your daughter a liar.'

'How dare you—'

'Be quiet, Betsy,' her grandmother thundered.

'I know nothing about your brooch or perhaps I have my suspicions,' she said looking her cousin full in the face and seeing it change to a dull red. 'The pearls were a gift for being bridesmaid to a friend of mine. As for the brooch,' the voice that had been steady began to shake, 'be kind enough to give it to Mrs Craig.'

Now decidedly uneasy, Betsy handed it to her grandmother.

For a long, long time the old lady kept her eyes on the brooch and then in a voice hoarse with emotion she said.

'Where did you get this?'

'From my mother.'

'Your – mother?' The dropping of a pin could have been heard.

'Yes. My mother was your daughter, Amelia.'

Maud gave a funny little cry and signalled for Mrs Anderson to leave. The housekeeper went quickly and quietly. Betsy was backing to the door, looking terrified and desperate to escape but no one tried to stop her.

'Amelia's daughter,' Mrs Craig shook her head from side to side. 'I should have known—'

Rachel felt the sudden pain take her breath away as she saw her grandmother, that proud, unbending woman, struggling with the tears that filled her eyes then rolled unchecked down the worn cheeks. 'There was something about you, your voice, movements of the head that brought back memories.'

Maud who had been silent all this time now spoke.

'My sister was small and fair and you are so dark.'

'I take after my father,' Rachel said shortly.

'Then he must have been a very handsome man,' her grandmother had recovered a little and spoke in her usual voice.

'You wouldn't know, would you? You couldn't bring yourself to meet a common working man.'

'Bitterness doesn't become the young, my dear.'

'My father was – is a proud man. He wanted to do the right and honourable thing and ask for your daughter's hand in marriage but he didn't get beyond the gate of your Dundee home.'

'Maud, I'd like to be alone with Rachel if you please, and you can tell Betsy and Mrs Anderson that I will deal with them later.'

'Very well,' she got up reluctantly and before leaving looked pleadingly at Rachel. 'It is a lot to ask, I know, Rachel, but try not to hate Betsy. At heart she is a good girl.'

Rachel nodded.

Left alone, her grandmother patted the chair beside her and Rachel, after only the briefest hesitation, went to sit beside her.

'You have a lot of explaining to do, Rachel.'

'So have you and I'd like to hear you first,' Rachel said unsmilingly.

'Very well,' her grandmother said tiredly, 'but it was all such a long time ago.' She sighed but Rachel wasn't helping her. 'Amelia, your mother, was an adorable child and badly spoilt. She was your grandfather's favourite and he didn't hide it. Doing what she did almost broke his heart and he never got over it, my dear.'

'Couldn't he have found it in his heart to forgive her?'

'No, she had done the unforgiveable.'

'And you, Grandmother—' she managed the word this time and was rewarded by a smile and a nod of the head— 'could you find no forgiveness in your heart?'

'My dear, I was caught in the middle and oh, yes, I was prepared to forgive. I wanted my daughter back but my first loyalty had to be to my husband. In these modern times that may sound strange but I am part of a bygone age when a wife obeyed her husband. What I did do, however, was make sure that Amelia was safe and well. Forgive me, but I am not going to tell you how I went about that.'

'Did you know about me?'

'Yes, I knew that Amelia had a daughter and then much later—' her voice broke.

'You heard of her death?'

'Yes, that was a dreadful time. Your grandfather was in a terrible state and it brought on a stroke leaving him paralysed and his memory gone. I sat by him almost constantly until he died.'

Rachel pictured the scene and felt a lump in her throat. Impulsively she reached out and took her grandmother's paper-dry hands in hers.

'We've all suffered, each one of us, and it makes me want to cry to think how little it would have taken to avoid the heartache. My mother missed you, missed her family, I knew that though she said very little.'

'Thank you, my dear.'

'Leaving me your address showed that she wanted me to get in touch. She had my father's promise that he would give it to me when I was old enough to understand.'

'That was good of him, he could have destroyed it and who could have blamed him?'

'He wouldn't have done that, my father is an honourable man.'

The old eyes were pleading. 'Tell me a little about them. Was she happy, my little Amelia?'

'Very happy,' Rachel said softly, 'they adored one another. I was nine when she died but I have only happy memories of those years.'

'The brooch, tell me about it.'

'It was in a little rosewood box, the brooch and a few other pieces. My father said the brooch was valuable, that it had been an eighteenth birthday gift and that I must take great care of it.'

'He said that?'

It wasn't altogether true, she tried to recall his words and knew there had been reluctance to hand over the box with her grandmother's address but why add to the pain? 'Something like that but though he didn't say so I knew that he would have preferred to have me go on believing my grandparents dead. I didn't want to get in touch, didn't think I ever would.'

'What was it that made you change your mind?'

'Let me tell you it in my own way. With the help of a very dear neighbour, we managed quite well, or so I thought. I was too young to understand how deeply my mother's death had affected him and how lonely he was. You see, I thought my company should have been enough for him.'

'My poor child, let me guess, your father eventually found someone else and you resented her.'

'At the time I didn't recognise it as jealousy. You see Peggy was so different from my mother and I couldn't understand what he saw in her. Neither of us made much effort to get on together and in a rebellious mood I decided to leave home without telling anyone.'

'Like mother, like daughter,' she said softly, too softly for Rachel to hear.

'I wanted to hurt my father the way he had hurt me.'

'Yet all he did was take another wife.'

'No, he broke his promise to me and that I could not forgive. I wanted to go to college and the money was there until Peggy arrived on the scene and she wanted this and that and my father seemed unable to say no to her.'

'Poor you, what did you do?'

'Served as a dressmaker's assistant until the business closed and it was then that I made up my mind to see what my mother's people were like.'

'But I don't understand why—'

Rachel smiled. 'Grandmother, I was brought up in a tenement and seeing Duncairn House for the first time terrified me. I couldn't bring myself to go up to the front door and introduce myself as Amelia's daughter.'

'You could have written to me.'

'No, I wasn't prepared to do that in case you tore the letter up.'

'As if I would have done such a thing,' she said indignantly.

'I wasn't to know that, was I?' She smiled as she remembered that day. 'What really happened, Grandmother, was that I found myself at the back door with another girl. Someone, it was Mrs Anderson actually, waved to me to come along quickly and I found that I was being interviewed for the job of maid.'

Her grandmother was wiping the tears of laughter from her eyes. 'My dear, this gets better by the minute but do go on.'

'I was about to tell Mrs Anderson of her mistake when the thought struck me that it was the ideal way to find out about my family without them knowing who I was. If I liked you I was to tell you my true identity and if I didn't then I would stay until I found another position.'

'What was your verdict on us?'

'I grew to love you, Grandmother, though I thought you very intimidating at first. This you will find hard to believe but I had decided this very day to tell you but I wanted Peter to know first.'

'Peter?'

'Peter McGregor,' she said shyly, 'we are engaged to be married.'

Mrs Craig beamed. 'My dear, I couldn't be more delighted. I'm very fond of Peter – oh, dear me, I am just beginning to understand, not that there can be any excuse for that appalling exhibition, but jealousy is a dreadful disease. It makes even good people do something completely out of character. Poor, silly Betsy imagining that Peter was interested in her. Maud, another silly girl, was almost as much to blame, encouraging it the way she did. There was no spark, anyone could have seen that. Peter, kind lad that he is, was only acting as escort because of the family pressure.'

'You won't be too hard on Betsy, we all make mistakes.'

'Not of that magnitude, she made you out to be a thief.'

It had been horrible and she was still a bit shaken. 'Did you believe it of me?'

'Not for a single moment, but to remain quiet is to find out more and I was curious as to the reason behind it. For the moment let us forget it. I must see to an engagement party for you and Peter and try in some way to make up for all those wasted years.'

'I should be hard at it in the sewing-room, do you realise that?' Rachel said tongue in cheek.

'To think that my granddaughter – words fail me. This very night you will remove yourself to one of the guest rooms.'

'No hurry.'

'Oh, but there is. My poor Amelia loved pretty clothes and her daughter, I am sure, is the same.'

'My father saw that she got them,' Rachel said proudly, 'and she was very good with a needle.'

'Good with embroidery, I remember, and no doubt she had the talent to pick up dressmaking.' She was silent for a long time, just gazing ahead and Rachel was becoming alarmed.

'Grandmother—'

'It's all right, child, I was just coming to a decision. Go and see your father, my dear, make your peace with him and if it isn't too late for an old woman's apologies, he has them.'

'Peter said that too.'

'Then go together; that way it will be easier for you.'

'Yes, I feel I want to go. I've missed him.'

'No doubt he's missed you too and for all you know your stepmother as well. She, like you, has had time to think and realise that there were faults on both sides.

'You look tired,' Rachel said anxiously.

'I am rather but before I go and rest will you promise me something, my dear?'

'You know I will.'

'Forgive my selfishness but let me have you with me for a while before Peter takes you away. What I'm asking is a longish engagement if Peter will agree to that.'

Rachel laughed. 'Depends what you mean by longish.'

'Six months at the very least.'

'It'll probably take that to find a suitable house in Perth. Peter wants to live near his surgery.' Her grandmother's eyes were almost closing though she was trying hard to hide the fact. 'Let me help you to your room.'

After Rachel saw her grandmother settled, she went along to her own room. She had a desperate need to be alone and think back on all that had happened on this momentous day but as soon as she turned the knob she knew that someone was there. Betsy was sitting on the bed her eyes red and swollen.

'What are you doing here, Betsy? Haven't you done me enough harm?' she said harshly, hardening herself against Betsy's distress.

'I'm very ashamed, Rachel, and I don't expect you to forgive me but I want you to know that I'm very, very sorry, not only for the brooch.' She paused and said through her tears, 'I destroyed two letters, I knew they were from Peter I recognised his writing.' She couldn't bear to admit that she'd opened them. 'I was so jealous of you and thinking of you as a maid made it worse. I knew how fond Grandmother was of Peter and I wanted to please her and my mother,' she gestured hopelessly and bowed her head.

'Love isn't made to order, Betsy.'

'No, and if I'm honest, I wanted Peter but I'm not sure if I loved him. Oh, it's all such a horrible mess and Grandmother is going to hate me. She'll send me away, I know she will.'

'No, she won't. You'll get a severe scolding and you deserve it but it won't be more than that.'

She looked genuinely surprised as if just making a discovery. 'If I was to be sent away the person I would most miss would be Brian. Now, isn't that strange?'

'I don't find it in the least strange nor would anyone else.'

'I've always liked him but I looked on him as a brother, he sort of is, but without us being blood related. My stepfather, that awful toad, wanted a match between us so that he could get his hands on Duncairn House, but my mother surprised us all by giving him his walking ticket.' She dropped her eyes in confusion. 'That was another awful thing I did to you. The way his eyes followed you around I knew that he was interested and I gave him a hint that you might be—'

'Attracted to him. Yes, that fits in with what happened.'

'Was he very objectionable?'

'To me he was, but he got rather more than he expected. I gave him an almighty kick on the leg that almost crippled him.'

She was smiling. 'Good for you and I remember now that he was limping and sending me filthy looks.'

'Which again you deserved.'

'I know. I wish we could start again,' she said wistfully.

'Then why don't we? We are cousins and we can be friends.'

'I'd like that very much.'

'Right now, I'm going to throw you out. I need to be on my own to get used to all that has happened.'

She got off the bed. 'I'm just going.' She began to giggle.

'What is so funny?'

'Dinner tonight. I can't wait to see Janet's face when she sees you at the table.'

'You know, I hadn't given any thought to that though I rather think Mrs Anderson may have told her and Hetty. Wonder what I'll wear,' and in the moment she said it she knew that it just had to be the skirt and blouse from Miss Reid. The newness had long gone from both garments but they had kept their shape and somehow it was fitting that she should wear them on this very special evening.

'You'll need lots of new clothes and you must let me help you choose them. I really would love to do that.'

'And so you shall but – out—'

She gave Rachel a broad smile then went out.

# Chapter Twenty-Seven

Rachel found she was shivering in spite of the warmth of the September day. 'Peter, I'm scared,' she said in a small voice.

'No, you aren't. Apprehensive perhaps but no more than that.'

Whatever it was her stomach was churning with nerves and with each mile bringing her nearer to Dundee it was getting worse.

Peter took his eyes off the road for a moment to give her a quick smile. 'Relax, my darling, your father will be relieved and happy to have his daughter back and that could well apply to your stepmother.'

'I don't think I could have done it on my own, Peter, I need you with me.'

'You need never do anything on your own again. Blast! Did you see that idiot overtaking on that hill? He could have involved more than himself in an accident.'

She hadn't, she had been too busy with her own thoughts. Peter had slowed down but now he increased his speed and with it being a Sunday traffic was light. Rachel had enjoyed two shopping sprees with Betsy who had gone out of her way to be as helpful as possible. The outfit she wore had been Betsy's choice and Peter's eyes had widened in appreciation. It was a pale blue button-through dress with a matching blazer-style jacket with embroidery on the pockets. The price had shocked Rachel but Betsy had dismissed it as nothing. She had been ordered by her grandmother to spare no expense and that Rachel was to get anything she wanted.

They were going through Inchture and Longforgan where the first touches of orange and brown were tinting the leaves but Rachel barely noticed, she was reliving the day when she had turned her back on Dundee for an uncertain future. Never in her wildest dreams had she imagined herself working as a maid in her grandmother's house. The thought made her smile.

'What brought the smile on?'

'Just thoughts. You know, Peter, no matter how many regrets I have at the manner of my leaving home, I can only feel glad that I did. You see, my darling, if I hadn't I wouldn't have met you.'

'Don't you believe it, it was written in the stars that we would meet, and pay attention, will you? You are supposed to be giving me directions.'

'Sorry! Sorry! Carry on for a bit yet but keep your speed down.' Very soon they were in the west end of Dundee and on to Blackness Road. 'Nearly there, Peter,' she said with a tremor in her voice. 'Blackford Street is the next on your left and twenty-three is about halfway along.'

Peter stopped just outside the close and Rachel got out and waited for him to lock the car door. She didn't look about her, she didn't want to be recognised.

Seeing her strained look, Peter gave her arm a reassuring squeeze then together they went up the stone stairs. The paintwork in the close and on the stairway was drab, some of it peeling, but the brass plate with the name G. M. DONALDSON had been polished.

Mutely she looked at Peter, she couldn't bring herself to knock, and it was he who gave a sharp rap on the door. When she heard the heavy footsteps Rachel unconsciously stepped back. The door opened.

In that split second when father and daughter looked at one another, her first thought was that he hadn't changed. It was much more likely that he would see a change in her.

'Da,' she said nervously.

He didn't utter a word, just held out his arms and she went into them. His woollen cardigan smelled faintly of the tobacco she remembered so well and she held her face into it fighting back the tears. They remained like that until Peggy's voice reached them.

'Geordie, who is it?' They heard her hurrying feet.

Peter was standing on the door mat and Rachel held out her hand to bring him in. He smiled at her and closed the door behind him. They were all together in the narrow lobby. Peggy's mouth fell open, then like Geordie she held out her arms. Never one to do things by halves she promptly burst into tears and it was Rachel who was comforting her.

'Sorry, lad, you're being ignored and we're making an exhibition of ourselves and what am I thinking of having you standing here in the lobby, come away into the kitchen.' He was nervous not pausing for breath and went on, 'Away and put the kettle on, Peggy.'

'Da, this is Peter, Peter McGregor, my fiancé. We – we're engaged to be married,' she said breathlessly.

'That it was something of the sort crossed my mind,' he smiled and held out his hand to Peter then shouted to Peggy hovering at the scullery door. 'Come and be introduced before you put that kettle on.'

'I'm happy to meet you, Mrs Donaldson,' Peter said with his ready smile.

'Me too – I mean I'm pleased to meet you,' she said flustered then looked at Rachel. 'You won't mind sitting in the kitchen, will you, the front room is cold without a fire?'

'As I well remember,' Rachel smiled. 'The kitchen was always homely and still is.' It was nerves of course but Rachel started to giggle and once started she couldn't stop.

'How about sharing the joke?' her da said and shaking his head at Peter.

'Just remembering something – you wouldn't see the joke but Peggy would.'

'Me! How would I see it?'

'That time when the old range came out and I arrived from school to find you covered from head to foot in grey dust.'

'Oh, I mind, and the mess, will I ever forget it! Yon,' she said looking at Peter, 'was the nearest we've been to a divorce.'

'You're right there and now, woman, that kettle won't boil in your hands.'

'Forgot what I was doing, I'm that excited.'

'I'll leave you two to chat and I'll give Peggy a hand.' Rachel went into the tiny scullery and it could have been yesterday she had been there, nothing had changed.

'There's only gingerbread, bought needless to say, and Abernethy biscuits,' she said apologetically. 'And it being Sunday—'

'Peggy, that will do very nicely.' She closed the door and her stepmother turned after bringing the cake tin down from the shelf. Keeping her voice down, Rachel said, 'I'm older now with a bit more sense and I'm sorry for what I did. Was Da very upset?'

'Nearly out of his mind and he wasn't the only one. Believe it or not I was in a state mysel'. You did wrong, no doubt about that, but I was a lot to blame.'

'Most of it was my fault. Looking back I suppose it was jealousy.'

'Daft when you think about it, it was jealousy that was the matter with me too.'

'We'll begin again. I'd like that if you would.'

'I'd like it fine,' she beamed. Her voice dropped. 'That's a fine lad. You've landed on your feet and he's doin' all right for himsel' too.'

Rachel shook her head. 'You're just the same old Peggy.'

'What does he do? I want to hear all about him.'

'I'll tell da and you together. Are you going to infuse that tea or am I?'

'You do it and I'll set the things on the tray.'

The tray was on the table, the tea poured and the cups handed round and when everyone had something to eat Rachel exchanged a smile with Peter.

'There's such a lot to tell you I scarcely know where to begin.'

'Is it to be a long or short engagement?'

'It all depends on how long it takes to get a suitable house, Mrs Donaldson.'

'Make that Peggy seein' as you'll soon be family. And if you don't mind me askin', what do you do?'

'Peter is a doctor,' Rachel said, not hiding the pride in her voice.

Peggy looked suitably impressed which she was.

'Where will you be living?' George asked.

'Perth and as near to the surgery as possible. It's more convenient that way and saves a lot of time in useless travel.'

'A bonny place, it's years since I was there,' Peggy said wistfully.

'It is very pleasant and once Rachel and I are settled in our home you both must come and spend a few days with us.'

'That would be grand, wouldn't it, Geordie?'

'Da,' Rachel swallowed, 'there's so much I have to tell you but first let me say how very sorry I am for all the worry I caused you.'

He nodded. 'I would have been more worried if I hadn't known where you were.' He paused. 'I guessed where you had gone and Mary confirmed it.'

They were all silent and Peggy reached over for the plate of gingerbread.

'Another piece of gingerbread, Peter?'

'Yes, please, I enjoyed it.' He took a piece and avoided Rachel's eye. She knew that gingerbread was not a favourite with him.

'It wasn't quite as you thought, Da. I worked in my grandmother's house as a maid.'

He almost dropped his cup. 'You what?'

'I fell for her first in her little frilly apron and white cap,' Peter teased. 'Sorry, darling, you go on with your story and believe me it is some story.'

Rachel did her best to relate all that had happened since she left Dundee.

'I became very fond of my grandmother, Da, and once she explained I could see how difficult it was for her. One day I'll tell you that part but there isn't the time just now.' She paused and looked at him pleadingly. 'She said that she hopes you will accept the apologies of an old woman and let bygones be bygones.

He didn't say anything, just nodded.

'Da, I didn't have the courage to come here myself, it was Peter and Grandmother who insisted that I did.'

'And a good job too,' Peggy said as she caught Rachel's left hand. 'Let me see your ring.'

Obediently Rachel showed off her ring with its three diamonds.

'Lovely, just lovely,' she breathed. 'I like the diamonds squint like that instead of straight across. Is it to be a big wedding?'

'Nothing has been arranged as yet, but I want, I mean I hope – Da, you will give me away, won't you?'

Peggy answered for him. 'Of course he will. He's your da, isn't he?'

'Da?'

'I take it it'll be in the Craigs' place, Duncairn House?'

'Yes, Grandmother would like it there and Peter's parents live nearby.'

'I don't know, lass, I'd feel like a fish out of water.'

'If I may say something, sir, that is complete nonsense. You and Peggy would be made most welcome. Indeed it would be a very great disappointment to us all if you weren't to be present.'

'Da, I don't just want you there, I need you.'

Peggy had disappeared and when she came back she had two gift boxes in her hand. 'You want them, Geordie?'

'No, you carry on.'

'Your da forgot your birthday once and he said it would never happen again. We knew you'd come back one day. Here,' she said putting them in Rachel's lap, 'open them and see if they are to your likin'.'

It took a supreme effort to hold back the tears as she undid the wrappings. In one box on cotton wool was a silver bracelet and in the other a fine silver chain.

'Oh, Da, I love them,' she said going over to hug him. 'I'll treasure them always.'

'Can't take all the credit,' he said gruffly, 'Peggy did the choosing.'

'Chose well, didn't I?' she said smugly.

'You did, Peggy.' Life was full of surprises, Rachel thought. A few years ago she would not have thought this possible.

She carefully closed the boxes. 'How is Mrs Rodgers? Do you ever see her?'

'Slowing down but otherwise just the same Mary,' her da said.

'That family of hers have taken a thought to themselves and not before time. She's havin' a wee holiday with the one that's gone to live in Tayport.'

'I want Peter to meet her, we'll have to arrange something.'

Her da nodded and turned to Peter. 'How well do you know Dundee?'

'The town centre, that's about all. At one time my father knew it quite well and was horrified to read that the Pillars was to be demolished.'

'Tell your father from me that I and many like me fought tooth and nail to save the Pillars.'

'Miss them dreadfully, Peter, I mean that was the meeting place; all Dundonians used it to shelter under and now there is just a big draughty square,' Peggy said as she collected the cups and saucers and put them on the tray.

'Tell you, Peter, lad, I despair. Progress is what they call it but to me it is criminal. In years to come the folk will have only anger for those responsible for destroying what should have been their heritage.'

'That's Geordie on his soap box.' Peggy winked at Rachel.

'Did I not read somewhere that Dundee received high praise for its building programme?'

'Oh, aye, that was said – see if I mind—' His voice was heavy with sarcasm. 'A paragon of civil excellence and a fine example to other municipalities.'

'Ah, come on, Geordie, be fair, yon corporation houses are a great improvement on the tenements, I wouldn't mind one mysel'.'

'Here we go,' George said but he was smiling, 'but before I get off the topic you two young ones mark my words. In twenty years, could even be less, it'll no' be the Dundee we know. Rumours are that there are plans to wipe out the Overgate and other places I cannae bear to mention.'

'Geordie, there are places in the Overgate not fit to live in, crawlin' with vermin and bairns brought up in that.'

'No reason to raze it to the ground, all it needs is a bit of cleaning up.'

Peter looked at his watch then at Rachel and she nodded.

'We'll have to tear ourselves away,' she said.

'You'll come back, though,' Peggy said anxiously, 'and let me know and I'll have a meal ready.'

'That is very kind of you, Peggy,' Peter smiled, 'but next time we come we'll take you out for a meal.'

Peggy beamed. What a lot she would have to tell her friends.

George lumbered to his feet. 'You've got the road now. How did you come?'

'Peter's car is at the end of the close.'

'Fine to have your own transport but then you being a doctor you need it.'

They all trooped down the stairs and George and Peggy, both in carpet slippers, saw them off and waved until the car was out of sight. A few people were about and Peggy smiled broadly to them making sure that they knew that the occupants of the car had been visiting them.

'Peter, you'll never know how worried I was and there was no need.'

'No need at all,' he said changing gear.

'You did like them?' she said anxiously.

'Very much. Your father is a fine man and a real character too and his happiness at having you back was a joy to see. Peggy is a character too and for the short time I was with them I would say that is a good marriage. They are well suited.'

'I would never have admitted this to myself before but I know what you say is true. It brings back too what my father once said to me. He told me that he loved my mother very much, would have done anything for her but that he was more comfortable with Peggy.'

'He could be himself.'

She smiled. 'With my mother he had to watch his ps and qs. Young as I was I do remember how particular she was, whereas Peggy—'

'Muddles along.'

'That's about it.'

# Chapter Twenty-Eight

Owing to circumstances beyond their control the friends rarely saw each other but they corresponded regularly and it was the latest letter that had Agnes feeling depressed. Happiness leaped off the pages as Rachel brought her up to date with events. Her writing was small and neat yet there were pages and pages of it and as Agnes read through the letter she could understand why. Such an amazing tale of events were unfolding that she had to go back and back again to read them. Amidst it all Peter's name cropped up on almost every page. Agnes, she had written, I didn't think it possible to love like this. Peter is my whole world and the days when I don't see him, thankfully there aren't many, are grey and empty. To me it is nothing short of a miracle that he can love me in the same way.

'It was very obvious the girl was of good family, Agnes,' Gerald said infuriatingly, as she read out passages to him. Gertrude, when she heard, said something similar.

That night she wept into her pillow. She was neither fish nor fowl, didn't belong with anyone. Once out of sheer loneliness she had risked Gerald's wrath and gone in search of Beatrice and Madge but the get-together hadn't been a success. Each in their own way had tried but it was soon obvious that they had nothing now in common.

The bitterness welled up inside her as she faced the truth. What she most wanted was out of her reach. She wanted Gerald to love her, to want her as she wanted him but he had no such feeling for her.

As her mother would have said, she had made her bed and she must lie on it and it was true that she had gone into this sham marriage with her eyes wide open. Her dream had materialised, she had everything she had ever wanted, a lovely home, beautiful clothes, jewellery, her position as Gerald's wife and Gerald was a fascinating and intelligent man.

When had she first realised that she loved Gerald? It had happened slowly but the first stirrings of desire had become a longing in her that was becoming too strong and the strain was making her irritable and bad-tempered.

To fill in her day Agnes had begun to write down her children's stories and had quite a selection ready to be typed. A typist in Perth was prepared to do them and rather than post them Agnes decided to deliver them herself. It would also give her the chance to visit a bookseller's and take a note of the address of a suitable publisher.

'Gerald, I am not asking permission to go into Perth. I am telling you that I am taking the bus in.'

'What do you want in Perth?'

She could so easily tell him but she was blowed if she would. She didn't want to. 'Nothing in particular, just a look around.'

'Don't you have enough clothes?'

'I have more than enough of everything, Gerald, except –' she stopped.

'Go on, I'd like to hear the rest – except what?'

'Except freedom.'

'Do I keep you locked up?'

'Don't be ridiculous, of course not.'

'You are meeting someone, aren't you?' he said accusingly.

She stared at him. 'Who on earth would I be meeting?'

'You tell me.'

'There is no one, Gerald,' she said wearily, 'and if you want a detailed account of my intentions I am taking the bus into Perth town centre, having a look at the shop windows, having afternoon tea somewhere and getting the bus back.'

'Sounds like a waste of time and I don't like you using the bus.'

'As regards my driving lessons I'm either a slow learner or Bannerman is a poor instructor. My own opinion is that he isn't keen for me to learn in case I take over from him.'

'Nonsense, there's no danger of that. You'll get a small car for your own use and Bannerman will continue as before.'

'Then let him know that.'

'I may do just that and as there is nothing urgent about your visit to Perth wait until Gertrude is free to take you in.'

'No, my mind is made up, I'm going to get the bus.'

'Then go,' he said coldly.

She sat well forward in the bus taking her into Perth and now that her anger had cooled she was regretting all the fuss. She could have delayed it but on the other hand why should she?

The day was bright and sunny but there was a cold wind and Agnes was glad that she had decided to wear her camel jacket over a tweed skirt. In them she felt both comfortable and smart. Her first call was to the office where the typist seemed to know exactly what was needed and a date was arranged for the work to be collected. Browsing round the bookshop was pleasurable and she spent some time studying the children's section. In her notepad she copied down the addresses of a couple of publishers then left the shop. The rest of the afternoon was hers to do as she wished.

When she had no money, window shopping had been enjoyable but now that she could afford to buy what she wanted it ceased to interest her. She was just considering taking an earlier bus home when she heard someone call her name. She swung round and found herself face to face with Tommy Kingsley.

'What are you—' they both began then broke off and laughed.

'Hardly recognised you, Agnes, you look absolutely marvellous,' he said, admiration in his eyes. 'What are you doing in Perth?'

'Having a look around, nothing special. What about you?'

'Saw a good second-hand van advertised and thought I'd take a look at it.'

'Was it any good?'

'Just what I was looking for but didn't let them know that,' he winked and touched the side of his nose. 'No flies on yours truly.'

'Kidded on that you had others to look at and got the price down.'

'Same old Agnes, quick on the uptake. You got time for tea or something?'

'Yes.' It would put in a little time, she thought.

They began walking until they came to a tearoom advertising afternoon teas with home-made scones and pastries. 'This do?'

'Yes, fine.'

They were shown to a table and their order taken. While he spoke to the waitress she studied him. She didn't like his loud-checked suit but perhaps the old Agnes Boyd would have thought it smart. The tea came and she poured, handing him his cup.

'Ta.' She had put milk in but it wasn't enough and he lifted the milk jug and added so much that it slopped into the saucer but he didn't seem to notice.

She buttered a scone. 'Business thriving, is it?'

'Sure is. New houses going up our way and that means families and families need butcher meat. Coining it in, Agnes. You and me could have done all right.'

She smiled. 'Are you married, Tommy?'

'About to be but then I might change my mind.'

'Can't be all that keen on her then, can you?'

He shrugged. 'Had a few but come to think about it you were the only one I really fancied. You're married,' he said looking at her left hand.

'Yes.'

'Seem to remember you were aiming high. Got what you wanted, did you?'

'I'm happily married if that is what you mean,' she said coldly.

'You fancied me just as much as I fancied you.'

'You're letting your imagination run away with you.'

'I'm not and you know it. He paused. 'Easy for you to get into Perth is it?'

'It means a couple of buses but I get a run in occasionally .'

'With your husband?'

'No, my sister-in-law.' Then she couldn't resist showing off. 'Actually,' she said with studied carelessness, 'I'm learning to drive and then I'm getting my own car.'

'Good for you. Must be a catch though. All that money, is he old or crippled or something?'

He saw her face go pale.

'Touched on the truth, did I?' There was a hard look on his face. 'You and me were meant to be together, and why not? Shouldn't be difficult to arrange something, nobody would be any the wiser, I would see to that.'

He didn't know that she was too angry to answer and took her silence as encouraging. 'Life is too short, so why deny ourselves some pleasure?'

She got up. 'Thank you for the tea and as to the rest you are quite mistaken. I am very happily married and now I must get home. Goodbye, Tommy, and good luck.'

She almost ran from the tearoom. How could she ever have imagined herself in love with Tommy Kingsley? He was brash, ill-mannered and full of himself. Had he always been like that and was the change in herself? The change was in herself, it must be. She was Mrs Gerald Patterson. Gerald had moulded the new Agnes and it was the way she wanted to be. She glanced at her watch and hurried to catch her bus.

On the way home she had the strangest feeling that something was wrong. She tried to shrug it off but the uneasiness persisted and all she wanted was to reach Drumoaks. The local bus was just leaving but stopped for her. Getting off just short of the gate she all but ran the rest of the way and as she reached the drive she saw Gertrude on the steps and the uneasiness gave way to panic.

Gertrude made to speak but Agnes tore past her and into the house. Gerald, something had happened to Gerald. Oh, please God, don't let there be anything wrong, she prayed. She burst into the sitting-room and he was sitting in his chair. The relief was so great that she threw herself on him, her arms going round his neck. 'I thought something awful had happened to you.' She was shaking and he held her close to him. It was the first time she had been in his arms and held close and the feeling was of coming home at last, of feeling safe.

'My darling,' he loosened her hold but held on to both her hands, 'you must be brave, there is bad news. 'A car mounted the pavement and your brother-in-law Sam was killed outright and your sister is—'

'Meg, what about Meg?' she whispered.

'She's badly hurt—'

'Where is she? I must go.'

'The infirmary, D.R.I. Bannerman is ready to take you there and Gertrude got the maid to pack a case for you, overnight things.'

She nodded too choked to speak and looked dazed as he picked up a bundle of notes. 'Put that in your bag.'

'I have money in my bag.'

'Take it,' he said putting it in her hand, 'you don't know what you'll need.'

She had a sudden thought. 'How did you get the news?'

'From the police. Your parents gave them this address.' He broke off and she saw his despair. 'If only I could be of assistance, I feel so damned useless.'

Just then Gertrude came in with the case in her hand and gently took Agnes's arm. 'Bannerman is waiting in the car.'

'Thank you, you're all very kind,' she whispered.

'Agnes?' It was Gerald. 'Stay for as long as you are needed and Bannerman is at your service, he'll do whatever you require of him.'

Her lips quivered but she managed to give him a smile before going with Gertrude to the car. She got in the front seat and Gertrude put the case in the back.

Since her marriage Bannerman had been addressing her as m'am but that was forgotten. 'Try not to worry too much, Agnes,' he said, but even as he said it he recognised the uselessness of the words.

'Do you know how to get to Dundee Royal Infirmary?'

'Yes and I'll get you there as quickly as I can.'

It was in record time that they drove up the steep hill and in through the gates of the hospital.

'I'll let you out here and I'll find a parking place then wait for you just inside the entrance.'

'You don't need to, Bannerman, I can quite easily take my case and you can get back.'

'No, I'll wait and take whatever message there is to Mr Gerald.'

She looked about her not knowing where to go and when a nurse appeared she asked directions. A porter was nearby and offered his services.

'I'm going that way, I'll take the lady.'

Agnes smiled gratefully and hurried along with him. The smell of disinfectant was getting stronger as they went through a maze of corridors.

'This is it.'

She didn't need to be told. Two people sat on a bench in the passageway outside the ward. 'Thank you,' she said to the porter's departing figure.

'Got here at last then!' The woman raised her eyes to Agnes but the man didn't.

'I came as soon as I got the message, Ma.' She swallowed painfully. 'How is – how is Meg?'

Her mother's face was grey but she was very composed. 'She's not goin' to make it but she's been askin' for you.'

Hearing the voices a nurse came through the door. 'Excuse me,' there was the rustle of a starched uniform, 'are you the patient's sister?'

'Yes, she's Agnes,' her mother answered for her.

'If you would just come this way, please. She's very weak but keeps asking for you.'

Dear God, this isn't happening, not Meg. You can't take Meg. It took her a moment or two to realise that the figure in the bed surrounded by a curtain was her sister. Her head was heavily bandaged to the eyebrows and one hand lay outside on the cover. Agnes took it gently in hers. 'Meg, it's me, it's Agnes.'

Her eyes opened and her lips moved.

'Don't talk, don't tire yourself.'

'Must. Sam's gone – won't say – but I know—' The voice was a thin whisper but Agnes could feel the urgency. Her fingers clutched at Agnes. 'Ronnie – want you – take him. Not Ma, promise not Ma. Look after my baby—'

'Yes, Meg, don't worry, please don't worry.'

'No! No!' she was getting agitated. 'Promise, say it, promise.'

It was like when they were children, Agnes thought. Cross my heart and hope to die. And Meg was dying. She would have to promise and if it was a promise it would have to be kept.

'Agnes, please—'

'I promise to look after Ronnie—'

'Like he was yours.'

'As if he were my own child,' Agnes said and as she heard her own voice she wondered how that could be managed. Gerald would never – couldn't be expected – she thrust the thought aside and bent over to hear what were to be Meg's last words.

'Thank you from me and Sam.' There was the ghost of a smile, a long drawn-out sigh, and Agnes knew that her sister had gone to join her husband.

'Nurse!'

She came quickly, looked at the bed and silently drew Agnes away.

'She's gone?'

There was sympathy and understanding in the soft brown eyes. 'Yes.'

Mrs Boyd looked from one to the other. 'It's over.' It was a statement not a question. 'Mebbe she's better where she is.'

'Come into the office, I'll get a cup of tea brought to you and the doctor will be along directly.'

She saw them seated in the small office then left.

'Where's Da?'

'In the pub. No use lookin' like that,' she said harshly, 'he took it bad and he needs a drink. 'Greetin' like a bairn he was, she was his favourite.'

'Meg was everybody's favourite, Ma,' Agnes said unsteadily.

'Funny like how the good are always taken first.'

There were no tears but Agnes guessed her mother had gone beyond them. Tea was brought to them but neither of them touched it and after about ten minutes with the doctor they walked together along the corridor.

'Good thing wee Ronnie was with Sam's ma or we might have lost him too. Her havin' the shop she won't be able to look after the wee soul but I'll take Meg's bairn.'

'Meg made me promise that I'd take Ronnie.'

'That won't come to pass,' she said dismissively. 'I'm havin' him, he'll be best with me.'

'I won't break my promise to Meg, Ma.'

'You don't want him, he wouldn't fit in with your life.'

In the midst of her grief Agnes felt outraged. 'You have no right to say that.'

'I know you too well, lass. You'll always put yourself and your ambitions first and that fancy family you're married into won't want anything to do with Meg's bairn.'

Agnes swallowed the hurt knowing that some of it was true, but she felt a flash of anger. 'My husband, part of that fancy family as you call them, happens to pay your rent and a bit besides or would you rather forget that?'

'No, it's a help I grant you that, and to ease your conscience about the bairn you could pay towards his upkeep.'

'I'm taking Ronnie.' Agnes's defiant look was met with a small grim smile.

'Huh! Time will tell.'

They were in the main corridor and Agnes saw Bannerman in conversation with one of the porters. He was seated and had a cup of tea in his hand which he put down when he saw Agnes and got to his feet.

'Do you want a run home, Ma?'

'No, ta, I'll need to get hold of your da.'

'Do you know where he'll be?'

'I'll find him, if he's no' in the first pub he'll be in the second.' About to move away she stopped. 'Needin' a bed for the night are you?'

'No, I'll go and see Sam's mother in Barnhill.'

She nodded. 'To tell her about Meg, yes, you'd best do that.' She gave a strangled cry. 'Give the bairn a hug from me.'

The animosity between them was forgotten as Agnes put her arms round her mother. 'I'm not takin' it in, Agnes, I know it's happened but I'm not believin' it.'

'It's the same for me, Ma. I want to waken up and find it all a nightmare.'

'Makes you wonder if there is a God in heaven.' She paused and there was a pleading look on her face. 'The arrangements, Agnes – your da wouldn't know where to begin.'

'I'll see to everything, help Sam's mother as much as I can.'

'Mebbe I haven't been fair to you, you're no' a bad lass at heart.'

Agnes watched her mother walk away, her shoes were down-at-heel but then she and Agnes didn't have the same size of foot. Agnes occasionally sent off a parcel of her clothes, some seldom worn. She had such a lot, and she liked to think that the Boyd family were better turned out than they used to be. The herringbone coat looked well on her mother and on the whole Agnes thought that she was taking more interest in her appearance.

Once her mother had gone Bannerman came over. 'Are you all right, lass?'

'My sister is dead but thanks to you I saw her – saw her before the end.'

'Life can be cruel, lass, but it must have been His will. There is a reason for everything though I'll grant you it's not easy to understand.'

She hadn't known that Bannerman was a religious man and she wasn't sure that she agreed with what he said. Where was the sense of taking Meg and Sam and leaving a three-year-old orphan? She wanted a good cry but the tears refused to come. Her mind kept going back to Spinner's Lane and to the poverty and harshness they had endured and to their dreams of a better life. Both Meg and she had managed it but in her sister's case it had been for such a short time. A cruelly short time. Was it any wonder, she asked herself, that Meg had used her dying breath to try and secure a better life, a better future for her son? Agnes couldn't blame her but her head ached abominably as she tried to picture the scene when she arrived at the Laurels with a three-year-old boy.

Times like these brought out the best in people, Agnes thought.

Bannerman couldn't have been kinder as he settled her into the front passenger seat. He seemed to sense that she didn't want to talk and he remained quiet throughout the journey to Barnhill.

Agnes closed her eyes and imagined herself talking to Meg.

'Meg, you and Sam up there have nothing to worry about. I gave you my word that I'd look after Ronnie and you know me well enough to know I'll keep that promise. It won't be easy but whatever the cost to me and my marriage Ronnie stays with me.'

'Agnes, I'll need directions now,' Bannerman said apologetically as they approached Barnhill.

'Yes, of course,' she said looking about her. 'Straight on to the garage at the corner then left and it's the shop at the far end.'

The car drew up outside the shop door and in the window was a handwritten notice stating that owing to a family bereavement the shop would be closed until further notice. Agnes read it and mentally adjusted it to double bereavement. The house door was separate from the shop and Agnes knocked. It was opened almost immediately by Sam's mother. They had only met once briefly since the marriage and after Agnes left Kerne House but Mrs Robson knew her immediately. Mutely she beckoned for her to come in but Agnes had turned to Bannerman who was behind her with her case.

'Mrs Robson, would it be convenient for me to stay the night with you?'

'I'll be glad of your company, lass, and if the gentleman would like a cup of tea he's very welcome.' There were black smudges under her eyes and a weariness about her but the smile was warm.

'That's kind of you but I'll have to get back.'

'You'll tell my husband—' she hesitated and they were both aware as they looked at each other that Mrs Robson didn't know of the death of her daughter-in-law.

'I'll do that.'

She nodded, aware that she was nearer breaking down now than she had been in the infirmary. 'Tell – tell my husband that I'll phone him when – when I have news for him.'

Bannerman got back into the driving seat and Agnes went inside with Mrs Robson. It was a small comfortably shabby room with a brightly burning fire that made Agnes realise that she was cold. The day had been coolish but the evenings could be chilly with autumn giving way to winter and the first early frost appearing. She shivered.

'Take that chair and get yourself a heat. I'll make a cup of tea.'

The tears that wouldn't come before came now in painful racking sobs and Agnes found herself held against a warm soft body.

'Meg – she's dead.'

'I know, lass, I knew as soon as I saw your face.' They clung together, their tears mingling and the comfort she hadn't been able to get from her own mother she got from Sam's.

The harsh sobs had ceased and Agnes was crying quietly now. 'Where is Ronnie?' she managed to ask.

'Through the wall and sound to the world. Poor bairn to be robbed of both parents in the space of a day.' Her eyes filled and she turned away.

Agnes had taken off her camel jacket and put out her hands to the heat. The door to the scullery was open and Mrs Robson busied herself making tea then cutting bread to make a few sandwiches with meat paste. With one hand she pulled out a small table and set it before the fire then put down the plate of sandwiches. She finished setting the table then sat down.

'Come on now, lass, you must eat something.'

'I couldn't.'

'You'll eat to please me and I'll try and get something down me too.'

Agnes lifted a sandwich and began eating it surprised that she could then she remembered that she'd had nothing since that scone in the tearoom with Tommy Kingsley. It seemed like another life.

'I was with Meg when she died,' then added unsteadily, 'she wanted me to have Ronnie, Mrs Robson, made me promise that I would bring him up.'

'That would have pleased Sam too, he had a great admiration for you, Agnes, and it would be better for the bairn to be with young people.' She stopped and looked at Agnes thoughtfully. 'A promise is difficult to break and not something you would do lightly I know, but if it is to cause trouble in your own marriage then I'll take the bairn. He'll be fine with me, I'm no stranger to him and we get on well.'

'You have the shop.'

'It won't be easy but where there is a will there is a way.'

'No, Mrs Robson,' Agnes said quietly but firmly, 'Ronnie is my responsibility and I couldn't live with myself if I broke my promise to Meg.'

She nodded. 'I'll miss him,' she said simply.

'I know that but I'll write and let you know how he is getting on and once I feel he has settled I'll bring him to see you.'

'You're a good lass, just like your sister was.'

'She was happy with Sam I know that.'

'They hadn't long but they were happy the pair of them and doted on their bairn. Maybe fate had a hand in it because by rights he would have been with them but I was baking when they came in and by his way of it he wanted to help me.'

'My mother wanted Ronnie,' Agnes said abruptly, 'but Meg didn't want her to have him.'

'Meg was right,' she said carefully, 'with a handicapped daughter your mother has enough to do.'

The fire was down, almost out, but the room was warm. Agnes yawned and she had difficulty keeping her eyes open.

'Time we were both in bed, Agnes. It's just a fold-down bed I have in the front room but I think you'll be comfortable enough.'

'Thank you, I'm sure I shall.'

'Do you want a peep at Ronnie?'

'Better not in case it disturbs him.'

'I doubt that but you'll see him in the morning.'

It was a well-attended funeral. The double tragedy had left everybody stunned and all wanted to pay their respects. Close relatives returned to the house where helpful neighbours had tea and sandwiches ready. Ronnie was with other neighbours who kept him until evening. Agnes undressed the sleeping boy, put on his pyjamas and tucked him into his small bed which had been brought down from his own house.

From a call box Agnes made two phone calls, one to tell Gerald the funeral arrangements and the other once it was all over. Gerald's concern and sympathy flowed across the line and almost she blurted out that she would be bringing Meg's little son but she held back.

'Everyone here is concerned about you, dearest, and I'm missing you very much.'

'Thank you,' she whispered.

'Bannerman will come for you and bring you home.'

Bring her home! It had a lovely sound. Until a short time ago the Laurels had been a beautiful house in which she was fortunate to live but now it was truly home. All she wanted was to be there with Gerald.

Ronnie was a sturdy little boy with light brown curly hair and big baby blue eyes wet with tears.

'Don't want to go.'

'A wee holiday with your Auntie Agnes, of course you do.'

Agnes, usually at ease with children, was too upset and worried as to the kind of reception they would get at the Laurels. Her nephew's clothes and toys were packed in two cases and put beside Agnes's own case.

'Grannie come too?'

'And who would look after the shop, tell me that, my wee man?'

His lips quivered. 'I want my mummy and daddy.'

'That's the car, Agnes,' Mrs Robson said as she moved the curtain the better to see.

'Come on, Ronnie, and see the car.' She took his hand. He turned round.

'Kiss,' he said to his grandmother.

She kissed him and held him close to her. Agnes could see how much the parting was costing her but she was smiling bravely.

'You'll be a good boy?'

He nodded and then they were on the pavement.

'This is Ronnie, Bannerman,' Agnes said, 'he's coming to the Laurels with us.'

'Hello, Ronnie, would you like to sit in the driver's seat before we go?'

The tears about to begin were forgotten in the excitement of sitting in the front and pretending to drive. Agnes smiled her appreciation to Bannerman. She was amazed at just how good he was with the child answering his questions at length and taking them seriously.

'The lad has an enquiring mind, m'am.'

'So I'm discovering.'

Just before they reached the Laurels Ronnie's eyes flickered then closed. His breathing was regular, his head resting in the crook of Agnes's arm as the car stopped beside the house.

'Leave him on the seat, I'll carry him in once I get the cases inside.'

'Thank you.'

Gently extricating herself and leaving the sleeping child comfortable, Agnes went indoors. Gerald was in his usual chair and had heard the car stopping. As she entered he held out his arms and she went into them feeling that she had truly come home. For those precious moments she had forgotten about Ronnie, then just as she was bracing herself to tell him Bannerman came in with the sleeping child in his arms.

Quickly Agnes moved away from Gerald.

'On the sofa, please, Bannerman, he'll be all right there,' she said as she arranged a cushion for the child's head.

'The cases, m'am?'

'Put them in my room and thank you for – for everything.'

'Glad to be of service.' He left and closed the door.

She swallowed nervously. 'Meg's little boy.'

'Poor little mite, we must all try and keep him amused and happy for the time he is to be here.'

For the time he was to be at the Laurels – Agnes breathed a little easier – it was a reprieve saving her saying anything for the time being. She put her jacket on the back of the chair and sat on the sofa beside Ronnie.

Gerald, the practical, was arranging things. 'A small bed will have to be brought down from Drumoaks but Brenda can see to all that. You look exhausted, my dear,' he said with concern in his voice. 'It must have been a dreadful ordeal.'

'It was, Gerald, I wouldn't like to live through that again.'

'A little brandy might help, Agnes.'

'No, I'm all right, really I am, and Ronnie had better sleep with me for a few nights. He knows that something is wrong and I'm going to be the one who has to tell him and I don't know how I am going to do it.'

'How old is—?' He nodded to the sleeping form.

'Ronnie is three and a half and I had better get him upstairs.'

'He's too heavy for you.'

'No, he isn't. You forget, Gerald, that I had to carry my little sisters and brothers around.'

He ignored the shake of her head and rang for attention. Brenda came running. 'You wanted me, m'am?' she said when she saw Agnes. Her eyes widened when she saw the child.

'Get my bed prepared and open up the cases. You'll find pyjamas on the top, I think.' She picked up the child who whimpered then settled again, smiled to Gerald and went through the door which Brenda had opened.

'He's lovely, m'am,' Brenda said as between them they undressed the child and got him into his pyjamas. 'If you want I'll keep an eye on him, I like kiddies,' she added shyly.

'You stay with him until I come up. I'm going to have an early night.'

'If you'll pardon me saying so, m'am, you look done in.'

'That's the way I feel.'

'You're too tired to talk, my dear. What you need is a good night's unbroken sleep and drink this, I insist you do.' Gerald had poured a little brandy in a glass and obediently she drank some and made a face.

'Get it over, the taste isn't as bad as all that,' he smiled.


Wakening up in the big strange bed, Ronnie looked about him with frightened eyes and his screams for his mummy and daddy could be heard through the house. Brenda was in tears as she came into the bedroom and it was a battle to get him washed and his clothes on but at last Agnes's soothing words reassured him. She would have her breakfast in the kitchen with him, Agnes decided, as she dragged an unwilling boy with her.

Brenda had gone ahead to warm Mrs Yuill, the cook-housekeeper, of their arrival and she was ready with a welcoming smile.

'Hello, little love, what would you like for breakfast?'

He scowled and went behind Agnes.

'Brenda, did you see a little boy a minute ago?'

'Yes, but I don't see him now.' She made a great show of looking all over the kitchen and was rewarded by a laughing little face peeping out.

They were both so good with him and it was a huge relief to Agnes who was becoming more worried by the minute. They stayed in the kitchen until Gerald had some time with his morning papers, then with Ronnie's hand in hers they went through to the sitting-room. Gerald was sitting in his chair with his crutches by his side.

'Good morning, Ronnie,' he smiled.

'Say good morning to – to – Uncle Gerald.'

He mumbled something after a little persuasion but his eyes were on the crutches.

'Come over beside me, Ronnie.'

Agnes was surprised when he obeyed but it was the crutches that he was interested in.

'What are those for?'

'To help me walk.'

'I can walk and I can run fast.'

'I'm sure you can.'

'Why can't you walk?'

'Because I had an accident and hurt my legs.'

For a while he looked at Gerald's legs then went down on his knees.

Agnes's heart was in her mouth. Gerald, she knew, couldn't bear anyone to touch his legs. Should she say something or would it make matters worse? She waited and watched. The little arms went round one leg and he placed his cheek against it.

'Poor leg, all better soon.' He did the same with the other leg then got to his feet.

'Thank you, Ronnie, it's a nice thought.'

'What's that?' he said pointing to the wheelchair in the corner.

'That is my special chair to get me to places.'

'It's got wheels.' Something must have reminded him of his parents and his lips quivered. 'When is Mummy and Daddy coming for me?'

Agnes looked at Gerald helplessly and his arm brought Ronnie closer.

'Ronnie, I know that you are a clever boy and a brave one too.'

The little head nodded in full agreement.

'Do you know about heaven, Ronnie?'

'Mummy told me, it's where the angels live.'

'That's right and that is where your mummy and daddy are.'

His little arm shot up. 'Way, way up in the sky?'

'Yes.'

He looked uncertain. 'How will they get down?'

It wasn't a question he had been anticipating and as their eyes met she saw the pity in his.

'Your mummy and daddy are happy with the angels and they want you to be happy too. Shall I whisper something, it's a secret and not even Aunt Agnes knows?'

'Tell me! Tell me!'

'I know a place where there are lots of toys.'

'Where?'

'Not far away but Aunt Agnes will take you.'

'She doesn't know, it's a secret.'

Gerald laughed. 'Good for you! Agnes, this is a bright little fellow.'

Agnes smiled, happy that things were going so well. 'Uncle Gerald will have to tell me, won't he?'

'Drumoaks. There's plenty in the attics and some of Mark's toys must be up there too.'

'One for you, Agnes,' Gerald said picking a letter out of the bundle. They were sitting together in the breakfast room. After four weeks Ronnie was settling in well, only at night was he tearful and those times were getting less frequent. Brenda considered herself nursery maid and another girl had been taken on to help with the kitchen work. All in all life at the Laurels was cheerful with childish laughter ringing out.

Rachel and she corresponded regularly and she expected it to be a letter from her friend but the typed address showed that it wasn't. Trying not to raise her hopes but with growing excitement, nevertheless, she tore it open then closed her eyes postponing the moment when she would know its contents.

She wasn't aware that Gerald had raised his eyes and was watching her.

The writing blurred then cleared, the colour rushed to her cheeks and her eyes were sparkling.

'My! My! You must have got good news.'

'Read it,' she said giving it to him then watching his expression as he read it.

He was beaming. 'Many, many congratulations, my dear, this is perfectly splendid. We now have a budding authoress within the family.'

'In a very small way,' she said shyness overcoming her. It was a new and welcome experience this feeling that she had done something worthwhile.

'I heard about the stories you told Mark and Mary but—'

'It was Olive who suggested I try and get them published,' she interrupted. 'That day I wanted to go to Perth – would she ever forget that day – 'it was to take them to be typed.'

'Why did you keep it from me?' he sounded hurt.

'I didn't expect them to be any good and if they weren't I didn't want anyone to know.'

'The publisher obviously likes them and wants more. Children's stories are in great demand, Agnes, and who knows your name may be well-known one day.'

She smiled at that. 'Do you know what I am really, really pleased about?'

'Not until you tell me.'

'Well, I'm the cuckoo in the nest, no don't deny it, I am.'

'I deny it most strongly and I am going to tell you something, my girl, so put that ridiculous idea out of your head. When you were away do you want to know what Adrian said?'

'If you think I can stand it.'

'He said I miss that wife of yours about the place, she sort of grows on you.'

'He said that? You're not making it up?'

'Why on earth should I do that? You belong, Agnes, and now I feel I have to ask this. How long is Ronnie to be here? I only ask because we are all becoming very attached to him and the child seems very contented. The longer it goes on the more difficult the separation.'

'Would you miss him, Gerald?'

'The child has come to mean a great deal to me and yes to your question, I would miss him very much.'

She went over to kneel by his chair. 'I should have told you before but I couldn't, I was so afraid.' She swallowed. 'Before Meg died she made me promise to look after Ronnie. She was dying, Gerald, I had to give her my promise.'

'Of course you did,' he said his fingers going through her hair. 'Tell me though what you would have done if I hadn't wanted the child, refused to have him?'

'I didn't know what I was going to do, only that I wouldn't break my promise to Meg.'

'I would have expected no less from you but now I can put your mind at rest. Ronnie will be ours and that means legally. He shall have my name,' he said smiling, 'added on to his own.'

'Ronald Robson Patterson. Sounds all right. Thank you, Gerald, you are very good to me.'

'I think we are good for each other and I've asked Bannerman to remove himself to Drumoaks and just to come here when he is required.'

She blushed. 'That means—'

'That means we will be sharing a room if you are still agreeable.'

'Perfectly agreeable,' she said demurely.

'Oh, God! that woman is never away.'

'Language, darling, remember there is a child in the house.'

Agnes knew to whom he was referring but went to the window just the same. Gertrude gave her a wave.

'Where is my little friend?' she said coming in without ceremony.

'You'll see him in a few minutes, meantime we have news for you, in fact you are the first to know,' Gerald said.

She raised her well-shaped eyebrows. 'Come on then, has Agnes had more of her stories accepted?'

'Better than that,' Agnes laughed, 'but as a matter of fact I have and Gerald is to get me a typewriter so that I can learn to type.'

'We are adopting Ronnie, Gertrude, and I want everything legalised as quickly as possible.'

Gertrude sat down heavily. 'I can't tell you how pleased I am, that little rascal is a heart-stealer. This has been a happier house since he came.'

'I couldn't agree more,' her brother said, 'and my temper has improved which must be a great relief to everyone.'

No one disputed that.

'Have to see about getting him his own pony although Mary raises no objections to sharing Brownie.'

'Thought that would be your first priority.'

'The younger the better and he's keen which is more than the other two were at that age. Excuse me, you two, and I'll go and find him.'


'Ronnie?'

'What?'

'Aunt Agnes is going to be your mama and I am going to be your papa. Papa and Mama are much easier to say, aren't they?'

He was giving the matter some thought then smiled brightly. 'Auntie Ger – trude Mama too?'

'Heaven forbid.'

'Gerald!' Then she began to giggle. 'Come here, rascal, and I'll explain.'

He ran to her. 'Auntie Gertrude is still Auntie Gertrude but I am going to be your mama and—'

He turned a beaming face to Gerald. 'You my papa. Mama, Papa, that's funny.'

'It isn't funny, that's what I called my mummy and daddy when I was little.'

Mummy and daddy had disturbed his memory but the tears didn't come. Agnes had kept her word and Sam's mother received an occasional letter which judging by her replies were greatly appreciated. In a month or two she would take him to see his paternal grandmother but it would be much later before she took him to see her own family in Dundee. She felt no guilt. It happened in some families that they got on better apart. Their rent continued to be paid and a few pounds sent periodically but not once had there been a letter of thanks.

As Christmas approached the weather deteriorated and a thin coating of snow lay around the Laurels but inside was warmth and laughter. An excited Ronnie was helping or more truthfully hindering Bannerman as he began decorating the drawing-room with holly from the gardens and tinsel and decorations from the attics at Drumoaks. Agnes, helped by Brenda, was busy with the Christmas tree and Agnes was anxious that everything should be right. It was Gerald's suggestion that the family Christmas lunch should be at the Laurels and the kitchen was busy with the preparations. Mark and Mary were frequent visitors to the Laurels and very often took their little cousin back with them to Drumoaks. Sometimes Agnes was afraid that such happiness couldn't last and confessed her fears to Gerald.

'None of us knows what life holds for us, Agnes, but we must just enjoy each day as it comes. Once my spirits were so low that I didn't know how I would get through the long endless days, then you came along and suddenly life became precious and each day valued.'

'You taught me how destructive envy could be and now I envy no one, I have all that I could ever want. A loving husband, a darling son and a supportive family.'

'Five pages of news from Rachel,' Agnes laughed as she waved the sheets towards Gerald.

'She must have a lot to tell you.'

'She has. They've managed to get a house near Peter's surgery, a big old-fashioned house that needs a lot done to it, and the wedding is arranged for July. Are you listening?'

'Of course I am, I'm reading and listening at the same time.'

'That's impossible.'

'No, it isn't, my brain accepts the important facts and ignores the trivia.'

'I'll tell Rachel what you said.'

'You wouldn't be so mean.'

He laughed and put aside the paper. 'You now have my undivided attention.'

'Glad to hear it,' she said with mock severity. 'The wedding is to be at the village church and the reception at Duncairn House.'

'The old lady, Mrs Craig, making a splash of it, is she?'

'Obviously, Rachel doesn't say that but I imagine there will be a fair number there. Our invitation will come in due course but she would like Ronnie to be a pageboy.'

Gerald looked horrified. 'My son is not wearing a velvet suit.'

'Who said anything about a velvet suit?'

'Well, isn't that the usual attire?'

'I wouldn't know, but Peter and his best man are to be in Highland dress.'

'Wearing the kilt, now that's different! Ronnie is a sturdy wee lad, he'll suit the kilt. You can see to that, Agnes, get him measured for one, the full outfit and it has to be the Stewart tartan.'

'Why the Stewart?'

'My mother belonged to the clan Stewart and Adrian and I always wore their tartan.' A look of sadness crossed his face. 'Believe it or not, I used to have the legs for the kilt though I say it myself.'

'I know, dear,' Agnes said gently. 'Gertrude showed me some family albums and snapshots and if you promise not to let it go to your head, I thought you were by far the most handsome.'

He grinned. 'Limited competition in our family but enough of that. You, my dearest, must get something extra special for this wedding. I want everyone to see what a sweet, charming and beautiful wife I have.'

'You'll have me blushing. I've been called lots of things and sweet, charming and beautiful weren't included.'

There was to be no battle, Gerald was to attend the wedding and hopefully it was the gradual return to a social life after the painful years of hiding himself away.

# Chapter Twenty-Nine

The village church was packed and well-wishers crowded round the gate, all anxious to get a good look at the bride. Tall and regal with a froth of white net over her satin gown Rachel looked breathtakingly beautiful and felt unbelievably calm. Not so her father, she could feel him shaking and she gave his arm a reassuring squeeze as they entered the porch. There they were met by the bridesmaid looking pretty as a picture in pale apricot. Little Ronnie Patterson, cute in his Stewart tartan kilt and green jacket, looked on solemnly as Betsy dealt with the bride's train.

The joining together of the popular young doctor and Mrs Craig's newly-found granddaughter was an occasion few were prepared to miss.

It was over. They were man and wife. In the grounds of Duncairn House and in the hot July sun everyone was happy to be outdoors and strolling around, chatting and admiring the gardens before going in to drink to the young couple's happiness and enjoy the magnificence of the meal that awaited them.

On the church steps the photographer had taken pictures of the bridal party then a family group. Peter's parents had taken charge of Peggy until George was free to do so and now Peggy stood with her husband looking flushed and proud. For this very special occasion she wore a shocking pink suit with matching wide-brimmed hat decorated with a large feather pointing like an arrow.

Tired of being arranged this way and that Ronnie was glad to be released from his duties and made a beeline to where his papa and mama were. Gerald was in his wheelchair with his crutches leaning against it and he greeted his son with a broad smile.

'Papa, I had my photo tooked and tooked and tooked,' he said excitedly as he jumped up and down.

'Taken,' Gerald corrected him as Agnes went into helpless laughter. She wore her favourite colour, lime green. The silk dress was plain but beautifully cut and made her look taller as well as showing her nicely rounded figure to advantage.

Rachel's eyes roved the grounds for Agnes and Gerald. 'There they are, Peter. I don't want to upset Gerald but I would so like a photograph of them.'

'He'll oblige, I'm sure, the way he looks at his wife he'll want to please her.'

'They are in love,' she said softly, 'just like us.'

'Impossible. No one could be as much in love as we are,' he said smugly.

As she looked at her husband Rachel's eyes were like stars. 'No one,' she agreed.

Agnes was openly admiring. 'Rachel, you make a beautiful bride, everyone is raving about you.'

'May I add my piece,' Gerald said in his clear diction, 'and say that I agree with every word my wife says.'

'Thank you,' Rachel blushed, lowered her eyes then raised them. 'Peter and I would love to have a photograph of you both for our wedding album.'

'Me too,' Ronnie said outraged at being left out.

'No show without Punch,' his papa laughed.

Agnes looked at him her expression showing that it was entirely up to Gerald.

'Not in this contraption,' he said firmly as the photographer took a step forward. 'I'll take my crutches, Agnes, if you please.'

Once he was ready, Agnes stood beside her husband with Ronnie in front and as the camera clicked they were smiling happily. It was a photograph that was to take pride of place at the Laurels.

While Peter and Gerald were talking, Rachel and Agnes had a few minutes together.

'Do you ever think back to our schooldays, Rachel?'

'Strangely enough just this morning I thought of that day in the playground when we became friends. Such a lot has happened to us and the best of all was falling in love.'

'Especially that,' Agnes agreed and her eyes went to Gerald who at that moment looked over and smiled to her.

Peter was moving away. 'Time we were going in, darling, your grandmother is trying to attract our attention.'

'A royal command, Peter,' Rachel said mischievously as they took their leave of Agnes and Gerald.

Mrs Craig looked well in her coffee-coloured lace dress and beside her was a gentleman. She took her granddaughter's hand. 'Rachel, my dear, this gentleman will introduce himself. He would like a word with you, and you, Peter, can look after me.'

He didn't move, just looked into her face. 'So you are Amelia's daughter,' he said softly. He had a nice smile, his hair was thick and pure white which probably made him look older than he was, Rachel thought.

'You knew my mother?'

'Very well. Indeed had your father not come on the scene we would most likely have been married.'

'Oh, dear, were you very heartbroken?' It was difficult to know what to say.

'Upset and worried like everyone else but not brokenhearted. You see, my dear, Amelia and I were childhood sweethearts and both families expected us to marry.' He smiled. 'When your father came on the scene Amelia fell in love just as I did with the lady who is now my wife.'

'Thank you for telling me, Mr—?'

'Charles Adamson. Your grandmother thought I should tell you.'

'I'm so glad you did.'

'I mustn't keep you any longer as I'm sure your husband is impatient to have you back with him.'

'What was all that about?' Peter asked as the guests began to move towards the house.

'Tell you later,' she whispered as they followed the old lady into Duncairn House to begin the celebrations.

Life stretched before them full of hope and promise and with so much love how could they go wrong?

A Woman of Spirit

To Bill and Raymond

# CHAPTER ONE

O n that last day of January 1885 a bitterly cold, contemptuous wind swept through the Lanarkshire village of Aranvale, flattening outhouses and sending slates crashing to the ground. Perched on the highest ground, Aran Heights braved the storm to suffer no more than a broken stable door left hanging drunkenly by its one remaining hinge.

Hamish MacFarlane, owner of the Aranvale Papermill, had had the house built to withstand the elements. Aran Heights was a grand mansion house without in any way being pretentious. Curved stone steps led up to the heavy oak door. The windows followed a precise pattern even to those in the attic and no unnecessary embellishments or fussiness of stone work detracted the eye from its classic simplicity and grace. Hamish MacFarlane was proud of his home and it would have surprised him greatly to know that his wife, Sarah, found it cold and forbidding. Only their daughter, Susan, shared her father's love of Aran Heights.

Hamish MacFarlane considered that he and his family were indeed fortunate to have the best of both worlds. Aranvale had all the attractions of a village with its low houses, small shops, its kirk and manse, two public houses and a railway station, yet was no more than fifteen miles from Glasgow. None would deny that this city of contrasts had some of the finest buildings in Scotland. The rich lived in splendid mansions in spacious streets while the poor were housed in disgusting hovels. Slowly these were disappearing and tenements taking their place, but with the owners demanding rents that most could not afford there was a great deal of bad feeling.

Years before, Samuel MacFarlane, Hamish's grandfather, had come to this part of Lanarkshire and seen the potential

1

for a papermill at Aranvale. With a little money and a great deal of enthusiasm Samuel and a small band of helpers had worked from morning light until darkness to erect a jumble of rough buildings near to the artificial reservoir. Shrewdly he had recognised that the controlled flow of water would ensure a constant supply for manufacturing purposes.

When his son, Thomas, took over, the mill was already showing a healthy profit. New buildings had replaced the old and modern machinery had been added. With more and more orders coming in a larger workforce was needed. The papermill had become the life-blood of Aranvale and the surrounding villages. Now with Hamish in charge the Aranvale Papermill was one of the finest in the country. Even so society was not yet ready to open its doors to the MacFarlanes. The new rich were not yet accepted.

Overnight the wind had almost worn itself out and a weak sun slanted through the curtains of the room where Susan MacFarlane was at the window and her mother warming her hands in front of the log fire.

'Did the storm keep you awake, Mama?'

'Of course it did. As you very well know I have difficulty getting to sleep at the best of times. But we were not discussing the storm.' Then she added irritably, 'Come away from that window.'

Susan moved slowly away to join her mother at the fireside.

In her younger days Sarah MacFarlane had been considered a beauty but now only a faded prettiness remained and despite a daily battle with ever tighter laced corsets her figure had spread.

Half a head taller than her mother, Susan was slimly built with a lovely figure. She had high cheekbones, a velvety smooth skin and eyes of a deep blue but perhaps her real claim to beauty was the glorious silver fairness of her hair.

'I'm only nineteen, Mama,' Susan said quietly.

Seeing her daughter looking so composed brought the angry colour to Sarah's face.

'You'll soon be twenty,' the voice shrilled. 'At your age I was married to your papa.'

'Yes, Mama.' Having heard it all before Susan made the mistake of allowing weariness to creep into her voice and, hearing it, Sarah's fragile control snapped. From where she was standing her raised hand caught Susan's face a stinging slap and Susan, taken aback, stared at her mother in wide-eyed shock.

All the colour had left Sarah's face, leaving it grey and a shaking hand went up to cover her mouth.

'I'm sorry, so very sorry,' she mumbled, 'but it was your manner, your insolence.'

Expelling a shaky breath Susan touched her inflamed cheek. No one had ever raised a hand to her before and she was both outraged and humiliated.

Sarah's ample bosom rose and fell and when next she spoke her voice was softer and a hint of pleading had crept in.

'Edward Brodie would make an excellent husband.'

'For someone else I'm sure he would and don't misunderstand me: I don't dislike Edward, in fact I quite like him but I don't want to get married.'

'Did you tell him that?'

'Yes, I did,' Susan said spiritedly. 'Better to tell him the truth surely.'

'Really, Susan, you are quite impossible. At your age I wouldn't have dared disobey my parents.' Her lips curled. 'Would you rather end up a spinster like your Aunt Rachel?'

Susan didn't take the trouble to answer. Her mother and Papa's sister had never got on but Susan had a very real affection for her eccentric and often embarrassingly outspoken aunt. Rachel MacFarlane could have married but didn't. She was a practical, intelligent woman full of energy and she led a full and independent life.

Abruptly Sarah sat down on the couch and leaned her head against the plump upholstery, managing to lose a hairpin in the process.

'Believe me, Susan, you'll have to learn and learn quickly that your own inclinations are unimportant.' She bit her lip.

3

'John and Lilian Brodie are going to be very upset at your dismissal of Edward and small wonder.' She paused and looked bleak. 'My own position is going to be difficult. Mrs Brodie may decide to exclude me from further invitations to Croft House.' There was a pinched look about her mouth and Susan guessed that that was what concerned her mother most. The Brodies were accepted by society and through Lilian Sarah was edging her way into that exclusive circle.

'Surely Mrs Brodie wouldn't do that, Mama?'

Sarah's eyes darted to the marble clock on the mantelshelf of the splendid Italian fireplace and she gasped. 'Oh, dear, I almost forgot. Your papa wants to see you in the library at ten. Get up there now, it's almost that,' she said warningly.

The warning wasn't needed. Hamish MacFarlane demanded punctuality and Susan had no wish to incur more wrath than that which she had little doubt awaited her. The hand moved to three minutes before the hour.

Checking her face in the mirror and relieved to see no tell-tale signs of her earlier distress, she moved to the door then spoke hesitantly.

'Mama, how is Papa this morning?'

'Your papa has a touch of bronchitis and Dr Sullivan insists that he remains indoors for the next week or two.'

With the closing of the drawing-room door Sarah continued to sit where she was. Much of the room's magnificent splendour was due to her unrestricted expenditure. The exquisite gold-inlaid escritoire, Hepplewhite table and delicate Venetian glass were in perfect taste. Paintings and tapestries adorned the walls and in a locked cabinet, on glass shelves, were placed crinoline figures and other treasured pieces of porcelain. The drawing-room at Aran Heights was a showplace. Sarah loved it and spent as much time as possible there but the rest of the family much preferred the more comfortable and smaller rooms at the back of the house.

In those early days Hamish had been loath to curtail his wife's spending and indeed had admired her choice of furniture and furnishings. Much of the pleasure derived from such a fine display disappeared as the bills began to arrive. Sternly he had

4

reminded Sarah that money did not grow on trees and that one never knew what lay ahead. Sarah had agreed tearfully to exercise restraint in future but it angered her, knowing as she did that the paper-making industry was enjoying a boom in trade.

Amidst all this splendour, as always, her eyes went to the mantelshelf – drawn there to the face smiling out from the gold frame. She could never look at it without her lip trembling and wondered anew if the pain would ever lessen. Here in this same room the news had been broken to her, and closing her eyes she relived the horror of that cruel icy day in January, a year ago now, when tragedy had struck.

Only that previous week her handsome, darling, first-born son had celebrated his twenty-first birthday with a magnificent party. A superb horseman, no one knew how it could have happened but somehow Ralph had been thrown from his horse and in the fall his head had smashed against the stone dyke. The riderless horse had returned to the stables and that same night a distraught and grief-stricken father had ordered the beast to be destroyed.

# CHAPTER TWO

**B**efore entering, Susan gave a light knock on the library door.

'Good morning, Papa.' Knowing it would only irritate him she didn't ask after his health.

'Good morning, Susan,' he grunted, turning away from the window.

'Mama said you wished to see me.'

He nodded, his expression stern. For some time he kept her standing and with each passing moment her apprehension grew. Only now was she beginning to realise the enormity of what she had done and her mouth went dry. She had dared to disobey her parents, gone against an arrangement made by two powerful men to unite their families. Worse still, Edward had been agreeable, more than agreeable. She shivered.

Though heavily built there was a refinement about Hamish MacFarlane and a certain grace to his movements. He had a square-jawed face framed by a beard and sideburns and his dark brown hair, just beginning to grey, was still plentiful and curled to his collar.

Keeping his daughter standing had not been entirely to add to her discomfort. Hamish was enjoying looking at her, proud of her beauty and at other times he would have been secretly amused at her stubbornness, a trait she had inherited from him. However her refusal to become betrothed to Edward Brodie had come as an unpleasant shock. The marriage would take place, he would see to that, but meantime he would go easy on her. Susan, like most women, could be led but not driven. He would do well to exercise patience.

Carefully lowering himself into the spacious leather chair,

7

he motioned for Susan to be seated and she sat down gratefully in the nearest chair.

'Well, young woman,' he rasped, 'what have you got to say for yourself?'

'I'm sorry, Papa,' she whispered.

'And so you should be.' He frowned, drawing his brows together. 'This is going to cause embarrassment between our families. Your mother is most upset.'

'I know.'

'What's wrong with Edward?' he demanded.

'Nothing.'

'You'll soon be twenty as your mother has reminded me, time you were settled.'

Her stomach was churning with nerves but she had to ask now.

'The last thing I want to be, Papa, is a burden to you and that's why' – she faltered – 'may – may I ask something?'

'Go on.'

'I – I know how much you miss Ralph, we all do – ' She saw the pain her words had produced but hurried on. 'Papa, please let me take on some of the responsibility Ralph was shouldering. More than anything I want to learn about the mill.'

He was silent for so long that she thought he wasn't going to answer at all. Then she saw that he was struggling for control but whether it was anger at her temerity or grief for Ralph she couldn't decide.

'Don't be ridiculous,' he said at last, 'the very idea is outrageous.'

Before her courage failed she plunged on. 'It's thanks to you, Papa, that I'm well educated. Sharing lessons with Matthew has given me a knowledge of subjects most girls aren't allowed to study.'

My, but she was a plucky one bringing that up, Hamish thought as he hid a smile. If the truth were known he hadn't been particularly interested in his daughter's education but he wasn't one to waste money. Having the twins educated by one tutor made economical sense.

'Oh, you have an aptitude for figures, I won't deny that. It's just a pity your brother wasn't similarly blessed.' He gave a deep sigh. 'Instead I have a son of great charm, little brain and absolutely no ambition.'

'Papa, that's not fair!' Susan rushed to her twin's defence. 'Mr Clapperton is very impressed with Matthew and says he has the makings of a fine farmer.'

'I'm well aware where Matthew's interests lie,' he said irritably, 'and at one time I may have agreed to his taking up farming, but surely even he must see that it's out of the question now. Matthew's place is in the mill with me and the sooner he realises that the better.'

'Then my education has been a complete waste,' she said angrily and beyond caring now. 'And you who always say how much you hate waste.'

He glowered across the desk and pointed a stubby finger. 'If you filled your days with ladylike pursuits it would be better for all concerned. From what your mother tells me you have few accomplishments and your needlework is a disgrace.'

Susan felt a suffocating tightness in her throat.

'That's because I hate it and I couldn't bear to spend my life as Mama does.'

His expression softened but he gave a shake of his head.

'A woman's place is in the home, my dear, bringing up a family and organising the servants. Maybe one day society will look at it differently but it won't be in my time.'

'You employ women,' she said accusingly.

'Women of that class need to earn money.'

'But Papa – '

'Not another word, young woman, my patience is exhausted.' To show it and hasten her departure he lifted his pen and dipped it into the inkwell.

Sick at heart, Susan stumbled from the library, almost colliding with a startled maid in her rush for the privacy of her own bedroom. Once there she gave in to a storm of weeping, pounding the pillow with her clenched fist. It wasn't fair, nothing was fair. Just because she was a female so many doors were closed. Marriage seemed to be the only escape and in time she was pretty sure that would become its own prison. As she grew calmer she felt ashamed at her outburst and got up from the bed. The covers were in disarray and she smoothed them then went over to the jug on the marble slab. A little water remained, cold now, and she poured it into the china basin and splashed her face. A brisk rub with the towel brought back her colour. Glancing in the mirror above she saw a mouth set in a stubborn line. Nobody, but nobody would force her into a marriage she didn't want. But even as she thought it she wondered how long she could hold out against her parents' wishes.

Hamish MacFarlane allowed himself a tired smile. The lass had a lot of character and a good head on her shoulders but that was no answer to his own problem. Hunched over his desk his eyes were troubled and to add to his difficulties he felt drained of his usual energy. Sarah's insistence on calling Dr Sullivan had resulted in him being confined to the house but truth to tell he didn't feel able to face a day's work at the mill.

'Ease up, man,' Dr Sullivan had said in his blunt manner, 'or you'll drive yourself into an early grave.' The two had been friends since their youth and believed in plain speaking.

'A touch of bronchitis is hardly likely to prove fatal,' Hamish said scornfully.

'With sensible precautions I quite agree but when have you ever been sensible where that mill is concerned?'

'Huh!'

'February is a treacherous month so you keep yourself indoors for the next week or ten days then we'll see.'

'Good God, man! You know that's impossible.'

'Nonsense. Takes a bit of rearranging that's all. Nothing to hinder you having the work needing your personal attention brought to you at Aran Heights and have enough confidence in your staff to delegate the rest.'

'Well, maybe –' Hamish said doubtfully.

'No maybe about it.' His finger pointed to a bottle of brown liquid. 'Don't be treating that as an ornament, the dosage is marked, see and take it regularly and I'll get on my way.'

Overweight and without the height to carry it, the doctor heaved himself up. 'Mistake to sit too long, Hamish. Could be that age is catching up with us,' he said cheerfully.

'Speak for yourself,' Hamish growled. He didn't like to be reminded that he was already well into middle age.

# CHAPTER THREE

By late afternoon Susan was anxious to get out of the house and the disapproving atmosphere. Putting an old cloak over her plain dark gown that she wore in the mornings and should have changed, and a bonnet to cover her hair, she let herself out of the side door and into the cobbled courtyard. Aran Heights, set high on the hilliest part of Aranvale, seemed to grow out of the stark and harsh landscape of the hills and caught the full blast of the north wind which for much of the winter months howled and shrieked through the fields. As she moved across the courtyard a single frisky wind caught at her cloak and whipped it about her legs.

Keeping to the paths around the gardens Susan didn't at first hear the carriage and only when she heard her name shouted did she turn to see Matthew hurrying after her.

'Where are you off to?' Then he grinned. 'No, don't tell me,' he said, falling into step. 'You're in the dog-house.'

In spite of herself she giggled. 'You're an idiot, Matthew, and what are you doing home? Shouldn't you be hard at it in the mill?'

He scowled. Matthew was over six feet tall, loose-limbed, handsome and well aware of the effect his fair good looks had on young women.

'Chalmers was bringing some ledgers and stuff for Father and I decided to accompany him home.'

'You're absolutely hopeless, Matthew, no wonder Papa despairs of you.'

She saw his boyish face darken and then he burst into a sulky tirade.

'Would you believe this?' He sounded horrified. 'Father is insisting I familiarise myself with each stage of paper-making.

13

Heaven knows the office is bad enough but that God-awful clanking of machinery will slowly but surely drive me mad,' he said, clapping a hand to his brow.

'Try to stick it, Matt. After a while you'll hardly notice the noise and in any case you'll be spending most of the time in the office with Papa. He wants you ready to take over and you can't blame him for that, the mill is his whole life.'

'Exactly! As you so rightly say the mill is his whole life. He enjoys it, he got what he wanted and it would have been the same for Ralph.' He kicked viciously at a mound of frozen snow. 'Why did Ralph have to be so stupid as to go and get himself killed?'

'Matthew!' Susan was shocked.

'Sorry, I was thinking out loud. But can't you see, can't anyone see I'm different?' He spread out his hands in a gesture of hopelessness. 'I'm not interested in the mill or in making huge profits.'

'You're quite good at getting through your allowance,' she said tartly.

He glared angrily. 'Whose side are you on?'

'Matthew, I'm not taking sides.'

'Yes, you are.'

She forced a laugh. 'You don't know how ironic this is. What you are rebelling against is what I want. More than anything I want to work with Papa.'

'Wrong sex,' he said bluntly.

'No. Not the wrong sex just the wrong attitude from yours.'

He looked surprised and not a little put out.

'You're beginning to sound just like those females – you know, the ones fighting for God-knows-what.'

'They know what they're fighting for, the right to make use of their talents.'

While walking they had wandered away from the grounds of Aran Heights and Matthew stopped suddenly. 'This far enough for you?'

'I'm in no hurry to get back.'

'Come on then, we'll go round by Moorend.'

'Where else but Clapperton farm?' she said, amused.

'We needn't call in.'

'We won't be calling in,' Susan said firmly as she went ahead to take the road forking away from the farm road. She thought of Winnie Clapperton so obviously in love with Matthew and he only giving her the time of day because of his interest in the farm. Frowning at her thoughts, she turned to look at her brother and was surprised by a look of naked longing in his face as his eyes roved the peaceful country scene. Until that moment she hadn't fully realised just how deep went his passion for the land. Whatever the future held she couldn't see Matthew settling in the mill.

'You gone deaf or something?'

'Sorry, Matt.' She laughed, 'I was miles away. What were you saying?'

'One day Winnie will have all this.' His hand swept the surrounding acres and acres of fields and she heard his sigh. 'Pity she's so plain but I suppose it's a small price to pay for all this.' He gave his sister a sidelong glance.

'Stop it, Matthew,' Susan said sharply, 'Don't make use of people for your own ends and certainly not Winnie. I happen to be fond of her.'

'I wasn't serious.'

'I'm not so sure. I wouldn't put it past you but remember this, Matthew MacFarlane, I don't want Winnie hurt. In fact I might go as far as warn her.'

'Calm down for any favour and she wouldn't, you know – get hurt I mean. She'd be getting exactly what she wants,' he said smugly.

'Don't be so disgustingly sure of yourself. Winnie is no fool.'

'That I do know. When it comes to the farm she's almost as knowledgeable as old Clapperton and I happen to know that there isn't very much done without first discussing it with Winnie.'

Nothing more was said as they walked the rough pitted road. In the distance they could see smoke coming from the chimneys of the Old Mill House where Hamish had been born and where his unmarried sister, Rachel, lived with her housekeeper and a small staff of servants.

'Susan!' Matthew gripped her arm. 'I've had an absolutely brilliant idea.' Then as she looked at him enquiringly he loosened his hold. 'No, I haven't, you've mucked it up by refusing Edward.'

'Mucked up what?'

'Edward hates playing second fiddle to that pompous ass Thomas.' He paused for Susan's reaction but there was none. 'What I'm trying to say is that Edward would be happier with some responsibility in the papermill rather than the way he's placed in the distillery.'

'Thomas is not a pompous ass, the description pompous applies more to Edward. Thomas is the elder son and naturally he'll succeed his father; Edward's trouble is that he doesn't like taking orders from anyone. That said, where is this supposed to be leading?'

'Nowhere,' he said morosely, 'unless you decide to marry Edward after all.' He brightened. 'Why not, Susan? Edward's all right, plenty after him and you could do worse.'

'You're the absolute limit, do you know that?'

'Just realistic. Married to you Edward becomes family and Father would welcome him with open arms, he'd be an asset to the mill. Later the pair of you will no doubt produce the longed-for grandson and all our troubles will be over.'

'Meaning you get what you want?'

'You won't come out of it so badly.'

'You're right I won't because, my dear brother, I have no intention of marrying Edward,' she said sweetly.

'Could be you'll have to, but speak of the devil, isn't that the Brodie carriage drawing up in the yard?'

She craned her neck and saw with a sinking heart that it was indeed the Brodie carriage. Even at that distance she could make out Edward's broad figure moving away from the carriage and walking towards the front entrance.

'What does he want here?' she muttered crossly.

'Come! Come! Susan, you must know that someone as persistent as our Edward won't be disheartened at the first

rebuff. Take it from me he won't be so easy to shake off.'
Seeing her expression he sobered. 'Why shouldn't he call?
Much more embarrassing if he didn't.' He grinned wickedly.
'Think of poor Mother if the Brodies were to shun Aran
Heights. She'd be inconsolable if her climb into society were
to be so cruelly halted.'

'That's going too far, Matthew,' Susan said coldly. 'Mama
has a wide circle of friends.'

'Agreed, but they're still way behind the high and mighty
Brodies.'

They were hardly inside and closing the vestibule door before
Sarah MacFarlane, in a pale lavender gown that rustled as she
moved, greeted her son warmly and turned to Susan.

'I do wish, Susan, that you had the good manners to tell
me before you go out,' she said petulantly. 'Edward is here,
he's with Papa at the moment.'

'My fault, Mother, don't blame Susan,' Matthew said
carelessly as he shrugged himself out of his coat. 'We were
both in need of a spot of fresh air.'

'Very well, but hadn't you better hurry and change?' she
said, looking with distaste at Susan's outdoor clothes.

'I was about to, Mama,' Susan said, anxious to make her
escape but it wasn't to be. The drawing-room door opened
and they heard Edward taking his leave of Hamish. Then,
catching sight of Susan, his eyebrows shot up and he was
smiling as he took the few strides along the passageway to
where they stood in the large square-shaped hall.

Moving away from the heat of the fire, Sarah excused
herself with a sweet smile to Edward and a warning look
in her daughter's direction. After a few pleasantries Matthew
followed his mother out.

Left together, Susan's first thought was that no matter
when one saw Edward he was always immaculately dressed.
Sarah liked such attention to appearance but Susan was
slightly put off by it. To her Edward just stopped short of
being a dandy.

Reaching for her hand he squeezed her fingers gently.

17

'Susan, let's not be awkward with one another; you were perfectly entitled to give me the answer you did.' He frowned as a maid arrived to add more logs to the hall fire. 'Couldn't we take a short stroll since you're dressed for outdoors?'

'Like this?'

He smiled. 'Not your best I gather but I have to be on my way shortly.'

At twenty-four Edward had the easy assurance of his class and was proud of his family history. His forebears had been Glasgow merchants engaged in the tobacco trade with the American colonies. Huge fortunes had been made and when trade declined the 'tobacco lords' as they were called bought other concerns. Seeing potential in the Granton Distillery, Joseph Brodie set about acquiring it and once it became his property began a programme of expansion. Pouring so much money into the hugely competitive whisky trade had not been without its risks, for though popular locally the Granton blend was virtually unknown outside Lanarkshire.

Aggressive marketing spread its fame and the Granton blend became known and approved. Profits soared and the Brodie family became one of the richest and most influential in Lanarkshire.

Once Susan and Edward were clear of the house Edward took her arm.

'Let me make one thing clear, Susan, the suddenness of my proposal was in no way influenced by your parents or mine.'

She felt laughter bubbling up in her throat. 'Come on, Edward, be completely honest, it had a good deal to do with it.'

'You're wrong about that.' His eyes met and held hers. 'Ralph knew how much I admired you. I even told him that you were the girl I was going to marry.'

'And what did Ralph have to say?' She couldn't stop herself asking.

'I'm happy to say he approved.'

And that was probably true, she thought. Ralph thought a lot of Edward, and Edward had been devastated by his friend's death. But it didn't alter anything as far as she was concerned.

'I wish it were different,' she said softly, 'but it's better to be honest. I like you but I don't love you.'

'That would come.' And when she didn't answer there was alarm in his voice. 'There isn't anyone – I mean you're not – '

She shook her head. 'No, Edward, there is no one,' she said truthfully.

His face relaxed. It was a nice face with well-defined features and light blue eyes but the mouth was too thin and could twist into a cruel line. Both Thomas and Edward owed their sandy colouring to their mother but that was all the brothers had in common. Whereas Thomas was small made with narrow shoulders Edward was built like his father and stood just short of six feet.

'That's a relief, you had me worried.' And as she made to speak he held up his hand. 'Don't worry, I'm not going to keep badgering you but at least I can go on hoping you'll change your mind.'

'You're a dear, Edward,' she said impulsively, 'and I know that for most girls marriage is the most important step in their life. One day maybe I'll feel that way too.'

'But not yet?'

'No, not yet. Before that I mean to do something with my life.'

'Such as?' His eyes were amused.

'Such as persuading Papa to give me some responsibility in the mill.'

Edward looked even more shocked than Papa had.

'Mr MacFarlane would never agree to that. Take my advice and don't suggest such a thing.'

'I already have,' she said haughtily.

'May I ask what he had to say?'

'Oh, he'll take a bit of persuading,' she said airily, 'but I don't give up easily.'

'Susan, I'm not suggesting that you are not intelligent – '

'How kind of you,' she said sarcastically, 'and how strange that one of my sex should be credited with brains.'

His face darkened with anger. 'All I meant was that business is a man's world and there is no place in it for a woman.'

'Why not? Are we fit only to do the master's bidding and bear his children?' she flashed back.

'Most women seem well satisfied with their lot,' he said grimly.

'What choice have they? I'm in a different position. Matthew wants to take up farming so Papa may have need of me.'

He nodded, some of his former annoyance evaporating. 'Yes, I know of Matthew's reluctance to be involved in the mill and how worrying it is for Mr MacFarlane. We were just discussing that.' About to say more he checked himself and in a blinding flash Susan saw it all. Matthew's brilliant idea hadn't been his alone. She could see that it would be to everyone's advantage if she were to marry Edward. Papa would welcome Edward into the mill but only as a son-in-law. Matthew wouldn't be under the same pressure and, last, but certainly not least, Mama's place in society would be assured if the families were united through marriage.

Well, she wouldn't let herself be used. She would stand up against the lot of them and if life became intolerable there was always Aunt Rachel. Aunt Rachel would understand as no one else would. The light of battle was in her eyes as she said frostily, 'I'm beginning to feel chilled, Edward. This is far enough and I'd like to return home now.'

# CHAPTER FOUR

In the library, a very masculine wood-panelled room where Hamish MacFarlane had ruled out any interference from Sarah, Susan sat stiffly in a chair across from a desk littered with papers. On the floor on either side of her father's chair was a stack of ledgers and, seeing the questioning look in her eyes, he gave one of his rare smiles.

'You could say the office has been transferred to Aran Heights.'

Not knowing the reason for her summons some of the unease lifted and she smiled in relief.

Placing his elbows on his desk and with the tips of his fingers pressed together, Hamish looked at his daughter thoughtfully.

'I hadn't quite dismissed your suggestion of assisting me. No, don't get carried away,' he said as she leaned forward eagerly. 'Your presence in the mill is out of the question.'

'Then how can I – '

'Kindly stop interrupting.'

'I'm sorry,' she murmured, looking down at her clasped hands.

'Quite! Now if you will allow me to continue. It occurred to me that working from Aran Heights, though tedious and unsatisfactory for me, could be the answer in your case and since you are so keen to learn you can take on some of the work here at home.'

'Thank you, Papa.'

He frowned. 'Let me add that this is all very much against your mother's wishes and it might be prudent if you were to spend some of your time following the pursuits of a normal,' he stressed normal, 'young lady.' His eyebrows beetled and he growled. 'That shouldn't be beyond your capabilities.'

'No, Papa,' she said demurely. 'I'll promise to try and please Mama.' Inwardly she was doubtful of success but at least she would try.

'Good!' he said as if that disposed of a tiresome problem. Rising from his chair she took as a signal for her departure and got up hastily.

'No, don't go just yet. This seems as good a time as any to initiate you into the business your great-grandfather founded.' He waved a hand. 'Bring your chair forward and we'll make a start and if you prove yourself useful I may consider having a desk brought in for your own use.'

Her father proved to be a good teacher. In a clear and unhurried manner he began to explain how a papermill functioned, emphasising the importance of each worker no matter how humble. She listened carefully, even venturing some questions and those he answered at length. She could sense that he was pleased. Time flew and too soon for Susan, her father closed the ledgers.

'Enough for one day, young woman.'

'I'm not a bit tired,' she protested.

'I dare say,' he said drily, 'but I am.'

Guiltily she remembered then that he was convalescent and, looking, she saw the tiredness etched on his face. She bit her lip. 'I ought to have remembered that Dr Sullivan – '

'Dr Sullivan is an old woman. A lot less fussing and I'd be a deal happier.' Then seeing her face and the concern there his voice softened. 'Teaching an able student is no hardship; my one regret is that you were blessed with the MacFarlane brains rather than Matthew. However that's the way it is,' he ended heavily.

'When may I come back?'

'Mmmmm. Mornings straight after breakfast, I think. I'll set you some work and – ' his eyes went to the bookshelves. 'You're not obliged to read them but if you're interested in the history of paper-making by all means take those you want.' His head went down and she knew that the time allotted to her had expired. Quietly she went out, closing the door behind her. Hardly had the door closed than her mother's voice reached her.

'Susan, come down here at once.'

'Coming, Mama.' Hurrying along the corridor and down to the dining-room Susan found her mother inspecting the polished furniture for traces of dust and, finding none, turned to her daughter.

'Where have you been all this time?' she snapped.

'With Papa, I told you.'

The dining-room was almost as big as the drawing-room and was used only when there were guests. The family dined in the breakfast-room or the small dining-room at the back of the house and nearer the kitchens.

'You think you've got your own way,' she smirked.

'Papa wants me – '

Sarah cut her off. 'What possible good it will do you is beyond me and what our friends would have to say if they found out – '

'Why should that matter?'

'Because, you stupid girl, well-brought-up young ladies do not interest themselves in such things. I'm surprised at your papa, more than surprised.'

'All I'll be doing is spending a few hours in the library and I would like to please you,' Susan said quietly, remembering her promise to her father.

'Then you may remain with me while I discuss the week's menus with Mrs Doig.'


Working closely with her father Susan got an insight into the real man. Not the harsh disciplinarian some saw but a man who had the good of his workers at heart. On self-inflicted troubles he poured out scorn but to those of his employees in genuine need he turned a sympathetic ear and there were many who had reason to bless the Master of Aranvale.

Loudly protesting yet recognising the necessity in this damp and foggy weather, Hamish MacFarlane extended his time at home. Each morning after breakfast Matthew left for the mill and Susan joined her father in the library. Early on they had come to an agreement that outside the time allocated to her she would make no demands, ask no questions. For Susan this was no hardship; what she failed to grasp she took note of for their next session.

A lot of her day was spent closeted with her father in the library and if he noticed the lengthening of the day he made no remark. After all, having her own desk and working area meant no more than the scratching of two pens instead of one.

Before long Hamish was involving her in discussions or rather, she supposed, he was thinking out loud and happy to have an interested listener. On the last of these days Susan looked across to where her father sat and felt a wave of depression.

'You can't imagine how much I'm going to miss all this.'

'Some work will continue to be brought to you but it's high time I was back, Susan. Even the most conscientious workers need supervision.' He nodded his head knowingly. 'Human nature being what it is, when there is no one to oversee, slackness invariably happens. And another thing, no matter how much they grumble the workers recognise the need for strict and fair supervision, in fact they welcome it.'

'I'm sure you're right, Papa, but is there no chance – '

'Of working alongside me? Absolutely none so let's have no more of that. Instead consider yourself fortunate that I have allowed you this far.'

'I am grateful.'

He smiled. 'An intelligent interest I expected but you have surpassed my expectations and there is just the possibility that someone will be instructed to come to Aran Heights to teach you our method of book-keeping. That is if I can spare a clerk.'

It was around ten o'clock on a Wednesday morning that Susan crossed to the shelves for another book on the history of paper-making. On the way to her desk she glanced out of the window and at that angle could just make out the figure of a young man before he disappeared round to the side of the house. Idly she wondered whom he might be. Not a visitor or he would have arrived by carriage and there was no carriage in the courtyard. Mrs Dunbar, the housekeeper, would deal with him and if not she would have to go down. Mrs MacFarlane was indisposed with a headache and likely to keep to her bedroom for most of the day.

Turning the pages of the book before beginning serious reading, she was interrupted by the maid announcing that a Mr David Cameron had an appointment with Miss Susan MacFarlane.

'Indeed! Did he state his business?'

'No, Miss Susan. I put him in the mornin' room like the mistress told me. Did I do right?' she asked anxiously.

'Yes, Polly.' Susan nodded kindly to the new maid. 'I'll come down right away.'

When she entered the morning-room the stranger turned from his study of the view and as their eyes met Susan's heart fluttered and she had the strangest sensation that nothing would ever be quite the same again. It was alarming and ridiculous and to hide her confusion she drew herself up and spoke more haughtily than she intended.

'Kindly state your business, Mr Cameron.'

He gave a small bow and spoke with icy politeness.

'My business, Miss MacFarlane, is to spend two hours twice weekly teaching you the basics of book-keeping.' He managed to convey that the task ahead afforded him little pleasure.

Embarrassed at being caught out and angered at his tone she faltered.

'I – I beg your pardon. No one warned me of your coming.' She shouldn't have used the word 'warn' but really this common and forward young man was having such a disturbing effect on her. 'In any case,' she rushed on, making matters worse, 'I would have expected my father to engage an older and more senior clerk.'

The dark almost black eyes looked at her steadily.

'Miss MacFarlane, the task is not of my choosing and it so happens that the more elderly clerks are not accountants.'

25

Her lips tightened. He was, she thought, quite the most odious and at the same time the most handsome man she had ever met. Tall and very dark, he held himself with a soldierly erectness yet without stiffness. His features were regular, his chin determined and his eyes, darkly lashed, appeared almost black in a clean-shaven face.

'Am I right in assuming that your duties begin immediately, Mr Cameron?'

'Whenever you are ready,' he said mockingly.

'Then be good enough to follow me to the library,' she said crisply.

Very conscious of those dark eyes following her, Susan was glad when they reached the library. Once inside she saw his eyes move quickly round the room then linger on the book-laden shelves and widen in appreciation.

'Where do we work?' he asked politely.

Quickly she went to her desk and sat down. 'Bring a chair for yourself.' She pointed to one.

Without a word he picked up the heavy high-backed chair as though it were a lightweight, set it well apart from her and sat down. From the folder he had been carrying he extracted a bundle of papers and proceeded to spread them across the desk.

'Am I correct in assuming you have no knowledge of the subject, Miss MacFarlane?' he asked but the answer was there in his voice.

Susan set her lips and didn't answer. Let him find out, she thought.

'Very well, we'll begin at the beginning.'

'Where else?' she said sweetly, earning herself a dark look.

Clearly and precisely he gave his explanations and in a manner that would have been acceptable to someone of limited intelligence. Not having to dwell on the content, Susan studied his voice instead. Pleasant enough, she conceded and well modulated but his articulation was too careful and shrewdly she recognised that here was someone trying to rise above his station and to do so he was obviously emulating

others. As he moved his head she frowned in concentration.
For a fleeting tantalising moment he had reminded her of
someone, then it was gone and she saw that he had stopped
talking. Putting down his pen he leaned back in his chair and
she saw a nerve twitch.

'For at least five minutes, Miss MacFarlane, you haven't
heard a word I've said. Either I'm not making myself clear and
you fail to understand or you already have some knowledge
of the subject.'

She knew she'd angered him, deserved his reproach and
she tried to redeem herself. 'Revision is seldom wasted,
Mr Cameron, and I have to admit that some of it is familiar.'

'Then had you taken the trouble to inform me,' he said with
icy coldness, 'your time and mine might have been saved.'

'I'm sorry, I do apologise,' she said, having the grace to
blush. 'Allow me to show you the stage I have reached.'
Taking out some of her own workings she put the neat
columns of figures before him and saw his start of surprise.

'You did these?'

Feeling absurdly pleased she nodded. 'You seem to find it
unusual in a female but figures have always held an interest
for me. My brother and I shared lessons so I had a good
grounding.'

'Forgive me saying so but your brother couldn't produce
that kind of work, not with any amount of tuition.'

'Perhaps not,' she said coldly, feeling he was overstepping
himself, 'my brother's talents take another direction.'

'I'm sure they do.' He selected another paper and began
doing calculations while she looked on.

After he'd gone Susan felt her legs suddenly weak and sat
down in the chair David Cameron had vacated. Her hands
went to her hot cheeks and she wondered what was happening
to her. Nothing or no one had ever made her feel this way and
it was humiliating that a brash young man, a mere employee
at the mill should have this effect on her. Then she tried to
make excuses for herself, blaming it on the unexpectedness
of his arrival.

Nevertheless it was the young accountant's mocking dark eyes she remembered as she lay awake well into the night.

David Cameron's first impression of Susan MacFarlane was of a spoilt and pampered young woman very much aware of her position and not likely to let him forget it either. As they would any full-blooded young man her beauty and poise had attracted him but it was her quick mind that had him captivated. In his short experience of the opposite sex beauty and brains seldom mixed yet here at Aran Heights he found that combination. Far from dreading his next visit to Aran Heights he found to his surprise that he was looking forward to teaching Miss Susan MacFarlane.

Taken aback by Mr MacFarlane's request – not a request, an order – to teach his daughter some book-keeping, David had resigned himself to the boredom of imparting information to someone incapable of understanding the first thing about such a complex subject. How wrong he had been to imagine that the master of the mill would indulge even his own daughter unless it were to prove profitable.

That had him wondering as he walked home to the humble cottage he shared with his mother. With the elder son dead and the other so obviously unsuited to follow his father, the master must be worried. Was it possible that Miss Susan MacFarlane was being coached and trained to become the controlling influence with her twin merely the figurehead? David had a shrewd suspicion that it could well be the case. What other explanation could there be?

A clever, ambitious young man, David had every intention of going far. The fact that he had been born out of wedlock did not greatly trouble him. Indeed after what he'd had to put up with it had prepared him to stand up for himself and given him the ruthlessness needed to succeed.

All that he had ever learned from his mother was that he had been fathered by a gentleman. Natural curiosity had urged him to ask more but his questions had been met with a tight-lipped refusal. For all her gentleness Eliza Cameron was a strong-willed and deeply religious woman. To her a vow such as she had made was a sacred promise and nothing would make her break it. Only her sister knew and the secret was safe with her.

Employed as a table-maid in one of Lanarkshire's finest houses, Eliza's fresh young beauty had not gone unnoticed by the master of the house and as her figure blossomed into the shapeliness of womanhood so his interest in the young maid had increased.

More flattered than repulsed by the attention of a man old enough to be her father it had never occurred to Eliza Cameron to do other than obey. Wasn't he the master and hadn't her mother, fearful of her daughter losing such a sought-after position, drummed into her repeatedly the need to be obedient at all times?

Finding herself pregnant the sixteen-year-old Eliza had been terrified. With no one to turn to and only too well aware that her strict parents would show her the door, she had blurted out her condition to the master. Not that she expected any help from that quarter, indeed it could only hasten her departure from his house but he had noticed her distress and demanded to know the reason for it. As she stammered out the awful truth his face had grown grave and his long silence had unnerved her, bringing her to the verge of hysteria.

What was to become of her? Where could she go? From gossip in the kitchen she was vaguely aware of the method used by some girls who found themselves in this position and wanted rid of their unwanted babies. But that was a sin and Eliza Cameron had a healthy fear of the wrath of God and His punishment.

Not an unkind man, the master had drawn her gently to him and looked into her swimming eyes. Of course, he'd said gently, there was no question but that she must leave his employ and quickly but not without some support. How grateful she had been for those gold coins. A fortune in her eyes. Between sniffs and sobs she had poured out her gratitude, only too happy to agree to his terms. In return for such generosity she was to move away from the area and give him her vow of silence. No one must know that he was responsible for her condition. Everything he said had been agreed to willingly and, no doubt relieved to be rid of her so easily, he had pressed a further sum to help her educate the child if it were a boy.

Eliza Cameron had guarded that money for her son's education and even when she was at her wits' end as to where their next crust of bread was coming from she had never been tempted to dip into it. Now she was reaping her reward. David was a good son and he had worked hard at his studies, gaining praise from his teachers. Eliza was bursting with pride when he secured a position as junior accountant with the Aranvale Papermill and when he had insisted that she no longer took in washing or went out scrubbing she had been touched. Reluctant at first, she had eventually given in to his wishes. With careful budgeting, and she was used to that, his salary would cover their needs.

# CHAPTER FIVE

Other than a Sunday morning, breakfast at Aran Heights was most often eaten in silence or at best in whispered conversation. Mr MacFarlane disliked talk at this time in the morning and indeed the family seldom sat down together. More and more in recent weeks the lady of the house was having a tray sent up to her bedroom and Matthew, always a late arrival for breakfast, allowed himself only sufficient time to swallow a few mouthfuls before joining his father in the carriage which would be ready and waiting for them in the drive.

This morning for some reason the entire family was to breakfast together. Susan was humming under her breath as she helped herself to breakfast from the hot plates on the dresser.

'Someone's happy,' Matthew whispered as he piled bacon on to his plate.

'Maybe I am but what's come over you? All of ten minutes to eat your bacon and eggs, that's unheard of.'

He grinned. 'Spring is in the air tra-la.'

'Susan,' her mother said plaintively, 'did you have a caller yesterday? I thought I heard voices but my head was pounding so painfully that I couldn't be sure.'

'A Mr Cameron from the mill called –' Susan began.

'Sarah,' her husband said irritably, 'you knew Mr Cameron was expected. Damn it, I told you to tell Susan.'

'I'm sorry, Hamish, it completely slipped my mind.'

'Must have been a bit of a surprise for you, Susan?'

'Yes, it was.' Hastily she dropped her eyes as she felt her colour rising.

'Not overgifted with patience our Mr Cameron but a good

31

head on him so pay attention and you'll learn a lot.'

'Really, I must object to this nonsense,' Sarah said sharply, putting down the finger of toast she had been nibbling. She touched her lips delicately with a corner of her napkin. 'This is complete folly and it has gone far enough. What possible use can Susan be to you?'

'At one time I would have said none, my dear, but I have the future to think about. I won't always be here – '

'Don't talk like that,' Sarah interrupted sharply, 'it upsets me.'

'Then it shouldn't. We all have to leave this world one day and I want a MacFarlane ready to take over when that day comes.'

'Of course I understand that and by then Matthew will be ready to do so.'

'Unfortunately Matthew has shown himself to be completely useless.'

Matthew had half risen, his face had gone white and his eyes smouldered with anger.

'Useless in the mill, Father! Yes, I couldn't agree more. I hate the place and I'm beginning to suffocate in that vile atmosphere.' His eyes switched to Susan. 'By all means teach Susan; it's what she wants. You'll find her a willing and I don't doubt able student and think about it, Father, if you haven't already done so. If, or is it when, she marries Edward Brodie you'll have a good team: two business heads instead of one.'

Susan rounded on him furiously. 'You've no right to say such a thing.'

'Why not?' her mother said, opening her eyes wide. 'As regards Edward, Matthew is only stating what your papa and I have agreed is best for you.'

'Papa, it's not true.' Her eyes were pleading. 'You wouldn't make me marry Edward?'

'You're too young to know what is best for you,' he barked angrily and scraping back his chair strode out of the room, leaving his breakfast unfinished. Three pairs of eyes watched his departure then Mrs MacFarlane spoke warningly.

'Matthew, dear, you had better hurry.'

Drawing a hand through his unruly fair hair he sighed resignedly, gave Susan a ruefully apologetic grin which she ignored and, rising from his chair, followed his father out. At that moment, to Susan's intense relief, the maid arrived and stood hesitantly within the doorway awaiting instructions.

'Yes, you may clear up.' Sarah signalled to the table with a flurry of a white hand. Then without a glance at Susan she got up and swept from the room.

Susan watched the maid for a few minutes then collected an old coat from the stand in the hall and went out into the garden for a breath of fresh air and to get a grip on herself. The mist was lifting from the hills and a glint of sun peeked out to give the promise of a fine day but Susan scarcely noticed. She felt betrayed and hurt yet honesty forced her to see it from her father's position and in her heart she couldn't blame him. What other course was open to him? Both sons had failed him – Ralph by his untimely death and Matthew by his reluctance to work in the mill. With his own health giving cause for alarm was it any wonder that he now turned to his daughter to make a suitable marriage. And Edward would be eminently suitable. His background was excellent and he had a keen brain, just what the papermill required.

In a fit of depression she thought perhaps it would be wiser just to fall in with everyone's wishes and marry Edward. Respect and liking were quite enough for marriage as both her parents had been at pains to point out. And it could be worse, much worse; some girls were forced into marriage with someone old and repugnant and Edward was certainly neither of these. Why then, as she almost decided her fate, did a pair of mocking eyes rise up to taunt her?

In rather less than an hour David Cameron was due at Aran Heights and still Susan hadn't made up her mind as to what she would wear. Four gowns lay in an untidy heap on the bed, having been discarded for various reasons. Finally she decided on a skirt of black taffeta and a crisp white blouse with a high frilled neckline and fastened down the front with tiny pearl buttons.

Ten minutes before the appointed hour saw Susan behind her desk. Her silver blonde hair was swept up into a pompadour and secured with two tortoise-shell combs, leaving a slender column of neck above the frilled neckline. There was a soft tell-tale flush on her cheeks as she bent her head in a pretence of working. All the time her ears were alert for the sounds of Mr Cameron's arrival.

David Cameron was prompt; he would not have dared be otherwise. Remembering Miss Susan's instructions, careful instructions, the housekeeper had the maid show David to the library immediately on his arrival. The task was very much to the liking of the saucy young maid who eyed the strikingly handsome young man with bold, inviting eyes. But the boldness fast disappeared when she met his cold stare. With a tightening of her own lips she saw his curl in disgust and she gave an angry toss of her head. Walking ahead of him with an exaggerated swing to her hips she led the way along a passage with a stone floor and drab painted walls to stairs which divided the servants' quarters from the main house. Where the carpet began huge oil paintings dignified the impressive staircase and the length of wall to the library.

Susan answered the sharp rap on the door and, dismissing the maid with a curt nod, David entered. At that precise moment the grandfather clock in the hall boomed out the hour and Susan smiled with amusement.

'Good morning, Mr Cameron, you are prompt.'

'Good morning, Miss MacFarlane,' he said gravely. 'I take great pains to be punctual but seldom manage it to the minute.'

She gave him her warm smile then laughed. 'Believe me, I do know of my father's insistence on punctuality, it extends to his family as well.' She indicated the vacant chair next to her own. 'Please sit down then we can get started.'

Behind hastily lowered lashes she watched his tall figure cross the room and felt the quickening of her heartbeat as he took his seat beside her. At once his eyes went to the papers neatly placed on his end of the desk and a ledger open to display a completed balance sheet.

'Very good! You've done the work I set you?' He managed to sound both pleased and surprised.

Her delicate eyebrows shot up. 'Didn't you expect me to do it?'

'Thought maybe I'd overdone it – shades of the classroom!'

'Not at all,' she said stiffly, 'you're here to teach and I to learn and I may add that my father will expect results.'

'That I don't doubt.'

She looked at him quickly but he had turned his attention to her workings and she saw him frown. When he put a question mark in the margin she said, 'Why? What have I done wrong?'

'Nothing at all, you've arrived at the right answer.'

'Well then?'

'It was a long laborious way to get there. Let me show you.'

He took her each step of the way, occasionally looking up to see if she were following. At the end she said apologetically, 'How very much simpler and how stupid of me.'

He put down his pen and regarded her unsmilingly. 'There was nothing stupid about it. This is merely a way of saving time and effort and now we'll get on with the next part. I can see with the progress you're making that my services will very shortly become unnecessary.'

'I'm sure I still have a great deal to learn,' she said hastily, then, seeing his amusement, coloured and looked away.

An hour later she rubbed at her neck, feeling a stiffness.

'Too long holding your head in one position. I used to suffer from that,' he said sympathetically.

'A short break will do us both good, Mr Cameron.' She had a sudden, urgent need to learn more about Mr David Cameron.

'What made you decide to be an accountant?'

He thought before answering. 'There's security in this type of work and figures fascinate me just as they do you.'

'So your ambition has been realised?'

'Not at all though you may well be right.' He paused. 'A

friend I studied with has written recently to tell me of the good opportunities there are down south. He's doing well and suggests I should join him.'

'But you wouldn't?' she said swiftly. It was ridiculous the depth of disappointment she felt at the thought of him leaving Aranvale.

'I'm not free to go otherwise I most certainly would pack my bags and seek my fortune.' He stopped. 'If it's not an impertinence may I make a personal remark?'

She nodded. Of course she shouldn't encourage him, she knew that well enough, but she wanted to hear what he had to say.

'You have beauty and intelligence, something rarely found together.'

She blushed. 'Thank you but your view is limited. Many women are gifted but have no outlet for their talents.'

'Is it possible that one day the Aranvale Papermill may have a woman at its head?'

'Would that be so terrible?'

'Any departure from the normal is looked on with suspicion,' he said carefully.

'You for one wouldn't welcome it?' What was she thinking of, talking like this to an employee of her father?

'I didn't say that. In my opinion it would be far better to have a capable, intelligent woman in a position of authority than a man lacking in those qualities. Problem would be getting the respect from the workers.'

'Yes, you're probably right,' she said, opening one of the ledgers. For the remainder of the two hours the dark head and the fair head were bent over papers bearing the crest of the Aranvale Papermill.

'Time is up, Miss MacFarlane.' Did she detect a note of regret or was it wishful thinking?

'You're not finding the task too arduous?'

'On the contrary it has been a privilege and a pleasure.'

Getting to her feet she disturbed the papers on the desk and a few fluttered to the floor. Simultaneously they made a grab and in doing so their fingers touched. Susan drew back as though she had been scorched and for a long moment they both seemed to be holding their breath. In that short interval she could have sworn he was equally shaken but if so he quickly recovered and she was left wondering if she had imagined it. What wasn't imagination was the alarming effect this young man had had on her right from the first moment of meeting and suddenly she was afraid . . .

Those electrifying moments had shaken David Cameron more than he would have believed possible. Only by a supreme effort had he conquered an overwhelming desire to take her in his arms and crush her to him. That she was not totally indifferent to him he knew by the shock in those startlingly blue eyes. Yet what a ridiculous situation. He would do well to remember his place if he wished to remain in the employ of the Master of Aranvale.

Embarrassment had brought out her frostiness and as he prepared to leave she gave him a cool smile of dismissal.

'I'll get the maid to see you out.'

'No need for that, Miss MacFarlane,' he said, matching her tone for coolness. 'I have mastered the geography of the servants' quarters and can very well see myself out.'

Once outside, his folder beneath his arm, David gave in to an impulse and walked round to the front of Aran Heights where a broad sweep of gravel gave ample room for a carriage to turn. At the wide open ornamental gates he stood and looked in and for him the joy of this magnificent structure lay in its stark simplicity, its compelling beauty. Here was classic undertstatement. The precision in the spacing of the windows, in the tall stately chimneys and weather-beaten stone walls. Uncluttered with mouldings and innocent of decorative patterns, each window had a long, graceful line which continued to the windows of the attics. A forest of trees and olive green firs gave protection to the house from the worst of the weather. In the distance he could see the bobbing heads of the gardeners hoeing the ground and hear the trundling of barrows.

To dwell in such a house! To have servants to do one's

bidding and a carriage for convenience. Susan MacFarlane had all this, this was where she belonged. Thinking of the humble, damp cottage he shared with his mother David almost laughed out loud. Miss MacFarlane might occupy his thoughts but that was all it would ever be.

A lane behind the main street of Aranvale led to a row of badly maintained cottages and the end one was home to David and his mother. It was a but and ben and Eliza's bed was in a hole in the wall covered during the day by a curtain. Waxcloth worn in places covered the stone floor. The carefully black-leaded range gleamed in the light from the gas mantle. Because of the dampness the fire was never allowed to go out even in the summer. Each night it was banked up with dross and left to slow burn. In the middle of the room was a wooden table covered in a green plush cloth and under it two kitchen chairs. Here David and his mother ate their meals. As a schoolboy and later as a student it had served as a desk for his books and on washing days old blankets were spread on it to iron the clothes. This was done with a flat iron heated at the fire and spat on to test for the correct heat. Eliza was a dab hand at ironing, her expertise gained by years of ironing for the well-to-do who paid little but expected much. Two shabby cushioned chairs sat either side of the range and on the opposite wall stood a dresser with a wally dog on each side.

A door gave directly into the other room where David slept.

At the sink in front of the curtained window Eliza Cameron, wearing a coarse apron over her skirt, scraped at a potato with a kitchen knife. Then she added it to the others in the thick black pot and closed her eyes until the sharp pain reduced to a small, nagging annoyance. Her brow was beaded in sweat and she used a rag to wipe it away. Wearily she started on the carrots and turnip. David needed a good nourishing meal when he got home. Once it was under way and the table set she'd settle down in the chair for a rest. It would help her get through the rest of the evening without alarming David. She didn't want him to be worried about her health.

David lifted the sneck and let himself in. The sound was usually enough to bring his mother but not tonight. He hung up his coat on a hook attached to the wall and called out, 'I'm home, Mother.'

She was asleep in front of the range where two pots spluttered and steam rose from the heavy black kettle. For a few moments he looked down at her. Her head was bent forward and some of the grey hairs had escaped the coiled plait and hung loose and untidy on her neck. Blue-veined, papery hands that had done a lifetime of scrubbing and cleaning rested in her lap. Suddenly she gave a snort, her head jerked up and she looked at him with startled, uncomprehending eyes.

'It's only me, Mother,' David said gently.

She roused herself. 'Dearie me, I must have dropped off. You're early,' she said accusingly as she made to get up.

'No, Mother, it's my usual time but stay where you are. I'm perfectly capable of serving my own meal.'

''deed and you'll do no such thing and you been workin' all day.' Pushing his arm away she staggered to her feet then held on to the back of the chair to regain her balance. 'Some would be sayin' your mother's had a drop too much,' she said with an attempt at humour.

'Folk know better than that, Mother.' He frowned. 'I'm worried about you and after we eat I'm going for Dr Anderson. This has gone on long enough.'

'You'll do no such thing, my lad. Can't a body be tired without all this fuss,' she said with a spurt of anger.

'All right,' he said soothingly, 'but promise me you'll see the doctor if this continues?'

'Take your meal while there's some good in it and stop worryin'. The Lord won't take me afore my time.'

# CHAPTER SIX

M r Cameron was seldom out of her thoughts and Susan felt strangely excited. She couldn't understand it or the sensation which twisted her stomach and sent her heart beating wildly. Getting up and wandering over to the window she watched the gardeners weeding and hoeing and replanting the flower-beds for the summer and longed to be out of doors.

'Susan, what is the matter with you?'

'Nothing, Mama.' She turned from the window as her mother put down the embroidery she had been working on. Then, after folding it carefully, put cloth, threads and scissors into a drawer of the small table and glanced at the clock.

'It's time I was getting ready. Susan, go and tell Mrs Dunbar to have the carriage brought round.'

Susan thought depressingly of the social calls ahead which played such an important part in her mother's day and, as if reading her thoughts, Sarah added, 'You won't be required to accompany me this afternoon.'

'In that case may I visit Moorend?' she asked, hiding her relief.

'By all means go over and spend some time with Winnie. Poor girl, her aunt can't be much company.'

It never ceased to surprise Susan that her mother encouraged the visits to Moorend when her own papa and Winnie's father barely spoke when they were in the same room.

Less than a mile from Aran Heights, it was a pleasant walk to Moorend. Sometimes she took the short cut across the fields but in the sunshine she decided on the longer route that took her past the kirk and the manse. Strains of organ music reached her ears from the open door which would be Mr McKay practising for the Sabbath worship.

Moorend, or Clapperton country as it was sometimes called, was by far the largest of the farms in the district and straddled the outward road. Like Hamish MacFarlane he was a fair employer and well respected by the farmhands.

From the window of the farmhouse Winnie Clapperton had spotted her visitor and she was at the door to meet Susan, her plain face wreathed in smiles. She was a tall, ungainly girl who looked older than her twenty years. Her face was sallow and framed by light mousy brown hair scraped back unbecomingly from her high forehead. Her eyes were of a soft velvety brown with amber flecks and hidden under the drab grey skirt was her only claim to beauty – her long, shapely legs hinted at only by the occasional glimpse of a neat ankle.

On the doorstep the two girls embraced then went indoors. 'Susan, how lovely of you to call and you couldn't have come at a better time,' Winnie said delightedly. 'Papa has just left for the market and Aunt Tina is in the village visiting one of her lame ducks so we can have a decent chat without interruptions.'

Susan was glad that Aunt Tina was not at Moorend. Not that she disliked Winnie's aunt, far from it; she was a kindly soul but with a tongue that would clip clouts as Papa once said on the one and only occasion she was at Aran Heights.

Shabby by Aran Heights' standard the parlour into which Winnie led her was a good-sized room with two large windows. From one could be seen the spire of the kirk where both the MacFarlanes and the Clappertons put in an appearance most Sabbath days. From the other windows the tall chimney of the papermill loomed high against the distant hills.

In protest against the violation of her comfortable quarters, Tabby, one of the farm cats, unfurled herself, mewed resentfully and slunk away to take refuge under one of the two leather armchairs drawn close on either side of the hearth. The rest of the furniture in the parlour was good and solid but here at Moorend polishing was an occasional rather than a daily event. Nevertheless its faded elegance never ceased to please Susan. Here was homeliness, something her mother had never achieved at Aran Heights. In her book tidiness came next to Godliness and even the smallest ornament out of place offended her eye and had to be corrected immediately.

Neither of the women at Moorend was particularly house-proud and as a consequence few alterations had been made since the time that Winnie's mother had been its mistress. Betsy Clapperton had been a frail, sweet-faced woman and her death at the age of twenty-nine had been a devastating blow to Euan Clapperton and a bewildering loss to the nine-year-old Winnie.

A widower and a well-to-do one at that, it was expected that Euan Clapperton would be deluged with offers of help from the unattached ladies of Aranvale and beyond but their hopes of becoming the next mistress of Moorend were rudely shattered when his outspoken and embarrassingly tactless spinster sister, Tina, arrived to take charge of her brother and his little daughter. Some said sourly that but for Tina Clapperton her brother would have taken to himself a second wife if for no better reason than to give him a son to inherit Moorend.

That he would have welcomed a son there was no denying but his hopes were now firmly pinned on Winnie making a suitable marriage and in time presenting him with a grandson. When that day came Euan Clapperton would be a contented man.

Susan grinned with amusement as Tabby re-emerged to stretch herself and rub against Susan's skirt before taking up her rightful position in the middle of the hearthrug.

'Rules the house that one does,' Winnie said, giving the cat a playful dig with her foot. 'Give me your cloak, Susan, and I'll tell Lydia we're in the parlour. She can bring in tea later.'

Susan sat back contentedly in the comfortable softness of the armchair, only sitting forward when Winnie took the seat opposite.

'If it gets uncomfortably hot in here tell me and I'll have a window opened.'

43

'I'm very comfortable,' Susan said, shifting under the other's steady scrutiny.

'Something different about you.'

'What makes you say that?'

'I'm not sure,' Winnie said slowly, 'you seem keyed up and just not yourself.'

'You know me too well, that's the trouble,' Susan said ruefully.

'We're friends, talk if you want, I'm a good listener but if you prefer not to I won't probe.'

'I do need someone to talk to.' She swallowed. 'Edward proposed but maybe Matthew told you?'

'No, he didn't but isn't this a call for celebration?'

'I refused him.'

'Oh!'

'Does that surprise you?'

'I suppose so. You two seemed so well suited and he is nice.'

'That's not enough. I'm not in love with him.'

'How do you know?'

'I just do. He doesn't excite me in the least.'

'Well, that could be because you've always known him. Don't tell me you're waiting for someone to sweep you off your feet,' Winnie teased. 'If it comes to that aren't we all but that's the stuff of romantic novels not real life.'

'Maybe it does happen, Winnie, and not just in novels.'

'You've met someone, haven't you?'

'Of course not.'

'Then why are you blushing?'

'I'm not.' Then was furious with herself when she felt her cheeks hot.

'Susan, I'm only teasing.'

'There isn't anyone, not in the way you mean.' Her eyes flew to the door as if expecting someone to come in. Her voice dropped to a whisper. 'If I tell you something do I have your solemn promise that you'll never breathe a word to anyone?'

'You should know better than ask that,' Winnie said, sounding hurt.

'Of course I trust you it's just that – well – it's so stupid I know you're going to laugh.'

'I promise I won't.'

'You do know I'm doing some work for the mill?'

'Matthew mentioned it and I'm delighted.'

'Papa has arranged for an accountant to come to Aran Heights and teach me.'

'And this accountant is responsible – '

'It's awful, Winnie,' Susan said miserably. 'Mama would die if she knew and Papa would do something awful but I can't help myself. I think of him constantly yet he's rude and arrogant and quite common. Honestly, do you know he actually had the nerve to tell me he considered his time wasted though later he did concede that I wasn't the feather-brained female he'd expected.' She took a deep breath. 'What do you think of that?'

Winnie tried to stifle a giggle. 'Surely it was a compliment. Poor soul, he was probably petrified and putting a brave face on it because, if you'll forgive me saying so, you can act the haughty young miss when you have a mind to.'

'He has to be kept in his place.'

'You sound like your mama but tell me, what is this disturbing young man's name?'

'Mr Cameron – David Cameron,' she said dreamily. 'He's very dark and as tall as Matthew and unbelievably handsome. The proud way he carries himself – I mean if I hadn't known him to be an employee of Papa's I might well have mistaken him for a gentleman.'

'Depends on your interpretation of a gentleman,' Winnie said drily.

Susan studied the floor. 'Winnie, I can only tell you this but even just speaking about him I feel – I can't describe it – but they are wicked feelings and I'm ashamed.'

'Nothing wicked about them,' Winnie said matter-of-factly, 'you're just more honest than most in admitting to them.'

'You're not just saying that,' Susan said, looking uncertain and embarrassed.

'I'm a farmer's daughter, Susan,' Winnie said gently. 'Much

45

of what is unspeakable in your world is not in mine. But,' she added warningly, 'feelings like that can be dangerous so don't be foolish and meet this young man secretly.'

'How do you know – well – about that kind of feeling?'

'I'm a woman.' She smiled. 'We all have our dreams, even plain old me.'

'I wouldn't dream of meeting him secretly,' she bristled.

'Then there's nothing to worry about. Incidentally has Mrs MacFarlane met this David Cameron?'

'No, and it's highly improbable she ever will.' Susan grinned mischievously. 'Papa told her he was sending an accountant but she believes him to be one of the mill's elderly clerks and anyway he comes straight to the library by the servants' wing and Mama never goes near the library.'

'Susan, don't take this the wrong way but it could be because he doesn't belong to your circle that you find him so attractive. Blame it on that rebellious streak in you.'

'It isn't that, I know it isn't.' Susan thought it was time they got off the subject of Mr Cameron. 'Tell me, what's been happening at Moorend?'

'Precious little. Unlike you, handsome young men don't fall over themselves seeking my company.'

'A little encouragement might help.'

'I doubt it,' she said wistfully. 'If you but knew the times I've looked in the mirror and wept floods of tears. Why instead of resembling the Clappertons couldn't I have looked like my mother?'

Susan felt sympathy but exasperation too. 'You make no attempt to make the most of yourself. Mama says few women are born beautiful but the clever ones play up their good points. For a start you take no interest in clothes and scraping your hair back that way makes you look severe.'

Susan saw the slow colour spread into the sallow cheeks and when she spoke it was hesitantly unlike her usual brisk tones.

'Strange you should say that. Papa has been complaining that I don't spend enough on myself and I'd made up my mind

to splash out on a whole new wardrobe.' she paused. 'I'll get
Aunt Tina to help me choose – '

'Over my dead body.'

Winnie giggled. 'Meaning her dress sense is as appalling
as mine?'

'Your aunt dresses to suit her age,' Susan said dismissively,
then broke off as Lydia knocked and entered with a tray. Once
tea had been dispensed and Lydia taken her leave, Susan took
up the subject of clothes again. 'Do let me help you choose,
I'd love to.'

'Would you, Susan? Would you really? I mean this ugly
duckling isn't going to turn into a swan and I'm not expecting
miracles.'

'There are times when I could shake you,' Susan said with
mock severity. She played with her lip the way she did when
she was thinking. 'I could try and persuade Mama to come, she
adores ordering new gowns and she does have good taste.'

'I know she always looks wonderful and I do know that Papa
would be pleased. He has a great admiration for your mother.
In fact,' her voice dropped to a conspiratorial whisper, 'Aunt
Tina let it slip one day that my papa was once very sweet on
your mama.'

'Really! That's news to me but she certainly has a soft
spot for you. Maybe she sees you as the daughter she may
have had.'

'And breathes a sigh of relief she had you instead,' Winnie
said with a peal of laughter.

Susan giggled. 'Funny but it's difficult to think of one's
parents doing – well, you know what I'm trying to say.'

'No, I don't.'

'Yes, you do. I mean falling in love and then all the
rest of it.'

'I don't find it difficult. My papa and yours don't like each
other, have you noticed?'

'Yes.'

Winnie looked thoughtful. 'Does Mr MacFarlane object to
Matthew calling so often?'

'I don't imagine he knows.'

'You see, Susan,' Winnie said slowly, 'until recently Matthew came to Moorend to talk farming with Papa but it seems I'm the attraction now.'

The silence lengthened then Susan said unhappily, 'Matthew can be the limit, Winnie. Much as I love my brother I'm not blind to his faults.' She stopped. 'There isn't an easy way to say this.'

'Then let me say it for you. Matthew's interest can only be in the farm not in me?'

Susan was genuinely distressed. 'I wasn't going to say that at all. Matthew has a great admiration for you and that is true.'

'In my knowledge of farming, yes, I think he does, but listen to me, Susan. Offers of marriage won't come flooding my way unless from those with an eye on Moorend and I'm well aware that Matthew falls into that category.'

'Don't let him do that to you,' Susan said harshly.

'Why not if it happens to be what I want too?'

Matthew's words exactly, Susan remembered. She would be getting what she wants was what he'd said and here was Winnie confirming it.

'You'd be taking a big risk.'

'A calculated risk. You see,' she said softly, 'I've always loved Matthew and I want to get married while I'm young enough to have a family, the larger the better. Papa's dearest wish is to have a grandson and he's made it clear to me that he would welcome Matthew as a future son-in-law.'

Susan was unprepared for her own anger.

'That takes care of Moorend but what about the papermill?'

'Matthew's heart is in the land, Susan, he would never be happy in the mill.'

'That's beside the point. His place is in the mill and Papa is only having me trained to help behind the scenes.'

'Matthew wouldn't be any good in the mill and he'd be miserable.'

'And what is my father supposed to do?'

Winnie smiled. 'Much the same as mine. Just hope that his daughter makes a suitable match.'

48

'Now I see why you're so keen for me to marry Edward. It would suit you both. Well I'm not going to oblige,' Susan said, her blue eyes flashing dangerously.

'Whether or not you marry Edward has nothing to do with me but I will tell you this, if Matthew proposes marriage I shall accept.'

'Do you imagine he'll remain faithful?' she asked scornfully. 'Matthew has never been short of girls, beautiful girls,' she said cruelly.

'Don't be so naïve, Susan. Do you think I don't know that? Anyway I wouldn't be alone. How many husbands do we both know who look elsewhere for their comforts?'

'Then you wouldn't mind?'

'Of course I'd mind, I'd mind terribly but I'll have the good sense I hope not to make a scene.' She smiled. 'Maybe by that time I'd have a child or two to fill my life.'

'How little we really know each other,' Susan said wonderingly. 'You're really quite calculating.'

'Realistic, Susan, but I would never willingly hurt anyone, least of all you. We've been friends since we were small and I'd hate that to end. In any case Matthew may find marriage to me too big a price to pay for Moorend.'

There was the sound of a door opening and voices.

'Wheesht! Here's Aunt Tina,' Winnie said warningly as a stout, rather aggressive-looking woman stuck her grey head round the door and, seeing Susan, came in.

'How nice to see your bonny face, Susan.' She smiled then took the lid off the teapot. 'Tea still drinkable, Winnie?'

'No, I'll ring for Lydia.'

'Don't bother her just yet, she's busy instructing that young scullery maid and by the look of the lass she's none too bright.'

'How are you, Miss Clapperton?' Susan asked when she could get a word in.

'Thankful to be off my feet, Susan,' she said, sitting down heavily. 'Some folk can be so trying. No matter how helpful one tries to be one's efforts are invariably looked on as interference.'

'I'm sure they are grateful,' Susan said dutifully but with some sympathy for those people. Aunt Tina was like a small steam-roller and folk took a while to recover from her visits.

'Then all I can say is they have a queer way of showing it.' She wheezed and patted her bosom. 'Winnie's not neglected these days,' she said with a knowing smile. 'That brother of yours is just about making this his second home.'

Winnie frowned with annoyance and Susan, anxious to get away, stood up.

'You will excuse me, Miss Clapperton, but I've been here longer than I intended and Mama will be expecting me back.'

'I'll come part of the way with you,' Winnie said, disappearing and returning with Susan's cloak and her own coat.

Goodbyes said, the girls walked along the cart track where the ground bore the imprint of cattle and horses' hooves. Both of them were silent and for the first time uneasy with each other. Anxious to get back to their old friendly footing Winnie put her arm through Susan's.

'I've been too outspoken and upset you.'

'No, some of it is my fault.' She shrugged. 'I suppose it will all work out for the best.'

'Our friendship will survive?'

'Of course it will.'

'May I say one last thing?'

'I'm listening.'

'Whatever you feel for Edward he does love you, it's obvious the way he looks at you. Believe me I'd give anything to have someone love me for myself,' she said wistfully. Then in her usual brisk fashion added, 'Edward could get tired of waiting for you and look elsewhere; with his looks and position he can take his pick.'

'Then I wish he would.' But did she? She didn't want him herself but – everything was impossibly difficult and she didn't know what she wanted. A visit to Moorend should have helped but instead she was more confused than ever.

The roads diverged and Winnie stopped. 'About the spending spree, will you mention it to Mrs MacFarlane? But no pressure, mind, and only if she wants.'

'Mama is never pressurised into doing something she doesn't want but I'll let you know.'

'Thank you.'

With a final wave they took leave of each other just as a threatening dark cloud hovered overhead. Seeing it darken further, Susan quickened her pace to a half run. As Aran Heights came into view she felt the first large splashes of rain which almost at once developed into a downpour and, lifting her skirts, she raced to the entrance just as a carriage hurtled through the gates, sending a shower of muddy water over her. Fuming at the carelessness of the coachman and in her bedraggled state, she altered course and sped round to the side entrance.

Once in her room she stripped out of her wet clothes, leaving them on the floor, and changed completely. A bonnet had kept the worst of the rain off her hair but some of it was wet and she dabbed at it with a towel. Then she went in search of her mother and found her in the drawing-room, embroidery on her lap but her hands idle.

'Sorry I'm late, Mama, I stayed longer than I intended at Moorend and then I got caught in a downpour.'

'That's quite all right, dear,' Sarah said, without a trace of a reprimand. 'You missed Mrs Brodie. She called unexpectedly and fortunately I was at home.'

'So that's who the carriage belonged to! I got half drenched the way it hurtled past and didn't see who it was.'

'That doesn't surprise me. Why the Brodies keep that coachman I'll never understand. I wouldn't care to risk life and limb.'

Whatever had transpired between the ladies must have pleased Mama, Susan thought. She looked almost smug.

'Did you change out of your wet clothes?'

'Yes, I had to.'

'Have you told one of the maids to remove them for laundering?'

'Not yet.'

'Go and do it now.'

Susan went in search of a maid and returned in a few minutes. 'Lottie is on her way up.'

'Very well. Now sit down, I want to talk. You can't begin to know the relief it was to me to see Mrs Brodie. There was no awkwardness at all. In fact,' she preened herself, 'I have been invited to accompany her to select a few new gowns. Apparently she admires my taste.'

'Everyone does,' Susan said generously, 'and I know that Winnie would value your guidance too. Mr Clapperton has been urging her to spend more on herself.'

'And not before time, but where do I come in?'

'She was to ask her aunt to accompany her and I had to do something.'

'I should think so. Tina would be completely useless,' Sarah said aghast, 'she wouldn't have the least idea how to advise a young lady on dress.'

'I thought perhaps you would advise Winnie.'

'Let me consult my engagement book but I should be able to fit something in and knowing Mr Clapperton he'll be more than generous.'

'Winnie will be delighted.'

'Poor girl, she hasn't had your advantages.' She broke off as if at a sudden thought. 'I wonder what brought this on! Undoubtedly there will be a few young men and perhaps a few not-so-young who will be looking hopefully in Winnie's direction. Let's hope she chooses sensibly. Do you know if there is anyone special, has she mentioned any young man?'

Susan shook her head but wondered what her mother would say if she knew that Matthew was the young man Winnie had set her heart on.

'She'll tell you when she's ready to do so.' She smiled. 'This is going to be quite a challenge. Winnie with the right clothes and a little poise may surprise us all and herself most of all.'

'She goes on about being plain but does nothing about it.'

'You can help by encouraging her to change her hairstyle.'

'You're fond of Winnie, aren't you?'

'Yes, I am. I want a good marriage for her. Mr Clapperton made a mistake in his choice of wife. Betsy was quite unsuitable.'

'I understood that he was heartbroken when she died?'

'Of course he was. Betsy was a pleasant girl but unsuited to be mistress of Moorend. Even before marrying Euan she was in delicate health and giving birth to Winnie nearly cost her her life. After that there was no question of her bearing more children. Such a disappointment not to have a son to carry on the farm.'

Next morning it wasn't just a headache, Mrs MacFarlane complained of feeling very unwell and the coachman was hurriedly despatched to bring back Dr Sullivan. Susan's offer to sit with her was declined; her mother just wanted to be left alone. While the doctor was with her mother Susan went out into the garden and walked between the rose beds. The gardens were at their best during the summer months with climbing roses, pink and blue rhododendron bushes and the sweet smell of honeysuckle was all around. One corner had been given over to the native heathers with their purples just beginning to show. Susan was complimenting the head gardener on the lovely show when she saw the doctor looking over in her direction. Excusing herself she hurried to join him.

'How is Mama, Dr Sullivan?'

'Nothing serious, my dear, a touch of indigestion that's all. Painful and disagreeable though it is, it'll pass and I've given her something to help.' He stood back and gave her a lengthy look which from anyone else would have angered her. But as well as being the doctor who brought her into the world he was also a family friend.

'The picture of health and bonnier by the day.'

'Flatterer.' She laughed but then she saw his face turn grave and all the banter gone.

'Susan, I don't want to alarm you – '

She felt a sudden, cold chill. 'What is it?'

'It's about your papa – '

She paled. 'Papa's not ill again?'

'He will be if he doesn't ease up.'

'You mean – '

'He's worried, Susan.' He sounded exasperated. 'I try to reason with my patients, let them see that worry is a killer. Get that across and a doctor's load would be halved. It doesn't make one whit of difference to the problem, all it does is damage the health.'

'But how do we stop Papa worrying?' she said despairingly.

'You can't, only he can do that. What you can do, however, is make sure he isn't upset needlessly, otherwise, my dear . . .' He shrugged his shoulders and left the rest unsaid.

Susan clutched at his arm. 'He isn't going to – I couldn't bear it if anything happened to Papa,' she choked.

'There! There! Don't be upsetting yourself, it isn't as bad as that. Your father has a lot of good years ahead of him if he would just try and remember that a man of his years can't expect to do what he did twenty years ago.'

'I'll try, I'll do my very best, Dr Sullivan.'

'That I know, that's why it's you I'm telling. Your mother would just get herself into a state.' He smiled and patted her arm. 'Between us, lass, we'll look after him and now if you'll excuse me there's some others needing or thinking they need my attention.'

Biting back the tears Susan watched him get into the carriage and it move away, then slowly she turned back to the house. It must be serious. Dr Sullivan was not one to spread alarm, and thinking back she could recall the tell-tale signs, the irritableness over trifles, the way in unguarded moments his hands would clench, and a terrible fear gripped her. Life without Papa, the thought was too awful to contemplate.

Mrs MacFarlane and the two girls left the station and went out to where a few carriages were lined up. At a signal the nearest coachman got down from his perch, touched his cap and listened to Mrs MacFarlane's instructions.

54

'You know, Susan, it's ages since I was in Glasgow,' Winnie remarked.

'Then you sit at the window and I'll be piggy in the middle.'

'Susan, really!' But her mother was smiling and shaking her head.

They moved off and soon were trundling over the cobbles into West George Street and on to Buchanan Street with its fashionable shops. A cart had toppled and there was a hold-up until it was righted, then they were into St Vincent Street. Soon they were in Gordon Street and stopping outside the premises belonging to Charlotte Beattie. The coachman was paid and dismissed and the three ladies went inside. The young assistant, recognising Mrs MacFarlane and her daughter, asked them to be seated while she went in search of Miss Beattie.

The owner arrived slightly out of breath. She was a short, dumpy woman with a pronounced double chin, sharp intelligent eyes and the clear complexion enjoyed by so many auburn-haired women. Born into poverty but with a determination to better herself and a firm belief that she had the talent to do so the young Lottie had worked long hours, much of it in bad light, learning to be a seamstress. The pitiful wages were barely enough to survive but very early on she began to recognise her worth as the more exacting work came her way. The demand for more wages had been a bold step and a grave risk but in the end her stubbornness had paid off and her request grudgingly granted.

From then on Lottie had studied fashion, used her creative talent and against all the difficulties, and they were many, she had become a top designer, an astute business woman and a demanding though fair employer.

Civilities over, the ladies were seated on blue padded chairs in the perfumed room where floor-length velvet curtains in a darker shade of blue were partly drawn over the window. An otherwise dull corner was brought to life by a beautiful display of flowers in a tall oriental vase.

'We're here, Miss Beattie, to find something for Miss Clapperton but perhaps I, too, may be tempted.'

Miss Beattie acknowledged that with a smile then turned

her trained eye on Winnie, noting her sallow complexion, her gaucheness and the unbecoming clothes she wore.

'Miss Clapperton, would you mind standing, please?'

Winnie got up and as the moments grew so did her embarrassment but at last Miss Beattie nodded and she sat down. Later she was to confess to Susan that in those moments she had felt herself examined like a prize animal at an auction.

'Be proud of your height, Miss Clapperton, and don't be tempted to stoop, a common fault with tall young ladies. Anna,' she beckoned to her assistant, 'take this lady to the cubicle and help her out of her gown while I take a look through my stock.'

Showing a marked lack of eagerness, Winnie followed Anna and once they heard the sound of the curtain rail being drawn, Susan took a fit of the giggles.

'Hardly enthusiastic is she?'

'Behave yourself, Susan.' But her own lips twitched as she turned to examine some materials.

Winnie came slowly towards them and at Miss Beattie's request she pirouetted for them. The warm shade of pink removed much of the sallowness of her skin and the flowing line of the russet silk with just a hint of bustle took away the heaviness of her figure.

'Winnie, it's lovely and you do suit it. Doesn't she, Mama?'

'Yes, Winnie, that's very nice.'

Winnie's eyes shone. 'I'll have it, I do like it.'

'Tut-tut!' Miss Beattie looked shocked. 'The colour is good but the neckline is too fussy. Tell me, is this for a special occasion?'

'Oh, no, I'm just replenishing my wardrobe,' but there was a faint flush on her cheeks.

'Perhaps three day dresses and two more for formal occasions. What do you think, Winnie?' Mrs MacFarlane asked.

'That would do very well.'

'Now that I know what is required.' Miss Beattie spoke to her assistant: 'Anna, after you help Miss Clapperton out of that gown hurry along to the workroom and bring the green silk and the yellow brocade.' She saw Mrs MacFarlane examining the samples of materials. 'Our new designs are on the table should you care to look at them.'

'May I see them with you, Mama?'

'Of course, I had intended that you have a new gown.'

If only Mother were always like this, Susan thought. She could be so charming when she wanted.

After some swithering a delighted Winnie decided on a stylish gown in rose pink and another in a brilliant green silk. The pink needed a small alteration and the others were to be made up in a different material with slight adjustments to the style.

Then it was Susan's turn and when she came out in the golden yellow gown it was as if they all held their breath.

'Well, what do you think?' Susan said, not at all sure what the silence denoted.

'Lovely,' breathed Winnie, 'absolutely perfect on you.'

'Mama?'

A smile played around her mother's mouth. 'Many years ago I had a gown in just that shade. Yes, Susan, you must have it.' Miss Beattie departed to the workroom.

'I adore it and it is such a lovely surprise. Thank you, Mama.'

'Only to be worn on special occasions but I have a feeling we won't have too long to wait.' She looked coyly at Winnie. 'Perhaps two special occasions?'

The girls exchanged startled glances but Mrs MacFarlane had forgotten them. Miss Beattie had arrived and she was too absorbed in selecting a gown for herself.

She was much more difficult to please and Susan marvelled at the patience Miss Beattie displayed. If she was wearied she didn't show it though Anna was visibly drooping from the many visits paid to the workroom where busy hands were putting the finishing touches to the season's collection.

Out in the street Mrs MacFarlane touched her throat. 'I don't know about you two but I'm parched and I seem to remember a delightful teashop nearby.'

'Just round the next corner, Mama. I remember too.'

'You know I'm really enjoying this day out,' Winnie said as she looked about her. 'I must do it more often.'

'I remember Papa taking us to George Square when we were little to see the statue of Sir Walter Scott. It was supposed to be a statue of King George III and that is why it's called George Square.'

'Fancy you remembering all that, Susan, I don't.'

'You weren't there, we left you with your dressmaker.'

'That explains it,' she said as they entered the shop and were immediately shown to a table.

'I'm decidedly peckish,' Susan announced. 'What about you, Winnie?'

'Now you mention it I am rather.'

'What it is to be young,' Mrs MacFarlane sighed as they waited to be served. 'We'll see what they have to offer but I must refrain.'

'Why, Mrs MacFarlane?'

'Because, Winnie, dear, when my new gown arrives I should like it to fit and at my age it is extremely easy to put on weight and very difficult to lose it.'

'Very trim and stylish is how my papa describes you,' Winnie said mischievously, 'his words exactly.'

'Coming from your papa that is quite something, he was never one for flowery speeches.'

The tables in the Willow Teashop were covered with snowy white damask tablecloths. Fashionably dressed matrons and a sprinkling of younger women were engaged in whispered conversations as they sipped tea from the fragile china cups. A waitress in a stiffly starched white square of apron arrived at their table and took their order.

Teapot, sugar and milk arrived on a silver tray followed by a plate of sandwiches cut in dainty triangles. There were two kinds of cake, seed and fruit, sponges filled with jam and cream and a selection of biscuits.

'That should take the edge off your appetite,' Mrs MacFarlane said gushingly as she weakened and reached for a sandwich. Halfway to her mouth it was arrested by a voice and she swung round.

'Caroline, my dear, it's you!' Putting down her sandwich she said, 'Do come and join us.'

'Yes, do, Caroline,' Susan joined in.

'I'd love to but I can't. My friend was just paying the bill when I caught sight of you, Mrs MacFarlane. How are you keeping?'

'I have my good days and my bad days but this is one of my good days I am happy to say. But let me introduce you to Winnie. Winnie, this is Caroline, a friend of Matthew's. Miss Caroline Beverley – Miss Winifred Clapperton,' she said formally.

As they shook hands Winnie managed a smile but Susan saw the sparkle leave her eyes as she looked at the newcomer. The contrast could not have been greater. Caroline was small made and perfectly proportioned. Her luxuriant blue-black hair fell in tumbled curls to her shoulders. Long silky eyelashes fringed the deep blue of her eyes and she had a dazzling smile.

'Did Matthew tell you I've been in Bournemouth with Mama?'

'Yes, he did. I hope she benefited from the change.'

Caroline made a face. 'Difficult to know with my mother but I'll tell you this,' she said gaily, 'I certainly didn't. It was deadly dull just taking Mama for walks and keeping her company in the hotel in the evenings. Oh, that's Kirsty looking for me, I'll have to go. Heavenly to have seen you both and to meet you, Miss Clapperton. Be sure to give my love to Matthew, Mrs MacFarlane.' Then she was gone in a whirl of skirts with a few heads turning to watch her departure.

Mrs MacFarlane bit into her sandwich, took a sip of tea then shook her head in mock relief. 'Like a whirlwind, Winnie, a little of Caroline and I'm exhausted.'

'And the only one of Matthew's friends who can charm Papa,' Susan added then wished she hadn't.

'Mr MacFarlane sees a very shrewd young woman behind all that excitable chatter. Matthew needs a steadying influence and he thinks Caroline could give him that.'

# CHAPTER SEVEN

In those weeks since Dr Sullivan had warned Susan about her father's health she had done everything possible to protect him from petty annoyances, smoothing over difficulties wherever she could. It had helped and Hamish seemed much more relaxed of late.

'Papa is much improved isn't he, Dr Sullivan?'

'He is that, my dear. Could be the man's getting some sense at last and what is this I'm hearing?' he said, raising his bushy eyebrows.

'What have you heard?' She smiled.

'Learning the business no less and why not? Told Hamish it was a sensible move having you brought in.'

'I'm not acceptable in the mill.'

'No matter, lass. That doesn't have to be such a drawback. It's not where the work is carried out it's how that counts. Quite a turn-up for the books if you'll excuse the expression. It's not only times that are changing – it's Hamish too!' He went off shaking his head and chuckling.

Those same weeks had established a routine. David Cameron arrived at ten o'clock on Tuesdays and Thursdays for two hours and so often in that time Susan blessed her good fortune that Sarah had never caught a glimpse of the handsome young man.

Confident in the belief that her daughter's tutor could only be one of the elderly clerks, Sarah had dismissed the whole tiresome business from her mind.

On this, his last morning at Aran Heights, David greeted Susan with quiet courtesy as he took his customary seat.

'You probably know, Miss MacFarlane, that this is to be my final visit,' he said, turning his dark eyes on her.

'Yes, Papa told me,' she said, feeling absurdly close to tears.

'I knew it couldn't go on much longer. After all you do have a good understanding of the financial side of the business.'

'And you to thank for it.' Her eyes were over-bright and the smile she gave him held such sweetness that his heart turned over.

What had started out as an attraction was so much more now. Susan MacFarlane was constantly in his mind. That she was lovely enough to disturb any man he knew, but for him it was so much more than that. He was in love with his employer's daughter and had been, he supposed, ever since that first morning when she had been so proud and aloof. Only then he had been too annoyed at her haughtiness to recognise it.

Whatever the future held for him he knew with absolute certainty that Susan MacFarlane would be the only woman he could ever truly love.

Through the corner of her eye Susan glanced at David surreptitiously while arranging and rearranging the papers. What were his feelings now? she wondered. Was he too feeling regret that their time together was to end?

'I'm going to miss this – miss you,' she said simply.

'I too,' he said gravely. He mustn't show his real feelings, at all costs he must avoid that.

Their eyes met and held. For the first time Susan saw that his eyes were blue but so dark that they appeared black. For him he saw something else that tore at his heart. For all the proud haughtiness she sometimes displayed there was an innocence and a curious vulnerability about her that moved him deeply.

Before he could stop himself he reached out and took her hand bringing it to his lips then, realising what he had done, he dropped it, and his blood rushed to his face.

'I'm – I'm sorry,' he stammered. 'I shouldn't have done that.'

The feel of his lips on her hand, the unexpectedness of it made Susan catch her breath.

'It – it's all right, I'm not angry,' she said unsteadily.

They stared at each other.

'It was unforgivable of me, Miss MacFarlane, and my only excuse is that I couldn't help myself. You are very beautiful,' he said softly.

His dark, charismatic eyes were on her and she half turned to hide her confusion. For all those weeks she had lived only for the precious hours spent together in the library and she couldn't bear the thought that they were to end. Guilt and longing struggled for control. Papa had trusted her with this young man and she hated to deceive him but this agony of longing was proving too strong.

She swallowed. 'We are both in Aranvale, perhaps we may see each other.'

'There's nothing I'd like better but I think it unlikely.'

'Oh, I don't know. You like walking?'

'Very much, I do a great deal of it.'

'Then we could arrange to meet by chance.'

'Accidentally on purpose,' he said laughing.

'My aunt lives at the Old Mill House and I do visit her from time to time.' She bit her lip. 'If I left her house earlier than usual you could accompany me part of the way back to Aran Heights.' Not wishing to hurt his feelings but knowing he must be made to understand she added hastily, 'We would have to leave each other before I reached home in case – '

'We were seen together?'

She lowered her eyes but not before she had seen the glint of anger in his. 'Try to understand,' she pleaded. 'I don't have a great deal of freedom and if my parents got to know . . .' her voice trailed off.

'A sharp reprimand for you and the end of my career at the Aranvale Papermill,' he said with an attempt at humour.

'I'm sure my father wouldn't go to that length but he would make sure I was closely chaperoned with even less freedom than I enjoy now.'

A chill of fear hit David. That it would be instant dismissal and probably without a reference he was in no doubt. For himself the risk was one he was prepared to take but there was his mother.

Something of his misgivings must have shown on his face as he became conscious that she was looking at him far too intently.

'Perhaps you consider my company not worth the risk?' she said coldly.

'I'd risk a great deal more.'

Reassured, she gave him a brilliant smile. 'Then from today and only when we are alone together we'll dispense with formality. I shall call you David and you may use my Christian name.'

'Thank you – Susan.'

Warning bells were ringing in Susan's head but she ignored them. What she couldn't ignore was the delicious new excitement surging through her.


That first arranged meeting had posed no problems. Mrs MacFarlane had given her permission to visit Aunt Rachel. Though she, herself, was seldom in her sister-in-law's company she had never raised objections to her family visiting their aunt.

The drawing-room of the Old Mill House where Susan and her aunt were sitting was filled with an assortment of chairs, sofas and little tables crowded with ornaments and family photographs. A huge oil painting of the first Master of Aranvale had pride of place above the wooden mantelpiece. No drastic changes had been made since the death of Susan's grandparents and only in the last few years had the dark green wall covering been changed for an embossed paper in sky blue with patterned curtains of the same shade hanging at the windows.

'Susan! I've never seen you so anxious to escape,' Aunt Rachel said reproachfully. 'That must be at least the fourth time you've looked at the clock in the last half hour.'

Susan flushed at the rebuke. 'How rude of me and I do apologise,' she said guiltily.

'Are you so anxious to be away?'

'No, of course not, at least – ' She stopped. There was no use trying to hoodwink Aunt Rachel. 'I've arranged to meet someone that's all.'

'Meet someone?' Her lined face was thoughtful and her eyes questioning as she saw that her niece was covered in confusion. 'Only a young man could put you in this state and most certainly he isn't Edward Brodie. Child, what is it you're getting yourself involved in?'

'Nothing Aunt Rachel, honestly it's nothing like that at all. He's just someone – someone – '

'Yes, I'm sure he's that,' her aunt said tartly.

'Listen, please just listen.' She took a deep breath before continuing. 'Papa had an accountant come to Aran Heights,' Susan began desperately as the clock struck the half hour.

'Yes, I do know about that, your papa told me. Very sensible since Matthew is not shaping up. But not quite so sensible, my dear, if you are having clandestine meetings with this young man.'

'I'm not,' Susan said indignantly. 'This is the first time and my interest in Mr Cameron is purely business. Papa terminated the lessons too soon, I have a lot to learn.'

'Certainly I would endorse that last bit. You do have a lot to learn. No doubt he is an excellent accountant and you have enjoyed his tuition – '

'That's it exactly,' she said eagerly. 'I have enjoyed his tuition and if we've become friends there's nothing wrong with that.'

'Susan, my dearest, you have been protected all your nineteen years. This young man of whom you think so highly may have hopes and ambitions above his station. Hopes centred around you. Far better to discourage him now before it gets out of hand. You will both recover if you avoid each other and whatever the attraction it will die a natural death.'

'It's not like that at all,' Susan protested.

'It's always like that, Susan. I may be an old spinster but I can still recognise the signs.'

Susan smiled at that. 'Aunt Rachel, why didn't you marry? You were pretty, I've seen photographs of you.'

'Passably pretty! Yes I suppose I was and had I wished I could have married.' She hesitated. 'Marriage isn't for everyone, Susan. I never wanted a husband though I confess I would have liked children.' She laughed. 'Since one is undesirable without the other I content myself with my niece and nephew, both of whom I love dearly.'

'You're a darling, Aunt Rachel,' Susan said impulsively. Then with another despairing look at the clock she got up, collected her cloak from where it lay on the sofa and pulled it around her.

Aunt Rachel got up too. She was tall and straight and scraggily thin.

'Take care,' she said worriedly as Susan hugged her.

'You won't say anything to Papa?' Susan said fearfully.

'No, I won't, though I'm not at all happy; in fact I'm worried.'

'No need to be, I'm not a child you know.'

No, she thought after Susan had departed. You're not a child and that is what worries me. What you are is a lovely warm-hearted girl who doesn't know the dangers. Maybe I'm wrong not to warn Hamish. She sighed as she went to the table for her book.

Not until she was well clear of the Old Mill House did Susan allow herself to search the long winding lane. Seeing it deserted her heart plummeted, disappointment flooded through her and her footsteps faltered. Had he waited then gone away, thinking she wasn't going to honour their arrangement or had he decided the risk was too great and hadn't turned up at all? Just as she was deciding that that was the more likely she saw his dark head appear in the dip in the road and disappointment and hurt swiftly changed to relief and happiness and only by a supreme effort did she keep to a ladylike walk. With David's long strides they were soon drawing level.

'Good evening, Miss MacFarlane,' he said gravely but there was a smile lurking at the corner of his mouth.

'Good evening, Mr Cameron,' she said demurely. 'How strange that we should meet.'

'Just what I was thinking and if you would allow me it would be a privilege to escort you to Aran Heights. I take it that is where you are heading?'

As they fell into step she said hurriedly, 'Did I keep you waiting very long? It was difficult to get away.'

'I was prepared to wait a good deal longer.'

'My aunt knows.'

David looked startled.

'I'm afraid glancing at the clock too often gave me away but you are not to worry. Aunt Rachel may not approve, indeed she doesn't, but our secret is safe with her.'

David certainly hoped so, then his misgivings evaporated, her sudden smile was so enchanting.

'All we are doing is walking side by side. What could anyone have to say about that?'

'You'd be surprised,' he said drily as his brooding eyes sought hers. 'I'd be a lot more comfortable if we could meet openly.'

'So would I but we both know that is impossible.' She looked at him wistfully. 'David, surely we can just be friends, enjoy each other's company and forget the difference in our backgrounds?'

He thought that impossible but nodded.

'I know nothing about you,' she said lightly, 'even to where you live.'

'That is easily remedied,' he said, taking her arm and pointing to a cluster of cottages, tiny specks at that distance. 'The far end one is my home.'

'Your parents live there?'

'Just my mother,' he said abruptly, then added after a pause, 'You might as well know now that my mother is unmarried and I know nothing of my father.'

All the time he was speaking she knew he was watching her face, studying its expression and she lowered her head, but even so she was quite unable to disguise the shudder or hide the shock his words had evoked.

'Excuse me, David,' she faltered. 'I'm sorry, I shouldn't have asked.'

'Why not?' he demanded harshly. 'It was a perfectly natural question to ask and surely it is better that I should answer it truthfully. Strangely enough I had expected better from you,' he said bitterly, 'though I should have known with your upbringing that was impossible. Without knowing anything of the circumstances you are prepared to condemn my mother.'

'That is not true, how dare you say that to me,' she said hotly, coming to a standstill. Facing him her colour had risen and her eyes flashed. 'You are the one who is drawing conclusions and though I cannot deny the surprise the rest is only in your imagination.'

'Is it, Susan?' he said quietly. His eyes were bleak but there was a proud lift to his head. 'You might as well hear the rest.'

His sensitive face had set in a grim mask as he continued: 'Some of your so-called gentry consider girls in their employ to be fair game and don't try telling me the girls have a choice because it is no choice at all. Either she satisfies her master's desires or she finds herself thrown out in the street, bag, baggage and penniless. You've never gone hungry so you don't know what that means.'

'Is that what happened to your mother?' Susan asked in a small strained voice.

'Something of the sort,' he said heavily. 'My mother is tight-lipped. For a few gold coins she gave her vow of silence and, knowing her, she'll go to the grave with her secret.'

Susan felt a clammy coldness. Though not well informed on the subject she did know enough to recognise that what David was saying could be the truth. They were within sight of Aran Heights but she was reluctant to let him go like this. Her fingers touched the sleeve of his jacket.

'There's enough time to go round by the churchyard.' He turned with her. 'Please, David, don't look like that. I do understand about the wickedness that goes on. Your mother must have been a very brave woman.'

'Hardly a woman, Susan, she was only seventeen when she had me.'

'How dreadful!' She drew in her breath sharply. 'How ever did she manage? Was her family supportive?'

'Supportive!' He gave a short, humourless laugh. 'My grandparents disowned her but her married sister was more charitable. Her house was overcrowded with her own family but they managed somehow and that's where I was born. Later, we, that is my mother and I, came to Aranvale and until recently she was scrubbing and cleaning and taking in washing. Thankfully there is no need for that now though had I not insisted she would be slaving yet. A very independent woman, my mother.'

'And you a son to be proud of,' Susan said gently.

There was a white, pinched look about his face as he turned to her.

'What I am I owe to her.'

Leaving the grassy slopes for the narrow cinder path they were both silent until David gave a rueful smile.

'Blurting out all this was the last thing I intended. Now you know my history you won't want anything to do with me.'

She tucked her arm in his and he looked at it in surprise.

'How little you know me, David Cameron, if you think that. My first reaction was inexcusable but it was the unexpectedness of it, that was all. Neither you nor your mother has anything to be ashamed of.'

'My mother would agree with you there. She has always held her head high. In a strange way she is proud that I should be the son of a gentleman. Don't ask me why, it is quite beyond me.'

As a farmhand approached she withdrew her arm but unhurriedly.

'This is where we must part,' she said.

'I suppose this is the end?'

'It doesn't have to be.'

'You mean I can see you again?'

'Yes.'

'Not if it is out of misplaced pity,' he said savagely.

'Don't be so tiresome, David,' she said, sounding like her mother. 'Why should I pity you? You seem to be doing quite well. Papa has a high opinion of your work and he is not given to idle praise. Just stop being so prickly.'

'That's me put in my place.' He laughed. 'When will it be possible?'

'My parents are leaving after church on Sunday to visit friends which should mean I'll be free all afternoon.'

'Where shall I meet you?'

'Oh, David, I don't know. Beside the bridge would be best, I think. Make it three o'clock but don't wait any longer than half an hour. Mama may have arranged something for me.' The words came out staccato and she seemed flustered.

'Susan, I've been honest with you and I'm not stupid. You have no intention of being there, admit it. This is just your way of letting me down lightly and I don't need it.'

'Then you're wrong again, Mr Smart Alec.' But he wasn't, she thought with a rush of shame, it had been her intention. She was remembering Aunt Rachel's warning and her own heart told her that it was dangerous to go on seeing David.

'Are you quite sure, Susan?' he said quietly.

He's giving me every chance, she thought desperately, but I can't just let it end like this, I can't. She took a deep breath.

'David,' she said slowly, 'if I'm not there beside the bridge between three and three thirty it will be because I have been unable to get away. You can believe that or not as you please,' she said as a parting shot, then she was running through the wide open gates and across the lawn. He stood watching until she was out of sight and for a long time afterwards.

Would she come? David couldn't be sure and wondered if it would not be better if she did not show up. After all, why keep tormenting himself? Better that it should end now before it had properly begun. She was not for him, never could be and to think otherwise would be foolish.

Even so he was standing before the mirror, pleased with his appearance. The cut-away coat and dark check trousers fitted comfortably. His mother had been right as usual. It wasn't enough to sound like a gentleman, one had to dress the part too was her excuse for what he considered until that moment to be an unnecessary extravagance.

'Don't know when I'll be home, Mother,' David said as he stood tall and straight in the doorway.

Eliza Cameron felt the familiar pride. 'That's all right, son. It's a lovely day and I'll mebbe take mysel' over to see Mrs Johnson. She's been that poorly of late.'

David frowned. 'Let that lazy good-for-nothing husband of hers lift a hand to help, you're not to, Mother.'

'I'm only goin' tae see the body,' Eliza said mildly.

'So you say. Anyway I'm off.'

The door closed and Eliza smiled to herself. That there was a lass in David's life she was sure but she would never ask. In his own good time he would tell her. Of one thing she was sure: it wasn't anyone from around here. David was ambitious. He would choose well.

Those loitering about the street, an area of the decayed dwellings that drew them, watched the well-groomed young man shut the door and move smartly away. Those who shouted a greeting he acknowledged with one of his own, well aware of the sneers that would follow his progress. But it was a matter of indifference to him. They had nothing in common. And it was this very indifference that angered and irked some. Eliza Cameron's bastard son had no right to such airs and graces.

The June day was just as Susan had laughingly forecast. The sky was a clear blue without a cloud in sight, the air was deliciously warm and the ground below baked hard in the sun. Well before he reached the bridge he reduced his pace. He didn't want to linger and draw attention to himself but found there was no fear of that. Smiling foolishly he watched her coming. Even at that distance he could recognise the proud tilt to the head and the youthful spring to her step. In a blue and white polkadot gown and a lightweight cape on top she looked like a breath of summer. Her hair, that he had only seen swept up and secured with combs, now hung in soft curls to her shoulders.

She waved happily and as they walked towards each other he saw that her face was flushed and her eyes sparkling.

'You didn't expect to see me? Be honest, you didn't?'

'Then why am I here?'

'Why are you?' she teased.

'There was hope in my heart when I set out.'

She thrust a package into his hands. 'In case we get peckish.'

'What is it?'

'Apples. Mrs Dunbar won't notice. Anyway there's always plenty.'

'Where would you like to go?' he asked.

'Had you anywhere in mind?'

He shook his head. 'You decide and it'll suit me.'

'I do know a lovely spot; it's over at the other side of the reservoir then a climb after that. Matthew and I used to have poor Nanny puffing and blowing long before she reached the top. Later on we came by ourselves and Matthew found a sheltered heavenly spot.'

He was smiling as she rattled on. 'I know this walk, I've done it many times.'

'I'm sure you have but I bet you missed our little hideaway.' The sun caressed the soft curves of her face as she chatted animatedly. Her voice had a lovely lilting quality and he felt he could have gone on listening for ever. A little tentatively, he took her arm to help her across a rough stony patch.

'How much further?' he asked, pretending to wilt in the heat.

'Almost there, lazybones.' She laughed as she ran ahead to an area of short grass almost hidden by the trees. By her expression he knew that she was waiting for him to say something.

'Now why is it I missed a paradise like this?'

Looking pleased, she discarded her cape and spread it out

on the grass before sitting down on it and leaning her back
against the tree trunk.

'David,' she said patting the place beside her.

'Not on your cloak!'

'Of course on my cape, why not?'

She opened the paper bag while he settled himself then
handed him an apple. In a companionable silence they ate
their apples down to the core then, smiling to each other,
they leaned back, squinting through the branches into the
strong sunshine.

'Isn't this heavenly?' Susan said dreamily. 'We could be
alone in a little world of our own.'

'That's because few people have the energy to come this
far,' he teased.

'But you are glad I brought you here?'

'Very glad,' he said softly.

She turned her face to him and a tremulous smile touched
her lips. He was so dark and good-looking but there was
so much more to David than a good appearance. She could
sense the restlessness that spoke of ambition but how could
that ever be satisfied? The right family background could open
so many doors but for someone like David they would remain
firmly shut.

His eyes flickered and she became aware that he had been
watching her through eyes only half closed and two spots of
colour stained her cheeks. Hastily she moved her back to a
more comfortable position and stared straight ahead.

'That must be painful through your thin gown.' He hesitated. 'Lean against my arm if you would be more comfortable.'

'Yes, David, thank you, I'll use you as a pillow.' She
managed to say it lightly as she moved into the curve of
his arm but her heart was racing. She was so aware of him.

'Is that better?' He gave her a smile that made her heart
hammer and lurch.

'Lovely.' Few people frequented these hills and she prayed
that no one would come and spoil the delicious thrill of being
alone with him. Was he as acutely aware of her as she was

of him? Surely he must feel something too. 'David, if you had a wish what would it be?'

'To be rich and successful,' he said without hesitation.

'More than anything else?' she asked, feeling let down.

'If I were rich and successful we could be together without all this secrecy,' David said quietly, 'and it is possible to rise from humble beginnings you know.'

'Of course it is,' she said stoutly and watched his face as he moved. Something in the angle of his head reminded her of someone but like that other occasion it remained just long enough to tantalise her then was completely lost.

'One day I may go to London to try my luck.'

'Would you leave Aranvale?' she asked in a low voice.

'Not as long as my mother needs me.'

A kind of desolation swept over her. Aranvale without David? She didn't want to think about it. 'It's perfectly ridiculous that I have to steal out this way to meet you.' She pouted like a spoilt child.

'No, it isn't, Susan. I can quite understand your parents wishing to protect you.' He paused and there was a sinking feeling at the pit of his stomach. 'No doubt they have a suitable young man in mind.'

She thought of Edward. 'If they do and I don't want to marry him then I won't.' She paused and her voice softened. 'I want to marry for love.'

'Even if that person were totally unsuitable, someone like me?' He sighed. 'No beautiful home, Susan, no servants.' Lightly he touched the hem of her gown. 'I very much doubt if my year's salary would stretch to the cost of your gown and cloak.'

They were playing but he was giving her a strong warning of what it would be like.

For a long time her fingers pulled at the grass. 'It's a great deal to give up, David, and I know I couldn't do it.' Then she brightened. 'If you did go to London would it take you a very long time to get rich? I'm being silly, of course it would.'

'Yes, I'm afraid so. A very long time if ever.' He frowned. 'No, that isn't what I believe. Given the chance and that is all I need then I would be a success. Money grows, Susan, once you have some you make it work for you.'

'And we'd be old before that time. I'm not brave, David,' she whispered. 'I love my family and I love Aran Heights.' Her blue eyes were swimming with tears and with a hoarse cry he gathered her to him.

'Oh, God, I have no right to say it but I can't help it. I love you, Susan, more than I thought possible to love anyone,' he said shakily.

'David! Oh, David!' She clung to him and as their lips met she could feel the rapid beating of his heart. Hardly aware of what she was doing her arms tightened round his neck and encouraged by her response his kisses became more urgent, more demanding. Time stood still. All about them was the fragrance of summer and a faint breeze whispered through the beech leaves. Somewhere a bee hummed and a flock of birds, alarmed at some noise rose as one and with a frenzied flapping of wings flew into the sky.

What was wrong with her? Why didn't she push David away? Her upbringing, everything she had been taught, screamed that what was in danger of happening was wrong and all it needed to save it going any further was a small show of resistance. It would give her the chance to show her disgust and blame it all on his lack of control then she could end the relationship and they need never meet again.

Her unbuttoned gown was falling from her shoulders, she could feel it, yet her only move was to slip her hands beneath David's shirt to touch the smooth skin. She heard his quick indrawn breath, felt his warm hand close round her breast and was totally unprepared for the flame of desire that took hold of her.

There was a confusion of pain and ecstasy then in the moment that David's weight shifted from her, it changed to an agony of terror. She must be bad, she must be wicked or how else could she have allowed this awful, dreadful thing to happen to her? She was trying to adjust her clothes, fumbling with the buttons, uncaring that they were incorrectly fastened and all the time she hadn't looked at him.

They sat well apart. David had his elbows on his knees, his face hidden in his hands, appalled at what had happened.

'Susan,' he whispered unsteadily, 'I'm so sorry, so very, very sorry.'

She gave no sign that she had heard. Her back was to him and she kept staring ahead like someone in shock. Desperately he wanted to reach out and comfort her but the archness of her back warned him against that and at last he got up and began brushing the grass from his trousers. Some of it was in her hair and with a dogged persistence he picked out each one. Still she didn't move.

'Susan,' he said helplessly.

She got up, her back still to him and he bent down for her cape, shaking it clear of grass and it was then that he saw her expression. It would live with him for a long time. Her eyes were huge in a chalk white face and she looked like a terrified child.

'Susan, please –' The choking feeling in his throat made it difficult to speak. 'Oh, God! I shouldn't have let it happen.'

'Don't say anything, just don't speak about it,' she said harshly, then she was running ahead, falling and stumbling through the bracken in her need to escape.

With his long strides he drew level with her while she kept up the same punishing pace until her breath was coming in painful gasps. Only then did she slow down. The despairing silence lasted until Aran Heights came into view.

'Goodbye, David.' Susan tossed the words over her shoulder and in those words he heard the finality.

Sick at heart he watched her go.

In a panic and desperate to reach her own room before anyone saw her, Susan raced round to the back of the house, almost knocking to the ground a startled Polly.

'I'm sorry –'

'Miss Susan! Miss Susan! Don't go. I was comin' to look for you. When you wasn't in the library or your own room Mr Brodie thought you might be in the garden.'

'Mr Brodie,' Susan said faintly.

'Mr Edward Brodie, he's in the mornin' room, Miss Susan, least that's where I left him.'

Susan took a deep, shaky breath. 'Tell Mr Brodie I'll be down once I've changed.'

Polly's brown eyes were full of concern. 'Miss Susan, you not comin' down with somethin'. You look all white.'

'Too much sun that's all it is, Polly, I've been silly.' Then as Polly made to go she gripped her arm. 'After you tell Mr Brodie bring water, plenty of hot water to my room and be quick, please.'

'Ever so quick I'll be,' Polly said as she hurried away.

Once in her room Susan stripped naked and put on her robe then went over to her wardrobe. Fiercely she held other thoughts at bay, concentrating solely on what she would wear for Edward. In the end she decided on a salmon pink gown and had it off its hanger when Polly arrived out of breath and carrying two jugs of hot water which she put on the marble top.

'Mr Brodie is quite happy, Miss Susan. He said to take your time.' Her eyes fell on the bundle of clothes on the floor. 'These for washing, Miss Susan?'

'Yes. No.' She swallowed. 'What I mean is yes they are to be laundered. Polly – '

'Yes, Miss Susan.'

'Are you handy with a needle?'

'Oh, yes, ever so neat I am.'

'Then you could alter that gown for yourself couldn't you? It's not a particular favourite of mine,' she lied 'so you're welcome to it.'

Her brown eyes widened in her pointed little face. 'You wants me to have it?' she said in wonderment.

'Yes, take it away and you may as well have the cape to go with it.'

'Thanks ever so, Miss Susan, I've never ever had anythin' that pretty.'

'Off you go then,' Susan said impatiently. 'You can come back later and tidy up.'

'Yes, Miss Susan,' Polly said, sweeping up the bundle and making for the door.

Alone again, Susan began washing herself with thoroughness as though she could wash away the memory of the afternoon. After towelling herself dry she slipped into fresh undergarments and pulled the salmon pink gown over her head. Carefully she examined her face, not knowing why but expecting to find some difference there. Reassured that she looked much as usual apart from being paler she took a tip from her mother and pinched at her cheeks with her fingers to bring some colour into them.

The earlier events crowded in again and she had to bite her knuckles to stop crying out. Somehow she had to act normally. Stiffening her shoulders and taking a shaky breath she went down to meet Edward. A touch of welcome normality greeted her. Edward was reclining in a deep armchair and looking very much at ease. At the sound of the door opening he sprang up and looked at her admiringly.

'A long wait but definitely worth it.' He grinned.

'My apologies, Edward, for taking so long but this heat doesn't encourage hurrying.' She held up her cheek for his kiss.

'Where were you? The maid had almost given up.'

'In the garden,' she lied. 'Stupid of me but I stayed too long in the sun and no doubt I'll pay the price.' To her own ears the words sounded ominous and an icy shiver went through her.

'It doesn't seem to affect your skin so think yourself lucky. A little of it and I go like a beetroot.' He looked at her quizzically. 'I take it you don't feel like a walk?'

'To be honest, Edward, I don't.'

'The carriage – a drive somewhere, does that appeal?'

'No, but I could do with something to eat.'

'I'll keep you company. A little sustenance would be welcome and we can't have you falling apart.'

Already normality was returning, thanks to Edward. If she didn't think about it, refused to allow herself to think about it, then maybe she could make herself believe it had never happened.

'I'll just go and see Mrs Carson. Excuse me, Edward.'

\*　　\*　　\*

Two places were very quickly set in the small dining-room and Polly brought in a selection of cold meats, crusty bread and a salad. Food had been the last thing on Susan's mind but she felt that conversation with Edward over a meal would be easier than sitting together when every expression could be analysed and remarked on. Nothing much missed Edward.

To her surprise she enjoyed the meal and felt the better for it. After they had finished Edward suggested a stroll in the garden and she agreed.

'Get yourself a hat, one with a brim.'

She laughed. There was something very solid and reliable about Edward. 'You're beginning to sound like Mama and incidentally what brought you here?'

'Charming,' he said drily. 'Just a whim, Susan, and the need to see a pretty face. And let me hasten to add that I didn't know that you'd be on your own.' He smiled. 'That was a bit of luck.'

'Well, I'm glad you came,' and surprised herself by meaning it. 'Just let me get that hat.'

She made no objection when he took her arm and put it through his. They walked the paths admiring the colourful borders, stopping to smell the honeysuckle and chatting comfortably.

'By the way I had a long chat with Matthew's lady love.'

'Who? Oh, you mean Caroline. I'm not sure how that relationship stands, it blows hot and cold. Matthew doesn't say much but I do know that she hasn't been near Aran Heights for some time.'

'Then all I can say is that Matthew had better look out. Caroline is a strikingly beautiful young woman and not the type a chap can afford to be careless about.' He grinned and looked pointedly at Susan. 'If a certain young woman of my acquaintance keeps me waiting too long then I may try my charms with the very delectable Caroline.'

'I don't think she is your type, Edward,' Susan said a little sourly then was immediately ashamed.

There was a satisfied smirk on Edward's face as he took

out his pocket watch. 'I'd love to stay longer but I have your reputation to think of. Since your parents are not here and Matthew isn't around they may consider this not quite proper.'

Susan stiffened at the word reputation but she managed to smile as she accompanied him to the courtyard where Donald was tending the horses.

Edward sprang up and gathered the reins. 'Give my regards to Mr and Mrs MacFarlane. See you sometime,' he said carelessly.

She raised her hand in farewell and wondered why she should be disappointed at his cavalier departure. Exasperated with herself she went back into the house.

It was a long, long, day. Would it never end! She was tired, her brain wouldn't even function properly. If only she could lie down, let sleep claim her but her parents would expect her to wait up for them.

It was to be a very long time indeed before any of them got to bed that night.

# CHAPTER EIGHT

Her needlework was on her lap when the carriage bringing her parents passed the window and drew up at the entrance. As soon as she heard voices in the hall Susan picked up the work and began stitching. Minutes later Mrs MacFarlane bustled in and Susan raised her head to smile.

'I didn't expect you for another hour, Mama. Did you have a pleasant day?'

'Very pleasant but your papa looked so tired that I made our excuses and came away.' Her voice dropped to a warning whisper. 'Not a word to your papa, you know what he's like.' Then as if suddenly becoming aware of Susan's busy fingers she said in a shocked voice, 'On the Sabbath day, Susan! Put that sewing away at once.'

'I'm sorry,' she faltered. 'I forgot what day this is.' Hastily she folded up the cloth and put it and the threads in the work basket.

Hamish came in, grunted a greeting to Susan and sank down gratefully into his chair.

'Getting too old for all this gallivanting, not that I ever had much time for these social affairs. Inane gossip and poor quality port is about the strength of it,' he added peevishly.

'There was a heavy shower of rain in Airdrie just before we left.'

'Not here, Mama, it's been lovely.'

'How did you spend your day, Susan?' She looked over to her husband and frowned. 'You could so easily have been with us. Beatrice Wakeham was there with her parents. Such a plain girl with nothing to say for herself yet she's managed

81

to get herself engaged to some army captain in the – what was it, Hamish?'

'Artillery.'

'Edward was here, Mama.'

'Edward! Now that was nice,' her mother said, visibly brightening. What did you do, go for a walk?'

'No, we had a meal together. Mrs Carson prepared something cold and Polly served it.' She stopped when she heard the outside door shut, heavy footsteps across the hall then Matthew came in. Susan saw the suppressed excitement and some nervousness and wondered. Like most twins they were attuned to each other's moods.

'Matthew, dear, this is early for you,' his mother exclaimed. 'We just got in ahead of you.'

'I know, I saw Donald putting the carriage down the drive. I – um – have something to tell you – an announcement actually.' He remained standing with his hands on the back of a chair.

'An announcement,' Sarah repeated wonderingly. 'You make it sound like an engagement. Have you and Caroline – ' she began.

'No, Mother, not Caroline.' He paused and put his weight on the other foot as all eyes settled on him. 'After getting Mr Clapperton's approval I proposed to Winnie and she has honoured me by accepting,' he said stiltedly.

There was a moment's stunned silence then Hamish spoke.

'All right, Matthew, let's hear the rest of it. There's more to come, isn't there?' he said bitingly.

'Yes, Father, I was coming to that,' Matthew said quietly, swallowing nervously. 'Once we are married I shall be taking up farming. I'm sorry I'm disappointing you, Father, but I've never hidden from you my dislike of working in the mill.'

'Instead you are prepared to marry that plain, dull daughter of Euan Clapperton to get your hands on Moorend. You are despicable, do you know that?'

Matthew's face was flushed and he was scowling. 'Whom

I decide to marry is a matter for me and I'm not prepared to let you or anyone else dictate.'

'That is no way to speak to your father, Matthew, and you, Hamish,' she said angrily, 'have no right to speak so disparagingly about Winnie. I'm just as surprised as you at the news but there was no call for that remark, it was most unkind.'

'Oh, of course,' Hamish sneered, 'Winnie is special to you; she'd have to be, she's Euan Clapperton's daughter after all.'

Sarah's face went pale then a dull red.

'You used the word despicable to Matthew and it is exactly what this is, Hamish.' She was breathing hard and Susan and Matthew exchanged startled glances.

Raising a shaking finger to his son Hamish shouted, 'Loyalty, you don't know the meaning of the word.'

Matthew started to speak but Sarah's voice cut short the words.

'Enough has been said, we will not discuss this any further if you please.'

'Why not?' Hamish roared as he got up from his chair. 'Have you no loyalty to the mill either? Let me tell you this, Sarah, it's what my grandfather began all those years ago that has allowed you the extravagances that you think of as your due, if you bother to think about it at all – '

They saw him stagger, his face turn an alarming shade of grey, a hand clutch at his chest then he collapsed on to the floor.

Susan screamed, 'Papa! Papa!' as she leapt out of her seat but Sarah was over and thrusting her roughly out of the way.

'Matthew, get Dr Sullivan.'

With an agonised look at the still figure, his own face as white as a sheet, Matthew ran out of the room and they could hear him shouting for the coachman. Donald must have been at hand for they heard the sounds of the horses and the crunch of the wheels as the carriage tore down the drive.

A calmness had come over Mrs MacFarlane as she took complete control.

'Susan, get Mrs Dunbar then get Polly to help you bring a pillow and blankets.'

'Mama – '

'Do it, don't waste time.'

Mrs Dunbar was quickly on the scene. Sarah had loosened Hamish's necktie and unfastened the buttons of his shirt. Carefully, with Mrs Dunbar's help, she lifted her husband's head on to the pillow and tucked the blankets around him.

''Tis better to leave him, m'am, until the doctor gets here.'

'If only he were here now; it's dreadful to feel so helpless.' She looked at Susan in mute appeal and with a sob Susan went into her mother's arms.

For those who waited it seemed an eternity before Dr Sullivan was kneeling beside Hamish. With an impatient movement of his arm he indicated that he wanted everybody out of the room. Sarah was reluctant to obey but after another look at the figure on the floor she followed the others into the morning-room. Polly had already poured out cups of tea and with Mrs Dunbar's coaxing they each reached for a cup.

'It was my fault,' Matthew said, clattering down his cup and spilling some of it. 'If he dies – ' He gulped.

'He won't, not Papa,' Susan sobbed as she put her arms around her twin. 'Dr Sullivan will pull him through.'

'We must all be brave,' Sarah said unsteadily, 'and blaming yourself isn't going to help, Matthew.' She smiled. 'Your father is a fighter, he's going to get well, he must.' Her hands were clenched.

Dr Sullivan's face was grave as he beckoned to Sarah. He lowered his voice but they could all hear what he said.

'An upstairs bedroom is out of the question. A bed will have to be brought down here and put in a couch or something for me. I'll remain with him.'

'Is he – ' Sarah said fearfully then, pulling herself together, said in a normal voice, 'How is my husband?'

He shook his head. 'The next few hours – all we can do is wait and hope,' he said quietly then he addressed Matthew: 'Once the room is ready you can help me move your father.'

Matthew nodded. 'Please, I want to sit with him.'

'No, lad.' Something in the young man's drawn face and anguished eyes made him change his mind. 'Yes, well perhaps that would be helpful. That way I can snatch a little sleep and you can waken me the moment there is any change.'

'Thank you.'

'May I – is there anything I can do?' Susan wavered.

'Prayer, my dear, you could try that,' he said. It was surprising coming from Dr Sullivan who was not renowned for his appearances at the kirk.

'We'll all be doing that,' Sarah said quietly before going with Mrs Dunbar to supervise the transfer of bed and bedding.

Afterwards Susan was to remember how they were all drawn together, family and servants, as if together they could will the master to recover.

Sleep for anyone that night was fitful if at all. Susan prayed as she never had before. Everything else was banished from her mind. Her only thoughts were of her beloved papa and how desperately ill he was.

'Mama, have you had any rest at all?'

'Yes, I had a few hours.' She smiled sadly. 'Sleep seems so unimportant just now but I have promised Dr Sullivan to try and get some rest.

'You must, Mama. Is there anything – '

'No, dear, there is nothing you can do.'

Aunt Rachel arrived and any coldness between the sisters-in-law was forgotten in their shared anxiety. Later in the day Edward and his parents arrived and were shown into the drawing-room. Tall and well built, John Brodie held himself very stiffly erect and was a fine-looking man though there was the beginning of a paunch. His dark hair was peppered with grey and the long sideburns nearly white. Lilian, his wife, was small and stout and being pear-shaped was the despair of a succession of dressmakers. Her auburn hair had faded to a dull blonde and weak blue eyes blinked frequently. Susan liked them both.

'Sarah, my dear.' Lilian kissed her friend and her voice was full of concern. 'We were so terribly distressed to hear – how is Hamish?'

'Holding his own according to Dr Sullivan.' Sarah bit her lip to stop its trembling and Lilian patted her hand.

'There! There! He's in good hands and Hamish will put up a fight.'

'No doubt about that.' John Brodie came from behind his wife to take both Sarah's hands in his own. 'By God! If anyone can put up a fight it's Hamish. Mark my words, lass,' he said with a brusque kindliness, 'he'll be all right.'

Susan turned from the window and seeing the stark misery in the young face Lilian went over to take the girl in her arms, clucking soothingly as if to a child.

'Susan, my dear, your papa has always declared you to be a true MacFarlane. He wouldn't like to see you giving way like this. Now would he?'

Susan raised eyes bright with unshed tears and tried to smile.

'I know, Mrs Brodie,' she said unsteadily. 'I haven't been much help and Matthew and Mama have been wonderful.'

'When it's needed, dear, we all get that extra strength.' Her voice dropped to a whisper. 'Your mama has always been capable but like most women she has kept it hidden until something like this happens.' Her eyes moved to watch her son go over and say a few words to Sarah. Then she turned her attention back to Susan. 'The young are ill at ease where there is illness and Edward is no exception. He's deeply upset, Susan, and wanted to call and see you before going on to the distillery.' She gave Susan a small push. 'Let him take you outside for a breath of air, it will do you good.'

Edward had overheard. 'Mother's right, Susan. Why don't you come outside for a few minutes?'

Like an obedient child she went with him and once they were down the steps he asked about Matthew.

'He was up all night sitting with Papa to let Dr Sullivan snatch a short rest. Then this morning he went to the village to bring the nurse. She's with Papa.' The lump in her throat was almost choking her. 'Poor Matthew was almost sleeping on his feet and we had a job persuading him to get some rest.'

'He's in bed now?'

'Yes, Mama looked in and he's dead to the world.'

'What brought on the attack or don't you know?'

She hesitated then said evasively, 'Mama said they shouldn't have gone visiting yesterday. She didn't like his colour but he was adamant he was all right. Mama did make some excuse to leave early and we were just together talking – when it happened.'

'Think how much worse it would have been if he had collapsed away from home,' Edward said, putting a comforting arm round her shoulders.

'That's just what Mama said. He was warned to take things easier but you know Papa.'

He nodded. 'Doesn't take too kindly to that kind of advice.'

'He should have, it was foolish of him. This coming on top of his bronchitis, he'll just have to resign himself to a shorter working day.'

'Probably will. Once he gets over this he won't want a repeat performance.'

She looked at him gratefully. He really was a dear. Sensing that she didn't want to talk he lapsed into silence.

In the house, in the atmosphere, she had found it difficult to think but out here it was easier. That Matthew's announcement had triggered off her papa's collapse she was in no doubt though that ugly scene between her parents must have contributed. It had been so out of character. Like all married couples they had their differences but there had never been anything like that. Maybe she was more to blame than Matthew or Mama. Had she agreed to become engaged to

Edward none of this need have happened. Matthew was no asset to the mill, Papa knew that better than anyone. He would have been little more than a figurehead and someone to sign papers. Her thoughts were becoming feverish. She could still – maybe it wasn't too late.

'Edward – '

'Mmmm.'

'Edward, your proposal, I mean, if you still want – ' she stammered and looked at him helplessly.

'Was there ever a time I didn't? Of course I want you. I love you and I want to marry you.' Surprise and something more shone out of his eyes. 'You're trying to tell me you've changed your mind?'

'Yes.'

'We can be married just as soon as you wish,' he said softly.

'Thank you, Edward.' Her nails were digging into the palms of her hand.

Turning her to him and uncaring whether they could be seen his lips brushed her cheek then moved to her mouth in a kiss that would have lingered had she not moved her head away. More than anything else she wanted to escape, to get away. It was all wrong that they should be kissing at a time like this, she thought resentfully.

'Susan, I'll never give you cause to regret it and I promise to make you happy,' he said huskily, then, almost in the same breath, 'When shall we make the announcement, make it official?'

Her startled eyes told him that he was going too fast for her.

'Not yet, Edward. When Mama is alone I'll tell her and you can inform your parents later, can't you? It seems so out of place just now.'

'I think you're wrong but I bow to your wishes.'

'Once Papa is well enough to hear the news then we'll make it official.'

'Mr MacFarlane won't object to me as a son-in-law.'

'No, you'll be welcomed into this family.'

Her eyes strayed to the courtyard where another carriage was drawing up. In a moment she saw Euan Clapperton help Winnie down, then together they walked to the door.

'That's Winnie Clapperton and her papa just arrived, Edward. Matthew must have gone over last night to tell them. You will excuse me but I must be on hand to help Mama.'

'Of course, my dearest, and I imagine the parents will be ready to leave now. Chin up, darling, our news might just help your papa's recovery.'

Once Edward and his parents had departed Susan went in to find Euan Clapperton and her mother in earnest conversation. Winnie was sitting a little apart but sprang up when she saw Susan.

'Susan,' she said urgently, 'is there some place where we can talk privately?'

Susan looked at her unsmilingly. 'I suppose so,' she said ungraciously and, turning her back, left Winnie to follow. She stopped at the door of what had once been the schoolroom but was now little more than a storeroom for unwanted furniture. Being at the back of the house the sun only reached there in the late afternoon and at this time it was chilly and cheerless. Engaged in moving two chairs in order that they could face each other, Susan was struck by the other's appearance. Winnie had dressed with care and she was wearing her hair in a softer and more flattering style.

'This will have to do, I'm afraid,' Susan said with a wave of her hand. 'Most of the downstairs rooms are in use, three of them are being used as temporary bedrooms.'

'I understand and this is quite satisfactory. What I have to say won't take long.' She appeared composed but her voice was jerky.

'Very well, I'm waiting,' Susan said coldly.

'When Matthew came to tell us about Mr MacFarlane, Susan, he was in a terrible state. He blames himself for what happened and of course I must share some of that blame.' Her eyes didn't waver as they met Susan's. 'Matthew has given up all thought of going into farming,' she said very quietly. 'He sees now that his place is in the papermill.' She paused to moisten her lips with the tip of her tongue. 'All this has changed Matthew, Susan. Given time I'm sure he'll acquire whatever qualities it needs to control the mill.'

It was a long speech for Winnie and one which had obviously been prepared. Susan didn't take it in, not at first. Then she grasped it. Matthew was to remain in the mill. Matthew had had a change of heart, a belated loyalty to the mill. That was what Winnie was telling her. She closed her eyes. There had been no need to tie herself to Edward, no need to enter into a marriage she didn't want. But it was too late. She had offered herself and been accepted. There was no going back.

Winnie was looking at her strangely. 'Susan, are you all right? Oh, I see what is worrying you,' she said with a strangled laugh. 'Well, you needn't worry any longer, I won't hold your brother to his promise of marriage.'

Susan saw the hurt. 'I'm sorry, Winnie, so much is happening you must excuse me.' Then as Winnie's sacrifice got through to her she shook her head. 'We all seem to be trying to do the right thing but your sacrifice and Matthew's turn-about have come too late for me.' Without another word she ran out of the room leaving a stricken Winnie to find her own way to the drawing-room.

Aran Heights was quiet, the late hour making it beyond the likelihood of callers and Mrs MacFarlane sighed with relief. The genuine concern shown by friends and acquaintances was comforting but the constant need to repeat oneself to each caller became more wearisome as the day dragged on.

Seeing the tiredness in her daughter's face she put it down to the same reason and smiled sympathetically.

'It becomes quite a strain doesn't it, dear?'

'Yes. Mama, there's something I want to tell you.'

Her tired smile turned to Susan.

'I've agreed to marry Edward.'

'That is quite splendid, my dear,' Sarah said, her tiredness temporarily forgotten. She kissed Susan warmly. 'I'm so delighted and I know how pleased your papa will be.' Then she frowned. 'You don't look very happy and the word agreed seems a peculiar choice.'

'Not really, I'm marrying Edward to please you both but mostly in the hope that it will help Papa get well.'

'No, Susan, don't go,' as Susan made to get up. 'I want you to sit down and listen to me.' She took a deep breath. 'First, I must explain about your papa's outburst and his mention of Mr Clapperton,' she said, the colour coming and going in her face. 'You are entitled to an explanation.'

'There's nothing to explain, Papa wasn't himself.'

'I have nothing to hide and nothing to be ashamed of but you may as well hear the facts now.' She paused. 'There was a time when I might have married Mr Clapperton and your papa hasn't forgotten it.'

Susan smiled in spite of herself. 'I find it hard to see you as a farmer's wife.'

'That was the problem, I couldn't either. Moorend then was nothing like it is today.'

'Then Papa came on the scene, you fell in love with him and married him. Was that how it was?'

She didn't give a direct answer and there was an odd look on her face.

'Love can grow out of liking, my dear, and it is possible to love more than once.' She paused and there was a look of regret on her face. 'We have never been close you and I and that was my fault. A mother gets wrapped up in her sons but that is no excuse. I should have been more sensitive to your needs.'

'It doesn't matter now,' Susan said awkwardly.

'You weren't entirely blameless but I'm straying,' she said, putting a hand to her brow. 'What I wanted to say was that in time you will learn that the secret of a successful marriage is to work at it and that very much depends upon the woman.'

'Yes, I suppose so.'

'Believe me, my dear, if we hadn't thought Edward to be right for you we would never have encouraged the union.' She looked steadily at Susan but Susan's face was expressionless.

'You like Edward and liking will blossom into love and the marriage all the stronger for it.' She smiled. 'Tomorrow morning, Susan, you must tell Papa yourself and after that I'll see about the announcement of your forthcoming marriage going into the newspapers.'

'Surely there is no need for all this rush,' Susan said, alarmed at the way everything was being speeded up.

'Nonsense, it is what your papa would want.'

Everything was crowding in on her and with a mumbled excuse Susan almost ran from the room.

When she did eventually sleep Susan dreamed of David Cameron, a confused dream that made her blush but by the time she was fully awake her thoughts were only of her papa.

The morning was dull, not like a June morning. There was hardly a movement in the trees. The air was clammy inside and out and the maids looked fatigued as they went about their duties. Matthew had left the house early and Susan and her mother were breakfasting together.

'What about Papa?'

'Dr Sullivan is quite pleased and now that we have a night nurse he feels he no longer requires to remain overnight.'

'But he'll come each day?'

'Of course. Papa is still a very sick man.'

Susan was outside the sickroom and waiting for Dr Sullivan when he came out.

His brows shot up. 'There you are, Susan. Your papa has taken some nourishment and there's a wee improvement.'

'If I promise not to tire him may I see Papa for a few minutes?'

'Can't see why not. Keep it short, he's very weak.' He turned back, opened the door and beckoned Susan to follow him. Tiptoeing in she was shocked at the change in her papa. His cheeks were sunken, his face grey and propped up with pillows he looked an old man. Her distress must have shown on her face.

'Don't look like that, Susan, I'm still in the land of the living and not ready to leave it just yet,' he said in a voice she had to strain to hear.

'Five minutes, Susan,' Dr Sullivan gave as his parting shot.

Hamish muttered something under his breath as she bent down to kiss his brow.

'Papa, you're some better,' she said unsteadily but it was hard to believe by looking at him.

'Up and about in no time,' he whispered.

'Here's something to cheer you. I'm going to marry Edward.'

She saw relief in the sunken eyes as his hand fastened on hers.

'He'll make you a good husband.' The effort of speech had cost him and he closed his eyes but his grip on her hand tightened. The nurse, out of earshot but watching, came to her patient and rearranged the pillows. Her starched uniform seemed to crackle with professional annoyance.

'The patient is not to be encouraged to talk,' she admonished severely but moved away at Hamish's ferocious glower.

'Old battleaxe,' Hamish grunted and it was so like her papa that Susan had to stifle a giggle. His speech became telegraphic.

'Matthew – misjudged him – says he'll stay on in the mill.'

'You must be pleased about that?'

'Lying here – time to think – no good, Susan – with the best will in the world he'd be no good. Better he should go into farming.'

'Don't tire yourself, Papa,' Susan said, alarmed.

'Don't you start. Edward now – capable – good head for business.'

He lay back exhausted and she was about to go but he held on to her hand.

'Get married quickly – let me get my affairs in order.'

Bristling with annoyance, the nurse almost propelled Susan from the room.

\*   \*   \*

Matthew had slept his exhaustion away and even after a full day in the papermill he looked remarkably fresh. Sarah had felt one of her headaches coming on and had returned to her room leaving brother and sister together.

'Matthew, I had a few minutes with Papa and he was saying you are prepared to stay on in the mill.'

'What choice had I after what happened? Mind you, come to think about it, he wasn't as relieved as I would have expected. Still, that could be attributed to the way he is just now.'

'I've decided to marry Edward,' she said quietly.

He looked at her sharply. 'When did this come about?'

'Yesterday.'

'Nothing would please him more. How did he take it?'

'As you would expect. It came as a great relief and Matthew, he appreciates your offer but he said as much to me that it isn't necessary. Edward will take on much of the responsibility and presumably I'll be allowed to make some contribution.'

His relief was almost comical. 'You're sure about that, I mean really sure?'

'That's what Papa said, Matthew.'

'Look, Susan,' he said awkwardly, 'I know what I said before but I wouldn't like to think of you marrying Edward just for the sake of the mill.'

'Rest assured, Matthew, there was no pressure, the decision was mine. And if you want over to Moorend hadn't you better get a move on?'

'You're right. She's a good sort, Winnie is, wasn't going to hold me to the marriage.'

'How about you, would you have gone through with it?' she asked him as he prepared to go but he made no answer.

Susan knocked first then went into the darkened bedroom.

'No, you're not disturbing me. I was just about to get up,' her mother said as she removed the net cap from her head. 'Is Matthew still downstairs?'

'No, he left for Moorend a few minutes ago.'

She smiled. 'Now that he has Papa's blessing to go

into farming everything is working out after all. Mind you, Matthew and Winnie making a match of it takes some getting used to.'

'Wasn't she looking smart?'

'Just what I thought. The sudden interest in clothes must have been for Matthew's benefit. Quite a dark horse our Winnie.'

Susan wandered over to the window to open the curtains a fraction then turned back to the bed. 'Mama, I'd much prefer to wait until Papa's a lot stronger but he wants the marriage to take place as soon as possible.'

'Then we must fall in with his wishes.' Her brow puckered. 'There's such a lot to arrange,' she said worriedly. 'Edward and his parents must come over to let us get started. And I must see Hamish,' she said, swinging her legs out of bed. 'Miss Beattie, I must get in touch with Miss Beattie and persuade her to stop everything else and do a rush order. But of course she will, after all we are valued customers.'

Susan could almost see her mind dart from one thing to another. There was a feverishness about her and Susan saw life becoming very difficult from now on. She would have to try and act the part of the happy bride yet all she could feel was a dreadful reluctance to tie herself to Edward Brodie. Leaving her mother, she went outside across the lawn and sought refuge in the summer house which Mrs MacFarlane had had built for her but seldom used. No one would worry her here and she had a great need to be alone with her thoughts. Gazing ahead without really seeing, Susan shivered and tried to banish the memory of those dark anguished eyes and her own panic-stricken flight. Shame mingled with guilt as she remembered her own conduct. David hadn't forced her. Her own body had betrayed her with its sudden, shameful, urgent desire and she knew her nearness had aroused him.

Well, it had happened and there was no turning back the clock. She had been foolish but now she must forget all about David Cameron. And in time she would, she must.

# CHAPTER NINE

'**D**on't be wishing her back, lad,' the doctor said as he sat down with a weariness that had nothing to do with age. 'Your mother had only pain ahead of her. This way, going in her sleep, she is spared that.'

Dr Archibald Anderson was thin-faced and wore waxed moustaches. Years ago he had come to this practice in Aranvale with all the energy and optimism of the newly qualified doctor only to find that the fashionable Dr Sullivan had creamed off the top families leaving him to take his patients from those families on the poverty line and under, who could ill afford his fees and a fair number who could but preferred to keep the publicans in business. The constant battle to make ends meet had soured and prematurely aged him.

'I pleaded with her to see you,' David said brokenly.

'And so she did, a long time ago and I only told her what she already knew.'

David's hands moved in a gesture of hopelessness. 'Why didn't she tell me? Why didn't she?'

'Her way, David, she wouldn't want to upset you.' Sighing, he took out a watch dangling from a chain across his middle and frowned. 'I'll need to be getting on my way,' he said, getting up. 'Do you have someone to stay with you, help you through this?'

'I've sent word to an aunt; she'll be over. Don't worry about me, Dr Anderson, I'll manage.'

'I dare say. You were a good son to her and now you must look to yourself,' he said kindly. 'You have your whole life ahead of you.'

'Yes.' From the dresser David picked up some coins and handed them over.

'This is more than my fee,' Dr Anderson grunted.

'Take it, you've been very kind.'

'Very good of you, lad,' he said, pocketing the money. 'Not many about here would do that.'

They shook hands. The door closed. David was alone, yet not alone. Behind the curtain lay the cold, still body of the mother who had suffered slights and cruel jibes yet had managed to hold her head high and devote her life to the son she had loved so dearly.

His eyes went to the empty chair which had always been hers. The sagging cushion was askew and automatically he went over to right it. On a corner of the table, neatly folded and ready to put away in the drawer, was his laundry, the shirts carefully ironed as she had once done for the gentry. She had been so particular about his clothes, so anxious that he should always be well turned out.

'Oh, Mother,' he whispered brokenly. The pain of loss was indescribable and for the only time in his adult life he gave in to his grief with great racking sobs that shook his body.

Tears were unmanly. He could imagine her reproachful eyes and he half smiled. Unmanly perhaps but the storm of weeping had left him calm and more able to face what had to be done.

The water in the big, black kettle was still warm and he used it to wash at the sink. The fire was low and he added some kindling then once it caught he rearranged the hot cinders and put on more coal. The chill of death was in the house and he shivered.

He couldn't eat but he made himself tea and drank it then went next door to the McDonalds. He could leave it to them to inform the neighbours. Those in the mill would know there would be a good reason for his lateness. Time off would be no problem. Though Mr MacFarlane lay ill at Aran Heights his rules regarding illness and bereavement would be carried out to the letter. There would be offers of help, he knew that and it comforted him.

Aunt Meg, his mother's sister, was in the cottage when he got back. She had the table set and the kettle on the boil.

Neither were demonstrative but they hugged each other. She made him eat a meat pie she had brought with her and he surprised himself by enjoying it. Like his mother Aunt Meg knew when to be silent. Later they would talk but the time wasn't right. He felt restless, not knowing what to do with himself.

'David, lad, take yourself for a long walk, you'll feel the better for it.'

'I can't leave you alone with – '

She knew what he meant and smiled sadly. 'We loved them in life, why should we fear them in death is what I always say.'

David walked with long strides until he was out of the village and following the burn which wound its tortuous way through the countryside until it flowed into the River Clyde. From Clapperton's farm he could hear the pigs squealing for food and the sounds of carts rattling up the farm track. The sun had slunk behind a cloud and in the distance the hills looked like purple shadows. The lonely figure of a shepherd could be seen with his flock and on other slopes the cattle grazed. Aranvale could pull at the heart, David thought with a pang, yet all he wanted was to get away from it, far away. There was nothing for him here.

In the short space of a week he had been dealt two crushing blows. The death of his mother was a devastating and unexpected loss. The other had not been altogether a surprise but it had left him low-spirited and depressed. The local newspaper had made a big splash of the forthcoming marriage of Susan MacFarlane to Edward Brodie, the younger son of John Brodie, owner of the Granton Distillery.

Thinking back to that Sunday David had only self-disgust for his behaviour and the guilt weighed upon him heavily. That she had done nothing to discourage him was no excuse. She was young, four years his junior and so vulnerable, so in need of protection and instead – he shut his eyes to blot out the memory. The past was dead. Very soon he would leave Aranvale never to return.

\*     \*     \*

Only a handful of mourners stood in the drizzling rain to see Eliza Cameron laid to rest in the graveyard behind the kirk. At the end of the short service one or two mourners shook hands with David, offering sympathy but with a clumsy awkwardness. David Cameron was something of a mystery. He had always preferred his own company to hanging around with others his own age.

Leaving them to find his own way back to the cottage, David wondered what was expected of him. Should he invite any of the neighbours in? Perhaps it was the custom yet he recoiled from it. How many had shown kindness to his mother during her lifetime?

He only wanted Aunt Meg and she was waiting for him, looking worried.

'I should have been asking if you'd be bringing anyone for a bite.'

'No, I don't want any of them.'

'Get a good send-off, did she?'

'A few turned up and it was a nice service.' There was a catch in his voice and she busied herself at the fire.

'There's broth and bannocks, we'll both be the better of something.'

'I'm not hungry.'

'Nor am I but we have to eat.' She was a small, stout woman not a bit like his mother. Only when she smiled did the resemblance show.

David ate to please her and she to encourage him.

'What are your plans, lad?'

'Once I've settled everything I'm going to London.'

Her eyebrows rose in perplexity. 'Don't rush into anything, lad, think on it well.' She shook her head. 'So many of the young seek their fortune in London and a lot of them find only loneliness and heartbreak. Besides which you'd be givin' up a good job.'

'I have a friend there, Aunt Meg, and accountants don't have too much trouble finding work.'

'If your mind's made up then that's that.'

'As long as Mother was in Aranvale I would have stayed

but now I want a change.' He smiled. 'A suitcase is all I need so please take anything from the house you want.'

She was on the verge of weeping. 'I wish you'd just bide here.'

David put his arms around her. 'Mother would have wanted you to have her things and if you have no use for them then give them to someone.'

'Oh, I'll find a home for them, never fear.'

There was something he had to ask, he'd been waiting for an opportunity and perhaps this was it.

'Aunt Meg, you were always closest to Mother and you were the one who came to her rescue when she was in trouble.'

Her face darkened. 'Your grandparents, good livin' by their way of thinkin' but hard as nails. They were the sinners not Eliza.'

He swallowed hard. 'You must know who my father is?'

She was silent for a long time. 'She told you nothin',' she said at last.

'Nothing.'

'Gave her word and being Eliza she wouldn't break it.'

'You could tell me,' he persisted.

'I didn't take an oath on it but I don't know – ' she said slowly.

'I believe I have a right to know, Aunt Meg.'

'Maybe you do at that.' She moved her flabby body in its too tight black gown and settled into a more comfortable position.

'See if you can squeeze another cup out of that pot, there's a lad.'

David got up to make a fresh pot of tea, taking glances at his aunt while he waited for the kettle to boil. She was looking straight ahead and David tensed with excitement. At long last he was to hear who had fathered him and abandoned his mother.

Taking the cup gratefully she drank from it then put it down.

'I'll tell you as much as I remember but mind, my memory isn't what it used to be.'

101

'Please, Aunt Meg, you remember very well and I must know.'

'She wouldn't want you taking your revenge. Whatever it was between them there was no hatred in her heart. He was a gentleman, she said to me as if that explained it all.' She paused. 'I'll be needin' your word, David, that you'll cause no mischief.'

'How could I? Haven't I just told you that I'm off to London?'

'Now then, where do I start?'

'At the beginning and leave nothing out.'

She sighed. 'I hope I'm doin' the right thing.'

June became July and with the wedding day coming ever closer Aran Heights was thrown into a frenzy of preparation. Ever fearful of another attack and anxious that his affairs should be in order, Hamish MacFarlane had shamelessly used his poor health to insist that the young couple be married within the month. And under the watchful eye of Dr Sullivan Mrs MacFarlane had had to agree. All the while she was frantic, wondering how an important occasion such as their only daughter's wedding could be arranged in such a short time. In the end she had gained one week and the date was firmly fixed for five weeks ahead.

Susan carried out the tasks allotted to her and tried to show some enthusiasm when the bride and bridesmaid's gowns were discussed but it was all such an effort. Nothing seemed real, they could have been discussing someone else's wedding.

She had always enjoyed good health but now it had deserted her and she seemed drained of energy. Then there was that awful nausea and the retching. Pre-wedding nerves her mother would put it down to. Thankfully the nausea was easing a little but at breakfast all she could face was dry toast, even the weak tea she could not stomach.

No one noticed. Mama had a tray in her room and Matthew had gone before she came down.

In the early days of his illness the life of the household had kept pace with the faltering strength of the master but as he gradually grew stronger the services of the night nurse were considered no longer necessary. Scorning the help of the day nurse he would get up and stand at the window looking over at Aranvale.

Lilian Brodie was a great help to Sarah at this time and the two friends, equally delighted at the coming union of their children, were frequently closeted together.

Today, Susan, Edward, Sarah and Lilian were seated in the small sitting-room. Lilian was having difficulty in containing her excitement as she turned her head to face her future daughter-in-law.

'Susan, dear, I think I have come up with the perfect solution and Edward agrees but only,' she added hastily, 'if it meets with your approval.'

Susan smiled politely. 'I'd like to hear it.'

'The matter of a home for you – to find one of your own in the short time available and have it furnished is quite, quite out of the question. I think we are agreed on that. But,' she paused, 'the Templetons, I hear, are going down south for six months and closing up their house.' She stopped, looked at Edward and he took over.

'Mother feels, Susan, that she could persuade the Templetons to let us occupy Hillview, rent it furnished – '

'How perfectly splendid,' Sarah interrupted. 'Susan! Edward! That would give you breathing space to look around for what you want and Hillview though small is quite charming.'

'That sounds fine and I'm perfectly agreeable,' Susan said, trying to infuse some enthusiasm into her voice.

'Are you sure, Lilian, that the Templetons would agree to this?' Sarah said doubtfully.

Lilian pursed her lips, nodded and dropped her voice. 'The business term, I believe, is financially embarrassed. John knows something of the circumstances and thinks they will be glad of the money and of course the staff can be retained.'

'Splendid! That takes care of that,' Sarah said briskly.

The carriage left with Mrs Brodie and her son and Susan and her mother returned to the drawing-room.

'Wasn't that just a little bit thoughtless of you, dear? I'm sure Edward would have appreciated some time with his bride-to-be. There must be things you wish to discuss in private.'

'Sorry, Mama, I didn't think about that, it was just that I didn't feel like a walk.'

'You're not unwell are you?' she asked anxiously.

'No, just tired.'

'Oh, well, just one of your difficult days I expect,' Sarah said in a hushed voice as she sat down at the Regency desk with pen and paper and a worried expression.

'This is all very awkward for me, Susan. Some of our friends are going to be greatly offended not to receive an invitation, particularly those who have invited us to weddings in their families.'

'Surely not, Mama. With Papa ill they must realise the position.'

'They will, my dear, they will, just until they find out that someone close to them is invited then jealousies arise and the whole thing becomes difficult, very difficult indeed.'

Susan looked over her mother's shoulder. 'Mama!' she burst out. 'That can't be the final list of guests, it's supposed to be a quiet wedding.'

'Mrs Brodie can't reduce her list and I'm not doing any further trimming of ours,' her mother said with a finality that brooked no argument.

Headaches were a thing of the past, Mrs MacFarlane had no time to suffer from one. Every minute of every day was occupied. Top priority were the visits to Miss Beattie who had given over her entire staff to the making of Susan's wedding gown, her trousseau, the bridesmaid's dress and the outfit for the mother of the bride. An ever more excitable Sarah had Susan shunted here and there and Susan did as she was bid without complaint, hiding her tiredness and lethargy as best she could. She marvelled at the amount of energy her mother was displaying while she herself had never felt so low-spirited and drained.

With his days in the mill numbered, Matthew was spending more time there than had ever been his custom and those who had previously written him off as lazy and virtually useless were now admitting, albeit grudgingly, that he was putting his back into the work in his father's absence.

'Matthew's very quiet these days, have you noticed, Susan?'

'Yes, I have. Papa's collapse was a terrible shock and it affected him dreadfully. Winnie has noticed the difference too.'

'Mmmmm.' Mrs MacFarlane gave a deep sigh. 'Once you and Edward are married I must see Mr Clapperton and his sister. Neither will have a clue as to how to go about arranging a wedding and I rather think the bulk of the work will fall to me. Not that I mind but I would like time to draw my breath after yours.'

'Winnie would hate fuss.'

'Even so her father will want to do the right thing by his only child and that reminds me of the shopping trip the three of us had,' she said, flitting to another subject. 'How very fortunate that your buttercup yellow gown hasn't been worn.'

'There was no occasion to wear it.'

'True. Entertaining has been far from our minds these last few weeks. Of them all that gown remains my favourite, the colour is perfect for you and I'm sure Edward will be quite dazzled when he sees you in it on your honeymoon.'

At the mention of honeymoon Susan felt her throat constrict. Until now she had managed to block from her mind that she wasn't going to Edward as an innocent young bride but as a woman who had shamelessly sinned. Busy with her own thoughts, Mrs MacFarlane noticed nothing amiss as she poured tea from the silver teapot.

'Susan, we really must spare an hour to visit Moorend. Winnie will have received her gowns from Miss Beattie and may want our opinion as to which to wear for your wedding.'

'Perhaps she's had something else made up. After all Winnie is taking more care over her appearance.'

'And about time. Still, we must go over before Hannah descends on us, then truly we won't have a minute.'

Susan laughed. 'Hannah's a darling, I'm looking forward to her coming.'

'Apparently she's over the moon about being your bridesmaid but the child is such a chatterbox.'

'Hardly a child, Hannah's seventeen.'

'She doesn't act it. Maybe I made a mistake asking your aunt and uncle to bring her here a week before the wedding.'

'No, mama, she'll be a great help and don't worry she'll be quiet enough when Papa is around.' She raised her eyes to the clock. 'Papa should have had his rest by now?'

'Yes, off you go.'

Hamish was sitting up in bed propped up with pillows and with papers strewn over the bedcover when Susan went in.

'Well, you do look more like yourself.' Susan smiled and kissed his cheek.

'Rarin' to be up and about, Susan.'

'Just don't be overdoing it. In fact,' she said severely, 'we are all going to make sure you don't.'

With her nursing duties about to end the stern-looking nurse – Hatchet Face, Hamish nicknamed her – was busy tidying bottles and stacking them neatly into a medicine cabinet. Looking up she muttered something and left father and daughter together.

'Got her trained now that she's leaving,' Hamish said, catching Susan's eye and grinning wickedly.

'Be fair, Papa,' Susan reproached. 'Nurse Robertson has looked after you very well.'

'So she has,' he agreed quietly. He raised himself and pointed to a porcelain figure of a crinoline lady. 'Fancies that thing, I'm sure she does, seen her looking at it often enough. In case I forget to tell your mother see that she gets it along with her wages and get yourself a chair, you can't stand there and I'm not having you sitting on the bed,' he said irritably. 'We have things to discuss.'

'Yes, Papa,' Susan replied as she brought a chair across to the bed and sat down.

'Preparations well in hand?'

'Mama is doing everything almost single-handed.' She laughed.

'In her element she'll be.' He smiled and sobered. 'Susan, I'm having my solicitor draw up a new will.'

Feeling uncomfortable at this turn in the conversation Susan bit her lip and looked away then turned back to face her father.

'Matthew shall have his inheritance now. I have no wish to have a son of mine dependent for his living on Euan Clapperton and this way Matthew can buy additional land, land which will belong to him and in time to his family.'

'He'll appreciate that, Papa.'

'So he should,' he grunted.

'He'll make a good farmer,' Susan said gently.

'But will he make a good husband?' His eyes were bleak. 'Matthew's getting married for all the wrong reasons. Still, that's his problem.' He sighed. 'Thankfully I've no such fears for you and Edward but that is not what I want to discuss.' He paused and looked at her searchingly. 'The mill, does it still mean as much to you?'

'The mill is a part of me, Papa, and I'm hoping you will allow me a share in its management.'

He smiled and there was a hint of moisture in the blue eyes as he patted her hand.

'I hoped you'd say that, lass.' He coughed and took a short rest. 'Lying here with time to think I'm seeing things much more clearly. What I'm saying or about to say is no disrespect to Edward. He is a fine lad with a good brain and a great hankering after responsibility but we have to be careful. Edward must never have total responsibility. He has a touch of his father's ruthlessness which some would admire but it isn't my way. John and I respect each other but his ways are not mine and what is tolerated in the distillery would not be in my mill.' He paused and moved his position. 'Workers are human beings, never lose sight of that, Susan. There could come a time when their loyalty could be crucial to survival.'

He was deadly serious, she could see that.

'Don't misunderstand me, my dear, this marriage is very important to me. When your marriage to Edward was being considered we had quite a talk. At that time I expected Matthew to become the eventual owner of the mill and Edward to be second in command and that seemed to satisfy him.'

'By refusing Edward I upset your carefully laid plans.'

'Not at all. Your mother and I never doubted but that you would change your mind and in the event we were proved right. Now where was I – oh, yes! Don't be alarmed but we must face facts. Heaven forbid that I should suffer another attack like this one but should it happen I'm well aware it could be fatal.'

'Papa!' Susan cried in distress. 'Don't talk like that, please.'

'Tch! Tch! Come, Susan, you are no longer a child and I'm in no hurry to leave this world but I do want to be prepared.'

'I wish you wouldn't – '

'I am treating you like an adult, kindly act as one,' he said sternly.

'I'm sorry.'

He glowered and continued. 'When I do go the papermill will become your responsibility,' he said, his eyes on her face.

'Papa!' She stared at him.

'You heard correctly. I am leaving the mill to you in the firm belief that you are capable of its management,' he said quietly.

'I can't believe this.'

'Let me go on. Many, perhaps your husband-to-be among them, will resent taking orders from a woman and to deal with the situation you will need both tact and firmness.'

She made to speak but he silenced her with an impatient move of his arm.

'Once I'm no longer here Edward may decide that my methods are old-fashioned and be anxious to make sweeping changes. You must decide their worth, Susan, and if you have doubts be strong enough to voice them. He cannot act without your authority. Remember that, Susan. *You* have the final say.' He smiled then. 'Edward is not likely to be difficult and one day, God willing, you will bear Edward's child and the mill shall pass to my grandson.' He lay back exhausted.

'You've tired yourself.'

'Talking tires me but I needed this conversation.'

She swallowed painfully and gave herself a few moments before speaking.

'Whatever lies ahead you have my promise that I shall carry on the way you taught me.'

'I know that. If I hadn't been so sure I would have held on to Matthew.'

'He was prepared to stay in the mill.'

'Yes, I know I was too hard on the lad.' He frowned. 'Perhaps I haven't explained myself very well. Don't think I'm against change – far from it. Change is healthy when the tried and trusted is replaced by something better but not when it is just for change itself.' He broke off for a drink from the covered glass and after a few sips pulled a face. 'Something a bit stronger than water would be welcome but I suppose I'll be denied it until I'm on my feet and can get it for myself.'

'You're not allowed it so don't look at me.' Susan laughed.

'All right, back to what I was saying. You must decide, Susan, what changes would be to the mill's advantage and not be talked into something that goes against your better judgment.'

'I do understand that.'

'Make time to read the journals, find out what is new and if it would be profitable in the long term. A time will come when you will need to install new machinery, nothing stands still. Occasionally, Susan, a calculated gamble is necessary to keep ahead of one's competitors. All this you will learn in time.' He sounded weary. 'Go now, Susan, I'll have a rest.'

Susan got to her feet, kissed her papa and left the room quietly.

So much was going through her head that she felt quite

dazed by it all. The need to be by herself, to go over in her own mind what Papa had said, was strong and taking a lightweight cape from the hallstand she went out into the warmth of the day. The old gardener, turning over the soil, raised his cap while the simple-looking youth with him watched Susan with his mouth hanging slack. She turned away hurriedly towards the tree-lined path with her head down. She was barely able to grasp at the enormity of the responsibility that would one day be hers. Everything was happening too quickly and it worried her. Such a short time ago she had been fighting to gain a small foothold in the mill and now she was to prepare to be at its head one day. Fervently she prayed that that day was far off. And of course it would be. Wasn't Papa getting stronger every day and just so long as he was there to advise – strange that he should feel this way about Edward, she mused. She, herself, had felt a bit apprehensive recently, in fact since Matthew had made his decision to become a farmer. Her stomach lurched. Hadn't she just of late had the distinct impression that Edward was smugly satisfied? And why not? With Matthew out of the way he must see himself as the future Master of Aranvale Papermill.

Dressed in a gown of pale green silk trimmed with gold thread, Susan looked both fresh and pretty. An unbroken night's sleep had left her refreshed, her colour was back and she was looking forward to the arrival of her cousin, Hannah, and her aunt and uncle.

When the carriage arrived with Mr and Mrs Forrester and their daughter, Hannah was first to fling herself into Susan's outstretched arms before Uncle George and Aunt Millie stepped into the hall and looked on with the amused indulgence of parents of an only child. Hannah was as tall as Susan but thin, shapeless and deeply concerned that her figure had failed to fill out despite repeated assurances from her mother that in time it would do so.

'Oh, it isn't fair,' Hannah wailed. 'Every time I see Susan I'm green with envy. Mama, how did you manage to produce such an ugly duckling?'

'Not an ugly duckling just a silly goose.' Susan laughed as she greeted her aunt and uncle. 'And just wait until you see your bridesmaid's dress, it's lovely and you may well steal the show.'

'Your Miss Beattie managed with the measurements?' Aunt Millie asked as she turned to embrace her sister who had just come into the hall.

'My apologies,' Sarah said as she moved from Millie's arms to turn her cheek for George's kiss. 'A small emergency in the kitchen which needed my personal attention. Come along to the sitting-room, it gets the sun at this time and while the meal is being prepared we can catch up on each other's news. The maid has just put a tray in and I'm sure a cup of tea will refresh you after your journey.' Gracefully she led the way and after the ladies were seated George sat down.

'Mama, Aunt Millie was asking about Hannah's measurements.'

'Miss Beattie managed with them. Incidentally she is coming with one of her assistants to Aran Heights for the final fittings. That is tomorrow but if Hannah needs more than one that can be arranged,' she said indulgently and with an upward glance as she poured tea and Susan handed it round.

'How is Hamish?'

'Very much better, Millie, I'm thankful to say, though nothing like his old self.' She sighed. 'One tries to be optimistic but I very much doubt if he ever will get his health fully back.'

'Rest and freedom from worry can work wonders,' George said in his kindly way then turned to Susan. 'Getting a bit nervous are you, Susan, now that the big day draws near?'

'I'm being kept so busy that I haven't time to be nervous.' She smiled.

'Really it's all been so sudden I don't know how you are managing, Sarah. I mean between the worry about Hamish and the preparations for the wedding. Even thinking about it and I'm exhausted.'

'It hasn't been easy but it was the only way to keep Hamish

calm. He worries about the mill you see, George,' she said, bringing her brother-in-law into the conversation, 'and he wants Edward as family as soon as possible.'

'What about cousin Matthew?' Hannah piped in.

'Yes, well, Hannah my dear, things don't always work out as we would like. Of course your Uncle Hamish would have preferred his own son in the mill but he has come to accept that Matthew would only be happy in farming.'

'It's decided then?' Millie enquired as she replaced her cup and declined a fill-up.

'Yes, Matthew is – oh, dear, this isn't quite official but there is the likelihood of an announcement soon and you are family – '

'That delightful girl, Caroline – '

'No, Millie, there was no serious attachment there,' Sarah said firmly. 'The young lady is Euan Clapperton's daughter, Winnie.'

'Never!' Millie's eyes widened with shock, then seeing Sarah's frown she hastened in with, 'I mean, Sarah, Matthew is such a good-looking and sophisticated young man and Winnie is – well – homely and hardly his type I would have thought.'

'Matthew's gorgeous,' Hannah said dreamily, 'and if I'd thought he would fall for someone plain like Winnie Clapperton I would have set my cap at him ages ago.'

They all laughed. 'Sarah, what am I to do with this child of mine, the outrageous things she comes away with?'

The arrival of the maid to announce that the meal was ready saved a reply.

Following her aunt, Susan thought how attractive she looked yet she must only spend a fraction of the money her mother spent on clothes. She was much slimmer, which gave her an immediate advantage but in colouring the sisters were alike and each had neat features. Hannah to her disgust had inherited her father's blunt features but this was in part compensated for by a bubbling personality.

George left most of the talking to the women but the way

his eyes rested on his wife and child it was easy to see he adored them.

With his sister-in-law George was never completely at ease, knowing that she had always considered him a poor match for her sister. Perhaps sensing this, Hamish was at pains to put him at his ease on the rare occasions the two met but even so George felt a bit out of his depth.

A snowy white damask cloth covered the long dining-room table and each place was set with the heavy silver cutlery which had been kept for special occasions in Hamish's parents' time but was now in daily use at Aran Heights. The empty chair at the head of the table emphasised the absence of the master of the house and all eyes went to it as they sat down.

'Hamish sends his apologies. Though getting up for longer periods each day he prefers to have lunch in his own room but you'll see him before you go,' Sarah explained as Polly and another maid began serving from the silver dishes.

'Will he be well enough to take Susan down the aisle?'

Sarah smiled. 'In his own words he'll be there to give his daughter in marriage as long as he can put one foot in front of the other.'

'Sounds as if he's anxious to get you married and off his hands, Susan,' George joked but the remark didn't bring forth laughter and Hannah's questioning eyes went to her cousin. In an unguarded moment she saw the bleakness in Susan's face and something like resignation.

'I can just imagine Hamish saying it in his dry way and Hannah, dear, you will remember Uncle Hamish tires easily and be on your best behaviour?'

Hannah looked outraged. 'I'm not a child, I know how to behave.'

'Of course you do,' Sarah said soothingly, 'and I know you're going to be a great help to Susan. With gifts coming in all the time it's so important not to get the cards mixed. You can write out the names and the gifts alongside and that way we'll have a double check.'

'All those thank-you letters,' Aunt Millie said feelingly. 'You have my sympathy, Susan. Lovely though it is to receive so many gifts, penning a note to each and trying to think of something new to say is bound to be a trial.'

'I'm afraid they will be all more or less the same.' Susan smiled.

'Men get it easy every time,' Hannah butted in. 'About all they have to do is put in an appearance at the wedding.'

'Shows how much you have to learn, young lady,' her father answered.

Later, when Hannah's parents departed, Susan accompanied her cousin to the guest bedroom nearest to her own and helped her unpack.

'Polly would have done this.'

'And have her see my wardrobe!'

'What's wrong with your wardrobe?'

'What's right with it?'

'Aunt Millie has excellent dress sense.'

'For herself but when it comes to buying for me,' she raised her eyes to heaven, 'you would think I was still in the schoolroom.'

Looking at the woebegone expression Susan wanted to giggle. Poor Hannah had such swings of moods. 'Tell you what, my gift to you for being bridesmaid and helping will be a new gown from Miss Beattie.'

'No!' Hannah was scandalised. 'You can't do that. Whatever would Aunt Sarah and my mama have to say and who would pay for it?'

'I will, otherwise it wouldn't be a gift from me, would it. I do have some money of my own. Aunt Rachel encouraged us to save so we got money for Christmas and birthdays with instructions that it was to go into the bank.'

'Lucky you.'

'That's not your real gift of course. Edward will have the pleasure of seeing to that and the bridesmaid's gift is usually a piece of jewellery.'

Hannah's eyes shone. 'Really, I had no idea.'

'And the gown, it will give me a lot of pleasure, so please no arguments.'

'You're a darling and I'm going to miss you, Susan,' she said, dangerously close to tears. 'Aran Heights won't be the same without you. I mean we're more than cousins – '

'I know,' Susan said gently, 'more like sisters.'

'And friends – '

'But not for long,' Susan joked, 'if you don't lift your idle hands and hang up your gowns while I put this underwear in the drawer.'

They got the job completed. 'Better put in an appearance downstairs.'

'Not yet, Susan, I want to ask you something.'

'Ask away then.'

'Everyone expected you and Edward to make a match of it one day.'

'But not you, Hannah?'

'Don't get me wrong,' she said hastily, 'Edward is nice and good husband material as Mama once said.' She caught Susan's eye and they both giggled. 'But I thought you would fall in love with someone new who would be gorgeous and exciting.'

'Edward can be very entertaining,' she said lamely.

'Hardly the same.' The freckles stood out on her pale skin and her face was deadly serious. 'Edward loves you, no doubt about that but then who wouldn't, you're so lovely. You're not in love with him and I'm so afraid for you.' She paused and whispered, 'What happens if one day you fall in love, deeply in love and you're married to Edward?'

'That won't happen and the only reason I'm not dancing about with excitement is because Papa has been so desperately ill.'

'And desperate to see you married to Edward,' she said quietly. 'You're marrying Edward to please Uncle Hamish and you can't deny that, not to me.'

To change the conversation Susan said, 'Edward's cousin is to be best man.'

'What's he like?'

'I don't know, I haven't met him but Edward is bringing Samuel – Samuel Hargreaves is his name – to Aran Heights tomorrow evening to meet everybody and you in particular. All I can tell you is he's two years younger than Edward, very shy and apprehensive about his duties as best man. Edward, I may say, is looking to you to bring him out of his shell.'

'He won't like me, young men don't because I haven't got a bosom.'

'Hannah! For goodness sake!' she exploded. 'Whatever will you come away with next?'

'It's all right for you saying that but I'm as flat as a pancake.'

'Nonsense! You do have a little. Don't you?'

'Hardly any.'

'There's still time to develop, you're only seventeen.'

'All my friends have bosoms. Katie, you know Katie, she's quite magnificent.'

'I don't agree. Last time I saw her I thought she looked top-heavy.'

Hannah let our a squeal of laughter. 'If she fell flat on her face she'd bounce back, is that what you mean?'

'It is not, you horrible creature.' Arm-in-arm they went downstairs to find Sarah ordering the servants to be careful how they carried the wedding gifts through to the room made over for that purpose.

'At last! I was beginning to wonder when you two were to show face. Now that you are here you can open these gifts carefully and take a note of the senders.'

'We'll do that, Mama and we'll be very careful. Matthew's late isn't he?'

'No, he told me he'd be delayed. There are a few acres of land adjoining Moorend that have just come on the market. Euan had his eye on it and the farmhouse. It was to be his wedding present but your papa will have none of it. Apparently Matthew is to get his inheritance now so that he can offer for it himself.'

'I think Papa's right and Matthew will be happier about it too. He'll want to stand on his own feet rather than have everything handed to him from his in-laws-to-be.'

A touch of anger crossed Sarah's face. 'Euan is not blind

to that, Susan, though why any of this should be a problem I can't understand. It is no different from John Brodie giving Thomas and his wife the Laurels as a wedding gift and I imagine Edward will be treated with the same generosity.'

'You're wrong there, Mama. As the younger son Edward will get a lot less.'

She looked surprised. 'Perhaps you're right. Your papa wouldn't have differentiated between Ralph and Matthew but then John has his own ways and maybe feels the younger son is not entitled to the same amount,' she said vaguely.

'Edward resents it, I do know that.'

'Hardly surprising but with all this talk you nearly put it out of my mind.'

'What?'

'Rumour has it that the Templetons will have to sell.'

'That won't alter anything, it's only temporary as far as we are concerned.'

'I shouldn't bank on that.'

'I haven't even seen the house,' Susan said indignantly, 'and I think I should have some say in the matter.'

'Don't be silly, of course you've seen it.'

'From the outside and I've always thought it very low-lying and there can't be many rooms.'

'Compared to what Edward and you have been used to of course it is small,' Sarah said patiently, 'but adequate to start off with. In any case Edward and you can come to your own decision.'

'He's coming over tomorrow so we can see over Hillview then.' Susan turned to Hannah. 'You must come too and meet the best man. Edward is bringing Samuel.'

'I'd love to come.'

The following day was packed with activity, everyone dashing around and getting in each other's way. Miss Beattie and her assistant set to with a will and, satisfied that the bridal gown and the mother-of-the-bride's outfit were perfect in every detail, turned their attention to the bridesmaid.

Standing before the mirror with Miss Beattie rearranging

the bodice to add fullness and a nimble-fingered assistant undoing the tacking thread where it failed to please the critical eye of Miss Beattie, Hannah was turned this way and that.

Susan had chosen her favourite shade of blue for the bridesmaid's dress. The material was a fine taffeta with a delicately raised flower pattern decorating the skirt. Appreciating Hannah's shortcomings, Miss Beattie had deftly added darts to the ruched bodice and a suggestion of a bustle to give her a new shapeliness.

'Is that quite comfortable?' Miss Beattie mumbled, her mouth full of pins.

'Yes, thank you, but even if it weren't I'd suffer gladly to look like this.' Then turning to the bride, 'Susan, it really looks as if there is a bosom under all this.'

'You look lovely,' Susan said gently.

'I do, don't I? Mama won't recognise her daughter and from now on I'm going to refuse to wear those ghastly girlish gowns she buys me.'

'Now! Now! Hannah, I heard that,' her aunt said as she returned to the fitting-room.

'Well, it's true, Aunt Sarah and you should have a word with my mama. She may listen to you.'

The assistant's mouth quirked and Miss Beattie, her mouth now free of pins gave her tinkle of a laugh.

'Don't ever think of yourself as thin. You are slim which is a much more attractive description. Stout and heavy-hipped young ladies have difficulty in camouflaging their figure faults and never totally succeed. You, on the other hand, require no more than a stiffener in the bodice and some padding at the hips.'

'That's an expert's opinion, Hannah, so stop complaining.'

'No more complaints, Susan, I promise,' she said with a faint flush on her usually pale cheeks.

Earlier in the day Susan had spoken to her mother about her wish to give Hannah a gown from Miss Beattie's collection and was rewarded with a smile.

'How very thoughtful of you, dear. Hannah does have a genuine grievance and Millie is not good at selecting clothes for her. Once you're on your honeymoon I'll arrange a visit to Miss Beattie and if Millie doesn't get on her high horse I'll chose a day gown for Hannah as well. Millie most certainly won't accept anything for herself.'

'She doesn't need to, Mama, she dresses beautifully,'

'And fortunate for her that she can get away with buying from the cheaper stores. Your Uncle George doesn't have the money to allow for the small luxuries we take for granted.' She sniffed. 'If I live to be a hundred I'll never know why she married George Forrester.'

'Mama, they are very happy and it shows.'

'Happy! She could have been rich and happy. Your aunt had looks, still has and she could so easily have been the wife of a very distinguished gentleman instead of throwing herself away. There was plenty of opposition to George from your grandparents but she just went ahead and married him.'

'That must have taken a lot of courage.'

'Stupidity more like.'

Susan said no more but she wondered if her mother had switched her affections to the son and heir of the Aranvale Papermill and had chosen for greater security. That she had been a good and faithful wife was not in dispute but there had been that uncharacteristic outburst from her papa that had shown all too clearly that Euan Clapperton was still a shadow between them.

Like her father, Susan had a great love of the stark, almost savage beauty of Aran Heights and though she found Hillview a pleasant enough house and the gardens attractive she was by no means taken with it. The others were loud in its praise and she smiled and nodded as the elderly housekeeper took them on an inspection of the house. Susan and Edward went ahead, leaving Hannah and Samuel to follow.

Samuel was a slight, very young-looking man with fair-ish, wispy hair, skin that flushed easily and eyelashes so fair that one had to look closely to discover if he had any at all. For Hannah it had been an uphill job getting through his painful shyness but she was getting there and discovering behind it an interesting and intelligent young man.

After a thorough inspection of the rooms and a look in at the servants' quarters, Edward declared himself satisfied and looked to Susan for agreement.

'As a temporary home it seems perfectly suitable and it has the advantage of not being too far from the mill.'

'Just what I thought,' he said eagerly, then becoming aware of the housekeeper hovering nearby he gave her a dismissive nod and a murmured 'thank you.'

She inclined her head, opened the vestibule door, waited for them to enter, closed it then crossed the floor to the main door. With it open she stood stiffly. Susan smiled her thanks as did Hannah. Samuel for all his shyness said, 'Thank you for all the trouble you've taken.' Edward gave another nod then they were all outside and into the fresh air. As they walked down the stone steps to the gravel drive they heard the bolts being shot into place.

'Hannah and Samuel, would you mind making yourselves scarce? Susan and I have matters to discuss.'

'Delighted to oblige,' Hannah said pertly. 'We shall inspect the gardens and don't hurry on our behalf,' she called back as Samuel, greatly daring, touched her elbow, hesitated and immediately Hannah slipped her arm in his.

'Wonders will never cease, we've all but despaired of Samuel but then possibly he's never met anyone like Hannah.'

'Interesting to see if it develops.' Susan smiled.

Reaching the summer house Edward flicked his handkerchief over the seat before allowing Susan to sit down, then joined her. 'I'm glad you like Hillview,' he smiled, taking her hand in his and separating her fingers with his own.

'As a temporary home.'

'Only as a temporary home?'

Her tone sharpened. 'Edward, is there something I should know?'

He nodded uncomfortably. 'Susan, there are some decisions that have to be made quickly without time for discussion.' Her eyes didn't move from his face. 'The thing is the

Templetons have decided to let Hillview go and a quick sale without the trouble and expense of putting it on the market would suit them very well.'

'I see.'

'Our solicitor got the price down provided it was an immediate acceptance.'

'So Hillview is ours whether I like it or not.'

'But you've just said you like it.'

'Only because I assumed it to be a temporary dwelling.'

'What don't you like about it?' She could hear the barely suppressed anger.

'It's too small and it has no character.'

'No doubt we could make alterations, add another wing but I fail to see how that would be necessary until we start a family.'

'Perhaps this is the time to tell you, Edward, that I intend continuing to assist Papa with the paperwork and that means I shall require a room where I can work undisturbed and my desk and other necessary working equipment will have to be brought from Aran Heights.'

'What nonsense you do talk, Susan.' His eyes glittered with anger and he was having difficulty in hiding his impatience. 'Foolishly, in my opinion, very foolishly, your father weakened and gave in to your whim but that ceases now. There will be no question of you continuing in any capacity whatsoever. My future father-in-law has already expressed his confidence in me – indeed Matthew being permitted to follow his own inclinations bears proof to that.' The ready colour suffused his face as he went on. 'I am not disputing your ability, far from it, but for a woman and a young woman at that to be involved in business is ludicrous.'

He had made an attempt to laugh it off but one look at her set face and his laugh took on a hollow sound.

'Edward,' Susan said in a dangerously quiet voice, 'you are quite mistaken. Papa made it clear to me as recently as two days ago that it was his wish that I continue to take a part in the management of the mill.'

'Management! Really, Susan, I gave you credit for some

sense. Your father is ill and rambling on. It takes some people that way and later they have no recollection of saying any such thing. What do you know about management? You've never as much as stepped inside the mill.'

'That isn't to say I won't one day,' she said spiritedly.

A little alarmed at the way things were going, Edward put his arm round her waist drawing her near but she kept her back rigidly straight.

'I see I'm going to have quite a time taming you, my love, but I'm rather looking forward to the experience. Nothing more do I enjoy than a challenge and two await me.'

She looked at him quickly.

'The smooth running and greater prosperity of the mill will be my first aim then taming the lovely creature very soon to be mine will be second.'

Susan shivered and thinking it was caused by the cooler breeze which had sprung up his hold tightened.

'If you're getting cold we'll go in a few minutes but we came here to discuss Hillview and we've rather strayed from that. Truly I do regret that it had to be a snap decision but I was awkwardly placed.' He frowned. 'Instead of the cheque I expected, my parents decided that Hillview would be their wedding gift to us.'

'I didn't know that, Edward, and I do apologise. Indeed there was little else you could do and of course it is extremely generous of them.'

'I'm glad you think so, I certainly don't,' he said bitterly. 'Compared to the Laurels I would say Hillview is modest in the extreme but of course good enough for the younger son.'

'Edward,' she said gently, 'try to think of it this way. If you had been the elder son would you have expected an equal share with Thomas?'

'Maybe not but Thomas is not a natural leader.'

'Whereas you are?'

'Yes, I am and Father, if he weren't so blind, would see that.'

Feeling sorry for him but sorry too for Thomas who must find it difficult to give orders to someone so unwilling to take them, her eyes softened. 'We'll be quite comfortable at Hillview and I'm sorry that I was so awkward.'

'Understandable,' he said generously, 'and to be honest I had thought with a decent cheque from both families we could have bought something superior.'

'My parents haven't said what their gift will be but in all likelihood it will be money and with it we can furnish Hillview.' She smiled. 'Once we have our own choice of furnishings the house will look very different.'

'You'll see to that side of things and you know, Susan, when we are married your days will be completely occupied with your wifely duties.' He paused and smiled. 'That means doing all you can to give comfort and pleasure to your husband.' It was said teasingly but there was no doubt that he meant what he said.

Susan swallowed hard and held herself in check. Now wasn't the time but later Edward must be made to understand. In fact it might be better coming from Papa. Edward would not dare raise objections if it was voiced by Papa that she was to have a hand in the management of the mill. She shook her head. No, Papa must not be worried, this was something she had to do herself. With shrewd insight she knew that if anything happened to Papa Edward would do all in his power to shut her out, keep her away from the mill.

Just then Hannah, accompanied by a more relaxed-looking Samuel, strolled into view and stood on the terrace facing the summer house. They had been intending to descend the steps but at sight of Susan and Edward, their heads close together and apparently deep in conversation, checked themselves and turned away.

Susan sprang up, anxious to be gone. 'Let's go, Edward. Hannah and Samuel have been very patient but we should be getting back to Aran Heights.'

He rose but reluctantly and tucked her arm into his. 'Very well, but we do have more to discuss.'

'Such as?'

'Our honeymoon.'

'That was the last thing on Susan's mind. 'Edward, just a

few days, please; the way Papa is I don't want to be away any longer.'

'I can understand that, my dear, and since it is to be just a few days what about Edinburgh?'

'Or Helensburgh? When we were children we had lovely holidays there.'

'Then Helensburgh it is.'

'Thank you, Edward.'

A warm breeze wafted in the open bedroom window and caressed Susan's face. Leaning over the sill she watched the moon peeking out from between the dark sombre hills and felt the tears sting the back of her eyes. Tonight she would sleep in this room for the last time, the room that had been hers for all the years she could remember. Slowly she turned, went over to the bed and undressed. Between the cool sheets she lay with her hands behind her head and looked across to the wardrobe. On top was her collection of dolls looking at her with their beady eyes and on the shelf the little knick-knacks, inexpensive gifts from Ralph and Matthew, chosen so carefully and paid for out of their pocket money. Poor, poor Ralph, once so full of life and now lying in the family burial ground behind the kirk where tomorrow she would take the solemn vows of marriage – to love, honour and obey.

Oh, Ralph, Susan wept silently, if only you had been spared none of this would be necessary. Below the sheet her hand clenched and unclenched. Soon her body would belong to Edward and she felt herself recoiling from what that meant. Yet maybe Mama was right and love would grow out of liking. But if it didn't – she closed her eyes and drifted into an uneasy sleep.

She awoke as the house began to stir and, throwing back the bedcovers, padded over to the window and parted the curtains. Down in the courtyard the horses were being groomed and she could hear the mingled sounds of men and beasts. With her head resting against the cool windowpane Susan looked up at the sky and the dark, ominous clouds and wondered if it were an omen. Happy the bride the sun shines on.

After a freshen-up Susan put on her clothes, pulling over her head the gown lying to hand. That she was expected to breakfast in bed she knew but she wasn't hungry. She would go down for tea and toast. When she reached the breakfast-room Matthew was alone. The porridge plate was empty and he was tucking into eggs and crispy bacon.

'Susan! Good morning!' he said, springing up to give his sister a bear-like hug. 'Surely you're breaking with tradition. The bride should be breakfasting in bed, her every whim catered for.'

'I couldn't lie any longer.'

'Then allow me to do the honours,' he said, standing to attention, a white napkin draped over his arm. 'Pray what is her ladyship's pleasure?'

Susan gave a nervous giggle. 'Stop fooling, Matthew, I'm not in the mood and if you want to be helpful, toast please but nothing cooked.'

'Never get through the day on that. Bet Edward's enjoying a hearty breakfast,' he leered.

Levelling a dark look at him she stretched over for a few fingers of toast. 'You can pour me some tea.'

'Certainly.' They both turned as the door opened and Mrs MacFarlane came in followed by Hannah, her hair hanging limp though she had pinned it up the previous night.

'Good morning, Mother and cousin Hannah,' Matthew said with exaggerated formality.

'Susan,' her mother said severely, 'you should be in bed taking all the rest you can.'

'No, really, I'm better up.' She looked over to the window. 'Not a blink of sunshine.'

'I know, it's very disappointing.' Mrs MacFarlane sighed.

'That was the one thing Mother was unable to organise,' Matthew said cheekily.

The mother of the bride knew that there would be great excitement in Aranvale and disappointment at the dullness

125

of the day. The MacFarlanes were Aranvale and the entire village and beyond would be lining the route to the kirk. The outfit of every guest would be remarked upon and discussed while the bride's gown would be remembered and talked about for a long time. None would be disappointed, Mrs MacFarlane had been determined upon that.

'Polly's on her way up to you with a tray, Susan,' her cousin stated.

'Hannah, dear, you go up and tell her.'

'All right, Aunt Sarah,' Hannah said, darting out of the door.

'Has Susan eaten, Matthew? She seems to be just picking these days.'

'Mama, I'm quite capable of speaking for myself.' She shot Matthew a warning look. 'I've had a good breakfast.'

'I'm very glad to hear it. Ah! there you are, Hannah.'

'She's taking it back to the kitchen and I suggested she bring fresh toast and replenish the bacon. I'm famished.'

'Can't have the bridesmaid fainting for lack of sustenance.' Matthew grinned.

'Aunt Sarah, you'll have to do something about that boy,' Hannah said primly as the maid arrived with more bacon and a basket of toast.

'Rather late for that, dear,' her aunt said absently as she studied Hannah's hair. 'A session with the tongs for you. As soon as you've had breakfast see the hairdresser and have yours done first.'

'Goodness is she here already?'

'Yes, Susan, she's here and so is Miss Beattie's assistant to help us dress.'

'That include me?'

'Matthew, will you stop it.'

'Bet he won't be so chirpy when it's his big day.'

'Men have fewer worries on these occasions, Hannah, and yes, please, I'll have a finger of toast though I doubt if I can eat anything.' She put a hand to her head. 'Did someone mention the weather?'

'Mother, we've already dealt with that subject.'

She took a drink of tea and clattered the cup back on the saucer. 'I never closed an eye last night for going over everything and I just know there is something I've forgotten,' she said worriedly.

'Not much you can do about it now,' Matthew said cheerfully.

'I get sick when I'm excited,' Hannah announced as she carefully put down her knife and fork on the empty plate.

'You're not going to be – '

'No, no, it doesn't always happen, thought I'd just mention it.'

Matthew got up. 'This is all getting too much for me, I'll go and see how Father is bearing up.'

'You'll do no such thing. I'll go up presently.'

'Mama, I hope all this excitement isn't going to put him back.'

'It won't. He's had a sharp lesson and with Dr Sullivan at the wedding we can all relax.'

'I've had a peep into the dining-room and it looks absolutely gorgeous.'

'Thank you, Hannah. The hotel will do the main catering but relatives and close friends will end up here.'

Hannah was over at the window. 'There's a glimmer of sun.'

'I'm quite sure it'll clear up to a fine day and now, Hannah, please, see about that hair of yours.'

'Goodness, yes.' She bolted.

'That child is in a state of nerves and you are far too composed, Susan. It is your wedding day.'

As if I didn't know, Susan thought resentfully. 'Better to stay calm, surely.'

'Yes, I'm sure it is but few brides manage it. While Hannah gets her hair seen to we'll go along to the sitting-room and have a little talk.' Suddenly her mother looked uncomfortable. 'This is all such a dreadful rush and so different from what I would have wanted for you. Has Papa mentioned our gift to you and Edward?'

'Not exactly – '

'Our reason for delaying,' she interrupted, 'was because we thought both families would share the cost of buying and furnishing a home for you. Your papa was most upset about the purchase of Hillview. Like you he thought it suitable until something larger and more prestigious came on the market.'

'You were in favour of Hillview.'

'That's true, I find it quite charming but then I don't see any advantage in a huge barn of a place. Your father had Aran Heights built and I had no say in the matter. Something smaller and cosier would have suited me; however that is beside the point. Our wedding gift to you is to be money, a substantial sum. Your papa has been very generous but he'll tell you about it himself.'

Susan swallowed the lump in her throat. 'Everyone has been so good and as for Aunt Rachel – ' She shook her head and her eyes misted.

'Matthew and you are all she has and she wanted you to have the benefit of the money before she is kicking up the daisies – her words, I need hardly tell you.'

'And as for you, Mama, you've done so much and I am very grateful.'

Her mother's eyes swam.

'What have I said? What is the matter?'

'Nothing, I'm just being silly.' She sniffed into a wisp of handkerchief. 'I didn't think it would affect me so much – you getting married then Matthew so soon after. Aran Heights is going to be so quiet, just your papa and – and he isn't always the best of company.' She blew her nose and managed to look both aggrieved and sorrowful. 'I'll be virtually alone, he'll take himself off to the library or hide behind his newspaper.'

'Mama, I'll need you,' she said gently, 'You've reminded me often enough about how little I know about supervising the housekeeping.'

'With cause.' She brightened. 'I'd enjoy that and I must say the staff at Hillview are not acceptable now that it is to be your permanent home. That dour-faced housekeeper has to go.'

'I entirely agree.' Susan breathed a sigh of relief. 'May I leave it to you?'

'Yes.'

'I'd very much like to take Polly with me. It would be one known face and I like her.'

'That could be arranged I'm sure. Mrs Dunbar will train one of the others to replace her.'

'Thank you.'

Mrs MacFarlane looked at the clock. 'We still have a few minutes. Susan, there are things I haven't mentioned, not forgotten, just that I considered it unnecessary.' She paused and her eyes went beyond Susan as if she were addressing the wall. 'Don't worry too much about what will take place, you understand what I mean. Before I married your papa I knew nothing at all and I don't believe it mattered. Just accept that it is something you have to put up with.'

Susan felt her colour rising and wished she could escape but her mother was still addressing the wall. 'To begin with you may experience – embarrassment, awkwardness but that is quite normal.' She frowned. 'I'm not making a very good job of this but I wanted to put your mind at rest and free from worry.' At last she removed her eyes from the wall and settled them on Susan's face.

'It's all right, Mama,' Susan mumbled.

Glad to have that out of the way, Mrs MacFarlane picked up a sheet of paper, neatly ruled off at various points, put on her spectacles and studied the writing.

'This is my timetable which I do need if things are to run smoothly.'

'Don't worry, Mama, they will.'

'I sincerely hope so.' She smiled. 'Off you go, dear and lie down for half an hour. I'll get my hair done next and let's hope the tongs have made some difference to Hannah's locks.'

# CHAPTER TEN

T he rain, never far away, had kept off and a weak sun
   showed behind the clouds as carriage after carriage drew
up at the Aranvale kirk where that morning professional hands
had arranged the magnificent floral display. The guests,
smiling and murmuring among themselves, were shown into
the pews by the ushers.

His music in place, the organist began playing a selection of
church music while fashionably dressed ladies and handsomely
attired gentlemen nodded to acquaintances before carefully
seating themselves.

At a hidden signal the organist ended his recital, flexed his
fingers and crashed into the rousing tune of the Bridal March.
Susan, pale and lovely, walked slowly down the aisle on her
father's arm while the bridesmaid, pretty in blue, showed her
nervousness in the way her teeth caught at her lower lip.

Holding himself stiffly erect Hamish looked straight ahead.
Susan could hear the wheeziness from his chest and unconsciously she tightened her hold on his arm as they walked
down the red-carpeted aisle to where the minister in his
robes and holding the bible watched their progress. The
groom stood easily, a smile on his lips, as he watched the
bridal procession in the mirror above the organ. The best
man was beside him standing rigidly to attention.

That she felt so calm amazed Susan. It was almost as
though she were a spectator at her own wedding. At every
stage of the way villagers craned their necks for a better view
of the bride. Rather than the traditional white Miss Beattie
had suggested a cream shade would be more flattering with
Susan's fairness. The rich material had an embossed pattern
of roses and the style had been kept simple. As always

Miss Beattie's creations were understated, depending for their elegance almost completely on the cut of the material. Her advice had also been taken on what would be the most suitable hairstyle and the hairdresser, working to a sketch, had swept Susan's hair high on her head with tendrils of curls escaping at the brow and at her ears to soften the effect. Firmly set into the thick fair hair nestled a silver and pearl headdress and flowing from it the long veil in exquisite lace which had been handed down to brides on her mother's side of the family.

As Hamish MacFarlane moved away to join his wife in the first pew Edward turned to get his first proper look at his bride. She smiled and she saw him swallow as if the sight of such loveliness had momentarily affected him.

Clearing his throat the minister began the solemn task of joining the two young people in holy matrimony. In a break in the sing-song voice he raised an eyebrow to Samuel who hastily reached into his pocket for the ring.

She was married! She was Mrs Edward Brodie and suddenly the uncertainties and anguish of the last few weeks were swept away in a flurry of excitement. Edward loved her and suddenly she felt a rush of real affection, perhaps it was even love, for the man who was now her husband.

In the large reception room at the Grand Hotel in Airdrie, the market town nearest to Aranvale, bride and groom stood together to receive the good wishes and congratulations from the long line of guests while waitresses circulated with trays of glasses and discreet enquiries as to the preferred drink. Hamish MacFarlane, without a flicker of annoyance, obeyed Dr Sullivan and sat down in one of the red plush chairs carried over by a waiter. That the occasion was taking a lot out of him was noticed and later remarked upon.

'Papa, are you quite sure that you're all right?'

'Just fine, Susan. Don't worry about me.' He took her hand in his and she saw that his eyes were moist. 'There was never a bonnier bride,' he said unsteadily, 'and no father could be prouder than I am this day.'

She kissed him. Then it was mother and daughter hugging

each other in an unusual display of affection. All the while Edward was smilingly accepting congratulations on winning such a prize. After her new in-laws it was Matthew's turn with a quietly radiant Winnie at his side.

'Be happy, Susan,' Matthew said huskily, 'and Edward, you look after my sister or you'll have me to reckon with.' There was banter but seriousness behind it.

'Your sister is in safe hands, Matthew,' he said, putting his arm around his wife and drawing her close.

Winnie hugged her. 'You look beautiful and I know you are going to be very happy.' Then she turned to Hannah. 'You're looking very pretty.'

'Thank you.' Her eyes went to Winnie in her lovely rose pink gown, her hair softly waved and a tell-tale flush on her cheeks. 'You look quite marvellous yourself.' Then she grinned. 'Just shows what we plain ones can do when we try.'

Mrs MacFarlane had heard and said in a shocked voice, 'Hannah, that was a dreadful thing to say.'

'I'm sorry, have I offended you, Winnie?'

'Not in the least.' Winnie laughed good-naturedly. 'Being outspoken myself I can hardly complain about it in others.'

After the wedding feast where champagne flowed like water the best man rose to his feet and amid much laughter stood silently until the noise stopped.

With the help of a few notes and an encouraging smile from the bridesmaid, Samuel delivered a well-prepared and fitting speech before sitting down to a storm of applause. Then the bride's father rose and there was a stillness in the room. All eyes were on the man who had aged so suddenly in the last months. An excellent speaker, it came as a shock to those seated away from the top table that they had to strain to hear his words.

He spoke without notes. First he welcomed the guests then went on to describe incidents in his daughter's early life which had obviously amused him at the time though he had been at pains to disguise it. Susan's lips twitched; she was remembering being severely chastised along with Matthew and in the shared memory brother and sister caught each other's eye and grinned.

After the laughter Mr MacFarlane bent down to take a sip from his glass then turned to Edward. 'My wife and I feel we are not losing a daughter, Edward, but rather gaining another son.' There was some clapping and he waited until it had died down. 'Our daughter is very precious to us and now she belongs to you, Edward and I know that you will love and protect her. May God bless you both and give you many years of happiness together.' He picked up his glass. 'Ladies and gentlemen, will you be upstanding and join me in a toast.'

The guests rose. The murmur went round. 'Susan and Edward.'

After the applause Edward got to his feet and in a firm and clear voice began, 'On behalf of my wife and . . .'

It was all over. A good many of the guests had driven to Aran Heights and were now on the lawn as the newlyweds made their escape through a shower of rice and rose petals. Edward had changed from his formal wedding suit into a perfectly tailored lightweight grey. For her going-away outfit Susan had favoured a peacock blue skirt and jacket and under the jacket a cream lacy-patterned blouse with a plain neckline and a double string of cultured pearls. Perched on her head was a saucy feathered hat in the same shade of blue. The maids were clustered at an upstairs window and seeing them Susan gave a wave.

The bride and groom were in the coach taking them to the station. Looking frail and tired Mr MacFarlane lifted his hand in farewell with his wife protectively by his side.

Edward frowned. 'You look worried.'

'I am, Edward, Papa looked exhausted.'

'Hardly surprising, it was quite an occasion after all, but a good night's sleep and I'm sure he'll be all right.' He paused and added, 'Regarding the mill your father can stop worrying. After all I have a lot more to offer than Matthew.'

Susan was nettled at his high-handed dismissal of Matthew.

'Matthew has worked very hard since Papa's illness,' she said sharply.

His mouth touched hers in a light kiss. 'He did what he could but I intend increasing profits,'

'My father won't want changes.'

'Don't worry your pretty head, I'll do nothing to upset your father.'

Susan was becoming increasingly uneasy. 'As long as my father draws breath he'll make the decisions and he means me to be involved.'

'I hadn't forgotten but a sick man does not always make wise decisions and that is when the business is most at risk, but I intend minimising those risks. Anyway this is us,' he said briskly as they stopped outside the station.

The newlyweds and those others travelling first class enjoyed a comfortable journey with soft leather seats to cushion the jolts and jerks, but for the third-class passengers huddled together in the overcrowded wooden-seated compartments it was a different story, though judging by the hilarity they didn't seem to mind.

A horse and carriage belonging to the Imperial Hotel stood outside the station awaiting Susan and Edward and on their approach the coachman lifted his hat and opened the door for them to climb in. Susan arranged herself in a corner and Edward moved up beside her. The luggage was put in beside the driver and then they were off.

Earlier Susan had wondered if she'd made a mistake suggesting Helensburgh. The resort on the north bank of the Clyde offered little more than pleasant walks and beautiful scenery whereas in Edinburgh, as Edward had suggested, the evenings could have been filled with a visit to the theatre or a concert.

Soon they joined the procession of coaches heading towards the seafront and at one point the coach lurched perilously over a deep rut in the road and Edward muttered a string of mild expletives.

Susan turned to him and burst out laughing. 'That was naughty, Edward.'

'I know. My humble – ' but he didn't finish. Instead he cupped his hands around her face and gently, oh, so gently, kissed her mouth. The moment was so tender, so unexpected that it brought the hot stinging tears to her eyes.

'Tears, Susan, surely not?'

'Tears of happiness, Edward,' Susan said tremulously. 'We are going to be happy, aren't we?'

'How else could it be?'

She nodded, her spirits lifting more by the minute. Edward was a dear, at least most of the time he was. If only he would be more understanding about the mill and her place in it. Still, she wasn't going to think about that and spoil their honeymoon.

Perched on a rocky hill overlooking the Gareloch the Imperial Hotel enjoyed the finest view in Helensburgh but the steep hill put a strain on horse and coachman. Inwardly relieved that they had made it to the top, Susan got out and inhaled the fresh, clean air. The porters busied themselves with the baggage but Susan was in no hurry to go indoors. There was a pleasant cooling breeze and tucking her arm in Edward's she looked about her with interest.

'Edward, do you know how Helensburgh got its name?'

'No, but then I was never curious enough to ask.'

'Then let me complete your education. Sir James Colquhoun designed Helensburgh and named it after his wife. Wasn't that lovely?'

'Who gave you that gem of information?' he teased.

'Papa. Matthew used to complain that no matter where we went Papa always made a history lesson of it.'

The room they were to share was large with a four-poster bed and immediately they were on their own Edward settled his weight on it and declared himself satisfied. Susan was embarrassed and to hide it she admired the bowl of flowers on the dressing-table. Mingling with their scent was a faint aroma of beeswax coming from the polished furniture.

Edward opened the communicating door to a dressing-room. 'I'll make use of this, Susan. Do you want a maid to help you unpack?'

'No, thank you, that won't be necessary. Incidentally what time do we go down for dinner?'

'Just as soon as we are ready. Feeling peckish, are you?'

'Yes, I ate very little at the reception.'

Susan hung up her gowns and was grateful to Edward for respecting her privacy. He was to change in the dressing-room. She had already decided what to wear and had spread out on the bed the pale blue gown with the tiny sprigs of white flowers decorating the skirt.

Edward's eyes rested on his wife approvingly as they went down the graceful stairway and across the panelled hall to the dining-room. Soft music was playing and there was a quiet elegance everywhere from the delicate, wrought-iron chandeliers to the large gilt-framed mirrors on each wall.

'You look beautiful, my darling,' Edward whispered. 'In fact I think that we look a really handsome couple.'

'I saw you admiring yourself in the mirror,' she teased.

'Wrong, I was admiring us, my dear.'

Some guests were already dining and eyes were briefly raised from the food to follow the attractive couple who were being shown to a window table. The service was pleasantly unhurried to allow time between courses and the appreciation of good food.

After a delicious meal which they both enjoyed they rose and went outside for a breath of fresh air. When it grew too cold for comfort they went in and sat in the lounge until Edward looked pointedly at the clock.

'Yes, it is getting late,' Susan agreed and wished her colour hadn't risen. She was all but sure by the quiet smiles on the faces of the few remaining guests that they realised they were on their honeymoon.

Edward was undressing in the adjoining room and giving her ample time to be in the big four-poster bed. In her lovely, lace-trimmed, shell pink nightdress Susan looked like a bride.

Only she didn't feel like one. How could she? She should have been coming to her husband as a virgin and what if he suspected? After all he would be looking for the proof of her innocence and when there was none what would be his thoughts? That some violent exercise when she was young or something of the sort was responsible? Yes, of course Edward would think that. She shivered. What if he ever found out the truth? But how could he? David Cameron was no longer in Aranvale, she had found that out, and there was no chance of their paths crossing.

The door opened and Edward came through in his silk dressing-gown. Susan smiled from her side of the bed, successfully hiding her nervousness.

Her fears were unfounded. Edward was gentle with her, taking no more than she was prepared to give and she was caught in conflicting emotions. She didn't want to remember David Cameron but couldn't stop herself. Though she looked back on that day with self-loathing she remembered how natural it had seemed, a drawing together of two people caught up in a passion that was too strong for them. She wondered if it had been David's first time.

With Edward there had been no gaucheness, indeed she supposed him a skilful lover and only experience, she decided, could have made him that. It made her realise how little she knew of the real Edward. The boy she had partnered on so many occasions was far removed from the sophisticated and worldly man to whom she was married. The thought of those other women did disturb her, then she tried to dismiss them. Young men were expected to sow their wild oats before they married and settled down and Edward was a man of the world but now that he had a wife all that would stop. Susan vowed to herself there and then that she would do all in her power to make Edward happy, be a good wife to him and by doing so make up for her wrongdoing.

On the evening before their departure a charity ball was being held in the hotel and for the occasion Susan decided to wear her golden yellow gown. As she began her preparations she was smiling happily. Helensburgh had been a good choice after all. Edward had said so and he had enjoyed the walks as much as she had. Best of all had been the tramp over the moors, an easy tramp, and at the end of it the unbelievable beauty of Loch Lomond. Her colour heightened as she remembered how Edward had folded his arms around her and she had leaned into him. In those moments surrounded by such beauty she had wanted Edward as much as he wanted her and only the sound of distant voices had prevented them making love in the soft grass near the banks of the loch.

'What are you smiling about?' Edward asked as he came through from his dressing-room.

'Pleasant thoughts, Edward, that's all,' she said as she made another attempt with the hooks. 'Do me up, please, dear, I can't get them in.' She held in her breath until he had the last one in place.

'My darling wife, your dressmaker hasn't left much room for manoeuvre. Not that I'm complaining; it accentuates your curves and I'm sure every male in the ballroom will wish himself in my shoes.'

'Flatterer,' she said, but as she said it she felt the first twinge of unease. The gown had fitted comfortably. Miss Beattie wouldn't have let it pass otherwise. Forcing the uneasiness to the back of her mind she whirled round, eager for his approval. 'This is Mama's favourite.'

'Mine too I think. You look ravishing,' he said softly.

The ball was an occasion that brought out the top families. Away from the dance floor and fanning themselves, the more elderly ladies eyed the young, perhaps remembering with nostalgia when they too had danced the night away before age and its accompanying weaknesses had taken over their bodies. Ruby and diamond necklaces gleamed and glistened between the fleshy folds of their aristocratic necks or hung disconsolately from a scrawny stem.

It was a colourful scene with so many beautiful gowns. Susan and Edward made a handsome couple as they circled the floor in time to the orchestra playing from a raised platform. Having danced together on many occasions their steps fitted perfectly and many eyes followed their progress. Though her gown came in for a lot of admiration it was the girl herself who caused something of a sensation. Her facial beauty may have been equalled but not her hair. The silver fairness was unique and she wore it piled high in the way her hairdresser had taught her.

As the evening wore on Susan put a cloak over her gown and they strolled arm-in-arm along the paths circling the rose gardens. It was a still evening with the lingering scents of summer. An evening for lovers and Edward drew her closer.

'Happy?'

'Very,' she said softly.

'A perfect honeymoon would you say?'

'Quite perfect.'

From where they were walking they could hear the strains of music, hauntingly beautiful. The moonlight threw the lawn in shadow and suddenly, without warning, Edward stopped and swung her to him then with a bruising fierceness brought his mouth down on hers. 'Blame that on looking so desirable,' he said thickly as she tried to draw away.

'Edward,' she faltered, 'the – the ball isn't over – '

'For us it is,' he said, steering her through the entrance and over to the stairway. Their rooms were on the first floor and he almost pushed her in. Suddenly she was afraid, afraid of the stranger he had become. He was breathing heavily and was the worse for drink. She had lost count of the number of times his glass had been replenished.

He was asleep, his breathing regular but Susan had never felt more awake. Looking down at his face flushed in sleep she thought back to when they were children. Edward had a quick temper but he always apologised afterwards. His charm and good manners were never more in evidence than when adults were present. She remembered Ralph grinning knowingly. 'Trust Edward,' he'd said, 'he knows when to turn it on.'

The bed moved and, alarmed that he was about to waken, Susan kept quite still. But he merely grunted, mumbled something and flung an arm across her. Carefully, so as not to waken him, she moved herself as far over to her own side as she could. Then she lay with her eyes wide open.

There was a cruel streak in Edward and last night or rather this morning he had been brutal, ignoring her protests, her unwillingness. She had been sickened and humiliated by what she had been made to endure. At the memory her lips curled in disgust. And on top of that the nagging worry had returned and was refusing to go away.

Was it two months since – why hadn't she taken a note? But she'd never been regular and she was panicking needlessly. Once she'd approached her mother on the subject but Mrs MacFarlane had been dismissive, the mention of such matters distasteful to her fastidious nature. 'Being irregular is of no consequence,' she'd said, 'I was like that myself.'

Susan grasped at the straw then found it giving way. Mama had meant a week, two at the outside but she was well beyond that. Her head ached. If only she weren't so ignorant, but all she knew was from girlish chatter and her friends knew little more than she did.

What were the symptoms? More tired than usual? That had passed; she cheered up. Goodness hadn't she danced the hours away without feeling in the least exhausted? Mentally she deleted the tiredness and lethargy. Morning sickness? A sinking feeling – she had been troubled with nausea. And the yellow gown, measured for her some months ago and now too tight. Girls put on weight for other reasons – other reasons than pregnancy.

There it was out! She was actually considering the possibility. She crammed a knuckle into her mouth to stifle her cry. No! No! No! she screamed inside. It can't be, no one conceives the first time. She'd heard that somewhere or was it that it was not impossible just unlikely? Going hot and cold with fear she tried to get a grip on herself. Drawing the bedcovers to her chin and staying as far away from Edward as possible she prayed that her fears were unfounded. Then she fell into a troubled sleep.

\* \* \*

In the morning Edward looked haggard and she saw him eyeing her uncertainly as she folded her clothes. Her lovely yellow gown was torn where he had ripped it and she had it already in the trunk. Keeping her face averted she continued with her task.

'Susan?'

'Yes, Edward,' she said coldly.

'Was I – um – objectionable last night?'

She didn't answer, just took a blouse off its hanger and began fastening the buttons.

'Your silence speaks for itself. I was. Was I?'

'Yes.'

'I'm sorry, you have my humble apologies and, Susan, you must know it was completely out of character.'

'How should I know that?'

'Don't be so damned ridiculous,' he said, moving his head and the action causing him to grimace. 'Haven't I always been considerate?'

'Yes.'

'Your trouble is that you don't like that side of marriage.'

She stopped packing and looked across at him. 'That isn't true. When you were gentle – '

'You enjoyed it,' he smirked.

'Perhaps I did.'

'Then what has changed?'

'You know perfectly well,' she said, giving a small shiver. 'Drink played its part but you were disgusting and to me it is very obvious that you have experience of women – a certain type of woman.'

'What exactly do you mean by that remark?' he said, deadly quiet.

For a moment she faltered, thinking she had gone too far then she held up her head proudly. 'I meant what I said, Edward. Perhaps you don't know me as well as you think. Being your wife does not give you the right to abuse me.'

'Drink was the cause of my lack of control but your attitude is all wrong. Believe me, my dear, you have a lot of growing up to do.'

She returned his gaze but remained silent.

'You belong to me, Susan, and what gives me pleasure should be pleasurable for you. In time you'll find it true.'

'No, I won't.'

'We'll see.' Suddenly he grinned and his manner changed. 'Drink may be the curse of the working classes,' he groaned loudly, 'but it has a pretty devastating effect on management too. My tongue feels like leather and my head is thumping.'

'Serves you right,' she said but she was laughing. 'You look awful.'

'Forgiven?' he begged, holding out his hand.

'This time, yes.' She ignored his outstretched hand.

'Thank God I'm out of the dog-house.'

'You'll be in trouble with someone else if you're not careful. Didn't I hear you arrange for our trunks to be collected after breakfast?'

He got up and reached for his dressing-gown. 'I'll dress, pack my trunks and settle the account.' He sat down heavily on the bed. 'Can you face breakfast?'

'Very easily,' she said sweetly, 'I wasn't drinking.'

'You'll have to go down on your own.'

Most of the guests had already breakfasted, their tables cleared and fresh tablecloths in place for luncheon. One elderly gentleman looked above his newspaper and nodded a greeting as she passed his table. Susan felt conspicuously alone. The waiter was already behind her chair and saw to it that she was comfortably seated before opening out a starched linen napkin and placing it across her knees. In the mirror she could see herself in her navy two-piece costume with its white piping round the collar.

'My husband won't be coming down.'

'Would the gentleman like something sent up to his room, madam?'

'No, thank you.' She paused. 'I'll have a lightly boiled egg, toast and tea.'

Breakfasting alone Susan thought of the previous night and Edward's behaviour, his roughness. He had apologised and obviously remembered little of what happened. But she did and she was uncomfortably aware that she hadn't been entirely honest. Certainly she had been disgusted but there had been some of the time when she had been roused and it shamed her to remember that.

She glanced out of the window, thinking how quickly the weather changed. Large raindrops splattered on the pane sending rivulets down the wide sill. Soon they would be on their way home yet she couldn't bring herself to think of Hillview as home. It was comfortable enough but home was Aran Heights.

Edward kept up a brooding silence for much of the journey to Aranvale and she didn't try to engage him in conversation. That his stomach was upset was all too evident by the greyness of his face. Eventually he smiled. 'I think the worst is past.'

'Maybe talking will take your mind off it.'

'Then let us talk about Hillview.'

'Yes, all right. There is money from my parents and Aunt Rachel to buy furniture.'

'That is your department.'

'We should choose together or maybe I'll get something you don't like.'

'Then I'll have to live with it.'

'What about the removal of the Templetons' furniture?'

'No problem. Once you have a delivery date I'll have them remove their belongings or failing that have it put in store.'

'With our own furniture around us and our lovely gifts Hillview will seem much more like home.'

'What else is there to arrange?'

'Neither Mama nor I like the housekeeper so I want her replaced and new staff engaged.'

He looked alarmed. 'You had better stop your mother from overdoing it. Hillview isn't Croft House or Aran Heights.'

'Even so it needs adequate staffing,' Susan said firmly. 'To hear you, Edward, one would think we had to look to every penny. Papa is very much against extravagance but he wouldn't think a well-run house an extravagance.'

'Duties properly allocated, that's what is needed. It applies in business as well as the home and as mistress of my house it will be your duty to see that the maids are fully occupied and money not frittered away.'

Susan was shocked into silence. Edward, she could see now, would be driven by a need to accumulate wealth and if he ever got his hands on the mill his first undertaking would be to reduce the workforce yet expect the same output at the end of the day.

'If I didn't know you better I'd think you had a mean streak.' She kept her voice light and smiled into his face.

'Not mean, my dearest Susan, just careful.' He paused. 'The mill has marvellous potential you know but it needs someone with drive to get it out of the rut.' He saw her scandalised expression and hastened in with, 'That was an unfortunate choice of expression, your father has done wonders but it needs a younger man to take control. My father is doing that, leaving more and more to Thomas but unfortunately Thomas is totally out of his depth.'

'What works in the distillery would not be acceptable in our mill.'

'Why not?'

'Our business methods are very different.'

'The distillery makes a greater profit.'

'Not in dispute. It is a bigger concern.'

'The papermill could grow, expansion is the way forward.'

'You overlook one important thing, Edward. We have a contented workforce and the same can't be said for the Brodie concern. There are always rumblings of discontent from the distillery workers.'

'They don't voice them where it matters.'

'They wouldn't dare but the discontent is just below the surface.'

'That type spend their entire life grumbling, it is second nature to them.' He smiled. 'What are we arguing about? We are on the same side and all my energies will be devoted to the papermill. Indeed one day I fully intend us to have a profit greater than the distillery.'

Edward's colour had improved and he looked much his normal self when the train reached Aranvale. The carriage was waiting and soon Hillview was in sight. As they drew nearer Edward groaned. 'Oh, God! A reception committee – I could have done without that.'

Susan craned for a better view then looked daggers at him. 'Don't be so disagreeable, Edward, our parents have got together to welcome us home and I think that was a lovely thought.'

She needn't have worried. Edward took her arm and was all smiles as both sets of parents waited to greet them.

'Papa, you look so much better.' Susan smiled. His face was less hollow-cheeked and he looked stronger.

'I'm just fine.'

Susan looked about her. The vestibule had been dull and drab but now pots of healthy-looking geraniums covered the octagonal table and on the broad window ledge there were small pots of African violets and yellow primroses. Decorating one wall was a hanging basket with greenery cascading almost to the floor.

'Mama, this is simply lovely.'

Mrs MacFarlane looked pleased. 'Flowers, I always think, bring life to a house and I got our gardener to raid the greenhouse for these.'

'Very thoughtful of you,' Edward said as he ushered the ladies out first.

'How was the weather?' John Brodie asked. 'Or didn't you notice?' he added with a wink to Edward.

'We did notice.' Susan laughed. 'It was fine and warm and the hotel was excellent.'

'Susan, I wondered what to do about the wedding gifts then decided not to have them brought over until I knew your plans.' She turned to Edward. 'Once the Templetons get their furniture away you'll want the decorators in?'

'That is Susan's department.'

'Quite right, son, that way you can't be blamed. I left all that to your mother.'

Hamish MacFarlane spoke quietly, his eyes on his daughter. 'Susan will manage but she has other qualities that shouldn't be overlooked, Edward. Since my illness she has been a great help to me, in fact I don't know what I would have done without her.'

'Brains and beauty,' John Brodie barked. 'Don't know how lucky you are, my boy.'

They were comfortably seated in the drawing-room before Edward answered. 'You are wrong there, sir, I do appreciate my luck.' Then, showing a smiling face to his father-in-law he spoke firmly. 'Susan has been a wonderful help to you, sir, but she can safely step aside now knowing that I am in a position to give you every assistance.'

Lilian Brodie beamed over to her son. 'There you are, Susan, you have nothing to worry about. Edward will be on hand to see that your papa doesn't overdo it. And you are a married woman with responsibilities in the home.'

'Mrs Brodie,' Susan said quietly but firmly, 'Edward and I have already discussed this and he knows that I have no intention of stepping aside.' She saw Edward's mouth harden and her own mother gave her a reproachful look.

'Mama, what about the meal?' Susan whispered. 'shall I go and see – '

'No, dear, everything is in hand.' She excused herself and returned to announce that the meal was ready to be served. They trooped into the dining-room, the one room that Susan found acceptable. It was a good size with a large bay window and two smaller ones overlooking the lawn and beyond to the flowering shrubs.

'That was a very enjoyable meal, Mama.'

'Can't fault the cook,' Edward said as he leaned back.

'Will she stay on, Mama?'

'Yes and we'll discuss the housekeeper once the gentlemen remove themselves for a glass of port.'

'Finding a good housekeeper is not easy, Susan,' her mother-in-law said. 'Anyone not already engaged must be

147

viewed with suspicion but I feel sure you will be satisfied with Miss Wilson. She is very refined and kept house for her father until his death. Now she is alone she must earn a living.'

Susan nodded politely.

'I have every confidence that she will meet with your approval but not having been in service before she is understandably nervous so do make allowances.'

'Yes, of course, but if she doesn't meet my requirements I take it I can look around for an experienced housekeeper?' Susan said, nettled at having everything arranged for her.

'I don't think it will come to that and she is a decided improvement on her predecessor,' Lilian Brodie said, sounding both hurt and peeved.

'You've been very kind,' Susan said, feeling ashamed and to make amends rushed in with, 'Mama is helping me to choose furniture and I'd be happy if you could come along too.'

'I'd be delighted and Susan, my dear, we can't have you calling me Mrs Brodie.'

'I know, but what do I call you?'

'Vexing question.'

'How does Elizabeth address you?'

'Before the children I don't recall her addressing me as anything. Now I'm Grandmama to them all.'

'What about Mama Brodie?'

'That'll do very nicely.' They all looked over at the door as John Brodie poked his head around.

'Lilian, we should be getting on our way and in any case these two young people will be anxious to be on their own.'

'We won't be long behind you but I want to introduce Miss Wilson to Susan.'

'She's here?'

'Yes, we thought it better that you saw her right away.'

The Brodies departed and Susan accompanied her mother to interview Miss Wilson.

'I feel most inadequate, Mama,' Susan said worriedly.

'And whose fault is that? You would occupy yourself with

other things instead of what would prove useful to you in the future.'

'I'm ready to learn now.'

'If you do decide to engage this Miss Wilson make it clear from the start what her duties are to be.'

'Do I do the interviewing?' Susan asked nervously.

'Of course and for goodness sake be dignified, you are the mistress.' She smiled to take the sting out of the words before opening the door to the morning-room. A woman had been sitting at the window and got up hurriedly.

Mrs MacFarlane sat down and Susan did too. 'Do sit down, Miss Wilson.' She indicated a chair facing them. The woman was very tall, exceptionally so for a woman and there was a proud lift to her head. She may have come down in the world, Susan thought, but she was accepting her new status with dignity. Her tired grey eyes didn't blink under Susan's scrutiny.

'If you should decide to engage me, m'am I shall do my utmost to give satisfaction,' she said in a quiet well-modulated voice.

Susan inclined her head. I like her, she thought. She's nervous under that calm look and she needs the position. 'My own duties as mistress are new to me and if you were to be housekeeper at Hillview much of the smooth running of the house would rest on you.'

Miss Wilson bit her lip. 'I prefer to be completely open with you, m'am. My only experience of housekeeping has been on a very small scale. I kept house for my father until his death.'

'In the circumstances, Miss Wilson, I am prepared to give you a trial period. We'll say three months.'

'Thank you, m'am.

Mrs MacFarlane gave a dismissive nod and Miss Wilson went out quickly.

'You handled that very well, Susan.'

'I liked her.'

'Someone with more experience would have been preferable.'

'At the end of three months we'll see.'

'Don't let your heart rule your head, Susan. If Miss Wilson doesn't meet your requirements get rid of her at the end of the trial period. No doubt by then I will have heard of someone.'

'Mama, I've a feeling she's going to be perfectly suitable,' Susan said and swiftly changed the subject. 'I worried about Papa when I was away but he does look so much better.

'What is it?' Susan asked fearfully when the silence lasted too long.

'This goes no further, my dear, not even to Edward.' Her voice dropped. 'Dr Sullivan saw me and said that I wasn't to bear the burden alone, that Matthew and you had a right to know.'

Susan felt her chest tighten. 'Know what?'

'Susan, you must learn to hide your feelings,' she said gently, 'and remember it is very much worse for me, I have to hide my concern all the time.' She took hold of Susan's cold hands. 'Your papa's heart is very weak and the bronchitis is causing breathing difficulties. God willing, we could have him with us for a long time but we have to be prepared. His heart could give out at any time.'

'Oh, Mama,' Susan said brokenly, 'I can't bear it, I can't bear the thought of – of – '

'You must be brave, we all must.' Her mouth pursed in a disapproving line but there were tears in her voice. 'Dr Sullivan is making a serious mistake agreeing to Hamish going into the mill even for an hour or two.'

Susan shook her head. 'No, Mama, I don't agree with you. I think Dr Sullivan is right and he understands Papa so well. Keeping an active interest in the mill, going in for a short time, an hour or two, will keep him from fretting and worrying at home.'

'Well, I suppose I expected you to take that attitude but I hadn't expected it from Matthew.' She paused. 'Maybe I am wrong but I'm certainly not happy about it.' She looked about her as if anxious to get away from any further discussion of her husband's failing health and said too brightly, 'This room is shabby and depressing, Susan, but once it is freshened up and your own possessions in place it should be quite charming.'

Susan murmured her agreement but her mind was on this fresh worry about her papa.

She and Edward went out to the carriage.

'Thank you for all you've done, Mama.' She smiled to them both and waved until the carriage was out of sight.

# CHAPTER ELEVEN

Those first few days at Hillview were pleasant and Edward, though not very forthcoming about his time spent in the mill, seemed well content.

'How did the shopping spree go?' he asked as they sat together in the dying hours of the evening.

'Come out from behind that newspaper and I'll tell you.'

She heard the sigh but he obliged by folding his paper and dropping it at his feet. 'I'm waiting.' He smiled indulgently like an uncle with a favourite niece and she wanted to laugh.

'Hectic, exhausting but successful I think and I was thankful to have both mothers with me.' She grinned mischievously. 'That way we were guaranteed a majority verdict.'

'So you're quite happy?'

'Yes, I am and I'm sure you'll approve. Incidentally in case you don't know, your mother heard that the Templetons intend selling their furniture rather than have it sent on and have instructed their solicitor to get what he can for it.'

Edward frowned. 'Knowing that you went ahead and spent my – our money on new furniture?'

'Most certainly I did. Surely you do not expect me to start my married life with second-hand furniture?' Amazement was written on her face.

'If it is good and most of it is, whyever not? We are paying rental for it already.'

'That doesn't matter.' Her arm waved round the room. 'None of this is my choice and in any case our wedding cheques will more than cover the bills.' None of it, she added silently, is coming out of your pocket.

'Can't you get it into your head that that money could have been set aside and used for some other purpose? Really, for

153

someone who saw herself as a budding business woman you are quite hopeless. Not your fault.' He gave her a quick smile. 'Women don't have the right mentality or quick-wittedness so necessary to succeed in the cut-throat world. Well-known fact, my dearest.'

'Some of us lack ruthlessness, I would agree with that, but ruthlessness isn't necessarily a recipe for success. Papa's dealings with everyone have always been fair and honest.'

'And he is losing hand over fist.'

'That is absolute nonsense,' she shouted angrily. 'Until quite recently I was doing the books with my father and there was no cause for concern. Quite the reverse in fact.'

'That could change tomorrow. What is needed is a whole new approach and for a start I'd turf out that doddering old fool – '

'To whom are you referring?'

'McNeil – Murdoch McNeil.'

'Mr McNeil is a trusted employee, my father holds him in high esteem and, Edward, if I were you, I wouldn't make your opinion known – '

'Give me credit for some sense.' He put his hand up. 'That is enough, we were discussing furniture. Have you refurnished completely?'

'No, the servants' quarters need to be inspected to find out what is required.'

'Without an inspection I can tell you that whatever is there will remain. Anything else?'

'The guest rooms I hadn't decided on the colour scheme,' she said stiffly.

'I have a feeling your extravagance is getting completely out of hand.'

His eyes narrowed into slits. 'For your own good I have decided from this moment to monitor the household expenses until such time as I can trust you to be moderate in your outlay.'

She got to her feet and she was shaking with anger.

'How dare you! Just whom do you think you are addressing?' she said haughtily, her blue eyes flashing dangerously.

'I am addressing my wife,' he said calmly, 'and just you remember, my dear Susan, that I am master in my own house and you will do as you are told.'

She sat down. 'And if I don't?' she said quietly, the nails digging into the palms of her hands.

'But you will.' He paused. 'Think how upsetting it would be, fatal even, if things were seen to be awkward between us. Your father needs me and was quite desperate to have me as a son-in-law.'

'What has happened to you, Edward?' You were never like this.'

'I'm still the same person.'

'Not to me.'

'All right,' he said grimly. 'I intend being successful.' His eyes glittered. 'All my life I've had to play second fiddle and do you know what that is like? To know that you have a superior brain but by an accident of birth Thomas takes over the distillery when Father dies.'

'Your father isn't a fool. He must have confidence in Thomas.'

'The old fool sees what he wants to see.'

'You care about the distillery, don't you?' Susan said gently.

He shrugged. 'Waste and inefficiency in any form distress me. However, Thomas can sink or swim, it is nothing to me.' He seemed to have forgotten her. 'One day the mill will be mine, mine to control and when that day comes I'll double the profits and expand the premises.' He gave an embarrassed laugh. 'Susan, my love, I have great plans. I'm not criticising your father, he's a shrewd enough business man but his methods are old-fashioned and his outlook out of date. The mill is stagnating.'

Only by taking a deep breath did she keep her temper in check.

'My father is a shrewd business man and because of that he is wise enough not to overstretch. He considers he has a duty to his workforce as well as to his family and he wouldn't gamble with the well-being of either. It distresses me to say this but I have a feeling that all you care about is power and you won't care who suffers just so long as you get what you want.'

'Power!' He repeated the word, savouring the sound. 'Yes, you are absolutely right. I want power and I mean to get it.' He paused. 'I haven't changed, Susan, you didn't know me as well as you thought, that's all.'

'I'm just beginning to realise that.'

'All I want is to prove to my father how wrong he was.'

'Bitterness only brings unhappiness and if you carry on in this way all you will be doing is building up misery for everyone and destroying yourself into the bargain.'

'As if you cared?'

'Of course I care, Edward. I care very much.'

'Then help me. Together we can do so much but if you attempt to thwart me,' he said threateningly then laughed. 'You wouldn't do that; after all, my success is yours.' He opened the newspaper and folded it ready to read, but changed his mind. 'There is one area where you can't but shine.'

'I'm glad to hear it,' she said, not hiding her sarcasm. 'You are going to tell me I suppose?'

'Entertaining our friends and business associates. You are blessed with charm when you choose to exercise it and you have beauty and intelligence. No one could ask for more in a hostess. Thomas is less fortunate. Elizabeth comes from a good family but she is an empty-headed chatterbox.'

'I don't know Elizabeth all that well but she struck me as a pleasant, friendly girl.'

'Oh, she's that,' he conceded, 'but she never has anything of interest to say.'

'With your tight hold on the purse-strings how could we possibly afford the lavish entertainment you appear to have in mind?'

'That is a necessary expense and one that is likely to pay a dividend. A lot of contracts are secured over a glass of port after a good dinner.' He smiled. 'You won't find me stingy there nor with your dress allowance. Be lavish to those who may be useful and don't look so disapproving. The end result will be a healthier order book.'

'You are infuriating and insulting. Anyone listening to you would think the mill a second-rate business. And another thing, if you have such a low opinion of the mill why were you so anxious to get a foot in?'

'That's the spirit. You look magnificent when you're roused. Now to answer your question. I didn't see Matthew as a major stumbling block. He would have left the decision-making to me and with clever marketing the money would be there for expansion.'

'My father would be appalled to hear all this. He believes that by putting too much emphasis on quantity, quality invariably suffers.'

'Rubbish and typical of his old-fashioned thinking.'

'He doesn't use people.'

'Your mother does though,' he said, raising an eyebrow.

'What do you mean?' she asked sharply but she had a horrid suspicion of what was coming.

'My mother has never been blind to the fact that her friendship was cultivated to improve your dear mama's social standing. As it happens they have become good friends.'

When she made no reply he rustled the paper. 'Now, maybe, I'll get a chance to read this.'

After Edward left for the mill Susan rang the hand-bell. It was answered by Mary, a pretty, dark-haired maid with a curvaceous figure who had worked for the Templetons.

'You rang, m'am?'

There was a touch of insolence in the voice.

'Tell Polly I want to see her and straighten your cap.'

An anxious-looking Polly arrived. 'Is there somethin' wrong, Miss Susan – I mean m'am?' she said, flustered.

'What makes you think there is something wrong?'

'Mary said – '

'What did Mary say?'

'Nothin', m'am, it was just the way – ' She bit her bottom lip and worked it with her teeth.

'Sit down, Polly.' She gestured to a chair and Polly sat down on the edge of the seat.

'How would you like to be my personal maid?'

Polly's eyes widened incredulously. 'Oh, m'am!'

'Then I take it you would?'

'Ever so pleased I'd be.' She was flushed and her eyes were shining like twin stars.

'I'll see Miss Wilson about relieving you of some of your duties. Sewing is going to take up a lot of your time and I know you are good with a needle. A few of my gowns are uncomfortably tight.'

'If the material is there the seams can be let out a wee thing or – '

'Yes, yes, I'm sure you'll manage. There's a small room presently used as a store I'm told. That can be cleared and you must consider it your workroom.'

'That's ever so kind, m'am.'

'Did you mind leaving Aran Heights?'

'Not when I was to be with you, Miss Susan.' She blushed. 'Beggin' your pardon, m'am, I keep forgettin'.'

'Don't worry about it,' Susan said kindly. 'There are times when I forget myself. Off you go then.'

For a long time Susan sat staring ahead and seeing nothing but her mind was working feverishly. This uncertainty had to end before she went mad. She shrank from consulting Dr Sullivan or Edward's doctor. No, it had to be someone unknown to her and she had the glimmer of an idea of how she could go about it. Tomorrow morning immediately after the coachman had driven Edward to the mill she would be dressed and waiting, then she would get him to take her to the station. And if everything worked to plan there would be ample time to catch the train to Glasgow. Never before had Susan gone anywhere alone except in Aranvale but she was a matron, she reminded herself, and Glasgow was not unknown to her. With it being so near to Aranvale there had been frequent trips to the city to see the sights when they were young and then more recently the journeys to Miss Beattie's salon. And it was on one of those journeys with her mother that she had seen it. Not long after leaving Queen Street station the coach had been held up and with nothing to do but gaze about her Susan recalled seeing the big brass plate belonging to a doctor's surgery. Apart from Buchanan Street and Sauchiehall Street she had never paid attention to the street names and without the name and address of the doctor she could hardly take a cab. Anyway the short walk was the least of her worries.

With that planned Susan felt calmer and, taking a book, went out to the garden. The first blooms had gone from the roses and some of the petals lay untidily on the black earth. Summer was slipping away, soon it would be autumn with the leaves fluttering from the trees. The seasons had a pattern, nothing changed, everything predictable – well, apart from the weather. But in life nothing was predictable. She closed her eyes. If only – if only David Cameron hadn't come into her life but it was too late for thoughts like that. Of one thing she was sure, David Cameron wouldn't be suffering, the David she remembered would be too busy trying to make his fortune.

After the first bewildering two weeks David Cameron settled happily in London. True to his promise his friend from student days had fixed up temporary accommodation. Young qualified accountants were in demand and David was overjoyed to gain a position with Hamilton & Hargreave, an established company with an excellent reputation and with offices in all the major English cities. One of his colleagues was leaving at the end of the month and David was fortunate to get the room he was vacating which was walking distance from the office.

Morning seemed a long time coming. She both welcomed and dreaded it. Like her father Edward disliked conversation so early in the morning and recently she had been glad of it. She saw him to the door, held up her face for his kiss and went indoors only after the carriage moved off. In an agony of impatience she awaited the return of the carriage and hearing it in the courtyard she went out quickly. Ramsay had already jumped down.

'Good mornin', m'am,' he said, taking off his cap and twisting it in his hands. -

'Good morning, Ramsay,' Susan said crisply. 'I want taking to the station and there is little enough time to catch the Glasgow train.'

Without wasting time on words Ramsay saw his mistress seated then set the horses to a spanking pace. There had been a gradual change in the weather. The early morning had been sunny but now there was a slow hazing of the sky and the hills were shrouded in mist. At the entrance to the station Ramsay brought the coach to a halt. He seemed anxious to speak but hesitated.

'What is it?' Susan said impatiently.

'Beggin' your pardon, m'am, but I wouldnae be venturin' far in this. That mist's goin' tae thicken, tak' my word for it.' He was sturdily built, had fathered six healthy youngsters and had a kindly way with him.

Susan glanced at the sky. 'You may well be right but I have only a very short journey at the other end. Expect me back on the late afternoon train and now I must hurry.'

'Ye've time enough.'

She began to walk away then stopped. 'Ramsay.' She forced a smile and a light tone. 'Don't mention this journey to my husband, he would only worry.'

'Can't say as I blame him but I'll say nothin'.'

She left him shaking his head and looking perplexed. A real nice lady she was that, but her and her kind were none too keen on taking advice.

He had been with John Brodie for many years, employed in the main for odd jobs but he was capable of taking the place of the coachman when necessary. It had been Lilian who had suggested to her husband that Edward should have the second coach as part of their wedding settlement and Ramsay had been only too delighted to take over the new position of coachman at Hillview.

Passengers were few at this time of day and Susan found

herself sharing a compartment with one other lady. After a brief smile and a remark about the weather, her fellow passenger buried her face in a book and was engrossed in it for the rest of the journey. Thankful that polite conversation wasn't called for, Susan closed her eyes and by concentrating on one thing at a time was managing to remain calm. She had the route pictured in her mind. Left coming out of the station and then not too far on, it was left again. At the corner was a double-fronted shop with fruit and vegetables piled high in one window and the other was a hatter. The incongruity of it had struck her at the time.

As the train steamed and puffed into the station the woman closed her book and put it in her bag. She was ready when it pulled up with a squealing of brakes. Doors up and down the train opened and people spilled out on to the platform.

'I hate fog and one doesn't expect it at this time of year,' the woman remarked as she hastened away and was soon lost from sight.

Other trains had arrived in Queen Street station and Susan was caught up in a mass of moving bodies impatient to reach the exit. Some had baggage and were none too careful of the comfort of others as they jostled for position.

Susan held back until the worst of the crush was over then she too was outside and without warning enveloped in a fog that slopped over the high buildings, successfully obliterating those landmarks on which she was depending.

In Aranvale Susan had experienced fog but she had never been alone in it and this was Glasgow. She shivered with fear. This was smog – a mixture of thick smoke and fog – and it caught at her throat, almost choking her. Stupid to rush out until her eyes became accustomed to the greyness. She waited until she imagined the fog to be less thick and stepped out, thinking that if others could cope then so could she.

Far away she heard the barking of a dog, a lonely sound, then coming closer the eerie clanging of trams. She let out a thin scream as she felt a violent push at her back. She would have lost her balance had a hand not steadied her.

'Sorry, hen. Cannae see sae weel in this pea-souper. I hevnae hurt ye, yer a'richt are ye?'

'Yes, thank you,' she whispered. She was trembling with fright and near to tears but not at the voice. It had been couthy, holding concern not malice.

Clutching her bag to her Susan strained her eyes, finding it marginally easier to make progress. Had she gone too far? It was so difficult to judge, she could make out nothing in this swirling mist. Then just as she thought she would scream she saw it, the shop, the double-fronted shop. Hats of all descriptions sat on their stands like disembodied ghostly apparitions in the blurred light. Almost sobbing with relief she quickened her pace. The fog was less dense here as though there were pockets of fog and this part had escaped the worst.

And there it was – the big brass plate and she had so nearly missed it. Going closer she looked at the lettering. Dr E. R. Skinner. There was more but she had seen all she needed.

With her heart beating like a sledgehammer, Susan pulled at the bell sharply. An echoing sound reached her followed by light footsteps, then the door opened.

'Yes?'

'May I see the doctor, please?' Susan asked, her voice wobbling with nervousness.

'There's plenty waitin' but if you've a mind to you can wait.'

'Thank you.' Susan stepped in gratefully, aware that the woman was eyeing her curiously but she said nothing more and Susan followed her along a passage with worn brown waxcloth. Stopping at a door she opened it and ushered Susan in.

'Move up and make way for this lady,' she said in a no-nonsense voice. There was a shuffling of feet and a space was made for Susan.

It was a square-shaped room with green painted walls chipped in places and a long wooden bench down two walls. The stench of unclean bodies and stale perspiration mingled with the smell of disinfectant. With the first onslaught Susan thought she was to be physically sick. She took out her handkerchief and held it to her nose. Around her were people with dry, racking coughs and one with the same kind of wheeziness as her papa. He was struggling for breath but holding on to an empty pipe in his gnarled hand. One old man hunched forward, his eyes fixed on one spot in the worn waxcloth. So still was he that he might have been carved in stone.

The patients were thinning out; no one was getting much time from the doctor. A whimper broke out and Susan looked at the boy in sympathy. He could have been no more than seven years of age. A woollen scarf was wound round his head and under his chin and Susan could see a huge swelling on his face. Gently the woman drew him towards her and it was her eyes that were filled with pain.

'He's tae get it lanced,' she said, seeing the sympathy in Susan's face.

They were from very different walks of life but as the woman and her child went out the two women exchanged sad smiles and Susan touched the boy as he went by.

A little later there was a piercing scream followed by another, then silence. Later still came the murmur of voices then the receptionist was telling her that she was next.

'Is the little boy all right?' she found herself asking.

'Right as rain. You've to be cruel to be kind and the doctor had a sweetie for him. He's good with bairns.'

The smell of disinfectant was stronger in the surgery. It was a small room with a desk, three chairs, a sofa covered with a blanket and a set of drawers.

The man behind the desk had his head bent and he was writing on a pad.

'Sit down.' The head didn't rise but an arm indicated the chair opposite.

Even in her worry and distress Susan still felt outraged at this appalling display of bad manners. She didn't move and his head went up slowly. In those moments when they looked at each other she saw that he was a man perhaps in his late thirties. He was clean-shaven, heavy featured and with smudges of tiredness under the grey eyes.

'Sit down,' he repeated then added, 'I haven't all day.'

She sat down.

Susan had dressed in the most sober outfit she could find in her wardrobe but it was still obvious that she was out of place in this surgery.

If he was surprised by her appearance he concealed it admirably.

'What can I do for you?' It was a pleasant voice with a hint of impatience as if already he had wasted enough time.

'I think I may be pregnant,' she said quietly.

'If this is an unwanted pregnancy,' he said harshly, 'you've come to the wrong place.'

She stared at him and moved her hands as if at a loss for words.

'You do wear a ring so perhaps I misjudged.'

She swallowed nervously. 'I want to have it confirmed or otherwise.'

'Very well,' he said brusquely, 'you had better answer a few questions before I examine you.' He leaned forward placing the palms of his well-shaped hands together. 'When was your last . . .'

Embarrassed at all the personal questions, she stammered out the answers while he kept nodding.

'Remove your jacket and blouse and undo the rest.'

Susan put her bag against the leg of the chair and her gloves with it. He was watching her and it made her clumsy and slow but at last she was ready. It was an impersonal, professional examination and he engaged himself elsewhere while she dressed. She bent down for her handbag and gloves and wished he would put her out of her misery.

Her eyes were huge in her white face. 'Please tell me,' she whispered.

'The signs all point to the fact that you are pregnant, Mrs . . .' He waited for her to fill in the name but she ignored it and with a slight shrug he picked up a pen, dipped it into an inkwell and did a swift calculation on his pad. 'Middle

March give or take a week either way. Difficult to be more precise, particularly with a first baby.'

He saw the panic in her eyes and he looked at her kindly. 'For God's sake don't believe all the stories you hear. You're a healthy young woman so there should be no problems. Just remember it is a natural function of the body. Is there anything else you want to ask?'

She saw his impatience. 'No, nothing else.' She opened her bag. 'What is your fee?'

'My receptionist deals with that,' he said curtly.

I'm going to have a baby, she thought wildly as she got up. The room swam then steadied. He was holding the door open, the receptionist was ushering in another patient.

'Good day,' he said politely then the door was closed. She paid the receptionist, amazed how little was asked, but had she known it was more than double the usual fee.

Then she was outside with no conscious thought of where she was going. Visibility had improved though fog still lingered. The air was warm and clammy and there was a film of moisture on her forehead yet Susan felt icy cold and dreadfully afraid.

What was she to do? Dear God, please help me but she didn't expect her prayers to be answered. She had sinned and now she had to pay the price. And what would that price be? Disowned by her husband; Edward would show no mercy, of that she was sure. But worst of all what would it do to Papa? Her heart filled with black despair and death would have been welcome. She didn't deserve to live but somehow she had to face what lay ahead.

Who would she turn to and for how long could she keep her secret? The questions hammered at her brain then she stopped suddenly as a new panic seized her. Where was she? She had been walking aimlessly and for how long? Her frightened eyes were taking in the shabbiness of the area, the hovels, the filthy middens – did people live in such dreadful conditions? But of course they did. Abruptly she wheeled round and walked a few yards then turned down another road. She blundered on, feverishly looking for some sign and seeing a blurred light she went towards it. With her heart thumping painfully she rubbed the misted glass with her glove and almost cried out in relief. It was a teashop. She was safe. She would go in and order a pot of tea then ask for directions to the station or better still a cab to get her there.

The wooden handle turned, a bell clanged and a girl came forward, a floor brush in her hand.

'We're just closin'.'

'Please, if I could just have a pot of tea?'

'There's nothin' much left to eat.'

'That doesn't matter.'

'In that case sit yersel' doon, onywhar yer like.' Her brush went against the wall and she dusted her hands with the skirts of her gown before going over to the dresser heaped with thick white china.

Susan sat at one of the small tables; the cloth was stained where soup had been spilt and there were tea stains but Susan was past caring. She was just too thankful to be inside. The girl was quick bringing milk and sugar and setting a place with a cup and saucer. When the large brown teapot arrived it had a chipped lid. Susan tried to pour tea into the cup but her hand was shaking so much that she had to replace it.

'My, but that's a fair state yer in. Here let me dae it.' The thin wrist lifted it as if it were a featherweight. 'Milk?'

'Yes, please.'

'Sugar?' But before Susan could answer she was spooning in a liberal quantity. 'It's shock yer sufferin' frae by the looks o' ye and sweet tea's the best thing fer that.'

Susan tried to smile but her lips were stiff. 'You're very kind.'

The sweet tea did help. Used to fine china the lip of the cup felt strange but she drank from it thirstily. The girl halted her cleaning to see if she wanted her cup refilled but Susan shook her head.

'No more, thank you but that has helped. I feel much better.' She smiled. 'If you could tell me how to get to Queen Street station I would be very much obliged. I seem to have lost myself. Is it possible to get a cab from somewhere nearby?'

The girl opened her eyes wide and stared. 'There's no cab hereabouts but the station's no' that far. Tak' the short cut – no, mebbe no, yer could be losin' yersel' again.' She bawled through to the back shop. 'Mind the shop, Bella, I'll no' be lang.'

Hauling a knitted cardigan from a chair she put it on. 'If this is summer Gawd help us in the winter.' She grinned.

Susan had her purse out and handed over some money.

'A meenit and I'll get change.'

'No, the rest is for yourself.'

'It's ower much.' She was swithering but there was a hopeful look on her thin narrow face.

'Please take it,' Susan said shakily. 'You can't know how helpful you've been.'

She took Susan's arm and led her through a warren of back alleys, careful to avoid the piles of decaying rubbish.

'Naebody will harm ye. Fowk hereabouts dinnae deserve the reputation they get.'

In a remarkably short time one of the alleyways brought them out almost at the station.

'Cannae lose yersel' noo.' But she kept Susan's arm until they were right into the station.

Susan glanced at the clock and sighed with relief. 'Thanks to you I'll catch my train.'

'Cheerio and remember nothin's ever as bad as it looks.'

'Thank you again.'

The girl waved then hurried away.

Utterly weary, Susan dragged her feet across the station and over to the platform where the train was already waiting. Returning shoppers had made the train busy and Susan found herself having to share a compartment with three well-dressed ladies who were chatting animatedly. Thankful that none was known to her she gave them a polite smile and sat down. A few efforts were made to draw her into their conversation but her reluctance to participate eventually discouraged them and she was left in peace.

Peace – as if she would ever know peace again.

Slowly and in a cloud of steam the train moved out of the station and as it began to gather speed Susan closed her eyes. Another time the rhythmic sound of metal clanging against metal would have been pleasant but now it was like a hammer in her head. Her plight was so dreadful that her brain could no longer cope. With so many stops the train never got up much speed and Susan had always liked to watch life in the small villages as they passed and she determined to do this and keep her mind occupied. She saw the rolling, purple-tinted hills in the distance, a stark contrast to the miners' rows of ugly brick houses. Opencast mining had provided the only means of livelihood until the opening of the Aranvale Papermill. The scars where the seams had been worked out were well hidden by the long, rough grass and bracken. In spite of herself a smile tugged at Susan's mouth as she watched the barefooted children egging on two boys as they raced their bogies down the slope in an attempt to keep up with the train. Susan knew what a bogie was, as a boy her papa had had one. It was made from the base and wheels of an old pram with a wooden box for the driver to sit.

She must have dozed off and it was a change in the rhythmic motion that brought her awake. In a few minutes they would be in Aranvale station and Ramsay pacing the platform, no doubt relieved to see her safely back.

The ladies were going further on and she wished them good day as the train squealed to a halt. They answered but coldly; her standoffishness had offended them.

Another time and she would have laughed at the look on Ramsay's face.

'My, but I'm that glad tae see ye, m'am,' he said as they walked to the carriage. 'Proper tizzie I've been in.'

'There was no need, Ramsay,' Susan said gently, touched by his concern. 'The fog was patchy and I managed very well.'

Before taking the turning to Hillview Susan looked across to the grey splendour of Aran Heights standing aloof and proud in its commanding position and her eyes filled. If only – oh, if only she were back there and all this a bad dream. She, like her papa, loved its wild ruggedness yet at times she knew that she had likened it to a prison. A place where she had been over-cosseted and protected and her rebellious nature had stormed against it. And where had it landed her? Those secret, stolen hours with David Cameron had ruined her whole life. Why, oh, why, had she been such a fool? Aunt Rachel had seen the dangers and warned her against furthering an acquaintance with a young man so totally unsuitable but she had chosen not to listen.

Susan swallowed nervously as the carriage turned into the drive and sat still until Ramsay opened the door and helped her down. With a murmured 'thank you' she went through the doorway that was still unfamiliar and into the vestibule with its flowering plants from Aran Heights.

Mary, the maid, was in the hall and at the sight of her mistress her mouth fell open and she stared.

'What are you gaping at, girl?' Susan snapped. 'Don't you have work to do?'

'Yes, m'am,' she muttered as she scuttled away.

'I'm getting rid of that girl,' Susan decided. 'I can't stand her, there's something about the creature I find loathsome.'

Once in her bedroom Susan let out a shuddering sob and, catching sight of herself in the full-length mirror, she had to admit that it was small wonder that the maid had gaped. Her face was chalk-white, her boots filthy and the hem of her skirt bespattered with mud.

Really she would have to get a grip on herself. She had almost two hours before Edward returned from the mill and in that time she must tidy herself, act normally through the meal then later . . .

First she must get out of these clothes and wash herself thoroughly. There was no telling what she may have picked up in the waiting-room. Just thinking about it the disgusting stench was with her. Her stomach heaved and she stood quite still until the nausea wore off then she was conscious of another ache, an ache of emptiness and she remembered that she hadn't eaten since breakfast and then only sparingly.

Polly! She could ring but that might bring Miss Wilson or Mary. Better to go along herself. The passage was quiet and when she went to what had once been a storeroom, she found Polly stooped over a gown and painstakingly unpicking the seams.

'M'am!' she said springing up.

'Polly, I'm afraid I've got myself into a filthy mess.' She tried to make a joke of it but it ended in a gulp.

'I'll get hot water and bring it right away.'

'And get Mrs Carson to prepare a tray, just a sandwich and tea. I'll be dining with the master later.'

Back in her bedroom, Susan stepped out of her clothes, kicking them aside before reaching for her robe. Slipping her arms into it she was tying the belt when the idea came to her. She stood stock still. It was so simple she couldn't think why she hadn't thought of it before. Babies were born prematurely, she could be having Edward's baby or rather she could pass it off as Edward's. All she had to do was hide her condition and that shouldn't be too difficult. She would watch her posture and Polly was letting out the seams of her gowns. And the looser style, though not to her liking, was fashionable.

Even as all this was going through her mind and a part of her was grasping at it she knew that she could never stoop so low. How could she cheat Edward so shamefully and live with herself? Her head went up. She would be honest, and delaying her confession would only add to her torture. The decision made, she felt a calmness and a new strength flow through her veins to help her face the ordeal.

Polly arrived panting from the exertion of carrying the ewer brimful of hot water. In her usual quick fashion she filled the basin, checked that there was soap and placed two folded towels on the edge of the marble slab.

'No, don't go, Polly. Get me fresh underclothes and a gown – the blue sprigged one I think.'

Polly turned her back while Susan sponged herself all over.

She took the underclothes from a drawer then drew along the hangers and took out the gown her mistress wished to wear. Very carefully she spread it over the large double bed.

'M'am, I told Mrs Carson. Mebbe it's ready and if that's all you'll be needin' – '

'Wait! Get rid of these.' She gave a backwards kick with her heel. 'Put them in the furnace,' she said with a shudder.

'M'am!' Polly was scandalised.

'Do as you're told,' Susan said sharply then regretted her tone. 'They are old and dirty and I have no further use for them.'

'There's many that would be glad of them, m'am,' Polly said stubbornly.

'You want them for yourself? Haven't I given you enough?'

'No, m'am, not for mysel',' she said, sounding hurt. ''tis a shame to waste what could be put to good use that's what I'm sayin'.'

'Very well, do what you like with them, just get them out of my sight.'

'I'll be seein' about the tray now,' she said as she scooped them up in her arms.

In the dining-room they sat at either end of the long table saying little to each other. The maid served the meal from the silver dishes and Susan was vaguely aware of Edward's eyes following her movements around the table. When she had gone his eyebrows rose.

'I see we have a change of table-maid.'

'Yes, Polly is an accomplished needlewoman and I had Miss Wilson reorganise the duties to allow her some time in the sewing-room.'

'Very good, you are learning, my dear, and with a little practice that young woman has the makings of a good table-maid.'

'You may be right, Edward, but I don't care for her. I don't like her manner.'

'Give the girl a chance, she's probably nervous.'

Nerves were the last thing Susan thought Mary suffered from. When she had finally departed Edward dropped his voice.

'Adrian Beverley – you know – '

'Caroline's father?'

'Yes.' He paused. 'He's committed suicide.'

'Surely not!' Susan said, shocked. 'But why, what on earth had come over him?'

'Rumours have been going around for some time that he was in financial difficulties and it would appear he couldn't face the disgrace of bankruptcy.'

'Poor man, I'm very, very sorry. What about his wife, poor soul, she's a bag of nerves at the best of times?'

'Gone to make her home with her widowed sister.'

'Where did you get all this information?'

'I had occasion to go into Airdrie and met Henry McCall, but don't ask me where he got his information.'

'That leaves Caroline on her own. She's an only child, you know.'

'From all accounts she's staying calm and intends seeing to the winding up of her father's affairs.' There was admiration in his voice. 'Caroline is not just a pretty face.'

'Papa always said that.'

With the meal over they moved into the sitting-room and Edward waved a hand. 'Won't be long before we have our own furniture. Have you thought how you are going to arrange matters?'

'We can make use of the guest room while our bedroom is being redecorated.'

'Is that really necessary, the redecoration I mean?'

'I would have thought so. Better now than having another upheaval.'

'We could stay with my parents until we are all square.'

'Aran Heights would be more convenient, nearer the mill.'

'True, but your father is a semi-invalid and I'm not particularly keen.'

'Very well, we'll stay here.'

Edward lowered himself into the chair, stretched out his

long legs and reached for his newspaper. 'Now, if you please, Susan, let me read this in peace.'

Susan sat on the edge of the horsehair chair, her fingers tightly locked together. 'Don't open your paper just yet, Edward, there's something I must tell you.'

'You had every opportunity at the table.' Edward's expression tightened into irritation. This was the time he liked to get up to date with the financial news and Susan should know that by this time. Still, she was looking a bit tense, he thought, better hear what she had to say and get it over. Some domestic detail no doubt, women got into a state about such trifles.

'Very well, Susan, you have my undivided attention.'

She moistened her lips, tried to speak but no words came.

'It can't be that bad surely?'

'I'm pregnant, Edward,' she blurted out.

His lips twitched then slapping his knees he hooted with laughter.

'My poor, sweet innocent, we haven't been married a month yet. Darling, if it should prove to be the case I'll be absolutely delighted but you can't know for some time yet. Heavens! Didn't your mother tell you anything?'

'Edward, I am not totally ignorant and I have been to see a doctor.' The desperation in her voice got through to him.

'When? Where? A doctor, what on earth are you talking about?'

She was shaking badly but she had to go on. 'I was in Glasgow today and saw a doctor there.'

His eyes bulged and he said incredulously, 'Are you trying to tell me you went to Glasgow on your own?'

'Ramsay drove me to the station. The – the doctor confirmed that I am pregnant.'

'I never touched you before we were married.'

'No.'

'Who was it?' His voice cut like steel and Susan flinched. 'I'm waiting for an answer.'

What could she say? Papa had let drop that David Cameron

was no longer employed at the mill. No doubt, she thought bitterly, he was seeking his fortune in London.

'No one you know, Edward, I can assure you of that and no one I shall ever see again.'

'You'll tell me who it was,' he said threateningly, 'or do you want me to force it out of you?'

Susan felt near to fainting. 'His name would mean nothing, he's no longer in this country and I only knew him for a very short time.'

'Long enough apparently – and you acting Miss Innocent on our wedding night.' The words were tumbling out but Susan caught an edge of bewilderment and pain.

'Edward, I'm so very, very, sorry.'

'Is that all you can say?' He was out of his chair and there was something frightening and menacing in the way he was bent, like an animal about to strike and Susan shrank back in terror.

As if getting a grip on himself he moved back with his mouth curled in disgust. 'Don't worry about your physical safety, my dear wife.' He spat the words. 'I've never struck a woman in my life but God knows I've never been nearer.' He moved unsteadily and slumped back into his chair.

'You must believe me, Edward,' she said despairingly, 'I didn't know. Had I even thought it a possibility I would never have married you.'

'I can hardly bring myself to look at you. My God! Do you know what you've done? You've sunk to the lowest trick a woman can play, trapping me into marriage to give your bastard a name and save your precious reputation.' He continued with some more choice expressions and she was sickened by his coarseness.

'It's not true,' she shouted hysterically. 'I swear I didn't know, you've got to believe that and if you just think about it, Edward, you would realise I couldn't possibly – '

'Oh, granted, you couldn't be certain but you knew it to be a possibility and you were taking no chances.'

'No. Oh, why won't you believe me?'

'Tell me this – that sudden change of heart, that decision

of yours to propose marriage and that is what you did. Was it because you decided that you loved me after all or was there another reason? Be honest, Susan, you owe me the truth.'

She tried to be completely honest and haltingly she began to explain that it had been to put her father's mind at rest regarding the mill. But as she faltered to a close it sounded hollow even to her own ears.

'Of course he wanted me for a son-in-law, my presence is needed in the mill. You knew that and used it for your own ends.'

Susan was resigned now. 'It really doesn't matter what I say, Edward, does it? You've made up your mind not to believe me.'

'You've used me and that is something I'll never forgive. But the question is where do we go from here, tell me that?'

'That rests with you and whatever you decide I shall abide by it,' she said very quietly.

Getting up abruptly he walked to the door and when he reached it he stood still with his back to her then slowly turned and for a long moment looked at her.

'How could you, Susan? How could you do this to me?'

She shook her head. What more was there to say?

'I need to be alone, need to think,' he mumbled. The door closed and she was left alone.

A strand of hair fell across her face and she pushed it behind her ear. What punishment would Edward exact? He was a proud man reeling under a heavy blow and forgiveness did not come easy to him. But how could she expect forgiveness, hadn't she sinned in the most terrible way by proposing marriage to Edward while David Cameron's seed was growing inside her?

Fires were lit in the evenings when the weather turned unseasonably cold. The kindling was already there and all Susan had to do was ring for a maid to put a light to it, wait until it caught then add coal. Two or three times her hand went to the bell but each time she drew back. Time went on, midnight was approaching and a bone-chilling coldness settled over her. As she got up weariness and a numbness of the limbs had her catching at the furniture for support. She would go up to bed, she decided and was almost at the door when it opened and Edward stood there blocking her path.

'Get back to your chair,' he thundered. 'You'll leave this room when I tell you but first you are going to hear what I have to say.'

Even before she smelt it on his breath Susan knew that he had been drinking. She had steeled herself for another verbal lashing but now she was much more nervous. Drink unleashed the devil and she had already experienced what it did to Edward.

She hastened back to her chair and watched him stumble to his. After sitting down and crossing his legs the palms of his hands went together as in an attitude of prayer. Drink hadn't slurred his speech only made it slower, each word carefully articulated.

'I have done a great deal of thinking – '

She waited and her tiredness vanished as a new kind of terror took hold. What was he going to do to her? He was keeping her waiting, playing cat and mouse. 'Say what you have to say,' she said harshly.

'Ah, a great relief to you, my dear. You see I have decided to give your bastard my name though God knows what tainted blood it may inherit.'

'Not that word, Edward. Please, not that word,' she whispered.

'Why not? A child conceived outside marriage is a bastard. I didn't invent the word. And now if you will allow me to go on. Let's call it *it*. It is to have my name but that is all. Never shall I accept it as mine so don't make the mistake of believing that time will change that. Nothing will.' There was a grim finality in the words.

'It is more than I expected and I am grateful.'

'You should be. It is far more than most men would be prepared to do but I am not finished. No one makes a fool of Edward Brodie – '

'I didn't – '

'Be quiet,' he thundered. 'I repeat, no one makes a fool of me and that is what I would be made to look if this ever came out. Apart from that there is my position in the mill.'

'Papa would never make you suffer for my mistake.'

'Maybe not but I am not prepared to take that chance and in any case it is bound to sour relations and be awkward. No, my dear wife, my mind is made up.' The blow to his pride drove him on remorselessly, bitterness and resentment pouring from him in an unleashed torrent. 'You and I shall continue to behave towards each other as a happily married couple for the benefit of relatives and acquaintances.' His speech was becoming slurred, some of it almost unintelligible. 'That maid, the table-maid, what did you call her?'

'Mary.'

'I told her to move my clothes and other things into one of the guest bedrooms where I propose to remain until your bastard is born. After you have recovered we shall share a bedroom only until such time as you bear me a son. After that I shall have no further use for you.'

She swallowed hard and a spot of colour burned in each cheek.

He saw it and his mouth twisted in contempt. 'In other words the less I see of you the better.' With that he got up abruptly, too abruptly, lurched unsteadily, righted himself and then with a venomous look in her direction opened the door and was gone.

The guest rooms in Hillview were located in the east wing, a corridor and a half separating them from the main bedroom which they had shared until tonight.

After giving him ample time to reach his new sleeping quarters she left the sitting-room and crept upstairs like a thief in her own house. Mary had done a hasty job of transferring Edward's belongings, leaving the bedroom untidy but Susan barely noticed. All she wanted was to be alone and to have somewhere to lay her head.

She undressed as quickly as her tired limbs would permit and got into bed. Lying between the cold sheets she curled her feet up in her nightdress for warmth. She shivered,

177

missing the familiar warmth next to her. Beyond sleep but with her body resting, Susan found her mind clearer than it had been all day.

Papa need never know and for that she was deeply grateful to Edward. A shudder went through her as she thought of the shame and disgrace she would have brought on the family. Mama, she guessed, would have taken to her bed, distanced herself from her friends, unable to cope with shame. Mercifully her parents were to be spared the pain and humiliation. Edward, for his own reasons, was determined to show the outside world that they were an affectionate loving couple and she would willingly play her part.

How badly she had let Edward down and she had deserved everything he said. He had treated her gently, reverently; only that one time when he'd had too much to drink had he taken her ruthlessly. And now he would seek his pleasure with other women.

Sleep eventually claimed her and it was like a drugged sleep, taking her some time to adjust when she awoke. The warmth of Edward's body was missing and she stretched out her hand to the emptiness before it all flooded back. She had slept late but it was a matter of indifference. So much easier to breakfast alone than try to make conversation.

What would the maids think? Separate rooms so soon, so early in their marriage. It was humiliating to think of the whispers and giggles that would go on in the servants' quarters. She remembered her mother once saying, half in annoyance, half in amusement, that the servants knew more about the affairs of their employers than the employers themselves.

As she brought fresh tea and toast into the breakfast-room Mary's expression was inscrutable. But what had she told the others? Still, what did it matter what any of them thought, they were only servants.

Day followed day with monotonous regularity. Edward said only the minimum and she felt if she didn't have something to do she would go out of her mind. Occasionally she had afternoon tea with her mother but her mother had a busy social life and not a great deal of time to spend with her daughter. Now Susan had a new routine. Hamish had changed his hours in the mill. Before, he had gone in the afternoon, now it was morning. And he had been pleased when Susan suggested she come over most afternoons to Aran Heights and help with the paperwork.

Ramsay had just deposited her at the entrance to Aran Heights and after leaving her cape with one of the maids she went along to the drawing-room to find her parents sitting together.

'Here comes the worker,' Hamish said jovially.

Susan kissed them both and marvelled at the change in her mother. No longer did she look disapproving when she and her papa disappeared to the library to discuss the affairs of the mill. Hamish treated her as a partner and seemed content when she was with him. Edward's name was seldom mentioned and sometimes she wondered if all was well between them.

'Susan, Winnie is being very tiresome.'

'That doesn't sound like her.'

'She wants a quiet wedding and I went along with that. About the same number of guests as at yours I suggested.'

'Mama, my wedding was anything but a quiet affair.'

'Nonsense. With more time for arrangements your wedding would have been a much more elaborate occasion. You only had one bridesmaid.'

'Hannah was enough.' Then Susan giggled. 'I didn't mean that the way it sounded. I only wanted one bridesmaid and Hannah was my choice. Who has Winnie decided on?'

'A cousin on her mother's side.' She gave a deep sigh. 'A mere handful of guests is all she wants – indeed all she'll have. When she makes up her mind Winnie is a very determined young woman.'

'What does Mr Clapperton have to say?'

'It's Winnie's day and if it is her wish so be it.'

'Then be pleased, Mama, it'll save you a lot of worry and work.'

179

'But I would have enjoyed arranging something special,' Mrs MacFarlane said regretfully. 'Admittedly yours was a worry but this one I could have enjoyed because it wouldn't have been entirely my responsibility.'

'I give up.' Susan smiled.

'I did a long time ago,' her father grunted as he got up gingerly. 'We'll get along to the library, lass, and leave your mother free to try more persuasion on Winnie.'

'Waste of time but I will pay a visit to find out how the work is coming along at Holmlea.'

'When I spoke to Matthew and Winnie they seemed delighted with the renovations to their new home.'

'Much needed renovations, I can tell you. Nothing has been done at Holmlea for years and the interior is a disgrace.'

'Which is why the price was so low,' Mr MacFarlane said, pausing at the doorway.

'And now they can do it up the way they want,' Susan added.

'Yes, I suppose there's that.'

# CHAPTER TWELVE

Keeping her secret had been easier than she had dared hope but as was inevitable the day came when Susan felt herself being studied surreptitiously.

'I'm wondering, Susan dear, if you're keeping something from me?'

Susan had herself well prepared. 'No, Mama, but I wanted to be sure.'

'And you are?'

'Yes.' She gave a smile she hoped would pass for a happy mother-to-be. It must have been convincing because Sarah got up and hugged her daughter.

'How lovely, I'm absolutely delighted. Maybe I shouldn't say this but I can't help hoping your first-born is a boy. Your papa would be overjoyed.'

'Then I hope it is a boy,' Susan said quietly.

'What is Edward saying? He must be over the moon.'

'Prospective papas usually are,' she said lightly but she had to bite her lip to keep her mouth from trembling. This should have been such a wonderful time and it would have been if only she had been carrying Edward's child. In truth the dreadful atmosphere at Hillview was getting worse by the day and she was finding it more and more difficult to put on an act. Edward, on the other hand, would have made a good actor she thought; he could switch on the charm for the benefit of others and wipe it clear once they were on their own.

'Lilian and John will be pleased at the news though of course they are already grandparents so it isn't quite the same thrill for them as it is for us.'

'No, I suppose not.'

'You'll be seeing Edward's doctor?'

'Yes. Edward has arranged for him to visit regularly.' That part was true and showed a little regard for her well-being.

'You are keeping well? No problems with sickness?'

'A little nausea earlier on but I'm all right now.'

'Then think yourself lucky. I had quite a dreadful time with the three of you.' She paused. 'You must be careful, try to eat sensibly and take plenty of rest.'

'Mama, you're fussing already,' Susan said, laughing, 'and it's early days.'

'With cause, you've never been very good at taking advice and I'm not taking any chances with our first grandchild.' She gave a little laugh. 'I must say you and Edward haven't put off much time, have you?'

Susan could feel the colour creeping up her neck and, unable to look at her mother, fell to admiring the needlework with an unusual display of interest. 'This is quite lovely, Mama, and something I could never do.'

'More's the pity but with the coming baby you must take less interest in the affairs of the mill and concentrate on your other duties. If you don't Edward will be putting his foot down and I for one wouldn't blame him.'

'Mama, Miss Wilson is very efficient and everything at Hillview is running smoothly. In truth there is very little for me to do.'

'That will change when the little one arrives.'

'I can't imagine why. The nurse will deal with all that surely.'

'Don't be silly, I wasn't referring to those duties but rather to such things as engaging extra staff.'

'Dr Walker spoke about a midwife and he is to do the arranging.'

'Good! I might have known that Edward would have seen to everything well in advance.'

'Hardly an onerous task, Mama. All Edward did was approach Dr Walker,' Susan said a little sourly.

'You must have an approximate date?'

'He – he was quite vague, Mama. According to him first babies seldom arrive when expected.'

'A week or two either way,' her mother said matter-of-factly. 'What about the nursery? Have you decided which rooms to prepare?'

'No, I haven't given it any thought.'

'Then you should start thinking about it now.' She pursed her lips, a habit she had when she was considering something of importance. 'South-facing rooms would be best and yours being smallish means that bit more planning.'

'Surely that can wait,' Susan said impatiently. The strain of continually acting a part was taking its toll and there were times when she wondered if she could go on deceiving everybody, but then reminded herself that she had no choice. If Papa had been in robust health maybe she would have been brave enough to face up to the consequences. No, that wasn't true, she would have clutched at any straw to hide the truth.

Her weariness must have shown for Mrs MacFarlane was suddenly all concern.

'Susan, you are not to let the thought of childbirth worry you. It's natural to be apprehensive but just remember I'll be at hand to help you.'

'Thank you, Mama,' Susan said unsteadily. 'I know I'm going to need you.'

'Once Matthew and Winnie are married and settled in Holmlea you'll have me all to yourself. Believe me, my dear, you are approaching the happiest and most satisfying time of a woman's life.'

'You surprise me, Mama,' Susan blurted out, unable to stop herself. 'There were times when I was quite small that I felt myself positively unwanted.'

'What a dreadful thing to say to your mother,' Sarah said sharply, the angry colour flooding her face. 'You were never unwanted, indeed I was proud to have such a lovely daughter. Admittedly I found you difficult and wilful.'

'That was my reaction to feeling unloved and insecure,' Susan said, her voice harsh. 'You didn't show me much affection.'

Mrs MacFarlane looked taken aback and deeply offended.

'I never realised you were so sensitive, it certainly never showed.' She frowned. 'This isn't the first time you've hinted that I favoured the boys but why bring it up now?'

'I don't know why I'm doing it,' Susan said, distressed, 'it just all came out. I'm sorry, very sorry that I said all that.'

'You've been dwelling on imaginary slights and that is unhealthy. We all make mistakes,' she said unsteadily, 'and I'm sincerely sorry that you believed yourself unloved. Nothing could have been further from the truth.'

'Let's not say any more about it, Mama,' Susan said wretchedly. 'I don't know what is wrong with me.' Then she burst into tears.

'There! There!' Mrs MacFarlane said soothingly and bending her head she touched her cheek to Susan's. 'Pregnancy plays strange tricks and it's a time when some of us do and say things that are completely out of character.'

Susan gave a watery smile. 'I'm glad there's an explanation.'

'You'll feel better in a few minutes.' She touched her forehead delicately. 'I feel one of my headaches coming on and a cup of tea will help us both. You're nearer, ring the bell, dear.'

'My fault,' she said getting up to ring for the maid.

'No, it's been a niggling ache all day and I don't want it to develop.'

'You must lie down.'

'I should I know but I'm not sure when your papa is coming home and I like to be downstairs when he gets in.'

Susan got up and wandered over to the window. The familiar scene had a soothing effect. This was home, this would always be home. The maid arrived and after giving her instructions, Mrs MacFarlane joined Susan at the window.

'This is what I miss, Mama. There is hardly any view from our sitting-room window.'

'But then Hillview –'

'How they settled on that house name I'll never understand, a misnomer if ever there was one.'

'True, but being so low-lying you are spared the worst

of the weather. Here as you know we get the full force of anything that is going. The very thought of winter, wind, snow and the freezing cold – ' She gave a mock shiver.

Tea arrived and the next few minutes went to the serving of it. They sipped the weak tea, Susan quiet and her mother thoughtful. Of a sudden she seemed to make up her mind and putting down her cup she sat with her back rod straight.

'I think it would be better, Susan, if we cleared the air completely with no more misunderstandings. Perhaps then you will see my seeming lack of affection in another light.'

'Mama, I have apologised, isn't that enough?'

'In this instance – no, it isn't. Far better that we should talk it through.' She took a sip of tea before continuing. 'Has it ever occurred to you that the boys, particularly Matthew, may have resented the attention you got from Papa?'

'I don't recall getting more.'

'We see what we want to see,' her mother said tartly. 'Matthew was always made to feel inferior. You had the better brain and of that he was constantly reminded. Sharing Matthew's tutor was a grave mistake and something I was against from the start.' She moistened her lips and her voice hardened. 'Was it any wonder that he lost heart with his lessons? Some of us are slower to learn but what we do learn we retain.'

'Mama – '

'Let me finish then there will be no reason ever to bring this up again. When it comes to his family your papa does not easily admit to a mistake but I believe he only has himself to blame. Handled differently Matthew may well have taken his proper place in the mill and what's more made a success of it.'

'And my marriage of convenience would not have been necessary or should I say less pressure would have been put on me,' Susan said angrily.

Mrs MacFarlane was staring at her.

'Blame it on my condition,' Susan said flippantly, wishing she hadn't said it but she could see her mother wasn't going to let it pass.

'Aren't you and Edward happy?' Mrs MacFarlane asked. 'You always appear to be.'

'We get along all right.'

'Is that all?'

Susan moved uncomfortably. 'Maybe I was expecting too much.' It was all she could think to say.

'A bit of give and take, Susan, you'll both have to learn that.'

'Mama, be fair, you know perfectly well that I entered this marriage to ease Papa's worries about the mill. You can hardly deny putting pressure on me.'

'I admit to encouraging the union.'

'Oh, you did, Mama.' Then she smiled. 'I haven't much to grumble about.'

'My dear, you're suffering from a form of melancholia which is not uncommon in pregnancy though it is usually after the birth. Anyway, Susan, once the baby arrives it will bring you closer and I can imagine Edward a doting father.' There was a timid knock at the door.

'Yes, what is it?'

The door opened a fraction. 'M'am, the carriage for Mistress Brodie – what'll I tell him?'

Susan got up, anxious to get away. 'Tell Ramsay to come to the front entrance. I'm just leaving.'

'Aren't you waiting to see Papa?'

'No, I'll see him tomorrow afternoon. And, Mama,' she said hesitantly, 'Edward and I get along well enough, don't worry about us.'

'I assure you I'm not in the least worried.'

Susan put on her cape and her mother accompanied her to the door.

'Take care of yourself,' she said, kissing her cheek.

'I'll do that.'

After waving from the window of the carriage Susan leaned back exhausted. So much had come out in that talk, each learning a lot about the other. Looking back she saw a clearer picture and her mother could have been right about Matthew. She had been thoughtless and selfish; compared to Matthew she had always been so much quicker to learn. What had been so simple to her had taken Matthew such a long time to grasp and she had been eager to move on to something more advanced. But that was no excuse, she could have waited for her brother to catch up. She sighed. It was too late for regrets.

As the weeks slowly dragged on and summer faded into a browning and mellowing autumn the gardens at Hillview were constantly being cleared of the crimson and brown leaves blown into the damp earth by the frivolous wind. Today the sun did not shine, it was grey and depressing like her spirits. She turned from the window to seat herself at her desk and, picking up her pen, decided to answer the letters long overdue a reply. She wondered what to say.

It was hard to sleep. Susan tossed and turned and closed her eyes as if to shut out the suspicions. She could not have said when they had first been aroused though looking back she saw significance in what had then seemed innocent, unconnected incidents. There was the way that maid Mary stood unnecessarily close to Edward when serving him at the table. The secretive smile on her face – not quite a smile – a mere twitch of the lips as if something amused her. And that provocative swing to the hips, was it becoming more pronounced or was it all in her imagination? Maybe she would have settled for that had it not been – she smiled grimly. Fate must have played into her hands or how else at that precise moment would she have looked over the banister and seen a disappearing hemline. No more than faintly curious she had moved on to a bend in the stairway where they were in full view. She stood and watched.

Edward was quite a bit taller than the maid and he had to stoop down to whisper something in her ear. Whatever it was had her giggling and to stop her he had raised his hand to land a playful slap on her skirt.

Susan's anger, part humiliation, was in danger of boiling over but she forced herself to remain calm. An unladylike outburst would be unwise and only make Edward believe her jealous. Or then perhaps not; he didn't feel she had any affection for him. Was she jealous, she asked herself? No, just furious but in all honesty she knew it was more than that.

Next morning Susan had her breakfast brought to her in bed. Once she heard the carriage leave with Edward she would get up.

There was something magical about impending motherhood, Susan thought. Even in her unhappiness there was a creamy bloom to her skin and a healthy shine to her hair. She dressed with care, checking her appearance in the mirror. What she was about to do needed confidence but she didn't doubt her ability to carry it out. With her thick fair hair coiled elegantly and her head held high she was every inch the mistress of Hillview as someone was to find out.

With her hand on the banister she went down the graceful stairway and into the wide hall. Mary was leaning over the gleaming surface of the exquisitely carved table which had once graced the Old Mill House and which Aunt Rachel had insisted on Susan having. The maid's elbow was raised and her hand was busy with a polished cloth. She did not raise her eyes.

Standing there, Susan had to fight an urge to hurl the book she was carrying and strike that hateful creature. She took a deep breath.

'Mary!' she said sharply, expecting an instant response but instead the head went up slowly and the eyes were insolent.

'M'am?'

'Leave what you are doing and go along to the dining-room. At once, girl. I will deal with you directly.'

A lot of the insolence had gone to be replaced by a startled wariness and was there also fear? It had been the tone of voice more than the words that had brought on the change and Susan felt a glow of satisfaction as she swept through the archway to where the housekeeper had her own sitting-room. Miss Wilson was there, it was her time off.

Alarmed at seeing her mistress, she got up quickly and her prim features were troubled.

'M'am, is something the matter?'

'Only that I am about to dispense with Mary's services.'

'Oh!'

'She is in the dining-room awaiting me and when I ring I want you to come.'

'Yes, of course, I'll come right away.'

Mary was standing with her back to the window and her hands clasped in front of her when Susan entered. Sweeping past, Susan went to the head of the long, mahogany table and drew out her husband's chair. She turned it round to face the girl before sitting down. Now that the moment had come she didn't feel the least bit nervous, rather she was enjoying the other's discomfort.

'How long have you worked at Hillview?'

'Over – over a year, m'am,' she faltered.

'I see. Maybe you satisfied your previous mistress but I find you far from suitable.'

'I'm a good worker.'

'You may well be but your manner is insolent and I will not tolerate it for another day. Your dismissal is immediate, though I have decided to pay your wages for the full week.'

Mary looked dumbfounded and her face was grey with shock. But just as Susan was beginning to feel a small twinge of sympathy the girl began shouting.

'That's it,' she almost spat, 'wantin' rid of me and for what? Tell me the real reason but you can't, can you?' she screeched.

'I am not required to give an explanation for my actions. I am mistress of this house and I strongly object to your disgraceful manner.'

'Huh! We'll see what the master has to say about that,' she said, her eyes narrowing down on Susan. 'He won't have me thrown out, I can tell you that now.' A sly look came out on her face. 'Seein' as you're not a proper wife to him like – '

'How dare you! You – you slut of a girl,' Susan screeched, white to the lips.

'That went home,' she sneered. 'See, I knows what goes on and if the master fancies me for a bit of – '

Almost knocking the chair over in her haste, Susan went across to the hand-bell and gave it such a tug that it was in danger of coming apart.

Miss Wilson was with them within moments. Her eyes went from one to the other.

A few deep breaths and Susan was sufficiently recovered to greet the housekeeper.

'Thank you for coming so promptly.' She turned to look at the maid as if she were some particularly revolting garbage. 'This creature is no longer in my employ, Miss Wilson. Pay her her wages until the end of the week but I want her out of Hillview now. Is that understood?'

'Yes, m'am.' Miss Wilson's smile was one of quiet satisfaction.

All the bravado had gone and Mary now resorted to noisy tears.

'What'll happen to me?' she blubbered. 'Weren't my fault the master fancied me.' She turned imploringly to Susan. 'Give me another chance, m'am, please. I've no place to go – you can't just throw me out. I'm sorry, m'am, please . . .' she snivelled.

'Don't waste any sympathy on this young woman, m'am, her kind will always survive.' Then with a remarkable show of strength Miss Wilson took hold of the maid and frogmarched her out of the room.

After they had gone Susan sat down and closed her eyes. She had not expected such an ugly scene and it had upset her more than she had expected. Then there was Edward to face later on.

Miss Wilson approached her after Susan had eaten a light meal. 'She's gone, m'am, bag and baggage and we'll all be the better for it.'

'If her work was unsatisfactory,' Susan said coldly, 'it was your place to report the matter to me.'

'That was the problem, m'am, her work couldn't be faulted.
It was the disturbing effect she had on the others that was the
trouble but I felt I should be able to deal with that.'

'Yes, I see your difficulty.' Susan smiled wanly. 'Now we
have the problem of engaging another table-maid.'

'May I make a suggestion, m'am?'

'Of course.'

'One of the kitchen maids is a bright and intelligent girl and
I believe with a little training she would prove satisfactory.'

'Very well, give the girl a chance and I imagine it is easier
to replace a kitchen maid.'

'It is, m'am, and thank you.'

The day's happenings had taken a lot out of Susan and she
was glad to lie back on the couch with her feet up.

She wasn't really worried but she did wonder what Edward
would say. She decided she would say nothing and leave it
to him. Maybe a guilty conscience would keep him silent.
Anyway she was ready for him if he did comment on the
change of table-maid.

The book on her lap slipped to the floor, her head nodded
and soon she was sound asleep. Miss Wilson came in, picked
up the book, placed it on a table then very quietly went out,
closing the door gently.

Flushed and nervous to hear of her unexpected promotion
to table-maid, the carrot-haired Agnes carefully followed
Polly's instructions as she started to serve the food. Susan
stole a glance at Edward but he showed no surprise at seeing
a new maid being trained. Only when they were finishing the
meal did he make mention of it.

'Why have we a new table-maid?'

Susan was saved answering by Polly coming to see if
anything else was required.

'No, Polly, we're quite finished,' Susan said, putting down
her napkin and getting up. Edward rose too and with his
impeccable good manners waited until she was ready to
precede him out of the room.

Once in their customary chairs he resorted to his habit of

placing the palms of his hands together and looking thoughtful before speaking.

'Why the change of table-maid? The other one seemed very efficient to me. Where is' – he tut-tutted – 'Whats-her-name?'

'Oh, Come! Come! Edward, you can do better than that, the girl's name can't have slipped your memory.'

'What exactly do you mean by that remark?' he asked but his eyes swerved away.

'You have no idea?'

'Where is she?'

'Dismissed.'

'On whose authority?'

'Mine of course. I am mistress of this house and the servants are my concern.'

'You mean you dismissed Mary – just like that – without any warning?'

'That's right. Aren't you going to ask the reason for her dismissal?'

'Unsatisfactory work I should imagine.'

'Not at all. Her work was well up to the expected standard.'

'Then there was no reason to dismiss her.'

Susan's self-control broke. 'No reason!' she said scornfully. 'You have the nerve to say that! Listen to me, Edward, I am well aware that there will be women in your life and I don't care just as long as it isn't someone from under the same roof. Obviously you are not very particular when you stoop to taking one of your own maids.' She was breathing heavily. 'That was despicable and if you think you have a meek and submissive wife it is time you knew otherwise.'

'Meek and submissive,' he roared. 'That is what you should be. And who are you to talk of anyone. However low I stoop it will be far short of the wrong you did me.'

What could she answer to that?

He got up and poured himself a whisky. 'Do you want anything?'

'No, thank you.'

'Of course, unwise in your condition. I should have remembered.'

He finished off his drink then went out, slamming the door behind him.

With Mary's departure Susan's relationship with Edward drifted into darker waters and she became more unhappy by the day. Her ballooning figure made her feel clumsy and unattractive and it was in this mood that she sat down to read Hannah's letter. There were pages and pages of it but with Hannah's large and well spaced writing it added up to about an average letter.

My dearest Susan,

How are you? Well, I hope and obeying instructions to take care of yourself. Knowing Edward he will see to it that you do. The gowns arrived from Miss Beattie and I am almost swooning over them. The peach-coloured, your generous gift to me, I am keeping for Matthew's wedding. It is to be a quiet affair I hear but being family I take it we are invited. You can tell Matthew I fully intend to be present anyway. Aunt Sarah, bless her, finally wore Mama down and now I have a new day dress which is quite lovely. It is a silvery grey, a colour I would never have chosen but your clever Miss Beattie was right as usual and it really does something for me. May I whisper something? The bosom, Susan, there is a definite improvement, I'm sure of it. Mama says it looks the same to her but then I'm the one who should know.

Susan giggled and wiped her eyes. What she would give to have Hannah beside her – no one could be in her company for long and remain in the doldrums. She went back to the letter.

Samuel wrote a letter to me which was little better than the thank-you note one sends to an acquaintance who has provided afternoon tea. Such a pathetic effort got no reply from me I can tell you.

I'm terribly depressed, feel life is slipping by me and nothing to show for it. Do you think I would make a good nurse? I read somewhere that young ladies from very good families – one or two anyway – are training to become nurses. The need, I believe, is very great. Mama is so upset and fearful that I may do something about it that she hardly allows me out of her sight which brings me neatly to the next bit – could you bear to have me come and stay for a few days? Mama says newlyweds prefer to spend their time together and if this is the case with you then you must be honest and tell me. On the other hand if you could persuade Edward that you needed company during the day then he may be agreeable to a visit from me. Please try, dearest Susan, I really am very low.

Your affectionate and loving cousin,<br>
Hannah

Edward had taken to spending most evenings away from home. He didn't say where he was going and she didn't ask. The only time they conversed was over dinner or for a short time in the sitting-room. Susan had Hannah's letter with her as they sat down to dinner.

'Edward, I have just had a letter from Hannah and she would like to spend a few days with us if you are agreeable.'

'Quite agreeable,' he said between bites. Then added surprisingly, 'She will be company for you.'

'Just what Hannah said.' She smiled.

He looked at her sharply, his brow drawn in a frown.

'Company during the day, Edward,' she said gently. 'She knows nothing of the circumstances.'

'Yes, well, as I said, invite her by all means.' He lapsed into silence but he was obviously deep in thought. 'Hannah's parents will be coming with her?'

'I would expect so. Very likely Uncle George and Aunt Millie will stay overnight at Aran Heights.'

'In that case we had better offer hospitality by having your parents and your aunt and uncle at Hillview for dinner.'

Susan was pleasantly surprised. 'That would be very nice.'

He smiled faintly. 'May I mention, my dear, that your performance in company of late has been far short of convincing.'

'I'm so sorry,' she said sarcastically, 'but I promise to make a greater effort for I am no more anxious than you to show anyone the true state of our relationship.'

The dinner party at Hillview was a pleasant occasion with everyone contributing to the conversation. Even Uncle George, so often tongue-tied, had opened up. With Mr MacFarlane he was more relaxed but then, Susan thought, her papa had mellowed since his illness and his manner was much less brusque and impatient.

'Edward,' Aunt Millie smiled to her host, 'you have a lovely home and I feel almost envious of you both with your life ahead of you.'

'Millie, that is most depressing – '

'Well, we have to face it, we are getting older – '

'I'm only too well aware of that and I don't like being reminded of it, particularly since I am some years older than you.'

'You've nothing to worry about, Aunt Sarah, you always look nice.'

'Thank you, Hannah.'

She gave a deep sigh. 'I wish I were pretty – '

'Hannah – '

'No, Susan, it's true. Appearance is very important.'

'No, it's not – ' Susan began but Edward interrupted.

'Hannah is right, looks are important and it is foolish to suggest otherwise – '

'See – '

'No, Hannah, let me finish. Looks attract but personality is just as important and you, young lady, have an abundance of that.'

Hannah blushed and looked pleased and Susan shot Edward a look of surprised approval.

\*　　\*　　\*

Hannah's natural high spirits brought much-needed relief to Hillview and in the evenings Edward remained at home and teased her mercilessly but she took it in good part and gave as good as she got.

'By the way, Samuel told me he wrote to you but you didn't favour him with a reply.'

'What a nerve! What a cheek! Edward, I should have brought the letter and let you read it. Goodness knows there was nothing personal in it.'

'But you did keep it,' Susan grinned.

Hannah ignored her.

'Surely you didn't expect him to pour his heart out,' Edward teased, 'poor Samuel wouldn't know how.'

'A little encouragement from you, Hannah, may have helped.' Susan smiled.

'Edward, do tell me, please, I want to know, was Samuel really upset at not getting a reply?'

'Devastated.'

'Don't tease, just tell me,' Hannah said quietly.

Edward smiled kindly. 'Yes, Hannah, I honestly believe he was disappointed but he was at pains to hide it. Samuel may have been afraid to tell you his feelings lest he frighten you off or, worse, have you laugh at him.'

'I would never do that, laugh at him I mean.'

'You do like him, don't you?'

'Yes, Susan, that's why I was so disappointed. I thought it was just a thank-you letter for being kind to him at the wedding.'

'Then put him out of his misery and write a note from here.'

'Yes, I could do that.' She turned to Edward. 'I could hug you, you really are a pet at times.'

'No running away to be a nurse now?' Susan said softly but Edward had heard.

'What's all this about nursing?'

'Nothing,' Hannah said hurriedly, 'it was just something said in fun.' She glared at Susan.

All too soon the holiday was over and after Hannah's

departure Susan made every effort to keep the atmosphere from deteriorating to its former chilly coolness and for a while she succeeded.

On a bitterly cold day in January with the frost still thick on the ground, Matthew and Winnie were married quietly in the church where Susan and Edward had taken their vows. Only close relatives and friends, shivering in their finery, had been invited for the occasion.

In a classically simple white gown with a short veil the bride looked tall and regal and serenely happy as the minister began the ceremony. And as they were pronounced husband and wife there was a radiance about her that made her truly beautiful.

Those who had not seen Winnie since her engagement to Matthew were having difficulty in equating this handsome young woman with the gauche, plain daughter of Euan Clapperton.

During the ceremony Susan stole a sideways glance at her husband, wondering what his thoughts were. Such a short time ago they too had made their vows before God. Edward must have been conscious of her eyes on him for he gave her a faint smile before turning his attention to the minister.

The words of the service were only a background to Susan's thoughts. Would her brother's marriage turn out to be happy? First-hand knowledge of the misery and despair the other could inflict had her praying silently that these two would find happiness together. Certainly Winnie would play her part and more, and Matthew would try to be a good and faithful husband for a time at least. But in restless moments what then? Would he remember with an aching longing what might have been? Caroline so delicately beautiful with such a sparkling personality and somehow so right for Matthew, the two names linked together for so long. Her papa had approved of Caroline, recognising the strength behind all that light-hearted nonsense but Matthew's head had ruled his heart.

197

# CHAPTER THIRTEEN

A s a harsh winter eased its icy grip the snowdrops bravely heralded another spring. Soon the whole countryside would awaken to the joyous sight of young lambs frisking in the fields but Susan was uncaring. Physically and mentally she felt weighed down and longed for the relief of shedding this burden and having her body her own again. There were times, more frequent now, when she hated the life growing inside her and hated herself for thinking the thoughts she did. Far less important to her now were the remarks the baby's early arrival would bring. People would believe Edward and she had anticipated marriage – well what if they did? It made no difference.

After that first embarrassing visit she had seen the folly and the uselessness of being vague with Dr Walker, a stocky, red-faced, middle-aged man with a brisk professional manner.

That the baby's 'premature' arrival would cause ripples through their circle she was in no doubt. There would be whispers from some and raised eyebrows, heavy with disapproval, from others. She managed a grim smile as she wondered how they would cope with the stark truth – that she was not carrying her husband's child.

That night, like so many other nights, Susan was alone in the sitting-room where a cheerful log fire burned. She raised her head from her book when the unmistakable noise of the heavy front door opening reached her. She heard voices too subdued to recognise and glancing at the clock wondered who could be calling. It had gone ten, too early for Edward who would let himself in noiselessly or nearly so; he'd had a lot of practice of late.

On the point of investigating, Susan was on her feet when after a light tap on the door it opened and she looked into Matthew's chalk-white face.

'Edward! Where is he?' he asked sharply, looking about the room as if he should find him there.

Startled as well as apprehensive she shook her head. 'Edward is out, Matthew, I don't know when he'll be home.'

'Susan –' He stopped, unable to go on and she knew with a dreadful certainty what she was about to hear.

'Papa! It's Papa!' she whispered, willing him to deny it but knowing he wasn't going to.

'Susan, you've got to be brave – '

'No! No! No!' she screamed and as the noise hit the room she was conscious of Matthew beginning to move, saw his blurred figure take on a grotesque shape and as the room began to spin alarmingly her hand went out and clutched at air – then she was falling – falling – falling. The sharp edge of something, the corner of the table, digging into her had her gasping, then an agonising, hot, fierce, brutalising pain shot through her followed by a piercing scream and after that only blackness and blessed oblivion.

She drifted in and out of consciousness and through it all pain, searing agonising pain that had her gasping as it held her in its terrifying grip. A white figure, two white figures, an army of white figures floated before her eyes, a face hovered near to hers and she tried to push it away but her arms were too heavy. Something cool wiped her forehead and whispered consultations went on around the bed, then came the blessed relief of sleep. Sleep from which she never wanted to awaken.

But those monsters in their white coats were pulling her back, trying to force her awake and she was deriving a curious comfort from refusing to co-operate. She had a choice but they didn't know that. Two doors were opening for her. To enter one was to invite more pain and unhappiness and she was so tired, so dreadfully tired and too weak to fight. But the other was drawing her ever nearer and from it she could hear soft, hauntingly beautiful music. Could these be the gates of heaven opening for her? Was she dying? She felt no fear just a longing to be safe but she must hurry – if she could just reach – but it was too late. With a gentle click the gates closed and there was the sound of a door closing.

Her eyes flickered open.

'She's coming round.'

'Thank God! Oh, thank God!' That was Papa's voice but it wasn't Papa standing looking down at her. It was Edward. She moved her head from side to side, she didn't want Edward, she wanted Papa. Her mouth opened, she tried to speak but she was too weak, too weak even to keep her eyes open.

'She'll be fine now, the crisis is past.' The doctor's voice was gruff but satisfied. 'What she needs is rest, plenty of it and I'd advise you both to get the same.'

'Dr Walker is right, Edward, you should go and lie down. I'll sit with Susan for a little while then I'll go home.'

That was Mama but where was Papa? Why wasn't he here? Maybe he'd gone to the mill. She could hear Edward's reluctance to go but at last he did agree. Only when she heard the click of the door did she open her eyes.

'Mama,' she said weakly.

'Oh, my darling.' The tears were coursing down her face and her mouth was quivering. 'You've been so very ill and we've all been so terribly worried.' Susan felt the wet cheek touch her own, then fear took hold of her and her hand went to the flatness that was her stomach.

'My baby!' Her eyes were wild as she tried to struggle up. 'What have they done?'

Mrs MacFarlane and the nurse exchanged looks then the nurse got up and walked away to the other end of the room. Susan's eyes followed her every movement. She saw her bend down to lift a shawl-wrapped bundle from the cradle and carry it over to the bed. Very gently she placed the baby in its mother's arms then with a smile to Mrs MacFarlane she left the room.

'Susan, dear, you have a beautiful son, he is quite, quite perfect,' she said softly.

Susan's eyes melted in wonderment as she looked into the tiny, crumpled face. Gently she touched the little hand with its perfectly formed fingers and felt an indescribable rush of love. Nothing had prepared her for the fierce protectiveness she was experiencing for this tiny scrap of humanity. Her son, her own child and in those moments she vowed that no harm would ever come to this child of her flesh.

'Mama?'

'What is it, darling?'

'Papa will be so happy, he wanted a grandson and now he's got one. My son is beautiful, isn't he?' she said proudly. 'I can't wait to show him to Papa.'

Sarah gave a sob. 'Susan, oh my dear, you must remember. Matthew came to tell you. It was the shock of that and you falling that brought on the baby. Darling, we've lost Papa.'

Susan looked at her mother with rising concern. What was that she was saying? Lost! How could Papa be lost? She puckered her brow trying to concentrate but she didn't seem able to keep her mind on anything and nothing was making sense.

'You're not well, Mama, you should go and lie down. And why are you wearing black? You know Papa doesn't like you in dark colours,' she said, before dropping her gaze to the still sleeping infant. 'If only he would hurry,' she said wistfully.

Her mother mumbled something, got up, opened the door and called for the nurse.

'Take the baby back, please, nurse.'

'I'll take him now, Mrs Brodie.' She lifted the baby with practised ease and settled him in the cradle. When she returned to Susan she had a bottle and a spoon. 'A little of this and just let it slide down your throat,' she said, pouring a spoonful of the mixture.

Susan opened her mouth like an obedient child, made a face at the taste and gave a slight shudder. Soon a pleasant drowsiness washed over her and in a few minutes she drifted off to sleep.

Edward was dozing in the chair at the bedside when Susan

awoke. She was studying him dispassionately when he opened his eyes and a broad smile lit his face.

'How are you feeling, Susan?' He got up and bent over the bed to kiss her brow. He touched her hand then sat down.

'I'm fine, much better,' she said unsteadily.

She saw with surprise that he was fighting some emotion and when he spoke there was a catch in his voice.

'You've been so very ill,' he said huskily, 'and you had us all desperately worried.'

'Were you, Edward? Were you really worried?'

There were dark shadows beneath his eyes and she saw the pain in them but she didn't wish the words unsaid.

'More worried than you would believe possible.'

'There's no need to worry now.' Her voice was weary.

'Is there anything I can do for you? Anything at all you need?'

'Nothing, Edward, nothing at all. All my needs have been taken care of.'

'Then I won't tire you by talking.' He smiled. 'The mill hasn't seen me for a while but I'd better put in an appearance now.' His lips brushed her cheek, his breath fanned her face then he was gone. Tears filled her eyes and ran down her cheeks. Neither of them had mentioned the baby.

Her next visitor was Matthew. He hugged and kissed her.

'Thank God you're more like yourself. No one will know what I went through, blaming myself – '

She put out her hand and he pressed it. 'I've quite recovered.'

'You're certainly coming on. Winnie's all dewy-eyed about that babe you've produced,' he said gently, 'and as for me I feel ten feet tall being an uncle.'

'Papa wanted a grandson, Matthew.'

'Yes, I know.'

'Why doesn't he come?' The tears rolled down her cheeks.

'Susan, you are only making matters worse for yourself,' he said, looking distressed. 'Blocking it off in your mind won't bring him back.'

'Papa wouldn't leave me,' she said brokenly.

'Stop it, Susan,' he said sternly. 'Father died peacefully in his sleep. It was an easy way to go. Try to think of it that way.'

She couldn't bear it. Not to see her papa again, her beloved papa. She gulped, then Matthew was holding her and she was sobbing her heart out.

'Get it out, don't fight it, Susan. Far better to give way to your grief now.'

Exhausted but more at peace, Susan lay back on the pillows. Tears were like the rain, they helped to wash away the agony. And it was strange but in those moments when she had given in to her grief she had felt her papa very near.

'Poor Mama, she'll be so lost and lonely.'

'She's coping, Susan. Mother's a very capable woman when the need arises. Perhaps worrying about you gave her less time to think of her loss.'

'Is someone with her?'

'Winnie has been spending a lot of time at Aran Heights and Aunt Millie is there. Poor Hannah is full of the cold otherwise she would have been over but she sends her love to you and the babe.'

'Matthew, what about . . .' She faltered and her eyes closed.

'Friday at two o'clock. The mill is closing for the half day to allow as many of the workers to attend as wish.'

'They'll all turn out for Papa.'

'Yes. I wish it could have been different, Susan. I feel so guilty yet I know I would never have been a success in the mill.'

'Don't torment yourself, Papa came to realise that. None of us can alter the way we are made. You are a farmer and you are going to be a good one.'

'Yes, I mean to be a good farmer,' he said confidently. 'The trouble is, things haven't worked out as Father hoped.'

'What do you mean?'

'We talked a lot, you know, these last weeks. At first he was reluctant to discuss Edward and please don't think I am being disloyal, far from it. Edward works hard, he doesn't spare himself.'

Susan propped herself up on the pillows and tucked the sodden handkerchief underneath. 'You'd better tell me, Matthew.'

'Nothing very serious, it's only that he seems to rub the workers the wrong way and the sad fact is they haven't taken to him. Father tried to be tactful, advise him.'

'But he wouldn't listen, that's Edward all right,' she said with a touch of bitterness. 'Papa hinted something of the sort to me when he was ill that last time.' She sighed. 'Edward uses the distillery as an example of how a business should be run and as he never tires of reminding me my father-in-law's workforce is better disciplined and works the harder for it or they know they are out of employment.'

He nodded. 'The rule of fear works for some, I suppose, but Father believed in a contented workforce being more reliable and conscientious and I'd go along with that.'

'Tell me what to do, Matthew. I want to keep my promise to Papa but I'm placed in an intolerable position.'

'I can understand that. Edward should listen to you, Susan. He knows you had Father's confidence and that you are well up on the management side.' He smiled. 'Added to which you are a MacFarlane. Give the workers time to get over the shock of seeing a woman in a position of authority and I do believe you would come to be accepted.'

'Am I hearing right?'

'Difficult to accept after what I've said in the past and maybe Winnie has something to do with that. She's a woman and she's capable enough.' He paused and looked at her thoughtfully. 'Once you're stronger why not get into the mill for an hour or two, get them used to seeing you about?'

'Edward would never stand for it. He thinks it is bad enough that I work at home.'

'Well, he is your husband after all.' He shrugged. 'It's up to you but forget all that just now and concentrate on getting well. And now tell me, what name have you decided to give

205

the wee lad? When I asked Edward he said he was leaving it to you.'

'I gave it some thought before you arrived so you are the first to hear. Paul because I like the name, MacFarlane for Papa rather than Hamish.'

'I'll keep it under my hat until Edward knows.'

'It wouldn't bother him.'

'Perhaps not. Too relieved that you came through what you did. The man was nearly out of his mind when we came so close to losing you so he is to be excused if he isn't showing too much excitement at becoming a father.'

She didn't answer, there was no answer. She smiled sadly and lay back feeling exhausted.

'Oh, dear, I've stayed too long and tired you out and here is the nurse ready to throw me out.' He got up, giving the nurse his lopsided grin.

'Sorry, nurse, I know you said just a few minutes – '

She looked at him reproachfully.

'Don't scold my brother.' Susan smiled. 'His visit has done me the world of good. And once I've had a rest I'm sure I'm well enough to get up for a while in the evening.'

'We'll see. Rest now and perhaps an hour downstairs and a walk around the room. Dr Walker isn't one for keeping his patients in bed longer than necessary.'

Friday, the day of the funeral, began cold and bright but by afternoon there was some warmth in the sun. When one o'clock struck the machinery in the Aranvale Papermill came to a grinding halt and the workers made haste to their homes to change into Sabbath suits and stiffened collars. In shambling fours they walked in silence ahead of the wreath-covered hearse drawn by black-plumed horses. A very large turnout of sombre-dressed business acquaintances joined relatives, friends and workers to follow the cortège to the cemetery.

All mourned the passing of Hamish MacFarlane but for the workers apprehension overshadowed their grief. The old master had been strict but fair and had earned their loyalty. With the son-in-law, Edward Brodie, in charge jobs that had once been secure seemed less so now. Already he was showing his hand by attempting to increase the workload of each worker, causing worry and resentment along the way.

After the funeral it was arranged that close members of the family should make their way to Hillview. The highly esteemed solicitors who handled the widow's affairs had expected the reading of the will to take place at Aran Heights but Mrs MacFarlane, on the advice of Dr Walker, had this changed to Hillview. Susan, he felt, was well enough to be up and dressed and sitting in her own drawing-room but not sufficiently recovered to venture out of doors.

Mrs MacFarlane, heavily weeded, the black accentuating her pallor, had been with Susan for much of the day supervising the arrangement of chairs and had a table brought through to the drawing-room for the convenience of the solicitor. Susan marvelled at her mother and wondered how she could have suppressed her own capabilities, but supposed women of her mother's generation would consider it an affront to their husband to do other than remain in the background.

By late afternoon they were assembled in the pleasantly furnished room with the sound of desultory conversation being carried on between folk ill at ease in the unnatural atmosphere.

Matthew and Winnie sat with Aunt Rachel between them. The old lady seemed to have aged in the last weeks and the death of her brother had affected her deeply. Edward sat on his own and Susan next to her mother.

Mr Joseph Weatherspoon's arrival put an end to the murmurings and Edward got up immediately to show the solicitor to his chair behind the table. He was a short, pompous elderly man who caused hidden irritation the way he kept rearranging the papers and taking time to polish his spectacles before replacing them on his blue-veined, bulbous nose. He cleared his throat and proceeded with the reading of the will.

Hamish MacFarlane had left his wife well provided for during her lifetime. Mrs MacFarlane turned slightly to exchange a wan smile with Susan. The droning voice went on . . .

'Aran Heights is to remain the property of my wife, Sarah, for as long as she has need of it. Thereafter it passes to my daughter Susan.'

Having known of this beforehand, Susan stole a glance at her husband. In that sombre room where emotions were kept in check she thought she detected quiet satisfaction. But then love of Aran Heights was something they shared. Edward had always expressed admiration for both the house and its commanding position.

'My son Matthew who has already received his inheritance in full is to have those of my personal possessions he cares to make his own.' There was a short pause and a rustle of paper then a noisy clearance of the throat. 'After my death the ownership of the Aranvale Papermill is to pass to my daughter, Susan. Her authority is absolute and only her decisions legally binding. No changes of any nature may be carried out in the mill without her written consent.'

Matthew's eyes sought and held his sister's and he gave an almost imperceptible nod before they both looked over to Edward. That he was taken aback and outraged was evident by the hard line of his mouth.

Hamish MacFarlane had been generous to various charities and to those who had served him faithfully, including Dr Sullivan who was to benefit by a small legacy. The only moment to lighten the proceedings had come when the solicitor made mention of Hamish's sister Rachel.

'To my dear sister, Rachel, I leave sufficient moneys in the sincere hope that she will use same to purchase for herself a carriage to replace the existing one which is, and has been for a considerable time, a danger to life and limb.'

Everyone smiled. It had been a joke for many years that Aunt Rachel, generous to a fault, had refused point blank all suggestions that she replace the shabby and dilapidated carriage which she declared would last her very well for the rest of her days. She laughed with the rest but there were tears in her eyes and Matthew put an arm around her.

\* \* \*

With everyone gone, Susan and Edward moved from the drawing-room to the smaller sitting-room.

'Susan, since you're not retiring I think we should talk.'

'What about?'

'Your father's will surprised me.'

'In what way?'

'It would have been more convenient and sensible if he'd left the mill in our joint ownership. Still, I'll make sure you're not troubled and such papers and documents that require your signature I'll have brought to you here.'

Her blue eyes regarded him steadily. 'Edward, I think my father made his wishes very clear. Indeed he discussed the mill with me on several occasions and left me in no doubt that he wished me to take control.'

'That is absurd, the man was sick and unable to make rational judgments.'

'That happens to be untrue and I'll tell you here and now that I intend to take an active part in the running of the mill.'

'Has it escaped your memory,' he said sarcastically, 'that you have an additional responsibility?'

'No, I haven't forgotten nor am I likely to,' she said icily. 'This is the first time you've even mentioned the baby, can't you bring yourself to?' she said bitterly.

'No, I can't. And you can hardly blame me for that. Instead you should be humbly grateful that he is to have the protection of my name.'

'Oh, I am I assure you, but people are going to think it strange if you never mention the baby. Are you sufficiently interested to want to hear the names I have decided for my son?'

'Of course.'

'Paul MacFarlane – Brodie,' she said slowly and distinctly.

'Any particular reason for the choice?'

'Paul because I like the name. MacFarlane – after all that is what he is and Brodie by your gracious consent.' She felt the sweat on her brow and her hands were moist but she couldn't stop herself adding, 'One day, should the truth come out, Paul can drop the Brodie.'

'And be known for the bastard he is?'

'There are times when I wonder if it wouldn't be better.'

'You don't think that at all.'

'How cruel and uncaring you can be, Edward.'

'You are so wrong, my dear. The truth is I care for you deeply and it is because of that that I can never come to terms with what you did to me.'

'Yes, Edward, I know. If only I could turn the clock back and this marriage of ours had never taken place.'

'I don't wish that at all but I can never accept your son. In the circumstances my terms were generous as most people would agree. And you could go some way to make amends by giving me control of the mill or at the very least joint control.'

'Never! That would be breaking my promise to my father and that I won't do.'

'Who is to look after your child?'

'Who looked after you and Thomas when you were small? Certainly not your mother, she left that to trained staff just as I mean to do.'

Slowly he began pacing the floor then came to stand in front of her.

'I would work very hard to see that the mill flourishes.'

'I know you work hard, Edward and nothing would please me more than that we should work together.'

'No, that's out of the question.'

'Why?'

'Because my position would be intolerable if I need your permission, a woman's permission, for everything I do.'

'Not everything. You have a great deal of responsibility, far more than you enjoyed at the distillery and I wouldn't dream of changing that.' She paused. 'That said, I intend taking up my rightful position at the earliest possible time.'

'Then don't come running to me when things go wrong.'

'Don't worry, I'm not likely to do that and now if you'll excuse me I'll say goodnight, it's been a long and trying day.'

'Of course,' he said, suddenly all solicitude. Swiftly he was over to open the door but before doing so he gave a half smile. 'Soon you'll be well enough for my company.'

She looked uncomprehending.

'Not until Dr Walker declares you fit. I wouldn't trouble you before you were completely well. You do remember our agreement?'

'Yes, I remember.'

'Susan, I want a son.'

'Yes, I do know that, Edward, but I would like a breathing space.' Why couldn't he have waited before talking like this? she thought resentfully. The horror of her experience was still fresh and she couldn't think of another pregnancy without a shudder. She made a move but before she could escape Edward had taken her arm and guided her back to her chair before sitting down himself.

'A few more minutes won't make much difference then you can go up.'

'What is it, Edward? Why can't it wait?'

'It is important to me to have a son and heir and as quickly as possible.'

Warning bells were ringing and she looked at him sharply. 'Paul is the first-born and it is he who will inherit the mill.'

He shook his head. 'That is where you are wrong. Paul may have my name but that doesn't alter anything. He is still a bastard.'

The colour rushed to her face. 'You delight in using that word knowing how it distresses me.'

'The truth can be cruel.' Then he smiled and leaned forward. 'Later on you'll feel differently when our son is born, yours and mine, Susan.'

She got up and almost ran from the room.

Undressing quickly, Susan got below the covers and lay rigid, staring into the darkness. How could Edward possibly cheat Paul? It was her mill, she was the legal owner. What had she to fear? Yet the unease persisted. It was a man's world and the law would bend backwards to accommodate its own. Should Edward be able to show her as incompetent, unable to manage her affairs, or if the workers refused to have a woman in charge . . . Surely it would never come to that, but if it did he would have a fight on his hands. She would fight him tooth and nail. She wouldn't fail her father. According to Matthew Edward had not endeared himself to the workers and provided she was strict and as fair as her father had been she would get the same loyalty. It was a challenge and she was ready to meet it. In two weeks whether or not Dr Walker declared her fit she would make her first entrance into the mill. She liked Matthew's suggestion of an hour or two to begin with. That settled in her mind, she turned to the matter of her marital obligations. To be pleasurable that side of marriage needed love and respect and both were in short supply in her marriage. He was desperate for a son. Thinking about it now she decided to forget her fears. The sooner the better, she wanted it over.

Paul MacFarlane Brodie gave only a tiny whimper during the christening service and only when the minister took him in his arms and splashed holy water on his head did he give a howl of outrage. Throughout it all Edward was very correct and very wooden but no one appeared to notice. Paul was the centre of attention and all eyes were on him. Hannah, much to her delight, had been given the honour of carrying the baby and declared to one and all that Paul was absolutely gorgeous and she wished she could run away with him.

In the days that followed, Edward was careful to put on a convincing show as the visitors began to arrive to see the baby and leave their gifts. Both grandmothers called frequently as if they couldn't allow a day to go by without seeing this new addition to the family.

'He is absolutely adorable, Susan,' her mother-in-law enthused as she and Mrs MacFarlane joined Susan in the drawing-room.

'Such a good baby, we left him gurgling away happily,' Susan's mother added.

'No question about whom he resembles,' Lilian Brodie gushed. 'Paul's a Brodie. John was very dark when he was younger with the same almost black eyes. He is very much John's grandson. You did see the resemblance too, didn't you, Sarah?'

'Well – yes – a little but there is quite a bit of Susan too. The shape – '

'Of course there is a little of Susan too,' Mrs Lilian Brodie conceded generously.

The maternal grandmother managed a smile but Susan could see that she was decidedly piqued.

# CHAPTER FOURTEEN

The cold April sun shone brightly and the walk to the village then back by the farm road had put the colour in her cheeks. Not ready to go indoors Susan lingered in the gardens and then, seeing Nanny Ferguson leaving the house and wheeling the high pram, she hurried to meet them.

'Good morning,' Susan said, but her attention was on the sleeping babe. After breakfast she'd gone to the nursery and gazed at the fuzz of dark hair which covered her baby's tiny, perfect head and felt her heart swell with love and pride.

'Good morning, m'am.'

The infant stirred, his eyes flickered then closed and he settled again.

'Good as gold,' Nanny Ferguson said in her throaty voice that was at odds with the soft hazel eyes and homely face. Miss Morag Ferguson could have been any age with her round figure, ample bosom and hair beginning to show salt and pepper but Susan knew her to be only in her thirty-eighth year.

'Don't venture too far,' Susan warned with an anxious glance at the sky which had darkened.

'I won't, m'am, though there's no harm in a soft April shower and Master Paul won't get wet. There's a rain cover under the quilt if it should be needed.'

Susan was annoyed with herself, she didn't want to fuss, something she deplored in others. 'Yes, of course you're well prepared,' Susan said as she turned away.

Daffodils withered and disappeared as spring gave way to summer but Susan barely noticed. The truth was she was bored and restless. She wasn't needed, the house almost ran itself. Dr Walker, though pronouncing her fit, insisted she take plenty of rest. The daily visits were unnecessary and she had annoyed him by saying so.

For something to do she went over her wardrobe with Polly. Gowns that Susan would have carelessly cast aside were quickly examined and hummed and hawed over.

'Hardly worn it is, m'am and such lovely material.'

'It's too slack.'

'That's 'cos I let out the seams. I can take them in again.'

'If I allow myself to listen to you, Polly, I'll never have anything new. All right, this once then. Take them with you to the sewing-room and if I'm satisfied I may wear them once or twice.'

Edward had a drink by his side and was reading the business news.

'I told Dr Walker that there was no need for these daily visits.'

'Wasn't that rather rude? He's been most attentive.'

'I certainly wasn't rude and he can spend more time with patients who do need him.'

'Well, I'm glad to hear that you have recovered.'

'Well enough to go into the mill for an hour or so. I want to accompany you tomorrow and have you introduce me.'

'You must be out of your mind! The answer is no, a very decided no. However, if you feel you must contribute more than your signature then I dare say I can arrange to have a little work brought here.'

'Don't be so patronising,' she snapped. 'To hear you one would imagine you owned the mill.' She took a shaky breath. 'Whether we travel together is up to you but I intend taking my place in the mill and if, as I suspect, you are already established in my father's office, then kindly vacate it and return to your own. And make no mistake, if you don't I'll take steps to have you removed.'

'As well as edging on the hysterical this is absurd,' he spluttered, the pages of his paper scattered on the floor. 'Everyone accepts me as being in charge.'

'Then the sooner they realise that you are merely standing

in for me the better.' She paused to moisten her dry lips. 'You have always been so anxious for our marriage to appear a success and our difficulties kept private but that can't go on if you are to take up this attitude.'

'More important for you I would have thought,' he sneered.

'Not any more, Edward,' Susan said quietly. 'Now that I am financially independent I can face up to the consequences of my mistake.'

'You couldn't stand the disgrace.'

'That was true when my father was alive but I could face it now.'

She hadn't intended saying that but now that she had she knew it was true.

'Very well,' he said, stumbling to his feet with his face twisted in anger. 'You can have your damned office and with you in charge we'll be facing ruin in no time.' Not bothering to pick up his newspaper he got up and halfway to the door turned. 'I'm going out, a change from your company will be more than welcome.'

'What about tomorrow?' she shouted after him. 'Do we travel together or not?'

'Go to hell.'

Susan gaped at the closed door. No one had ever sworn in her presence. Papa, she knew, had occasionally said damn but as her mother explained, that word was permissible from a man under a considerable strain.

Susan was shaking with anger. How dare he speak to her like that! She would show him, show everyone, that under her guidance the mill would go from strength to strength. It needed determination but she wasn't short of that. By putting her back into the work she could only gain the respect of the workers, for above all they wanted security of work and a living wage and who better to give them that than herself.

Her mind made up to defy Edward she went upstairs and began to look out the most suitable clothes for her first time in the mill. Being still in mourning reduced the choice. The black gowns she put aside as unsuitable and finally selected a skirt in dark grey with enough fullness to allow her freedom of movement and with it a black silk blouse.

Her anger, quick to rise, seldom lasted long and with it gone she felt a twinge of guilt. Maybe a child of Edward's would lessen the bickering which was tearing them apart and making them both miserable. She would rather like another child herself. In that mood she had even toyed with the idea of having her husband's belongings brought back to her bedroom then dismissed it. If she knew Edward he would be consoling himself with drink and the sympathetic ear of some woman. Tonight it was unlikely he would have need of her.

Morning came and Susan was keyed up. Edward overslept and she had finished breakfast before he appeared. With the maid fussing about they greeted each other civilly. She was standing dressed in cloak and bonnet and fastening her gloves but he made no remark. After a hasty breakfast he scraped back his chair and left the breakfast-room without a look in her direction. It would be undignified to follow but she could feel her lips twitching in amusement. They were both acting like children.

To pass the time before Ramsay's return Susan went along to the nursery. Paul was awake and rather timidly she bent down to take her baby in her arms. She thought he was going to protest and looked over to Nanny Ferguson in alarm.

'The wee mite won't object to a cuddle, m'am. More than likely he'll raise a rumpus when you put him down.'

Feeling the endearing warmth of the tiny body Susan cuddled him closer.

'My own precious darling,' she murmured and touched the petal-smooth cheek to her own. 'Nanny, how soon do babies recognise – I mean how soon before he knows me?' She felt foolish asking the question but Miss Ferguson only smiled kindly.

'From the very beginning, m'am, a baby knows its own mother.'

'Really?' She smiled in wonder. 'I must go,' she said handing Nanny her precious bundle.

'A proper charmer Master Paul is going to turn out.'

'I shouldn't wonder,' Susan said proudly as she left.

Nanny Ferguson watched her go then spoke to her young charge. 'Your mama loves you dearly, my pet, but as for your papa – ' She shook her head. 'Unnatural I call it, proper unnatural. Not once to my knowledge has the master come near the nursery.'

Baby Paul MacFarlane Brodie gurgled his complete indifference.

'Where to, m'am?' Ramsay asked as he helped his mistress into the carriage.

'Holmlea Farm, Ramsay, please.'

The roads were thick with dust. Everyone seemed short-tempered and she wondered if the long, dry spell was responsible.

'How long do you think this dry spell will continue?' she asked Ramsay as they approached the farm track and she asked him to stop.

'I feel a change, m'am.'

'I hope you're right. Don't wait, Ramsay, Mr MacFarlane will bring me back.'

'Very good, m'am.' He waited until she reached the gate into Holmlea Farm then he set the horses to a trot.

Susan closed the gate behind her and walked slowly along the hard, uneven path to the house. To right and left of her was a wide panoramic view of rich farmland but in the oppressive heat the countryside had a tired look. Already the shaws were drooping in the potato fields and the only splash of colour was in the hills, bright yellow with broom and touched in patches by the pale purple of heather not yet showing its full colour.

She hadn't noticed Matthew until he shouted. She waved and he waved back then, after saying something to the farmhands, he hurried over to meet his sister.

'This is a nice surprise,' he said, giving her a brotherly kiss, 'and how are you?'

'Absolutely fine, Matthew.' She smiled. 'Except for the

heat, but I have it from Ramsay that there is a change in the air.'

'Let's hope he's right.' He wiped his brow. 'It's got to break sometime.'

Holmlea was a substantial two-storey, stone-built house with no claim to splendour but since Susan's last visit a tub of flowers graced each side of the doorway. Winnie had the door open, a welcoming smile on her face.

'Susan, how lovely, come along in.'

'Just for a minute then.' She looked apologetic. 'Actually I came to see if Matthew would take me to the mill, that is if it isn't inconvenient,' she said glancing at his heavy boots and working togs.

Winnie gave a peal of laughter. 'Don't be misled by appearances. To look at him one would think he was to tackle the farmhand's job instead of just giving orders.'

'And let me tell you, my good woman, I am no stranger to manual labour,' he protested.

Susan laughed with them and felt real envy. This was how marriage should be.

'Before we say any more how is my nephew?'

'He's gorgeous, Matthew,' Susan said softly.

'And now what is this all about, Susan?'

'It can't be any surprise to you that Edward is against me setting foot in the mill and I can hardly go in by myself. I mean I'd feel a fool not knowing where to go.'

'Did you ask Edward?'

'He refused.'

'Matthew, go and change and Susan can give me all the news about little Paul.'

At the end of the recital Winnie sighed. 'I just hope you appreciate how lucky you are,' she said enviously.

'Your turn will come.'

'I hope so. It won't be for want of trying,' Winnie said without a trace of embarrassment, then saw Susan's shocked look. 'Sorry! Sorry! Sorry! We farming folk are much too outspoken but why it should embarrass you, a married woman, I don't know.'

Matthew came in soberly dressed. 'I'm ready.'

'Stay a bit longer next time,' Winnie called as Matthew had the carriage brought round.

'Oh, I shall.' She sat down beside her brother. 'I'm nervous.'

'Don't be. We'll find Mr McNeil. Father had a great respect for him and there's not much he doesn't know about the mill.'

Matthew could see that Susan was tense and kept up a flow of conversation. 'Many's the time he's covered up for me and I had reason to be grateful.'

'Edward thinks he's an old fool.'

'He's anything but that.'

Crossing the yard Matthew stopped. 'A word of brotherly advice.'

'I'm listening.'

'Edward is going out of his way to be awkward but don't be too hard on him. I have yet to meet the man who would enjoy taking orders from a woman and remember your husband has more than his share of pride.'

'But I thought you were in favour – '

'I am but you have to be careful how you go about this. The mill needs you and so does the workforce though they don't know it. Edward isn't a success, he's resented but even so they may prefer him to working for a woman.'

'Then I have to prove myself.'

'That's the spirit.'

'Matthew, I hate the way things are.' She paused and swallowed painfully, 'All I want is for us to work together but it's hopeless.'

'Things must be pretty rough for you at home.'

'Let's say they could be a lot better.'

'Don't rush things and when I think the time is right I'll have a quiet word with Edward – man to man – after all he has to accept the situation sometime. He was there at the reading of the will and Father made it clear enough that you were to be in charge.'

'You're happy, aren't you, Matthew?'

'Yes, Susan, I am. Winnie is right for me.'

'I envy you both.'

'Things will work out for you two and of one thing you can be sure. Edward loves you, Susan; if it isn't obvious to you it is to everyone else.'

'We'd better go in.'

The elderly man sweeping up the debris watched them cross the yard and go in to the mill. Matthew MacFarlane he recognised as the old master's son but only when they got closer did he see that the fine-looking woman was young Mistress Brodie. There had been plenty of rumours going about, some of them plain daft. Whoever heard of a slip of a lassie taking control of the likes of the Aranvale Papermill!

A clerk weighed down with ledgers murmured, 'Mornin', Mr Matthew, sir,' then flushed crimson. 'Beggin' your pardon, Mr MacFarlane, sir.'

Matthew smiled but made no remark. They walked along the corridor to where the offices were. Taking Susan's arm Matthew stopped opposite a door with a large brass plate, highly polished and bearing the late master's name. Seeing it brought a lump to Susan's throat and she could see Matthew was affected too. Matthew opened the door and Susan went in first. She walked to the centre of the room, a spacious room, and looked at the large mahogany desk placed across the length of window with a leather chair behind it. Cabinets lined the office but even so there was an overspill on the floor. There was a framed parchment on the wall and she went over to read it.

> Rags make paper
> Paper makes money
> Money makes banks
> Banks make loans
> Loans make beggars
> Beggars make rags.

Matthew came up behind her. 'Good, isn't it? It dates from the eighteenth century and Grandfather had it put on parchment. Later on it was framed. Father was very proud of it.'

Susan smiled. 'You know it reminds me of when we were children. Don't you remember Aunt Rachel having us stand on a box so that we could see the wagonloads of rags going into the mill?'

'You remember that too?'

'Of course, it was the highlight of our day. She told us about the clothes being sorted and all the buttons and fastenings being removed before they could be put in the boilers.'

'And that, my dear Susan, was known locally as the Buttony.'

'The what?' She giggled.

'It's true. The Buttony produced some high quality buttons which managed to find their way to the cottages. Father knew that it went on and he turned a blind eye but he often said that the villagers might be shabbily dressed but most of them sported a fine row of buttons.'

'I miss him terribly, Matthew.'

'I know,' he said gently, then pointed to the desk. 'Try it for size.'

'What?'

'Sit behind the desk and get the feel of your new position. I'll see if I can find Mr McNeil.'

Sitting in the chair that had once been her father's brought him very close but not in a tearful way. She had shed her tears, now she was going to do the job she had been entrusted with.

Mr McNeil was well beyond middle age with a face devoid of any healthy colour. He was a small man who held himself stiffly erect as if in defiance of his advancing years.

Susan came a little self-consciously from behind the desk and joined her brother. After the introductions Matthew said, 'My sister is to be in charge of the mill, Mr McNeil.'

'Father spoke very highly of you,' Susan said quietly.

'T'was a sad day for the mill when he went. The maister was a man among men.'

'We would be better sitting,' Matthew said, bringing three chairs together. He straddled his own and leaned forward.

'Mr McNeil, Mrs Brodie would be glad of your assistance until she gets settled.'

'A privilege, m'am.'

'As you probably know, Mr McNeil, I've been trained in financial matters but I'm completely ignorant about the rest and my husband is tied up with – with other matters.'

His blue-veined hand went to stroke his chin and his eyes were thoughtful.

'You see problems?'

'Oh, I do but 'tis better to face up to them than pretend they don't exist. The maister liked plain speaking and I'd be thinkin' a daughter of his would be like-minded?'

'Please go on.'

'There are some who thrive on causin' unrest and the ithers are like sheep – easily led.'

'I'm aware of the difficulties. Because I am a woman I am not accepted.'

'They'll be wary. To them you'll represent an ambitious young leddy with a few new-fangled ideas. But you've this to mind too, they've no choice but to accept you but it could be a grudgin' acceptance.'

'How would they show it?'

'A machine breakin' doon for no apparent reason, orders held up, that sort of thing.'

'That's not going to help them either and surely they'll give me a chance before resorting to that,' she said impatiently.

'Mebbe aye and mebbe no.'

'Working together is for our mutual benefit.'

'Give them time to get used to you.'

'Then let's hope they don't take too long about it,' she said crisply.

'Oh, I see a day when they won't just accept you. Mark my words, Mistress Brodie, they'll not only accept but respect you.'

'I can only hope that you're right and I'd like to meet those you feel I should meet.'

'Arrange a meeting, Mr McNeil. No need to give an explanation, just make sure they attend.'

He winked. 'The auld maister knew the value of involving the charge hands,' he said slyly. 'It gied them an inflated sense of their own importance and output improved because of it.'

Matthew hooted with laughter and Mr McNeil got up stiffly.

'I'll be gettin' back then but afore I go may I say how fine it is tae see that seat about to be occupied by a MacFarlane.'

'Even a female MacFarlane?' she teased.

'When she's a MacFarlane I mak' an exception.'

'Quite a character, our Mr McNeil.' Susan smiled when they were alone.

'And fiercely protective you'll find him. Even with me he was. No one knew better than Mr McNeil just how hopeless I was but heaven help anyone else who dared suggest it.'

# CHAPTER FIFTEEN

'Edward, are you to be present?'

They had just finished the main course and Edward placed his knife and fork side by side on the plate before answering.

'No.'

'Then I'll make your apologies.'

'Do that.'

The rice pudding, browned on the top the way Edward like it, was served and when the maid had gone he shook his head as if in exasperation.

'If you would only listen to reason, Susan. I am thinking of your welfare.'

'My welfare?'

'Yes. If you insist on being in charge then it means visiting all departments and some are positively hazardous.'

She smiled. 'I do know that, Edward, and I'm assuming you mean the Beater House. My father explained to me about the boiling of the rags, the pulp being spaded into the beaters and that the floor was always awash. He likened it to a giant wash-house.'

'Well, then – '

'It's not all like that, the machine-house by contrast is clean and dry but my place is in the office. My father spent most of his time there leaving the chargehands to look after their own areas of work. And now won't you give me your support?'

'No.'

'Very well, I'll give the reason as pressure of work,' she said sweetly.

In truth Susan was relieved, knowing that his presence would only add to her nervousness.

* * *

When eleven struck Susan took her place at the head of the highly polished oval table. She looked cool and in control but her hands in her lap and out of sight were tightly clenched. The faces round the table seemed lengthened with disapproval but she told herself that could be imagination. Maybe they always looked grim and forbidding.

Somehow she had to get the right mix, show a reasonableness and at the same time assert her authority from the start.

In his slow and precise manner Mr McNeil had introduced each one by name and occupation but little of it registered. Her mind was on what she was going to say.

Mr McNeil took his place on her left but before doing so frowned deeply at the accountant, the youngest there. Faced with such beauty and poise young Mr Harper was experiencing great difficulty in keeping his mind on business. If the more mature were similarly affected they hid it behind their long faces as they sat stiffly upright in the matching brass-studded high-backed chairs.

That she made a very attractive picture in that solemn room Susan was completely unaware. Her aim had been to look neat and businesslike but the contrast between the black of her mourning and her own fair beauty was quite startling.

She took a deep breath.

'Gentlemen,' she began and wondered if that was how she should have started. 'Now that I have taken over my late father's position in the mill I wanted this opportunity to meet you.' She was glad her voice was firm and clear and paused for a moment but there was no alteration in their expressions. 'The continued prosperity of the mill depends, among other things, on a good relationship existing between management and workers. My father did not underestimate its importance and while training me for this position, stressed its value. You have that same duty to those under you.' A few heads nodded, the accountant beamed his approval.

'Changes will only be made where these are shown to be an aid to efficiency and smooth working and will in no way constitute a threat to the workers. In all matters I intend to follow the example set by my father and I hope that the same loyalty you gave to him you will now extend to me.' She smiled. 'That is all, thank you.'

No one spoke as they shuffled out. Some bowed stiffly, others merely nodded and the accountant looked at her with undisguised admiration. Mr McNeil, at her request, remained behind.

She bit her lip. 'Is it always like this, Mr McNeil? Don't any of them make a comment?'

Mr McNeil looked shocked. 'If ye'll forgive me sayin' so, m'am, ye've a lot tae learn but you were fine, just fine,' he said hastily. 'What you said was enough to keep them from worrying, but Mistress Brodie, when ye want their opinion ye hae tae ask for it. That aside it's nae often the likes o' them is invited tae the boardroom, but ye'll mind it was Mr Matthew's orders.'

She smiled. 'It's a good thing I have you by my side to keep me from blundering.'

'We'd a' tae crawl afore we could walk, m'am,' he said with a twinkle in his faded blue eyes.

'Before you go, Mr McNeil, I want you to arrange for some-one – no, on second thoughts make that someone yourself – to show me the mill and each process of paper-making. In theory I know it, in practice I want to see it.'

Murdoch pursed his lips in disapproval. 'Some of it, m'am, if it's insistin' ye are, but a lot o' it is no' fit for a leddy tae enter.'

'Why should that be?'

'The stench, m'am, frae auld dirty rags and the boilin' o' them would hae ye reelin'. My ain stomach's been turned at times.'

'Mr McNeil,' Susan said severely, 'if my workers can spend whole days in such unpleasantness surely I can put up with it for a few minutes.'

'I'm nae sae sure,' he said stubbornly.

'Nevertheless, I intend going through with it. Indeed some improvements in their conditions may be possible if it is as bad as you suggest.'

After Mr McNeil had left Susan stared at the door that he had gently closed behind him and smiled with satisfaction, then she went through to her own office. There was a spring in her step as she walked to the cabinet, used her key to open it and carried the ledgers over to her desk.

She felt the thrill of ownership and a new confidence in herself. Doubts and uncertainties were now cast aside; she had inherited her father's shrewd business sense and the only risks she would consider would be those carefully calculated. A gambler took chances but she wasn't that way inclined. She would use her judgment and not be inhibited by those too unimaginative to see the long-term advantages.

Susan would never forget that first visit to the rag house. Mr McNeil had warned her but even so she was unprepared for the stench that almost stopped her breathing. Piles and piles of rags lay about the floor and on small stools women sat snipping away with scissors, the discarded buttons and fastenings falling at their feet ready to be swept up and emptied into containers. The women, most of them elderly, looked up at their visitors, their faces grey with tiredness but eyes bright with curiosity.

Hiding her shock and with physical sickness a distinct possibility, Susan left the premises quickly and Mr McNeil followed, looking at her with concern.

'Shouldnae hae let ye go in,' he muttered.

'You had no choice. Just give me a minute or two in the open and I'll be all right.' They went out to the yard and when she felt sufficiently recovered she shook her head. 'Mr McNeil, how can they stand it?'

'Fowk get used tae onythin' in time. Yon wimen mak' no complaints and if they did there's ithers ready and willin' tae tak' their place.'

'Surely a few improvements could be made without incurring too much expense?'

'Time enough when they seek it. Ye've enough on yer plate withoot lookin' for mair.'

'You could be right at that.' She paused and looked a little shamefaced. 'Regarding the other areas of the mill we needn't rush and do them all at once.'

'No, m'am.' Mr McNeil hid a smile.

The days became weeks and the weeks months, but Susan was hardly aware of the passing of time. Her days were fully occupied, her brain active as she put heart and soul into the work. No longer did Edward object to sharing transport in the mornings and at the least encouragement she discussed the day's events with him. Perhaps he was accepting the situation or at least making the best of it. Certainly she welcomed the thaw in their relations and now that they were sharing a bedroom she tried to be a loving wife. Not that he made it easy with his swift changes of mood, she thought, but would she ever understand her husband? He could be so gentle and tender and she could feel herself responding, then without warning he would change to a rough, demanding, frightening stranger and she would recoil from him.

Working in her office longer than usual, Susan looked up when Edward walked in unexpectedly and flung himself in a chair.

'You've done it now and don't say I didn't warn you.'

Annoyed at the interruption she frowned. 'Don't be tiresome, Edward. If something has happened then tell me what it is.'

'Number two machine, Dry End number two has broken down again and if we can't keep to our delivery dates we'll lose the order altogether.' He looked smug. 'If you'd paid attention in the first place and allowed me to order a replacement machine for that one and – '

She interrupted. 'Don't you find it strange, Edward, I know I do, that the machinery should break down so frequently?'

He shrugged. 'It's old but are you suggesting carelessness?'

'Or perhaps more than that,' she said carefully.

'Deliberate?' He looked thoughtful. 'Possible, I suppose, but it would be difficult to prove. Could be their way of bringing the problem to your attention. In any case,' he said impatiently, 'we can afford new machinery so why not replace it now?'

'I quite agree the machinery is old and no longer dependable and the matter has been receiving my attention.'

'Well, then, what do you intend to do?'

'Have you studied this article?' She handed him a trade magazine with a pamphlet keeping the place.

'No, I haven't. I've neither the time nor the inclination.'

'Then I suggest you stay where you are and read it. After that we can discuss the subject of new machinery.'

He gave her a dark look but settled down to read and she continued with her own work. Once she looked over at him briefly and seeing his raised eyebrows smiled to herself.

'Mmmmmm!' he said at last. 'Very impressive.'

'German-made but my father had a healthy respect for their workmanship and when their representatives were over here a year or two back they declared themselves very impressed with a design improvement our head machineman had thought out. Since then we've kept up the contact and should we decide to order we could be guaranteed a respectable discount and early delivery.'

'That may well be so, Susan, but this is a revolutionary design and even with a generous discount we still couldn't afford that kind of money. Far better to settle for a replacement, it has served us well in the past – '

She leaned forward eagerly. 'But don't you see, Edward, if we do that and our competitors go for this German invention we are going to lose out.'

'I see the possibility and getting in first would give us the edge – '

'Exactly. In time we could double our production,' she said excitedly. 'We have to act now and not miss this opportunity.'

'How do you propose to pay? Get the bank to finance it?'

She shook her head. 'The cost of borrowing is too high. No, I've worked it out and my figures have been checked by the accountant. We can manage – just.'

'Leaving nothing? Cleaned out?' he said aghast.

'Using my own money would let us have a small working capital.'

'Count me out, I like a bit of security at my back.'

'Quite right too,' she said briskly, 'and anyway it isn't needed.' She looked at him steadily. 'What I want, what I need is your co-operation; you can help if only you will.'

'If it is for our mutual benefit I am not likely to refuse,' he said stiffly.

'We both want what is best for the mill.'

He smiled. 'What sort of help is it you require?'

'Let the workers know that new machinery is ordered but that in the meantime we cannot afford stoppages. In fact, go as far as to tell them that their own jobs are only secure if production is kept up.'

'Quite the business woman, aren't you?' But he wasn't sneering.

'Yes, Edward, I am and I enjoy this life.' Her face softened. 'This is perhaps not the right place to announce it but we are alone so why not? I'm pregnant.'

'You are? You're absolutely sure?'

'Yes, I've seen Dr Walker.'

He got up and grasped her hand. 'When?'

'Late September.'

'You can't even begin to know what this means to me,' he said unsteadily.

'I think I do.'

'You must stop working, give all this up,' he said anxiously. 'We can't take any chances with our first-born.'

She stiffened and withdrew her hand. 'Our second,' she said coldly, 'or had you forgotten Paul?'

'He doesn't count, he isn't mine,' he said dismissively. 'This one will be a Brodie, my own flesh and blood.'

Susan gave a deep, resigned sigh. Nothing was ever going to change his attitude to Paul and quarrelling about it only set them at each other's throat.

'You must take care of yourself.'

'I shall do nothing foolish but having a baby is not an illness as every doctor is at pains to explain. It is perfectly all right for me to work so stop worrying. When the time comes and I'll know when that is, then I'll cease coming to the mill and instead work from home.' She paused and looked at him steadily. 'Once the baby is born and a few weeks to regain my strength then I'm back to working in my office in the mill.'

'I appear to have no choice in the matter but at least promise me that you won't overtax your strength.'

'I can promise you that and you can reduce my workload by seeing to the ordering of this German machine.'

'Leave it to me. Heavens! I feel like celebrating.'

She laughed. 'Just keep your mind on your work. I'm not exactly throwing you out but I have a lot to do and I work better on my own.'

'Hint taken, my dear,' he said without resentment. Then, picking up the trade magazine, he sketched a salute and departed.

Susan allowed herself to sit back for a moment and her mouth curved in a gentle smile. From now on things are going to be better, she thought. Edward is thrilled at the thought of the baby and one day soon he'll forgive me and accept Paul and we can settle down to a happy life. Without warning the sun went behind a cloud, darkening the window and some of her optimism vanished. Wishful thinking was all she was engaged in. Forgiveness for her perhaps but what chance had Paul of ever being accepted?

Shortly after Paul had celebrated his first birthday with a nursery tea-party Winnie gave birth to a son, whom she called Duncan. Such excitement that followed had never before been witnessed at Moorend. Matthew's own delight was enormous but Euan Clapperton could not contain his joy, his face was suffused with it. The farm manager right down to the most humble of the farmhands were sent to the huge kitchen at Moorend for a wee dram to drink the health of his grandson.

Susan was having a trouble-free pregnancy and only gave up

going into the mill when her condition could no longer be disguised. Throughout the months Edward had been quietly attentive to her needs and when she was at home he took time to discuss the day's happenings, knowing how much it pleased her. The order for the new machinery had been confirmed, its transport arranged and sooner than expected was in position in the Aranvale Papermill and working perfectly. In the weeks and months that followed efficiency was much improved with the workers taking a pride in the latest machinery. Delivery dates were cut, resulting in an upsurge in new orders and this in turn meant engaging more workers.

The benefits filtered through to the village with the shops doing more business and the public houses doing even better. If Susan did not receive the credit she was due, at least she was accepted as being no longer a threat.

On a mild September morning Susan's daughter was born and all she could feel was an overwhelming disappointment. She had been so sure it would be a boy. But if Edward wanted a son, he was delighted when he looked at the tiny rosebud mouth and the fan of thick lashes that lifted from eyes that stared into his own. He drew in his breath, almost ashamed of the rush of tenderness which filled his heart.

'I'm sorry, Edward,' she whispered.

'Whatever for?'

'You wanted a son so much,' she said, tears of weakness spilling over.

Bending over her he took up her hand and kissed it. 'Don't upset yourself, darling. She's lovely, absolutely beautiful, our little daughter. Thank you, Susan.'

She felt a sudden rush of love and clutched at his hand. 'I love you, Edward, and next time I promise you a son.'

'That is the first time you have ever said that to me, Susan.' He was about to say more but the doctor came in.

'Mr Brodie, your wife needs a rest after all that hard work so I must ask you to leave.'

He seemed reluctant to go and stopped beside the baby's cot.

'She's a little beauty, isn't she?' he said, gazing adoringly at the tiny face peeping out from the snowy white covers.

'Quite perfect,' Dr Walker agreed in a voice that suggested he was taking full credit.

From that first peep at his daughter Edward was besotted and visited the nursery each day. As with Paul both grandmothers were frequent visitors.

'Such a lovely name, Susan,' her mother-in-law said. 'Who decided on Victoria?'

'Edward did and we both decided Lilian for her second name.'

'I'm very honoured.'

Victoria Lilian Brodie, according to Mrs MacFarlane, was just like Susan at that age except that Victoria's hair was turning to a reddish blonde.

'Yes, Sarah,' Lilian Brodie agreed, 'this one is a MacFarlane, no doubt about that. She's going to be a beauty like her mother and her grandmother.'

Sarah demurred but blushed with pleasure at the compliment.

'Paul, now,' Mrs Lilian Brodie continued, her hand on the banister as they came slowly downstairs from the nursery, 'is getting more like John each time I see him. John doesn't see it but he's very proud just the same.'

'Paul's adorable.'

'He is and you're so lucky,' she said turning to Susan. 'It's such a pity Thomas doesn't have a son, that's three girls and a miscarriage and Elizabeth seems disinclined to have more.'

'And who could blame her,' Susan said, feeling real sympathy for the unfortunate Elizabeth. 'After going through all that it's hardly surprising.'

'Oh, one quickly forgets all that,' her mother-in-law said with a wave of a plump hand, then added with a knowing smile, 'I don't imagine she'll have too much say in the matter.'

Back at the mill work had been accumulating in her absence and Susan was kept busy getting up to date. Edward got

through a power of work and his manner when dealing with
employees had improved of late. Victoria's arrival seemed to
have mellowed him and relations were much better with the
foremen and managers.

Each day without fail Edward paid a visit to the nursery
and lifting up his daughter he had her squealing and gurgling
with delight as he played with her but the dark-eyed toddler
who looked on silently was totally ignored. Once Paul had
ventured a hand on Edward's leg but the cold look he received
had him running back to Nanny Ferguson, his lips trembling as
he buried his head in her lap. Miss Ferguson cuddled him and
her lips tightened in anger as she led her darling charge away.
There was something far wrong when a father treated his
little son like that and drooled over his daughter. She vowed
there and then to have a word with the mistress and risk the
consequences.

'Yes, of course, Miss Ferguson, I've time to see you,' Susan
said, inviting her to be seated.

'It's about Master Paul,' she began nervously.

A cold hand touched Susan. 'There's nothing wrong? Paul
isn't unwell, is he?'

'No! No! He's in good health.'

'Then what is it? I don't imagine Paul causes you too much
trouble?' she said with a smile, wondering what this was
all about.

'None at all, m'am.' Miss Ferguson bit her lip. 'It's just that
Master Paul, young though he is, he's sensitive . . .'

'Yes?' Susan prodded.

'If you will excuse plain speaking, m'am, the way the master
ignores his son and makes such a fuss of Miss Victoria, well,
m'am, that can be real harmful, especially to a sensitive child.'

'I see,' Susan said slowly. 'It was good of you to bring this
to my attention and I'll have a word with my husband. I can
assure you it is unintentional. You don't seem to understand,
Miss Ferguson, that some fathers make a fuss of their daughters but feel it is bad to lavish too much attention on a son.'

'Then it's wrong, m'am, that's all I can say,' Miss Ferguson said spiritedly. 'Maybe when they are older that may apply though I am not so sure it does but when they are small it is cruel.' She paused and looked at her mistress, knowing she had gone too far but unable to stop herself. 'Children should be treated alike and that way they feel equally loved.'

How very true, Susan thought, her mind going back to her own childhood. Miss Ferguson knew what she was talking about, but even so she had to be loyal to Edward and show Nanny that she was overstepping the mark.

She drew herself up, her back straight and looked like her mother at her most disapproving.

'That is quite enough, Miss Ferguson,' she said sharply. She stood up to show the interview was at an end and Miss Ferguson got up, her face flushed and alarmed.

'I'm very sorry, m'am, no disrespect intended I assure you.'

'Very well, I accept that you have the interest of your charge at heart and will overlook your outspokenness this time.'

'Thank you, m'am.' She gave a bob and all but fled from the room.

After she had gone, Susan sat on, thoughtful and deeply worried. There was cause for anxiety, of that she was certain. It had taken a lot of courage on Miss Ferguson's part to speak out. Surely if Edward was made to realise the seriousness of his callous treatment of Paul he wouldn't continue to ignore him. Tonight she would tell him of Miss Ferguson's fears, plead with him if necessary but surely it wouldn't come to that.

'I enjoyed that, it was delicious,' Susan said, touching her lips with the napkin and looking down the length of the table to her husband.

'Mmmm. Very nice but for myself I prefer the meat less well done.'

After finishing the meal they went through to the sitting-room where a recent addition of fresh logs had the fire spluttering and crackling.

'Shall I put up the guard?' Edward asked.

'No, it hides the fire and I think it's settling.' She waited until he had poured himself a drink and taken his usual chair. 'Nanny, Miss Ferguson, came to see me.'

'About what?'

'About Paul.'

Deliberately he put down his glass and reached for the newspaper.

'She's very worried about your – your indifference to Paul and its damaging effect in later years. Before Victoria was born you never went near the nursery.'

'Are you objecting to my visits there?'

'Of course not, quite the opposite. It's just that you make such a fuss of Victoria and Paul is bewildered – he's just a little boy and he cannot understand – ' She stopped.

'Have you quite finished?'

'Edward, please – please don't do this to Paul.'

'Your memory can be conveniently short when it suits you.'

'But –' she said desperately.

'No. Do I have to repeat it again?'

'No, you don't, I remember it very well including the rest.'

'The rest? What rest?'

'Once I give you a son you will have no further use for me.'

'That was said in anger.' He managed a smile. 'That side of our marriage is perfectly satisfactory.'

'Then I hope from our union that I am already with a child and pray to God that it will be a boy. Then, Edward, we can live our separate lives and I no longer will have to feign pleasure from your advances.'

It was cruel and not altogether true but it had gone home. His face was a dull red. 'Indeed you won't for I shall look elsewhere for my pleasures.'

Her lips curled. 'Before we were married you had women and you still have. I imagine that the only difference will be that you'll take a mistress instead of spreading your favours.'

'How dare you speak to me like that!' He looked on the point of springing at her but she knew he wouldn't and she didn't flinch.

'The truth can be cruel as we both know.'

He took up his paper but whether to read or hide his anger she could not tell. Her own book was open but not to read. It was something to occupy her hands while she stared at its pages. She knew only too well that the fragile improvement in their relationship was smashed beyond repair. Too much had been said, too much bitterness existed between them. But that was unimportant compared to Paul's happiness. The innocent must not suffer. Yet she was not without blame; the mill had been claiming more and more of her time and energy but it should be possible to change that now. Business was good and the order book healthy – she'd achieved more than she had dared hope. It was time to delegate some of her work on to others and two of the senior clerks, one in particular, had impressed her. Yes, she could and would rearrange her day so that more of it could be spent with her children. She would make more visits to Holmlea. Little Paul adored his Uncle Matthew's farm and shrieked with joy when Matthew carried him shoulder high to see the animals.

Edward was still reading when Susan looked across but now as she turned the pages of the book the words made sense. Her immediate problems were partly solved, at least for the time being. For what remained of the evening the only sounds were the ticking of the clock, the occasional movement of logs settling to a new position and the turning of the page.

# CHAPTER SIXTEEN

T hat winter there was no snow until after Hogmanay and then a darkening sky let loose a fluttering of snow to cover the hills like a feather pillow. In the middle of January a storm lashed the west coast, sending boats scuttling for shelter and the full force of its fury was felt as far inland as Aranvale. Some said its like hadn't been experienced since January 1885.

Impossible though it seemed, by morning the storm had spent itself and in the uneasy calm that followed folk ventured out to see the extent of the damage and assess the cost.

Edward was in his heavy outdoor clothes when Susan met him in the hall.

'I've just been out to check,' he said, blowing on his hands, 'but apart from a few broken slates lying about and a bit of devastation in the garden we appear to have escaped. Comes from being so low-lying.'

'Yes, it must have helped and we must be thankful. I've never heard anything like it. Never!' she said, giving a shudder.

'You were terrified.' Their glances met.

'Yes, I was,' she admitted, then remembering how she had clung to him during the worst of the storm she turned away and spoke too quickly. 'The children – I've seen Nanny Ferguson and they both slept through it. Unbelievable isn't it?'

'Children sleep through anything, I suppose. Take my tip, Susan, and stay indoors today anyway; a rest won't do you any harm.'

It was a change to feel protected and rather nice she had to admit. Though she could quite easily have accompanied him, she decided against it.

'I'll take your advice.'

'That's a change.' But he was smiling. 'I'll deal with anything urgent.'

'Thank you and remember if you are busy get Mr Lamond to assist; he is proving very dependable.' She laughed at his look of disbelief. 'I'm learning to delegate.'

'And not before time.' He hesitated.

'What is it, Edward?'

'To put your mind at rest I'll call in at Aran Heights and then see Matthew before going on to the mill.'

'I'd be grateful but don't forget Croft House – your parents.'

'No, I won't but I'm not going to get much done at the mill, am I?'

'Never mind that, it can wait. To be honest I am anxious about Mama being on her own. A storm like that gets her in a bit of a panic.'

'Like most women.'

She smiled at him with genuine tenderness and before he left she turned her cheek for his kiss, the first in a very long time.

Edward was a strange mixture. Would she ever understand her husband? For weeks hardly an unnecessary word had been exchanged yet here he was putting himself out for her. Matthew would be busy enough with the animals to settle and maybe unable to get to Aran Heights until later. Edward would see that her mother was all right and of course Mrs Dunbar was there.

She spent longer with the children but Nanny Ferguson had her routine and she was upsetting it. What was there to do? How empty her life would be without the mill.

Miss Wilson approached her. 'Good morning, m'am. I'm afraid we're short-staffed, two of the maids haven't arrived yet.'

'After such a night it's hardly surprising. Have you heard if there is much damage in the village?'

'Ramsay says a fair bit but it's mainly slates and the like.'

'Bad enough if it lets in the rain and there'll be a lot of

clearing up to do.' She paused. 'Miss Wilson, keep work to a minimum today and tell Mrs Carson a simple, easily prepared meal will do very well.'

'I'll do that and thank you, m'am.'

Susan watched her departure and thought back to Miss Wilson's appointment as housekeeper. Then she had lacked confidence but then so had she. They had both grown together and Miss Wilson had proved her worth. She was good with the staff, not over-friendly and not over-strict. There was a pleasant atmosphere and at least on the domestic front she wasn't troubled by conflict. Not since the departure of that slut Mary.

By evening she was looking forward to Edward's return and when he appeared she had to hold herself back from bombarding him with questions.

'Well, tell me,' she said impatiently.

'The roof of the cutting-house is damaged.'

'Badly?'

'A gaping hole but it was all hands on deck, everybody got stuck in to see it rainproof and it should hold until the job can be properly done.'

'Excuse me, m'am, the meal is ready to be served.'

'Thank you.'

Susan kept the rest of her questions until they were seated and the first course served.

'We must get someone on to it as quickly as possible.'

'Don't worry about it,' he said, picking up his cutlery, 'the mill will get priority. And now for the rest of the news.' He swallowed a mouthful of food and had the next prepared on his fork. 'Someone must have been very concerned about your mother. Euan Clapperton was a very early visitor, I just missed him.'

Susan smiled. 'That comes as no surprise, Mr Clapperton is very attentive to Mama. You found her quite well then?'

'Oh, she made the most of it, you know your mother. She said she was petrified but Mrs Dunbar left her own room to sit with her. Needless to say your mother had the comfort of her bed and Mrs Dunbar was huddled in a chair wrapped in a blanket.'

Susan giggled. She could picture the scene. 'Good, she's all right then?'

'Quite perky and oh, before I forget, your mother is paying you a visit tomorrow.'

'Coming here you mean? When?'

'Late afternoon and she expects you to be here and not in the mill.'

'Of course I'll be here when I know she's coming. My mother can be the limit. A social visit or is it something more?'

'Haven't the foggiest.'

'Did you manage to see Matthew and Winnie?'

'I did and there is quite a trail of damage. Matthew was doing some clearing up and using some very colourful language.'

'Mama wouldn't need to hear him. Is the damage really bad?'

'Winnie says it is nothing like as bad as your brother is trying to make out. She is very matter-of-fact and as she so rightly says the buildings can be repaired and she is just thankful that the livestock escaped injury though they could hear the animals whimpering with fright.'

Mrs Sarah MacFarlane arrived at Hillview in a cloud of lavender perfume, a little overdone Susan thought. Greeting each other she got a strong whiff. After seeing her mother comfortably settled in the sitting-room Susan rang the bell, the signal for tea.

'This is a lovely surprise, Mama.'

'Hardly a surprise, I told Edward to tell you I was coming.'

'Oh, he did.' Susan smiled. 'I don't recall seeing that gown before and that shade of dull rose is very becoming to you.'

'Thank you, my dear, and no, you won't have seen it. After so long in black I felt the need of something new and Miss Beattie suggested this as being pretty and not too bright.'

She's on edge, Susan thought, watching the nervous movements.

'Mama, what is it? Is it something you have to tell me?'

'Is it so patently obvious?' she said turning pink then, recovering, pointed to the tray which had just arrived moments earlier. 'That tea will be getting cold and you know how I dislike tea that isn't fresh. Are you pouring or am I?'

'Sorry, I'll pour.'

Nothing more was said until Mrs MacFarlane was nibbling at a biscuit and sipping at the tea. At last she put down the cup and leaned back.

'You must be honest with me, Susan. Should I decide to remarry would it distress you?'

'Mr Clapperton – '

'Yes,' she said, colouring like a young girl. 'Euan has proposed and I have promised him his answer just as soon as I have your approval and Matthew's.'

'Mama,' Susan said gently, 'you don't need our approval – ' Then seeing her mother's face hastened in with, 'I mean of course you have my approval. You are entitled to your happiness and it is not as though you are going off with a stranger.'

'Well, I'm glad that is over. This has been quite an ordeal for me. You and your papa were so close and I didn't want you to – to – it's no disrespect to your father's memory.' Her voice faltered and Susan got up to give her a warm hug.

'Papa would want you to be happy so don't feel guilty.'

'There are some who won't be so generous.'

'Does it matter?'

'No, it doesn't,' she said firmly. 'I won't let it.'

'That's the spirit and I assure you Matthew won't object.'

'No.' She laughed. 'In fact he and Winnie were getting quite hilarious about the complicated relationship. Cheeky too! Says he can stand me as a mother but is less certain how I'll measure up as a mother-in-law. Until he mentioned it I hadn't considered the complication.'

'Didn't occur to me either but now that I think about it it is amusing. When is the big day?'

'It won't be, it'll be very quiet and quite soon.' Her delicate eyebrows shot up. 'What is the point of delaying at our time of life? We are both lonely and last night's storm – well, that's when he asked me.' She blushed. 'Tina told me it was all she could do to keep her brother from going out at the height of the storm to see if I was all right.'

'Oh, Miss Clapperton, I had forgotten about her. Isn't this going to put her nose out of joint, you becoming the mistress of Moorend?'

'Susan,' her mother reprimanded, 'that was a most unlady-like expression.' She sniffed. 'No doubt being a business woman you think it acceptable but I can assure you it is not.'

'I apologise,' Susan murmured, trying to keep her face straight, 'but you haven't answered my question.'

'Tina is not in the least put out, she made that very clear to me. There is a vacant cottage in the village and Euan means to buy it for her. It is walking distance from Moorend and she is quite looking forward to settling down in a house of her own.'

'Then our approval was anticipated?' Susan teased.

'Euan foresaw no problem,' she said tartly, 'and now to the piece that concerns you. Once I move to Moorend Aran Heights becomes yours, you hadn't forgotten had you?'

Susan's face paled then flushed and her eyes were bright. 'I hadn't thought – hadn't realised – but it's true, isn't it?' she stammered. 'Aran Heights will be mine,' she said wonderingly. 'Mama, how can you bear to leave it?'

'Very easily.' She gave a short laugh. 'That big barn of a house! And don't look so shocked. All those years I put on an act, a convincing one and your father never suspected. Aran Heights never meant to me what it did to your papa and you. My dear, you are very welcome to it.'

Susan's eyes misted. She was going back to Aran Heights but different this time. It was to be hers. Her children would grow up in it and perhaps one day another son or daughter would be born there. Aware suddenly that her mother was watching her Susan gave an embarrassed laugh. 'I'm sorry, I'm just so thrilled.'

'And I'm happy for you. You've never liked Hillview, I've known that.'

'Because my heart was in Aran Heights. You think I am being ridiculous about a house, don't you?'

'No, you are a bit of a romantic. How will Edward take the news?'

'He'll be delighted.'

'We should discuss the furniture.' She made a face. 'As you can imagine everything will have to go at Moorend. Tina will take what she wants, Winnie too and the rest can be disposed of.'

'You'll be able to furnish Moorend from Aran Heights.'

'Some of it,' she said carelessly. 'I rather fancy buying new.'

'And I think Mr Clapperton will give you anything you set your heart on.'

'And why not? The money is there and Euan has prepared himself for my expensive tastes.' She needled her brow in thought. 'There was something else I had to tell you, now what was it?' Her face brightened. 'How could I have forgotten that?'

'Forgotten what?'

'Hannah and Samuel have announced their engagement and your Aunt Millie said in her letter that Hannah would be writing to you herself.'

'That's lovely news. I'm really delighted and I think they are perfectly matched. She will bring Samuel out of his shell and he'll have a restraining influence on her. You're pleased too, aren't you?'

'Very pleased. Samuel has a good family background and though he is a strange young man – '

'He isn't, Mama, not when you get to know him. He's shy, that's all. Is it to be a long engagement?'

Mrs MacFarlane drained the rest of her tea but declined another cup.

'I don't think so but there is no date fixed as yet.'
She got up.

'You're not going so soon?'

'I must, but a few minutes with my grandchildren first.'

Susan was humming under her breath when Edward breezed in.

'Someone is happy by the sound of it.'

'I am, I've got marvellous news.'

'So have I. You'll never guess but our Samuel has proposed to Hannah, or come to think about it it may have been the other way round; anyway they've got themselves engaged.'

'I know.'

'Oh!' he said deflated.

'Mama told me.'

'So what is your news?'

'My mother and Mr Clapperton are to be married.'

'That comes as no surprise, I thought there was something in the wind.'

'You do realise what it means?'

'I suppose you'll be gaining a stepfather and God knows what it makes Matthew.'

'It means, Edward, that Mama will be going to live at Moorend.'

'And Aran Heights becomes ours or should I say yours?'

'Ours, Edward, and I'm so happy I could cry. You won't mind leaving Hillview will you?'

'Not in the least. Hillview has served its purpose but it is a doll's house compared to Aran Heights.'

'Oh, come, that's a bit strong.'

'A good time, Susan, the house market is buoyant and it should be possible to get a good price for Hillview.'

Six weeks later there was a small gathering at the church. Susan sat with Edward in one of the front pews along with close relatives to witness the joining of Sarah MacFarlane and Euan Clapperton in marriage. It had been a unanimous

decision that the children should have a tea-party at home
with Nanny Ferguson.

Before the actual marriage it had been easy to give her
blessing but now as they stood before the minister Susan
could only feel sadness and resentment. How could she? How
could her mother marry this burly man who had suddenly
become an intruder? The light glinted off the stained-glass
windows and tears pricked at the back of her eyes, forcing
her to blink fiercely. She could feel Edward's eyes on her and
she turned to smile but it was a poor effort.

'What's the matter?' he whispered.

'N-nothing, I was just thinking about Papa.'

After the ceremony the new Mrs Clapperton looked
serenely happy and Euan Clapperton, nervous throughout
the service, smiled as if he had come through an ordeal and
was now ready to claim his prize.

Carriages took the guests the three miles to the recently
opened Burnbank Hotel where a splendid meal awaited them.
There was only one absentee from the family. Aunt Rachel
had given no excuse for declining the invitation, instead
writing a note to Susan wishing her niece and family every
happiness at Aran Heights.

Knowing how devoted Aunt Rachel was to her brother,
Susan could readily understand her feelings, her own were
similar, but even so she wished her aunt could have forced
herself to put in an appearance even for a short time. Though
her mother would never admit it she must have felt hurt at
the slight.

When Hillview reached the market it attracted a large number
of prospective buyers and Miss Wilson was kept busy showing
the various interested parties around the house then, something Susan had insisted on, leaving them the freedom to
walk about the gardens at their leisure. She apologised for
the additional work but Miss Wilson dismissed it.

'M'am, I am only too happy to assist. It is such a relief
to know that I am to work at Aran Heights. I've been very
worried.'

'Then I do apologise and indeed I would have been greatly distressed had you not been prepared to come.' She smiled. 'You thought Mrs Dunbar would be staying – '

'Yes, I did.'

Susan shook her head emphatically. 'My mother couldn't do without Mrs Dunbar.'

Polly passed by with an armful of linen and when she was out of earshot Susan said, 'Polly was at Aran Heights and appears quite excited at the prospect of returning.

'Yes, she is, she has told us.' Miss Wilson spoke with the weary air of someone who had heard it all too often.

'Susan? Where are you, Susan?' Edward called out as he hung his coat on the hallstand.

'I'm here,' she said, appearing at his side.

'In here,' he said, leading her through to the sitting-room and closing the door.

'Whatever it is it must be good by the look on your face.'

'I've made a substantial profit on the sale of Hillview.'

She noted the 'I' but smiled. 'Glad to hear it.'

'The joy of an unexpected windfall, we timed it beautifully.'

'What do you propose doing with it?'

'Banking it of course. Why? Have you any suggestions?'

'Well, it is found money, Edward. I'd be inclined to have a little flutter, buy shares, study the stock market, have a little excitement.'

'And risk losing it? Certainly not, I like security.'

'So do I and it's true you could lose. But on the other hand you could also gain substantially.'

'It's going in the bank until I find something without a risk and a guaranteed return.'

'Unfortunately there's no such investment.' She laughed.

Later Edward was to wish he had taken Susan's advice but then no one could have guessed . . .

The west of Scotland was bathed in sunshine when Mr Euan Clapperton, smart in a grey suit, and his wife, dressed in a dark blue travelling habit and matching bonnet, took themselves off to the Lake District for two weeks to escape the workmen.

Moorend had never seen such an upheaval; dust was everywhere. There were alterations, redecorating, the laying of carpets and the movement of furniture. Servants deplored the rate of progress and itched for them to finish so that they could climb up the ladders to hang the curtains. Mrs Dunbar, with so much responsibility placed upon her, grew ever more worried and excited. She began giving orders and contradicting them in the same breath. Panic developed when after ten days instead of the arranged fourteen the master and new mistress of Moorend arrived at the farmhouse.

Mrs Dunbar apologised profusely for what was in no way her fault and the new mistress of Moorend graciously accepted her apologies. Apparently torrential rain for much of their stay in the Lake District had eventually dampened their enthusiasm for sightseeing and shortened their honeymoon.

An amused Matthew and Winnie came to the rescue and the honeymooners spent the next three days at Holmlea.

Much less traumatic was the move from Hillview to Aran Heights. All that Susan decided to take was the furniture gifted by her parents and of course the other wedding presents. The new owners had shown a cautious interest in the remaining furniture and furnishings and Susan, anxious that they got it cheaply, reminded Edward that they had no use for it. After a show of reluctance Edward let it go at what he thought a ridiculously low figure.

The children's voices were high with excitement as they charged about the house they still thought of as Grandmama's.

'Mama, am I getting Uncle Matt's bedroom?' Paul asked, pink with pleasure.

'Yes, dear, and I really think now that you are a big boy that you should start saying Uncle Matthew.'

'Uncle Matthew,' Paul repeated, 'all right.'

'Yes.' Susan smiled, delighted at his enthusiasm. And Victoria will get the one I had when I was a little girl.

251

Long used as a storeroom the schoolroom was to revert back to its original use. Her plans she would discuss with Edward but with or without his approval she would go ahead. Then she stood still and pondered the change in herself, some of it not to her liking. It was one thing to be a business woman but was it at the expense of her femininity? She was so used to making decisions in the mill and now she was doing the same at home. Then she shrugged and gave a satisfied smile. No, she hadn't lost her femininity, she told herself, she still had the assurance that sprang from seeing desire in the eyes of men at those functions and dinner parties she attended with Edward. She was woman enough to get a glow of pleasure not only from that but from Edward's obvious pride in her appearance.

People changed, circumstances altered but Aran Heights alone defied time and the elements. Looking down from the top of the stone steps her eyes roved the scene. Summer brought a pastoral and gentle beauty filled with tranquillity. Pinks and mauves spilled forth from the magnificent rhododendron bushes and beds and beds of roses flowered for the second or third time.

In this house I grew up and now my children will enjoy it and for the rest of my life it is to be my home. Susan hugged the thought as she went indoors and up to the library, the room that drew her as no other did. As a rebellious child she remembered the atmosphere portentous with brewing storms, her papa's stern warnings when she had gone too far. Then he had seemed huge and terrifying as she suffered the harsh rasp of his voice. Suitably cowed she had promised tearfully to behave herself and give her mama less trouble and before dismissing her he had patted her on the head as if to take some of the sting out of his words.

The library looked strangely naked and on an impulse she sat down in her father's chair and surveyed the room. Her own desk, the instrument of her changing fortunes, was back in its position and for a fleeting moment she pictured someone else there. Where was he now? That young man she had once loved and whose son would one day inherit the mill and Aran

Heights. Had he prospered? She would never know. She came out of her daydream and gave a small shiver. In Paul, the growing boy, she was seeing the resemblance to David Cameron becoming more pronounced and it was disturbing.

How impressed David had been with the shelves and shelves of books; she remembered the longing in his face. Her father had been an avid reader and she had shared his love of books. Paul was going to be the same, she was sure of that.

In the hall the grandfather clock chimed the hour and she rose to go, closing the door quietly behind her.

# CHAPTER SEVENTEEN

There was a breath of spring in the air when Susan gave birth to her second son but it was a false spring, one that occasionally comes in February or early March, raising the spirits but cheating the land so that the buds begin to sprout then blacken and be killed off when the severe frosts return.

Paul was almost seven, a tall nice-looking boy though too serious for his years. His sister Victoria was a bouncy, precocious child with a mop of reddish fair curls and given to temper tantrums when she didn't get her own way.

For much of the time with this pregnancy Susan had felt unwell but with Dr Walker assuring her that there was nothing to worry about she had tried to keep as much as possible to routine, spending a few hours most days at her office in the mill.

As if to make up for it the birth itself was easy, so easy that Susan couldn't believe it was over. But the baby was small and frail with barely enough strength to suck milk and when his birth weight dropped alarmingly it was feared he would not live.

Edward had been anguished.

'Why?' he demanded of the doctor. 'Why is he like this when my daughter was – ' He broke off and looked at the doctor then the nurse but she turned away.

'Both your children,' the doctor corrected him, 'were healthy babies. No one can say why it happens this way but in many families there is one child weaker than the others.'

In bed a few feet away from them Susan listened and could only feel guilt as she heard the rise and fall of their voices. Edward had been over the moon when told he had a son but that had quickly turned to disbelief verging on anger when he gazed upon the pitifully weak infant with his fragile hold on life.

Susan put out her hand and he came over. 'Edward, our son is going to be fine, all he needs is careful nursing and he'll get that.' Her blue eyes were soft and appealing and he nodded, forcing a smile.

'Yes, he'll get that.' Then added softly, 'If it's enough.'

'Don't think like that, Edward, I'm not, I'm going to will my baby to live and you must too.'

'That's the spirit, Mrs Brodie,' Dr Walker said approvingly. 'I've seen some underweight babies thrive against all the odds.' He went off and beckoned to the nurse to follow, leaving Susan and Edward alone.

'We should get the baby baptised as soon as possible,' she said quietly, nervously plucking at the bedcover.

'Yes.'

'The name we chose – ' She hesitated. 'John after your father?'

His face twisted in pain. 'No, I don't want him called John. Had he been – ' He left the rest unsaid.

'Then what name, Edward?'

He looked at her bleakly. 'You said you liked James.'

'I do.'

'Then call him that,' he said, getting up. 'You'd better get some rest.'

'I'm all right,' she said tonelessly, wanting him to stay but knowing he wouldn't.

James did live though he wailed plaintively, causing consternation to those around. Susan had arranged for the nurse to stay on in order that the baby should have special care. Both grandmothers called but they were subdued, neither rushing to claim a family resemblance with this one.

Gradually though, James began to take a little interest in his surroundings and in those early weeks Susan spent a lot of time with her baby, nursing and cuddling him as she had never done with Paul and Victoria. Eagerly she watched for some improvement and when it came she took a personal pride in each small achievement.

'He is coming on, Nurse?'

'His progress, m'am, is what one expects in any underweight baby. Each stage is slow and you must accept that.'

'Oh, I do, but surely now that he is feeding well and gaining in weight he'll come on?' she said anxiously.

'Perhaps,' she said, but without conviction. The nurse, brisk and efficient, did not believe in raising false hopes, rather she was of the firm opinion that parents were better equipped to deal with a situation if they understood it.

Susan was aware of this and gave a sad little smile.

'I'm not looking for miracles, Nurse, but that doesn't mean I'm not hoping. Compared to my other children Master James is backward but as long as he is happy and contented.'

'That is the best attitude to take,' the nurse said approvingly, as with a slight nod she disappeared with the baby in her arms.

James was painfully slow in every way but Susan wouldn't go beyond admitting that James was backward and was angered when Edward hinted that their son was more than backward, that he was severely mentally retarded. One day she had come on him in the summer house sitting on a low chair, his elbows on his knees and his head in his hands. Her heart went out to him in his silent agony but their relationship was such that no words of hers would give comfort.

Edward continued his visits to the nursery but James was not responsive and when he began whimpering Edward would turn to Victoria and scoop her up in his arms until she was squealing with delight. Paul, used to being ignored, would go over to the cot and comfort James in his childish way. He was fiercely protective of his little brother and James seemed to settle when Paul was near.

One morning on the way to her own bedroom Susan heard the sound of quarrelling coming from the nursery and went along to investigate. She had opened the door and could hear them though they were unaware of her presence.

'Papa doesn't love you, he only loves me and James,' Victoria said in her childish treble, her curls bobbing as she tossed her head.

'I don't care,' Paul said with his mouth set in a stubborn line, but his eyes belied the words. Susan saw the hurt and misery and closed her eyes, feeling his pain hers.

Oh, my darling, you do care and it is breaking your heart. Her own guilt returned to torment her but her hatred was levelled at her husband. Only a monster would treat an innocent child as he was doing. Walking into the room she was fearful that she would strike her daughter and kept her hands rigidly at her side.

'How dare you, Victoria! How dare you say such a wicked thing!' Susan spoke with a harshness never before heard in the nursery. She was shaking with rage. 'You will apologise to your brother at once. At once! Do you hear?' she said, her voice rising to a shout.

Victoria stared back at her mother, her feet set apart, and looked mutinous. Had Susan but known it it was a stance she too had taken and Victoria and the young Susan looked very alike in those moments.

'I'm waiting,' Susan said with a dangerous quietness.

Just then the door opened and Nanny arrived, breathless from hurrying.

'M'am, I'm so sorry but I had to see Mrs Carson about the children's menu.'

'That's perfectly all right, Nanny, you cannot be expected to be with them every minute.' Susan tried to modulate her voice but her eyes were smouldering.

'Is there something wrong, m'am?' Nanny asked, taking in the scene. Paul stood silently, his eyes downcast and Victoria was backing away looking a little afraid.

'Yes. Miss Victoria has been rude to her brother and refuses to apologise. See that she is put to bed half an hour earlier than usual and without supper.'

'Mama! No!' Victoria wailed. 'I'm sorry, I'm very, very sorry.'

'Your apology comes too late, young lady,' Susan said

coldly, then with a smile she turned to Paul. 'Come along with me, dear.'

The air was warm with a gentle breeze and the sky was so penetratingly blue that its shimmering clarity had one blinking. Together Susan and her son walked along the path with its neatly trimmed hedges and Paul kicked at a stone and said awkwardly, 'It's true, Mama, Papa doesn't like me. What Victoria said is true.'

'Of course it isn't true, Paul,' she began, then stopped herself from going on. It was no use, his face made it all too clear that he was well aware that Edward held no love for him. To change the subject she said brightly, 'Tomorrow is Saturday and you have no lessons. Would you like to go over to Aunt Winnie's and see the new baby? You could play with Duncan.'

'Oh, yes, please, Mama, and will Uncle Matthew be there?'

'I expect so.' She smiled.

'I wish Uncle Matthew was my papa,' he said wistfully.

'Paul,' she said gently, 'it's wrong to say that or even to think it.'

'I can't help if I think it,' he said reasonably.

'Don't keep kicking the stones, dear, or you'll ruin your boots,' Susan said, fighting her tears.

'Have you got to go to the mill, Mama?'

'Yes, Paul, I must, there is a lot of work awaiting my attention.'

'All ladies don't work, why do you, Mama?'

'I enjoy it, Paul.'

'Will I work in the mill when I'm big?'

'I hope so.'

'Duncan is going to be a farmer like Uncle Matthew.'

'That's nice. Now run along, dear, or Nanny will be annoyed at me for keeping you so long.'

She watched him run over to the side door then turn and wave. She waved back then went in search of Ramsay. He was in the courtyard.

'Bring the carriage round in ten minutes, Ramsay.'

Once in the mill and behind her desk Susan began to tackle the backlog of work. Both before and after the birth of James she had given less of her attention to the mill and she was uncomfortably aware that Edward was taking on more and more responsibility and making decisions she was only advised about once the changes had been adopted.

All that was going to cease. She was back in command.

In a light grey costume, with touches of white at neck and cuffs, Susan looked neat and businesslike and her manner matched her appearance. Her fair head was bent over the columns of figures which at a quick glance appeared to be in order and she put them aside. Next to receive her attention was the accounts ledger and here her frown deepened as she studied the entries and compared them with the previous month's. After jotting down some names she rang the bell which sounded in the main office where the clerks sat on high stools at their desks. The insistent ring, jarring the silence, brought the most junior clerk to Susan's office.

'Have Mr Lamond come here immediately,' she ordered, glancing up briefly.

'Yes, m'am.' He hurried away. When the lady boss spoke like that it was trouble for someone and that could be Mr Lamond. He grinned. Having been severely reprimanded that very morning for untidy figures the young clerk saw no reason to warn his superior that Mrs Brodie was on the warpath.

'Come in.'

'You wished to see me, m'am?'

'Yes, I think you have some explaining to do.'

His grey eyes blinked nervously and he licked his lips.

'I'm afraid I don't understand, m'am,' he stammered.

'Neither do I, Mr Lamond, which is the reason I sent for you,' she said icily. She turned the ledger to face him. 'Kindly explain why these accounts haven't been settled? Has it been an oversight?'

'Not at all, m'am. I mean, it wasn't an oversight, it's the new policy.'

'Really!' she said sarcastically. 'Do go on.'

'Well, m'am, these customers know they will be paid and won't push for early settlement. By waiting a few more weeks the money can be working for us – begging your pardon – for the mill I mean,' he said hastily.

'And you think that makes good sense?'

'Oh, yes, m'am.'

'Who authorised this?'

'Mr Brodie,' he answered as if it were a foolish question. 'I see.'

He smiled with relief and shifted his feet. Susan was holding in her anger with difficulty. Mr Lamond had only been obeying instructions, not hers to be sure, but then he would assume Edward to have full authority in her absence.

'There have been a few misunderstandings, Mr Lamond, which need to be cleared up now that I am back in charge. Perhaps there is wisdom in delaying payments but it has never been the policy of the Aranvale Papermill and it is not mine.' She tapped the ledger. 'See that these accounts are settled today and a letter of apology for the delay enclosed with each. Have this done immediately and brought for my signature. Is that understood?'

'Yes, m'am,' he said meekly.

'And in future kindly remember that your instructions come from me and no one else. Have I made myself clear?'

'Yes, m'am,' he repeated, bowing himself out.

Susan put a hand to her brow and stared down at the desk. She would make no mention of this to Edward, there was no need. Mr Lamond would be extremely careful in future. Should he fail to do so she would have him dismissed and this possibility would undoubtedly have occurred to him.

By evening her mind was on Paul and her rage was at boiling point. It was all she could do to restrain herself until after dinner. As usual Edward's first move was to the drinks cabinet.

'May I get you something, dear?'

'No, thank you and I do wish you would stop offering, you know perfectly well I do not drink.'

'On your high horse are you?' He smirked as he poured himself a whisky.

She ignored the remark, took a deep breath and her eyes bored into him. 'Your precious daughter, that precocious child, has been goading Paul with the remark that you only love her and James.'

'An observant child.'

'She's becoming impossible.'

'You don't like your daughter, you never have.'

Susan was taken aback. 'That is ridiculous and totally untrue. I love my children but I do not like the child Victoria is becoming and it is your fault. You have her absolutely ruined.'

'Exaggerating as usual.'

Her hands were shaking. 'Edward, can't you see that what you are doing to Paul is monstrously cruel and unless you – you change your attitude to the child I am going to tell him the truth. Once he realises that you are not his natural father then he will find your attitude towards him easier to understand.'

'And when he is old enough to understand how that came about, what then? What will he think of his mother?' he jeered.

'I'll have to take that risk but perhaps he will be more charitable and forgiving than you,' she said bitterly.

Leaning against the mantelpiece and sipping his drink he looked at her thoughtfully and shook his head.

'Don't think I wouldn't carry it out, Edward. Don't think that for a moment. Paul is my son and means the world to me whilst you are my husband in name only.'

The glass was arrested before it reached his mouth and he was looking at her oddly, seemingly at a loss for words. She saw it and felt satisfied with her performance.

Among the passengers getting off at Queen Street station was Matthew MacFarlane. Until recently Euan Clapperton had attended the market but now he had confidence in his son-in-law and Matthew was only too happy to take his place. He enjoyed farming talk and frequently joined a group who continued their discussions over a refreshment in a nearby hotel. Today Matthew declined their invitation as he had promised Winnie to call in at Morton's in St Vincent Street. His father-in-law's birthday was on Sunday and Winnie wanted special tobacco that only Morton's stocked.

Leaving the shop he found himself face to face with Caroline Beverley, only now, he had to remind himself, she was Caroline Saunders. For an instant they stood staring at one another, each startled by the change read in the other's eyes. Caroline saw a tweed-suited man still with his boyish good looks but now there was an air of confidence lacking before. For his part Matthew saw a strikingly lovely woman in a cherry red costume with a nipped-in waist accentuating her dainty figure. The colour was superb with her blue-black hair and dark eyes but the soft appealing look that had been so much a part of Caroline had gone.

'Matthew! Well, hello,' she said, holding out a gloved hand. 'It's been a long time.'

'Yes, it has. You're looking very well, Caroline.'

Matthew secretly marvelled at his good luck; he had been wondering how he could get in touch and here she was.

'I was about to ask you what you are doing here but of course it's market day and may I say you look every inch the successful farmer.'

Did he detect a hint of sarcasm or was it just his imagination? 'Yes, Caroline, I've been at the mart and now I'm on my way to get a bite to eat before heading home.'

'May I invite myself?' She smiled into his face. 'I haven't eaten.'

'I was about to invite you. The Royal all right?'

'Yes.'

It was a short walk to the hotel and once inside the entrance hall they took the left passage leading to the red and gold dining-room. Small tables were set for luncheon and they were shown to a vacant one in the corner then supplied with menus and left to make their choice.

Caroline barely glanced at hers. 'I'm not very hungry. Do you think I could just have a lightly poached egg on toast?'

'I imagine so.' He beckoned for the waitress, ordered for Caroline and something more substantial for himself. The dining-room was filling up and the occupants of one table were taking a great interest in the couple at the corner table.

Caroline leaned forward, an elbow on the table and a hand supporting her chin. 'This is like old times, isn't it?' She smiled.

Matthew gave an uncomfortable smile. 'Caroline, I was very,' very sorry to hear about your father. I wanted to write – '

'But in the circumstances you didn't know what to say,' she said harshly. She paused and said bleakly, 'I found him you know, he would know I would. He chose a time when my mother was staying with my aunt.'

The waitress came to adjust the cutlery and Caroline leaned back.

Matthew waited until they were alone. 'That must have been dreadful for you.'

'Oh, it was, Matthew, it was I can assure you.' She had been speaking softly but her voice dropped to a little above a whisper. 'He shot himself, Matthew. Hard to believe, isn't it, that my strong, God-fearing father should take his own life.' There was the hint of tears in her voice. 'I needed someone so badly but there was no one. No one to help. I had it all to do and face up to the fact that my father left nothing but debts. Matthew, I needed you, needed you so badly but you weren't there.' She gave a half sob. 'You treated me very shabbily.'

'Caroline, we weren't engaged, I made no promises,' he said defensively but only too aware that he had behaved badly.

'Everyone expected us to marry. I expected it, Matthew, after all we'd been to each other.'

'Caroline, you're married.'

'Oh, yes, Matthew, I'm Mrs Charles Saunders. Like you I married for the wrong reasons. You married that clumsy girl Winnie to get your hands on Moorend and I married a man more than twenty years older for security. Charles was a widower with no children and a large bank balance.' Her eyes glinted. 'One day I'll be all right but meantime he keeps a tight grip on the purse-strings.'

'You're wrong about Winnie,' Matthew said, the angry colour showing on his face. 'I happen to love my wife and our two little sons.'

'Very cosy,' she said as their meal arrived. In silence they each ate a few mouthfuls then Caroline put down her fork and knife and pushed back the plate.

'In the beginning,' Matthew said, striving to be honest, 'Moorend was the attraction but not any more. You may believe it or not but it happens to be the truth. Winnie is a lovely person and I am very lucky.'

'Well, I'm not. Charles is old, dull and I hate it when he touches me.' She shuddered.

Matthew discovered he wasn't hungry and was only eating to save the waitress asking if there was something wrong with the food. Before Caroline left him he had to find out.

'Caroline, are you seeing Edward Brodie?' he asked abruptly.

'What if I am, what business is it of yours?'

'I don't want Susan hurt.'

'Coming from you that's rich. My feelings weren't important when you dropped me.'

'Edward Brodie is a married man.'

'So he is,' she said sarcastically, 'but from what I gather that too was a marriage of convenience.'

'You used to like Susan.'

'I do like Susan and unlike you she managed to write me a letter and somehow she found the right words.'

'Would there be anything else?' the waitress asked politely.

Matthew looked at Caroline and she shook her head.

'No, thank you, just bring the bill in a few minutes.'

Caroline reached over and took hold of his hand. 'I'm sorry if I've sounded bitter, Matthew, but life hasn't been all that kind to me.' She kept hold of his hand and said playfully, 'Edward is a pet but I'd give him up like a shot if we could meet sometimes. It shouldn't be too difficult and it would make my life just bearable.'

'No, Caroline,' Matthew said firmly. 'I have a good marriage and I don't mean to do anything to spoil that or hurt my wife.'.

She snatched back her hand and stood up. 'Then I'll say goodbye, Matthew. I've just remembered some shopping I want to do.'

He sat and watched her trim figure walk away and what did he feel? Relief, sadness and oh, yes, the shameful reminder of how little consideration he had given to his one-time love.

It was a beautiful but cold autumn day when Susan and Paul set out for Moorend. Unlike her brother Victoria was afraid of the animals and made no fuss at being left behind.

Paul was warmly dressed and laughing as he waded through the mounds of gold and brown leaves before leaving them to turn into the village Main Street. The cottages were of old standing but had been added to by room and kitchen houses built on either side of the road to meet the needs of the influx of Irish workers for the mines and quarries.

Next they came to the school. The classrooms were on the ground floor and upstairs was occupied by the dominee and his family with access by an outside stair.

Soon they were into Clapperton land with the cows lifting their heads from grazing to watch their approach, then Holmlea farmhouse was in sight and Paul took to his heels. The dogs began to bark excitedly and Winnie appeared to subdue them. She came to meet them and the sisters-in-law kissed.

'Winnie, I'm not being a nuisance bringing Paul, am I?'

'Of course not as you very well know.' She bent down to Paul. 'Hello, Paul, fancy your mama suggesting that you could be a nuisance.'

Paul grinned. 'Hello, Aunt Winnie, where's Duncan?'

'Not far away. Look, there he is,' she said pointing to a small figure pushing a wooden barrow. Paul ran across to his cousin and Susan and Winnie went indoors.

'And now tell me how is baby Peter?'

'Sound asleep, he's a night bird and chirpiest when all good people are in bed.' They tiptoed through to an adjoining room and over to the cradle.

Susan very gently moved the cover to get a better look at the sleeping babe. 'He's gorgeous, Winnie,' Susan said, taking another lingering look. 'Peter resembles your side I think.'

'Not so likely to be a heart-throb then, is he?' Winnie said bitterly and Susan looked at her quickly. Now that she was studying her properly she could see that something was wrong. Since her engagement Winnie had been particular about her appearance but her hair today was lank and she wore an unbecoming gown.

'What is it, Winnie? Something's troubling you?'

'Nothing is and do sit down,' she said when they were in the sitting-room. 'I'll go and see about tea being brought through.'

She made to go but Susan caught her arm. 'Later, Winnie.'

Winnie sat down, her hands in her lap. 'How is James?'

'He's well enough I suppose.' Susan sighed.

'He'll come on, just try not to compare him with Paul and Victoria.'

'I know.'

'You've accepted the situation, Susan, but Edward hasn't, has he?'

'Having a backward son isn't easy to accept.'

'No, it can't be.' They lapsed into silence.

'Winnie, don't try putting me off. I know there is something wrong and if it was the other way you would force it out of me.'

'You may as well know, it'll be common gossip before long. Matthew is seeing Caroline Beverley or rather Saunders.'

'That I do not believe, not for a moment.'

'Then you should, you of all people. You warned me before our marriage that this could happen.'

'That was a very long time ago and we were both young and silly,' Susan protested. 'Matthew is a very different person now and a very contented husband and father.'

'Susan, I got it from a very reliable source.' Her face twisted with pain.

'Have you tackled Matthew?'

'No, and I don't intend to.'

'Why not for heaven's sake? He probably has a very good explanation.'

'They dined together, even holding hands at one stage I believe.' She laughed mirthlessly. 'Now I know why Matthew is always so keen to attend the market and save Papa.'

'Caroline is married.'

'That doesn't appear to be a hindrance. She married someone old enough to be her father and is no doubt bored with him and looking for a bit of excitement. Probably Matthew is bored with me and they are consoling each other.'

'It doesn't make sense to me.'

'Then it should. Matthew married me for the farm, I knew that, you knew that and I accepted it. With having the children I thought,' her voice broke, 'thought it would be enough.'

'But it isn't?' Susan said gently. 'You need Matthew?'

'More than I believed possible, yet I've always known it was Caroline he loved and would have married if things had been different.'

Everything Winnie said was true or had been but even so she couldn't believe Matthew would do this. There had to be another explanation for seeing Caroline.

'Try not to worry, Winnie, I'm sure things will work out.'

'Perhaps, we'll see.' She brightened. 'I must tell you about Duncan but for goodness sake don't tell your mother.'

'What's the little monkey been up to?'

'Aunt Tina drops in and takes Duncan for a walk, usually into the village.'

'Is she still doing her "good works"?'

'Yes, she is and it was the turn of the McGregors to get some advice and a basket of goodies. While they chatted Duncan went outside to play with the children.'

'Did you mind?'

'Not in the least, good for him. Anyway after a while Aunt Tina went outside to see what all the hilarity was about.' Winnie laughed. 'There he was, the young master, barefooted and tramping the blankets with the others.'

'Tramping the blankets?' Susan said, mystified.

'You wouldn't know of course. Well, to enlighten you it's a yearly event or perhaps twice yearly when the blankets are washed. A tub is filled with soapy water, the blankets put in and the family, adults first, jump up and down to get them clean. The children then get a turn and it makes sense you know. Washing by hand isn't nearly so effective or perhaps I should say doesn't get so much of the dirt out.'

'And that's what young Duncan was doing?' Susan laughed.

'Having the time of his life according to Aunt Tina and she had quite a job tearing him away.'

'Did you tell Matthew?'

'Yes. He thought a lot of people in Aranvale would have clean feet for a change.'

'Cheeky.'

'And now that tea. Just let me ring for Edith.' Winnie pulled at the bell and a rosy-cheeked girl knocked and opened the door.

'Tea, please, Edith and some scones.'

'How are the love-birds?'

'Happy as the day is long. Mind you, Susan, I thought Papa might have rebelled at some of the changes at Moorend but not a bit of it. He doesn't seem to mind just as long as your mother is happy.'

'I'll drink this then I must go. There's a mountain of work to be done.'

'I hear you are well thought of in the mill.'

'Thank you, Winnie, thank you for telling me that. I do know that I've been called that bossy young woman and that description I could do without.'

'Don't let it bother you. In your position you have to assert your authority. Forgive me asking but how does Edward feel about taking orders from his wife?'

'I do very little ordering and though the position isn't to his liking Edward has come to accept it.' She shrugged. 'He has to, after all.'

The tea arrived and Winnie poured. The scones were delicious and still warm and Susan couldn't resist another.

'Before I go, may I say something and please don't be offended.'

'I'll try not.'

'Don't let your appearance go. You've been looking marvellous but just now your hair is a mess and do get rid of that gown.'

'You are a bossy boots and a real little madam, but all right I'll take your advice. It was just that I couldn't be bothered when – '

Susan hastened in with, 'That makes it doubly important. Now I really am going. Tell Paul to be good and maybe Matthew will bring him home.'

'Yes, he'll do that.'

When the carriage from Holmlea trundled up the drive Susan was at the door awaiting it. Paul was tired but happy and needed no prompting to run indoors to Nanny.

'What's this? Aren't I being invited in?'

'Could we take a walk, Matthew? I need to ask you something?'

Was that unease she saw? She couldn't be sure.

'Fine by me,' he said as they fell into step.

She didn't waste time. 'Is it true that you are seeing Caroline?'

'Whatever made you ask that?'

'Is it true?' Susan persisted.

'I've seen her, yes,' he said guardedly.

'You dined together.'

'Suppose you tell me what this is all about. And who has been gossiping?' He sounded distinctly annoyed.

'I have no idea but I do know that it has reached Winnie. How could you, Matthew? How could you hurt Winnie like that? She worships you and the children.' Her eyes flashed dangerously. 'You are my brother, more than that, my twin, and I love you dearly but if there is any truth in this, about you and Caroline, then I am not only disappointed but I'm disgusted.'

'Have you quite finished?' he said icily.

'Matthew, I don't want to believe it.'

'Then don't.'

'Are you saying that you haven't been seeing Caroline?'

'No, not exactly, we had a meal together that was all.'

'But why, Matthew? You must have known that if you were seen together tongues would wag. Remember, you two were practically engaged.'

'We were not.'

'Then there is nothing between you?

'Nothing. I'm not in love with her and to be honest, Susan, I don't think I knew what love was until I married Winnie. Caroline is beautiful and her gaiety is infectious but exhausting and now it's all a bit forced.'

'Then you do love Winnie?'

'Yes, I do,' he said quietly, 'She is the best thing that ever happened to me.'

'Then you stupid, stupid boy tell Winnie that. She still thinks you married her for the farm and but for that Caroline would have been your wife.'

'Maybe at the beginning that was true but she must know. Surely she still doesn't think,' he said incredulously, 'she can't – '

'She does, I can assure you of that and it's up to you to put things right between you. Incidentally I'm curious, why did you have a meal with Caroline and what did you talk about?'

His eyes fell. 'I can't tell you that, I'm sorry.'

Susan raised her eyebrows in surprise. Why the secrecy? But she didn't pursue it. 'Make sure you tell Winnie if you can't tell me. It isn't good to have secrets from her.'

He smiled. 'Just as soon as I get home she shall be told all.'

Matthew put off no time in getting back to Holmlea; he was shaken by what he had just heard but he managed to wait until Duncan was in bed and asleep. He wanted no interruptions.

'Winnie, come and sit down.' He indicated the space beside him on the couch.

'I'm busy, I have things to do.'

'Leave them, this is important.'

'Very well,' she said, sitting down but in the chair opposite.

'I've been talking to Susan and she tells me – '

'Susan had no right, what was said was in confidence.'

'Thank God she did tell me.' He paused. 'You have been a bit strange recently but I thought you were just off colour. Winnie MacFarlane,' he said slowly, 'I love you, I love the life we have together and I adore our two little sons. Is that enough for you?'

Her lips were trembling. 'No, Matthew, it isn't enough. I have to know about Caroline. I can't, I won't share you.'

'Come over here, woman.'

After some hesitation she got up and sat beside her husband but sideways so that she could look at him.

'Tell me why you were with Caroline. The truth, Matthew, you owe me that.'

'Yes, I owe you that. All right here it is. I happen to know that Caroline and Edward are seeing each other.'

Winnie stared. 'Oh, Matthew, and all you were doing was trying to put an end to it.'

'That's right and I wasn't successful I'm afraid. Caroline isn't the girl she used to be, she's an embittered young woman.'

'Hardly surprising,' Winnie said, feeling generous now that her own happiness wasn't at risk. 'Her father's suicide and then marriage to a man so much older.' And losing you, my darling, she added silently.

Matthew's arm went round her, drawing her close and she snuggled in.

'I love you so much, Matthew, life without you would be meaningless.'

Very gently he eased himself away and got up to close the curtains and in the dim light from the one oil lamp they made love.

Winnie's arrival at Aran Heights surprised Susan.

'Matthew said I would catch you, that you only work a half day on a Wednesday.'

'As a rule,' Susan smiled. 'And I'm delighted to see you.'

'I believe I would have ventured into the mill if you hadn't been at home.' She laughed, her happiness brimming over.

'You look wonderful,' Susan said approvingly. 'Now tell me what has brought on this change.'

'As if you didn't know,' she said softly.

'Matthew has made his peace with you?'

'More than that, he has explained everything. Caroline means nothing to him and it's true, Susan. Matthew loves me,' she said wonderingly, 'he really does.'

'Of course he does and you had better believe it. And now forgive me for being a nosey parker but why was he seeing Caroline? He wouldn't tell me.'

'Nothing important, really it wasn't, they just had a chat,' Winnie said evasively and glanced away so that she didn't meet Susan's eyes.

'You can tell me, I'm no gossip.'

'I know that but I'm afraid I can't tell you.' She was beginning to look agitated.

'This gets curiouser and curiouser.' Susan laughed. 'Anyway, just as long as you are satisfied with his explanation.'

'Oh, I am,' she said and Susan had the uncomfortable feeling that she was getting an oddly sympathetic glance.

Tea arrived and after being refreshed they went upstairs to the nursery. James was lying on cushions on the floor surrounded by soft toys which held no interest for him. He was staring at the ceiling and didn't move his head as they came over. Susan felt the familiar tightness in her throat as she looked at her child, her poor, damaged child as she thought of him.

'Come on, lazybones,' Winnie said, scooping him up and kissing his cheek. His eyes were a very pale blue, almost colourless and his fine hair was gingery fair.

'Here, he's a solid weight, Susan,' Winnie said as she put him back on the cushions.

'I know. Nanny is trying to get him to walk a little but so far without success.'

'Paul and Victoria are in the schoolroom,' Susan said as they walked towards the main stairway.

'That's what I meant to ask. Are you satisfied with the governess?'

'She is quite excellent, Winnie. Appearances can be very deceptive. She looks so severe, mannish almost but she's very good with children. Victoria needs a firm hand and she gets that from Miss Loudon. I expected ructions from that young lady but strangely enough she gives Miss Loudon no trouble.'

'What about Paul?'

'He's very good and very quick. Before another year passes I must see about engaging a tutor. I had the advantage of sharing Matthew's and I consider myself very fortunate. Should Victoria show a willingness to learn she'll get every encouragement. She'll continue with the governess for a few years then we'll see.'

'And James, can anything be done?'

'Very little but there is a light at the end of the tunnel. Miss Loudon is beginning to spend some time with him, she's had some experience with handicapped children and slow learners and once the other two are through her hands she'll take on James.'

'That's a big relief. Duncan isn't all that keen on schooling.'

'Like Matthew.'

'Yes, like Matthew but it doesn't really matter. Duncan wants to be a farmer like his papa and his grandpapa. And now I must go, I hadn't intended staying this long.'

'I've enjoyed it, we must try and do this more often.'

'Yes, we must and, Susan, thank you for – for everything.'

It was Susan's day for checking the ledgers and she didn't welcome the interruption.

'Yes, Edward, what is it?' she said, trying to hide her impatience.

'Letter from Frankfurt,' he said, putting it down in front of her.

'From Herr Wilhelm Rolfe?'

'No, his son, Helmut.'

'What does he want?'

'An order I expect. The fellow is to be in Scotland and would like to pay us a visit if we are agreeable.'

'Quite agreeable but put him right concerning an order, there'll be nothing in the forseeable future,' she said, glancing over the letter and then shaking her head. 'No, Edward, he's not after an order it's no more than a courtesy visit.' She smiled up at him. 'Be a dear and reply to it and offer whatever hospitality you feel necessary.'

'Yes, all right and it is to be hoped he speaks English as well as he writes it.'

'I'm sure he will. His father and mine exchanged the occasional letter – in English of course,' she added.

It was March, but a bitterly cold day with a blustery north-west wind beating gusts against the windows of Aran Heights as the carriage took Edward to the station to meet Herr Helmut Rolfe. Susan had brought work home so that she could be at Aran Heights to meet their German visitor. Edward had suggested that after a light refreshment he would take Herr Rolfe to the mill and show him around. Then about one o'clock they would return to Aran Heights for luncheon. Hopefully their guest would have departed by early afternoon and Edward saw no reason to alter his appointment.

To receive her guest Susan wore a deep blue gown with a stand-up collar and a double row of real pearls at her throat. She thought that the total lack of fussiness made it suitable for a luncheon where, she imagined, the conversation would be mainly about business. What Susan failed to realise was that the gown's sheer simplicity showed her slender figure to advantage.

Her ears caught the sound of the carriage stopping in the drive then a little later she heard masculine voices but only when the door opened did Susan get up from her seat at the fire and go forward. Edward made the introductions and at the touch of the German's hand Susan raised startled eyes

275

and saw her own awareness mirrored in his. She turned away sharply as a tingle of excitement went coursing through her body.

What, she wondered, is the magical formula that instantly draws two people together? Herr Rolfe was far from being unattractive but her own husband was more handsome. The German was shorter with broad shoulders and a slim athletic body and like most of his countrymen he was fair. His dark blond hair was longer than convention dictated. It was very thick and a lock of it fell on to his wide forehead. The face was squarish, denoting strength, the nose straight and the eyes a light blue.

Not quite recovered and feeling her colour high, Susan was glad of Edward's ease with guests. He talked while she rang for the maid. Coffee was served and as is the British custom the conversation centred around the vagaries of the weather.

'You didn't pick the best day for your visit, Herr Rolfe.' Susan smiled.

'The cold does not trouble me, Mrs Brodie,' he said in a voice only lightly accented, 'but the wind!' He gave a mock shudder. 'If it is like this now what, I ask myself, is it like in the depth of winter?'

'Very much worse.' Susan laughed. 'But we are quite snug here. My father had Aran Heights built to withstand the elements.'

'And it certainly does that,' Edward added. 'During one of the severest storms we've had in this part of the country there was hardly a building that didn't suffer damage yet Aran Heights, in the most vulnerable position, got off with losing a few slates.'

Herr Rolfe turned to Susan. 'My father was deeply upset to hear about Mr MacFarlane's death and I do know he misses the occasional letter they exchanged.'

'Thank you.' She paused. 'Does Herr Rolfe keep well?'

'Father is slowing down and becoming forgetful but otherwise, allowing for his age, he is remarkably well.'

'Your English is so good, isn't it, Edward?'

276

'Excellent and I feel ashamed that apart from a smattering of French I speak only my own language.'

'Forgive me, Mr Brodie, but we call that the arrogance of the English, expecting everyone to speak their language.'

'That lets us out, Herr Rolfe,' Susan said mischievously. 'We are Scottish and some of the English have great difficulty understanding us.'

They all laughed.

'Look at that, a blink of sun!' Susan said as a shaft of bright sunshine came through the parted curtains. 'By afternoon the wind may have dropped.'

As the maid cleared away the coffee cups Edward got to his feet. 'I think we should get on our way, Herr Rolfe. Among other things you'll want to see your own machinery working.'

'Indeed I would and I trust you have no complaints.'

'On the contrary,' Susan answered, 'we are very well satisfied.'

Anxious to be gone, Edward moved to the door and the German followed him. 'We should be back by one, Susan.'

Alone, Susan took herself to task. She was being utterly ridiculous, acting like a lovesick seventeen-year-old instead of a married woman and the mother of three children. Well, she would get down to some work and that would put this nonsense out of her head, only it didn't. She found that she couldn't concentrate and, sighing, put aside the papers and sat in unaccustomed idleness dreaming impossible dreams.

They were punctual, a few minutes before one o'clock but everything was prepared. Game soup was to be followed by slightly underdone roast beef with garden vegetables and roast and boiled potatoes, and the sweet was an almond pastry. Edward had selected the appropriate wines.

Earlier Susan had remarked to Edward that perhaps they should have made it a light lunch but Edward hadn't agreed. 'Germans have hearty appetites, my dear Susan.'

They were using the main dining-room and dining three people at such a long table posed problems. Susan solved it by making use of the top end of the table. Edward sat in his customary place and she and Herr Rolfe sat opposite one another. The conversation during the meal had been general but Susan had a burning curiosity to know more about this German.

'Are you married, Herr Rolfe?'

'Yes, I am married and we have a small daughter. Marlene will be seven next month. And you, you have a family?'

'Two sons and a daughter.'

She saw his face cloud. 'How I envy you both. I was a one child – is that how you say it?'

'An only child,' Susan said gently.

'I was an only child and I did not wish that on Marlene. I felt too much was expected of me but then,' he shrugged, 'it was natural that my father would want his only son to take over the business.'

'You would have preferred to do something else?'

'Perhaps, Mrs Brodie, but I cannot be sure. Painting, unless one has exceptional talent, should be no more than a hobby and honesty forces me to confess that I fall into that category.'

Edward was frowning and his eyes kept going to the clock.

'Edward, I'm sure Herr Rolfe will excuse you.' Then to the German. 'My husband has an appointment.'

'Then I must not keep – '

'No, there is no hurry for you, Herr Rolfe. My wife will look after you and our coachman will be ready to take you to the station when you wish to leave.'

Herr Rolfe was on his feet. They shook hands. 'I am indebted to you for your kindness and maybe one day you will bring your charming wife to Germany. We have a very beautiful country and the journey is less tedious than it used to be.'

'One day I hope to do just that and now you must excuse me.'

With Edward gone Susan suggested they return to the drawing-room.

'That was a delicious meal,' Herr Rolfe said as he sat in the chair near to hers.

'I'm glad you enjoyed it,' she said breathlessly. His nearness was affecting her and she rushed in with the first thing that came into her mind. 'My elder brother was killed in an accident and my other brother had no interest in the mill. Matthew always wanted to farm and now he has got his wish. You would see the farm on your way here.' She was babbling.

'Yes, your husband pointed it out. He also said that one day both farms would be his.' He grinned. 'Your brother married a farmer's daughter and very sensible too.'

'They are very happy,' Susan said defensively and wondered what Edward had been saying.

'I do know quite a lot about your family, Mrs Brodie. Your father gave a glowing account of his daughter's capabilities and frankly I was in awe of meeting this exceptional woman.' His voice dropped. 'One thing he could have added was beauty: you are very beautiful, Mrs Brodie.'

'And you know how to flatter. I'm sure your wife – '

He didn't let her finish. 'My wife never recovered from the birth of our daughter. I believe your term for the condition is melancholia.'

'Oh, I am sorry, that must be very distressing for you.'

'Yes. Very distressing. Poor Helga was a lovely, lively girl but now she has no interest in anything. No interest in her daughter and no interest in her husband.'

'How do you cope?'

'Eva has been our salvation. She is my wife's sister and unmarried and I persuaded her to come and live with us.' His face softened as he spoke of his sister-in-law and Susan felt a sudden stab of unreasonable jealousy.

'Is she beautiful, your sister-in-law?'

'Eva beautiful? No, far from it but she is good and we all love her. That is not to say she is plain, she has – ' He seemed to be struggling for a word.

'An interesting face,' Susan finished for him and he let out a guffaw of laughter.

'An interesting face! I like that and it is true, I shall tell Eva and I know she will be much amused.'

If his marriage was dead a man like Helmut would need a woman, Susan thought and wondered if Eva supplied what was missing in his marriage.

'Are you and your husband happy or is that a question I should not ask?'

'No, you shouldn't. But why do you ask it?'

'Perhaps I notice more than I should; forgive me, we'll say no more about it.'

'We have our difficulties but that is all I am going to say,' Susan said firmly.

'Mrs Brodie,' he said abruptly, 'I am to be in Glasgow for a little time. Is it possible that we could meet?'

She shook her head weakly.

'Why not?' he said softly. 'You must know that something has happened between us.'

Yes, she thought, I do know. Raising her eyes, she felt the full power of his magnetism. Without taking his eyes from her Helmut Rolfe got up and drew her gently to her feet. She didn't try to pull away when his arms went around her and when his mouth found hers it was a kiss that transported her to another world. Sighing, she moved out of his embrace and went over to the window. After a while he joined her and they stood looking out at the gardens and beyond to the hills.

'It amazes me that you are surrounded by such peaceful countryside yet a few miles away is Glasgow, a city of such contrasts.'

'Yes, my father always said we had the best of both worlds, but you can't know Glasgow well?' She turned to him and as if by common consent they went over and sat on the couch.

'I have seen some of its impressive architecture and magnificent buildings but I have also seen its squalor and the hovels where some must live. We, too, have that in Frankfurt. It is an unfair world, Mrs Brodie, but happily you won't have seen that side of Glasgow.'

She smiled and shook her head but in those moments she was remembering a time when, sick with worry, she had stumbled into its mean streets and only chance had taken her into a dreary teashop and safety.

He touched her hand. 'You were miles away and I was asking you about shopping, surely you could make some excuse?'

'It's true I do shop in Glasgow occasionally.'

'Well, then – ah, I see, perhaps you are not permitted to travel alone?'

Susan frowned. 'Herr Rolfe, I do not require my husband's permission. I am a matron not a young girl.'

'A woman of spirit is what you are, Mrs Brodie, and that I admire.' He gave a slow smile. 'This formality is it not ridiculous? Please, I would like you to call me Helmut and may I address you as Susan?'

'Yes.' She smiled, amazed that in a few short hours they should be so at ease with one another.

'You promise to come to Glasgow but when?' he persisted.

A recklessness came over her. 'Tuesday would be best.'

'Tuesday and at what time?'

She thought for a few minutes. 'In the late morning. The train gets in to Queen Street at eleven fifteen.'

'And must you return the same night?' he asked, so softly that she almost didn't hear.

Her own gaze dropped in confusion and as if sensing a withdrawal he spoke quickly. 'Please do not misunderstand, the accommodation would be as you wish. You have nothing to fear.'

She nodded, knowing that she could trust him but wondering if she could trust herself.

'And now,' he said regretfully, 'it is time I left for the station.'

'Yes, it is,' Susan said, and with a glance at the clock pulled at the bell.

'You rang, m'am?'

'Yes. Tell Ramsay to bring the carriage round. Herr Rolfe is ready to leave.'

Sitting back in the carriage taking him to the station Helmut Rolfe's thoughts were only of Susan Brodie. He had to keep reminding himself that she was another man's wife but it didn't stop the strong desire he felt for her. It had been a very long time since a woman had aroused in him such a hungry passion. His wife never had. Pretty, spoiled Helga had hated the intimate side of marriage and had never pretended otherwise. Her mother had had a lot to do with that, he always thought. They had been very close and Helga would never have questioned anything her mother said.

He frowned in perplexity. What was wrong with the Brodie marriage? Susan had been genuinely surprised that he had noticed something amiss. It was no light tiff but something deep-rooted and he guessed correctly that Susan would never speak of it. Even so, it continued to intrigue him. Edward Brodie was a fortunate man indeed for his wife had everything, beauty, poise, charm and a keen mind. Then his thoughts went to Tuesday. Would she come? Would she keep her promise? Yes, he was almost sure she would. Susan Brodie would not readily break her word.

Soup was not served that night. Susan had requested a two-course meal with biscuits and cheese to follow. Edward, concerned at what he thought was the beginning of a paunch, made no complaint.

'Rolfe got away then?'

'Yes.'

'Seemed favourably impressed with everything, do you agree?'

'Yes and I think he enjoyed his day.'

With the German dismissed from his mind Edward was unusually talkative about a business deal which had left him in a pleasant mood. Once they'd moved to the sitting-room and before he reached the business section of the paper, Susan had decided to broach the subject.

'Edward, I'm planning to do some shopping in Glasgow and Tuesday seems most convenient,' she said in a casual, offhand manner.

'Mmmmm.'

'I may decide to stay overnight rather than rush the shopping in an afternoon.'

He looked up. 'In that case you can pop into Browns and see if the book I ordered has arrived.'

'Yes, no trouble.'

'You remember where it is?'

'That lane off St Vincent Street.'

'Yes, that's it.' His attention went back to the paper and after a few minutes Susan excused herself and climbed the stairs to the library. To protect the books the room was always heated and comfortable to sit in and Susan was spending more and more of her time there rather than the sitting-room. With her elbows on the desk and her chin resting on her hands she marvelled at how easy it had been. Edward hadn't questioned her at all. Of course he would assume that she would be staying overnight with Agnes and Duncan Stewart. On the occasions when they made a foursome for the theatre or went to a concert Susan and Edward remained overnight at the Stewart home in Maryhill. Other than that they rarely saw the Stewarts so she had little to fear. And if she felt the faintest touch of guilt she had only to remember how often Edward left her alone.

It was Tuesday and Susan felt a growing excitement and was amazed how everything had worked for her. Even the weather, by one of those sudden twists so common to the west, had become warm and springlike. Dressed and ready, Susan took one last look in the mirror and smiled at her reflection. Her costume was fashionable with the jacket nipped in at the waist and the shade of soft rose pink set off her fair complexion. To complete the outfit she wore a saucy hat with a long feather. Some time ago Charlotte Beattie had closed her salon but even before that, Susan, like so many of the ladies of her acquaintance, was shopping in Buchanan Street and Sauchiehall Street. Glasgow, it was agreed, was very nearly as good as London for stylish clothes.

Ramsay drove Susan to the station and saw her safely on the train. Then as they moved off suddenly and unexpectedly,

Susan was full of doubts. Until then she had carried the memory of Helmut's face but now she couldn't remember what he looked like. Was he, too, experiencing doubts? Would it be politeness that brought him to the station? Well, that needn't be a problem, they didn't have to go through with it, did they? Herr Rolfe would understand and no doubt be relieved when she told him that she had changed her mind. Then she could do a little shopping, collect Edward's book and return home. That settled in her mind, she sat back and tried to enjoy the rest of the journey.

The train puffed into Queen Street station a few minutes before its scheduled time of arrival and Susan joined the others walking along the platform. Of Helmut Rolfe there was no sign. Relief, disappointment and a damaging blow to her pride were battling for place. Then just as suddenly her whole world changed. Helmut was coming towards her, almost running, his face wreathed in smiles and her own face lit up. The hug he gave her was quick, satisfying and completely natural. Just two people so happy to meet again. Relieving her of the bag, he tucked her arm in his and together they walked out into the spring sunshine. They stopped on the pavement and Helmut looked at her with eyes full of admiration.

'You look enchanting, my dear Susan, and do you know I was in torment fearing you would not come.' He laughed and she smiled at the boyish gesture as he pulled his fingers through his hair. 'You cannot begin to imagine the joy it was to see you walking along that platform.'

Should she tell him of her earlier doubts? she wondered but decided against it. They were together and that was all that mattered. Oh, there was risk and danger, she was aware of that but somehow it only added to a sense of adventure.

'Helmut, I want to do something before I forget. My husband ordered a book and I said I'd collect it.' She was sorry to bring up Edward's name so early but Helmut didn't seem troubled.

'But of course, we will get a cab.'

'No, really, it isn't far and I would enjoy the walk.'

They strolled happily along West George Street saying little, just content to be together. When they reached Browns bookshop with its small bow-fronted window Helmut remained outside until Susan appeared with the wrapped package.

He took it from her. 'And now?' He smiled.

'I'm quite thirsty.' She didn't tell him that she'd been too excited to eat breakfast. 'And I do know there is a teashop a few doors away.'

Miss MacGregor's Teashop was famous for its home baking. The wonderful smell of hot loaves and pastries made Susan realise how hungry she was. They were shown to a table with a fresh white tablecloth and in the centre was a pot containing a few sprigs of white heather.

The waitress arrived and Helmut ordered a pot of tea and a selection of pastries.

'That is white heather, Helmut, and supposed to be lucky.'

'Then I must have a bit,' he said, taking a sprig of heather and fixing it in his buttonhole.

Putting down the plate of pastries and a pot of tea Susan saw the waitress glance at the heather and raise an eyebrow.

'You must charge the gentleman for that.' Susan smiled. 'My fault, I told him it's supposed to be lucky.'

'And so it is.' She smiled. 'But the gentleman is welcome to the white heather and there is no charge.'

After serving the other tables the waitress, who looked to be in her forties, hovered nearby. The couple interested her. Not young lovers but lovers all the same, she thought with a pang of envy. A married lady, she wore a ring, but the gentleman she was with was not her husband. She could always tell the married couples. They seldom made eye-to-eye contact and for much of the time they sat in a comfortable silence. The lady was very, very pretty and a toff, that was easy to tell. The gentleman was handsome enough and though his English was good she was quite sure that he was a foreigner. The generous tip he left was very welcome and a boost to her meagre wages.

Susan felt completely happy and carefree as they walked and talked and had lunch at a restaurant. Helmut signalled for a cab and they had a short tour of the city then at Susan's suggestion they dismissed the cab at the Suspension Bridge and arm-in-arm walked across it. How safe it looked at this time of day with people coming and going but Susan knew from her father how different it was when darkness fell. A sudden need to warn Helmut made her clutch at his arm.

'Helmut, you must promise me never to come here at night.'

He smiled. 'Thank you for your concern, my dearest Susan, but I have more sense. All cities have their unsafe areas and bridges are a magnet for undesirables.'

'My father told my brothers and me that at night drunken beggars sleep here and half-starved, barefooted children roam around begging for pennies.'

'Poor little wretches. We live in an unfair world, Susan.'

'Yes, I know, but there is little we can do about it.'

'Now I cannot agree with you there; we should all make some effort to improve conditions.'

'How?'

'Cheaper houses and basic education for all.'

'My father would have agreed with that. I do too though I am ashamed to say I haven't given it a great deal of thought.'

He was silent for some moments then when he spoke again it was hesitantly. 'You do know I have been staying at the Majestic?'

'Yes, you said so in your letter.'

'So I did.' He paused and Susan, knowing what was coming, avoided his eyes.

'As I said before you have nothing to fear. It would, of course, be unwise for us to stay there and I have booked accommodation at the Park Inn. The food there is very good or so I am told and I have booked a table for dinner.'

'That sounds lovely.'

They had eaten an excellent meal with Susan taking more

wine than she was used to but even so it didn't dull her mind. Instead it left her with a feeling of euphoria. She was here with Helmut, enjoying the company of a charming and intelligent man. Their table was in one of the alcoves and she supposed that had been at Helmut's request.

When she put down her coffee cup he caught her hand and kissed it with passion. 'You are very beautiful, my dear Susan,' he said softly, 'and I speak the truth when I say I have never wanted a woman as much as I want you.'

Susan saw the longing in his face and feeling her own body responding she dropped her eyes in confusion. Not certain of what it meant, Helmut sat back in his chair and she saw him bring out a key and place it between them on the white tablecloth.

'I am a gentleman of my word, Susan, and if you wish to spend the night alone that is your key.'

For a long time Susan looked at it. She didn't deny to herself that she wanted Helmut and what harm were they doing? she asked herself. One precious night, that was all it would be. They would never meet again, no one need ever know. Helmut would return to Germany to his unsatisfactory marriage and she to the coldness of hers.

She shook her head and Helmut put the key back in his pocket. Then they got up and climbed the stairs. Helmut unlocked the door and she went into the comfortably furnished room with its large four-poster bed. Coming behind her, Helmut turned her to face him then put his arms around her. His mouth came down on hers and she was aware of the strength of his body and could feel his heartbeats blend with hers. When he began to undo the buttons of her blouse she made no attempt to stop him. She felt no shame, only shivering with desire when his hands touched her bare skin.

Across the breakfast table Helmut gazed at her adoringly but there was sadness in his expression.

'I shall always remember you, Susan, and those precious hours we shared gave me more happiness than I have ever experienced. In English I do not have the words to tell you but you understand?'

'I understand, Helmut,' Susan said almost in tears. 'For me it was very special too but now,' she said, fighting for normality, 'time is short and we have shopping to do. I can't go home empty-handed. I must buy gloves for myself, ribbons for Victoria, a book for Paul and a toy for James.'

'Don't forget you promised to help me with mine.'

'I hadn't.'

Inside the large store Susan looked at Helmut enquiringly. 'You'll have to give me some idea.'

'Marlene is no problem. She likes adding to her collection of dolls.'

'Good, the children's department is on the ground floor.'

The assistant was very helpful, showing dolls of all sizes. 'You choose, Susan.'

'I like this one, it has such a lovely face,' she said, touching the china doll.

'That one then,' Helmut told the assistant.

'I shall tell Marlene the doll's name is Susan,' Helmut whispered when the assistant was out of earshot.

'I'm honoured.' Susan laughed as she left Helmut to pay and went off to select something for Paul and James.

'So far so good, now what do I get my wife?'

'Does she sit about a lot?'

'Most of the time.'

'Then I suggest a fine-knit shawl.'

'Excellent,' he said when that was purchased. 'And now my sister-in-law.'

'Something to wear?'

'I think not.'

They had moved to the china department. 'What about a little Wedgwood dish?'

'Yes, that would do very nicely.'

'Helmut, I'm going to leave you here while I do some shopping on my own, then we can meet at the entrance.'

'That is fine, I shall arrange for these to be sent to the hotel.'

Susan bought two pairs of gloves, a selection of hair ribbons for Victoria and at a sudden thought bought some for Helmut's daughter.

He was there at the entrance watching the faces as the customers came out and when Susan appeared he was over quickly, taking the packages from her.

'Those are ribbons for your little girl,' Susan said, handing him the small packet. 'If she's anything like Victoria she'll be for ever losing them.'

'Yes, she does and that was very thoughtful of you. And this is for you.'

'Oh, no, Helmut, you shouldn't, I didn't want – '

'It is only perfume, Susan, something you may well have bought for yourself.'

She looked at the beautifully wrapped box and felt close to tears. 'I have nothing for you.'

'My darling, you gave me the greatest gift of all, you gave me yourself.'

So engrossed were they with each other that they were unaware of eyes watching them until they heard the voice.

'Susan, it is you, for a moment I wasn't sure.'

Seeing who it was, Susan found it difficult to hide her dismay.

'Hello, Beccy,' she said, knowing she looked guilty. Beccy and Adrian Brownlea were friends of Edward's and occasionally joined their circle of friends. Though Adrian was pleasant enough, Beccy had a sharp tongue and a nose for gossip.

'Herr Rolfe is a business friend from Germany,' Susan said after making the introductions.

'Really!' she said, fixing Helmut with her green eyes. 'And how do you like our country, Herr Rolfe?'

'Very much and I am indebted to Mr and Mrs Brodie for their hospitality and to Mrs Brodie for helping me with the difficult task of choosing gifts to take home.'

Susan breathed more easily, grateful to Helmut for his quick thinking.

'Is this trouble for you, Susan?' Helmut said worriedly as Beccy disappeared into the store.

'No, not at all, I'm sure your explanation satisfied her.'

Susan wished that she were as confident as she sounded but when three weeks went by she relaxed, though she should have known better.

As usual Edward waited until they were in the sitting-room.

'Adrian mentioned that Beccy met you in Glasgow in the company of that German, Rolfe.' His eyes narrowed. 'How did that come about?'

Susan's stomach was churning with nerves. How much did Edward know or guess?

'Strangely silent, aren't you? Incidentally I took the trouble to find out from the Stewarts if you had remained the night with them. Apparently you hadn't.'

Susan's nervousness vanished and anger took its place.

'How dare you check up on me.'

'You are my wife.'

'That doesn't stop you having other women.' Her blue eyes were flashing dangerously. 'This is the first time I have been unfaithful to you and yes, I'll be happy to tell you all about it.'

'Have you no shame?' he shouted, his face purple.

'No shame at all, Edward.' She smiled. 'Helmut Rolfe made me feel young and desirable and those hours with him in Glasgow were the happiest I have had in a very long time.'

'Love at first sight,' he said sneeringly but behind the sneer there was uncertainty and she could see that he was shaken.

'No, not as strong as that but I was very, very attracted to Herr Rolfe.'

'What about his wife, had you given any thought to her?'

'It would not affect her. Helmut has returned to Frankfurt to his unsatisfactory marriage and I am back to the sham that is ours but don't worry, Edward, life will carry on as before.'

# CHAPTER EIGHTEEN

No other institution is regarded with the same respect as the bank. From the humble depositor of a few coppers to the giants of industry all use its services with complete confidence and its solid reliability is never in question. For a variety of reasons a small business or one of its larger sisters may go to the wall but for a bank to fail is beyond comprehension. Yet in that year of 1898 it happened to the Lomond Bank.

Virtually disregarded were the first faint rumblings that preceded its collapse. Though the City was nervous no one seriously doubted but that the position would steady. There was no cause for alarm.

When its collapse did come the whole country was shaken and repercussions were felt far beyond its own doors. Other banks were quick to realise that if they were to survive, withdrawals must be kept to a minimum. Ugly scenes followed as customers, rushing to get their hands on their savings, were refused.

In the Aranvale Papermill the machines were silent, the workers gone home but a gas lamp still burned in one of the offices. All day there had been rumours and counter-rumours. Too disturbed to settle to anything, Edward had gone by train to Glasgow to see the position for himself. Barely had he arrived than the news broke. The horrified groups hanging around saw the heavy wooden doors of the Lomond Bank close, heard the massive bolts snap into position. There was a surge forward to read the notice posted on the outside. With their worst fears confirmed, the more hysterical among them made to break down the doors. Hurriedly more police were drafted to the scene before it got completely out of hand.

Edward was pale and shaken when he returned.

'My God! You wouldn't believe what I saw, Susan, it's mass hysteria.' Backwards and forwards he walked the floor and Susan's worried eyes followed him.

'Edward, we mustn't let ourselves panic and overreact. Undoubtedly the bank has serious problems but the fact that they have seen fit to shut out the public may only be to assess the true position.' It was bravely said but she didn't believe it herself.

'The true position!' Edward repeated bitterly. 'What might that be?'

'A panic to withdraw, Edward, they have to avoid that, no bank could stand . . .' She trailed off.

'It's the end, Susan, it's ruin for us and others like us.'

Susan was pale but spoke firmly. 'I refuse to think along those lines. The full facts are not available yet and until such time as they are – '

'You'll go on hoping?'

'Yes.'

Flinging open the cabinet which had at one time lodged a variety of bottles, he stared at the office paraphernalia which now occupied the space. The door banged shut.

'Why the hell don't you keep this place stocked? Your old man did. Right now what I need is a good stiff drink.'

'What we both need, Edward, is to go home and try to get some rest. Tomorrow the news may be better and even if it isn't we'll be better able to face it after a night's sleep.'

He smiled at that. 'Cool as always, aren't you? Maybe I envy you the ability to distance yourself from reality.'

'If you believe that you'd believe anything,' she said tartly. After locking the cabinets she picked up her belongings. 'Are you coming?'

'I suppose so.'

Tomorrow confirmed their worst fears but Susan was anxious that it should be business as usual. A workforce plagued by uncertainties and worried about the security of jobs would not give of its best and it was vitally important that the wheels of industry keep turning.

'Edward, I'm calling a meeting of the chargehands right away,' she said, having made up her mind that moment.

'What do you intend telling them? That there is no money and they can whistle for their wages.'

'It hasn't quite come to that,' she said quietly. Edward didn't look like removing himself and she wanted to be alone. 'On your way out, Edward, would you mind asking Mr McNeil to come and see me?'

'What for?'

'To arrange the meeting. Incidentally, do you want to be present?'

'I do not.'

'Very well,' she said to his departing back.

'This is a richt bad business, Mistress Brodie.' Mr McNeil's expression was serious and his eyes troubled.

'Yes, Mr McNeil, this is something no one could have foreseen.' She paused. 'I feel I should see the chargehands, speak to them personally. The others I can talk to at a later date.' Her eyes went to the clock. 'Will you arrange it for – say – eleven thirty in the boardroom?'

His eyebrows rose when she said boardroom.

'I know! I know! Mr McNeil, but it suits me better and these are special circumstances.'

'I'll grant ye that.'

In an unguarded moment Susan closed her eyes and Mr McNeil saw the strain and tiredness in her face.

'You're a fighter, Mistress Brodie, you'll come through.'

'If only my father were here,' she whispered, 'he would have known what to do. I thought I was equal to the responsibility but I'm not so sure now.'

'Tch! Tch! What kind of talk is that comin' from a MacFarlane? I've found the maister gie low at times but he pulled through and you'll do the same, never fear.'

'I hope you're right, it would break my heart if I failed.'

'There's no such word.'

Susan looked with affection at the old man who had been both employee and friend to her father. 'What would I do without you, Mr McNeil?'

'Ye'd manage I dare say but could I gie ye a word o' advice?'

'Say whatever you have to say.'

'Maist fowk like tae feel needed. My advice is, dinnae haud back. Let the workers know the true position, that survival is possible if a'body pulls th' gither,' he said gruffly. 'Test their loyalty and I dinnae think ye'll find it wantin'.'

'Thank you, Mr McNeil, I was thinking along those lines myself.'

The chargehands filed into the boardroom looking ill at ease in such hallowed surroundings but when Susan addressed them the posh upholstery was forgotten and she had their undivided attention.

She took a deep breath before beginning. 'Gentlemen, you are all aware of the gravity of the position. I don't need to emphasise it.'

There were murmurs and nods.

'It is my firm belief that honesty is the best policy and I want you all to know the position.' She had been standing with her hands splayed on the table but now she sat down as her legs threatened to buckle. She had made some notes on a pad but she didn't refer to them.

'Due to the collapse of the bank we have suffered a crippling blow and we are quite unable to meet all our debts. However we do have one advantage.' She paused and looked at the faces turned her way. 'My father preferred to pay his accounts promptly, believing that should we ever be in financial difficulties we would be treated more sympathetically than those others who chose to wait until the last minute to settle.'

A thin-faced, anxious-looking man raised a hand tentatively and Susan acknowledged the movement with an encouraging nod.

'A word, m'am, if ye'd be so kind,' he said, glancing nervously around the table as if searching for support.

'Comments are welcomed.' She smiled.

With a calloused hand he brushed the moisture from his moustache and lumbered to his feet.

'Is it likely ye'll be payin' aff some o' the workers?' he asked worriedly, then sat down quickly, drawing his brows together. All those present had wanted to ask the same question and were grateful that one of their number was bold enough to voice their concern.

'I very much hope not,' Susan said quietly, 'the very last thing I want to do is that.' Leaning forward she spoke earnestly. 'To avoid such a measure I need your help and those under you. Uncertainty is bad for business, bad for everybody. It is absolutely essential that you reassure the workers about their jobs. Let them know that for the foreseeable future their position in the mill is secure.' She paused to sip from the glass of water thoughtfully placed there. 'Unfortunately and I very much regret this, but it may become necessary to cut their wages. Not just theirs,' she hastened in with, 'each and every one of us will be called on to make sacrifices.'

Another chargehand begged to be allowed his say. This man was older with a scalp speckled like a thrush's egg.

'M'am, I dinnae think I'm speakin' oot o' turn when I say that a cut in wages, unwelcome though that is, is preferable to nae job at a'.' His eyes sought the approval of those round the table and he got it in the murmurings that followed. 'There wis a time when, like mony mair, I had ma doots aboot a woman, beggin' yer pardon, m'am, takin' o'er frae the maister.' He swallowed noisily and cleared his throat. 'I hope I'm man enough tae admit I've bin proved wrang. Ye've earned oor respect, m'am, and ye'll get frae us the same loyalty we'd hae gi'en tae the maister, rest his soul.' It had been a long speech and his colour had risen before he finished.

Susan was having difficulty with a lump in her throat.

'Thank you, each and every one of you. I am deeply moved and I hope I'll always be worthy of that respect.' She tried to smile but her lips were trembling too much. 'My confidence has been given a boost now that I know we are facing this together,' she said unsteadily.

Recognising how near Mistress MacFarlane was to breaking down, Mr McNeil took it upon himself to bring the meeting to a close and Susan escaped to her office. Once inside she turned the key, went to her desk and sat behind it, staring at the wall opposite. Once she felt more composed, she sent for the accountant. They would go over the books again.

Neither she nor Edward had an appetite for the food placed before them, merely picking at it. For much of the time they had been silent, each engrossed with thoughts that could not be shared.

Later on they sat in the sitting-room and Edward poured himself a drink.

'God! I wish I'd taken your advice, Susan, and invested the money from Hillview. Even a gamble would have been a spot of excitement,' he said, staring moodily into the amber liquid. 'As it is I might just as well have poured it down the drain.'

'Surely you'll get a small percentage, they'll be able to pay something.'

'So small it'll be negligible.' His face darkened as he put down his glass then his fist crashed down on the table, disturbing his drink and splashing some over the rim. 'Susan, I hear myself saying all this yet deep down I'm not believing it has happened.'

'I know, Edward, I'm the same. The enormity of it hits me one moment and in the next I am hoping to awaken from a nightmare.'

'We'll have to cut down expenses. Get rid of some of the servants and make the others do a bit more for their wages.'

Her blue eyes resting on him were cold and hostile.

'Maybe that will come but it will certainly not be our first economy, but I can tell you what that will be.'

'Then do.'

'The first to feel the pinch and I apologise for the unfortunate choice of expression, will be your mistress.'

'What the devil – ' he spluttered.

It was a shot in the dark but since Winnie's evasiveness she was becoming more and more convinced that she was right. 'Caroline is too expensive, Edward, she is a luxury you can no longer afford.' Her lips curled. 'Unless of course, the lady is sufficiently taken with you to supply her services free.'

Edward's face had turned a mottled red. 'You bitch,' he breathed. 'Brother Matthew's doing I suppose,' and followed nastily with, 'Resents someone else having a bit of fun when he has to be content with that cold fish of a wife.'

With difficulty Susan kept her temper. 'Wrong on both counts. Matthew and Winnie happen to enjoy a particularly happy marriage and I did not hear about you and Caroline from Matthew or indeed from anyone.' She paused to let her words sink in. 'It was a chance remark which aroused my suspicions and you, yourself, have just confirmed its truth. I recall you once saying how attractive you found Caroline.'

'I do believe the lady is jealous!'

'Wishful thinking on your part, Edward. I am not in the least jealous. Caroline is a decided improvement on that slut of a maid.' She gave an exaggerated mock sigh. 'Sadly though, the Carolines of this world do not come cheap.'

Edward threw back his head and laughed heartily.

'Susan, you never cease to surprise me. Who would have guessed that the innocent maiden, protected from the harshness of life, would become such a very worldly and outspoken young matron.'

She laughed with him, glad that it hadn't deteriorated into a slanging match as it so often did. 'Let us just say that I had a lot of growing up to do in a very short time.'

He had positioned himself at the window and she heard him groan.

'Oh, God! Your Aunt Rachel is about to descend upon us.'

Susan hurried across to the window. 'So she is!' For a moment she considered going out to greet her aunt then instead waited for her to be announced.

Rachel MacFarlane was not given to making unexpected visits, preferring to await an invitation. She came in hurriedly, refused to part with her cloak, planted a kiss on Susan's cheek and offered her own to Edward who obliged with a brush of his lips. Waving away the offer of a comfortable chair she chose instead one with a hard back, declaring she would have difficulty getting out of the other.

'How are you, Aunt Rachel?'

'Well enough or I wouldn't be here. But never mind that. How bad is it? And don't treat me as if I were senile. Kindly remember that I am a daughter of the mill and what happens to it is of concern to me.' Her eyes bored into Susan.

'Our losses are substantial, Aunt Rachel, I won't hide that from you,' Susan said quietly. 'All we can do is hope that somehow we'll battle through.' She bit her lip. 'It's going to be a struggle.'

'If you have the determination – '

'Needs more than that,' Edward put in bluntly as he drained his glass.

'Drink dulls the intellect, Edward,' Aunt Rachel said severely. 'I hope this is not you drowning your sorrows.'

'Not at all,' he said stiffly, 'a small stimulant increases one's thought processes.'

'Does it indeed! We're always learning.'

Having dealt with Edward she turned her sharp gaze back to her niece.

'Susan, I want to help – '

'No, Aunt Rachel – '

'Kindly do not interrupt your elders.'

Susan murmured an apology.

'What I have will one day be shared between you and Matthew. However as your need is now – '

'No! You are not drawing on your money, I won't have it,' Susan said stubbornly.

'False pride will get you nowhere, my dear, and now be good enough to allow me an uninterrupted hearing.' She placed her feet in their tightly laced boots a little apart and looked down pointedly. Remembering then that her aunt liked a footstool, Susan hurried to bring one over.

'Thank you, that's much more restful. And now to what I

was saying. You, Susan, are not the only female member of this family to have a head for business.' She almost smirked. 'Against all well-intentioned advice and it is never in short supply, I invested my money in various enterprises. All were not successful I must admit but others paid a handsome dividend. An occasional flutter may not be considered ladylike but who was to know,' she twinkled, 'and from it I derived a great deal of enjoyment.'

Edward guffawed and Susan couldn't keep herself from giggling.

'Those misspent years mean that I am in a position to help you, Susan, but don't go imagining that I'm noble enough to risk becoming penniless in my old age because I am not. I'm too fond of my creature comforts.'

'May I say something?' Susan said meekly.

'You may.'

'Some capital would be a godsend but if I accept it, it has to be on my terms.'

'Go on.'

'This is to be a business transaction, the equivalent of a loan from the bank – '

'That's a bad joke,' Edward muttered.

'The Lomond Bank as it was and will be again,' Susan said, annoyed at the interruption. 'It means, Aunt Rachel, that the money is a loan and to be repaid with interest at the earliest possible date.'

'From one business woman to another I accept your terms,' she said smartly. There was a smug look on her face as she turned to Edward. 'Have no fears, Edward, just so long as there is a MacFarlane at its head, male or female, the papermill will survive.'

'I'm more than grateful,' Susan said as Aunt Rachel named a sum, 'but we should get by with less.'

'Very possibly but confidence will be quickly restored in the mill and out of it when you are seen to be paying your accounts at the normal time,' she said shrewdly.

'How very true, Aunt Rachel.' She hugged her aunt. 'You and I should have been partners.'

'Nothing would have suited me better, my dear, but I'm a bit long in the tooth for that now.'

At that moment the maid arrived to announce the arrival of Matthew and Winnie. There were kisses and hugs and a show of pleased surprise at seeing Aunt Rachel.

'Isn't this a dreadful business!' Winnie exclaimed, looking from one to the other as she loosened the buttons of her costume jacket.

'We're still reeling from shock,' Edward commented as he moved a chair forward for Winnie. 'How bad is it with you two?'

'Never have much in the bank, Edward,' Winnie answered for both of them. 'Most of what we have goes on stock.'

'Lucky you.'

'What about Moorend?' Susan enquired.

'Papa's a bit white about the gills, Susan, but that's delayed shock thinking what might have been.' Winnie smiled. 'Thankfully all the alterations and new furniture have been paid but as to how much they have lost I wouldn't know.'

Matthew took up the story there. 'Winnie's father is very close about what he has lost but neither he nor Mother seem too shattered. Why we really came over was to find out about the mill.'

Aunt Rachel moved her feet and managed to knock over the footstool and while this was being restored to its upright position, she spoke for Susan.

'Matthew, your sister has been telling me that the mill has lost heavily,' she said briskly, 'and a very worrying time it is for Susan and Edward too.'

Matthew nodded. 'That I can well believe and just because I opted out of the mill doesn't mean I don't care what happens. On the contrary I would be devastated to see the mill in real difficulties.' He smiled across to his wife. 'We discussed this before leaving home and we can raise some capital.'

Susan shook her head.

'Yes, Susan,' Winnie said gently, 'we do want to help.'

Susan swallowed hard but couldn't hold back the tears. 'Everyone is so kind,' she sobbed. 'Thank you from the bottom of my heart but it won't be necessary. Aunt Rachel has – '

'There! There!' Aunt Rachel said soothingly as if to a child. 'It's a woman's privilege to shed tears,' she said fiercely then swivelled to face Edward. 'Give your wife a handkerchief, there's a good boy, that apology she has in her hand is quite useless.'

Edward obeyed instantly, handing over a clean folded handkerchief and while doing so exchanged a look of resignation with Matthew. Shaking it open, Susan dabbed at her eyes then blew her nose and looked up shamefacedly.

'Sorry, everybody, I can stand the odd hard knock but too much kindness is my undoing,' she sniffed.

'Matthew and Winnie,' Aunt Rachel smiled to them, 'that was a very generous offer but I am in a better position to help. Anyway,' she added in her usual forthright manner, 'you farming folk are for ever pleading poverty, if not you're moaning about the weather, always something.'

The laughter that followed eased the strain for Susan and had Winnie wiping her eyes.

'When I found you here, Aunt Rachel, I rather thought you would be giving Susan a bit of help just as you did – '

'That is quite enough, Matthew.' She glared at him fiercely. 'That was strictly between us.'

Susan had suspected that their aunt had been financially supportive when Matthew was contemplating the purchase of Holmlea. Like her brother she hadn't wanted her nephew to be dependent on Euan Clapperton.

Refreshments were offered and declined. Aunt Rachel declared that she wanted home before darkness fell and shortly after her departure Matthew and Winnie decided it was time they went too.

'The old dear's bark is worse than her bite,' Edward laughed. 'My relatives would have offered sympathy but not much more whilst the old lady comes up with the hard cash.'

'She's a dear. Matthew and I have always adored her.'

'And she dotes on the pair of you.'

'Edward, shouldn't you be going over to Croft House?'

'Why?'

'Surely the fate of the distillery means something to you.'

'Under different circumstances it would.' He shrugged. 'Let Thomas and the old man get on with it.'

'I was just going to say that I would have gone with you but if you've made up your mind – '

'I have.'

'Then if you'll excuse me I'll retire. It's been a long day and I'm worn out.' But it hadn't finished yet.

'Unless I'm very much mistaken that is brother Thomas's voice I hear.'

They were both startled to their feet as Thomas barged in unannounced leaving the maid open-mouthed. He looked on the point of collapse. Like his brother he was normally fastidious about his appearance but his coat had been flung on and his necktie was askew. Though the night was chilly, sweat sat in beads on his forehead. And on his chalk-white face the freckles stood out like a disease. He stood in the middle of the room and babbled.

'We're ruined, everything's gone. Oh, God! Edward, can't you understand, we've lost everything. We haven't a hope in hell – begging your pardon, Susan – ' The words were pouring out and there was a froth of spittle at the corners of his mouth.

Edward looked at him with distaste. 'Get a grip on yourself, Thomas.'

'Susan.' His reddened eyes sought hers. 'S-sorry – ' His hand went out and she caught it in hers then began leading him gently to a chair.

'Edward, get Thomas something to drink,' she ordered, then to her brother-in-law, 'Don't try to speak for a few moments.'

Edward handed his brother a drink but Thomas's hand was shaking so much that he was in danger of spilling it and Susan guided the glass to his mouth. After a while he gave a shudder and a little colour reached his face. He tried to smile as he began to apologise.

'It's understandable, Thomas, we are all in shock.' Then added, 'Have you eaten at all today?'

'Eaten?' He seemed to be pondering the meaning of the word.

'Are you hungry is what Susan is asking.'

'No, I'm not,' Susan snapped. 'I asked if he had eaten which is quite different.'

Thomas looked from one to the other. 'I haven't but I couldn't anyway. Susan, what about the mill?'

'It's too early to say,' she said carefully, 'but I believe with a bit of luck we'll come through.'

'Luck,' he said bitterly, 'we'd need a miracle to get out of our mess.'

'Maybe things aren't as bad as you imagine.'

'Oh, they are I assure you, Susan, as bad as they can be. Tell me, what happens when one can't pay the workers?'

'They walk out,' Edward volunteered calmly.

'Surely you can raise –'

'Nothing, Susan, we can raise nothing,' he said hopelessly. 'Everybody is clamouring for what is due them, there's no goodwill left.' He cradled his chin with his elbow on his knee. 'We could have been all right; well, not all right but in a position to carry on. It was that hiccup with the new machinery and we refused to pay any part of it until the fault was corrected.'

'Which is precisely what we, ourselves, would have done,' Susan said.

'Is it working satisfactorily now?' Edward wanted to know.

'It has been for months but Father felt they should be penalised and withheld payment longer than I, personally, thought to be reasonable.' He shrugged. 'That has always been Father's way.'

'Hence the mess you are in now!'

'You are hardly in a position to speak,' Thomas said heatedly. 'If I recall correctly you favoured that policy yourself.'

'That is perfectly true, Thomas,' Susan said calmly. 'Edward tried to introduce it in the mill but I put a stop to it.'

Thomas smiled and looked at his sister-in-law with unconcealed admiration. 'You take after your father. I was a great admirer of his, you know.'

She was surprised. 'Thank you, Thomas.'

He turned to his brother. 'Life plays queer tricks. Don't think for a moment that I haven't known all these years that you resented the position I hold in the distillery. Well, thanks to Susan, you're sitting pretty while I and my family face ruin,' he said bitterly.

'How is your father, Thomas?' Susan hastened in with.

'Difficult to say,' he said broodingly. 'Look, I'm sorry for the ass I made of myself but I was feeling almost suicidal.' He looked at Edward. 'We don't all react in the same way.'

'Thomas, I am ringing for the maid. I insist you have some food inside you. On second thoughts I'll see Mrs Carson myself. Excuse me.'

It was a chance for her to get out of the room and leave the brothers together. For all his brother's boorishness Edward would want to be of assistance. She left Mrs Carson preparing sandwiches from the cold roast and the maid waiting to bring them.

'That's taken care of,' Susan said as she closed the door quietly behind her.

Thomas smiled as she sat down. 'Father has a bit behind him, Susan, but he is keeping quiet about it.'

Susan nodded. 'Sensible in the circumstances I would have thought. No use calling on reserves until it becomes absolutely necessary.'

Edward laughed. 'Take it from me, Father won't risk his all. He'll keep what he has to see himself and Mother in reasonable comfort for the remainder of their days.'

'Forgive me asking, Thomas, but does Elizabeth have money of her own?'

'A little but it's earmarked to pay for the alterations. The extra wing we had built is only just completed. In fact we were in the middle of arranging to have all the family over to see it.'

'You are having it hard. How is Elizabeth bearing up?'

'She is as worried as I am, Susan, but she tries to hide it from me. Elizabeth is quite marvellous really.'

The maid arrived with a tray and Susan served Thomas then poured a cup of tea for Edward and herself. As well as sympathy for Thomas and Elizabeth, Susan felt a helpless pity for all those small depositors whose dreams had been shattered like the fragments of a valued article lying in pieces at their feet.

'Thank you, that was very nice,' Thomas said after eating one small sandwich.

'Thomas, try to eat, please.'

'No, really, that was just fine.' He finished off the tea then stood up. 'I must get back to Elizabeth.'

'What is the next step?' Edward asked, getting up from his chair.

'You tell me! What does a bankrupt usually do, apart from committing suicide?' he said with an attempt at humour.

'Sell off.'

'And that, believe me, is a real possibility.' He kissed Susan and surprisingly Edward shook his hand. 'Susan, you look exhausted.'

'We all are, Thomas.'

Edward put his arm on his brother's shoulder. 'Anything I can do that doesn't require cash and you'll find me more than willing.'

'I'll take you up on that. If you can manage it, call at the distillery tomorrow and see for yourself just how bad things are.'

'I'll do that.'

In the weeks that followed the commercial life of the west of Scotland and beyond came to a virtual standstill. Warehouses and factories put up their 'For Sale' signs. And those firms struggling along were laying off workers. Trade dwindled, the small shops were feeling the pinch as customers' spending power dropped alarmingly. No one escaped, forced sales became the order of the day. It was a buyer's paradise. Those selling had to accept a fraction of the real value of their premises. For many no buyer could be found.

The Aranvale Papermill struggled on. Wages had fallen to just above an unacceptable level but no worker was paid off. At Aran Heights, Miss Wilson enthusiastically carried out Susan's wishes. Food bills were almost halved and unheard-of economies were now taking place in the kitchen. Surprisingly, Edward made no complaints; indeed he declared that some of the meat dishes, favourites with the servants, were tastier than the more expensive cuts of beef. Polly was kept busy altering gowns and even cutting up one to make a dress for Victoria. New clothes were not even considered.

'Well, Edward, did you see your father and Thomas?'

'Yes. Everything's in the hands of the solicitor.'

'You mean,' she said aghast, 'the distillery is to be sold?'

'Yes,' he said heavily and she saw by his face that he, too, was shocked.

'It's so sad, it's a tragedy. One just can't imagine the Brodie name disappearing from the distillery. I could weep.'

'After that exhibition of Thomas's – '

'Unkind, Edward, very unkind.'

'Wait for it! I was going to say that he's remarkably calm considering the possibility that no buyer may come along.'

'Nonsense, its name alone will bring the buyers.'

But it didn't. The Brodie name was not enough and fears were growing as day after day went by without a genuine enquiry.

Susan's fair head was bent over papers and she frowned as the door opened and her concentration was broken. There was no need to look up. Edward was the only one who entered without first knocking.

'Busy?'

'As you can see.'

'Thought you'd want to hear the news. Thomas informs me that there is a prospective buyer for the distillery – maybe that is over-optimistic but a firm enquiry has been made.'

Her blue eyes widened with genuine relief. 'I'm so glad, but I knew it was just a question of time. One enquiry usually leads to others.'

'Father said something of the sort.'

'I feel sorry for your father but it is Thomas who has my real sympathy. He stands to lose most whatever happens.'

'And he's a born worrier.'

Edward perched himself on the corner of the desk and turned the top paper to read it. 'What is all this?'

'I'm authorising the wages clerk to restore the workers' pay to what it was.'

'We're not out of the wood yet. A bit premature I would have thought. Weren't you going to repay your aunt first?'

'All other economies will continue, Edward, but I want wages restored. The workers have been very supportive all this time but I don't want their hardship to continue.'

'Well, you're the boss,' he said, getting up from the desk. 'I'll go and get my head down too.'

The change in Thomas was unbelievable. He was almost jubilant when he called at Aran Heights.

'Who is it? Who is interested in the distillery?' Edward asked.

'Can't tell you that,' Thomas said, accepting a whisky. 'The information we have is that an English firm of solicitors is making enquiries on behalf of a client.'

'Someone looking for a bargain,' Edward muttered.

'More than likely but beggars can't be choosers,' Thomas said, pushing back his unfinished drink. 'Need to keep a clear head anyway.'

Susan nodded her approval and as if in silent protest Edward drained his glass.

'The arrangements are tentative,' Thomas continued, 'but I expect to be showing the prospective buyer round the distillery on Tuesday and then Father suggested we invite him to Croft House if it looks promising.' He smiled. 'You'll be kept in the picture.'

\*   \*   \*

True to his word Thomas arrived at Aran Heights with the latest news, choosing a time when both Susan and Edward were to be at home.

'Thomas, you look a lot better.' Susan smiled as they moved into the sitting-room.

'Hope, however slim, has that effect and I've discovered the identity of the interested party.'

'Who is it?' Edward asked.

'Percy Carruthers.'

'The cotton king? Edward said disbelievingly. 'What would that lot want with a distillery?'

'It's the son-in-law who is interested; apparently he comes from these parts.' Thomas looked at his brother. 'I'd appreciate it if you could be there.'

'Of course you must go, Edward.'

'You, too, Susan. Father made special mention of that and Mother would be glad of your assistance.'

'Won't she have Elizabeth to help her?'

'Didn't Edward tell you?'

'Sorry, my humble apologies, I forgot,' Edward muttered.

'Elizabeth went over her ankle rather badly, Susan, and she's having to keep the weight off it for a few days.'

'I'm sorry to hear that. You could both do without that at this time. Poor Elizabeth.'

'You'll come?'

'Yes, of course I'll come, Thomas.'

# CHAPTER NINETEEN

C roft House, home of the Brodies, was a large mansion on the fringe of Airdrie with a view of Airdriehill, the town's highest point and from which Arran, fifty miles away in the Firth of Clyde, could be seen on clear days. The house was surrounded by trees and set in spacious well-kept gardens, but for all its grandeur it lacked the commanding position enjoyed by Aran Heights.

Over the years Lilian Brodie had paid out a small fortune on clothes yet never even approached the look she was striving for. So it was with her home. Whatever took her fancy she purchased without thought as to how it would appear with the existing furniture and furnishings. An example was the Brodies' drawing-room. Large and well proportioned, it had a magnificent frescoed ceiling, priceless Persian carpets and a handsome Italian fireplace. Yet for all that it looked cluttered and untidy and there was the constant danger of falling over small spindly legged tables or embroidered footstools.

Susan and her mother-in-law were alone and sipping tea in the drawing-room.

'I don't see much of your mama these days.'

'I don't see a great deal of her myself.'

'That new husband is getting all the attention,' she said plaintively, 'and her friends have to take a back seat. I must say I'm surprised, Susan, Hamish was such a fine man.' She paused. 'Speaking for myself I could never replace John and I'm sure you must feel the same way about Edward.'

Could she replace Edward? Would she want to? No, she thought, Edward and I are often at each other's throat, we've hurt one another unbearably, yet I'd be lost without him. It was a comforting thought and she smiled.

'Yes, Mama Brodie, of course I do, feel the same way I mean.'

Just then the door opened and John Brodie came in followed by Edward.

'Good of you to come, my dear,' the elderly man said, kissing Susan on the cheek.

The weather was cold for late autumn but a fire took the chill off the room. Susan had given a lot of thought as to what she should wear and finally had decided on a costume in a lightweight material, thinking if the room got uncomfortably hot she could discard the jacket. The slightly full skirt was in royal blue and with it she wore a cream silk blouse with pleats down the front and leg-of-mutton sleeves ending in a tight-fitting cuff. Her hair was still her crowning glory but now it had darkened slightly and she wore it plaited and coiled in the fashion of the day.

For all his determination to appear at ease Susan thought that her father-in-law looked defeated, the broad shoulders drooped and his eyes were tired.

'Terrible times we live in, Susan, and this is a sad day for the Brodies,' he said heavily.

'I'm sorrier than I can say,' Susan said gently. 'I just can't believe that the Brodie Distillery is to be no more.'

'Only the name, Susan,' Edward corrected her, 'and that is only if anything comes of this.' His tone suggested his hopes were not high.

'Negotiations wouldn't have gone this far unless someone was really interested. Do try to be optimistic, Edward.'

'Like John I'll hate to see the Brodie name go,' Mrs Brodie said, 'but Thomas seems quite resigned to seeing the distillery in other hands.'

'Mother, has he an alternative?' Edward asked. 'After all, he is the one most affected.'

'Of course it is hard on Thomas,' his father said, fixing him with a baleful stare, 'and if I sense criticism you are rather too quick to allocate blame. My God!' he exploded. 'The bank, who would have believed it? The whole affair needs a thorough investigation and those responsible for this disaster put up against the wall and shot. Criminal incompetence, that's what it is.'

His wife looked shocked. 'John, what a dreadful thing to say!'

'Father is absolutely right, Mother. Personally I could cheerfully see someone swing for it.'

To change the subject Mrs Brodie turned to Susan and pointed to the cabinet. 'That is the most recent photograph, Elizabeth sent it over. Aren't the girls sweet and the baby is a little darling.'

'I must have a proper look.' Susan crossed to the cabinet and was remarking about the middle girl's resemblance to Elizabeth when Thomas arrived with his guest. Before turning round Susan carefully replaced the framed picture. Then she froze.

For a moment she gazed wildly round the room as though looking for an escape. She had to be dreaming, this was a nightmare, it couldn't be happening. She felt numb with shock and swallowed convulsively. Gooseflesh ran up her arms and she gave a shiver. The years had only enhanced his dark good looks and given him poise and assurance.

The voices carried – Thomas was doing the introductions, introducing Mr David Cameron first to his parents then to Edward. Thomas looked over to where she was. They were coming over and she felt a fluttering in her chest like a trapped bird.

'Mr Cameron, I would like you to meet my sister-in-law, Mrs Edward Brodie.'

In the moment their eyes met, his slightly amused, Susan knew instinctively that David Cameron was leaving it to her. What should she do? Claim to have met – suggest a vague remembrance of someone of that name having been employed as an accountant by her father? No, she couldn't bring herself to do that. In any case he had the advantage; just this possibility must have occurred to him.

She managed a thin polite smile as to a stranger and he bowed stiffly. Both his manners and his clothes were impeccable, the old David had gone. This one was smoothed and tailored by success.

She was only dimly aware of Thomas speaking: '. . . owns and manages the papermill, we are all very proud of her.'

Susan smiled to her brother-in-law, inclined her head to David Cameron and watched them move away. That was the moment tea arrived. Quietly and efficiently the maids poured the Indian blend to requirements, handed round plates of small cakes and biscuits then at a nod from the mistress of the house withdrew. During this time the conversation had been mainly of the vagaries of the weather.

'I believe you know this part of Scotland, Mr Cameron,' his hostess said.

'Yes, Mrs Brodie, I do.' A smile played round his mouth. 'This house was once well known to my mother.'

'Really!' Lilian Brodie's eyes widened. 'How very interesting. I don't recall the name but one meets so many people socially then sadly one loses touch.'

'My mother did not meet you socially, Mrs Brodie,' David Cameron said quietly. 'She was a maid in your service.'

'Oh!'

There was an awkward pause while Lilian Brodie recovered but she quickly rose to the occasion. 'Perhaps if you told me the name,' she said uncertainly.

'Cameron, Eliza Cameron.'

'Eliza – yes, I think – ' Her eyes were puzzled. 'Your mother's service at Croft House would be before her marriage.'

'My mother was unmarried.' Turning abruptly to face John Brodie he said, 'The name should mean something to you, sir.'

Susan caught her breath. What was David Cameron saying? What was he implying? A picture of the young David danced before her eyes. She remembered almost running to meet him from Aunt Rachel's and as they'd walked together he had pointed out the tiny speck of a cottage that had been home to him and his mother. And the rest – she was afraid of what she would hear – afraid of what she was just beginning to think. Her father-in-law's voice brought her back to the present.

'Hardly, young man, the servants were and are my wife's concern,' he said dismissively.

Dark smouldering eyes levelled on the older man and remained there. There was a stillness in the room as though everyone were waiting. Edward sat beside the window, Thomas a little apart and nearer to where David Cameron sat. Susan had deliberately chosen a chair some distance from the others. Mrs Lilian Brodie looked in bewilderment from the stranger to her husband.

'My mother should have been very much your concern, sir,' David Cameron said slowly and deliberately.

The elderly man had been sitting in an armchair but now he stood up and his hands were clenched fists.

'How dare you insinuate anything improper in my house,' he said in a peculiar breathy quiver.

Without haste David got up to face him.

'For a few paltry coins, sir,' he laid emphasis on the sir, 'you bought my mother's silence.' He paused but his eyes never wavered. 'You got her pregnant then all you cared about was getting rid of her as quickly as possible.'

In that room the silence was absolute. Susan could feel the hammering of her own heart. Beyond the curtains the rain lashed the windows but no one noticed. Those present watched the colour drain slowly from John Brodie's face. With an enormous effort he fought for control but Susan thought she detected a silent plea as he allowed his eyes to settle briefly on his wife. If she was aware of it she gave no sign. Her face was as white as his.

Locked in battle there was a strong similarity in the way each held himself. Both were powerfully built with the same jawline and each was engaged in weighing the other up.

It was in a blinding flash that it came to Susan. Dear God! Of course, that fugitive sense of recognition that had always just eluded her during those hours in the library with David. He had reminded her of someone but it had been too fleeting and it had drifted away. Now she knew that someone was her father-in-law.

Another thought struck her and its impact had her almost

crying out. No wonder Paul resembled the Brodies. He – was – a – Brodie. Paul was John Brodie's illegitimate grandson. Too much was happening, there was a buzzing in her ears and her mouth felt parched.

'This is absurd, young man,' John Brodie spluttered. 'Servant girls are all alike, get into trouble with one of their own kind and try to blame – ' He stopped at the look on David Cameron's face. There was hatred and contempt.

'You'd better be careful what you say,' David said threateningly, his eyes glittering with a dangerous light. 'For the sake of your health I'd advise you to sit down for you are going to hear the rest.'

Almost choking with rage and was it fear, John Brodie did sit down and once he had David returned to his own chair.

'My mother was incapable of lying, Mr Brodie.' He paused and leaned forward. 'Look at me! Go on, look at me closely. I look more like you than your two legitimate sons.' He laughed mirthlessly. 'The law of genetics is not to be ignored.'

No one could deny it, Susan thought, seen together the likeness was striking.

The face that had been the colour of porridge took on a purplish tinge.

'What do you want?' he rasped.

David threw him a glance of utter contempt, ignored the question and continued.

'My mother kept her vow of silence and took her secret with her to the grave. All she ever told me in answer to my questions was that my father was a gentleman. I find that amusing I must say but perhaps I do you an injustice, sir. Many in your place would have put a servant girl out in the street with nothing. You, in fact, handed over a few gold coins and a little extra to educate – excuse me, ladies – the bastard she was about to bring into the world.' He paused for breath and Susan could see that this was costing him too. He swallowed before he continued. 'My mother guarded that money and worked her fingers to the bone to add to it. Her only concern was that I should be well educated.' His voice cracked. 'No one could have had a better mother.'

314

No one spoke. No one took their eyes away and after a moment he was composed enough to carry on. 'My grandparents wanted nothing to do with a daughter who had disgraced their name. Fortunately an aunt was more charitable and she was the only one in whom my mother ever confided. After my mother died my aunt saw no reason why she should remain silent and it was she who told me the identity of my father.'

With a strangled sob Lilian Brodie got up and without looking at anyone went out, closing the door behind her. Susan made as if to follow but Edward shook his head warningly and she sat down again.

'Do you see what you've done, you've upset my wife.'

'Yes, but her suffering will be considerably less than that which my mother had to bear,' David said harshly.

'How much are you trying to get out of me?'

David laughed. 'Out of you? Do you imagine I would touch a penny of yours even if I were starving?'

'You don't really have an interest in the distillery, do you?' Thomas said bleakly.

'But I do, a very real interest I assure you. It is always prudent to have an additional financial concern.' He smiled but without malice. 'As you know to your cost there is no such thing as certainty in business.'

'No offer of yours will be considered,' John Brodie shouted. 'We have others –'

David shook his head. 'According to my sources and they are reliable, you have had no offers and in the present climate none seems likely.'

'That's quite true,' Thomas said quietly. 'False pride may suit you, Father, but it won't keep my wife and family.'

Edward was the most relaxed, almost as though he were enjoying the scene.

'Thomas is right, Father.'

'How long before –' Thomas began anxiously.

'My solicitor will be in touch.' He got up and spoke directly to John Brodie. 'I am no more anxious than you that our relationship is known and should it go further than this room it won't be through me.'

John Brodie opened his mouth to speak, changed his mind and just nodded.

Before leaving the room with Thomas, David's eyes rested on Susan for a long moment then he was gone.

Shocked by all the disclosures yet amidst it all feeling a rush of compassion for her father-in-law, Susan went over to put a comforting arm around his shoulders. He acknowledged it by patting her hand.

'Skeletons in the cupboard, Susan.' He sighed. 'And I'm too old, the fight's gone out of me.'

'Why fight a losing battle, Father? You haven't denied his claim, couldn't really, not with the resemblance.'

'Damn it, he could have faced me without dramatising it in front of my family.'

'And forego his moment of glory! In his position I would have done the same thing.'

'I'm quite sure you would, Edward,' he said cuttingly.

'Yes, Edward, you would be as ruthless as your half brother.'

'He's certainly a success story.'

'You two had better get on your way and I'll go and make my peace with Lilian, try to anyway.'

They saw him square his shoulders before going through to his wife.

Edward was flushed and his eyes bright as they left Croft House. The rain had stopped but there were puddles everywhere and a darkened sky suggested more rain wasn't far away.

'Quite an afternoon wasn't it?'

Susan's head was throbbing and all she wanted was to get home and be on her own. 'Yes,' she said wearily, 'quite an afternoon.'

'It's incredible! Who would have believed it? Mind you, Susan, it could be well worth while cultivating a friendship with my new-found half brother. Just think of the connections. He must be rolling in money.'

She didn't answer but he didn't seem to notice as he went on. 'After all he can't hold us responsible for Father's small peccadillos.'

'Edward, even if Mr Cameron were to take over the distillery, and I'm not all that sure he will but just supposing he did, the likelihood is that he would put in a manager and return to his own interests.' That was wishful thinking. She wanted David Cameron as far away as possible lest one day he met his own son.

# CHAPTER TWENTY

With Caroline gone from his life, Edward turned again to Susan and though at first the shared nights gave her little pleasure, gradually she forgot his other women and warmed to a satisfying relationship.

Edward was asleep beside her, his breathing regular and she was able to think about those hours at Croft House. All her fears were for her son. Was there any threat to Paul? But how could there be? With her brain now working clearly she could see she had been worrying needlessly.

David would never know that his son was at Aran Heights. How could he? It was her secret, hers alone. David was out for revenge on the Brodies. What was he planning? Remembering how fiercely protective he had been towards his mother she should have felt more sympathy but curiously enough her heart had gone out to that broken old man.

David Cameron's arrival on the scene had affected them all. In David Cameron John Brodie had met his match. Edward was impressed, perhaps even envious. Rags to riches. Poor Thomas's only hope of selling the distillery. And what of herself? Sleep was beginning to overtake her but before it did her last waking thought was of David's wife. What was she like? Was she beautiful or had the attraction for David been the immense fortune that would one day be hers?

In a hotel in Hillhead, the aristocratic west end of Glasgow, David Cameron was also having a disturbed night. With his hands clasped behind his head he gazed into the grey dark and wished for the morning. For so long he had lived for this moment when he could humiliate John Brodie and had marvelled at his incredible luck in reading about the Granton

319

Distillery and the Brodies' financial difficulties. Later when the business came on the market he determined to get it whatever the cost.

Percy Carruthers had a great respect and liking for his son-in-law and with no son of his own he was involving David more and more in the running of his empire. There was little chance of the cotton industry falling into bad times but even so there was no harm in acquiring other interests. On that they both agreed.

When David spoke about the distillery in Scotland, Percy Carruthers had been surprised but then again the lad belonged to those parts so perhaps it was natural. In any case he raised no objections.

Now with everything working out as he had planned David could could only feel regret and sadness. Why hadn't he just kept in the background and used the Carruthers' name to acquire the distillery? That should have been enough but it was too late for regrets. Then his mood changed and his brow darkened. This was the revenge he had promised himself for his mother and he determined not to weaken. In his hand was the perfect tool. On him rested the future of the distillery. He could watch the proud Brodie empire topple, the ruined buildings all that would remain of a once prosperous concern or he, the bastard son of the owner, could take it over. How would John Brodie feel then? How would he feel about Eliza Cameron's son being the new owner?

If only he didn't keep on seeing Susan's face. It worried him that he couldn't stop thinking about her yet he'd accepted the possibility of seeing her on some occasion. Once she had been his youthful torment but gradually her memory had faded as a new and exciting life had claimed him. Seeing her again had surprised an ache in him. There was something about her, a proud dignity that set her apart and the passing years had only made her more beautiful.

His aunt was dead, her family scattered and away from Aranvale. But of course he would never set foot in the village that had once been home. And he would never go near the papermill, there was no reason why he should. He smiled. Somehow he didn't think anyone would connect him with the raw country lad he had once been. The distillery was far enough away and if he should decide to take up accommodation for part of the year then he'd buy a house in Airdrie or nearby.

The bed was too narrow and he moved restlessly, wishing he could reach for Gwen. Having her near, her warm body pressed to his, he wouldn't be thinking of Susan Brodie. A thought struck him and he smiled. Married to his half brother, Susan and he were related. There he was thinking of Susan again and it must stop. Gwen was the best wife a man could have and she was the one person in the world he would never hurt.

When Edward came down for breakfast, Susan was already seated at the table. Apart from a reference to the brightness of the morning they ate in silence until the maid went out.

'Did you get any sleep?' He smiled.

She laughed. 'It didn't keep you off yours. I was long in getting over.'

'What were you thinking about?'

'Thomas mostly,' she lied. 'I wonder how he'll come out of this.'

'Will Cameron offer him a position?'

'What do you think?'

Edward shrugged, examined the bacon on his fork then popped it in his mouth. 'He'll need someone who knows the business. A come-down for Thomas taking orders but as he said beggars cannot be choosers.'

Before the end of the week Thomas was at Aran Heights and looking happier than he had done for weeks.

'How is Elizabeth?' Susan asked as they joined Edward in the sitting-room.

'The ankle's improving and she can take the weight on it for short spells.'

'Oh, that's good but she'll have to go carefully.'

'You're looking cheerful, good news is it?' Edward asked

as he went to the drinks cabinet and began pouring whisky into two glasses. Susan shook her head to his unspoken question.

'Yes, Edward, the deal's gone through and though he must have known he could drop us further he didn't.'

'Not a complete rogue then our half brother?' Edward grinned as he handed Thomas a glass.

'He is an astute business man, that's evident by the conditions he's had drawn up.'

'What conditions?'

'Nothing that in his position I wouldn't have insisted on myself.'

'What are Mr Cameron's plans?' Susan found herself asking.

'He's bringing his wife and if she likes the area he'll consider buying a house and spending part of the year here.'

Susan felt a sinking sensation. No matter how often she told herself there was nothing to fear she couldn't rid herself of a feeling of impending danger. 'What about your own position, Thomas?'

'I'm to carry on with the day-to-day running and financially I'm to be better off than I dared hope.'

'What about Father? How is the old man?'

'Ignoring the whole situation, maybe feels it is the only way. And – wait for it – for the first time in his life he's allowing Mother to make the decisions and she thinks they should get away for a long holiday.'

'Best thing they could do,' Susan said approvingly.

# CHAPTER TWENTY-ONE

For those companies fortunate enough to survive the collapse of the bank there was a gradual upturn in fortunes. Hard lessons had been learnt and those lessons would not be easily forgotten. Foremost among the survivors was the Aranvale Papermill. The undercurrents of discontent had largely disappeared and Susan was now respected by management and workers alike. She was the 'boss lady' but it was said with affection, for hadn't she fought to keep the mill going and shared in their hardship.

Now that she was sensible about delegating work, Susan was spending more time at Aran Heights and she had just come downstairs to find a letter from her cousin Hannah. Picking it up she took it through to the small sitting-room where a log fire gave out a welcome heat. She was anxious to know what Hannah had written, apprehensive too. Hannah and Samuel had been married for almost fifteen years but to their great disappointment the union had not been blessed with children. And now, wonder of wonders, Hannah was pregnant but amidst the joy there was worry. Hannah wasn't strong, she was in her mid thirties and early on there had been two miscarriages.

Susan slit open the letter, scanned it quickly then gave a sigh of relief. Hannah was well though tired, the doctor was pleased and Samuel, a worrier at the best of times, was much more relaxed. Susan went back to read the letter properly. Happiness leapt out of each page and Susan felt a lump in her throat. Please, God, she prayed, make everything go well.

Putting down the letter she began thinking of her own life. For eighteen years of it she had been married to Edward yet in spite of all its ups and downs there had been happiness

323

between the dark times. And the family was growing up; well, not James. James would always be a child but sometimes looking at him Susan thought he was probably the most contented. It took so little to please him and his affection for them, in particular Paul, was touching. She supposed Nanny was right. James didn't have enough intelligence to worry, his own little world was secure and that was all that concerned him. Pretty vivacious Victoria was very different to the spoilt, pampered child she had been. True, there were still occasional tantrums when she would toss her red-gold curls in rage but these outbursts were quickly over and she was always sorry afterwards.

When her thoughts turned to Paul, Susan's eyes softened and her heart turned over with pride. At seventeen Paul was a tall, handsome boy and according to his tutor a very able student. Just recently Susan had seen a surprising change in Edward. It was as if he were anxious to get on a better footing with Paul. Only the other evening at dinner he had gone as far as seek his opinion and had been disconcerted by Paul's polite but cold response. Keen to help matters along Susan decided to discuss Paul's future education with Edward.

'Edward, are you to be at home tonight?' she asked as the clock chimed eight and he'd made no move.

'It would appear so. Why?'

'I'd like your opinion on Blackhall College.'

Lowering his newspaper he leaned back, looked at her and when he answered his tone was thoughtful. 'One of the Lansdown boys was there and did well.'

'That's encouraging. I've been impressed with what I've read but I wanted to be sure that it is educationally sound.'

He shrugged. 'As far as I know they teach the usual academic subjects but the main aim is to prepare the students for future responsibility.' He paused. 'Would do Paul good and give him more confidence to deal with people.'

'Y-yes. Of course he may hate the idea.'

'Or again he may be glad to get away from Aran Heights for a bit and have a chance to mix with others.'

Glad to get away, she didn't like the sound of that. 'Perhaps.'

'Leave it to the lad himself,' Edward said dismissively. 'And now to a change of subject. When are you going to buy yourself some new gowns? You've been to the Urquharts' twice recently in the same one. Surely the penny-pinching days are over?'

'Yes, of course they are and I do apologise if I've appeared careless about my appearance.'

He frowned. 'I didn't say that.'

'But you are absolutely right and it is high time I renewed my wardrobe and Victoria could do with some really nice dresses. She's only fifteen but she's getting so many invitations.'

'Break a few hearts that one,' Edward said fondly.

'But she'll do it gently.' Susan laughed. 'Deep down she's quite tender-hearted our Victoria.'

'Another snippet of news for you.'

'Oh!'

'David Cameron has bought the Beeches.'

Susan's heart plummeted. With the passage of time she had been lulled into a false security, convincing herself that David's wife would be unwilling to leave her friends to settle among strangers even for part of the year.

'It's not too far from the distillery or Croft House for that matter.'

'The house has been empty for months and needs a lot done to it but apparently an army of workmen are about to descend on it.' He paused. 'It would be a nice gesture on our part, Susan, if we were to invite the Camerons to Aran Heights. Make it a dinner party with the Maxwells and the Urquharts.'

She was playing for time. 'Edward, wait until they are settled in for a while before asking them.'

'That's just an excuse not to invite them. You don't like him, do you?'

'If you want the truth I think he's ruthless and he's made an old man of your father.'

325

'That's going a bit far,' Edward said reasonably. 'Cameron has only been making short trips up north and the two have never clapped eyes on each other since that day at Croft House.' He paused to throw a log on the fire. 'In his heart I bet the old boy is proud of his illegitimate son and if there's a ruthless streak in David Cameron where do you think he gets it from?'

'Your father, yes, I suppose you're right.' Edward and David had the same ruthlessness, Susan thought. She was beginning to see similarities in the half brothers. Thomas was the odd one out.

'We don't invite them?'

'Not yet. I'd much prefer if we waited.'

'Paul, when you've finished your lessons come along to the sitting-room. I have something I want to discuss with you.'

'Do I get a clue?'

'No, you don't.'

Susan was amused to see Paul take Edward's chair and stretch out his long legs in much the same way Edward did.

'It's about your education, Paul. This is just a suggestion and if you are not keen then you can continue with your tutor for another year or two.'

'What is the alternative?'

'There is a college in York, Blackhall College. I've made enquiries and your father and I thought two years there might be good for you. I'll let you have the literature to look at – ' She broke off. 'Paul, we want what is best for you but if you'd rather stay here – '

'No, Mother,' Paul put in swiftly and firmly. 'Two years at this Blackhall College would suit me very well.'

Susan felt unreasonably hurt. 'Aren't you happy? Is that why you want away from Aran Heights?'

'No, Mother,' he said gently, 'it isn't that at all. I love Aran Heights but I want to – I need to – broaden my life. Surely that's not wrong?'

She shook her head. 'Not in the least wrong and I'm just

being selfish. College would be good for you but I'll miss you so much and as for James – '

'You'll all have to spend a bit more time with him,' Paul said with a new outspokenness. 'Viccy knows what I've been doing with him and she can take over.'

Susan felt a rush of guilt whenever James was mentioned. It wasn't that she neglected him, she told herself, not a day went by without her seeing him either in the nursery or the garden but her visits seldom exceeded fifteen minutes. The truth was she hadn't the patience and was only too happy to hand over to others. It wouldn't do though, she must make a bigger effort.

'Then that's settled,' she said in a tone she would have used in the mill and was unaware of it until Paul laughed.

'Yes, m'am.'

'Oh, dear, I really must leave my office manner behind.'

Victoria was picking at her food and eventually pushed her plate aside.

'Why does Paul have to go to that hateful college? I don't want him to go.'

'That's because you'll have no one to fight with,' Paul grinned, his own appetite in no way affected.

'We haven't had a fight for ages.' She turned to Susan. 'Why are you making him go?' she snapped.

'Calm down, Victoria,' Edward said sternly, 'and don't use that tone of voice to your mother. Paul had no pressure put on him.'

'Well, it isn't fair and what about James?'

'James will miss Paul for a week or two then he'll begin to forget,' Susan said gently. 'Children like James have very short memories.'

'I don't want him to forget me.'

'He won't,' Edward said surprisingly. 'And for heaven's sake let's keep things in perspective. Paul will be home for Christmas and no doubt he'll find a spare minute to write home.'

'Will you, Paul? Will you write to me?'

'If you promise to reply.'

'Of course,' she said, her cheerfulness returning as well as her appetite. She brought the plate back. 'Might as well eat this.'

Blackhall College took in its new students in September and Susan was busy ticking off the items on the list, a very long list. Quite amazing, she thought, how much a student at Blackhall College required.

Like her father before her the family accepted that Susan did not wish to be disturbed when she was in the library and she was surprised to get a visit from Paul.

'Am I disturbing you?'

'Not at all.'

Before sitting down he looked appreciatively at the shelves of books and at the large desk.

'This is rather nice. I don't blame you disappearing up here.'

'I've loved it since I was quite small and kept it much as your grandfather had it.' She smiled over to him. 'One day it will be yours, Paul, but now I can see you have something to say.'

'Yes, Mother.' She could see that it was taking an effort for him to begin and suddenly she felt uneasy. 'I couldn't bring myself to ask this before but now that I am going off to college – ' He bit his lower lip. 'There's something, isn't there? I mean there has to be a reason for the way Father treated me.'

'Paul, your father has gone out of his way to be pleasant to you and you haven't responded.'

'Maybe he's just waited too long, Mother.' He was pale and sitting forward in his chair. 'I used to hear the maids discussing me.'

'What do you mean?' she said sharply.

'They could hardly fail to notice the difference. I mean he made a big fuss of Viccy, even James came in for some attention but I was ignored.'

'What did – they say?'

'Between giggles – that someone other than Father must have – must have fathered me.' She could hear the tears in his voice and he gave an angry brush to his eyes. 'At the time I was too young to understand but I remembered.' His dark eyes were anguished. 'There has to be a reason, Mother, I'm seventeen and I have a right to know.'

Susan's fingers began nervously pleating the material of her skirt. What she had always dreaded was happening and she was totally unprepared.

A wave of fury towards Edward swept over her. Damn you, Edward Brodie, damn you! she swore silently. If only you'd shown some compassion and not ignored the child this wouldn't be happening. But it was happening and Paul was waiting, his eyes on her face.

Unconsciously squaring her shoulders, Susan looked into that young, vulnerable face for a few moments in silence then she let out a small sigh.

'I had prayed this would never be necessary, Paul, but in this world sooner or later one must pay for one's mistakes. Other than to say I was very young and innocent I'm not going to make excuses for myself.'

Paul seemed to be holding his breath waiting for her to go on.

'Your – '

'My real father,' he said gently.

'Yes, your natural father and I were totally unsuited and perhaps that was where most of the attraction lay. Anyway we began to meet secretly, not often – '

'But you must have been in love?' It was dragged out almost pleadingly and she knew what he wanted to hear.

'Yes, Paul, we were in love but it was an immature love, mine was anyway. Much as I imagined myself in love I couldn't give up all that was dear to me – my family and Aran Heights – and make no mistake about it I would have had to give them up.'

He got up and began moving about the room restlessly.

'It was the time my father fell ill and he knew himself that it was serious, that he might not have long to live. You see,

Paul, it was his dearest wish to see John Brodie's son and his daughter married.'

'You could have objected, told him,' he choked.

'I did object at the beginning but you can't know how difficult it was for a girl to go against her parents' wishes.' She gazed ahead, thinking back to that time and for the moment forgetting Paul.

'Don't stop there, Mother, go on,' he said irritably.

'Try to be patient and try to understand. I adored my father, more than anything else I wanted to please him. I thought he might get better if I agreed to marry Edward and it did make him very happy. Then he couldn't get us married quickly enough. He wanted all his affairs in order before he died and my mother was barely given enough time to make the arrangements.'

'What about – '

'He must have seen the engagement and forthcoming marriage announcement in the newspaper because shortly after that he left Aranvale.'

'You never saw him again?'

'Never,' she lied. She gave a small shiver. 'What I didn't know, Paul, was that I was already carrying you before I married Edward.'

He looked stunned. The colour had left his face. Before he had been pale but now his face was chalk white and she felt sick inside herself.

'Not something I'm proud of, Paul, but I would never have married Edward if I had known.'

'What would you have done?'

'Confessed and taken the consequences.'

He tried to smile. 'In a way I feel better and there's a lot I can understand, about Father's attitude to me I mean.'

'Paul, remember this. Your father was a fine and an honourable man and he never knew about you.'

'A bit of a shock for – for my adopted father and no wonder he couldn't stand the sight of me.'

Susan gave a small hysterical laugh. 'Oh, yes, it was a dreadful shock for Edward.'

'Decent of him allowing me to take his name and of course that way he spared you – ' He broke off, appalled at what he was going to say.

She finished it for him. 'The disgrace. Yes, Edward spared me that,' she said flatly.

Paul got to his feet awkwardly.

Susan felt drained. 'I'm sorry, Paul, sorrier than I can say that you've had to learn all this.' She swallowed the lump in her throat, determined not to break down but it was costing her. 'You must be very disappointed in your mother.'

'No, really, honestly I'm not. All the pressures, I mean it couldn't have been easy for you.'

Susan gave a sad smile and nodded but they both knew that something precious had gone. Before he reached the door she stopped him. 'Paul, about Victoria – '

He looked surprised. 'Viccy won't hear it from me – no one will.'

'Thank you, Paul.'

Paul closed the door behind him and leaned against it. His mother! How could she? How could she have given herself like some cheap – he stopped, appalled at his thoughts yet powerless to shut them out. For miserable moments he felt something very close to disgust. It would pass, she was his mother and he still loved her, adored her, but just now his feelings couldn't be denied.

Yet deep down hadn't he suspected something of the sort but hoped desperately that there would be some other explanation? The secret was between the three of them but did that make it any easier to bear? He knew what he was and would carry the stain for the rest of his life. A maid looked at him standing there and, moving away, he went quickly outside. He needed the fresh air. He needed to get away from Aran Heights. College! How he welcomed it.

Long after her son had gone Susan remained where she was. She knew something of what he was feeling. Suspecting the truth yet hoping, always hoping for a different explanation. Sitting there she saw herself through

Paul's eyes. She looked the same. Like a painting, she thought, one that had an imperfection pointed out and no matter how one tried to forget it the eyes were drawn there.

# CHAPTER TWENTY-TWO

In those last weeks before leaving for college, Paul had been very conscientious about visiting relations and friends and Susan found herself wondering if it were deliberate, a way of spending less time at Aran Heights, then dismissed the thought as unworthy. Of course Paul would want to spend more time with his friends, it was only natural.

When Edward suggested that Paul's tutor should accompany him to Blackhall College and see him settled in, Paul readily agreed. Mr Erskine, with three weeks to spare before taking up his next appointment, was only too happy to oblige.

The night before his departure Susan organised a dinner party. Those present were Edward's parents, John and Lilian Brodie, Susan's mother and her stepfather, Euan Clapperton and Matthew and Winnie.

September was only a week in but already the evenings were shortening. Susan had the heavy plum-coloured curtains closed in the dining-room and the candle-light gleamed on the silver dishes and crystal glasses. There was game soup, white fish, saddle of lamb with garden vegetables and, to follow, apple pie, a favourite of Paul's.

After the meal Mrs Carson had been summoned and complimented on the splendid meal. In her great white apron and with her round face wreathed in smiles she had accepted her due.

'T'was for Master Paul,' she said, her small beady eyes seeking him out. 'For what he'll be gettin' to eat in one o' them establishments I wouldnae like tae think.'

Paul grinned. 'Don't worry, Mrs Carson, if it's too dreadful I'll sneak out a letter and you can send me – '

"deed and I will,' she said, not letting him finish. 'And now I'll be getting on.'

'She's a gem, Susan,' her mother said once the door closed.

'Yes, she is.' Susan laughed. 'And quite a character too.'

With a chilly wind blowing no one lingered in the courtyard and once the carriages were down the driveway the family went indoors. Victoria skipped away to see Polly about an alteration to a gown and Susan, Edward and Paul went along to the drawing-room. Here too the curtains were drawn and a fire burned brightly.

After some small talk Edward turned to Paul and said heartily, 'Bit of a change for you, lad, but I'm sure you'll soon settle down and begin to enjoy the life.'

'Yes, sir, I'm sure I shall.'

Edward frowned. 'Paul, just because you're going off to college there is no need for this formality. To be honest I don't much care to be addressed as "sir", at least not in my own home.'

Paul gave a slight smile that was not lost on Susan. 'Since you are not my father what do you suggest I call you?'

Edward's eyes bulged then he turned abruptly to Susan. 'You told him!' he said incredulously.

'I asked Mother,' Paul hastened in with. 'I've known for a long time that there was something about me – all Mother did was confirm my suspicions.'

Susan looked from one to the other. Paul was pale but at ease and she saw with a grim satisfaction that Edward looked absolutely shattered.

Her lips curled and she said with an icy calm, 'If you find this upsetting, Edward, you have no one to blame but yourself.'

'I don't blame you, sir. I mean accepting someone else's son can't have been easy and I should be grateful to you for giving me your name. No,' he shook his head, 'that wasn't what I wanted to say at all. I am grateful.'

Edward cleared his throat but his voice was oddly hoarse. 'Yes, Paul, I did treat you badly and I'm sorry about it now, but it wasn't for the reason you imagine. What I wanted was to hurt your mother as she hurt me and the way to do that was through you.'

'You can believe that,' Susan said bitterly.

Edward ignored her. 'Paul, if only you knew how often I've looked at you and wished you were my son instead of that – that idiot we have upstairs.'

'How dare you call James an idiot,' Susan shouted, her blue eyes glittering with anger. 'He's slow, he's backward but he's not – '

'Susan,' Edward said patiently, 'you can call James slow, mentally retarded, it all comes to the same thing, he'll always be a child.' He paused. 'Maybe you've learned to accept it but I haven't. God forgive me, he's my own son but I'm ashamed of him.'

'You're both ashamed of him, that's the trouble,' Paul said quietly. 'You can hardly bear to look at him that's why you spend so little time with James. Well, he has feelings too, you know, and thoughts too; no one knows what goes through his head. He's someone to me. I love him and that's why he's happiest with me.'

'Very noble, Paul, and I'm sure you genuinely believe it. But you can't know and I hope you never do know what it means to have a son like James. To be told that you have a son, all your hopes and dreams centred on that new life then to be told that he'll remain a child all his life.'

'I do understand, I understand only too well. If James had been born normal then he would be the heir, the rightful heir.'

'No! No! No!' It was torn out of Susan. 'The mill was your grandfather's and now it is mine. Mine to hand on to you. James's birth wouldn't have altered that.'

'You're wrong, Mother. I'm afraid you're wrong. Illegitimate sons have no claims, I do know that.' He walked out of the room.

A minute or two later Edward went out too. Susan didn't know that he had gone to Paul's room.

\* \* \*

The bookshelves had a number of spaces.

'You're taking some reading matter with you?'

'Yes.'

'Paul?' Edward extended a hand. 'We can be friends, can't we?'

'I hope so.' The handshake was firm.

Uninvited Edward sat down. 'As a favour would you drop this 'sir' nonsense?'

'That shouldn't be difficult, I've had seventeen years of calling you Papa or Father.' He smiled. 'It would be difficult to change now.'

'Thank you – son.' He got up. 'You'll have some last-minute packing to do so I'll leave you to get on with it. See you at breakfast. Goodnight, Paul.'

'Good night, Father.' Paul watched the door closing. Tomorrow he would be gone and it was for the best. They all needed a breathing space.


Susan was busy checking the household accounts while Victoria stood at the window looking out. Quickly tiring of that she began to move restlessly about the room.

'Victoria, can't you settle to do something?' Susan said in much the same tone of voice her own mother had used when she had been that age.

'There's nothing to do and I miss Paul.'

'You could reply to his letter.'

'I've done that but I won't see him until Christmas and that's ages and ages.'

Susan sighed. After three attempts at the same column of figures she gave up and put down the book. The child did look miserable and remembering the dark storms of her own girlhood she looked at her daughter with an exasperated sympathy.

'Darling, haven't I just bought you two lovely new gowns, that should make you feel on top of the world.'

'When am I going to wear them?'

'You've never been short of invitations.'

'I'm going to be now,' she said sulkily.

'And why should that be?'

'Oh, Mama, you don't know anything,' she burst out. 'They all wanted Paul because he's better looking than the other boys but they couldn't invite him without me.'

'What nonsense. You're very pretty and well you know it.'

'And that's why – oh, never mind, you'd never understand.'

Susan smiled to herself. She knew well enough that the less attractive daughters of their friends envied Victoria her beauty and it was possible they were none too keen to invite competition. Then she laughed out loud. How ridiculous! Fifteen-year-olds and jealousy already rearing its ugly head.

'What are you laughing at?'

'You! Paul has never been keen on parties but you made such a fuss that he only went to please you.'

'I know.' She made a circle on the carpet with her toe, examined the mark left until the pile recovered. 'Mama, do you know what I really wish?'

'What do you wish, Victoria?' her mother said kindly.

'That Paul wasn't my brother then one day we could get married.'

'Now that is just silly.'

'It's not silly, I love him.'

'We all love Paul.'

'Not that way,' she said scornfully. 'I love him, you know – different.'

'Then all I can say is you've changed. As a young child you were positively horrid to Paul.'

'Only because Nanny and everybody liked him better than me. Not Papa though,' she said thoughtfully. 'Why was that, Mama?'

'Lots of fathers don't fuss over their sons.'

Victoria had her mother's full attention now and wanted to make the most of it even though she looked a bit wary when she said, 'Mama, you won't be angry if I ask you something, will you?'

'I don't know until I hear it.'

Her eyes dropped to the floor and her voice was little more than a whisper. 'Why is it Papa and you sometimes use different bedrooms? Rachel said her parents always use the same one and Mina said hers do too except when they have a quarrel.'

Susan was appalled. 'Victoria, I sincerely hope you do not discuss your parents. That is a private matter.'

'Well, I had to say something so I told a lie. I said you did – all the time. But why don't you?'

Losing her temper would be a mistake, this had to be handled delicately. It was obvious what they had been discussing. Rachel was older and possibly her mother had decided the time had come for that kind of talk. Informing Victoria of what lay ahead was something she had hoped to put off for a year or two.

'I am a business woman with very different interests from Rachel's mother or Mina's.' What on earth was she going to say?

'I know you need to be on your own to think out the day's problems,' Victoria said importantly.

Susan clutched at it. 'That is exactly it, my dear,' she said, relieved to have the matter settled so easily.

'You don't want any more children after James, that's another thing, isn't it?'

'Victoria, I do not like this conversation.'

'Then you're not like Rachel's mama, she says mothers have a duty to tell their daughters about babies and everything in case they get themselves into trouble.'

'I'm aware of my duties and we'll discuss these matters when I consider the time right.'

'I know most of it anyway,' Victoria said as she went out the door.

# CHAPTER TWENTY-THREE

T he gilt-edged invitation was on the mantelpiece; putting it there was a habit Susan had picked up from her mother. She knew Edward would be pleased, he always was when an invitation came from Robina and George Walker. Very comfortably off, the Walkers entertained lavishly and although Susan enjoyed their company she often felt sorry for George. Love of money, not of George, had been the attraction for Robina, almost a head taller than her slightly built husband. They looked an ill-matched couple and neither seemed to have much to say to the other.

That Robina was attracted to Edward, Susan was in no doubt, but whether those feelings were reciprocated she didn't know. Edward liked women and Robina was undoubtedly a fine-looking woman though there was a hardness about her mouth that made her look calculating. Somehow she didn't see Edward seducing his best friend's wife though on the occasions he did tease Robina the invitation in her eyes was plain enough.

One of the new gowns was laid out on the bed and after a leisurely soak in the perfumed bathwater Susan dressed with care. The perfect cut allowed the gown to mould to her figure rather than cling and the vivid blue was startling against her fair hair and creamy skin. The choker of real pearls, a gift from Edward's mother, added the final touch.

Edward's face lit up with pleasure when he saw her. She knew that she was looking her best but she still liked to hear Edward's opinion.

'Yes, I do like that, it's perfect on you. Now aren't you glad I persuaded you to get something new?'

339

'Yes, of course I am,' she said, half turning to get a view of the back. 'Let me look at you. Yes, very smart.' She flicked a tiny speck from his shoulder.

There were more than a dozen people in the Walkers' drawing-room when Susan and Edward arrived. Susan had only taken a few steps into the room when her fingers dug into Edward's arm and hearing her startled gasp he looked at her quickly.

'What's the matter?'

'You might have told me,' she hissed.

'Told you what?' Then enlightenment dawned. 'Oh, the Camerons! I didn't know they were to be here but what of it? To hear you one would think you had a personal grudge against him.'

'I'm totally indifferent to Mr Cameron,' she said frostily.

'Doesn't look like it the way you carry on. For heaven's sake, Susan, David Cameron had a perfect right to do what he did and it looks as though they are to be in our social circle so you had better try to be a bit friendlier.'

'Darlings, lovely to see you,' Robina enthused as she kissed Susan then, raising her face, waited for Edward's kiss on her cheek. Her vivaciousness wrapped them in a closeness Susan found slightly ridiculous. After the greetings Robina studied Susan's gown. 'This is new? But of course it is and quite, quite charming.' Her eyes swivelled. 'Your wife has excellent taste, Edward. And now come along and let me introduce the newcomers, Mr and Mrs Cameron.'

'Robina, Susan and I have already met Mr Cameron.'

Robina clapped a hand to her mouth like a child caught out in a moment of naughtiness. 'How silly of me, George did mention something about Mr Cameron and the distillery but any talk of business bores me, goes right over my head. We're not all like you, Susan,' she said waspishly.

Edward's fingers touched the bare shoulder.

'You could introduce us to Mrs Cameron. Neither of us has had that pleasure.'

'Then come along. She's a sweet little thing,' she said

dismissively, then when Edward was passing a remark to a couple who had just come in, Robina whispered to Susan, 'She's nothing but isn't he gorgeous?'

The Camerons were at the far side of the room but as if on cue David Cameron turned. Their eyes met and Susan found herself unable to look away.

'He is, isn't he?' Robina nudged her.

'S-sorry – '

'Having that effect on you too, my dear, I can see.' Then playfully, 'Don't be greedy, Susan, you have a handsome man of your own.'

'Robina, you make the most outrageous remarks.'

'Oh, I'm quick, Susan, that's my trouble. I can interpret a look,' she said meaningly.

Susan drew in her breath sharply but was saved an answer by Edward's reappearance. Robina took Edward's arm and tucked it in hers then marched him across the room with Susan a step behind. Everything about this evening was beginning to irritate Susan. Normally Robina's over-possessiveness didn't trouble her but just now she needed Edward. The prospect of being in David's company had her feeling curiously defenceless.

Gushingly Robina made the introductions and would have lingered had not George joined them. The talk became general until Robina said pointedly, 'George, have you seen to everything?'

'I very much doubt it, my dear, but we'll both go and check. They moved away and Edward immediately engaged David in conversation. The two women looked at each other and smiled. Gwen Cameron was small and fragile with large brown eyes and the sweetest of smiles.

'Do you think you'll like living here, Mrs Cameron? It must be a big change for you.'

'It is but I think I'll settle all right. David spent his early years in this area. Not that he's told me much about it but you know what men are.'

Edward and David broke off their conversation. 'We're not likely to be eating for some time so I suggest we find ourselves a place to sit.' Edward's eyes went to four chairs and with David's help he placed them so that they could converse easily.

Once seated Gwen spoke in her soft voice. 'Do you have a family, Mrs Brodie?'

'Yes, we have three. Two boys and a girl.'

'Our eldest, Paul, is seventeen and in his first term at Blackhall College,' Edward said with all the pride of a father.

'We have two lovely daughters and a son to complete the family was our dearest wish but it wasn't to be,' Gwen said wistfully.

'These things can't be made to order.'

'No, Mr Brodie and more's the pity.'

'How old are your daughters?' Edward asked.

'Sylvia is fifteen and Amy is nine and as different as chalk and cheese. 'Aren't they, David?'

'Our Amy is a fighter, she'll hold her own with the best of them,' he said with the lopsided smile Susan remembered. 'Should have been a boy my father-in-law says.'

Gwen Cameron took over. 'Sylvia is inclined to be reserved and she's going to miss her close friend. We're hoping she'll find a companion of her age, someone to bring her out of her shell.'

'Look no further,' Edward said, deliberately avoiding Susan's eyes. 'Victoria has just turned fifteen and full of life, too full at times.'

Gwen's face lit up. 'How nice if the girls could meet.'

'That should be quite easy to arrange,' Edward said with a smile to Gwen.

Mrs Cameron looked at Susan.

Susan was beginning to feel panicky, everything was getting out of hand but she strove to hide her disquiet. 'Of course your daughter must come to Aran Heights and meet Victoria.' Then felt forced to add, 'Indeed you must all visit us one day.'

'That would be an honour,' David Cameron said gravely and she flushed. Did she imagine it or were those dark eyes mocking her?

'I'm afraid it's going to be a long time before we have our house-warming party, there's such a lot to do. But we very much hope that you and your family will come.'

'We'd be delighted,' Edward said warmly, 'and *I* speak for us all.'

'How much of the year are you to be spending in Scotland, Mr Cameron?'

'Quite a lot I expect, Mrs Brodie. There's much to be done and expansion is very much on the cards. However, once everything is running smoothly and I have someone trained to take control then we'll see.' As if it had just occurred to him David turned to Edward. 'If you are worrying about your brother's position then don't. I need someone with his experience.'

'But not the one you had in mind to –'

'Take over?' He shook his head. 'With due respect your brother is not decisive enough.'

'Don't you mean ruthless?' Susan shot at him.

'Perhaps I do, Mrs Brodie, but there are degrees of ruthlessness and to succeed in business a measure of it is essential. In your position you should appreciate that.'

'You may have gathered from that, Mrs Cameron, that my wife is a very competent business woman.'

'I had heard.' She turned to Susan. 'You can't know how I envy you. To succeed in a man's world is a great achievement.'

'Once one cuts through the prejudice, Mrs Cameron, it isn't so difficult and I was fortunate. My brother's interest is in farming and my father had me trained to take over from him.' David's eyes were on her; she could feel them but her attention stayed with his wife.

'David has engaged a tutor for Sylvia and I can tell you that raised a few eyebrows back home.'

'Did you object?'

'Not at all, I backed him all the way. Sylvia has a good brain and with no son to take over it seemed a sensible idea. There's no pressure on Sylvia but at least she'll be properly educated.' She grimaced. 'All I'm capable of is sewing a fine seam and giving a moderate performance on the piano.'

'My wife underestimates herself. She is as shrewd as they come.' David laughed. 'Enough about us, you mentioned another son. How old is he?'

Susan had been expecting the question and her face shadowed. 'James is the youngest and I'm afraid he – he's backward,' she said, getting the words out with difficulty.

Gwen Cameron became flustered and looked helplessly to her husband.

'A great tragedy but these things happen,' David said, quietly sympathetic. 'At least you have the means to care for your child.'

'Unless one has first-hand experience one cannot begin to understand the anguish,' Edward said drily.

They were silent, an uncomfortable silence and it was a relief to all when their hostess came in to announce that they should go through to the dining-room.

For the remainder of the evening Edward and Susan were claimed by their friends.


Back at Aran Heights Susan and Edward went through to the sitting-room to discuss the evening.

'Enjoyed it I must say, though Robina is a bitch the way she humiliates poor George and embarrasses everyone else.'

'She annoys me,' Susan said, 'I often wonder how George puts up with it.'

'He won't for much longer.'

'Why? Is there something I don't know?'

'I got it in confidence a few months ago but no harm in telling you now. George has been seeing a young widow, seems pretty taken with her and this one isn't after his money. She has more than enough of her own.'

Susan's eyes widened. 'You mean George and Robina are parting?'

'Seems likely.'

'I know Robina has only herself to blame but I can't help feeling sorry for her. Do you think she suspects?'

Edward guffawed. 'Robina! She would never dream that George would look elsewhere.'

'When the blow falls she'll need a shoulder to cry on.'

'Don't look at me, I'm keeping my distance.'

'I'm very glad to hear it.'

Susan was beginning to feel guilty at the way she was neglecting her mother and with work well forward at the mill she decided to take the day off and visit Moorend. She wore a burgundy corduroy costume and a small matching hat and looked both attractive and warm. The day was cold and bright and pleasant for walking. Arriving at Moorend she was welcomed in by Mrs Dunbar.

The cluttered homely look had gone from Moorend to be replaced by quiet elegance. Even its owner had a new look. Long gone were the comfortably shabby suits and now Euan Clapperton wore fine tweed for the house, rough tweed out of doors. He was a gentleman farmer and should look the part as his new wife pointed out.

Susan kissed them both and dutifully remarked on the pleasing appearance of the drawing-room which had recently been in the hands of the decorator. It was the same room where she and Winnie had so often sat and chatted with the tabby cat stretched out before the warmth. There was no sign of a cat now. With no gift for small talk Euan Clapperton made little contribution to the conversation. Fortunately that morning a letter from Paul had arrived at the farmhouse and the talk centred round it. After a little over an hour and promising a longer visit next time Susan took the short cut across the fields. Matthew saw her and broke off what he was doing to greet his sister.

'Don't mind the back door do you? We're very informal here.'

'I don't.' she laughed. 'But I bet you don't bring Mother in this way.'

'Oh, no, it is the red carpet for her ladyship.'

She stood on the stone floor watching him use the scraper for his muddy footwear and change into other boots.

'Winnie has you well trained.'

'Henpecked.' They went through the door and into the kitchen where at the sink a girl in a coarse apron was cleaning vegetables. Along the passage Matthew opened the door of a square-shaped room dominated by a desk and a pile of papers clipped together.

'Winnie does the accounts here. Like you with the library this is her den and out of bounds to the rest of us.' They went out and into the sitting-room.

'Where's Winnie?'

'In the village. Aunt Tina is poorly and Winnie is suggesting she closes up the cottage and come to us at least for a while but she wants to hang on to her independence.'

'Matthew, they're all getting old; sad, isn't it? For a long time they seem to remain the same then suddenly you notice them ageing. Mother's slowing down.'

'Can't say I've noticed,' he said carelessly. 'Sit down and give me the news. How is Paul?'

'Enjoying life or says he is anyway. He'll be home for Christmas.'

'Young Peter thinks his big cousin Paul is marvellous. He's made up his mind he's going to college too. Could be he's like you; he certainly isn't interested in the farm.'

'But Duncan is so you've nothing to worry about.'

'Incidentally you didn't tell me the new owner of the distillery is that accountant chap who gave you the occasional lesson at Aran Heights.'

'Didn't think it would interest you.'

'I like to know what is going on. Have you met him?'

'Briefly and in company. I'm not sure if he recognised me or not. Anyway I didn't say anything about him having worked for Father.'

'Prefers to forget it?'

'Perhaps, perhaps not; anyway it isn't important.'

'Funny though, you have to admit. I mean why a distillery in this area when their main concern is in England?'

'Saw a bargain and snapped it up.'

'More to it than that I think. Here's Winnie,' he said as she

346

tapped at the window. The back door opened, they heard her voice then she was with them.

'Susan, how lovely! Has your big brother offered you a refreshment?'

'Sorry, the thought never occurred to me.' He got up. 'No rest for the wicked. I'll leave you to your gossip.'

'Notice, Susan, how men talk and women gossip?'

'True though.' Matthew grinned.

'On your way out tell Edith or Annie to bring in tea.'

'How is your Aunt Tina?' Susan said when her brother had departed.

'Quite chirpy but at her age it isn't easy to throw off a chill. I pop in most days and oh, isn't it lovely news about Hannah! Your mother came over to tell us.'

'A little daughter, very tiny but gaining weight.' She paused. 'I'm very honoured and proud that the baby is to be called after me.'

'Congratulations! No surprise though, I mean you two were always like sisters.' She turned her head. 'Thank you, Annie and no, don't pour I'll give it a little longer.'

During the drinking of the tea the talk was of babies and family matters then Winnie put down her cup. 'Susan, that Mr Cameron at the distillery, is he your one-time heart-throb?'

'He was the accountant who came to Aran Heights,' Susan said stiffly.

'I know, Matthew mentioned it.' She looked at Susan in surprise. 'Sorry! Sorry! If I said anything out of place it was only intended as a joke.'

'No, you didn't. It's just a little embarrassing remembering the silly things I said to you at that time.'

'Well, you needn't be. Heavens! When I think of the times I've told you things I wouldn't want anyone else to hear. Have no fear, this is between us and no one else.'

'I almost fainted when I saw him.'

'You hadn't a clue?'

'No, the name was never mentioned – just a client and his solicitor.'

347

'Where did you meet him?'

'Croft House. Thomas introduced us and to be honest I knew that he was leaving it to me and I, coward that I am, decided to meet him as a stranger.'

'Maybe that suited him too?'

'I've a feeling it did.'

# CHAPTER TWENTY-FOUR

Having missed one week which would have been noticed by the minister, Susan and Edward braved the storm to attend the kirk. The sermon was long and uninspiring and the worshippers were glad to leave the poorly heated place of worship. Rachel's parents were there and Victoria went off to spend the day with them and their two daughters. After waving them off Susan and Edward hurried to their own carriage. In spite of the warmth of her cloak Susan shivered in the November damp and her fingers, locked together inside the fur muff, tingled painfully.

November was a dreary month heralding the cold, dark wintry days. The promise of snow was in the air and once it came the Shotts hills would be cloaked in white but just now they looked drained of colour, brooding and depressing.

The scalding hot Scotch broth awaiting them helped to take the chill away and after changing into more comfortable clothes they sat at either side of the huge log fire.

'We must discuss this dinner party, Susan. Have you thought about whom to invite with the Camerons?'

'Really, Edward,' Susan bristled, 'after the way Mr Cameron treated your father, and your mother too for that matter, I'm surprised that you should wish to entertain them.'

'And I'm surprised at your attitude, it's totally incomprehensible to me.'

'Then it shouldn't be.'

'Like it or not, Susan, David Cameron is my half brother and I for one intend – '

'To keep in with him because he is Percy Carruther's son-in-law. Had he been a penniless nobody it would have been a different story.'

'Granted, but then he isn't a penniless nobody and he happens to be the new owner of the distillery.'

Susan pursed her lips but said nothing.

'David and his wife are to be invited to Aran Heights, I insist on it, so there's an end to it.'

Still she said nothing.

'Before that you had better ask Mrs Cameron and the girls for afternoon tea or are you against that too?'

'Not at all,' she said frigidly, 'but I think it should have been left. At some stage the girls would have met in other company and decided for themselves if they wished to become friends.'

There was a dangerous edge to Edward's voice. 'I wish to God I hadn't mentioned the girls meeting and if that is the way you feel forget about it.'

'And be thought of as inhospitable? Certainly not. No, Edward, I'll go through with it though an afternoon away from the mill is an inconvenience.' With a kind of horror Susan listened to her own voice and felt a deep shame. Getting away from the mill at one time would have posed problems but not now. No wonder Edward was shocked and angry; she was behaving abominably. And it was all David Cameron's fault. Why did he have to come back to Aranvale? Hadn't he caused enough upset in her life? And then there was her secret fear, Paul's strong resemblance to David, what if it was remarked upon? Some days she felt that she would make herself ill with worry.

Edward knew that she liked entertaining and he must be wondering about her reluctance to have anything to do with Mr and Mrs Cameron. David's treatment of her in-laws was a good excuse and true to a certain extent but it wouldn't do much longer. She would have to watch her step and try to behave normally.

Feeling wretched, Susan was on the point of apologising but he had his face screened by the book he was reading and the moment passed.

*　　*　　*

Mrs Cameron and her two daughters were coming for afternoon tea. During the morning there had been intermittent squally showers and Susan saw to it that the maids kept up the fires. By afternoon the drawing-room was well heated and welcoming. Victoria was standing at the window and saw the carriage enter the wide gates.

'That's the carriage, Mama.'

'Then come away from the window.'

Some minutes passed before the maid announced the visitors.

Small though she was, Gwen Cameron held herself well. 'This is very kind of you, Mrs Brodie, and we have been looking forward to coming to Aran Heights.'

Susan smiled. She liked David's wife and wished the circumstances had been different. Introductions over they sat down, the three girls together on the Chesterfield sofa while she and Mrs Cameron occupied a wing chair on either side of the blazing fire.

'This is lovely and warm,' Mrs Cameron said, holding her hands out to the heat.

'The house takes a lot of heating, we are so exposed here.'

'Our other house is much warmer isn't it, Mama?'

'Yes, Amy, dear, but the Beeches lay empty and as your papa said, it takes a long time to get completely rid of cold and damp.' She turned away and spoke to Susan. 'Actually we are quite comfortable and I don't complain because David did suggest us waiting until the workmen finished but I prefer the discomfort and being with my husband.'

While Mrs Cameron chatted on about the alterations being made to the house Susan found herself studying David Cameron's daughters. The younger child, Amy, was by far the prettier. She had her father's blue-black curly hair and dark heavily lashed eyes. One day she was going to be a beauty, Susan thought.

The elder girl was very different and just escaped being plain. She was fair like her mother but without her gentleness. Sylvia's was an arresting face with hidden depths in the

351

grey-blue eyes. Her long fair hair was brushed back, showing her high forehead and she wore her hair secured at the back with a ribboned bow. What was so startling in such a young girl and what made Susan feel vaguely uncomfortable was the quiet dignified reserve. That same quiet reserve she remembered in the young David and for no reason at all Susan felt a disquiet and a curious foreboding of trouble ahead.

A disapproving look from her mother stopped Amy swinging her legs and with a deep sigh the child responded by fiddling with the sash of her dress. Catching Susan's eye, Victoria tried to turn a giggle into a cough and noticing it, Amy gave her an impish grin.

Susan laughed and bent across to touch Amy. 'Victoria is amused, Amy dear, because that's what she used to do when she got tired sitting still.'

'Oh, she isn't – ' her mother began anxiously but Susan stopped her.

'I can still remember how difficult it was for me to keep still when I was that age. It's just a pity this isn't the summer and we could be in the garden but never mind, once tea is over Victoria will find something to amuse you.'

'We could play hide and seek,' Amy said hopefully.

'No!' Mrs Cameron said firmly and shook her head to Susan as if to say please don't encourage her. It was obvious that she found her younger daughter a handful.

A welcome distraction came with the arrival of the tea things. Amy's eyes widened in anticipation. The doily-covered plates were filled with dainty three-cornered sandwiches, tiny buttered scones, macaroons, iced sponges and an assortment of biscuits.

If Mrs Cameron ate sparingly the girls made up for her. Victoria had a good appetite and a sweet tooth and seeing her tucking in was the signal for Sylvia and Amy to do likewise. The sheer joy of eating did more than anything to chase away reserve, Susan thought as she watched their expressions. By the time the plates had shed most of their load the three of them were at ease and anxious to be on their own.

'Victoria, take Sylvia and Amy through to the small sitting-room. It should be quite cosy and you'll get freedom to do as you wish.'

'Amy can be difficult,' Mrs Cameron continued after the girls had gone. 'She's a dear but gets too much of her own way. My father spoils her terribly and David gives them both a great deal more freedom than I think is good for them.' She smiled. 'David had quite a hard life and was used, even at an early age, to making his own decisions. That is something I have had to get used to, Mrs Brodie. David's upbringing was so different from mine and he is adamant that the girls will not be over-protected.'

'Victoria has quietened down but she was very rebellious and we had a difficult time with her.'

'She is very like you.'

'So everyone says. Your father must miss you all?'

'He does.' A frown puckered her forehead. 'My mother died some years ago and I'm an only child but, oh dear, I'm talking too much about myself.'

'You're not, I'm interested. But do excuse me while I ring for the maid to take away the tray.'

'Not much left to take away.' Mrs Cameron laughed.

'Mrs Carson will be delighted, she likes to know that her baking has been appreciated. Tell me, Mrs Cameron, as an only child were you lonely?'

'Not really but I used to feel guilty not being a boy.'

'Hardly your fault.'

'No, but you know the silly thoughts you have as a child.' She fingered the ring on her finger. 'David and my father get on famously and incidentally he is very impressed with the way you are managing the mill. I think he is putting you forward as an example to Sylvia.'

'I think if your daughter puts her mind to it she would succeed at most things. She strikes me as being very competent for one so young.'

'Thank you.' The warmth of the room had brought a faint flush to Gwen Cameron's cheeks. 'Why my husband decided to take over a distillery of all things I'll never know.'

'Didn't he tell you?'

Gwen shook her head. 'He had discussed it with my father and a decision was made to offer for it. Only after the offer was accepted did I learn of it.'

'I would have been furious. Weren't you annoyed?'

Gwen looked taken aback at the suggestion. 'Not annoyed, surprised yes, but when David explained to me that he had spent his early years in this district and liked the thought of having an interest here I quite understood. At one time he had relatives here but they are all dead or moved away.'

Susan smiled. 'So you didn't try to talk him out of it even though it was uprooting you all?'

'I wouldn't have dreamt of it but I think my father might have been less keen had he known that David intended to spend part of the year in Scotland. Like me he thought that my husband intended putting in a qualified person and returning periodically to see that everything was running smoothly.'

'Instead of which he decided to buy a house?'

'Yes, he now thinks that the distillery needs constant supervision for a year or so.'

'And he'll be anxious to learn the trade for himself,' Susan said drily.

Gwen Cameron looked unhappy. 'Forgive me, Mrs Brodie, but I can't rid myself of the idea that you don't much care for my husband.'

Rather than meet those searching eyes Susan got up to straighten a crystal vase that was only slightly out of position. 'Distresses the eye, don't you think? I'm getting to be as bad as my mother, she can't bear to see anything out of place.' She sat down, feeling more able to meet those questioning eyes.

'I'm sorry if I have given you that impression. I hardly know your husband,' she lied, 'but I imagine he is a very astute business man.'

'Oh, he's that all right but I expect Edward is too.'

'A frustrated one. My elder brother died in an accident and Matthew, my twin, wanted to be a farmer. That only left me, Mrs Cameron. I was desperately keen to learn the business and my father had me trained to take over. Edward has a lot of pride and for a long time he found it intolerable to have his wife at the helm.'

'It couldn't have been easy for you?'

'It wasn't.'

'Does your brother-in-law resent taking orders from my husband?'

'Far from it. Thomas is only too grateful to have a position in the distillery.'

The clock chimed and Mrs Cameron glanced at the mantelpiece. 'How time flies when one is enjoying oneself. Thank you very much for a very enjoyable afternoon but now we really must go.'

'I'll ring for the maid to tell the girls.' Susan smiled and held out her hand. 'I've enjoyed meeting you.' And it was true. Mrs Gwen Cameron was a genuinely nice person and an intelligent one too.

# CHAPTER TWENTY-FIVE

T he invitations went out to the Carmichaels, the Lawsons and the Baxters, all of whom had business interests in the area. Their acceptances came within the week as did one from David and Gwen Cameron. All were anxious to meet the daughter of Percy Carruthers and curious about the local lad who had made good.

The dinner was arranged for Thursday evening and on Monday Mrs Carson produced a menu. They went over it together but it was a mere formality and both knew it. Susan invariably agreed with Mrs Carson's suggestions. In the early days Susan's energies had been taken up with the mill and though she spent less time there now she saw no point in changing something that had worked so well in the past.

Miss Wilson continued to see to the smooth running of the house and Mrs Carson had a free hand in the kitchen. Proud of the confidence placed in her, Mrs Carson could be relied upon to produce a meal that would be hugely enjoyed on the night.

Seldom had Susan been in such a state of nervous excitement and Edward shook his head, puzzled by the change in her but wisely refrained from remarking on it, knowing that it would probably only make her worse. Women were unpredictable creatures.

What was David thinking as he prepared for this evening? Susan couldn't help wondering. Would he remember those other times when it had been the servants' entrance for him and then the back stairs to the library? Her lips curled into a smile as she stepped out of the perfumed bathwater and wrapped herself in the warm fluffy towel. Patting herself dry she stretched over for her robe and sat before the mirror studying her face and wondering how long her looks would last. Soon she would be forty. The thought both alarmed and saddened her. How would age affect her? Would her skin tauten or like her mother would her fate be the little pads of slack flesh? As if to reassure herself she touched the skin under her chin and felt its firmness.

Blue for so long had been her favourite colour but now she thought it suited her less well. It was too cold. Tonight she would wear the rose pink.

In the hall she met Edward on his way upstairs.

'Edward?'

Knowing it was his opinion she wanted he stopped and she twirled for his benefit. Desire quickened as he looked at her. She was still very beautiful and his eyes rested on the fragile material swathed over her firm breasts then to the gently nipped-in waist and the lovely full skirt.

'You'll do.' The words were nothing but his expression told her all she needed to know.

'Thank you.'

The Carmichaels could be depended upon to arrive first and when Edward and Susan heard the sound of the first carriage in the courtyard Edward grinned. 'Want to bet that's John and Lydia?'

'At least they never hold up the meal.' Susan laughed as they went along to the drawing-room to be ready to receive their guests.

'Surely we're not first!' Lydia said as she always did. She was a sallow-faced woman with a high nervous voice.

'Someone has to be, Lydia.' Edward smiled as he kissed her and shook John's hand. John Carmichael was a small dapper man who liked to flirt with the ladies but in a way that gave no offence. With charming old-world courtesy he raised Susan's hand to his lips.

'How very beautiful you look, my dear,' he murmured then, turning to Edward: 'Your wife has the kind of beauty that survives the years. I hope you appreciate her, old boy.'

'My wife's appearance has always been a source of pleasure to me,' Edward said smoothly.

'How lucky you are, Susan, to have a husband who still pays you compliments,' Lydia said plaintively. 'I can't recall the last time John paid me one.'

'Then he should be thoroughly ashamed of himself,' Edward said as he put an arm round her narrow shoulders which barely held up the flimsy straps of her burgundy gown.

They chatted together until Mark and Eleanor Lawson arrived, closely followed by George and Beatrice Baxter. George's booming voice and hearty laughter could be heard before he reached the drawing-room and Lydia gave a pained look.

'Fond though I am of George it must be dreadful to live with that voice. Poor Beatrice, she has my sympathy.'

'Sh-sh,' Susan said warningly, as both couples were about to enter. For the next few minutes there were shrieks of delight as friend greeted friend.

Susan was aware of Mark Lawson moving away from the others and waiting for her to do the same. But she didn't, she didn't want to give him any encouragement. Fond though she was of Mark it was no more than that, whereas he had made no secret of the fact that his feelings went deeper. His own marriage to Eleanor was dead. All they shared was a house and the children and occasionally a social occasion such as the invitation to Aran Heights. More than once Mark had said that he found it utterly inconceivable that Edward could look at another woman when he had a wife like Susan. At first his advances had amused her, he was never objectionable and she had been flattered at his persistence. Only once in a fit of depression when things had been particularly bad with Edward had she been tempted and how glad she was that she hadn't succumbed.

Mr and Mrs Cameron were barely inside the door when Edward was over to greet them. With a murmured 'excuse me' Susan followed.

'Welcome to Aran Heights, David,' Edward said heartily.

Then he kissed Gwen on the cheek and shook hands with her husband.

'Thank you, I'm delighted.to be here. You know, Edward, as a young lad I always admired Aran Heights, there was something about it that made it stand out from the others.'

'As far as my wife is concerned you've said the right thing. Mind you, I have a great affection for the old house myself but Susan loves it.' While he spoke he took Gwen by the arm and was leading her over to where the others had broken off their conversation to meet the newcomer.

It left Susan alone with David and as she brought her gaze up to meet his she was mesmerised by those dark eyes observing her with a cool concentration. She felt angry that he should be so much at ease when her own heart was thumping painfully. Then she saw a nerve twitch and there was something in his voice – embarrassment – apology – she couldn't tell.

He spoke very softly. 'I'm well aware that my presence in your house doesn't give you pleasure but don't worry, Mrs Brodie.' He smiled into her face. 'You chose to meet me as a stranger and I find that suits me too.'

'You had the advantage. I was taken aback,' she said shortly, then with an effort managed to adopt her hostess manner and with a charming smile touched his sleeve. 'Do come and let Edward introduce you to the others and I must see to my duties.'

In the dining-room the guests sat in high-backed chairs at the long table covered in stiff, pure white damask. The silver dishes glittered in the light from the tall candles and it caught too the facets of the crystal glasses. Edward sat with Mrs Cameron on his right. No one could be more charming than Edward when he made the effort, Susan thought, and he was making the effort for Gwen. That it was appreciated was evident when her smile widened and her lips twitched at some amusing remark.

George Baxter enjoyed good food and when he got it it received the attention it deserved. He put in a word here and there but largely left the conversation to others.

Knowing how snobbish Beatrice Baxter could be Susan was highly amused at the number of times she drew David into the conversation. That she was impressed with his quiet courtesy and good looks was not lost on her husband who looked over to Susan and raised an eyebrow. She smiled back then answered a remark of John Carmichael's who then called on Beatrice for her opinion. Lydia, feeling neglected, decided to get in on the conversation.

'Excuse me, Mrs Cameron, but how is your son getting on with his tutor?'

Gwen smiled. 'We haven't a son, Mrs Carmichael, David engaged Mr Beveridge to teach our elder daughter.'

'A tutor for a girl!' Lydia almost gasped.

'Why not, Lydia?' Susan laughed. 'Have you forgotten that I shared a tutor with Matthew?'

'No, I hadn't,' she said, flushing because she had then excused herself by saying, 'but then you're the exception.'

'Your father must have been very forward thinking, Susan.'

Susan shook her head and leaned back as the maid removed her plate.

'I'm not so sure about forward thinking, Beatrice. Two for the price of one made economic sense.'

Lydia wouldn't leave it alone though her husband shot her a warning glance.

'Advanced education may have some advantage if a girl is unattractive and unlikely to marry, though even then – '

Susan saw Gwen Cameron's flush of annoyance. David looked amused.

'Lydia, both Sylvia and Amy are nice-looking girls, indeed Amy is going to be a real beauty.'

Gwen gave Susan a quick smile and David looked both pleased and surprised.

'In that case it is beyond me. I know we are perfectly satisfied with our governess,' Lydia said huffily, then turned to Beatrice for support. 'You are too, aren't you, Beatrice?'

Beatrice leaned forward with a soft rounded thrust of bare shoulders.

'Perfectly satisfied but then Mary is very talented musically.' She dismissed Lydia and rested her eyes on David. 'Forgive me for not quite agreeing but don't you think that giving young ladies a broader education can only result in them losing some of their femininity?'

'For heaven's sake, Beatrice,' Mark said almost angrily, 'how can you say that? No one could call Susan anything but charmingly feminine.'

'Why, Mark! Thank you, that was sweet of you but Beatrice may have a point. Edward thinks I've developed a hard streak.'

'What a lot of nonsense you all talk,' George boomed. 'Surely it all depends on the girl and if she has brains.'

'See what you've started, Lydia,' John said with an edge to his voice. 'That's all right between us, we know each other so well but Mr and Mrs Cameron don't.'

'No need to apologise,' David said quietly. 'Another viewpoint is always refreshing.'

'Good! Then perhaps, Mr Cameron, you wouldn't mind answering this,' Eleanor said coyly, twisting the rope of pearls at her throat. 'Would you have bothered the same about your daughter's education if you'd had a son?'

'I sincerely hope that the answer to that is yes. You see, Mrs Lawson, in my opinion there will come a time when everyone, irrespective of sex, whether rich or poor, will be educated according to ability.'

'Then I sincerely hope it isn't in my lifetime,' Lydia sniffed. 'I detest those feminist demonstrations.'

'You may well be right, Mr Cameron,' George said as he wiped his mouth with his napkin. 'Perhaps we should all cultivate our intellects, male and female. The country needs brains and God knows there aren't too many of our politicians over-gifted in that department.'

'Now! Now! George, that's dangerous talk.' Edward laughed.

'Susan, is Victoria to have a tutor?'

'Unlikely, Beatrice, but if she wished then of course.'

'You go along with that, Edward?'

'I most certainly do not. I would have forbidden it.'

'What nonsense, Edward. You've never been able to deny Victoria anything.'

Edward threw up his hands. 'I give in, and now for any favour let us talk about something else.'

# CHAPTER TWENTY-SIX

Stifling a yawn, Victoria helped herself to bacon and scrambled egg and carried the plate to the table.

'Off porridge are you?' her father asked.

'I haven't taken it for ages, it's fattening.'

'It is not fattening, dear, and at your age you need a good breakfast.'

'By the look of what she's got there I wouldn't say she was doing too badly.' Edward grinned.

'This is from your brother, Victoria,' Susan said, waving a page of the letter.

'What is he saying?'

'He wants to bring a friend with him when he comes home for Christmas. Edwin somebody – ' She went back to the previous page. 'Edwin Martin. The boy's parents are in India and according to Paul he's going to find it a bit dull spending all his holiday with his grandparents.'

'And I know what that means,' Victoria said, pulling a long face. 'They'll go off on their own and leave me.'

'Then ask one of your own friends to spend a few days when this Edwin is here.'

'That's what to do, Victoria,' Edward said approvingly. 'Then if the young men are agreeable you can always make up a foursome.'

'Ask Mina, we're due her hospitality anyway.'

'Absolutely not, Mama, she's been sweet on Paul for ages and I can just see her making eyes at him, it would be sickening.'

'You'll have to resign yourself to Paul getting married one day, Victoria, and he could do a lot worse than choose Mina.' Her father grinned. Nothing delighted him more than teasing Victoria.

'I don't want her for a sister-in-law and she won't be if I can help it.' She frowned then brightened. 'I know, I'll ask Sylvia.'

'Why on earth do you want to ask Sylvia Cameron?'

'Why shouldn't she?' Edward bristled.

Now why had she said that? Susan could have kicked herself. She might have been able to dissuade Victoria if she'd handled it carefully but now Victoria had Edward on her side.

'I didn't mean it that way. I imagine the Cameron family will be going to Rochdale to spend Christmas there.'

'They're not. Sylvia's grandfather is coming up for Christmas and possibly staying for New Year too.'

'Then you go right ahead and invite Sylvia,' Edward said and was rewarded with a smile.

Susan bit her lip. No matter how hard she tried to keep distance between herself and the Camerons she wasn't succeeding. Victoria, looking smug, finished her breakfast then went out.

'I cannot understand you, Susan. Sylvia is a very suitable companion for Victoria, she's quiet and sensible. Her only fault seems to be that she is a Cameron.'

'Just leave it, Edward.'

'It must have been my imagination but I thought there was a thawing in your attitude to David.'

'He and his wife were guests in this house and I hope I know how to behave,' she said haughtily.

'Oh, you do, my dear, no one could be more dignified and charming. And may I add, though small and fragile, Mrs Cameron is astute; after all she is Percy Carruther's daughter and he doesn't miss a trick.'

'Astute about what? What do you mean?'

'She adores David and she must wonder what it is about him that you dislike.'

'You know, you don't have to wonder,' Susan said harshly. 'I don't suppose you've noticed but your father and mother have never got over that dreadful scene. That said, I have no objections to Sylvia coming here.' Susan got up, flicked a crumb off her skirt and left the breakfast-room.

\* \* \*

The December weather worsened then came a reprieve. The cold east wind dropped and a pale sun glinted through the clouds. Aran Heights had undergone its Christmas cleaning and everything was bright and sparkling. Susan avoided what she called the over-Christmassy look but she had the gardeners bring in armfuls of holly. In one corner of the hall a huge vase was filled with the deep red berries and with the log fire burning cheerfully it was a welcoming sight. The tree she and Victoria had decorated was in the drawing-room and pieces of holly were spread over the picture frames.

Late in the afternoon of the sixteenth the carriage drew up at the front of the house. There were voices and instructions given as the carriage moved away and Paul and his friend entered. Waiting in the hall to greet them were Susan, Edward and Victoria.

With a start of surprise Susan saw that Paul had grown in the time he'd been away and his great height made him look older. She was the first to step forward to greet her son. Paul, looking happy and relaxed, kissed her on the cheek then gave her a hug. 'Wonderful to see you, Mother.'

'Welcome home, Paul,' she said softly.

He crossed to Edward. 'Hello, Father.' They shook hands. 'God, you're stretching, you're as tall as I am.'

Victoria had been standing aside but as Paul turned to her she threw her arms round his neck and kissed him. A bit embarrassed, Paul extricated himself and brought his friend forward.

Edwin Martin was of average height with thick brown hair, a pleasantly rugged face and a ready smile. After bowing politely to Susan he exchanged a firm handshake with Edward then looked at his friend's sister with open admiration. Paul and Edward exchanged looks and both grinned. In her dark skirt and high-necked white lacy blouse, Victoria looked sweet and fresh. She murmured a conventional greeting but her colour had risen and her eyes were shining.

'Where is James?'

'In the nursery,' Susan said. 'I thought you would see him later.'

'No, I want to see him now and introduce him to Edwin.'

'I'll bring him down,' Victoria said with uncharacteristic eagerness.

'Mrs Brodie, I'm very grateful to you for having me.'

'Edwin, we're delighted to meet a friend of Paul's. Your parents are in India I believe?'

'Yes. They're doing a four-year stint. My grandfather has a jute mill in Dundee and my father is looking after the family interests in India.' He smiled across to Paul. 'I'm an only son and this college lark is supposed to prepare me to take on some responsibility.'

'And is it succeeding?' Edward laughed. 'Or are your parents and Paul's pouring money down the drain?'

'Oh, no, sir, truly the money isn't wasted. I mean we really do have to keep our nose to the grindstone.'

'Edwin's right, Father. If we manage to retain a third of what we are taught we'll be doing well.'

'Your son has natural ability, Mr Brodie, I'm just a plodder.'

A disturbance on the stairs made them all look up. Victoria was dragging a reluctant James who grunted angrily. Paul crossed over to take charge.

'What a way to treat your big brother,' he said with mock severity. 'James, it's me! It's Paul.'

'Paul,' James said uncertainly then raised his arms and Paul bent down to clasp the short awkward body.

'I missed everybody, James, but you most of all and I've brought someone to meet you.'

Edwin joined them at the foot of the stairs and without being the least bit embarrassed held out his hand to James who slowly put out his left hand and Edwin shook it gently. 'Hello, James, I'm pleased to meet you. I've heard a lot about you from Paul.'

James looked bewildered but happy as he looked from one face to the other. Edward had walked away; the sight of his son always distressed him.

Paul took his hand. 'Come on, James, we'll take you upstairs. Mother, Edwin is getting the room next to mine, is that right?'

'Yes, I think you'll be quite comfortable, Edwin, but if you want anything be sure to ask.'

'Thanks very much.'

Gwen Cameron was puzzled. 'I thought you would have welcomed a few days at Aran Heights.'

'Mrs Brodie doesn't want me, she's only asking me to please Victoria.'

'What nonsense, Sylvia, Mrs Brodie is charming.'

'She is to you.' She saw her mother frown. 'There's no use looking like that; it isn't imagination, I just know.'

'Well it would upset me very much if I had to write and decline the invitation on your behalf.'

'Oh, I'll go,' Sylvia said resignedly, 'just don't expect me to enjoy it that's all.'

'Of course you'll enjoy the company. Victoria's brother Paul is home for Christmas and Mrs Brodie mentions a friend – ' She broke off as other matters claimed her attention.

Paul had expected a friend of his sister's to be fun-loving and pretty and was disappointed to find that Sylvia Cameron was neither. Not that she was actually plain, he told himself, but rather that her appearance was unremarkable, someone who would go unnoticed in a crowd. Also that cool manner of hers was a bit off-putting. He could see the time ahead being pretty heavy going with Edwin going soppy on Victoria.

Sylvia wasn't too happy either. Far from needing her company Victoria seemed to want to spend all her time with Edwin. It threw Paul and her together and she wasn't sure that she particularly liked him. She distrusted his good looks and resented his slightly condescending manner. Just because he had been away at college he seemed to think himself superior. Still, she was a guest in the house and the warning from her mother still rang in her ears so she made the effort to be friendly.

Becoming aware that she had made very little contribution to the conversation and with Victoria busy pouring out tea and being mother, Sylvia turned to Edwin and began questioning him about college. Some of the questions surprised and baffled him and he appealed to Paul.

'You take over, pal, I'm getting out of my depth.'

Victoria laughed. 'Sorry, you two, I should have warned you. Sylvia has dispensed with a governess and has a tutor all to herself. She's going to be like my mother and run the business.'

'Are you, Sylvia?' Paul asked.

'I'm hoping to and my grandfather has promised me a position in the cotton mill.'

'Not the distillery?'

'Oh, no,' she said dismissively. 'Once my father is satisfied with the running of that he'll get someone to take over and we'll all return to Rochdale.'

'Presumably you'll get married one day.'

'It's a possibility, Edwin, but what of it?'

'Maybe your husband wouldn't approve of his wife spending her days in the mill.'

'His loss then. I wouldn't marry him.'

'Could work all right,' Paul said thoughtfully. 'It hasn't damaged my mother and father's relationship.'

'Yes, it has, Paul. Papa's never liked Mama going into the mill,' Victoria said with a toss of her head. 'I'm not going to be like Mama.'

'Couldn't be, you haven't the brains.'

'Beast.'

'I'd quite like to see round the papermill if that wouldn't be asking too much.'

'Mother would be delighted. If Father is available he'll show us round or get someone else.'

'May I come?' Sylvia asked.

'Of course. We'll all go.'

'What a bore.'

'You can stay at home, Viccy.'

'On my own? Certainly not.'

Sylvia turned to Edwin. 'If you'd be interested in seeing over the distillery I could arrange it with my father.'

'Great! I'd like that, thanks.'

Paul felt strangely hurt that Sylvia hadn't included him – yet why should she? The distillery, until recently, had belonged to the Brodies and he'd been inside it many times.

'Does the invitation include me?'

She looked surprised. 'But of course, Paul. I'm sorry, I just imagined you'd been in it often enough.'

'I have but I'd like to see the changes your father has made.'

She looked at him sharply and he realised his mistake.

'My Uncle Thomas has nothing but admiration for the way Mr Cameron handles the workers, Sylvia. They like and respect him and I'm afraid that couldn't be said for my grandfather.'

'Your grandfather was never a humble worker, my father was and because of that he can understand their worries.'

'He's got the distillery back on its feet and that's what is important.'

She was certainly impressing him. Most girls would have tried to hide their father's humble beginnings but she seemed to take a pride in mentioning it.

He really isn't so bad, Sylvia thought, in fact he was really rather nice.

The next day the four of them went out. Victoria and Edwin went on ahead leaving Sylvia and Paul to follow.

'You don't get this kind of weather in Rochdale?' he shouted against the wind.

'It gets its share of blustery weather but there is a wildness about here that's exhilarating and I like it.'

Sylvia was laughing, her cheeks flushed as a frisky wind whipped her skirt round her legs.

'I'm glad Victoria invited you, Sylvia, and not one of her other friends,' Paul said, wondering how he could ever have thought her plain.

'Why?' she asked in her direct manner.

'You're much more interesting.'

'And not at all pretty. Don't deny it, Paul, it's what you thought when you met me. It was written all over your face.'

Paul had the grace to blush. 'That was your fault.'

'How could it be my fault?'

'That abrupt manner would scare anyone off.'

'Yes, I know.' She sighed. 'I have an unfortunate way of talking as my mother keeps telling me.'

'No, you don't. It's only a bit off-putting at first. I think you're delightful and it's marvellous to be able to carry on an intelligent conversation with a girl. Poor old Edwin won't get that with Viccy.'

'That won't worry Edwin. Victoria is lovely, Paul, and more important, she is nice with it.'

'Certainly seem to be smitten with each other, don't you think?'

'I do and if there is such a thing as love at first sight I'd say it's happened to them.'

'Maybe I'm beginning to believe in it too,' he said softly, so softly that he didn't know if she had heard.

With Victoria and Edwin out of sight Paul decided to risk it. Sylvia had taken off her gloves and he caught her hand in his. A tingling sensation shot up his arm and made him draw in his breath. Bewildered by it he said shakily, 'Sylvia, may I write to you when I go back to college?'

'Yes.'

'But will you reply to my letters?'

'Of course I'll reply; what a stupid thing to ask.'

The young people were entertaining themselves and were no trouble. Finding herself unexpectedly busy at the mill Susan saw little of them apart from meal times and not always then. Edward was being helpful and made himself available to show Edwin the various departments in the papermill. Peter, Matthew's younger son, should have been with them, Susan thought fondly. Young though he was, he seemed fascinated by the machinery and each time he was there demanded full explanations to his questions.

*　　*　　*

Hearing of his daughter's request concerning the distillery, David Cameron sent the carriage for the young people. The girls, if they insisted on coming, were to remain in the office while the boys did a tour of the distillery.

In the carriage they were laughing and talking about the visit ahead.

'Your Uncle Thomas is very proud of the distillery, Paul.'

'He is and when you get him started talking about it there is no stopping him.'

'I like hearing about it.'

'I take it you know then that only the finest natural ingredients are used in the making of Granton whisky,' Paul said, sounding intentionally pompous.

Sylvia laughed. 'Making it one of the best?'

'Not one of the best. The best. Incidentally have you been round it?'

'Of course she hasn't,' his sister said scornfully.

'No, I haven't. My mother would have fainted at the suggestion and even my father couldn't be persuaded but he did tell me about it.'

'Come on, Sylvia, tell all,' Edwin said, 'and let me appear a little knowledgeable.'

'Ask Paul, he's been through a number of times.'

'Him! I'd rather hear it from you.'

'All right, I'll do my best. The smell, the rich aroma of fermentation is what hits you first.'

'Go on.'

'I'm thinking, Edwin. You'll be taken to see the raw whisky before it is transferred into oak casks for maturation.' She paused and Edwin nodded. 'Apparently that is the point when the distiller uses his skill to make the crucial judgment that determines the quality of the whisky,' She nudged Paul. 'You now.'

'Ah, yes, well, the oak casks are left in a darkened warehouse for at least ten years.'

Victoria yawned. 'When do we get there?'

'In a few minutes,' her brother answered.

The long street they entered was dreary and dirty and the

warehouses had windows thick with dust and most had the
added protection of iron bars across them. After another
turn they were through the gates and into a cobbled courtyard. From the carriage windows they could see workers
bent under their heavy sacks of grain and there was the
constant rumble of empty casks being rolled along the
cobbles. Further away could be heard the steady tapping
of a cooper's hammer on the iron hoops of a cask. These
the coachman, when he got down from his perch, informed
them were the sights and sounds of whisky. Remembering
his instructions, he led them through a labyrinth of corridors
to the offices. Victoria giggled and wrinkled her nose.
Before Edwin arrived on the scene nothing would have
dragged her into this smelly place but now she thought
of it as an adventure.

David Cameron sat in a swivel chair behind an enormous
desk where once John Brodie had ruled with a harshness
that he considered the only language the workers could
understand. David had contemplated clearing away all that
had belonged to its owner then he changed his mind, getting
a curious pleasure from keeping it as it was. The desk and
chair, together with the rest of the furniture, were very
much to his taste as were the watercolours of old Glasgow,
a reminder of a time when the Brodies were merchants and
made their fortune in the tobacco trade.

Walking to the window David saw the carriage turn into the
gates and a little later Mr Davies, the coachman, announced
that his daughter and her friends had arrived.

Sylvia came in ahead of the others and David noticed
that she looked flushed. She kissed him before making the
introductions.

'Papa, this is Victoria.'

Just for a second the clock was turned back and he was with
the young Susan MacFarlane. The girl was very pretty, he
thought, but now that he studied her he noted the difference.
She didn't have that gorgeous silver fairness, hers was a
reddish fairness and the seriousness, the quick intelligent
look, were missing.

'Delighted to meet you, Victoria, and may I say how charming you look.'

Victoria, smiling demurely, acknowledged the greetings and a tall, dark boy came forward.

'This is Paul, Papa,' Sylvia said, suddenly shy and David felt a quickening of interest. Gone was the brusque manner which her mother deplored, to be replaced with a softness that touched her face and was in her voice. David felt strangely moved at the thought of his daughter and Susan's son being attracted to one another.

'This is very good of you, Mr Cameron and much appreciated,' Paul said. They shook hands, each weighing up the other.

David liked what he saw. He liked this tall young man with his ready smile and the signs of strength in the firm chin. Sylvia was very precious to him but he would have no hesitation in trusting this boy with her happiness.

Paul, too, was favourably impressed. Mr Cameron was nothing like he expected and straightaway he liked Sylvia's father. Why his mother extended such a lukewarm welcome to the Cameron family was beyond him – beyond his father too. Edward got on well with them.

Edwin left Victoria's side to be introduced. 'Edwin is a college friend of mine, Mr Cameron.' For a while the conversation was about college then Thomas Brodie arrived.

'Hello, Uncle Thomas, are you going to do the honours?'

'Your uncle knows a lot more about the whisky trade than I do, Paul. For me every day is a school.'

Thomas smiled. He looks happy, Paul thought, there was certainly no bad feeling or even awkwardness between the son of the former owner and Mr Cameron and surely that spoke volumes.

'What about the young ladies?' Thomas hadn't expected to see his niece and David's daughter.

'They are going to stay in the office with me.' Then David began to laugh. 'If this is going to be a regular occurrence, Thomas, we'll have to do something about light refreshments.

As it is they are all too young to partake of the "water of life".'

'What is the water of life, Mr Cameron?'

'Whisky, Victoria.' David smiled.

Sylvia was no longer at Aran Heights. Her grandfather had arrived and she had returned home. She thanked her hostess rather stiffly for an enjoyable few days and left one young man feeling lost.

'Edwin, will you have to go to India one day?'

'I expect so.'

'Is it terribly hot?'

'Almost unbearable according to my mother but no one works during the hottest part of the day.'

'Does your mother enjoy the life?'

'Not much, Mrs Brodie, but she's in the minority, most of them do.'

'What is it she doesn't like?' Edward asked as he buttered his toast.

'She can't be bothered with the endless socialising and hates the emptiness of the life.'

'Then why does she go?'

'Considers it is her duty to accompany my father.' He grinned. 'He says it is to keep an eye on him.'

Edward laughed heartily and Susan smiled.

They were in bed.

'What do you think of Edwin, Edward?'

'Nice lad.'

'Victoria hangs on to his every word, have you noticed?'

'Does that bother you?'

'No, but I hope she realises that once Edwin is back in college that could be the end of it.'

'Somehow I don't think so. It may well develop.'

'Paul did very well entertaining Sylvia.'

'I don't think he found it a hardship,' Edward said drily.

'I'm afraid I've had to neglect them.'

'Probably glad to be left to themselves,' Edward muttered from under the bedclothes.

'You could be right. Incidentally where did they go on Wednesday afternoon? I forgot to ask.'

'Sylvia suggested her father show Edwin over the distillery but in the event they all went.'

Her heart stopped then raced. 'They – all – went?' Susan said stupidly.

'That's what I said. David sent the carriage and he looked after the girls while Thomas showed Edwin accompanied by Paul the magic of whisky-making. And now, please, do you think I could get some sleep?' Turning away, he dragged the bedclothes with him but Susan was too shocked to complain. A kind of fury born of despair seized her. The unthinkable had happened. Paul and David had met. Father and son had come face to face. She tried to visualise it and failed.

Did kinship show itself in some way? Was there an invisible bond, something that would draw them together? But of course not. They were strangers meeting for the first time and if someone remarked on a resemblance there was nothing to fear. Paul was a Brodie, he took after his grandfather. Her head ached, she longed for sleep and in the morning her face was pale and there were shadows beneath her eyes showing how little she had slept.

Christmas Day. Mrs Carson had excelled herself. It was the traditional Christmas dinner but cooked to perfection. Edwin looked blissfully content as they rose from the table to sit in the drawing-room. Paul and Edwin both flopped into chairs.

'Mrs Brodie, I've been a proper glutton and I do apologise but you have a cook in a million.'

'Yes, Mrs Carson is a treasure.' Susan smiled.

'The cook my grandparents have is an old dear but she's past it. A burnt offering is nothing new but the old folk eat so little they hardly notice.'

'I'm quite sure it isn't as bad as that, Edwin, but I do think it helps with our cook that I don't interfere. Mrs Carson has a free hand.'

\* \* \*

Paul and Edwin had gone. The house was quiet and there was the flat feeling of the end of a holiday. The postman had been and the maid arrived with letters on a silver tray just as they were finishing breakfast. Edward took them, glanced at the envelopes and handed two to Susan. He was well aware that Victoria was craning her neck to see the other envelopes.

'One for you, Viccy,' he said, examining the envelope and infuriating his daughter. 'Sloppy writing.'

'Papa, it's mine, please give me my letter.'

'Edward, give it to her and don't tease.'

'There you are.'

'Thank you.'

'Aren't you going to open it?'

She blushed. 'No, I'll wait I think.' Swallowing the rest of her breakfast she pushed back her chair and with an 'excuse me' hurried from the room.

# CHAPTER TWENTY-SEVEN

Winter had held the countryside in its grip until well into March but now the cherry trees with their delicate pinks overhung the large trumpeted daffodils and there were the first glimpses of early red tulips.

'I wish it were Easter,' Victoria said wistfully as she followed her mother down the steps to the terrace.

'Well, you won't have long to wait.'

'It'll be nice when Paul and Edwin come. You do like Edwin, don't you?'

'I seem to have answered that before but yes, I think Edwin is a pleasant, well-mannered boy.'

'I wish he was to stay all the holidays.'

'His grandparents would be offended if he didn't spend some time with them.'

Victoria gave a little skip and took her mother's arm. 'Edwin is the nicest boy I know and it's even better that he's a friend of Paul's.'

Poor dear, Susan thought with a pang, she just can't hide her feelings. 'Victoria, it doesn't do to show your feelings. Let the boy do the running and he'll respect you all the more for it.'

'All right, I'll try and Mama,' the tone had become wheedling, 'may I have a new gown? One with a low neckline, not too low of course.'

'It won't be, you're far too young.'

'I'm not and you're just old-fashioned. This isn't the Victorian age now you know.'

Susan hid a smile. 'I'm well aware that this is 1903 but that doesn't mean we have to let Victorian standards go.'

Her daughter smiled knowingly. 'I know why the Queen liked going to Balmoral.'

'Oh!'

'She wanted to be with her ghillie, John Brown.'

'That is gossip. Rachel, I suppose?'

'Her mother says it is common knowledge.'

'It is only gossip and it is unkind. The Queen may have been lonely and liked to talk to her ghillie and some people had to make the most of it.'

'Sylvia had a letter from Paul.'

Another moment of unease for Susan. 'Just politeness, Victoria, and hoping that Sylvia enjoyed her few days at Aran Heights.'

Victoria looked at her mother thoughtfully. Mama didn't like Sylvia very much so she needn't say that Paul and Sylvia were corresponding regularly.

The longed-for Easter holidays. Paul and Edwin arrived. All that morning Victoria had been up to high doh but she had calmed down and Susan couldn't have faulted the way Victoria smiled and greeted Edwin. She was learning.

That same evening Paul announced calmly that he was going to the Beeches to see Sylvia and all Susan could do was watch him going.

'Mama, we're going to Moorend and we'll see Uncle Matthew and Aunt Winnie at the same time.'

'That's fine, dear. Give them my love.' She turned to her son. 'You'll be going too, Paul?'

'Not today, Mother.'

'What are your plans?' she asked after the other two had gone.

'I'll be seeing Sylvia.'

Susan moistened her lips and strove to keep her voice steady.

'Paul, dear, aren't you perhaps overdoing it? I mean Sylvia may be reading too much into your friendship and her parents may not be happy about you calling so often.'

'On the contrary, Mother,' he said coldly, 'Mr and Mrs Cameron have been extremely kind and I couldn't have had a warmer welcome. And what's more,' he added, 'Sylvia would come here if you invited her but you haven't.'

'Paul, you are very young – '

'The same age as Edwin and that relationship doesn't seem to bother you.'

'You're all far too young to know your own mind.'

Paul's face relaxed. 'Mother, I'm not contemplating marriage.'

'I'm very glad to hear it,' Susan said almost dizzy with relief but it was short-lived.

'That doesn't mean we won't at some time. I love Sylvia and I know I won't change.'

Something sour and choking filled her throat. 'You can't be,' she said harshly, 'it's out of the question. Sylvia is not right for you.'

'Let me be the judge of that, please,' he said, looking at her with the eyes of a stranger.

'Judge of what?' Edward asked as he came in.

Paul turned to him with relief. 'Mother strongly objects to my friendship with Sylvia.'

'Don't let that bother you. Sylvia's a fine girl but your mother, for some reason of her own, has no time for the Camerons.'

Susan saw the sardonic smile on Edward's face and if something had been to hand she would have hurled it at him.

Paul left the room without another word.

'If you're trying to drive a wedge between you and your son then you're going the right way about it. And another thing, Susan, if it comes to a choice between you and Sylvia I think we both know whom he'll choose.'

She shot him a look of pure dislike and walked out, almost banging the door behind her. As always when she was deeply troubled Susan climbed the stairs to the library. Sitting behind the desk she knew black despair. She was losing her son, losing his love and his cold politeness was breaking her heart. If there was a God in heaven why did he allow the Camerons to come here and cause so much misery? She felt wounded and mortally hurt as she saw Paul turning more and more to Edward. To think that at one time she had prayed for such a closeness and now that it was happening she was jealous and miserable.

Next morning she went in to the mill earlier than usual. Work, plenty of it was what she needed to occupy her mind, and always before it had been successful but not this time. The problem was too big. It frightened her. What should she do? If she waited perhaps the attraction would die a natural death. They were at a romantic age. But if it didn't? She couldn't put it off much longer. Something would have to be done.

'Is Mother out?'

'Yes, Paul,' Edward said, looking up briefly from the paper. 'You're looking very smart.'

'I'm getting the nine fifteen for Glasgow.'

'Going on your own?'

'No, Sylvia wants to see Glasgow.'

'Cleared it with Mr and Mrs Cameron?'

'Just Mr Cameron. He said it was all right, that he considered me responsible enough to take care of Sylvia.'

'And so do I.'

'Thanks.'

'How are you for cash?'

'Not bad.'

Edward went into his pocket. 'Here you are, it doesn't do to be short when you are taking a young lady out for the day.'

'Thank you very much, Father, that is very generous.'

'I can recommend Green's in Gordon Street. It's a respectable place and the food is good.'

'I – um – haven't mentioned this to Mother,' he said awkwardly.

'Don't. If anything is said I'll handle it.'

'I'd better get going.'

'Enjoy yourselves but remember to behave.'

Paul grinned, feeling a surge of real affection for the man who had once treated him so badly.

'I can promise you that.'

Before getting on the train at Aranvale Paul bought three-pennyworth of Fry's creams from the small confectioners. And when the train drew in at Airdrie station Sylvia was on the platform looking anxiously the length of the train. He waved and she half ran towards him, looking fresh and pretty in a lime green dress and bolero. Soon they were sitting close together, Sylvia nearest the window.

'For you,' he said, dropping the paper bag in her lap.

'Oh, Paul, thank you. Fry's creams, I love them.' They looked at each other and smiled. A smile that told it all, happiness spilled out. They were together, a whole lovely long day ahead of them.

'Papa says it always rains in Glasgow.'

'Today it wouldn't dare.' He smiled as doors slammed, the guard blew his whistle, the green flag was waved and they were off. Sylvia watched the passing scenery and he watched her.

In what seemed a remarkably short time the rhythm of the train altered and they were slowing down before coming into Queen Street station. When it lurched to a stop Paul lowered the window on its leather strap, opened the door and they got out.

They hurried along with the other travellers until they were outside the station. 'Anything special you want to do, Sylvia?'

'Papa knew Glasgow well as a boy so I can leave the sightseeing to him. What's that place where the steamers sail from? Papa told me but I forget.'

'Broomielaw?'

'That's it,' she said, delighted.

'We can get a tram and go there after luncheon.' He touched the coins in his pocket. 'My father suggested I take you to Green's in Gordon Street.'

'Good, that's settled. Paul, let's just walk; anywhere, it doesn't matter.'

Arm-in-arm they walked along Sauchiehall Street busy with

shoppers. The windows were well stocked and pleasing to the eye. It would have been difficult to drag Victoria away but Sylvia barely gave them a glance.

They had a good lunch at Green's then they took the tram to Broomielaw. For a while the mist persisted then it cleared and the sun came through. With their fingers interlocked Paul and Sylvia watched the steamers and the swans circling the moored boats as if staking their claim. Others stood and watched and mothers grabbed at their children as if fearful of losing them.

'Paul, where did you go for family holidays?'

'It was difficult to get away for more than a few days with both my parents in the mill so we didn't go far. Gourock, Rothesay, Dunoon.'

'Lovely names.'

'Lovely places but I think I've outgrown them. I haven't been to London but I mean to put that right.'

'I've been several times. Papa worked there for some years so he was able to show us around.' She swung round to face Paul. 'Wouldn't it be wonderful to travel? Now when we're young, not wait as most people do until they are too old to enjoy it.'

'Which faraway places were you thinking of?'

'Oh, I meant Europe. Paris, Rome, Venice, Florence, so many places I've read about and would love to see and I'm lucky, Paul. My papa would never hold me back from something I really wanted to do.'

'What about your mother?'

'In the end she always gives in to my father.'

'Your mother is very gentle.'

'Not the right description. Beneath that gentleness there's quite a band of steel.' She dropped her voice and her eyes fixed on his face. 'I want to see your face when I say this.'

'Good gracious! You look serious.'

'This is serious. Paul, my father is illegitimate.'

'So?'

She laughed and did he hear relief? 'You mean you aren't shocked? Most people are. My father has risen above it or he pretends that he has. Deep down I know he does care, he cares terribly. Can you imagine what it must be like not to know who your father is? Whether he is alive or dead and worst of all what kind of person he could be to leave a young girl to bring up his child single-handed?'

Paul's face showed nothing of what he was feeling. Should he tell her, since she'd been so honest, that he shared the same fate as her father? Easier for him, he had a substitute father and a name to protect him. The urge to tell this remarkable girl was strong but he couldn't do it. The person to suffer would be his mother and he'd given his promise not to tell Victoria, not to tell anyone.

'A person is who he is and the accident of birth doesn't alter that.'

'I agree. You're like my father, Paul, maybe that's why I like you so much and my mother can't get over you being so dark. She says it is very unusual, almost unique, for both parents to be fair and produce such a dark child.'

'My grandfather, before he turned grey, was very dark and presumably that is where I get my dark good looks.'

'Conceited, aren't you?'

'No, I've nothing to be conceited about. Sylvia . . .'

'Yes?' she said as they began walking towards the tram stop.

'I've enjoyed everything about today.'

'And so have I. It's been wonderful.'

# CHAPTER TWENTY-EIGHT

Another night of broken sleep for Susan. With her nerves raw at the thought of what lay ahead she determined to keep to the usual morning routine. Ramsay brought her back to Aran Heights at noon and after a pretence of eating luncheon she went up to her bedroom to change. On the bed lay the day dress she had decided to wear. Without Edward's persuasion Susan doubted whether she would have chosen it – amber wasn't a colour she favoured but she trusted Edward. He always knew what suited her.

By three o'clock Susan decided he wasn't coming but by quarter past he was being shown in by the maid.

'Good afternoon, Mrs Brodie.' He was very smart and businesslike in a dark suit.

'Thank you for coming.' She waved a hand for him to be seated and sat down herself.

'I'm here at your request, Mrs Brodie, or was it a command?'

She didn't rise to the bait. 'My reason for asking you to come alone concerns Paul and Sylvia. You must know, David,' she deliberately used his Christian name, 'that a serious relationship is out of the question.'

'May I ask why?'

'That should be obvious. Edward and you are related.'

'That isn't generally known and it only makes us half brothers and the young ones half cousins. Marriage between half cousins is not unusual.'

'I don't want it.'

His eyes glinted. 'Now we're getting the truth. You don't want a daughter of mine marrying into your family.'

'I won't deny that, but it isn't for the reason you think.'

'Ah, but I'm sure it is.' He leaned forward, his eyes fixed unwaveringly on her pale face and a harshness crept into his voice. 'You had better get this into your head, Mrs Brodie: my daughter's happiness means a great deal to me and if – and that is all I am saying – if Sylvia and Paul wish to marry some time in the future they have my blessing and my wife's too. We are both fond of Paul and he's assured of a welcome in our home.'

'David,' she spoke slowly and clearly, 'I can only tell you that marriage between Paul and Sylvia is impossible, it can never be.'

He got up abruptly. 'I've said all I intend saying on the subject. Now if you will excuse me – '

Susan half rose. 'No, David, don't go. Please sit down and hear me out then you'll understand.'

For a moment she thought he was going to refuse but he sat down, his face set in a hard line and watched Susan put a hand to her throat. Her eyes were on him, those beautiful eyes pain-filled as she fought for control.

'Susan, what's wrong? What is the matter?'

'Sylvia is a delightful and intelligent girl and you do me an injustice. In different circumstances . . .' Her voice trailed off and she closed her eyes. For so long she had kept her secret but now . . . 'David,' her voice was a whisper, 'Paul is your son.'

He stared at her. 'What in God's name are you saying?' he said hoarsely.

'I'd hoped even to the last moment that it wouldn't have to come out.'

What he was hearing couldn't be true! His hand was pressed over his mouth. He felt numb, stupefied, incapable of thought or speech. When he could speak his voice came out thick, muffled, as if he were drunk.

'Now you can understand my anguish, seeing those two – ' She broke off and gave a mirthless laugh. 'I married Edward not knowing that I was carrying your child. Can you imagine that, David? Can you imagine what I went through?'

She heard his swiftly indrawn breath. 'What did you tell Edward?'

'The truth or what I believed it to be then – that the father of my child was someone I knew for a brief time and would never see again. He wanted a name but I never gave him one.' Anger touched her voice. 'If only you hadn't come back. Revenge was what you wanted and you got it.'

'Perhaps.' He was pale and shaken but there was a light in his eyes she didn't like.

'You have no claim on Paul,' she said quickly. 'He believes Edward to be his father and that is the way it is going to remain.' It wasn't true, Paul knew that Edward wasn't his natural father, but she didn't care.

David's breathing was still heavy but his colour had returned. 'Susan, if only I had known, if only – '

'You'd gone from Aranvale and I was married to Edward.' She didn't know if he was listening.

'You can't even begin to understand how much I – we – wanted a son. My daughters mean the world to me but a son, I needed a son, Susan.' He stopped and said slowly, wonderingly, 'Paul – is – my son.' Susan saw the longing, the naked agony of suddenly being told of a son but a son denied him.

'We all have our cross to bear, David. Trying to discourage this relationship has cost me the love of my son,' she said brokenly. 'I've lost Paul and hurt him badly.'

David got to his feet and squared his shoulders. 'For what you have suffered, Susan, I am deeply, deeply sorry. Now it is up to me. Somehow I have to protect those two and keep them apart.'

'No matter what you do they are going to be miserable.' She got up to stand beside him and he gave a small smile.

'Mercifully the awful anguish felt by the young doesn't last for ever. I speak from experience. It took me a long time to get over you, Susan. No, that isn't quite true. I never really got over you, I thought I had but just seeing you again – Once you were a lovely girl but now you are a very beautiful woman.'

It was a dangerous moment and they both knew it.

'You made a good marriage, David,' Susan said unsteadily. 'I like Gwen.'

'We both chose well, Susan. Edward must love you very, very much to accept and bring up another man's child as his own.'

She nodded. They both smiled and the tension eased. Even so they were so engrossed with one another that they didn't hear the door opening until Edward spoke and they both turned.

Susan hadn't realised that it was so late and she was taken aback to see Edward.

'Well, hello there! What brings you to Aran Heights, David?'

'I invited him,' Susan put in swiftly before David could answer.

David gave her a quick look then spoke easily. 'We were discussing the young folk and I agree with your wife that the relationship should be discouraged.'

'Why?'

'We are half brothers.'

'Is that the reason Susan gave – ?'

'No! Stop it!' Susan drew herself up and held her head high. 'David, it's time for the truth and Edward has a right to hear it.' She turned to her husband. 'It isn't often I suggest you have a drink but I think you may need one.'

'Thank you but I'll manage without.'

'Very well.' She paused. 'You've always been desperate to know the identity of Paul's father so now I'm going to tell you.' Her lips were trembling but she kept a grip on herself. 'Edward, Paul is David's son,' she said clearly.

'Is this some kind of joke?' he demanded but he looked sick.

'No joke. You knew that David worked for my father but you didn't know he came to Aran Heights to teach me the business.'

'Why the secrecy?'

'The fault was mine. I was too shocked that day at Croft House to think clearly. I thought it better to pretend we hadn't met. Later I regretted it but by then it was too late.'

'Edward, you must believe me I knew nothing about it – I had no idea,' David said quietly, looking ill at ease. 'That is the truth. What happened was my fault and I was then and I still am deeply ashamed.'

'Spare me the details,' Edward said savagely.

'There are no details, Edward,' Susan said quietly. 'It was the only time and we were never together after that. By the time I knew that I was pregnant David had left the mill and Aranvale and I was married to you.'

Edward opened his mouth but no words came and abruptly he turned his back and busied himself with the decanter. His hand shook and some of the whisky spilled. He was remembering that unguarded moment when he had seen the longing in David's face and a dreadful fear took hold of him. What were Susan's feelings? Had he lost her? Was her seeming dislike of David Cameron just a cover for her real feelings?

With a murmured excuse David had moved towards the door but turned before reaching it.

'Susan, you mustn't worry. I'll do what has to be done.' Then he was gone.

Edward drained his glass and poured himself another. With it in his hand he walked to the window. After a few minutes he said tonelessly, 'David's coming back.'

He came in without an apology. 'I can't leave it like this.' He sounded agitated. 'Paul is my son and I must, I have to do something for him.' His eyes fixed on Edward. 'The only way I can do that is through you.'

'What do you mean?'

'One day I want my son to take over the distillery but it can only be through you. It's thanks to you that Paul has a name and I'm grateful. More than anyone I know what that means.'

'Where do I come in?'

'I gather from Thomas that you've always hankered after the distillery. Well I want you to take control of it.'

'Control of the distillery?' Edward said incredulously.

'Already we're making a fair profit with the potential for a lot more. Once my father-in-law is repaid in full for his outlay then the Granton Distillery becomes yours. No strings attached, Edward. I'll have the necessary papers prepared by my solicitor and ownership transferred to you with Paul inheriting one day.'

'David, how are you going to explain all this to Gwen?'

'Don't worry about Gwen, Susan. She'll be happy to go back to Rochdale to be near her father and she isn't one for questions.'

'You'll have to tell her something.'

'Yes, I'll have to tell her something but I don't yet know what that is. Be assured it will be what I consider gives least pain to all concerned.'

'And Sylvia?'

'Poor Sylvia. Poor Paul.' He sighed. 'Sylvia has always longed to travel so perhaps that is the answer for her.'

'Yes.'

'Once we are back in Rochdale all this will be forgotten.' He didn't believe it, not for a moment.

She didn't either. She loved Edward and knew she would be lost without him but David would always have a corner of her heart. Didn't one always remember one's first love?

There was a light tap on the door and the maid put her head round. 'A Mr Ritchie – '

Edward glanced at the clock and frowned. 'He's early but I'd better see him. Excuse me, I shouldn't be more than ten minutes.'

Left alone, David went over to Susan and very gently put his hands on her shoulders. 'Thank you for making such a fine job of our son. He is a young man to be proud of and don't worry, nothing will change his love for you.'

Feeling his nearness and knowing this could be the last time she saw him her eyes filled. She blinked them away but not before he had seen them. With a groan he gathered her in his arms and for a brief moment they were locked in an embrace. 'How I wish things had been different,' he whispered.

Gently she drew away from him. 'No, David, don't wish that. You have a good marriage, you love Gwen and I love Edward.'

'I'll never forget you but I like to think of our son in Aran Heights, the house that always held such a fascination for me.'

'One day it will belong to Paul.'

'He's gone then?'

'Yes, Edward, he's gone.' She tried to read his expression but failed. 'You must be very happy about the distillery?'

'I'm not sure I've taken it in.'

'Ironic though, isn't it?'

'What is?'

'You getting what you most want and through my bastard son.'

'Don't, Susan, please don't.' His eyes were bleak and he didn't look like someone who had just got his heart's desire. 'You're still in love with him, aren't you?'

'No, Edward.' She shook her head. 'Once I thought myself in love with David but that was a very long time ago. People change, we all do.'

'I couldn't bear it if you left me,' he said brokenly. 'I love you, Susan. Those others, Caroline included, meant nothing. It was always you but you never seemed to want me and God knows I don't deserve you after what I made Paul and you suffer.'

'Paul has completely forgiven you. He likes and respects you.' She paused. 'And as for me what I did to you was dreadful, unforgivable, yet you stood by me,' she said quietly. They had been standing well apart and without being aware of what she was doing she held out her hand. Slowly he came towards her and she gripped his hand. 'Edward, I need to tell you something.'

'No,' he said harshly, 'I don't want to hear it.'

'But you do. I love you, Edward, love you very much and I'm just sorry it's taken me so long to tell you.'

'You do mean it? Oh, God! You do, don't you?'

'You should know by this time that I only say what I mean.'

'Then tell me about David – the truth, please.'

'This is the truth. I shall remember David with warmth and affection and perhaps I'll remain a little in love with him but only in the way one remembers one's first love.'

He drew her close and she knew that he was satisfied. She could feel the thudding of his heart and a lovely warm feeling enveloped her. Life for them both had been fraught with difficulties but they had overcome them. Now she couldn't bear the thought of life without him. She hadn't known it at the time but her parents had been right. They had known that Edward was right for her.

'I've just had a thought, Susan. Paul will have to choose between the papermill and the distillery.'

'No, he won't. Paul is a Brodie and that changes everything. His place is in the distillery and maybe fate has taken a hand. Peter likes nothing better than wandering about the mill.'

'Matthew's son. That's fitting. So it will still be the Brodies and the MacFarlanes.'

Susan moved away from him to look into his face, her own worried. 'Tell me, Edward, am I doing the right thing or should Paul know that David is his father?'

'He should know,' Edward said firmly. 'Paul should know that the distillery becomes his in his own right and not through me.'

'And then he would understand about Sylvia?'

'Yes.'

With her head resting on her husband's shoulder Susan felt at peace, the burden of guilt gone. All the trauma, the fears and the heartbreak were in the past and buried forever. What lay ahead no one could say but together they would face it.